ABOU

website a[illegible]aobrien.com.

Praise for NO RESERVATIONS:

'You'll devour this in one sitting . . . Grown-up, intelligent fiction. She just gets better and better.' Cathy Kelly

'A fascinating tangled web is woven by Fiona O'Brien in this fast-paced book . . . An engrossing summer read.'
Irish Independent

'The right mix of heartfelt emotion and upbeat humour'
Image

ALSO BY FIONA O'BRIEN

None of My Affair

NO RESERVATIONS

FIONA O'BRIEN

HODDER

First published in Great Britain in 2009 by Hodder & Stoughton
An Hachette UK company

First published in paperback in 2010

1

A CIP catalogue record for this title is available from the British Library

ISBN 978 0 340 96233 6 (B format)
ISBN 978 0 340 99857 1 (A format)

Typeset in Plantin Light by Palimpsest Book Production Limited, Grangemouth, Stirlingshire

Printed and bound by Clays Ltd, St Ives plc

Hodder & Stoughton policy is to use papers that are natural, renewable and recyclable products and made from wood grown in sustainable forests. The logging and manufacturing processes are expected to conform to the environmental regulations of the country of origin.

Hodder & Stoughton Ltd
338 Euston Road
London NW1 3BH

www.hodder.co.uk

For Kate Thompson,
who convinced me there was life beyond slogans and jingles, and who, over a memorable lunch, persuaded me to write that first full page A4.

Prologue

'Problem at table twenty-two,' the young French waiter murmured discreetly in Dom's ear.

'So deal with it.' The handsome proprietor smiled in greeting as a well-known actress and her new husband swept past him en route to their table.

'They're asking for you.' The waiter kept a smile fixed on his face.

'On a scale of one to ten?' Dom continued to glance through the reservations list.

'Twelve.'

'We've never had a twelve.' Dom raised an eyebrow.

'We do now.'

'What is it?'

'WUT.' This was restaurant shorthand for Woman Under Table. Dom had learned the lingo during the many years he'd spent working in the restaurant business, honing his skills until he'd finally realised his dream of setting up on his own.

'At table twenty-two?' Dom did some quick mental arithmetic. The table in question comprised an elderly heiress, Mrs Randolph Fitzgerald, and her son and daughter, both in their sixties – they were regulars. No love was lost between them and they had been drinking steadily since they arrived. The heiress, celebrating her eighty-ninth birthday, had been putting away an impressive number of double gin and tonics.

'How bad is it?' Dom glanced towards the table, where, sure enough, only the man and woman were visible. They looked remarkably unperturbed and were continuing with their meal, the place between them vacant. The immaculately starched white linen tablecloth that reached to the floor clearly concealed their absent mother. Dom was glad he'd decided on long tablecloths. They were not only elegant, but also convenient, it turned out.

'Never settle for anything but the best,' his mentor, Marco, had told him in L'Aurelius on the Place des Vosges, Paris. L'Aurelius was one of France's great restaurants, with three Michelin stars, where Dom had earned his restaurant stripes.

'How bad is it?' Dom asked now.

'Pretty bad.' The waiter fingered his collar and coughed. 'She was complaining of chest pains.'

'Oh, shit.'

'Precisely.'

'Is there a doctor in the house?' Dom's eagle eye swept the room. Everything was just as it should be. It was Friday and they had a full house, as usual. The perfectly choreographed staff were weaving their way between tables, discreetly serving and taking away the dishes that were effusively referred to as the best food in Dublin in the hottest new restaurant. So far, nothing appeared to be amiss, and that was the way Dom intended to keep it.

'Yes, P.J. O'Sullivan, table three. I've mentioned we might need his help.' The waiter indicated the doctor, who made eye contact with Dom. He was ready to act.

'Thank Christ for that!' Dom took a deep breath. At least that was something. 'You've called an ambulance?'

'It's on its way, five minutes, no sirens.'

'Good. No disturbances, you know the drill. Code Red. Alert all staff.'

'This is a first.' Small beads of sweat broke out on the waiter's forehead.

'That's what this business is all about,' Dom smiled grimly. 'Just follow the drill. Have Tanya take over on the desk.'

As he moved smoothly towards table twenty-two, nodding

and smiling at well-known diners, no one in the restaurant could have guessed that beneath his cool exterior, the much-admired proprietor had a cold trickle of sweat running down his back.

Dom Coleman-Cappabianca was charm personified. He was kind to girls, decent to men, gave money to beggars and couldn't pass a charity ticket seller without buying two. Dogs crossed the street to be petted by him. He was, as his mother never ceased telling him, a big softie. He was also utterly professional. This particular Friday evening, he was going to have to employ both qualities to the very best of his ability.

I

'Watch it, lady!' yelled Carla Berlusconi, skipping nimbly aside and narrowly avoiding being drenched by a passing SUV. The driver, blonde, imperious and unconcerned, mouthed into her mobile phone, cruising through the vast pothole, spraying water and pedestrians alike in her wake. 'Bitch,' Carla muttered, pressing on quickly, the cold November rain making her feel more irritable than usual.

Dublin, she had decided, was not a good city for pedestrians. Oh, sure, you could walk most places, but there were way too many cars. In her native New York, people used the subway, although granted, there was no decent public transport here. It was cool, though. She liked to walk. It reminded her of Rome, her spiritual home. Carla could never understand why her parents had moved to New York, both of them, before they had even got married; it was where they had met each other. If you could live in Italy, where else was there? In Rome, young people walked everywhere or raced around on scooters, but here, it was four wheels or nothing.

It was just as well she lived centrally and liked to walk, and it did keep her toned. Carla would never be one of those skinny girls. She was all Italian curves. She had inherited her mama's hourglass figure and that was just fine with her. Too bad Gino, her erstwhile boyfriend, had mentioned he preferred thinner girls. Was he history or what! Carla loved her food and wasn't going to play the skinny game for anyone. Anyway, she was through with men, which was one of the reasons she'd come to Dublin. Her father was the other. She'd had to get out of New York if she was ever going to strike out on her own, and Dublin had seemed as good a place as any to get some space.

Carla liked Dublin and the people, who were friendly, but also curiously shy. She also liked the fact that people didn't pigeonhole you according to what you did for a living or where you came from. Just as well in her case, Carla smiled. If they'd known about her background, she would never have got away with her present job, waiting tables in the hottest restaurant in town.

That wasn't the only hot thing about it – the proprietor, Dom, the guy who'd interviewed her and given her the job, was drop-dead gorgeous. She smiled, remembering the interview just over six weeks ago, when forcing herself to be positive despite the gloomy economic forecast, she had walked in off the street determined to get a job. Answering his questions, it had been all she could do to stop herself from staring at him he was so beautiful. He made her think of the Italian statues she'd seen when she'd visited her grandparents in Italy. He had dark brown eyes, with a slightly hooked nose and dark hair that fell over his forehead. He was half Italian too, on his mother's side, which would account for the olive skin. But looking at Dom was as much as she was going to do. She'd had it with men and careers. Neither had worked for her so far. Apart from Mr You Could Lose a Couple of Pounds, the few serious relationships she'd had thus far had all bitten the dust because of her dedication to work and the unsocial hours it had demanded of her. Getting to the top of the heap career-wise had left her lonely and frustrated and had culminated in the spectacular family row that had seen her leave New York.

Carla sighed. She'd had enough. No men and a complete career break were what she had decided. She had told Dom that she had worked in restaurants pretty much all her life, and that, at least, was true.

'When can you start?' he'd asked her.

'Right now, if you like.' She couldn't help smiling at the way his face broke into a wide grin.

'That's the spirit I like in my staff.' He had shown her around the restaurant and introduced her to the others. She had allowed herself to wonder if that was all he might like about her, but only for an instant. This was work, she reminded herself.

Dominic's had been the right choice. It was fun and her co-workers were great – everyone, that is, apart from Tanya Sherry, Dom's girlfriend. It hadn't taken Carla more than one minute in Tanya's presence to work out that the manageress was a tough cookie and was one of those women who viewed all other women as competition. Carla hated that type of thing. Tanya reminded Carla of those icy New York women with perfect manicures on the lookout for a man to bankroll them. But that aside, something told her Tanya wasn't quite what she seemed, that beneath her perfectly groomed exterior, she wasn't as assured as she appeared. Nobody that uptight could be.

Tanya was a public relations executive who had somehow assumed the front of house position. This seemed to mostly involve entertaining her friends and contacts on a regular basis and reminding Dom just how indispensable she was to him. The staff loathed her almost as much as they loved Dom. Privately Carla had come to the conclusion that far too much of Dom's profits were being eaten up by Tanya comping her friends for lunch and dinner. But who was she to comment?

All the same, yesterday Tanya had noticed Carla looking speculatively at a table of her friends as yet another bottle of good wine was sent over – none of it paid for. Tanya had quickly sent Carla to the storeroom on an errand, dismissing her with a steely smile. Mind you, Tanya's ice-cold demeanour had come in useful last week when that old lady had died. The poor woman had had a heart attack right at the table – or was it after she had slipped under it? Apparently she had been so comatose with alcohol she wouldn't have felt a thing, the doctor had said. He'd been really nice, the doctor, kind and concerned, preserving the old lady's dignity right up to the end. Her family, on the other hand, had been horrible about her. They hadn't even seemed upset. That was the trouble with family feuds, she thought sadly – you could take them too far. Nothing was worth that.

She thought affectionately about her own family: her old-fashioned, fiercely protective father and her three handsome, hot-headed brothers. She was still furious at their outdated and downright stupid machismo attitude towards her proposition. Well, that was their problem. They would find out just how much she had done for them in their own good time – without her. She was going to stick to her guns come what may, but all the same, she hadn't bargained on missing them quite as much as she did.

Reaching the restaurant, she ran down the side alley and keyed in the security code that let her in through the staff entrance. At ten o'clock in the morning, Dominic's was already a hive of activity. Carla avoided the kitchen and its cacophony of shouts and crashing pots and pans and made for the staff room. She was deliberately early for her shift and enjoyed the twenty minutes or so of calm before the inevitable storm began.

'Howya, gorgeous?' Paddy, the elderly kitchen porter looked up from his paper, grinning at her as she stowed her coat and pulled off her boots, replacing them with her work shoes.

'Wet,' Carla said, pouring herself a cup of steaming coffee and hungrily eyeing the plate of pastries that Astrid, the Austrian pastry chef, put down on the table.

'Have one.' Astrid pushed the plate towards her. 'I've tweaked my recipe.'

Carla sat down, bit into a feather-light puff and shook her head. 'Oh my God,' she sighed. 'This is divine. What did you put in it?'

Astrid smiled. 'I could tell you, but then I'd have to kill you.'

'You're killing my waistline for sure. I've put on at least ten pounds in the last month.'

'Nothing wrong with a few curves on a woman,' Paddy interjected. 'In my opinion, women only slim for other women. Men like something to hold on to.'

'Yeah, well, I'd quite like to hold on to my figure, or what remains of it.'

'At least your skin doesn't suffer,' Astrid said moodily. 'Mine has gone berserk since I started working here. Dry one day, greasy the next, and look at this!' She pointed to an offending spot on her forehead.

Privately, Carla had to agree Astrid wasn't looking her best. She had lost weight, her fair colouring had become sallow and deep purple shadows nestled underneath her beautiful eyes.

Despite Astrid's protestations, Carla knew full well it had little or nothing to do with work, and everything to do with her on-again, off-again relationship with the larger-than-life Rollo, Dominic's temperamental and egotistical head chef.

'Full house again?' Carla asked.

'Yes, both sittings,' Astrid said. 'Thankfully I get to escape this afternoon, my weekend off. I don't think I could stand another moment of Tanya sticking her nose in and getting under everybody's feet. I have no idea what purpose she serves here.'

'Search me,' said Carla, agreeing with Astrid's bewilderment, 'but Dom seems to think she's vital.'

'Pah,' Astrid scowled. 'He's a man, what would he know? In any of the restaurants where I trained, someone like Tanya would have been thrown out faster than yesterday's leftovers.'

As if on cue, they heard the *click clack* of stiletto heels that heralded Tanya's arrival. She popped her freshly blow-dried head around the door and despite her bright smile managed to look disapproving. 'Ah, there you all are. I was wondering where you were hiding. Paddy, somebody's parking in one of our spaces, be a dear and shoo them off, would you? And Carla, *Socialite's* booking has increased by three, see that the place settings are organised, will you? They're at the corner table, as usual.'

'It's already full. We'll have to move them.'

'Nonsense, I've promised them the corner. There's plenty of room for three more, just whoosh them all up a bit. They won't mind being cosy.' She pointedly checked her watch. 'Whenever you're ready, of course,' she added briskly before disappearing.

'That's crazy,' Carla muttered. 'They're going to be packed in there.'

'They won't care,' Astrid said witheringly. 'All that crowd wants to do is drink for the afternoon. Food is wasted on them. It's the same every Friday. Anyway,' she said, getting up, 'I'm out of here. See you Monday.'

When Paddy and Astrid had gone, Carla cleared away the pastries and changed quickly, putting on her working outfit of freshly pressed black shirt and tailored trousers covered by an immaculate white apron. She pinned her hair up, cursing at the fact that it was frizzing nicely thanks to the earlier shower she had got caught in. Then she went to work setting and checking her tables.

The restaurant interior, she had to admit, was spectacular. In its previous incarnation, Dominic's had been an old furniture shop and storeroom. It was impossible to believe now, after being lavishly refurbished by the celebrity Italian architect, Lorenzo Benadutti. The ambience was understated and modern. Gleaming terrazzo floors and cool white walls formed a uniform palette for the array of simple but beautifully designed walnut tables. Cleverly disguised and adjustable lighting ensured just the right ambience at midday or in the evening. The walls were hung with modern Irish art belonging to some serious collectors, on loan from their owners for public exhibition who thereby enjoyed the generous tax break it allowed them. Cleverly positioned mirrors ensured diners could discreetly see and be seen.

At the back of the room and to the left was the *pièce de résistance*, the state-of-the-art bar where every type of alcohol known to man was arranged in tiers against a mirrored wall. The designer bottles stood row upon row in a pyramid effect, backlit by a host of changing coloured lights, giving rise to its name, Chameleon. The bar, in contrast to the stark styling of the main restaurant floor, was intimate, with an array of comfortable tub chairs and sumptuous sofas, covered in opulent silks and velvets, the low tables in between lit by pretty candle lights.

Satisfied that her tables were in order, Carla risked poking her head into the kitchen.

'Hey,' she said, ducking out of the way as Pino, a Latvian sous chef, rushed past, a tray of garnishes held above his head as he made for his station.

'Not a good time,' he muttered as Carla followed him. 'He's depressed today. Says it's the fucking rain, but he and Astrid are fighting again.' He glanced meaningfully in Rollo's direction, who was shouting at a new assistant, the poor boy cowering in fright.

'What's new?' Carla said. 'That looks good.' She sniffed at a whole salmon gently poaching in a fragrant court bouillon. 'I didn't think salmon was on the menu today.'

'It's not. It's for that stupid party we're catering tomorrow,' Pino said as he chopped a row of spring onions with vehemence. 'I come to learn from an acclaimed chef and end up doing party food a monkey could prepare.'

'Shit. I forgot,' Carla said, her visions of her Saturday night off at the movies shattered.

'Yup. You and me, babe, and the assistants we'll have to babysit. The latest three don't even speak English.'

'Last I heard, speaking wasn't a requirement. What was it Dom said? Perfect food and drink, perfectly timed, perfectly served, and we are to glide seamlessly through the rooms, catering to every whim of our host and hostess.'

Carla had been surprised when Dom agreed to cater this particular party, given by one of Dublin's elite business tycoons to celebrate his fiftieth birthday. Dominic's didn't usually cater, unless it was for a valued customer or a close friend of Dom's, but on this occasion, according to Astrid, who had overheard the conversation, Tanya had been adamant.

'It's such a high-profile gig, Dom. Money's no object and half of Dublin's invited, or so I hear,' Tanya had said. 'Television coverage too, lots of media types. It'll be a good PR exercise. I'll be there, of course, to make sure everything's up to scratch.

'All right,' Dom had acquiesced, 'just as long as it doesn't interfere with the rest of the kitchen – and no matter what, I will *not*, under any circumstances, have to attend said party.'

Tanya had pouted. 'Oh, Dom. Just for a half an hour or so – it would be such fun.'

'Not a chance. I can't stand the man, he's an ostentatious git. In fact,' he'd scowled, 'I'm not sure we should be having anything to do with it. It's not exactly the type of image I want Dominic's to be associated with.'

'We need the money, Dom,' Tanya had said, playing her trump card.

'Fine, whatever,' he'd sighed. 'You organise it.'

'She totally manipulates him,' Astrid sighed when she relayed the conversation to Carla. 'He's too nice a guy for her.'

The discussion about the fiftieth birthday party had been weeks ago and Carla had clean forgotten that she and Pino had signed on to head up the team of staff that would cater the function. If nothing else, the extra money would be useful.

'What time's kick-off?' Carla asked.

'We have to be at the house at ten tomorrow morning. I'll pick you up. Make sure you don't forget your costume.'

'Costume? What are you talking about?'

'For the party – it's themed, you know, fancy dress.' Pino grinned as he whisked a béchamel sauce. 'Luckily for me, I'm a chef and already wear a uniform – I refused on health and safety grounds to wear anything else. You, on the other hand, are a mere . . . what was it?' Pino frowned in mock concentration. 'Ah yes, a serving wench – that was what Tanya said. I believe she is collecting your costume as we speak.'

'Don't bullshit me, Pino!' Carla laughed, well used to his wind-ups.

'No bullshit, Carla,' Pino grinned evilly. 'The theme of the party is the Tudors. That means you and the rest of the staff will be dressed as medieval serving wenches. I look forward to seeing you in your outfit. I'm sure you'll look adorable.'

Carla was about to protest when she was silenced by a roar and the sight of Rollo bearing down on them, meat cleaver in hand. At six feet two inches of well-built muscle, he was an intimidating prospect.

'Nobody speaks in my kitchen without permission!' he roared at Carla. 'Get out! I won't have my chefs disturbed.'

'Oh keep your hair on, Rollo,' Carla replied, slipping into fluent Italian, his native language. 'I was only checking the menu, and then I got distracted by those fabulous Capelletti,' Carla said, referring to the cones of pasta stuffed with chicken, cheese and eggs she had spied at the other end of the kitchen. 'How can a girl stay out of the kitchen when there's such temptation inside?'

Rollo's face creased into an enormous smile. 'My little Carlita with the J-Lo body! Always you can make Rollo smile, eh?' He put an arm around her shoulders and bent down to whisper conspiratorially in her ear. 'But Astrid, she no make me happy.' He shook his head emphatically. 'Astrid makes me sad, and that is very bad for Rollo. Sad chef, he make sad food.'

'You could never make sad food, Rollo, even if you tried,' Carla said. 'And Astrid is just a bit depressed because of the weather. I think she's a little homesick too.'

'Why she not say that to me?' Rollo demanded. 'To me, she say that I no love her.'

'She doesn't want to worry you. You know Astrid would never do anything that might stress you, she knows how important your role is, how crucial the kitchen is to you. How we *all* depend on you.'

Pino and the other sous chefs within earshot hid their smiles as Carla expertly stroked Rollo's enormous, but eggshell-fragile, ego.

Rollo nodded earnestly. 'Yes, yes, you are right as usual, my Carlita. I will talk to Astrid this evening, maybe take her for a weekend home.' His face lit up at the idea. 'Then she will be happy, yes?'

'That's a great idea. Just make sure you give Tanya plenty of notice. Losing her chef and pastry chef for a whole weekend could be traumatic for her.'

'I don't speak with Tanya!' Rollo banged his fist on the counter. 'I answer only to Dom. He will understand that my Astrid needs holiday.'

'Sure he will. Just don't tell him it was my idea.'

'My lips are sealed, Carlita,' Rollo grinned. 'Now, tell whoever is out there that no one comes into the kitchen before lunch until I say so.' He swatted her on the behind with a tea towel.

'Whatever you say, Chef!'

Just then, Tanya came through the swing door. 'Carla,' she began crossly. 'I've been looking—'

'I said no one!' Rollo roared, advancing ominously in her direction. 'Out! Everybody, *out*!'

Tanya rapidly obliged, followed by a grinning Carla.

* * *

Upstairs, in his apartment above the restaurant, Dom put down the phone to his mother and shook his head despairingly. He didn't know what had got into her, and her move from the family home into the mews at the bottom of the garden was bewildering, to put it mildly, not to mention upsetting. Although he loved her dearly, she seemed to be going through what he could only describe as some sort of midlife crisis. Probably better if he stayed out of it, as his father had advised him to. In Dom's experience, marriages were best left to their own devices, even if the one in question was his parents'.

Dom Coleman-Cappabianca adored women – simply because he had no justifiable reason not to. And the feeling, by all accounts, was mutual.

It was hardly surprising. His mother, Cici, a noted beauty with sloe eyes and the seductive gaze of Goya's naked Maja, doted on him, and his younger sisters, Sophia and Mimi, practically hero-worshipped him. Dom had inherited his mother's dark Italian looks and his father's height and broad-shouldered, lean build. His looks, together with his affable, laid-back personality and his genuine delight in female company, ensured that women everywhere loved him right back – some to distraction.

It had always been that way. Even in his exclusive all-male boarding school run by an order of Benedictine monks in the heart of the Irish countryside, Dom had attracted affectionate looks and lingering, indulgent glances from teachers, matrons and cleaning ladies alike, not to mention the local village girls. On Valentine's Day and his birthday, Dom's post had grown to such unseemly proportions as to warrant the abbot bringing the matter to the attention of Dom's parents, explaining that the 'fan mail', for want of a better description, had become a rather inappropriate and indeed unfair distraction to the other boys.

His mates, on the other hand, thought it was hilarious.

Dom was completely unaffected and great fun, and

although highly intelligent, his dyslexia meant academics were an obvious struggle. He wasn't annoyingly obsessive about sport either (apart from his beloved polo, which he played in the holidays), and, most important of all, he was more than generous when it came to setting the guys up with his numerous female contacts. As a result, his popularity only increased.

School holidays were spent travelling abroad with his family when he was younger – both Cici and James were adamant about encouraging their children to learn about different cultures and languages. Later, when Dom's interest in food and wine became evident, summers were spent working in private vineyards in France and Italy, the US and Argentina, where he was able to improve his already competent polo playing. It was on one of these happy, sun-filled working holidays that Dom was initiated into what was to become the other great passion of his life.

Eagerly encouraged by girls his own age and several considerably older and more experienced ones, Dom became a willing and naturally talented student eager to be shown and instructed in the age-old skills of how to please a woman, happily discovering in the process that he had a God-given talent he effortlessly excelled in. It was a talent that would bring him equal measures of delight and bewilderment and not a little bother over the years.

On his eighteenth birthday, working at a chateau in the Loire and at the height of a passionate six-week affair with his employer's wife, the very beautiful and experienced *comtesse*, their liaison was discovered and Dom was unceremoniously discharged and packed off home after a flurry of disgruntled emails from the cuckolded *comte*, leaving a tearful, but not at all remorseful, *comtesse* mourning his departure.

James, Dom's father, was furious with him on hearing the news. Cici, his mother, had been philosophical and not a little amused. 'What do you expect, James? He is a beautiful and eager young man, and half Italian,' she had said to her horrified husband. 'Just be thankful it's Dom, and not one of our daughters.' She had laughed at the horrified look on James's face at the prospect.

Unwilling at the time to face his father's inevitable lectures and warnings, Dom had hopped on a train to Paris, spent what he had left of his hard-earned wages renting a tiny studio apartment off the Rue Saint-Denis and got a job as a *plongeur* working under a female chef who liked the look of him. It was there, in the sweltering, electrically charged, stressed atmosphere of the kitchen, that Dom discovered his real calling. He vowed then that he would open a restaurant of his own and set himself a goal of ten years from that day to do it.

Now, strolling through that very restaurant to take his mind off things, Dom smiled with pleasure. They had just completed their first year in business and already Dominic's was a thundering success with diners and critics alike. It hadn't been easy – he and the rest of the staff had worked relentlessly – but it was finally paying off. He looked around methodically, checking every detail as if for the first time. There was no letting up in this business, where the tiniest slip could cost a restaurant dearly, and even though his staff were the best, the buck stopped with him. Today, in preparation for Friday lunch, one of their busiest sittings, everything seemed to be in order. The tablecloths were pristine and starched, the cutlery and glasses gleaming. Over in the corner, he watched as the new girl he had hired, Carla, worked quietly and efficiently.

She had been a real find, though initially he hadn't been sure about her. At the interview she had seemed almost too polished, too competent to be applying for the job of waitress, but then, he reflected, those were exactly the qualities he was looking for in his staff. She was cheerful, too, and had proved a real hit with her co-workers and diners alike.

She also bore an amazing resemblance to Jennifer Lopez, which was going down well with the male diners. Dom grinned. Having a pretty girl around never hurt, and Carla certainly was very pretty. Gorgeous, even. She looked up suddenly, caught him gazing at her, and flashed him one of her ear-to-ear smiles. Dom beamed back at her.

Even her working outfit of black shirt and trousers, covered by the traditional white apron, failed to hide her curvaceous body, and Dom found himself wondering just what those delicious curves would look like without it – then pulled himself up abruptly. That was the kind of thinking that got a man into trouble, and Dom didn't have time for that kind of trouble any more. Besides, he was her employer. It was completely unacceptable for him to flirt with her. Those days, he sternly reminded himself, were well and truly over.

Dom had had many romances, but sooner or later every girl had begun to put pressure on him, with one or two taking it to quite frightening levels. He remembered one girl in particular who had rung him and told him she'd taken an overdose after he had gently ended their relationship. Although it had only been a few of her mother's Valiums and it hadn't been serious, Dom had rushed over and called an ambulance. He still shuddered to think of the awful day. No matter how nice or gentle he was about it to women, they just couldn't seem to cope when he felt it was time to move on and reacted with varying degrees of petulance or hysteria. So Dom had decided women were off the menu – at least for a while – until he'd met Tanya.

Tanya was different from his other girlfriends. She was attractive, naturally, but was also cool, calm and very collected. She never shouted at him or threw hissy fits if he was late or was unavoidably detained by work. She made things easy for him too, organising the decoration of his flat, which he had never got around to, and making sure he didn't forget his mother's or sisters' birthdays. She was also doing an amazing job with the PR for the restaurant – the reviews they were getting were consistently fabulous. Although Dom knew they were deserved, he also knew a lot of it was due to Tanya's relentless work on his behalf. And so far, she seemed perfectly content to take their relationship one day at a time, which was only about as far as Dom could think lately. Their relationship was very civilised, he reflected. No demands, no screaming at him, no tempestuous outbursts. It was a nice change.

The restaurant began to fill promptly at quarter to one, with a seemingly automated file of glamorous patrons processing through the doors. There were a few early birds, not regulars, who had taken their places at half past twelve to get ahead of the rush so they would be seated comfortably to watch the parade of beautiful, high-profile diners guaranteed to make an appearance every Friday.

Dom was there to greet them all.

There was the usual crowd, of course – Tanya's weekly group of PR people and journalists, jovial, enthusiastic, back-slapping guys and thin, hungry-looking, accessory-laden women. They would eat little, consuming only who was in attendance, who they were dining with and whether or not they were worth writing up. Food would be toyed with, many bottles of champagne and wine ordered, and at some stage of the afternoon, they would stagger on to either the Shelbourne Hotel or Doheny & Nesbitt's pub, possibly followed by the Four Seasons Hotel to bolster their stamina for the long Friday night ahead.

The real diehards would continue clubbing. Reynard's for the older set, and Krystal for the young celebrity wannabe's: models, actresses, sports personalities, all who would be photographed outside looking nonchalant and spend what remained of the wee hours eagerly awaiting the Sunday papers and glossies that would hopefully feature them. To his left

Dom noticed a famous Irish rock star, clearly on a visit home as he lived in London. He was accompanied by a very attractive blonde, not his wife, who was stealing surreptitious glances in the mirror to make sure people had noticed them.

Dom was annoyed. Tanya should have tipped him off, and she hadn't. Rick Waters expected special treatment, and that included an obsequious welcome on arrival. He always reserved a table under his code name, and it would have been in the book. Dom made a mental note to check the database – these kinds of slip-ups could cost a restaurant dearly.

'Mr Waters!' Dom greeted him respectfully, although of course they were on first-name terms. 'To what do we owe this honour? Haven't seen you in a while, can I get you a drink?'

'Howya, Dom.' Rick smiled up at him and winked. 'Champagne's already on the way, thanks. This is Melanie.' He waved towards his companion by way of introduction. 'She's my new sound engineer, aren't you, love?'

Melanie smiled obligingly. 'I've been dying to come to Dominic's,' she said, clearly overawed. 'I couldn't believe it when Rick said he was bringing me here. It's not even a special occasion or anything.'

'I can think of two good reasons, eh, Dom?' Rick stared pointedly at her generously displayed cleavage nestling in a black, fluffy, low-cut jumper and laughed loudly at his own humour.

Dom's smile didn't quite reach his eyes. He hated men who treated women like accessories to be flaunted, even if the woman in question, as was clearly the case here, was more than happy to oblige.

Luckily the champagne arrived just then, followed closely by Tanya. 'On the house of course, Mr Waters,' she murmured as the waiter poured a tasting glass.

'Good girl,' Rick said, delighted to see that Melanie, his date, was clearly impressed.

Dom made his escape. 'Enjoy your lunch. If you need anything . . .'

'Don't worry, mate, I'll holler.'

I don't doubt for a minute you will, thought Dom, smiling as he moved away.

He made his way through the room greeting customers, appearing for all the world like the delightfully charming host he was. But behind the welcoming words and gracious manner, he was alert, constantly monitoring the apparently effortlessly choreographed show that unfolded before him with military-like precision.

Dominic's had attracted the fun crowd for sure, but the food was taken seriously.

Food was Dom's passion. Ever since he could remember, Dom had been in love with good food. He understood it, so much so that he realised early on in his training that although he could cook well himself, he lacked the extra five per cent that would have made him a great chef, and Dom wouldn't settle for anything less. In the kitchen, he firmly believed, as he had been taught, that 'good is the enemy of great', and Dom wasn't afraid to admit he didn't have what it took. He didn't have the fierce determination, the drive, the particular kind of genius that makes a revered chef. Dom's strengths lay in motivating the team that made up his kitchen, seeking out unusual ingredients, fusing together ideas, techniques and styles and, of course, dealing with the public, who adored him. In short, Dominic Coleman-Cappabianca was too nice to be a great chef, but he made a fantastic restaurateur. Which was just as well, because he certainly wasn't cut out for the family business.

James Coleman, Dom's father, had made a fortune in computers in the early 1980s. One of the few successful entrepreneurs who held on to his business and didn't sell out to the big guys, he had become one of the big guys himself through diversifying into software and other techie stocks.

Not unnaturally, it was his father's dream, or rather assumption, that Dom would follow him into the rapidly expanding business that was Coleman Technologies Ltd. But it wasn't to be. Apart from being dyslexic, Dom loathed studying, although he had loved school, and had graduated with little in the way of scholastic results, but with a great deal of laid-back charm. This, coupled with his stunning, dark good looks, made him a happy target for every young woman in Dublin upon his graduation. And Dom was willingly seduced by what was to become the *other* great passion in his life.

Now, focused as he was on the job in hand, Dom, as usual, was unaware of the female diners whose glances trailed him as he wove through the tables. Today, wearing an immaculate charcoal grey Jermyn Street suit and a crisp, pale pink open-necked shirt that set off his dark colouring beautifully, he looked more handsome than ever. His hair, freshly washed and damp around the edges, was just beginning to wave, the unruly forelock falling into his eyes at regular intervals. It made more than one woman present want to reach up and tenderly brush it back.

He was chatting briefly with an up-and-coming politician and the journalist who was buying him lunch in the hope of garnering an interesting political titbit when the occupant of a table to the side caught his attention.

There was no mistaking P.J. O'Sullivan, the infamous doctor. He was well built, with shoulders like a prop forward, a handsome, craggy face and shaggy, greying hair. It seemed that half the restaurant knew him and were waving hello. Rick Waters, the rock star, had even left his table to go over and greet him.

P.J. was a friend of Dom's father, and although he had only met him once or twice socially, he had done Dom a great favour in helping him out so discreetly last week when the unthinkable occurred and Mrs Fitzgerald had departed this world, slipping elegantly underneath her table right there in the restaurant. Dom would never forget it. He made a mental note to make sure P.J. got a very good bottle of whatever he was drinking on the house. By any standards he was a good-looking man, if dishevelled. He was a little heavier, maybe, a little worn looking, but nothing a bit of TLC wouldn't take care of. Then Dom remembered hearing that he had lost his wife to cancer about five years back. That would account for it. They had adored each other. He seemed slightly uncomfortable too, which wasn't like him, as if he felt too big for the table he sat at, hiding behind his menu and taking a quick swig of the glass of red in front of him. In fact, if Dom hadn't known better, he'd have said he was nervous, but that was ridiculous. Or was it? As the doctor's lunch companion strolled into the restaurant and joined him, Dom realised that it was Alex O'Sullivan. They were father and son, although he would never have put the smooth, suave financial adviser and P.J. O'Sullivan together. It just went to show.

Dom glanced over at the other corner table, today set for eight. It was already full except for one vacant seat, and its occupants were chattering ten to the dozen. Today, they were a gay milliner, whose outrageously chic hats were the crowning glory to every outfit; a property developer; not one, but *two* members of Viper, the biggest band on the planet; a well-known social diarist; a sports commentator; and a model turned vocalist who was enjoying a number one hit single in the UK. The champagne had arrived and there was an air of eager anticipation around the table. Dom checked his watch. Of course she'd be the last to arrive. It was all part of the theatre.

As if on cue, a slight hush descended as the whole restaurant looked up for a split second to acknowledge her arrival.

The Sophia Loren lookalike stood at the top of the steps and paused for just enough time to show off her outfit, which was, Dom had to admit, magnificent. A figure-hugging midnight blue silk suit clung to every curve, the scooped out neckline of the jacket showing off her décolletage to perfection. The skirt was to the knee and tight. The collar and cuffs were trimmed in matching navy fur, and a pair of navy suede high-heeled boots encased the famous legs. On her head sat one of the aforementioned milliner's creations: a midnight blue, wide-brimmed hat that curved dramatically around her face, emphasising the already spectacular bone structure. No one else could have carried it off.

'Cici!' the milliner cried, leaping up from the table and rushing to greet her. 'You look fabulous.' He air kissed her on both cheeks.

She sauntered down the steps, nodding and smiling to staff and friends alike until she reached Dom, when she paused again, making a great show of removing her navy silk gloves and proffering her cheek to him, which he duly kissed.

'Hello, darling,' she beamed at him. 'Don't *you* look nice today. That shade of pink is divine on you.' She patted his cheek fondly.

Embarrassment crawled all over him. 'Hello, Mum.'

'Well, aren't you going to escort me to my table, darling?'

'Sure,' he said glumly.

Now the real work would begin. If Cici had arrived, then Friday lunch at Dominic's had officially begun.

'Damn,' James Coleman cursed under his breath as he sliced his third drive of the day.

'You'd want to get that shoulder of yours seen to,' his partner, Mike, said, shaking his head. 'Your game's shot to pieces, and in case it's slipped your memory, the club championship's less than three weeks away.'

'You're right, and I haven't forgotten. I'm going to pull out.'

'Don't be ridiculous.' Mike's swing stopped in mid-air. 'We've won it for the past four years. One more and we get to keep the trophy. Just get your bloody shoulder sorted.'

If only it were that simple, thought James.

'Let's call it a day,' Mike said, not pushing it. 'I'll see you back at the clubhouse?'

'Sorry,' James turned away and slotted his driver into the bag. 'I've got a meeting. Have to dash. I'll call you tomorrow.'

'You work too hard, you know that?' Mike looked at him quizzically. 'Should take things a bit easier, James. You're not yourself these days. Surely the company can survive without you for a while? You should take a holiday, take that gorgeous wife of yours away somewhere exotic and chill out – after the championship, of course.' He chuckled. 'How is Cici, by the way?'

'She's great.'

'Tell her I said hello. We should have dinner soon, just the four of us. It's been too long. I'll tell Janet to organise it.'

'Sure, great, whatever.'

'Well don't sound so enthusiastic.' Mike sounded hurt.

'Really, Mike, I've got to go.' James was already making long strides towards the clubhouse, golf bag slung over his shoulder. He turned briefly. 'Dinner would be great.'

Mike shook his head as he watched his friend walk away. Something was up. James Coleman was most certainly *not* his calm, courteous, collected self these days. He wondered what it could be. Not business problems anyway; James's company was *huge* and doing better than ever. He was worth millions. Normally the man was utterly unflappable, but lately his behaviour seemed distracted at best, strained at worst. In fact, Mike reflected, it was downright worrying. He thought about calling him now on his mobile and pinning him down, asking what the hell was going on with him. Instead he shrugged. Who was he to be nosy?

James turned his sleek black Mercedes 600 coupé into Wellington Square and pulled up outside number 15. The car had been chosen only after careful consideration, the same consideration that he applied to everything in his life. James Coleman was not a man who rushed into things. On the contrary, whether in his personal life or his business dealings, James moved with the utmost deliberation only after analysing every minute detail and nuance of the matter in question. It made for a straightforward life. Consequences to potential actions had to be anticipated or mayhem ensued. The Rules applied at all times, and if you followed them, desired results were achieved – or at least they had been up till now.

He walked up the steps to his home and reached for his key, taking a barely perceptible breath before inserting it in the lock and turning it.

Inside, the long hallway greeted him as always. The warm timber floors, polished to perfection, were covered by an intricately patterned Persian runner leading to the base of the stairway. The narrow Edwardian hall table held a large silver salver containing the day's post, and a vase of elegantly arranged flowers stood in pride of place. The large mirror that ran the length of the table had been found at an auction at Adam's and hung now above it, dutifully enhancing the width of the rather narrow space. James caught sight of himself in it now and frowned. His face seemed shrunken to him, pale and rather pinched against the bold dark red backdrop of the walls. He took off his long navy cashmere overcoat and threw it on a hall chair, not bothering to hang it, and watched it slither to the ground. He walked into the drawing room, straight to the drinks cabinet, and poured himself a large gin. He sat there, sipping it mechanically, for fifteen or twenty minutes before realising the room was in complete darkness. He turned on a table lamp and tried, for the umpteenth time, to make sense of the mess that had become his life.

If there had been warning signs, he certainly hadn't seen them. Looking back, he still saw nothing that would have alerted him that all was not as it should be. In fact, as far as he could tell, things had been good, better than good even.

'Darling,' Cici had said to him one evening after dinner.'I think the mews could do with a makeover. It's looking a bit tired these days. I was thinking of redecorating it. What do you think?'

'I think that's a great idea.' He had looked up from his laptop and smiled at the enthusiasm in her voice. 'Go right ahead, I'm sure you'll do a wonderful job. Just don't expect me to get involved, you know how I hate all that stuff.' He went back to his share portfolio. 'Only please, no builders around the house, I beg you.'

'Of course not, sweetie. It will be my little project. You won't even know it's being done. I'll surprise you with the finished result.'

'Cici, you never cease to surprise me, as you well know. And you're right, redecorating the mews will be a good investment. Maybe we can rent it out. It's silly to have it lying there empty, unless one of the children wants it for a while, of course.'

'Unlikely, darling. Dommy has to be near the restaurant, and the girls, well, they're gone for this year at any rate. It's just you and me now,' she had said.

He remembered, with a rueful smile, the first time he had set eyes on her. He had wandered into the Shelbourne Hotel after a boring business pitch over dinner at his club nearby and made straight for the famous Horseshoe Bar, where a friend of his had arranged to meet him. There was no sign of the friend, but sitting at the bar was a stunning young woman gulping champagne as she endeavoured, in heavily accented English, to tearfully relate to the barman, who was listening, enthralled, the story of her first miserable day in Ireland.

Perhaps it was the fact that she was in evening dress that

intrigued him, or that the white chiffon confection plunged in a Grecian neckline to enhance the most incredible breasts James Coleman had ever seen that made him approach her and ask if he might join her and buy her a drink.

She had turned towards him then and the slanting, chocolate brown eyes had surveyed him, looking up at him from under thick, curling lashes. Suddenly she smiled and crossed her legs, allowing the dress, which was full length, to shift, revealing a thigh-high split that displayed long, shapely, olive-skinned limbs.

'I'd be delighted,' she said.

After that, everything had happened very quickly.

They'd had a few more drinks, champagne for Cici, but when James had been about to order a martini, Cici had interjected.

'Please, let me choose for you.' She had let those eyes rove over him again and a playful smiled curved suggestively. 'A Carpano, for my new friend,' she instructed the amused barman. 'An Italian drink for an Irish gentleman, yes? A martini is too . . . James Bond. Too predictable. And you, James, I think are not so predictable as you would like me to think, no?'

James, captivated and wildly flattered, had no intention of disillusioning her. And he hadn't been predictable, not that night.

'Has anyone ever told you that you look remarkably like Sophia Loren? A very young Sophia Loren,' he added hastily.

'All the time.' It was true; there was no mistaking the resemblance. 'But you,' she said, 'you are too aristocratic looking to be a movie star.'

'Well I can assure you I am not an aristocrat, and much as I wish I had a magnificent castle in the depths of the country to lure you away to, I'm afraid I do not,' James said equally playfully. 'How long are you here for?'

'I had planned to stay for a week, but now I must go back to Italy tomorrow. I would go sooner if I could,' she scowled.

'What on earth for?'

'My boyfriend, he is . . . how you say . . . a Don Juan, a cheat, a liar.'

'Then why go back to him?'

'He is here. I came over to be with him. That is the problem.'

James listened as she related her romance with the handsome army officer who was now a famous member of the Italian show-jumping team. James wasn't well up on things equestrian, but even the dogs on the street knew it was Horse Show week in Dublin. The yearly event brought traffic to a standstill and was the highlight of the social season every first week of August, when, after the day's competitions, a series of glamorous balls were held in various hotels in Ballsbridge, close to the Royal Dublin Society, where the Horse Show was held.

'But . . .' he racked his brain to remember, 'today was the Aga Khan trophy, the Nation's Cup. The Italians won, didn't they?'

'Yes, they did, and as we speak he and the rest of the team are celebrating at the ball that I left.'

'But why did you leave?'

'He didn't know I was coming. It was to be a surprise. I arrived at the hotel and went to the bar, where they were drinking before the ball. I could tell by the faces of his teammates that it was a mistake. And then I saw him with the girl who was supposed to be his ex-girlfriend. He had invited her to the ball.'

'What did you do?'

'I picked up a drink and I threw it in his face. Then I left. But now,' she grinned defiantly, 'now I am glad that it happened. Otherwise I would not be sitting here with a very handsome Irishman.'

'I'm very glad it happened too. He may be an accomplished horseman, this boyfriend—'

'Ex-boyfriend,' she corrected him.

'But he's clearly a complete fool in every other sense.' James checked his watch. It was half past ten, almost closing time. 'Have you eaten?' He was suddenly ravenously hungry.

'No. But perhaps I should, so much champagne . . .'

As it was Horse Show week, James knew they would have no chance of getting into a restaurant at that late stage.

'I live quite close by,' he risked. 'If you want, we could have something to eat at my place. I can't say I'm a good cook, but I'll fix us something.'

'But I am.' Her eyes lit up. 'I am a very good cook. We go to your place and I cook for you, yes?'

So they had. James had automatically gone to look for a taxi, but when Cici learned that his flat was in nearby Baggot Street, she insisted on walking.

'But you can't,' James protested, 'not like that, in your beautiful dress and those sandals.'

'Of course I can. Come, let's go.'

So he had taken off his jacket, placed it around her shoulders and they had strolled the ten-minute walk to the Georgian house where he had his flat. And she had cooked for him – she made the best spaghetti puttanesca he had ever tasted in his life.

He had somehow persuaded her to stay on for the week in his flat. There was nothing inappropriate; James was far too much of a gentleman to suggest anything untoward. Cici stayed in the second bedroom and they spent a wonderful week together as James showed her around Dublin and proudly introduced her to his clearly astounded and envious friends. Before she left, he proposed to her and she accepted. She went back to Rome to make the appropriate arrangements. Her parents, she informed him, had been killed in a car crash and she lived with an elderly aunt who would not be sorry to see her go, and the feeling, she assured him, would be mutual.

They were married three months later, in a quiet ceremony

in the Irish College in Rome and returned to Dublin, where James set about building his fledgling computer business and Cici, in true Italian fashion, settled down to babies and cooking, embracing domesticity as passionately as she did everything else in her life.

They had three children: Dominic, Sophia and Mimi. All of them had inherited their parents' dark good looks, but it was Dominic who was most like his mother in temperament. The girls, on the other hand, took after their father. They had done well at school and were presently abroad, Sophia studying art history in Florence and Mimi travelling the world on a year out from her political science degree at the Sorbonne in Paris.

Dominic, of course, had his restaurant, where by all accounts Cici was spending far too much time in the company of the kind of people James would rather not think about. It wasn't that he was jealous as such – he was too hurt, too miserable, too genuinely bewildered at the extraordinary turn events had taken. Why had his beautiful, devoted and adored wife, at forty-nine years of age, suddenly announced she wanted a trial separation? And had plotted to conduct that same separation in their newly revamped mews house under his very nose? It was . . . James searched for the appropriate word and failed. Bizarre was the closest he could manage.

What was he supposed to do? What would he say to people? *My wife has left me and she's living at the bottom of the garden.* If it weren't so bloody tragic, it would be funny.

He drained the remains of his drink and wandered down to the kitchen. He wasn't hungry, but he knew he should force himself to eat something, and the fridge, as always, would be well stocked by their Filipina housekeeper, who was carrying out her duties as usual. If she knew of her mistress's whereabouts, she made no mention of the matter. James was thankful for that at least. It was bad enough to come home to and wake up to the relentless loneliness of a house he had once regarded as a happy, love-filled home without fielding embarrassing questions.

Despite himself, he felt the familiar siren call of the kitchen window, which looked out onto the back garden and from where he could see the downstairs windows of the mews. He knew he shouldn't, but he couldn't help himself. He peered out and saw the mews lit up, looking warm and inviting, the outlines of several people moving about, glasses in hand. Cici was in residence, and obviously entertaining. James wanted to feel angry, enraged even, but all he could feel was the knife twist of loneliness that cut him to the quick. Then the curtains were pulled.

Just at that moment, his mobile rang.

'Dad?' he heard Dominic's voice. 'If you, er, don't have any plans, Tanya and I were wondering if you'd like to join us for a bite to eat this evening?'

Trying to inject a semblance of levity into his voice, James assured his son that he would be delighted to.

Never, for as long as he could remember, had an invitation been so welcomed.

2

P.J. O'Sullivan was not a man made for sleeping alone.

Yet this was exactly what he had been doing for the past five years.

Today, another bleak late-November morning, was, as he knew it would be, the worst – the one he steadfastly resisted waking up to.

Every year it was the same. No matter how much he drank, how late he stayed up or what kind of pill he took, he tossed and turned, dreaming fitfully. Sometime towards dawn, the gnawing emptiness would invade his artificially induced sleep and consciousness would return. Then he would feel keenly, as always, the sense of loss afresh.

Today would be her fifth anniversary.

Five long years without Jilly. A sixth about to begin.

He shoved the palms of his hands into his eyes and groaned. A headache was hovering if he thought about it and he had a crick in his neck. Hardly surprising when he realised the awkward angle he'd been sleeping at – on his stomach, one arm caught under his rib cage, the other stretching out across the empty bed as if reaching for her would bring her back.

Not to think, that was the trick. Definitely not to think.

He would focus on the throbbing in his temples, taste the bitter dryness of his mouth, dismiss the erection that deserted him as quickly as his dreams of her.

He would not think about the amazing life they had had together. The chaotic, colourful life that had been his – his and Jilly's. Nothing else had mattered. Together they had been an island of their own.

Wonderful, warm, spontaneous, exuberant Jilly. Wife, lover, soul mate. A woman who made everybody happy, and without whom life was unbearably lonely. No, he would definitely not think about that.

The alarm clock beside his bed told him it was 6:30 a.m. It was earlier than he usually woke, but this wasn't a bad thing. The sooner he got on with it, the sooner this day would be over, and he truly hated this day.

Downstairs, he opened the door to the kitchen and was greeted by Bones, his golden Labrador, who at ten years of age was, like himself, overweight and out of condition. Neither of them cared. P.J. let him out and made the first of the many cups of coffee he would drink that day.

Back inside, after his morning amble, Bones sat beside him, alert now, looking wistfully at the toast P.J. spread thickly with butter, which Jilly would have reproved him for.

'Don't listen to what they say, Bones,' he said, throwing his dog a piece he caught deftly and wolfed down, 'cholesterol is great.' Bones thumped his tail in agreement.

Mind you, P.J. thought, it had got the better of that poor old dear who had pegged it in Dominic's last night. He shook his head at the memory of the bizarre turn events had taken the previous evening in his favourite restaurant. He had to hand it to Dom – he and his staff had handled the whole thing superbly. Without a hint of the drama unfolding, they had managed to resurrect the old lady from under the table and prop her up, and while staff had gathered discreetly to conceal the activity, P.J. and Dom had managed to hold her up between them and get her out to the ante room, where the paramedics took over. She had been pronounced dead from a massive heart attack. P.J. had been rather impressed. As a way to go, eating and drinking with gusto in a first-class restaurant before slipping quietly under the table showed a certain amount of brio. Very convivial, really – by all accounts, it was the way she had conducted most of her life.

P.J. and his dog sat there for a while companionably, long-time breakfast partners taking comfort from the ritual that began their day.

The kitchen had been Jilly's favourite room, 'the heart of the house', she said, where they had retreated to cook, eat, drink, laugh and entertain and, when they couldn't make it upstairs, have wonderful sex.

The spacious old room had captivated her and responded eagerly to the hours of painstaking restoration she had undertaken with the help of various workmen, students and friends. Lino had been pulled up to reveal impressive flagstones, walls stripped and replastered and painted warm colours. Original brickwork was exposed and cleaned and, best of all, a hidden stone fireplace unveiled.

The ramshackle larders had been stripped out and a large, American-style stainless-steel fridge-freezer installed along with a huge, comfortable sofa. The old cream Aga had also been overhauled and proclaimed functional. It sat now, as it always had, radiating heat between the two large picture windows that looked out onto the square.

'Won't it be awfully posh?' A note of worry had crept into Jilly's voice despite her excitement at the thought of moving into the wonderful old house.

'Not once *we're* installed,' P.J. had retorted, grinning.

It had come as a complete surprise that his dotty old maiden aunt, Barbara, rumoured to have been a hell-raiser in her day and who studiously avoided all her relatives bar P.J.'s late father, her brother, had left him her splendidly decaying old house in Wellington Square upon her death. And so, ten years ago, with their two children, Alex, twenty, and Bella, just ten, they had become the latest residents of the elegant and much-sought-after location that was Wellington Square.

Even then, riding on the back of the soaring Celtic Tiger,

the prices the houses fetched were thought ludicrous at five, even six million. Now you wouldn't get one for ten. Some of them had a mews at the back, which made them even more valuable. Theirs also had a granny flat to the side.

Along with the house, his aunt had left P.J. a decent sum of cash, which meant that with a loan on top they could actually manage to undertake most of the work needed on the old place. Of course, it wasn't nearly as grand as some of the houses on the square, all recently renovated as they changed hands or long-time residents took advantage of increasing their ever-escalating property interests, but he and Jilly had achieved the home they had dreamed of, even though it had meant living in what felt and looked like a building site for a long time, managing with a kettle and a microwave in an upstairs bedroom.

It had been fun. But then, everything had been fun with Jilly.

From the moment he had set eyes on her, he knew she was the one.

Knebworth House, 1979, Led Zeppelin belting out across the grounds, but P.J. was hearing a different kind of music. Catching sight of her, dressed in wellies and a charmingly inappropriate vintage summer dress, she was a vision of loveliness amongst the crowd of heavy metal rockers and early punks. Taking in her masses of long copper and blonde-streaked curls, her golden skin, the wide sensual mouth, head thrown back as she laughed uproariously at something her mates were saying, P.J.'s breath caught. The girl was sex on long, lissom legs. She had turned suddenly then, caught him gazing at her, and smiled at him. He left his friends and walked over to her. She seemed a little out of it, and so was he. He took her hand. It felt like the most natural thing in the world.

She was a psychology student, had just taken her final exams and was waiting for results. When he told her he was a med student, she had laughed and said he looked far too sexy.

'That makes two of us,' he replied.

'I like you,' she said, her eyes crinkling at the corners when she smiled.

They split from the others, walked, talked, got high, talked some more, got hungry and grabbed a burger and chips from a catering van. They spent the night in his tent, and the next, and though the rock concert had come to an end, P.J. knew something much, much better had begun.

He didn't want to leave her, but he had to get back. One of his mates had a car and they were heading back to Holyhead to catch the ferry.

'Can I have your number?' he'd asked her.

'Sure.' She pulled a piece of paper from the back pocket of her jeans and wrote it down.

'Don't you want mine?' he heard himself bleat.

'If you want to give it to me,' she grinned.

'Come to Dublin,' he said.

'Maybe I will.'

'I'll call you.'

'Of course you will.' She had kissed him then, lightly, and turned, swinging her backpack over her shoulder.

P.J. felt as if someone had kicked him in the guts.

Back home, he told himself he would forget about her, that in time she would fade into one of the many hazy, happy, soft-focus memories that formed his summer breaks.

She didn't.

His mates gave him a hard time. Rugby-playing students like himself, they took full advantage of this rare opportunity to wind him up mercilessly. He thought he was hiding it well. They told him he was pathetic.

He tried, he really did. There were other girls, other nights. University resumed and he made the Rugby Firsts, but he never stopped thinking about her.

'She's really got to you, hasn't she?' his best mate, Joey, said, looking at him quizzically. 'Pity she's English. I mean, if she was *here,* there'd be some hope,' he went on as P.J. scowled at him, 'but what's the point? You'll probably never see her again. Best forget her, mate.'

She called him that night.

'I'm in Dublin,' she said. 'I think we'd better meet. I'm pregnant.'

He met her in town. She was standing, as they had arranged, outside the Bailey, a pub off Grafton Street that was considered way too posh and expensive for any of his student mates to frequent. He saw her first, as he turned the corner.

She didn't look pregnant. She looked beautiful, her slim, long legs encased in flared jeans, a multicoloured woolly hat pulled over her blonde curls and a matching long, skinny scarf wound around her neck. When she saw him, her face lit up and suddenly nothing mattered, nothing at all.

'I wasn't sure you'd come,' she said, pulling back finally from the lingering kiss their initial tentative peck had become.

'Try and stop me,' he grinned. 'C'mon, let's go inside, we can talk.'

At three in the afternoon, the pub was fairly empty.

'I'm sorry about this,' she began.

'Don't be,' he said. 'It's not your fault.'

'I was on the Pill, but I'd had food poisoning. I suppose that did it. It must be an awful shock for you.' A line of worry creased between her eyes.

'For you too.' He wanted to reach out and stroke the line away. 'How, um, how far along are you?' *Stupid question!* his brain screamed. *Do the maths! You're studying to be a doctor, for Christ's sake.* 'Sorry, sorry, stupid question – I didn't mean—'

'No, it's okay. Two months, a couple of weeks ago.'

'Two months eleven days then?' he grinned.

'You've been counting too?'

'I couldn't get you out of my head. I can't stop thinking about you.'

'Me neither.'

'Have you told your parents?'

'Yes. They're okay, they're cool.'

Cool parents? It was an oxymoron, a thought he couldn't quite get his head around. Not when your twenty-one-year-old daughter suddenly announced she was pregnant.

'Have you?' she asked. 'I mean, will you?'

'Not yet. I thought we should meet first.' He didn't want to contemplate that prospective discussion – not yet.

'That's what my parents said. That I should tell you and we should talk it over, see, um, what we want to do. They'll support me whatever we decide.' Her eyes were clear and certain.

'That's, er, very decent of them.' It was – decent, sensible, considerate. P.J. tried to imagine these liberal, calm-sounding people and couldn't.

'Will your parents . . . be upset?' she ventured.

He tried to search for the appropriate word and couldn't. 'It'll be a surprise,' he said brightly. 'They'll get used to it.' It was time for the million-dollar question. 'What *do* you want to do?'

'I don't want to get rid of it – you know, have an abortion.'

'No, no, of course not.'

'I don't want to get married either. That would be silly. I don't mean, you know . . .'

'No, I know what you mean.' He didn't know anything, really, but he hastened to assure her, this beautiful creature with her wide, innocent gaze and clear thinking, who was – the thought both terrified and beguiled him – carrying his child.

'What about you?' she asked. 'This can't have been on your list of things to do before you're thirty.' She smiled, but she was searching his face. 'What do *you* want to do? I mean it's crazy, you don't even know me.'

'But I want to.' He didn't have to think about it – he just had to say it. 'I want to get to know you.'

The concern left her face and was replaced by something light and hopeful. 'That's good, because I want to get to know you too.'

He reached across the table to take her hand, and they sat there, grinning foolishly, like the young, idealistic people they were, with their whole lives stretching before them.

His parents were not cool about it. Astounded, dumbfounded, disbelieving, certainly. Not cool.

'She's trapped you, you stupid boy,' his mother cried. 'This – this girl, whoever she is. She's ruined your life.'

'You bloody fool!' His father shouted. 'You're a medical student for God's sake! What were you thinking?' He was pacing up and down the drawing room.

'For Christ sake stop crying Maureen!' He snapped at his wife, who was perched on the edge of a Chippendale chair, wringing her hands.

His father's voice was cold. He was an intimidating man at the best of times but now, angry and taken aback, P.J. sensed for the first time that he was not someone to be crossed.

'Do something!' His mother was hysterical now. 'You're a doctor aren't you – a surgeon. You have contacts – can't she . . . you know . . .'

'No!' P.J.'s voice surprised him, sounding as firm and decisive as it did. 'That's out of the question. Jilly is – we . . . we're having this baby.'

'And how, precisely, are you proposing to support a wife, and a child, as a fourth year medical student?'

'That's another thing, we're not getting married either. It would be stupid.'

'Oh, sweet Jesus,' his mother moaned. 'The girls, your sisters, what an example to them – they'll be ruined. Tell him, Charlie, *tell* him. You'll *have* to get married if you're having this child, it's the only thing you can do.'

'We don't and we won't.' P.J. was feeling weary now. He was all out of fight.

'You've got it all worked out, haven't you?' His father leaned against the mantelpiece. 'Well I wish you luck young man, I really do. You're going to need it.'

'We'll manage.'

He left home the next day.

There wasn't much to pack. His books were the biggest problem. Otherwise, he just needed some clothes and his guitar. Joey had borrowed a small van and was waiting outside as arranged, looking sheepish.

'That's it.' P.J. said, hoisting the last of the boxes in. 'Hang on for a mo' will you, I've just got to go back inside to . . . you know.'

P.J. went upstairs and knocked on his parent's bedroom door. His mother had taken to bed and had not been seen or heard all day.

'Mum,' he called, softly. 'Can I come in?'

There was no reply. He sighed. 'I'm off now, Mum, I'll be in touch, okay?' He thought he heard a sniff, but he wasn't sure. He went back downstairs. His twin sisters were standing in the hall still in their school uniforms, silent, for once, looking worried and much younger than their seventeen years.

Shit, this was going to be worse than he had expected.

Lydia, the younger of the pair, by five minutes, opened her mouth to say something and then, to his horror, began to cry.

'You'll come back, won't you?' blurted Jane, the elder. 'I mean, it's not like you're gone for ever or anything?'

'No, no, 'course not. Don't be mad! C'mere.' He hugged them awkwardly.

Just then the door to his father's study opened and his

father emerged looking grim and, P.J. noted with a pang of guilt, as if he had aged overnight.

For a moment they regarded one another.

'You're off then?' his father said.

'Yes, Dad, I am.' He met his father's eyes and saw something flicker briefly, something he didn't recognize.

'Right. Well, then.'

His father reached into his jacket pocket and withdrew an envelope. 'Take this P.J.' He held it out.

'No, Dad. Thanks, it's good of you, but I . . . I can't.'

'Of course you can, man.' His father was brusque but P.J. could see the emotion in his eyes. 'Dammit, this is no time for pride. You have a child to support now, and the rest of it. It's just to get you on your way. I still think you're a fool, but you might as well learn the hard way, if that's what you want. Don't give up on your studies, son.' His voice almost caught. 'You're a born doctor.'

'Thanks, Dad.' P.J. croaked.

'And P.J.?'

'Yes?'

'This has all come as a terrible shock to your mother but if you get into difficulties . . .' He paused. 'You know we're always here for you. You can always come home – the three of you.'

For a horrible moment P.J. thought he was going to cry, as the full implications of what he was doing hit him. And then, thankfully, his father retreated back inside his study and closed the door.

Outside, P.J. climbed into the van.

'Are you right?' asked Joey.

'Yeah, let's hit the road.'

'Was it heavy?'

'Yeah.'

'Jaysus, I don't envy you, P.J. I mean, sorry – that's not what I mean, y'know . . . Did the folks throw the head?'

'Yup. Big time.'

Joey shook his head in awe, 'Respect, man. I mean, it's tough stuff, y'know, we're all behind you mate.' He shook his head again. 'Jaysus, I hate to think what my folks would do to me. Ma, well, she says she thinks you're mental but you know what mothers are like.'

'Yeah,' said P.J., darkly. 'I do.'

Things happened very quickly. They found somewhere to live through a friend of a friend's mother. The parent network had gone into action, it seemed, fuelled either by genuine sympathy or the huge collective relief that it wasn't one of *their* children having to negotiate this unfortunate turn of events. Sympathetic enquiries were made about the young couple, genuine advice offered and many knowing looks exchanged across dinner tables. To their credit, not one parent ever came out and said 'I told you so' or 'now you see why we're always telling you to be careful. They didn't have to – they could see the sobering effect this sudden visitation of adulthood and its attendant responsibilities produced on their own offspring. Besides which, everyone was inordinately fond of P.J. He was bright, funny, respectful and totally unaware of his good looks.

In fact, the only real tragedy, it was agreed among the womenfolk, was that P.J. was a terrific catch and more than a few mothers had harboured hopeful ambitions to acquire him as a son-in-law, an ambition their daughters had happily concurred with. Now, the disappointment was palpable.

'It's such a *waste*,' said Clodagh McLaughlin, Joey's mother, as she doled out a chicken casserole with more force than usual. 'He would have made some girl a wonderful husband, and from such a good family too. His parents must be devastated, poor things, I must ring Maureen this week, see how she is.'

'He *is* making someone a wonderful husband, isn't he?' Her husband interjected.

'Oh they're not getting married, dear, just living together, you know, shacking up, isn't that what you young people call it?'

'Same thing,' Vicky, Joey's sister, threw her mother a resentful look. 'She's got him hasn't she? So much for your warnings about playing fast and loose Mum, hasn't done this Jilly any harm.'

'It won't last kissing time.' Clodagh McLaughlin sniffed. 'Mark my words, they'll be history before the baby's a year old. And he can say goodbye to his career. She's ruined him, that's what she's done, that English tart.'

'Why don't you just shut up! All of you!' Joey stood up angrily from the table. 'Jilly's a lovely girl, and stunning looking, P.J. couldn't be happier. I for one would consider myself more than lucky if I could meet a girl half as fabulous as Jilly.' And he stormed from the room.

'Well!' exclaimed his mother, 'I knew it, I just *knew* that all this would be a bad example for the rest of them.'

Vicky opened her mouth to protest but her mother glared at her.

'I think the less mentioned about young P.J. and his circumstances the better, for the time being at any rate,' said her husband, his mouth settling in a thin line of disapproval.

It shouldn't have worked, but it did.

Once he had organised a flat, P.J. borrowed a van and got the ferry to Holyhead and drove down to Oxford to pick Jilly up.

He had found his way easily to the picturesque, orderly village on the outskirts of Oxford. Their house was just as she had described it: a pretty, regency home overlooking a weir where swans glided by serenely.

Jilly opened the door to him, grinning, and brought him

inside. In the sitting room, her parents rose to greet him, if not effusively then with considered interest. There was no chilliness, no undercurrent of resentment.

Jilly's mother was Swedish, a teacher, and had passed on to her daughter her Scandinavian good looks. Her father was good-looking too, in that aristocratic, even-featured English way, and was a professor of classics. By the time lunch was served, everyone had relaxed a little.

'I can see what Jilly sees in you,' her mother said to him matter-of-factly in her lilting accent as she regarded him. 'You have a lot of sex appeal.'

P.J. nearly choked on his roast beef, although there had been no trace of suggestiveness in the remark.

'Er, thank you, I think,' he said colouring and feeling hugely embarrassed.

Her husband allowed himself a smile. 'Really Freda! Steady on old girl! Young P.J. won't be as used to your direct manner as we are.'

'But I am right, no?' she laughed at them as she and Jilly got up to clear the table.

Then it was time to set off. Jilly's belongings were loaded into the van and goodbyes were said. As Jilly hugged her parents warmly and kissed them both, P.J. was again astonished at how unlike his own family they were. How unaffected, demonstrative and loving they were, and so generous to him, a stranger, taking away their only daughter.

'Good luck,' said Jilly's father to them. 'Be kind to each other.'

And then they were waving to them, to the receding village, to the landscape they were leaving behind as they set out for Dublin, and their first home together.

Their flat was in the basement of a rundown house in Leeson Street, owned by an elderly and very deaf widower. What it lacked in mod cons, it made up for in spaciousness, consisting of a reasonable bedroom, a small bathroom, a tiny galley kitchen and a sitting room. There was no furniture, precious little light and far too much noise, particularly late at night, when the basement nightclubs on either side of them pulsed music through the walls.

To Jilly and P.J., it was complete heaven.

The arrangement suited everybody. The widower, Billy, was happier with a young couple below him in the house, particularly a medical student. In exchange for keeping an eye out for him and Jilly doing his shopping now and then and listening for the doorbell he couldn't hear, the rent was minimal.

They were the envy of all their friends, who, still stuck at home and mostly studying, thought the dark, dimly lit flat terribly exotic. Their bed was a large mattress on the floor, orange crates made perfectly acceptable bedside tables and, thanks to a tip-off from a hospital porter, P.J. was able to salvage a table, some chairs and a few stools destined for the dump. Three evenings a week, he worked in a bar and Jilly got a job as a temporary secretary, and between them they made ends meet. Weekends were spent painting and decorating, their friends lending a hand. Exhausted, they would open some cans, send someone out for pizzas or burgers, then sit around the rescued hospital table, laughing and talking and playing music long into the night.

The baby arrived bang on time. On 1 June 1978, Alexander Charles Patrick O'Sullivan made his entrance to the world. Everything had gone perfectly according to plan. P.J. had been rather disappointed about that – he'd envisaged a dramatic dash to hospital, breaking traffic lights and possibly a police escort. Instead, Jilly woke up at six o'clock with mild contractions. By lunchtime, they took her packed case and got a taxi to the hospital.

Despite her calmness throughout the pregnancy, Jilly was suddenly uncharacteristically nervous.

'It's okay, I'm here. Everything's going to be fine,' P.J. reassured her, looking into her eyes, wide with worry. She had refused to attend the hospital on a private basis, although she could have, and now greatly missed the presence of a familiar and trusted gynaecologist.

By four o'clock, she was exhausted. Then, alarmingly, the baby's heartbeat faltered. The monitor set off a flurry of action.

'Baby in distress.' The stern voice of the midwife cut through the delivery room.

P.J., having watched hundreds of deliveries and assisted with several himself, now felt as terrified and helpless as Jilly looked.

'Oh, please,' she whimpered. 'Don't let anything happen to my baby, please.'

Suddenly the swing doors burst open and a tall, gowned figure strode towards Jilly's bed. 'Thank you, Nurse, I'll take over now.'

P.J., relief coursing through him, recognised the clipped, confident tones of his father's golf partner, one of the most respected gynaecologists in the country. P.J. had never been so glad to see anyone in his life.

'Mr O'Gallagher!' The midwife looked surprised and not altogether pleased. 'You're not listed as being on call this evening.'

'A happy coincidence, Nurse. Just happened to be passing by. Now, let's see what the problem is here.'

Jilly began to cry as Tony O'Gallagher examined her and assessed the situation quickly. When he spoke, it was with kindness but there was urgency in his voice.

'Forceps,' he commanded. 'And suction. You're doing splendidly well, Mum, just another minute or two, good girl . . . here we go, stand back please, people, let's give Dad a ringside seat . . . ready P.J.?'

And suddenly everyone was cheering and slapping him on the back, and Jilly was holding their perfect new baby in her arms.

Not far away, in his consulting rooms in Fitzwilliam Square, P.J.'s father smiled into the phone. 'Thank you, Tony, I appreciate that. It was good of you to make yourself available to keep an eye on things.'

'Nonsense,' replied his old friend, 'Worth it all to see you the first granddad on the block! Hope it improves your game. Congratulations old chap, give my best to Maureen.'

'Will do.'

Then Charles Richard Ignatius O'Sullivan poured himself a large tumbler of Jameson's finest, leaned back in his chair, and, with an impressive surge of emotion, drank a toast to his first grandson.

It is a well-known fact of life that babies are great peacemakers and Alexander Charles Patrick O'Sullivan was no exception. A model child from the outset, Alex embraced routine the way other children resist it. He fed when he was supposed to feed and slept when he was supposed to sleep, so soundly and so still that sometimes Jilly woke him up to make sure he was still breathing.

He looked remarkably unlike either of his parents. This further endeared him to his four doting grandparents, who spent many an hour speculating upon, and claiming, every emerging feature as one of their own.

And all the while, P.J. and Jilly grew closer and fell more deeply in love.

What had started off as a haphazard, blinding haze of attraction developed into a mutual appreciation and dependency that grew stronger every day. It wasn't all plain sailing, of course. They had their ups and downs like every young couple, the most memorable of which was when P.J. disappeared for three days to play with his mates in their band. He had negotiated a free pass for one night, but it inexplicably turned into three.

At first vexed, then genuinely worried, Jilly had tracked him down to an inner city 'studio', where Viper, his mates' burgeoning band, was writing and recording.

Joey let her in. Through the haze of smoke and alcohol fumes, Jilly spied P.J. lying against a wall, his arm protectively resting on his beloved guitar and a silly smile on his face.

'You fucking selfish bastard!' she screamed in fury. 'I thought something had happened to you!'

The silly smile got bigger. 'Hey, babe,' he said sleepily. 'It's beautiful of you to find me. Really beautiful.'

'That's it!' Joey shouted, joint dangling from his lips as he scampered to the keyboard. 'That's the lyric! Fucking brilliant, guys!'

As he played a haunting riff, Jilly sat down beside P.J. and, taking a swig from the vodka bottle, gave up the fight and began to hum along with the tune.

It was Viper's breakthrough single, and 'Beautiful to Find Me' went on to be a hit.

A few years passed, and suddenly it seemed like all their mates were getting married and settling down and having babies too. The earlier drama they had caused felt like another lifetime. Now everyone was in the same boat. The guys moaned to P.J. about sleepless nights and the girls were glad to have Jilly to confide in and seek advice from as someone who had been through it all before.

They were happy days.

P.J. eventually qualified and won a place at M.D. Anderson, the renowned medical establishment in Texas, to pursue his chosen specialty of oncology. It was there that Bella arrived unexpectedly. The spitting image of her mother, the longed-for second child had surprised and overjoyed them. In an ironic twist of fate, despite Alex's instant arrival, they had been unable to conceive thereafter. 'Unexplained infertility' was the diagnosis, though neither Jilly nor P.J. had been unduly upset. They had Alex and, of course, each other. Jilly had resumed her psychological studies and qualified as a counsellor. By the time she discovered she was pregnant with Bella, Alex was almost ten.

An orderly and precise child, Alex was as unlike his parents as it was possible to be.

'Do you think they gave us the wrong baby leaving the hospital? P.J. asked Jilly more than once, shaking his head as he watched Alex methodically tick off a to-do list.

Jilly grinned. 'It won't hurt to have one organised member in the family.'

'Guess what?' Jilly had said to Alex one warm May Texas evening, ruffling his hair as he came in from tennis practice.

'Mom, don't do that,' he'd moaned, ducking his head, although he grinned as she hugged him in a vicelike grip. 'I don't like guessing. What's cooking?'

'Big, juicy steaks,' P.J. said.

'Great.' Alex looked approving. 'Can Freddie come over?'

'Sure, there's plenty,' said Jilly. 'Alex?' Jilly called as he made to run to the phone.

'Uh huh?'

'We're having a baby, honey. You're going to have a little brother or sister. How about that?'

'How about that indeed!' added P.J., looking pleased as punch.

'When?'

'December. It'll be our big Christmas surprise. Isn't that fantastic?'

'I don't like surprises, and I've already made up my mind what I want for Christmas.'

Alex turned away quickly, but not before P.J. had caught the mutinous expression that crossed his face.

Three years later, they returned home to a very different Dublin. The city was alive, vibrant and confidently about to clamber aboard the back of the Celtic Tiger. P.J., whose medical credentials were spectacular, had been offered, amongst other positions, a consultant post in St Edmund's, one of the three big teaching hospitals in the city.

He and Jilly bought a nice house on the south side, near the hospital, and Alex attended his father's old school, Blackrock College, where he studiously avoided rugby and attained top grades in everything, especially mathematics, which he excelled in, finding satisfaction in intricate and foreign calculations that P.J. couldn't come close to understanding.

He'd hoped that moving back home might bring Alex out of himself a bit more, help them bond. It was silly, he knew – as if Alex going to his old school would bring them closer, help Alex understand him better because they'd walked the same corridors, run around the same muddy playing fields in the same jerseys. But it hadn't happened. Whatever way he looked at it, he and Alex were just too different, and finding common ground was becoming more and more difficult.

Bella, on the other hand, was a three-year-old bundle of energy who looked just like her mother and was showing signs of having her father's personality. She adored P.J. and worshipped her big brother, following him around at every opportunity, a pastime Alex found, and failed to hide, profoundly irritating.

There was only one problem. P.J. wasn't happy. It wasn't his domestic life; that couldn't have been better. It was work. Not medicine per se, but rather hospital politics. He loathed the game-playing, the wasted hours arguing with the Board, and he hated the Health Service most of all, the lumbering, blood-sucking, inefficient body that was the common symptom in every illness.

'You're not happy, are you?' Jilly asked him one night, stroking his hand as they sat quietly in the kitchen, sharing a joint.

'That obvious?'

'How bad is it?'

'The pits,' P.J. smiled ruefully. 'I thought I could cope with it, you know, enjoy the bits I liked and ignore the rest, but it gets to me so much. I don't want to be a property developer masquerading as a physician, I want to be a bloody doctor – someone who can help make sick people better, and when that's not an option, make them as comfortable as they can be, by whatever means are at my disposal.' He let out a long, angry sigh.

'Then why don't you do that?'

'What? You mean give it – all this – up?'

'Why not, if it's making you miserable.'

'Wouldn't you be disappointed? I mean, all those years of training, Texas, the exams, having no money. Jesus, it must have been so hard for you, and now, just when I could reap all the rewards, to chuck it all in?'

'You wouldn't be chucking anything in. Your training will always stand to you, and to your patients, probably more so if you can use it the way you want to. Set up your own practice, hon, a general practice. Go back to what you enjoy – being a doctor. On your own terms.'

So he did, and never regretted it for a moment. It had been the right move to make.

From then on, things got better and better.

They converted the garage of their semi-d. P.J. had his surgery downstairs and Jilly had a room upstairs, where she saw her clients.

Word spread quickly about the practice, about the wonderful young doctor with the kind and sympathetic manner who was more like someone you'd want to have a pint with than a remote, judgemental member of the medical profession. The word on the street was that he was open-minded too, and creative in his prescriptions. Best of all, it was said, Dr P.J. O'Sullivan could work out what the hell was wrong with you when no one else could. His diagnostic skills were legendary. The more superstitious among them said he had the 'gift'. More than one consultant had been pulled up in his tracks when P.J. had spotted a rogue symptom they had overlooked or dismissed. It made him inordinately popular with patients, but not with the medical establishment. Dr. P.J. O'Sullivan was a maverick. In other words, he was trouble.

Patients came to him from all over the country, and he never turned anyone away. If you could afford it, he charged top dollar. If you couldn't, you didn't pay or you made a donation at your discretion to the Cancer Fund.

Rock stars, actors and stressed-out whizz-kids attended him. He didn't lecture anyone about their lifestyles or tell them to shape up or he wouldn't treat them. 'Look, I smoke and drink myself. What would I be doing giving you a hard time about it? They'll kill you more likely than not, but we all have to die of something, don't we?' he'd chuckle.

He could as easily be found playing doctor on stage behind the scenes at one of the many rock concerts he was invited to (his old band, Viper, was now a famous rock group) as making a house call to a frightened, vulnerable pensioner.

No one ever came empty-handed to the surgery. Whether it was a bone for the dog, a bunch of flowers for Jilly or a leg of lamb for the freezer, even the most hard-up patients brought something for their dearly loved doctor and his gorgeous wife. P.J. and Jilly never wanted for anything.

Then his aunt died, and they inherited the wonderful house on Wellington Square. P.J.'s surgery was moved to the mews, and Jilly counselled her clients from a cosy room at the back of the house.

They never changed. P.J. still looked like a reject from the 1970s, according to Alex, and Jilly was as unaffected and natural as ever.

They had five years in Wellington Square, five blissful years, before the cancer struck, and when it did, it was quick.

Metastatic lung cancer. No warnings, just a niggling pain in her back and a devastating diagnosis. Six weeks later, Jilly was dead.

They had considered everything. No treatment plan had been unexplored, no centre of excellence ruled out. But P.J. knew, the way he always did, instinctively, that this was a losing battle. The specialists were kind, but adamant – there was nothing to be done, nothing that would save her or extend her life. Examining the evidence for himself, P.J. had to agree with them.

Gavin, one of their oldest friends, now an eminent Cedars-Sinai-trained oncologist, had sat with P.J., head in his hands, and watched helplessly as his dearest friend picked up a glass from a sideboard and flung it against the wall, where it shattered. Then he sobbed inconsolably.

For the short time that remained to her, she was kept out of pain.

Her last words were 'Love you, baby,' whispered, barely caught. She died in his arms seconds later, at home, Bella beside her on the bed crying softly, and Alex, stern and white-faced, who waited till the end, then turned and left the room quietly.

People had been kind, unbelievably kind, but for P.J., nothing would be, could ever be, the same again.

He continued with his practice, of course, drank a little more, smoked a little more than was good for him, but he kept it together. He had to, for the children. Bella was devastated, and fourteen was too young for a daughter to lose her mother, especially one as wonderful as Jilly. He worried about that – about her first date, about buying the right clothes, her wedding even, all without Jilly.

Alex was a worry too, in a different way. He seemed to be coping, but he never referred to his mother and seemed exasperated if P.J. tried to. He continued to be as remote, as controlled and as much a mystery to his father as he had ever been.

But they had managed.

Five long years without Jilly. P.J. shook his head. It didn't get any easier.

He left the kitchen, went upstairs, showered and dressed, then grimaced at the reflection that peered back at him. Alex was right; he did look like a relic from the 1970s. But was that such a bad thing? Mick Jagger, Ronnie Wood, plenty of guys way older than him wore their hair long – he felt lucky to still have any. It was greying now, but still there. Anyway, Jilly had liked it long. His face still looked pretty much the same – a few more creases, the hooded eyes maybe a bit heavier and, he had to admit, blearier. Sure, he could do with getting a bit more exercise, losing a bit of weight, but why? And he was comfortable with his gear, even if Alex wasn't. Jeans were acceptable at any age. Maybe the sweatshirt was pushing it a bit for work, but God, it was comfortable. And ankle boots had come back into fashion again – he had read that somewhere – even if he had never realised they had been out of it. That was one of the best things about working for yourself – you could wear what you liked.

Downstairs, he collected Bones and they set off for the morning surgery. All the way down the garden to the mews. 'Ready old chap?' he said to his adoring dog. 'Let's see who's on the list today.'

He tried to motivate himself, he really did. He tried to remember the gratitude of so many of his patients, the challenge of decoding a trail of tricky symptoms, the genuine pleasure of helping and seeing someone get well.

But underneath it all was the nagging reality. *What the hell use was it being a doctor, a good one, when you weren't able to help the one person in the world who meant everything to you?*

3

Candice Keating regarded herself in the full-length mirror of her designer bedroom and smiled approvingly. The tight, elaborately worked corset pushed up her boobs to make them look twice their normal size and had sucked in her waist by at least three inches. The heavy, full skirt of the dress was a bit cumbersome to walk around in, but who cared? The effect was fabulous.

'You look amazing, Candy, really amazing,' her friend Katy breathed admiringly, trying to get a glimpse of herself unsuccessfully in the mirror Candy was monopolising.

'I do, don't I?' Candy turned sideways, appraising her reflection from this new and engaging angle.

'Is my hair all right?' Emma fidgeted with a blonde tendril.

'Leave it, Em, it's fine.' Candy turned to her friends, both dressed as ladies-in-waiting. 'You'll ruin it if you start pulling at it. Dylan's the best hairdresser in the city. He didn't spend all afternoon here for nothing. Don't undo all his good work.'

'It feels weird, up like this,' grumbled Emma.

'You both look fine. Now remember what I said – no messing and no getting pissed, at least not until we're on our own later. There's going to be loads of press people and I know at least one TV station is covering it. And if *she* comes over to us, you're to ignore her, got it? Unless Dad's with her, in which case you can nod, but no smiling or simpering and playing up to her.'

'I can't wait to see her, though – up close, I mean,' Katy said, a note of awe creeping into her voice.

Candy scowled. This was exactly the kind of attitude she was at pains to discourage. 'She looks exactly like she does in her photos. Like a slut.'

Her friends' eyes widened and they giggled. Candy Keating might be a bossy, stuck-up, spoiled, opinionated pain in the ass, but she more than made up for it by her advantageous associations. Her father was one of the wealthiest men in the country and by all accounts was happy to spend that money in as obvious and extravagant a manner as possible, which included, among other things, catering to Candy's every whim. Since Katy and Emma, as her two best, and possibly only, friends were regularly included in many of these dubious demands, they felt that such glamorous outings and events more than made up for their friend's other shortcomings – which were multiple.

Tonight would be the best of all, when they would be going to the party of all parties: the fiftieth birthday party thrown by Candy's multimillionaire father, Ossie Keating, and his model girlfriend, Shalom deLacey, bane of Candy's life, would be there. Anyone who was anyone was going, including loads of celebrities. It didn't get any better.

'D'you think they'll get married?' Emma mused, adding a final coat of pearlescent midnight blue to her nails.

'Not if I have anything to do with it.'

'Why do you hate her so much?' Katy was curious.

'I don't hate her. She just makes me sick, that's all.'

Emma and Katy exchanged looks.

Before the subject could be debated further, the bedroom door opened and Candy's grandmother poked her head in. 'Are you decent, girls?'

'Come on in, Gran.'

'Well, don't you all look splendid. You could have walked straight from a film set.'

'Hi, Mrs Searson,' the girls chorused.

'How many times do I have to tell you to call me Jennifer?'

she said fondly to Emma and Katy before turning to her granddaughter.

'What a perfect young queen you make, Candice.'

'Thanks, Gran.'

Emma and Katy made wild eyes at each other and tried not to laugh. They loved Candy's gran. She was terribly posh and a bit scary, but she said the most outrageous things and didn't give a hoot about what the recipient of her acerbic remarks might think. A glamorous seventy-six years of age, she had trouble with her hip and since her hip operation had taken to walking with a silver-topped cane, which she didn't hesitate to bang on the floor or indeed prod people with if the situation warranted. Now, dressed in a fuchsia pink quilted satin dressing gown and full make-up, she lowered herself regally onto Candy's bed, crossed her legs and took a sip from the gin and tonic she clutched in her hand.

'My feet are killing me.' She rotated her ankle and stretched out one of the offending feet, encased in her favourite gold ballet slippers, before returning her appraising gaze to Candy. 'I must say, it was well worth getting those costumes over from Paris. At the time I thought that stylist creature was off her rocker, but that rig-out does wonders for you, Candice. Although I do wish you wouldn't cover up your lovely freckles with that mask of make-up,' she frowned. 'Still, you look wonderful, dear, and your lovely red hair makes you a perfect young Elizabeth.'

'It's strawberry blonde.' Candy looked at her coldly as her friends tried not to snigger.

'Yes dear, whatever. Your father will be so proud of you. He won't have eyes for anyone else.'

Candy was slightly mollified. 'I do wish you were coming, Gran. Won't you change your mind, for me? There's still time.'

'Yes, Mrs – I mean, Jennifer,' Katy encouraged. 'Do come.'

'I'd rather have bamboo shoots inserted under my nails than accept such a vulgar invitation.'

Candy glared at her while Katy and Emma collapsed into giggles.

'It's not vulgar, Gran. It's going to be brilliant, and loads of celebrities will be there.'

'Exactly,' Jennifer said. 'And your mother shouldn't be going either. I told her, but of course she wouldn't listen to me.'

'What did you tell me, Mother?' Charlotte Keating appeared at the door, smiling, but her tone was deceptively light.

'Good God!' Jennifer's mouth dropped open. 'Tell me, I *beg* of you, you are not going in that – that regalia.'

'Why not? It's entirely appropriate, I think, and even you, Mother, approve of me in black.'

The girls were riveted.

Jennifer looked outraged and the temporary plate the dentist had given her until her implants were ready, began to slip as she searched for words. 'But you're going as . . . as . . .'

'Catherine of Aragon. Yes, Mother, I am. I'm chronologically spot on – after all, I *am* the first wife.' She tilted her head to one side. 'What's wrong with that? It's a fancy dress party – it's all in good fun.'

'Are you out of your mind?' spluttered Jennifer. 'You'll be a laughing stock.'

'No I won't. If anyone's laughing, it will be me.' She looked at the girls approvingly. 'You look terrific, girls. If you're ready, we should get going, the car's outside.'

'I think you look brilliant, Mrs Keating.'

'Thank you, Katy.'

'Fantastic,' added Emma.

'Now come along. Mother, will you be all right?'

Jennifer harrumphed loudly. 'Of course I'll be all right. It's you who needs your head checked.'

Downstairs, standing in the hallway, the girls watched as Charlotte descended the stairs, followed by Candy, who was looking mutinous.

'She looks amazing, doesn't she? Who'd have thought it?' whispered Emma.

It was true. Charlotte Keating was a very good-looking woman. She had inherited her mother's pale skin and black hair, which tonight was caught up gracefully in a Spanish headdress from which a black lace mantilla flowed. Her dress, which was in period, was fitted with a billowing skirt and made her already slim figure look even more dramatic. The black corset top accented the pearly white skin of her décolletage and arms, which were tantalisingly covered by a sheer veil of black chiffon. The whole effect was both dramatic and startlingly elegant.

'She looks better than any of us,' Katy agreed wonderingly.

As Charlotte picked up her black pearl-encrusted evening bag from a chair, she checked for her keys and then hurried the girls out and into the waiting chauffeur-driven car.

'Hurry up, Candy,' she said to her daughter, who was taking a last, lingering look in the hall mirror.

'All right, all right, I'm coming.' She brushed past her mother angrily. 'Gran was right,' she hissed at her. 'You look like a crow. Why do you always have to get it so wrong?'

Charlotte took a deep breath and slid into the front seat of the car. She had been looking forward to the party, but now she wasn't so sure. Perhaps her mother was right after all. Maybe it was a mistake to go. But why? She and Ossie had a perfectly civilised post-marital relationship – everybody knew that. She was genuinely happy for him, for his new relationship. She only wished her daughter, and indeed her mother, could be too.

'What do you mean, he's in property?' her mother had asked archly after Charlotte had introduced Ossie to her parents all those years ago. 'He doesn't even have a house, he only rents that place he's in.'

'He's investing in property, speculating. He'll have a house of his own soon, it's just that now he has to spread the risk on other stuff, offices and things.'

'He's not right for you, Charlotte. Mark my words, he'll lead you a merry dance, a chap like that. I know the type well. Social climbers, want to marry the perfect girl so they can run a perfect house and provide a perfect family for them to cover up their own inadequacies. Then the minute they make the big time, they're off without so much as a backward look. You won't listen to me, I know, you've got that stubborn look on your face, but if you marry that chap you'll be throwing yourself away. Remember, Charlotte – origins will out.'

'Your mother's right – for once.' Her father had looked up from *The Irish Field* he was studying intently. 'He's not our type – not yours either.'

And that was all that had been said on the matter.

But it was too late. Charlotte was already in love with the funny, witty, larger-than-life character who was, as her parents pointed out, so unlike anyone she had ever met before.

Up until then, her life had been an orderly, diligent affair that ran mostly as it was meant to. She had grown up, along with her two older brothers, on the stud farm in Kildare, an hour or so from Dublin. Secondary school was spent boarding at an exclusive convent where she had excelled at sports and made many good friends. This was followed, despite protestations (her parents had insisted) by a stint in finishing school at St Mary's Ascot.

After school, she had applied successfully for a post as a trainee estate agent in Dublin, and it was there, showing one of her first properties, that she had encountered Ossie Keating.

'Just what do you think you're doing?' she had whispered angrily, anxious not to attract attention from other viewers inspecting the three-storey-over-basement house.

The tall young man with brown wavy hair a shade too long, wearing a camel-hair coat over jeans and shiny, pointy-toed boots, took not a jot of notice of her. He continued to pull at and eventually removed a large chunk of damp wallpaper and held it up for inspection. 'See?' he grinned infuriatingly. 'Rot – and lots of it,' he added loudly. 'You'd need plenty of dosh and a builder who owes you more than one favour to get this place anywhere close to liveable. It's way overpriced.' Then, with a nod and a further dismissive glance around the property, he had disappeared, and most of the other viewers had promptly followed.

Charlotte had been livid. The ignorant, arrogant oaf! She checked her clipboard for his name. Ossie Keating. Sure, the house was a bit run down – a lot run down, actually; it hadn't been lived in for over twenty years – but the proportions were wonderful and its location in the old world, elegant Wellington Square, so close to town, was second to none. At £120,000, it was a seriously good buy. The auction was the following week.

Despite the recession, there was a fair amount of interest in the property, and bidding began briskly with three eager parties. Charlotte, sitting beside the auctioneer, looking neat and composed in her pleated skirt and Laura Ashley blouse, was keeping written track of bids. It went quickly to reserve price and then on to £140,000, where two parties dropped out and the remaining bidder waited expectantly for the auctioneer to close the deal. Then another bidder entered the fray. As the price reached £150,000, the property was proclaimed sold. Charlotte looked up from her notes to inspect the buyer. He was standing at the back of the room leaning against the wall, wearing his camel-hair coat and a cheeky grin. He waved up at her. It was none other than Ossie Keating.

'Have a drink with me,' he said to her after everybody had shaken hands and Ossie had signed the various deeds of sale. 'I think this calls for a celebration, and I don't have anyone else to celebrate with right now.' He'd looked at her expectantly.

'I have to get back to the office to finish the rest of the paperwork,' Charlotte had said.

'No need, Lottie,' her boss said, happy at the unexpectedly high price they had achieved. 'Go right ahead. See you tomorrow.'

'Allow me to introduce myself,' he had said with mock gallantry. 'Oswald Keating. Delighted to make your acquaintance. And you are . . .?' He held out his hand.

'Charlotte Searson.' She took his hand and he shook hers firmly.

'Well, Charlotte Searson, you shouldn't allow your boss to call you Lottie.'

'Why not?' she had asked.

'Because you're definitely a Charlotte.'

They had gone for a drink in the nearby Shelbourne Hotel, and before she left to go home, Charlotte had agreed to have dinner with him the following Friday.

He took her to a good restaurant in an upmarket hotel. Charlotte was nervous and shy, but Ossie was engaging company and she soon found her natural reserve disappearing as she laughed at his stories and escapades. He was generous too, and always paid in cash and tipped heavily. He was well known in these restaurants and the waiters and maître d's were always happy to see him and greeted him warmly, sometimes, Charlotte felt, with overfamiliarity. After dinner, they would sometimes go to a nightclub, where more people would greet him, and there would be shouts of laughter and winks from his mates.

Her parents kept a house in town, on nearby Merrion Square, and Charlotte had a flat in the basement. Ossie had been impressed. She had always taken her upbringing for granted, but with Ossie, she began to see it through new eyes. After two months of dating, she had introduced him to her parents, who had been polite – overly polite. Charlotte knew immediately what that meant – they didn't approve.

Thankfully, Ossie seemed unaware of the undercurrent and was his usual laid-back self. He had dressed up for the occasion without any prompting on her part and wore a pair of dark green corduroys with suede laced-up shoes. His shirt was brushed cotton and checked and his jacket was a bright green and brown tweed. A red tie covered in horseshoes completed the outfit. He'd even had a haircut. Looking at him, he could have been auditioning for a part in *The Irish R.M.*, and Charlotte's heart went out to him. She'd have preferred if he'd worn his jeans and cowboy boots, but clearly he had gone to great trouble on her behalf and she told him he looked terrific.

'Only the best for my girl,' he'd winked at her. 'Told you I cleaned up nice, didn't I?'

He was chatty and respectful to her parents and complimented her mother heartily on the pheasant served at lunch.

'Nice place you have here.' He waved his knife to illustrate his enthusiasm, and Charlotte cringed inwardly as she saw her mother all but flinch. 'Charlotte tells me you're big into horses, Mr Searson,' he went on, chewing rather excessively, Charlotte noticed for the first time. 'I'm a fan myself. Got an eye for a good filly.' He winked at Charlotte.

'I've bred some of the best bloodstock in Europe, yes,' her father said pleasantly.

After coffee, Charlotte said they had to go, otherwise they would hit all the Sunday evening traffic.

The next morning, Charlotte rang her mother to thank her for lunch. No mention was made of Ossie. Hating herself for it, Charlotte couldn't help asking.

'Well, what did you think of him, Mummy?'

There was the briefest of pauses. 'Revolting. And your father agrees with me. He said there'd be no use telling you, but you know me, Charlotte, I'm your mother and I'm not one to mince words. You're obviously in the grip of some sort of sexual excitement or something, but I would strongly advise you to look elsewhere. Good God, Charlotte, his table manners alone are appalling and he was dressed like a bookie, for heaven's sakes.'

For the first time in her life, but not the last, Charlotte had hung up the phone on her. Her hands were trembling.

Her mother had hit on at least one home truth. Charlotte was having ecstatically satisfying sex, and was enjoying every delicious minute of it.

Ossie noticed how subdued she was in the following days. 'They don't like me, do they, your folks?'

When she had protested, he silenced her with a kiss and seemed not at all put out about the situation. 'Don't worry about it, babe. When they see us surrounded by half a dozen kids and all the millions I'm going to make, they'll know you made the right choice.'

'What?' Charlotte almost dropped the cup of coffee she had just poured.

'You heard me.' He stood in front of her, smiling, confident. 'You *are* going to marry me, aren't you?'

'Ossie . . . I . . .'

He took the cup from her hand and placed it on the counter behind her. 'Because if you don't . . .'

Charlotte gasped as his hands found their way under her skirt and reached up until they had found her panties, which were then unceremoniously pulled off. 'Because if you don't,' he was lifting her onto the countertop and pushing himself between her legs, 'I'm going to have to tell your parents what a naughty little convent girl you really are.' He was holding her hair back and kissing her neck, undoing his jeans with his free hand.

'Won't I, Miss Searson?' He opened her blouse, unhooked her bra, and flicked his tongue lightly across her nipple. 'Well?'

'Oh yes!' Charlotte murmured, winding her arms around him. 'Yes, Ossie, yes, yes, yes.'

* * *

The wedding was an elegant affair, held, of course, at home, on the stud farm. They were married in the little village church, where Charlotte and her father arrived in a horse-drawn carriage.

Afterwards, three hundred and fifty guests partied long into the night in a vast, chiffon-lined marquee and the newly-weds made their getaway to Dublin, from where they flew to London and then on to an island-hopping tour of the Caribbean.

They arrived back three weeks later, sunburned and sated, to Charlotte's flat, where she set about making them a late-night snack before going to bed. But Ossie had a surprise in store for her.

'Don't unpack just yet, Mrs Keating,' he said. 'There's something I want to show you.' He collected his car and she slipped into the front seat as he drove off.

'What on earth is all this about?'

'Wait and see.' He turned into Wellington Square, in darkness apart from the street lights and a few night lights that shone from elegant sash windows.

'Remember I told you yesterday I got the go-ahead to develop the Cabinteely site?'

'Yes.'

'Well, it means I won't have to turn this place into flats like I was going to.' He pulled up outside number 42. 'It's all yours, Mrs Keating. It may be a wreck, but if you'd care to take on the task of turning it into the elegant family home for us that I know you would, money will not be an object.'

'Oh, Ossie, really? Really and truly?'

'It's all yours, Charlotte. That's the first bit of good news you can give those disapproving parents of yours!'

So she did. It took two long years while number 42 was gutted and painstakingly rebuilt, and once the builders had finished, Charlotte went to work. Six months later, a home that spoke of generations of good taste welcomed its new owners. For once, her mother had nothing negative to say – after all, she had been consulted and much involved in the decorating project.

Nine months after they had moved in, almost to the day, their daughter was born.

'What about Candice?' Charlotte asked, cradling her newborn while Ossie cracked open the champagne.

'Call her whatever you like, darling,' he beamed, looking proudly down at the small pink face that hiccupped loudly at him. 'She'll always be Princess to me.'

Those were the happiest times, Charlotte always thought later. She had relished homemaking and looking after Ossie and their little daughter and ran a fabulous house. Nothing fazed her. No last-minute surprise sprung by Ossie that he had to entertain a dozen people at short notice or throw a party for such-and-such was a bother. Charlotte came from a long line of capable, confident women and had the upbringing to match. Their parties, when they threw them, were the talk of the country – for all the right reasons.

All the while, Ossie's property interests flourished and he made more and more money. He even won her parents over, bit by bit, particularly when he bought his first racehorse. Trips to Cheltenham, Royal Ascot and local courses were a regular part of their calendar, and now they were doing it in the best corporate style.

The fact was, it was impossible to insult Ossie. He took everything in great good humour whether or not it was intended as such. He was clever too, and slowly but surely, the flash clothes were replaced by more subdued, stylish ones and his table manners and sometimes raucous behaviour were modulated. When he appeared one day, ready to take them to the Grand National, sporting a Barbour jacket, trilby and racing glasses, Jennifer murmured to her daughter, 'I've seen it all now. Who'd have thought it?'

Charlotte hunted every season, as she always had, until

one cold, unforgiving November day, when she had the fall that preceded her first miscarriage, and the four that were to follow.

Ossie was marvellous. No one could have been better to her, more concerned, more understanding, but the loss, the desperate, fluttering hopes that were dashed time and time again, left Charlotte bereft in a way she could never have anticipated.

She blamed herself constantly and never got on a horse again. Instead, she threw herself even more into her role as the perfect wife, doing course after course, fund-raising for endless charities and entertaining royally for the husband she felt, but couldn't bear to acknowledge, slipping slowly but surely away from her.

She didn't blame him. Ossie had always wanted a big family and had never made any secret of it – nor had she. He was larger than life himself and never happier than when he was organising and amusing great crowds of people. Ossie was a provider, a fixer, a builder of empires. It did more to him than he knew that he couldn't help, fix or provide the one thing they both longed for.

Eventually, she was advised to stop trying for the sake of her health, both physical and psychological, and she reluctantly agreed to have her tubes tied. By that stage it didn't matter. Something inside her, something nurturing, life-giving and hopeful, had already withered away.

It was in May 2004, shortly before their twentieth wedding anniversary, that Ossie told her that he was leaving her, that he had met someone else and was in love. Charlotte sat down and listened as a great vacuum inside threatened to consume her. She took deep breaths and resolved not to make a scene. She sat up straight in her chair and folded her hands on her lap, remembering from somewhere in the dim and distant past a voice telling her that deportment was everything, even in the most unlikely of situations.

'I see,' she said quietly. 'When will you be leaving?'

Ossie looked uncomfortable. 'Well, over the next couple of days. I thought . . . that is, we have to talk to Candice, explain it to her.'

'Yes, yes we do. They say it's better for both parents to sit down and talk about . . . it. Although I think I'll leave most of the talking to you, if that's all right. I – I wouldn't really know what to say.'

'Charlotte, please.' Ossie looked wretched. 'I never meant for this to happen. I never meant to hurt you. You've always been a wonderful wife and mother. We've just grown apart. Things move on – life, people move on.' He looked at her hopefully.

'It certainly would appear so.'

'Look, I know you must be angry with me, hurt. You have every right to scream at me. Please, say something.'

'I think you know by now that's not my style,' Charlotte said quietly. 'But I will say this – if you're going, I'd like you to leave now, tonight.' She had to stop herself from offering, out of habit and despite the roaring in her ears, *Would you like me to pack for you?*

'But—'

'Tonight, Ossie. That's all I'm asking.'

He sighed deeply. 'Whatever you say.' He got up from his chair. 'Don't you even want to know who she is?' He seemed puzzled, unsure now.

'I imagine I'll find out in good time.' Charlotte gave a little smile. 'What's important now is that we tell Candice. I'll go into the kitchen and make some coffee. You'd better call her down.'

In the kitchen, she went mechanically about her task, grinding fresh beans, putting them into the coffee-maker and watching the dark liquid filter through as if she was seeing it for the first time, a thing of wonder. She poured three mugs, adding vanilla essence to Ossie's, just the way he liked it.

Then she sat down and sipped her coffee and watched as Ossie appeared at the door, followed by Candice, looking put out to have been dragged away from her bedroom, her iPod and her endless emails. And then the surreal scene began to unfold as Ossie haltingly began telling Candice how much they both loved her.

'Princess, you know how I – how much we both – love you, don't you?' he looked at her beseechingly.

He didn't get any further. The expression on Candice's sixteen-year-old face said it all – a flicker of bewilderment, followed closely by horror, then disgust. 'You're getting a divorce, aren't you?'

'Princess, please, let me explain.'

'Darling.' Charlotte reached out for her hand across the table, which was instantly snatched back. 'Let Daddy talk for a minute.'

'There's someone else, isn't there?' Her eyes were blazing. 'You've met someone else and now you're leaving us.'

'Please, Princess, just let me—'

'Shut up!' she shouted, jumping up from the table. 'Shut up! I don't want to hear this.'

'Please, Candy.' Charlotte was appalled. 'Please sit down and listen.'

'To what, exactly? How much you love me, blah, blah, yeah, right. How people grow apart? Give me a fucking break. I've heard it all before. I watch television. I know how the script goes.' She was shivering now.

'Please, Princess.'

'Stop calling me Princess – I hate it. I hate you both!'

Charlotte and Ossie watched immobilised, frozen as their daughter fell apart.

'And you,' she spat at Ossie. 'Don't think I don't know about these things. You've been seeing someone, haven't you? Sleeping with some . . . some *slut* and you haven't even got the guts to come out and say it!'

'Candy, that's enough!' Charlotte's voice was sharper than

she intended, but she could hardly take in the scene of horror that was unfolding.

'Who is she? Who is she?' Candy screamed.

Ossie sat speechless, stricken. His mouth opened but no words came out.

'I knew it. I just knew it. You've been different. You've been dressing funny and using stupid trendy words. You think you're so cool, don't you? Well, you're pathetic. Just a pathetic old man having filthy sex with some tart. Well go on, go! I never want to see you again! And don't think you're any better!' She regarded Charlotte with utter contempt. 'This is all your fault! I bet you never even noticed anything. You're always so busy playing Mrs Perfect. Doing your stupid charity stuff and courses and telling me how I should behave. Well it hasn't got you very far, has it?'

Ossie tried one more time, getting up awkwardly to reach for her.

She backed away from him as if he were about to strike her. 'Don't come near me! Don't touch me! Don't you even dare try.' Tears were pouring down her face. 'You disgust me!'

And with that she ran from the kitchen, up the stairs and into her room, where they heard the door slam and the thumping sound of music begin. Charlotte looked at her husband as he sat with his head in his hands and took a shuddering breath.

'It was never going to be easy,' she said quietly. 'She adores you, she always has. It's hard for her. You're her knight in shining armour. And you indulged her dreadfully. We both did.'

He looked at her, still shocked and numb. 'I thought I was just loving her. She was all I . . . all we had.' His voice caught.

'Don't, Ossie.' Charlotte felt the twist of pain begin. 'Not now.'

'What will we do?' He seemed helpless.

Charlotte sighed. 'I think it's best if you go now. Take an overnight bag; you can get the rest of your things later. I'll talk to her when she's calmed down. It'll take a while, but she'll come around.'

'She hates me.'

'No, she doesn't. She adores you. That's the problem.'

Charlotte sat and listened as her husband went upstairs, packed a case and came back down to her.

'Charlotte?'

'Yes?'

'You know the house is yours, don't you? I would never . . .'

'Thank you, Ossie, I appreciate that. I suppose the lawyers will sort out everything else.'

'You won't want for anything – ever. You have my word on that.' And then he turned and walked down the hall and out of her life.

Outside, she heard the gravel crunch as he drove away. She poured herself another cup of coffee and sat down again, moulding her hands against the cup for warmth, hardly noticing the trembling in her fingers.

Had she somehow always known this day would come? Was that why she was so calm, so controlled? Or was she in shock? Why, at this moment, when this bombshell had been dropped in their lives, why was it her daughter and not her who was behaving like the wronged wife?

Later, as Charlotte wearily made for bed, she stood outside her daughter's bedroom, which was now silent, and knocked gently. 'Candy? Can I come in?'

There was a shuffle, and then the door opened. Candy stood there in her pink pyjamas, clutching her favourite teddy. Against her white, blotchy, woebegone face, her freckles stood out more than ever, and her eyes, red from crying, regarded Charlotte with accusation. She looked about twelve years old. Seeing her, Charlotte's heart constricted.

'I know this seems awful now, but I promise you, we'll be

all right, really we will. Daddy adores you. You'll always come first in his life, whatever happens. You're the most important person in both our lives. Nothing will ever change that.'

Candy looked at her mutely.

'Try and get some sleep, darling. We'll talk about it in the morning.'

'There's nothing to talk about, is there?' Her tone was flat, matter-of-fact, but Charlotte could see the pain in her eyes. 'He's gone. And,' she added, with a sudden look of loathing, 'I bet you never even tried to stop him.' With that, the door closed.

In her room, Charlotte undressed, put away her clothes and cleaned her face. Looking at that face in the mirror, she marvelled that it could seem so normal, so unchanged, when inside she felt as if an earthquake had struck, destroying the familiar landscape she held so dear and rearranging it with jagged, harsh cracks and ridges she could no longer recognise or negotiate.

She climbed into bed, turned off the light and lay very still, knowing with sudden clarity that this must be her destiny – to be alone and to try with every fibre of her being to make that aloneness bearable, endurable. Most of all, to convince her stricken, terrified daughter that life as she knew it would go on, would continue to be full of new and exciting adventures, and that her father, wherever he might go and whoever he might be with, would always provide a life that would include her, first and foremost.

It was then that she allowed herself to cry, great, heaving sobs that wracked her body. She cried for herself, for Ossie and for Candy. For her broken dreams and for her lost babies, and most of all she cried because yet again, her mother had been proved right.

Sometime towards early morning, she fell into an exhausted sleep. When she awoke at half past eight, she was resolved. Whatever it took, however monumentally difficult it might be, she was going to make sure this divorce would be amicable and civilised. She would be the perfect ex-wife. There would be no drama, no self-pity, no recriminations. Satisfied that she had another sensible task to devote herself to, Charlotte showered, put on her minimal make-up and dressed briskly. She listened briefly at Candy's door, from which there was no sound, and decided to let her sleep or keep to herself for as long as it took for her to appear. Then she went down to the kitchen and made herself some strong coffee and toast. She would need fortification, she reflected, to get through today, and a good breakfast had always stood her in good stead. Then, taking a deep breath, she prepared for the first, most daunting of the tasks that lay ahead. Picking up the phone, she dialled and waited for an answer.

'Mummy, she said, 'there's something I have to tell you.'

In the event, Jennifer's reaction had been restrained and as sympathetic as she could manage. Her concern, along with Charlotte's father, had been the effect this would have on Candice.

Eventually, of course, things did settle down. The separation and divorce moved smoothly enough and everyone breathed a sigh of relief when the last Is were dotted and the Ts crossed. Her parents took her and Candy to lunch in Guilbaud's when it was all final.

'At least you've got the house,' Jennifer said.

'That was never in question.'

'You never know. Make sure you hold on to it. These days they can go back at any time and try to change arrangements, you know.'

'Thank you, Mummy, but let's discuss something else for a change, hmm?' Charlotte said lightly.

In the following months, Ossie became Enemy Number One in Jennifer's books. It was more than just motherly support for her newly single daughter, Charlotte suddenly realised. Over the years, Jennifer had become fond of Ossie. She had let her guard down with him. She had also come to enjoy the privileges associated with having a multimillionaire son-in-law, not least of which was talking about him to her friends. In a flash of insight, Charlotte understood that her mother, of all people, was feeling deserted and abandoned too, and unlike her daughter or granddaughter, she made no bones about the fact that Ossie Keating had made a big mistake in taking this course of action – one that, she, Jennifer, of course, had predicted many years ago.

Two years after the divorce, Charlotte's father had died of a heart attack. Jennifer had found him, thinking him to be dozing in his chair, his half-moon reading glasses perched on the end of his nose, a copy of *The Irish Field* on his lap and an unfinished tumbler of whiskey on the table beside him. It was only when she tried to rouse him and his two beloved Jack Russells, Bonnie and Clyde, sitting at his feet in front of the fire had begun to howl that she realised he was gone.

Ossie had been wonderful. He had been there at the funeral, alone, standing discreetly in the pew behind Candy and Charlotte. Afterwards, he had offered to and gladly taken on the monumental task of selling the stud farm and disposing of the bloodstock, making sure every mare and foal fetched their rightful market price. This was almost too much for Jennifer to bear, but Charlotte was intensely grateful to him. By the time the estate was finalised, Jennifer was left a very wealthy widow. She came to stay with Charlotte, along with the dogs, for six weeks, and despite her protestations, Charlotte knew she was glad of the invitation.

'I refuse to be a burden to anyone. I'm quite capable of managing on my own, you know.'

'Of course we know that, Mummy. It's just until you get used to things. Then we can find you somewhere nice of your own.'

It turned out to be a happy arrangement, more so than anyone could have imagined. When Charlotte discussed the possibility of turning the basement into a separate apartment for Jennifer with Ossie, he declared it to be a marvellous idea and once again the builders were brought in to number 42.

Jennifer pretended to be furious when the idea was put to her.

'Don't be ridiculous, Charlotte! All mothers and daughters irritate the pants off each other. I'd drive you mad, and you me.'

It was only when Candy appealed to her that she made a great show of relenting.

'Please, Gran, for me? I'd love to have you here in the basement, and you'll hardly know Mum is in the house. We can all meet up for Sunday lunch or by appointment.'

Charlotte hid a smile as she saw her mother wrestle with the invitation she was dying to accept.

'Candy's right, Mummy. It would be good for her, and for me.'

'What about the dogs?' Jennifer was suspicious.

'Naturally you can have the dogs. Candy and I love dogs, you know that. The only reason I never had one in the house was because Ossie wasn't keen on them.'

'Well, as long as we all live independently and I have my own separate entrance to come and go through, and my own house rules . . .'

'Absolutely.'

'I suppose we could give it a try. But I won't be beholden to anyone, Charlotte. I'll pay my own way. I'm a very independent woman.'

'Of course, Mummy. Let's just see how it goes.'

And it went very well. The basement was converted into two bedrooms, a sitting room with a small dining area and a small, cosy kitchen with its own bright red Aga. This was extended to include a small conservatory leading onto a private patio where Jennifer could continue to enjoy her gardening. And every Sunday, as arranged, they met for lunch either upstairs, when it was Charlotte's turn, or downstairs when Jennifer cooked, and, as it turned out, on many other days of the week as well.

Charlotte realised with a start that they were almost there. The car had sped along the motorway as she was lost in thought, and the girls had been chattering away in the back – now, they couldn't be more than five minutes away. Suddenly, for no reason at all, she felt a fluttering begin in her stomach.

'Will we be on TV?' Katy was asking. 'And how will we know? My mum is dying to see anything and she warned me to text her.'

'If you are,' Charlotte said, 'it will probably be tomorrow. I imagine they'll do a slot on one of the entertainment programmes, you know the ones?'

'Maybe I'll finally be discovered,' Emma said. 'My sister's dead jealous.'

Moments later, they turned off the motorway and onto a slip road that climbed steadily, then another left turn, where up ahead, an impressive pair of wrought iron gates came into view.

'Look!' cried Katy. 'TV cameras at the gate, and loads of paparazzi.'

She was right. As they turned through the gates of Windsor Hall and past the pretty gate lodge, a flurry of flashes went off – but that was just for starters.

Charlotte knew Ossie never did things by half, but this was extraordinary.

Along the half mile leading up to the old manor house, the drive was lined on either side with blazing effigies of martyrs, interspersed with the odd faux head on a pike, producing squeals of horror from the girls.

They drew to a halt a little way before the house as a dark figure emerged in medieval dress. 'No cars beyond this point, order of the King.' Another three figures appeared and opened the car doors. 'From here, my ladies, you will journey by sedan chair.'

Charlotte and the girls emerged and were guided to separate sedan chairs, which were duly lifted and transported the remaining distance, where they were set down.

'Ready girls?' Charlotte smiled at their barely contained excitement. Even Candy, who was trying to be nonchalant, was goggle-eyed. As they were ushered into the house, still more people were arriving on horseback.

They were escorted through the main hall on through to the back of the house, where steps led down to french doors thrown open into the biggest marquee Charlotte had ever seen. It must have been the size of a football pitch, and brilliantly disguised as a great medieval hall. It was simply spectacular – there was no other word for it. Stepping into it, one was transported into another world. Everywhere, from elaborate table arrangements to garlands hung from the walls and ceilings, were the fabled white Tudor roses. Lute players strolled among guests, acrobats formed human pyramids, tumblers frolicked and jesters in lurid colours played to their delighted court. Tables groaned with every kind of food, dwarfed by whole boars and even swans.

'Some refreshment, my lady?' a rather embarrassed waiter in hose smiled at her, proffering a selection of drinks from his tray. Charlotte avoided the mead and asked instead for champagne, although there were no glasses of it to be seen. When the waiter indicated a pewter tumbler, she laughed. Only Ossie would provide pints of champagne. She looked around. The girls had already deserted her, and there was no sign of their host. Tumbler in hand, she made to enter the fray. She was stopped by the royal proclaimer, who shouted loudly, 'My lords and ladies, Her Majesty, the dowager queen,

Catherine of Aragon!' Before she could move any further, at least three photographers were clamouring for a shot. She posed and smiled obligingly and then excused herself as she saw the TV cameras and crew about to bear down.

'Charlotte!' A male voice greeted her and laughed loudly. 'What a fabulous outfit. Wonderful choice, my darling. You look amazing!'

Charlotte recognised a familiar voice, although it took her a second or two to work out who was disguised as the elegant figure of Sir Francis Drake. She recognised a good friend of Ossie's, Philip Carter, who she was very fond of. 'I can return the compliment, Phil. I must say, you're looking very dashing yourself. Back from your travels?'

'Sent to singe the King of Spain's beard and all that!' he chuckled. 'Actually I'm just back from a spot of golf in Portugal, but close enough. Quite a production, this, isn't it?'

'I'll say. Speaking of which, where is Ossie? Have you seen him?'

'Oh, the King is not here to greet the guests, Charlotte. We're here to greet *him*. In fact, according to my source, they should be appearing any moment now. Come with me.'

Charlotte followed him towards the back of the marquee, where everyone was heading. Outside was just as spectacular. Bonfires and braziers blazed, roasting ox, pigs and sheep.

'Better behave yourself,' said Phil, pointing at an executioner at his station looking menacingly out at the crowd.

'If I haven't lost my head by now,' Charlotte grinned, 'I think I'm probably safe. I'm much more likely to end up over there.' She pointed to a set of stocks, where an old hag was being pelted by her husband.

'In the stocks? Why?'

'According to my mother, my choice of outfit will make me a laughing stock. Let's just say she didn't approve.'

'I think it's a marvellous choice – very droll – and Ossie will think it's hilarious.'

'I hope so.' Charlotte felt suddenly nervous.

'Speaking of losing heads,' Phil scowled, looking serious, 'we all think he's off his rocker, you know. It was mad enough to leave you, but this . . . this girl, well . . .'

'That's kind of you to say so Phil, but it's all water under the bridge now, really, and I'm glad Ossie's happy.'

'What about you, Charlotte?' He looked at her keenly. 'Anyone special in your life?'

'Not at present, no,' she said lightly.

'There should be. If it wasn't for Jackie,' he said, referring to his long-time wife, 'I'd be in there like a shot!'

'No you wouldn't,' Charlotte laughed. 'You're incorrigible, but thank you.'

Suddenly a loud gong boomed and a voice called for silence. 'My lords and ladies, prepare for the imminent arrival of His Majesty, the King!'

As a fanfare of trumpets went up, Charlotte gazed, along with everyone else, as her ex-husband, dressed as Henry VIII, held out his hand to escort his rather younger queen.

As they processed regally towards the marquee, the TV crews and cameras fought for coverage. Taking their place at the head of the top table, Ossie welcomed his guests and ordered the dining to commence: 'Eat, drink and be merry, my friends!'

Wandering to her table, Charlotte was glad to see she was seated with Phil and Jackie. As far as she could see, the top table where Ossie and Shalom, his partner, sat was mostly made up of celebrities. She recognised one newsreader, several actors, a few members of Viper and what she supposed to be many models. Ossie's new friends seemed to be made up entirely of Shalom's set. Charlotte certainly didn't spot any familiar faces among them. As she chatted to Jackie on her left, who was eager to catch up with her, Phil, on her other side, nudged her. 'Interesting choice of costume for Ossie's queen, don't you think?' he murmured. 'She's dressed as Jane

Seymour, beloved wife number *three*, when technically speaking, she should have come as Anne Boleyn.'

'Perhaps,' Charlotte grinned, 'she was being sensitive to the implications.'

'What?' Jackie asked. 'Losing her head? Oh, I don't think so. Far too late for that,' she giggled.

'Hey, wench! Over here!'

Carla scowled as Pino thrust a platter of poached salmon at her. 'How's it going?'

'Hideously well, as far as one can tell. At least there haven't been any catastrophes yet. Although there's way too much food. I've never seen anything like it.'

'At least we didn't have to worry about the big stuff. Can you imagine?'

'No, I can't. I thought hiring a "historical culinary expert" sounded off the wall, but looking at those medieval barbeques, I'm very glad they did. There are whole animals being roasted out there!'

'A truly medieval barnyard, I believe,' Pino agreed. 'Terrible waste, though. There's no way this crowd will get through it.'

'No, but I know of at least three homeless shelters who'll be only too thrilled to take the leftovers, and as it's part of our contract to clear away *everything*, I've organised for the catering trucks to drop them off tonight.'

'Clever girl.' Pino looked at her admiringly. 'Now get going with that salmon, or the only hot thing will be you in that *very* delectable costume.'

Carla struggled up the stairs from the main kitchen, cursing her outfit, which was becoming unbearably sticky. Although it was November, the heating inside and outside had been a priority and she was beginning to perspire profusely. In the marquee, she deposited the salmon on the main banqueting table and made her way outside for a breath of fresh air.

Fishing in her voluminous skirts for the pocket she had been relieved to find, she extracted her cigarettes and lit up. From here, she was able to watch what was going on inside relatively unobserved. The main course was now pretty much winding up and the staff were busy taking away plates from diners who were obviously working on getting plastered. Gallons of the finest wines and champagnes had been freely flowing all night, and there was no sign of things letting up. There was only the desserts to go, followed by coffee and liqueurs, and then the dancing would begin. By that stage, the clearing up would be in full swing and the worst would be over. Carla smiled wryly. It sure was one hell of a party. She couldn't even begin to think how much it had cost this Ossie guy. He'd seemed nice enough when she'd been briefly introduced to him earlier, if a bit over the top. But then, anyone who wanted to dress up as an overweight medieval king had to have issues. Clearly spending the annual income of a small country on a fiftieth birthday party and inviting the national press and television stations to cover it said something – though quite what, Carla wasn't sure. She wasn't keen on his partner though. Sure, she was pretty in that fake, plastic kind of way. Earlier in the day, in her clingy velour tracksuit, airbrushed, perfect make-up and lacquered ringlets, she hadn't looked bad, but tonight, in that Tudor outfit, her breasts looked as if she'd stuffed a baby's bottom down her corset. And the name! Who in their right mind called themselves *Shalom*? Of course, Carla knew it meant 'peace', but that was pushing it. She was some 'piece' all right – piece of work, more like. Carla watched her now from her vantage point. She hadn't taken her eyes off Ossie all night, simpering and cooing at him, and like all men he was lapping it up. Typical, thought Carla. As long as their enormous egos were being stroked, men like Ossie were happy to bypass the other, considerably smaller parts of their anatomy, such as their brains.

'Carla!' The sharp voice made her jump. She wheeled around, fag in hand, to see Tanya regarding her coldly. Although she was in evening dress, Tanya was not, interestingly enough, dressed in party mode for the Tudors theme. Instead, she wore a strapless column of black silk jersey, which was strikingly simple and looked as if it cost a fortune.

'You are not being paid to stand around outside smoking. What are you thinking? Get back inside immediately. Dessert is about to be served and you should be in there supervising. I might remind you that you are representing Dominic's tonight, and that kind of behaviour is not what we expect from our staff, particularly when they're meant to be on duty at one of the most prestigious social events of the year.' She was almost quivering with anger.

'I was taking a break and getting some fresh air, that's all.' Carla finished her cigarette and stubbed it out under her foot, counting to ten slowly. 'Everything is perfectly under control.'

'Is that so?' Tanya's voice dripped sarcasm. 'Then perhaps you'd be good enough to ensure it remains that way. And if anything happens to that costume you're wearing, cleaning or repairing it will come out of your salary.' She turned on her heel and walked away.

Carla was furious. Who the hell did Tanya think she was? And why, oh why, had she caught her on the one and only five-minute break she had taken all evening? For some reason she couldn't work out, Tanya definitely seemed to have it in for her, and Carla's patience was running out. She didn't give a damn what Tanya thought of her, but she did enjoy working at Dominic's, and if Tanya had her way, Carla was pretty sure she'd have her fired in the morning. Carla couldn't understand what Dom saw in her. Tanya was overbearing, rude to the staff and clearly knew little or nothing about how to run a restaurant. Yet Dom, who had a first-rate training behind him, seemed to rely on her and trust her advice. It didn't make sense. Tanya was one of those women who bulldozed their way into a man's life and simply took over, and by all accounts that was what she was doing with Dom. They hadn't been together long, according to Astrid, but already Tanya had taken over Dom's apartment, reorganised his social life and had somehow persuaded him that her public-relations duties involved floating around the restaurant and generally getting in everybody's way, not to mention getting their backs up.

'Don't worry,' Astrid had said to Carla, 'it won't last for ever. She's determined to marry him. That's why she won't let him out of her sight. Once she's got the ring on her finger, she'll disappear to play Mrs Society Wife. Then she'll be out of our hair.'

For some reason, that hadn't made Carla feel any better.

Now, she hurried back inside, where, right on cue, Pino was lining up the desserts to coincide with what Carla hoped would be the final spectacle of the evening.

Medieval kings were apparently fond of a surprise pie, so a giant one had been duly constructed on Shalom's instructions. Instead of four and twenty blackbirds being sprung on an unsuspecting audience, a flock of fifty doves were to rise up out of the pie. This was greeted by great shouts and applause from the guests and followed by a well-known boy band weaving in and out of the tables, quite unsteadily at this stage, singing 'You Raise Me Up'.

As he sat watching it all unfold, Ossie was quite clearly delighted. Looking at him as he leaned over and kissed Shalom, Carla couldn't help smiling as she saw a girl at a nearby table, dressed as a young Queen Elizabeth, pretend to put her fingers down her throat in disgust for the benefit of her two friends, who giggled with delight.

Ossie rose to his feet and welcomed his guests as Shalom sat gazing up at him, hanging on his every word. He kept it short, thanking everyone for being with him to share his fiftieth birthday and congratulating Dominic's on providing such wonderful food for the event.

'But tonight isn't just about me,' he continued, looking down at Shalom, an expression of tenderness softening his face. 'I ask you all to raise your glasses to my partner, Shalom, who worked so hard to make tonight special for me,' he paused, 'and to the baby she and I are expecting next June. Who could have thought of a more perfect birthday gift? My darling, you are simply wonderful.'

As people raised their glasses and toasted their hosts, a round of applause broke out among some of the rowdier groups in the room.

At Charlotte's table, Jackie noted the pain that registered on her friend's face before she stapled a smile to it and raised her glass along with everybody else.

'You didn't know about this, did you?' she murmured sympathetically.

'No,' Charlotte replied, 'I didn't.'

'The bastard!' Jackie whispered furiously. 'That selfish, insensitive bastard. He should have told you first. I can't imagine what you must be feeling.' She quickly poured more champagne into Charlotte's glass, but Charlotte wasn't listening. She was watching, with horrified comprehension, as Candy, frozen to her seat for the announcement, now got up from the table and walked around until she stood in front of her father, then picked up the nearest plate of dessert and flung it straight into his face. As Shalom's mouth dropped open and she cringed backwards, Ossie, covered in what appeared to be pavlova, gasped in shock while a flurry of flashes went off to capture what was later widely agreed to have been the highlight of the night.

Jennifer was still watching television in the upstairs sitting room and enjoying a little nightcap when she heard the front door slam and footsteps clumping across the hallway. 'Charlotte?' she called. 'Surely you're not home this early?'

'It's me, Gran,' Candy said, pausing on the stairs.

'Candice? What are you doing back at this hour?' She checked her watch, which pointed to eleven p.m. 'Come in here at once!'

Candy sighed and trudged back downstairs and into the sitting room, where Jennifer was propped up in her favourite winged armchair.

'Is your mother with you? Where are the girls?'

'I left them behind. They're still there, at the party.'

'Did you tell them you were leaving?'

'No. I assume they'll have guessed as much though.' Candy plonked down onto a sofa.

'Well that wasn't very sensible, was it?'

'She's having a baby.' Candy looked mutinous, but Jennifer could tell tears were threatening.

'Well.' Jennifer sat up a little straighter in her chair. 'I can't say that comes as a huge surprise. Here.' She held out her glass to Candy. 'Be a dear and top me up, would you? I think I'm going to need some fortification before your mother gets back.'

'Me too.' Candy got up and filled two glasses, pouring herself a vodka and tonic. 'I only had one glass of champagne at the stupid party anyway.' She handed Jennifer her gin and tonic and sat back down, taking a mouthful of her drink.

'Do you mind, about this baby?' Jennifer regarded her shrewdly.

'Mind? It's disgusting. He's fifty, for heaven's sake.'

'That's not a deterrent, apparently. Anyway, that's his problem, not yours.'

'It'll be twenty, no, twenty-one years younger than me. It's obscene.'

'Precisely. You'll be far too busy having an exciting life of your own to even notice a baby. Just be thankful it isn't living *here* – then you'd know all about it. Take it from me, Candice, babies are extremely overrated. I know, I've had four of them.'

'That's it, though, isn't it?' Candy blurted. 'That's the end. He'll have loads of babies with *her* and he won't have any time for me.'

'Don't be ridiculous, Candice. Really, you're blowing this all out of proportion.

'Am I?'

'Yes. Babies are a novelty. The first one is a lovely fantasy until it arrives, and then it's bloody hard work. I can't imagine your father relishing sleepless nights and changing nappies – he's not that sort of man, not at any age. And this isn't his first baby – *you* were. Give him three months and he'll be tearing his hair out – and extremely grateful to have a daughter he can actually converse with.'

The first glimmer that disaster might yet be averted flickered in Candy's face. 'D'you really think so?'

'I'm sure of it. Now, if you take my advice,' Jennifer took a swig of her drink, 'you'll tell everyone you know that you're thrilled with the news.'

'It's a bit late for that.' Candy looked sheepish. 'I threw a plate of pavlova in his face. Everybody saw me.'

'You what?' Jennifer looked appalled.

'He announced it, when he was making his stupid speech, in front of all those people. I couldn't help it. I wanted to kill him. I wanted to wipe the smug look off her stupid face.'

'Well,' said Jennifer, inhaling deeply, 'I imagine you did that all right.'

'It was such a shock.'

'Yes, yes, I can see that.' Jennifer was thoughtful. 'What about your mother? What did *she* do?'

'I don't know. After I threw the pavlova at him, I ran out. There were loads of cars and drivers outside, I just got in one and came home.'

'I see.'

Candy started as they heard the front door open.

'That'll be your mother. We're in here,' Jennifer called to her.

Charlotte came in, looking pale and drawn minus her head-dress, which she carried under her arm. She flung it on the sofa. 'Candy,' she said, sitting down beside her daughter and putting an arm around her shoulders. 'I wish you hadn't run off like that. You gave me a terrible fright. Are you all right?'

'Of course she's all right, stop mollycoddling her. She's twenty, not ten years of age. Isn't that so, Candice?'

'It must have been an awful shock for you. I don't think Daddy thought it through very well, how to break the news.'

'What's new?' Jennifer was withering.

'Please, Mummy.' Charlotte gave Jennifer a warning look.

'Gran's right, Mum,' Candy sighed. 'I'm sorry I, um, over-reacted like that. It was silly of me. I'll apologise to Dad tomorrow.'

'You'll do no such thing!' Jennifer was adamant. 'Your mother will have a little talk with him, won't you, Charlotte? Just like Candice and I had a little talk before you came in, and we've decided it's very good news about this baby. At least that's the line we'll be taking with anyone who's nasty enough to enquire about it. Don't you agree, Charlotte?'

'Do I have a choice in the matter?'

'Candice, go up to bed and get out of that ridiculous costume. Everything will seem much better after a good night's sleep.' She proffered her cheek for a goodnight kiss. 'I might say the same applies to your mother,' she said, looking meaningfully at Charlotte, 'but first I'd like a word. So good-night, Candice dear, sleep tight.'

'Goodnight, Gran. And thanks.' Candice closed the door softly behind her.

'I need a drink.' Charlotte made for the drinks trolley and poured herself a brandy.

'I'm not surprised.' Jennifer looked at her keenly. 'How do you feel about it?'

'Ghastly, if I'm honest. I suppose I knew it was inevitable, but to announce it like that, it was such a shock, such a . . .'

'Slap in the face?'

Charlotte nodded miserably. 'Ossie always wanted a big family. Frankly, I'm surprised they waited as long as they have. I'd sort of steeled myself to expect it, but still . . . it hurts.'

'Ossie always wanted a big family with *you,* Charlotte,' Jennifer said gently but firmly. 'He may discover that children with this other creature will be *quite* a different kettle of fish. Very few women – none that *I* know, at any rate – have your talent for seemingly effortless yet exquisite homemaking. I'd wager Ossie's missing that more than he lets on.'

Charlotte smiled gratefully. 'Sometimes, Mother – not often, mind – you say just the right thing.'

'I have my moments.' Jennifer hauled herself out of her chair. 'Now, let's get to bed. I suspect we'll need to be on top of our game to deal with that daughter of yours tomorrow.'

Charlotte groaned. 'Oh, God, if you'd seen her . . .'

'I rather wish I had,' Jennifer said, chuckling.

In her bedroom, Charlotte undressed slowly, struggling to unhook herself from the elaborate corset-topped dress. It was funny, she thought, stepping out of it, it was the little things you missed a man for. Right now, she'd give anything to have someone undo her dress and help her out of it, laugh about the bizarre evening and climb into bed and cuddle up with.

Now she hung the dress up carefully on its special hanger and regarded it fondly. It was sentimental to have kept it all these years, but every time she had tried, she just hadn't had the heart to give it away. When the invitation came for the party, with the instructions for guests to come appropriately dressed as Tudors, Charlotte had immediately known what she would wear. While stylists everywhere were bombarded with requests from frantic guests the minute the invitations had landed and were scouring every theatre supply company in the country and beyond, Charlotte had simply unearthed her beautiful wedding dress, feeling a little thrill of satisfaction that she could still fit into it, and had it professionally dyed black. No one, not even Ossie, had recognised it. The dress had served her well on both occasions. Tomorrow, she resolved, she would take it to one of the charity shops. After all, she reasoned, wedding dresses, current *or* vintage, were not part and parcel of a divorced wife's wardrobe.

Collapsing into bed, Charlotte fell asleep almost immediately and dreamed of Catherine of Aragon, locked in the Tower, existing solely on pavlova pies.

After everything had been cleared away, the kitchens tidied up and the catering trucks sent off, stocked with leftover food for the shelters, Carla decided to go for a stroll. Apart from anything else, she needed to find a loo, and the car that would be taking her and Pino back to town wasn't due for another forty-five minutes. Pino was on his phone, presumably relating the events of the night in rapid Latvian to a friend, accompanied, not surprisingly, by bursts of laughter.

Making her way up from the basement, Carla found herself in the main hall of the house and paused, tilting her head to admire the soaring ceilings above her, with their ornate decorations, and the great sweep of curving staircase that rose ahead. Impulsively, she made her way upstairs, past regal portraits of men and women who regarded her haughtily. Presumably the ancestors, she guessed, although they looked far too formidable to belong to the Ossie guy or his consort, but hey, who knew? Popping her head around the doors of a few sumptuously decorated bedrooms that looked as if they had featured in the pages of a glossy interiors magazine, she kept going until she found a separate guest bathroom, hurried inside and locked the door.

What a night! She shook her head, thinking of the spectacular display of daughterly rage they had all been treated to, courtesy of the young Princess Elizabeth, who turned out to be Ossie Keating's only daughter – to date, that is. Clearly, her reaction to the news that she was about to have a baby half-brother or sister in her life didn't exactly thrill her, and considering the way the news had been delivered, Carla couldn't say she blamed her. It was a hell of a stunt to pull though. Ossie's face covered in pavlova had just about made everyone's night. After the gasps of shock, people had found it impossible to keep a straight face. It was just way too funny – although presumably not for the family involved. Still, she thought, straightening her skirt, washing her hands and splashing some cold water on her flushed face, that was life – the old had to make way for the new. Not that you'd know it as regards her *own* family, she scowled, remembering the angry scenes she had left behind her. She missed her brothers, and her father – but she wouldn't think about that now.

Instead, she regarded her reflection in the mirror and almost laughed out loud. With all the fuss and hard work, she had almost forgotten the costume she was wearing. Now, with her cheeks flushed from heat, tendrils of hair escaping to curl around her face and her breasts pushed up in the red silk corset lined at the neck with a white pleated silk ruffle, she could have taken her place beside any of the portraits she had passed adorning the staircase. Pino had been right – she looked just like a lusty medieval serving wench, straight out of central casting. It was a good look, she acknowledged, if you liked that kind of thing, though thoroughly impractical. Even coming up those stairs had left her fighting for breath, and her waist was cinched in so tightly it was all she could do to take in tiny gasps of air.

She had just dried her hands when the handle on the door

turned. 'Just a minute,' she called out, hoping it wasn't Tanya, following her around again. 'I'll be out in a sec.' Making sure she had left the bathroom just as she found it, down to straightening the hand towel with military precision, she made her exit.

For a moment, she thought she was alone, that whoever had turned the handle had gone away, and then she saw him leaning against the wall, glass of champagne in hand.

'Carla,' he said, straightening up and taking a step towards her.

'Dom,' she breathed, suddenly feeling both awkward and guilty. She hadn't known he was coming to the party.

'You look . . . gorgeous.' His eyes roved over her appreciatively, resting for a split second on her décolletage, which, she felt sure, was now suffused with the slow flush of embarrassment that had started in her cheeks. God, he looked sexy. He was in jeans, and the pale blue shirt open at the neck set off his dark skin beautifully. He pushed his hair back from his face and smiled, shaking his head slightly as if to clear it. He was obviously a little worse for wear. She'd never seen him even slightly tipsy in all her time at Dominic's. He was so adamant about professionalism, unlike some restaurateurs she had known in her time.

'I was just . . .' She paused, feeling beyond stupid. What was she doing? She didn't have to justify herself to anyone. She raised her eyes to his and saw only amusement, and something else, something warm that locked with her eyes and then flared between them.

'Just what?' He was grinning now, leaning towards her with a gorgeous, inviting, lopsided grin.

'I was just about to . . .' And then she did it. She couldn't help herself – she reached up and kissed him. She didn't think about it, she just did it, impulsively, and suddenly he was kissing her back, quite fiercely, one hand cradling her head, the other around her waist, pulling her closer. And she kept kissing him, just as he kept kissing her, as he moved backwards, taking her with him, until he had pulled her into one of the bedrooms she had passed, kicking the door shut with his foot. When he came up for air he flicked on the light.

'Christ, you're sexy,' he murmured in Italian, and the sound of it, of her native language, aroused her even more. She didn't care that she was in someone else's house, that she was in this ridiculous costume or even that he had a girlfriend – a girlfriend who was possibly searching for him at that very moment, prowling the house. All that mattered was that she was with him and he was kissing her.

Suddenly she gasped, laughing. 'Wait a minute. I can't breathe, really. This corset is so restricting.'

'Then let's do something about that,' he said, untying the silk bow that laced it together at the back, allowing the tightly boned material to give finally. She took a deep breath and gasped again as Dom's hand found her breast, cupping it, caressing it exquisitely, and he was kissing her again, kissing her neck, his thumb tracing her lips. And then his mouth trailed downwards, his tongue tracing circles on her skin, and then finally his lips closed on her nipple and he was sucking and licking and holding her, moulding her to him and she never wanted him to stop. And then—

'Dom?' The unmistakable voice called from the corridor. 'Dommy? Where are you?'

She froze as Dom wrenched his lips away. 'Shh,' he whispered, holding her still, and then the voice became fainter as its owner moved on down the corridor in her search. For a moment, they looked at one another, desire written all over their faces, and Dom pulled away abruptly. 'I'm sorry,' he said, running his hands through his now-dishevelled hair. 'That was unforgivable of me.'

'No, no,' she heard herself saying as she fumbled to haul her corset back to its original position. 'It was my fault. I shouldn't have. It was . . .' Oh God, this was awful, it was dreadful. It was agonisingly awkward and – worst of all – it was over. The glorious moment had been broken.

'Let me help you with that.' Dom was behind her. She could feel his hands trembling as he pulled the ribbon ties together, drawing them tighter. 'There,' he said, letting out a long breath. 'Not my finest example, but one of the advantages of having sisters is becoming adept at doing up tops.' He was trying to make light of it. That made it even worse, and Carla felt her face flame. He turned her around gently to face him and put his hand under her chin, tilting it until she met his eyes. 'I *am* sorry. You must believe me. And it most certainly was not your fault, it was mine, every bit of it. Will you forgive me?' He searched her face.

Carla pulled herself together. Tanya was his girlfriend, it was *her* he was interested in, and he was clearly embarrassed by what had happened. How could she have encouraged him to kiss her? He was the drunk one; *she* should have behaved better. 'Of course.' She forced herself to smile. 'There's nothing to forgive. These things happen. We're both adults. This has been quite a party and we've all had a lot of wine – don't give it another thought. I won't.' She was giving him her brightest, fakest smile now and willed him to go. She was still finding it hard to breathe and it had nothing to do with her corset.

He seemed reluctant to leave her, then opened the door softly, his eyes still locked on hers. 'Are you okay?' He seemed genuinely concerned.

'Sure. You'd better go.'

'It had nothing to do with the wine,' he said quietly. 'I want you to know that.' And then he closed the door behind him.

'Oh God,' she whispered to herself when he had gone. How could she have been so stupid? How could she even have tried to fool herself? She was crazy about him, and now he'd think she was just a slutty waitress who'd stuck her boobs out at him on purpose. 'Oh no,' she moaned, sitting on the bed, putting her face in her hands as tears ran down it. 'Why did I ruin everything?'

Dom hadn't been planning on attending the party – in fact, he'd been determined to avoid it at all costs, despite Tanya's protestations. But it had been a long week and at the last minute, satisfied that Dominic's final orders had left the kitchen, he had decided to jump in a taxi and have a look in, even if it *was* late. Judging by Tanya's incessant text messages, it was a spectacular event that absolutely *had* to be seen to be believed. At this stage, the formal dinner would be over, so he wouldn't have to sit through that, and it wouldn't hurt to have a few drinks and relax for a change – he'd been working like a dog. And, as Tanya was always reminding him, it was important to be seen at social events to keep up a high profile for the restaurant. It was the one area of contention between them: Dom absolutely refused to be a 'couple about town'. He believed that if the food was good enough and the atmosphere pleasant enough, Dominic's would attract the right clientele. But Tanya didn't give up easily and continued to pester him, and tonight, for a change, he had given in. In more ways than one, it turned out, with possibly disastrous consequences. What on earth had he been thinking? To follow Carla upstairs (well, not really follow, more trail helplessly after her, despite every warning bell that was sounding in his head), waiting until he could strategically bump into her, and then – well, he just couldn't take his eyes off her in that sexy outfit, that corset moulded to every delicious curve, her flushed cheeks and shining eyes, locked just as firmly with his. And then she had kissed him and there had been no stopping himself. It had been madness, sheer madness. What if Tanya had walked in on them? She didn't deserve that, and thank God it hadn't come to that. But it had been a close shave.

Tanya could be irritating, but she meant well. She was incredibly organised and made sure all the annoying little things he didn't have the time or inclination to deal with got done. In short, she made his life easy – not interesting, but Dom had had enough of interesting. In his experience, it meant drama – particularly where women were concerned – and he had had quite enough of that. Tanya was a refreshing change, always pleasant and unperturbed, although sometimes Dom almost wished she would lose her rag with him and lose control. But even in bed, Tanya was calmly proficient and capable, always taking care of his needs before her own. Dom shrugged – and he was complaining? There wasn't a guy he knew of who wouldn't be very happy with that arrangement.

But he couldn't get Carla or that kiss out of his head. He would have to pull himself together. His womanising days were over. What he had done had been incredibly irresponsible. Carla was his employee, for heaven's sakes, and now they would have to face each other in the restaurant. He shuddered, but it wasn't only with apprehension, he realised. There was a definite sense of delicious anticipation lurking there as well at the thought of seeing her again.

TAKE THAT! screamed *The Irish Sun.*

CANDY, WARRIOR PRINCESS! proclaimed *The Irish Star.*

TUDOR FEAST ENDS IN FACE-OFF! *The Irish Daily Mail* led with.

GOB SMACKED! quipped *The Echo.*

The shot under every headline was the same: Candy, wearing an expression of rage and triumph, Ossie, face splattered with pavlova, and Shalom, diving for cover, hands protecting her face, mouth open in horror.

The papers lay carefully arranged on the kitchen table and Jennifer was perusing them one at a time while she had her toast and coffee. She didn't usually read the tabloids, but this morning, having reflected on the amount of media presence at Ossie's party, she had correctly guessed that Candice's spontaneity might well have been captured. She had rung the newsagents and had their delivery boy bring them over. She wasn't disappointed. She checked her watch: 8:30 a.m., not too early to ring her daughter.

'Yes, Mother?'

'I know it's a trifle early, Charlotte, but I think you should know this whole episode with Candice and her father has been covered by the tabloids in glorious Technicolor. I have them here.'

'Come on up, I've just put some coffee on.'

'I'm on my way.'

Armed with the evidence, Jennifer lowered herself onto the stair lift that stood at the bottom of the stairs. Normally she avoided using it, but when she had a drink in hand or had to carry her walking cane or, as at present, something awkward, she was glad of it. She settled herself in, pushed the button and sailed upstairs to the door that separated her basement flat from the main house. Safely deposited at the top of the stairs, she got up and went into the kitchen, where Charlotte, already dressed, sat at the table. She poured another coffee for her mother.

'I thought you'd better see for yourself.' Jennifer put the papers down and sat opposite her.

'How bad are they?'

'Not *that* bad. The shot's the same in every one. Actually, there's a very nice one of you and Ossie earlier in the evening in the great hall.'

'Oh dear God,' Charlotte murmured as she leafed through the pages. 'This is frightful.'

'Depends what spin you put on it,' Jennifer pronounced.

'Spin?' Charlotte echoed, looking at her incredulously.

'Yes, spin. That Max Clifford person makes a fortune out

of it. I've seen him lots of times on television. He does an awful lot of charity work too, you know. Apparently it's all about how brazen you can be about things. Luckily for Candice, I would have thought that's rather a forte of hers. She takes after her father in that respect. Speaking of whom,' Jennifer advised, 'you shouldn't speak to him until we've got this sorted out. His behaviour was barbaric.'

'To be fair, he did try and take me aside once or twice in the evening, and he mentioned he had something he wanted to talk to me about, but someone or other always interrupted us.'

'Shalom, no doubt.'

'Well, yes, now that you mention it.'

As if on cue, Charlotte's phone began to ring beside her on the table. Picking it up, she saw Ossie's number on caller display.

'Don't answer it,' Jennifer commanded.

Charlotte held the phone in her hand and chewed her lip.

'Really, Charlotte, I mean it. His behaviour was appalling, both to you *and* Candice. You've got to stop jumping every time he clicks his fingers. It'll be on *her* instructions, you know.'

'What on earth am I going to say?' The phone stopped ringing. 'I'll have to deal with it sometime.'

'Yes, but not just now, dear. We have to think about this, think about what's best for Candice and how to salvage the situation to her advantage.'

'Salvage what situation, exactly?' Candice stood in the doorway in her dressing gown.

'You've made rather a splash in the newspapers this morning. Not entirely unexpected, I suppose,' Jennifer said. 'It really was monstrously ignorant of your father to invite the media. You do know, of course,' she said as she regarded Candice directly, 'that a lady's name should appear in print on only three occasions?'

'What occasions?' Candice had sat down and was already engrossed in the first headline.

'On her birth, her engagement and her death. That is the official line, and the correct one. Anything else is vulgarity personified.'

'Well, it's a bit late for that, isn't it?' Candice grabbed a bit of toast and poured a mug of coffee. 'If you don't mind,' she said, gathering up the papers, 'I'd like to look at the rest of these upstairs. See you later.'

'How extraordinary,' murmured Charlotte, looking bewildered. 'She didn't seem in the slightest bit distressed. I thought there would be a major tantrum at the very least.'

'That,' said Jennifer, pursing her mouth, 'is a bad sign. A very bad sign indeed.'

Upstairs in her bedroom, Candy got back into bed, flicked on the TV for background noise and settled herself down to read every single word.

'Poor Little Rich Girl', the first article was headed, and the others were variations on the same theme. The articles, which were sketchy on hard facts, had at least grasped the general details that her multimillionaire father had left her and her mother for Shalom almost four years ago. Best of all, though, one paper had been more thorough than the rest and had correctly named Shalom as Sharon, which was her real name, or had been until she'd changed it by deed poll. It also gratifyingly painted her mother as a woman of immaculate taste and dignity, implying that Shalom, along with her new name and shop-bought body parts, was anything but.

Candice was described as an aspiring actress, according to 'sources'. 'If her performance last night was anything to go by,' said the *Mail* reporter, 'I don't doubt an Oscar-winning role is imminent!'

Candice grinned. This was even better than she could have hoped for.

Her phone rang, interrupting her reverie. Looking at it, she saw her father's number flash on screen and deftly pressed the 'reject' button. He could piss off! There was no way she was going to talk to him now. Gran was right about that at least.

It rang again almost instantly. Candy cursed under her breath and picked it up crossly, until she saw that it was Emma calling.

'Candy,' she said breathlessly, 'why on earth did you run off like that? We had a brilliant time. Katy got off with Eamonn from Guyz, he's been texting her all night, and I've got an audition to model lingerie on a spot for *TV 2000*!' Emma could hardly contain her excitement.

'Really?' Candy sounded bored. 'Clearly you haven't seen the newspapers then?'

'What do you mean?' Emma was on her guard. 'We didn't say anything except good stuff about you. After you left, they bombarded us.'

'Good,' Candy said. 'That's just as well. And if they ask you anything else, say nothing until you've cleared it with me first.'

'What's going on?'

'You might say I've become an overnight celebrity,' Candy said.

'Ohmigod,' Emma breathed.

'Exactly. We need to discuss strategy. Meet me at three o'clock in Dundrum. Coffee at Harvey Nicks will be on me. Oh, and Emma?'

'Yes?'

'Make sure you and Katy look the biz, okay?'

4

'The doctor will see you now, Mr O'Reilly,' Sheila O'Connor said imperiously, drawing herself up to her full height of five feet ten inches. She peered suspiciously at the prospective patient now crossing the path she guarded so vigilantly between the waiting room and the confessional that was the doctor's office.

A newcomer to the practice, the man looked simultaneously chastened and apprehensive, without quite knowing why.

'Take a seat,' Dr P.J. O'Sullivan stood up from behind his desk and shook his hand, indicating the battered leather tub chair in front of him, which the man sat on gingerly, twisting his cap in his hands, still under the watchful gaze of Sheila.

'Your next two patients are waiting, Doctor.' Her tone was heavy with meaning. 'Mrs Kelly was *particularly* punctual. I've already explained to her that you're running twenty minutes late.' Sheila frowned, clearly disapproving.

'Yes, thank you, Sheila. As I've said many times, a doctor's surgery cannot be run with the precision of a Swiss railway station, much though we would all like it to be. I'm sure Mrs Kelly will understand. I will give her my full and undivided attention when I see her.'

'If you could just shave off five minutes on the next two patients, Doctor, it would greatly—'

'Thank you, Sheila,' P.J. nodded firmly to her. 'That will be all.'

Sheila reluctantly retreated and closed the door behind her.

The patient checked his watch anxiously and was now looking rather alarmed.

'Take no notice of her,' P.J. grinned. 'I don't. She's well used to it.'

'I really don't want to be taking up any more of your time than is absolutely—'

'Nonsense.' P.J. waved a hand. 'I have all the time in the world, and so do you. Sheila – that is, Ms O'Connor – is a first-class secretary in many ways, but she also suffers from OCD, with a touch of bi-polar thrown in.'

'OCD?'

'Obsessive Compulsive Disorder.'

'Oh,' said the patient, sounding not in the least reassured.

'In other words, she means well, but is rather more driven by a longing for orderliness than the rest of us. I have to admit I take an unkind delight in pushing her buttons.' P.J. smiled. 'Now, Mr O'Reilly, if I may take a few details . . .'

The man automatically answered the usual perfunctory medical history queries, and while P.J. took notes, his patient took in his surroundings.

The room was not quite like anything he had ever seen before, certainly nothing that resembled a doctor's office. Patrick O'Reilly had heard a lot about the infamous Dr P.J. O'Sullivan and had imagined his surgery to be a clinical cross between a squash court and a recording studio. Certainly judging from all the famous people who went to see him and spoke so glowingly of him, he never expected anything like this.

The mews P.J. ran his surgery from was a delightfully quaint converted coach house. Inside was a bright, spacious waiting-room area, open plan, with two large picture windows, plenty of single chairs and armchairs and two large sofas that had seen better days. They were all covered in various patterns of faded but immaculately clean chintz. A real fire crackled in the centre of the room, in front of which sat a large wicker dog basket. A vast array of magazines (in fairness, some of them up to date) from *Golfer's Monthly* to the *Sacred Heart Messenger* to *Vogue*, *Harper's* and other high fashion bibles sat in meticulous order on various tables. Fresh flowers and a few interesting plants perched on windowsills, and the resident cat, Psycho, lounged in a corner of the sofa, purring loudly. Presiding over all sat Sheila O'Connor at her pristine receptionist's sentry just inside the door.

Inside, in the surgery, was a whole other story. Paddy O'Reilly had seen untidiness in his time, coming as he did from a small farm shared with a widowed father and four feckless brothers, but this . . . well, this was something else.

Behind the doctor, as he scribbled his notes, was a set of floor-to-ceiling shelves that ran the whole wall, groaning with paperwork. Real paperwork, mind, not neat, typed, orderly stacks of it, but handwritten, unwieldy *masses* of the stuff, like something from a bygone era. His desk, too, obviously antique (if you could manage to see the tiny patch of visible leather-topped mahogany), was covered in more of the stuff. There was paper everywhere – and no rhyme or reason to any of it, apparently. More extraordinarily, the cat that had been sleeping in the waiting room had obviously slipped in through the open door while Sheila had been dispensing instructions. It sat now, a handsome marmalade creature, on the desk, imperiously kneading a pile of handwritten notes for all it was worth. The doctor, Paddy was unnerved to see, paid not a jot of notice.

At the far side of the room was a real log fire, in front of which basked the fattest Labrador Paddy had ever seen. The dog looked at him now, groaned and wagged his tail. He seemed doubly incongruous beside the standing real-life skeleton that inhabited the corner, sporting a trilby, a scarf and a cigarette clenched between his teeth. To cap it all, the strains of some rock band were playing on the sound system.

'You don't mind animals, I hope?' P.J. asked pleasantly. 'I find they have a remarkably therapeutic effect on people. And Psycho here,' he said, indicating the cat, 'provides a first-class filing system. All I have to do is find the paper with the most hairs on it, and I have to hand my most recent notes.' He beamed.

Paddy felt a bit weak but swallowed and nodded, a watery smile on his face.

'They also provide me with the perfect introduction to my cat scan and lab test jokes,' P.J. chuckled. 'Now, what is it I can help you with?'

For an awful moment, Paddy felt the whole room come to a standstill. All movement ceased. Sound faded. The cat had paused in his activity and was regarding him with an accusatory stare and the dog was ogling him, his mouth open and panting. Paddy felt his head begin to swim. He tried to speak, but no words came out. He looked at the cap in his hands, crushed in his clutches.

'Paddy,' P.J. began. 'May I call you Paddy?'

Paddy nodded mutely.

'You must remember that there is nothing – absolutely *nothing* – you could divulge to me that I haven't heard or dealt with before. I realise that doesn't make it any easier for you, especially at a first consultation,' he continued, 'but for what it's worth, I am completely unshockable and resoundingly resilient. And I'm fairly sure that once you share your problem with me – whatever it is – I'll be able to help you, or if not, I'll direct you to someone who can.' P.J. paused to draw breath, hoping against hope that Sheila would not avail of this opportunity to knock discreetly on his door, three times in a row, to remind him he was over time. It was one of many signs that usually indicated she was becoming lax in her medication, and at times such as this, it could have disastrous results. P.J. waited patiently and held his breath.

'It all started about eleven months, two weeks ago, to the day. I'm an accountant, so I remember dates and things like that. I'm very precise.' The cap was fairly spinning in his hands.

P.J. added to his notes and nodded encouragingly.

'Well,' Paddy took a rasping breath, 'there's no other way to say this, Doctor . . .'

'Yes?' P.J. was beginning to feel as agonised as his patient.

Just then, Bones, the Labrador, farted loudly and thumped his tail in approval. The sound made Paddy jump.

'I, er, beg your pardon,' P.J. risked, 'on his behalf.' He grinned. 'As you can see, this is a place of free expression. You were saying?'

'Ican'tgetitupanymore.' The words tumbled out in a rush. Paddy looked first startled, and then as if he might cry.

'A common occurrence, if an inconvenient one,' P.J. nodded knowingly. 'I've suffered from it myself,' he lied. 'Show me the man who hasn't and I'll show you a liar.'

Before his eyes, Paddy expelled a shuddering sigh and regained five, if not ten years. His face, which had been taut, was flooded with relief and he sat up straighter in his chair, an expression of hope and interest replacing despair.

P.J. listened now as the floodgates opened and Paddy related the story of his boardroom barracuda of a wife and her increasingly dissatisfied views of their marriage and indeed their four young children. He wrote him a prescription and took mental notes. It was a textbook case: ambitious, dissatisfied, resentful wife, bewildered, emasculated and increasingly anxious husband.

'We'll have to rule out obvious physical indications, but as you don't smoke or drink, it's unlikely to be a factor.' He handed him the prescription. 'Take these and come back and see me in two weeks. The results of the tests will be back then and we can investigate further if necessary. And remember, Paddy,' he said, tapping his head, 'problems in the bedroom are almost always about what's up here and not about what's down there. That applies to both men and women. If I had a penny for every man who came in here with similar confidences . . .'

Paddy got up and shook his hand heartily. 'Thank you, Doctor, you've been a tonic. I feel better already.' He made for the door.

'Oh, and Paddy?' P.J. regarded him sternly.

'Yes?'

'I think it would be not only appropriate, but thoroughly advisable for you and your wife to abstain in the intervening period until you see me again. Do you think you can manage that? Doctor's orders, if anyone asks.'

The look of relief that crossed his patient's face was positively celestial.

'Whatever you say, Doctor. Whatever you say.'

'Be sure to reassure relevant parties that your emotions are steadfast and that you are merely taking time out to unravel a stressful situation, one which, unresolved, will only contribute to further marital confusion. I have no doubt, no doubt whatsoever, that this situation is entirely resolvable. I wouldn't say that if I didn't believe it. We'll talk further next time.'

'Thank you, Doctor. Again, you have no idea what a load off my mind that is.'

'Take care, Paddy, good to meet you.'

As P.J. went back to his notes and took a gulp of a very cold cup of coffee, another new and hopeful patient took his leave and vowed to tell everyone he knew that it was true, this Dr P.J. O'Sullivan was the real deal, every bit of it. He was halfway down the street in his new BMW, whistling a happy tune, when Paddy realised he had forgotten to offer any kind of payment for the consultation, and, more astonishingly, not one person had prompted him for it – not even the Sheila person, who had very pointedly looked at her watch on his departure. He resolved to write a very generous cheque on his return. It was the least he could do.

For the rest of the day, P.J. continued to see patients, dealing with the usual ailments that presented at this time of year:

flu, a couple of respiratory infections, stress, depression and, interestingly, a rash on an attractive young woman that he strongly suspected might be syphilitic. A few of his regular cancer patients checked in to have him monitor their progress and have their oncologist's ongoing treatment plan explained to them. Nothing too out of the ordinary, and thankfully no bad news to break. He had a cup of coffee and a banana for lunch and by the time he saw his last patient out, he was both tired and ravenous.

'You work too hard, and left to yourself your eating habits are appalling.' Sheila stood at the door, shaking her head.

'Keeps me out of mischief, Sheila, you know that. And don't I know you'll have a lovely dinner waiting for me up at the house.'

Sheila allowed herself a smile. 'It's your favourite, roast chicken with all the trimmings.'

'What would I do without you?'

'Seven o'clock sharp, mind.'

'On the dot, you have my word. Bones and I will go for our evening constitutional and I shall be thinking of chicken every step of the way.'

Sheila checked her watch. 'What time do you have?' She looked at him suspiciously.

'Two minutes past six, exactly.'

She nodded, satisfied. 'We're in sync then.'

'Now don't let me delay you, Sheila. Your duties here finish at five thirty, there's no need to be waiting around here for me.'

'It's no bother.' Sheila was looking longingly at the mound of papers on the desk. 'If you'd just let me tidy that lot up for you . . .'

'Now Sheila, you know the drill.'

'Just the once. I hate to think of—'

'I know my filing system is unorthodox, but it all works perfectly well the way it is.'

'But the Lord only knows what's lurking under that pile. What your patients must think.'

'They think I'll help them to feel better, and that's what I try to do to the best of my ability.'

'And animals in the surgery.' Sheila was edging in now. 'You'll be reported any day now.'

'Sheila.' P.J. was firm. 'If you don't get going, I'll be late on my walk, and then dinner will be delayed, won't it?' He played his trump card.

She looked torn and backed out reluctantly. 'Well, if you're sure.'

'Don't worry, I'll lock up.'

When Sheila had gone, P.J. heaved a sigh of relief. It was always touch and go, finishing up. Sheila kept the house and surgery religiously organised, but P.J.'s office was strictly out of bounds to her. It was the only way the arrangement could survive. The upside was he got to maintain his unbelievingly untidy office just the way he liked it. It had always been the same, ever since he had been a student: P.J. was reasonably tidy with everything else, but his paperwork was sacrosanct. He lived happily with great disjointed mountains of the stuff, covering every possible surface, and was able to find exactly what he wanted at any given moment, even notes dating back years. It gave him an inordinate sense of triumph. He also claimed it was good training for continued mental alertness. He didn't need any of those awful computer games to test his skills, he simply had to think about a particular set of notes and somehow an instinct would arise and he would be drawn unfailingly to the exact piece of paper he wanted. The downside was that he had to do his own dusting and hoovering. It was a small price to pay. The streamlined-looking computer that sat on his desk was used purely for internet research purposes. The only exception he made was to allow Sheila, under his supervision, to clean out and reset the fire. Other than that, unless he was there himself, he kept the office locked.

It drove Sheila mental. Well, it would have driven any woman mental, P.J. supposed, but then, Sheila was not your average woman.

She had come into their lives eight years ago, an anxious, troubled woman of indeterminate age in a well-worn but immaculate overcoat and headscarf. He remembered the day well. She sat down in front of him, plucking at the strap of her handbag, and P.J. had noticed her hands were rubbed raw. It turned out she lived with an elderly and demanding aunt as her carer in return for bed and board. P.J. had correctly diagnosed Obsessive Compulsive Disorder. An intelligent and reasonably well-educated individual, Sheila had begun and been fired from a succession of jobs earlier in life due to her various eccentricities.

Organising her treatment, however, had proved rather more difficult. 'Oh, I don't believe in medication,' she had pronounced. 'It can lead to dependency, and I'm a very independent person.'

'I don't doubt it for a minute, Ms O'Connor.'

'I'd just like to be able to relax a bit more, not get so upset about things and how they should be.' The look of despair that flitted across her face had moved him.

'This medication will help you to do just that. I'd also like you to see my wife, Jilly, for some talking therapy.'

'Talking?' She was wary.

'Yes, counselling. It will help.'

'Isn't that expensive? You see, I don't think my medical card will cover—'

'No need to be concerned about that at present. Look, I'll make a deal with you,' P.J. reasoned with her.

'What's that?' He had her attention.

'If you take these tablets for two weeks and have an appointment with my wife, and if you're still against the idea of medication at your next visit, we'll do it your way.'

'My way?' She looked suspicious.

'You're the boss. That's the way this surgery is run.'

'Well then, I suppose, for two weeks . . .'

And the pills had helped, just as he knew they would. So, of course, had a few sessions with Jilly, who had proclaimed her adorable. 'She *is* funny,' she had said, laughing over dinner that night. 'Sometimes it's all I can do to keep a straight face with some of the things she comes out with.'

Eager to make a bit of extra money, Sheila had put forward the possibility of coming in on a Saturday morning to help with a bit of cleaning and typing, and took to it with relish. The old aunt had eventually died and left her home to her son in America, who promptly sold it. Not a penny went to Sheila. Homeless and jobless, Jilly and P.J. took her on full time, insisting she would be invaluable to them, as long, of course, as she agreed to live in the adjoining granny flat. The arrangement proved to be a successful, if unpredictable, one.

Sheila adored them. This adoration was demonstrated not by any obvious outward affection, but rather a relentless and determined effort to organise and protect Jilly and P.J. from the hazardous possibilities that lurked everywhere. People (the postman was terrified of her), especially patients, were considered a particular threat. She would regard them suspiciously, interrogate them imperiously if unsupervised, and watch with an eagle eye while they sat in the waiting room, silently daring them to touch or move so much as a magazine. It was an uneasy alliance, seeing as they were the sole source of income for her employers, but it made for many hilarious episodes, and as far as his patients were concerned, she only added to the appeal of P.J.'s practice.

Sheila had been a lifesaver, though, since Jilly's death. She kept house and mealtimes as if her life depended on it, which, in a way, P.J. supposed it did. They quite simply would never have managed without her. And now, well, with Bella away studying music in Florence and Alex married, P.J. was glad of Sheila's regular, if eccentric, presence. She was a good cook too, and although P.J. was himself, he knew he would never have bothered about regular meals on his own.

Outside, P.J. and Bones set off for the park a short stroll away. He usually enjoyed this time of day, getting a bit of fresh air and laughing at Bones's enthusiastic efforts at retrieving, which preferably involved hurling himself into the lake, where he would swim powerfully, returning with his trophy. Today, though, P.J. was lost in thought and not as attentive as he might have been.

'Sorry, old chap,' he said to his dog, who was looking perplexed and had dropped his ball at P.J.'s feet for the third time without a response. 'I was miles away. Here you go.' He flung the ball back into the water.

Why was it that Alex always had that effect on him? P.J. frowned. He would have loved to have a good relationship with his only son, to be able to do all the man-to-man stuff, going to rugby matches and having the occasional pint. But Alex wasn't into rugby and favoured smart wine bars over familiar pubs.

It wasn't that they had a bad relationship, as such; he just didn't know how to relate to him. Alex made him feel uncomfortable, and for the life of him P.J. couldn't work out why. Take last week, for instance, when they had met for lunch in that trendy restaurant, Dominic's. It had started off well. P.J. had been deliberately early and had ordered a good bottle of red, a very expensive bottle of red, one that even Alex would approve of. He had made an effort, too, to dress properly and had even had a haircut – well, a trim at any rate. He had stayed away from any incendiary topics and let Alex steer the conversation. Then a couple of people – well, perhaps four or five, maybe – had come over during the course of lunch to say hello to him, including the proprietor, and Alex had positively bristled. To cap it all off, Alex had recounted his latest investment scheme at length, which sounded remarkably risky to P.J., if possibly very profitable. He had listened, nodding encouragingly, and made all the right noises, and then Alex had said, 'Well, that's good. I was hoping you'd be one of the first to come on board.'

P.J. had had to say that he had suggested no such thing, and that he would not be investing in this or indeed any other of Alex's business interests, on family principle. The rest of lunch had passed in relative silence and Alex had made a speedy and resentful exit.

P.J. sighed now, thinking of the day. He had taken the afternoon off especially and had been left with a hefty bill (although he had insisted on paying) and the remains of the bottle of red, which he'd finished.

He wondered if he had been wrong. Should he have invested in the scheme anyway, just as a vote of confidence in his son? Somehow, he didn't think it would have made any real difference. Whatever he did, Alex seemed to think it was always exactly the wrong thing.

'Come on, Bones!' P.J. called his dog. 'Let's go home.'

As Bones galloped towards him, ears flying and soaking wet, P.J. grinned.

'Just as well we have each other, isn't it, old chap?' he said, setting off home. He checked his watch. It was ten minutes to seven. Sheila would not be disappointed.

'Why don't we have your dad to Sunday lunch this week?' Catherine, Alex's wife, suggested. She sat down on the sofa beside her husband and put her feet up, rubbing her growing bump tenderly.

'Not a good idea,' Alex replied sourly.

'Why not?'

'I told you about how he wouldn't even invest in my proposition.' Alex looked irritated.

'Oh, that.'

'What do you mean, *oh, that*? This is what I do,

Catherine, this is how I make my living. He won't even endorse or support me in that. Nothing I do is good enough for that man.'

Catherine sighed. It was a phrase she'd got used to whenever Alex talked about his father. She wished she could get to the bottom of his bitterness with his dad, but no matter how often she tried to talk about it, Alex refused to have any real discussion about it, apart from muttering that they were different.

Only once, on a night when they'd been out with friends, one of whom had been talking fondly about their own father, had Alex said anything.

'He's an old hippie. All free love, act first, think later. I can't stand that type of thing. Besides, he's not—' He'd broken off, as if he'd been about to say something, then thought better of it.

'He's not what?' she'd asked.

'Nothing,' he'd said.

Catherine thought she might never get to the bottom of it. She understood that not everyone adored their parents the way she did; she was lucky. But it pained her that Alex, who she loved so much and who she knew to be kind, could be so cold to his poor father.

'You know that isn't true, Alex,' she said now. 'He really cares about you. I know he does.'

'The only thing he cares about is himself and his bloody practice. He never had any time for me; neither of them did. If they weren't working, they were getting high and mooning at each other across the kitchen table. It was pathetic.'

'Doesn't sound very pathetic to me.' Catherine reached for his hand. 'What's wrong with adoring your wife, might I ask?'

'I do adore you.' Alex softened momentarily. 'You know that. And I know we'll both make wonderful parents.'

'I hope so, but they don't come with a manual, you know. No matter how much you read, no one can teach you how to be a good parent. We'll just have to do the best we can,' she sighed.

'It'll be a cinch,' Alex said. 'I'll just do the exact opposite of everything Dad did.'

Catherine didn't push it. She was tired, and as she was pregnant, she wasn't drinking. The thought of having to listen to Alex begin a well-rehearsed rant about his father without a soothing glass of wine in her hand didn't appeal.

'Honestly,' he began, 'you should have seen him. Before I'd even sat down he'd ordered practically the most expensive red on the list. He didn't even think to enquire as to what I might have fancied. Then all through lunch the most ghastly people kept coming over to interrupt us. Joey and Sharkey from Viper, some awful rock star, Rick something or other—'

'Rick Waters?'

'Yes, that's the one.'

Catherine's eyebrows shot up. 'Rick Waters doesn't talk to anyone. He's notoriously rude.'

'Oh, Dad probably cured him of some horrible dose of the clap or something, no doubt. And then of course that twit that owns Dominic's came over to fawn over him – well of course he would, having just offloaded one of the most expensive bottles in the restaurant,' Alex scowled. 'I've never seen anyone crave attention like my father. It's really quite extraordinary.'

'I'm going to have a bath, hon.' Catherine got up. She hated seeing Alex like this, angry and bitter. 'See you later.'

'What? Oh, fine, darling, I won't be long.'

'No rush. I'm looking forward to a nice long soak.'

Catherine went upstairs and wondered for the umpteenth time what P.J. could have done to make his son resent him so much. She was fond of P.J. and she knew he wanted to have a close relationship with his son, but there wasn't an awful lot he could do. The reason, she reflected, was pure and simple. Her husband was quite clearly consumed with jealousy of his father, and neither father nor son cared to confront or even acknowledge the fact.

'Two hundred and forty-eight, two hundred and forty-nine, two hundred and . . . fifty.' Tanya collapsed back onto the floor and pulled her knees into her chest. It didn't get any easier, but two hundred and fifty stomach crunches was the way she began her morning and so had her mother before her. The reward was a flat-as-a-board tummy and a figure a model could be proud of. What other way was there? Tanya couldn't understand people who didn't look after themselves. That was the way to flabby middle age and other unthinkable possibilities. She didn't bother with a personal trainer either. That was for wimps. If you could push yourself, then what was the point of paying someone else to? Although it would be nice, she mused, to have some tasty piece of eye candy to help relieve the tedium of working out. All in good time, she reminded herself. When she was married to Dom, she could have all the personal trainers and other perks she was looking forward to that rich women took for granted. Right now, it was an inconceivable expense.

Tanya's attitude to spending was strangely skewed. She would be ruthlessly mean with herself in some ways, and then in others, like shopping, particularly for clothes, she would splurge uncontrollably. After all, she reasoned, she took care of herself, kept herself in terrific shape all the time; she deserved to treat herself occasionally. Like that fabulous dress she had bought for Ossie Keating's Tudor party Dominic's had catered. Tanya had no intention whatsoever of dressing up in some ridiculous Elizabethan number that wouldn't show off her slim figure or long, toned legs. Instead, she had bought herself a fabulous strapless designer gown. It had cost a fortune, even with the generous discount the designer had allowed her in return for like favours when she booked at

Dominic's. Quid pro quo. That was the way it worked. Girls in business understood each other.

Mopping her face with a towel, she headed for the treadmill and began to pound her way through three miles. The smart flat tucked away in a discreet development off Stephen's Green complete with treadmill had been a godsend. A rich banker friend of her mother's was newly divorced and decided to relocate to the States for a year. Not wanting or needing to rent out his ultra-modern, no-expenses-spared apartment, he had been looking for someone suitable to 'house sit' and take care of it in his absence. Tanya's mother had pounced on the opportunity for her equally ambitious daughter to avail of, and now she had the home of her dreams, albeit temporarily – and she didn't even have to pay a penny. If Tanya had believed in good fortune, she would have said she was blessed. But she didn't believe in luck. As the heaving shelf of self-help books in the spare bedroom was testimony to, Tanya was firmly convinced that you made your own luck. She had visualised and believed that the perfect flat would find her – and it had. Better still, so had the perfect man.

She had hardly believed her eyes when Dom had strolled into the polo grounds in the Phoenix Park that Saturday afternoon where she had been organising the PR for a charity function a friend of hers had been involved in. Tall, dark and impossibly handsome, he had, unbelievably, been on his own, clearly meeting a couple of male friends who were equally well dressed and hosting a boys-only table at the summer barbeque.

She didn't waste a minute. Waiting until the food had been served and finished, she kept an eagle eye on the table. The moment one of the guys had gone up to the bar, she seized her chance. Slipping into his vacated chair on the pretext of selling raffle tickets she had purloined from one of the young girls employed to do exactly that, she went into action, flirting and flattering them all shamelessly. The boys, who had been hitting the Pimms steadily since arriving, were in great form and gentlemanly enough to insist she join them in a glass or two while they fought over who bought the most tickets. When Dom mentioned he was opening a restaurant the following month, she had immediately advised him on the vital importance of PR for the occasion and had generously offered her services.

'Really,' she had said in the low, sultry voice she had practised so carefully, 'it would be a pleasure. I've just gone out on my own too, and although my company has taken off hugely, I've never done a restaurant launch before. It would be a feather in my cap, and,' she lowered her voice to a whisper, 'I wouldn't dream of charging you anything like full rates until you were up and running and I had proved myself. Why don't we discuss it over lunch?' She handed him her card.

'Well, thanks, er, Tanya,' he had said, genuinely pleased. 'That's awfully decent of you.'

'Not at all. Now, I must get back to work,' she had said, getting up from the table, making sure she left him with an impression of her attention to efficiency and a good view of her long, shapely legs. 'Call me on Monday and we'll set something up.'

They had met for lunch and Tanya had sized Dominic up. Like many handsome, well-bred young men, he was, she correctly guessed, heavy on charm but not terribly astute. His education had been expensive and well rounded, but clearly he was no academic and happily lacked the killer punch and drive that would have made him a ruthless businessman. On the contrary, Dom appeared to be kind, creative and totally absorbed in his passion for food and the restaurant he was about to open. And best of all, he was single and his family was loaded.

Not being terribly organised either, Dom had been happy to let Tanya oversee all the irritating aspects of the opening night – and she had made sure it was a blinder. Calling in all favours and her not inconsiderable contacts, she had made sure that Dominic's got absolutely rave reviews and was regularly referred to in newspapers and magazines as the current and indeed only place to dine, or to see and be seen in. From there, it had been easy. She simply moved from organising the PR to organising his life. The apartment he lived in above the actual restaurant had been converted, but Dom had never got around to properly decorating it or making it into any kind of a home. With the help of an interior decorator friend, Tanya had accomplished in weeks what Dom had happily left unfinished for months. She had arranged a woman to come in twice a week to clean and iron for him and, having been introduced to his friends, began to host a series of casual dinner parties in her flat for him, away from the relentless demands of the restaurant. Soon, Dom began to wonder how he had ever managed without her. She made sure he ate properly, worked out and even stored all his family's birthdays and relevant dates and anniversaries on her computer so she could remind him what was coming up and to purchase the appropriate gift or flowers.

After gentle but insistent nudging on Tanya's part, it wasn't long before he introduced her to his parents. Tanya had been slightly worried about that. Although she was enormously pleased at this crucial move forward in the development of their relationship, she realised how important it was that she pulled it off to her advantage. She had met Dom's parents, Cici and James, briefly at the restaurant, but to be invited to their elegant home in Wellington Square and be presented as his girlfriend – well, that was a whole other ball game. And she had prepared assiduously for it. All the same, Tanya had found the experience intimidating and not a little unnerving. She had dressed carefully for the occasion in an immaculately cut knee-length wool pencil skirt teamed with a white, pintucked designer shirt with double cuffs. At her neck she wore a string of discreet pearls with matching studs in her ears. She had her roots done, her hair trimmed and blow dried. Black Prada medium-heeled pumps and a matching handbag completed the ensemble. The whole effect was polished, yet demure, she decided.

She had been welcomed warmly upon arrival by James and ushered straight down to the enormous kitchen, where Cici and the girls were chattering away ten to the dozen.

Cici, Tanya was rather alarmed to see, was clearly a fabulous cook and one of those women who made throwing together a delicious yet deceptively simple meal seem utterly effortless. Tanya was quiet and carefully polite throughout dinner, answering when she was spoken to and watching her table manners. She was relieved not to be bombarded, as she might have been, with any overly intrusive questions about her life and background, and complimented Cici warmly on her cooking and her beautiful home. The whole thing, she felt, beginning to relax as she took a sip of her Chianti, was going very well. Seated beside James, who was charming, she enquired about his business and appeared fascinated as he recounted the latest wonders of technology with enthusiasm.

As Dom and the girls cleared away plates, Tanya excused herself and escaped to the loo to freshen up. Inside, she smiled at her reflection. She looked every inch the elegant career girl, calm, poised and together. No one could ever guess about the uneasy interior. The Coleman-Cappabiancas were as far removed from her own family as it was possible to imagine – charming, accomplished and with that annoying confidence that only the very rich and educated exuded. Of course, being half Italian helped, she thought grudgingly – it gave Sophia, Mimi and Dom that whole understated glamour thing.

Tanya's own upbringing had been vastly different. Things had not been easy for her, an only child, when her father left her mother when Tanya was only three years old. He had fled to America with his secretary and left a mountain of debts in his wake. The house had to be sold and a much smaller one acquired in a less-than-desirable suburb, and her mother unwillingly went back to work as an air hostess. She had impressed upon Tanya from an early age that men were not to be relied upon unless they had substantial amounts of money to make up for their other, more obvious drawbacks.

There had been no glamorous schools or holidays for Tanya, but she hadn't been afraid of hard work, figuring her cool, blonde good looks and frightening determination would supply what life had taken away from her – the right to claim her place in a world of class and luxury, where she would never have to worry again.

Working as a secretary, she had found her way into PR and had risen rapidly through the ranks, stepping consciously on any offending toes that happened to be in her way. Along with passing her exams and acquiring the industry qualifications, she had attended every evening course she could find on fine art, antiques and wine-tasting. All that eluded her was the man who would be her ticket into that other, rarefied world, and now he had finally turned up.

On her way back to the kitchen, Tanya paused for a second, listening to the sound of voices engaged in lively discussion. She took a chance and slipped into one of the huge, double reception rooms, flicking on the light and having a quick look around. The room was decorated beautifully and the furniture and paintings had to be worth a fortune. Solid silver frames stood on every available surface, encasing photos of happy family gatherings and many of Cici, looking gorgeous, in what Tanya supposed was her native Italy.

'Are you lost?'

Tanya started guiltily as Sophia stood smiling in the doorway.

'I must have taken the wrong turn,' Tanya replied, 'and then I couldn't resist looking at all these lovely photographs. Silly of me – I have no sense of direction.' She moved smoothly past her.

'An easy mistake to make,' Sophia replied genially. 'It could happen to anyone. Let me show you the way back, it's just down these three little steps.' She was still smiling, but her eyes were cold.

Back in the kitchen, coffee was being served and the others didn't seem to notice that her absence had been longer than usual. But as Dom poured a cup for her, she heard Sophia rattle off a rapid fire of Italian to her mother. Did she imagine it, or did Dom's pouring falter ever so fractionally?

So what if his stupid sister had caught her having a little look around? Dom had never mentioned the incident to her, so clearly it hadn't bothered him. That had been over a year ago and she had been in the house many times since, and now, thankfully, Sophia and Mimi were both studying abroad. Mind you, Tanya thought, pounding away on the treadmill, she wasn't at all happy about recent events in the Coleman-Cappabianca household. She frowned, thinking of the unorthodox arrangement that was in place at the moment, with Cici living in the mews at the bottom of the garden and behaving for all the world as if she was single, and James, as the song went, drinking doubles at the thought of it. It wasn't an ideal state of affairs at all as far as Tanya was concerned. Quite apart from anything else, parents on the verge of splitting up were not at all conducive to hastening a son towards a timely and eagerly awaited proposal of marriage. Something would have to be done, but just what Tanya hadn't yet figured out. Still, she reasoned, at least the restaurant was doing well. It kept Dom's mind off other, more disconcerting events. And Tanya loved being involved with it all.

There was only one fly in the ointment. The books, despite chock-a-block bookings, were showing a distinct loss. Eric, the accountant, had been rather concerned about it. Tanya had briskly instructed him not to worry Dom with it at the moment, as he had so many more important things to deal with.

If she was honest, she wasn't altogether surprised. She had been comping her PR friends to beat the band. But it was all for a good cause, she reassured herself. How else had Dominic's got to be so well known and well spoken of, and so quickly? Of course, the food lived up to the reviews, but it was only because of Tanya's relentless pursuit of publicity that they appeared so frequently in all the best columns, and that required a lot of favours in the shape of reduced bills and many free bottles bestowed. Speaking of which, his own mother, Cici, wasn't above showering champagne on her 'friends', and Tanya hadn't once seen her pay for it. Oh well, it wasn't her problem. Not yet anyway. Dominic's was going from strength to strength and the staff were worked off their feet.

Thinking of staff, Tanya scowled. They were all fine, except the chef, Rollo, who was an arrogant and temperamental bastard, but Dom claimed he was the best in the business. Then there was that Carla girl. Tanya didn't like her, not one little bit. She was far too uppity. Sometimes, to watch her, you'd think *she* ran the restaurant. And men adored her. She had that Latin American vibe going on, people were always saying she was the image of J-Lo. And she'd seen the way she looked at Dom when she thought she was unobserved. She fancied him big time and she flirted with him, weaving that sinuous body of hers in and out of tables and wiggling her bottom whenever he was around. She'd seen Dom looking at her too – what man wouldn't with all that sashaying going on under his very nose? It would all but make you dizzy. Still, Tanya reflected, that was the least of her worries. Dom's parents' marital situation was a far more serious impediment to her hopes of procuring an engagement ring any time soon. Carla and her carry-on was just a silly irritation. After all, what would a man like Dom ever see in a ditzy, New York waitress with an ass to match her clearly inflated self-opinion?

5

Cici examined herself in the full-length mirrors of her dressing room. Every morning, after a leisurely bath, she assessed her naked body from every angle. That way, there were no sudden shocks. Approaching fifty, it was holding up pretty well, all things considered. She was, as the French say, comfortable in her own skin. Cici didn't believe in being neurotic about ageing; she fully intended to enjoy every bit of herself that worked and tolerate and encourage the bits that didn't. All the same, she had done well in the gene pool. At five feet eight inches, she was reasonably tall and her long legs were still shapely, especially in high heels, which she favoured, not just for the inches they added but for the way they made a woman walk. How a woman carried herself was so important. It said more about her than words or any amount of money ever could. Her breasts were still impressive, despite fighting an ongoing battle with gravity, but at least lying down, they were splendid, and when she was upright, the situation was helped by fabulous underwear – another vital weapon.

After three children, her waist was no longer what it had been, but her softly rounded tummy simply added to her overall femininity. She wasn't entirely happy with her arms, but so what? Anyway, they were easily covered up. Her face, thanks to fabulous bone structure, was still striking, and her olive skin supple. She maintained it with occasional shots of Botox and fillers but was rigorously vigilant about looking natural, in no way altered. That was the trick. The minute a woman looked in any way 'done' was the minute you saw fear on her face – and nothing, but *nothing* was more unattractive, whether you were seventeen or seventy.

She wondered what to wear. She was lunching, of course, in Dominic's, but today it would be a table just for two. Thinking of her lunch date, she smiled. He really was too adorable: tall, blond, good-looking, terribly intelligent and with that particular brand of earnestness that only the young could carry off without appearing totally idiotic. Not that he was *that* young, she reflected; at thirty, he was two years older than her own son, Dom.

She had met him at a press reception to announce details of a fund-raising event in aid of a local children's hospital, where he had approached her, quite directly, and told her she was the most stylish woman he had ever set eyes upon. He edited a popular women's magazine she knew well, called *Select*, a contemporary mix of style bible and current affairs, and for the rest of the evening had remained glued to her side, much to her delight and to the dismay of many other, much younger, women who threw regretful glances in their direction. After the reception, she had agreed to have dinner with him (why not?), and he had chosen a nearby Italian place that Cici hadn't been in for at least twenty years. It was cheap and cheerful, the food good, if predictable, and the charming waiters greeted her as a long-lost friend.

She told him about coming to Ireland from Italy and how strange and unfamiliar she had found it all at first, especially the men, who, she had been astonished to discover, did not *look* at women – at least not the way Italian men did, lingeringly, assessing almost all of them favourably.

'In Italy, men celebrate women, all women – young, old and in between. It was a severe culture shock for me to arrive here and be deprived of all that attention I took so much for granted,' she laughed. 'Luckily, my husband was very supportive and understanding.'

'What a lucky man, your husband,' he said enviously.

'Oh,' she demurred, suddenly flustered under his intense gaze, 'I'm not so sure he would share those sentiments.'

'You *are* still married?' He looked questioningly at the large solitaire diamond and wedding band she wore.

'Yes, yes, in a manner of speaking . . .'

'Separated?' Hope flickered in his eyes.

'Well, yes, sort of . . . it's complicated.'

'Of course, I'm sorry.' He was genuinely contrite. 'It's absolutely none of my business.'

'No, you have every right to ask. It is I who must apologise for seeming so indecisive, but that's just it, you see. I'm not at all sure whether I *want* to be married or not any more.'

'Ah, I see.' He looked amused. 'Then for tonight at least, let's pretend you're not.'

'I'm afraid I must warn you that I can be very good at pretending,' Cici said flirtatiously, back on safer ground now that she'd been honest.

'Good,' he grinned, 'so am I. I've always thought too much reality can be a little harsh for the soul.'

She had found him endearing, and interesting. He had a double first from Trinity College and a Masters in English from Oxford. During his student years, he had worked, among other things, as a barman, a carpet cleaner and a general dogsbody at a national newspaper: 'That's where I caught the bug, when I realised newspapers, publishing, was for me.'

He had earned his stripes at several London broadsheets, most recently on the *Sunday Times*, and his rise through the English media had been meteoric.

Intrigued, Cici asked, 'Why did you—'

'Throw it all away to edit a women's glossy?' he finished her question. 'There was a girl . . . it went wrong, a misunderstanding that got blown totally out of proportion.' He shrugged self-deprecatingly. 'She was unbalanced, became a bit obsessed, you know the kind of thing. It was easier to move away. Anyway, I was restless, curious to come home again, see if I could hack Dublin. I put out the word and *Select* approached me, made me a very decent offer, actually. That was three years ago. The rest, as they say, is history.'

'You've packed quite a lot into your history.' Cici looked at him admiringly.

'When I want something, I go after it with a vengeance.'

'And when you have it?'

'Then I savour it.'

Something in his tone, or was it his expression, made Cici swallow suddenly. She dabbed the corners of her mouth with her napkin and checked her watch. 'Goodness, it's late,' she said. 'Let's get the bill.'

He had insisted on paying, had walked her to a taxi rank and very much wanted to see her home.

'That's sweet of you, but thank you, no. I've had a most unexpected and enjoyable evening.'

'Then we must do it again.'

'Perhaps,' she said enigmatically, slipping into the taxi.

'Here's my card. Call me next time you're pretending not to be married.' He smiled briefly and walked away.

She hadn't called him, of course, although she had thought about it – and him – quite a lot.

But she did meet him again. He seemed to be at every function she had attended over Christmas. Cici had many young friends of both sexes, and although she flirted outrageously with the young men who admired her, she wasn't really attracted to any of them. They were amusing and fun to have at her Friday lunch table in Dominic's, but that was as far as it went – until Harry.

It didn't matter where she was or how many men of whatever age she was surrounded by, he would wait, patiently, intently, studying her, until one by one they left and only he remained, this strangely beautiful young man who had eyes only for her. And so she had agreed to meet him for a drink once or twice, and then lunch once or twice, maybe three times, and today, Cici smiled, today would be the fourth.

He intrigued her. He never pressed her, had never, since that first dinner, enquired or referred to her marriage, and he was terrific company. There was something about him, something she couldn't define, that made her feel alluring again, in a way she hadn't felt for years.

She decided on black, which was unusual for her, as she generally preferred complementing her looks with brighter colours that local Celtic complexions struggled with, but today she wanted to look dramatic. Black cigarette pants, a clinging, silk jersey T-shirt and a long, knee-length wraparound cardigan. Black high-heeled ankle boots completed the outfit. Her hair had been recently restyled, slightly shorter than usual, with a sexy angled fringe and flicked out at the back, very sixties. She picked up her newest oversized handbag, slung it over her shoulder and took a final approving look in the mirror, checked she had her phone and made for the door. Downstairs, on the hall table (always handy, which meant she never forgot), she picked up the bottle of Chanel No. 5 and dabbed some at her wrists and behind her ears. She was ready.

He was there before her, waiting eagerly, and noticed her the moment she walked through the door, standing up immediately from the table to greet her. As it was a Tuesday in January and they were meeting at three o'clock, Dominic's was pleasantly quiet, most people already winding up their lunches and heading back to work or home. Dom was nowhere to be seen, and then Cici remembered he was away on business, sourcing and selecting a variety of new organic cheeses from France. Before Cici reached the table, Tanya appeared at her side as if from nowhere and feigned surprise and delight at seeing her.

'Cici, how lovely to see you. We weren't expecting you.' She sounded puzzled.

'That's because I haven't booked, Tanya,' Cici beamed, 'but I can see my table and indeed my lunch companion is waiting.' She walked smoothly past her to her table, where Harry bent to kiss her cheek.

'Oh,' said Tanya, 'of course, how silly of me. Let me get you a glass of champagne.'

'It's already on the way, thanks,' Harry said, never taking his eyes off Cici as she sat down opposite him.

'I see. Well, if you need anything . . .' She hovered, disapproval seeping from every pore.

'If I need anything,' Cici gazed back at Harry, sounding amused, 'I'm sure it will be taken care of.'

'We'll let you know.' Harry looked up at Tanya, dismissing her with a nod.

Cici giggled as Tanya glided away. 'She makes me feel like a naughty schoolgirl, caught playing truant.'

'Aren't you?' Harry grinned. 'Although you're far more delectable than any schoolgirl I ever came across.'

'You're incorrigible.'

Just then the champagne arrived, poured deftly by Carla, and they ordered quickly, not needing to see the menu.

'Shall I tell you today's specials?' Carla asked.

'No thank you, not for me,' said Cici. 'I'll have the grilled chicken Caesar salad.'

'And for you, sir?'

'Fillet steak, rare, and a salad.'

Over lunch, Harry suddenly became serious. 'I was wondering,' he ventured, 'how you would feel about doing a photo shoot.'

'A photo shoot? What for?'

'A special issue of *Select*. I want to do a feature on Ireland's most stylish women. If I had my way,' he smiled, 'I would devote the whole section to you, but that would be unfair.' He watched as Cici's face softened. 'But I'm hoping that you'll agree to allow us to at least feature you?'

'What would that involve, exactly?'

'Ideally, we would shoot you at home in a selection of different outfits, which you would, of course, have complete control over. The interview – the article, that is – would cover how you live, your innate sense of style, the kind of clothes you like to wear, how you entertain, that sort of thing.'

'Hmm, interesting.' Cici took a sip of champagne. 'Would I have final approval on the shots?'

'That goes without saying, and I myself will be doing the interview and naturally would supervise the whole thing. We'd recommend hair and make-up people that we usually use, but if you prefer your own people, then that can be arranged.'

'It sounds like fun.' Cici sat back in her chair and smiled. 'I don't see why not.'

'I was hoping you'd say that.' He raised his glass to her. 'I can see the spread already. You'll be our most beautiful and intriguing subject.'

'I hope you're not planning on asking me any inappropriate questions.'

'How could anything at all about *you*, Cici, be inappropriate?'

Cici gave a throaty laugh. 'I see what you mean about going after something you want with a vengeance.'

'It's the only way.' His eyes held hers, and she didn't flinch, not even when he took her hand across the table and brought it gently to his lips and his leg brushed hers, for a second longer than could be considered accidental, under the table.

Shalom was doing something very unusual. She was eating. Rather a lot, actually, even more than for two. She hadn't bargained on feeling constantly ravenous, having long ago suppressed her overly eager appetite into complete submission. The fact that it was making itself felt again in such a demanding, insatiable manner had come as a complete surprise. But not as big a surprise as the fact that she was humouring it – indulging it, even – searching for ways to appease it even *before* the hunger pangs struck. This morning, and it was only eleven o'clock, she had already put away five slices of buttery toast, two doughnuts and three squares of Toblerone, and that was *after* her freshly blended morning smoothie, which was all she usually allowed herself.

It was all Candice's fault, of course. Since the fateful night of Ossie's party before Christmas and the horrific pictures and unflattering press coverage Shalom had been subjected to, she had been in a state of shock.

She had been thoroughly disgruntled to discover that once his initial anger had blown over, Ossie had proclaimed the whole incident to be laugh-out-loud funny and had even declared that Candice had displayed great 'spirit' to have acted in the manner she had. That all changed, though, when he discovered that Candice was freezing him out. Over Christmas she had refused to take a single one of his calls and it had drived Ossie to distraction.

'Darling,' Shalom had risked advising him after she had listened to him leave yet another pleading voice message on Candice's phone, 'you mustn't let her upset you like this. It's so bad for you, for your stress levels. Really, it's Candice who should be apologising to *you*.'

'She's only a child, Shalom,' Ossie had retorted, exasperated. 'My only child. This is difficult for her. It was a mistake not to explain things to her gently. I should have told her and her mother beforehand, at an appropriate time, together.'

Shalom had been livid but instead had said reproachfully, 'It's not a "thing", our baby, and there was never going to be an easy way to tell Candice, or Charlotte. You have a new life now Ossie, and you owe it to me and our baby not to let anything else distract you.' Two big tears rolled down her face. 'After all, I'm doing my best, and it's all terribly upsetting for *me*.'

'Sweetheart,' Ossie was immediately contrite, 'I'm so sorry, please don't cry. You know I can't bear to see you upset.'

He had put his arm around her. 'Every time I open my mouth these days, I appear to put my foot in it.'

Shalom sniffed.

'Why don't you go out and buy yourself and the baby something lovely? I have to go to the office, I'm late already, and I hate leaving you like this. Promise me you'll forgive me?'

'Of course I forgive you, darling. I know you didn't mean to upset me. I suppose I'm just sensitive at the moment, you know, a bit emotional.' She had smiled tremulously through her tears.

'Good girl,' he said, sounding relieved as he picked up his briefcase and made for the door. 'I'll see you later.'

Shalom hadn't forgiven him at all, but she was determined not to allow Candice and her carry-on to upset her relationship with Ossie.

Shalom couldn't stand Candice. The girl treated her with thinly veiled contempt at best and at worst was downright rude to her. Charlotte, on the other hand, on the few occasions she had met her, had been friendly and polite, almost disinterested. Shalom didn't really know what to make of Charlotte; she had never met anyone quite like her. She had seen photos of her, of course, in the society pages, organising this or that charity event. Ossie had always said she was a formidable fund-raiser. But in the flesh, Shalom had been taken aback to find that Charlotte was really very beautiful. She was tall and thin – she had a great figure, actually, only she didn't show it off the way she could have in all those boringly elegant clothes she wore. She had beautiful, pale skin, enormous dark eyes, and her hair, still dark and silky, fell in a mass of natural waves to her shoulders. She didn't wear enough make-up, in Shalom's opinion. If she did and got herself some funky, figure-hugging gear, Charlotte could be a real head-turner. Shalom didn't understand why she didn't get herself a stylist and a proper makeover with all that money she had. No wonder she hadn't got a man since Ossie left her.

After meeting Charlotte for the first time, Shalom had been intrigued. She would never in a million years have put Ossie and her together. She couldn't for the life of her think what Ossie would find attractive about her. She had even asked him about it later, when they were in the car.

'Did you ever really fancy Charlotte?'

'What?' Ossie seemed taken aback. 'What sort of a question is that? Of course I fancied her.'

'How?' she probed. 'In what way, exactly?'

'Charlotte's a very beautiful woman, obviously, but it wasn't just her looks. There was something fresh and unspoiled about her. She was terribly prim and proper and had no idea how sexy she was. I never thought she'd look at me, really. I used to love shocking her. She was so easy to wind up.' He laughed. 'I fancied her rotten.' A wistful look had come over his face and Shalom had quickly changed the subject, knowing instinctively that she had been heading for dangerous territory. After that, she stopped asking about Charlotte.

Their daughter, Candice, was another matter altogether. Ossie and Shalom had officially been together for over a year before he agreed to introduce them. Initially Shalom had just assumed he'd been being protective of her, and then she discovered that it was Candice who was refusing to meet *her*. When she had finally agreed to the introduction (and even Shalom didn't know that it had required clearing Candice's considerable credit-card debt and an increased limit on the same card), the encounter had been excruciating.

They had agreed to meet in the lounge of the Four Seasons Hotel for afternoon tea. The plan was that Ossie would pick Candice up from home and they would get there first, then after a respectable fifteen minutes or so Shalom would join them. This way, Ossie and Candice would have time to chat and relax. After all, she reflected, at seventeen and twenty-seven, a ten-year gap was really nothing between girls. Once Candice realised that Shalom wasn't an evil stepmother type but a glamorous, fashion-conscious young woman, she would relax and realise that they probably had a lot in common. She would be able to talk to her about clothes and hair and make-up, advise her on a style to cultivate – something Candice's own mother clearly had no intention of doing by the looks of things.

Shalom almost felt sorry for Candice. She had seen photographs of her and caught a glimpse of her once or twice when she had followed Ossie in the early days (unbeknownst to him) and parked across the road in a borrowed car, wearing a wig and sunglasses, so she could get a look at the women in his life. Candice, she was secretly relieved to discover, had not inherited her mother's dark beauty. In fact, from what Shalom could see, Candice was the living image of her father. It was almost comical. She even walked the same way, with a rather ungainly gait, and stood with her two legs planted firmly apart and her arms folded, particularly when she was making a point. Her colouring was fair, she had nice skin, and her light red hair was silky and poker straight. Shalom had assessed her shrewdly. She was no looker, but it was nothing that couldn't be improved upon. First of all, the girl was overweight by a good stone and a half. Puppy fat, maybe, but Shalom would have got rid of it, sharpish. Her face was quite pretty, really, and on the rare occasions when she smiled (mostly in photos, as far as Shalom could tell), she was like another person, the sulky mouth upturned and sweet, revealing straight, even teeth achieved by the braces that Charlotte insisted she wore in her early teens. Either way, Shalom had reckoned, Candice wouldn't be a problem. She had worried that she might be a younger, frostier version of her mother, with a snooty manner and the kind of bone structure achieved from generations of good breeding that no surgeon, sadly, had yet managed to replicate.

The girl she saw from her car window was really nothing but an awkward teenager. Once they got to know one another,

Candy would be relieved to find she had a sympathetic friend who would be able to help her with things her mother wouldn't or couldn't. With these reassuring thoughts in her mind, Shalom drove off home to her mother (she was still living at home at that stage) to report on the evening's findings. 'The daughter', as Shalom's mother, Bernie, referred to Candice, would not be a problem.

Her pleasing fantasies had come to an abrupt halt upon officially meeting Candice that first time, a year later.

Shalom had thought long and hard about what to wear, and in the end she decided to go for a funky, if more casual than usual outfit. As it was mid-summer, she chose her favourite pair of white Dolce & Gabbana skinny jeans, matching white high wedge sandals and a clingy black strappy T-shirt which revealed her toned stomach and cute little navel ring.

'There, you can't go wrong in black and white.' Bernie surveyed her daughter proudly. 'No point in hiding that figure of yours, pet, it's what he fell for in the first place, don't forget.'

Shalom had shown up late, as arranged, attracting not a little attention as she breezed into the hotel and joined Ossie and Candice in the lounge.

'Ah, here she is.' Ossie stood up to greet her, rather awkwardly, Shalom felt, and said to his daughter, 'Princess, I'd like you to meet my friend Shalom.' He had looked hopefully at Candice.

Shalom had held out her hand politely and said as she had practised in front of the mirror, 'Charmed to meet you. I've heard so much about you.' She kept a smile fixed on her face as Candice looked her up and down disbelievingly and took her hand gingerly, as if it might be infected.

'How do you do,' she said. And that was all she had said – to Shalom at any rate – deliberately excluding her from the conversation as she chatted away to Ossie, telling him about school, horses and how Jennifer, her grandmother, was going to show her and two friends how to pluck and cook a pheasant. 'Gran says it's a crucial part of a young woman's culinary training. "No good having manicured hands if you don't know what to do with them!"' Candice said in a perfect imitation of Jennifer's plummy tones. Ossie had roared with laughter while Shalom sat, still smiling politely but quietly simmering with rage.

Eventually, the strain had become too much even for Ossie, who got up, muttered something about settling the bill and said, 'I'll leave you two girls to have a little chat.'

'Candice,' Shalom leaned forward and began her well-rehearsed worst-case-scenario speech. 'I know this must be difficult for you, but can't we at least try to be friends? You know—'

'Shut up.' Candice's voice was dangerously quiet. 'What makes you think I'd want to be friends with a tart? Just because you're sleeping with my father doesn't mean you've pulled the wool over my eyes. You'll never weasel your way into my family, not if I have anything to do with it. And there's nothing friendly about you either. You've broken up a marriage and broken up my family. As far as I'm concerned you're just a gold-digging slapper. And you look like – like a stupid drag artist.' That last bit she had heard from Emma, who had reported that those were the words *her* mother had described Shalom with after seeing her picture for the first time in *VIP* magazine.

Just then, Ossie came back, smiling broadly. 'Come along, girls. Time I got you back home, Candy.'

And Candy had smiled sweetly and said, 'Thank you for tea, Daddy, it was lovely, and very nice to meet you too, Shalom.'

The drive home had passed in ominous silence, with Candice sitting in the back sending and receiving endless text messages, which appeared to be the cause of much giggling.

'Bye, Daddy,' she chirped, getting out of the car. 'See you soon. Take care, Shalom.' And she ran eagerly up the steps to her home.

'At least one of you seems to be in good spirits,' Ossie said, seemingly oblivious to the undercurrent. 'I must say,' he continued, 'I do think you could have made a bit more effort, Shalom. You didn't say one word to her the whole way back.'

Shalom had turned to him in fury. 'Don't you even dare!' she cried. 'That girl is a monster. I tried my very best. I was charming to her and she said the most horrible, horrible things to me when you left the room.'

'Really, sweetheart,' Ossie sighed. 'I think you're exaggerating. You must be imagining it. I thought she was very civil to you. You mustn't be jealous of her. You know I'm mad about you, but Candy is the most important person in my life. This is difficult for her. You have to understand and make allowances for her. She's only seventeen. It's an awkward age. She's just a child, really.'

It was a phrase Shalom was to become very familiar with over the following months – years even.

Since then, any thoughts Shalom had had about winning Candice over were well and truly knocked on the head. She supposed it was better this way. At least she knew where she stood. The battle lines had been drawn, and if Candice wanted to play it that way, that was fine by her. Shalom knew she had a fight on her hands, but whatever it took, she was *not* going to let Ossie's daughter come between them.

Anyway, soon they'd have a baby of their own, and that would change everything. Ossie adored children. He'd always assumed he'd have a large family and now she would give him another chance at fatherhood. Not that she had any intention of having a brood – one, maybe two, and that would be it. A boy and a girl would be nice, she mused. Her mother was usually right, she reflected, and she said it gave a woman a whole different standing in a relationship when she was the mother of her partner's child. And if Candice didn't like it, well, she'd just have to get used to the fact. It was positively ridiculous the way she expected to be babied by her father. And Ossie was as bad, still calling the girl Princess as if she was six years old.

'For heaven's sake, stop calling her that,' Shalom had said in an unusual burst of irritation not so long ago, after another hostile encounter with Candy.

Ossie had looked astonished. 'But it's what I've always called her. It's just habit, that's all.'

'It sounds pathetic. She's a grown woman now, I bet she hates it. I've seen her friends sniggering when you do it.'

'Oh,' Ossie sounded hurt. 'I didn't think . . . yes, I suppose it would be embarrassing. I must try to remember not to.'

'Come here, darling.' Shalom had immediately wound her arms around him. 'You're too good – that's your problem.' She kissed him and began to unbuckle his belt, feeling him grow hard at her touch. 'Little girls grow up,' she said in a cute baby voice, 'but never in their daddy's eyes.' She opened her blouse to reveal a low-cut balcony-style bra that her breasts threatened to escape from at any moment. Ossie groaned and bent to lick the nipple she exposed. 'Come to bed, big guy.' She pulled away and led him by the hand, laughing softly.

As Ossie followed her eagerly into their plush bordello-style bedroom, Shalom wriggled out of her jeans and draped herself provocatively on the bed. Seconds later he was on top of her, inside her, thrusting intently as she gazed, breathless and adoring, into his eyes. When he came, she held him, cradling his head against her breasts, and smiled.

The battle might have gone to Candice, but Shalom would win the war. After all, as Candice had rightly pointed out at that first meeting, she was sleeping with her father.

As strategies went, it was a pretty foolproof one, and Shalom knew just how to keep a man happy in that respect.

'No potatoes for me, Gran, thanks. Just eggs and bacon.'

'What? None of my special-recipe sauté potatoes? Are you sick?'

'I'm fine,' Candy assured her, 'I'm just cutting back a bit. Eggs and bacon are fine. Protein is good,' she said knowledgeably.

'You're not on one of those awful diets, are you? Ruinous to the hair and skin, you know.' Jennifer dished up the eggs and bacon on plates and added her special potatoes to all but one.

Charlotte was out at a committee meeting and Candice and her pals, Emma and Katy, were having a late breakfast with Jennifer.

'Nope. I've just been training at the gym.'

'Training for what?'

'Training – you know, working out, getting fit. That's all.'

'I must say you *are* looking well. And now that you mention it, yes, you've definitely got slimmer.' Jennifer passed the plates over.

Candice was pleased. The personal trainer she had signed up with was putting her through hell, but he was worth every tortuous minute if it meant losing weight and getting in shape – and she was. Even Gran had noticed now.

'Of course in my day,' Jennifer sat down at the table, 'nobody needed to diet. Food was a luxury we had to do without.'

'Gran grew up in Gloucestershire when the war was on,' Candice explained.

'Didn't have have to do any of this keep-fit nonsense either. No petrol. We had to cycle or ride everywhere. Lot to be said for it.'

'Was it as romantic as it looks in all those old movies?' Emma asked wistfully.

Jennifer smiled. 'I used not to think so, but now, well, when you get to be my age, everything looks better in retrospect. It did make situations and people more intense, I think.'

'Gran was proposed to lots of times, weren't you?'

'Oh, I had my admirers, to be sure, but I only had eyes for Flinty. Until I met your grandfather, of course.'

'Flinty was Gran's first fiancé, wasn't he?'

'Yes. It was love at first sight for both of us. I was only sixteen and I had snuck out with my sister to a local dance. I thought with my lipstick and powder I looked very grown up, but really I was just a terribly innocent and excitable young girl.' She paused, remembering.

'Go on.'

'Well, once we got into the hall, there were all these wonderfully good-looking men everywhere – Yanks, of course. All the girls were terribly keen on them, but I found them a bit forward, really. I was terribly shy, you see, and I suppose I looked older than my sixteen years. I was still awfully skinny, but even at that age I had quite a bust. Good bosoms, you know – all the Wilding women did – runs in my side of the family. Candice, bless her, takes after her father's side.'

Emma took a gulp of her Buck's Fizz and tried not to splutter as Katy caught her eye.

Candice watched them, daring them to so much as smile, her 34A measurements being the cause of much resentment on her part.

'Anyway, where was I? Well, a few of them surrounded me, and my sister was swept off, and a rather pushy chap asked me to dance. I was brought up never to refuse an invitation to dance, terribly impolite, unless the chap in question was drunk – which this chap clearly was. Didn't like the look of him anyway – smarmy type.'

'What did you do?' Katy was agog.

'I said, "No, thank you very much, I'd rather not. I think you've already had too much to drink."'

'Then what?'

'He didn't like that at all. Clearly wasn't used to being turned down – he became quite nasty, really. As I'm always telling Candice, and you girls should take note, origins will out.'

'What do you mean?' Emma asked.

'It means that someone's background and upbringing will always show through eventually, however much a person may try to suppress or avoid it. No avoiding the genes.'

'Anyway, what happened?'

'He looked me up and down, then said, "You're right, honey, I must be drunk. Who'd want to dance with you? I've seen better legs than yours on a piano."'

There was a gasp from the girls.

'To which I retorted, taken aback though I was, "And I've seen a better face than yours on a clock!"'

'Ohmigod!' said the girls, gasping with laughter.

'Quite. Then I heard this wonderful deep voice say, "Stand back, please, I'll handle this," and the owner of the voice stepped in and punched the Yank's lights out.'

'Brilliant!'

'Yes, he was, rather. Anyway, that was how I met Flinty, all six foot four gorgeous inches of him. Blond, blue-eyed and cheekbones I'd have killed for. We corresponded for four months. I only saw him on leave once, when he proposed and I accepted. Then the letters stopped and I received word from one of his squadron that he'd been killed in action over Germany. I had to come clean and tell my parents, who'd had no idea of my secret romance. I don't think I came out of my room for weeks.'

'What did you do?'

'What everybody else did – I got on with things. There were so many girls and women mourning lost lovers and husbands. The war was over, it was a time of huge upheaval, everyone had to help each other – it was the only option.'

'So how did you meet Candy's grandfather?'

'Over a horse.' Jennifer chuckled. 'It was all because of dear old "Fruity" Nesbit. He was one of the gang in London – you know, a chum. I was about twenty-two, an apprentice at Sotheby's. Fruity was terribly well off and his family had a flat in Cadogan Square. One night, we were all a bit squiffy, and someone found a bottle of peroxide in the cleaning cupboard. One of the chaps dared him to dye his hair blond, and by the end of the night his hair was flaxen. His parents came to town the next day and it didn't go down at all well with his father. He threw a complete fit, said he was going to have him sent out to Malaya to work on the plantations. Poor old Fruity did a runner and caught the mail boat to Ireland. A few of us went over for a weekend to console him, and he was having the most wonderful time hanging about the race-courses and gambling and he asked me to look over a horse he was thinking of buying so down we all went to Kildare to this lovely stud farm. As we watched this three-year-old being put through his paces, I was aware of this chap behind me talking, and then I realised he was talking to me!' Jennifer paused for effect as the girls listened, enthralled.

'What did he say?' asked Emma.

'"He'll fall at the first fence, mark my words – won't stay the pace, just like his predecessors – and I'll wager most of your suitors too." That was dear old Jeremy,' Jennifer laughed. 'Cut straight to the chase. I was intrigued, of course, and, luckily for me, he looked as nice as he sounded. We fell madly in love and were married six months later.'

'That's so romantic,' Katy sighed.

'You must miss him,' Emma ventured.

Jennifer smiled. 'Yes, I do miss him, of course I do, but he's around, you know. I can tell when he's around. The dogs know too. Animals are more finely tuned than we are. Just because someone dies doesn't mean they're not keeping an eye on you.'

As if to illustrate the point, Bonnie and Clyde emerged from under the table and began to bark, tails wagging.

'It's time for their walk. It's important to keep to a routine,' Jennifer said, getting up from the table.

'We'll clear away the dishes, Gran,' Candy said.

'Thank you so much for breakfast, Jennifer,' Katy and Emma said.

'It was a pleasure to have you girls. I hope I didn't bore you with all my talk of the past.' Bonnie and Clyde sat quivering with excitement as Jennifer produced their leads.

'It's much more exciting than anything that's happened to us so far.' Katy sounded glum.

'You never know what's around the corner.' Jennifer set off with the dogs, walking stick to hand. 'Cheerio, girls – and don't tell your mother there was Buck's Fizz with breakfast, she'll lecture me about how I'm setting you a bad example.'

'Bye, Gran,' Candy called after her.

'Are you really sure about this Candy?' Emma asked after they were sure Jennifer was gone.

'Of course I'm sure.'

'What time's your appointment?'

'Two-thirty.'

'Chinese dentist time,' quipped Katy.

'Very funny,' Candy said, giving the table a final wipe. 'Come on, let's go back upstairs. Dad got the *Sex and the City* movie downloaded for me ages ago. Anyone for cosmos?' she laughed as her friends followed her.

6

P.J. was woken by the unusual sound of Bones barking downstairs. Even more unusual was that it was bright outside. He checked the clock: 9:30 a.m. He sat up with a start. He must have overslept. And then he remembered – it was Saturday and there was no surgery. All the same, he was usually awake hours before this. No wonder poor Bones was barking, he must have been dying to get out for a pee, and being the well-trained animal he was, he'd rather explode than make a puddle on the floor, particularly if Sheila were to come across the evidence and find him responsible. P.J. couldn't say he blamed him.

That was it! No wonder he had slept in. Sheila had left yesterday to go on a weekend pilgrimage to visit some religious shrine or other and the house was blissfully quiet, apart from Bones protesting from the kitchen. Normally Sheila didn't believe in time off and came in on Saturday, just as she did every other day, to keep hearth and home pristine for her beloved employer. In fact, because she didn't have her surgery duties to distract her, Saturday was the day she got down to the *really* thorough cleaning assault.

P.J. had long since become used to being roused from a reasonably pleasant dream or slight hangover stupor by the strains of the industrial-sized hoover Sheila wielded outside his door. *Errmm, errmm, errmm* it would drone until it seemed as if it was right inside his head, and P.J. would give up any hope of returning to sleep for a well-earned lie-in. What would happen if he were ever to bring a woman home didn't bear thinking about. 'Sorry, hon,' he'd imagine saying as a noise to wake the dead began any time around seven a.m. – from the hoover outside the door, to the clatter and banging of windows and floors being attacked, to pots and pans being brandished. 'The good news is, there's a cooked breakfast waiting for us downstairs.' And then he and his lady friend would stroll downstairs, hungry after a late night of love-making, saunter into the kitchen and he would say, confidently, with a look that brooked no nonsense, 'Sheila I'd like to introduce my lover, Mrs X, and honey, this is my mad housekeeper, Sheila.' The fantasy, for some strange reason, always stopped there.

But today P.J. stretched lazily before leaving his comfortable bed. Today, there would be blissful peace with not a single soul to bother him. He would have to make the most of it.

Downstairs, he released a grateful and forgiving dog into the garden and set about making coffee and toast. He was about to retreat upstairs, cup and plate in hand, when Bones bounded back inside looking dismayed that he was about to be abandoned again.

P.J. relented. 'All right,' he said, grinning, as he jerked his head towards the kitchen door. 'I won't tell if you won't.' Bones dashed past him and shot upstairs, where, as he fully expected, P.J. found him looking both adoring and guilty as he sprawled on the bed.

Climbing back under the covers, P.J. flicked on the television and checked the sports results. There was a Grand Slam rugby match too this afternoon, he reminded himself. Ireland were playing away, in Edinburgh. P.J. had had two tickets for the match (a gift from a patient) but didn't fancy going. These days, a rugby trip took longer and longer to recover from. Instead, he had given the tickets to Alex, hoping he might suggest going with him, which he *would* have considered. Instead, Alex had said, 'Thanks, Dad, they'll come in handy. Just in time too, a client of mine will kill for them.'

'Big supporter, is he?' P.J. had enquired.

'What? Oh no, she's a girl. But she's after a rugger bugger and apparently Edinburgh's one of the more fun away games to go to.'

'It is,' P.J. said, feeling deflated. Those tickets were like gold dust, virtually unobtainable. It wasn't that he resented them going to this girl, whoever she was, but they probably wouldn't even be used for the game. They would likely go to waste while the girls got dolled up and staked their claim in the pub or hotel of choice and waited for the boys to come back, geared up and ready for action.

He thought of all the matches he and Jilly had gone to over the years, at home and away. She had enjoyed them all as much as he had, particularly England v. Ireland, where she would insist on shouting for England even in the midst of the Irish supporters. For some of the bigger home games, they would have a pre-match lunch, eagerly attended by all their friends before setting off to the game or settling down to watch it at home in the kitchen, as P.J. would today. He thought of Jilly now, as he always did, and wondered if she could see him and what she would think of him and how he had done without her.

He was lonely. He let the thought roll around his head for longer than the usual millisecond he allowed it. He knew Jilly would definitely not want that for him. They had discussed it on several occasions, even before she had become ill, that if anything were to happen to either of them, they would each want the other to find happiness with someone else, never dreaming for a moment that the unthinkable occasion was so much closer than they could have possibly imagined.

'Just as long as you know that if the bedposts are rattling in protest, it's me from wherever I'll be watching – and not your new lover,' P.J. had grumbled, joking.

'I wouldn't want you to be on your own – really,' Jilly had said seriously. 'You wouldn't do well. I'm not saying you wouldn't cope,' she added, seeing the look of objection on P.J.'s face. 'But you're a man who *needs* a woman, it's what you're made for – and some very lucky woman out there will need you too.'

'The only need I have right now,' he had retorted, tired now of the mournful nature of the conversation, however theoretical, 'is for my gorgeous, sexy wife to attend to her conjugal duties – immediately.' He climbed on top of her and kissed her lingeringly. 'I'll give you rattling bedposts,' he had laughed, coming up for air.

P.J. smiled, remembering, then jumped as his elbow was firmly nudged, and Bones (who had been edging artfully up the bed towards his master) thrust his big face under his arm and snuggled down beside him, sighing happily, his head resting on P.J.'s hip.

'Looks like you're my only prospect for bedroom company, mate.' He ruffled his dog's head. 'I mean, who on earth would take us on?' he asked as Bones yawned widely. Thirty seconds later, they were both asleep.

He was awoken for the second time that morning by his dog. This time, Bones was licking his hand assiduously. 'What the . . .?' P.J. began, then collapsed back on the pillows again. Good Lord, it was ten to twelve; he'd been asleep for almost two hours. He leapt out of bed, hit the shower, skipped shaving and dressed speedily. 'Come on, fella, it's time we got some fresh air. I'll take you for an extra-long walk now, then we can veg out and watch the match. How about that?' Bones hurtled downstairs ahead of him and by the time P.J. reached the hall was already sitting with his lead in his mouth, his tail thumping eagerly against the floor.

Outside, the bracing January Saturday was clear and bright. P.J. inhaled the crisp air and felt himself revive. He really must try and get more exercise, he thought, but somehow there just never seemed to be enough time. A daily stroll or two to the park with Bones just didn't do it – his waistbands were beginning to feel particularly tight these days.

Inside the park gates, he let Bones off the lead and headed for the riverside so that he could throw Bones's favourite rubber toy into the water. He was laughing at Bones, who, soaking wet, emerged up from the riverbank, shook himself heartily, panted heavily and did his typical Labrador victory parade before replacing the toy at his master's feet. P.J. was bending down to pick it up when he heard a clipped, accented and very disapproving voice.

'You're an absolute disgrace!'

P.J. straightened himself up and looked around, expecting to see a naughty child being reprimanded, but the park was quiet. The voice came again from behind him, louder this time.

'You there! Yes, you!'

P.J. wheeled around to see an immaculately turned-out elderly woman leaning on a park bench, regarding him with derision. She was wearing a green padded Barbour jacket, tweed herringbone skirt, green Hunter wellingtons and what he'd bet was a Hermés headscarf tied elegantly under her chin. She looked like a slightly taller and more glamorous version of the Queen – and just as forbidding. As she brought a dog whistle to her lips, two white and tan Jack Russells hurtled out of the undergrowth, raced to heel and sat at her feet obediently.

'I'm sorry,' P.J. looked around again, perplexed, checking if there was some mistake, 'but are you talking to *me*?'

'I certainly am,' the woman said. 'I don't see anybody else around, do you?'

P.J. walked towards her slowly, wondering if she was a bit of a loony. Perhaps she wasn't meant to be out alone or needed directions home – but then, the dogs were obviously hers.

He tried again. 'You were saying . . .?'

'You heard perfectly well: you're a disgrace.'

'Might I enquire why, exactly?'

'That unfortunate creature belongs to you, I take it?' She pointed a walking cane at Bones, who was lying down, gnawing happily at his toy.

'That's my dog, yes. What is unfortunate about him, I have no idea. Do you have some kind of objection to my owning one?'

The woman snorted. 'I should think so. Look at him! He can hardly walk, never mind run. The poor animal is obese. It's outrageous to let a dog get that fat. I've a good mind to report you. I'll have you know I'm very well connected, and the animal-rights people would take a very dim view of this, a very dim view indeed. When was he last at the vet? Surely he or she must have said something to you?'

'Not that it's any of your business,' P.J. was counting to ten, slowly, 'but Bones has regular veterinary check-ups. He's in perfectly good health.' He was embellishing the truth a bit on this last point, as his vet had pointed out (tactfully, mind you) that Bones was very, very overweight.

'Bones!' The woman showed the first signs of mirth and laughed heartily. 'Well, that's surely a misnomer.'

On hearing his name, Bones came over to investigate and sniffed at her with interest.

'Sit!' she commanded. And he did, responding immediately to the authority in her tone, although he looked worriedly towards P.J.

He was rewarded by an examination worthy of a Crufts judge. 'Just as I thought,' the woman proclaimed, examining his teeth. 'Magnificent dog. Beautiful head. Damned fine pedigree, I'll wager.'

'Well, now that you mention it, his grandfather, or maybe great-grandfather, was a field champion, actually,' P.J. said, vaguely remembering his pedigree papers lodged in some long-lost pile of paper in his office.

'What's the matter with you?' She looked perplexed, then held out her hand. 'Jennifer Searson. I live across the square.'

'You do?' P.J. took the proffered hand and shook it, feeling decidedly wary.

'Number 42.'

'I thought that was . . .' P.J. trailed off.

'Yes, it used to be Ossie Keating's house, but it's my daughter's now – actually, it always was. I live in the basement. Converted flat. Suits us both.'

'How do you do. I'm—'

'I know who you are. You're that doctor chap everyone's always talking about.'

'Is that so?'

'I must say, it's pretty typical.'

'What is?'

'Physician heal thyself and all that.'

'I'm not sure I follow you.' Definitely early Alzheimer's or dementia. P.J. was mentally running through possible diagnoses.

'You're clearly no stranger to the knife and fork yourself!'

For once, P.J. was lost for words.

'And if I'm not mistaken,' Jennifer continued, giving him an unapologetic once-over, 'and I rarely am, Doctor, you're a good-looking man if you'd care to keep yourself in any sort of shape. Can't bear people who let themselves go to seed. Shows dreadful lack of character. But no need to inflict your lack of discipline on this fine animal. Is this the only walk he gets?'

'Well, sometimes we get out in the morning.'

'Sometimes? And for a stroll like this? That's not good enough.'

'Bones and I are perfectly happy with the arrangement. Now if you'll excuse me, Jennifer, it was very nice meeting you.' P.J. made to walk away.

'He'll be dead before the year's out,' she called after him. 'Mark my words. Then you'll be sorry.'

P.J. stopped in his tracks and turned around. It had been a long time since he'd lost his temper, and when he did, he was fearsome. He didn't want to do it now – she wasn't worth it.

'I'll tell you what,' she said, oblivious to his rising blood pressure. 'My daughter takes these two,' she indicated the Jack Russells, who were now racing around with Bones, who was doing his best to keep up, 'three times a week to Sandymount Beach for a proper run, an hour at least. I'm sure she'd be glad to take Bones along. Three months of proper exercise and you won't know him. He'll love it. What do you say?'

Before P.J. had a chance to reply, she continued.

'Monday, Wednesday and Friday, seven a.m. sharp. That too early for you to have him ready?'

'Certainly not.' For some inexplicable reason, P.J. felt it imperative to rise to the challenge.

'Jolly good, then. I'll tell her to pick him up on Monday. Come along.' She blew again into the whistle and her dogs dashed back to her, leaving Bones looking deflated.

'Cheerio, Doctor!' And with that she was off, although P.J. noted the limp and the grimace she fought to conceal. She was probably in a good deal of pain with that hip, he deduced, but not as much as he'd have liked her to be in. Shaking his head, he threw a few more balls for Bones, then made for home himself.

'Holy Mother of Divine God,' he said aloud. 'What do you make of her?' He looked at Bones, who was, now that he cared to admit it, panting alarmingly and plodding along rather slowly. P.J. was suddenly overcome with guilt. 'I have let you get appallingly fat, old chap. The old bat was right, we do need to shape up. But that's all about to change – you'll hit the beach and I'll hit the gym. And,' he reflected mournfully, 'I expect we'll have to take a look at our respective diets, too.'

And then another thought hit him. If the mother was anything to go by, the daughter was *bound* to be a complete harridan. Oh well, who cared? He would have Sheila hand

Bones over and reclaim him. Sheila would be able for any amount of them.

With that potentially awkward encounter resolved, P.J. set off for home feeling considerably better about the forthcoming arrangement.

Carla sat in the small baroque-style church and closed her eyes, letting the uplifting strains of the choir wash over her. She certainly hadn't intended on going to mass – she couldn't even remember the last time she'd been to church at home in New York – but for some reason it had seemed like a good idea this Sunday. In one of the guidebooks she had read, she remembered the church being described as a gem, and it didn't disappoint. Built in the gardens beside and behind number 87 St Stephen's Green, the church was the work of the late Cardinal Henry Newman. Known locally simply as University Church, the correct title was in fact Our Lady Seat of Wisdom. Carla smiled at that – she could sure do with a bit of wisdom.

She had woken up that morning at eight o'clock in the little one-bedroom basement flat she had rented in Wellington Square and had known immediately that she wouldn't get back to sleep. It was one of those dark, grey, misty January mornings and already a light drizzle was trailing against the window. Despite the weather, Carla had suddenly felt the need to get out – anywhere. She pulled on her sweatpants, trainers and a top, put on a baseball cap and set off. Walking briskly, she reached her destination, Sandymount Beach, in about twenty minutes, and once she was down on the sand, she began to run. That was something she hadn't done in a while either, and she felt the better for it. At home, she used to run at least three times a week, sometimes more.

Home. That's why she'd had to get out. If she'd stayed one more minute in the flat, she would have been tempted to pick up the phone and dial home, and that was the one thing she was not going to do. Not yet, anyway, not even when she was feeling this homesick – *especially* not when she was feeling this homesick. Looking around her, she wasn't sure whether the general greyness helped or not. The sky was grey, the sand was grey, and the sea, or what she could see of it, the tide being so far out, appeared to be grey as well. But it wasn't New York grey. Still, it felt good to get out, to run, and, good to watch other early souls out and about, walking their dogs or playing with their kids.

Afterwards, she picked up the papers on her way home and, after a long, hot shower, settled down to read them. Except she couldn't settle. That was when she'd decided to go into town, go to church and afterwards meet Liz for a pizza. Liz was her neighbour and shared the flat across the hall with another Slovakian girl. They were both studying hotel management and had jumped at the chance for an exchange year in Dublin.

Pino, her usual companion, was on duty and Astrid was away for the long-promised weekend in Vienna with Rollo, so instead of relaxing at home on her one Sunday off in the month, Carla found herself back in town, sitting in a church of all places.

She closed her eyes now and remembered all the times she had gone to mass with her mother, father and three brothers. The ritual had always been the same for as long as she could remember: her mother singing, making pancakes in the kitchen, chasing them to get clean and dressed, and her father, drinking coffee and saying without fail from behind his newspaper, 'You can't beat real Italian coffee, nothing like that dishwater the Americans swallow.' And then they would set off in their Sunday best, all of them in the car, the boys – Marco, Paulo, Bruno – and herself, squabbling in the back.

After mass, they would return home and her mother and one or more of her mother's many sisters would gather in the kitchen to prepare the wonderful lunch that could include anything from eight to eighteen friends, neighbours and various relatives and, of course, the parish priest, Father Barbero. They would eat and talk and laugh and argue long into the evening, until Carla would climb onto her father's knee and fall asleep. Later her mother would put her to bed and read to her, telling her stories of when she had been a little girl in Italy. Carla never tired of these stories and eagerly looked forward to the time when, as her mother promised, they would go to Rome, just the two of them, to shop and sightsee and visit family. Only it never happened that way.

One Sunday, everything changed.

The Sunday her mother had complained of feeling dizzy before mass and then had collapsed on the floor with a sickening thud. The Sunday she had been rushed to hospital in an ambulance and Carla had been rushed to her room and kept there, watched over by her fretful aunt. The Sunday when Father Barbero came over and the other, younger priest. When the house was full of people, but everyone was crying, not laughing. The Sunday her mother died. The Sunday that had been Carla's eighth birthday. When everything had changed for ever.

After that, she had never liked Sundays much. Oh, life went on. The old brownstone house was always full of people, and her three older brothers grew up and so did she. Her father didn't remarry. He didn't have to, really. Carla's many aunts and uncles made sure he was never alone, and that seemed to be enough for him. He threw himself into the family business, and, one by one, her brothers joined him. Except it was Carla who outshone them all.

At first, she had gone along with her father's wishes. She had worked hard at the private convent school she attended, and, despite her protestations, she had gone to a prestigious finishing school in Switzerland, where she perfected her French, learned how to arrange flowers and recognise a good painting and listened politely at the cookery classes, just about managing to hide her monumental disinterest.

When she returned home, her father had her career all mapped out for her – an apprenticeship with Gerard Matteus, the renowned gemologist, after which she could take her pick of positions in any firm of jewellers, or indeed consultancies, in New York, or wherever she chose.

It was then that she put her foot down. Carla wasn't interested in diamonds, sapphires or rubies. She understood what her father was trying to do – provide his daughter with what he imagined to be the most glamorous, feminine and sought-after career any girl could want. But like many a father before him, Antonio Berlusconi had underestimated his daughter.

Carla's passion was, not unnaturally, food. From the age of thirteen, she had cooked competently and efficiently, helping with and sometimes preparing the weekly Sunday lunches and evening dinners, quickly finishing her homework so she could join the productive, comforting atmosphere of the kitchen, fitting in seamlessly and learning effortlessly from her aunts, father and various household cooks. By fifteen, she was scouring New York's food markets the way other girls scoured flea markets, creating and collecting recipes and then constantly improving them, instinctively knowing just the right ingredient or twist to add that vital *ooomph* to a dish. By eighteen, her aunts were standing back and learning from her.

At first, her father thought it amusing, touching. Of course he was glad, proud even, that Carla was such a good cook – it reflected well on him, seeing as he ran the most successful chain of Italian restaurants in New York. But as a career? Certainly not. He had no intention of allowing his only daughter to engage in the fiercely competitive, fiendishly aggressive and downright cut-throat world of the kitchen. That was the arena in which her brothers would compete and carry on the family tradition. So far, two of them were doing very well, and the other, Paulo, who failed to show the family flair in the kitchen, had become an accountant, also vital to the family business.

Carla begged and pleaded, to no avail.

'I will not have my daughter working like an immigrant pauper in some hellhole of a kitchen,' Antonio fumed. 'Why can't you just *try* the gemology apprenticeship – for me?' he tried cajoling.

'Because I don't even *like* jewellery – I never have!' Carla screamed.

'Forget the jewellery then! Think of the career, the people you'll meet from educated, aristocratic backgrounds. Men who appreciate the finer things in life, who show finesse, discernment – not some idiot, arrogant chef who will work you to the bone just for the pleasure of it, especially because of who you are!'

'Don't worry,' Carla had replied scathingly, 'they can't all be like you.'

'How dare you!'

'Very easily – just watch me.'

After that particular scene she had packed a suitcase, and, with the help of the money in the savings account her mother had left her (for the shopping trip to Rome) she had caught a flight to Paris, stayed in a hostel and from there had done her research. Within a week she had secured her first position in the kitchen of her choice.

She started off as a plongeur, washer-up and general dogsbody, but within a year she was the most requested sous chef in the kitchen. After Paris came Switzerland, then London, where working under an infamous French establishment chef, she was part of the team that obtained the restaurant's third Michelin star.

She went home once a year, and her father eventually accepted defeat. Six months after that, she was back. A year on, heading up the kitchen at the trendy new M Hotel, she was listed among America's top five chefs to watch in *Time* magazine.

Her brothers were not altogether happy. The family business was doing well and they were due to expand and add another restaurant to the chain, this time in Manhattan. Carla saw her chance. She had always dreamed of running her own restaurant.

'Let me head it up, Papa,' she begged her father. 'Berlusconi's needs a newer, modern flagship. I know I could do it.'

Her father hemmed and hawed and finally agreed to at least consider the idea. 'Let me talk to your brothers.'

They were adamantly against the idea.

'So what?' Carla cried. 'It's what *you* say that goes, Papa. What does it matter what they think?' she fumed. 'Marco has always been threatened by me, and Bruno's a lazy chef.'

'That's no way to talk about your brothers.'

'It's the truth! You know it is.'

'What if it is, Carla? Is that so bad? Why must you be so . . . so driven? You're nearly thirty now.'

'Twenty-eight.'

'Exactly! Don't you want to find a nice man, settle down, have some *bambinos*?'

'I want a restaurant of my own. And if you won't help me, I'll do it without you.'

'Carla,' he reasoned, 'please, this is your *family* you're talking about, your own flesh and blood. Nothing is worth creating friction and bad feeling between family. Besides,' he gestured helplessly, 'if you won't do it for me, at least think of your mother – think of what she would have wanted.'

'She'd have wanted me to have a fulfilling life of my own – that's what she would have wanted, not to be running around after a household of selfish men all my life like she did!' She got up, pushing her chair back angrily from the table. 'You can shove your restaurant! And tell my brothers they're welcome to their out-of-date, third-rate brand of dining. The word on the street is that Berlusconi's is in trouble. When was the last time you checked the figures, Papa? Is Paulo as good an accountant as Bruno is a chef?

If I were you, I'd make sure the books weren't the only thing being decently cooked in the *family* restaurant.'

'Now you have gone too far, Carla.' His voice was quivering with anger. 'My sons would never be responsible for such a dishonourable act.'

'Is that so?' Carla looked pityingly at him, her arrogant, handsome, pig-headed father, too proud to even contemplate that his sons could be letting things slip, withholding vital information, that they would be too afraid to admit the truth to him.

'Just remember that you heard it from me first. I could have turned things around for you. Good luck, Papa. I hope you work things out.' She began to walk away.

'Come back here! I haven't finished talking to you.'

'We have nothing more to say to each other, Papa. Say goodbye to my brothers for me – neither they nor you will be hearing from me for quite some time.'

'Where are you going?'

'What's it to you?'

Truthfully, Carla had had no idea what she was going to do. She was shocked at her brothers' resentment and at her father's lack of support for her and his total disregard for her wishes, despite all her hard-won achievements. Everything had to be on *his* terms – which meant, as usual in her family, that the men got to run the show, even if it was turning out to be a very lacklustre production.

She handed in her resignation with regret at the M. Carla knew she had to get away from New York again, away from her family and their antediluvian, masochistic behaviour.

She never really knew what made her choose Dublin. Perhaps it was because she had not one drop of Irish blood in her, no long-lost relatives, no ancestors, no roots. She simply knew that one night she found herself in an Irish hotel in Manhattan called Fitzpatrick's, where her friends were meeting other friends, visiting from Ireland. When she mentioned that despite all her travels throughout Europe she had never been to Ireland, not even when she had been living in London, outrage was expressed. Instructions were issued, addresses written down, Guinness and oysters extolled, poetry and pubs eulogised, *craic* mightified, and suddenly it had all seemed like a very good idea. A week later she had a one-way ticket on an Aer Lingus flight to a city where nobody knew her, and better still, where nobody knew she could cook – there was something wonderfully liberating about that. She called it her year of being invisible – a gap year in more ways than one. She rented a small flat, got herself a job as a waitress and settled in to forgetting all about drive, ambition and career advancement.

That had been three months ago and she hadn't phoned home once, except to leave a message to say she was safe and was taking a year out to travel. But it still got to her – or rather, *they* got to her – even across all the miles.

Rousing herself from her thoughts, Carla realised that mass was over. The priest said the final blessing and people began to file out of the church. She waited a minute, until the church was almost empty, and went over to light a candle and to say a silent prayer to her mother. Sometimes she missed her more than ever. Perhaps it was because today was Carla's birthday, and this was probably the closest thing to a celebration she was going to get.

She'd have loved to be able to talk to her mother about how lonely she got sometimes.

It was odd, but when she felt very lonely, the only person who sprung to her mind was Dom. If she was with him, she wouldn't be lonely. But since the 'incident', he was assiduously keeping his distance and Carla made sure to be equally aloof around him, even though she knew she was being stupid. What would her mother tell her to do? What would she say to her? *Oh Mama, I'm falling for a guy that doesn't have the slightest interest in me apart from a drunken kiss which he clearly regrets, since he can barely look me in the eye any more. And all because I threw myself at him. I'm a mess.*

Outside, the rain had stopped and she walked quickly across the Green and onto nearby Dawson Street, into the pizza place where she was meeting Liz. Inside, it was jammed, although Carla quickly spotted Liz waving to her through the throngs of people from a table at the back.

'*Ciao, bella*,' she grinned as Carla sat down. 'Red okay?' she asked, pouring Carla a glass. 'It's that kind of Sunday, don't you think?'

'Perfect,' Carla agreed, feeling suddenly more cheerful. 'God, it's nice to be waited on for a change,' she said as the pizzas arrived.

'So, how's Dublin's smartest eatery?'

'Exhausting.'

'I'm looking forward to the DVD,' Liz grinned.

'What DVD?'

'Pino says he got a friend to copy the footage from that Tudor party you were at. He says you look adorable in it! He's having us all around next Thursday for a private viewing.'

'It was something else, all right. Unbelievable. Oh shit,' Carla muttered, shrinking back in her chair.

'What?'

'I've just seen someone.' There was no mistaking the blonde, blow-dried hair and the smiling, determined expression, head bent towards her dining companion as she talked intently while signing the bill.

'Who?'

'Oh, it's nothing,' Carla brushed it off. 'Just someone I work with and would rather avoid. It's okay, she looks as if she's just about to leave.'

And she did – walking briskly through the tables and towards the exit, giving a frosty smile to the manager who held the door open for her. There was no mistaking Tanya, but it was who she was lunching with that interested Carla.

It was Eric, Dominic's accountant, and he was looking anything but happy.

Carla felt her professional antennae vibrate. Something was up, and she'd bet her bottom dollar it had to do with Tanya and her cavalier attitude to entertaining her friends at Dominic's. Few established restaurants, let alone a new one, could cope with all that comping. Despite what had happened between them, Carla suddenly felt a wave of concern for Dom. He was so good at what he did, so trusting – was it possible he was unaware of what Tanya was doing?

'I have to say something to Dom,' Eric persisted as he scurried to keep up with Tanya's lengthening strides. 'It would be remiss of me not to. I've only held off this long because you asked me not to, but really, Tanya, he needs to know. Something has to be done.'

'Just one more month, Eric, that's all I'm asking. Four weeks. That won't hurt – can't hurt – surely? Dom has a lot on his plate right now, if you'll excuse the pun,' she smiled. 'I'm sure even you have noticed that his parents' marriage is under quite a lot of strain at the moment. He really doesn't need any extra concerns right now. Anyway, it's nothing I can't take care of. A few more reviews, a mention or two in the right columns . . .'

'Tanya, this is way beyond the bounds of playing PR games. Dominic's is in real trouble. I don't think you're quite grasping the fact.' Eric was frustrated, his small, thin mouth pursed in disapproval. 'As for Dom's parents, well, Cici herself is responsible for quite a large chunk of the deficit, not to mention you and your PR chums.'

Tanya had grasped it all right. 'Look, I have a plan. There's always a way round these things if you just keep calm and think laterally. If you tell Dom now, he'll just go into a spiral of panic and then we really will be in trouble. Just a month, that's all I'm asking.' She flashed him her most beguiling smile. She had no intention of letting Eric ruin her plans.

'Well . . .' Eric was reluctant. 'I hope it's a plan that ends in four zeros, because that's what it's going to take to get him out of the red. One month, Tanya, that's all I can promise. After that, it'll be out of my hands.'

'You won't regret it,' Tanya beamed and kissed him on the cheek. 'You'll see.' She waved goodbye to him as she slipped into the taxi at the head of the queue on the Green.

Once she was home, Tanya switched on the gas fire and slipped into her favourite cashmere hoodie and lounging trousers. She thought about ringing Dom and then decided against it. He was lunching with his father in the Royal Irish Yacht Club, and although he had invited Tanya, she had encouraged him to take the opportunity to have a good man-to-man talk to his father and find out what exactly was going on with him and Cici.

'I mean, it's ridiculous, Dom,' she had said to him last week when they were heading upstairs after a late night in the restaurant. 'Moving into the mews, living at the bottom of the garden and carrying on as if she was a – well, certainly not a wife and mother of three, not to mention pushing fifty.' Tanya couldn't help the nasty little jibe escaping. Her own mother was the same age and had followed Cici's 'career', as she snidely called it, since her arrival in Ireland all those years ago, when she had snared one of the most eligible bachelors in the country seemingly overnight.

'Hmph,' her mother had said. 'No wonder they got married in Rome. It was the talk of Dublin at the time. James Coleman's parents were *not at all* happy about their son marrying an Italian showgirl.'

'Was she really a showgirl?' Tanya had asked.

'She claimed she was an actress – well she would, wouldn't she? But no one here has ever seen or heard of any films she was in.'

'Please, Tanya,' Dom said, 'not now. I have no idea what's going on with my mother, and I'd say Dad knows even less. But I'd really rather not think about it at the moment, if you don't mind.'

Tanya knew when to back off. 'Of course, lovey, I'm sorry. It's absolutely none of my business. It's just that I hate to see your dad so, well, helpless, and he seems so desperately unhappy.'

'That's probably because he is,' Dom sighed. 'Look, like I said, I really don't want to talk about it – she's probably just throwing a few parties, taking a bit of space. You know what she's like. It's not as if she's having an affair or anything, is it?'

Tanya chewed her lip. 'Look, I probably shouldn't say this, but you know what this town is like, and in my business, well, I get to hear more than most people. I'm sure there's nothing in it, but . . .'

'But what?' Dom was frowning.

'Like I said, I'm sure it's nothing, but Cici has been seen around a lot with Harry McCabe. I've seen them myself, lunching in Dominic's at least twice. People are beginning to talk.'

'Harry McCabe!' Dom exclaimed. 'But he's only . . . he can't be more than—'

'Your age,' Tanya finished. 'Exactly.'

'That's impossible.' Dom looked horrified for a moment.

'I'm sure you're right, babe. I'm sure it's just gossip, but if your father gets to hear of it – or perhaps he already has – it won't help things.'

'No,' Dom agreed, 'it certainly will not. I'll have lunch with him on Sunday, sound him out, find out what's going on.'

'I think that would be a very good idea.' Tanya looked sympathetic. 'It can't be easy for him, poor man.'

Now, at home, sitting with her feet curled under her on the large modern sofa, Tanya cursed Dom's mother for her appalling timing, never mind behaviour. And as if that wasn't bad enough, now she had this financial mess in the restaurant to worry about too. At this rate, marriage would be the last thing on Dom's mind, even though they had been getting on better than ever these past few months. Tanya had made sure of that. She frowned, lost deep in thought. Things were not going her way. Indeed, they appeared to be conspiring against her. But that was ridiculous. That was the way losers thought, and whatever else she was, Tanya was not a loser. Still, for the life of her, she couldn't think what to do. *Make it happen*, the voice whispered in her mind. *Take control.* But how?

She loved Dom, of course she did. Who wouldn't? He was handsome, charming, funny, kind and thoughtful. But it was more than that. She didn't just love Dom, she loved everything he represented, everything he was a part of – everything, in short, that she wasn't. It was something Dom couldn't possibly understand, even if she had been able to find the words to explain it to him. How she longed to be a part of his world – that cultivated, rarefied world of careless elegance and throwaway, confident remarks that were the product of enviable educations and glamorous backgrounds, unimaginable advantages that the people upon whom these blessings were bestowed seemed to take for granted.

But Tanya never would. She would enjoy every hard-won, exquisite minute of belonging to that world, precisely because she knew what it was like to look in at it from the outside.

She often tried to remember her dad. Sometimes she thought she could. If she looked at a photograph for long enough, sometimes she thought she could remember his face, his smile. Sometimes she thought she remembered his smell, a vague combination of tobacco and aftershave, or his voice, a comforting, gravelly reassurance, but then she would wonder if it was all in her imagination.

When she asked her mother about it, she was bitterly

dismissive. 'I'm not surprised you can't remember him – he was never around,' she had laughed.

'But he must have been, some of the time at least,' Tanya persisted.

'Not in my version of events, sweetheart. He was working, or so he claimed, and when he wasn't working he was on the golf course. Both pastimes were followed by a stint in the pub – *she* encouraged it, of course. It was because of her he remortgaged the house – to pay for *her* expensive tastes. You and I didn't warrant such consideration.'

'But he must have had some decent qualities,' Tanya pressed. 'I mean, you married him, didn't you? There must have been something.'

'He was charming, I suppose,' she admitted grudgingly. 'In the beginning. Attractive and charming – weak men often are. But he lied to me, pretended he was much more successful than he actually was. I had no reason not to believe him initially.' She grimaced. 'Then even the lies became third rate. By the time I decided to find out just how bad things were, he had conveniently run off with his secretary to America. Such a cliché. I don't think that man ever had an original thought in his head. Then, of course, I was left with the whole pack of cards tumbling down around us.'

Tanya knew the rest of the story by heart. It had been recounted many times, with varying degrees of anger, bitterness and contempt. To listen to her mother, you'd think that *she* was the only one who'd suffered, who'd gone to superhuman lengths to salvage any sort of home and upbringing for her young daughter. Not that Tanya denied it – she knew she had an awful lot to thank her for – but sometimes she felt as if her mother almost relished the delicious victimisation of it all.

Tanya had known since she was very little that something was amiss in her family. It wasn't just that she didn't have a daddy, and when other children asked her, as they did, she would say, as she had been coached to, 'My daddy lives in America. He has a very important job there and I fly over for holidays to see him.' That usually inspired equal measures of intrigue and awe, followed closely by enquires about Disneyland and whether or not she had been.

'Of course I have,' she would say and would relay in impressive detail descriptions of rides, roller coasters, castles and queues. For a child who had never been there and wasn't likely to go, she knew more about it than many of its bona-fide visitors. But she had watched numerous videos of it, mesmerised by the one and only letter she had received from her absent father, in which he had promised to come for her and take her for a special holiday in America and they would go, just the two of them, to Disneyland. That the invitation never materialised, just as her mother predicted, year in and year out, made the fantasy somehow all the more important to her, and so she would embellish it in minute, exquisite detail until it was so vivid, so word perfect, she almost believed it herself.

That was when she had been very young.

When she got to be about ten or twelve, she merely said, if asked, that her parents were divorced and that her dad lived in Florida. By then she had gathered, without ever having the matter properly explained to her, that her father had not only been absent, but somehow had been *lacking*, even in the short time he had lived with her mother, when she, Tanya, was a baby. She sensed a certain triumph in her mother, that this lack, having been diagnosed like a case of measles or mumps, had indeed manifested itself in such a noteworthy and lasting legacy. All Tanya knew, though, despite the clucking reassurances of her mother's few family members and female friends, was that her father, however unreliable and lacking he may have been, had left her – and much, *much* worse, had never once come back for Tanya.

After that, everything else had been easy: living in a smaller house in not nearly as nice a neighbourhood or not having new, up-to-date clothes like the other girls in her class. She had learned later that the nuns at the exclusive convent day school she attended had reduced her school fees considerably upon learning of her mother's predicament. She worked hard and was reasonably bright, although not terribly clever, and did well enough. Otherwise, she kept pretty much to herself. It was easier that way. She learned to dissemble, to manipulate the truth just enough to appear interesting but without arousing suspicion or jealousy. She was pleasant to the other girls, but not overly friendly or confiding, and as a result was left to her own devices, which suited her.

So when the time came and boys entered the equation, Tanya was poised and ready. At sixteen years of age, she was finally able to salvage something from the wreck that was her paternal heritage. As she grew up and into her coltish, blonde good looks, it became apparent she was taking after her father's side of the family. The gene pool, at least, had been kind to her. Now, she finally had something advantageous to work with.

Cool, disinterested and playfully insincere, she attracted guys effortlessly and just as effortlessly dispensed with their affections when they no longer suited her. Tanya wasn't interested in romance – that was for kids. She had no time for girly exchanges, analysing and poring over every minute detail of a boyfriend's text messages or phone calls. Tanya was after something much more important. She was after a life, one that had been cruelly taken from her, one that rightfully should have been hers – and she fully intended to reclaim it. She had spent far too long looking in from the outside. Now it was her turn to enter that world of wealth, glamour and society. And she had finally found the man who would help her do it.

Only he wasn't showing any signs of moving their relationship on to that vital next level. If anything, Dom seemed distracted and absorbed in affairs of the kitchen. Rollo, their chef, was having a particularly good run, and Dom, who made no secret of the fact that winning a coveted Michelin star for the restaurant was his ultimate goal and passion, was doing everything he could to humour Rollo and keep him sweet, including paying for this latest trip to Vienna for him and Astrid so they could rekindle their volatile relationship.

It was all very vexing. He should have been concentrating on keeping their own relationship on track, but of course men didn't think like that, Tanya had to remind herself. She flicked on the television and channel-hopped for a bit, hoping to find an old movie she could settle down to, when a segment of an American chat show caught her attention. *Women Who Make It Happen*, the clip was titled. She paused, remote in hand, watching idly as a housewife from Virginia related how she had turned her hobby of making accessories for shoes into a multimillion-dollar business. This was followed by the presenter introducing a more romantic angle to the discussion.

'Women everywhere,' she began, smiling broadly, 'will identify with my next guest, Cindy, who was fed up waiting for her boyfriend of eight years to propose, so when a leap year came around, Cindy leapt at her chance!' Cindy, it turned out, had proposed to her boyfriend, who had responded with a resounding yes and was on the show to share the story, along with their four picture-perfect children, of his wife's 'management' of the commitment issue.

'That's what I love about Cindy,' her rather sappy-looking husband gushed. 'When she wants something, she sure as hell goes after it till she gets it. In my case, I just thank my lucky stars she did.' The camera pulled out as they kissed and their four kids giggled nervously. But Tanya was sitting up straighter now.

It wasn't such a bad idea, she thought. Not ideal, of course, not by any means, but where did ideals ever get a girl?

And this year *was* a leap year. She pulled her diary out of her handbag – the twenty-ninth of February was a Friday. Naturally, Tanya would have preferred if Dom had taken matters into his own hands and organised a romantic and thoughtful setting in which to surprise her with the longed-for request, but if he wasn't going to get around to it, she would. It was as simple as that. Otherwise, God knows what would happen. With Cici acting so inappropriately and now Eric, the accountant, being such a pain in the neck, if something wasn't done about things, and done quickly, well, things could take a very different turn altogether, and Tanya was not going to allow *that* to happen.

She *had* considered, very briefly, getting pregnant. It was the obvious thing to do, really, and Dom adored children. He was brilliant with them whenever he was around them. Being half Italian helped, she supposed, but whatever it was, they appeared to adore him too. He could play happily with them for hours, thinking up new and ridiculous games that made them shriek with delight. He would make a wonderful father.

That was another thing that featured highly on her list of necessary qualities in a husband. She would not subject a child of hers to what she had gone through. Having an available, hands-on, devoted father would be vital – particularly since she was rather afraid of becoming a mother herself.

It wasn't that she didn't *like* children; she just wasn't very comfortable around them. She wasn't sure what exactly was required of her. She supposed it was because she was an only child and hadn't had any brothers or sisters to tumble around with, to rail and argue against. Nobody had ever picked her up (that she could remember) and swung her around to delighted, excited shrieks or cuddled her or chased her around the garden playing tag or hide and seek.

But something made her recoil from simply getting pregnant. It was such an old trick. After all, it wasn't as if she wouldn't make Dom a wonderful wife. She shouldn't have to trap or persuade him into marriage, just hurry him up a bit, make him see what a fabulous opportunity was under his nose, and might not be there for much longer if he didn't get his act together. A leap-year proposal gave her the perfect opportunity. She would make sure it would be whimsical rather than pushy. It would be rather endearing, in fact, if she handled it the right way – and that was the only way *to* handle it. She would leave nothing to chance. It would have to be absolutely perfect, and she had four weeks to make sure it was.

7

'I'm thinking Audrey Hepburn in *Roman Holiday*, Anita Ekberg in *La Dolce Vita*, and of course lots of Sophia Loren.' Erin, the art director, rifled through the racks of clothes brought by the stylist before setting off to prowl around the mews for the umpteenth time. 'Fantastic,' she muttered, alighting upon room after tastefully decorated room. 'It's perfect, just perfect.'

Wanda, the make-up artist, was methodically laying out the tools of her craft. Bob, the photographer, and his assistant were busy setting up shop in the corner of the sitting room, and perched in splendour in the middle of it all, sitting on a stool wearing a red silk robe with a head full of curlers while two hairdressers circled her, working their magic, was Cici.

It was only eight o'clock in the morning, but already the mews looked like a film set with all these people scurrying around, checking the light, steam-pressing already pristine clothes and barking instructions into mobile phones. Cici was loving every second of it. She hadn't enjoyed anything as much in almost thirty years, not since her last (well, her only) movie in Rome, when she had been just eighteen, the year before she had come to Dublin and met James. It had only been a small part, a walk-on part as a waitress, where she got to take a surly detective's order in a small café and be swatted on the behind by his dining companion as she turned away. She had been discovered by the producer of the same movie, a small, fat, balding individual, in a men's clothes shop, where she worked behind the counter, and he had approached her, telling her to come to the audition. He had handed her his card and told her to be at the studios at seven a.m. sharp. He had then proceeded to breathe heavily down her cleavage when she auditioned, declaring she was perfect for the part. The director predicted she would be the next Sophia Loren, and Cici, in a daze of unimaginable excitement, had rehearsed her one line religiously, and after fifteen diligent takes, completed her dramatic debut. In a cruel stroke of fate, her part was axed and she ended up on the editing floor instead of the silver screen. The movie went on to become a resounding flop, and her fledgling career likewise. Despite numerous auditions and a genuine talent, Cici was proclaimed to be either too similar to Sophia Loren or not enough like her – too old or too young, her breasts too big or not big enough. A few uninspiring television commercials followed, and eventually even those parts dried up as hordes of thinner girls with longer legs and frail, fragile looks became the vogue.

'You have the most amazing bone structure,' Wanda, the make-up girl, was saying now as she expertly applied foundation with her blending brush. 'And your skin is really unbelievable—' She had been about to add 'for your age', but stopped herself.

'Thank you, darling,' Cici purred. 'I'm afraid I cannot take any credit for either. I was simply lucky enough to have good-looking parents,' she laughed.

She closed her eyes and let Wanda chat away as she worked, only half listening, and tried to quell the fluttering in her stomach every time someone mentioned Harry's name, which seemed to be frequently. So far, there had been no sign of him, but he had said he'd be there at some stage during the day. Cici rather hoped it would be *after* her hair and make-up had been done.

She had done the interview earlier in the week with him, also at the mews, where he had arrived punctually at three o'clock, leather satchel slung over his shoulder, from which he produced a notebook, digital recorder and bottle of champagne.

'You shouldn't have!' she said as she took it from him, although she had plenty in her fridge, already on ice.

'Let me open it,' he said, twisting the cork from the bottle until it gave way with a satisfying pop. 'To you, Cici,' he said, raising the glass she had filled, 'and to an intriguing and I hope revealing interview.' His eyes locked with hers.

'I'm all yours,' she said playfully. 'But you must promise not to twist anything I say – I know what you journalists can be like.'

'Not a word, I promise,' he grinned. 'I can't think of a single thing I would alter about you. Now let's get started.' He switched the recorder on, sat it on the table in front of them and leaned in towards her. 'If you want to stop at any time and take a break, just say so.'

But she hadn't. He made it easy. Talking to him, recounting her early life in Rome, then her impressions of Ireland, of living in Dublin and making the inevitable adjustments that followed, her life had sounded glamorous, exciting. She had her three lovely children, and of course had been a stay-at-home mother, but Cici had never lost sight of the fact that she was first and foremost a woman. She couldn't help it, it was in her blood – she thrived on attention, particularly from men. Luckily, in the circles she and James mixed in, a full and busy social life had been part of the package. There was never any shortage of parties to attend, where she had always been openly admired, and she had cut a dashing figure on the fashion circuit, her dark, exotic colouring and bold, frequently flamboyant style making her the darling of Dublin's couturiers. One of them even referred to her as his muse, and, although flattered, she refused to favour only his creations, as most women would have done, preferring to play one designer off against the other at whim.

James had always been a thoroughly generous husband in that respect, and a significant monthly allowance was deposited in her bank account without fail, which she quickly became accustomed to and took for granted. So far, six months out of the family home and living in the mews, the same arrangement seemed to be holding up. She had been worried about that and had assiduously avoided any reference to things financial, counting, as always, on James's innate sense of gentlemanly fair play. Thinking of him now, she felt another flicker of guilt. Any time Harry's beautiful, sensual face floated into her mind, James's questioning, confused and bewildered one would appear and hover insistently behind it. It was spoiling everything.

In the interview, she had taken great care to skirt around the issue of her marriage, and Harry had diplomatically allowed her to. How was it he had referred to her? *A woman on the brink of discovering a new phase in her life, glorying in all her many and accomplished dimensions*. Cici had liked that enormously, although she wasn't quite sure what it meant. But then, if she was honest, she wasn't quite sure about anything at all any more.

'Why? Just tell me *why*,' James had pleaded, his face paling, that awful evening she had told him after dinner, when she had dropped her bombshell.

'I need some space, James.' She had rehearsed the speech so often, but now, in the presence of his awful bewilderment, it deserted her, failing to sound as reasonable and plausible as she had anticipated. 'I need to . . . to find myself, to figure out what I want from my life, from myself . . .' She had trailed off.

'But why can't you do that here?' He was aghast. 'Take a holiday, go on a retreat, whatever you like, Cici, travel around the world if you must, but moving out – I don't understand.' He had sat down suddenly, as if all the energy that had been keeping him upright had suddenly been sucked from him.

'I'm so sorry, James,' she said lamely, 'it's just something I have to do.' And she had fled from the room and into one of the many other, now empty bedrooms, where she had lain that night, tossing and turning, hearing him eventually climb the stairs and go into their bedroom, where he had softly closed the door.

Why?

That was the million-dollar question, of course, the one she had wrestled with day after day and night after night. She didn't know why. She just knew that she needed to explore, to test one last time, to push the boundaries, to have one more go – before it was too late. How *could* she explain? How could she put into words what she didn't understand herself? That no matter how confident she thought she was, how comfortable she had always been with her looks, with her life, that recently another, wheedling, pleading, sometimes sinister voice had been whispering to her. A voice that told her she was losing it – that every day, a little bit of her was slipping away. A new wrinkle would appear and have to be fought, a favourite dress or outfit would no longer look appropriate on her or give her the required boost or lift that she so depended on. One day, she would enter rooms full of people chattering, laughing, watching, where heads would turn to check her arrival, but their gaze would no longer linger on her, enviously and admiringly, quite the way they once had. The prettier, fresher, younger girls, glossy and dewy in their beauty, who wordlessly assessed her, then returned their attention to their partners, triumphant and confident that she, Cici, would not distract them the way she once would have.

How could she explain this to James? Poor, straightforward, honourable James, who would no more have understood what she was talking about than she did herself. 'But I adore you, Cici,' he would have said, laughingly. 'You know that.' And she did, of course she did. But she needed more than that.

What the exact nature of that 'more' was, she didn't know, but she did know she needed to get away from these horrid, stealthy, undermining feelings and remember what it was to inspire passion, to inflame a heart and mind, to command attention, before – the thought occurred with increasing terror – before it was too late and the chance slipped away for ever. Before she felt tempted to turn into one of those pitiable women who succumbed to surgery and endless, relentless dieting and exercise until they looked as desperate and whittled away as the empty emotions inside them.

Just for a little while, she reasoned. Just a little while to have one last adventure, one last bite of the cherry, and perhaps then she could resign herself to the onslaught of invisibility, of old age, of expanding waistlines and settled folds on her skin, of warm, kindly glances instead of longing, lingering eye-to-eye exchanges. In a little while, but not just *yet*.

'Okay, everybody,' Bob, the photographer, called out. 'Let's go with the *Roman Holiday* shot first. Kerry?' He turned to his assistant. 'We're all set up, right?'

'Sure are, just waiting for hair and make-up.'

'Ready in five.' Wanda held up her hand, spreading her fingers wide.

Cici marvelled at how calm they all seemed. Bob Clarke was an über-hot English photographer with an über-hot temper if his well-known impatience wasn't immediately pacified. Yet Wanda and the rest of the team refused to be flustered and just grinned and kept on rigorously doing what they were doing. Just listening to Bob, never mind looking at his thunderous expression, was enough to make Cici quiver. But the team from *Select* were obviously used to this – after all, it was what they did for a living. All the same, Wanda told Cici, when Erin, the art director, had heard they were getting Bob Clarke for the shoot, she'd almost passed out with disbelief.

'It was Harry who swung it,' Wanda whispered. 'I don't think anyone else could have. Bob's incredibly hard to get hold of these days, and he charges an absolute fortune.'

'What do you think persuaded him?' asked Cici, intrigued.

Wanda shrugged. 'Who knows? Ireland's still hot at the moment, and there was talk that Bob has his eye on a new young model here he saw cast in a stocking ad. Harry also managed to get *Vibe* magazine to commission Bob for a fashion shoot in Connemara, so two birds with one stone and all that.'

'He certainly went to an awful lot of trouble.' Cici pressed her lips together to seal the just-applied lipstick before Wanda blotted it with a tissue.

'When Harry wants something, he usually makes sure he gets it.' Wanda dusted a final veil of powder over Cici's face and proclaimed her done.

'Great,' Cici said, although she felt a sudden shiver of apprehension as what Wanda said ran through her – or was it anticipation?

Before she could decide, she was hustled into a pretty V-necked shirt, a tightly belted swirling cotton skirt and flat pumps and ushered outside, where a bright red 1950s scooter stood, polished until it gleamed. Philip, the male model who was Cici's foil for the shots, stood in a beautifully tailored single-breasted suit, looking tall, dark and handsome, just like Gregory Peck, but unlike Mr Peck, he had a sulky, bored expression. Understandable, really, thought Cici, feeling vaguely amused, considering he was probably twenty-five years younger than her. How awful, she thought, to be a male model, all that standing around doing nothing, and then the girls got all the good shots! Mind you, when Bob appeared and looked through his lens, Philip suddenly perked up and a bright, friendly smile quickly transformed his sullen appearance.

'Okay.' Bob was in command as a respectful hush descended

on the small gathering. 'Cici, on the scooter, Philip, you too – behind her, that's it. Arms around her waist. Somebody spread that skirt out a bit! That's it.' He was still looking through his lens intently. 'Now Cici, lean back into Philip, that's it, and look back up at him.' Cici did as she was told, looking flirtatiously at Philip, who, to be fair, looked straight back at her with camera-ready lust. 'Great,' Bob enthused. 'Chin down a tad, Cici, and a hint of a smile, that's it, good girl.' And he was off, moving around them, bending and arching as the camera whirred and clicked, taking shot after shot.

'Good work, guys, we're done. Let's move on to the Sophia set-ups now, then we can break for lunch.'

Cici clambered off the scooter and was ushered off to make-up again. She was shocked. She'd had no idea just how much work went into setting up a photo shoot and was already feeling quite tired. Apart from that, it was absolutely freezing. Not that that seemed to count. The light was good, and that was all that mattered – to Bob, at any rate. The crew were well equipped with coats, gloves and woolly hats, but she and Philip had to stand for as long as it took in the outfits for each shot. The next set was to feature her dressed as Sophia Loren in her famous movie *The Fall of the Roman Empire*, which meant a whole new backdrop was set up outside in the courtyard patio. This was achieved by the placement of some fake Roman columns and steps and three amazingly convincing pieces of painted scenery, the arrangement of which looked as if it would take some time, particularly as Bob was a maniacal perfectionist.

In the meantime, Cici was back in wardrobe and make-up, dreading slipping into her next outfit, which was an elegant white Grecian-style evening dress that plunged and draped around her in all the right places, but in this cold, she might as well be standing stark naked. She hoped her nipples wouldn't be too obvious through the thin material; they were standing to attention already.

Wanda must have been reading her mind, as she instructed Cici to raise her arms, then deftly arranged her breasts with the aid of two stick-on patches that supported them from underneath. 'Tricks of the trade,' she grinned, applying nipple tape as the final touch. 'There. You're respectable.'

'God, I used to think I'd enjoy modelling,' Cici grimaced. 'I had no idea it was such awfully hard work.'

'Nobody does,' agreed Wanda. 'Not until they actually have to do it – or at least until they get to work with models. I can't say I'd enjoy it myself. Rather be on this side of the camera any day. Glamorous it is *not*. Still, very few models ever get to work with Bob. Most of them would give their right arm to. If nothing else, you're going to have a fantastic portfolio of shots to show off.'

To who? Cici found herself suddenly wondering.

'Pity your girls aren't here, or your son,' Wanda continued. 'Bob's a control freak while he's on the job, but he would have taken some great family shots afterwards – no chance you could get any of them here? It's such a shame to miss the opportunity.' She was deftly applying a thick layer of eyeliner along Cici's lashes and winging it up and out dramatically.

'No, unfortunately not,' Cici murmured. 'My girls are both abroad this year and my son, Dom, never leaves his restaurant for a moment.'

'Never mind. They'll get even more of a surprise when they see the spread.'

'Yes, I expect so.' She smiled, although inside her stomach lurched uncharacteristically. Cici hadn't actually told anyone about the shoot. She wasn't quite sure why. She was sure her girls would be thrilled for her, and Dom . . . well, you never really knew with sons, they could be so proprietorial about their mothers. And as for James . . . Cici swallowed. It wasn't as if he was a regular reader of women's magazines, but he would hear sooner or later. Someone was bound to mention it to him. She would tell him, of course, at an appropriate time, when she could casually drop it into conversation. She wouldn't think about that just yet.

'Okay people,' called Kerry, Bob's assistant. 'Take your positions please, models!' She smiled at Cici. 'You look beautiful, Cici. You really are a dead ringer for her – it's incredible.'

Cici had to hide a grin when she saw Philip dressed as a gladiator – he could have given Russell Crowe a run for his money any day.

'Philip,' Bob barked. 'Stand next to the column, that's it, and put your foot up on the step. Cici, I want you seated at his feet, looking up at him passionately. And . . . that's it, let's go, lovely.' And he was off again. Forty-five minutes later, Cici was blue with cold and trying not to shiver. Finally, thankfully, it was over.

'Okay, lunch break,' Kerry announced. Cici hadn't thought about food, but now she found she was starving. Rushing back inside, she pulled on a fleecy robe and tried to regain sensation in her limbs, which were completely numb. Lunch, she was pleased to see, had been taken care of by a local catering outlet, and the current gofer on *Select* had collected some very welcome food. There was wine too, although no one had the nerve to pour any while Bob was still in working mode. Cici helped herself to some steaming lasagne and salads and tucked in.

It was after lunch, when the team were still chatting over coffee, that Erin whispered something in Bob's ear and led him away from the table. They disappeared for a few minutes and then came back, looking pleased and hopeful.

'Cici,' Erin began, 'we've had an idea, a change of plan, if you'll allow it?'

'What's that?'

'The next shots, the *Dolce Vita* ones, we were just going to do them down here, in the sitting room.'

'Yes?' Cici listened expectantly, wondering what was coming next.

'Well, that was before we knew you had that wonderful sunken bath up there,' Erin went on excitedly. She was referring, of course, to the magnificent marble creation in Cici's master en suite that resembled a small swimming pool, with a mural of Venus rising from the waves painted on the surrounding walls. 'If you wouldn't object, Bob and I thought that if you wore the black velvet dress, you know the strapless, boned one, and we did the shoot with you standing in the bath, full of water and bubbles – you know, like the fountain shot in the movie – well, it would be just fantastic.' She held her breath.

'It'd be totally cool,' Bob nodded emphatically.

'I don't see why not,' said Cici, thinking that whatever else transpired, at least she could make sure the water was hot. These fashion people were odd, but as long as it got things over with quickly and she didn't have to be cold again, she would have agreed to almost anything.

'Brilliant. We'll get the lights rigged up straight away.' Kerry flicked open her mobile phone to tell the lighting technician.

'And just who is going to pay for that Valentino original that's about to be destroyed?' Valerie, the stylist, asked archly.

'Don't worry about it, Val,' beamed Kerry, 'I've cleared it with Harry. He thinks it's a great idea. He's on his way over now.'

Once again, Cici was led away to hair and make-up. Philip, having served his purpose in the former shots, was finished for the day and allowed to go. Cici envied him. Really, this was too tiring. She would go out of her mind if she had to do this sort of thing every day.

Wanda went to work quickly, cleansing and reapplying a lighter, beige-toned base and the palest of pink blushers to add a slight flush to Cici's cheeks. Pale pink lipstick, which she never, ever wore, was applied, and then the *pièce de résistance* – the long, ash-blonde wig, which completely transformed her. It was quite extraordinary. She wriggled into the black velvet strapless creation with the full skirt, and only then turned to look at her reflection. It showed off her spectacular curves to perfection. She really could be Anita Ekberg in the famous movie.

'Well,' she said, shaking her head, 'I don't know what to say. I feel as if I've had a whole body transplant.'

'As bodies go, Cici, yours is pretty delectable.' Val, the stylist, arranged the boned bodice of the dress one final time. 'I'd give anything to have breasts like those. Come on upstairs with you. After this, we're done.'

It was rather surreal to walk into her bathroom, which was now full of people, and see the mysterious blonde beauty who looked out at her from the mirrors. Lights were being adjusted and readjusted and the huge wide lighting umbrella angled and coaxed into position. Kerry was handing Bob a succession of lenses, which he was trying and then discarding, frowning, looking through the frame, lost in concentration. When he looked up and saw her, he gave a long, low whistle. 'This is just about as good as it gets. You look *fantastic*, Cici. Good job, Erin, and great hair and make-up.' He was all business again. 'Watch out for steam, people, make sure that water isn't too hot. Okay, Cici, into the bath, please.'

She was helped into the foaming mass of bubbles by Kerry, while Val helped hold up the hem of the dress above the water. 'I still can't believe we're doing this. It's sacrilege. Once it's soaked, that's it.' She shook her head.

'Okay, let the dress go,' Bob instructed. 'Now Cici, hoist the skirt up at the front, that's it, and let's see those legs of yours. Run your other hand through your hair, okay, fantastic.'

And it was. Cici felt faintly ridiculous, but she could tell from the expressions on their faces as the rest of the team watched intently that they were more than pleased with what they saw. She kept moving as instructed from pose to pose, gradually becoming more daring as Bob encouraged her, flattering her, coaxing her, and soon it seemed there was just her and him, working seamlessly, effortlessly as the room full of people ceased to exist.

'Okay, just a couple more, we're nearly there. I want you to kneel down, Cici, let the dress billow out behind you. Val, would you get that? Good, good. Now lean in towards me, you can hold onto the marble edge. There, yes, good, just a bit more, Cici, I want to get lots of cleavage for this one. Wanda, get that wisp of hair, would you? Okay, now grab a handful of bubbles and hold them out in the palm of your hand as if you're going to blow them straight into the camera, that's it, come on, you can look naughtier than that, Cici. That's it. Great.'

Cici thought her shins were going to crack, kneeling as she was on the hard marble, but she did as she was told and finally was allowed, with help, to stand up.

'Last one, promise. Don't move, Cici. Stay right where you are.'

She had been about to clamber out of the bath, thoroughly fed up now with a soaking wet, heavy velvet dress clinging to her.

'Okay, turn around, back to me, that's it. Val, unzip it, would you? I want a nice open V down to the waist. Actually, make that down to the bottom of that very gorgeous spine. Don't worry,' he grinned as Cici threw him a look of alarm. 'Come on, Cici, nothing wrong with a naked back. This will be very tasteful, trust me.'

Bob found himself getting quite turned on as he looked through the lens. He recognised a great shot when he saw it. It was tasteful, all right. Christ, Cici had almost hand-drawn perfect proportions, and the sensuous curve of her back against the unzipped bodice of the dress that fell open to just above her bottom was framed perfectly. Tasteful, definitely, but also wonderfully, almost unbearably erotic.

'Okay, that's it, guys. It's a wrap!' Bob finally called it a day. 'Good work, everybody. I think we're all going to be very, *very* pleased with the finished results. Well done, Cici,' he smiled warmly at her. 'I know that can't have been easy for you. Now you know why good models are so highly paid!'

She stepped out of the bath, helped again by Wanda, who took her hand, and with her other hand, she held the unzipped bodice of the dress to her breasts, covering them as best she could. She looked up, and it was then that she saw him, lounging in the doorway, a half smile curving his mouth. His eyes held hers, boldly, as he flashed her a look of what could only be described as pure, unadulterated lust.

'Hello, Harry.' Bob had only just noticed him as well. 'Didn't see you there. Very good day, very good indeed. Productive. Got exactly what I wanted. I'll be in touch next week, when we can look at the contacts.'

'Good stuff.' Harry was upbeat, professional, congratulating everyone on a job well done. 'I look forward to seeing them.' His eyes roved around the sumptuous bathroom, taking in every detail. 'Just thought I'd stop by and make sure everything was going to plan. As it is,' he checked his watch, 'I can see you've all managed admirably without me.'

'There's some delicious grub downstairs that we hardly made any inroads into, and wine, of course,' Erin said. 'Come and join us for a drink. I'll just pour some glasses downstairs.' She made for the door.

'Love to, but I'm afraid I can't stop.' He made a face. 'Got to do an interview with Rick Waters at his place in half an hour. I was really lucky to get him. Better make tracks, you guys have a good time – looks like you've earned it.' And without so much as a backward glance, he was gone.

Cici suddenly felt as deflated as the wet dress that clung to her.

While everybody was clearing up, lights were taken down and equipment put away, Cici went into one of the other bathrooms to take off all the make-up and have a long, hot shower. She was absolutely exhausted. They had started at eight that morning, and it was now half past five. How did these people do it, day in and day out? Feeling hugely relieved it was all over, she dried herself off and hurried back to her bedroom, where she slipped into her favourite jeans and pulled on a soft white V-necked sweater. She didn't bother with make-up, just ran a brush through her hair, twisted it and pinned it up and went downstairs to join the others, who, by the sounds of it, were beginning to unwind and let their hair down. Someone had found a Cuban mix CD and, over it, the sounds of raised voices and laughter filled the mews.

'Come on, Cici, where's your glass?' Erin was proffering a bottle of white wine. 'After all, you're the star of the show.'

She found one and held it out to be filled. 'If I'd known what terribly hard work it would be, I wouldn't have volunteered my services quite so eagerly,' she laughed. 'Oh, by the way,' she said to Val, who was putting away the clothes used on the shoot, 'I left the dress upstairs, in the smaller bathroom. It's hanging on the back of the door. I meant to bring it down and completely forgot.'

'No worries, Cici, I'll get it in a jiffy.'

'Thanks, Val, that would be great. I really feel my legs would give way for good if I had to go back up those stairs again. Kneeling on the marble bath floor has done them in.'

Soon, everything was packed up, and after an hour or so they had polished off what was left of the food and had drunk most of the wine. 'Here, take it with you, I insist,' Cici said, forcing the remaining bottles on Val, Kerry and Wanda, which were eagerly accepted. 'I have tons more in the fridge, really.' People began to filter out, saying warm farewells. Even Bob had let his guard down and done some hilarious imitations of supermodels he had worked with.

'I'll be in touch when I have something to show you,' he promised Cici, kissing her on both cheeks.

It was only eight o'clock, and closing the door behind them, Cici sat down, turned on the television and poured herself a glass of wine. She was relieved it was over and rather apprehensively excited about the results, which she would not be privy to for another couple of weeks at least. Now, without the cheery company of the crowd that had just left, she felt suddenly rather glum. She watched a couple of soaps, put on the dishwasher and at nine-thirty decided it might be time for an early night. She had a good book that she was enjoying, and the long day had left her feeling weary.

She was just about to go upstairs when the doorbell rang. She jumped. Who could it possibly be at this hour? James, maybe, she wondered, suddenly fearful. Perhaps he had seen all the cars and comings and goings and would be demanding to know what was going on. It wouldn't be any of her friends, or even Dom; they would always have rung first to check if calling around suited her. She waited for a moment while the bell sounded again. Oh sod it! She would just have to go and find out who it was.

He turned around as she opened the door and gave a slow, wide grin. 'I was about to give up on you,' he said, standing there as if it was the most natural thing in the world.

'Oh,' she said, momentarily taken aback. 'Well, I'm glad you didn't.'

'May I come in?' He had a suit carrier and his satchel was slung over his shoulder.

'Of course. It's, er, just that I wasn't expecting anyone. It's a bit of a surprise.' Cici stood back to let him in.

'A nice surprise, I hope?' His eyes roved over her. 'They've all gone?'

'Yes, yes, a while ago.' Cici felt flustered. 'Can I get you a drink?'

'I'll have whatever you're having.' He looked at the empty glass on the table beside where she had been sitting on the sofa.

'Oh, I can do better than that.' She moved towards the kitchen. 'How about some champagne? It's chilled.'

'Great.' He put down his bags and followed her, taking the glass she held out to him while she poured one for herself.

'Well,' he said, watching her, amused at the slight tremble she tried and failed to conceal as she poured the fizzing liquid, 'aren't you going to ask me why I'm here?'

'Should I?' she countered, smiling, brushing past him and back into the sitting room. She hoped she sounded amused, confident, although her heart was thudding alarmingly. 'How did your interview go – how was Rick Waters?' she asked, trying to sound nonchalant, although her voice sounded distinctly high pitched. She was nervous, unsure of herself, alone with Harry now for the first time – *in her house*. The thought both excited and terrified her.

'It went well, but he's not nearly as fascinating a subject to interview as you are. In fact,' he said, following her, 'I wound things up early so I could come back and see you.' Without warning, he hooked a finger into the waistband of her jeans, pulling her up in her tracks as she wheeled around.

'Harry, what?'

He kissed her then, suddenly, briefly, one hand hooking around her neck, pulling her into him, his tongue slipping into her mouth deftly, easily, perusing her.

'Harry, really!' she protested, pulling back and laughing nervously, putting her glass hurriedly on the mantelpiece. He did the same, but not before he took a swig of his drink. Then he was kissing her again, sharing it with her, as the sweet taste of champagne trickled into her mouth, his tongue lazily exploring, searching, demanding.

She pulled away. 'Harry,' she laughed, 'really.'

'Yes, Cici. Really.' He was definite, looking down at her intently. He took her upper lip between his own and sucked it lightly, then pulled back, leaving her desperately, foolishly wanting more. 'I've brought something for you,' he said, smiling enigmatically.

He made his way over to the door, where he had left the suit carrier lying against the wall.

She had wondered about that – what did it mean? God, was he planning on staying the night? Suddenly she wasn't at all sure what to do – it was all so unexpected. *No it isn't*, the small voice was whispering to her, scornful, taunting. *You've been wanting this to happen since you first laid eyes on him*. But now, she felt panicked.

He opened the suit carrier and took out something long and black, throwing it over his arm and turning towards her with that slow, lazy smile again. 'Put it on.'

'What?' For a moment she was confused, and then with a flash of comprehension she understood and panic gave way to even more panic and then sheer, and rather shameful, excitement.

'But – but—' she flustered, gazing, transfixed, at him. 'It's still wet.'

'Exactly,' he said. 'I watched you earlier. That shot in the bathroom was the sexiest thing I've ever seen. Now I want a repeat performance, but this time, just for me. Go on. You know you want to.' His eyes challenged her. He handed it to her, followed by the long blonde wig. 'Put them on, for me, and I'll see you upstairs. I'll be waiting in the bathroom.' He walked past her and up the stairs, confident, certain that she wouldn't disappoint him.

For a moment she was paralysed, standing there with the dress and wig lifeless in her arms. She could stop this right now. She could laugh and tell him he was out of his mind to think that she had the slightest interest in collaborating with this ridiculous carry-on. And then she remembered the look in his eyes, heard his voice again. *You know you want to*. And she did.

She undressed then, hurriedly, pulling off her jeans and

jumper with trembling hands, throwing her bra and panties aside carelessly, and slid into the heavy black velvet once again. She zipped it up as best she could, although she couldn't quite manage the hook at the top – but that didn't matter. Then she pulled on the wig, fixing it in the large mirror over the mantel, pulling down a tendril or two so they curled under her chin, just as Wanda had done earlier, while the rest fell in a heavy sheet down her back. She was momentarily shocked again at the sensual, blonde vision that looked back at her, mockingly, tauntingly, daring her to bring her to life. And then, very slowly, she took a few deep breaths and, holding the skirt up carefully, made her way upstairs.

He was waiting for her, just as he had promised, leaning against the mirrored wall, his arms folded, wearing a slightly amused expression. The vast sunken bath was already full, mountains of foaming bubbles rising and falling gently in frothy peaks. A thin layer of steam filled the room, making the atmosphere humid and sultry, coating the mirrors in a fine mist. He turned and wrote on one now, lazily tracing the words. *You are so, so sexy.*

She gasped, trapped suddenly in his gaze, shivering with desire, waiting, anticipating his next delicious instruction.

'Get into the bath.'

And she did, letting the skirt drop, watching it billow out, feeling its weight dragging at her, the water and bubbles caressing her bare legs.

Still he looked at her, then slowly came over and stood at the edge of the bath.

'Turn around.'

He unzipped her, tracing a slow finger all along her spine, until the dress fell away and she was completely naked. He kissed her then, on her neck, her shoulders, his cool hands stroking her, and finally turned her around to face him.

'God, you're beautiful.' He began to open his shirt and pull off his jeans, and suddenly she was helping him, tugging urgently at buttons, belts and zips. Marvelling at him, standing there before her, taut, sculpted, impossibly lean and so . . . *young*, his golden skin covered with a dusting of burnished, copper hairs.

'Come,' she said breathlessly, wanting him now, unable to be separate from him for a single moment longer. Then he was beside her, kissing her hungrily, laughing as a sea of bubbles flew up around them, displaced by their urgency. 'Lie down,' he commanded, and she did, giggling as her new blonde hair trailed around her and he slid down beside her, pulling her on top of him until she straddled him, giddy now and helpless with desire.

'Cici,' he murmured, reaching up to stroke her face and trailing his other hand slowly, tantalisingly along her thigh. 'You are every man's living, breathing fantasy. You are a *goddess*.'

And she believed him, understanding in that instant that she had always known it, had always been waiting, hoping, *longing* to hear those very words uttered.

Then, in that languorous, luxurious, erotically charged moment, the fantasy became real.

8

It took much, *much* longer than she thought it would. How did anyone sit through this every, what, two to three weeks? It was so incredibly boring. If she hadn't had her phone and her iPod with her, she'd have gone mental.

'Are you absolutely sure about this?' the colourist, Tracy, had asked her, sounding concerned. 'It's a rather drastic change, and not exactly what I'd have recommended for your skin tone. Your own hair is really lovely. If you're bored with it, we could just take it up a shade, or maybe I could add a few copper and caramel highlights, much better for the condition too.' She ran her fingers through Candy's hair, but her client had been adamant.

'No. I want it exactly like *that*. Exactly.' She held open the magazine and pointed to the photograph of Shalom, attending the opening of some new yoga studio.

'But,' Tracy tried again, 'the girl in that photo, well, she's older than you, and her style is, well, sort of flamboyant.' She struggled to find the appropriate words. 'Wouldn't you rather get something more natural-looking? And it's going to be very time-consuming to maintain. You'll need your roots touched up every two to three weeks, conditioning treatments, too. It'll be expensive,' she warned.

'Look, you're supposed to be the hottest salon in Dublin.' Candy was getting impatient. 'Are you going to do as I ask or not? Because if you're not, I can easily go somewhere else.'

'Of course,' Tracy backed down. 'Whatever you like, love.

I'll be back in a moment, just have to mix up the colour. Tea or coffee?'

'Coffee, please,' snapped Candy. 'And don't call me love.'

Bloody hell! This was one snotty little bitch she was saddled with for the afternoon. Tracy shook her head as she walked towards the cupboard where the range of colour mixes was kept. She had seen her come in, looking surly and discontent before she had barely set foot in the salon, wearing designer jeans tucked into platform boots she could barely walk in. Her handbag, too, was D&G and would have cost the better part of Tracy's monthly salary. She didn't look more than eighteen or nineteen either, despite her uppity manner. Just to be sure, Tracy decided to have a word with the manager, Gary, before she committed herself. She didn't need some outraged mother coming in gunning for her, accusing her of ruining her daughter's virgin hair.

She interrupted Gary and explained the situation, nodding discreetly in Candy's direction, where she sat in her chair, reading a magazine.

He looked over at her and shrugged. 'Go ahead, do what she wants. She can obviously afford it. Anyway, you've done your best, pointed out all the obvious reasons not to, haven't you?'

'Course I have. She wasn't interested. Got quite stroppy, actually.'

'Well then, we've been responsible about it. If she wants to be a bleached blonde, then we've got to carry out her instructions. The customer's always right, remember?' he winked at her.

'Righty-oh. Just thought I'd run it by you.'

'You did the right thing,' Gary nodded. 'Good luck. I look forward to seeing the finished result.'

'Just five more minutes,' Tracy said and checked the colour. 'Then we'll get you shampooed.'

Thank God for that, Candy had wanted to scream. She had already read every magazine in the place, and looking at the vile-smelling purple goo on her head was beginning to make her feel sick. Instead, she smiled pleasantly and said thank you. It would all be worth it in the end, she reminded herself. She checked her watch. It was a quarter past five and she'd been in there since two-thirty. Her dad was picking her up at six-thirty outside the Shelbourne Hotel as she'd instructed him. She had decided to spend the weekend with him and Shalom and she had left her weekend bag in the hotel, where she could pick it up after her hair appointment. He'd been caught off guard when she had suggested it to him on the phone last week, just as she had known he would be, but he was pleased too. Her sudden change of tack would have come as a surprise, particularly since she hadn't been speaking to him – not since that awful, awful night more than two months ago. But Candy had been doing a lot of thinking lately, along with Katy and Emma.

She'd done everything she could, but her dad had still chosen Shalom. He'd left her and Mum and gone to live with *her*.

'Maybe he prefers blondes,' Katy had quipped, and that's when the idea began to take hold. Clearly the kind of woman a man wanted looked like Shalom did, and not like her mother. After that, it had all seemed easy.

They had decided that there was no point in Candy fighting with her dad about Shalom or the new baby. Instead, it was much easier to work the situation to her advantage. Anyway, Candy was tired of spending so much time with her mother and Gran. They were great, of course, but she needed a bit more freedom now, more room to manoeuvre, particularly in light of recent events. Since her photo op at the Tudor party, Candy had got a taste for celebrity – now people recognised her. She'd had her photo taken on a few other occasions at openings and fashion shows she had gone to and decided she liked it. Emma and Katy were right, she reflected, even if they could be a bit of a pain at times. She would start being nice to Shalom, the stupid cow. It wouldn't do any harm, and perhaps just the opposite. She would start by imitating her sense of style. That would show her dad that she understood, that she could see why he left. She would become like Shalom, the kind of woman men looked at and wanted – and she would make sure that no man ever left her like her father had left her mother.

After her shampoo and conditioning treatment, another, younger girl set about blow-drying her hair. When Candy sat back down in front of the mirror, she got quite a shock. Even totally wet, just patted with a towel, her hair was, well, quite *white*. Against her pale golden brows and eyelashes, it made her look very different.

'It's a big change, isn't it?' the stylist said, a wide grin on her face as she began to wield the hairdryer and brush.

'It's exactly what I wanted,' Candy said pertly, studying her magazine and avoiding interaction.

'You'll have to rethink your make-up and get your eyebrows and eyelashes tinted, otherwise you'll look like a bit of a ghost, won't you?' She seemed pleased with the observation.

'My father's partner is a make-up artist. I expect that'll come in useful. That's her there.' Candy pointed to the photo of Shalom she had used as an earlier example.

'That's your dad's partner?' The girl's mouth dropped open. 'Wow, she's like a celebrity, isn't she? I've seen her photo loads of times.'

'Yes, I expect you have.'

'Didn't know she was a make-up artist though.'

'Well, I think that's what she was. She wears enough of it. Did a bit of part-time modelling as well, underwear and stuff. Anyway, she doesn't have to work any more, now that she's with my dad.'

'What, is he loaded or something?'

'Yes.' Candy allowed herself a grin in the mirror. 'Totally loaded.'

'Some people have all the luck.'

The traffic wasn't too bad for some reason, Ossie thought, as he cut across town in his new Bentley, heading from Christchurch towards Stephen's Green and the Shelbourne Hotel, where Candy had told him to pick her up. It was dark, of course, and cold, and people were scurrying into buses or the Luas to make their way home after a bleak February day.

He had been taken completely by surprise to get her phone call. She'd been refusing to take his calls ever since the party, and it had been worrying him greatly. Charlotte had told him to give it time, that she would come around. Shalom had been impatient with him at first and then downright cross and told him to let her stew.

'Stop ringing her, Ossie, you're playing right into her hands. That's exactly what she wants you to do. Can't you see? If you stop ringing and pleading with her, then she'll get a wake-up call and stop treating you so unfairly. *Then* she'll be on the phone quick enough.'

He hadn't been able to heed either set of advice and had been thoroughly miserable about the whole situation. Guilty, too; enormously guilty. He couldn't believe how insensitive he'd been about announcing Shalom's pregnancy the way he had, that awful night at the party. What had he been thinking? He had tried once or twice in the weeks leading up to it to mention it to Charlotte on the phone, but every time something in her voice, or something in his heart, had stopped him. Then on the night itself, when he had seen Charlotte looking absolutely radiant in that magnificent period outfit she had worn, talking and laughing with old friends . . . he just hadn't had the heart to say anything. The words he had rehearsed so often just didn't seem to ever be appropriate. Then when he made his speech at the top table and was about to skirt around it, Shalom had prodded him, quite hard actually, and whispered to him sternly. Talk about being between a rock and a hard place! So he had blurted it out – and the rest was history. Of course he was thrilled about the new baby, but it seemed to Ossie that before it had even arrived in his life, things were becoming distinctly problematic.

For starters, there had been Candy's extreme reaction. It had genuinely startled Ossie, quite apart from the awful pie-throwing incident. Ossie had thought that Candy would have been thrilled to have a new little brother or sister on the way. It was Charlotte he'd been worried about. But Charlotte had taken the news calmly, bravely even, and with her usual magnanimous generosity had congratulated him and Shalom and wished them well. He wondered, briefly, how she really felt about it, considering everything they – well, *she* really – had gone through, all the doomed pregnancies Ossie could hardly bear to remember, even now.

Charlotte was extraordinary, really. He felt another swift stab of guilt. It must have been so hard for her when he left her for Shalom. But at the time he'd been having such fun, light-hearted, naughty, giddy fun, the kind of fun that made him forget all the pain and sorrow that he couldn't fix. It had lain there between him and Charlotte and grown until it had become a chasm he could no longer even think of broaching, let alone closing. Shalom had made him feel young and carefree again, and the sex, well, of course it had been amazing. Not that sex with Charlotte hadn't been wonderful – it had – but that had all seemed so long ago. Towards the end, the sadness seemed to even follow them there, in their most intimate moments, until eventually they avoided each other more and more.

With Shalom, everything seemed possible again. It was like being given a second chance. A second chance to spoil someone, to be irresponsible and not have to exist with that mantle of vague misery that seemed to always be there when he was with Charlotte.

It wasn't that she ever said anything or blamed him in any way; nothing could have been further from the truth. But despite Ossie's great success and wealth, he always felt he was something of a disappointment around Charlotte's crowd, particularly her parents. He always felt he had to prove something. And Jennifer – what a mother-in-law! He'd actually become very fond of her over the years. She was a tough old bird, no doubt about it, but she had a good heart and a great eye for horses. They had spent many a happy day at the races, he and Jennifer, and returned home a little squiffy and almost always considerably richer. She was incredibly knowledgeable and interesting too, and he had learned a lot from her. Underneath her brusque manner, she was kind and perceptive.

Like that time at Royal Ascot, when he had had his first runner, a wonderful three-year-old called *Johnny Come Lately*, who had, totally unexpectedly, won the Gold Cup, beating the Queen Mother's horse, the out-and-out favourite, by a nose and a half. Ossie, in an uncharacteristic fit of nerves, had almost been paralysed with fright at having the cup presented to him by the Queen.

'What's the matter? Got stage fright, Ossie? Surely not!' Jennifer had grinned evilly at him. Then said, with her usual forthrightness, 'you don't want to be intimidated by that lot – they're just a bunch of blow-in Germans, remember? Had to change their name from Saxe-Coburg-Gotha to Windsor! The ones you want to watch out for are the dukes – proper aristocracy. Speaking of which, there's Nottingham now! Oi,' she had called out to a portly looking man with a remarkably weather-beaten face, 'Biffy! Over here.'

The tall man in immaculate tails and silk top hat had peered at her, and then shouted joyfully, 'Jennifer, I don't believe it – good God you look wonderful, haven't changed a day!'

Then Ossie and Charlotte had been presented with the wonderful trophy (Charlotte looking utterly beautiful in a Bellville Sassoon shell-pink silk suit and a wonderful matching hat) and the Queen had congratulated Ossie heartily. After that, they had all gone back to Biffy's, or rather the Duke of Nottingham's, ongoing picnic in Car Park One, and got very drunk. He had even met Princess Diana, who had been looking very beautiful, and very pregnant. "Far too neurotic,' Jennifer had whispered to him, covertly, nodding in the Princess's direction, decidedly squiffy by this stage. 'Just like her mother. *Always look at the mother*, Ossie,' Jennifer had counselled. 'That's what they say, you know, *look at the mother before you take on the daughter.* Although in your case, better not look too closely, eh?' and they had both roared with laughter. It had been one of the best days of his life.

He never would have imagined all those years ago, on that first disastrous meeting with Charlotte's parents, that he would ever have got on so well with them down the road. And he had. He'd been genuinely saddened when Jeremy, Charlotte's father, had died, and even now, if he was honest, he missed Jennifer's outrageous remarks and remorseless good company more than he would have ever imagined.

His first meeting with Shalom's parents, on the other hand, couldn't have been more different. It had taken place a month or so before he had managed to get Candy to agree to meeting Shalom (and what an awful day *that* had been), when Shalom had pronounced it was time she introduced him to her parents, who, she claimed, were a bit worried about her and this mysterious man she was involved with who never seemed to materialise. Although Ossie could have done without it, he admitted that it was unfair for Shalom not to be able to produce her 'boyfriend', as she referred to him, to her parents.

So he had gone along good-humouredly that night in August, wearing a casual blue linen suit and a more colourful shirt than normal, a rather deep pink that Shalom had bought him earlier that week and which Charlotte would have cringed at. He felt peculiarly uncomfortable in it. Pulling up in his Bentley outside the small terraced house on the north side of the city, Ossie had felt, as well as seen, more than one net curtain twitching at their arrival.

They had been welcomed with open arms (literally) by Bernie, Shalom's mother, who, Ossie had been alarmed to find, was clearly about the same age as he was, give or take a year or two. She was also quite large, very made up and very blonde. She wore a tight white denim skirt, a sequinned cerise top with a deep V-neck that showed off a rather disturbing amount of deeply tanned cleavage and high-heeled bright pink shoes. Her father, Dessie, had been less effusive, looking uncomfortable and slightly sweaty in a clearly unworn shiny suit and unpolished, scuffed shoes with suspiciously high heels.

Bernie had grabbed the two bottles of good red that Ossie had brought and clearly forgot about them, as they never reappeared. Dinner was lukewarm stuffed peppers and chicken Kiev – 'Marks & Spencer's best!' Bernie had proclaimed cheerily. 'I can't be expected to cook as well. After all, I'm the businessperson in this family.' It had passed easily enough, served in the lean-to kitchen extension. Bernie, Ossie learned, had her own hairdressing salon in the local village. 'Wouldn't want to be relying on him,' she nodded at Dessie, who ignored her, tucking into his food. 'He never lifts a finger. Got no ambition and never did, did you? Of course, his bad back did for him. He was doing well in Bus Éireann up until then, weren't you, love? He had a nasty incident in one of those buses, didn't you, Dessie?'

'Shower of ungrateful gobshites,' Dessie said with considerable feeling, coming to life suddenly. 'Give 'em a life's work and they let you go without so much as a year's salary.'

'Ahem,' Bernie cleared her throat warningly. 'Wine or beer, Ossie?' she asked brightly.

'I'll, ah, have a Heineken, thanks,' Ossie plumped quickly for beer in favour of the Spanish plonk open on the table. 'Have you been away?' Ossie enquired politely. 'You have a very good tan.' This was true, although Dessie's fleshy face looked pale and pasty.

'Dear me, no!' trilled Bernie. 'God knows I'm due a holiday, but summer's my busiest time. I just go on the sun bed every day, works a treat, although I'm planning to get away to Gran Canaria in September with the bingo club.'

Dessie took his leave immediately after dinner. 'Can't hang about, got an appointment,' he winked. 'Nice to meet you, Ossie.'

Ossie jumped to his feet. 'Yes, yes, delighted to meet you too, er, Dessie.'

'Hope our Sharon's looking after you?'

'Shalom,' Shalom interrupted. 'My name is Shalom. You know that perfectly well, Dad.'

'Yes, yes, very well, very well indeed,' Ossie smiled. 'She's a credit to you both.'

'Looks like she's taken to the high life, too. Hope you can afford her – if she's anything like her mother, only the best is good enough,' he laughed heartily before disappearing out the door.

Shalom had been livid.

'Don't mind him,' Bernie had said. 'Appointment, my arse! He's off to the pub to meet his cronies.' After an hour of listening to Bernie's incessant chatter, Ossie rather wished he could have joined him.

After that official introduction, Ossie had been relieved not to have to meet them on a regular basis. Shalom, it appeared, was more than happy to spend time alone with her mother and met up with her frequently, often popping into the hair salon for a chat. Other than birthdays and Christmases, Ossie managed to claim business appointments. 'It's just nice for them to know you, darling, and see what good care you're taking of me,' Shalom had told him. *In-laws!* Ossie thought to himself. *Who needed them?*

Then there was the other little problem. Shalom had, not very discreetly, been dropping large hints that a marriage proposal would be timely. 'We'll be a proper little family now, darling, and Mummy and Daddy are a bit old-fashioned about things like that,' she had said, more than once. 'I think they're expecting an announcement any day soon.'

For some reason, this had thrown Ossie into a dilemma, one he wisely kept to himself. He had told Shalom many times, right from the very start of their relationship, that he wouldn't be getting married again. He had done it once, and that was all there was to it. Shalom had never seemed to mind or be put out about it. 'Of course, Ossie,' she had said. 'I'm so young still, it's not something I think about, really.'

Now, she appeared to be taking a different tack. He wondered why he still felt reluctant. He was happy, wasn't he? He was delighted to be having another baby after all this time – why shouldn't he take the plunge? But something, he was never quite sure what, just didn't feel right about it. There was a stubborn little voice that told him he didn't want to be pushed into anything. If – and it was a very big if – Ossie wanted to get married again, only he would decide when. All the same, it was there, like an undercurrent between them now, and Ossie knew Shalom expected a wedding – sooner rather than later.

He wouldn't think about it now. His darling daughter was spending her first proper weekend with them. He would concentrate on making it as pleasant and as much fun as possible.

He was on the Green now and pulled up outside the Shelbourne Hotel. Luckily there was a space right in front, just behind the taxi rank. He turned off the engine and waited, as Candy had told him to, in the car. He checked his watch: six-thirty on the dot, but there didn't seem to be any sign of Candy. The only person he could see was a bleached blonde girl, her curled ringlets trailing down from underneath a beaded cap, wearing tight jeans tucked into ridiculously high platform boots, talking intently into her mobile phone. She looked like a plainer version of Agnetha, from Abba fame, in her Waterloo outfit. Suddenly she began walking towards the car. For a moment he wondered if she was a young hooker and was about to wave her away, when unthinkably she opened the car door and – it couldn't *possibly* be! Surely *not*! But the voice, at least, was unmistakeable.

'Hi, Daddy!' She laughed at the look of disbelief on his face. 'What do you think of my new hairdo?'

Shalom parked her white convertible 911 Porsche Carrera and went into Bernie's hair salon. She was greeted with equal looks of awe and envy by the stylists and various clients, who had either clocked her car or recognised her from various celebrity society photos. She sat down in a vacant chair in the waiting area until Bernie had seen a client off and got one of the juniors to man the reception desk, then made a great fuss of ushering her daughter into the back staff room.

'Hello, love,' she kissed her. 'What a lovely surprise, wasn't expecting you today. Tea or coffee?

'Tea, and a muffin, if you have any.'

'Only these chocolate biscuits, pet, will they do?'

'Great.' Shalom took the cup of tea Bernie poured.

'How's our little baba?' She patted Shalom's burgeoning bump. 'Getting bigger every day.' Privately, Bernie noted, that wasn't the only thing getting bigger. Shalom's already enhanced breasts had become alarmingly large, and together with her five-month bump were beginning to form a rather solid-looking land mass. The floaty smock top she was wearing over her jeans did nothing to conceal it. Her arms, too, were losing their slenderness and she was developing a distinct double chin. Bernie wondered if she should comment and decided against it. She was bound to put on a bit of weight during the pregnancy, but still, she'd have to watch it . . .

'Didn't you have any lunch, pet?' She asked brightly as her daughter mindlessly reached for her third biscuit in as many minutes.

'Not really. I didn't feel like food. I just had a Danish or two. The baby seems to like them.'

'Well you put your feet up there and have a little rest. How's Ossie? I hope he's spoiling my girl rotten?'

'It's not Ossie that's the problem,' Shalom scowled. 'The daughter's arriving today to stay for the weekend. I told him I wasn't up to it, not in my condition, but he wasn't having any of it. Said he was picking her up and we'd all have great fun together.'

'The daughter!' Bernie's mouth settled in a grim line of disapproval. 'I thought he wasn't talking to her. Proper order too, after that disgraceful outburst of hers.' Memories of the offending newspaper coverage came flooding back, when more than one client, not to mention the staff, had been found sniggering over the pictures. 'I don't know how he can allow her in the house. Did she even apologise to you?'

'Are you joking? All she had to do was pick up the phone to him and he was ecstatic. He's playing straight into the little madam's hands. I can't believe it.' Shalom's lip wobbled petulantly.

Bernie stirred her tea and thought quickly. No point in fanning an already incendiary state of affairs, not when they'd come this far. 'Look, it's you he's with, pet, not her. So what if she has to visit the odd time? She's what, twenty?'

'Going on six.'

'Whatever. Maybe she's had a change of heart. Just be nice to her. Forget all about the other horrid business and offer to give her a make-up lesson. God knows she could do with one if those pictures were anything to go by. She'll love that. If it all gets too much, just say you're not feeling well and go to bed. In a few months he'll have forgotten she exists, he'll be so besotted with *your* baby.'

'I hope you're right,' Shalom said darkly.

'Course I am, pet,' Bernie said chirpily. 'When have I ever been wrong about Ossie? I know what a man like that wants, and he's got it in you. Then, when the baby arrives, maybe a bit before it even, I'll come and stay to help out. He or she is going to want Nana Bernie there!'

'Oh, would you, Mum?' Shalom brightened. 'I hadn't thought of that. It would be great. And there's loads of room in our house – I even get lost in it still,' she giggled. 'Although of course there'll be nannies and things, even though we've got loads of staff already. Ossie's determined I'm not to have too much to do – I couldn't cope on my own, you know.'

'Of course you couldn't. Who'd expect you to?' Bernie was indignant. 'But all those foreigners must be annoying, under your feet all the time, and nobody knows how to make your favourite smoothies like I do, do they?'

Shalom shook her head and smiled ruefully. 'I do miss our little chats, Mum.'

'So do I, pet, but like I said, I'll make sure I'm there to help out, and your father can manage perfectly well here on his own. If not, he can get up off his arse and make himself useful for once in his life. He could help out in the garden or do a bit of driving for Ossie – he'd probably even put him on the payroll, wouldn't he?' Bernie's eye's lit up.

'Maybe.' Shalom wasn't so sure about that.

'Anyway, if Ossie's moving family members in on a weekend, it's only right you should have yours around you now and again for a bit of moral support – that's all there is to it.'

'Oh, Mum,' Shalom smiled gratefully. 'I don't know what I'd do without you.'

'Hopefully, pet, you won't ever have to. Another biscuit? Oh dear, they're all gone. Never mind.'

'What do you think?' Candy did a twirl in her matching underwear, a new lacy thong with a cute little diamante decoration at the back and a black and red push-up padded bra. Her skin was a deep tan and her nails and toes had been manicured and painted a deep rouge noir.

'Wow, you look amazing. You've really lost weight since you've been going to that personal trainer,' Emma said.

'The spray tan makes all the difference, Shalom says. And you only have to have it done once a week to keep it up.'

'Your hair is just wicked. It makes you look really sophisticated, *much* older.' Katy was in awe.

'Are you sure you don't want her to do your make-up too? She said she would.'

'Um, no thanks, we'll just watch if that's okay?'

'Whatever – she's just getting all her gear together now.' Candy pulled on a short satin wrap and tied her hair back in a ponytail.

The weekend was going well. On Friday, they had gone out to dinner in the posh new Ritz-Carlton Hotel, and Candy had been chatty and pleasant, asking all about the baby and telling Shalom that she was so excited and couldn't wait to have a brother or sister.

'It was just a bit of a shock that night,' she ventured, smiling sheepishly at her dad. 'I overreacted a bit, I'm afraid.'

'That's all water under the bridge, isn't it Shalom?' Ossie had looked meaningfully at her. 'Shalom and I are just delighted you've decided to spend a bit of time with us, Princess – aren't we, Shalom?'

'Delighted,' murmured Shalom, taking a sip of water. She couldn't take her eyes off Candy's hair, which was rather spookily like her own.

'If it's all right with you, Daddy,' Candy continued, 'I thought

I might go shopping tomorrow. I need some new gear to go with my new look. I was wondering, Shalom, if you'd come along and help me choose some stuff. If we went in the morning, Daddy, you could meet us for lunch?'

'I think that's a great idea, don't you, Shalom?'

'Er, yes. Yes, of course.'

'Great,' Candy beamed. 'Then, if you don't mind, I thought Katy and Emma might come around about four o'clock. I'm going out with them to a party and I told them it would be fine if they came around and we could all get ready together, then you and Shalom can have a nice evening to yourselves.'

'Of course they can,' Ossie said. 'I'll make sure Eddie is available to drive you. Just let me know what time you want to leave and he'll drop everyone home after as well. You must promise me, Prin— I mean, Candy – that's the only condition. I won't have you taking any lifts from anyone, not even your friends – it's too much of a risk. And there's no guarantee you'll get a taxi if you're late.'

'Of course not, Daddy, you have my word.'

'I'm starting with a slightly warmer base, girls, because of Candy's new hair colour, and of course because it's a night-time look as opposed to daytime.' The girls watched intently as Shalom got to work. 'Now I'm mixing a bit of bronzing cream with the foundation on my hand, see? That's a good tip.' Another layer of bronzing powder was whisked over Candy's face and then some more 'contouring' under her cheekbones and 'shading' for the sides of her nose. 'Now a bit of blusher. I think we'll go for quite a dramatic look, and some highlighter on the cheekbones and just under her brows, see?'

They were riveted.

'Now, smoky eyes, I think.' She began wielding a dark navy shadow over Candy's lid and in the socket, and with a kohl liner pencil began outlining and emphasising her eyes, followed by three coats of mascara over a few added false lashes. She then applied a spice lip-liner and lipstick, which managed to change the shape of Candy's mouth completely, followed by a heavy gloss, which completed the look. Shalom stood back to admire her handiwork. 'Okay, take down your hair, Candy, and have a look. What do you think, girls?'

Transformation was too small a word.

'Unbelievable,' said Katy.

'Awesome.' Emma shook her head.

'Perfect,' said Candy.

Half an hour later, they were ready. They popped their heads around the door into the vast television room with the giant screen where Ossie and Shalom were watching a movie. 'Bye, Daddy, bye Shalom. See you later – don't wait up!'

'Bye Mr Searson, bye Shalom,' said Katy and Emma. 'Thanks so much for letting us get ready here.'

'Not at all, girls,' said Ossie, looking a bit shell-shocked. 'Have a great time.'

He was having trouble taking in the very made-up young woman in the tight top revealing the top of a very obvious bra and the very short skirt, who sounded like his daughter but looked decidedly different. Beside her fresh-faced friends, she looked much older.

'Bye, girls, have a great night,' Shalom smiled at them.

As the front door closed behind them, Shalom snuggled down beside Ossie on the sofa. 'She looks great, doesn't she?'

'Yes, it's just a bit of a shock, that's all.' Ossie struggled with unfamiliar feelings. 'She looked a lot . . . older.' He sounded worried.

'Darling, she is almost twenty-one. All girls her age have to experiment with different looks. Anyway, it's what she wanted. You have to let her grow up sometime, you know. At her age, I was really into my make-up too.'

'But the other two looked just the same as ever, just . . . prettier.' He sounded miserable.

'Katy said her mother would kill her and Emma said she was allergic and had to stick to her regular make-up. Candy's lucky to be able to have someone like me to show her how to work a look.'

'I'm sure you're right.' Then a thought struck him. 'Of course, it's obvious what she's doing,' he grinned. 'She's imitating *you*. She's obviously impressed with how glamorous you are.'

'I'll take that as a compliment.'

'I imagine it's just a phase,' Ossie reassured himself.

'What's that supposed to mean? You like the way I look, don't you?'

'Of course I do. I just think . . .'

'What?' A sharp note had entered Shalom's tone.

'It was just a bit of a shock, that's all.' Ossie wisely decided to say no more on the subject.

'I think it's a real improvement,' Shalom proclaimed. 'She looks hip and funky now, just like a girl her age should. You don't want her dressing like Charlotte, do you? That's not what men like, boys neither, and that's what it's all about at Candy's age. They'll be queuing up for her now.'

Ossie felt a twinge of worry, and something else, something he couldn't quite articulate. All he knew was his fresh, freckle-faced, silky-haired daughter had somehow morphed into a stranger – a very tarty-looking stranger. He couldn't deny anything Shalom had said; it made sense, in a way. She was probably right. He was just having a hard time seeing Candy grow up. It was just that he'd never imagined her growing up quite like *that*.

9

Dominic's was buzzing with every table in the house already claimed or waiting for the few remaining diners to be seated. Alex checked with the desk and was told his lunch guest was waiting in the Chameleon Bar, as instructed, and had arrived about fifteen minutes ago. Although Alex was absolutely punctual (it didn't do to appear *too* eager), he had correctly guessed that Frank Casey, one of the managers of Eurocorp, would be there well ahead of him. He had kept tabs on his career since their schooldays, when diligent, plodding Frank, not a star on the rugby field, or indeed any sport, had devoted himself to his studies and obtained a good degree in commerce and economics from University College Dublin, and through sheer determination and application had carved out a surprisingly successful, if uninteresting, path in finance and now held quite a covetable position with one of the substantial European banks that had set up shop in Dublin during the past ten years. A country boy at heart, Alex deduced that Frank would be suitably impressed and, with a bit of luck, distracted by the glamorous surroundings of the hip restaurant. As far as he could remember, lunch for Frank usually consisted of a sandwich at his desk, even when his position and indeed salary could have afforded him a prominent table at any restaurant of his choice.

Alex checked his watch – two minutes to one exactly. Perfect. He had been lucky to find a parking space almost right outside the restaurant and had carefully manoeuvred his precious red Ferrari into it, enjoying, as always, the envious and admiring glances it attracted. That car meant a lot to him, not just because of its brand name, but because of everything it represented, everything that Alex had fought and struggled for. It almost, but not quite, made up for all those other, awful years . . .

Lately, Catherine, his wife, had been suggesting he change it for something more suitable for a young couple expecting their first child. She was right, of course, they did need something more suitable, so he had surprised her and traded in the baby Mercedes he had bought her for her last birthday for a Range Rover Sport. 'Plenty of room for all of us now,' he'd proclaimed, delighted at his creative solution to the problem.

'Oh my God, Alex,' she had gasped, astonished as he led her to the front door and told her to close her eyes. 'It's gorgeous, but are you sure? I mean, can we really afford it? It seems a bit excessive, that *and* your Ferrari.'

'Of course I can afford it.' He had been rather annoyed at the question. 'The company's doing brilliantly. Anyway, in my line of business, it's important to keep up a high profile. People are hardly going to trust me with their investments unless I look like I'm doing well myself, are they? Particularly since I'm the same age as a lot of their kids.'

P.J.'s reaction to his car had been rather different that day last year when he had called around in the brand-new Ferrari to his father's house in Wellington Square on the pretext of picking up some post for his sister, Bella, who he was seeing the following in week in Florence, where she was studying.

'Hi, Dad,' he had said, moving past him into the hall and perusing the tray of mail that sat on the hall table. 'What do you think of my new set of wheels?' He nodded towards the gleaming red machine that sat in the driveway beside P.J.'s ten-year-old Jeep.

'I dread to think what that does to the gallon.' He shook his head. 'Ten? Eleven, maybe?'

'That's not why anyone buys a Ferrari,' Alex had snapped, irritated that P.J. had actually been spot on at eleven miles to the gallon.

'No, I shouldn't imagine it is. Well it's very nice, very . . .'

'Obvious?' Alex's mouth tightened. 'You think it's flash, don't you? Why don't you just come right out and say it?'

'Because I wasn't going to,' P.J. replied lightly. 'Actually, I was going to wish you all the best with it, happy driving and all that, if you'd care to give me the opportunity.'

Just then, Sheila had come up to see what the commotion was about. 'Jesus, Mary and Joseph, what's that?'

'It's my new car, Sheila.'

'It looks like a spaceship.'

'Come on, I'll take you for a spin,' Alex said, deliberately excluding P.J. from the invitation.

Sheila looked anxiously at her watch. 'I'd love to, really I would, but I've only just started cleaning the oven – the stuff has to be left on for fifteen minutes exactly.'

'I'll have you back in ten.'

'Just let me get my gloves, I wouldn't want to catch anything.'

Minutes later, Sheila and he were cutting quite a dash, swishing out of the square and onto the main road, Sheila clutching tightly onto the passenger handle. 'How do you stand the noise of it?' she shouted as the engine roared into life.

'It's part of the attraction,' Alex grinned. 'Sort of like your hoover. It's meant to sound like that.'

'Oh, right.'

Alex had a soft spot for Sheila, despite her idiosyncrasies. He identified with her driven sense for orderliness, and even as an awkward teenager had appreciated the rigorous predictability her presence had brought to their home. At least with Sheila, you knew that if it was Monday, it would be shepherd's pie for dinner, that Wednesday was laundry day or that on Thursday afternoon there would always be freshly baked scones on offer. Alex had liked that. He liked the reassurance of that comforting, methodical presence in a household and indeed life which for him had become unwieldy and unpredictable.

Plucked from his safe, familiar American schooling and surroundings at thirteen, Alex had been deeply suspicious and later resentful of the unexpected move back to Ireland. Deposited in his father's (and indeed grandfather's) alma mater, Blackrock College, Alex was to learn that an awful lot was expected of him – a lot, he quickly discovered, that he couldn't deliver. For starters, he loathed rugby, a veritable religion at the school. 'Another O'Sullivan,' the form priest had boomed with delight on his first day, as Alex had sat conspicuously at the front of the classroom, where the only free desk was left (Jilly had been late getting him off and had then lost her way, making him later still). 'Excellent! Remember your father and grandfather well, played for Ireland,' he informed the rest of the year, who were sizing Alex up with interest. This was only half right. His grandfather had indeed played rugby for Ireland, whereas P.J., although he had captained the school team and had been a noted star, had turned up for the Leinster trials still drunk from the previous night and had been sent off in disgrace, to much hilarity. It was a story he (and his friends) still told with relish, although Alex wanted to scream every time he heard it. 'No doubt you'll be carrying on the family tradition,' the priest continued. 'We'll be expecting great things from you, O'Sullivan.'

The great things had never materialised, at least not on the rugby field, and Alex had even given up competing in tennis, which he'd been good at. Seizing on his inability to fit in, the other boys had quickly started teasing him about his Texan accent, his apparent studiousness and his small, skinny frame. He was quickly christened the Milky Bar Kid from the TV spots about the goody-goody child cowboy who distributed the white chocolate bars, and from then on, life, as far as Alex was concerned, became miserable. It wasn't that he was bullied as such, but he was definitely not one of the crowd. He didn't understand their accents, their humour or their blinding obsession with rugby. For the first time in his life, Alex couldn't play by the rules and refused to try to learn these new, confusing ones. Instead he threw himself into studies, which he excelled at, and kept pretty much to himself.

Jilly asked him occasionally if he'd like to invite some friends around from school, but he always made an excuse. Instead, he made friends with a couple of kids down the road and a French boy whose father was a diplomat and who seemed to find these Irish boys as perplexing as Alex did. He never divulged his misery to his father. He already felt like too much of a failure, but admitting it to his outgoing, multi-talented, popular father would have been the ultimate defeat. Instead, he shored up his misery, gritted his teeth and vowed that one day he would show them all.

And the day did come. His qualifications were first-rate and he was considered to be a financial whizz-kid. In Catherine, he had married an exceptionally pretty, clever girl, also with a background in finance, and last year he had bought his Ferrari. There was something about it that had just been the icing on the cake. Alex was quite good-looking, tall and thin with reasonably broad shoulders, dark hair and eyes and pale skin. Girls had never been a problem. It was other men who never seemed to rate him. But pulling up in a Ferrari changed all that that and made up for all the years he had spent feeling painfully inadequate. Soon he would have his first son or daughter. He was excited and proud of that, and no matter what happened, he or she was going to have the perfect father. He would make sure of it.

'Frank!' he greeted his old school friend heartily. 'Great to see you. Let's go straight to our table. Hope I didn't keep you waiting? Just had to park the Ferrari.'

'Ferrari?' Frank's eye's opened wide. 'Crikey, business must be good then.' They sat down at their table and Alex ordered drinks. 'Couldn't be better, actually, things are going really well. In fact, that's what I wanted to talk to you about.'

'Oh yes?'

'The new development, the one in Sheffield – I might need your guys to up the investment just a tad,' he smiled reassuringly. 'Absolutely nothing to worry about, just a few punters taking longer than usual to get their acts together – you know what you bankers are like!' he laughed easily.

'How much?' Frank wasn't laughing quite so easily.

'About ten per cent.'

'Hmm,' Frank was reticent, although the very pretty waitress who came to take their order had got his attention. 'I'll have a word, Alex, that's all I can say. Things are tight at the moment. It's the same for all of us.'

'Of course.' Alex quickly ordered the day's special. 'But this one's a sure win. You'll be sorry if you get left behind.'

'Like I said, I'll have a word.'

The rest of lunch passed in discussions of shares, portfolios and interest rates. Alex was hard pushed to remember when he had been more bored. Bankers were all the same – they lacked any vision or imagination, always wanted a safe bet. But that wasn't the way you made big money. You had to stick your head above the parapet and take the bullets when they came, and when you managed to avoid them, reap the rewards of your timing.

'Thanks for lunch, Alex.' Frank sat back while Alex signed the bill. 'I've been wanting to come to this place for ages, I've heard a lot about it. Best food I've had in a long time.'

'You're welcome, Frank, good to see you. Remember to let

me know by next week, will you? Otherwise I'll have to approach some of my other clients – they're queuing up.'

'I'll be in touch.'

They went their separate ways, Alex's stomach churning in a most unusual manner, which had absolutely nothing to do with the lunch he had just consumed.

Dom felt vile. It had started at about ten o'clock that morning, when his eyes began to sting and his throat felt ominously scratchy. By four o'clock he had a throbbing head and his limbs felt like lead. He was also beginning to perspire profusely. It was Friday, and as always there would be a full house, but by four-thirty he knew it was a losing battle. He was rarely sick, and on the few occasions he succumbed to the odd cold, he usually managed to fight it off or at least weather it, but this was something more sinister. There was a particularly nasty flu virus doing the rounds and it had clearly decided to seek out his company. So weary and weak he could hardly walk, he gave in and went up to his apartment above Dominic's and collapsed into bed, reminding himself to ring Tanya and apologise for cancelling the late dinner date they had arranged at her place. Once a month, Dom allowed himself a Friday night off, and although he would be in the restaurant to greet clients, he would leave at about nine or nine-thirty, when one of the many other capable members of staff would be in left in charge. This evening, Astrid had briskly stepped into his place and happily agreed to begin her duties earlier than previously arranged, ordering him straight to bed and saying she would have Rollo have his special-recipe chicken soup sent up, which everybody knew had enormously curative properties, due in no small part, Dom had heard on the grapevine, to rather generous amounts of some magic ingredient that was bracingly alcoholic. Dom had declined the offer, saying the thought of any kind of food made him feel infinitely worse. Agreeing to notify the kitchen if he had the slightest requirement, he had made his escape. Now he just had to give the bad news to Tanya.

She was going to keep the whole thing very low key, simple, not in any way premeditated, as if the idea had just popped into her head. They often had a late-night supper at her place, so there would be nothing unusual in that. She made sure she was looking her best, but that was a pretty much constant discipline anyhow. She had thought about setting up the whole romantic dinner thing. Although she would be far too nervous to cook, she could have ordered something gorgeous from many of the designer grocery stores that catered to the thousands of young, busy people like herself, leading demanding, executive lifestyles. And then she reminded herself – tonight was about Dom, not her, and he liked nothing better than a takeaway from their favourite Indonesian restaurant. That was the easy bit. Rehearsing what to say and, more importantly, how and when to say it was proving to be a minefield. If she overdid it, she would appear at best silly, at worst desperate. If she was too light-hearted, he might think she was joking and then the moment might be lost for ever. Her mind was spinning with various scenarios, so much so that she was brought back to earth with a bump when she realised that she had just chewed through the nail of her little finger, painted a delicate frosted caramel. She cursed rather vehemently, which was most unlike her. Really, she would have to pull herself together.

Just then, her phone rang. She almost didn't pick up. She really wasn't in the mood for chatting to anyone, especially her mother, whom she hadn't confided in, although she knew she would have endorsed and heartily encouraged Tanya's choice of action. For some reason, she preferred to keep the whole idea to herself. The only thing that needed to be broadcast was the result itself. The manner in which it would have been achieved would remain her and Dom's little secret.

She checked the number that flashed on her screen. Oh God, it was Dom. Please, oh please, she thought, don't let him be cancelling – not tonight of all nights.

'Hi sweetie, how are you?' She answered the call in her brightest voice.

'Awful,' he croaked. 'That's why I'm ringing. Tanya, I'm sorry, but I really can't make it this evening, I've got this awful flu that's going around and I can barely stay upright. I'm afraid I wouldn't be much use to you, never mind any company.' He broke off as a fit of coughing took hold of him.

'You poor, poor darling, you do sound dreadful. Don't move, I'm coming right over.'

'No, really,' he wheezed, 'there's no need. You've no idea, this thing's a real bugger. I'd hate for you to get it, and, like I said,' another fit of coughing began, 'I'm really feeling pretty vile. I'm just going to crash out.'

'Nonsense,' Tanya said crisply. *Don't panic*, she told herself, *do* not *panic*. She searched for exactly the right blend of sympathy and matronly firmness. 'You can't possibly be on your own when you sound like that. I'm coming straight over. What would happen if you collapsed or couldn't breathe or something? I'll sleep in the spare room even, but Dom, sweetie, I wouldn't have a minute's peace of mind here knowing you were lying there that sick and weak. Don't worry about a thing. I'm on my way.'

She clicked off her phone.

Even if Dom had had the strength, which he didn't, he wasn't given a chance to dissuade her.

Damn it anyway, she thought. What was it her assistant had said to her that morning? Something about Mercury being retrograde, upsetting the best-laid plans and all that. Tanya wasn't superstitious – she was on a mission, and it would take more than an uncooperative planet to get in her re the big guys. As for the others, a lot of them lding under the pressure. He just hoped Alex t be one of them.

ghed. He had tried to advise him, but Alex would sten to him, always took offence. It was almost as s waging some personal battle between them, deter- ie would win – that he would somehow 'show' P.J., P.J. had ever wanted for him was that he be happy. a lovely, pretty, clever wife and a new baby on the : had everything any young man could possibly dn't he? Yet Alex always seemed to be dissatisfied, l in some way. Still, P.J. thought, looking on the ide, at least he hadn't invested anything in Alex's cheme. Things weren't looking too good on that

e bloody hell Dominic's?' Alex had stormed, flinging oat as he came in on Wednesday evening and going kitchen to pour himself a drink.

's the matter with you?' Catherine had asked. 'Why ninic's? We always go there. You love the place, we all the best restaurant in Dublin.'

ick of it, that's why. And I don't particularly want to on Friday. I've been working my ass off, it's been a a week and if anybody had bothered to ask, I was forward to spending a quiet night in with my wife.'

it's all arranged now. Your father's booked a table, e continued firmly, despite the thunderous expres- husband was wearing, '*I* would like to go out on We haven't been out for ages, Alex, and I'm tired of oped up in the house here waiting for Junior to arrive. ut there meeting people, having lunch wherever you haven't been to Dominic's in ages.' There was an edge to her voice. 'It'll be fun.'

ighed. 'Sorry, babe, I didn't mean to have a go at you.

way. She felt in her jeans pocket and reached for the little piece of paper she had been carrying around all week. *Who makes it happen?* It read. *I make it happen.* And she would. She couldn't afford not to.

Astrid was happy and refreshed after her weekend with Rollo in Vienna. They'd had a wonderful time visiting her home and meeting her parents, who had approved of him greatly. Now, at the end of her first week back, she was happy to take on the extra Friday night shift as front of house and even happier that Tanya was nowhere in evidence, poking her nose in where it wasn't wanted and breathing down everyone's necks. Astrid had informed Rollo of Dom's sudden illness and, as she knew he would, he insisted on whipping up his famous chicken soup, even though Dom had shud- dered at the thought of eating anything. She would just go and check on things in the kitchen and make sure everything was going according to plan.

Dom lay in bed feeling sicker by the minute. His head ached, his limbs ached and now he was in the grip of escalating waves of nausea. He *really* didn't want to see anybody. He had dosed himself with Paracetamol and only wanted the blessed oblivion of sleep. He was just about to drop off when he heard Tanya's key in the door. The sound of it suddenly irritated him profoundly. Although he had pushed the thought to the back of his mind (he had so much else to deal with, after all), he'd lately been regretting giving her a key so easily. Normally he was reticent about such things, but it had made sense at the time, especially when Tanya had been overseeing the decoration and organisation of his flat. She'd been quite adamant about it, actually, and he had to admit he would never have got around to it without her. It was just that lately she'd taken to popping in and out at any time of the day, or indeed night, that suited her, and now he wasn't sure it had been such a good idea. That was the trouble, Dom reflected, just as his teachers always told him at school – he never really thought things through or considered the implications. Much as he hated to admit it, Dom now felt he would rather have his key back, but he was in no condition to have that particular conversation now.

'Only me, sweetie,' she called from the hallway.

God, his head ached. Even his ears hurt, which was ridiculous, and the *click clack* of Tanya's heels on the wooden floor and the scratching of her overnight wheelie case seemed to penetrate every hair of his head. When she came in, he tried to smile weakly. He knew she meant well, but . . .

'Poor darling,' she cooed, sitting down on the edge of the bed beside him, 'you really do look rough.' She smoothed his hair back from his damp forehead. 'I'm just going to get settled and then I'll come and take your temperature. You're burning up, you poor pet.' She smiled determinedly. 'Then I'll decide whether or not we need to call the doctor.'

'No. No doctor,' it was a croak, but Dom's scowl was unusually bad-tempered, Tanya thought. 'If I'm not feeling better tomorrow, maybe. Please, Tanya, I just want to be left in peace.'

'Well, all right. I suppose you've every right to feel grumpy, Mr Bear Head. But we'll see what the thermometer says anyhow.'

One hundred and three degrees, said the thermometer.

'That's it, I'm calling the doctor.'

'Tanya, I couldn't stand it. Look, it's just the flu,' Dom muttered. 'Tomorrow, if I'm not better, then . . .'

'You really are being awfully silly – and stubborn,' she frowned. Then she had a brilliant idea. 'Don't worry, darling, I'm just popping downstairs for a moment, there's something I have to check on.'

It was Friday night and the chances of getting a doctor were zero to none – not for hours, anyway – but she was

almost sure she had noted a bookin
of P.J. O'Sullivan, for a party of f
doctor and a regular at Dominic's,
With any luck, he'd be in the restau
sure the booking had been for eigh
perfect opportunity.

Dinner had been Catherine's idea.
P.J. when she called him on the pho
doing, as she and Alex hadn't seen
'Great idea,' he had proclaimed. 'I
book Dominic's. Does eight-thirty s
'Perfect.'
'And I'll bring Sheila, if that's all r
a hot date, that is,' he chuckled.
'What could be a hotter date than
'My son is a very lucky man, Cat
'And I'm a very fortunate daug
smiled down the phone.
'How is Alex, by the way?' P.J. enqu
form last time I had lunch with him
'Oh, he's fine. A bit stressed with
he'll enjoy a night out. It'll do him g
too hard lately.'
'Good. Well, I'll look forward to s
'See you Friday then.'
P.J. put the phone down thought
was stressed, as Catherine had put i
was in free fall and the banks we
certainly wasn't a good time to be
luxury hotel, spa and golf complex
together didn't appear to be movi
Not that he was an expert in the
P.J. heard a lot through his patients, an
in property were having to tighten thei

they w
were f
wouldn
He s
never
if he w
mined
when a
He ha
way. H
want,
resent
bright
latest
front.

'Why
off his
into th
'Wh
not Do
do – it
'I'm
go out
bitch
lookin
'We
and,'
sion h
Friday
being
You're
please
unusu
Ale

I'm just tired, that's all. And I really don't fancy a night out with Dad throwing his weight around, doing his utmost to hold court in any restaurant. But if that's what you want, I'll be on my best behaviour. I wish it was just you and me, that's all.' He came over and put his arms around her.

'It'll do us good to get out, and it'll be good for your dad too. Oh, he's bringing Sheila.'

'Is he? Oh good,' Alex brightened. 'If she's at the table, then even Dad will be upstaged.'

Catherine laughed, but she was really very worried. Alex was becoming even more touchy than usual, snapping and taking imaginary offence at the slightest thing, although he was always immediately remorseful afterwards. She also knew he wasn't sleeping. She was awake herself at night a lot with the baby, both of them tossing and turning, and more than once she had awoken to find Alex's side of the bed empty and, calling softly to him, had found him downstairs, poring over figures in his office, or worse, the time she had found him with his head in his hands, a large brandy beside him.

He had always been rather highly-strung and sensitive, but he was clearly terribly stressed. She hoped it was just about the baby's fairly imminent arrival. Alex was such a perfectionist, he would want every eventuality planned down to the most minute detail for his new son or daughter, preferably for the next twenty-one years. But life wasn't like that, Catherine knew. You couldn't plan or protect people – even your own family – no matter how much you wanted to.

All the same, they needed to sit down and have a good talk about it all – and Alex's development scheme. He had been unusually evasive about it when she had asked him lately, saying everything was just fine, though the banks were being a bit of a pain, but investors were queuing up. As an accountant, and a good one, Catherine had a good grip on such matters. It was just that with Junior's arrival growing ever closer, figures, except her own expanding one, were far from her mind. And when she did try to make sense of them, they didn't add up at all.

Alex sat down beside Catherine, determined to relax and to try to chat and vaguely follow the plastic-surgery programme she was watching with interest. It seemed to him almost as surreal and grotesque as his week was proving thus far – and it was only Wednesday. Why Dominic's of all places, and this Friday? Of all the bad luck. He would rather die than be seen in there and have to smile and meet and greet that arrogant twit Dom as if nothing had happened. And it wasn't as if he could explain to Catherine, tell her what had transpired, not with the baby nearly due, and certainly not with all the other, far more worrying scenarios that could follow . . . it didn't bear thinking about.

He'd thought it was such a brilliant idea – and it was. More importantly, so did the banks – it was what had sold them on the Royal Alexander Golf and Health Resort. The deciding 'hook' was that he would get Dominic's to open a second restaurant there. It was already proving a crowd-puller in Dublin and it was widely tipped to win a Michelin star any day now.

So he'd approached Dom. He knew him vaguely; their families lived on the same square – their parents would have been contemporaries and Dublin was such a small place anyway, socially speaking. He had asked him to meet him for a drink, said he had something he wanted to seek his opinion on. Dom had agreed, as he knew he would, and Alex had suggested meeting in the Royal Dublin Society, where he was a member. *That should impress him*, Alex thought. Those posh Glenstal Abbey boys loved going to all of their various clubs. And Dom had been there on the dot of six-thirty as arranged, looking casual and effortlessly elegant beside Alex's very carefully thought out and rather stiff outfit. Alex had ordered faces, 'we have a little emergency, and it's so fortunate to see we have a doctor in the house. I won't take him away for long, I promise.'

'I really do appreciate this, Dr O'Sullivan. The wine and any drinks you've had will be on the house, naturally.'

'Not at all,' said P.J. as he followed her out and up the stairs to Dom's apartment. 'I wouldn't hear of it. You're quite right to come and get me. One can never take any chances. I'm delighted to help.'

'Dom, sweetie,' Tanya called to the covered shape in the bed of the master bedroom, 'there's someone here to see you. I'll wait outside, of course,' she murmured to P.J. 'The bathroom's just there if you need to wash your hands.' And she discreetly closed the door behind her.

'Dr O'Sullivan!' Dom croaked. 'What on earth?'

'A happy coincidence, Dom. I was having dinner downstairs, and please, call me P.J. I hear you're a bit under the weather?'

'No, I'm fine, really. It's just this flu that's going around.' He struggled to sit up.

P.J. washed his hands briskly and returned with the medical bag he had retrieved from the car on the way up.

'Well, let's just have a look at you old chap. Never hurts, you know.'

Fifteen minutes later, P.J. emerged and found Tanya waiting in the sitting room.

'How is he? I was so worried.'

'He'll live,' P.J. grinned. 'He was right, it's just a dose of this horrid flu that's doing the rounds. He's doing the best thing he can, plenty of sleep, plenty of fluids, a couple of Paracetamol when he needs them. Call me tomorrow and tell me how he's doing. He should be right as rain in forty-eight hours, if a bit weak, but nothing a bit of TLC won't take care of,' he winked at her.

'I'm so relieved. I was afraid it might have been something

serious. That was so kind of you to come and check on him. Let me show you back down.'

'You go and tend to your patient, I can see myself out. Mind you, I suspect he won't be much company tonight. Probably best to let him sleep and sweat it out.'

'Yes, yes, of course. Thank you again, Doctor. I – we're really most grateful.'

'Pleasure,' said P.J., looking forward to getting back to the sirloin of beef he had ordered.

Dinner was going very well. P.J. rejoined his table and smiled as he listened to the good-natured banter.

'What was it you ordered, Sheila?' Alex asked.

'What I always order. Chicken. Plain and roasted, nothing fancy.' She looked disapproving as a selection of dishes were brought to the table the minute P.J. rejoined them. Nestling under their silver covers, the table waited in anticipation as the immaculately choreographed waiters lined up and, with military precision, whipped the covers off to reveal and then distribute the art-directed array of wonderful food.

'Bon appetit.' They faded away in perfect unison.

'Thank you,' everyone said, salivating at the delicious-looking concoctions. Even Sheila's roast chicken breast seemed to have acquired a wonderful caramelised luminosity, and the fresh green runner beans and mashed potatoes were arranged in a meticulous design that even she couldn't fault.

Alex was in good form for a change, although he had looked strained on the way in, but once he had sat down and had a good look around, he seemed to suddenly cheer up. Clocking the financier at a nearby table, the restaurant suddenly seemed to meet with his approval again.

'No sign of Dom,' Catherine, said. 'Must be his night off.'

'No indeed,' P.J. said. 'That's who I was just called away to check on. He's feeling thoroughly miserable, poor chap, got this awful flu that's going around. Nothing serious though.'

Pity, thought Alex. He turned to P.J. 'Enjoying the wine, Dad? I think it was a good choice, don't you? A client of mine imports it.'

'Excellent choice, Alex. It's going down a treat.'

'Good,' Alex said, resolving to sit back and enjoy dinner. Now that Dom was out of the way, there was absolutely no reason why he shouldn't.

'To your very good health, everybody,' P.J. said, raising his glass.

In Dom's apartment, things were not going according to plan at all. Time was running out for Tanya. It wasn't just the matter of timing, of it being the twenty-ninth of February and a leap year, the acceptable time for a woman to propose marriage – there was the other, considerably more pressing matter of her financial situation. Her credit-card bills were huge and there was no way she could pay them. Tanya didn't just want to get married to Dom – she needed to, particularly before he discovered how freely she had been dispensing favours to her friends and contacts. But what else could she do? It had been the only way. Dominic's had been her major account – it had been a real coup to win it – and naturally she had had to give it her all, at the risk of neglecting her other, considerably less important, clients, who despite what she had intimated to Dom were pretty low-rent stuff. And if she was representing Dominic's, she had to look the part. Tanya couldn't afford designer clothes, but she liked wearing them. What she couldn't buy, she borrowed. She simply developed a close relationship with one or two designers, who were only too happy to loan her outfits or evening dresses for a special occasion if she guaranteed them a good table at the now impossible-to-book restaurant – and an appropriate discount on the bill.

Then there had been the decoration of Dom's apartment. Tanya had chosen only the best of everything, and it didn't come cheap. She had been loath to bring the matter of bills up to Dom (it was so unromantic), and she had simply managed to stall for a while and pay a few crucial amounts here and there by persuading Eric to advance her the cash from accounts, assuring him that Dom would settle up with her later.

Now, though, she was beginning to panic. She hadn't always been a spendthrift, not until she had started earning money, and even then, in the beginning, she had been careful. But then she would get the craving, the compulsion to purchase something lovely and relish the warm, comforting glow of satisfaction it gave her. It was the one area of her life she couldn't seem to keep under the rigorous control she managed otherwise. When Dom found out what the whole lot had come to, he would flip. Maybe even dump her. She took a deep breath. That wasn't going to happen.

She had left Dom to sleep as he'd requested, rather brusquely actually, after P.J. had left. She had felt pretty miffed that he hadn't exactly thanked her for her Florence Nightingale display of wifely concern. But then, that was men for you; they were always a nightmare when they were sick. Since then, she had been in the sitting room trying unsuccessfully to watch television. Now it was nearly eleven o'clock and she was beginning to panic. What disastrously bad luck for Dom to be sick tonight of all nights, February the twenty-ninth – D-Day. The day she had planned and prepared for so assiduously. But Tanya was used to life throwing her curve balls. She had negotiated them before and she would do so now. There simply wasn't any other option. It was far from ideal, but on the positive side Dom was weak and vulnerable. Even if romance wasn't on the menu, he would have to appreciate her obvious devotion to him. Taking a deep breath, she dabbed some more perfume on her wrists and at her neck, then got up and softly opened the door to his room, which was in darkness.

She flicked on the lights. 'Dom, sweetie?' She went over to him and sat on the bed. He was out for the count, breathing deeply, his mouth relaxed. She looked at him, thinking how handsome he looked, even sick as he was, his aquiline profile resting on the white pillow, accentuating his dark skin and hair, his sensual lips, ridiculously long eyelashes and strongly curving brows that made him seem like something carved by Michelangelo. She felt his forehead with her hand. It was still damp, but definitely cooler than it had been. His temperature was obviously dropping.

'Dom, darling,' she said, a bit louder this time, leaning in close to him, willing him to wake up.

'What?' He woke with a start, then struggled to sit up. 'You gave me a fright. I thought I might be in Casualty.' He rubbed his eyes, looking like a confused little boy. 'Why are all the lights on?'

'I just wanted to check on you, make sure you were all right.'

'Well I was. I was having rather a nice dream, actually.'

'Dom, there's something I need to say . . . to ask you.'

'What, now?' He gave a low groan. 'Tanya, can't it wait? I'm really not—'

'Dom, listen to me.' Her tone was sharper than she intended, but it was now or never. Her heart was thudding alarmingly and she felt like she would faint if she didn't get the words out.

He looked at her searchingly. 'What is it? What's so important? Has something happened?' He sounded worried. 'God I feel sick,' he moaned, collapsing back on his pillows.

'Dom, you know how much I love you, don't you? How we love each other?'

'What?'

She took his hand in hers and looked at him tenderly. 'I love you, Dom, more than anything in the world.'

'Tanya—'

'Just listen, Dom. I love you so, so much, and that's why, because it's February twenty-ninth . . .'

He was looking at her strangely.

'Because it's, um, a leap year, you know . . . I'm asking you to marry me. Dom, will you? Marry me? You're everything I've ever wanted in a husband, a life partner, and I would be so honoured to be your wife. I'd love and cherish you just like I'm doing—'

A look of comprehension mixed with something else, something urgent, flitted across his face, then he flung the covers off and almost pushed her out of the way.

'Dom!'

'Sorry, Tanya,' he spluttered, 'I think I'm going to be sick.' The bathroom door slammed behind him.

When he reappeared ten minutes later, looking pale and drawn, she was still sitting on the bed. 'Are you all right?' she whispered, fear suddenly seeping into her very bones.

The silence as he climbed back into bed was screaming in her ears. 'For God's sake, Tanya,' he croaked, 'can't you just leave me alone? We'll have to talk about this, but not now.'

She knew she should stop, back off there and then, but she couldn't. 'But you only have to say yes, Dommie, just one little word.' She felt her heart constricting.

'This isn't the time or the place, Tanya. Please, don't do this to yourself.' He looked chalk-white now.

And then she heard a discreet cough, and a knock on the bedroom door. Tearing her eyes from Dom's distraught face, Tanya's head snapped up to see Carla standing in the bedroom doorway, with a bowl of something steaming that smelled delicious.

'Excuse me,' she said, 'but the door was open. I did knock, but no one answered.' She chewed her lip awkwardly. 'Rollo sent this up. We were all so worried about you, Dom.'

Tanya mustered every ounce of self-control she had and forced herself to smile brightly. She got up and walked over to the door. 'Thank you, Carla. I'll take that.' She took the tureen of soup from her. 'You can tell everyone there's no need to worry. Dom's just got a bad bout of flu, but he mustn't be disturbed for the next forty-eight hours by *anyone*. Doctor's orders,' she said firmly. 'Thank Rollo, of course, it was very thoughtful of him.' She stared at her hard, watching Carla pull her glance away from Dom, who was looking right back at her. 'You can go now, Carla. Dom needs to rest.'

'Of course,' said Carla. 'Goodnight.'

'Thank you, Carla,' Dom croaked as he cleared his throat. 'That was kind of you, I appreciate it.' He gave her a heart-breaking smile.

'Not at all, I – we're concerned about you. I hope you feel better soon.' And she was gone.

'I take it you're not hungry,' Tanya said, turning back to him, her voice tight.

'No, I'm not. You have it. I'm going back to sleep. We'll talk tomorrow,' he said wearily.

'Fine. Sleep well,' she said and closed the door behind her. Her hands were beginning to tremble, the spoon rattling against the tureen. This was not the way it was supposed to turn out. And that bloody Carla, sneaking in, sly and speculative. How much, if anything, had she overheard? In a sudden fit of spite, Tanya poured the chicken soup down the kitchen sink. She couldn't look at it. Not now, not tomorrow. She didn't think she could ever eat again. Her stomach was clenched in a hard, terrifying knot of fear.

10

It was out, on newsstands everywhere, right on the front rack. There, on the front cover of the March issue of *Select* magazine, blowing a kiss to the camera with the stunning black velvet dress billowing around her in the water, was Cici, leaning out of her marble bath, surrounded by bubbles and looking very seductive indeed. *Ireland's Sexiest Woman* was the cover line that blazed across the shot.

After she had recovered from the shock (and it had been a shock), Cici had been thrilled and delighted, although it was very naughty of Harry not to tell her. The photo shoot she had done, along with the other five women featured, was also, unbeknownst to her, a competition of sorts, and a handpicked group of judges had voted her the winner. It was now official. According to *Select* magazine, Cici Coleman-Cappabianca was Ireland's sexiest woman.

She had received an advance copy a week before the actual magazine was on sale to the public. It had arrived courtesy of a special courier and she had taken the large brown envelope and bouquet of magnificent flowers inside, wondering what the occasion could be. When she opened it and saw the cover, she had to sit down. There was a note, of course, in Harry's now familiar scrawl: *Just sharing what I knew the minute I first set eyes on you with the rest of the country. Your adoring, number one fan, Harry.*

She had smiled then and flicked through the rest of the article. She had to admit it read well, and Bob's shots were fabulous, the best one, of course, being the one of her with her back to the camera, the bodice of the dress falling away in a perfect V to reveal her wonderful curves. It was quite simply stunning, very sensual, yet utterly tasteful. All the same, Cici had a sudden shiver. What would James think of all this? She'd better tell him before someone else did, but how? He was bound to hear. She chewed her lip. James wasn't keen on publicity of any kind, even at the best of times. Normally she would have discussed something like this with him, sought his opinion, but it had all happened so quickly. She wouldn't think about it now. She would call him up in a couple of days and tell him.

To be fair, James had been behaving impeccably. He never rang or pestered her about a decision. He had given her her space as she had requested, and every month, her personal account was topped up as usual. Cici couldn't help feeling terribly guilty about that. It wasn't as if she was running the family home any more. She assumed their housekeepers were taking care of groceries, flowers and so forth, much as they did when she had been in residence, but at least she had always supervised everything. And cooked. Cici loved to cook. She had often thought she was happiest in the kitchen, with her family around her, all laughing and bickering and helping out with the chores, just like any family. She felt a pang thinking about it. Poor James. He must be so lonely. With Dom gone and the girls away, no matter how well the house was run, it must be awfully empty there just on his own. Well, they had plenty of good friends, she reasoned. Not that she had heard from many of them lately, she mused. They were probably all horrified at her behaviour, at putting James through this seemingly unnecessary and painful separation.

But lately she'd been too busy to even think about it. She was simply having too much fun. Harry was like a drug to her. She knew she was in denial about the whole thing, that sooner rather than later she would have to take responsibility for her actions, but somehow, even when she tried to force herself to think about it, her mind would wander and take a delicious detour away from the highway of harsh decisions and down one of the many scenic back roads, meandering through romantic, sensual encounters with Harry, where she could bask in his adoration of her, which appeared to be utterly genuine and without guile. It was like discovering an age of innocence, a time gone by filled with love letters, notes and flowers left hidden in places where she would later find them and, of course, long, languorous hours of lovemaking.

With Harry, Cici found herself discovering her body anew, as if resurrecting some wonderful instrument from a hidden place and relishing it, appreciating it as it came to life in the hands of a talented, eager musician. And they did make sweet music together. How could they not? With Harry, nothing was ever rushed or perfunctory. He believed in setting the scenes as carefully as he embraced the act that followed.

They never went to his place. What was the point? Quite apart from the fact that Harry had temporarily moved back into his father's house while he was searching for a place of his own to buy.

'Dad's on his own in the old place and he enjoys having me there, particularly since Mum's gone,' he had told her. Harry's mother, Cici learned, had died tragically when he was just fifteen. After routine surgery, a post-operative infection had set in, and weak as she was, she was unable to fight it despite the desperate efforts of the hospital staff and every cocktail of antibiotics imaginable. Other than relating the incident, Harry rarely discussed her.

Poor boy, thought Cici with a rush of tenderness. It must have been terrible for him. Boys were so attached to their mothers, and at that awful, in-between age, so unable to relate to them or untangle their own inarticulate, confused emotions.

Thinking of which, Cici realised, she hadn't heard from Dom in the past week or so. She must ring him, have him to dinner or at least drop in for a drink – if she could prise him away from the awful Tanya. Cici didn't like Tanya. Neither did her girls, who had discussed her with their mother at length. James had thought her perfectly charming, but then, James was a man. He wouldn't understand or pick up the subtle signals long ingrained in the feminine psyche that alerted women to a predatory female. Not the man-eating kind; that wouldn't have bothered Cici in the slightest. They were open and straightforward. No, it was the closed, carefully composed ones who appeared harmless and innocuous on the surface and almost always harboured inner complications and turmoil, visiting unwarranted anxieties and tribulations on hitherto carefree and untroubled families and relationships. As far as Cici was concerned, Tanya might as well have had Trouble tattooed on her forehead with a capital T, and she was patently wrong for Dom. Cici sighed. There was absolutely nothing she could do about it. She would just have to sit back and hope against hope that her only son would discover the fact for himself. Knowing Dom, that wouldn't necessarily be any time soon. Much as she adored him, Cici was not oblivious to each of her children's various shortcomings, and Dom's, in the emotional arena at any rate, was quite simply laziness, a very dangerous laziness that might just lead him into a long-term relationship that would be very hard work indeed – for all of them.

She checked her watch and hurried upstairs. Harry would be arriving in a little under an hour, and she felt the familiar rush of excitement. She would just have time for a quick shower and shampoo. Undressing quickly (only to get redressed and then undressed *again*), she padded over to her dressing room to wonder, with delicious anticipation, what outfit she would wear to greet him.

Flicking through her racks of clothes, Cici thought they seemed unusually crowded. She was meticulous about her wardrobe and always made sure to get rid of something old whenever she acquired a new item of clothing. Several charities had done very well out of this sensible, ordered habit of hers. Now she was perplexed, until, reaching the end of the rail, the reason for the crowding revealed itself. There, at the left-hand side of the rack, were four hangers of Harry's suits and jackets, and beneath them, on a shelf, were two stacks of neatly folded shirts, jeans and underpants. Her own tops, which had been kept there, had been moved to another, already occupied shelf to the right. She shook her head and smiled. How sweet. He obviously wanted to leave some spare clothes there, which was entirely reasonable and sensible, she supposed. But she had never noticed him bringing them in, and he had never mentioned it to her. Well, that was men for you. When did a woman's shelf space or clothes, for that matter, ever take precedence over other, more important matters? All the same, she would have liked him to ask her first, as a matter of courtesy.

She reproved herself. Really, how old-fashioned of her! She was turning into an old nag, just like those women she despised. Young people never thought about such things or considered anything other than the urgency of the moment. Wasn't that what she loved about Harry? His spontaneity, his exuberance and how he made her feel? She would have to learn to be flexible, unconcerned, to go with the flow. She would mention it to him later, playfully, when she was lying in his arms, drowsy, happy and sated.

'James?' Angela, his long-time PA, popped her head around the door of his office.

'Yes?' He looked up from the papers he was studying. 'What is it?'

'I thought you'd want to see this, although you probably have already.' She held the magazine out to him. 'It's wonderful. I'm sure you've all been so excited about it,' she continued tactfully. 'I was in town at lunchtime and I thought I'd pick it up for you, it's only out today. Cici must be thrilled.

Do tell her I think she looks amazing, won't you? I'll bring you in your coffee in just a mo,' she said, smiling, and left the magazine on his desk, closing the door behind her.

Phew, she thought. *Poor James*. He had never said a word about his wife leaving him, but it was the talk of the office, particularly since Cici had been spotted on more than one occasion around town with a tall, blond, handsome and decidedly younger man, young enough to be her son, people were saying. Angela shook her head. She couldn't believe it when she'd heard the rumours. Cici and James had been one couple she would have bet her life on lasting the distance. They had always seemed so happy together. James adored his gorgeous, glamorous, Italian wife and made no bones about it, and she had appeared to return that adoration. And they made, or *had* made, such a handsome couple. It was a shame. Just went to show you never could tell. And now, with that magazine out and Cici being proclaimed Ireland's sexiest woman, well, that would really put the cat amongst the pigeons, Angela thought. She had guessed, shrewdly and correctly, that James probably had no idea about it, but already the office was humming with the latest gossip. Angela had thought it only fair to let him know as discreetly as she could. She hoped it wouldn't cause any trouble. She was desperately fond of James and had worked for him now for almost fifteen years. He was looking wretched, poor man. He had lost weight and looked pale and tired. Probably wasn't sleeping a wink. Still, it wasn't her place to ask any intrusive questions. These things sorted themselves out sooner or later.

He had resisted for as long as he could. Now, draining his coffee, James took a deep breath and picked up the magazine. Looking at the cover, taking it in and perusing the main article inside, and the other seemingly endless shots of Cici, the outside world receded and eventually stopped altogether. All that was real, or rather, weirdly *surreal*, was that he appeared to be sitting in a chair, holding a magazine in his hands, reading about the woman he called his wife as she related her life to another man. A man who, by all accounts (James was kept updated on events), she was seeing on a regular basis. A man young enough to be her – *their* – son. He looked earnestly at it, studying the pictures in a kind of daze. He admired their beauty, *her* beauty, as if the woman in them were a stranger. And so she was – to him at any rate. This wasn't the warm, exuberant, loving woman he knew. This wasn't the mother of their children, who had looked after them, loved them, and him. This was a stranger who talked about her life as if he didn't exist, as if their family had somehow been some obscure accident of fate. This creature in her blonde wig, her make-up and her witty, throwaway expressions was someone he didn't know. She certainly bore no resemblance to his beloved wife.

He wasn't jealous. James had always celebrated Cici's beauty, had always willingly shared her company and time with whoever she chose to bestow it on, even when he longed to be alone with her. All the endless trips, parties, house guests – he had allowed her anything her heart desired. He would have, *could* have put up with anything – but not this. This was too much. Not the publicity itself – that was the least of it – but the awful, twisting, unrelenting pain he felt. To have to stand back, silent and unobtrusive, while he watched his life, *their* life, their *family* for God's sake, disintegrate.

He had done his best for the past six months, he really had, hoping against hope that she would get this thing out of her system, that it was all some midlife crisis that would burn itself out. But he couldn't take it any longer – the sympathetic phone calls from friends, the knowing glances. James Coleman was a patient man, a kind man and a surprisingly intuitive man. He was also a brilliant man, ruthless in business when he had to be, and he did not suffer fools gladly. And that was what he felt himself to be now, in a sudden, blinding flash of admittance. He had sat back and played the waiting game for too long. Now it was time for action, however deeply unpleasant that action might be. It was time for him to talk to Cici, to confront her and sort this awful mess out with as much dignity as could be mustered.

With a sigh that came from the very depths of his being, James picked up the phone. He never entered the fray without making sure of the rules of the game. It was what had got him to where he was today.

'James,' his old friend and solicitor, Malcolm Stokes, boomed into the phone. 'What corporation are we taking on this month?' he chuckled.

'I'm afraid this isn't a business call, Malcolm.' James didn't bother with niceties. 'I wish it were that simple. I need you to get me the best divorce lawyer in the country.'

As soon as he had made the call, he felt immediately better. At least he was taking action, however ghastly and painful the consequences might be. Then, with another sigh, he made another reluctant phone call.

'Mike?'

'James, good to hear you, thought you'd slipped off the radar altogether,' his understanding and abandoned golf partner said.

'Mike, you know that charity ball you and Janet invited us to?'

'I do.'

'I'd be delighted to join your party. Unfortunately, I will be joining it alone.'

There was a beat.

'Marvellous!' proclaimed Mike. 'That's great news, James, Janet will be thrilled. I'll email you the details. See you Friday.'

In his office in town, Mike put down the phone and immediately rang his wife.

'Excellent news, Janet. James is joining our party after all.

No, not Cici. He's finally appearing to see sense at last. I was beginning to seriously worry about him.'

'Is it true?' Sophia asked Dom from the small apartment she shared with two other girls in Florence, both studying art history like her.

'Yes, I'm afraid it is,' her brother sighed as he heard the bewilderment in her voice.

'But why? How?'

'Who knows? She won't discuss it with anyone. She moved into the mews saying she wanted space. Now she's Ireland's sexiest woman and is having an affair with some guy who's barely two years older than me.'

'Eeeuuuuw.'

'Exactly. Although,' Dom added ruefully, 'I can't exactly sit in judgement, since I was even younger than Harry when I had my little liaison with the *comtesse*.' Dom fully understood now how hard it was to be on the other side of the older woman/younger man divide. He'd been the younger man several times and had been taken aback at how upset and angry his lovers' sons were about their mothers' affairs. Now he understood why.

'Dad has been as patient as he can be,' he continued, 'but now he's had enough. He's already talking to lawyers.'

'I can't believe it. I have to talk to her, make her see sense. She must have gone mad.'

'I wish you luck.'

'She'll listen to me, she always does.'

'I wouldn't be too sure, Sophia. Anyway, it's better you know. It's the favourite topic of conversation in Dublin at the moment, or so I'm reliably informed.'

'Poor you. How are you anyway?

'I'm fine.'

'And Tanya?'

'She's fine too.' There was a pause.

'And? Come on, Dom, this is your sister, your intuitive, wonderfully perceptive sister.'

'Tanya and I have split up.'

'Oh, Dom. I'm sorry.' Sophia fought to keep the glee from her voice. 'But none of us thought she was right for you, you know – just think of all those gorgeous women out there who'll be queuing up for you.'

'Funny,' Dom sounded glum. 'That's exactly what some woman said to Dad last week.'

'It's a man's world,' Sophia said knowingly. 'No amount of post-feminism is going to change that.'

'You could have fooled me. You've been out of Dublin for too long,' Dom grinned.

'You know what they say in Rome . . .'

'What?'

'"The world is old". Nothing happens that hasn't already happened before and will happen again. You just have to roll with the punches.'

'Tell me about it. I gotta go. Take it easy, Sis.'

'Bye, Dom, and don't worry. I'll talk to her, get her over here, see what's really going on. *Ciao*.'

Sophia put down the phone thoughtfully. So it was true. She knew something was up when her mother had moved into the mews, claiming it was just so she could have a little change of scenery while she was working on renovating the interior. Sophia just assumed her parents had had a row and were taking time out to cool off. Then she had begun to hear the rumours, the veiled questions from friends mentioning that their parents hadn't seen Cici and James out and about as usual, coupled with her father's evasiveness on the phone the few times she had brought it up. Now she understood. But another man? A younger man – much younger. Ugh! What had got into her mother? Everybody, even Sophia's friends, always commented on what a handsome couple her mum and dad made and how happy they seemed. What the hell was going on?

Florence was beautiful in March but today she felt unseasonably cold. Grabbing her long cardigan and pulling it on over her T-shirt and jeans, Sophia headed out to meet her friends at the local café for a glass of wine and a slice of pizza. She thought about texting her younger sister, Mimi; last time she'd heard from her, she was in Buenos Aires, doing South America. Then she thought better of it. What was the point? It would only upset her. She would call her mother later that night and get her to come over to Rome for a couple of days, for a bit of shopping and to catch up. Then she would find out exactly what was going on.

P.J. was up bright and early, ready to set off for the gym. He hated to admit it, but he was actually enjoying getting fit again, and the results were beginning to manifest in a very satisfactory manner. He had already lost a stone in a month and was feeling fitter and more energetic than he had in years. His personal trainer, Pip, a strapping young South African, had been putting him through his paces three times a week and was pleased with P.J.'s progress.

'Muscle memory, P.J.,' he told him, weighing him and taking his measurements. 'We might forget what our bodies can do, but they don't. The fact that you played so much rugby, even if it was a long time ago, will stand to you. Your muscles remember all that training, and as long as you put the work in, which you have been doing, it can be surprising how quickly the body responds. Well done, mate. We'll increase the weights next week, concentrate on some explosive lifting and intensive interval training, and you'll be back in shape in no time.'

'Whoa!' P.J. was alarmed. 'I'm not as young as I used to be. I'm not sure I like the sound of all that.'

'Nonsense, you're well able for it. Your body won't change unless you force it to. That's what you're paying me for, isn't it?' Pip had grinned.

All the same, P.J. thought, catching sight of himself in the bathroom mirror, it was gratifying to see the beginnings of some impressive muscles again. Just then, the doorbell rang. He checked his watch; it was ten to seven. He'd better make tracks or he'd be late, and Pip didn't take kindly to being kept waiting. Hurrying downstairs with his gym kit, the doorbell sounded again, this time longer. Who could it be at this hour? He hoped it wasn't an emergency, and where was Sheila? He opened the door and found himself face to face with a very good-looking woman.

She smiled and held out her hand. 'Dr O'Sullivan, I presume? I'm Charlotte Keating.' Seeing the perplexed look on his face, she added, 'I'm here to collect Bones for his walk?'

'What?' P.J.'s manners deserted him as confusion was replaced by something else, a curious feeling, one he couldn't quite get his head around. Then he remembered himself. 'Of course! You must be Jennifer's daughter. Come in, please.'

She stood in the hall, looking amused at his obvious confusion. 'I hope I'm not disturbing you. I'm a few minutes early, but I like to set off before the traffic gets too heavy.'

Just then the kitchen door opened and Bones hurtled up, a considerably slimmer Bones, P.J. had noticed of late, followed, hot on his heels, by Sheila.

'Oh, Mrs Keating,' she said. 'I'm so sorry, I didn't hear the bell. I was hoovering, you see.'

'Not at all, Sheila, I've just arrived. Dr O'Sullivan let me in.' She reached down and put a lead on Bones, who sat obediently and looked adoringly at her. P.J. could well understand why.

'Well, then, we'll be off, right Bones? Nice to meet you, Dr O'Sullivan.'

'P.J., please.'

'I'll have him back at the usual time, Sheila. See you later.'

'Er, just a moment,' P.J. heard himself saying.

'Yes?' she turned questioningly.

God, he had never seen such beautiful, enormous brown eyes. 'You're going to the beach?' He cursed himself for sounding like a halfwit.

'Yes, we always go to Sandymount Beach. Is that a problem?'

P.J. could feel Sheila's eyes boring into him with disapproval.

'I was just after a bit of exercise myself. Would you mind if I joined you?'

'Aren't you off to your gym?' Sheila said accusingly.

'I was,' P.J. smiled at Sheila, 'but a bit of fresh air is what I need, now that I think of it.' He thought he saw a twinkle in the big brown eyes.

'I'd be delighted,' Charlotte said.

'Good,' P.J. said, dumping his kit under the hall table. He would text Pip to cancel his workout. He'd earned some time off anyway, and it wasn't as if he wouldn't be exercising. Walking was the best exercise of all. He recommended it to his patients all the time. And he would be doing it, if appearances were anything to go by, in the company of a beautiful and very charming woman.

'There's a pile of wellies in the back of the car,' Charlotte said, loading Bones into the rear of the station wagon, along with the two Jack Russell terriers P.J. recognised from his meeting with Jennifer. 'I'm sure one of them will fit. Pity to spoil those new trainers of yours. It can be a bit mucky if it's been raining. Do you go to the gym a lot?'

'Only in the past month.' P.J. settled himself into the passenger seat. 'I was very out of condition, you see, out of practice.'

'You look pretty fit to me.' She glanced at him, manoeuvring the car out onto the road.

P.J. had to stop himself from staring at her, this apparition who, astonishingly, lived across the square from him and who he had never set eyes on.

'Let's just say I'm a work in progress,' he grinned. 'Rather like Bones here,' he added, listening to his dog panting gleefully in the back. He sounded as excited and eager as he felt himself.

Candy loaded her parcels into the brand-new, black, two-seater BMW convertible that was an early twenty-first birthday present from Ossie and slid in behind the wheel. She was exhausted. Two and a half hours at the hairdresser (again), just to have her roots touched up, then lunch in town with Emma and Katy (although they'd had to rush back to lectures) and some enthusiastic shopping had left her drained. Being a glamorous girl about town was hard work, but definitely worth it, she thought, tilting her head back to get another look in the rear-view mirror at her shiny, platinum hair. It was amazing the difference it had made. Since she had gone for the complete colour change, she had also had extensions added. Now she and her waist-length platinum ringlets and catwalk-worthy make-up were turning heads. It was true, she decided. Blondes definitely did have more fun. Men were looking at her now, properly – younger ones, older ones and a good few in between, but not as much as they were going to. She had almost, but not quite, finished her transformation. She had lost weight, not too much, and thanks to her regular workouts with her trainer had toned up nicely, enough to be slim but not skinny. Her new look was sophisticated. She looked much older and worldly, with quite a Paris Hilton vibe going on, actually. There was no sign of the gawky, rather insecure young girl that had looked back at her from mirrors in the past. She had been well and truly left behind.

Not that things had been easy of late; quite the contrary, in fact. But no pain, no gain, Candy reminded herself. It had been difficult, much harder than she could have anticipated, standing her ground. She still didn't like to think of her mother and grandmother's faces when she had appeared back home that fateful day four weeks ago. Even after a couple of vodka and tonics with Emma and Katy to bolster her resolve before facing the music, Candy had been taken aback. Jennifer's expression alone had been thunderous, and that was before the storm had broken.

She had come back in the evening after her weekend with her dad and Shalom and gone into the sitting room where Charlotte and Jennifer were watching *Gone with the Wind.*

'We're in here, sweetheart,' her mother had called, hearing her come in the front door. 'Have you eaten? There's plenty left over if you haven't.'

When she walked in, there had been a stunned silence.

Jennifer had been first to speak. 'Is that a wig you're wearing under that cap?' she asked, looking curiously at her.

'No, Gran, it's not,' Candy had said, glaring at her, feeling her courage deserting her as she looked from her gran to her mother's comprehending and distraught face.

'Oh, Candy.' Charlotte's hand flew to her mouth. 'Your hair, your beautiful hair. What have you done?'

'What does it look like I've done?' she snapped. 'I've gone blonde, that's all. It's not a crime, is it?'

'But those clothes,' Jennifer spluttered. 'That frightful make-up. You can't possibly be serious. She's not, Charlotte,' Jennifer went on disbelievingly. 'It's a fancy dress or something, isn't it – she's having us on. You've come from a party, is that it?' Jennifer was looking at her as if she had grown antlers.

'I was at a party last night, yes.' Candy wandered over to the drinks cabinet and poured herself another vodka and slimline before sitting down and crossing her legs. 'But this has nothing to with that. This is my new look, and if you don't like it, you'll just have to get used to it.' She took a sip of her drink, enjoying the drama she had unleashed.

'Your father's behind this, isn't he?' Jennifer sounded mutinous.

'Don't be ridiculous, Gran. Not that it's any of your

business, but he and Shalom think I look fabulous. Shalom did my makeover for me, in fact. She was very good to me all weekend. She's not nearly as bad as I thought she was. She's quite nice, in fact. You were right, Mum, I just hadn't ever given her a proper chance. The three of us got on very well, actually.'

Candy wasn't sure why she was deliberately imparting this spiteful and not altogether true information to her mother, but seeing the look of pain on Charlotte's face and feeling Jennifer's simmering outrage were making her feel strangely elated, powerful, even.

'Well,' said Jennifer dryly. 'That explains a lot.'

'Please, Mother.' Charlotte had recovered her power of speech. 'Let's not talk about this now.'

'She looks like a tart. A cheap, trashy tart. Look at her!'

'Mother.' Charlotte threw her mother a warning look, but it was too late.

'If you won't say it, I will.' Jennifer's face had turned puce with rage. 'If you've any sense, Candice, you'll wash that clownish muck off your face right now and go straight into a hairdresser first thing tomorrow and get that awful platinum blonde toned down. It makes you look like an old woman.'

'The only old woman around here is you!' Candy said nastily. 'You're completely out of touch, and so are you.' She turned on Charlotte. 'Look at you both, sitting in here. This place might as well be an old folks' home. You need to get over yourselves, get with the programme – and you need to get a life, Mum. Gran is having a very bad influence on you. At least Dad and Shalom know how to have a good time. What would either of you know about what's fashionable now? You're both stuck in some weird time warp. Well, you're not going to drag me into it. I think you're both sad, the pair of you. No wonder Dad left you, Mum! What man would possibly want you? You're no fun, and you're not going to turn me into some pathetic replica of you either,' she ranted. 'I've seen how it works. Men want a girl who's fun and who looks hot, and if you don't like the way I look, then that's too bad. I don't have to stay here, you know.' And then she'd fled from the room, run upstairs and slammed her door.

She was furious, furious and horribly confused and upset. Not because of the rumpus she had caused – she had been prepared for that – but what had shocked her, frightened her, was that she had made her mother cry. Tears had suddenly begun to slide down her face, even though she had tried to hide them. Candy had never seen her mother cry, not even when Dad had left. She had always been calm and controlled, annoyingly so. Now, seeing her like that, so openly upset and hurt, was making Candy feel very strange indeed. But she couldn't think about that now. She would think about it tomorrow – wasn't that what Scarlett O'Hara had said in the movie they'd been watching?

She had to get out. She couldn't stand another minute of this place, of her mother's silent reproach and Jennifer's equally vociferous disapproval. What did they know anyway? Candy suddenly felt very tired. She had never had a row with her mother, not really, not like this. She got out of her new clothes and flung them on the floor, then went into her bathroom and ran a hot bath. Taking off her make-up (it took ages to do it properly, with all the different oils and cleansers Shalom had made her buy), she peered at her face in the mirror. Devoid of make-up, she was unusually pale, her white-blonde hair making her look almost ethereal. She twisted it up into a knot and slid into the comforting bubbles, closing her eyes. She hadn't meant for things to turn out like this, to say what she had to her mother, but she had to stand her ground. She was almost twenty-one, for heaven's sake – a sussed and savvy young woman. If her mother and gran couldn't see that, at least her dad could, and did. And that was all that mattered, wasn't it?

11

'You have to talk to him, Charlotte, it's as simple as that.' Jennifer was firm. 'Put a stop to this nonsense once and for all.' They sat in her kitchen beside the bright red Aga after a Sunday lunch of roast lamb that had seemed terribly lonely without Candy.

'It's not that simple, though, is it?' Charlotte sipped her glass of red miserably as she looked across the table at her mother. 'I mean, she's almost twenty-one. She has a mind of her own and we know what she thinks of me – I can't see her listening to anything I say.'

'That's not the point and you know it. She's playing you off, one against the other. It's textbook behaviour for children of divorced parents. I've seen it many times on all those American chat shows, and whatever age she is, and whatever you may think of her, Candy is just a very mixed-up young girl in many ways.'

Charlotte was all too well aware of that fact. She had hardly slept since the awful row. The sight of Candy's hideously dyed platinum hair had dismayed her, but she had felt powerless to say anything. Candy was so like Ossie; that was a major part of the problem. She did exactly what she wanted and up until now had got away with it. Charlotte still felt so guilty about the divorce and the effect it had had on Candy. She knew she felt hurt and betrayed and in some confused way was trying to win her father's attention and love. Charlotte just desperately hoped it was a phase she might grow out of.

'She blames me for her father leaving,' Charlotte said quietly, 'and maybe she has a right to.'

'That's piffle and you know it. Whoever she blames for it – and I don't think even Candy is aware of who that is – you and Ossie are allowing her to turn into a complete monster.'

'You think I don't see that?' said Charlotte angrily. It was so simple for her mother, who saw something wrong and fixed it, never thinking about the sensitivities underneath the hard shell that Candy had put up to hide the vulnerable centre. She'd be devastated if Charlotte told her she looked like a slapper. Jennifer was always blunt, and Charlotte herself had suffered the consequences over the years. She'd always vowed to be a different kind of mother. Now she didn't know anything, except that bawling Candy out wasn't going to help anything.

'Well, what are you going to do about it?' Jennifer prodded.

'I don't see what I *can* do. Since she's moved in with her father, it's up to him and Shalom, I suppose, and what they're prepared to put up with under their roof. What I say isn't going to make an awful lot of difference.'

'That's where you are very wrong.' Jennifer poured some coffee. 'Let's leave Candy out of this for a moment. She's seeking attention, particularly from her father. That's as plain as the nose on her face. Ossie won't see that, but he *will* listen to you, Charlotte, I know he will. He has huge respect for you, whatever may have transpired since your marriage, and he *will* listen to you, particularly with regard to your daughter.'

'I don't see what I can say, really.' Charlotte chewed her lip. 'I mean, imagine it: "Hello, Ossie, I'm very concerned our daughter is turning into a carbon copy of your girlfriend and it's freaking me out and it should be freaking you out."'

'Don't be ridiculous,' Jennifer scowled. 'Of course that's not what you're going to say. Ossie will see that quite clearly for himself. It just might take him a while to acknowledge it.'

'And in the meantime he encourages it?'

'I didn't say that. We have to move carefully here. Candy's well-being is at stake and that's all that matters. As dear Jeremy would have said, she's difficult to load, but it's nothing we can't resolve if we keep our heads.'

Charlotte grinned despite herself at her mother's turn of phrase, 'difficult to load' referring to a highly strung horse who required a lot of coaxing into a horse box. 'That's rich coming from you, Mummy. As I recall, it was you flying off the handle that sent her storming off to her room and now she's gone.'

'I'm sorry about that, but I'm not sorry for what I said. Every bit of it was the unvarnished truth, and Candy needed to hear it. She *does* look like a tart.'

'Much as I hate to agree with you, you're right. But I can't say that to her.'

'Mark my words, whatever you say or don't say, Ossie isn't going to like it.'

'According to Candy, he already does.'

'That's nonsense – he's just humouring her. No father wants to see their daughter trussed up like a cheap hooker.'

'Mother!' Charlotte protested. 'There's no need to go quite so far.'

'There's every need, Charlotte, which is why you have to talk to him. You have to make him realise what he can't quite admit to himself – that he's made an awful mistake with that Shalom creature. Men have terrible double standards, Charlotte. Just because he may be having sex with Shalom doesn't mean he'll want his own daughter to turn out like her. Quite the opposite, I should think.'

'It's a bit late for that.'

'It's never too late,' Jennifer smiled. 'Now how about planning something nice, something non-confrontational? Why don't you suggest having dinner with him, on Friday perhaps, just so you can discuss things.'

'I can't.' Charlotte had almost forgotten. 'Not on Friday. I already have a dinner.'

'A dinner party, how nice.' Jennifer was pleased for her. 'Who's giving it?'

'It's not a dinner party.' Charlotte was suddenly looking uncomfortable, almost shifty even. 'Just, um, dinner.'

'Dinner? With whom? Why are you beating about the bush like this?'

'Dr O'Sullivan has asked me to have dinner with him this Friday.' There, she had said it.

'Dinner! With the doctor! Charlotte, why didn't you tell me? What fun!' Jennifer exclaimed.

A wave of guilt washed over Charlotte. How could she even be thinking of going out and having fun when all this was going on with Candy? Charlotte had been thinking of nothing but Candy and had been phoning her constantly, both on her mobile and even Ossie's landline, but Candy was refusing to take her calls. It hurt more than Charlotte could have imagined.

'It will do you a world of good,' Jennifer went on. 'Candy was right about one thing, Charlotte – you do need to get out and about a bit. Dinner with the doctor's just the ticket. Wait till Ossie hears about that! He's very eligible, you know. I've heard all about him on the grapevine, a sort of modern-day Robin Hood.'

'Well, you certainly know more about him than I do. And it's only dinner.'

'That'll do for starters,' Jennifer grinned. 'Speaking of which, have you anything decent to wear, Charlotte?

'I'm glad to see you're still your ruthlessly practical self, Mother.'

Let's go into town tomorrow, shall we? I feel like spending some money. After all, I'm a woman of considerable means, and what better way to spend it than buying your daughter a wonderful outfit for your first date in how many years?'

'It's not a date. Really, Mother, you're making me nervous.'

'That's what they all say.'

Friday evening came around as usual, harbinger equally of wonderful possibilities and doomed expectations. Dom, for one, was glad. It was their busiest night in the restaurant and he needed to throw himself into it completely, to be totally absorbed so that he wouldn't have to think about the ghastly two weeks that had preceded it. He had more or less recovered from his flu, although he still felt pretty weak, but it wasn't so much the physical symptoms that were bothering him as the emotional ones.

What a nightmare! It had all started when he had come down with the awful dose that was doing the rounds. Then the unthinkable, unimaginable drama with Tanya had unfolded. To say Dom had been surprised was an understatement. He had been pretty out of it anyway when she had sprung her leap-year proposal on him, barely coherent with a raging temperature. The whole thing had been absolutely horrific. Dom was not in the business of hurting people, but what had transpired had taken him so much by surprise that he had been more abrupt than he'd meant to be. The result had been a very angry and resentful girlfriend.

Dom sighed, thinking about it all. What the hell had got into her? The Tanya he knew had been cool, calm and always reassuringly in control, both of her career and her emotions. The woman who revealed herself that night had been on the verge of hysteria. And even before her surprise proposal, there had been the appalling incident of her approaching and interrupting a customer. That was strictly against restaurant rules – a doctor in the house was entitled to enjoy his time off just like any other guest, unless of course it really *was* a matter of life or death, as had been the case with Mrs Fitzgerald. But to drag poor P.J. O'Sullivan away from his family dinner on a Friday night on the pretext that he, Dominic, had been mortally ill – well, that had been the final straw as far as Dom was concerned. Of course P.J. had been charming about it – he was always charming, he was that kind of man, he wouldn't know how to behave otherwise – but it was a monumental black mark against Tanya for her to abuse her position like that. And Dominic had told her so in no uncertain terms the following morning. It hadn't gone down well.

After that, pointing out their basic unsuitability as a long-term couple had been relatively easy. Still, the whole thing had pulled him up in his tracks smartly, and he'd been doing a lot of thinking, taking stock of his life. But marriage? That had been the last thing on his mind. He was only twenty-eight for heaven's sake, and even if he had been contemplating it, which he hadn't, he had never, at any point in their relationship, hinted to Tanya at a long-term commitment.

Mind you, that wasn't quite how Tanya had seen things. After the tears and pleading, when she realised he was serious about ending their relationship, she had thrown the most enormous wobbly.

'You miserable bastard!' she had screamed in fury. 'After all I've done for you!' She'd picked up a silver photograph frame and flung it at him across the room. Ducking quickly, he had just avoided it. That was when he had asked her to leave, instantly, telling her that he would have anything else of hers sent around to her apartment – and there wasn't much, he had been relieved to see, just the few items of clothing and toiletries she had left in the spare room. The whole incident had left Dom feeling shaken. Women! He would certainly avoid them for the foreseeable future. His restaurant was what was important to him now and he would focus on that.

That was when he had got the second, much nastier shock.

Eric, his accountant, had rung him, requesting an urgent meeting. When Dom had seen him, coming into his office at the back of the restaurant, his lips pursed and acting unusually twitchy, he had immediately known that something was wrong. And it was. Dominic's was almost twenty thousand euro in the red. That was when Dominic had *seen* red.

'What the hell were you thinking?' he had said through clenched teeth, looking at the figures that laid it all out in black and white. 'Why didn't you let me know about this immediately?'

'I did try.' Eric was white. 'But Tanya was adamant that you shouldn't be told about it just yet – that you had, um, rather a lot on your plate, so to speak. She wanted a little more time.'

'What the hell has Tanya got to do with it?' Dom demanded. '*I* employ you. You're *my* bloody accountant – you should have come to me.'

'You, um, didn't seem all that concerned with accounts,' Eric had protested. 'I did try to approach you once or twice.'

'Not hard enough.'

'Tanya is a very persuasive girl, Dom. She gave strict instructions that you were not to be disturbed by any of this, that it was more important to get the restaurant up and running and keep the positive reviews coming in. I did say I was going to give her a little more time and that was all.'

Dom sighed, suddenly feeling terribly weary. 'Well, Tanya is well and truly out of the picture now, Eric.'

Eric coughed politely. He had heard, of course, from the staff; it was the talk of the restaurant. 'It's not quite as bad as it seems, Dom. If you stop all the comping and the freebies and maybe cut back on a few areas in the kitchen, with the staff, we should be able to turn it around in a few months.' He looked sheepish.

'At the expense of Dominic's,' Dom said, chewing his lip. 'This situation should never have been allowed to develop, Eric. I'm very, very angry.' And he was, but truthfully, Dom knew he was the one at fault. He had been carried away by the enormous success of Dominic's, by their wonderful clientele and the constant rave reviews they were getting and had made the biggest mistake that a restaurateur could make – falling for his own publicity at the expense of hard economic facts. Now he was going to have to pay the price.

'Leave it with me for a few days,' Dom said. 'I'll have to get my head around this, talk to the bank, consult with a few people before I make any permanent decisions. And from now on, you talk to me and to me only – got that?'

'Absolutely.'

It had been a huge wake-up call for Dom, and a timely one. But things could have been worse. At least the situation was redeemable, although it would take a lot of hard work. But he had been lucky – it wasn't too late. He could turn things around, he knew he could. His restaurant was the overriding passion in his life, and he was going to make sure nothing, but nothing interfered with that.

He checked the bookings for tonight. It was a full house, a lot of their regulars and a few high-profile names, a politician bringing a party with a visiting dignitary and a well-known actor booked under his code name. It was a good mix for a Friday night. Dom headed to the kitchen to give a sterner than usual pep talk. He had been lackadaisical of late, but that was all about to change.

Striding across the restaurant floor, he couldn't help noticing Carla, busily polishing tables. She looked up and for a second their eyes met, although she immediately resumed her study of the table. Despite himself, Dom felt the same powerful surge of attraction followed by the embarrassing but delicious memory of their encounter in the bedroom that night at the party. If he was honest, it was never very far from his mind.

Carla was tired and her arms ached. She had been busy keeping busy, which was all she did whenever Dom was around. All the same, despite the tension that was evident and the speculation amongst the staff that there was some kind of trouble afoot, there was an air of general elation at the news that Tanya was gone.

Carla had seen Eric coming out of Dom's office looking pale and had shrewdly guessed that Tanya's comping and whatever else she had been up to had come to light. Dom's face when he strode past her and into the kitchen confirmed her suspicions. He looked absolutely furious. She remembered someone trying once to scam her father in New York and the resulting furore. She felt sorry for Dom – it was every restaurateur's worst nightmare. She was glad, in this instance, that she was on the other side of the kitchen doors. Stress levels in any restaurant were always worst in the kitchen.

'You can almost see your reflection in that table, Carla.' It was Astrid, coming over to chat. 'There's no need to look so busy now that the wicked witch has gone.' She grinned evilly. 'Isn't it a lovely surprise? Even I couldn't have expected such a rapid exit for our manageress.'

'Tough for Dom, though.' Carla paused in her polishing.

'Nonsense, he's much better off without her,' Astrid proclaimed. 'Speaking of which, he could hardly keep his eyes off you just now. I think he fancies you.' She raised a speculative eyebrow.

'Don't be ridiculous.' Carla felt herself blushing.

'What's ridiculous?' Astrid demanded. 'You'd make such a cute couple. I'm surprised it never occurred to me before.'

'I'm a waitress, Astrid. Dom is my employer,' Carla said patiently, hoping she didn't sound as flustered as she felt. And then, not sure why, she lied, 'Besides, I've met someone. I'm seeing him tonight as a matter of fact.'

'Astrid?' Dom came out of the kitchen and called to her. 'You're wanted inside, Rollo wants a word with you.'

'Coming, Dom,' she said, walking towards the swing doors, then turning back to Carla she called, 'Enjoy your hot date tonight, I'll want all the details tomorrow.'

Nothing in Dom's expression indicated that he had heard the comment, but he couldn't not have. Yet again, Carla wished she could keep her big mouth shut for once in her life.

It's not a date, it's not a date, it's not, it's not, it's not. Just dinner, that's all, dinner with a nice, friendly, educated, entertaining (and oh, all right, very attractive) man. Someone who lived across the square. Someone who would be a friend, someone nice to talk to, good company and her own age group. No ex-wife, no strange habits and someone who had, by all accounts, a steady, reliable career and had asked her to have dinner with him. What was the big deal? Oh, God, was it a date? She was going on a date with a man when her daughter was in a crisis, all because her ex-husband had fallen in love with a phony bleached blonde. And now Candy had moved in bag and baggage with her father and Shalom.

For a moment, despair threatened as Charlotte wondered what Candy was doing – was living with Ossie and Shalom what she wanted? Maybe she was having so much fun she never even thought about her mum. Had she lost her lovely, headstrong, mixed-up daughter for good? She dragged her mind away from the unthinkable and focused on the job at hand.

Charlotte was uncharacteristically nervous. What would she talk about? How did one behave these days on a date? The questions and possibilities were flying around her head. And worst of all, what should she wear? At least that was a practical problem, one she could apply herself to and concentrate on.

The shopping trip with Jennifer had been productive, if nerve-wracking. They had gone into town early and headed for Brown Thomas, and in the end Charlotte had come away with several new outfits, although Jennifer had been miffed when the assistant had looked at her blankly when she had announced she wanted everything on approbation, saying, 'I've had an account in this shop since 1950.'

'There's no need, Mummy,' Charlotte had said. 'I can always come back and exchange them if they're wrong, and I'm pretty sure we've made some good choices.'

'Yes, but you never know until you get home, do you? Things can look quite different in front of your own mirror. The lighting in these places is designed to make *everything* look nice. And why is everybody foreign?' she whispered loudly. 'None of them speak proper English, it's disgraceful.'

'They speak perfect English, Mummy. Now let's get out of here and go have a nice lunch.'

'Good idea.' Jennifer was flagging and her hip was killing her, although she had managed to try on three lovely suits and purchased two of them.

Charlotte had lingered briefly at the designer jeans section they passed, thinking of how she used to love taking Candy shopping. It seemed ages ago since they had, and now Candy certainly didn't want to go with her. Even if she did, Charlotte reflected, she would probably want some awful-looking stuff, if her new image was anything to go by. She was probably going shopping with Shalom these days, and that made her feel even worse. What was she to do? Was it better to let Candy work it all out herself, or should she confront her more persistently? But maybe that would drive her even further away.

Now, appraising herself in the mirror, Charlotte had to admit she looked well. She had opted for a soft, black, knitted wool dress that moulded her willowy figure perfectly, with a nice V-neck that was low enough to be interesting without being obvious. The dress came to just below knee length and looked very well with the black opaque tights and her new black suede, high-heeled boots that fit like gloves. A wide black leather belt with a large silver buckle completed the outfit. It was elegant, but definitely casual. She had had her hair trimmed and blow-dried and it fell in soft waves around her face to just below her shoulders. Her hairdresser had persuaded her to leave it longer than usual, saying, 'It suits you this length, and you've got the hair for it.' And she had been right. Actually, she felt rather glamorous for a change. If only she didn't feel so ridiculously nervous. When her mother came into her bedroom, she jumped.

'Only me!' Jennifer grinned. 'I must say you look very nice, Charlotte, very nice indeed.' Jennifer sat on the bed and regarded her approvingly.

Charlotte smiled at her, despite her nerves. Jennifer was in her evening attire of her favourite quilted dressing gown, gold elastic-heeled ballet slippers and full make-up, although she had pin-curled her hair and had her hair net on.

'Do you ever take your make-up off, Mummy?' Charlotte asked, shaking her head. 'I don't think I've ever seen you barefaced. I bet you even sleep in it.'

'If you mean do I use all those insanely expensive cleansers and potions, no, I do not. Nothing wrong with my Pond's face cream and a good facecloth. Make-up was my generation's armour. There's nothing you can't face if you've got your lipstick and powder on. In moderation, of course.'

'I wish I didn't feel so nervous.'

'What on earth are you nervous about?' Jennifer demanded. 'He's a nice chap, isn't he? I think you'll have a good time.'

'It's been so long, I suppose.'

'All the more reason to enjoy it. Actually, I'm envious of you.'

'What?' Charlotte was startled. 'Why?'

'Why do you think?' Jennifer looked mulish. 'I'm only seventy-five. I'm not in the grave yet, you know. I'd love to be going out to dinner with a nice man to a lovely restaurant. I like men's company – always did. Not that I don't enjoy all my women friends, but there's nothing quite like the excitement of getting ready and dressing up to go out on a nice date, is there? Be honest.'

There it was, that word "date" again. Charlotte quailed inside and then felt immediately remorseful.

'You're right, Mummy. I *am* looking forward to it. I just feel out of practice.'

'It's like riding a bicycle; it'll all come back to you. I'd swap places with you in a jiffy.'

'Oh, Mummy.' Charlotte sat down beside her on the bed. 'I'm sorry. How selfish of me. I never realised.'

'No one does,' Jennifer said ruefully. 'Not until you're in the same position yourself. I know I'm an old woman, really, but I'd love to have a nice man friend to go out to dinner with occasionally, have a bit of fun with, you know. People think because you're a certain age, or a widow, that all that sort of nonsense goes out of your head – and it does, most of the time. But inside, part of us always remains a young, hopeful girl. I know that sounds ridiculous, but it's true.'

'It doesn't sound ridiculous at all,' Charlotte hugged her. 'You've been wonderful, so brave, and you must miss Daddy dreadfully.'

'Oh, it's not so bad. I'm just feeling a bit maudlin, that's all,' she said, returning to her usual brisk self. 'And be careful, Charlotte, you'll ruin your make-up.'

'Oh God, there's the doorbell.' Charlotte looked alarmed.

'Well go on, hurry up.' Jennifer gave her a prod. 'Have a lovely time, and don't talk about your divorce or your lack of a social life.'

'I have a very full social life, by any standards.' Charlotte was indignant.

'You know what I mean,' Jennifer replied ominously. 'And if he asks you out again, which he will, tell him you're not free for at least a week – that you're inundated with suitors.'

'Really, Mummy, now you *are* being ridiculous,' Charlotte laughed. 'I'd better go. Will you be all right?'

'Of course I'll be all right. Aren't I always? And Charlotte?'

'Yes?' Charlotte paused at the top of the stairs.

'You look lovely. You're a very good-looking woman. I don't think I ever told you that – not properly. He's damned lucky to be taking you out to dinner. Now get going.' She waved dismissively at her.

'Bye, Mummy, see you later.'

'I hope not – I shall be fast asleep with any luck, with or without my make-up. We'll catch up tomorrow – or whenever.'

It was pathetic to feel this nervous. It was only dinner. Only getting into a taxi, going to a restaurant, picking up a knife and fork and eating and talking, like normal people did every day of the week. All the same, P.J. wished someone would answer the bloody door. He felt very peculiar standing there at the top of the steps in his new suit, and a very nice new suit it was. He had treated himself to it as part of his new slimmer image. His tailor had been impressed, not just at the long-overdue visit from his long-time client, but at his new, improved measurements. 'Well, well, well, P.J.,' he had said. 'You're an inspiration to the rest of us. You're a fine figure of a man – I haven't seen you looking so well in years. It'll be a pleasure to kit you out in a few new suits. You'll be a grand advertisement for me.'

And it had been fun. He'd commissioned three. The one he was wearing now was an elegant, dark navy, single-breasted number, with a bright red lining, just for fun. He was glad now he hadn't worn a tie, just a crisp, white, open-necked shirt. He fingered the collar now, chewing his lip. He'd give it thirty more seconds, then he was out of here. He wondered if he'd got the day wrong. He was capable of anything, but he was sure he had said eight o'clock on Friday. At the bottom of the drive, the taxi waited patiently.

Suddenly the door opened, and there she was.

'I'm so sorry, I don't think I heard the bell the first time,' she said breathlessly. 'I hope I didn't keep you waiting?' She looked anxiously at him.

'Not at all,' he grinned, taking in the vision that stood in front of him. 'But I was just about to lose my nerve. It's been a long time since I've, um, asked anyone out to dinner.'

'Oh,' Charlotte sounded relieved. 'Me too. I almost had to have a drink for Dutch courage.'

P.J. thought it best not to divulge that he had almost cancelled out of nerves. 'You look fantastic,' he said truthfully. 'I ordered a taxi, shall we go?'

'Absolutely,' Charlotte beamed. 'Just let me make sure I have my keys before I close the door. I'm a bit flustered.'

Just then a voice floated down from upstairs.

'Charlotte?' P.J. recognised Jennifer's voice, calling loudly.

'Yes, Mummy?'

'Remember, no sex on a first date – I don't care how old you both are.' It was followed by a throaty chuckle.

'Oh, God.' Charlotte put her hands to her face. 'I do not believe she said that. The woman's a witch.' She closed the door, and then they both began to laugh.

'She's quite a woman, your mother,' said P.J., taking her arm as they went down the steps and to the taxi, where he held the door open for her as she slid in, then got in himself around the other side. 'If you have half her spirit, it should be an interesting evening.'

'I must apologise for her – she's incorrigible.'

'She's only having a bit of fun,' P.J. grinned, 'and isn't that what life's about?'

'You're right,' Charlotte agreed, 'it is, and I for one haven't been having nearly enough of it.'

'Me neither,' P.J. said. 'What about we start making up for lost time then? Tonight, fun will be on the menu, first and foremost.'

'You're on,' said Charlotte, rising to the challenge. And

suddenly she didn't feel nervous at all, just comfortable, and a little bit giddy.

'Good,' said P.J. approvingly, and then to the taxi driver, 'Dominic's restaurant, please, and don't spare the horses.'

Further across town, in the Mansion House ballroom, James Coleman was also having a surprisingly good time. He had been dreading going to the charity ball alone, even if it was in the company of his good friends Mike and Janet. But despite his misgivings, the evening was proving very enjoyable. Their party of ten were a lively bunch and included, seated to his left, a beautiful, recently divorced blonde whose husband had been involved in a less than desirable paternity suit with a young Danish actress. The tabloids had had a field day with what was widely referred to as the Danish Pastry Affair, and his wife, a former model, had sent him packing. James remembered meeting her a couple of times over the years, although not at such close quarters, and was finding her to be charming and amusing company. She appeared to be equally captivated by him. By the time the band started up, James found himself asking her to dance and they were cutting quite a dash on the floor. Around the ballroom, people were watching and commenting with discreet interest. As the grapevine went into action, more than one available, and many other *not* so available women, felt a definite thrill to hear that it was true: James Coleman was almost certainly on the market again.

One person was not having a good Friday night. In fact, it was the worst Friday night of her life. In her (borrowed) flat off Stephen's Green, Tanya sat in her living room in semi-darkness, the television on but muted. As a series of pictures flitted across the screen, she watched, numbly, as people moved, conversed and went about everyday, normal actions as she sat, alone and silent. It had been more than two weeks since the unspeakably dreadful night of her leap-year proposal to Dom. How she had managed to get through it, she didn't know – sheer, automated habit had got her up every morning and into the shower. The face that she looked at as she applied her make-up had looked the same, but surely could not belong to her. She felt as if nothing did, or ever had. She had done the bare minimum at work, avoided her mother and finally, the equally dreaded and desired weekend had arrived, where at last she could be left alone and could lock herself in her flat and stop the pretence that life as she knew it could possibly continue in any realm of normality.

How could she have done it? How could she have been so abysmally, profoundly stupid? What could have possessed her? How could she have blown her romance, her life, sky high? The questions as much as the memories tormented her. Up until then, everything had been just fine. She was sure it had. If only she had waited – if only she had played it cool – if only she had got pregnant – *anything* at all except the disastrous action she had taken that had unleashed this unimaginable result. And she had planned it all so carefully – but not carefully enough. She hadn't asked herself the unanswerable question of what she would do if Dom turned her down because it was unthinkable to her. She couldn't, wouldn't, contemplate such a thing. But then fate had intervened, the fate she had fought against every single day of her life, and now, just as she thought she had triumphed, it had caught her out. And no matter what she said or did or how many times she thought things over from every conceivable angle, there didn't seem to be a single thing she could do about it. She had lost him. Dom Coleman-Cappabianca was gone from her life.

Even her money problems paled into insignificance. She may have been broke, but Dom was special – he would have looked after her, taken care of her, she knew he would have.

Putting her head in her hands, Tanya sobbed and sobbed.

It didn't make her feel any better, but it did make her feel calmer. And then she felt something else, something so real, so all-consuming it almost took her breath away. It was pure, unadulterated, primeval rage, and it coursed through her, wave after wave of it. This was something she could relate to, could allow herself to feel, unlike the dreadful, bereft feeling of loss and emptiness, which she could do nothing about. This was palpable, this rage. It would motivate her, inspire her to function, to act. Did Dom Coleman-Cappabianca think he could dispose of her, abandon her without so much as a backward glance, turn her out of his apartment, take away her key? Tanya laughed out loud, the sudden sound almost shocking her. Tomorrow was another day, and she was going to make that bastard Dom pay for robbing her of her dreams, her life. He would rue the day he ever crossed her.

She sat up straighter and turned on the lamp beside her, then flicked the remote until she found the shopping channel. Her mother was right – all men *were* bastards. But there was always something you could do to cheer yourself up. For Tanya, that was shopping. So what if her credit cards were nearly all maxed out? She deserved to buy herself something. She didn't need to splurge – just a little present or two for herself, it always made her feel better. She needed it now more than ever.

12

April was Cici's favourite time of the year in Rome. She was shown to her suite in the chic Hotel de Russie on Via del Babuino and sat down gratefully on the bed, kicking off her shoes. It was so good to be back. She would have a quick shower, then spend the day shopping and wandering around before meeting Sophia. Her daughter was coming down from Florence that evening and they would spend the time catching up and having a good heart-to-heart. She couldn't wait to see her and to hear all her news. On the phone, Sophia had sounded concerned, but Cici had reassured her that everything was fine, really, that she would explain things to her when she saw her.

Truthfully, things were very far from fine – which was another reason Cici was glad to be out of Dublin and back in her native Rome, even if it was only for two all-too-brief days. It would give her time to think. It had been so much fun in the beginning, but now, facing the facts she knew she would have to face sooner or later, Cici could see that her fling with Harry was just that – a fling. A delicious, exciting one to be sure, but it had no future, none at all. He would see that too, she was sure, when she explained that they would just have to remain friends from here on out. For now, though, she wouldn't think about it – she would enjoy Rome and its delights and cherish the short time she would have with Sophia.

Cici adored her children. They were everything she had hoped for and more, bright, kind, funny and generous. Even

Dom hadn't been judgemental about it when she had dined very obviously several times in his restaurant with Harry. If it had bothered him, he had never said so – although it must have, she thought with a stab of guilt. And that lovely young waitress who had served them, what was her name? Oh yes, Carla – Cici had noticed Dom gazing at her several times. She was sure he fancied her, and if the lingering looks Carla had thrown in his direction were anything to go by, the feeling was certainly mutual.

Cici smiled. Carla reminded her of herself when she was younger, and she would be a far better girl for Dom than the awful Tanya. Thank God that was over – or so Sophia had told her on the phone. Cici had wisely said nothing to Dom about it – one never knew with young people. She hoped it *was* over, but what if they got back together? She sincerely hoped not, but in the meantime she would keep her opinions to herself. After all, it wasn't as if she had any right to advise anyone on their love life at present. But all that was about to change. She would sort things out calmly and with dignity on her return home.

She would break things gently to Harry when she got back to Dublin. He would be upset, of course, but he would understand, see the sense of it. After all, he was a brilliant journalist, a writer – he knew how the script went. And there would be no shortage of young, eager girls to console him. She smiled rather sadly, thinking of it, but it was the only way. She had just wanted a bit of fun, really, one last, naughty love affair. Hadn't she said at the very outset that she had been good at pretending? And he had entered into the whole spirit of that fun.

The past six weeks *had* been fun, she thought, allowing the powerful jets of water to sluice over her as she washed off the flight, but when he had begun to move his clothes in and then, to her horror, had set up a fax machine in the spare bedroom, and then that rather awkward moment when he had suggested she give him a key . . . well, she had known that it was time to put a stop to things. The weekend away had come just in time to avoid the 'we need to talk' conversation, but she was sure that he had guessed, and being the delightful, well-mannered young man he was, he would take it all in his stride.

Lately, too, she'd been missing James. This had surprised her. Not because she didn't love him – she did, hugely – but because she had assumed they'd drifted apart the way so many couples did even in the midst of being so together. James, she often thought, was married to his work and golf had become his mistress. That was true from a certain perspective, but from another, truer one, she realised how that very togetherness, however mundane it may seem, had a physical presence of its own. She missed his quiet, thoughtful, determined devotion, his unstinting support for whatever she did, particularly in this case, which he didn't, couldn't possibly, understand, and which must be so terribly painful for him. But it was all she had needed, this trial separation, this foray into irresponsibility, this last taste of freedom, of things forbidden. She wondered what he was doing now and smiled, thinking of him. He had been so strong and clever, really, to leave her alone as she had asked of him. There had been no pestering phone calls, no demands to know what she was doing and with whom, no nasty manipulating or turning the children against her, which he could so easily have done. She had worried about that. She knew she was pushing it being seen around town with Harry, but no one could prove anything. James was definitely not the type of husband who would have her watched or spied on. He was far too much of a gentleman and had too much integrity, an integrity that she very much respected him for.

James, she realised, as she had suspected that night in the Horseshoe Bar so long ago, was a man in a million. She just had to tell him that, and she would, repeatedly. She would make it up to him. She would tell him how wrong she'd been, how easily and stupidly she had trifled with their marriage, their family. She knew now, without a shadow of a doubt, that that was the only thing that meant *anything* to her, that wonderful, extraordinary unit that she and James had created, that had been, that *was* her strength, her raison d'être for all those years when she had thought herself to be slipping away, becoming invisible – now she knew it was the only tangible thing that made her what she truly was: a wife, a lover, a mother. The most affirming roles to the feminine psyche – the ones that no career, no amount of freedom, publicity or celebrity could possibly provide – and she had taken them so much, so shamefully, for granted. She belonged with James, with her family. Every fibre of her being told her so.

Feeling calmer and happier about her decision, she dressed quickly, slipping into a cool pink linen trouser suit and a pair of flat black patent Tod's she could traverse the cobbled streets in as comfortably as possible. The phone, when it rang, startled her.

'Señora Coleman-Cappabianca?' the voice from the front desk enquired.

'Yes?'

'There is someone to see you in reception. Shall I say you will come down?'

'Of course, I was just on my way. Who is it?'

There was the slightest pause. 'I am instructed to tell you it is a surprise.'

'Oh, I see.' Cici smiled into the phone. Sophia must have arrived earlier than she'd anticipated. She had probably caught an earlier flight. How wonderful. Now they could go for a lovely long lunch. 'I'll be down right away. I'm leaving now.'

Catherine placed the tiny wicker chair in the corner of the newly decorated nursery and almost laughed aloud. It was so small! Ridiculous, really, like a doll's chair, but she had been unable to resist it when she had come across it in the village shop. It was a brightly coloured pink and blue, with a bit of yellow thrown in for good measure. Set in the corner, it looked adorable. She tried to imagine a little person sitting in it and shook her head. Bending down to move it ever so slightly to the left, she felt the first sharp twinge. Startled, she gasped and straightened up, rubbing her back where she had felt it. Gosh, if labour pains were a lot worse than that, then she really wasn't looking forward to it. She focused instead on the excitement, just under eight more weeks, and it wouldn't be a minute too soon. She was fed up now and dying for the pregnancy to be over. She felt tired now almost all the time, and she was bored too. Wandering downstairs, she decided to make a cup of tea and watch some lunchtime TV, anything to take her mind off things. Alex was away for the day in London, talking to some bank or other, and he had been even more tetchy and jumpy than usual. Actually, it was a relief not to have him around. He was beginning to make her more nervous than she already was.

She was three steps from the bottom when the next pain hit her, harder and swifter, almost taking her breath away. She grabbed the handrail for support and suddenly felt frightened. It was a false alarm, surely. It couldn't be happening – not now. She was only thirty-three weeks, babies weren't supposed to arrive until forty. She got to the kitchen before another band of pain contracted around her middle, almost doubling her over with the force. Reaching for her mobile phone, she quickly called an ambulance. Oh please, please, let this not be happening, not now when Alex was away, when she was alone. She dialled Alex's number, but it went to voicemail. She left a brief, breathless message. Then she called P.J.'s surgery and prayed for someone to answer.

'Dr O'Sullivan's surgery,' Sheila's clipped tones answered.

'Oh Sheila,' Catherine gasped, the phone trembling in her hand. 'Something's wrong. Tell P.J. the baby's coming and

Alex is in London. I've called an ambulance, but – ohhh,' she groaned as another contraction hit. 'Please, just tell him.'

Almost crying with relief, she managed to open the door to the ambulance crew. 'My bag,' she cried, 'it's upstairs, in the front room.'

'Don't worry, love,' said the paramedic. 'We'll have it in a jiffy.' He helped her to a chair as she groaned again. 'How far along are you?'

'Thirty-three weeks.' She looked stricken.

'We'll have you there in no time. Just try to relax. Tom,' he yelled to his colleague who had run upstairs to get the bag, 'make it sharp, looks like we have an early arrival here.'

'Oh God. My husband – he's not here.'

'Don't you worry, love.' He helped her into the ambulance. 'We'll get in touch with anyone you need to call. Which hospital is it?'

'Holles Street,' she gasped.

'We'll have you there in no time. Right, Tom, Holles Street – full steam ahead,' he nodded at the driver jovially, although Catherine could see the seriousness in his expression. As the sirens started to wail, tears began to roll down Catherine's cheeks. She had never felt so frightened in her entire life.

P.J. was writing a prescription for anti-anxiety medication to a very charming, if neurotic, twice-divorced woman who had been a patient of his long before her first marriage, when the phone on his desk rang.

'If only all men were as understanding as you are, Dr O'Sullivan,' she beamed at him adoringly, 'I'm quite sure the divorce rate would halve overnight.'

'Excuse me please while I take this.' He tried not to sound impatient, but Sheila knew never to interrupt him mid-consult – not unless it was serious. However, 'serious' to Sheila, if she was having one of her days, could mean that he wasn't hustling patients through on what she considered to be a time-efficient schedule. Though that hadn't happened in quite a while.

'I see. Right.' His voice was grim. 'Cancel all patients for this afternoon, we'll reschedule for tomorrow.'

'An emergency?' The divorcee looked simultaneously hopeful and impressed.

'Yes, I'm afraid so, one I must attend to immediately. Sheila will see you out.' He terminated the visit abruptly, handing her the prescription.

'Oh,' said his patient, sounding disappointed. 'Yes, of course. Good luck with it.'

'I should think we'll need quite a bit of that – and thank you.' P.J. stood up as she left the room, then he grabbed his phone and strode out of the surgery, leaving Sheila to give the few waiting patients the bad news.

Cici took the lift down to reception and strolled towards the front desk.

'Ah, Señora Coleman-Cappabianca,' the concierge smiled, 'your guest is outside, in the terrace. Champagne is already on its way.'

Champagne! Well, it *was* a quarter past twelve, Cici supposed, although it was rather unlike Sophia to order it. She wandered outside, where her gaze drifted to one of the occupied tables in the shade of the umbrellas that were dotted around the famous terrace, and then her smile froze as the champagne arrived and was duly set down and poured. It wasn't Sophia who raised a glass to salute her – but Harry.

He stood up to greet her, his face alight, but suddenly Cici was gripped with foreboding. This was going to be difficult. *Look on the bright side*, she told herself. At least she was alone. Imagine if Sophia had been with her, which could so easily have happened. She would have to play this carefully.

'Well,' she said, allowing him to kiss her on the cheek and hug her, 'this is certainly a surprise.' She sat down and took a much-needed sip of champagne.

'A good one, I hope,' he grinned playfully. 'I couldn't resist it. Well, that's not quite the truth,' he looked at her meaningfully. 'Actually, I couldn't bear the thought of being without you for a whole weekend, and you in Rome, alone . . . I just had to.'

'Harry,' she began gently.

'I thought maybe we could stay on for a while, together, you know, when your daughter goes back. I told them to leave my luggage in your suite.'

Oh, God. This was worse than she could possibly have imagined. Cici bit her lip. 'Harry, darling Harry, I'm afraid that is impossible, and it wasn't a good idea at all for you to come here.'

'What do you mean?' He looked surprised. 'Nothing's impossible. I'm here, aren't I? I'm looking forward to meeting Sophia. Isn't that her name? We can all have a lovely time, then when we're alone . . .' He reached over to stroke her cheek and suddenly she felt a spasm of anger. How dare he follow her here? How dare he spoil a weekend she had planned with her daughter?

'Harry,' she said sharply, 'listen to me.' She had his attention now. He slouched back in his chair, his face sulky and (how had she never noticed this before?) unattractively child like. 'I told you I was coming to Rome to meet my daughter to catch up with her, do some shopping. I never in a thousand years dreamed you'd follow me here. It's unthinkable.'

'Why?' he asked, a sneer lacing his voice. 'Why is it so unthinkable?' He looked at her speculatively. 'You've done a lot of unthinkable things with me, haven't you? As long as they're on your terms, you seem to find them perfectly acceptable. *More* than acceptable, I would go so far as to say.'

He smiled nastily, while Cici, almost lost for words, felt a slow blush creeping up her neck and flooding her face. She wasn't sure if it was induced by mortification or rage. She tried to keep her temper.

'Be reasonable, Harry. I'm here in Rome to see my daughter.'

'So you've said.'

'If I had wanted or thought it appropriate for you to be here, I would have asked you to be here. This,' she waved her hand, 'is totally inappropriate.' She took a deep breath. 'It's out of the question for me to introduce you to Sophia. She doesn't even know about you.'

'Us,' he corrected her. 'She doesn't know about *us*.' He was leaning in towards her now. 'There are, in case it has slipped your memory, Cici, two of us in this relationship.'

'Not any more.' The words escaped her before she could stop them.

'I'm sorry?'

'So am I, Harry. I never anticipated this, but then, you never gave me a chance to.' She took a deep breath. 'I'm afraid I'm going to have to ask you to leave.'

'To leave?'

'Yes, Harry, to leave. I didn't want to have this conversation, certainly not here, and certainly not under these awful circumstances, but you leave me no choice.'

'And what if I don't?'

Cici felt her throat constrict as a fresh wave of panic gripped her. She mustn't let him see it or sense how flustered she was – no, make that frightened. 'Then you will be making things unnecessarily awkward for yourself.'

'For myself?'

'Yes, Harry, for yourself. There was no need for any of this. If you had only talked to me, consulted with me—'

'Consulted!' He almost spat the word as he stood up, pushing the chair back angrily. 'I have to consult with you?

The woman who threw herself at me, begged me, pleaded with me, night after night? "More, Harry, oh yes, Harry, don't stop, Harry,"' he mocked her.

'Please,' she whispered, bringing her hand to her mouth. 'Please don't do this.'

'What's that, Cici?' He put his hand behind his ear. 'I didn't quite hear you – a little louder, please. You were asking me something. Sorry, *begging me*, weren't you? You appear to be very good at that at least.' He came around and leaned into her neck as she recoiled.

'You don't understand.' She was almost sobbing now. 'You should never have come here.'

'Don't worry,' he hissed at her, his eyes blazing. 'I'm going. But you haven't heard the last of me. Nobody, least of all some pathetic, middle-aged woman whose husband can't even be bothered to fight for her, tells me what to do.' He laughed a hard, bitter laugh. 'He was probably glad I took you off his hands for a while.'

'How dare you!'

'Very easily, Cici. Who do you think you are, anyway? You're just a sad woman pushing fifty, desperate for some young flesh. You're all the bloody same. Don't think you're any different. You disgust me!'

And with that he strode away, attracting not a few interested glances to their table in his wake.

She sat there, stunned, immobile, and then remembered where she was – in public. Anyone at all could be watching. Summoning all the acting talent that had failed to get her to the silver screen in the past, Cici regained her composure, at least outwardly, sat back in her chair and took another sip of champagne. Never had it tasted quite so bitter. As if on cue, the waiter arrived with the bill to sign. 'Señora,' he placed it discreetly in front of her, then gestured questioningly at the empty glass opposite her. 'Take it away,' Cici said, signing her room number with a flourish, although she felt as if she might faint. What the hell. A wasted bottle of Krug was the least of her worries.

P.J. parked his car in an almost legitimate space opposite the National Maternity Hospital. Who cared about clamping at a time like this? He had called Alex, of course, who had left his meeting in London immediately and was desperately trying to make his way to Heathrow and get the first flight he could. P.J. had told him not to worry, that he was on his way to the hospital.

'Thanks, Dad.' Alex was grateful. 'I really appreciate it.'

'Don't worry, everything will be fine, I'm sure of it. Holles Street has the best neonatal staff in the world. Whatever happens, Catherine and the baby will be in the best possible hands.'

'Ring me the minute you know anything.'

'Will do.'

Now P.J. ran across the road and in through the doors of Holles Street and was instantly transported back to earlier times, when Alex, his own son, had been born.

'Catherine O'Sullivan?' he asked at the front desk. 'She's a patient of Dan Collins. I'm her father-in-law, Dr P.J. O'Sullivan. She was admitted about an hour ago?'

'Just a moment, Dr O'Sullivan, I'll check for you now. Take a seat.' P.J. waited for what seemed like an interminable amount of time with other excited or weary relatives. Just then, the girl he had spoken to approached him. 'Catherine is in the recovery room. I spoke to Dr Collins's registrar and you can go down now, they're expecting you.'

Getting out of the lift and walking down the corridor, P.J. immediately recognised Dan Collins talking to one of his staff. He looked up as P.J. approached. 'P.J.,' he exclaimed, smiling, 'good to see you.'

'Dan, we're all worried sick. What's the story?'

'It all went very well.' He patted his old friend on the back reassuringly. 'We did an emergency section. Catherine's coming around now but she's very groggy. The baby's in neonatal intensive. Why don't you go in and see her, then I'll take you over.'

P.J. went over to Catherine and pulled up a chair. 'Hey,' he said, taking her hand. 'Hello, Mum, how're you doing? You gave us all a fright.'

Her eyes fluttered open and she smiled. She was still very out of it. 'P.J.,' she murmured. 'The baby . . .?'

'It's all right, Catherine, everything will be just fine. You just need to rest now.'

'Alex?' she whispered.

'He's on his way. He should be here in a couple of hours, he's at Heathrow.'

'But my baby . . . where?'

'The baby's in neonatal,' he told her, leaving out the 'intensive'.

'Will you . . .?'

'I'm going there right now. You just get some rest. I'll be right back.' She was already fast asleep.

It was only when he rejoined Dan and they made their way over to the hushed area of neonatal intensive care that P.J. stopped in his tracks. 'Dan, I forgot to ask – boy or girl?'

'Congratulations, Granddad,' he smiled, 'it's a boy!'

As the doors opened and they were allowed in, P.J. felt his throat constrict that his first grandson, Alex's boy, would have to make his foray into the world in such a tenuous, precarious manner.

'Don't look so worried, P.J.,' Dan said. 'He'll have the best possible care here, you know that. He's thirty-three weeks, a little earlier than we'd have liked, but he'll do fine, just you see.'

P.J. looked down at the tiny figure in the incubator and shook his head. Around him, the highly trained team were working in their quietly efficient manner. He was already on a ventilator and a drip was being inserted into his scalp. It was all routine procedure, nothing P.J. hadn't seen a hundred times before, but now he felt so completely helpless. He felt a huge rush of affection for this little chap who couldn't be held by his parents and was struggling so bravely all alone.

'Come on, old chap,' Dan said quietly. 'Let's get back to Catherine, she'll need someone to be with her. They'll keep a good eye on him here.'

'I know they will,' P.J. said, reluctantly tearing himself away. 'It's just all been a bit of a shock.'

They were almost at the door when P.J. noticed one of the nurses look back sharply in the direction of the baby's incubator. He followed her glance to the Registrar, who was bending over and checking the drip on his grandson. His expression had changed from one of concern to urgency. He looked up and beckoned. 'Over here *now*, guys, *quickly*. Looks like we've got a bleeder.'

'Come on, P.J.' Dan was sympathetic but firm as P.J. froze. 'They know what they're doing. Go back to Catherine, I'll keep you updated. *Go*.'

Cici had returned to her suite as nonchalantly as possible, although inside she was frantic. Passing reception, there was no sign of Harry, and she hoped against hope that he had gone and hadn't somehow wangled his way into the room. She opened the door slowly. There were no signs of anything untoward. Just to be sure she checked everywhere – cupboards, bathroom, even under the beds. Then she reproved herself. This was madness! Of course his luggage wasn't here! All the same, she felt terribly nervous. She wondered if she should phone him, then decided against it. Really, he had behaved appallingly. He knew full well that she had come to Rome specifically to catch up with Sophia, have a heart-to-heart and do some shopping. She had never even hinted that he should join her.

She sat down on the bed suddenly, putting her face in her hands. She had seen another side to Harry now, a rather unpleasant, unnerving one. His reaction hadn't been in any way apologetic or even conciliatory. He had been livid the moment he realised she was serious about asking him to leave, livid and unnecessarily vicious. His hurtful remarks were still reverberating in her head. The whole thing had left her shaken. But it was a lesson, she told herself, a good lesson, and thank God Sophia hadn't been around to witness it. She would never allow such a near miss to happen again.

Pulling herself together, she left the suite and took the lift down to reception, where she left strict instructions that she was expecting her daughter to join her that evening at about seven o'clock and that she alone was the only visitor she would be entertaining. The man at the front desk told her he understood completely and informed her that her previous visitor had left and taken his luggage with him. Harry seemed to have gone on his way.

Feeling considerably better about things, Cici left the hotel and paused for a moment, deciding where to go. Instinctively, she turned left, strolling up Via Babuino, hardly noticing its discreet art galleries, exclusive antique shops and furnishing stores, heading for her favourite stomping ground of the Spanish Steps and Piazza di Spagna. Absorbing the sights and smells of her native city, she began to feel better, its familiar, bustling ambiance restoring her with every step. She checked her watch; it was a quarter to one. Suddenly she discovered she was ravenously hungry. She grinned to herself – drama always had that effect on her. She needed lunch, and she knew exactly where she was going to go. Turning right into Via della Croce, she made her way to her favourite restaurant, Fiaschetteria Beltramme, the hugely trendy place for fashion and media people in Rome. As Cici walked past a queue of ordinary mortals and tourists and into the interior that could have passed for an Italian grandmother's front room, she was welcomed instantly in a similar fashion by Toni, one of the long-time staff. 'Señora Cici!' He rushed over to her, beaming from ear to ear. 'How wonderful to see you. You are dining alone?'

'Yes, Toni, just a table for one, if you can fit me in?'

'There is always a table for you here, Señora,' he said warmly, showing her to what she knew was one of the most enviously coveted tables in the house.

'Thank you, Toni,' she smiled up at him as she slid into the chair. 'It's good to be home.'

James heard his mobile phone bleep twice and saw he had a message. He knew who it was from too. He opened it, smiling. He wasn't used to receiving messages. He mostly used his phone to make or take a quick call whenever needed, but lately, his phone had been the bearer of some very nice, and for a change, endearing, communications. It was from Sarah, the beautiful blonde divorcee who had been quite unabashedly chasing him since they had sat together at the charity ball. James was finding it quite disconcerting, really, but in a very nice way. *Dinner at my place tonight? 8:30? Do say yes. Longing to see you! Sarah xx*

James thought about it for a minute, then texted back. *Love to!* He put his phone back in his pocket and smiled. Why not? He didn't have any other plans for the evening.

He thought about Cici. He knew she was in Rome and that she would be meeting Sophia for some mother–daughter catching up. He could just imagine the pair of them hitting the shops. He was almost caught by a swift pang of regret, but with enormous self-will told himself he was doing the right thing. The papers had gone out today. On her return, Cici would discover that he had decided to file for separation and divorce.

He gave a deep sigh and forced himself to concentrate on the sales figures in front of him, suddenly very glad of the surprise dinner invitation. Sarah was amusing company, and she had been through the mill herself over the past year or two and understood the ravages a prospective divorce unleashed on someone. He was looking forward to dinner with her. At the very least, it would take his mind off his own immeasurably sad domestic situation.

P.J. was suddenly overcome with tiredness. Sitting in his kitchen with Bones at his feet, he realised he hadn't eaten since breakfast. He decided to throw on some pasta and open a bottle of red. What a day! Poor Catherine. She'd been terribly upset, not unnaturally, at the turn things had taken. Thank God Alex had got back, though, and once he had turned up and rushed to her side, Catherine had burst into tears of relief and, P.J. supposed, sheer exhaustion. He had left them alone then, and his good friend Dan Collins had been marvellous, sitting with them and explaining everything to them and taking them to see their newborn son. Charlie, they were going to call him. They were a proper little family now, the three of them. P.J. felt quite emotional just thinking about it. Seeing her face light up as Alex had come into the room, concern and love written all over his face for her, P.J. was thankful that his own son clearly had a wife who adored him, as he did her. It was what every marriage – every family – should be.

Thinking of family, he suddenly remembered. In the midst of all the drama, he had clean forgotten to tell his sisters, and indeed his own father the news that he was a great-grandfather. It was only seven-thirty, P.J. checked, not too late to ring him. At eighty-five years of age, Charles O'Sullivan was still in good health, if a little frail. His wife, Maureen, P.J.'s mother, had passed away three years ago after a series of strokes. Charles still lived in their small regency villa just ten minutes from Wellington Square in the care of two full-time

Filipino carer nurses. It was a perfect arrangement, as Charles made no secret of the fact that he would hate going into a residential home, preferring to take his chances and go 'with his boots on', as he put it, in the comfort of his own home. P.J. was in the happy position of being able to help him to do so, financially at any rate. His father was under the illusion that he was paying for the nurses entirely from his own capital resources – if he had known the true cost of employing them, which P.J. contributed to considerably, he would have keeled over on the spot. He answered the phone now in the less robust, but familiar tones, which by turns had both comforted and terrified P.J. as a young boy.

'Dad, it's me.'

'P.J. How nice to hear from you.'

'Are you sitting down?'

'I rarely do anything else these days,' he chuckled. 'As a matter of fact, I'm just reading the *Medical Times*. Why do you ask?'

'Well, the good news is you've just become a great-grandfather. The bad news is that makes me a grandfather.' P.J. grinned at his end.

'How marvellous! Congratulations, P.J., I'm so pleased. But I thought, or am I being dopey, the happy event was still some weeks away?'

'No, you're spot on, Dad. The little grey cells are still as efficient as ever. He's a preemie, arrived at thirty-three weeks. Dan Collins was looking after Catherine, did a wonderful job.'

'It's a boy then!'

'It certainly is.'

'Well, well, well, another O'Sullivan. With a bit of luck he might even be a rugby player, eh?'

P.J. paused. 'I'm not so sure about that, Dad.'

'What? Why?'

'He's a bleeder,' P.J. explained. 'The tests came back late this evening, Von Willebrand's.' P.J. knew his father realised the implications. 'They were alerted when they put the drip in.'

'Of course, of course,' his father tutted. 'Oh dear, that must have been worrying for Alex and Catherine, poor things. But just as well they know. It's easily treated and monitored these days, the drugs are first rate. Shouldn't affect the little chap at all, they'll just have to be careful with surgery and dentists, of course. But I see what you mean, contact sports probably aren't a good idea. Still, we must be thankful for small mercies. At least he made the trip here safely. When can they take him home?'

'All going well, Dan Collins thought two weeks.'

'Good, good.' Charles sounded thoughtful. 'Von Willebrand's certainly isn't in our side of the family – you realise that, don't you? Jilly must have been a carrier and not known it – unless Catherine is, of course.'

'Yes, I was thinking that.' P.J. rubbed his chin distractedly.

'Well, I'm sure they're doing the full profile of tests. Marvellous what they can pinpoint these days. Medicine has come so far since my time. All the same, you should all get yourselves tested. There's Bella to consider, she should know if she's a carrier.'

'She's coming home next week. I'll discuss it with her, but right now she's just over the moon about having a new nephew.'

'How wonderful. I'm looking forward to seeing her. Do give her my love.'

'Oh, and Dad?' P.J. saved the best bit of news till last. 'They're calling him Charlie, after you.'

'Well, well, well, how very kind.' P.J. thought he heard tears in his voice. 'Tell them I'm delighted, absolutely thrilled and delighted. In fact, I'm going to have a small glass of whiskey the minute I put the phone down.'

'In that case,' P.J. smiled, 'I won't delay you.'

'Thank you for ringing, P.J., I appreciate it, and congratulations again. It's quite a feeling becoming a grandfather, isn't it? I remember the day well myself, one of the proudest moments of my life.'

'Goodbye, Dad. Bella and I will see you when she's home.'

'I shall look forward to it.'

As P.J. put the phone down, he was lost in thought. His attention was captured by the pasta he had put on, which was now boiling over, water cascading and spitting onto the cooker. Rushing to turn down the gas, the unsettling, unarticulated thought that had begun to surface in the back of his mind was, for the present moment, forgotten.

He was just about to tuck in when his phone rang. It was Charlotte, of course. He had meant to ring her too; she was waiting for news.

'Charlotte!' he said. 'I'm so sorry, I completely forgot to call you back.'

'Never mind that.' He could tell she was smiling. 'Quick, tell me what happened.'

'It's a long story.'

'Well, are you or aren't you a grandfather?'

'As a matter of fact, I am,' P.J. said proudly. 'I have a beautiful grandson called Charlie.'

'Oh, P.J.,' she gasped. 'How wonderful. What are you doing?'

'Sorry,' he gulped, 'I was just shovelling some pasta into my mouth. Haven't eaten since this morning.'

'You mean you're sitting there on your own with a bowl of pasta when you should be celebrating?'

'Well, yes, I suppose so.'

'I've never heard anything so ridiculous in my life. Come over here right now, I've got champagne on ice and a lovely fresh salmon poaching.'

'I'd love to, if you're sure.'

'Of course I'm sure. It'll be a novelty for me. I've never had dinner with a grandfather before,' she chuckled.

'In that case, I don't see how I could possibly refuse.'

'And bring Bones if you want to, he shouldn't be left out either.'

P.J. smiled. 'We'll see you in ten.'

Cici looked at her daughter sitting across from her and smiled.

'What are you thinking, Mum?' Sophia pushed a glossy dark ringlet over her shoulder and looked at her mother speculatively as she bent to take a sip of her cosmopolitan in the stylish stemless cocktail glasses that sat in tumblers on their very own beds of ice.

'I'm just thinking how beautiful you are, and how very happy I am to be here with you,' Cici sighed.

'Me too,' grinned Sophia. 'And you look beautiful too, Mum. You always do.'

She had arrived, as arranged, at seven o'clock with a flurry of hugs and kisses, chattering ten to the dozen. After examining the suite thoroughly and proclaiming it perfect, she had taken a shower and they decided to have a drink in the bar downstairs before dining in the hotel or perhaps heading up to one of their favourite restaurants near the Spanish Steps. Tomorrow they would go shopping. Now, Cici listened happily to Sophia's accounts of university and her student life in Florence.

'Let's have another, shall we?' Sophia suggested as the waiter came to take their glasses.

'Why not?' smiled Cici. 'It's been far too long since we've chatted like this. I could listen to you all evening. Tell, me,' she asked, 'have you heard from Mimi?'

Sophia nodded. 'She's having a brilliant time. She's in Buenos Aires right now. Her Facebook accounts are scintillating,' she grinned.

'I dread to think what she's up to.'

'Oh, nothing much, just a lot of partying and sightseeing.'

Sophia chewed her lip, thinking of the phone call from

Dom and wondering if she should broach the delicate subject that was her parents' marriage. 'Mum, I don't mean to pry, but what's going on with you and Dad? It's just that Dom was talking to me and he seemed worried.'

'There's nothing to be concerned about, darling.' Cici was immediately consumed with guilt. She knew her children knew about the temporary separation, but other than that, both James and she had agreed not to say anything further on the subject. 'Daddy and I needed this time apart. Sometimes couples do, just to, well, reassess things.'

'I don't think Daddy needed it.' Sophia looked at her mother astutely. 'It's just that everybody always thought you and Daddy were so happy together.' She bit her lip anxiously. 'Aren't you?'

'Oh, darling.' Cici was flooded with remorse. 'Of course we were – *are*. I think this time apart was a good thing, really I do. And yes, you're right, I'm sure Daddy wasn't keen on the idea, but he's been wonderful, very understanding. He's allowed me my space, and I realise now that that was all I needed, just a bit of time on my own to have a little look at the world again, see what it feels like to be myself again and not just somebody's wife or somebody's mother.'

'So you're not getting a divorce then?'

Cici put down her drink and looked at her incredulously. 'A divorce? Of course not. Whatever put that thought into your head?'

Sophia thought it best not to mention what Dom had said. Perhaps he'd got it wrong. Maybe Dad had just been angry when he'd been talking to him.

'It's quite the opposite, actually,' Cici smiled ruefully. 'I've realised in the past few weeks just how much I love your father, and I'm going to tell him so the minute I get back home, and every day after that too.'

Sophia smiled. 'That's more like it, Mum. I was beginning

to think you'd taken leave of your senses. You'll never find another man like Daddy, you know.'

'I do know, darling. And I'm going to make it up to him, I promise.'

'Good,' said Sophia, finishing her drink. 'Now let's go for a stroll and find somewhere lovely to have dinner.' She felt a lot better after talking to her mother. Dom had obviously got the wrong end of the stick, which was typical of him. And this Harry person he had spoken of clearly didn't figure in her mother's plans at all, thank God. She hadn't even mentioned him to her. Linking her mother's arm in hers, they walked out of the hotel and decided to stroll to Piazza di Spagna.

'Isn't it brilliant that Dom has broken up with Tanya?' Sophia said. 'I couldn't stand her. There was something awfully sly about her.'

'I must say I couldn't warm to her at all,' Cici agreed. 'Poor girl, though. I'm sure she's terribly upset.'

'Not as upset as we'd be if Dom had married her,' Sophia said emphatically.

'Perish the thought,' Cici laughed.

'You know,' mused Sophia, 'I always thought Dom would go for someone more, well, passionate, sensual. A bon viveur, someone who loved their food, loved life and wasn't afraid to show it. Someone like—'

'Us, you mean?' Cici finished for her, laughing.

'Exactly.'

Sophia was right, Cici thought, that's exactly the type of woman Dom needed. And she was right under his nose – because those were the very words she would have used to describe Carla. Although she didn't know her well, it was the impression Cici had of her from the restaurant, and it wasn't for nothing all the staff and customers were mad about her too.

They strolled along happily, pausing on the Via Condotti

to admire the wonderful wares in the traditional designer clothes shops, where Sophia spotted and fell in love with a fabulous handbag. Cici, delighted to be on happier ground as regards her family, immediately insisted on purchasing it for her. 'I want to, *cara*,' she insisted when Sophia protested at the price. 'A beautiful handbag for my beautiful daughter. Now come, let's eat.'

At the top of the street, they entered the Piazza di Spagna, quirkily described as being shaped like a crooked bow tie, which it was, and surrounded by houses painted in muted shades of ochre, cream and russet. It was crowded, as always. Ahead lay the Spanish Steps, and to the right, another little tucked-away restaurant that Cici favoured. They found a table easily and were seated with welcoming smiles by the waiters, who were happy to escort them to one where they could see and be seen easily.

'I'm ravenous,' Sophia said as the waiter arrived and poured the wonderful Barolo from Tuscany that Cici had ordered.

Cici raised her glass. 'To family,' she said, smiling fondly at her daughter.

'I'll drink to that,' Sophia retorted warmly.

They had finished their meal and were just planning their shopping itinerary for the following day over coffees when a voice interrupted them.

'Cici, darling. And this gorgeous creature,' he said, his eyes roving over Sophia appreciatively, 'must be Sophia. I'm *so* sorry I'm late, but I only got away from my meeting just now. I hope you've ordered something delicious for me.'

As she looked up in utter disbelief, Cici saw Harry, who swiftly pulled up a chair from the table beside them and sat down, smiling confidently.

'Allow me to introduce myself. I've heard so much about you,' he said to Sophia, whose coffee cup had frozen on its way to her mouth. 'Harry McCabe.' He signalled to the waiter for a glass to be brought and helped himself to some wine.

For once in her life, Cici was lost for words, too horrified and shocked to take in the scene that was unfolding before her.

Sophia, on the other hand, was not. She looked disbelievingly from one to the other, and then, ignoring Harry, she turned on Cici with a horrified sob.

'Mum – how could you? How *could* you?'

'Darling, please,' Cici protested in vain while Harry sat there, looking calmly interested.

'I don't believe this.' Sophia looked at Harry with loathing.

'I'm sorry,' he enquired innocently, 'have I said something to upset you? Your mother assured me you were looking forward to meeting me, and I was – and indeed *am* – very much looking forward to meeting you.' He appeared bewildered and rather hurt.

'Harry!' Cici wanted to scream but her voice emerged as a whisper. She reached out to put a comforting hand on Sophia's arm, but it was too late. She had jumped up from her chair and was looking at Cici as if she were a stranger.

'You set this up!' she cried. 'Both of you! You never wanted to see me at all, it was all just a horrid excuse to introduce your – your lover boy to me.' She almost spat the words, then she ran from the table and pushed her way through the crowds, tears running down her face, and disappeared down Via Condotti.

Somehow, Cici found her voice. She looked at Harry, fury blazing from her eyes, but he remained smilingly unperturbed. 'You vicious, horrible, nasty human being. How could you?' she asked incredulously. 'What have I ever done to you to deserve this?'

'I did warn you, Cici,' he said calmly, though onlookers from neighbouring tables were beginning to take a distinct interest in them. 'I don't take kindly to being dismissed on a feminine whim. You treated me very shabbily back at the hotel. Now I'm afraid you're going to have to face the consequences.' He smiled infuriatingly.

'You're a monster. I don't know what I ever saw in you.' Cici was rigid with shock. 'I despise you.' She pushed her chair back and stood up from the table, pausing only to pick up Sophia's new handbag, which she had left behind.

'What a fickle creature you are,' he said nastily, watching her carefully. 'One minute it's James you don't want, the next minute it's me.'

'Don't you dare bring my husband into this – or any of my family.'

'Why not? I can do pretty much exactly as I please, Cici. You see, I don't have a wife or children, for that matter, to answer to. You, on the other hand, do. But I'm very disappointed in you Cici, very disappointed indeed.' His mouth was set in a thin line and his eyes were strangely alight in his face. 'I've done an awful lot for you, and you're really quite extraordinarily ungrateful.'

'Stay away from me,' she hissed, 'and stay away from my family.'

'Or what?' he asked blithely. 'It seems to me that you're finally out of your depth. You shouldn't have messed with me, with my affections. And now it seems there's really not a lot you can do about anything, is there? While I,' he said as he brought his glass to his mouth and took a drink of wine, 'can do exactly as I please.'

She had heard enough. She wouldn't listen to another word from this insane man who looked and sounded like Harry, but couldn't possibly be him. Fleeing the restaurant, Cici ran to the nearby taxi rank and flung herself into a car. 'Hotel de Russie,' she gasped to the driver. As the car pulled away, the tears began, and even then, she kept looking behind her, out the window, as if Harry could materialise before her yet again, determined to ruin everything she held so dear.

Reaching the hotel, she paid the driver, put on her sunglasses to hide her ravaged face and quickly went inside.

The man behind the front desk coughed discreetly as she tried to hurry past reception to the lift. 'Señora?' he queried.

'Yes?'

'Your, er, most recent guest, she has departed.'

'What?' Cici was aghast.

'She checked out just ten minutes ago and left instructions for me to inform you of her change of plans.' He seemed apologetic. 'You have just missed her.'

'Oh – oh, I see.' Cici forced a smile. 'Thank you so much.'

'Will you be expecting any other guests?'

'No, I won't, thank you. And I'm afraid I've had a change of plan myself. I need to get on the first available flight to Dublin. Will you arrange that immediately please?'

'Right away, Señora.' He seemed disappointed.

She fled to her suite, locked the door and sat, immobile, on the bed. She hardly noticed the tears streaming down her face. She was suddenly cold and began to shiver. What in the name of God was going to happen now?

In number 42 Wellington Square, P.J. had just finished some delicious poached salmon and asparagus, washed down with a particularly nice bottle of white. He and Charlotte were sitting in her kitchen. Bones had joined Bonnie and Clyde in their basket and was now snoring loudly. 'Thank you, Charlotte,' he said. 'I can't remember when I had a nicer piece of salmon, or a nicer evening, for that matter.'

'It has been nice, hasn't it? I'm so glad you came over.'

'So am I.'

And it *had* been a lovely evening. He had arrived over as instructed, with Bones, and they had celebrated his new-found status as a grandfather with some ice-cold champagne and not a little hilarity, although Charlotte had been concerned to hear about the baby.

'It's not serious,' P.J. reassured her, 'not in Charlie's case. It's just a mild bleeding disorder. It often doesn't even show up until much later in life, when one has to have surgery or dentistry. In a way, they're lucky he's been diagnosed now. It means they can keep an eye on him.'

'What about Alex and Catherine? Do they know yet how he inherited it?' Charlotte was curious.

'They'll run all the usual profile of tests. We should find out in a few days.' P.J. yawned. 'If Alex has it, I must say I'll be surprised, although it's perfectly possible. I do remember him bruising quite a lot as a youngster, now that I think of it, and getting a lot of nosebleeds, but most small boys do. I'm afraid we doctors are always rather dismissive of our own children's symptoms. Comes with the territory. We're notorious for being unsympathetic to family members unless something's life-threatening,' he grinned. 'I must get myself tested, just out of curiosity.'

'As long as little Charlie isn't in danger, then that's all that matters.'

'You're right – and he's not. All going well, they should be able to bring him home in about two weeks.'

'Poor Catherine. How awful to have such a worrying time with your first baby. I can't imagine. Candy, thank God, was robustly healthy when she arrived, and even then demanded relentless attention. Come to think of it, she's been doing that ever since,' she smiled ruefully.

'Why only Candy?' P.J. enquired. 'Didn't you want any more kids?'

'It's a long story.'

'I'm not in any rush.' His eyes were warm as he topped up their glasses.

So she told him all about the fall she'd out hunting, about her first miscarriage and the four that had followed in the intervening years. He listened attentively, never once interrupting her.

'I can't imagine how devastating that must have been for you.'

'It was,' she said quietly, 'and for Ossie too. He – that is, we – had always wanted a large family. But it wasn't to be. Except . . .'

'Except that Ossie gets to have another chance with someone else,' P.J. finished the thought for her. 'It's horribly unfair.'

'Yes,' she smiled sadly. 'It did seem unfair at the time, but that's life. You men can go on reproducing forever. It's not so easy for us women.'

P.J. sighed. 'Life isn't fair, that's for sure. When you're in my line of business, you come across a lot of people who've been dealt unfair hands. You just have to make the best of the good stuff when it comes along.'

'You're right, of course. And I have Candy – or at least I used to,' she said, sighing. 'She's moved in with her dad for a bit. There was a disagreement. She needs some space . . .' She trailed off, thinking of all the recent drama with Candy, but she didn't want to say any more about it – not yet – although she felt she could have told P.J. anything.

'Tell me about it,' P.J. said wryly, shaking his head. 'My son Alex thinks I come from another planet. I should go.' P.J. checked his watch. 'It's late and I'm keeping you up. But thank you, I really can't think of when I've spent a nicer evening.' He paused. 'That's not entirely true, I can – it was the last time we had dinner together.' He smiled.

'Oh, P.J.' Charlotte went a little pink. 'What a nice thing to say – I think so too.'

'Do you want me to go?' He held her eyes, hopefully. 'I *could* stay . . . that is, if Jennifer doesn't appear to chase me out.'

'My mother is safely in bed in the basement. Which is where I should like to keep her locked a lot of the time.'

'Then I think we should go to bed too . . . what do you say?' P.J. took her hands in his, hardly believing what he was suggesting, but they had to broach the subject sometime, and it felt right to do it now, to stay, and not right at all for him to go back alone across the square and end this lovely, warm and comforting evening.

She hesitated for only a second. 'Yes. Let's go upstairs.'

So he followed her, holding her hand, as she led him up to her bedroom, and he took her in his arms and bent to kiss her, marvelling yet again at the softness of her lips, and how they yielded so perfectly to his.

While she was in the bathroom, P.J. quickly discarded his clothes, putting them on the sofa that sat across the foot of the large double bed. He kept on his boxer shorts and snuck a quick peek at himself in the mirror before slipping in between the cool cotton sheets. All that training had paid off. He wasn't looking half bad. Either that, or the wine was affecting his reflection. All the same, he was nervous. He knew it was ridiculous, but it had been so long, over five years, since he had made love to anyone. He had almost forgotten what it felt like. He hoped he would remember what to do.

When she emerged, naked, from the bathroom, her dark hair in a cloud around her shoulders, smiling nervously at him, she took his breath away. Her figure was stunning, slender and gently curvaceous in all the right places. When she slipped in beside him he pulled her close, breathing her in. 'You are so beautiful, do you know that?' he said, stroking her hair back from her face and looking into the depths of those huge dark eyes.

'Oh, P.J., I know it's silly, but I – well, I haven't – you know – it's been a while.'

'Me too,' he murmured. 'All the more reason to enjoy it. Let's just take it slowly, hmm?'

So they did. Wonderfully slowly. And he hadn't forgotten, he realised, and neither had she. And even if he had, his body was reminding him, urging him on, in the most deliciously memorable way.

It was true, he thought, losing himself in her kiss, in her

wonderful, arousing caresses. There were some things you never forgot. Just like riding a bicycle – except much, *much* nicer . . .

Would the night *ever* end? Cici had tossed and turned miserably, alternating between tears and terror, completely unable to sleep. Now, at six o'clock in the morning, she gave up trying and hauled herself out of bed, feeling like death warmed up.

She had been unable to get back to Dublin the day before, as she had so desperately wanted to. The two flights had been completely full. She could have gone back via London, but she couldn't have stood hanging about in Heathrow, and it wouldn't have got her back that much earlier. Instead, she was on the lunchtime flight today. Only six more hours, six interminably long hours, and she would be at Da Vinci Airport, hopefully about to board a flight for home.

Home. The word reverberated in her mind. After Harry's hideous stunt yesterday, she doubted if she would have any kind of home at all to return to. She certainly seemed to have lost a daughter. Cici had been trying Sophia's phone incessantly, but it had been turned off – she couldn't even leave a message. Thinking of her, her heart constricted again. She would never, as long as she lived, forget the look of bewilderment and betrayal on Sophia's face when Harry had turned up.

And then she would think of him, of Harry, and be gripped with an anger so devouring it threatened to consume her, the raw, primal anger of a mother thwarted in protecting her vulnerable, innocent child. Then she would relapse into fear. Where was he now? If he had been capable of setting up that spiteful scene he had pulled off so successfully, what, if anything, would his next move be? The questions tormented her. She desperately wanted to talk to someone – anyone – but who? Sophia wouldn't take her calls. There was no point in calling Dom, who would no doubt be on the receiving end of Sophia's version of events. And James . . . oh God, if only James were here. If only she could talk to him and explain, he would know what to do. No matter how awful things were, he would fix them and make them better. She thought about calling him, even now, and held her phone in her hand. All she had to do was punch in his number, but her fingers began to tremble so violently she abandoned the task before even attempting it.

What would she say? 'Please, James, come and get me, my insane lover is trying to destroy me and our family.' Just thinking about it made her blood run cold. If James knew, if he got to hear about Sophia and what had happened, he would be incandescent with anger. And what's more, she knew he would have every right to be. He would never forgive her, *could* never forgive her, and she didn't blame him. She was a wicked, selfish, irresponsible woman who had risked her marriage and family for a series of cheap thrills, thrills from which she now not only recoiled, but whose memory, and that of their instigator, left her reeling with nothing but shame and awful, chilling foreboding.

She passed the hours with gritted teeth, forcing herself to have a massage in the spa, followed by a blow-dry in the hairdresser's. When the masseuse had commented on how tense her muscles were, Cici had wanted to relieve that very tension by punching her. Instead, she had muttered something about stress and willed the girl to revert to silence. The hairdresser hadn't been much better. A chatty, cheerfully gay coiffeur had regaled her about her resemblance to Sophia Loren and his obsession with her and Cici had wanted to kill him. But still she smiled and murmured encouragingly, comforting herself with the thought that she would soon be on her way.

The hotel staff bade her a respectful farewell, and at last she was in the taxi, on her way to the airport. She had never wanted to get out of Rome so fast in her life. She never wanted to see the place again.

The flight, thank God, was on time. Boarding it, she tried Sophia's number one last time before switching her phone off. At least this time it went to voicemail. 'Please, Sophia,' Cici begged. 'Please ring me, *cara*, I have to explain to you. I beg you, ring me. What happened was a terrible thing – it wasn't how it looked, I promise you. I had no idea. He – Harry – followed me over. I would never, never—' She was cut off. She hung up miserably.

The flight, too, seemed interminable, although they landed on schedule in Dublin in the midst of a gently rolling mist. Cici reclaimed her case from the baggage carousel, and before getting a taxi, stopped in the airport shop to pick up some fresh milk and a couple of magazines. Once she was home, she didn't want to have to go outside her front door. Not now.

'Wellington Square, please,' she told the driver.

'Been anywhere nice?' he asked cheerily. 'Hope you've had better weather than you left behind.'

'I'm sorry, I'm very tired.' She leaned back and closed her eyes, not caring if she sounded rude. Thankfully the traffic was light, and they made good headway. Safe in the assumption that the driver wouldn't engage her in further conversation, which she would have been incapable of, she opened one of the magazines. Leafing idly through its pages, she barely registered the new colourful summer fashions or the many smiling, handsome couples that stared out at her from various glamorous functions. Until one photograph caught her eye. She looked again, carefully, blinking, squeezing her eyes shut and opening them again. But there was no mistaking it. No mistaking the handsome face, the dark hair greying at the temples, swept elegantly back from the aristocratic brow, the mouth she knew so well relaxed in a wide, happy smile. It was James. *Her* James. And beside him, looking equally happy, her head thrown back and laughing, was – oh, God, it was Sarah de Burgh, the fabulously beautiful, fabulously wealthy, blonde, *divorced* Sarah de Burgh. They had been attending a ball in aid of the Grosvenor Foundation, held in the Dorchester Hotel in London. Cici closed her eyes again. She thought she was going to pass out, or at the very least be sick. Thankfully, the taxi pulled up at Wellington Square, outside her house – James's house.

'You all right, love?' The driver handed her her case. 'You look a bit peaky. I could give you a hand in, if you like.' He seemed genuinely concerned.

'No, thank you, I'm all right.' She tipped him generously. Trailing her case on its wheels along the side path and down to the mews, she took a few deep breaths. *Just keep breathing*, she told herself. *You're almost home, almost inside.* She twisted the key in the lock, and mercifully the door opened. She dragged her case inside, shut the door and pulled up the blinds, which had been left drawn, blinking as her eyes adjusted to the late afternoon sunlight streaming through the window. Then she turned towards the mirror over the mantelpiece and froze, her hand flying to her throat. There, scrawled in bright red lipstick, was one solitary word. *Whore*, it screamed at her.

For a very long moment, she stood stock still, like an animal transfixed, then cold, hard reasoning tugged at her brain. She hadn't given Harry a key, she was sure of it, but she had left one out for him on one or two occasions. He must have had it copied. How could she have been so stupid? But now was not the time for recriminations. Moving as if through a bad dream, she forced herself to walk through the house, upstairs, wanting with every step to flee, to escape, but to where? To who? This was something she had got herself into and now had to get herself out of.

'Hello?' she called hesitantly, her voice sounding eerily

unreal. Upstairs, she went into each room, methodically, and there it was again, on the mirror in her bedroom and in the bathroom. *Whore.* That appeared to be the extent of the damage.

Searching everywhere, in the cupboards (at least his clothes were gone; he must have taken them) and under the beds, Cici realised, relief flooding through her, that she was alone – at least for the moment. Then fear gave way to anger and she picked up the phone. 'Get me the number of an emergency locksmith,' she instructed directory enquiries. Then she went downstairs, found some glass cleaner and a cloth and proceeded to wipe away the horrible evidence of Harry's vitriol.

By the time the locksmith arrived, the mews looked as it always had. She felt better having taken action. She might have been naive, but this was nothing she couldn't sort out. She had to believe that – had to. One step at a time. The locks would be changed and Harry would never set foot in her home or her life again.

While the locksmith went about his work, Cici unpacked, put on the washing machine and changed out of her travelling outfit – normal, sensible actions, even if they were undertaken by a woman who felt anything but.

Satisfied that her new locks were installed and working, she put her set of new keys carefully away, turned on the alarm and ran a hot bath, forcing herself to think as she sank into the soothing water. She would meet with James as soon as possible, tomorrow, hopefully. Tell him how sorry she was, how she had lost sight of everything, even herself. She would move back into their beautiful home and make everything right. They would sell or rent the mews and she would put this terrible part of her life behind her. He would understand and forgive her; he'd never been able to resist her. Getting out, she patted herself dry, slipped into a cashmere top and lounging trousers and suddenly found she was hungry. She went downstairs and fixed herself a light supper and poured herself a glass of wine.

Turning on the television, more for background noise than anything else, she wandered over to pick up the post that had gathered while she'd been away. There wasn't much. A few mail shots, a couple of bills and one rather official-looking letter, addressed to her, here at the mews. She was intrigued. She hadn't had her mailing address changed. Any post was dropped down to her from the main house by the housekeeper. She finished her supper and, curling up on the couch, took a sip of wine, finally beginning to relax. She opened the letter, barely registering the title and company address of the sender. She didn't need to – the first line after *Dear Mrs Coleman-Cappabianca* had got her attention. *We are instructed by our client, Mr James Coleman, of 15 Wellington Square, to inform you of his intention to initiate immediate proceedings for formal separation followed by divorce.* Numbly, she allowed her eyes to follow the neat, computerised script, advising her to consult with and appoint a family-law solicitor of her choosing and have them contact and enter into negotiations with Mr John O'Carroll, of McGregor, O'Carroll and Lawson, at her earliest convenience.

Cici felt the room spin around her. Clutching the letter, she seemed to be unable to move, watching it as it began to tremble in her hand. It couldn't be true, it *couldn't* be. There'd been some terrible mistake. James would never do something like this – not without telling her, warning her. And then she heard the small voice of truth whisper in her head. *You didn't exactly talk to or warn him when you decided to turn his life upside down.* That was the real truth, she knew, just as she knew that McGregor, O'Carroll and Lawson were the most feared divorce lawyers in the country. And John O'Carroll, the leading partner, was not known as 'The Rottweiler' without good cause. She sat there, stunned and suddenly very, very frightened.

13

'That was . . . you are . . . *amazing*,' said Candy, collapsing back on pillows that had seen better days. Beside her, Josh hauled himself upright, and leaving her in bed, made for the tiny kitchenette.

'So they tell me,' he quipped. 'Wanna beer, babe?' He opened one for himself.

'No, but I'd like you back here and right beside me as soon as possible.' She smiled in what she hoped was a provocative fashion as she watched him walk back towards her, his thin, hungry-looking body and slightly bandy legs seeming impossibly attractive to her. His skin was pale, his hair long and dark and when he looked at her, which wasn't often enough, his slanting cobalt blue eyes seemed to see right through her. She wasn't so keen on the wispy goatee he allowed to ruin his sensitive mouth and finely chiselled jaw, but it was a small flaw in the overall perfection.

Candy had never met anyone like Josh, and she certainly hadn't ever known anything approaching the skills he was capable of in bed, or indeed out of it. She smiled as he got back in beside her and watched him as he lit a joint, inhaling it slowly. Candy had only had a few boyfriends, nothing serious, just part of the crowd she used to hang around with, and Robbie, who her parents had loved because they knew *his* parents and he was a talented horseman, tipped to pick up an Olympic medal in the three-day eventing. Though he was awfully nice and really good fun, his aptitude in the saddle sadly wasn't matched anywhere else. Apart from a few fairly tame attempts at drunken fumblings on Robbie's part, Candy really hadn't understood what all the fuss was about sex.

That had all changed when she met Josh, and it had all been quite by accident. Her mother's new boyfriend (ugh!) or whatever she called him, that stupid doctor, had invited her mother and her to a Viper concert, the coolest band on the planet.

As the end of their latest world tour, they were wrapping up in Dublin with a mega-hyped performance and were threatening to take a break for quite some time after that, so tickets to the show in the Royal Dublin Society were almost impossible to get hold of. P.J., however, was doctor on stage at any, or indeed all of the venues they played at, if he so chose, worldwide. Apparently, they had all been mates from a million years ago.

Candy couldn't stand him. For starters, he called her mother *babe* or *hon*, and worse still, she even seemed to like it. When she was around P.J., her usually calm, aloof mother became like a pathetic, simpering teenager. If she hadn't seen it with her own eyes, she wouldn't have believed it. They were embarrassing, the pair of them. Even her father and Shalom were past that sort of stuff.

She had only gone to the concert with them because Emma and Katy had been so impressed. She had demanded that they be included, thinking that would put a fly in the ointment, but P.J. had said he would see what he could do and had been able to produce another pair of tickets. Not only that, but they were in the VIP area. Katy and Emma had almost fainted when they'd heard that. And better still, since P.J. was technically on duty as doctor on stage, they all got to go backstage and meet the band afterwards and go to the after-concert party to end all parties. Though she was grudging in her acknowledgement, even Candy had to admit it was a pretty cool gig, and one that was to prove very exciting for her, for it was that electric, unforgettable night that she met Josh.

'What's a gaggle of cute little schoolgirls like you doing in the VIP area then?' he had asked, his mouth curving in a lazy smile, aiming the remark mostly at Emma, who looked incredible in tight pink jeans and a floral smock top.

'We're not schoolgirls and I'm here with my mother,' Candy had retorted, flicking back her platinum ringlets. 'What's it to you?'

'Nothing really.' He turned to her and gave her a once-over, not seeming very impressed at all. 'Daddy with the band then?'

'Don't be ridiculous. My mother's with a – a friend. And my father is a property developer. You've probably heard of him,' she added for good measure, 'Ossie Keating.' There, that would put the arrogant jerk in his place.

'That figures,' he said, infuriatingly.

'What do you mean?'

'Poor little rich girl – it's written all over you, love.'

Candy was speechless with anger, but Emma and Katy had been reduced to helpless giggles. He grinned at them, then held out his hand by way of introduction. 'Josh McIntyre, video director.'

'Wow,' breathed Emma, 'you, like, shoot all the video footage?'

'And direct it. You're cute,' he added, 'want to be in a video? We could do some test shots sometime.'

Now it was Emma's turn to be speechless. 'Give me your numbers,' he instructed, although he hadn't so much as looked at Candy.

Nonetheless, she found herself offering her phone number to him along with Katy and Emma.

'I'll be in touch. Better not tell your mother, though,' he winked at Candy. 'Parents can get twitchy about their little darlings being filmed.' And then he had walked away, leaving them staring after him.

'Wow,' said Emma again. 'D'you think he was serious?'

'Doubt it,' Katy said. 'Anyway, he's, like, really old. Thirty-five maybe?'

'He's cute,' Candy said, her head tilted to one side. 'Really cute.'

Emma and Katy exchanged looks and shook their heads.

Candy was smitten. For a whole week after that she dreamed about him every night. She could hardly eat.

When he rang, she couldn't believe it. And it was *her* he rang – not Emma or Katy, but her.

'Meet me,' he said and mentioned a pub she didn't know, but pretended she did.

She agreed to meet him readily – too readily. She didn't tell Katy or Emma, and she most certainly didn't tell her mother. She wasn't really talking to her and had been avoiding all her invitations for coffee or dinner. Anyway, her mum had got a boyfriend now – if even *she* could get a man, then it was about time she had a love interest herself. Instinctively she knew both her mum and dad would have hated Josh, but so what? They didn't exactly consult her about their choices, did they?

He never took her out, not properly, not to dinner or anything, and when they met, those few initial times in obscure pubs (he had even stood her up once or twice), he had let her pay for the drinks. She'd been shocked, but automatically did what he told her. This was obviously the way the girls he went for behaved. She had never met anyone like him and had no idea how to play things. Sometimes he seemed miles away, as if he was in his own world. Other times he openly admired other girls, which infuriated her, although she pretended she didn't care. And then other times he would be kind and sweet to her. Like the first time he had invited her back to his flat. It was small, much smaller than she had imagined. She had assumed he lived in a smart chrome and black leather infested apartment, filled with boy toys and gadgets and a huge TV. What she found was a pokey one-bedroom flat with a rather flea-bitten carpet. It was in the city centre, she supposed, although in a less desirable part than she would have expected – but what did she care? She was inside the front door, at home with him – that was all that mattered, wasn't it? He told her to undress, and she did, quaking with excitement and apprehension, then feeling vulnerable and exposed as he made her wait, looking at her appraisingly from every angle. Then he had made love to her, slowly and carefully, until lying on the scratchy acrylic rug in front of the fireplace she writhed beneath him, breathless with excitement. Candy had never had a proper orgasm, not like this, and she was hooked, instantly. She only had to look at him and she was aroused, and in the weeks that followed, he made sure she had plenty of them.

It had been Josh's idea for her to get her boobs done, although she'd been toying with the idea for quite some time. But now she had a good reason to go ahead with it. 'You should do something about those,' he had said, tweaking a nipple playfully one afternoon when they were lying in his bed.

'What?' She'd been taken by surprise, not altogether pleasantly.

'Have your boobs done, love. Those aren't tits, they're fried eggs,' he had laughed.

'Don't you like me the way I am?' Candy had chewed her lip.

'I'd like you a whole lot better with a pair of 34Ds.'

'Well,' she said doubtfully, 'I had been thinking about it, but I thought maybe a B or C cup, not a D.'

'Why not? If you're getting them done, you might as well get your money's worth. And I know a good surgeon. He might even give you a discount. I send a lot of girls to him.'

'What girls?' Candy looked shocked.

'Models. Relax,' he laughed at her. 'In my line of business, girls are always getting stuff done – they have to, otherwise they don't get the jobs.'

'Oh,' Candy said, feeling better about it. 'Of course, I see.'

And the more she thought about it, the more it seemed like a good idea, so one day she picked up the phone and made an appointment to go for a consultation at the clinic Josh had recommended. She met with the surgeon, who wasn't very nice at all – he was rather brusque and spoke very little English. But she had gone ahead and had booked herself in for the breast-augmentation procedure two weeks from then, and told Ossie and Shalom she was staying with Emma for the week to check out a few courses she was thinking of doing.

She had felt miserable coming around from the anaesthetic. Katy and Emma were sitting exams, so they couldn't be with her. She hadn't told her parents, or even Shalom, who had clearly had her own breasts enlarged. And Josh, although he had assured her he would be there when she went into theatre and came around, hadn't even visited, saying he was on an important freelance gig. So she had come to, feeling nauseous and vulnerable and as if her chest was about to explode. 'What do you expect, love?' the clinic nurse had said cheerfully – a little too cheerfully. 'You've gone from a 34A to a 34D – those puppies are bound to be making their presence felt.' She had grinned as she refused to give Candy any more painkillers. 'Doctor's orders,' she'd said, then had left.

Candy had burst into tears. The next day, still feeling horribly tender, wearing bandages and a support bra, Candy and her new breasts were hustled into a taxi and she was taken back to Josh's place, where she arrived to an empty and very grim homecoming. Suddenly she wanted to be at home, to have her mother with her, or at the very least Emma and Katy. At least they could have examined the surgical results in combined awe. But she was here, alone in Josh's shoddy and, more to the point, empty flat. For a second, she thought about calling her mum. She thought of the time she'd had her tonsils out when she was ten, and how wonderful her mum had been to her, bringing her up ice cream and taking care of her when she was feeling miserable. But she couldn't back down now. Fighting back tears, she crawled into the unmade bed. She couldn't even curl up – she had to lie propped up on support pillows and hope for sleep. It was a more likely prospect than company, she realised.

It was late when Josh finally got back, and Candy was relieved to see him.

'Hey, baby!' He greeted her with a kiss, smelling of beer, which made Candy feel nauseous all over again. 'How're my girls?' He looked impressed at the size of her new chest.

'They're in agony,' she said, although just looking at Josh made her feel better.

'Poor you. Never mind. Think of the fun we're going to have playing with them, eh?' he grinned. 'Brought back a pizza, fancy some?'

'Maybe just a teeny bit.'

'Good girl. Heat it up for us, would you? I need to take a shower.'

'Sure,' Candy said, struggling to get out of bed. If she had thought the clinic unsympathetic, she certainly wasn't going to be treated like a recovering patient here, she thought miserably. Still, it would all be worth it in the end. She had a fabulous new figure, and a fabulously sexy man to enjoy it with, someone who needed her and wanted to be with her. A sore chest for a few days was a small price to pay.

It was late, but once Dom started, he wasn't going to stop until he worked all this out, even if the figures were beginning to swim in front of his eyes. Sitting in the back office, he poured another glass of Chianti Classico and realised he was almost three-quarters of the way through the bottle. He didn't care. His restaurant was in trouble and it was all his own fault for taking his eye off the ball. Since that awful day when Eric had broken the news about the accounts, Dom had been grappling with the situation every which way. Now he was going to have to pay the price and let people go and he could hardly bear it, especially when all the team had worked so hard to make Dominic's the success it had become, at least as far as appearances went. It was still the most popular place in town to eat, and the food was superb, although Dom couldn't help noticing, going through the books, that Rollo had been extraordinarily wasteful and unnecessarily extravagant a lot of the time. That would have to change. He was racking his brains, trying to work out how he should approach the whole thing, when he heard a noise and the door was pushed tentatively open.

'Oh, I'm sorry.' It was Carla, looking surprised to see him there. 'I left my phone behind. I don't have a landline so it's my only form of contact with the outside world – I get worried if I don't have it on me,' she gabbled. 'I saw the light on and just wanted to check everything was all right.'

'I wish I could say it was,' Dom smiled at her, pleased at the unexpected company.

'What's wrong?' She looked concerned.

'How long have you got?'

She shrugged, smiling back at him, looking very Italian. She reminded him in that moment of his mother and sisters, and suddenly he wanted to tell her everything.

'I'm not rushing anywhere.'

'Then would you join me in a drink? I think I might need to open another bottle anyway, there doesn't seem to be quite enough in this one.'

'I'll get it, you stay there.' She returned with a bottle and another glass, then opened the bottle expertly and poured two fresh glasses. 'Chianti is still my favourite,' she smiled.

'Reminds me of so many long Sunday lunches from a very long time ago.'

'Tell me about yourself, Carla. I really don't know anything about you.' Dom caught her eye and looked at her quizzically.

'You first,' she said. 'You tell me what the problem is, and then I'll tell you about me.' She pulled up a chair and sat down opposite him.

An hour and a half later, they had gone over every possible permutation. Dom had been astonished at Carla's grasp of the business.

'My family runs a restaurant – that is, my father and three brothers run it – but I know how it works,' she said, not quite telling the whole truth but not lying to him either. She was still cautious, still not sure how much, if anything, she should tell him.

'How come you're in Dublin?' he asked, not unnaturally.

She shrugged. 'It was a spur of the moment thing. There was a fight – a family thing. I needed to get away, have some space, so I decided to take a year off and Dublin seemed as good a place as any.'

'That bad, huh?'

She smiled. 'Families. Can't live with them, can't kill them, but I do miss them all – especially Dad.'

'What about your mum?'

'She died when I was eight.'

'I'm so sorry.' His eyes were full of sympathy.

'Yeah . . . well.' She changed the subject quickly. 'Speaking of mothers, yours is a beauty. She seems like fun too. She's always nice to me when she's in the restaurant.'

Dom's face clouded. 'They're always lovely when they're not your own,' he said wryly. 'They're splitting up, my parents.'

'Oh, I'm sorry. I didn't know.'

'Neither did we till quite recently. I thought my parents had the happiest marriage on the planet. Apparently Mum had other ideas. I'm sure you've noticed she hasn't been dining here with my father.'

Carla nodded. 'I know. That must be tough.'

'It's certainly weird to see your mother taking up with a guy half her age.'

'Is it serious? I mean, your mum and this guy?'

Dom shrugged. 'Who can tell? She's like a different person these days. She looks like Mum, sounds like Mum, but she's sure as hell not behaving like Mum. She used to be great – you'd have loved her,' he said without thinking.

'Maybe she's just going through some stuff – you know, trying to find herself. It's tough for a beautiful woman to face getting older.'

Dom seemed surprised. 'Maybe you're right,' he said thoughtfully. 'I never thought of it in that light.'

He looked at her, and as their eyes met all the past awkwardness and embarrassment melted away. But suddenly Carla was frightened. This was getting personal, and Dom had wanted business advice, not a lecture on families. It was time to get back to the subject in hand.

'You can lose two waiters, that's it,' she proclaimed. 'You are front of house. Astrid or I will take over when you can't be there. She won't ask for much of an increase, and it's cheaper and easier than hiring someone new.'

'And you?'

'I'll do it as a favour,' she grinned. 'Then you'll owe me one.' She paused. 'The real problem is Rollo. That's where you have to cut back.'

'I can't let him go – the restaurant depends on him, on his reputation.' Dom looked worried.

'That's only partly true. And maybe you won't have to let him go, but you can ask him to take a cut in salary. Explain the situation, and if he won't agree, then he'll leave anyway.'

'Then what will I do?'

'Let's worry about that when we come to it,' Carla said, yawning. 'The kitchen is running like clockwork anyway. If they have to, the sous chefs will manage without an executive chef for a little while. You can go in and shout at them in the meantime.'

'It's almost midnight,' Dom said, looking at his watch. 'Thank you for listening to me, and for your advice. I hate doing it, but it's the right thing to do.'

'We work in a precarious business,' she said, clearing away the glasses and the second bottle. 'It's always touch and go.'

'Speaking of going, it's far too late for you to be off out there on your own. And it's a horrible night.' It was: a wind had got up and rain was driving against the window. 'Why don't you stay the night in my place?' he heard himself saying. 'It's only upstairs, and as you know, I have a spare room. I promise I'll behave, though to be honest, I'd like very much to misbehave with you.'

She coloured slightly. 'I could get a taxi,' she ventured.

'You could.' Dom was moving towards the window and looking out at the lack of cars on the street. Then he paced back and was standing in front of her. 'But don't you think that would be silly when you can just grab a bed upstairs?'

'I – I don't know what to say.'

'Then don't say anything.' He moved closer, and then his arms were pulling her to him and his hands were moulding around that amazing bottom. And she wasn't pulling away. Then he bent his head and did what he had been longing to do ever since he had done it the last time. He kissed her, slowly and thoroughly, and as she kissed him back, he thought he had never tasted anything quite so delicious.

Carla never made it to the spare room. They barely made it upstairs. Shedding their clothes, they clung to one another, hungrily discovering each other's bodies long into the night. When she awoke, sometime towards dawn, in a tangle of limbs, Carla extricated herself gently, propping herself up on an elbow and looking at Dom's beautiful face as he lay sleeping. She slipped out of bed and padded to the kitchen to get a drink of water, suddenly thinking again of her family, her father. He had always told her she would know when she met the right man – now she knew what he meant. He would be happy for her, happy she had finally found him – although possibly not quite so happy that she was in bed with him and had had such abandoned sex with him *before* marriage. She smiled at the thought and went back to the bedroom, where she slipped in beside Dom and snuggled up to him, breathing him in and kissing his shoulder as he stirred briefly in his sleep.

'*Cara*' was the word he murmured as he hooked his hand around her thigh. Italian for *darling*.

Carla had never felt so happy.

James Coleman was sitting very comfortably in the spectacular drawing room of Sarah de Burgh's mansion that looked out over Dublin Bay. She had just given a most enjoyable dinner party for fourteen people and had entertained them all impeccably. She really was a charming hostess, James thought, smiling at her as she topped up his glass of red. The others had all left, Sarah's housekeeper was clearing up in the dining room, and it was just the two of them now, enjoying a nightcap.

'You look beautiful tonight, Sarah,' he said truthfully as she joined him on the sofa. And she did. The black dress she wore was elegant and showed off her superb figure, which she obviously kept in meticulous shape. Her blonde hair was loosely waved and her blue eyes shone in the firelight. Her skin, too, was beautiful, pale and luminous. No wonder she had been Ireland's most successful model. As far as James could tell, she hadn't changed a bit. Plus she was charming and kind. James wondered why on earth her husband had been mad enough to leave her – although naturally he didn't say so.

'I really enjoyed this evening, it was wonderful. You went to an awful lot of trouble,' he said, smiling as she leaned against him and wrapped his arm around her shoulders. He had been seeing quite a bit of her, and was becoming more and more fond of her, but . . .

'A penny for them?'

'I should go, it's late. I'll call my driver.'

'Oh, Jamie, don't be such a spoilsport,' she pouted prettily, then giggled. She was a little tipsy, and so was he. The selection of wines had been first rate and he told her so.

'Then stay and have another glass.' She slanted up at him, then pulled back and sat up. 'James?'

'Er, yes?' He didn't have to ask; he knew what was coming next. He cleared his throat awkwardly.

'Don't go – there's no need to. Stay here. You can leave in the morning,' she said huskily, leaning in to kiss him. He had kissed her before, of course, many times – but nothing more. It wasn't that he didn't want to sleep with her, it was just that it felt like crossing a line of some sort, one there would be no coming back from, and part of him, an irritatingly reluctant part of him, just didn't feel ready for that.

'Please?' she said, batting those huge blue eyes. 'I really don't want to be alone tonight, and I don't think you want to be either, if you're honest.'

'I'm sorry, Sarah.' He stood up. 'I really do have to go, I have a terribly early start tomorrow,' he lied. 'Another time, I'd love to.'

'When?' she asked, petulantly. 'All you've ever done is kiss me – is there something wrong with me? Something unattractive?'

'Sarah, darling, you know perfectly well you're beauty personified. Look, it's late, we'll discuss this another time. I really must go.'

'Of course you must.' She smiled suddenly, but her eyes were hard. 'That's what all you men do, isn't it? Go, eventually.'

'Sarah,' James gestured helplessly. 'It's just not the right time. It would spoil things between us, and I don't want to do that.'

'What *do* you want?' The question hung menacingly in the air. Sarah folded her arms and regarded him, her many diamonds glinting on her fingers and wrists. 'You're still in love with that wife of yours, aren't you?' she said bitterly.

'Really, Sarah, this isn't the place or the time.' He suppressed a flash of anger.

'So you keep saying.' She was hurt now, and angry. He couldn't say he blamed her.

'I'll call you tomorrow.' He bent to kiss her cheek, then let himself out and called his driver to meet him on the road outside. Loosening his collar, he took a deep breath. He must be mad. He had one of the most beautiful women in the country offering herself to him on a plate and he had turned her down. What the hell was the matter with him?

Back inside one of the most beautiful homes in the city, one of the most beautiful women in Dublin was asking herself the very same question. What the hell was the matter with James Coleman?

He was charming, considerate, handsome and very, *very* rich – and he hadn't so much as made a move on her, apart from kissing her – very well, actually, perhaps too well. It was driving Sarah mad. And they made such a wonderful couple, all their friends were saying so – they were the talk of the town. She knew he had feelings for her; he was too gentlemanly to waste her time otherwise. She looked at herself in the mirror, at the outfit she had taken so much time selecting, at her appearance, which she'd gone to so much trouble with. She looked great, she knew she did – everyone was always telling her she looked ten years younger than her forty-eight years. And she was rich too, so no one, least of all James, could accuse her of being after him for his money. And it had given her ex-husband something to sit up and take notice of! He'd had to take another look at her, through the eyes of another man – a man even more successful than he was in many ways. Sarah had loved showing him that she wasn't on the scrap heap just because he had thrown her aside in favour of a younger, more likely racier, model. Word on the street was he was put out, jealous even. Well, it served him bloody right.

Still, Sarah flung her clothes off angrily. Just what, exactly, did he have to be jealous of? It had been four weeks now, more or less, since James had been asking her out, and although she knew he was embarking on a painful divorce, it really shouldn't stop him from moving their relationship on a bit, particularly in the bedroom. Why was he hesitating? She assessed her naked body in the mirror critically. Didn't he fancy her? Was that it? Wasn't she sexy enough? Alluring enough? Was it because she had already been abandoned by one man? Used goods? A series of debilitating questions began to crawl around her mind – the needy, unanswerable questions of the abandoned wife or lover. *Why me? Why am I not enough?* Beautiful as she was, and the envy of most women who knew her, Sarah de Burgh went to bed lonely yet again and cried herself to sleep.

14

'Bella!' P.J. swung his daughter off her feet as she fought her way through the waiting crowds at Arrivals to meet him.

'Hey, Dad!' she laughed. 'You're looking good.' She was impressed. 'You're half the man I left behind.'

'I wasn't *that* bad,' P.J. protested, taking her case and leading the way out to the car park.

'I know, I'm only teasing. But you *were* out of shape. That trainer of yours must be good, you're looking really fit.'

'And you look as beautiful as ever.' P.J. regarded her proudly. She was beautiful in a natural, unaffected way and was becoming more like her mother every time he saw her. She was tall and slim, and her long, golden blonde hair hung in waves down her back. Her skin was golden too, with a smattering of freckles across her nose and cheeks. Her smile could light up a room. 'How's college?'

'It's great.' She slid into the car while P.J. stowed her case.

'Hope all those Italian men aren't distracting you from your studies?'

'Actually, I've met a very nice English guy, we've been seeing each other for a couple of months now. You'll like him – his name's Tim.'

'Any chance of meeting him?' P.J. raised an eyebrow.

'Sure, I'll bring him home one of these days, or you can always come over for a visit – you could even bring your girlfriend.' She looked at him wickedly.

'What – I – who?' P.J. spluttered.

'It's okay, Dad,' Bella grinned. 'The Wellington Square network has gone into action. There's not a lot those sash windows miss. Actually,' she continued, 'it was Sophia Coleman-Cappabianca who mentioned it. She's in Florence too, you know. We all meet up quite a bit, the Irish crowd. When I was talking to Sheila, she confirmed it.'

'Sheila!' P.J. was shocked.

'Don't worry, Dad, she approves. So do I, by the way. It's time you got out there again, had another female friend. It's what Mum would have wanted, she told me so. And if this friend of yours . . .?'

'Charlotte.'

'If Charlotte is good enough for Sheila, then she must be a very special woman.' Bella looked mischievous.

'She is. I'd like you to meet her, if you want to.'

'Of course I would. I'm looking forward to it.'

'Good.' P.J. was pleasantly surprised.

'But I'm dying to meet my new nephew. How's he doing, little Charlie? Alex is so uncommunicative, and I didn't want to upset Catherine by asking any awkward questions. Tell me everything.'

'He's doing fine, he's a terrific little chap.'

'Oh, that's great, I'm so pleased. Is he . . . will he be all right?'

'He *is* all right! He's fine, he just arrived a little early, gave us all a bit of a fright.'

'But this Von Whatsit?'

'Von Willebrand's. It's not a big deal, really. It's a fairly common, and luckily in Charlie's case, mild bleeding disorder. It often goes undetected, actually. It shouldn't be a problem or restrict his life in any way. Contact sports probably aren't a good idea but apart from that, surgery and dentistry are the only things to be careful with, and the drugs these days pretty much take care of that anyhow.'

'Isn't it an inherited thing?' Bella looked concerned.

'Yes, it is.'

'And?'

'Alex is the carrier, all the tests have confirmed it. Catherine was negative.'

'That means . . .' Bella chewed her lip.

'Yes, sweetheart.' P.J. was sympathetic, seeking to reassure her. 'It means you could be a carrier too. If you want to, we could have the tests done while you're home.'

'Definitely.' Bella looked worried. 'I'd want to know. Might as well find out as soon as I can.'

'It's really nothing to worry about, honestly, and just because one sibling has it doesn't mean another will. Anyway, there's someone else who's dying to see you,' P.J. said, changing the subject. He couldn't bear to see Bella looking so worried.

'Who?'

'Granddad, of course. He's beside himself with excitement. I told him we'd call around tomorrow, if that's okay? Maybe take him out to dinner?'

'That would be lovely, Dad, I'm dying to see him too.' Bella smiled as they pulled into Wellington Square and drove up to number 24, where she leapt out of the car and ran up the steps. She had no sooner reached the top when the door opened and Sheila stood there, in her working outfit of a buttoned overall and a shower cap on her head, which she had recently taken to wearing. Her face was scrubbed and red, as always, but when she set eyes on Bella, it almost cracked in two with smiles. 'Well, well, well,' was all she could say.

'Sheila!' Bella hurled herself at her and threw her arms around her, and Sheila tried to look disapproving.

'Now, that's enough of that. You know I'm not a tactile person,' she said, patting Bella gingerly on the back with her surgical gloves.

'Oh, look!' cried Bella, 'it's Bones, darling Bones! A much slimmer Bones!' And then there was a lot of people tripping over one another as Bones raced to bring Bella as many retrieving gifts as he could find to welcome her back.

'Will you look at that dog,' said Sheila. 'He's got an envelope in his mouth now, he's been at the post tray. It could be something important.' She tried to catch him, but Bones was hurtling about with delight at his beloved family member's return.

'A bill, with any luck,' said P.J., lugging Bella's case inside.

'I have the dinner on,' said Sheila. 'Seven o'clock, on the dot?' She tapped her watch.

'Why seven, Sheila?' P.J. asked innocently.

A look of alarm crossed her face. 'It's always at seven.'

'I know that – I was just checking.' He grinned wickedly at her.

'Pay no attention to him, Sheila, he's winding you up,' said Bella.

'He never does anything else. How you ever became a doctor, I don't know. You should have been a comedian,' she scowled as she retreated to the safety of the kitchen.

'You're appalling,' Bella grinned at him.

'Nonsense. She loves it. Fancy a drink?'

'I'd love one.'

'Good. So would I, and we have exactly twenty-three and a half minutes to enjoy one before dinner.'

'It's good to be home, Dad,' said Bella, giving him a hug.

'Good to have you home, sweetheart.'

Tanya was in the hairdresser's and was so angry she could hardly sit still.

She had walked the long way around, of course, as she had been doing ever since the débâcle, so she would pass Dominic's and might have a chance of running into Dom either going into the restaurant or coming out of his apartment. So far, she had managed to do neither. Occasionally she would sit at the window seat in the small coffee shop across the road and monitor the situation discreetly over a skinny cappuccino. Then, this morning, she had seen *her.*

Tripping out gaily at eight o'clock, practically luminous with delight, from Dom's apartment, Carla had run around the corner and into the restaurant. She was followed a respectable five minutes later (Tanya had waited, and watched) by Dom himself, looking equally chipper. Tanya had thought the cup in her hands was going to break, she was clenching it so tightly. *How could he? How could he?* It was all her fault, of course, the scheming little bitch. Tanya knew she'd been dying to get her claws into Dom the minute Carla had sashayed past her in the restaurant, wiggling that bottom of hers. She had always known she was trouble. *And what was she doing here anyway*? Tanya mused, suddenly intensifying her speculating. There was something odd about it all. Sure, Carla was all New York attitude and Italian gesturing. Rollo adored her and so did Pino – make that most of the staff. But still, there was something about her that didn't add up. She was too cool, way too sure of herself to just be a waitress from the Bronx. All Tanya's instincts were screaming that there was a story there somewhere, and she was going to get to the bottom of it, whatever it was. She sure as hell wasn't going to sit back and let Carla walk off into the sunset with her boyfriend.

Because that's what he was, Tanya reminded herself. Dom was hers – and no one else's. She had ordered him from the universe and the universe had obliged. This awful misunderstanding they had had was merely a test to see how badly Tanya wanted him. She had read about things like this happening. Tanya wasn't giving up – not now. She'd sooner die.

'All right, love?' queried the colourist, looking at her strangely in the mirror.

'What?' Tanya snapped.

'You were miles away. I was just asking have you got any nice holidays planned?'

'Yes,' answered Tanya. 'As a matter of fact, I do. I was just thinking about my honeymoon.'

'I didn't know you were engaged.' Her eyes widened.

'I'm not. Not yet.' Tanya smiled up from her magazine. 'But it's only a matter of time.'

'Yes?' James was more brusque than usual, but he was developing a healthy respect for the phone, particularly since picking it up seemed to elicit some rather intense reactions these days.

'James? John O'Carroll here. Is it a good time? If it's inconvenient I can always call you back later.'

'No, no, not at all,' said James, recognising the brisk voice of his family-law solicitor. 'Go ahead.' He tried to sound pleased to hear from him, but his spirits began to sink.

'Well, James, this is a very unusual situation I find myself in.' There was a long pause.

'I'm all ears, John.'

'You're going to find this hard to believe, James, as I did, but you see, the thing is, you're not really married at all.' Now the pause was audible. 'Hello? James, are you there?'

'Yes, yes, of course I'm here. Would you mind repeating that?'

'You heard me! I could hardly believe it myself, old chap – you must be the luckiest man alive! That marriage ceremony in Rome . . . well, it turns out there's a loophole – a very significant one, actually. You didn't fulfil the residency requirements. The religious ceremony was genuine, of course, but legally, here in Ireland, I'm afraid it doesn't qualify at all.'

'Are you telling me . . .' James was processing every syllable. 'Are you saying that the woman I exchanged vows with, have lived with for thirty years, have had three children with – are you telling me that this . . . this *loophole* gives me an out?'

'Well, I wouldn't say that, exactly, but it sets a precedent, a very interesting precedent, point of law and all that. Of course, we'd have to be careful how we presented it – wouldn't want to come across as callous or opportunistic, but a judge, well, there's no doubt—'

'Don't even think about it.'

'I beg your pardon?'

'I said, don't even think about it.'

'But James, I don't think you understand. You see—'

'I understand perfectly, just as I hope *you* understand and are listening very carefully to me now.'

Silence.

'If you think that I would avail of such a cheap and shoddy blow as to suggest, however justifiably, that my marriage to Cici was in any way, shape or form invalid, then consider yourself off the case. Whatever has transpired – and I don't doubt your team has come up with a valid point – anyone who thinks that I would shirk my responsibilities or make a mockery of a relationship that has been the cornerstone of the better part of my life because of an unfortunate *loophole*, as you put it, is sadly misguided. Clearly you have gathered the wrong impression of what kind of man I am, but let me tell you now: I married my wife – and that is what she is – with every intention known to man, honourable or otherwise. Anything to the contrary that has come to light is an unfortunate, profoundly sad revelation, and one, I most assuredly advise you, not to be used in court, or indeed my case. Do I make myself clear?'

'Absolutely.'

James let out a long breath.

'I imagine this has come as quite a shock.'

'I'm becoming rather accustomed to sudden shocks and revelations, John. I don't know if you can appreciate that.'

'I understand completely. And may I say, your reaction is most refreshing, and there is not a hint of patronisation in that observation. You see, I happen to have an enduring marriage of my own spanning thirty-three years, which I owe, I might add, to a wonderful and, er, challenging woman that I am fortunate enough to call my wife. Contrary to popular opinion, obtaining divorce decrees for my clients gives me little satisfaction, except, of course, where there is real sadness and mutual misery.' He paused significantly. 'Despite the, er, current storm in a teacup, I suspect this is *not* the case between you and your wife. You have been quite articulate on the subject, revealingly so. You might want to consider that – or perhaps even *reconsider* your intentions.'

'I take your point, John, and thank you. But for the moment, consider yourself on the case. I haven't quite dispensed of your services yet, although your observations are uncannily astute,' James couldn't help smiling.

'You're the boss.'

'I still like to think so.'

'I'm here if you need me.'

'Thank you, John, I'll be in touch.'

'Oh, and James?'

'Yes?'

'What I've just told you . . .'

'What of it?'

'Don't dismiss it completely out of hand. It may have its uses, significantly advantageous uses if it were to be, ah, sensitively employed, if you get my drift. Just a little man-to-man advice, you understand? Or should I make that man to *woman*.'

'I hear you.'

'All's fair in love and war – you don't need a lawyer to tell you that, I hope.'

'I imagine this phone call has cost me dearly already,' said James. 'Rest assured, I shall put its content to good use.'

'In that case, I won't detain you any further.'

'Thank you, John, and I mean that.'

'My pleasure. Do let me know how things work out.'

'You'll be the first to know.'

Sensations streamed through her body. Ebbing and flowing, rising and falling, rivulets of exquisite pleasure flooded her senses. As Josh's hands roved freely over her, then inside her, searching, stroking, expertly coaxing her to the brink again and again, Candy thought she would die of pleasure. It was wonderful, it was amazing, it was . . . awfully bright. 'What's with the lights?' she gasped, squinting. 'They're practically blinding me.' She pulled away from him fractionally.

'I like to look at you, baby, you know that,' he mumbled, his mouth fastened on a nipple, eliciting another set of delicious sensations.

'Can't you turn them down? It's like a bloody operating theatre in here.'

'Quit the running commentary, will ya, you're wrecking my buzz.' He entered her swiftly, taking her by surprise.

'Oh . . . oh,' she said.

'I'm not hearing any complaints now,' he said, grinning, as he rolled off her ten minutes later.

'Oh, Josh, baby, you're the best.'

'I keep tellin' ya.'

Candy stretched languorously, basking in her post-orgasmic glow. 'Can we turn the lights out now?' she murmured, snuggling up beside him. The effects of the enormous joint he had given her earlier were kicking in and she was feeling almost comatose, if still giddy.

'Nope, we haven't finished yet.'

'You're insatiable.' She giggled. I can't take any more.'

'You don't have to – it's my turn. Now you get to do the hard work.' He told her in no uncertain terms what he wanted her to do to him.

Candy would rather have just relaxed for a while, but she couldn't help herself. If Josh was issuing the instructions, then

Candy did exactly as she was told. 'And make sure you let me know just how much you enjoy pleasuring me, Miss Rich.'

Candy hated it when he called her that, but she didn't tell him. Her tongue was employed busily and, by all accounts, very effectively elsewhere.

Later, Candy heated up the remnants of last night's Chinese. Josh lounged on the couch, flicking the remote. When she handed him a plate and a bottle of beer and sat down beside him, he looked at her appreciatively. 'You're getting quite good at this,' he grinned. 'I'll make a sex kitten of you yet.'

Candy scowled. 'Quite good' wasn't what she wanted to hear. They watched a Mad Max movie, or rather Josh did while Candy sat quietly beside him. 'Can I stay over, Josh? It's late.'

'Nope. Got an early start.'

'So what?' Candy whined. She hated leaving him, hated the way he turfed her out into the night.

'So, no, you can't stay over.' He kept his eyes fixed on the screen.

'Why not?'

'Because I say so.'

'I don't want to go.' She really didn't. She hated sneaking into her dad's house at all hours, not that he or Shalom seemed to notice, or if they did they didn't comment. She still hadn't told anyone about Josh, not even her girlfriends.

'What you want doesn't work in my world, Miss Rich.'

'Don't call me that – I hate it.' Candy stood up and picked up the plates, fearful suddenly of the tears that threatened. Why was Josh so mean to her sometimes?

'No you don't, you like it – I could call you anything at all and you'd like it. Isn't that so?' His voice was gravelly, his tone suggestive, and worst of all he was right. And he knew it.

'No, it's not so. I hate it.' Candy was petulant, but the

thought of leaving Josh and going out into the cold, windy night made her want to cry.

'Baby.' He got up and pulled her to him, stroking her hair and holding her close. 'You can stay at the weekend, maybe.'

'Promise?'

'I never make promises, baby.'

It was as good as she was going to get. Candy forced herself to smile. It was a straw, a fragile straw, but it was something to cling to.

'Okay,' she said in a small voice.

She was just at the door when he pulled a piece of folded paper from his jeans. 'Sweetheart?'

She looked up, surprised. That was a definite improvement.

'Yeah?'

'Put your name on that for me, would ya?' He grabbed a pen from the table.

'Why? What is it?' she stalled, loath to go, but hating him for letting her.

'I need a second signature. It's just a witness thing, you know, a lease for my landlord.' He smiled lopsidedly at her, making her heart constrict. She would do anything for that smile, for any sign of approval. 'Here.' He handed her the pen and pointed to where her signature was required.

It looked like a normal kind of form, but the print was very small and she couldn't really read it. She knew you should never sign anything without reading it fully, but she was tired, and Josh was smiling at her . . .

'C'mon.' He tapped his foot, irritation a heartbeat away.

She put the paper on the table and leaned over to scrawl her name. Nothing happened. 'It's empty.' She shook the pen and tried again. It was no use.

'Sorry,' she said, and then, because she couldn't resist it, 'you should have let me stay. I have a pen somewhere in my bag, but I don't have time to look for it right now – I'll have to run if I'm to get a cab out there.' She opened the door and stepped into the cold hallway, shivering. 'Bye.'

'Never mind, I'll get someone else to do it for me.' His eyes were cold behind the smile. 'See ya.'

The minute she was outside, she felt desolate. Who would the 'someone else' be? Another girl? One of the models, maybe? She should have done as he asked – and she absolutely shouldn't have made that last parting remark. She had pissed him off. Displeasure had been written all over his gorgeous face.

15

'We need to talk about Candy.'

'I was just about to ring you with that very suggestion,' Charlotte said grimly at her end of the phone. 'I take it she's still with you. I haven't heard from her in over a week. If I'm lucky I get the odd text message.'

Charlotte was seriously worried. She had left at least ten messages on Candy's phone and even several with a woman who said she was Shalom's mother when she had rung Ossie's house. Now she wondered if they had even been passed on to Candy.

'In a manner of speaking.' Ossie sounded tired. 'She comes and goes whenever she pleases. In the beginning it was all right, but now I'm pretty sure there's a guy involved.'

'Who?' Charlotte felt her anxiety rising. She'd let Ossie take care of their daughter and look what was happening.

'I have no idea. She tells me she's staying with a friend.'

'A friend! Who?' demanded Charlotte. 'Ossie, she's twenty years old, she's never lived away from home. Her best friends haven't seen her either – I rang both Katy and Emma's mothers yesterday. What the hell is going on?'

'Don't tear strips off me, Charlotte,' Ossie said defensively. 'I'm as concerned as you are. She was here last night, but not every night.'

'We'll have to sort this out.'

'Are you up to lunch? I'm free today, or whenever suits you.'

'Today's fine. You can come here. I'll see you at one?'

'If it wasn't because our only daughter is causing such havoc, I'd say it would be a pleasure,' Ossie sighed, trying to make light of things.

Candy was proving a force to be reckoned with. And how, he grimaced, was he going to tell Charlotte about Candy's boob job? She would have a fit. He paled at the thought. He hadn't noticed it himself, not until Shalom had taken him aside and pointed it out. Then, when he had looked properly, he wondered how he could possibly have missed it. But then, it wasn't exactly as if he was supposed to scrutinise his own daughter's figure, was it? When he had confronted her about it (he had tried to get Shalom to talk to her – he was embarrassed to – but she was having none of it), Candy had been quite snotty.

'So what if I have?' she had said nonchalantly. 'There's nothing wrong with a bit of self-improvement.'

'Did you discuss it with Mum?' He fervently hoped she had.

She sighed, exasperated. 'No, I didn't. I'm over eighteen, Dad, I don't *actually* have to discuss anything with you *or* Mum. I bet Shalom didn't discuss it with anyone when she had *her* boobs done – unless, of course, it was after she met you.' She had let the comment hang in the air accusingly.

Ossie had been furious but had kept his mouth shut. The conversation was heading for dangerous territory and he wasn't going to go there.

'I'll see you at one.' Charlotte put the phone down and tried to take deep breaths.

Ossie had sounded weary. Well, it was hardly surprising. What did he expect? He had spoiled Candy beyond all reckoning and now he, or rather they, were paying the price. And whatever was going on, Candy clearly had the bit between her teeth. The more she thought about it, the more furious she became with Ossie. But then, she hadn't exactly tried to stop him from spoiling Candy, had she?

Charlotte suddenly felt terribly defeated. There was no point attacking Ossie. It wouldn't get her anywhere. She would make a nice lunch for them both, then hopefully they could work this thing out.

Opening the fridge, she had a good look at the contents. There wasn't an awful lot of food, but there was a nice bottle of Sancerre chilling. She would pop out to her local deli to pick up some treats and some nice fresh bread. They would have . . . what did P.J. call it? An indoor picnic. Thinking of him, Charlotte smiled. He made her laugh. And that wasn't all he made her do. He made her feel sexy, desirable, almost wanton. He was a fantastic lover. When she was in bed with him, she became someone else entirely, and they had been spending more and more time there . . .

More importantly, he seemed to be a fantastic father. Suddenly, she wished she could talk to him about all this instead of Ossie. P.J. would know what to do.

It was about three o'clock that day when Jennifer spied P.J. walking across the road heading for number 42 with a large parcel under his arm. She pulled up in her ancient Mini Clubman and wound down her window. 'Hello, P.J., what have you got there?'

'Oh, hello, Jennifer, didn't see you. I was miles away,' P.J. grinned at her. 'It's a fine brace of pheasant a patient of mine gave to me. I've finished up early today. Bella, my daughter, is home for a few days. I was wondering if Charlotte would like them.'

'She'd love them!' Jennifer said immediately.

'Shall I give them to you to give to her?'

'No, give them to her yourself, she'll be delighted to see you. Why don't you come in now for a cup of coffee?' Jennifer nodded towards the front door before turning her car into the driveway, pulling up beside the large silver Bentley that was parked at the bottom of the steps. P.J. followed her on foot and waited as she got out of the car.

'How's the hip?' he asked.

'Super. I feel like a youngster,' she laughed.

'Let me,' he said, insisting on taking out and carrying the bags of groceries she had bought. 'Er, Jennifer,' P.J. rubbed his chin, 'I'm not sure I should come in. Charlotte appears to have company.' He nodded at the Bentley. 'Nice car.'

'Yes, it is rather. Shame about the plonker who drives it, though.' She grinned evilly. There was no need, Jennifer thought, to mention it was *Ossie's* Bentley. P.J. would find that out for himself in just a minute. In fact, it was a perfect opportunity, she reflected: nothing like two men meeting up over a mutual woman to spur on a bit of action. Jennifer was pretty sure Ossie still had feelings for Charlotte, and though she was fond of him in her own way, despite his appalling behaviour on the marital front, she felt that Charlotte was still too much under his influence. She needed to see him up against a real man – a man like P.J., Jennifer thought astutely. And it wouldn't do P.J. any harm either to see that Ossie was still hovering in the vicinity. Men were proprietorial creatures when it came to the women in their life – nothing like a bit of competition to make the chase more interesting – and Jennifer was very definite about who she wanted to win.

'Look, I really don't think—'

'Nonsense, she'd love to see you.' She looked at him meaningfully. 'We'll be arriving just in time, I'd bet my last dollar on it.'

'Well, if you're sure.' P.J. followed her first into her own flat in the basement, where he left the parcels, and then, still carrying the pheasant, followed Jennifer upstairs. Without pausing to knock, Jennifer walked into Charlotte's kitchen, where she was greeted with varying degrees of surprise.

'Mummy!' said Charlotte.

'Hello, Jennifer,' said Ossie, standing up to greet her.

'Hello you two.' Jennifer was smiling broadly. 'I've brought a visitor.' She indicated P.J., who had followed her in and was now standing rather awkwardly with his gift.

'Sorry to barge in. I thought you might like these, Charlotte, and then I ran into your mother. P.J. O' Sullivan,' he held out his hand to Ossie by way of introduction, who shook it firmly.

'Oh, how silly of me.' Charlotte sounded flustered. 'Ossie, this is P.J. O'Sullivan, you know, the doctor who lives across the road. And this is Ossie,' she said to P.J. 'My, er, my . . .'

'Her ex-husband,' Jennifer finished for her. 'Now that we've got the introductions out of the way, any chance of a cup of coffee?'

'Of course, I'll just make another pot.' Charlotte jumped up, glad to busy herself with the task. 'Please, sit down.' She indicated a chair to P.J., who was eyeing the remains of the very nice lunch and the bottle of Sancerre. 'I really don't think I should.'

'Nonsense,' said Jennifer. 'Tell him, Charlotte – we're not interrupting anything, are we?'

'Of course not.' Ossie seemed uncomfortable. 'Actually, I was just about to leave.'

'You'll do no such thing,' Jennifer insisted. 'At least have a cup of coffee with us before running off.' She managed to make it sound as if he was a naughty schoolboy.

'I didn't mean to imply I was running off.'

'Then sit down,' Jennifer smiled.

So they did. Charlotte poured some fresh coffee and handed around some homemade brownies and everyone made particularly polite conversation.

It was P.J. who eventually made the move. 'I really must go. My daughter is home on a visit and I have to be getting back. Thank you for the coffee, Charlotte.' He stood up to go. 'Good to meet you, Ossie.'

'Yes, yes,' Ossie said heartily. 'Very good to meet you too!' He thought he managed to hide his surprise very well, considering. First Charlotte was being unreasonably angry with him about Candy's behaviour and now this handsome doctor chap breezing in . . .

'Do bring Bella over before she goes back,' said Jennifer. 'We'd love to meet her – wouldn't we, Charlotte?'

'Yes, of course,' agreed Charlotte, 'but I'm sure she has a very full social calendar, Mummy. She won't want to be meeting old fogies like us.'

'Actually,' P.J. turned and looked at Charlotte from the door, 'Bella is really looking forward to meeting you.'

'Oh – well.' Charlotte was taken aback. 'That's great. I – we'd love to meet her too.'

'We'll sort out the details later.' Jennifer was sitting at the table, looking very pleased with herself.

As Charlotte saw P.J. out, Jennifer proclaimed to nobody in particular, 'He's a thoroughly nice chap, that doctor. *Thoroughly* nice. Very handsome, too, and doesn't know it either. They're the best sort.'

'He certainly seems like a nice bloke,' Ossie said. 'Widower, isn't he?'

'Yes. Lost his wife five years ago to cancer – dreadful business. Lives all on his own in that big place across the road. Very sad.'

'I remember her, now that you mention it. Blonde girl, stunning-looking. That *is* sad,' Ossie said.

Why had she done that? Charlotte banged about the kitchen in a manner most unlike her, throwing things into the dish-washer and swiping a cloth over the counter surfaces with unnecessary vehemence. Why, when she had been having an important discussion with Ossie about Candy, had Jennifer decided to roll into the kitchen accompanied by P.J. of all people? The whole thing had been excruciatingly awkward for them all – apart from Jennifer, of course, who had seemed to find it all thoroughly amusing. She had disappeared swiftly afterwards, anticipating her daughter's wrath, and was hiding out downstairs in her flat, having a little 'lie-down', as she called it.

Ossie had looked tired when he came in. They had begun as they intended, talking about Candice, agreeing that her behaviour of late had become quite unacceptable and that, as Jennifer and others had quite rightly pointed out, she was turning into a little monster.

'I don't know what to do, Charlotte,' Ossie had said, despair flitting across his face. 'She's a force to be reckoned with. I don't know where she gets it from.'

'She's like you,' Charlotte smiled ruefully, 'a chip off the old block. And she adores you. I think she's just trying to get your attention.'

'But she's always had my attention.' He seemed bewildered.

'I know that.' Charlotte took a deep breath. She would have to tread carefully here. 'But fathers and daughters have a special relationship. I'm afraid we spoiled her dreadfully, Ossie.' She looked up at him from those enormous brown eyes. 'And it's got to stop. That, and the fact that she seems determined to do whatever it takes to keep winning your attention. Take her recent, um, makeover.'

'She looks like a tart!' Ossie spoke with feeling, failing to realise the irony. 'I got an awful shock. She's ruined herself, her lovely hair, and all that awful make-up.'

Charlotte said nothing.

'Don't *you* think she looks awful?' he asked, looking concerned.

'Well, yes,' Charlotte said, biting her lip. She had refrained from screaming, *can't you see she's turning herself into the spitting image of your plastic slapper of a girlfriend? That's who she's imitating, for God's sake – that's how badly she's trying to get your attention.* Instead, she said, 'Have you tried talking to her about it? She won't listen to me or Jennifer, told us we're living in the Dark Ages.'

'I did think about it, but when I mentioned it to Shalom, she said that all girls that age are really into the make-up and hair thing.'

Charlotte fought to keep her mouth shut, but because she couldn't, *wouldn't*, remain mute on the subject, said, 'I imagine it's much easier to watch when it isn't actually your *own* daughter you're talking about.'

Ossie looked at her for a long moment, then nodded. 'You're right, of course,' he said miserably. And then, steeling himself, he told her. 'There's something else.'

'Oh God, what?' Charlotte held her breath.

'She's had a boob job.'

'What?' Charlotte gasped. 'When?'

'Ten days ago, apparently. I didn't notice, not at first. It was, er, Shalom who pointed it out. She was wearing a lot of baggy jumpers and stuff, and, well . . .' He paused, looking at the horrified expression on her face.

Charlotte put her face in her hands. 'I don't believe this,' was all she could say. 'How could you let this happen?'

'She *is* nearly twenty-one. She's not a child,' he said gently.

'I suppose you paid for that too.'

'I knew nothing about it.' Ossie looked hurt.

'No, of course you wouldn't.'

'Charlotte, that's not fair.'

'My girl was perfectly beautiful just the way she was. Poor, poor Candy,' she whispered, shaking her head. 'What next?'

Ossie looked even more uncomfortable. He had no idea what to say.

Charlotte got up to clear some dishes away. She couldn't look at him. She was afraid of what else she might say.

When she sat down again, Ossie had tried to reassure her, but it was too late. He could already see the tears she had tried to wipe away.

He had taken her hand then. 'Charlotte?'

She had swallowed, her throat constricting.

'It's not that bad, really. It's probably just a phase.'

'She's craving male attention, Ossie,' Charlotte said. 'That's a phase that can go on for a long time, with disastrous consequences for a girl – *our* girl,' she added miserably.

'I'm sorry, Charlotte, so sorry for everything. Truly, I am.' Ossie sounded equally miserable. 'I don't think I ever told you . . . that is, I don't think I ever said how much I appreciate your handling of all this, since I left. It must have been hard for you. I often think about that, and I just wanted to say I think you're pretty amazing.'

She got up then, quickly, and turned on the kettle, unsure suddenly, her normal composure deserting her yet again. 'I'm not amazing,' she heard herself saying. 'If you must know, I cried myself to sleep that night, and for a great many nights after that. I just had to keep things together for Candy, and now I wonder why. It doesn't seem to have done any good. Sometimes I think she hates me, blames me for everything. Maybe she's right.'

'Don't say that. You *are* amazing, you've always been amazing. I always knew you were too good for me, but I had hoped Candy would take after *you*, be lovely and gentle and feminine and, well, you know, posh, I suppose. And instead she has to go and take after me.' He looked wretched. 'You're right, she *is* a chip off the old block, God help her!'

And suddenly, looking at the expression on his face, Charlotte had begun to laugh. They laughed and laughed and then suddenly, hearing the drone of the chair lift, pulled themselves together as Jennifer had appeared in the doorway – followed, unthinkably, by P.J.

Charlotte had hardly been able to believe it. Of all the worst possible timing. Why had Jennifer chosen that moment to invite P.J. in? Even she couldn't be that oblivious to the sensitivities of the situation, but she certainly had appeared to be. It hadn't taken a feather out of her, and in fact she seemed to have enjoyed the whole encounter tremendously, while she, Charlotte, had cringed through it, the collective awkwardness of herself and both men almost palpable in the room.

And P.J.! Poor P.J. had looked as if he would rather be anywhere else than there. She had seen him as his eyes roved over the table, taking in the remains of the lunch and indeed the empty bottle of Sancerre that she had quickly cleared away, how he had stood looking supremely uncomfortable with his gift of the pheasant until Jennifer had relieved him of them and told him to sit down.

Ossie had looked equally uncomfortable and suddenly quite guilty, as if he were a naughty schoolboy caught playing truant, and all the while they chatted about ridiculous things like the weather and even the Lisbon Treaty while Jennifer sat back, looking delighted with herself. Thankfully P.J. had put an end to the embarrassing torment by getting up to leave. She had felt dreadful then, afraid that he would read the wrong thing into her and Ossie's meeting and that she would never see him again. But then he had said that his daughter was looking forward to meeting her, and she'd been almost speechless with surprise and delight. That must mean he had spoken to Bella about her, that she mattered to him. It must mean— *Oh, stop it!* Charlotte told herself. She was becoming ridiculous, worse than a teenager, going over every word and trying to decipher every hidden meaning behind perfectly normal conversations. It was just that when she had seen the look on P.J.'s face, the sudden uncertainty that had flitted across it before he could hide it, her heart had constricted. She couldn't bear for him to be hurt or upset. He was the one person in the world who had been kind to her and she was having such fun being with him. She couldn't have survived what she was going through these past few weeks without him.

And Ossie had certainly noticed it. Before P.J., she would have found the meeting with Ossie intimidating and depressing. She would have felt inadequate and been distraught at the thought of Shalom and their baby on the way. Instead, she had been able to be strong and confront Ossie. Or was that a bad sign? Was she being a bad mother? She had tried, she really had, in every possible way, but now maybe it was time for Ossie to take more of a fatherly responsibility than he had done to date. There was more to being a father than just doling out unlimited amounts of money – and that had been Ossie's solution to everything. As far as she was concerned, there was nothing more she could do except be there for Candy if or when she needed her.

She wondered when, or indeed if, she would hear from P.J. Should she ring him and apologise? But for what? What could she say? *I'm sorry you walked in on me and my ex-husband having lunch*? She would look pathetic. But what if he didn't ring? What if seeing her and Ossie together had put him off, given him the wrong impression? What if she never heard from him again? Charlotte put her face in her hands. She couldn't bear it. What a mess, what a stupid, stupid mess, and it was all Jennifer's fault!

'It's always much worse first thing in the morning,' the glamorous thirty-something career woman was saying. 'Particularly, funnily enough, on a Monday morning. On a Friday, I hardly have any symptoms at all. Why do you think that might be? Doctor? Are you listening to me?'

'Yes, yes, of course I'm listening, I was just thinking about what you were saying, running a few ideas through my head.' P.J. was brought back to earth with a bang. These were the kind of patients he found it the hardest to sit through. They weren't really sick at all – not in the conventional sense – just self-obsessed and wanting to go over every minute detail of their mostly imagined symptoms with a professional that they would listen to and then disregard if the forthcoming diagnosis wasn't pleasing.

The woman in question was as healthy as an ox. She had

decided she was depressed in the wake of yet another relationship break-up and, in this instance, a run-in with her boss. P.J. sympathised greatly with both parties. He'd bet she was a nightmare to work with or live with. Now, she was suggesting a course of anti-depressants, which he had put her on several times before, and P.J. was almost ready to write her the prescription just to get rid of her, but he stuck to his guns. Anti-depressants had a real and positive place in modern mental-health issues, but they were not medicinal sweeties to be handed out on demand, and certainly not in a case such as this, where they would merely be masking and prolonging a personality problem that would have to be dealt with sooner or later.

'I'm prescribing a course of CBT.' He wrote the details down and handed them to her.

'CBT? I haven't heard of those before.' She looked pleased. 'Are they new?'

'CBT stands for cognitive behavioural therapy, which is what I think you need, not anti-depressants. We've tried them before and they haven't made much difference, have they?'

'But I—'

'We're talking about a behaviour pattern here, Lisa, not a depression. That's why you'll find CBT very helpful. I've referred you to a therapist who is an excellent practitioner. I'd like you to make an appointment as soon as possible.'

'I'm not sure I think—'

'I'm telling you what *I* think, Lisa. That's what you pay me for, for my professional opinion, and that's what you've got. Now, if you don't mind, I have a lot of very sick people out there waiting to see me.'

'Well, really!' Lisa slung her designer bag over her shoulder. 'So much for bedside manner. You're just like all the rest of them, can't take our money quickly enough and then want to write us off! You won't be seeing me again, Doctor!' She flounced out of the office.

P.J. sighed. He hadn't meant to be sharp with her, but

sometimes you had to be cruel to be kind. He certainly wasn't doing her any favours encouraging her to believe her own interpretation of the matter. The girl needed therapy, it was as plain as the nose on her face, and all he could do was point her in the right direction.

He was interrupted by Sheila, carrying in a cup of tea and a muffin. 'You've a twenty-minute break,' she said triumphantly. 'Mr O'Riordan cancelled and Mrs Clancy isn't due in until twenty past, so make the most of it.'

'Thank you, Sheila, that muffin looks good.'

'Maggie O'Neill left a bag of them in. I have the rest up in the house.'

'That was kind of her.'

'I doubt kindness had anything to do with it – she's just trying to outdo my recipe,' Sheila sniffed. 'But I said I'd give you one.' She stood, waiting for the verdict.

P.J. bit in dutifully. 'It's excellent, Sheila, really excellent, but, between ourselves, not a patch on your own.'

'I thought as much.'

P.J. shook his head as she returned to the surgery. What was a little white lie when every patient between now and closing up would benefit from the beatific happiness that Sheila would radiate? Satisfied he had at least performed one good deed for the day, he set about enjoying one of the most delicious muffins he had ever tasted. It wasn't that Sheila's muffins weren't good – they were – or rather, they had been. But since she had taken to wearing those surgical gloves, all her muffins had begun to taste of rubber. It was just that neither he, nor anyone else, had the heart to tell her.

Telling, or indeed withholding, the truth, P.J. reflected, was one of life's great dilemmas. Speaking of which, it had come as a surprise to him just how rattled he'd been to see Charlotte with her ex-husband, having what had patently been a very cosy lunch until they'd been interrupted. It wasn't that he disliked the fellow – Ossie had been perfectly pleasant – he just would rather not have met him, and certainly not under those circumstances. P.J. tried to examine his feelings. Charlotte and her ex-husband were as entitled as anybody to have whatever relationship they chose with one another, and of course they had a daughter, and P.J. knew more than most people just how big a tie family was. People could say what they liked, but the old saying held true: blood is thicker than water, and rightly so.

No, P.J. didn't begrudge Charlotte her relationship with Ossie, such as it may be. It was just that he was pretty sure Ossie hadn't been thrilled to see *him*. Oh, of course he'd been polite, friendly even, a nice bloke, but P.J. had picked up immediately on the distinctly speculative evaluation Ossie had directed towards him. It was a man-to-man thing, suitor assessing suitor. And that was it – that was what had been niggling him, he realised. He had assumed, rightly or wrongly, that Charlotte and Ossie were over, ancient history. Charlotte had told him as much and P.J. had no reason to doubt her, but he had seen with his own eyes that Ossie quite clearly still had feelings for Charlotte, and he hadn't looked at all happy at meeting P.J., or indeed at hearing any of the references Jennifer had made (which had been plentiful) to his relationship with Charlotte.

The whole incident had been very ill timed, really. It was an awful pity he had run into Jennifer the way he had. Otherwise the unfortunate meeting would never have happened at all and he wouldn't be feeling so . . . what was he feeling? Perturbed? Perplexed? Uncomfortable? Yes, but there was something else, something more annoying. P.J. scowled. He was jealous. That was it, pure and simple. He was having a very bad case of the green-eyed monster, and as far as he knew there was really no cure for it. He wouldn't think about it now. It was ridiculous – at his age! What was he even thinking of?

Anyway, he reminded himself briskly, he had his own family

to be concerned about. There was Bella, for instance. She was looking forward to meeting Charlotte, she had told him so, but now he wondered about it. When Jennifer had suggested bringing her over, Charlotte had seemed to pooh-pooh the idea of meeting her, although when he had said that Bella was hoping to meet her (he had watched Ossie's reaction to that too), she seemed to be pleased. To tell the truth, she had seemed a little on edge herself. He hoped Ossie hadn't done anything to upset her. Charlotte had been through enough on that front already.

He wondered what he should do. Should he just tell Bella that Charlotte was busy, or should he suggest a dinner maybe? Either way, he would have to talk to Bella. The tests had come back, and thankfully Bella was clear – she wasn't a carrier of Von Willebrand's. P.J. had hoped as much. Interestingly enough, his own test had also come back negative, which meant he wasn't a carrier either. It could mean a number of things, but Jilly, bless her, was not there to confirm matters, or indeed be tested herself. She must have been a carrier, or else . . .

P.J. forced himself to focus on the facts in hand. What mattered was that Alex had the disorder, and his new baby Charlie too. That the rest of the family was clear was a blessing. He would talk to Bella about it this evening. She would be relieved.

And then they would have to talk about Alex.

Ossie slammed his fist on the horn. 'Look where you're bloody going, mate!' he shouted out the window of his Bentley at the guy who had sauntered across the road without looking, daring any motorist to so much as touch him.

'Look out yourself!' the guy yelled back. 'What's your problem? You're just another prick in a fancy car.' He gave him the finger for good measure.

Ossie forced himself to take a few slow breaths. He shouldn't let it get to him, but recently he was feeling increasingly under pressure, though just why, he wasn't sure. Business was tough, of course; times were tough for everyone in property, but he was still holding up, although no one could take anything for granted in the current crash. It was all uncharted waters at the moment. He truly felt for the others, the first-timers particularly, young chaps who had ventured into the market at the worst possible time, some of them up to their necks in debt. And the financial situation was dire. Still, at least that was something he could handle. His domestic situation was quite a different kettle of fish, and one which he increasingly felt less and less able to cope with.

Candy taking up residence had changed everything. Initially he'd been happy to have her stay while she took some time out and decided what she wanted to do with her life. She had dropped out of university last year where she had begun to study drama and literature and pronounced it boring. From there, she had said she wanted to pursue a career in acting, and decided a modelling course wouldn't be a bad idea to start off with. That had proved futile, and the acting career didn't seem to be materialising either, although Candy assured her father that these things took time. Time indeed, and as it turned out, a lot of it spent on his payroll. Ossie didn't even like to think about how much he had coughed up on Candy in the past couple of months. He would have to take her to task and stop her allowance, even though it upset him to have to even think about that. She would have to learn the hard way, as everyone did eventually, that she either supported herself or got back into some kind of educational system that would provide a career at the end of it. And her behaviour of late was becoming increasingly worrying.

He and Charlotte had gone over the various possibilities of what might happen, the most likely scenario being Candy being pursued by someone entirely unsuitable for her, after her, or rather her father's, money. And what if she were to marry such an unscrupulous sort? Children and an objectionable son-in-law to support indefinitely . . . it didn't bear thinking about.

Shalom was also beginning to get fed up with having Candy around and made her feelings felt on the subject. 'She's big and bold enough to get a job of her own and be paying for her own place. I was at her age,' she said.

She was becoming increasingly moody with him and incessantly reminding everybody of the imminent birth of the baby in six weeks' time. Her mother, Bernie, seemed to be visiting more and more lately. Initially Ossie had been unperturbed about this, thinking it was good that Shalom had some company and someone she could talk things over with, but increasingly Ossie was coming down to find Bernie bustling about in the kitchen first thing in the morning, when he wanted some breakfast – in peace and quiet. Listening to Bernie's shrill train of chatter and whizzing blenders of smoothies were beginning to do his head in. Shalom had even begun referring to one of the many spare bedrooms in the west wing as 'Mummy's room', and Bernie seemed to be spending more and more time in it. Why only last week he had turned away a delivery van of some ridiculous instrument only to learn from a highly indignant Shalom that Mummy's sun bed was taking up too much space in her house and she, Shalom, had told her she could keep it here for as long as she wanted. Ossie sighed. He would have paid quite an obscene amount of money to send both mother and daughter away – quite far away, actually – to get the real thing.

And then there had been that lunch with Charlotte last week. He'd been quite nervous about the whole thing, and not just about Candy. He had pulled into the driveway, parked his car and walked up the steps, just as he used to do, and had been welcomed by Charlotte, looking (he had to admit he had been taken aback) absolutely stunning in a pair of skinny denim jeans tucked into dark brown soft suede knee-high boots. Her hair hung about her shoulders in a dark cloud, and her face, her skin . . . she looked lit up from inside. Radiant. Younger too, somehow, and much more carefree. It had taken his breath away.

She had put on a really lovely lunch and they had tackled the matter of their wayward daughter. When he told her about Candy's boob job, she'd been terribly upset, as he'd known she would be. But she had been quite tough on him, he felt, unfairly so, as if the whole thing had been *his* fault. But then they'd begun to laugh, really laugh, about something silly, and he had looked at her, laughing, tears of mirth pouring down her face, and he'd wanted to leap across the table and take her in his arms. It was as if the past twenty years had been wiped away, all the tragedy, all the hurt – and then Jennifer had come in. Unannounced, of course, accompanied by that doctor chap. Handsome bloke.

It had spoiled everything. Oh, they had all sat down on Jennifer's instructions and had coffee and made small talk, but the mood had been broken. P.J., or whatever he called himself, had come over on the pretext of bringing a brace of pheasant to Charlotte (who on earth brought a brace of pheasant as a gift these days?). Ossie sighed – he'd never understand their lot. Posh people really were a law unto themselves, no matter how much money you had. Clearly he'd become quite a friend, maybe more.

Ossie scowled. He had said something about introducing Charlotte to his daughter; Ossie had picked that up right away. It had been said for his benefit, of course. Typical male behaviour, trying to stake out his territory. But what of it? Charlotte was entitled to entertain whomever she pleased in her house. There was clearly something going on between them, or if not, the doctor very much wanted there to be. Any fool could see that.

Ossie pulled into the impressive gates of Windsor Hall and

continued up the long gravelled driveway. He was in a bad mood, that was all. Who could blame him? Life got you down sometimes, that was all there was to it. Or was there? He certainly would pay no attention to the ridiculous voice that whispered in his head that he was jealous. He'd been the one to leave his marriage, hadn't he? All the same . . .

He saw Candy's BMW parked outside. That was good. She was home for a change. He remembered her mentioning something about that doctor and a concert he had brought Charlotte and her to. He would ask her casually about him and her mum. Very casually.

'Candy? Where are you?' Ossie called up from the huge square hall, his footsteps echoing on the boldly patterned Italian tiles.

Candy scowled. She was hiding out in her bedroom and hated being disturbed, especially now. It had been exactly a week since she had heard from Josh – or rather, not heard from him – and the silence was excruciating. Anything would have been better. If he had bawled her out, yelled at her, even if he had hit her she wouldn't have cared, but to leave her like this, to withdraw from her totally . . . she couldn't bear it. And he hadn't returned or even acknowledged a single one of her increasingly desperate and desolate text messages or voice messages, pleading with him, begging him to tell her what was wrong. She had cried for three whole days and nights, and now there were no more tears left, just the cold, empty, terrifying abyss she was looking into that would be a life without Josh. She wouldn't even contemplate it – couldn't. One day at a time, she kept reminding herself, just get through today. He'll ring tomorrow.

And now, just when she needed it like a hole in her head, her stupid dad was hollering for her. What the hell did he want now? Why couldn't they just leave her alone? Her mother had been hounding her with messages, and every time she had thought it would be Josh. She'd better go down, otherwise he might come up looking for her, to her room, where even he would notice something was up. Her room looked like a bomb had hit it. Clothes had been discarded all over the place and there were so many used tissues on the floor it looked like there was a carpet of snow. She pulled on some jeans, quickly ran into the bathroom and splashed some cold water on her face, rubbed in some foundation and concealer and hoped for the best.

Downstairs, she found Ossie in the kitchen. 'Hi, Daddy,' she said, heading for the fridge to get a drink.

'Hi, Princess, I was wondering where you were. What are you up to?'

'I've got the flu, I'm staying in bed. Don't come too close, I wouldn't want to give it to you.'

'Should we call the doctor?'

'No, I'll be fine, I'm just feeling horrible. If I don't feel better in a couple of days, I'll go to the doctor then.' She pulled out a snipe of champagne and held it towards him. 'Open this for me, would you?'

'Champagne? When you've got the flu?' Even Ossie looked taken aback. Candy didn't care.

'Well, you know what they say, drink plenty of fluids.' If she had her way, and she fully intended to, she would get completely smashed in the privacy of her own bedroom before the night was through.

Ossie raised an eyebrow but pulled the cork effortlessly. 'Well, go easy on it. Oh,' he paused, rifling through some papers on the countertop. 'Speaking of doctors, was it P.J. O'Sullivan who brought you and your pals to the concert with Mum a while back?'

'Yeah. Why?' Candy's antennae were up and she held her breath. Did he know about Josh? Was that what was coming next?

'Oh, nothing, just wondering. He's a neighbour of ours, that's all. Well, you know, in the old . . . in Mum's house.'

Candy looked at him strangely. 'If he's a neighbour, he's a very friendly one,' she said, taking a sip of her champagne. 'He might as well live in the place for all the time he spends in his own house.' There, that should shift any unwelcome scrutiny of her own social life at the moment. She watched as Ossie's face remained inscrutable. 'I wouldn't mind, but he brings the bloody dog too. That's part of the reason I moved out, actually.' Now she had his attention.

'Really? Well, it's nice Mum has a friend.'

Candy snorted. 'I'd say "friend" is a bit of an understatement. But yeah, she has every right to have a boyfriend – surprising it took her so long, actually.' And with that she retreated upstairs to her sanctuary of grief, where once she was behind closed doors she threw herself on the bed and feverishly examined her phone for signs of life. Seeing none, she took another gulp of champagne, swallowing the bitter, fizzing liquid. It made a change from the taste of her tears.

Suddenly she could bear it no longer. She would go to him. If she could only see him and talk to him, everything would be fine, she knew it would. She would make sure she looked great – it wouldn't take too long, just an hour or two – and then she'd drive into town and call around to Josh's flat. She didn't care who or what she found there, as long as she could talk to him.

Ossie closeted himself in his office. There was still an hour or two to go before dinner, and he really didn't want to be disturbed. There was no sign of Shalom and, better still, none of Bernie. They were probably out somewhere together.

So Charlotte and this doctor were clearly an item then. Well, what of it? It was all perfectly respectable. He was a widower and she was a – a divorcee. Why was that so hard to say? *Because you still think of her as your wife*, said the small voice in his head. And it was true, he reflected, he did. He couldn't help it; Charlotte would always be his wife. She was the one he had pursued, had exchanged vows with. How had it all gone so wrong? Did he still have feelings for her? *Of course*, was the answer to that. But was it possible that he was still in love with her? But that would mean . . . no, he would not follow this ridiculous train of thought. He was happy, happy with Shalom and a new baby on the way. Because if he wasn't . . . Oh, God. Ossie shook his head. This was the way to madness.

To distract himself, he booted up his computer and decided to run through his emails, anything to take his mind off the women in his life. There wasn't much; everything went to his head office for his secretary to screen. If anything urgent needed his attention when he was away from the office, then she alerted him. There were a couple from a few mates, a better than usual joke and one from his brother in Australia, asking when he was making an honest woman of Shalom. And then he noticed it. Marked urgent, with a red flag attached, was one from his secretary. That was strange – usually she called him if there was anything urgent. Then he remembered he'd put his phone on silent since the last meeting he'd had in town. Looking at it, there were five missed calls from her and several messages. He clicked on the email and simultaneously dialled his voicemail. Both messages began with varying degrees of urgency. 'Ossie, ring me the minute you get this,' said the voice message.

'Tried ringing, your phone's turned off. You need to see this,' the email said. Putting his phone down, Ossie scrolled down the email, which was from an unidentified address. It read simply: *Take a look at this, Mr Keating, and let me know what it's worth NOT to see your daughter having sex on the Internet.*

With a creeping feeling of dread mingled with disbelief, Ossie clicked on the attached mpeg. Before his eyes, the screen came to life and he watched three quick takes of a couple indulging in various sexual positions and activities, clearly just a sample of what was on offer in the full version. He had never laid eyes on the man, but there was no mistaking the young woman. He'd have known her anywhere. Quickly he shut the offending clip down then, feeling so angry he thought his head was going to explode, he strode out of his office into the hall. He didn't hear or seem to notice the front door open while Shalom and Bernie came in loaded with shopping bags. Ignoring them completely, he broke into a run, and taking the stairs three at a time, let out a roar of such magnitude that Shalom dropped her new D&G handbag and Bernie had to put her hands over her ears.

'*Candice*!' was the word that reverberated off the walls.

16

Cici couldn't remember when she last ate – for the past two weeks the thought of food revolted her. She hadn't been dressing either, not in the proper sense, and as for make-up, why bother? Why paint a pretty face on the outside when inside she felt beyond ugly? Where had it all got her? What was the point? Much easier to slip into her cashmere lounging suit, which then gave way to a succession of sweatpants and tops, and finally just her towel robe. Then the effort of putting on even that seemed pointless and she had just stayed in bed, venturing forth only to make an occasional cup of coffee. Her world had come to an end, so why pretend that life could be in any way normal? She had had a perfectly wonderful one, a marriage and a family, and she had screwed it all up royally. And now she was paying the price. Now she was being discarded by possibly the most loving, supportive (and now sought-after) husband that had ever existed. How could she have been so monumentally stupid? How could she have let her pathetic vanity, her ridiculous insecurities, her lack of conscience, destroy everything she held so dear? It had been sheer insanity. Now no one cared if she were alive or dead, least of all herself.

When her phone rang, she barely bothered to pick it up, particularly since Harry was still leaving the occasional nasty text message and voicemail, probably, Cici speculated correctly, under the influence of alcohol. Then, squinting over the sheets, she saw it was James. Lunging for the mobile, she tried to sound upbeat.

'Hello?' she said.

'Hello, Cici, it's me.' The voice was brusque, but it still belonged to him, that sorely missed and dearly beloved voice.

'James. How are you?'

'I'm well, thank you. I'll come straight to the point, Cici.'

Oh please, don't, she begged him silently. *No more points, no more clipped, punctuated finalities. Please, let's talk about anything else.*

'I assume you've received my, er, solicitor's instructions?'

'Yes, yes I did.' She managed to articulate the words and sound normal, when she really wanted to scream.

'Good. Well, there's something I need to talk to you about – to, ah, discuss?'

'Of course.' She steeled herself.

'I thought we should meet for lunch. Today, at my club?'

Anything could happen. She grasped the lifeline like a drowning woman.

'That would be lovely, James.'

'One o'clock?'

'I'll be there.'

'Good. Well, goodbye then.'

She hurtled out of bed. It was eleven o'clock. She had one and a half hours to try and make herself look vaguely human. Lunch was a good thing, a chance to meet and talk with her husband and hear whatever he had to say. It was a tiny ray of hope amidst the dark, all-consuming void she'd been living in since she'd opened that horrible envelope. Maybe God had answered her prayers and was going to give her the second chance she had begged Him for, even if she didn't deserve it. She could hope. There was nothing wrong with hoping.

Bingo! She'd hit pay dirt. She had just *known* there'd been something sly and underhanded about her. Well, her little fabrication was about to be blown sky high. Waitress, my ass!

Tanya had guessed as much. Carla Berlusconi was no waitress. She was, according to what the Internet had offered up, a world-class chef! It wasn't exactly what Tanya had hoped to discover about her, but nonetheless it was spectacular. The question was, why? Why on earth had she chosen Dublin – and indeed Dominic's – to conduct her incognito existence? It was probably something to do with her family's chain of restaurants in New York. But who cared? Whatever way she tried to explain or wriggle her way out of it, it wasn't going to look good. Nobody liked a spy in the camp, particularly in such a tightly knit group as a kitchen.

Tanya grinned, thinking of it, savouring the prospective shock and anger. Rollo would be outraged to be made a fool of by a woman, and one who was, by all accounts, a much more talented and acclaimed chef than he was. And as for Dom . . . Tanya's mouth curved in a smile. Who knew what the deceitful little witch's reasons were, but Tanya would bet her bottom dollar that Carla didn't have Dom's interests at heart, and Dom was passionately protective of his restaurant. To undermine it in any way would be seen as a personal attack on everything he held dear, and sneaking around pretending to be a waitress while Carla went about whatever unsavoury undercover business she was conducting would be seen as the worst kind of attack of all.

It wasn't going to go down well, but what a story. Tanya was so excited at the thought of leaking it to her press contact that her fingers were trembling as she punched in the number.

Dom was having trouble concentrating. He was trying to work out what to say to Rollo about the financial situation and how to approach asking him to take a cut in salary. He had already let two of the waiters go, and had found that incredibly difficult. Then he would think about Carla, her feisty determination and willingness to work so hard, and, more importantly, the absolutely amazing sex they were having. No wonder he was having trouble thinking about anything else. What else was there worth thinking about?

When she had stayed in his place that first night, he had woken up to find her gone from the bed, and found her in the kitchen.

'Coffee?' she had asked him, looking sheepish. 'I couldn't sleep.'

'Me neither.' He came over and dropped a kiss on her forehead.

'Would you like to try again?' he said, slipping his arms around her and pushing a stray tendril behind her ear.

'To sleep?'

'Something like that.' He had kissed her then, and it had been every bit as promising and tantalising as the night before.

'Yes,' she said, smiling up at him. 'I think I would.'

'I was hoping you'd say that.'

Since then they had been trying, not very successfully he suspected, to keep their blossoming affair to themselves – at least until they got used to the idea. It wasn't that everyone in the restaurant wouldn't be happy for them – they would – but just for the moment, they wanted it to be their own delicious secret. But they would have to say something soon, and then – Dom kept trying to avoid the awful thought – Tanya would be bound to find out. He should probably tell her, he thought, but then, they were over. Whatever way she found out, it was all perfectly legitimate – she was probably dating someone else herself by now, he reassured himself.

During the week, he and Carla slipped up to his apartment at every opportunity, and at the weekend, Dom would follow Carla to her basement flat in Wellington Square. He would have followed her anywhere, the realisation dawned on him slowly – he couldn't get enough of her.

Happily, she seemed to feel the same way about him. Neither of them had mentioned the 'L' word yet, he thought, grinning. They didn't have to. It was written all over their faces and expressed quite eloquently in many other ways, without them having to say a word.

Lunch was not going at all well. Cici had been meticulously punctual, arriving at the Royal Irish Yacht Club at five minutes to one, and had taken great care with her appearance, wearing a suit she knew James loved on her, though it felt as if it was two sizes too big – she had lost that much weight. She wasn't pleased when she looked in the mirror. She looked gaunt and drawn, with purple shadows under her eyes that no amount of concealer properly covered.

James had arrived precisely at one o'clock and they had gone straight to their table by the window. Cici had accepted James's offer of champagne but had then been dismayed when he ordered water for himself. They had chatted about the weather, business and the recession until Cici thought she would scream, she felt so awkward. But there was nothing she could say – James was calling the shots now and he was taking his time getting to whatever it was he wanted to discuss with her. What was there to discuss anyway, she thought miserably. Whether or not to go to court, or to arrange a dignified out-of-court settlement? Either way, she didn't care. She just wanted her gorgeous husband to tell her it had all been a terrible mistake and that he was still as much in love with her as he had ever been. She allowed herself this thirty-second fantasy, gazing wistfully out over the bright blue bay beneath them.

'Cici?'

'Sorry.' She was contrite. 'I was miles away.'

'My solicitor tells me you still haven't appointed a firm to represent you legally.' He looked at her patiently, but his face was unreadable.

'No, I haven't,' she said wretchedly.

'You'll have to sooner or later, and it might as well be sooner.'

No I don't, she thought. *I can lock myself away and hide in bed and never come out again and waste away and die. Why bother hiring solicitors?*

'You see,' James was toying with the salmon on his plate, 'something very unusual has come to light. About the case, that is.'

'What?' she said blankly, staring at the lamb she had barely touched.

'Well, the thing is . . . it turns out we're not actually married at all.'

Her head snapped up and she gasped. 'What?'

'That's exactly what I said.' James gave a little laugh and wiped the corner of his mouth with his napkin.

'If this is your idea of a joke . . .'

'No, I wouldn't, nor would my solicitor joke about anything this serious.'

'But what – how?' Her hand went to her throat. She could barely form the words, let alone the questions.

'Apparently we didn't fulfil the correct residency requirements in Rome prior to the marriage. While the religious ceremony was legitimate, it turns out that legally, back in Dublin, it doesn't stand up at all. So as I said, in the eyes of the legal system, we're not married at all. Extraordinary, isn't it?' James sounded thoroughly amused. 'So you see, you really must hire a solicitor as soon as possible so we can sort all this out. Then you'll be perfectly free to pursue this, er, young friend of yours – Harry, isn't that his name? – and we can all go our separate ways much sooner than we thought.' He looked pleased.

'But I don't want to,' she croaked.

'Oh really, Cici, even you must tire of playing games eventually. Don't be silly.'

'No, you don't understand. I don't want him – Harry. I want you, James!'

'Is that so? I must say you have a funny way of showing it.

Forgive me if I've lost my sense of humour, but I don't really find any of this amusing. I'll be glad to get it all wrapped up. This revelation about our marriage is a most welcome one and perfectly timed.'

'No, it's me who should beg for forgiveness,' Cici cried, the words coming out in a torrent. 'Please, James, I beg of you, give me a chance to explain.'

'Cici, don't do this. Leave us some dignity.' His voice was clipped and cold.

'I don't have any dignity! I don't want any dignity! Not if it means losing you. I love you, really I do, I've always loved you. I believe you know that deep down – you must!'

'Is that what you told Harry too?' His eyes were hard.

'No – never! I never loved him, James. It was stupid selfish, madness, but I never loved him.' She paused to draw a shuddering breath. 'But now – now I hate him! He's insane! He tried to upset Sophia. He followed me to Rome. You have to believe me.'

'Yes, I heard about that sordid little incident. Sophia was and *is* upset – upset and angry. I empathise entirely with her.'

'I'll make it up to her and to you.' She reached out to take his hand across the table, but he withdrew it. 'Harry is mad.' She began to cry, exhaustion and desolation making tears pour down her face. 'He followed me to Rome. I was going to finish with him before, but I did then, and ever since he's been threatening me and sending horrid messages to me. I know I deserve it all, I know it's all my stupid fault, but believe me, James, I have paid the price. If there was anything I could do, anything to turn back the clock and undo what I did, I would. But I can't.'

'That much at least is true.' He looked at her, unmoved.

'Please, James,' she whispered. 'Please can we go somewhere and talk properly? I beg of you, let me explain – please give me that chance.'

For a split second he seemed to waver, then he took a

breath and stood up. 'No, Cici, I'm afraid not. The only talking that will be done from here on out will be between our solicitors. Which is why I would urge you once again to appoint one. If not, I shall proceed with the divorce without you. It's your choice. I will, of course, accord you all the financial security entitled to that of any wife. We did, after all, live as husband and wife for a great many happy years – or so I foolishly thought.'

'James, please,' she said, barely audible.

'Thank you for meeting me for lunch, Cici. I'll leave you to make your own way home.' And with that, he walked away from the table and out of the dining room.

She wasn't sure how long she sat there, looking out unseeingly over the sea, grey now and bleak.

'Ahem.' It was the elderly waiter, clearing his throat discreetly as he removed her plate. 'Can I get you anything else, Mrs Coleman?'

The words plunged a knife into her very soul. *Mrs Coleman.* It was probably the last time she would ever hear them uttered.

Carla had just finished her afternoon shift and was looking forward to having a much-needed evening of pampering, including a long bath, then falling into bed – alone for a change. Dom was away for a couple of days, selecting and ordering some new wines for their increasing list. How Carla would have loved to go with him! As it was, they were tight staffed enough already. Instead, she was using the time to catch up on her sleep and beauty treatments and generally daydream. Every thought, every action, every fibre of her being was revolving around Dom. She could hardly believe what was happening and she couldn't think of anything else.

There was only one thing weighing heavily on her mind. She still hadn't told Dom the truth about who or what she was. She was scared he'd think she was sly and secretive, and then, when they had made love that first time, that amazingly wonderful time when she *should* have told him, she hadn't wanted to ruin the moment. She'd been trying to find the right time and there never seemed to be one, and the longer she left it, the harder it got. What would she say? *You know how you think I'm a penniless waitress? Well* . . . She just couldn't find the words somehow. And Dom was so kind and thoughtful. He had even said he thought she should go and see her father, that maybe they might go to New York together. She could talk about everything else with him, it seemed, but now she was consumed with anxiety about telling him the truth.

At home, she took off her coat and boots and went straight to the tiny bathroom to run a hot bath with generous helpings of aromatherapy oil. She put a conditioning treatment on her hair and sank into the silky water and wished Dom was with her. Afterwards, she did her nails and toes, dried her hair and slipped in between fresh sheets. She picked up the phone eagerly when it rang.

'Hello?'

'Hey, gorgeous.' It was Dom and her heart skipped a beat. 'What are you doing?'

'I'm in bed, having an early night for a change.'

'I wish I was in there with you.'

'Me too, although I could do with getting some shut-eye. I'm definitely sleep deprived. I got two orders wrong today, I've never done that.'

'That has nothing to do with lack of sleep, as you well know.'

'Is that so?'

'Absolutely. I'll prove it to you when I get back. Now I have to go down to this tasting dinner, which will go on for hours.'

'You're good at that.'

'Be careful, Carla, or I'll skip the dinner and stay up here having phone sex with you.'

'I'll settle for the real thing. When are you back?'

'Tomorrow, late afternoon. I'll see you then.'

'Good. I miss you.'

'I miss you too.'

'*Ciao, cara.*'

'*Ciao.* Oh, and Carla?'

'Yes?'

'I'm crazy about you. You know that, don't you?'

'Oh Dom, I've been mad about you since I first set eyes on you.'

'Sweet dreams, *cara.*' There was the briefest of pauses. 'I love you.' He hung up before she could say a word, but the warmth and smile in his voice were loud and clear.

He'd said it! Dom loved her. She had hoped, of course, dreamed of it in every waking moment, but to hear the words . . . She tried calling him back but couldn't get through, so she sent a text message instead. *I love you too – hurry home xxx*

Then she kissed the phone, bearer of such lovely tidings, and snuggled down to sleep. Tomorrow she would tell him, explain about why she had kept it all a secret. He wouldn't be cross. Dom never got cross.

It was the phone that woke her again, in what felt like the middle of the night. Fumbling blindly for the light switch, she picked it up. No number showed up on the caller display. Perhaps it was Dom again, calling from France, maybe from a landline, but it was five a.m. He was probably squiffy after his wine-tasting dinner and didn't realise what time it was.

'Hello?' she said tentatively.

'Carla?' she recognised the voice at once.

'Marco? How did you—?'

'Thank God. Listen, never mind how we got your number. You must come home right away. It's Papa – he's had a heart attack.'

'Oh my God, Marco, no!'

'Hurry, Carla. I'll meet you at JFK – just get yourself over here as fast as you can.'

'Is he – is he . . .?'

'He's still alive, but he's critical. He's asking for you.'

'Oh God, oh God, I'm on my way – I'll leave right now.'

'I'll pray you make it in time. Let me know your flight details when you can.'

She moved as if in a bad dream, methodically flinging things into a case, checking her passport, turning off lights and banging the door behind her, only just remembering to lock it. She hailed a taxi in the street and told him to get to the airport. Something in the tone of her voice and her ravaged face made even this most cheerful of Dublin taxi drivers refrain from asking if she was off somewhere nice. Instead, he nodded brusquely and drove intently through the early morning darkness until finally, the lights of Dublin Airport loomed ahead of them.

Tanya awoke with a thrill of anticipation she hadn't experienced for a long time. She didn't bother with her exercises, just showered and did her hair and make-up with even more care than usual. Donning a pair of slim black trousers and a long, slinky, black V-necked jumper, she slipped her feet into her new black suede ankle boots. Slinging her bag over her shoulder, she made for the door, took one last approving look in the mirror and headed out, humming 'These Boots Are Made for Walking'.

It didn't take her long to reach the fashionable coffee bar and deli where her breakfast companion was waiting for her.

'Just an Americano for me,' she said to the waiter. 'Well?' she asked the journalist, who was tucking into a full Irish.

'Take a look at this,' he grinned, handing her the morning edition of the paper. 'I think you'll like it.'

Tanya flicked quickly to his avidly followed gossip and entertainment column and consumed every syllable of the article. 'Excellent!' she proclaimed, shaking her head and grinning.

'You owe me one.'

'Yes, Owen, I most certainly do.'

It had been the longest three hours of her life.

The Aer Lingus staff had been kind and concerned, but the flight was full. She was on standby, and they were pulling out whatever stops they could. She rang her brother, who sounded battle-weary but confirmed that her father was at least still alive, still holding on. She had just finished the phone call when the ground hostess beckoned her to the desk. 'Good news, pet, we've got you on. You can go and check in now.'

Carla could only nod her gratitude. She couldn't speak, as tears were pouring down her face. 'Come on, love, I'll go with you,' said the sympathetic girl. 'It's your dad, is it?'

Carla nodded again and blew her nose.

'I'll say a prayer for you. Don't give up hope. Here,' she fished in her handbag and pressed something that felt like a coin into Carla's hand. 'It's never let me down yet. You'll get home in time, I know you will.'

Carla looked at the small silver medal and smiled. It was a miraculous medal, just like the one her mother had worn around her neck all her life.

'Thank you so much, but don't you need it?'

'Plenty more where that came from – my parents' house is full of them. God bless, pet, and safe journey.' And then she was disappeared into the crowds of tourists and holiday-makers all intent on making their way out of Dublin.

It was just as the flight was called to board that she remembered to call Dom. She was already on a couple of days' leave from work so there was no need just yet to call the restaurant – they wouldn't be expecting her.

She longed to hear his voice, but on the other hand she was afraid she would break down completely if she heard it, wanting him to be here now to hold her, reassure her.

She dialled his number and tried to keep her voice steady. It went to voicemail. 'Dom,' she began haltingly. 'I have to go home, to New York. It's urgent. It's my father. He's had a heart attack, and he's critical. I'll call you when I have news. I love you.' She switched the phone off as she boarded, already dreading turning it on at the other end, on the other side of the Atlantic, fearful of the devastating news it could bring her at any moment.

Back in Dominic's, they were going through the morning drill, preparing, as usual, for the lunch sitting.

The cutback in staff meant they all had to work extra hard, and everyone was feeling the strain.

In the kitchen, tempers and nerves were even more frayed than usual as Rollo was making no bones about the fact that taking a hefty cut in salary was affecting his creative instincts.

He had said as much to Astrid. They had both discussed their options carefully.

'It is only because I feel for him,' Rollo had said, shaking his head sadly. 'It was a bad day when he got mixed up with that Tanya woman – I knew she would be trouble.'

'We all did, for Dom at any rate, but I thought she was just a nuisance here. I never dreamed she would be taking liberties with the accounts. Although all the freebies – how could Dom not have noticed?'

'He is creative spirit, like me.' Rollo shook his head. 'He was building his restaurant, caring for his kitchen. His accountant is to blame.'

'But now look what's happened.' Astrid was mournful.

'I know. I told him I would stay for as long as I could on this pay cut, but only because I don't want to see him go under. I can't do it for much longer, Astrid, maybe a couple of weeks. Already I have had two offers after making discreet enquiries. And I think soon, I would like to go back to Italy.'

Astrid's face fell. 'To Italy?'

'Yes – home, to Italy.' He took her hands and grinned. 'But only if my Astrid comes with me.'

'Oh Rollo,' she beamed, all thoughts of Dominic's travails forgotten. 'Of course I will.'

It was Paddy, the kitchen porter, who saw it first. He'd been sitting in the staff room having his tea break and had paused when mid-mouthful he saw the headline. DOMINIC'S DISH OF THE DAY, it read, followed by a subhead. *What will debonair restaurant owner have to say?*

The article went on to speculate about 'riveting revelations' that sexy J-Lo look-alike Carla Berlusconi, a waitress who was a favourite with staff and clients alike, was, in fact, none other than an undercover plant. She was herself an acclaimed and talented chef who had worked in several single- and double-starred Michelin restaurants before heading up the kitchen at the famous M Hotel in New York.

Carla, it was pointed out, was the daughter of Antonio Berlusconi, head of the famous New York chain, noted for his aggressive expansion technique in taking over key restaurants and adding them to the family business. Clearly the beautiful Carla was on an undercover mission here in Dublin to glean the information needed before Dominic's presumably became the chain's first Irish flagship. Watch this space . . .

The article was accompanied by a shot of Dom, looking gorgeous at a polo match, and one of Carla, at work in the restaurant, plates in hand, looking stressed and cross. It had clearly been taken by a mobile phone. There was also a shot of Tanya, looking immaculate, with a sad smile on her face. She was quoted as saying, 'Unfortunately Dominic's is no longer a client of mine. In light of certain inexplicable discrepancies I no longer felt I could consciously represent them in my capacity as PR consultant, so I terminated our contract. Therefore I have no comment to make.'

Paddy almost choked on his morning pastry. Grabbing the

paper, he dashed onto the restaurant floor, gesticulating wildly. 'C'mere, lads, get an eyeful of this!'

They just about got through lunch.

No one could believe it, least of all Rollo, who was roaring and banging about the kitchen like a bear.

'To think I have offered my services practically for free to this – this idiot! And all the time he has a spy under his nose!'

'It's not Dom's fault.' Astrid shook her head. 'She's my friend, and even I had no clue. I can't believe it.'

'What does he think he's running? A restaurant or a TV reality show? What is she doing here? Why is she pretending to be a waitress?' Rollo was becoming more and more angry the more he thought about it, especially when he thought about how much he really did like Carla – or rather, *had* liked her. He had depended on her, confided in her. How could she ridicule him like this? And her credentials – they were even better than his! It was completely intolerable. 'Tonight.' He banged his fist on the counter. 'I will do one more night here – that's it. Then I go. I will not be humiliated like this by anyone. I don't care if it's not Dom's fault – he should know what's going on in his own restaurant – know his own staff, for God's sake! For all we know he could be part of it. He's probably in on it himself.'

17

Dom, as it turned out, wasn't in on it.

When he wandered into the restaurant at six-thirty that evening, he was smiling, happy and eager to get to work, especially to talk to Vincent, the sommelier, about the successful trip to the Loire and the fantastic wines he had selected. He was also counting the minutes until he could get away and go to Carla's place. He was so lost in thought about her, about how he had told her that he loved her and that she had texted back that she was in love with him too, that he failed to notice the strained, subdued atmosphere he walked into.

'Hello, Dom, how was your trip?' Astrid asked and smiled wanly.

'Great, thanks.' He headed for his office. 'How were things here?'

'Oh, fine.'

'Good. Tell Rollo I'll be in to see him in a mo.'

'Er, Dom . . .'

'Yes?'

'Have you, um, heard from Carla?'

He looked at her strangely. 'Why?'

'You need to see this.' She handed him the morning's paper, open at the offending article. 'I'll, uh, be in the kitchen.' She backed away discreetly.

For a moment he stood there, perplexed, as the combination of the shots of himself, Carla and Tanya – *Tanya?* – fought with the headline and subhead. Then, still reading, he went over to a table, sat down and studied it carefully. When he had finished, he looked up. The room was empty. Everyone had clearly retreated to the kitchen.

It was only then that he reached for his phone, which he had forgotten to turn back on after the flight. Sure enough, there were a couple of messages. The one from Carla, from last night, one or two texts and one telling him he had three voicemail messages in his mailbox. He dialled the number and listened, a myriad of emotions fighting for expression. One was from his mother, asking him to phone her, another was from his mate Paul, and then the one he really listened to, from Carla. 'Dom,' it began, 'I have to go home, to New York. It's urgent—' and then the rest of the message broke up. He listened to it again, replayed it twice and then deleted it, put his phone back in his pocket and headed for the kitchen to face the troops. He had never felt so foolish or betrayed in his entire life.

This was the woman he loved, who'd been sleeping with him, and all the time she had been keeping this huge secret. He'd never dreamed Carla was like that. Tanya, maybe, but Carla? And yet, if she was Antonio Berlusconi's daughter, why not tell him, and why flee back to New York? There could only be one reason – and it was staring at him in black and white.

The flight took for ever. Strong headwinds were against them, which meant a possible five hours turned into seven. Thankfully, Carla had a window seat, and the man beside her read assiduously, so she was free to put on her headphones and pretend she was listening to music or watching a movie. Of course, she could do neither – her mind was either racing or numbly frozen. She couldn't eat, either, so there was no whiling away the interminable hours. She tried to sleep, but found that every time she closed her eyes, another memory would float to her consciousness. She didn't need or want to watch the in-flight movie – she had one of her very own playing in her head.

Her father smiling as she, Paulo, Marco and Bruno helped their mother decorate the enormous Christmas tree.

Her father laughing and looking on proudly as she managed unsteadily to ride her first bike.

Her father ageing overnight, his grief palpable, at her mother's death.

And then the picture she had always shut out, that he always joked about, now almost unbearably painful to contemplate, of her on her father's arm, at some unknown time in the future, as he walked her down the aisle.

He couldn't . . . it wasn't possible – it would be too cruel. He had to make it, had to at least hold on until she got there and could tell him how sorry she was for everything and tell him how much she loved him. Tears began to roll down her face. She silently prayed: *If you're up there, please let me see him, let me talk to him one more time. Just one more time.*

'Where the hell is she?' Paulo paced the floor of the small private hospital room.

'How do I know?' retorted Marco, running his hands through his hair. 'She got the flight, that's all I know. She should be here any minute.'

'Any minute could be too late.' Paulo shook his head.

'Don't say that.'

'Why did she have to go away? Why couldn't she have just—'

'Coulda, shoulda, woulda,' Bruno looked at him. 'What's the point?'

They lapsed into silence, the only sound the bleeping of the monitor that told them their father's heart was still beating, although he hadn't spoken since last night, when he'd lapsed into unconsciousness. The nurse came in to check on him.

She looked at them sympathetically and shook her head. 'No change.'

Rollo was as good as his word.

He stayed for one night and one night only. There was no talking him round. Not even Astrid could persuade him. His ego was badly bruised, and fond though he was of Dom, he refused to stay on. Once the article had been published and the press in general got wind of the news, other journalists were soon on the scent of a good story and the phone had been going all day. It was infuriating, but they had to answer it in case it was a reservation. Several tabloid journalists had actually called to the restaurant hoping for a comment or revealing shot, and tempers and patience were fraying. Dom tried Carla's phone again and it went to voicemail. He knew it was churlish, but he couldn't help it. He left one message. *Nice one, Carla, you really pulled it off. I may have meant nothing to you, but I thought at least your colleagues would. I hope it was worth it.*

A patient of P.J.'s in property rang him with the news. 'I thought it was your boy, and thought you'd want to know before it's general knowledge.' Only minutes later, Catherine called him, in tears.

'P.J.,' she said, fighting to control her voice. 'I'm going to my mother's and I'm taking Charlie with me. It's Alex. The banks have pulled the plug and he, well, he's sort of lost it, really. He won't talk to me, to anyone. He told me to go, that we were better off without him.'

'I've just heard about it. I'll go over and try and talk to him.'

'I don't think he'll talk to you of all people. Sorry,' she gulped, 'I didn't mean it like that. It's just he's so defensive where you're concerned.'

'I hear you,' P.J. said. He understood all too well what Catherine was trying to say.

'But I'm really worried about him. He's not himself, and—' She broke into fresh sobs. 'Oh P.J., I'm so scared. I don't want to leave, but he won't listen to me, and I have to consider Charlie.'

'You're doing the right thing.'

'Will you ring me when you – if you . . .?'

'Of course. Let me know when you've got to your mum's – just text me.' P.J. put down the phone. What else could he say? Of course Catherine was worried – he was worried himself. More than worried, if he was honest. He should have seen it coming, and maybe he had. Some day, somehow, he had always known this situation was going to blow. The question was – how high?

It was only seven-thirty when he reached Alex and Catherine's place, but the house was in darkness. Catherine's car was gone and only Alex's red Ferrari sat in the driveway. P.J. got out of his jeep and rang the doorbell.

Nothing.

He took out his phone and called Alex's number, but it went to voicemail. He left a message anyway, knowing how unlikely it was that Alex might listen to it. 'Alex, it's me, I'm outside. Let me in will you? We need to talk.'

Still nothing.

He sighed, but his heart quickened. He had to get into the house. Alex was in there – he was sure of it – but what if he had done something stupid? What if he couldn't cope with this débâcle, this debt? What was it he had said to Catherine? That she and Charlie would be better off without him? P.J. fought to keep calm in the face of escalating panic.

He could call the Fire Brigade, he could call an ambulance, but it appeared the one person he couldn't call or talk to was his own son.

Sod this! he thought with a sudden surge of anger. *I'm getting in, whatever it takes.*

He thought about breaking a window, but then that would

cause a furore and the neighbours might get involved. He assessed the front door critically. It was solid oak. It was unlikely, even with the best of intentions, that he could shoulder it like they did in the movies. And even though he had powered many a scrum, he wasn't as young as he used to be. In the end, he decided to give it one more try, and opening the letterbox, bent down and yelled through it.

'Alex, I know you're in there. If you won't let me in, I'm going to make my own way in.'

Still silence. Now he was scared. There was nothing for it; he would have to break in. He thought one more warning was only fair. 'Fine. If that's the way you want it, Alex, I'm coming in.'

He was just about to force or break a ground-floor window when the door opened. Wheeling around, P.J. regarded the figure who looked back at him. He resembled Alex, a thinner, gaunt-looking Alex, but it was the face, the unreadable expression in his eyes, the curl of the mouth that were unfamiliar.

'I suppose you've come to gloat,' Alex said. 'Well, do come inside, Father dear. So tacky to have to make a song and dance on the doorstep, although we all know how you love an audience.'

P.J. realised immediately that whatever else, Alex was well and truly drunk. He stood there, swaying slightly, in a pair of well-worn jeans and a stained sweatshirt, his feet bare, his face unshaven.

'I will come in, Alex, if that's all right.' P.J. walked past him and into the hall. 'I'd like to talk to you.'

'I suppose Catherine has been on?' Alex smiled and arched an eyebrow. He closed the door and then headed towards the sitting room. 'I told her to go. Better off without me, Charlie and her. Can I offer you a drink . . . Father?'

'I'll have whatever you're having.' P.J. thought he'd need it.

'Of course you would – it's whiskey.' Alex waved the almost empty bottle in the air. 'I seem to have made quite a dent in it.' He reached for a tumbler and poured what was left into it. 'Cheers,' he said, handing it to P.J., then pulled another bottle from the press and proceeded to top up his own glass.

'How much have you had?' P.J. asked him levelly.

'Pretty much enough – on every front.'

'I can understand that.'

'Can you? Can you really?'

'Look, Alex—'

'I'd rather not, actually, if it's all the same to you. I've looked at it every which way and it – my life – seems pretty much screwed.'

'I want to help.'

'I'm sure you do. How noble.'

'Alex, I know—'

'You don't know anything. How could you?' He laughed bitterly. 'You've always got what you wanted, haven't you? School hero, rugby star. Got the career, got the girl, got all the adoring patients. How could you possibly know what it's like to not measure up?'

'Alex, can we just—'

'Just what? Talk? Make it all better? The answer to that is no. I don't want to talk, and certainly not to you. Frankly, you're the last person on earth I want to see right now.'

P.J. had a sharp intake of breath.

'Not so nice, is it, to be on the receiving end? How embarrassing for you, the great Dr P.J. O'Sullivan, to have a son who's such a sap, such a failure.'

'Shut up with this self-pitying drivel. You may hate the sight of me, but you're my *son*. I'm your *father*. We're family – we'll work this all out.'

'Actually,' Alex took a swig of his drink and smiled pityingly at him, 'that is where you're wrong – for once in your life.' He waved an admonishing finger at him. 'You see, this may come as a shock, but you don't actually know *everything*.'

P.J. sighed. He wasn't going to get anywhere – not with Alex in the state he was in – and yet he couldn't leave him alone, not like this. Even if he was the last person on the face of the earth Alex wanted to see.

'Contrary to your opinion of me, Alex, I'm actually quite well aware of that.'

'I beg to differ, P.J. – otherwise you wouldn't be referring to me as your son.'

'What?'

'You heard me.'

'What do you mean?'

'Just what I said. I am not your son. You are not my father.'

For a moment – a long moment – everything slowed down. P.J. opened his mouth, then closed it.

'What? Lost for words? That's a first.' Alex's eyes were hard. 'Maybe *you* could kid yourself for thirty-odd years, but I won't. I'm pretty sure you know, maybe you've always known, but the tests at any rate must have provoked an inkling of curiosity. Not on our side of the family, is it? Von Willebrand's? Catherine's neither.'

'Alex, that doesn't prove anything. Just because—'

'Shut up.' Alex was quietly derisive. 'She told me. Maybe she never told *you*, but Mum told *me*.' He looked P.J. in the eye. 'Funny what people confess to on their deathbeds, isn't it?' he said matter-of-factly, but his expression was bleak. Then realisation dawned. 'Don't tell me – how extraordinary. You really *didn't* know, did you?' Alex regarded him with something approaching amusement.

'Know what, exactly?'

'That there was someone else, shortly before you. Some other guy. She said she couldn't be sure initially, but the timing was right and apparently I'm the spitting image of him. She showed me a photo. He tried to contact her when he heard she was getting married to you, but by then she had set off for Ireland. I guess it must have weighed on her conscience. Or maybe it was the morphine at the end. Who knows? She said not to say anything to you, that it would – what were her words? Oh yes, that it would break your heart. That no father had ever been more thrilled with a son than you when I arrived. Ironic, don't you think? So you see, P.J., she was thinking of you right until the end. It didn't bother her that she might be upsetting me, her own son. It was always about you.'

'You can't be sure,' P.J. began.

'Oh stop it, will you? Bella agreed to have the DNA tests done while she was home. We are not, as I suspected, full siblings, which pretty much confirms Mum's story. Sadly, she's not around to fill in the details. Just as well, really. At least she doesn't have to see what a mess I've made of things. But the day she died, she took with her any hope I had of ever really fitting in. I know she loved me,' he said, looking defiantly at P.J. 'It's just that you were always in the way. You always took too much from her – there was never any left for me. Now I understand why. She was guilty, trying to make it up to you – even if she never told you. You must have known.'

'No.' P.J.'s voice was flat. 'I didn't.' True, there had always been the sliver of possibility, but it hadn't mattered. Now he didn't know what to say. He looked at the son who had always been a stranger to him and wanted to reach out to him.

'So you see, it's a wasted journey you've come on, P.J. I am not your son and there's no need for you to be here.'

'You're my son in every way that matters, Alex,' P.J. said quietly. 'I know we're very different people, and maybe I haven't been the kind of father you needed, but Mum was right about one thing – no father was ever more thrilled by your arrival, and whether or not you are my biological son makes no difference to me whatsoever. Perhaps I wasn't very good at showing it, but I have always loved you, always been proud of you and your achievements.' P.J. realised with every word he was saying that it was the truth.

'More importantly,' he continued, '*you* now have a son, a family of your own. Listen to me, for them if not yourself. I want to help, Alex.'

'There's nothing you can do.' Alex stood up, almost shouting. 'I've lost everything. I'm ruined. That's how good a husband – a father – I am.' He broke down, sobbing hoarsely. 'Go on, go – get out of here.'

P.J. looked at the stooped figure, the shoulders heaving with grief and defeat, and thought his heart would break. 'I'm not going anywhere, Alex,' he said quietly, going over to him. He removed the glass gently from his hand, then he put his arms around his son and held him as he collapsed against him and cried his heart out.

'I'm sorry,' Alex whispered hoarsely when he drew breath.

'So am I, son, so am I.' P.J. wiped his own face. 'Come with me – I don't think you should stay here and you certainly shouldn't be on your own.'

'Where are we going?' Alex asked anxiously, reminding P.J. of the small, uptight little boy he had once been.

'Home, son,' P.J. put an arm around his shoulders. 'We're going home.'

18

'Carla! Thank God.' Her brothers hugged her.

'How is he?' she whispered, almost afraid to look at the body lying so still in the bed, hooked up to machines.

'No change. He lost consciousness last night,' Marco said gently. 'Go sit with him.'

'We'll leave you alone for a little while. We've been taking it in shifts and I could do with something to eat,' Bruno said. 'We'll be in the canteen if you need us.'

Carla could only nod miserably, not trusting herself to speak.

'Come on,' Paulo said to his brothers, nodding towards the door. 'Call us if there's any change.'

'Papa,' she whispered, sitting down on the small chair beside the bed. 'It's me, Carla. I'm here.' She took his hand in hers. 'I'm here, Papa,' she said again, tears rolling down her face. She brushed them away angrily. She would not cry now – she would pull herself together, for him. 'I'm so sorry, Papa, for all our stupid fights.' She bit her lip. 'Please wake up. I need to tell you some things. I need to talk to you. I need to tell you I love you.'

The nurse came through the door quietly, and taking in the scene, slipped out again, equally quietly. No matter how many times she saw it, she never got used to watching family or lovers as their hearts broke, as they begged a loved one not to take leave of them.

Her brothers came back after half an hour. They sat through the night, talking, crying and laughing softly around the bed, lost in memories and recalling happier times.

Once or twice, Carla went out to check her phone. There were no messages. She had checked it, of course, immediately after arriving in JFK, terrified of bad news, that she might have been too late, but there was only a weird voice message from Dom, sounding accusatory. She had hardly bothered to listen to it, she was so desperate to get to the hospital. There had been another message from Astrid, asking her to ring her. Not a word from anyone about her father, enquiring as to how he or she was. At the time it hadn't really registered with her, but now, in the small hours of the night, it bothered her. Didn't Dom care? He hadn't sent so much as a text message. Carla was too upset to give it much thought, but all the same, it hurt. She tried his phone again, but he didn't pick up – it went straight to voicemail. She didn't leave a message. Because nothing mattered, she reminded herself, nothing mattered at all, as long as her father regained consciousness.

No one had ever seen Ossie so angry, not even Charlotte. When he had rung to ask if he could see her to talk about Candy, he had been abrupt and uninformative. She had duly agreed, wondering what Candy could have done now.

When he arrived that evening, she had been shocked. He was so angry he could barely speak. After making coffee and listening to his halting account, she could understand why. Worse still was watching the offending mpeg. Ossie hadn't wanted her to see it, but she had insisted.

'She's my daughter too, Ossie.'

'Not so's you'd know it,' he said grimly. 'I'm warning you, it doesn't make pleasant viewing.'

'I'd rather know the worst,' she said weakly.

After that, they'd had a drink and a very long talk about what to do.

Candy was frightened.

It took her a while to figure out she was scared, because

she had become so used to doing exactly as she pleased, causing maximum drama at maximum expense – generally everybody else's. But she had never experienced her father's anger – never even seen him angry, come to think of it – until that moment when he had roared her name so loudly the roof almost shook. He had barged into her room and told her in an ice-cold voice to get herself down to his study now.

'I'm going out.' Candy had looked at him as if he was stupid.

'You. Downstairs. In my study. *Now*.'

Candy's mouth dropped open.

He had looked at her strangely then. Something had made her obey him and not reiterate the fact that she was going out – indeed *had* to go out – to find Josh. She dropped the brush she had been about to put through her hair and heard it rattle on the dressing table as she left the room. Downstairs, he had all but propelled her into his study and closed the door. Candy would never forget the hideous moments that followed.

'Go over to my computer,' he commanded in a voice she had never heard before.

'What?'

'Do as I say.'

Candy walked over to the vast mahogany desk and stood behind it.

'Sit down.'

She did, wondering if her father had taken leave of his senses, only this dangerous, sinister tone he was using was making her very uneasy.

'Open the email in my inbox.'

Again, Candy did as she was told. Something about sex on the Internet? What was this?

'Read it. Carefully.'

Take a look at this, Mr Keating, and let me know what it's worth NOT to see your daughter having sex on the Internet.

Still she didn't get it. Was this some sort of joke?

'Now click on the attachment.'

She thought she was going to pass out. She sat there, frozen and sick, unable to speak. Eventually she managed to whisper, 'What are you going to do?'

'I'm going to think very carefully about this, Candice,' he said in the same strange, measured voice, 'and about you. You are going to do the same. As for the kind of people you are . . . mixing with . . .' He let the words hang in the air. 'Well, you can see what they think of you.' That hit her like a blow. 'You will go to your room and stay there. You may go down to the kitchen to eat, but consider yourself under house arrest. You will hand over your phone and laptop and have no access to phones or computers of any kind. I have my best security people on this, and if you so much as attempt to send out one text message, all hell will break loose. Do I make myself clear? Now get back upstairs to your room and stay there until you hear from me again. Your mother will have to be told about this. I imagine she'll have something to say about it too.'

'Please,' she whispered, 'not Mum.'

'Don't think it gives me any pleasure, Candice. I can only imagine how horrified and hurt she's going to be, but she must be told. Your behaviour leaves me no alternative. Your appalling carry-on may not only have destroyed your own life as you know it but is going to cause enormous distress to a wonderful mother. Whatever about you, she doesn't deserve this.'

That had been two days ago. She had stayed in her room – she couldn't even think about facing anyone – but today she had been faint with hunger and had tiptoed downstairs to get herself some breakfast. Shalom was in the kitchen when she got there. Neither of them said a word. Even Shalom looked shocked and uncomfortable. She avoided making eye contact and appeared relieved when Candy took her mug of tea and slice of toast upstairs with her. The silence had been deafening.

It was like awaiting execution, Candy thought, shivering.

And then came the summons. From outside her door, she heard her father's voice.

'Candice, you will come down to my study now. I want you there in no less than three minutes.'

Suddenly Candy wanted her mother. She wanted her calm, forgiving, loving presence, even though she was so filled with shame and self-loathing. She hardly dared think what her mum would make of this. Why hadn't she stayed at home with her and Gran? None of this would ever have happened. Why had she come to this awful house? Now she couldn't even phone her mum. And why, oh why, had Josh done this to her? For that was who was behind this – that much was clear. All she had been to him was an opportunity to blackmail her wealthy father. How he must have laughed at her. Running to the bathroom, she was horribly, violently ill.

She ran a facecloth quickly over her face, and with trembling legs made her way downstairs to her father's study. The door was closed. She knocked tentatively.

'Come in.'

She opened the door slowly and her throat constricted. In front of her, looking more wretched and upset than even *she* felt, was her mum, sitting beside her father on the large sofa. There were dark circles under her eyes and she had clearly been crying. She was sitting very straight and her hands were folded in her lap. Looking at her, Candy wanted simultaneously to flee the room and throw herself at her feet and beg for forgiveness, but she could barely meet her eyes. Her father, on the other hand, looked white-faced and grim, but sat with his legs stretched out, his feet crossed. He appeared to be deep in thought. Nobody said a word.

Candy closed the door behind her and waited, unable to drag her eyes from the floor.

After what seemed like an eternity, her father got up and strolled towards the window, then turned to face her. Finally he spoke. 'Your mother and I have given this distasteful matter a lot of thought and we have finally come to a decision.'

'What are you going to do?' she whispered, her eyes flitting from Charlotte's distraught face to Ossie's impassive one.

There was another pause and then he said, 'We're not going to do anything at all, Candice. You are.'

'What?' She looked astounded.

'You got yourself into this ugly mess, and you should get yourself out of it.'

'But how?' She paled.

'That's for you to figure out. You know this chap, we don't. And frankly, I have no intention of meeting him or entering into any sort of negotiations with him or his kind. You can tell him that for starters.'

'You mean you won't help me? You won't stop him from putting that . . .' she faltered, looking bereft.

'It's your life, Candice,' Ossie continued, 'as you are so fond of reminding us all. Now I suggest you go back to your room and figure out what your plan of action is.'

'But I – but he wouldn't take my calls.' She looked about six years old.

'I can't say I'm surprised,' Ossie continued in the same cold, matter-of-fact tone. 'What did you expect?'

'Mum?' It was a heartfelt plea as Candy looked imploringly at Charlotte, and it broke Charlotte's heart, but she had promised Ossie – no giving in.

'Oh, Candy,' Charlotte said, shaking her head helplessly, her face etched with grief. 'What have you done?'

'Go back to your room,' Ossie commanded, the first signs of tiredness entering his tone.

'I'm sorry,' Candy whispered. 'I'm so sorry.'

'I'm sure you are, but that's not a lot of help to anyone now, is it?' he said. 'Now go.'

So she did, creeping upstairs and back into her room.

She wasn't to know that the second she left the study, Charlotte broke down and sobbed while Ossie held her and tried to comfort her. 'It's only a scam,' he said, 'not serious blackmail. I'm pretty sure about that. But it's no harm for her to get a wake-up call.'

'But if it gets out . . .' She shook her head. 'Candy'll be ruined. It's unthinkable.'

'Let's not assume the worst just yet.'

'But I can't leave her like this, Ossie. Let me take her home, at least. She looks so shattered.'

'We've already decided,' Ossie said gently. 'It's time for me to do what I should have done years ago. The chips are down, now Candy and I will have to pick them up together. I know this is tough for you, but really, I'd prefer if you'd leave her here with me. There are a few new ground rules I need to enforce.'

'All right,' Charlotte agreed, sniffing. 'I'd better go.'

Ossie saw her to her car. From her bedroom window, Candy watched her mum's car pull away, then she crawled into bed and cried her heart out.

P.J. sat down at the kitchen table and opened a bottle of red. He was all done in. Bones, lying in his bed beside the Aga, lifted his head momentarily to watch him pull the cork, then stretched languorously, thumping his tail a few times before drifting back to sleep. Sheila popped her head around the door. 'Is there anything I can get you before I go?'

'No, Sheila, I'm grand, but thank you for everything this evening – you're a trooper. Join me in a drink?'

'As you well know, I'm a Pioneer.' She looked at him sternly. 'But I will have a cup of coffee with you before I turn in.'

'Of course,' P.J. smiled. 'How silly of me, I genuinely forgot. I must be getting old. You don't mind if I do?'

'After the day you've had, you're entitled to whatever you want,' she said briskly, 'but you're looking tired. Don't sit up too late.'

'I won't.' He sipped his wine while Sheila put on the kettle and clattered a few cups and saucers for good measure. She was upset too, he could tell.

He had brought Alex back an hour or so ago, a very weakened and feeble Alex, and Sheila had got a shock when she saw him. But she had immediately rallied and acted as if it was the most natural thing in the world that P.J. should bring his thirty-year-old son home, ask Sheila to make up the bed in his old room, then help him upstairs and undress him and put him to bed as carefully and tenderly as if he had been ten years old. Then he had given him a shot of sedative and sat on the bed beside him until Alex had fallen into a deep sleep.

Only then did Sheila see the tears he quickly brushed away. 'I'll take his clothes and put them in the wash,' she said quietly, picking them up off the floor. She hesitated for a second, then said, 'Will he be all right?'

'I think so, but he's been through a lot recently. He's been under a lot of strain. I'm going to keep him sedated for a couple of days and see how he is after a good rest. Then we'll take it from there.'

'What about Catherine and little Charlie?' Concern flooded her face.

'They're with Catherine's mother.'

'Don't tell me she's left him?'

'No, not at all. He told her to go, said she and Charlie were better off without him.'

'He never!' Sheila's hand went to her mouth.

'He's lost the business, Sheila. He wasn't himself. He's been under a terrible strain and carrying it and a few other loads all by himself.'

'Aren't they lucky they have you to turn to.' Sheila shook her head wonderingly.

'I didn't do enough. I should have seen this coming.'

'Now don't you go blaming yourself. You're a wonderful father – everybody says so.'

P.J. smiled ruefully. 'What would "they" know?'

'Well, I know it.' She was firm.

'Thank you. As I'm always saying, I don't know how we'd manage without you.'

'Your dinner's in the oven.' She exited the room rapidly. The conversation was taking far too emotional a turn for her comfort level. There was only so much a body could deal with. Instead she went down to the kitchen and began making rather a lot of noise.

After Sheila had left to go back to her flat, P.J. continued to sit at the table, with Bones snoring peacefully by the Aga. He refilled his glass and went over the day's events, and eventually a lot more besides.

He thought of the early days, of him and Jilly so much in love.

He thought of Alex, the excitement he and Jilly had both felt, the incredible rush of love when he had been handed to him that first time, a tiny bundle to hold.

And he remembered then the unspoken promise he had made to him, there in the ward, with the team of nurses and his father's best friend – the watchful gynaecologist who had delivered him, now long dead – standing back, tired and happy, thankful for the safe arrival of another new baby. 'Well, P.J.,' he had said, smiling broadly, 'another new arrival! You have a son, young man – that means you have to step up to bat. No better man!' he added, winking as he left them to it.

Hello, my son, P.J. had said in his mind, gazing at the tiny bundle in his arms as he rocked him gently. *My precious, precious son. Welcome to this mad, bad, wonderful world. I'm your dad, and I promise, here and now, to do the best I can for you, now and always. I promise to teach you to throw a ball, to ride a bike, how to look like you're listening in class when you're not, and later I'll teach you about girls, at least the little I know, and hopefully one day you'll be as lucky as I was and you'll meet a girl as wonderful as your mum.*

Where had it all gone wrong? He had meant every word of it. Still did. But somewhere along the way, he had let Alex down, and badly.

Had he always suspected he wasn't really his son?

Had he loved Jilly so much that he was blinded to the needs of the young, insecure, uptight little boy who looked to him for support, guidance, approval?

The questions, once asked, kept on coming.

Sure, Alex had always had the best of everything, and P.J. had always tried to, if not *actually*, make the parents' meetings, the plays, the tennis matches and the swimming competitions. But whenever he showed up, it always seemed to make Alex more nervous. Even Jilly had acknowledged that. Eventually, he had stayed away – it seemed to produce better results. When P.J. was absent, Alex won tennis matches, broke swimming records and generally did well. If P.J. was there, things just seemed to, well, fall apart. Alex lost out and everyone else felt bad for him, and somehow P.J. seemed to feel it was all because of him. And so a chasm had formed, and try as he might to forge a bridge across it, P.J. knew his son was slipping further and further away from him. When he tried to discuss it with Jilly, she would dismiss it, make light of it. Now P.J. knew why.

What a mess, he thought miserably.

'Jilly?' he asked aloud. 'What should I do? If you can hear me, wherever you are, help me do the best for Alex. He needs our help now, and I could do with a bit myself,' he added, shaking his head. 'Now I know I'm drunk,' he said to the almost empty bottle in front of him. Then, as the full enormity of her loss and what it had done to him and the children threatened to overtake him again, he put his head in his hands.

He hardly heard his phone ringing.

'P.J.,' said Charlotte when he picked up, 'I'm so sorry for not calling like I said I would. I'm in the car on my way home. I've had the day from hell.' Her voice sounded shaky.

'You too?'

'You wouldn't believe it.'

'Try me.'

'I don't even want to discuss it over the phone. It's Candy, and it's pretty horrible, actually.'

P.J. thought he could hear her stifling a sob. 'If it's any help, I've had a horrible day myself.'

'I'm such a failure, P.J.,' her voice broke. 'I'm such a pathetic, lousy mother.'

'You couldn't be, even if you tried. I, on the other hand, am an egocentric, self-obsessed man and the worst father any son could be unfortunate enough to have.' He hiccupped slightly.

'Are you mad?' Charlotte was roused out of self-pity. 'You're the success story, the stoic widower with two perfect, well-adjusted and successful children, and by all accounts the only man in Dublin who ever had a happy, loving marriage.'

At his end of the phone, P.J. smiled wryly. 'Where are you?'

'I'm about to turn into Wellington Square.'

'Well pull up outside my house and come in for a drink. I could do with some company.'

There was the briefest of pauses. 'So could I,' she said. And for the first time that day, they both smiled like they meant it.

'You first,' said P.J., handing Charlotte a glass of red wine, which she accepted gratefully, sinking into the big sofa in the kitchen.

'Oh God, P.J. I really don't know where to start.'

'Try the beginning,' he prompted her, sitting down beside her and resting his arm around her shoulders.

So she told him. About how Candy had been behaving since she'd left home as such and went to stay with her father and Shalom, about the boob job, and then finally, the awful video clip and blackmail threat.

'It's so unspeakably awful. I can still hardly take it in. I feel like such a failure as a mother.' Her voice wavered.

'Of course you're not,' he said gently. 'Kids go off the rails all the time, Charlotte, no matter what. Marriage breakdown is tough on everyone, and we've all indulged our kids at times.'

'Yes, but Ossie ruined her and I let him. I have to take responsibility for that.'

'How's Candy about all this?'

'Not good, as you can imagine. I think she's shattered, actually.' Charlotte bit her lip, visions of women in porn movies creeping into her mind. She shuddered, thinking of the emotional damage it would do to Candy if the video got out. She just wanted Candy home, safe with her. 'She admits nobody forced her to do it. She was crazy about this guy. That says it all, really. I mean, how badly have Ossie and I screwed up to make her fall for a sleazeball like that?'

'It happens,' P.J. sighed. 'So where is she now?'

'Ossie has been keeping her under house arrest until he's decided how to approach this.'

'Which is . . .?'

'Well, he had his top security people on it immediately when Candy finally admitted she had been meeting some guy called Josh McIntyre, I think his name is. Clearly he's behind it. The thing is, she met him, or claims to have met him, at the Viper concert we brought her to. He's got something to do with the band, video directing or something.'

'Not for much longer, he won't. What a vile thing to do.' P.J. was outraged.

'But we have to be careful. This thing could end up on the Internet at any moment. For now, Ossie says it's best not to do anything, to make Candy sweat it out. He says it'll be a good lesson for her. Personally, I'm not so sure.' Charlotte put her face in her hands. 'I felt so sorry for her. I thought she was going to faint. And Ossie was so cold, so angry, although I can't say I blame him. He's shattered too – we all are. It's like living with a bomb ready to explode at any second.'

'So what happened today?'

'Well, Ossie and I were sitting in the study, and Candy was called down. When she came in, it was so awful. She looked sick, and petrified, as if she were being thrown to a bunch of lions. When she saw me there, I thought she was going to die of shame. I just wanted to run to her and take her away from it all.'

'If only we could protect our children from themselves,' P.J. murmured, shaking his head.

'Ossie made her stand there, just like that, in front of us, without saying a word. It was excruciating.' Charlotte felt sick remembering the scene. 'After that, I left,' she said miserably. 'I really don't know what's going to happen next.'

'It *is* a bit of a nightmare all right. If I can help in any way . . .'

'Thank you, P.J., I appreciate that, but right now I think we just have to do what Ossie says.'

'Don't forget that my mates in Viper will have something to say about all this.'

'Don't say anything, not just yet – there are so many legal implications and so on. Anyway,' she added, 'here I am wittering on about my day from hell. What happened with you?'

P.J. sighed deeply. 'It's my son, Alex. He – well, he's lost everything on this investment scheme he was involved in. The banks have closed in and he's been under terrible strain. He sort of fell apart a bit, I suppose, hit the bottle, told his wife she and the baby were better off without him.'

'Oh, P.J., how awful. How is he?'

'He's here, upstairs, asleep. I sedated him. I'll keep an eye on him for a few days. My guess is he'll be okay after a good rest, then we can sort the other mess out.'

'How bad is it?'

'Five million, at a rough estimate.'

Charlotte paled. 'Poor Alex and Catherine. What will happen? What will they do?'

'I think I might be able to help.'

'But P.J., five million? You'd have to sell your house, wouldn't you?'

'I don't think it'll come to that.'

'Well, all I can say is they're jolly lucky to have you to help them. You're a wonderful father.'

'That's the second time someone's said that to me today,' P.J. mused.

'Well there you are.'

'But I'm not. I don't think any of us are. We just do the best we can with what we have.'

'Do you think,' mused Charlotte, 'they have *any* idea, any idea at all, how much we love them? How we'd do anything? How we worry about them?'

'Nope,' grinned P.J. 'At least not until they have their own.'

'You're right, of course,' Charlotte yawned. 'I'd better go.' She hadn't slept at all, worrying about Candy, and although she hated the situation, she knew Ossie was right and that Candy had to face up to what she had done herself. Part of the problem was that Candy had the money of a grown-up but none of the responsibilities. Charlotte blamed herself for that too. She should have put her foot down more when Ossie gave in to Candy's demands, but she hadn't, so now Candy was learning the hard way that there were consequences. Much as it hurt Charlotte, that was what had to happen. She would be there for Candy as long as there was breath in her, but Candy had to grow up. Charlotte just hoped and prayed that Ossie was right and it was just a scam, that this guy didn't really mean business – but they had no way of knowing that yet.

'You won't stay?'

'I'd love to, but my mother will be chomping at the bit, waiting for an update. She's horrified to be left out of the drama. We didn't tell her, not the full story at any rate. I just told her Candy had been put in a very compromising situation and was in deep trouble. I'd better get back to her.'

'I wish you were staying.' P.J. took her in his arms as Charlotte got up to leave.

'So do I.'

'Nothing like kids to get in the way of a romantic evening, is there?'

'Or parents,' countered Charlotte as they walked arm in arm to the hall.

Then P.J. kissed her, and kissed her, and they stood there at the front door, reluctant to say goodnight, for quite a long time.

At first she thought she was imagining it.

She and Marco were sitting with her father. Marco had fallen asleep sitting in the chair, his chin resting on his chest, dark shadows under his eyes. Paulo and Bruno were both checking in with their families; both had wives and young children. Carla and Marco were on the afternoon shift, although Carla hadn't left her father's bedside since she'd arrived two days ago, except to grab a coffee or a bagel from the canteen. She was gazing out the window of the small room, looking out over the sprawling suburbs of New York, when she heard it.

'Carla.' It was a rasp, a whisper, then louder as she wheeled around. 'Carla.'

'Papa!' she cried, rousing Marco from his snooze and throwing herself on her knees beside her father's bed. She grabbed his hand and kissed it. 'You're awake! Marco, he's awake! Oh thank God.' She began to sob while Marco leapt from his chair and whooped, searching frantically for his phone to give his brothers the good news.

19

James looked at his watch and sighed. Ordinarily he got unpleasant tasks straight out of the way as soon as he could, but he'd been putting this one off all week. There was no way around it. He'd just have to bite the bullet. He should meet her, he reflected, he owed her that, but the thought of it made his heart sink. Suppose she began to cry? He would feel like such a heel. Then what would happen? No, much better to do it over the phone. Cowardly, perhaps, but safer. After all, things couldn't go on as they were. It simply wasn't fair to her.

After that, he had another task to complete, one he'd been putting the finishing touches to for quite some time now, ever since he'd heard about the ghastly incident in Rome from Sophia, when she'd been so upset. James had been incandescent with rage and vowed there and then to put a stop to this nonsense once and for all. It had required quite a lot of time and effort, not to mention considerable expense, but he could afford it. The result would be well worth it. Contracts had been signed last week and all the legalities had been taken care of. Now he just had to do his bit – make it personal, so to speak.

First, though, there was the other thing. James took a deep breath and dialled her number.

'James!' He could hear the delight in her voice, which made what he was about to do infinitely more difficult.

He cleared his throat. 'Sarah, I'm so sorry, but there's something I have to tell you . . .'

* * *

Cici didn't think her level of misery could plummet much further. She had reached a stage now where she was sort of bumping along the bottom, some days only slightly less awful than others. She was seeing Dom that evening. At least he was speaking to her. Sophia was still giving her the cold shoulder, although at Dom's request she had allowed her mother to explain her side of the story. At least after talking to her, Cici could tell that Sophia was thawing a little. She had listened to her, taken her phone call. That was a positive sign. It would take a lot of hard work, but Cici would make it up to her. She'd had such a great relationship with her daughter up until this and she couldn't bear to be cut off from her. It was like having her heart ripped out.

She checked the spaghetti and meatballs and gave them a stir, then put the finishing touches to the salad. As she opened a bottle of Chianti, the doorbell rang. Dom was as punctual as his father, she mused with a pang.

She could tell he was shocked at her appearance, though he tried to hide it well. Although they had talked regularly on the phone, it had been a few weeks since he had seen her. She knew she looked dreadful.

'Oh, Dommy, you shouldn't have. How thoughtful of you.' She took the flowers he pressed into her hands and tried very hard not to cry.

'I thought you might need a bit of cheering up,' he said jovially, although she could see the concern in his face.

'Have a glass of wine. You pour, and I'll dish up.' She found a vase for the flowers.

'It smells good, whatever it is.' Dom sniffed the air appreciatively.

'Your favourite, mine too,' she smiled.

'Spaghetti and meatballs,' he grinned. 'Excellent. Nothing like home cooking.' He sat down at the table.

Over dinner, they effortlessly slipped into Italian, as they always did, and chatted away, Cici deliberately staying away from her current domestic situation. She was afraid if she said anything, she might break down and cry.

But Dom brought it up before very long. 'What are you going to do, Mum?'

The forkful of food paused midway to her mouth, and she sighed and put it down. 'I don't know, Dommy. What can I do? It's all such a dreadful mess.'

'You can get a lawyer,' he said gently. 'You have to, Mum. You can't stick your head in the sand about this any more. You have to have legal representation. Dad is going ahead with this divorce whether you like it or not.'

She forced herself to reply. 'You're right. I've been looking into it, and I've been given the names of a few good people. I intend to ring them next week, make an appointment to see them.'

'Good,' Dom sounded relieved. 'The sooner all this is sorted out, the better. I know it's horrible, Mum, really I do. None of us ever thought – well, you know.'

'I know,' Cici filled the awkward pause miserably. 'And it's all my fault. If I could turn the clock back, I'd do anything. *Anything*.'

'I know you would, but you can't.' He was firm. 'And now we all have to move forward and get on with our lives.'

She changed the subject. 'Speaking of which, Dommy, what's going on with you? Here we are talking about awful depressing things, like me and Daddy. Let's talk about you and the restaurant. How is everything? It's so long since I've been to Dominic's.'

Dom sighed and decided to be truthful. 'Actually, Mum, things are pretty bad.'

'What?' Cici was astonished. 'How do you mean?'

Taking a sip of his wine, Dom launched into the whole story. He told his mother about being in the red, the deteriorating accounts that Tanya had kept from him that he should have spotted, and then about Carla, about how he had almost fallen in love with her, until the awful moment a couple of days ago when he had returned home and Astrid had thrust the awful newspaper article into his hands.

'I couldn't believe it,' he said despondently. 'I still can't. And now, well, you can imagine. Things are completely crazy. Rollo has left. His pride was fatally injured – understandably. The kitchen was on a skeleton staff anyway, Carla has conveniently run off back to New York and I'm barely managing to keep the doors open. Of course, the most ironic twist of all is that the story has piqued interest in the restaurant, so we're getting more bookings than ever. But the food is deteriorating by the minute. I've already put word out for a replacement chef, but I'll never get anyone of Rollo's calibre, and even if I could, I couldn't afford it. So things, since you ask, are looking pretty bleak.' He paused to draw breath.

'Oh, Dommy – I can't believe it!' Cici was appalled, listening to his account.

'Well, there you go – that's pretty much where I'm at.'

'But,' Cici was thinking aloud, 'you and Carla, why didn't you tell me? Although I did notice the way you looked at her in the restaurant.'

'You did?' He was astonished.

'Of course I did, what do you take me for?' She grinned impishly, a hint of the old Cici coming through.

'Nobody else did, I hope.' He looked sheepish, then scowled. 'Anyway, now I know that was just a ruse. How could I have been so stupid?'

Cici patted his hand sympathetically. 'Don't blame yourself, sweetheart. Look at your mother.'

Dom managed a weak smile.

'But still,' Cici looked puzzled. 'Something about this doesn't ring true.'

'What, exactly?' Dom tried not to sound sarcastic.

'I don't know. It just doesn't feel right. I saw Carla often in the restaurant, and apart from Harry,' she said ruefully,

'I'm not a bad judge of character. I can't believe she would be that conniving.'

'Yeah, well, that's the way it is – believe me.'

'Oh, I do, Dommy, I'm not suggesting for a moment that you're exaggerating or making it up – you couldn't,' she laughed. 'No one could. But that's just it – it sounds almost too ridiculous.'

'Nothing ridiculous about it from where I'm sitting.'

'There is just one thing,' Cici paused.

'What?'

'You said that you were *almost* falling in love with Carla.'

'So?'

'In my experience, there is no "almost" falling in love. You either do or you don't. *Are* you in love with her?'

'A girl who would set me up? Betray me? Put my restaurant, my reputation, at risk? Are you mad?'

'You haven't answered my question,' Cici pressed. 'And we don't actually know that Carla did *any* of those things. I for one always liked her tremendously. She's a great girl, and Italian. That's what feels wrong about all this.' She paused, nodding her head emphatically. 'Yes, that's it. I don't for one moment believe Carla would do that to anyone, let alone the man she loved. And believe me, she has loved you for a long time, Dommy, any woman could see that, let alone your mother. It used to drive poor Tanya mad – I'm pretty sure it still does. Does Tanya know you and Carla are together?'

'*Were* together,' Dom corrected her. 'I suppose she could have.'

'And have you talked to Carla about all this?'

'She left a message on my phone saying she had to go back to New York, something urgent had come up. Well obviously it had – her cover had been blown, for starters.'

'And you didn't call her back?'

'I got her voicemail – I left a message.'

'Not a very nice one, I'm guessing.'

'There's nothing to say.'

'Dommy, listen to me, and listen carefully.' Cici was serious. 'You're my son, and I know you. For what it's worth, I think that you *are* in love with Carla.' She held up her hand to stop Dom objecting. 'Just hear me out. I think that you are in love with her and I *know* she is in love with you – a mother can sense these things. You are in love with each other. Do you know how important that is? How precious? To find someone you can feel that way about? I think there has been some horrible misunderstanding, but even if there hasn't, even if it turns out that all this undercover stuff is true and her intentions were dishonourable, don't you think you owe it to yourself to talk it over face to face? Surely it's worth that much. If you have any Italian blood in you at all, if you have a shred of the passion I know you have, if you have even the smallest bit of your father's integrity, you will go now to Carla. Fly to New York, do whatever it takes to find out what has gone wrong. Otherwise – believe me – you will spend the rest of your life regretting it.' Cici drew a long breath. 'I know what I'm talking about here. I may have made a horrible mess of my life, but you don't have to. I have managed to lose the person I have loved most in all the world. Don't let foolish pride and misunderstandings stand in the way of finding out the truth – however difficult that truth may be to face.'

Dom was silent, wrestling with a myriad of conflicting emotions. Eventually he sighed and got up. 'It's late. I'd better go. Thanks for dinner, Mum.' He put on his coat.

'At least think about what I've said, will you?' Cici said, patting his face fondly. 'I know I'm not a very good example of relationship counselling right now, but I just have a feeling about this.'

Dom hugged her. 'Maybe,' was all he would say.

'Let me know what happens,' Cici said.

When he had gone, she poured another glass of red wine and sat down alone at the table. She had been right to say what she had. She was sure of it.

She liked Carla – almost as much as she had *disliked* Tanya. Carla would no more hurt Dom than his own family would. Cici would bet her life on it. Every motherly instinct she possessed was telling her so.

Carla was in her old bedroom, still maintained just as it always had been, in her family home. The old Victorian brownstone with steep steps up to the front door in Brooklyn was unchanged, except now her father lived there alone. When her family bought the house in the 1950s, it wouldn't have been considered a particularly good neighbourhood, just your regular big, blue-collar Italian families. Now, because of its proximity to the financial district just across the river and the stunning views of the Manhattan skyline, it was considered very trendy.

Now that he was recovering and off the critical list, she had, on Marco's insistence, gone home to shower, change and get some rest. She was just undressing, almost incoherent with tiredness and relief, when her phone rang. It was Astrid.

'Carla!' she said, sounding both exasperated and relieved. 'Finally, I get hold of you. What the hell is going on with you?'

'What do you think is going on with me?' Carla snapped. 'And thanks for asking, but my father came out of his coma just hours ago. He still has a long way to go, but he's out of danger – only just.'

'What are you talking about?' Astrid was bewildered.

'What do you mean, what am I talking about? My father had a heart attack. He almost died. I've spent the past two days by his bedside while he hovered between life and death, and neither the man I thought loved me or anyone else I work with even had the decency to ask how he or I were doing. I thought I had a good working relationship with everybody in Dominic's, never mind the one I clearly *don't* have with Dom.'

There was a pause at Astrid's end of the line. 'A lot's been happening since you've gone, Carla.'

'Well, clearly it's more important, whatever it is.'

'Carla,' Astrid said, 'why didn't you tell anyone who you really were?'

'Excuse me? What are you talking about?'

So Astrid told her everything – about the newspaper article, Dom's reaction and, of course, about Rollo leaving. 'We're up the creek without a paddle, you could say.'

By the time Carla had finished listening to Astrid's account, she was pacing around the room. 'I don't believe this,' she kept repeating. 'I don't believe it.'

'It's true. Take it from me.'

'And you, Astrid? Do you believe I would do such a thing?'

There was a pause. 'No, I don't. But it's a pity you never told anyone about your background, your career. You can see how it could be construed unfavourably.'

'Only one person could construe anything unfavourable out of this, and that's Tanya. Everything about this smacks of her. But still, I can't believe that Dom would believe I'd do such a thing – nothing could be further from the truth.'

'He said he tried to call you, but he just got voicemail. That confirmed his suspicions.'

'Oh for God's sake!' Carla cried. 'My father was dying! Phone calls and messages, unless they were a matter of life and death, were not at the top of my list of priorities.'

'Look, you've had a shock, Carla, and I'm truly sorry to hear about your father. None of us had any idea, really.'

'I told Dom – I left a message on his phone.'

'All these messages,' Astrid sounded exasperated. 'There's some sort of crossed wires or something going on. Call him – better still, come back and talk to him yourself. He's miserable without you and hell to be around. I thought Rollo could be difficult, but . . .'

'Dom can go to hell! I've done nothing wrong except ask

for a little privacy in my life. So what if I'm a chef? Who cares? I just wanted to get away from New York, away from my brothers, my father and away from cooking. I wanted to be invisible for a while, and now—' Her voice broke. 'I'm sorry, Astrid. It's not your fault. It was good of you to call me. I just can't cope with anything else right now.'

'Of course.' Astrid was sympathetic. 'Is there anything I can do?'

'No, thanks. Look, I'll call you in a couple of days.'

'Take care, Carla. I miss you – we all do.'

'Sure you do,' said Carla. If she hadn't been so tired, she'd have flung the phone out the window. She was stunned, stunned and hurt. How could they? How could he?

She had left a message on his phone, telling him her father was desperately ill, and he hadn't even called her back except to leave some accusatory message on *her* phone. And this was the man she loved, who said he loved *her*? She had thought she meant something to him – that they had something special. Clearly she had been wrong – again. He was judgemental, selfish and unappreciative, just like all the other men in her life.

Fully intending to have another good cry, Carla climbed wearily into bed and was asleep before her head hit the pillow.

Since Carla had gone, Dom had been working around the clock. It wasn't just a necessity, given his increasingly fraught kitchen arrangements – it was the only way he could keep his mind off what had happened between him and Carla. How could he have been so wrong about her? How could he have been so easily taken in by her charms? Tanya had never liked her either. Perhaps she'd been right, womanly intuition and all that. But then he thought about what his mother had said the night before and when he started thinking about that, he started thinking about other things, like how he'd always fancied Carla rotten but for some reason never admitted it to himself. He remembered how concerned she'd been when he was sick and she'd brought the soup up to him, and the look on her face, the look they'd both exchanged, full of meaning, before Tanya had all but physically turfed Carla out. Then he thought of that first night, and the many other nights and days that had followed when their bodies had spoken so eloquently of what neither one would say – which was that they were falling more and more deeply in love.

Why hadn't she told him?

Sitting at his computer, Dom googled her again. Scrolling through mentions of her culinary achievements, he had to admit they were right up there. No wonder Rollo had been upset! She outranked him any day.

And then he saw it. Under the same name, Berlusconi, *The New York Times* excerpt, dated only three days ago, reporting that Antonio Berlusconi, owner of the famous chain of Italian restaurants, had suffered a serious heart attack and was in a critical condition. His three sons were by his bedside and it was hoped that his only daughter would join the vigil, despite a family rift rumoured to have forced Carla, former executive chef of the M Hotel, to leave the country.

Dom's hands froze over the keyboard. He was reading it again, checking the date, when Astrid came in, looking uncomfortable.

'I'm really sorry to interfere, and I know it's none of my business, but I've just been talking to Carla and I think you need to talk to her. It's her father – he's really ill. That's why she had to go back to New York. She said she left a message on your phone, but . . .' She held her hands out helplessly. 'I told her about the article, and of course, well, you know the rest. She's really upset about it.'

Dom ran his hands through his hair and let out a long breath. 'What a bloody mess,' he said, shaking his head, then he stood up. 'I know it's an awful lot to ask of you, Astrid, but do you think you could hold the fort here for a day or two? Just tell everyone to do the best they can. I need to go to New York.' He grabbed his jacket and was already on his way.

'Of course,' Astrid smiled broadly. 'I was hoping you'd say that.'

What a difference a day made! Or in this case, four days. Carla swung through the doors of St Vincent's Hospital with a broad smile now the hospital was no longer a place that held fear and anguish for her. Walking along the by-now-familiar corridors and nursing stations, Carla smiled and greeted the medical staff who had taken such good care of her father and had been so supportive of her and her brothers during that awful night when he hovered between life and death. Now, pushing the door open to his room, Carla was overjoyed to see the change. Antonio Berlusconi was sitting up, declaring they weren't feeding him enough and flirting with the two nurses who were monitoring his chart and checking the apparatus. He was still hooked up to a few drips, but the man who greeted her was definitely the father she knew and loved, even though they were both so alike they drove each other crazy.

'Well, well, well, if it's not my hot-headed daughter,' he grinned at her, indicating that she should come and sit beside him.

'Papa,' she said, dropping a kiss on his forehead, 'you gave us such a scare.'

'You keep saying that,' he grinned at her. 'If that's what it took to get you to come home, I'd do it all over again.'

'Don't say that. Nothing matters any more except that you're going to get better again.' She settled down to eat the take-out lunch she had brought from the deli. 'You're going to have to take it easy from now on, Papa. No more stress, no more drama. You're going to have to learn to be calm, go with the flow.'

'Look who's talking!'

'I'm serious.'

'So am I. But I'd rest a lot easier if I knew my only daughter would stop running around and settle down, find a nice man, have some children,' he grumbled. 'Marco, Paulo, even Bruno, all married.' He looked at her. 'Now don't go getting angry with me – it's only natural for a father to want those things for his daughter.' He patted her hand. 'I didn't check out this time, but who knows when I will, and when I do, I'd like to think I was leaving knowing you were happy and loved by a good man. There must be someone out there who's right for you.'

'I thought so too,' Carla said, for once not challenging him. 'And I thought I had found him, in Dublin.'

'An Irishman? Well, I suppose . . .'

Carla smiled at his expression. 'He's half Irish, half Italian.'

'Good,' he nodded, encouraged. 'So what's wrong with him?'

'Oh God, Papa, you wouldn't believe it if I told you.' She rolled her eyes.

'Try me.'

'It would take too long.'

'Do I look like I'm going anywhere?'

So she told him everything, from her first day in Dublin, to getting the job in Dominic's as a waitress. At this, her father's eyes bulged. She told him about Dom and how she'd fallen for him, and then the awful call she'd received from Marco to come home immediately, and then, finally, the unbelievable newspaper article and the misunderstandings and accusations that had followed.

'Let me get this straight.' Antonio hoisted himself further up on his pillows, his eyebrows knitted together in a manner she knew all too well. 'You fight with your father. You run away to a strange city. You get a job in a restaurant, where you masquerade as a waitress, misleading your employer and the rest of the staff. You then fall in love with the owner of this restaurant, never at any time telling him that you are a world-class chef and by the time some wise guy gets hold of the fact and runs to the newspapers with the story, you have disappeared to New York.'

'You were dying!' Carla cried indignantly.

'Listen to me, Carla.' He was glowering at her now. 'I don't know anything about this Dominic guy. I don't know if he's worth it or not. I don't know if you love him or not – only you know that. But I can tell you that if you do, you had better do something about it. Your mother, God rest her soul, was, unlike her daughter, a patient, understanding, forgiving woman. I loved her more than my own life. She would tell you what I am going to tell you. If you find love, real love, then you don't run away from it! You don't let any misunderstandings or secrets destroy it.'

'It wasn't my fault!'

'Do you love him, Carla?'

'I don't know.' She made a face. 'Maybe.'

'Did you love him before you left for New York?'

'Yes, but—'

'No buts. Then this is what you must do. This is one piece of advice you must listen to – even if it is from your father. You must go back, Carla, immediately.' He held up his hand to stop her protest. 'You must go back and tell him everything. It is the only honourable thing to do.'

'I can't go back, they all hate me. The chef has even left because of me.'

'Then who is running the kitchen?'

'Astrid, the pastry chef.'

'A pastry chef in charge of a kitchen?' He was incredulous.

'They're on a skeleton staff already,' Carla mumbled, feeling the force of his disapproval.

'No daughter of Antonio Berlusconi shirks her responsibilities and leaves a kitchen in chaos, never mind in the hands of a pastry chef! You must go back to Dublin immediately and help them out. Otherwise I will have another heart attack.'

'Papa, that's not fair!'

'Who said anything about fair?' he shrugged, but there was a gleam in his eye. 'I'm fine now, they're sending me home at the end of the week. I'll have full-time nursing at home until I'm back on my feet. It will help my recovery to know you are doing the right thing. Now go!'

'I won't.'

'It's what your dear mother would want.'

'Papa, don't do this to me,' she begged.

'I don't want to see you again until this mess is sorted out.' And with that, Antonio lay back on his pillows and pretended to close his eyes.

When his considerably confused and subdued daughter had kissed him and left the room, Antonio took the photograph of his late wife from the bedside locker and held it to him. 'Maria,' he murmured. 'If you could only see her. She is so beautiful, so like you, and is so clearly in love.' He sighed, shaking his head. 'Wherever you are, watch over her. Don't let her screw it up!' Then he kissed the miraculous medal of hers that he'd worn around his neck since the day she had died.

20

It was a beautiful, clear, sunny day in Dublin, and the bright blue sky made Harry feel more cheerful than he had in weeks. He was particularly sensitive to the weather and convinced he suffered from seasonal affective disorder, although his therapist had challenged him about this. Not that he had seen her for months, ever since he'd waxed lyrical to her about his relationship with Cici and she'd been nonplussed. He could tell, without her having to say a word. She just got that look on her face, like she always did when he talked about his love life. What did she know anyway? All sympathetic and supportive when he was down, and then, when he was feeling positively euphoric about life, she would rain on his parade, telling him to take things slowly and did he think it was wise in light of his past experiences? Clearly she didn't approve, though unfortunately, she had been proved right. Women! They were all the same.

Since the Rome incident, he'd been lying low, confining himself to sending the odd derogatory text message to Cici, and a few times, when he'd sat up late having a couple of drinks (he didn't tell his therapist about *that* either), he had left voice messages telling Cici in no uncertain terms what he thought of her. He was still stung to think of what had happened, but at least he had wiped the smile off her face when he'd followed her and turned up at the restaurant that evening with her daughter. The look on her face had been worth it.

He got a good laugh too over that article about Dominic's

he had read in the paper. Made her son look like a right eejit! Harry knew the waitress to see – she was hard to miss, sexy too, if you liked that sort of thing. He had never liked Dominic anyway, arrogant sod. He had always treated Harry politely, but he could tell he was looking down his nose at him – that kind always did. Still, who cared about the Coleman-Cappabiancas anyway?

The other thing that was making Harry whistle as he strolled towards the offices of *Select* was that he had an appointment to see the new CEO of Marquess, the publishing company that owned *Select* and a variety of other top-class publications. The surprise takeover had increased the share price considerably, and since Harry had taken *Select* from being a rather fuddy-duddy women's monthly to one of the hottest new style bibles, he was pretty sure he was in for a promotion. Stephen Friar, the CEO, was a slick Brit and appreciated bright, young, driven talent. Harry had taken even more care than usual with his appearance. The new biscuit-coloured linen suit with pale blue lining had cost a fortune. At the time, he had thought of it as an investment. He'd bought it especially for the Rome trip, thinking, as he had then, that when he would be living with Cici he would need an extensive wardrobe for all the wonderful places they would visit and stay in. He scowled again, thinking of what he'd been deprived of. Still, at least he was looking the part today.

He strolled past reception and went to grab a coffee. He still had ten minutes to spare and was just about to head into his office when Lucy, one of the PAs, caught up with him.

'Harry,' she said rather breathlessly, 'you're wanted in the boardroom now. He's early,' she said. 'Just as well you are too.'

'Thanks, Lucy, I'm on my way. Ditch this for me, would you?' He handed her the coffee.

He walked down to the end of the corridor and opened the double doors into the huge room, where the long walnut table held pride of place, gleaming now in the sunlight that streamed through floor-to-ceiling glass windows.

'Mr Friar!' Harry moved forward eagerly, holding out his hand to greet the tall figure who stood looking out at the view from the end of the room, then stopped in his tracks as the man slowly turned around, keeping his hands casually in the pockets of his pinstriped trousers, making no effort to return the greeting.

This wasn't Stephen Friar, Harry registered slowly, but there was something definitely familiar about the elegant, handsome figure who regarded him with something that approached disinterest. The warning bells and recognition began to tug at his consciousness simultaneously, and Harry faltered halfway across the room. The man in front of him was none other than James Coleman.

'Sit down, Harry.' James indicated a seat. 'This will only take a few moments.'

'I don't understand.' Harry's throat was dry. 'Where's Stephen Friar?'

'I'll make it simple.' James's tone was pleasant, although he remained standing. 'Stephen had other business to attend to. As I now hold a controlling interest in Marquess, I said I'd be happy to stand in for him.'

A cold trickle of sweat began to run down Harry's spine.

'I'm afraid we no longer require your services, Harry.'

'You can't do this,' he began.

'Please don't interrupt.' He waved a hand dismissively. 'In view of your acknowledged contribution to *Select*, which we have taken into account, we have a position to offer you in our Manchester office.'

'This is a joke!' Harry blustered.

James continued, unperturbed by Harry's outburst. 'A smaller position, but similar. A challenge, if you like.'

'I won't be—'

'Be quiet.' The voice was like steel. 'The choice is yours,

Harry. You have half an hour to collect your belongings and vacate your office, or I will be forced to involve the police – and I have much to involve them with. I would have sooner, of course, but in light of your rather *unfortunate* history, and indeed proven records of emotional instability, I'm offering you a discreet way out.'

'I have a lawyer,' Harry spluttered.

'I'm sure you do, but the time for fantasy is over, Harry. And I mean *over*. You're playing with the big boys now, and you've already lost.'

Harry felt a strange roaring in his head. 'Cici's behind this. She made you do this.'

'My wife knows absolutely nothing about this.' James Coleman leaned on the table, his eyes boring into Harry's. 'And if you ever – *ever* – contact, much less approach, her or indeed any of my family again, I will have you locked up for a very long time. I'm prepared to offer you this position in Manchester because I'm a reasonable man, and I appreciate that you may not, as it would appear, always be able to control your behaviour. But if you think for one moment that I will stand by and watch my wife and daughter be taken advantage of, stalked and harassed by a delusional young man, however unfortunate the circumstances leading up to that behaviour have been, then you are sadly mistaken. If I were you, I would see Manchester as an infinitely preferable option to remaining here and facing what are bound to be unpleasant and distasteful consequences.'

'Are you threatening me?'

'No, I'm merely advising you. As I said, I'm a reasonable man, unless my patience, which is considerable, is taxed, at which point I become extremely unreasonable. I have not risen to the position I hold today without taking necessary action, however unpleasant that action may be – when required. I will not hesitate to do so where you are concerned.'

Harry sat there, immobilised.

'You may go now.'

Somehow he got up and made it back to his office, his breath coming in rasps. His throat felt tight, constricted. With shaking hands, he scrolled through the numbers in his phone for the one he so desperately needed. He wished now he hadn't stopped taking his medication. It had affected his sexual performance, so he'd ditched it. He would have to come clean and tell her everything, all over again. He didn't care how annoyed she would be with him. If she would only pick up the phone, he would never disregard his therapist's advice ever again.

Jennifer was feeling like a new woman. What with her new hip and two new front teeth implants, she was feeling twenty years younger. It was wonderful to be pain-free after all those years of limping.

She had already met up with most of her old friends for lunch or bridge to show off all the new technology. Now, though, she was bored, bored and a little lonely. Charlotte was always out and about with P.J., which she was happy about. Jennifer was immensely fond of P.J. She felt as if she had known him for ever; he was that sort of chap. But now she found herself on her own a lot of the time. She missed Candy about the place too and hadn't heard from her in weeks. According to Charlotte, her granddaughter had got herself into some sort of unspeakable trouble – so unspeakable that nobody would tell her anything about it. It was thoroughly frustrating. She had even tried phoning Candy once or twice on her mobile, but just got the recorded message.

Now, on her way back from the hairdresser's, in her ancient Mini Clubman, she was surprised when her phone rang.

'Gran?'

'Candice! I was just thinking of you.'

'I can't talk for long, Gran, the money's going to run out.' Candy was breathless.

'What? Where are you?'

'I'm in a phone-box thingy.'

'What on earth are you doing in a phone box?'

'They've taken my phone, Gran, and my computer – I'm under house arrest.'

'What on earth are you talking about?' Jennifer swerved, narrowly avoiding a parked car.

'You sound funny, Gran. Have you been drinking?'

'Don't be impertinent! Of course not. It's my new teeth, I haven't got used to them yet. Where are you?'

'I'm at Dad's house, or I'm supposed to be – they've locked me up. I only escaped now to the village. You've got to help me. Will you come and get me, please?'

'Oh, Candice, really! What's going on?'

'I'll tell you when I see you. Just come and get me, will you?' She sounded desperate.

'Who's there? Is that Shalom creature at home?'

'And her mother, that's all. Dad's out. Please, Gran, hurry.' The phone went dead.

Shalom and her mother! So Ossie was moving the family in, was he? Whatever her granddaughter had done, it couldn't possibly warrant being locked up with that sort of people – why, that was what had started all this trouble in the first place.

Jennifer pulled up abruptly and did a U-turn, blithely ignoring the rude oaf in the lorry who made some vulgar hand signal at her, and headed straight for the Stillorgan dual carriageway. When she reached it and got through the traffic lights at Donnybrook church, she put her foot down. She didn't care what Charlotte might say. Charlotte wasn't who Candy had rung for help, she had rung her grandmother – and quite rightly, by the sounds of things. Tearing along the motorway, Jennifer hadn't felt such an adrenaline rush since she had last ridden to hounds.

* * *

Carla pulled the cushion and patterned throw off the old trunk that served as a window seat in her old bedroom and knelt down in front of it. Opening it, she inhaled the familiar, slightly musty smell, a combination of old papers, yellowing photographs, old letters and, of course, her notebooks. Taking them out carefully, one by one, and flicking through them, she was immersed in culinary memories. Her first, childish, carefully printed recipes for baking, painstakingly copied in red pencil, hastily scribbled notes of inspired combinations of flavours jotted on the back of an envelope on a backpacking trip through Peru, famous recipes from Michelin-starred restaurants and, of course, her family recipes, tweaked and added to down through the years – wives, mothers, grandmothers all adding their own magic ingredients, their own words of wisdom. She found the ones she needed and put the rest back carefully. Then she placed them in her hand luggage (she would never have risked losing them in a suitcase) and gathered the rest of her belongings. Five minutes later she was on the street, hailing a cab. 'Kennedy,' she said to the Rastafarian driver as he pulled off into the stream of traffic. She was on her way back to Dublin to face the biggest test of her life so far – both in the kitchen and out of it.

Twenty minutes later, Jennifer pulled off the motorway, taking the exit for Annaderry. She knew the country house Ossie had bought and lavishly refurbished well, although in her day it had been a smaller and no doubt significantly more tasteful home than the one she now approached. All the same, she had to admit it was impressive. Driving slowly up the long, winding driveway, she pulled up outside the front entrance and parked her car, taking good care to keep her distance from the white Porsche (undoubtedly Shalom's) and the hideous mustard-coloured car beside it with lots of bits sticking out of it. Taking one final look in the mirror, she adjusted her headscarf, rubbed some lipstick off her teeth and got out. She rang the doorbell and waited, tapping her foot. A voice whispered through the intercom. 'Gran? Is that you?'

'Of course it's me, Candice. Stop this nonsense and let me in at once.'

The door opened and Candice let her in, looking over her shoulder nervously. 'Shh,' she said, holding her finger to her lips. 'I didn't think you'd be so quick. I just have to get my bag, it's in the kitchen.' She darted through a door and reappeared with a holdall. They were just about to depart when a shrill voice beckoned. 'Candy? Just a minute, young lady, where do you think you're going? And who are you?' Bernie asked indignantly, emerging from the front living room.

Jennifer turned slowly, regarding the plump, blonde, overly made-up woman in the leopard-print top and tight white skirt from beneath arched brows.

'*I* am Jennifer Searson,' she said. 'And who might you be?'

'I'm Bernie. And she's under house arrest.' She pointed a blood-red nail at Candy. 'Ossie left strict instructions she was not to leave her room except to eat.'

'Is that so?' Jennifer was icily polite. 'Well, you may tell your employer, Bernie, that I have come to take my granddaughter home.'

'Employer!' Bernie shrieked. 'I'll have you know my daughter is the lady of this house – I'm Shalom's mother.' She stood with her hands on her hips.

'That explains a lot,' Jennifer smiled.

'C'mon, Gran, let's go.' Candy tugged at her sleeve.

'What's that supposed to mean?' Bernie's eyes narrowed.

'Never mind. You may tell my son-in-law that Candice is coming with me.'

'Ossie's not your son-in-law, is he? Not any more!' she shot back. 'And he's not going to be happy about this.'

'You're quite right on both counts,' Jennifer said breezily. 'I never did think he was good enough for my daughter, and yes, I dare say he won't be happy about this. But you may tell him to ring me – he has my number on speed dial. Come along, Candice, let's go.'

'You'll be sorry,' Bernie leered at them. 'I bet he'll send the police after you when I ring him. She's got herself into a right heap of trouble, the little tart! Ossie's furious. We all are.'

'Please, Gran,' Candy beseeched her. 'We need to go now.'

'If Candice's behaviour has been in any way inappropriate, it is because her father has encouraged and enabled it, not least through his own example – or rather, lack of one. You may tell him I said that too. Good day to you.'

'What a frightful woman,' Jennifer said to Candy, starting the car and setting off. 'Is she anything like the daughter?'

'Peas in a pod,' Candy confirmed.

Jennifer shuddered. 'Now Candice, you'd better tell me what's going on.'

'I – I don't think I can. I'm too ashamed. Bernie was right, I *am* a stupid tart.' A tear rolled down her face and she brushed it away.

'Stop that snivelling right now. Whatever you've done, whatever trouble you've gotten into, I'm your best chance of getting you out of it, but I can't help you unless you tell me everything – and I mean everything. Now I want every detail, right from the beginning. How bad can it be?'

A little while later, Jennifer almost wished she hadn't asked, but to her credit she kept her eyes on the road, only spluttered once and tried not to look too horrified.

'So you see, Gran? You can't help me, nobody can,' Candy said miserably. 'Not unless Dad pays up.'

'I sincerely hope he does no such thing. On this occasion, your father is absolutely right.'

'Then there's nothing anyone can do.'

'I don't know about that – but I know a man who will.' Jennifer turned off the motorway and headed into town.

'Where are we going?'

'To visit a friend of mine. If anyone can help you, he can.'

Minutes later, Jennifer and Candice walked into the opulent offices of Whitaker, Willoughby and Turnbull, Solicitors.

'Mr Whitaker's office?' she enquired of the receptionist.

'Third floor, the lift is on your left.'

Exiting the lift, Jennifer approached an immaculately groomed girl tapping away on a computer. 'I'm looking for Mr Whitaker's secretary.'

'That would be me,' the girl smiled politely. 'Can I help you?'

'I certainly hope so. I need to see him immediately.'

'Do you have an appointment, Mrs . . .?'

'Searson. Jennifer Searson. No I don't, but just tell him I'm here and that it's a matter of great urgency. I'm quite sure he'll see me.'

'I'm terribly sorry, but Mr Whitaker is in a meeting. Without an appointment, I'm afraid there's absolutely no chance of him seeing you. He's a very busy man,' she explained.

'I'm sure he is, and he has me to thank in no small part for that. His late father used to shoe our horses. My late husband was responsible for putting the very busy Mr Whitaker through college and arranging his apprenticeship. Now if you won't let him know I'm here, I shall sit outside, right here, until he appears – but he will not be happy to know I have been treated in this manner.'

Candy studied the floor, wishing it would open up and swallow her. And they called *her* brazen!

The girl's expression hardened, but she seemed to waver. 'Take a seat, please. I'll interrupt his meeting to let him know you're here,' she said disapprovingly. The girl picked up the phone and murmured discreetly into it. Then, with a forced smile, she said, 'He'll be with you in just a few moments. Can I offer you some tea or coffee?'

Five minutes later, a tall, thin, austere-looking man appeared from around a corner. 'Jennifer!' he beamed. 'How lovely to see you. Do come into my office.'

'Forgive me for being so insistent, Nigel. It's terribly good of you to see us like this. I'm afraid my granddaughter here, Candice, has got herself into a most undesirable predicament. I'm hoping you can help her – and time is of the essence.'

'I'll certainly try. It would be a pleasure. Sit down, do.' He indicated two very expensive-looking antique leather tub chairs in front of his desk. Then he sat down behind it, rested his chin on his hands and, looking directly at Candice, said, 'Tell me the facts, right from the beginning.'

Candice looked at Jennifer, who nodded affirmatively, and for what seemed like the umpteenth time, launched into her nightmare account.

His face remained impassive throughout. He made a few notes and asked for confirmation of a couple of details. 'Did you sign anything?' he asked pointedly. 'This is very important. Think carefully.'

'No – no I didn't.'

'Are you quite sure?'

'Yes. Well, I almost signed something.' She looked worried.

'Almost?'

'Josh did ask me to sign some lease or something, to witness it for him.'

'And did you?' Jennifer held her breath.

'I was going to, but the pen wouldn't work – it had run out. So I couldn't.'

'That's good, Candice, that's very good,' said Nigel, smiling for the first time. 'Now how about some tea or coffee, and I'll tell you what I suggest we do?'

'You mean you can help us?' Jennifer asked eagerly.

'Jennifer, I'm not the foremost show-business lawyer in the country for nothing, you know. Legally speaking, I can't promise anything, but I'm pretty sure I can help. Now here's what I suggest . . .'

Cici had only gone to the hairdresser to get her roots done. She had no desire to leave the house if she could avoid it, but she was depressed looking at her disintegrating appearance. Things were bad enough. She didn't need to see a wreck looking back at her every time she passed a mirror. And besides, old habits died hard. She had found the buzzing atmosphere of the salon vaguely unsettling, she had been out of circulation for so long. Her colourist, Raymond, had been pleased to see her at least.

'Cici! It's been a long time – that's not like you,' he said, running his hands through her hair. 'Been burning the candle at both ends I suppose?'

More like my bridges, she thought, but stapled a bright smile to her face. 'Just work some magic, Ray, and make me look glamorous again.'

'You always look glamorous, Cici, although you've lost a lot of weight and you didn't need to.' He looked concerned. 'Have you been ill?'

'I'm fine, I just had a bad bout of flu, couldn't eat a thing,' she lied.

'Wish I could lose my appetite.' He pointed to a burgeoning paunch. 'Never mind, we'll soon have you looking perky. I think we should be a little adventurous. Let's put a mixture of copper and dark gold through it, it'll look fabulous with your dark base.'

She let him rattle on, relieved not to have to talk. She would have let him shave her head if he'd suggested it. Settling back into her chair, she picked up a few magazines, leaving aside and shuddering inwardly at the March copy of *Select*, which featured the spread on her. She cringed now when she thought of it.

When she was done, she had to admit the finished result

was worth it. Her hair had been freshly restyled in flattering layers around her face, and longer, just brushing her shoulders. The copper and bronze highlights gave her a much-needed lift without appearing drastic. Her hair seemed to shimmer now when she moved.

It was only when she got back to her car that she realised she had a message on her phone. She dialled her voicemail and chewed her lip as she listened to James's voice.

'Cici, it's me, James. I was wondering would you pop up to the house this evening if you're free? I'll rustle up something to eat. There are a couple of things I'd like to discuss if it suits. I'll expect you around seven. No need to ring me back unless you can't make it.'

Dinner with James, in the house – their home. Oh God, she wanted to, but under such awful circumstances, how could she?

And then she made a decision. Enough with the self-pity crap. This flaky, pathetic, crumbling creature she had turned into was not the woman he had married (or rather, thought he had married). She would go for dinner. She would make herself look fabulous – whatever it took. She would laugh and be cheerful and stoic. She had thrown away her marriage, her wonderful life, and put her family in jeopardy, and she would face the consequences. At least she could make sure they would have a civilised, friendly relationship from here on out. Whatever he threw at her, she would accept it with dignity and resignation. She would not object, she would not plead, she would not resort to tears. She would leave them with one last dinner they could perhaps remember fondly one day. She would look on the bright side. At least it was in the evening – the lighting would be flattering.

P.J. was feeling better about things. They had all come through a rough week. Alex, thank God, was considerably better, although he was still pretty shaken. He had been seen by a psychologist who had confirmed, as P.J. had suspected, an emotional breakdown rather than a nervous one – stress induced, not surprisingly. Alex had liked the man and had found talking to him helpful, and to everyone's relief had agreed to see him on a regular basis until he was feeling stronger and had come through this crisis. Catherine had been at his side the moment P.J. told her he was ready, which was after three days of complete rest. She and Charlie had come to stay – there was plenty of room – and their house was put on the market. The Ferrari, too, had been sent back to the shop. Everyone agreed that a fresh start and a more modest set-up was the best course of action.

Sheila was delighted with all the company and having young people in the house again, and Bones had taken to nightly preambles, sneaking up from the kitchen and checking on newly inhabited rooms, where he would settle happily for the night, nudging their surprised inhabitants awake with an insistent wet nose thrust in their face come the morning.

Behind the scenes, P.J. had been to see his own accountant, and together they had arranged a meeting with the investors in the various banks who had put up the cash for Alex to deduce exactly what the damage was. Then he and his accountant and investment people had gone away to formulate their plan.

'It's a big deal, P.J.,' Jim, the accountant, warned. 'Four point nine million's a lot of money.'

P.J. nodded. 'It is, but at least I have it. Might as well give it with a warm hand, as they say. Alex and Bella will get it one way or the other. It might as well be when they need it – which in Alex's case is now.'

'It's a big risk, this hotel resort business. Times are tough. How confident are you about it?'

'The music industry has been good to me, Jim, and financially speaking, the whole world is in disarray. Now I have it to give, but next year, who knows? As for the scheme, I don't know – but I do know I have confidence in my son. Alex is a hard worker; he was just unlucky with the timing. An awful lot of people are going to find themselves in the same boat.'

'And they won't have someone like you to bail them out.'

'I prefer to think of it as giving him another chance. I've had plenty of them in my time. I didn't invest in this scheme when Alex asked me to before. I'd like to now.'

'It'll take a few weeks to release the capital, but we can start with the initial tranche right away.'

He was looking forward to telling Alex and Catherine the news.

He smiled, thinking back to his student days. If anyone had told him that mucking about with a guitar and a penchant for writing lyrics would have proved so profitable, he'd have laughed. But that was before Viper made it big and before some of his lyrics had become big hits, before one had become a movie soundtrack and he'd been asked to write another, and especially before ringtones. It really was extraordinary how one thing led to another.

Sure, P.J. did well as a doctor, but it was his beloved hobby that made him worth an awful lot more than anyone had ever imagined.

Cici waited at the top of the steps outside the front door of what used to be her home, feeling terribly ill at ease, but she was determined not to back out now. This had to be done, had to be endured, however painful it might be. She had taken great care with her make-up (thank God she'd had her hair done) and had discovered a beautiful coral wraparound dress in Sophia's wardrobe that accentuated her new overly slender silhouette, rather than drawing attention to her drastic weight loss. She had even brought a bottle of champagne with her, but her heart was in her mouth as James answered the door.

'Cici,' he said, his eyes roving over her. 'You look wonderful. Come in. And champagne – how thoughtful.'

Following him down into the kitchen, Cici wanted to cry. How bizarre was this, to be invited into her own kitchen and have her soon-to-be-ex-husband cook dinner for her? Looking around her at all the familiar nooks and crannies, the memories flooded back of all the family dinners through the years, feeding the children as they fought to hold a spoon in chubby, uncoordinated little fingers, teaching them to sit at table, and later to cook. Shared confidences, comforting favourite foods in the bad times, celebratory dinners in the good times, but always, always family. How could she have been so stupid to throw all this away?

'The champagne was a great idea, Cici,' James was saying as he dished up. 'I think we ought to make this a fun occasion. There's been far too much doom and gloom recently. To new beginnings,' he said, handing her a glass and raising his own.

'Yes, of course, you're absolutely right. To new beginnings,' she said with forced brightness. *To new beginnings with you and Sarah de Burgh*, she thought as a savage twist of pain gripped her. No wonder James was looking so cheerful. He was getting rid of his stupid, selfish, self-obsessed wife (or non-wife) and making way for the new woman in his life, who by all accounts would appreciate and value him as he deserved to be. Cici took a quick gulp of her champagne to stop herself from sobbing.

'Now, there we are.' James set down a dish of spaghetti puttanesca. 'I doubt it's as good as yours, but I did steal the recipe. After all, it was our first meal together, remember?' he smiled. 'I thought it would be nice . . . for old time's sake.'

Cici felt sick. Was he trying to torture her? If so, he was succeeding. She smiled weakly. At least he hadn't mentioned how thin and gaunt she was looking . . .

'You've got awfully thin, Cici. You're not sick, are you?'

'No. At least, I don't think so.'

'Good. Well, tuck in.'

Desperate to change the subject, she brought up the restaurant and asked him if he had heard the news.

'Yes, I did. Dreadful business. Dom told me all about it. I must say I was taken aback. I don't know this Carla girl well, but I always found her very pleasant. But then, you never can tell, can you?' He shrugged. 'I rather liked Tanya, but I always was partial to good-looking, charming women,' he grinned.

'I just want him to be happy,' Cici said.

'He's rushed off to New York now, so he must be keen on her.'

'He went to New York?' Cici asked, surprised.

'Yes, called me from the airport. I have no idea what's going on, but I never was very good at playing games with all this romantic business. I always preferred to put my cards on the table.'

She nodded dumbly.

They chatted amiably about other, inconsequential things when all Cici wanted to do was break down and beg James for one more chance.

And then he asked the dreaded question.

'I don't like to keep harping on about it, Cici, but have you appointed a lawyer yet?'

Her throat constricted. 'Yes – no – that is, I'm going to. I've been given some names, I just . . . haven't got around to it yet.'

He looked at her across the table with no sign of emotion or regret. 'Because we really must wrap this up, make it legal.'

'Yes . . . I do know that. It just seemed . . . ' How could she say that it seemed impossible, unthinkable? Now she *was* going to break down. She put her hand to her mouth and stifled a sob.

'Come on, Cici,' he said, reaching over to take her hands. 'It's not so bad. There's no point in upsetting yourself about this. We've just got to take the next step. It's only sensible, in light of what's transpired.'

She could only nod helplessly as two big tears rolled down her face.

'Which is why,' he continued gently, 'I'm asking you to marry me. What do you say?'

'What?' she whispered.

'You heard me. Will you marry me? Properly, this time?'

'Is this your idea of a joke?'

'I have only ever asked someone to marry me once before in my life. I was dead serious then – and I'm serious now.'

'But how? Why?' She was unable to absorb what she was hearing.

'Quietly is the answer to your first question, and the answer to your second question is because I love you, I have always loved you and I always *will* love you. Life without you is a bit like this house, just an empty, meaningless shell.' He smiled at her, really smiled at her, for the first time in a long, long time.

'But after everything I've done . . . how could you forgive me?' She couldn't go on.

'What? Because you had an affair? Because you weren't always a perfect wife? Cici, listen to me. You have always had a certain penchant for . . . how shall I put it . . . drama. That was evident the minute I first set eyes on you. It was part of what I fell in love with. You were so very different from me. I always knew we could hit a rocky patch at any stage – and frankly, I'm surprised it wasn't sooner. You gave up so much for me. I know you want life to be like it is in the movies, with men rushing around waving swords and killing their rivals, but life isn't like that. Do you think my love was dependent on you always loving me back? Do you think I'd let you go so easily? What sort of man would that make me? A pretty weedy one, I think. I know things haven't always been easy for you, and maybe I did play too much golf and take you for granted, but we can work all that out. Let's just wipe the slate clean and start over.'

'Oh, James.' She put her hand to her mouth.

'Is that all you can say?' He arched an eyebrow. 'You still haven't answered my question.'

'Yes,' she sobbed, 'yes, a thousand times yes. You have no idea how miserable, how wretched I've been. I was so stupid, so selfish. I was afraid nobody needed me any more. You were so successful, and the kids were all sorted. I was afraid of growing old, becoming old and invisible, when all that really mattered was that *I* needed *you*. It didn't matter if nobody needed me.'

'You! Afraid of growing old!' James gave a shout of laughter. 'I don't believe it.'

'But it's true, James,' she protested. 'I *am* afraid of growing old, losing my looks. They're what I've always relied upon, traded on, and now . . .'

'But Cici, I adore you. You'll always be beautiful to me, whatever age you are. Nothing could change that.'

'Are you sure about this? Are you sure it's what you really want?'

'Absolutely sure – sure enough, and perhaps presumptuous enough, to have booked the registry office for the 7 November . . .'

'The 7 November,' Cici gasped. 'But that's—'

'Our wedding anniversary, yes. Rather a nice touch, don't you think? I haven't completely lost my sense of romance.'

'What will we say?' She began to laugh. 'What will we tell the children?'

'We won't say anything at all to anyone – least of all the children. It's none of their damned business!'

'I can't believe this is happening,' she said, shaking her head.

'Neither can I – although I'm very glad it is.'

'This is the most wonderful surprise I've ever had in my life. I love you so much, James, more than ever. And I'm going to prove it to you every day of my life for as long as I live.'

'Good. Then come upstairs with me now, Cici. We have only six months left to live in sin. It may all become quite dull after that.'

'And you say *I* have a sense of drama.' She shook her head in wonder.

Josh was in the studio editing Viper's latest promo video when he got the call.

'Mr McIntyre?'

'Yeah?'

'This is Mr Nigel Whitaker of Willoughby, Whitaker and Turnbull Solicitors.'

'Uh-huh.' Josh put down the mug of coffee in his hand as a slow smile spread across his face.

'My client, Miss Candice Keating, has instructed me to set up a meeting to discuss the, ah, proposed use of her video images.'

'Is that so? I think I can manage that. When did you have in mind, Mr Whitaker?'

'Would tomorrow at three o'clock be convenient?'

'It's short notice, but I guess I can make it.'

'It would be in your interest to make it, Mr McIntyre.'

'Is that what she told you?' Josh's eyes narrowed.

'That is what I am merely advising you of.'

'I would say it's pretty much in your client's interest too, Mr Whitaker.'

'We can discuss just such matters at the meeting, Mr McIntyre, if you would be so good as to confirm you'll attend.'

'Sure, I'll be there. I'll be counting the minutes,' he grinned.

'Very good. I'll inform my client and give you directions to my office.'

Josh put the phone down and sucked in a long breath. This would be fun, just as he had known it would be. Very lucrative fun, by the sounds of it.

* * *

'Please don't make me go, Gran,' Candy pleaded. 'I don't need to be there, the solicitor can do it on his own.'

'Don't be ridiculous, Candice, of course you need to be there.' This wasn't strictly true, but Jennifer had her reasons, one of which was making sure her granddaughter got to look this snake in the eye in the cold light of day and see him for what he was. Otherwise she would be forever cowed by the incident, and Jennifer wasn't having that. Quite apart from the fact that Jennifer wanted to get a look at him herself – not just out of curiosity, although there was an element of that; it was more a protective instinct on her part. She knew his type, and they never scrubbed up well. Nothing like a bit of harsh reality to do away with the veneer of dangerous glamour Candy had no doubt attributed to him. 'It's not as if you'll be on your own. I'll be there too.'

'You can't!' Candy shrieked in horror.

'Oh yes I can,' said Jennifer grimly, 'and so can you.'

The imposing offices of WWT Solicitors were easy to find on Clarion Quay. Josh had decided he'd better look like he meant business and had unearthed the only suit he possessed, a beige double-breasted number he had appropriated from a shoot he'd done with a boy band two years ago. He teamed it with a black shirt, a white tie and left his hair long and loose. The whole effect was *don't mess with me.*

Now, waiting in reception for what felt like an unnecessarily long time, he was becoming impatient, drumming his chewed fingernails on the arm of the couch. Just when he was about to complain, the lift doors opened and a very pretty, prim-looking girl addressed him. 'Mr McIntyre, if you would like to come with me, I'll show you up to Mr Whitaker's office.'

In the lift, he gave her the benefit of his practised once-over, narrowing his blue eyes speculatively as he took in her black pencil skirt and slim high-heeled pumps, but if she noticed, she gave no sign of either registering or responding to his interest.

Exiting the lift, Josh felt as if he lost at least two inches as his shoes sank into the deep pile carpet that lined the corridor, off which solid mahogany doors concealed their secrets.

'Here we are.' The girl knocked discreetly before opening the door. 'Mr Josh McIntyre,' she announced, showing him in before leaving the room discreetly, closing the door behind her.

What was this, the Three Stooges? Josh was momentarily taken aback. He had expected the lawyer guy, for sure, who stood up now to greet him and indicated that he take a seat at the long table, but he hadn't banked on seeing Candy – a very pale, un-made-up and surprisingly vulnerable-looking Candy. And who was the old broad with the stony expression and the weird hat? He had thought this would be a man-to-man thing.

'Do sit down, Mr McIntyre.' Nigel Whitaker resumed his seat opposite him and smiled pleasantly. 'I'll come straight to the point. There seems to be a fundamental problem with your, ah, proposal.'

'I wasn't aware I had made any proposal – yet.'

'Then now is as good a time as any to point out that you appear to have neglected to offer a consideration to my client, Miss Keating, for your proposed use of these video images.'

'Are you kidding? *She's* supposed to offer *me* a consideration for them.'

'My client, as far as I am aware,' he looked to Candy for confirmation, who nodded, then continued, still in the same mildly bewildered tone, 'has not signed any formal release for these images.'

'So what?'

'That leaves us with a predicament on our hands.'

'You said it.'

'I understand you work for another of my clients, the rock band Viper. Isn't that so? In the capacity of director of promotional videos – would that be correct?'

'Yeah, your point being?'

'I would imagine that accounts for a large part of your earned income?'

'What's that got to do with anything?'

'Well that depends, Mr McIntyre, on how much you value your association with Viper.'

'What're you getting at?'

'It has come to my attention, Mr McIntyre, that your company, Windvest, is involved in selling pornography on the Internet, isn't that so? Videos are made available to the procurers of such entertainment by downloading and so forth for a fee.'

'Nothing illegal about that.'

'Quite. But legal or not, I'm afraid my clients, Viper, would find it very unappealing to be associated with any such practices. It wouldn't, as they say, be good for the image. They would be forced to disassociate themselves from any such activity, and as their lawyer I would advise them quite strenuously to do so, never mind what the PR people would have to say. I imagine there would be quite a lot of noise made about it. Very undesirable noise.'

'What are you getting at?' Josh growled.

'We are willing to pay you a consideration for the time and effort spent in producing these images of my client.'

'So you do want to buy it, right?' he grinned.

'Indeed. My client is prepared to offer you the sum of one euro.'

'Funny.'

'There is nothing remotely amusing about the offer, Mr McIntyre. If you do not accept it and make any attempt to launch these images, we will sue for infringement of copyright – and it will be a very substantial sum we will sue for, make no mistake about that.'

Josh's face was working. He looked at the lawyer guy, who returned his gaze steadfastly, and then at the old broad, whose mouth was set in a thin line. Then he looked at Candy, who was squirming in her chair.

'Keep your money, Miss Rich,' he spat. 'I don't need it.'

'Oh, but I insist,' the lawyer continued. 'This has to be a legal transaction. Candy?' Nigel looked at her as she bit her lip and fished in her pocket for the amount they had decided on. She put the coin on the table and Nigel pushed it across to Josh. 'There you are.'

Josh stood up and swiped it off the table. 'Fuck you,' he said and walked out the door.

'Well,' said Jennifer, 'I must say I really can't see what you saw in him, Candice. Can you, Nigel?'

Nigel smiled.

'Neither can I,' murmured Candice. 'Thank you, Gran. Thank you, Mr Whitaker – I won't forget this.'

'And I hope you won't forget the promise you made me either.' Jennifer looked expectant. 'Quid pro quo.'

'I haven't forgotten, Gran. The hairdresser's appointment is booked for four-thirty.'

'Jolly good. Now I think it's time you called your father and told him you've sorted out this unfortunate incident.'

'Feel free to use my phone,' Nigel said, leaving the office discreetly.

Dom hadn't been in New York for a few years, and he certainly never expected to be there on a mission such as he was.

Arriving at 2:30 p.m. after the six-hour flight, he was tired, and viewing the vast queue of passengers from all over the globe, he thanked God he had been able to clear customs in Dublin. He jumped into a cab at Kennedy and told the driver to go straight to St Vincent's Hospital. As always, it was bumper to bumper on the Brooklyn-Queens Expressway and the stop–start motion of the cab and jet lag began to lull him into a mindless trance. They took the Queensborough Bridge at 59th Street and Dom looked out at the panoramic view of Midtown Manhattan, which never failed to impress him. Finally, after what seemed like an eternity, with the driver hunched over the wheel muttering under his breath about the delay, they reached the hospital. Dom paid him, grabbed his bag and headed for Reception.

He asked for Antonio Berlusconi's room number and went straight up. Outside the door, he took a deep breath, knocked and went in.

'Excuse me,' he said to the old man sitting up in bed who looked straight out of central casting for a *Godfather* movie. 'I'm terribly sorry to barge in like this, but I've come to find Carla – there's something important I need to explain to her.' He paused to catch his breath. 'My name's Dominic Coleman-Cappabianca,' he added as two younger men sitting by the bed, obviously Carla's brothers, regarded him quizzically.

The old man looked at him for a beat, then folded his arms and nodded slowly. 'So you're the Dominic guy, huh?' He turned to his son and said, 'Marco, get this boy a cup of coffee and let him sit down. I hate to tell ya, but your timing is crap.'

'I do realise you've been very unwell,' Dom began, feeling beyond awkward, 'and I'm terribly sorry to intrude, but this won't take long. If you could just tell me where I might find her . . .' The brothers were looking at him strangely.

'You won't find her here,' Antonio said, his eyebrows knitting alarmingly.

'Then where?'

The brothers were shaking their heads.

'What is it with you young people?' Antonio exclaimed, throwing up his hands. 'All this technology you have – cell phones, computers – and you still can't communicate with each other.'

'I just need to explain—'

'Then you've come to the wrong place,' he glowered at him.

Dominic's nerve was beginning to desert him, but then the old guy began to chuckle. 'You've come to the wrong place because Carla has gone back to Dublin to explain things to *you*.'

'I don't believe this.' Dom ran his hands through his hair.

'You better believe it,' said Antonio. 'But since you're here, sit down and tell us a bit about yourself.'

Marco handed him a coffee and Paulo slapped him on the back, laughing. Then they sat back and listened expectantly.

'Start from the beginning,' ordered Antonio. 'And don't leave anything out!'

21

'As we are making our final approach into Dublin, please ensure your seatbelts are fastened and your seatback is in the upright position.'

Carla rubbed her eyes and looked out at the emerald green map unfolding beneath her, bathed in early morning sunlight. It was six-thirty a.m., and all around her people were rousing themselves, chatting and laughing, glad that the flight was over and that they were almost home.

Inside the airport, she collected her bags, got a taxi and headed straight into town. There was no time to lose.

'Early start, love?' the taxi driver asked.

'You bet,' she said, 'and it's gonna be a long day.'

'What is it you work at?'

'I'm a chef,' she said.

'Get away!' He was clearly impressed. 'Would I know where you work?'

'Have you heard of a restaurant called Dominic's?'

'Dominic's,' he mulled it over. 'I *have* heard of that place, right enough. Haven't been in it though. I've heard the food's very good there,' he said.

'It's about to get even better,' she grinned.

It was seven-thirty when she arrived at Dominic's. She dropped her case in the staff room, which was empty, then quickly fished out her uniform, put it on, tied back her hair and fixed her white chef hat, taking one final look in the mirror before heading for the kitchen. She paused for a moment before pushing through the swing doors, took a deep breath and prepared to face the music.

Thirty seconds passed before anyone actually realised she was there, but it was more than enough time for Carla to see that the kitchen was in complete disarray. At first glance, her eagle eye took in wilted vegetables, drab prosciutto and, to her horror, some packets of bought, dried pasta.

'Carla!' Astrid's mouth dropped open. 'Thank God you're here.' She ran to give her a floury hug.

Pino turned from a blazing argument with the other sous chef, grinned and shook his head. 'If I had known . . .' He waved a knife at her.

'Jaysus!' said Paddy, the kitchen porter, looking up from the pile of potatoes he was peeling, 'Who'd have thought it!' He beamed as if his face would split in two.

'Look,' Carla said. 'I know you all have a lot of questions, and believe me, I want to answer them, but there's no time now. Where's Dom? I need to talk to him.' And then, 'What's so funny?'

'Dom's in New York,' Astrid explained, 'looking for you.'

'I don't believe this.' She put her hands to her face and shook her head.

After she'd fully taken in the deteriorating situation, she brought them all together. 'Here's the deal: we still have a restaurant to run. I'm in charge now. Anyone got any problems with that?'

They shook their heads in unison.

'Good, because this kitchen's a disgrace!'

'We're running out of supplies. We can't possibly deliver the menu tonight.' Pino was stressed. 'Nothing's been ordered. It'll be all we can do to get through lunch.'

'We'll get through it all right,' she said grimly. 'For now, Pino, get that dried pasta out of my sight. Those vegetables can go into a country minestrone, with garlic and pecorino cheese and anchovy croutons,' she instructed, making her way into the cold room. At least there were some decent steaks hanging, and a couple of large sole. Apparently a new fish supplier had dropped them in on appro earlier. It wasn't ideal, but it wasn't a disaster either. With a lot of work and even more luck, they could make it – dinner, though, depended on the suppliers. Since Dom always insisted on using the best fresh ingredients, they naturally varied from day to day and week to week – and nobody had ordered.

First, though, there was pasta to make. Within minutes, she had set up a mini pasta factory, covering every surface in paper-thin sheets of dough, remembering her mother teaching her that making pasta is an art as much as a science – and Carla was an artist.

'Let's go, people! If we put our backs into it we can still make lunch. Forget the dinner menu for now – I'll do a new one. Gary,' she instructed the other sous chef, 'those steaks can be braised. We'll do a Tuscan-style hearty casserole with borlotti beans, red peppers and red wine – make that our best Chianti. No skimping on quality.'

'Yes, Chef.'

'I'll make saffron angel-hair spaghetti for the sole. Pino, use the heads and bones for a fish stock to cook the pasta in. Waste not, want not.'

'Right away, Chef.'

Then it was time to get on to suppliers. Offering up a quick prayer to St Macarius, patron saint of chefs, she held her breath and hoped against hope.

First was the fish. She tried the new supplier who had dropped in the sole earlier that day. One of his boats had come back unexpectedly early with engine trouble, but they had a bumper catch of Dublin Bay prawns, monkfish and some magnificent turbot. She took five kilos of the monkfish and four of the prawns.

The meat supplier had just had an order cancelled for a lavish party, but yes, Carla was more than welcome to it –

finest aged Aberdeen Angus steaks, racks of lamb and sweet veal.

The organic vegetable supplier had a huge crush on her and was more than happy to accept a late order. He was still out in his fields and polytunnels selecting his finest crops and would do his best for her.

The strange herb lady, Tessa, was very fond of Carla, especially since she had given her a delicious recipe for vegetarian lasagne, and was eager to help. Just that morning she had picked a fine crop of exotic herbs, wild edible fungi and greens and Carla was welcome to them.

Astrid, of course, had already baked the breads and made the desserts, so those weren't a problem.

Finally, studying what was on order, Carla sat down, sipped an espresso and prayed for inspiration. In the end, it came easily, just like it always had, her instinct, talent and love of great food arising naturally. She wrote the evening menu confidently, and studied it with approval.

They got through lunch by the skin of their teeth. By the time the evening menu was being prepared, the kitchen had become a hive of activity, everyone working methodically and purposefully as instructed, intent on giving it their best shot. Carla presided over it all, offering advice, checking, scolding and stepping in to finesse when necessary.

By seven o'clock that evening, when the first bookings arrived, the elegantly dressed diners who sat sipping cocktails in the Chameleon Bar had no idea of how close they had come to not eating at all.

Exhausted but exhilarated, Carla and her team worked through the night, preparing and delivering the inspirational dishes that more than one table described as exceptional.

On the floor, there was no evidence that they were understaffed. The fewer waiters and waitresses just worked extra hard, quietly and efficiently, even though their faces hurt from smiling as much as their feet did from covering twice as much ground. But it all worked. There were no disasters, no dropped orders or dropped plates. Nothing at all out of the usual. The crowd was as noisy and effusive as ever, so much so that no one had time to notice the small, balding man sitting at the corner table alone, glancing at his newspaper from time to time. 'Can I get you anything else, sir?' asked Therese, the small, relentlessly cheerful Lithuanian waitress.

'No thank you, just the bill,' he smiled. 'That was very good.'

When the last dishes had gone out, the kitchen was bare – they'd had just enough food to complete the service. Exhausted and elated, Carla finished up with another family tradition. Opening a bottle of grappa produced by her cousins in their ancestral region of Italy, she poured a shot for everybody. 'Well done, guys, I think we pulled it off. Here's to new beginnings.'

Charlotte and P.J. both agreed they had never had better food. Back at P.J.'s house in Wellington Square, they had a nightcap, enjoying the break from their respective family dramas.

Alex and Catherine had gone away for the weekend, leaving little Charlie with Catherine's mother.

Ossie had taken Jennifer and Candy out to dinner in Guilbaud's to celebrate the successful solution to the video débâcle, as it was referred to now. Charlotte had been invited too, but had declined, preferring to spend the evening with P.J. Alone now for the first time in weeks, or so it felt, they slipped up to bed like guilty teenagers.

'Do you think it's true what they say?' P.J. mused, propped up on his elbow as he traced the outline of her mouth. 'You know, about blood being thicker than water and all that?'

'I don't know.' Charlotte thought about it. 'I suppose so, but I do know that when you love someone – *really* love someone – there's no holding back.' She smiled up at him.

'Good,' he said, bending down to kiss her. 'I was hoping you'd say that.'

Epilogue: One Year Later

It was Viper's last-ever concert – again.

Seventy thousand people had filled the new Lansdowne Road Stadium in Dublin for what promised to be the hottest gig of the decade. As it was for charity, several other big acts had come on board to join them and the atmosphere was electric.

Cici and James were there with Mimi, Sophia, Dom and Carla. Afterwards, there would be a special dinner at Dominic's, invitation only, for selected guests. Since winning their first Michelin star, and rumoured to be gunning for a second, neither Dom nor Carla had had a night off – not together, at any rate, except for the magical trip to the villa in Tuscany last New Year's Eve, which had been work-related, of course, and where he had proposed to her.

They had gone for an after-dinner stroll in the crisp December air. Behind them, the villa stood in the moonlight, its time-mellowed stone guarded by rows of picture-perfect cypresses, surrounded by vineyards and olive groves. Walking hand in hand in the moonlight, they stopped to admire an ancient moss-covered statue of Bacchus, the god of wine. Dom had turned around and got down on one knee. 'Will you marry me, Carla?'

'Oh Dom,' her eyes were shining, 'you know I will. Yes, yes, yes.' She laughed as he got up and swung her around.

Encased in their bubble of happiness, neither of them could ever have guessed that theirs would be the *second* wedding in the family of late. As Viper launched into one of their huge ballads, Cici and James held hands and exchanged a secret smile . . .

Ossie and Shalom were there, of course, and Bernie, who stood up regularly to gyrate to her favourite numbers, singing loudly and tunelessly. Becoming a grandmother hadn't slowed her down at all. Ossie watched Bernie in her gold leggings and wondered what Jennifer would have said looking at her. He missed the old girl. Shalom was leaning against him, tired. Kylie was almost a year old and Shalom was pregnant again, which had come as a surprise, seeing as she hardly ever let him near her, she was so sleep-deprived. Shalom's dad had nudged him and made jokes on hearing of the second impending arrival and Ossie had felt a bit sick. He was sleep-deprived himself these days. Three weeks ago, the third nanny had left, saying politely but firmly that she couldn't work with Ossie's mother-in-law (as she politely referred to Bernie) interfering all the time. Ossie could understand why. He sighed. He had seen Charlotte earlier on the way in and she looked fabulous. He thought about her quite a lot these days – and nights – more than he would have liked to.

Ossie's wasn't the only baby-in-waiting in the audience. Alex and Catherine were enjoying a night out on their own, for a change. Charlie was in the safe hands of a babysitter, and the young parents were singing along as loudly as everyone else. Catherine placed Alex's hand on her tummy and laughed. She was sure the baby was kicking along in time to the music.

Charlotte was there too, having a blast with Candy and her pals Emma and Katy. After her brush with disaster, Candy, along with Jennifer, had embarked on a small business venture running courses advising and coaching men and women about social etiquette and speaking skills. Jennifer did the coaching (she was superb) and Candy videoed the participants so they could review their performance as Jennifer critiqued it. They were doing remarkably well and had a constant waiting list of prospective clients. 'Hardly surprising, given today's appalling lack of manners,' Jennifer had pronounced. She had declined the invite to the concert, preferring to stay at home and watch *Gone with the Wind* – again.

Along with the other members of Viper's families and entourage, Candy and Charlotte had the best seats in the house – right up front. P.J., of course, was doing his stuff behind the scenes, playing doctor on stage.

As they wrapped up the last act of the night and Viper disappeared behind a screen of smoke and laser lights, the crowd bayed for more, stamping their feet and screaming, *Vi-per, Vi-per, Vi-per!*

After what seemed like an eternity, there was a sliver of movement, and Joey, the lead singer, scampered out on stage. The cheers were deafening as the crowd went wild again. He shouted into the mike for silence, *'Ciúnas! Ciúnas!'* and quiet descended. 'It's been a great night, Dublin, but we've got one more number for you. Our final act tonight – and I mean final – belongs to an old friend of ours. We owe him a lot – not least for keeping a bunch of old farts like us on our feet. He started out with us but left the band to pursue a more respectable career. Our loss was the medical profession's gain. We know him as Doc,' he continued, 'and not a lot of people know he's written some of our best lyrics. Tonight we've persuaded him to dust down his old guitar and play one last gig with us.'

As Charlotte's hands flew to her mouth, she gasped as a murmur of curiosity began among the crowd. And then, as the band ran back on stage, there he was, walking on with his guitar, grinning sheepishly but looking very sexy. As he settled himself on the stool, tuned up his guitar and nodded at Rory on keyboard, he picked out the first deliberately unfamiliar chords of a haunting riff.

'Take it away, P.J.!' yelled Joey, slipping back to join Barry on base.

'This song is a very special one for me,' he began, keeping them guessing, 'and I know it is for all of you too.' He grinned as a roar of anticipation filled the stadium. 'I wrote it a long, long time ago, but tonight, I want to dedicate it to someone very special to me. I want to dedicate it to my wife.'

As the lights went down and a sea of hand-held lighters glowed and swayed in the darkness, he looked straight at her and said, 'Charlotte, this one's for you.'

When the band launched into the much-loved ballad and P.J.'s gravelly voice rang out into the night, a wild cheer went up as the fans recognised the famous track.

As he reached the chorus of 'Beautiful to Find Me', the great crowd sang as one.

Acknowledgements

Grateful thanks to Sue Fletcher of Hodder UK; Ciara Doorley and Breda Purdue of Hachette Books Ireland; Margaret Daly of Hachette; Louise Swanell, and my agent, Vivienne Schuster of Curtis Brown.

I am indebted also to Dr. Damien Rutledge for information on Von Willebrands disease and related medical implications.

And also to David Bergin of O'Connor & Bergin, for advice on family law.

If I have forgotten anyone, which is entirely possible; lunch is on me.

If You Like Happy Endings . . .

You have just come to the end of a book.

Before you put it aside, please take a moment to reflect on the 37 million people who are blind in the developing world.

90% of this blindness is TOTALLY PREVENTABLE.

In our world, blindness is a disability – in the developing world, it's a death sentence.

Every minute, one child goes blind – needlessly.

That's about the time it will take you to read this.

It's also about the time it will take you to log on to www.righttosight.com and help this wonderful organisation achieve its goal of totally eradicating preventable global blindness.

Now that would be a happy ending.

And it will only take a minute.

Fiona O'Brien supports RIGHT TO SIGHT and would love if you would too.

An

NDY SY

This is Andalucía

Often described as having one foot in Europe and one in Africa, Andalucía is quintessentially southern, with baking heat, vibrant dance and song, and intoxicating hedonism seemingly wafted on the breeze (with a tinge of orange blossom). Yet it's a far deeper, more complex place than you might expect. Layers of occupation over the millennnia have left a cornucopia of historical treasures and a rich culture resplendent with colour. And flavour: tastebuds are treated like visiting royalty down here. The salty tang of *manzanilla* wine, a cool, garlicky gazpacho in the summer heat, the freshest of seafood, the rich olive oils, the flavoursome ham and pork from the Huelvan hills. In Andalucía the emphasis is on fresh ingredients, with the local cuisine trumping more pretentious fare and creating a unique eating and drinking culture based around the region's greatest invention: tapas.

Scenically, there's an even wider range on the menu. Lush green hills around Grazalema are crowned with postcard-pretty white villages, while the desert-scapes around Almería have featured in many spaghetti westerns. You can kitesurf off the windy beaches of the Costa de la Luz, or ski in the Sierra Nevada, while the churches of noble Sevilla and Renaissance splendourof Baeza compete for your attention with the United Nations of birdlife in the Coto Doñana national park.

If you're looking for Spanish stereotypes, Andalucía's eight provinces have them all; yet the seeker of less-known cultural and natural jewels also still has extraordinary scope for fulfilling exploration here under the near constant sunshine.

Andy Symington

Best of Andalucía

top things to do and see

❶ Sevilla

Hot and hedonistic, Andalucía's capital encompasses all the romance and passion of the region, from the sombre glory of Semana Santa processions to the vibrancy and colour of its April festival. Most famous of a fistful of magnificent churches, its majestic cathedral overlooks a vibrant tapas scene. Page 34.

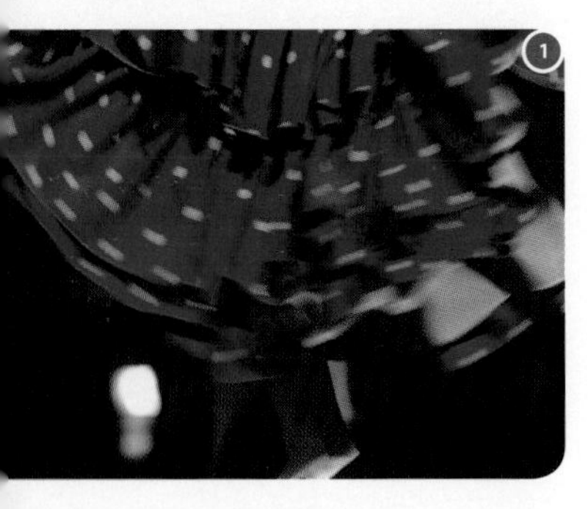

❷ Coto Doñana

This vast wetland national park is one of Europe's most important bird habitats, with a huge number of local and migratory species present, as well as important mammals such as the endangered Iberian lynx. On its edge, the Wild West-like town of El Rocío is the focus of Spain's liveliest pilgrimage. Page 108.

❸ Sierra Morena

These low hills that divide Andalucía from central Spain make a great base for walking, with plenty of low tree cover and intriguing villages spaced at comfortable distances. Rooting around for acorns here are Iberian pigs: the sublime pork and astonishing range of wild mushrooms make this an intriguing food destination too. Page 116.

❹ Cádiz

Gleaming in the sunlight, the promontory city of Cádiz has a fascinating maritime past and a strongly independent streak that manifests itself in its subversive carnival celebrations. Outside the atmospheric old town with its restored fishermen's *barrios* and sociable market, its magnificent beach stretches for miles. Page 131.

❼ Málaga

Far more interesting than the Costa del Sol resorts around it, Málaga is a fun, very Spanish city with plenty to see, including two excellent galleries: the Picasso and Carmen Thyssen museums. There's a very lively eating and strolling scene, a beach, pretty portside and one of Europe's biggest parties in August. Page 209.

❺ White Towns

Very North African in feel, this string of picturesque, blindingly bright hilltop settlements are a charming legacy of the region's Moorish past. Houses are typically built around interior patios, while the atmospherically narrow streets served as protection from both the sun and invaders. Page 168.

❻ Costa de la Luz

Andalucía's Atlantic coast has wild beaches, including some long, less-developed stretches. Tarifa has wind and waves aplenty for board riders of all types, with Morocco dramatically visible just across the straits. The Huelva coastline has appealing towns with good seafood and not an English breakfast in sight. Page 180.

❽ Antequera

One of the region's most interesting towns, this inland destination has an intriguing selection of monuments and fascinating, imposingly large prehistoric dolmens. Nearby are the bizarre, tortured rockscapes of El Torcal and an intriguing place to meet and learn about wolves. Page 248.

❾ Córdoba

A magnificent city from the zenith of Moorish might, Córdoba has an enormous old town replete with worthwhile sights, and houses whose elegant flower-filled courtyards are famously beautiful. Above the Guadalquivir river, the enormous Mezquita mosque is the glory of what remains of Muslim Spain. Page 267.

❿ Granada

In the shadow of snowy peaks, Granada's allure begins with the sumptuous Alhambra whose wistful beauty was the last flowering of Moorish culture, and continues in the evocative Albayzín district. Renaissance architectural sobriety, great tapas, lively North African culture, and the spirit of Lorca add to its siren-song. Page 305.

⓫ La Alpujarra

On the southern flanks of the Sierra Nevada, these fertile valleys are dotted with picturesque white villages with a rugged, historic local culture. The area is perfect for exploring by walking, with comfortable trails between villages and more demanding ascents to some of Spain's highest mountains. Page 345.

⓬ Sistema Subbética

Off the tourist beat, these rugged mountains make a great destination for outdoor activities or exploration of the area's traditional villages. Particularly enticing are Priego de Córdoba and Zuheros, friendly places full of hidden corners and local character. Page 292.

⓭ Baeza and Ubeda

In remote Jaén province, these towns surprise with their wonderful assemblage of beautiful Renaissance palaces and churches. Several palaces have been converted into hotels, marvellously characterful, relaxing places to hole up for a day or two. Pages 394 and 398.

⓮ Cabo de Gata

There's something special about this barren peninsula that meets the sea in a combination of astonishing cliffscapes and enticing beaches. Small settlements make for unusual, non-resort coastal escapes and there's a real magic in the air and sea here. Page 437.

EXTREMADURA
PORTUGAL
Belalcázar
Sierra Morena
CORDOBA
Baños de la Encina
JAEN
Aracena
Cazalla de la Sierra
Córdoba
Andújar
Ubeda
Baeza
HUELVA
SEVILLA
Almodóvar del Río
Guadalquivir
Jaén
Ecija
Campiña Cordobesa
Zuheros
Alcalá la Real
Ayamonte
Huelva
Sevilla
Carmona
Priego de Córdoba
Mazagón
Costa de la Luz
Parque Nacional Coto Doñana
Utrera
Osuna
Subbética
GRANADA
Sistema
Granada
Sierra Nevada
Sanlúcar de Barrameda
Arcos de la Frontera
Antequera
La Alpujarra
MALAGA
Cádiz
Jerez de la Frontera
Parque Natural Sierra de Grazalema
Ronda
Málaga
Nerja
Almuñécar
Torremolinos
Salobreña
CADIZ
Fuengirola
Marbella
Costa del Sol
Costa Tropical
Estepona
Atlantic Ocean
Tarifa
Gibraltar
Straits of Gibraltar
Mediterranean Sea
MOROCCO
1
2
3
4
5
6
7
8
9
10
11
12
13

N
20 km
20 miles

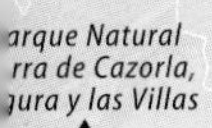

MURCIA

Vélez
Blanco

ALMERIA

Mojácar

Parque Natural
Cabo de
Gata-Nijar

Almería

14

osta del Almería

Fundada en 1.9

Route planner Andalucía

putting it all together

Andalucía is a sizeable region and a little time spent planning will reward you with more time for exploring monuments, beaches and tapas bars, and less time on the motorways. Southern Spain's rich historical and cultural heritage means there's an absolute cornucopia of intriguing sights and experiences; what you choose will depend on your own interests, but here we help out with a few suggested itineraries.

One week or less

Sevilla, Granada, Mediterranean and White Towns

You can comfortably spend a week in either **Granada** or **Sevilla** without getting bored, and Granada has the extra temptations of the **Sierra Nevada** and the **Alpujarra** within easy reach.

Fly to **Málaga** and head east along the Mediterranean, stopping at places such as **Nerja**, **Almuñécar** and **Almería** before exploring the rugged shores of the **Cabo de Gata** for a couple of days.

West from Málaga, and also easily reached from Sevilla or **Jerez de la Frontera** airports, the **Costa de la Luz** is Andalucía's finest stretch of coastline.

Learn to kitesurf in the laid-back resort of **Tarifa** then head north, investigating the Roman ruins of Baelo Claudia, tasting tuna at **Zahara de los Atunes**, and surfing at **El Palmar**. Head back south via the evocative white towns of **Arcos de la Frontera** and **Vejer de la Frontera**.

Right: Tarifa
Above right: La Calahorra castle
Opposite page: Barrio Santa Cruz, Sevilla

Two weeks

cities, sherry towns and Atlantic beaches

With two weeks, you could focus on Sevilla, Granada and **Córdoba**, spending a few days in each and also checking out nearby areas, such as the Alpujarra, the bird-rich wetlands of the **Coto Doñana**, or the rugged **Sistema Subbética** of southern Córdoba province. Smaller towns near these cities, such as **Antequera**, **Carmona** and **Priego de Córdoba**, make attractive bases for a day or two.

If it's summer, consider the quiet old-town streets of **Cádiz**, seafood meals in **El Puerto de Santa María** and sherry tasting in **Sanlúcar de Barrameda** and Jerez. From here head down to the Costa de la Luz, inland to the **Sierra de Grazalema** for some cool climate walking, or across to the fine beaches of **Huelva province**.

One month

off the beaten track

If architecture is a passion, make a point of visiting **Jaén province**, the stamping ground of one of Spain's finest Renaissance architects, Andrés de Vandelvira. You can

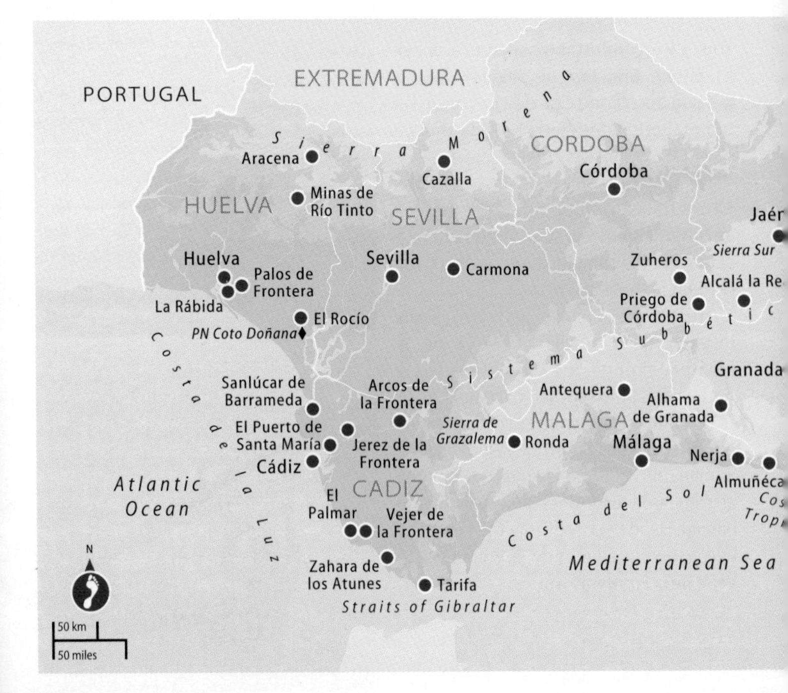

CASTILLA LA MANCHA
PN Sierra de Cazorla
Ubeda
MURCIA
GRANADA
La Calahorra
ALMERIA
Laujar de Andarax
Almería
Cabo de Gata
Costa del Almería

Top: El Puerto de Santa María
Above: Baeza

see his work in **Jaén** itself and the nearby towns of **Baeza** and **Ubeda**. From here, the **Parque Natural Sierra de Cazorla** beckons, then the Moorish splendours of Granada. After investigating the Alpujarra and Sierra Nevada, head westwards, stopping at the hot springs of **Alhama de Granada** before heading for the majestic dolmens of Antequera, the cloven town of **Ronda** and the numerous pretty white villages thereabouts. Once there, Sevilla, Cádiz and Jerez are but a skip away.

If you think a beach should be long, sandy and have proper waves, a short trip beyond Cádiz to the Atlantic tuna-fishing village of **Zahara de los Atunes** and the nearby Roman ruins of Baelo Claudia will not fail to impress. If birdwatching holds more appeal, the wetlands of the Coto Doñana will prove irresistible, as will the migratory route across the Straits of Gibraltar.

If getting away from the crowds is a priority, Huelva province will appeal. From Sevilla, head west, taking in the pilgrimage town of **El Rocío**, and the Parque Nacional Coto Doñana, before following in Columbus' footsteps to **Palos de la Frontera** and the monastery of **La Rábida**. On your way north to the peaceful hills of the **Sierra Morena**, stop by the moonscape mining operations of **Minas de Río Tinto** before reaching **Aracena**, the best base for exploring and walking. Head east from here to **Cazalla** and on to Córdoba, before basing yourself in pretty Zuheros. Spend a couple of days in one of the beautifully restored *casas rurales* in Priego de Córdoba's old town before turning east and visiting the castle of **Alcalá la Real** and the olivescapes of Jaén's **Sierra Sur**. From here, Granada is temptingly close; after spending time in the city, head east to the striking castle of **La Calahorra** and over the sierra to the Alpujarra. If the lesser known is still driving you, investigate the Almerían valleys around the friendly village of **Laujar de Andarax** and the Chalcolithic site of Los Millares. From here, Almería itself is close by.

Above: Alhama de Granada
Right: Zahara de los Atunes
Below: El Rocío
Opposite page: Serranía de Ronda

Six of the best fabulous fiestas

Semana Santa (Sevilla)
Sevilla's iconic Easter processions make it a most special time to visit Andalucía's capital. Religious brotherhoods, some hooded or carrying crosses, others bearing the significant weight of *pasos* (floats with sculptures of Christ or the Virgin), process from their home chapel to the cathedral and back, which can take over 12 hours. See box, page 46.

Romería del Rocío (Huelva province)
The Whitsun journey to the shrine at El Rocío is a boisterous affair of horses, revelry, flamenco music and the drinking of frightening quantities of wine. It's a riotous party as the figure of the much-adored Virgin gets manhandled around the sand streets of this atmospheric Wild West-like town. See box, page 110.

Carnaval (Cádiz)
The maritime city of Cádiz has always had a liberal, rebellious streak and its Carnaval, the Spanish mainland's best, reflects that, with groups of minstrel-like locals reciting political satire. Add fireworks, flamenco and fancy dress, and you have the ingredients for a memorable party. See box, page 143.

Feria del Caballo (Jerez de la Frontera)

Andalucía is a pretty horsey place, and Jerez de la Frontera is the capital of all things equine, so there are plenty of horses on show here at this May festival, as well as numerous *casetas*, marquees where groups of friends – all dressed to the nines in traditional costume – meet to drink *manzanilla* and dance the night away. See page 166.

Festival de los Patios (Córdoba)

Cordoban homeowners take great pride in their *patio cordobés*, and keep them very spruce with bright *azulejo* tiles and a stunning array of flowers. In early May the Festival de los Patio opens them in their full glory, with numerous courtyards, on show. See box, page 273.

Moros y Cristianos (La Alpujarra)

An intriguing historical relic celebrated in Las Alpujarras, the Moors and Christians fiestas are re-enactments of Reconquista battles, with spectacular costumes. The two sides usually march in a procession, before a ritual enactment of the battle. See pages 355 and 361.

Harvested cork, Tarifa

When to go to Andalucía

... and when not to

Andalucía has one of mainland Europe's most agreeable climates. Winters are mild with some rain, but plenty of sunshine; coastal temperatures in January average 15-17°C. It is colder inland, particularly in the mountains, where snow lies on the Sierra Nevada for much of the year. Be prepared for sub-zero temperatures in higher places inland like Granada and Ronda.

Summers are hot, especially inland, but the coast benefits from pleasant sea breezes, particularly along the stretch from Gibraltar to Cádiz, where the strong *levante* wind can last for days on end, much to the joy of windsurfers. In summer, it can seem like most of Spain and half of Europe is lined up along Andalucía's beaches. While the atmosphere is good, the crowding and overpriced accommodation might induce you to pick the June or September shoulder season, when there's still plenty of sun. In high summer, inland temperatures soar; it can hit 50°C in Sevilla, although the high 30s and low 40s are more normal. Apart from the obvious inconvenience of the heat, the fact that much of the population decamps to the coast removes much of the atmosphere of the inland cities.

Spring and autumn are ideal seasons to visit Andalucía. Spring is the best time for birdwatching and wildflowers, temperatures are warm but not extreme, and there are many important festivals, such as Sevilla's Semana Santa and Feria de Abril, or Córdoba's Fiesta de los Patios. Easter week is a major holiday in Spain and accommodation prices are very high. In autumn, the sea is still pleasantly warm and hiking conditions in the hills are at their best.

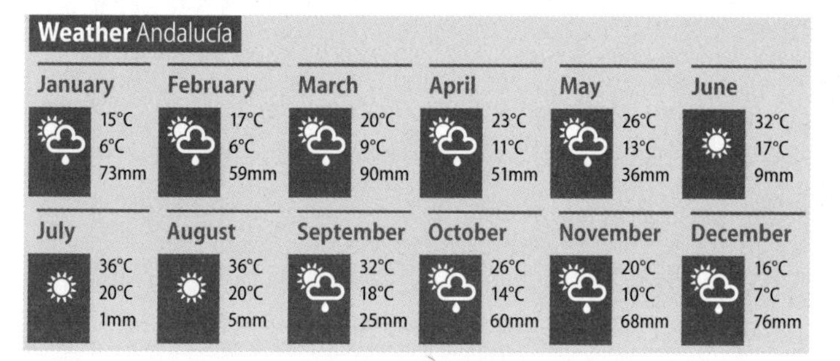

Weather Andalucía

January	February	March	April	May	June
15°C	17°C	20°C	23°C	26°C	32°C
6°C	6°C	9°C	11°C	13°C	17°C
73mm	59mm	90mm	51mm	36mm	9mm

July	August	September	October	November	December
36°C	36°C	32°C	26°C	20°C	16°C
20°C	20°C	18°C	14°C	10°C	7°C
1mm	5mm	25mm	60mm	68mm	76mm

Festivals

Even the smallest village in Andalucía has a fiesta and many have several. Although mostly nominally religious featuring a mass and procession or two, they also offer live music, bullfights, competitions and fireworks. A feature of many are *gigantes y cabezudos*, huge-headed papier mâché figures based on historical personages who parade the streets. In many Andalucían villages there's a *Moros y Cristianos* festival, which recreates a Reconquista battle with colourful costumes. Most fiestas are in summer; expect some trouble finding accommodation. Details of the major town fiestas can be found in the travel text. National holidays and *puentes* (long weekends) can be difficult times to travel; it's important to reserve tickets in advance. See also Public holidays, page 513.

Flamenco festivals

These are an excellent experience. There are many throughout the year: ask the local tourist office for details. The most popular are:

February/March Festival de Flamenco, in Jerez. Check dates at www.festivaldejerez.es.

June/July International Festival of Music and Dance, in Granada. One of Andalucía's biggest cultural events held in the Alhambra's Carlos V Palace, with classical music and ballet shows as well as flamenco. Check dates at www.granadafestival.org.

Late August Festival de Flamenco, Almería, www.almeriacultura.com.

September/October Bienal de Flamenco, Sevilla, held every even-numbered year. The most respected names in flamenco perform here, with more than 600 artists taking part. Check dates at www.labienal.com.

December Encuentros Flamencos, Granada. The biggest names in flamenco, with a different theme each year. For more information, see www.facebook.com/encuentrosflamencosdegranada.

What to do in Andalucía

activities from skiing to sherry tasting

Andalucía has a number of options for independent and organized special interest travel. See also destination chapters and Tour operators, page 516.

Archaeology

Andalucía has a rich archaeological heritage and you could plan a trip to include sites like the Cueva de Los Murciélagos (near Zuheros), Cueva de la Pileta (near Ronda) and the Cueva de los Letreros (near Vélez Blanco in Almería province). Not far from Almería itself, Los Millares is a large, important, and memorable Chalcolithic settlement; while the ancient dolmens of Antequera (north of Málaga) are breathtaking. There are several excellent Roman sites, such as Baelo Claudia (Bolonia, on the Costa de la Luz), Itálica (near Sevilla), Acinipo (near Ronda), and Almedinilla, a well-excavated villa near the town of Priego de Córdoba.

Birdwatching

Southern Spain is rich in birdlife, partly because it makes a handy bridge between Europe and Africa for the feathered species, and partly because it has some 100 protected areas covering nearly 20% of the region.

The absolute mecca is magnificent Coto Doñana National Park, one of Europe's premier wetland sites, stocked full of birds. One of the most spectacular aspects of Andalucían birdwatching is the twice-yearly migration, which you can observe in spring and autumn at locations around Tarifa and Algeciras in Cádiz province and the Upper Rock Nature Reserve, Gibraltar. Other good spots for birdlife include: the Marismas de Odiel (Huelva province); Las Salinas (on the Cabo de Gata coastline); Laguna de Medina (Cádiz); Campiña Cordobesa (Córdoba) for winter wildfowl on semi-saline lakes; Spain's largest protected area, the Parque Natural de Cazorla (Jaén); and the Sierra Nevada (Granada).

Football

Football is king. Most of Andalucía's cities have prominent football teams. Sevilla boasts two: Sevilla and Real Betis, while Málaga, Granada, Córdoba, Recreativo de Huelva and Almería have all been in the top division in recent years. Tickets are relatively easy to obtain on match days or the days leading up to them. Some clubs offer online sales. Games are usually played on Sat or Sun afternoon/evening.

Golf

There are over 100 golf courses in Andalucía, comprising more than a third of all courses in Spain. The better courses are of championship standard such as **Montecastillo**, Jerez, www.montecastilloresortjerez.com; **Las Brisas**, Marbella, www.realclubdegolflasbrisas.es; **Sotogrande**, Cádiz, www.golfsotogrande.com; **Los Naranjos**, Marbella, www.losnaranjos.com; **San Roque**, Cádiz, www.sanroqueclub.com; and **Valderrama**, Sotogrande, www.valderrama.com. Contact the **Federación Andaluza de Golf**, www.rfga.org, or **Golf Spain**, www.golfspain.com, for reservations, lessons and links.

For insurance reasons, to play golf in Spain, you will usually need a green card from your home club or be a member of the **Federación Andaluza de Golf** (see above).

Horse riding

Horses can be hired at numerous stables and equestrian centres; contact tourist offices for more information. Some of the best areas for horse riding are the Alpujarra, the Sierra Nevada, and the Sierra de Cazorla, while beach towns like Tarifa offer flatter shoreline riding. For operators go to www. andalucia.com/rural/horseriding.htm.

Skiing

Though it seems implausibly far south for snowsports, Andalucía is in fact an excellent destination for skiing. The lofty Sierra Nevada boasts the most southerly and one of the highest ski resorts of mainland Europe. It has plenty of sunshine, but a long season from Nov into early May. See also www.sierranevada.es.

Walking and hiking

Andalucía is one of the most mountainous regions in Europe and has a plethora of deep gorges, forests and picturesque lakes. The regional government has actively promoted tourism for walking (*senderismo*), and there's a good network of waymarked paths, especially in protected areas, complemented by *vías verdes*, former railways that have been turned into routes for walkers and cyclists. Spain's excellent network of marked walking trails are divided into *pequeño recorrido* (PR), short trails marked with yellow and white signs, and *gran recorrido* (GR), long-distance walks marked in red and white. The GR trails are planned so that nights can be spent at *refugios* (walkers' hostels) or in villages with accommodation. At weekends in summer the popular walking areas can become very busy. Descriptions of routes can be found online – www.wikirutas.es is a good place to start if you can manage a bit of Spanish – in bookshops or outdoor equipment shops. Tourist offices supply details of routes and *refugios*.

Some of the best *senderismo* in Andalucía can be found in the Alpujarra region. Here, Trévelez is the starting point for tackling Mulhacén, which, at 3479 m, is the highest mountain in

SIX OF THE BEST

Surf breaks

Most of Andalucía's best waves are on the Atlantic coast in Cádiz province.

Around Chipiona

Between Chipiona and Rota is Playa de Regla, a white-sand urban beach best at mid to high tide. On the same stretch is Playa de Tres Piedras, a dune-backed beach break with some rocks to the eastern edge. It has lefts and rights and works best at mid to high tide. Both need winds from the northeast or east and southwesterly or westerly swells. To the south a quality right-hander, Cien Metros, is a fast and powerful wave that breaks between mid and high tide.

Cádiz

Cádiz sits on the end of a peninsula, which has a huge expanse of sandy beaches. The town beach, La Playita, works best at low to mid tide. Las Caracolas works best on a mid to high tide. At the end of Playa de la Victoria is La Cabañita, a hollow, right-hand high tide wave. Torregorda and Campo Soto are both picturesque dune-backed beaches. Heading on towards Chiclana, La Barrosa has peaks that work best at low to mid tide; it's a fairly quiet spot with some shelter that needs a bigger swell to get going.

Roche

North of Conil de la Frontera is this popular beach break that is one of the region's most consistent waves. It has powerful, high-quality lefts and rights that are best from low to mid tide. It's busy in summer.

El Palmar

This long beach is a popular spot that can produce high-quality lefts and rights, with powerful and hollow waves breaking consistently on the sandbanks. It works on all tides with a high tide shore break, but is best from low to mid tide. It can get busy at peak times.

Barbate and around

Barbate is the region's most famous break. The river mouth currents sculpt a sandbar ready for when a good size swell hits, sending long, reeling lefts spinning through to the inside. However, it's not very consistent and is a low tide spot.

Tarifa

The magnificent Playa de los Lances has kilometres of sand broken only by the occasional rocky finger point. When the wind drops a decent swell can kick in. At the northern end is a right-hand point accessed in front of the Jardín de Las Dunas campsite. This stretch is offshore in a light northeasterly wind.

mainland Spain. Gentler walking can be found in Parque Natural de la Sierra de Aracena in Huelva province. Another popular area can be found amongst the *pueblos blancos* southwest of Ronda, around Gaucín and Grazalema. In the La Axarquía, there is good hiking, while the Parque Natural de Cazorla has a marvellous network of marked routes.

When walking in protected areas respect the rules and restrictions.

Watersports

Diving, sailing, parasailing, waterskiing and windsurfing are common right along the Andalucían coast. Tarifa in Cádiz province is Europe's mecca for windsurfers and kitesurfers, while the Cabo de Gata near Almería, is good for diving. There are surf schools at many places along the Costa de la Luz, and boats are available for charter and rental at most marinas. See also box, page 23.

Wine and sherry tasting

The most rewarding area to visit for wine tasting is the sherry triangle, bounded by Jerez de la Frontera, El Puerto de Santa María and Sanlúcar de Barrameda in Cádiz province. The historic and atmospheric bodegas are well set up for visitors. Another important denomination of origin is Montilla-Moriles, centred on Montilla, south of Córdoba. Outside the sherry region, it's best to call ahead, as the concept of cellar-door tasting hasn't wholly caught on.

Shopping tips

Andalucía is famous for its handicrafts, or *artesanía*, many of which developed in Moorish times. Pottery, leather goods, marquetry, textiles and wickerwork are all relatively cheap and widely available in craft shops and markets. In Granada, you can get marquetry boxes, trays and chess sets. Córdoba is by far the most important centre for finely made gold and silver ware, producing two-thirds of Spain's jewellery. Leather goods are available throughout Andalucía, but one of the best-known places for traditional leatherwork is Ubrique in Cádiz.

Made on hand-operated looms are *jarapas*, rugs and blankets of scraps of fabric and wool, sold in Almería province, although they are available in other provinces. The Alpujarras is famed for its Moorish rugs and *alpujarreño* cloth. Look out for hand-embroidered shawls, tablecloths, flamenco dresses and lace products.

The most common pottery products include colourful painted flower pots, decorative plates and bowls and terracotta ovenware. Moorish techniques and designs are still widespread; look out for Moorish-style tiles and, in Sevilla, copies of tiles with 16th-century designs.

Non-EU residents can reclaim VAT (*IVA*) on purchases over €90, see page 514.

Where to stay in Andalucía

from *casas rurales* to campsites

The standard of accommodation in Andalucía is very high; even the most modest of *pensiones* is usually very clean and respectable. At time of writing, for Spain the website www.booking.com is by far the most comprehensive. If you're booking accommodation not listed in this guide, always be sure to check the location if that's important to you – it's easy to find yourself a 15-minute cab ride from the town you think you're going to be in.

Environmental issues are an individual's responsibility, and the type of holiday you choose has a direct impact on the future of the region. Opting for more sustainable tourism choices – picking a *casa rural* in a traditional village and eating in restaurants serving locally sourced food rather than staying in the four-star multinational hotel – has a small but significant knock-on effect. Don't be afraid to ask questions about environmental policy before making a hotel or *casa rural* booking.

Types of accommodation

Alojamientos (places to stay), are divided into two main categories; the distinctions between them are in an arcane series of regulations devised by the government.

Hotels, hostales and pensiones

Hoteles (marked H or HR) are graded from one to five stars and occupy their own building, which distinguishes them from many *hostales* (Hs or HsR), which go from one to two stars. The *hostal* category includes *pensiones*, the standard budget option, typically family-run and occupying a floor of an apartment building. The standard for the price paid is normally excellent, and they're nearly all spotless. Spanish traditions of hospitality are alive and well; check-out time is almost uniformly a very civilized midday.

Tip…
Normally only the more expensive hotels have parking, and they always charge for it, normally around €10-25 per day.

A great number of Spanish hotels are well equipped but characterless chain business places (big players include **NH** ⓘ *www.nh-hoteles.es*, **Husa** ⓘ *www.husa.es*, **AC/Marriott** ⓘ *www.marriott.com*, **Tryp/SolMelia** ⓘ *www.solmelia.com*, and **Riu** ⓘ *www.riu.com*), and are often situated outside the old town. This guide has expressly minimized these in the listings, preferring to concentrate on more atmospheric options.

Casas rurales

An excellent option if you've got your own transport are the networks of rural houses, called *casas rurales*. Although these are under a different classification system, the standard is often as high as any country hotel. The best of them are traditional farmhouses or characterful village cottages. Some are available only to rent out whole (often for a minimum of three days), while others offer rooms on a nightly basis. Rates tend to be excellent compared to hotels. While many are listed in the text, there are huge numbers of them. Local tourist offices will have details of nearby *casas rurales*; the tourist board website www.andalucia.org lists a good selection.

Youth hostels

There's a network of *albergues* (youth hostels), which are listed at www.inturjoven.com. These are institutional and often group-booked. Funding issues mean that many now open only seasonally. Major cities have backpacker hostels with instant social life and every mod con. *Refugios* are mountain bunkhouses, which range from unstaffed sheds to cheerful hostels with a bar and restaurant.

Price codes

Where to stay

€€€€ over €170

€€€ €110-170

€€ €60-110

€ under €60

A standard double/twin room in high season.

Restaurants

€€€ over €30

€€ €15-30

€ under €15

A two-course meal (or two average *raciones*) for one person, without drinks.

Campsites

Most campsites are set up as well-equipped holiday villages for families; some are open only in summer. While the facilities are good, they get extremely busy in peak season. Many have cabins or bungalows available, ranging from simple huts to houses with fully equipped kitchens and bathrooms. In other areas, camping, unless specifically prohibited, is a matter of common sense. Don't camp where you're not allowed to; prohibitions are usually there for a good reason. Fire danger can be high in summer, so respect local regulations.

Prices

Price codes refer to a standard double or twin room, inclusive of VAT. The rates are generally for high season (June-August on the coast, March-May in cities such as Sevilla or Granada). Occasionally, an area or town will have a short period when prices are hugely exaggerated; this is usually due to a festival.

Breakfast is often included in the price at small intimate hotels, but rarely at the grander places, who tend to charge a fortune.

All registered accommodation charge a 10% value added tax; this is usually included in the price and may be waived if you pay cash. If you have any problems, a last resort is to ask for the *libro de reclamaciones* (complaints book), an official document that, like stepping on cracks in the pavement, means uncertain but definitely horrible consequences for the hotel if anything is written in it. Be aware that you must also take a copy to the local police station for the complaint to be registered.

Tip...

The most useful websites for saving on hotel rates in Spain are www.booking.com, www.hotels.com and www.laterooms.com.

Food & drink in Andalucía

In no country in the world are culture and society as intimately connected with eating and drinking as in Spain, and in Andalucía, the spiritual home of tapas, this is even more the case.

Food → *See page 522 for a glossary of food.*

Andalucían cooking is characterized by an abundance of fresh ingredients, generally consecrated with the chef's holy trinity of garlic, peppers and local olive oil.

Spaniards eat little for breakfast and, apart from hotels in touristy places, you're unlikely to find anything beyond a *tostada* (large piece of toasted bread spread with olive oil, tomato and garlic, pâté or jam) or a pastry to go with your coffee. A common breakfast or afternoon snack are *churros*, fried dough sticks typically dipped in hot chocolate.

Lunch is the main meal and is nearly always a filling affair with three courses. Most places open for lunch at about 1300, and take last orders at 1500 or 1530, although at weekends this can extend. Lunchtime is the cheapest time to eat if you opt for the ubiquitous *menú del día*, usually a set three-course meal that includes wine or soft drink, typically costing €10 to €16. Dinner and/or evening tapas time is from around 2100 to midnight. It's not much fun sitting alone in a restaurant so try and adapt to the local hours; it may feel strange dining so late, but you'll miss out on a lot of atmosphere if you don't. If a place is open for lunch at noon, or dinner at 1900, it's likely to be a tourist trap.

Types of eateries

The great joy of eating out in Andalucía is going for tapas. This word refers to bar food, served in saucer-sized tapa portions typically costing €1.50-3. In Granada, Almería and Jaén, you'll receive a free tapa with your drink. Tapas are available at lunchtime, but the classic time to eat them is in the evening. To do tapas the Andalucían way don't order more than a couple at each place, taste each others' dishes, and stand at the bar. Locals know what the specialities of each bar are; if there's a daily special, order that. Also available are *raciones*, substantial meal-sized plates of the same fare, which also come in halves,

SIX OF THE BEST

Gastro experiences

Tapas in Sevilla

Sevilla has the richest tapas culture, from *espinacas con garbanzos* (spinach and chickpeas) to *solomillo al whisky* (steak with whisky sauce). The most traditional places will tot up your bill with chalk on the counter as you graze. See page 70.

Iberian pork

You've never tasted pork like they do it here in Aracena in the hills north of Huelva. *Ibérico* is the word to look out for: it means the black-trottered porker has lived a free range life in the holm oak groves, gorging itself on their acorns. All the prime cuts are exquisitely flavoursome and juicy. See page 123.

Sherry in Sanlúcar and Jerez

Nothing beats the southern heat like a crisp cold dry *fino* sherry. Jerez de la Frontera does wine tourism very well, with wonderful tapas bars and restaurants and winery tours. The tangy, slightly lighter *manzanilla* is the perfect aperitif or seafood match. It's aged in barrels in the atmospheric town of Sanlúcar de Barrameda and is best drunk on a terrace by the mouth of the Guadalquivir. See pages 151 and 160.

Costa de la Luz seafood

Along the sometimes wild Atlantic shore of the Costa de la Luz, coastal towns and villages specialize in seafood. The crustaceans, from tiny *quisquilla* shrimps to portly Huelva prawns, are especially famous. See pages 105, 113 and 180.

Fried fish in Málaga

If you're along the Málaga coast, make sure you check out a *freiduría*, a simple seafood-frying place with a long bar of polished chrome serving cold beer. The classic dish is *pescaíto frito*, a mountain of tiny battered fried fish, but also delicious is *choco* (cuttlefish) or *chopitos* (little squid). See pages 217.

Back-to-basics in Las Alpujarras

In the valleys of the Alpujarra is gloriously unreconstructed cuisine. Hearty local staples– potato, pepper, ham, sausage – are cooked up in plenty of village olive oil. Accompanied by Costa wine – muddy in aspect, unconvincing at first sip, but curiously satisfying after half a jug – you'll soon have a warm glow in your belly. See page 345.

medias raciones. Both are good for sharing. Considering these, the distinction between restaurants and tapas bars more or less disappears, as in the latter you can usually sit down at a table to order your *raciones*, effectively turning the experience into a meal.

Other types of eateries include the *chiringuito*, a beach bar open in summer and serving drinks and fresh seafood. A *freiduría* is a takeaway specializing in fried fish, while a *marisquería* is a classier type of seafood restaurant. In rural areas, look out for *ventas*, roadside eateries that often have a long history of feeding the passing muleteers with generous, hearty and cheap portions. The more cars and trucks outside, the better it will be. In cities, North African-style teahouses, *teterías*, are popular.

Vegetarian food

Vegetarians in Andalucía won't be spoiled for choice, but at least what there is tends to be good. There are few dedicated vegetarian restaurants and many restaurants won't have a vegetarian main course on offer, although the existence of tapas, *raciones* and salads makes this less of a burden than it might be. You'll have to specify *soy vegetariano/a* (I am a vegetarian), but ask what dishes contain, as ham, fish and even chicken are often considered suitable vegetarian fare. Vegans will have a tougher time. What doesn't have meat nearly always contains cheese or egg. Better restaurants, particularly in cities, will be happy to prepare something, but otherwise stick to very simple dishes.

On the menu

Typical starters include gazpacho (a cold summer tomato soup flavoured with garlic, olive oil and peppers; *salmorejo* is a thicker version from Córdoba), *ensalada mixta* (mixed salad based on lettuce, tomatoes, tuna and more), or paella.

Main courses will usually be either meat or fish and are rarely served with any accompaniment beyond chips. Beef is common; the better steaks such as *solomillo* or *entrecot* are usually superbly tender. Spaniards tend to eat them fairly rare (*poco hecho*; ask for *al punto* for medium rare or *bien hecho* for well done). Pork is also widespread; *solomillo de cerdo*, *secreto*, *pluma* and *lomo* are all tasty cuts. Innards are popular: *callos* (tripe), *mollejas* (sweetbreads) and *morcilla* (black pudding) are excellent, if acquired, tastes.

Seafood is the pride of Andalucía. The region is famous for its *pescaíto frito* (fried fish) which typically consists of small fry such as whitebait in batter. Shellfish include *mejillones* (mussels), *gambas* (prawns) and *coquillas* (cockles).

Calamares (calamari), *sepia* or *choco* (cuttlefish) and *chipirones* (small squid) are common, and you'll sometimes see *pulpo* (octopus). Among the vertebrates, *sardinas* (sardines), *dorada* (gilthead bream), *rape* (monkfish) and *pez espada* (swordfish) are all usually excellent. In the Alpujarra and other hilly areas you can enjoy freshwater *trucha* (trout).

Signature tapas dishes vary from bar to bar and from province to province, and part of the delight of Andalucía comes trying regional specialities. Ubiquitous are *jamón* (cured ham; the best, *ibérico*, comes from black-footed acorn-eating porkers that roam the woods of Huelva province and Extremadura) and *queso* (in Andalucía, usually the hard salty *manchego* from Castilla-la Mancha). *Gambas* (prawns) are usually on the tapas list; the best and priciest are from Huelva.

Desserts focus on the sweet and milky. *Flan* (a sort of crème caramel) is ubiquitous; great when *casero* (home-made), but often out of a plastic tub. *Natillas* are a similar but more liquid version, while Moorish-style pastries are also specialities of some areas.

Drink

Alcoholic drinks

In good Catholic fashion, wine is the blood of Spain. It's the standard accompaniment to meals, but also features prominently in bars. *Tinto* is red (if you just order *vino* this is what you'll get), *blanco* is white and rosé is *rosado*.

A well-regulated system of *denominaciones de origen* (DO), similar to the French *appelation d'origine contrôlée*, has lifted the quality and reputation of Spanish wines. While the daddy in terms of production and popularity is still Rioja, regions such as the Ribera del Duero, Rueda, Bierzo, Jumilla, Priorat and Valdepeñas have achieved worldwide recognition. The words *crianza*, *reserva* and *gran reserva* refer to the length and nature of the ageing process.

One of the joys of Spain, though, is the rest of the wine. Order a *menú del día* at a cheap restaurant and you'll be unceremoniously served a cheap bottle of local red. Wine snobbery can leave by the back door at this point: it may be cold, but you'll find it refreshing; it may be acidic, but once the olive-oil laden food arrives, you'll be glad of it. People add water to it if they feel like it, or *gaseosa* (lemonade) or cola (for the party drink *calimocho*).

Andalucía produces several table wines of this sort. The whites of the Condado region in eastern Huelva province and those from nearby Cádiz are simple seafood companions, while in the Alpujarra region the nut-brown *costa*, somewhere between a conventional red and a rosé, accompanies the likeably simple local fare. In the same area, Laujar de Andarax produces some tasty cheapish reds. Jaén province also has red grapes tucked between its seas of olive trees, mainly around Torreperogil near Ubeda. Bartenders throughout Andalucía tend to assume that tourists only want Rioja, so be sure to specify *vino corriente* (or *vino de la zona*) if you want to try the local stuff. As a general rule, only bars that serve food serve wine; most *pubs* and *discotecas* won't have it. Cheaper red wine is often served cold, a refreshing alternative in summer. *Tinto de verano* is a summery mix of red wine and lemonade, often with fruit added, while the stronger *sangría* adds healthy measures of sherry and sometimes spirits to the mix. The real vinous fame of the region comes, of course, from its fortified wines; sherries and others (see box, page 29).

Beer is mostly lager, usually reasonably strong, fairly gassy, cold and good. Sweetish Cruzcampo from Sevilla is found throughout the region; other local brews include San Miguel, named after the archangel and brewed in Málaga, and Alhambra from Granada. A *caña* or *tubo* is a glass of draught beer, while just specifying *cerveza* usually gets you a bottle, otherwise known as a *botellín*. Many people order their beer *con gas* (half beer and half fizzy sweet water) or *con limón* (half lemonade, also called a *clara*).

Vermut (vermouth) is a popular pre-lunch aperitif. Many bars make their own vermouth by adding various herbs and fruits and letting it sit in barrels.

After dinner it's time for a *copa*. People relax over a whisky or a brandy, or hit the *cubatas* (mixed drinks); gin and tonic, rum and coke, whisky and coke are the most popular. Spirits are free-poured and large.

When ordering a spirit, you'll be expected to choose which brand you want; the range of, particularly, gins, is extraordinary. There's always a good selection of rum (*ron*) and blended whisky available too. *Chupitos* are short drinks often served in shot-glasses.

Non-alcoholic drinks

Zumo (fruit juice) is normally bottled; *mosto* (grape juice, really pre-fermented wine) is a popular soft drink in bars. All bars serve alcohol-free beer (*cerveza sin alcohol*). *Horchata* is a summer drink, a sort of milkshake made from tiger nuts. *Agua* (water) comes *con* (with) or *sin* (without) *gas*. The tap water is totally safe.

Café (coffee) is excellent and strong. *Solo* is black, served espresso style. Order *americano* if you want a long black, *cortado* if you want a dash of milk, or *con leche* for about half milk. *Té* (tea) is served without milk unless you ask; herbal teas (*infusiones*) are common, especially chamomile (*manzanilla*; don't confuse with the sherry of the same name) and mint (*menta poleo*).

Sevilla

magnificent architecture and buzzing tapas culture

Seductive, sun-baked and hedonistic, the sophisticated city of Sevilla, capital of Andalucía, in many ways embodies the romance of the region. First choice for many visitors to Andalucía, this is the brightest star in the south's tapas firmament.

The city has a post-reconquest architectural heritage unmatched in Andalucía, from the evocative Alcázar to the giant Gothic cathedral. Sevilla was the focal point of the Golden Age of Spanish painting, and many of the country's most memorable canvases are here.

The city's famed Semana Santa processions are the largest and best known of solemn Easter celebrations in Spain. Equally well known, the riotous Feria de Abril exemplifies many opposing features of the Andalucían character.

But as many as the temptations of Sevilla are, the rest of this landlocked province also commands attention. The agricultural settlements of the fertile Guadalquivir valley are a great contrast to the elegant bustle of the capital. Carmona was an important fortified town; further east, Ecija has an extraordinary number of Baroque churches, while the town of Osuna has many elegant Renaissance mansions.

Sevilla gets powerfully hot in summer, and many locals head north to the cooler regions of the Sierra Morena.

Best for
Architecture ▪ Festivals ▪ Nightlife ▪ Tapas

Sevilla

Footprint picks

★ **The cathedral**, page 39

Marvel at the sheer size of Sevilla's most famous building and climb the city's distinctive landmark, the Giralda tower.

★ **Real Alcázar**, page 43

Explore Sevilla's richly decorated Moorish-style palace.

★ **Parque María Luisa**, page 53

Visit the old exhibition pavilions and the city's archaeological museum.

★ **Triana**, page 56

Spend an evening trawling around the lesser-known bars in Triana, Sevilla, in search of down-to-earth flamenco.

★ **El Ayuntamiento**, page 59

Take a tour of Sevilla's town hall with its impressive carved stone function rooms.

★ **Carmona**, page 83

Descend into the enormous tombs of the Roman necropolis.

★ **Osuna**, page 87

Stroll around this attractive former ducal seat.

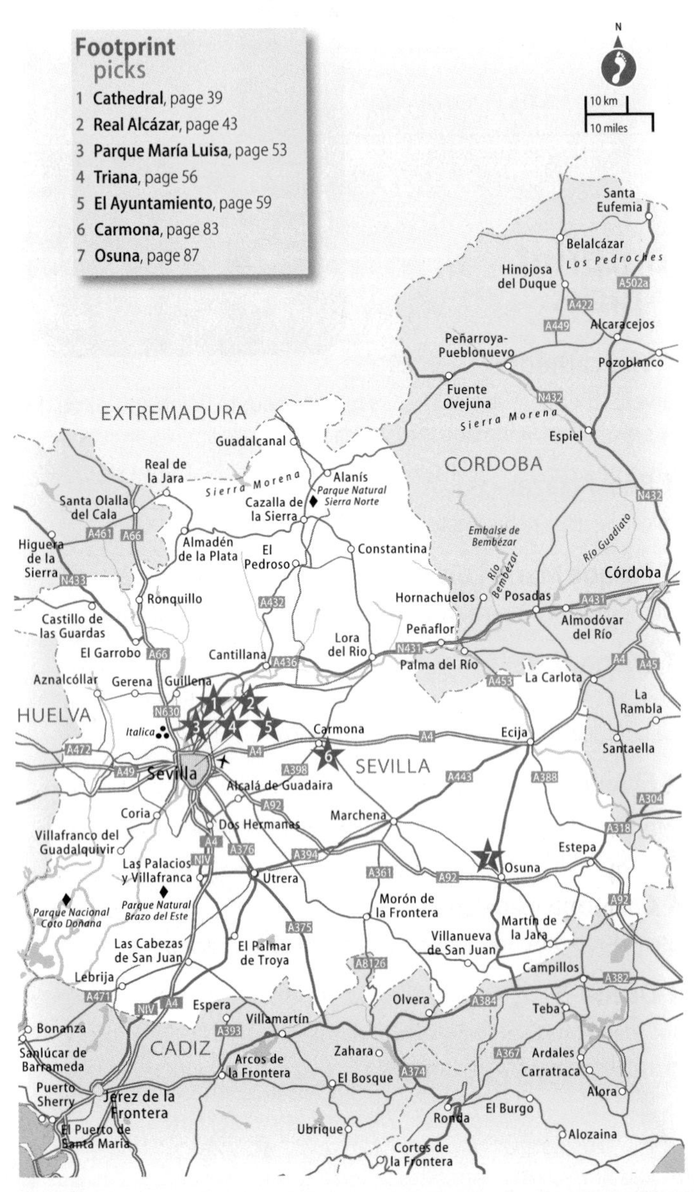

Footprint picks
1 Cathedral, page 39
2 Real Alcázar, page 43
3 Parque María Luisa, page 53
4 Triana, page 56
5 El Ayuntamiento, page 59
6 Carmona, page 83
7 Osuna, page 87
N
10 km
10 miles
EXTREMADURA
CORDOBA
HUELVA
SEVILLA
CADIZ
Sierra Morena
Los Pedroches
Parque Natural Sierra Norte
Parque Nacional Coto Doñana
Parque Natural Brazo del Este
Embalse de Bembézar
Río Bembézar
Río Guadiato
Italica
Sevilla
Córdoba
Santa Eufemia
Belalcázar
Hinojosa del Duque
Alcaracejos
Pozoblanco
Peñarroya-Pueblonuevo
Fuente Ovejuna
Espiel
Guadalcanal
Alanís
Real de la Jara
Santa Olalla del Cala
Cazalla de la Sierra
Higuera de la Sierra
Almadén de la Plata
El Pedroso
Constantina
Ronquillo
Castillo de las Guardas
El Garrobo
Cantillana
Lora del Rio
Hornachuelos
Posadas
Almodóvar del Río
Peñaflor
Palma del Río
La Carlota
La Rambla
Aznalcóllar
Gerena
Guillena
Carmona
Ecija
Santaella
Alcalá de Guadaira
Coria
Dos Hermanas
Marchena
Villafranco del Guadalquivir
Las Palacios y Villafranca
Utrera
Osuna
Estepa
Morón de la Frontera
Martín de la Jara
Villanueva de San Juan
Las Cabezas de San Juan
El Palmar de Troya
Campillos
Lebrija
Olvera
Teba
Espera
Villamartín
Bonanza
Sanlúcar de Barrameda
Zahara
Ardales
Carratraca
Arcos de la Frontera
El Bosque
Alora
Puerto Sherry
Jerez de la Frontera
El Burgo
El Puerto de Santa María
Ubrique
Ronda
Alozaina
Cortes de la Frontera
A502a
A422
A449
N432
A461
A66
N433
A432
A431
N431
A436
A4
A45
A453
N630
A472
A49
A398
A443
A388
A304
A92
A318
A376
NIV
A394
A361
A375
A8126
A382
A471
A384
A393
A367
A374

Sevilla city

The capital of Andalucía was accurately described in the 16th century as having 'the smell of a city and of something undefinable, of another greatness'. While the fortunes of this one-time mercantile powerhouse have waxed and waned, its allure has not; even within Spain its name is spoken like a mantra, a word laden with sensuality and promise. Delving beyond the famous icons; the horse carriages, the oranges, the flamenco, the haunting Semana Santa celebrations, you find a place where being seen is nothing unless you're seen to be having fun, a place where the ghosts of Spain walk the streets, be they fictional, like Don Juan or Carmen, or historical, like Cervantes, Columbus, Caesar or Joselito.

Sevilla has an astonishingly rich architectural heritage within its enormous old town, still girt by sections of what was once Europe's longest city wall. The bristling Moorish tower of the Torre del Oro, the Baroque magnificence of numerous churches; the gigantic Gothic cathedral and the *mudéjar* splendours of the Alcázar; these and much more are ample reason to spend plenty of time in Sevilla; you could spend weeks here and not get to see all the sights.

But the supreme joy of the city is its tapas. They claim to have invented them here, and they are unbeatable; you'll surely find that your most pleasurable moments in this hot, hedonistic city come with glass and fork in hand. *Colour map 1, C5.*

Essential Sevilla city

Getting around

Most of the sights in Sevilla are in the old town. As it was once one of the biggest cities in Europe, this is a fairly large area. However, large sections of it are pedestrianized and walking is by far the best way to get around.

Bus
To avoid the fierce summer heat, take one of Sevilla's air-conditioned TUSSAM city buses (see Transport, page 79). Bus C5 does a useful circuit around the centre of the city, including La Macarena.

Metro
Sevilla has a metro, www.metro-sevilla.es, with only one line operational until at least 2017. Line 1 links the satellite towns of Mairena de Aljarafe and Dos Hermanas with the city centre. Useful stops for visitors are Prado de San Sebastián bus station, Puerta de Jerez near the cathedral and Barrio Santa Cruz, Plaza de Cuba at one end of Triana, Parque de los Príncipes in Los Remedios, and Nervión, in the prime modern shopping area and near the Sevilla football stadium. However, most of the interesting parts of tourist Sevilla are not covered by the network. A single costs €1.35 for short journeys.

Best places to stay

Casa del Poeta, page 67
Corral del Rey, page 67
Hotel Amadeus & La Música, page 67
Las Casas del Rey de Baeza, page 69

Taxi
Taxis are a good way to get around. A green light on means they are available and they are comparatively cheap.

Tram
Sevilla has a tram service. Line 1 of Metrocentro, as the tram is known, handily zips between Plaza Nueva and San Bernardo local train station, via the cathedral, Puerta de Jerez and the Prado de San Sebastián bus station. A single ticket costs €1.40.

Best tapas bars

Ovejas Negras, page 70
Bar Alfalfa, page 71
Bodega Santa Cruz, page 71
Casa Morales, page 72
Yebra, page 73

When to go

High season, when prices are notably higher, in Sevilla is March to May, with the most pleasant weather and the two major festivals, Semana Santa and Feria de Abril. Summer is a quiet time as temperatures can be almost unbearable (hitting 50°C in recent years); autumn is a good time to visit, and winter is much milder here than elsewhere in Europe.

Time required

At least three days to see the main sights in the city of Sevilla.

The cathedral and around

vast Gothic cathedral and sumptuous *mudéjar* Alcázar

Plaza del Triunfo s/n, T954-214971, www.catedraldesevilla.es. Mon 1100-1530, Tue-Sat 1100-1700, Sun 1430-1800, you can prebook a free visit including audioguide on Mon 1630-1800. €8/€4 students under 26 and retirees. You can buy tickets online to avoid queues.

★Sevilla's bases of ecclesiastical and royal power, the cathedral and Alcázar face each other across the sun-beaten Plaza del Triunfo, once just inside the city's major gateway. They're both heavily visited, and with good reason: you should give plenty of your time to visit either and linger in a quiet corner while the tourist groups surge past. In the squares around, horse carriages sit under the orange trees ready to trot visitors around the sights of the town.

The fall of Sevilla to the Christians in 1248 was an event of massive resonance. While Granada's capitulation in 1492 marked the final victory, it was something of a foregone conclusion – the fall of Sevilla really represented the breaking of the backbone of Muslim Spain. After a while, at the beginning of the 15th century, the Castillians decided to hammer home the point and erect a cathedral over the mosque (which they had been using as a church), on a scale that would leave no doubts.

Santa María de la Sede is the result, which contains so many riches that most of its chapels and altars could have been tourist attractions in their own right; there are nearly 50 of them.

Several Moorish elements were happily left standing; the city's symbol, the superb Giralda tower, is the most obvious of these. Originally the minaret of the mosque, it was built by the Almohads in the late 12th century and was one of the tallest buildings in the world in its day. Although rebuilt by the Christians after its destruction in an earthquake, its emblematic exterior brick decoration is true to the original, although the famous weather vane atop the structure (El Giraldillo) is not.

Approaching the cathedral, try and start from Plaza de San Francisco, behind the Ayuntamiento. Taking Calle Hernando Colón, another Moorish feature will soon become apparent – the Puerta del Perdón gateway, with fine stucco decoration and a dog-toothed horseshoe arch. Turning left and walking around the whole structure will let you appreciate the Giralda and the many fine 15th-century Gothic doorways. You enter via the soaring Puerta San Cristóbal, next to the Archivo de las Indias.

It's impossible to list here all the works of artistic merit contained within the huge five-naved space. After passing through the entrance the first chamber is a small museum with several excellent pieces including a head of the Baptist by Juan de Mesa; a Roldán Joseph and Child; a San Fernando by Murillo; and a Zurbarán depicting the Baptist in the desert.

Around the chapels

Once into the cathedral proper, after catching your breath at the dimensions and the pillars like trunks of an ancient stone forest, turn hard left and do a circuit of

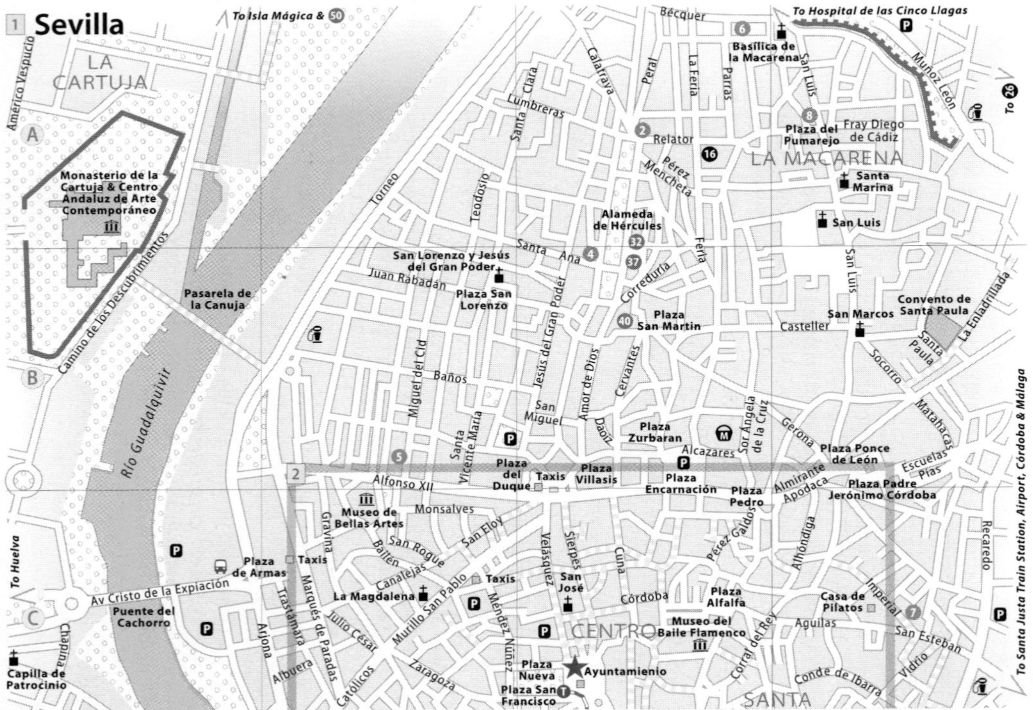
Sevilla
1
2
A
B
C
To Isla Mágica & 50
To Hospital de las Cinco Llagas
To 26
To Santa Justa Train Station, Airport, Córdoba & Málaga
To Huelva
LA CARTUJA
LA MACARENA
CENTRO
SANTA
Américo Vespucio
Monasterio de la Cartuja & Centro Andaluz de Arte Contemporáneo
Camino de los Descubrimientos
Pasarela de la Canuja
Río Guadalquivir
Torneo
Bécquer
Basílica de la Macarena
San Luis
Muñoz León
Calatrava
Peral
La Feria
Parras
Plaza del Pumarejo
Fray Diego de Cádiz
Santa Clara
Lumbreras
Relator
Pérez Mencheta
Santa Marina
San Luis
Teodosio
Alameda de Hércules
Santa Ana
Feria
San Lorenzo y Jesús del Gran Poder
Juan Rabadán
Plaza San Lorenzo
Jesús del Gran Poder
Correduría
Plaza San Martin
Casteller
San Marcos
Convento de Santa Paula
La Enladrillada
Santa Paula
Socorro
Miguel del Cid
Baños
Amor de Dios
Cervantes
San Miguel
Daoiz
Plaza Zurbaran
Sor Angela de la Cruz
Gerona
Matahacas
Santa Vicente María
Alcazares
Plaza Ponce de León
Escuelas Pías
Plaza del Duque
Taxis
Plaza Villasis
Plaza Encarnación
Plaza Pedro
Almirante Apodaca
Plaza Padre Jerónimo Córdoba
Alfonso XII
Museo de Bellas Artes
Monsalves
San Eloy
Gravina
Bailén
San Roque
Velásquez
Sierpes
Cuna
Pérez Galdos
Alhóndiga
Recaredo
Plaza de Armas
Taxis
Av Cristo de la Expiación
Canalejas
Taxis
San José
Córdoba
Plaza Alfalfa
Casa de Pilatos
Imperial
La Magdalena
Murillo San Pablo
Méndez Núñez
Puente del Cachorro
Trastámara
Marqués de Paradas
Julio César
Museo del Baile Flamenco
Corral del Rey
Aguilas
San Esteban
Chapina
Arjona
Albuera
Católicos
Zaragoza
Plaza Nueva
Ayuntamienio
Plaza San Francisco
Conde de Ibarra
Vidrio
Capilla de Patrocinio

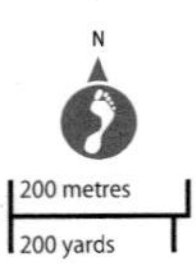
N
200 metres
200 yards

Taxis Reyes Pastor y Landero Castelar Gamazo Herando Colón Argote de Molina CRUZ Levies Santa María la Blanca Menéndez Pelayo
San Vicente de Paul Castilla Puente Isabel II (Puente de Triana) La Maestranza Paseo Cristóbal Colón Antonio Díaz EL ARENAL García de Vinuesa Arte Plaza Cabildo Cathedral Santa Cruz Fabiola Ximénez de Enciso Cruces Sta Teresa Plaza Santa Cruz Plaza del Triunfo
Plaza Callao Pagés del Corro Antillano Campos San Jorge Plaza de Altozano Archivo de las Indias Hospital de los Venerables Plaza Contratación López de Rueda Jardines de Murillo
Dos de Mayo Hospital de Caridad Teatro Maestranza Temprado Taxis Real Alcázar San Gregorio
San Jacinto Betis Pureza Capilla de los Marineros Rodrigo de Triana Santa Ana Plaza Puerta de Jerez Jardines de los Reales Alcázares Taxis
Leiria Evangelista Pagés del Corro Pelay Correa Almirante Lobo Torre del Oro & Museo Marítimo Puerta de Jerez Av Malaga Manuel Vásquez Sagastizabal
TRIANA Plaza Virgen Milagrosa Génova Taxis Av Paseo de Cristina Av Roma Antigua Fábrica de Tabacos Plaza Don Juan de Austria Taxis Prado de San Sebastián Prado
Plaza Cuba Puente San Telmo Palos de la Frontera Av Cid Plaza San Sebastián Av Carlos V
Juan Sebastián Elcano Paseo de las Delicias La Rábida Teatro Lope de Vega Av María Luisa Av Portugal
Av República Argentina Asunción Plaza de España Av Isabel la Católica
Parque de los Príncipes Niebla LOS REMEDIOS Puente del Generalísimo Parque María Luisa Av Pizarro
Turia Santa Fe Virgen de Luján Av Magallanes Av Pinzón
Fernando IV To Museo Arqueológico To Museo de Artes y Costumbres Populares

Sevilla maps

1 Sevilla, page 40
2 Sevilla centre, page 44
3 Barrio Santa Cruz, page 50

Where to stay

Alcoba del Rey **6** *A3*
Alfonso XIII **1** *E3*
Hostal Macarena **8** *A4*
Hostal Museo **5** *B2*
Monte Triana **3** *D1*
Patio de la Alameda **2** *A3*
Pensión Virgen de la Luz **7** *C4*
Sacristía Santa Ana **4** *B3*
TOC Hostel Sevilla **7** *D3*
Triana Backpackers **13** *D2*

Restaurants

Abades Triana **1** *E2*
Cervecería Yerbabuena **16** *A3*
La Blanca Paloma **8** *D1*
La Bulla **4** *D1*
Taberna Miami **6** *D1*
Yebra **26** *A4*

Bars & clubs

Antique Theatro **50** *A2*
Bulebar Café **32** *A3*
Fun Club **37** *B3*
Itaca **40** *B3*
Kiosco del Agua **41** *D2*
Puerto de Cuba **2** *E2*

Metrocentro Tram

the chapels. Don't forget to look up once in a while to appreciate the lofty Gothic grandeur and the excellent stained glass, much of it by Heinrich of Germany (15th century) and Arnao of Flanders (16th century). At the western end of the church, Murillo's *Guardian Angel* stands to the left of the middle door, leading the Christ child by the hand.

Turning on to the north side, see if you can barge through the tour groups into the chapel of **San Antonio**, with a huge and much-admired Murillo of that saint's vision of a cloud of cherubs and angels. Above it is a smaller Baptism by the same artist. An impressive Renaissance baptismal font here is still in use, while a 15th-century frieze of saints adorns the *reja*. These *rejas* are works of art in their own right – some of them take wrought iron to extraordinary delicacy.

Arriving in the northeast corner, take a break from chapels and climb the **Giralda**. You reach the top via 35 ramps (if they weren't numbered you'd think you were in a neverending Escher sketch), designed to allow sentries to climb the tower on horseback. The tower is 94 m high and the view from the top is excellent and helps to orientate yourself in this confusing city. There's a host of bells up here; the oldest date from the 14th century.

Coming down, the next chapel of **San Pedro** contains a *retablo* with nine good Zurbaráns devoted to the first pope's life. The inspiring **Royal Chapel** is often curtained off for services. The cuissons of its masterly domed ceiling contain busts of Castilla's kings and queens. In a funerary urn are the remains of the sainted conqueror-king Fernando III, while his wife Beatrice of Swabia (the inspiration behind Burgos cathedral) and their son Alfonso X (the Wise) are also buried here.

In the southeast corner, the treasury is entered through the **Mariscal Chapel**, which has a stunning altarpiece centred on the Purification of Mary and painted by Pedro de Campaña (Pieter Kempeneer), a Fleming of exalted talent. The **Treasury** contains a display of monstrances (one of which holds a spine from the Crown of Thorns), salvers and processional crowns. A fine antechamber and courtyard adjoin the Chapterhouse, adorned with vault paintings by Murillo.

The massive vestry is almost a church in its own right, with an ornate Plateresque entrance and three altars featuring fine paintings; a moving Descent from the Cross by Pedro de Campaña, a Santa Teresa by Zurbarán and a San Laurencio by Jordán. Two Murillos face each other across the room; they depict two of the city's earliest archbishops from the Visigothic period, San Isidoro and San Leandro.

Columbus' tomb stands proud in the southern central doorway, borne aloft by four figures representing the kingdoms of Castilla, León, Aragón and Navarra. It's in late 19th-century Romantic style, and some remains were deposited there in 1902, but nobody knows for sure whose they are – Sevilla is one of four cities that claim to have the fair-dinkum Columbus tomb. Columbus spent time praying in the next chapel, which features an excellent 14th-century fresco of Mary, in the place where the mosque's *mihrab* once stood. The later *retablo* was built around the painting.

The cathedral's principal devotional spaces are in the centre of the massive five-naved structure – the choir and the chancel. The choir itself is closed off by a noteworthy gilt Plateresque *reja* depicting the Tree of Jesse, while the ornate stalls feature misericords with charismatic depictions of demons and the vices.

The main *retablo* is a marvel of Christian art and has been the subject of several books in its own right. Measuring a gigantic 18 m by 28 m, it was masterminded by the Fleming Pieter Dancart, who began it in 1481; several other notable painters and sculptors worked on it until its completion in 1526. It is surmounted by a gilt canopy, atop which is a Calvary scene, and figures of the Apostles. The central panels depict the Ascension, Resurrection, Assumption and Nativity, while the other panels depict scenes from the life of Jesus and parts of the Old Testament.

You exit the church under the curious wooden crocodile known as El Lagarto (the lizard), probably a replica of a gift from an Egyptian ruler wooing a Spanish *infanta*. The pretty **Patio de los Naranjos** is another Moorish original, formerly the ablutions courtyard of the mosque. It's shaded with the orange trees that give it its name, as well as an irrigation system likely to trip you as your eyes adjust from the dusky interior. Admire the lofty Puerta de la Concepción (20th century, but faithful to the cathedral's style) before you exit through the Puerta del Perdón.

★Real Alcázar

Plaza del Triunfo s/n, T954-502323, www.alcazarsevilla.org. Oct-Mar 0930-1700, Apr-Sep 0930-1900. €9.50, students and retirees €2. The informative audio tour (Spanish, French, English, German, Italian) costs €3 and uses quotes from various kings responsible for the building's construction.

Even if the delights of tapas and the heat of the day are seducing your hours in Sevilla away from you, don't head for home without seeing the Alcázar, as you'll be derided by any friends who have. While you'll see horseshoe arches, stucco, calligraphy and coffered ceilings throughout, it's not a Moorish palace. It used to be, but little remains from that period; it owes its Moorish look to the Castillian kings who built it after the Reconquest: Alfonso X and his enlightened son Pedro I.

As well as being a magnificent palace, the Alcázar was once a considerable fortress in this impressively fortified city, a fact easily appreciable as you pass through the chunky walls in the dramatic red Puerta del León entrance gate, named for the tiled king of beasts guarding it. You emerge on to a large courtyard dominated by the impressive façade of the main palace of the Castillian kings. Before heading into this, investigate the Patio del Yeso to the left, one of the few remaining Moorish structures, where lobed arches face horseshoe ones across a pool surrounded by myrtle hedges.

Opposite, across the courtyard, are chambers built by Fernando and Isabel to control New World affairs. Magellan planned his trip here, and there's an important *retablo* from this period of the Virgen de los Navegantes. In the main panel by Alejo Fernández, the Virgin spreads her protective mantle over Columbus, Carlos V, and a shadowy group of indigenous figures (who might see some trouble coming if they could glimpse the side panel of Santiago, Spain's patron, who is gleefully decapitating Moors).

From this main courtyard, if you arrive early, it is possible to see some of the **upper floor of the palace**, still used when Spanish royals are in town. A series of elaborately furnished chambers are visited on the **guided tour** ⓘ *€4.50, you can prebook (advisable) online or on T954-560040*, which leaves roughly half-hourly.

2 Sevilla centre

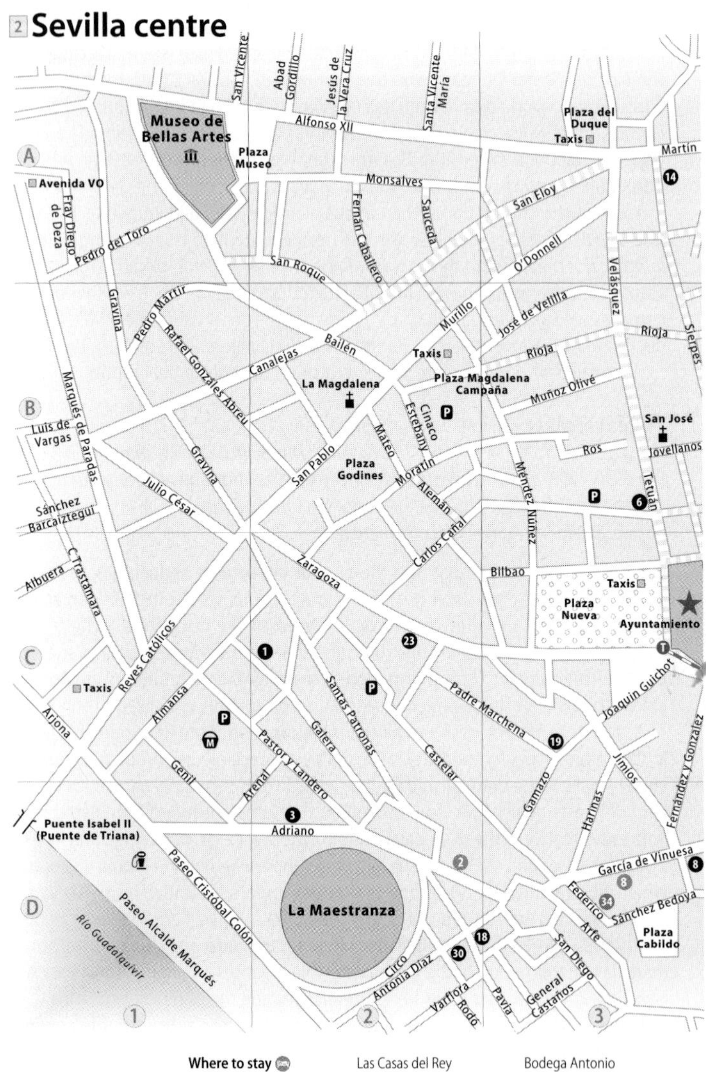

N

100 metres

100 yards

Where to stay
Adriano **1** *D2*
Alminar **2** *C4*
Corral del Rey **14** *C5*
EME Catedral **11** *D4*
Las Casas de los Mercaderes **6** *C4*
Las Casas del Rey de Baeza **9** *B6*
Simón **8** *D3*

Restaurants
Bar Alfalfa **2** *B5*
Bar Pepe Hillo **3** *D2*
Bodega Antonio Romero **30** *D2*
Casa La Viuda **6** *B3*
Casa Morales **8** *D3*
Casa Salva **15** *A1*
El Rinconcillo **20** *A6*
Enrique Becerra **19** *D3*

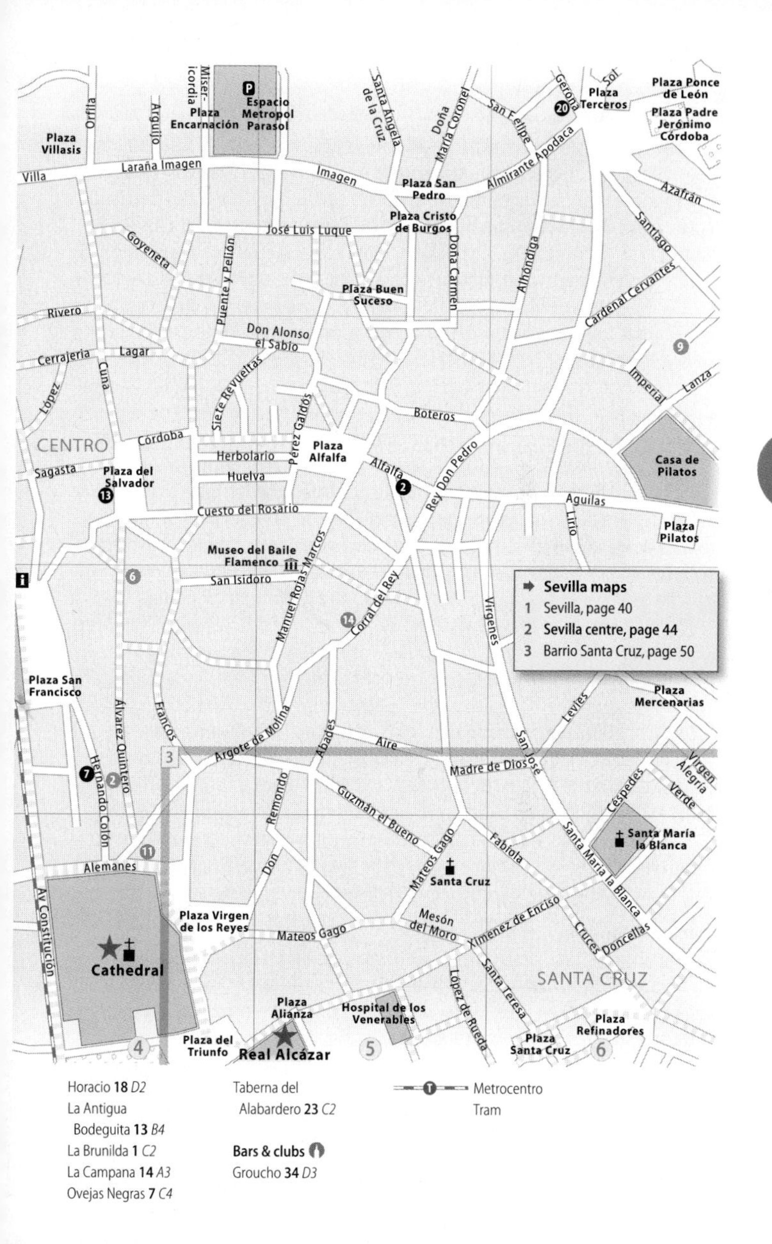

Horacio **18** *D2*
La Antigua Bodeguita **13** *B4*
La Brunilda **1** *C2*
La Campana **14** *A3*
Ovejas Negras **7** *C4*

Taberna del Alabardero **23** *C2*

Bars & clubs
Groucho **34** *D3*

Metrocentro Tram

Semana Santa

Sevilla's Holy Week processions are an unforgettable sight. Mesmeric candlelit lines of hooded figures and cross-carrying penitents make their way through the streets accompanied by the mournful notes of a brass band and two large *pasos*, one with a scene from the Passion, one with a statue of Mary. These scenes aren't unusual in Spain but what makes it so special is the *sevillanos'* extraordinary respect and interest for the event and devotion to the sculptures.

In Sevilla at least, the Semana Santa processions we know today evolved when the Spanish crown lurched into financial meltdown in the 17th century, and Sevilla, the economic hub of the country, went with it. The idea that the city was being punished by God took hold. Public displays of penitence, and a projection of the people's suffering on to the weeping Mary or agonized Christ developed.

Today, members of nearly 60 *cofradías* (brotherhoods) practise intensively for their big moment, when they leave their home church or chapel and walk through the streets to the *carrera oficial*, a route leading along Calle Sierpes to the cathedral and then home again. Some of the brotherhoods have well over 1000 in the parade; these consist of *nazarenos*, who wear pointed hoods, *penitentes*, who carry crosses and *costaleros*, who carry the *pasos*. Each *paso* is accompanied by a band that plays haunting brass laments and deep thuds of drums.

The first brotherhoods walk on Palm Sunday and the processions continue up until Easter Sunday, when a single *cofradía* celebrates the Resurrection. The most important processions are on the night of Maundy Thursday (*la madrugá*), when several brotherhoods go to the cathedral during the wee hours.

Sevillanos hold the processions in great esteem and a high percentage are members of a *cofradía*, even if they're not really religious. Everyone has their favourite sculpture too; the best-loved Marys are La Macarena and La Triana. The most admired Christs are El Cachorro and Jesús del Gran Poder, both supreme pieces of art. During the processions, it's not uncommon for people on the street or on balconies to launch into a *saeta*, a haunting flamenco-based song inspired by the *paso*; similarly, the Marys are often greeted with shouts of '*Guapa!*'.

What to take

Pick up a copy of the programme for the processions; it's available free in bookshops. Buy a map with a street index so you can track down exactly what route the processions take. Make sure you're dosed up with suncream if it's a hot day, but don't bother with an umbrella; the *cofradías* stay home if it's wet, as the rain damages the *pasos*. They have to wait until the next year.

What to see

If you're in Sevilla for the week, you'll see plenty of processions. Just pick a couple to start the week, and then go at it hard on the Thursday night. The busiest places are near the church and cathedral (although the *carrera oficial*, the last stretch into the cathedral, is seating only). There are less people on the *cofradía*'s return journey.

The seating along the *carrera oficial* is mostly occupied by long-time local subscribers, but there are some seats available, which you can nab by going in the early morning and paying the attendants. The price is usually €25-50. The view is great, but it can be boring sitting in one place; much of the excitement is in seeking out the *cofradías* or coming across them by chance in a narrow street. Some of the most interesting are:

La Paz (Palm Sunday) The first *cofradía* and a spectacular sight coming up Calle San Fernando, best seen from the fountain in Puerta de Jerez, where it passes around 1500.

San Esteban (Tuesday) Their exit (1500) and entry (2230-2330) from a church just behind the Casa de Pilatos is great to watch as the manouevring of the *pasos* is a difficult feat. Get there a long time before.

Las Siete Palabras (Wednesday) This 16th-century *cofradía* has an excellent Calvary as one of their *pasos*. Be in the Museo de Bellas Artes square from 2030.

La Madrugá Late on Thursday night, six of the most important *cofradías* make the journey. It's worth making the effort to stay up all night, as most of the city does. First up is El Silencio, a 14th-century brotherhood and one of the oldest. Although it's not completely silent, it's black-robed *nazarenos* are an eerie sight. See it from Plaza del Duque from 0100 and stay there for Jesús del Gran Poder, whose stunning Christ follows hard on their heels. Then trot north to the Alameda de Hércules, for the procession of La Macarena. At about 0430 try and be at the Puente de Triana to watch her great rival La Esperanza de Triana cross the river. If you're still on two feet, head to Plaza Encarnación to see Los Gitanos, the well-loved gypsy *cofradía*.

El Cachorro/La O (Friday) These two popular Triana *cofradías* simultaneously cross the Puente de San Telmo and the Puente de Triana on their way home at 2330 or so.

La Resurrección (Sunday) Leaving their Macarena home at 0400-0500, they reach the cathedral about 0800, where there's enough room to see them, the last of the processions.

Etiquette

Be silent when watching the *pasos* pass, and don't applaud unless other people are so doing. It is considered rude to cross a procession; definitely don't do it in front of the *paso* or among the band.

Timing

If you've got to be somewhere at a certain time during Semana Santa, allow plenty of it, as you're likely to get caught in crowds watching a procession. It can take ages to get even a short distance.

What to eat

Semana Santa food is *torrijas*, bread slices soaked in milk and honey and fried, *pestiños*, fried nuggets of honey and dough, and the offcuts of communion hosts.

BACKGROUND

Sevilla

While Sevilla legend attributes the founding of the city to Hercules, it is likely that the first permanent settlements on this site were built by the Tartessians in the first half of the first millennium BC.

The Phoenicians established themselves here shortly afterwards, and they extended and fortified the existing town. It became an important trading centre in the Western Mediterranean, and continued to be so after a Carthaginian takeover in the third century BC. In 206 BC the Romans defeated them in the battle of Ilipa, near the city that they named Hispalis. They also established the town of Itálica nearby, originally as a rest camp for mutinous Italian soldiers. The river in these days was known as the Betis. Caesar arrived here as administrator of the town and enjoyed his stay by all accounts. The people sided with him against Pompeii and were rewarded by being conferred full Roman citizenship. When Augustus created the province of Baetica, Hispalis soon became the capital, and both it and Itálica became very important Roman cities. The emperor Trajan was born in the latter and Hadrian grew up there. Christianity took early root in Sevilla and, after early persecutions, soon flourished.

The city was sacked by Vandals and Swabians as the Empire collapsed, but then prospered under Visigothic rule, with the wise historian and archbishop San Isidoro particularly prominent. The Islamic invasion in 711 put an end to the Visigothic kingdom; Hispalis was transliterated to Isbiliyya, from which Sevilla is derived, and the river was renamed *al wadi al kibir* (big river), or Guadalquivir as it is now written. Sevilla spent the first few centuries of the Moorish occupation under the shadow of Córdoba, but, on the collapse of the caliphate, became an independent *taifa* state and grew rapidly to be the most powerful one in Al-Andalus. Under the poet-king Al-Mu'tamid, the city experienced an exceptional flourishing of wealth and culture. Much of Sevilla's Moorish architectural heritage dates from the 12th century and the Almohad regime.

The palace façade is a fusion of Christian and Moorish styles that just about achieves harmony. Inscriptions about the glory of Allah (Pedro had a deep interest in Islamic culture) adjoin more conventional Latin ones proclaiming royal greatness.

This fusion is repeated throughout this whole section, centred around the stunning **Patio de las Doncellas**. Throughout the complex are azulejos, topped by friezes of ceramic decoration, while higher up, intricate stucco friezes are surmounted by a range of marvellous inlaid ceilings. Also worth admiring are the imposing doors, some elaborately inlaid. Among the rooms off this courtyard are the **Salón de Embajadores**, with a beautiful half-orange ceiling and a frieze of Spanish kings; and the chapel, where Carlos V married his first cousin Isabella of Portugal (one of many inbreedings that doomed the Habsburg line).

In 1248, Isbiliyya was conquered by Fernando III, and nearly all its Muslim population were expelled and their lands divided among noble families. In 1391, a massive anti-Jewish pogrom occurred in the city. Synagogues were forcibly changed into churches and the Jewish quarter virtually ceased to exist. The current cathedral was begun soon afterwards.

With the discovery of the New World, Sevilla's Golden Age began. In 1503, it was granted a monopoly on trade with the transatlantic colonies, and became one of the largest and most prosperous cities in Europe.

The 17th century, however, saw a decline, although this was the zenith of Sevilla's school of painting, with artists such as Zurbarán, Murillo and Velázquez all operating. The expulsion of the *moriscos* (converted Moors) in 1610 hit the city hard and merchants left to ply their trade elsewhere. A plague in 1649 killed an incredible half of the inhabitants, and in 1717, with the Guadalquivir silting up rapidly, New World trade was moved to Cádiz.

Occupied by the French from 1810-1812, Sevilla only really rose from its torpor in the 20th century. The massive Ibero-American exhibition of 1929 bankrupted the city but created the infrastructure for a modern town and many fine public spaces. In the Civil War, the oddball General Queipo de Llano bluffed his way into control of the city. Workers struggled against the rising and were brutally repressed, with much of Triana destroyed.

In 1982, the Sevillano Felipe González was elected the first Socialist prime minister since the Civil War, governing until 1996. The city, beginning to stir once more, hosted a World Cup semi-final and, 10 years later, Expo 1992, having already become the capital of semi-autonomous Andalucía. The event left the city with enormous debts but attracted some 15 million visitors and boosted Sevilla's international profile.

The city continues with urban improvements, with the metro and tram system recently inaugurated, and extensive pedestrianization of the old centre implemented. Unemployment, poverty and homelessness are still massive, if not always visible, problems.

Adjacent is the **Renaissance Palace**, heavily altered from the original Gothic by Carlos V and his descendants. In the chapel is an interesting Velázquez portraying a beautiful Virgin placing a chasuble over the shoulders of San Ildefonso. From here stretches the vast and fantastic garden; different sections filled with slurping carp, palm trees and a grotesque gallery built into a section of the old walls. Steps lead down to the picturesque covered pool known as **Los Baños de Doña María de Padilla**. The garden has featured in several films and series, most recently in *Game of Thrones*. You finally exit the complex through the vestibule where coaches and horses used to roll in, and you emerge in the Patio de Bandera. There are often small exhibitions in this last section.

Archivo de las Indias
Plaza del Triunfo s/n, T954-500528. Mon-Sat 0930-1645, Sun 1000-1400. Free.

This square and sober Renaissance building – "An immense icebox of granite guarded by lions, in which is housed the colonial past, every sigh and every comma, until the end of the world" (C Nooteboom, *Roads to Santiago*) – between the cathedral and Alcázar was once Sevilla's Lonja, where merchants met to broker trade with the New World. The cannons poking out from the roof echo the decks of Spain's ocean-going vessels.

In the late 18th century it was converted into the state archive, where all documents relating to the Americas were stored and filed, an intriguing record that includes everything from the excited scribblings of Columbus to the most mundane book-keeping of remote jungle outposts. There's a small display of

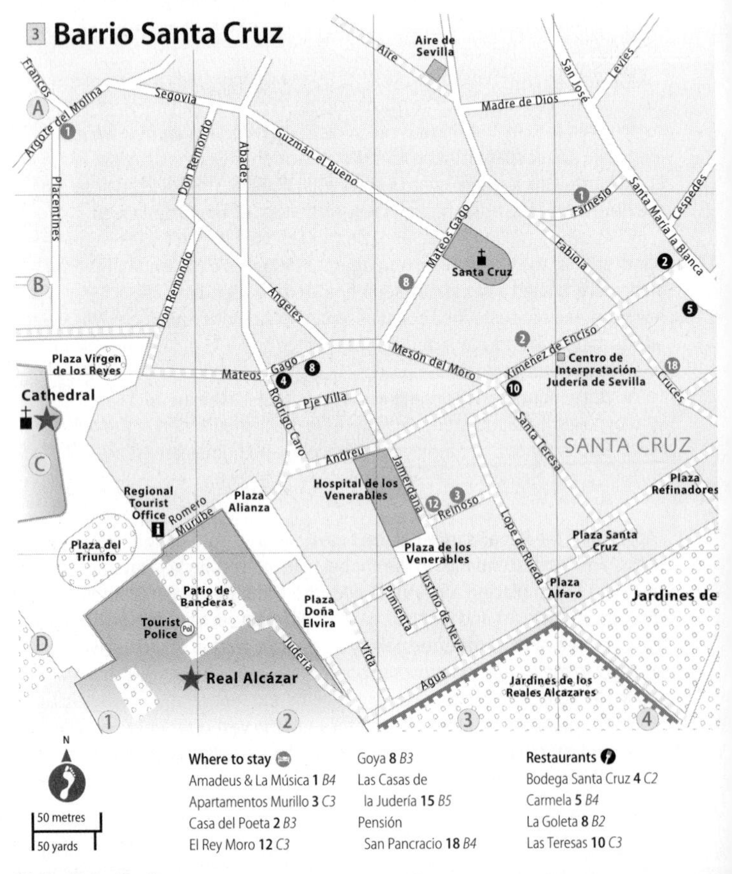

Where to stay
Amadeus & La Música 1 *B4*
Apartamentos Murillo 3 *C3*
Casa del Poeta 2 *B3*
El Rey Moro 12 *C3*
Goya 8 *B3*
Las Casas de la Judería 15 *B5*
Pensión San Pancracio 18 *B4*

Restaurants
Bodega Santa Cruz 4 *C2*
Carmela 5 *B4*
La Goleta 8 *B2*
Las Teresas 10 *C3*

the building's history on the ground floor, and upstairs, under the vaulted stone ceilings and among the polished shelves holding the archives are regular themed exhibitions and a couple of Goya portraits. Researchers can examine documents in the reading room, after filling in a form and showing ID.

Barrio Santa Cruz

Sevilla's most charming barrio: small plazas shaded by orange trees

Once home to much of Sevilla's Jewish population, atmospheric Barrio Santa Cruz has a web of narrow pedestrian lanes. Squeezed between the Alcázar, cathedral and a section of the old city walls, it's very touristy but thankfully not over-prettified, and there's a fairly standard tour beat that you can easily explore away from. There are excellent accommodation and restaurant options as well as several intriguing antique and handicraft shops; even the souvenir shops are comparatively tasteful.

Taberna Poncio **2** *B4*

Bars & clubs

The Second Room **1** *A1*

The best way to enter the barrio is from the Plaza del Triunfo by the cathedral; head through the gate in the Alcázar walls to the south into the pretty square of Patio de Banderas, floored with sand and lined with orange trees. In the opposite corner, duck through a small tunnel and twist and turn your way on to Calle Judería, one of the nooks with most medieval flavour.

A wander through the narrow lanes of Barrio Santa Cruz will reveal much. On one side, the area is bounded by a stretch of the old Almohad city walls, behind which is the public park of the Jardines de Murillo, centred around a monument to Columbus. Nearby, Calle Santa María la Blanca was once one of the city's entrances; the food markets used to be in this zone and farmers would enter here with carts piled high with meats, cereals, and vegetables. These days, it's more of a plaza than a street, with several sun-kissed terraces (go for Carmela ahead of any place with paellas on display). It's well worth visiting the small **church** ⓘ *Mon-Fri 1000-1300, 1600-2000*, that gives the street its name. The attractive toothed arch of the portal gives little hint of the Baroque fantasy inside – the central vault of the triple-naved church is carved with a riot of floral and vegetal decoration. In the left aisle you'll see a Murillo, a *Last Supper* that's not usually reckoned one of his best works but certainly deserves to be. A young, visionary Christ is surrounded by the wise, bearded old heads of his apostles. It's all the better for being in situ.

Hospital de los Venerables

Plaza de los Venerables 8, T954-562696, www.focus.abengoa.es. Daily 1000-1400, 1600-2000. €5.50, free Sun afternoon.

In the heart of Barrio Santa Cruz, and built at the end of the 17th century in a charitable vein, the Venerables refers to the old priests for whom it was originally intended as a hospital and residence. Now owned and managed by a cultural foundation, the building regularly holds good temporary exhibitions on Sevillian culture and history, but is also worth visiting for its church, a repository of fine painting of the late Sevillian school. The church is alongside the main courtyard, a noble space centred around a sunken fountain and surrounded by an arcade on marble columns. Stunning tilework completes the effect. Entry includes an audio tour.

Aire de Sevilla

C Aire 15, T955-010024, www.airedesevilla.com. Daily 1000-midnight, to 0200 weekends, tea room 1530-2400, 0200 at weekends. Visit with aromatherapy €26, with massage €41.

Located in a 16th-century palace, this luxurious Arabian-style bathhouse offers warm, hot, and cold baths as well as a steam room and massage facilities. The place itself is beautifully relaxing, with delicate lighting and stylish design. Only a certain number of people are allowed in at a time, so it pays to reserve a slot in advance by phone or via the website. Take a bathing suit; you can hire one if necessary.

Centro de Interpretación Judería de Sevilla

C Ximénez de Enciso 22, T954-047089, www.juderiadesevilla.es. Mon-Sat 1030-1530, 1700-2000, Sun 1030-1930. €6.50.

This is run by enthusiastic people and has a reasonable display on Sevilla's Jewish history, with information about various historical figures. It's set in a beautiful Santa Cruz house. They also run walking tours (€22 including museum entry) of the former Jewish barrio.

South of the cathedral

Sevilla's best park, superb museums and a historic landmark hotel

Much of this area is taken up with the large Parque María Luisa, donated to the city by the queen's sister in the late 19th century. It was used as the site for the grandiose 1929 Ibero-American Exhibition, an event on a massive scale that the dictatorship hoped would re-establish Sevilla and Spain in the world spotlight. The legacy of the exhibition is a much-loved public park, the monumental Plaza de España, and a beautiful series of the former pavilions. On Calle San Fernando, the massive and elegant Hotel Alfonso XIII was built to put up important visitors to the exhibition.

Antigua Fábrica de Tabacos

C San Fernando 4, T954-551000. Mon-Fri 0800-2030. Free.

Next door to the Alfonso XIII hotel stands what was once Spain's second largest building, surrounded by a fence and moat; the building was originally the cigarette factory and workers were carefully checked to make sure they didn't nick any fags. Visitors flocked to the cigarette factory in the late 19th century to see the girls at work, for it had been made famous by *Carmen* and other tales of the beauty of Sevilla's womenfolk. Despite poor conditions, the workers must have had no complaints about the building itself, with numerous elegant hallways and courtyards that suit it perfectly in its new function as a university building. It's a lively place and worth a visit to wander around its corridors.

★Parque María Luisa

Daily 0800-2400 summer (2200 winter). Free.

This beautiful and peaceful space is Sevilla's best park, again developed for the 1929 exhibition. It's full of quiet corners, even on busy days, and a series of informative plaques detail the huge range of exotic trees and plants on show; parts of the park even feel like an authentic rainforest.

Around the park are dotted various buildings erected for the 1929 exhibition. The most grandiose of these is the Plaza de España, envisaged as a second Giralda, a symbol of a new, dynamic Sevilla. The semi-circular area is backed by a massive brick and marble building that curves around to two proud towers. A small canal was once used for leisurely rowing and is crossed by four bridges. The most endearing feature is the row of benches, each one dedicated to one of Spain's provinces. A tiled map of each is accompanied by a significant historical event and some typical symbols. The buildings are used now for various government departments, but it's no surprise that the stunning ensemble has been used in several films, featuring as part of Cairo in *Lawrence of Arabia* and, more recently, Naboo in *Star Wars: The Attack of the Clones* and Wadiya in *The Dictator*.

At the other end of the park are two excellent museums. The **Museo de Artes y Costumbres Populares** ⓘ *Plaza de América 3, T954-232576, mid-Sep to mid-Jun*

ON THE ROAD

Feria de Abril

Sevilla's April fiesta is a lively counterpoint to the solemnity of the Semana Santa processions. Originally a gypsy horse fair, it took its present form in the early 20th century. It gets bigger and livelier every year; with the well-loved Los Remedios grounds being squeezed to the limit by well over 1000 *casetas*, the event is eventually scheduled to move to a new location in a few years' time.

The *casetas* are colourfully striped tents, venues for six days of socializing, eating, drinking *manzanilla* and dancing *sevillanas*. Most are privately owned, by social clubs, employers or families; bar a few public ones, entry is by invitation only. It's busy day and night; during the afternoon *sevillanos* dashingly dressed in riding suits and bright *flamenca* costumes parade by in colourful carriages, while the dancing and drinking action hots up at night. A large funfair adds to the attraction as do the season's biggest bullfights, held at the Maestranza.

Getting there The massive Feria gate is at the bottom of Calle Asunción, a 15-minute walk from the Puente de San Telmo. Shuttle buses run from Prado San Sebastián station. Cars are not allowed near the grounds. Taxis are, but you're much better walking home as the queues are horrendous. Or use the rank at the back exit rather than by the front gate.

Kick-off The Feria begins on the Monday night two weeks and a day after Easter Sunday (unless this would mean that it begins in May, in which case it's brought forward). Crowds wait until midnight, when the gate (a new one is built each year) is spectacularly lit up and the party begins. The Feria runs until the next Sunday, when a fireworks display east of the gate officially ends the revelry at midnight.

Casetas Grab a map from tourist information; most of the public *casetas* are clearly marked; these belong to leftist political parties and the local

Tue-Sat 1000-2030, Sun 1000-1700, mid-Jun to mid-Sep Tue-Sun 1000-1700, free for EU citizens, €1.50 others, is in the rather majestic *mudéjar* pavilion. The exhibition is a cut above the dreary displays that well-intentioned ethnographic museums often seem to become. The top floor is mostly devoted to what *sevillanos* wore through the centuries; there's a good blend of period paintings and costumes themselves. There's an excellent display on wheat farming, important here since the Stone Age, and a collection of Semana Santa and Feria posters.

In the massive basement are many items of furniture and household use, as well as reconstructions of typical workshops, including a guitar maker's, and a wine bodega whose smell permeates the level. The information is in Spanish but it's all pretty self-explanatory and a fascinating record of urban and rural Sevilla life.

Sevilla's **Museo Arqueológico** ⓘ *Pabellón de Bellas Artes, Plaza de América s/n, T954-232401, mid-Sep to May Tue-Sat 1000-2030, Sun 1000-1700, mid-Jun to Sep Tue-Sun 1000-1700, free for EU citizens, €1.50 otherwise*, should be good, considering the wealth of peoples that have lived and traded in the region since prehistoric times.

councils of the city. If you know a local that can invite you in to a *caseta*, well and good, but it's fairly easy to get in to some of the less exclusive ones; after all, many of them are happy to have a few extra punters paying for drinks and thus defraying their hire costs.

Dress respectably and ask the doorman politely in Spanish if you can enter; you'll get plenty of knockbacks but also plenty of entries, particularly (doormen being doormen) if a woman does the asking. Large groups of people speaking English will likely get in nowhere. Up until about 2100, there are no doormen, and many of the *casetas* can be entered freely.

Eating and drinking The best places to eat are the *casetas* themselves, which put on a range of good-value tapas and *raciones*. Drink *manzanilla* (usually served in a half-bottle) or *rebujito*, a weaker refreshing blend of the same with lemonade, served in a litre cup. *Pescaíto frito* (fried fish) is traditionally eaten on the first night of Feria.

In all the *casetas*, once the eating's done, people spend most of the night dancing. The *sevillana* is a relatively modern form with roots in both flamenco and Latin music. A dance has four distinct parts, all characterized by elaborate arms-aloft movements, partners stepping around each other, and stares of moody intensity. You'll experience another dimension of Feria if you manage to learn the basics.

Kicking on Unless you've hit a manic *caseta*, Feria winds down about 0300. If you want more, the best places are around the Feria grounds on and near Calle Asunción; the rest of Sevilla's nightlife is comparatively quiet during Feria. The biggest night at Feria is usually the Friday; Saturday isn't nearly as busy.

Toilets Queues in the public *casetas* are long, so you're better going in a private one, paying €1 to use one of the few public loos around, or dashing off to the trees at the edge of the compound.

And it doesn't disappoint, with a particularly rich Roman collection. Among a good selection of prehistoric finds and fossils the standout pieces are from Tartessian culture; a people that lived in the Guadalquivir valley from about 1100 BC onwards. Their best pieces, finely worked pottery, carved stone and gold jewellery, show clear influences from the Phoenicians, who began trading along this coast around 700 BC.

On the ground floor, after an imposing array of Iberian stone lions, come the Roman finds, mostly from nearby Itálica, but many also from the large necropolis at Carmona. There are several mosaics; one from Ecija depicting Bacchus and his leashed pards, and a later one showing the Judgement of Paris, with Aphrodite seeming keen to win the contest. Among the excellent sculptures on display are a second-century AD headless Venus, striding out of the waves at the moment of her birth, a slightly later Diana, the emperor Trajan in full heroic mode, and a fine depiction of the bearded Hadrian. There's a collection of citizens' portrait heads – a real rogues' gallery – and a fascinating room full of bronze law scrolls. There are English summaries at the entrance to most rooms, and a good printed handout.

Triana

backstreet flamenco bars, riverside restaurants and colourful tiles

★Many visitors find that Triana becomes their favourite part of Sevilla. It's redolent with history from every epoch of the Christian city as well as having a picturesque riverfront lined with terraced bars and restaurants. It was for a long time the gypsy barrio and as such the home of flamenco in Sevilla. Although most of the gypsies were moved on in the 1950s, its backstreet bars are still the best place to catch impromptu performances. Triana is also famous for ceramics; most of the azulejo tiles that decorate Sevilla's houses so beautifully come from here, and there are still many workshops in the area. It's also got a significant maritime history.

Entering the barrio across the Puente Isabel II, you arrive at Plaza de Altozano. From here, Calle Betis stretches to your left along the riverfront and is one of the top strolls in the city, lined with prettily coloured buildings, most of which are dedicated to eating and drinking.

Behind here, on Calle Pureza, is the **Iglesia de Santa Ana** ⓘ *C Pureza s/n, Mon-Fri 1030-1330, plus Tue-Wed 1630-1830, €1.50 donation requested.* The 'Cathedral of Triana' is believed to be Sevilla's oldest church, dating from around 1276.

Not far from here, at Calle Pureza 53, La Esperanza de Triana lives in an ornate *retablo* behind the big yellow and white façade of the **Capilla de los Marineros** ⓘ *Mon-Sat 1000-1330, 1730-2100, Sun 1000-1400, 1730-2030, free.* She and La Macarena are the two most-adored Virgins of the city, and there are few bars around without a picture up of one or the other of them. Her passages across the bridges in the wee hours of Good Friday morning are among the most emotional of the Semana Santa processions; see box, page 46.

On the other side of Triana, the **Capilla de Patrocinio** ⓘ *C Castilla 182, Mon-Fri 1030-1330, 1800-2130, Sun 1030-1330, free,* is worth a visit for the superb Christ inside, who is much revered across Sevilla. He is named El Cachorro, after a dead young gypsy that the sculptor is said to have used as a model. The sculpture is breathtaking; you can feel the sinews of the crucified Christ straining, while his face is a perfectly rendered mixture of anguish and relief.

El Arenal

Sevilla's bullring and a Moorish tower

If you look at a picture of Sevilla in the early 19th century or before, you'll see that from the Moorish Torre del Oro, the city wall recedes from the riverbank, leaving a large open area, El Arenal (meaning sandy spot). This was a haunt of thieves, swindlers, prostitutes and smugglers, who hung out near the docks where the action was. It was built over in the 19th century, and El Arenal is now one of Sevilla's most pleasant barrios, with some of the city's major landmarks.

Torre del Oro

Paseo de Colón, T954-222419. Mon-Fri 0930-1845, Sat-Sun 1030-1845. €3, free Mon.

The spiky battlements of this beautiful Moorish tower are one of Sevilla's primary landmarks and the building is powerfully evocative of the city's military and maritime history. The exterior was once decorated with bright golden ceramic tiles, from which it gets its name. The interior now holds a motley maritime museum with sharks' teeth and paintings of galleons and sea-dogs that aren't illuminated by any explanatory panels. It's worth going in, however, for the great river views from the top and for the old prints showing Sevilla in the late 16th century: Triana has its boat-bridge and castle, and the docks are bristling with ships.

La Maestranza

Paseo de Colón 12, T954-224577, www.realmaestranza.com. Daily Nov-Apr 0930-1900, May and Oct 0930-2000, Jun-Aug 0930-2300, except bullfight days (Sun in spring and summer and all week during Feria), when it's open 0930-1500, guided tours every 30 mins (English and Spanish). €7.

One of Spain's principal temples of bullfighting, La Maestranza is a beautiful building wedged into a city block, which accounts for its slightly elliptical shape. Started in the mid-18th century, it took until the late 1800s to finish it. It holds some 14,000 spectators, and sells out nearly every seat during the April Feria, when the most prestigious fights of the season are held. The Sevilla crowd are among the most knowledgeable of aficionados, and many of bullfighting's most famous names have been *sevillanos*. The guided tour is a poor substitute for the atmosphere at the corridas, and has no information on how a bullfight works. The main entrance, La Puerta del Príncipe, has an imposing wrought-iron gateway by Pedro Roldán; it's a 16th-century work that originally stood in a convent. If a *torero* has a particularly good day, he is carried out through this door. There's a small museum, which has some good pictures of the chaotic affairs that were early bullfights before the present structure of a fight was adopted in 1830. You also briefly visit the horse stables, but disappointingly not the bullpens. Nor are you permitted on to the sand itself. You do, however, see the small chapel, where bullfighters can pray before the fight, and the infirmary, a chillingly modern room where horn wounds are operated on.

Hospital de Caridad

C Temprado 3, T954-223223. Mon-Sat 0900-1300, 1530-1900, Sun 0900-1230. €5.

Behind the theatre is this *residencia de ancianos* (nursing home) still fulfilling its original charitable purpose. It was built as a hospital for the poor by Miguel de Mañara, a curious 17th-century *sevillano* often likened to Don Juan. After a scandalous youth of seduction and deceit he reformed completely when he saw a vision of his own death and dedicated himself to a life of charity and religion. He had a good eye for art; as a result of this, the hospital chapel has a collection of masterpieces commissioned by Mañara expressly to remind his brotherhood of the charitable virtues and the ultimate futility of worldly wealth and pride.

Two astonishing paintings stand above and opposite the entrance. They are the two finest, and most disturbing, works of the Sevillian painter Juan de Valdés Leal. The first one you'll see depicts a leering skeletal Death with a scythe, putting out a candle with one hand while trampling over objects that represent worldly wealth, power, and knowledge. The inscription *In Ictu Oculi* translates as in the blink of an eye. Opposite this is an even more challenging painting entitled *Finis Gloriae Mundi* (the end of worldly glory). It depicts a crypt in which a dead bishop and knight are being eaten by worms. Above, a balance is borne by the hand of Christ. On one side are symbols of the seven deadly sins, on the other side symbols of a holy love between God and Christ. 'Neither more nor less', read the words on the scales. Mañara commissioned these works in detail, and the face of the knight is thought to be his own.

After these grim warnings, the paintings of Murillo demonstrate the charitable life Mañara wanted his brotherhood to lead. Although four are missing (they were stolen by Napoleon's pillaging general, Soult, and are now scattered around the world; they include the impressive *Return of the Prodigal Son* in Washington), those that remain are exceptional examples of this artist's work. St John of God carries a sick man, while St Isabelle of Hungary cares for the afflicted. A Moses horned with light brings forth water from the rock, while Jesus feeds the multitude with loaves and fishes. In a *retablo* by Bernardo Simón de Pineda next to the pulpit is another Murillo painting, a depiction of the Annunciation. The sculptor Pedro Roldán is responsible for the figures in the intense *retablo* of Santo Cristo de la Caridad, with a Christ dripping blood flanked by cherubs. The main *retablo*, a Churrigueresque riot of cherubs and *salomónica* columns, is again the work of Roldán and Pineda; the former responsible for the emotive central tableau of the burial of Christ.

Juan de Valdés Leal painted the ceiling, of which the cupola is particularly fine, while Murillo also painted the small panels of the infants Jesus and John the Baptist above two other *retablos*.

Centro and San Vicente

Sevilla's shopping heartland

The busy Centro region is centred on the shopping streets of Sierpes, Tetuán, Velásquez, Cuna and O'Donnell. It's a fascinating stroll around this area, and there's an encouragingly low number of chain stores, giving the zone a particularly local character. Shops selling fans, shawls and other Sevilla fashion essentials abound. Worth looking for is the small church of San José, on Calle Jovellanos just off Calle Sierpes; the main *retablo*, an extraordinary sight: with its two side panels and bristling with cherubs, it could be a production of *A Midsummer Night's Dream* in gold.

★El Ayuntamiento

Plaza Nueva s/n, T954-590101. Mon-Thu 1630-1930, Sat 1000 (subject to change due to civic functions and other events). €4, free Sat. Bring passport or ID to enter. Closed Jul-Aug.

It's hard to miss Sevilla's town hall as it fronts two major squares, Plaza Nueva and Plaza San Francisco. It was formerly the site of one of Sevilla's most important monasteries; in the disentailment of 1835, it was demolished and the hitherto tiny Ayuntamiento expanded. As such, the building has two distinct sections, a Plateresque and a neoclassical (as well as some more recent annexes). From Plaza San Francisco, you can admire the superbly intricate stonework of the original 16th-century building. The architect of the newer structure thought he'd better continue with the Plateresque design to ensure harmony, but was stopped in his tracks by outraged neoclassicists appalled at the perceived flippancy; the Plateresque stonework thus comes to an abrupt and jagged end.

The interior, entered through the sober façade on Plaza Nueva, is a revelation. An excellent volunteer-guided tour (Spanish only, but worth doing even if you don't understand the commentary) visits the chambers of the original edifice, which has some breathtaking Renaissance stonework that still features some Gothic influences. The lower council chamber is entered through a dignified doorway crowned with a depiction of Fernando III; inside there's an amazing coffered stone ceiling with busts of 36 monarchs in the coffers, finishing with Carlos V himself in one corner, complete with imperial crown. There are several elegant rooms on the top floor; notable works of art up here include a Zurbarán *Inmaculada* and a sketch by Murillo.

Espacio Metropol Parasol

Plaza de la Encarnación, www.espacio-metropol.com. Viewing platform Sun-Thu 1030-0000, Fri-Sat 1030-0100, €3 including a drink. Museum Tue-Sat 1000-2000, Sun 1000-1400, €2.10.

This striking and controversial addition to central Sevilla opened in 2011 and has a viewing platform that is a magical place to be at sunset. Consisting of six giant interlinked parasol-like structures – dubbed Las Setas (the mushrooms) by locals – it was designed by Jürgen Mayer. The lower gallery holds the traditional food market and an archaeological museum based around the Roman remains discovered below street level. From here you can access the viewing platform in a lift. It's a spectacular series of walkways that puts you up among the city's rooftops, giving great views in all directions.

Casa de Pilatos

Plaza de Pilatos s/n, T954-225298. Daily 0900-1900, to 1800 winter. €6 lower floor, €8 both floors, free Wed from 1500 for EU citizens.

This stunning mansion is still partly inhabited by members of the family of the Dukes of Medinaceli, who built most of it in the late 15th to early 16th centuries. It owes its name to the story that the Duke, on a pilgrimage to Jerusalem, was so struck by the former residence of the Roman governors (including Pontius Pilate) that he decided to model his own house on it. The profusion of classical sculpture decorating the courtyards and gardens, some of it original, certainly gives the house a Roman air, but the architecture is principally an attractive blend of Renaissance classicism and *mudéjar* styles. Sensitive restoration has healed the damage caused during the Spanish Civil War, when the building was used as a hospital.

The highlight of the visit is the central courtyard, reached from the entrance by passing under a thriving purple cascade of bougainvillea. It's a stunning combination of azulejos and stuccowork; the Italianate central fountain is overseen by statues, including an excellent Athena Promachos. On the walls are mounted a series of Roman portrait heads, obtained by the dukes from Italy. The gardens are beautiful and peaceful; one even has a small grotto with tinkling water. The staircase to the upper level is a cascade of shining tiles topped by a majestic golden dome that owes some of its decoration to Moorish *mocárabes*.

Beyond here is accessed by a **guided tour** ⓘ *English and Spanish, tours leave every 30 mins from 1000-1830 except 1400 and 1430*. The tour takes you through furnished rooms with some excellent 17th-century coffered ceilings and a large collection of paintings, including a Goya of the Ronda bullring, and an Assumption by Murillo, not one of his better works.

Museo del Baile Flamenco

C Manuel Rojas Marcos 3, T954-340311, www.museoflamenco.com. Daily 1000-1900. €10.

This museum is devoted to flamenco, in particular the dance side of it, and involved renowned *bailaora* Cristina Hoyos in its development. Set in a lovely patioed building, it's a good spot to visit before you see some performances. While the entrance charge offers questionable value, there are stylish interactive displays on the world of flamenco dance, with an interestingly humanistic slant: dancers' lives are examined as well as the great performances. They have decent evening shows daily. There's also a shop and café.

Museo de Bellas Artes

Plaza del Museo 9, T954-221829. Mid-Sep to May Tue-Sat 1000-2030, Sun 1000-1700, mid-Jun to mid-Sep Tue-Sun 1000-1700. Free for EU citizens, €1.50 for others.

Sevilla's major art gallery is a must-see, picturesquely housed in a convent dating from the 17th and 18th centuries. This is appropriate enough, as most of the collection comes from the monasteries stripped of all their possessions in the Disentailment Act of 1835. The Sevillian school of painting was the dominant artistic force in Spain's Golden Age and is represented here in all its glory, offset by peaceful and pretty tiled patios.

The collection is thoughtfully laid out and thankfully uncluttered. Early pieces include a fine work from the monastery of San Agustín by Martín de Vos showing the awakening dead being sorted by angels and demons. In the same room there's also an El Greco; a good portrait of his own son.

In the early years of the 17th century, two distinct styles were evident in Sevillian painting, naturalism and mannerism, but these were gradually brought together as the century progressed. The latter style is well represented here by a selection of Francisco Pacheco's works. A portrait by the master Velázquez (Pacheco's son-in-law), of a gentleman against a brooding sky, is also in this section. Room IV has works of another mannerist, Alonso Vázquez, including, appropriately, a series on San Pedro Nolasco, who founded the original monastery on this site.

The former convent church is an awesome space with an elaborate painted ceiling. Here we see the evolution of the Sevilla school to its peak; the works of Zurbarán and Murillo. Although the former is represented here by an appropriately imposing heavenly Father and his large, famous Apotheosis of St Thomas Aquinas, there are more of his works upstairs; this room belongs to Murillo, whose statue graces the square outside the museum. Most of his works here are from the former Capuchin monastery. The city's patrons, Santa Justa and Santa Rufina, hold the Giralda in one renowned canvas, while a tender San Felix and child, *St Francis' Dream of the Crucified Christ*, and the famous *Virgin of the Napkin*, who holds a wide-eyed Christ child, are other noteworthy pieces. While mannerist traces remain in his early work, Murillo evolves into a complete Baroque style characterized by intense religious fervour, usually centred on a gaze or glance of striking power or emotion.

There are more Murillos upstairs and a long gallery devoted to Juan de Valdés Leal (1622-1690). Zurbarán, a little out of context, is represented in Room X. In the corridor outside is perhaps his most powerful work here, a crucifixion of incredible solitude and force, with Christ, head-down, seemingly chiselled from rock.

The 19th- and 20th-century rooms have works by Sevillian proto-Impressionist Gonzalo Bilbao as well as a portrait of the haunted Romantic poet Gustavo Adolfo Bécquer, famously and sensitively portrayed by his brother Valeriano, while two good portraits by the Basque painter Ignacio Zuloaga and a fiesta scene by Gustavo Bacarisas round off the superb collection.

La Macarena

working-class barrio with Sevilla's best markets and buzzing nightlife

The large barrio of La Macarena, once one of the poorest slums in the peninsula, is an enticing web of narrow streets and numerous churches and chapels, occupying the northern portion of the old town. One church is home to Sevilla's best-loved Virgin, La Esperanza de la Macarena. She gives her name to many of Sevilla's women, one of whom was the subject of the bestselling Latin hit of all time, by the ageing duo Los del Río. Still a working-class zone, La Macarena is home to much of Sevilla's alternative culture. It's still demarcated by a long section of the city wall, the best-preserved chunk of what was once one of Europe's mightiest bastions.

Walking tour of Barrio La Macarena

Heading into the barrio along Calle Santa Vicente María, you come to the **Iglesia de San Lorenzo y Jesús del Gran Poder** ⓘ *mid-Sep to mid-Jun Mon-Thu 0900-1330, 1800-2100, Fri 0730-2200, Sat-Sun 0800-1330, 1800-2100, mid-Jun to mid-Sep Mon-Thu 0800-1330, 1800-2100, Fri 0730-1400, 1700-2200, Sat-Sun 0800-1400, 1800-2100, free*, most notable for the 17th-century sculpture of Christ by Juan de Mesa in a side chapel. It's a focus of much local adoration and a breathtaking piece of art; Jesus looks utterly careworn and harrowed; the brotherhood's procession with the sculpture is one of the highlights of Semana Santa. Continuing down Calle Santa Clara, and then right up Calle Santa Ana, you reach the **Alameda de Hércules**. This long avenue lined with planes and poplars is the centre of Sevilla's alternative scene. Once a marsh, it was drained in the 16th century and adorned at both ends with Roman columns; upon the taller of the two were placed sculptures of Hercules, who is said to have founded Sevilla, and Julius Caesar, whose presence as governor of the province is considerably more certain. On Sunday mornings (and a little on Thursdays), there's a lively flea market here; while Sevilla's busiest and oldest market, El Jueves, takes place on Thursday mornings too, a couple of blocks away on Calle Feria, which is named after it.

From the Alameda, follow Calle Peral, and then turn right up Calle Bécquer. This will bring you to the **Basílica de la Macarena** ⓘ *C Bécquer 1, T954-370195, daily 0900-1400, 1700-2100 (Semana Santa 0900-1500 most days), free (€5 for museum)*, the home of Sevilla's most-adored Mary and a fairly recent construction; the first stone was laid by Pope Pius XII in the 1940s. The Virgin takes pride of place in the *retablo*; the Christ from the other *paso* stands in front of her. You can see the *pasos* themselves in the museum, along with various gifts that have been bestowed on the Virgin and a variety of her garments.

Across the main road from the basilica is the **Hospital de las Cinco Llagas**. Built in the 16th century, it is said to have been the biggest hospital in the world at the time. The sober façade is long and impressive but these days the patients have been replaced by politicians; it's the seat of Andalucía's regional parliament. On the main road here begins the best-preserved stretch of the city walls. They were originally at least partially Roman, perhaps built by Julius Caesar when he governed the region. The Moors made them formidable again; with the circumference of some 6 km defended by 166 towers, a moat and jagged castellation.

Back at the basilica, take Calle San Luis, which meanders its way back towards the centre of town. You soon pass **Plaza del Pumarejo**, a shady spot frequented by some real barrio characters, then the **Iglesia de Santa Marina**, with a *mudéjar* tower. Shortly afterwards, on the right you come to the **Iglesia de San Luis** ⓘ *C San Luis s/n, T954-214024, Tue-Sat 0900-1400, Fri and Sat also 1700-2000, closed Aug, free*, whose flamboyant façade will snap you out of any heat-induced reverie. Although the road's too narrow to really appreciate the architecture, the front is a Baroque masterpiece with scores of Churrigueresque features. Inside the circular interior are several *retablos*, the finest is the main one, inlaid with blue ceramic and centred around a small Madonna painting; look out also for the massive Zurbarán painting depicting the saint Louis XIV of France in his earthly days. The ceiling frescoes in the dome are also very impressive; an ornate mirror is on hand to help you appreciate them.

Further down the street, the **Iglesia de San Marcos** is a Gothic-*mudéjar* church that was once a mosque. It has a well-crafted façade, with a toothed Gothic portal, delicate *mudéjar* blind arcading above, and the bearded evangelist himself atop. However, it is most notable for its slim tower, which is very similar in style to the Giralda. It's adorned with attractive brickwork and a series of windows that increase in size as the tower rises. Cervantes was fond of climbing to the top. The interior features some horseshoe arches, preserved despite extensive Civil War damage.

Behind the church, along Calle Santa Paula, is the **convent** ⓘ *C Santa Paula s/n, T954-536330, Tue-Sun 1000-1300, €3*, of the same name. There's an air of mystery about a visit here; knock at the door and you'll eventually be admitted and get shown around by a knowledgeable old nun with a twinkle in her eye. It's the home of a few dozen nuns; the building dates from the 15th century and contains many pieces of art of varying quality and some fine faded, but wholly original, 15th-century *artesonado* ceilings. There's a gorgeous patio and a fine tiled doorway, a work of Pisano. On either side of the church is a pair of excellent sculptures by Martínez Montañés of the two Johns, while some Alonso Cano works are also present. Don't forget to buy some of the delicious marmalade made by the nuns.

La Cartuja

the city's contemporary art gallery and a theme park

The clay-rich Isla de la Cartuja was a centre for potters' workshops in bygone centuries but was more or less derelict until the city decided to make it the site of the World Expo in 1992. Predictably for such an event, costs skyrocketed, and the city was left with massive debts and a huge space filled with modern buildings that needed to be used. There's a popular theme park here, Isla Mágica; nearby the river is spanned by two bridges by the Valencian architect Santiago Calatrava.

Monasterio de la Cartuja

Av Américo Vespucio 2, www.caac.es, Isla de la Cartuja, T955-037070. Tue-Sat 1100-2100, Sun 1100-1500. €1.80 for permanent collection or exhibition, €3 for both, free from 1900 weekdays and all day Sat; audio guide €3.

The clay in this part of Sevilla meant that ceramics were made here from ancient times; it was in a pottery in the 13th century that the Virgin appeared and a shrine was built. It later became this important monastery, a favourite of Sevilla's wealthy and powerful in the Golden Age. Columbus came here to pray and contemplate his next voyages; when he died his remains lay here for 23 years.

In the Peninsular War, the arch-desecrator of Spanish cultural heritage, Maréchal Soult, stationed some troops here, and the buildings were badly damaged. Once the monks were expelled some 20 years later, it was in an extremely poor state and was picked up cheaply by Charles Pickman, a British businessman, who set up a ceramics factory on the site and lived there. Pickman generally respected the monastic buildings, though all were put to use, and the huge brick kilns and chimneys still dominate the site.

Renovated by the Sevillian authorities, it became the Royal Pavilion of Expo 92, and now houses a good contemporary art museum, the **Centro Andaluz de Arte Contemporáneo**. First visit the church itself, with a small cloister, a refectory with a beautiful coffered ceiling, and the well-carved tombs of the powerful Ribera family. Then access the galleries (the layout of the complex is confusing). The temporary exhibitions are usually good and the gallery spaces white, uncluttered, and relaxing.

The permanent collection (not all of which is always on display) has some excellent pieces, mostly by Andalucían artists. Look out for Guillermo Pérez Villalta's series on the four elements, which speaks powerfully about the fate of the Moors and their cultural contribution to Andalucía.

Itálica and Alcalá de Guadaira → *Colour map 1, C5.*

Roman ruins and a 14th-century monastery

Itálica

Santiponce (9 km from Sevilla), T955-996583. Mid-Sep to Mar Tue-Sat 1000-1830, Sun 1000-1700, Apr to mid-Jun Tue-Sat 1000-2030, Sun 1000-1700, mid-Jun to mid-Sep Tue-Sat 1000-1700, Sun 1000-1700. Free EU citizens, otherwise €1.50. To get there, take the Damas (www.damas-sa.es) bus from Plaza de Armas bus station to Santiponce, €1.20 each way (25 mins), every 20-30 mins weekdays and on Sat mornings, every hour on Sat afternoons and Sun, by car take the N630 north (following the signposts for Mérida) across the Puente Cristo de la Expiración.

It's hard to believe, wandering around the ruins of Itálica, that this was once one of the Roman Empire's largest and most important cities. In truth, little of it has been excavated; what you can walk around today is the partially revealed remains of the *nova urbs* (new town; a relative term these days), built by Hadrian in the early second century AD, while the *vetus urbs* (old town) lies under the village of Santiponce. It was originally built by Publius Cornelius Scipio in 206 BC; one of the Italian (not Roman) regiments of his army had a rough time of it during the battle against the Carthaginians at Illipa and he decided to build a settlement for them to let them heal up and ease the threat of mutiny. It grew rapidly and in time became the most important Roman city in the region, birthplace of the emperor Trajan and perhaps his protégé Hadrian, who certainly grew up here.

While it's a pleasant place to wander around, with birds, bees and acres of flowering weeds, there's not a huge amount to see (and the information given is paltry), but what's here is very good, particularly the huge amphitheatre near the entrance, which seated 20,000. Although much of the seating has been removed over the years, the terraces are still very clear, as are the stairways and the large sunken area in the middle (thought to have had a central dais erected over it for use in gladiatorial combats). One fascinating find is displayed in a side chamber: a bronze tablet inscribed with norms for gladiatorial combat imposed by Marcus Aurelius and his son (who else but Commodus, Russell Crowe's sworn enemy in *Gladiator*).

The other highlights of a visit are the mosaics on display on the floors of some of the excavated houses. The **House of Neptune** has one of these; the centre features sea creatures, including the god himself, while the outer edges depict a Nilotic hunting scene; it's not without its humour, as the large crane doing an injury to a hunter's backside attests. There's a statue of the god-emperor Trajan near here; it's thought that the whole of this section of the city was built by Hadrian in his predecessor's honour. The **House of the Birds** also has some excellent mosaics, two of which colourfully feature an array of the feathered tribe. The **House of the Planetarium** has perhaps the finest piece, with portraits of the seven divinities who gave their name to the Roman week.

It's hot out here, and there's not much shade, but thankfully there are several good bars and restaurants clustered around the entrance. If you're not exhausted yet, turn right out of the entrance and up the hill a couple of minutes to check out the partially restored Roman theatre (there's a tourist information point here). Don't bother with the small bathhouse nearby, but head straight for the monastery further up the road. The return bus passes the entrance to this, so you won't have to retrace your steps.

The **Monasterio San Isidoro del Campo** ⓘ *T955-998028, Wed-Thu 1000-1400, Fri-Sat 1000-1400, 1600-1900 (1700-2030 summer), Sun 1000-1500, €3*, was founded in 1301 by Guzmán El Bueno in the place where, by tradition, San Isidoro (StIsidore) had been interred until the removal of his remains to León. It's a sizeable monastery whose imposing walls attest to its double function as a fortress in those uncertain times. The place has had an interesting history; one of its monastic communities dabbled in translations of forbidden texts, not a healthy move in 16th century Spain with the Inquisition at the peak of its power and paranoia about Protestantism rife. Some of the monks fled the country, others burned for their bookish crimes. Guzmán and his wife are buried in the curious twin church, alongside a magnificent *retablo* by Martínez Montañés. One of the cloisters features unusual *mudéjar* frescoes.

Alcalá de Guadaira

Now basically a suburb of Sevilla, the friendly village of Alcalá is worth visiting for its huge, muscular Moorish fortress, constructed by the Almohads. It's very impressive, if a shell; little remains inside the walls. Buses run every 20 minutes from Avenida Portugal (after 2100 they run from Prado San Sebastián bus station); €1.20.

Tourist information

Junta de Andalucía tourist office
Plaza del Triunfo, T954-221005, www.turismosevilla.org. Mon-Fri 0900-1930, Sat and Sun 0930-1930.
Near the cathedral, Sevilla's most useful tourist office is always busy, but has good information and multilingual staff. Their former location on Av de la Constitución still resembles a tourist office but is actually a private business. There are also information booths at the airport and at platform 6 at Santa Justa train station. The tourist office sells the Sevilla Card for access to most museums and monuments, as well as free tour buses, river cruises, entry to the Isla Mágica theme park and discounts on flamenco shows. For a little extra it includes public transport. It costs €33 for 24 hrs or €53 for 48 hrs, slightly less online at www.sevillacard.es.

Where to stay

There's a wealth of choice of attractive and intimate lodgings set in attractively renovated old Sevillian mansions. The densest concentration can be found in Barrio Santa Cruz and in San Vicente, between the Plaza de Armas bus station and the Museo de Bellas Artes.

If you're planning a visit in spring, booking ahead is advisable. All places raise their prices massively during Semana Santa and Feria; sometimes double or more, although it's more commonly 50-70%. At some hotels, this increase is in place for the whole Mar-May period. Price codes here reflect high season (but not Semana Santa) prices.

At many hotels you can get good discounts online rather than reserving with the hotel directly.

The cathedral and around

€€€€ Alfonso XIII
C San Fernando 2, T954-917000, www.hotel-alfonsoxiii-sevilla.com.
One of Spain's most luxurious hotels, this huge neo-Moorish building was erected for the 1929 exhibition. Completely renovated recently, it's beautifully decorated with opulent patios. The hotel is 5-star in every sense of the word, but the prices are exorbitant at around €400-500 for a double, more during Sevilla's festive season. You'll get the best deals via the website.

€€€€ Eme Catedral Hotel
C Alemanes 27, T954-560000, www.emecatedralhotel.com.
This fashion-conscious modern hotel by the cathedral has brought a splash of colour and modern design to Sevilla's old centre. Certain humorous touches, undeniably attractive furnishings, and enticing features like the small rooftop pool and jacuzzi win it points; the rooms are stylish but perhaps lack features for this price. The location is wonderful.

€€€ Hotel Alminar
C Alvarez Quintero 52, T954-293913, www.hotelalminar.com.
On this likeable pedestrian street linking the cathedral with Plaza del Salvador, this hotel trades in warm personal service; with only 11 rooms, it feels like they've got time for all their guests. The rooms are spacious, modern, and

sparklingly clean, with efficient a/c and really good bathrooms. There's no parking particularly close.

€ TOC Hostel Sevilla
T954-501244, Miguel Mañara 18, www.tocsevilla.com.
It's hard to find fault with this brilliant spot slap-bang in the heart of the main monument area. It's got both private en suite rooms and comfortable dorms, all with upbeat modern decor and thoughtful design features. There's good security and staff have a helpful attitude. Great features include the reception desk and the back terrace. Recommended.

Barrio Santa Cruz

€€€€ Casa del Poeta
C Don Carlos Alonso Chaparro 3, T954-213868, www.casadelpoeta.es.
With a very discreet entrance in the heart of Santa Cruz (the street is a little cul-de-sac off Ximénez Enciso), this is another heart-stoppingly beautiful Sevilla patio hotel. Rooms are elegant and unfussily handsome – we loved the duplex one – and staff are professional and eager to please. Recommended.

€€€€ Corral del Rey
Corral del Rey 12, T954-227116, www.corraldelrey.com.
This boutique hotel has turned heads in the Spanish hotel world for its faultlessly realized restoration of an historic *palacio*, its irresistible romantic ambience, thoughtfully selected modern art, and its beautiful rooms, which are coupled with excellent bathrooms and equipped with all sorts of amenities. There's a gourmet restaurant here, and a small rooftop pool; the staff are commendably solicitous. Recommended.

€€€€ Las Casas de la Judería
Callejón Dos Hermanas 7, T954-415150, www.casasypalacios.com.
It's difficult to describe just how big this outstanding hotel complex is. It spreads across several old *palacios* in the Barrio Santa Cruz – all have been superbly renovated, with sparkling patios, pretty nooks, and hanging foliage. The rooms are sizeable, luxurious enough and agreeable, though not a patch on the exterior decor and a little dark and stuffy. Service is conscientious and there's live music in the piano bar every evening. A particular highlight of the hotel is the originally decorated underground passageway to the dining room. Recommended.

€€€ El Rey Moro
C Lope de Rueda 14, T954-563468, www.elreymoro.com.
Run by the restaurant of the same name, this excellent hotel that sits between 2 central Santa Cruz streets is built around a large 3-storey patio with wooden columns. The appealing rooms have beams, big beds and shiny modern bathrooms; some face inwards on to the patio, others face the street and the buzz of the Plaza de los Venerables restaurants. Staff are charming, and rent out Segways to explore town. Breakfast included.

€€ Hotel Amadeus & La Música
C Farnesio 6, T954-501443, www.hotelamadeussevilla.com.
A fantastic and original hotel occupying 2 adjacent buildings with a musical theme. The individually decorated rooms are named after composers; some have a piano, of which there are also a couple downstairs. All rooms have first-rate facilities. A highlight, apart from the charming service, is the spacious roof terrace with views

over the centre, including the Giralda. Highly recommended.

€€ Hotel Goya
C Mateos Gago 31, T954-211170, www.hotelgoyasevilla.com.
Located at the top of the street that is Sevilla's tapas epicentre, the Goya is a cool place with marbled floors and a/c. The rooms are large and fairly minimalist, with excellent bathrooms. Some have balconies overlooking this interesting street.

€ Pensión San Pancracio
Plaza de las Cruces 9, T954-413104, pensionsanpancracio@hotmail.com.
In a quiet nook of the barrio, this is a good cheap choice; a touch faded, but well-scrubbed and quiet. There are several room choices: they are all adequate, with attractive white calico bedspreads and light and air from a central patio. The bathrooms are shared and clean. Ground floor rooms are cooler, but those above have a fan; take your pick.

Self-catering

There's an ever-growing number of apartments around Barrio Santa Cruz; lots of them are listed online on sites like www.booking.com and www.airbnb.com.

€€ Apartamentos Murillo
C Reinoso 6, T954-216095, www.hotelmurillo.com.
The **Hotel Murillo** in the heart of Santa Cruz also runs these stylish modern apartments around the corner. There are 3 types, sleeping up to 5, and fitted out with kitchen, bathroom, TV and phone. Rates are reasonable for this location. Also rented on a daily basis.

Triana

€€ Hotel Monte Triana
C Clara de Jesús Montero 24, T954-343111, www.hotelesmonte.com.
With a barrio location in Triana but close to the bus station and bridge, this makes an appealing and somewhat secluded Sevilla base. Staff are excellent and the modern rooms are very well kept. The buffet breakfast is better than average too.

€ Triana Backpackers
C Rodrigo de Triana 69, T954-459960, www.trianabackpackers.com.
This backpackers' hostel stands out for its Triana location as well as traveller-friendly features such as free internet, breakfast, a roof terrace and a TV lounge. It's a sociable place with friendly staff and a welcoming feel. It's not the cheapest, and couples won't get value from the cramped doubles, but it's a great place to meet other folk.

El Arenal

€€€ Hotel Adriano
C Adriano 12, T954-293800, www.adrianohotel.com.
This boutique hotel has a great location near the bullring and in the heart of a great tapas and restaurant area. Decor is in keeping with the building's 18th-century origins, with antique furniture and gilt trim. There's parking available too; another pleasing feature.

€€ Hotel Simón
C García de Vinuesa 19, T954-226660, www.hotelsimonsevilla.com.
Long a Sevilla favourite, this is an attractive hotel built around a beautiful airy courtyard with a fountain. There are plenty of azulejos and neo-Moorish features. Rooms are smallish

but accommodating and decorated as thoughtfully as the rest of the establishment. It's not luxurious, but good value for the decor and ambience.

Centro and San Vicente

€€€€ Las Casas del Rey de Baeza
Plaza Jesús de la Redención 2, off C Santiago, T954-561496, www.hospes.com.
An enchanting place to stay near Casa de Pilatos, this old *corral de vecinos* has been superbly restored to be charming but not overdone. The patios are surrounded by pretty wooden galleries and the underfloor hessian mats are a great touch. The rooms are big, with huge beds and all facilities. Guests have use of a rooftop pool and terrace as well as an elegantly decorated library and lounges. The service is first rate. Recommended.

€€€ Las Casas de los Mercaderes
C Alvarez Quintero 9, T954-136211, www.aahoteles.com.
In the heart of the shopping district and a short walk from the centre is this beautifully renovated hotel. The tempting rooms are interestingly furnished and spacious, with all conveniences; the hotel is built around a striking arcaded patio. Elegant 19th-century furnishings in the public areas complete the classy but welcoming feeling.

€€ Pensión Virgen de la Luz
C Virgen de la Luz 18, T954-537963, www.pensionvirgendelaluz.es.
One of Sevilla's best-value cheapies, this pretty little place is near the Casa de Pilatos. The rooms come with or without bath; the latter (**€**) are of an unusually high standard and represent good value, particularly those on the lane, which have a small plant-filled balcony. The beds are welcoming, the bathroom spotless, and the patio decorated caringly with blue tiling.

€ Hostal Museo
C Abad Gordillo 17, T954-915526, www.hostalmuseo.com.
Offering excellent value for money, this clean and courteously run place is a short stroll from the bus station and very close to the art gallery. There are flawless, comfortable rooms, as well as a lift, not seen in many Sevilla *hostales*.

Self-catering

Sevilla Apartamentos
T667-511348, www.sevillapartamentos.com.
This organization has well-furnished apartments for short-term rental in different areas of Sevilla. Prices start at €266 for 2 people per week, which is very good value.

La Macarena

The Macarena barrio, particularly around the Alameda de Hércules, is a great spot to be based if you want to explore the untouristy parts of old Sevilla; there are great tapas and nightlife and no camera-toting hordes.

€€€ Hotel Alcoba del Rey
C Bécquer 9, T954-915800, www.alcobadelrey.com.
Close to the home of the Virgen de Macarena, this comfortable hotel offers cordial service and plentiful facilities at the western edge of the old town. The decor is Moroccan-inspired, with attractive imported furniture lending a North African ambience. Every room is stylish and distinct, with unusual bathroom arrangements providing plenty of romance and charm. The best of the rooms has a candlelit jacuzzi; a honeymoon special.

€€€ Patio de la Alameda
Alameda de Hércules 56, T954-904999, www.patiodelaalameda.com.
This classy apartment hotel makes a top-value place to stay. Built around a striking orange restored patio, it has excellent rooms with sitting room, kitchen and all facilities. The location right on the Alameda de Hércules is great for strolling and bar-hopping. Recommended.

€€€ Sacristía Santa Ana Hotel
Alameda de Hércules 22, T954-915722, www.hotelsacristia.com.
This boutique hotel is a sensitive and sumptuous conversion of a noble 18th-century mansion in a most appealing Macarena location. It's built around an elegant patio and has warm, personal service. The rooms have a classical ambience, with ornate headboards and tiled floors; you'll get some night noise at weekends from the ones at the front. There's also a restaurant. Recommended.

€ Hostal Macarena
C San Luis 91, T954-370141, www.hostalmacarenasevilla.com.
Great budget option on Plaza del Pumarejo; friendly, family run and set around a lovely atrium, with beautiful tilework and attractive furniture. Rooms come with or without bath.

Restaurants

There's little distinction between restaurants and tapas bars in Sevilla; most restaurants include an area to stand and snack, while at tapas bars you can usually sit down and order meal-sized portions (*raciones*). Accepted practice is to stand at the bar, have a couple of tapas and also taste what your friends are eating. A standard tapa will cost €2.50-5. Tapas portions and set menus virtually disappear during Semana Santa when restaurants and bars are full to bursting.

Most central restaurants offer traditional Sevilla cuisine; if you fancy finer dining, head out to the new town, where upmarket restaurants congregate around avenues like Eduardo Dato.

The cathedral and around

€€ Ovejas Negras
C Hernando Colón 8, T955 123811, www.ovejasnegrastapas.com.
Just around the corner from the cathedral but packed with locals as well as visitors, this buzzy modern bar keeps the quality high and the atmosphere relaxed. Fusion flavour combinations make for some stellar tapas plates, which are very generously proportioned. Wines are excellent also. Recommended.

Barrio Santa Cruz

The lovely Barrio Santa Cruz is an obvious place to eat, with its shady plazas and terraces. Unfortunately, a high percentage of the restaurants are aimed at tourists, and serve below-par food at inflated prices.

€€ Carmela
C Santa María la Blanca 6, T954-531432.
From 0900 onwards. One of the better of the terraced bars on this long plaza, Carmela serves good breakfasts, plenty of vegetarian dishes and snacks, and decent tapas (top gazpacho), as well as a *plato del día* that's good value for this area. It's also available at night.

€€ Las Teresas
C Santa Teresa 2, T954-213069.
Research indicates that 9 out of 10 people dredge up an image very

similar to this Santa Cruz local when they think the words 'tapas bar'. Hams: check, tiles: check, patina of age: check, gruff but lovable bar staff: check, mouth-watering smell of fried fish: check. Popular with locals and visitors. Recommended.

€€ Taberna Poncio
C Ximénez de Enciso 33, T954 460717, www.ponciorestaurantes.com.
Sashimi, ravioli or succulent pork medallions might come your way at this worthwhile Santa Cruz tapas restaurant. Eschew the high tables in the foyer for the more relaxing dining room or bench-top eating in the bar. Service is correct, and some dishes hit real heights. Portions are generous; 2 tapas per person is ample.

€ Bar Alfalfa
Corner C Alfalfa and C Candilejo, T654-809297.
On the square of the same name, this excellent Italian tapas bar is decorated with farming implements, earthenware jars and hundreds of bottles of wine. Enjoy a perfect *bruschetta* here, divine *bresaola* or a selection of Italian cheeses. You can order streetside on warm evenings. Recommended.

€ Bodega Santa Cruz
C Rodrigo Caro 2, T954-213246.
This busy and cheerful bar does some of Sevilla's choicest tapas and *montaditos*, with *cazón en adobo* or *pringá* particularly delicious. As the night wears on, the frantically busy bar staff wipe what they've run out of off the menus, which are chalked up at each end of the bar. Sees plenty of tourists but still very authentic. Also known as **Las Columnas**. Recommended.

€ La Goleta
C Mateos Gago 22, T954-218966.
Simple, tiny bar with loads of atmosphere. Run by a notable local character, it's an historic Santa Cruz watering hole. It specializes in a tasty orange wine; the tapas are limited but excellent. Humorous touches abound, and when the boss Alvaro's on form it's a one-man show. There's a more spacious extension open next door but the original is best.

Triana

C Betis that runs along the river is full of places to eat and drink, not all of them good. C San Jacinto is pedestrianized and has some reliably excellent options.

€€€ Abades Triana
C Betis 69, T954-286459, www.abadestriana.com.
A comparatively recent arrival to the riverbank in Triana, this restaurant occupies a hard-to-miss modern building that's all glass and light, offering wonderful views over the Guadalquivir and across to the old town. The food is high-priced, but there are some very tasty fish dishes and an inventive tapas degustation menu. The location is especially seductive at night.

€€ La Blanca Paloma
C Pagés del Corro 86, T954-333788.
This cheerful Triana venue was always one of the best tapas stops this side of the Guadalquivir. It has the same boisterous bar scene and also offers an excellent restaurant, with the same philosophy of originality combined with good humour and high-quality ingredients. Try the *bacalao al horno* (baked cod with a prawn sauce).

€ Taberna Miami
C San Jacinto 21, T954-340843.
A stalwart tapas bar with many tempting offers, decorated with photos of pilgrimages to Rocío and Santiago, as well as a couple of boars' heads. Portions are very generous; 2 tapas and you'll feel like you've had dinner. It's a cheery spot to be and is great value. Recommended.

El Arenal

€€ Bodega Antonio Romero
C Antonia Díaz 19, T954-223939.
Cheery waistcoated waiters man the bar at this warm and inviting venue. It's got a very typical feel, and serves up delicious tapas like grilled goat's cheese, as well as staples like thick tortilla and well-cut ham. There are several offshoots nearby.

€€ Enrique Becerra
C Gamazo 2, T954-213049.
A fabulous, traditional tapas bar and restaurant serving reliably excellent Andalucían specialities in pretty dining areas with rustic painted wooden furniture. The swordfish in amontillado sherry is especially good, but so is everything else, including an impressive wine list.

€€ Horacio Restaurante
Antonia Díaz 9, T954-225385.
On a street that's impressively stocked with quality eating choice, this has plenty to recommend it. Decorated with still-life canvases and soft yellow walls, it offers excellent, and fairly priced dishes – the grilled vegetables, avocado, prawn and walnut salad, and tossed tuna in soy sauce all impress – alongside warm service and decent wines.

€€ La Brunilda
C Galera 5, T954 220481, www.facebook.com/labrunilda.
Exposed brick and a backstreet location give this a romantic feel ... or they would, if it weren't the latest trendy Sevilla bar on the food hound circuit. The tapas are great, featuring fresh market produce with refreshing twists, but expect to queue: not just for a table, but even to get to the bar.

€€ La Bulla
C Dos de Mayo 26, T954-219262, www.facebook.com/labulla.
Reader-recommended, this buzzy modern tavern offers high-quality tapas, with beautiful presentation and great originality, all at a very fair price. Staff are helpful.

€ Bar Pepe Hillo
C Adriano 24, T954-215390.
A legend in its own tapas-time, this place is always full to bursting with animated *sevillanos* enjoying their tasty stews and *croquetas* among other goodies. A pork *solomillo* in sweet wine and raisin sauce is another star. High ceilinged, busy and buzzy, it's decorated with farming implements and no fewer than 10 bulls' heads lugubriously observe proceedings. There's a very attractive dining area out the back, away from the hurly-burly of the bar.

€ Casa Morales
C García de Vinuesa 11, T954-221242.
This great old place is in a one-time sherry bodega – the big jars in one of the 2 bars used to hold the stuff. The service is old style, with orders scrawled on serviettes and friendly chat. The tapas and *montaditos* are served on a wee wooden tray; the *guiso del día* (stew of the day) is often a tempting option. Recommended.

Centro and San Vicente

€€€ Taberna del Alabardero

C Zaragoza 20, T954-502721, www.tabernadelalabardero.es.

This hospitality school is also one of the city's best restaurants. It's pricey but worth it; the menu changes seasonally, but look out for house specials such as *corvina* (sea bass) with spinach, kidneys and grapes, or succulent beef fillet with blue *cabrales* cheese. There's a good-value *menú de degustación* for €65. For cheaper eats or a coffee, stay downstairs and head to the back, where *raciones* and *montaditos* are served. The building was once home of the Sevillian poet Covestany and also has a handful of well-appointed rooms available (**€€€**).

€€ Casa la Viuda

C Albareda 2, T954-215420, www.comerdetapasensevilla.es.

There's a thriving tapas scene in the streets north of the town hall at lunchtimes, where tourists and civil servants rub shoulders in a variety of bars. This is perhaps the best, with delicious and generously proportioned tapas at fair prices. They are innovative and beautifully presented, but it's not modern cuisine: think lots of sauces, spices and garlic. They offer interesting wines too.

€ El Rinconcillo

C Gerona 40, T954-223183, www.elrinconcillo.es.

An incredibly old bar that was founded in 1670 when the large-jawed Habsburgs still ruled Spain. It's an attractive place that's definitely worth a visit. The fittings are all wooden and the hams hanging over the counter look to be as old as the bar. The tapas are good and served until fairly late; the *croquetas* are particularly memorable.

€ La Antigua Bodeguita

Plaza del Salvador 6, T954-561833.

As long as the weather holds, the interior of this popular bar is just a place to order, as the crowd from here and the bar next door spills out on to the square. It's a great Sevillian scene in its own right, but the tapas are also worthy, particularly the seafood. Check out *mojama*, cured tuna meat, which will either delight or disgust.

Cafés

La Campana

C Sierpes 1, T954-223570.

An institution in this part of town, this place will seduce the sweet-toothed with its ice creams and pastries. During Semana Santa, when it's *the* place to have a seat booked, it has an impressive display of pointy caramel *nazarenos*. At other times, try the *yemas* or the *lenguas de almendra*.

La Macarena

€€ Yebra

C Medalla Milagrosa 3, T954-351007, www.yebrarestauracion.com. Closed Mon.

Just outside the walls beyond the edge of Macarena barrio, this is one of Sevilla's best tapas joints; a smart but relaxed place offering authentic and original gourmet tapas at around €3-4. It's not often that you'll see partridge or pheasant on tapas menus, but you do here. The only drawback is its popularity; getting an order in can be a nightmare.

€ Cervecería Yerbabuena

C Feria s/n.

The Macarena barrio has a real community feel to it, and there's nowhere better to experience it than in its picturesque food market. On Sat, locals and stallholders mingle at this bar at the corner of the market, enjoying a cold beer and tapa in the sunshine.

Bars and clubs

Sevilla's nightlife can't compete in terms of variety with Barcelona or Madrid, but you certainly won't be left sipping vodka in an empty bar. Sevilla folk tend to call it a night fairly early midweek and party until sun-up come the weekend, but there are plenty of zones that are always lively, particularly around Plaza Alfalfa in the old town and C Betis in Triana; both populated by a mixture of locals and tourists. The Viapol zone in the new town Nervión has a much more local scene, with heaps of bars and *discotecas*, and the character-packed Alameda de Hércules buzzes with a fairly alternative set.

Bars

Bulebar Café
Alameda de Hércules 83, T954-294212, www.cafebulebar.com.
One of several good choices on this long promenade, the **Bulebar** is colourfully decorated and has a great terrace. It's a popular meeting point for an alternative set and has a relaxed feel about it.

Kiosco del Agua
Paseo de Colón 10, www.facebook.com/kioscodelagua.
On the riverfront across the road from the Teatro Maestranza, this is one of Sevilla's best spots for an evening beer. Sit on the wrought-metal chairs and watch the sun set over Triana while bats and swallows flutter among the silhouetted palm trees. Good views of the floodlit Torre del Oro too.

Puerto de Cuba
C Betis s/n, www.puertodecubasevilla.com. Fri-Sun from 1700, daily at busy times.
It's hard to imagine a more romantic location than this garden bar right on the river below the **Abades** restaurant in Triana. Torchlight, designer couches, and palm fronds make this feel like an enclave of the Caribbean by the Guadalquivir; it's the perfect place for a stylish evening drink.

The Second Room
C Placentines 19, T603-628759, www.facebook.com/TheSecondRoom. Open 1500-0200 or 0300.
Great *copas*, cocktails and mojitos served by waiting staff who don't seem to have the usual attitude problem – in fact, they look pleased to be here. Top views of the Giralda.

Clubs

Antique Theatro
C Matemáticos Rey Pastor y Castro s/n, T954-462207, www.antiquetheatro.com. Daily Jun-Sep, Wed-Sun the rest of the year. Open 2400-0700, but don't turn up until at least 0300 unless you want the place to yourself. Cover charge €10-15 with a drink.
Sevilla's most upmarket nightclub, with an excellent sound system and committed DJs in one of the old pavilions from the 1992 Expo.

Fun Club
Alameda de Hércules 84, T636-669023, www.funclubsevilla.com. Thu-Sat 2400-0600 or so. Entry is around €5 or often free otherwise.
A music venue and *discoteca* with some serious alternative cred in these parts. There's often live rock, drum 'n' bass or good DJs.

Groucho
C Federico Sánchez Bedoya 22, T954-216039, www.grouchobar.com. Entry €10 including a drink.
This stylish *discoteca* is tucked away on an Arenal side street and is definitely one of the city's in spots to be seen. There are 3 rooms and 2 dance floors; be prepared to queue at weekends.

Itaca
C Amor de Dios 31, www.facebook.com/itacadisco.
Sevilla's best-established gay *discoteca*, always well attended, and with appropriately good dance music. There's a backroom and shows from Wed-Sat nights.

Entertainment

Your best guide to upcoming events is the magazine *El Giraldillo*, www.elgiraldillo.es. *Cultura en Sevilla* is another free publication worth checking out for cultural events.

Cinema

Check www.ecartelera.com/cartelera for what's on.
Avenida, *C Marqués de Paradas 15, T954-293025.* Original version films subtitled in Spanish.

Flamenco

Whether you're planning to spend every hour of darkness trawling bars in search of the most authentic *cante jondo* or just want to briefly experience what it's all about, it's likely that you'll want to see some flamenco when you're in Sevilla. While much of what's on offer is geared to tourists (although frequently of a very high technical standard), it's still possible to track down a more authentic experience.

There are essentially 3 ways to see flamenco in Sevilla. The *tablaos* are organized performances in set venues, with entry ranging from €15-30. The crowd at these is mostly tourists, the performers often well known and of a very high standard, and the emotion factor usually low.

Secondly, there are many bars that have dedicated flamenco nights; the quality varies according to the artist and the atmosphere, the cost is minimal and occasionally you'll see something very special.

Thirdly, in bars where flamenco enthusiasts hang out – and there are still plenty in Triana – you may see some impromptu performances. The tourist office has a fuller list of shows and flamenco bars.

Auditorio Alvarez Quintero, *C Alvarez Quintero 48, T954-293949, www.alvarezquintero.com.* Daily evening shows at 2100 that are among the most authentic of the *tablaos*. €18 entry.

Casa Anselma, *C Pages del Corro 49, Triana. Open 2000-0100.* A busy and beautifully decorated bar with free entry but expensive drinks. There's live music every night (except Sun when it's closed); it tends to be popular Sevilla ditties and *rocieras* (music associated with the pilgrimage to El Rocío in Huelva province) rather than pure flamenco, but it can be entertaining, particularly when Anselma herself is on form. At 2400 she belts out *Salve Rociera.*

Casa de la Memoria, *C Cuna 6, T954-029999, www.casadelamemoria.es.*
2 nightly shows of good quality at this venue in central Sevilla. They cost €18; this is good value, as the performers are usually excellent and the atmosphere intimate; be sure to book in advance as it's a small venue. You can book tickets

at the Centro de Interpretación de la Judería in Barrio Santa Cruz too.

La Carbonería, *C Leviés 18, T954-214460, www.levies18.com. Open 2000-0330.* Long-established, popular sprawling bar, a former coal yard (hence the name) where flamenco is performed at 2330 every night. It's very touristy, but there's sometimes a strong gypsy presence too, and some of the flamenco is very good. There's also a tapas counter, a beer garden and a front bar. Free (but the drinks are slightly pricier than normal).

Los Gallos, *Plaza de Santa Cruz 11, Barrio Santa Cruz, T954-216981, www.tablaolosgallos.com.* This is a touristy *tablao* but definitely one of the best of its kind, with high-quality performers who don't seem to be going through the motions. There are 2 shows a night; go to the later one. €35 including a drink.

Museo del Baile Flamenco, *C Manuel Rojas Marcos 3, T954-340311, www.museoflamenco.com.* Live performances by good artists every night, €20, 2 shows nightly, ticket includes a guided walk through Santa Cruz, book ahead.

Music

The main venues for classical concerts are the theatres (see below). For live music, see also Bars and clubs, above, and Flamenco, above. *El Giraldillo* is the best guide to upcoming performances.

Theatre

These theatres put on a range of drama, music and dance.

La Fundición, *Casa de la Moneda, C Habana s/n, T954-225844, www.fundiciondesevilla.es.* In the attractively refurbished complex that was once the royal mint, this has a variety of comedy, flamenco, dance, and other theatre.

Teatro Lope de Vega, *Av María Luisa, T954-590867, www.teatrolopedevega.org.* This lovely building built for the 1929 exhibition has some excellent theatre and music at bargain prices; some tickets are only €5.

Teatro Maestranza, *Paseo de Cristóbal Colón, T954-223344, www.teatrodelamaestranza.es.* This acclaimed modern building is Sevilla's main venue for opera, drama and dance. The ticket office is open daily 1000-1400, 1800-2100; it's a fairly dressy scene.

Festivals

It's well worth planning your trip to coincide with the solemn Semana Santa processions or the subsequent Feria de Abril, but you'll be paying more for accommodation and should reserve rooms well in advance.

5 Jan Cabalgata de los Reyes Magos, is a colourful night parade of the 3 kings through the streets. They travel in colourful carriages and toss sweets and gifts to onlookers.

Easter Semana Santa (29 Mar-5 Apr 2015, 20-27 Mar 2016, 9-16 Apr 2017, 23 Mar-1 Apr 2018). The most famous of Spain's celebrations is in Sevilla. Members of the city's 52 *cofradías* parade *pasos* of Christ and the Virgin through the city streets. See box, page 46.

Apr Feria de Abril is the major social event of the Sevilla calendar. Upwards of 1000 *casetas* (small pavilions) see a week of eating, drinking and parading their pretty horse carriages and *flamenca* dresses. See box, page 54.

Sep (even years only) **Bienal de Flamenco**, is a major flamenco event, held in various venues around the city. Check www.labienal.com for information.

7 Dec Fiesta de la Inmaculada, *tunas* (traditional student minstrel bands) gather at night in the Plaza del Triunfo to sing traditional songs. In the morning children perform the *Danza de los Seises* in the cathedral.

Shopping

Books

Antonio Castro, *C Sol 3, T954-217030, www.castrolibros.es.* Nice old second-hand bookshop in the old town with a respectable selection of English paperbacks.

La Casa del Libro, *C Velásquez 8, T954-502950, www.casadellibro.com.* Good large bookshop for any needs, including travel or English language.

Ceramics

If it's superb ceramics you're after, Triana is the place to go; there are dozens of attractively decorated shops; many have been family run for generations. Most of these shops are used to tourists and can arrange reasonably priced secure international delivery. If you're not an EU resident, pick up an IVA-exemption form with any major purchase, see page 514.

Cerámica Santa Ana, *C San Jorge 31, T954-333990, www.ceramicasantaana.com.* One of a few excellent ceramic shops in this area.

Pilar Márquez Pérez/Cerámica Aracena, *C Sierpes 36, T954-215228.* A good place to buy Sevillian tiles and other painted ceramics. Some are hand painted in the shop itself, which can be good to watch.

Clothes and fashion

Sevilla's main shopping zone is around **C Sierpes, C Tetuán, C Velásquez, C Cuna** and **Plaza del Duque**. This busy area is the place to come for clothes, be it well-priced modern Spanish gear, or essential Sevilla Feria fashion: shawls, *flamenca* dresses, ornamental combs, castanets and fans.

Head to the **Alameda de Hércules** area for more offbeat shopping, either in the lively markets, or the smaller shops along **C Amor de Dios, C Jesús del Gran Poder** or **C Trajano**.

Department stores

El Corte Inglés, *Plaza del Duque 7 and 13, T954-220931, Av Luis Montoto 122, T954-571440, Plaza Magdalena 1, T954-218855, C San Pablo 1, T954-218855, www.elcorteingles.es.* Spain's premier department store, with almost anything you could want to buy.

Food and drink

Baco, *C Cuna 4, T902-211313, www.baco.es. Mon-Sat 0930-1430, 1700-2100.* Spanish and foreign products, good for classy picnic fare.

Markets

Sevilla has some excellent street markets. A famous flea market takes place on Sun mornings in the **Alameda de Hércules**; there is a smaller one on Thu too. The big Thu event, **El Jueves**, takes place on nearby C Feria, when the whole street is filled with stalls of every description. **Plaza Alfalfa** has a curious Sun morning animal market. There are excellent food markets in **Triana** by the Puente Isabel II and in **La Macarena**, also on C Feria.

What to do

Bike hire

Bike stands are all over the centre, with a €13.33 weekly fee plus a small per-hire cost. See www.sevici.es (Spanish only) for details.

Bici4City, *C Peral 6, T954-229883, www.bici4city.com.* Rent bikes (€3 per hr, €15 for 24 hrs) and audio guides. Also have mountain bikes available and run guided tours.
Rentabike, *Pl Santa Cruz 4, T955-118228, www.rentabikesevilla.com.* Hires various types of bike (from €10 per day) and also has daily bike tours of the city.

Bullfighting

Although controversial, bullfighting is very popular in Sevilla; Andalucía is really the cradle of *los toros* (see box, page 258). Sevilla's bullring, **La Maestranza**, is the 2nd most prestigious in Spain and draws top fighters every year. Sevilla has around 28 bullfights a season, one every day in Feria, then every Sun until Sep. The highest standard can be seen at Feria and at the season's end, but you'll pay more for tickets, and they are harder to get hold of. For big fights, it's worth reserving several days in advance at the *taquilla* at the bullring, or at one of the agents on Puerta de Jerez or C Tetuán, who add on a small commission. Or book at www.taquillatoros.com.

Football

Sevilla's main sporting passion is football. While international matches, when they come to town, are mostly played at the Estadio Olímpico, the city's 2 main clubs, **Real Betis** and **Sevilla**, have their own stadiums. Going to a match can be a great experience; there's much more of a family atmosphere than in the majority of European countries. One of the 2 teams will be at home almost every weekend of the Spanish season. Games take place on Sat and Sun with one game on Mon evening. You can buy tickets at the grounds during business hours or before the match; they don't sell out unless they're playing Real Madrid, Barcelona or the volatile local derby.

Agencies on C Tetuán also sell tickets, for a small mark-up. Tickets are pricey, with the cheapest seats starting at about €25.
Real Betis Balompié, *Estadio Manuel Ruíz de Lopera, Av de la Palmera s/n, T954-610340, www.realbetisbalompie.es.* Traditionally representing the working class of the city, Betis play in green and white stripes. They have won the league only once, in 1935. In the second division at time of writing.
Sevilla FC, *Estadio Sánchez Pizjuan, Av Eduardo Dato s/n, T954-535353, www.sevillafc.es.* Play in white and red and won the league in 1946. In recent years have been one of the best teams outside the big two of Real Madrid and Barcelona.

Tours

There are 2 identical **open-top bus tours** of the city, with the usual multilingual commentary. Both leave from the Torre

Language schools

There's a huge number, and you're recommended to do lots of research. **Instituto de Estudios de la Lengua Española** (IELE), C García de Vinuesa 29, T954-560788, www.iele.com, is a popular school; **Lenguaviva**, C Viriato 24, T915-943776, www.lenguaviva.net, offers crash courses and longer options, various accommodation options and excursions; **CLIC**, C Albareda 19, T954-502131, www.clic.es, is a frequently recommended school with lively teaching, youngish students and packages including accommodation and excursions.

del Oro every 30 mins from 1000. They have the same stops and hop-on-hop-off system, free walking tour and 1992 Expo site tour. They cost €18 for a 24-hr ticket, but it's worth bargaining and checking for special promos.

For a cruise on the river, **Cruceros Turísticos Torre del Oro**, T954-561692, www.crucerostorredeloro.com, departs every 30 mins from 1100 to 2200 (1900 winter) from the quay by the Torre del Oro. It goes both ways along the river, and points out the sights, including the old quays where Magellan and others once set sail. Bar on board. €16, under-14s free, cruise lasts 1 hr. For a much more intimate experience, **Guadaluxe**, T661-278826, www.guadaluxe.com, offer personal cruises in a small boat, with a friendly skipper and good information on both sights and river wildlife.

There are several **walking tours** of Sevilla; contact the tourist information office for details. There are tapas tours, tours on bikes, walks in Triana, and guided visits to the cathedral and Alcázar. Try **Sevilla Walking Tours**, www.sevillawalkingtours.com.

Horse carriages can be found everywhere, particularly near the cathedral. Seating up to 5, they'll take you on a trot around the city; you can specify which things you want to see. Rates vary in season, and bargaining is useful; think €45-60 for a ride of 50 mins or so. Drivers provide a commentary of dubious accuracy.

Watersports

Pedalquivir, *T679-194045, www.pedalquivir.com*. Rental of rowing boats, pedalos and canoes on the river near the bullring.

Transport

Air

Sevilla's airport is 10 km northeast of the centre. A bus runs to central Sevilla (Prado de San Sebastián bus station) via the train station. It goes roughly every 30 mins Mon to Sat (hourly or better on Sun) and takes 30 mins (€4). A taxi to town costs a fixed €22.20 during the day, slightly more at night or weekends.

Easyjet and **Ryanair** connect Sevilla with several European cities including **London**, and there are many domestic routes run by **Iberia**, **Vueling** and others. For airport information, T954-449000.

Bus

The city of Sevilla is one of Spain's major destinations for interurban buses. They arrive at 2 stations, Plaza de Armas for destinations north and west, and Prado de San Sebastián for the south and east.

Local Sevilla's fleet of **TUSSAM** buses (T902-459954, www.tussam.es) provides a good service around the city. A single fare is €1.40 (drivers will give change up to a point), but you can buy a 1- or 3-day tourist card for €5/10 respectively. The most useful bus services are the circular routes: bus C5 does a tight circuit of the historic centre; buses C1 and C2 run via Santa Justa train station and the Expo site (C1 goes clockwise, C2 anti-clockwise); while C3 (clockwise) and C4 (anti-clockwise) follow the perimeter of the old walls, except for C3's brief detour into Triana. You can examine routes online, download a route map or pick up a map from the **TUSSAM** kiosk on Plaza Encarnación.

Long distance Sevilla has 2 principal bus stations. The larger, **Plaza de**

Armas, by the river near the Puente del Cachorro, T954-038655, www.autobusesplazadearmas.es, serves destinations to the north and the west of the city. These include **Madrid** (6 hrs, hourly), **Huelva** (½-hourly, 1 hr 15 mins via motorway, longer via main road) and 3 daily buses to **Asturias** via **Mérida**, **Cáceres** (these 2 are serviced hourly anyway), **Salamanca**, **Zamora** and **León**. There's a day and a night bus to **Lisbon** (6-8 hrs), remember that Portugal is 1 hr behind), and daily buses to **Faro** and **Lagos** in the Algarve. There are also buses to **Alicante**, **Valencia** and **Barcelona**.

The other bus station, **Prado de San Sebastián**, is near the Barrio Santa Cruz on Plaza San Sebastián, T954-417111. It serves destinations east and south of the city. There are buses almost hourly to **Jerez de la Frontera** and **Cádiz** (1 hr 30 mins), **Córdoba** (1 hr 45 mins), as well as **Granada** (7 daily, 3 hrs), **Jaén** and **Almería**. There are also connections to a number of smaller Andalucían towns.

For both bus stations, the biggest operators are **Alsa** (www.alsa.es) and **Damas** (www.damas-sa.es).

Car

Sevilla isn't a great place to have a car due to the narrow one-way streets of the old town, lack of parking, high car crime and the confusing layout. There are plenty of underground car parks that cost about €3 per hr/€25 per day, and most hotels have a car park or access to one.

Car hire There are major international firms at the airport, including **Budget**, www.budget.com, T954-999137, and **Hertz**, T954-514720, www.hertz.com. **Avis**, T954-537861, www. avis.com, have an office at the train station.

Motorcycle hire

Vespasur, C Júpiter 25, T954-417500, www. vespasur.es. Discounts for hire of 3 days or more. Near Santa Justa train station.

Taxis

A ride right across town, for example from the cathedral to the Puerta de Macarena, or Triana to the train station, will cost €6-10. Prices rise slightly after 2200, at weekends and during fiestas such as Semana Santa or Feria. T954-622222 or T954-580000 to book.

Train

Sevilla's modern train station, Santa Justa, is a 15-min walk from the centre on Av Kansas City.

For train information **RENFE** have a good telephone information line, T902-240202, and their website is www.renfe.com. There's a booking agent in the centre at C Zaragoza 29.

Sevilla is served by the high-speed AVE train, which cuts travel time to Madrid and Córdoba to impressively low levels. It's expensive, but a good option. If you travel *preferente* class, up to 50% more expensive, you get access to an a/c hospitality waiting room (free food and drinks). Groups can get a great deal booking a table for four in *preferente* class.

There are 10-15 daily trains to **Cádiz** (1 hr 45 mins-2 hrs), stopping at **Jerez** (1 hr). There are 3 daily trains to **Barcelona** (2 fast, 5½ hrs, 1 slow, 11 hrs), 1 to **Valencia** (8½ hrs) and lots of high-speed services to **Madrid** (up to 20 **AVE** fast trains daily, 2 hrs 25 mins). To **Córdoba**, there are 6 normal trains daily, 1 hr 20 mins; and up to 24 **AVE** trains, 41 mins.

Both fast and slow trains head for **Málaga** (2 hrs 40 mins/1 hr 55 mins). There are also trains to **Jaén**, **Huelva**, and **Granada**.

Around
Sevilla city

The bulk of Sevilla province is undulating farmland, and there's not a great deal of scenic interest. However, north from Sevilla are the low hills of the Sierra Morena, with lightly forested slopes and valleys making this a great walking destination.

A few small towns beckon through the heat haze east of Sevilla; Carmona with its excellent Roman graveyard, the spires of Ecija, and the elegant ducal seat of Osuna.

Sierra Morena → *Colour map 1, B6.*

gently rolling countryside, quiet and attractive towns and good walks

North of Sevilla, the Sierra Morena is a popular weekend trip from the capital. The region's main town is Cazalla de la Sierra, while nearby Constantina is the base for the Parque Natural Sierra Norte, covering much of this part of the province. Heading west, you can cross into the fascinating Huelvan section of the Sierra Morena, home to Spain's finest ham.

Cazalla de la Sierra

This pleasing whitewashed town is the most useful base for exploring the northern reaches of Sevilla's province. Once an Iberian settlement, it was controlled in turn by the Romans and the Moors, who named it thus (meaning fortified town). The town is now known for its production of *aguardiente*, including the much-imbibed *Miura* cherry-flavoured anis. The company has a shop in the centre of the village.

The town's church, **Nuestra Señora de la Consolación**, is worth a look; massive in scale, it's a real mixture of styles, with a keep-like main section featuring layered brick and stone walls; this is *mudéjar* and dates from the 14th-15th centuries, as does the belltower. Other parts were added in the 18th century. Inside, the chancel has elaborate late Gothic vaulting; the ornate *retablo* is a fine 17th-century work; look out for the beautiful 14th-century baptismal font still in use.

The town has a **tourist office** ⓘ *C Paseo del Moro 2, T954-883562, turismo@cazalladelasierra.es, Tue-Wed 1000-1400, Thu 1000-1400, 1600-1800 (1800-2000 summer), Fri-Sat 1000-1400, 1600-1900 (1800-2100 summer), Sun 1100-1300*, with limited material on the area.

Essential Around Sevilla city

Getting around

It's easy to get out of Sevilla by bus to the main towns listed in the text, although travelling by car would give you more freedom. There are trains from Sevilla to Cazalla de la Sierra in the Sierra Morena but Cazalla train station is 7 km away from the town, so is not very convenient.

When to go

The best time to visit is spring or autumn, because July and August are baking hot, although temperatures in the Sierra Morena are a bit cooler than elsewhere in Sevilla province due to the higher altitude.

Time required

Allow at least a day in the Sierra Morena, a few days for towns east of Sevilla.

There are several marked **walking trails** in the Cazalla area. One of the best is Sendero Las Laderas, which begins from the bottom of the street that runs through the Plaza Mayor past the old town hall. It heads down to the river Huéznar and doubles back through woodland to the town; it takes 1½ hours, but you can extend the walk or even follow the river down to **El Pedroso**, a livestock town with a good hotel; see Where to stay, below. Visit the tourist office for maps.

Constantina

This town, said to be named after the emperor Constantine, is a likeable village topped by a medieval castle with Moorish origins. In the narrow streets of the *morería* below are several fine mansions, while the parish church of Santa María de la Encarnación has a *mudéjar* tower and a Plateresque doorway. The town is the main centre for the Sierra del Norte natural park, which covers some 1650 sq km of the Sierra Morena. It's home to several species of raptor, as well as otters and wild boar. There's a visitor information centre, **El Robledo** ⓘ *T955-889593, Wed-Sun 1000-1400, 1600-1800 (1700-2000 summer)*, on the western edge of town. The office has leaflets on the marked walking trails in the area and in autumn run guided walks that focus on the astonishing variety of wild mushrooms in the area.

Listings Sierra Morena

Where to stay

Cazalla de la Sierra

€€ La Posada del Moro
Paseo del Moro s/n, T954-884858, www.laposadadelmoro.com.
This excellent and welcoming hotel is in Cazalla itself and is remarkably good value. It's got much rural elegance, with the emphasis on comfort, and has a pool, pretty garden, and a restaurant that will tempt you to prolong your stay. Recommended.

€€ Las Navezuelas
Ctra Cazalla-El Robledo s/n, T954-884764, www.lasnavezuelas.com.
Another charming rural establishment, set in a whitewashed *cortijo* with a restored olive mill and good pool. There

are 6 appealing rustic rooms and a variety of self-contained cottages. The price includes breakfast, and the owners can advise on walks in the area and arrange horse riding.

Constantina

€ Albergue Juvenil
Cuesta Blanca s/n, T955-035886, www.inturjoven.com.
This official youth hostel has fine facilities and twin rooms with bathroom. Funding issues meant that this was temporarily closed at last research.

Transport

Cazalla de la Sierra

Cercanía trains run 3 times daily from **Sevilla** (1 hr 35 mins) via **El Pedroso**, but the station is 7 km from town on the road to Constantina; taxis meet the train. There are also daily **buses** (1 hr 20 mins), which are more convenient.

Constantina

Several daily buses run from Constantina to **Sevilla** (1 hr).

Carmona → *Colour map 1, C6.*

sun-baked, sleepy agricultural town

★The small town of Carmona, encircled by formidable defensive walls, is an easy day trip from Sevilla, only 36 km east of the city, but couldn't have a more different feel. Outside the old town is one of Andalucía's most interesting archaeological sites, an excavated Roman cemetery. Carmona also offers a couple of excellent luxury hotels in the old town; see Where to stay, below, for details.

Alcázar de Abajo

Mon-Sat 1000-1800, Sun 1000-1500. €2, free Mon.

On arrival in Carmona, you'll immediately be struck by the bulky complex of the lower *alcázar*, looming over the narrow entrance gate known as the Puerta de Sevilla. Fortified by successive conquering powers from the Phoenicians to the Castillians, the fortress preserves structures and foundations from all these periods. After an audiovisual presentation, you can wander around the building, which sometimes has temporary exhibitions in one of its halls. There's an informative brochure that helps you pick out the different building stages of the walls. From the top there are worthwhile views over the town and the fertile plains below. The **tourist office** ⓘ *Mon-Sat 1000-1800, Sun 1000-1500, www.turismo.carmona.org*, is located in the Puerta de Sevilla. They can provide a town map and other information.

From here you should wander up through the whitewashed old town, peering into corners. Within this walled area are several churches; Santa María la Mayor preserves the former mosque's Patio de Naranjos and has a good 16th-century *retablo*, while San Pedro has an attractive *mudéjar* tower. Behind Santa María is a small archaeological and historical museum. The town centres on the shady Plaza de San Fernando; nearby the Ayuntamiento has a well-crafted Roman mosaic of

ON THE ROAD

Haciendas

Much of Sevilla province is taken up by huge farms that produce vast quantities of citrus fruit, olives, beef and fighting bulls. They are privately owned; this *latifundia* system derives from the days of the Christian Reconquest, when vast parcels of land won from the Moors in battle were distributed among the military leaders. These divisions are still in place and mean that in general local workers can't own their own land but must work as seasonal *jornaleros* on the *haciendas*. The system has contributed to large-scale social inequality in Andalucía and produced much rural unrest, not least in the years leading up to the Spanish Civil War.

The centrepiece of a *hacienda* is the farmhouse, or *cortijo*, which is usually a very grand affair, a complex of elegant whitewashed buildings that often includes a chapel. Many *haciendas* offer accommodation that is typically very luxurious. They are also popular venues for weddings and other celebrations.

For a full list, contact the Sevilla tourist office, see page 66. Some of the best are:

El Esparragal, T955-782702, www.elesparragal.com. Famous and fabulous hacienda in grassy grounds 23 km north of Sevilla in Gerena. Top restaurant and stylish fittings.

Hacienda Benazuza, T955-703344, www.elbullihotel.com. Fabulously luxurious and run by Ferran Adrià, the famous Catalan chef. In Sanlúcar La Mayor, 22 km west of Sevilla. Closed in winter.

Hacienda San Rafael, T955-227196, www.haciendadesanrafael.com. Run by same owners as the Corral del Rey in Sevilla. Lovely, with flowering plants, spacious rooms, and a great pool. South of Sevilla, halfway to Jerez. Recommended.

Medusa in its central courtyard. It's also worth seeking out Plaza de Abastos, an attractive hidden space dedicated to the morning food market.

Roman Necropolis

Tue-Sun 1000-1700. Free.

Walking down the hill from the Puerta de Sevilla, you'll come to a long square, Paseo del Estatuto (where the bus from Sevilla stops). At the far end of this, take the middle of the three streets, which after 10 minutes will bring you to this very rewarding site. A series of interesting tombs have been excavated; belonging to wealthy citizens, they were dug into the rock and crowned with marble or stone structures (none of which survive). You get disinterestedly guided about but can make your way down into many of them, including the massive Tomb of Servilia, daughter of the local governor, where fragments of wall paintings are conserved. Information is in Spanish and English; try and see the small museum before visiting the site as it puts the material in context.

Where to stay

€€€€ Casa de Carmona
Plaza de Lasso 1, T954-143300, www.casadecarmona.com.
A restored *palacio* in the heart of Carmona's old town, this is furnished in period style and has comfortable rooms, a restaurant and a pool, which is a godsend in this sun-beaten town. It's a little down in the dumps compared to past glories but still doesn't disappoint.

€€€€ Parador del Rey Don Pedro
C Los Alcázares s/n, T954-141010, www.parador.es.
The upper Alcázar, once used as a palace by the charismatic Pedro I, has been partially restored to house this, one of southern Spain's finest paradores. There are great views over the town and the plains below. Recommended.

€ Pensión Comercio
C Torre del Oro 56, T954-140018.
Right next to the impressive Puerta de Sevilla and tucked inside the walls, this is a spruce option that's good value for Carmona. It has rooms with or without bath, as well as a/c (if you thought Sevilla was hot, try Carmona). There's also a decent cheap restaurant and cordial management.

Restaurants

The accommodation options above all have restaurants that are recommended. Other options centre around Plaza San Fernando, where there are several tapas bars. The tourist office has a leaflet describing a tapas crawl around the town.

€€ Molino de la Romera
C Sor Angela de la Cruz 8, halfway between San Pedro Church and the Alcázar, T954-142000, www.molinodelaromera.com.
This restaurant is set in an old olive mill and serves good local cuisine on its terrace, which gives views over the plains below. The wide menu includes cheese platters, *revueltos*, and game dishes.

Transport

Buses run hourly on the hour weekdays and a little less often at weekends from the Prado de San Sebastián station in **Sevilla**, 50 mins. These drop you off and leave from the Paseo del Estatuto, just downhill from the Puerta de Sevilla. From the pretty Alameda nearby, there are a couple of daily buses to **Ecija** and **Córdoba**.

Ecija

→ *Colour map 2, C2.*

baroque churches and abundant *palacios*

Halfway between Sevilla and Córdoba, this place shouldn't be missed by those with a liking for Baroque architecture, although try to get there early, as the town is famous for its fearsome summer heat. Once an important Roman olive oil town named Astigi, it enjoyed great prosperity from the 16th to 18th centuries as the vast *latifundias* claimed in the Reconquest began to pay dividends to their inheritors, if not to the landless labourers that sweated to cultivate them.

This wealth is reflected the town's attractive *palacios*. Ecija is also notable for its 18th-century church towers, built after the 1755 Lisbon earthquake toppled the existing steeples.

Located in the centre of town is a **tourist office** ⓘ *C Elvira 1, T955-902933, www.turismoecija.com, Mon-Sat 1000-1400, 1700-1900 Sun 1000-1400*, with plenty to offer; the website is also good.

The grandest of Ecija's palaces is the **Palacio de Peñaflor** ⓘ *C Castelar s/n, listed for extensive renovation at time of writing*. The curved exterior is striking; it's known locally as the house of the long balcony, this feature being nearly 60 m long. The façade is decorated with frescoes, while inside is a fine staircase topped by a cupola with extravagantly decorative stucco work. The central patio has a marble fountain and a colourful dado of agate and different hues of marble.

Another stately residence near the Plaza de España is **Palacio de Benameji** ⓘ *Jun-Sep Tue-Fri 1000-1430, Sat 1000-1400, 2000-2200, Sun 1000-1500; Oct-May Tue-Fri 1000-1330, 1630-1830, Sat 1000-1400, 1730-2000, Sun 1000-1500; free*, which has been converted into a beautiful museum displaying Roman finds, as well as some exhibits on local culture, particularly horse breeding.

The churches are too plentiful to list in detail here, but you'll come across nearly all of them by strolling in the area around Plaza de España. Most of the towers are cheerfully coloured in bright yellow and blue ceramic tiles.

Listings Ecija

Where to stay

Ecija's accommodation options are limited.

€€ Hotel Platería
C Platería 1, T955-902754, www.hotelplateria.net.
Tucked away down a side road, the hospitable **Platería** has well-furnished modern rooms set around a central atrium. There's also an excellent low-priced restaurant. An all-round bargain.

Restaurants

€€ Las Ninfas
C Cánovas del Castillo 4, T955-904592.
This stylish restaurant occupying part of the same *palacio* as the museum is decorated with various objets d'art and offers well-prepared local cuisine, including some excellent steaks.

Festivals

Sep The town's **feria** takes place for 6 days in the 2nd week of the month. There's also a *cante jondo* **flamenco festival** night, which attracts excellent performers.

Transport

Bus
There are 10 weekday buses (4-5 at weekends) to and from Prado San Sebastián station in **Sevilla** (1 hr 15 mins). There are also 4 daily buses that run to **Córdoba** and a few to **Carmona** and **Osuna**.

Osuna → *Colour map 4, A5.*

beautifully preserved Renaissance town

★South of Ecija, this little-visited town is a ducal seat which owes most of its monuments to the wealthy Girón family, who held the title from the 16th century onwards. Osuna had been an important Iberian and then Roman town (Urso).

The town is situated on a steep hill; in the centre, in a characterful historic building that was once a brothel and theatre before being converted to the town grain store in the 18th century, stands the **tourist office** ⓘ *C Carrera 82, T954-815732, www.turismosuna.org, Tue-Sat 0930-1330, 1600-1800, Sun 0930-1330.*

The top of the hill is dominated by two buildings, the collegiate church and the old university. **Santa María de la Asunción** ⓘ *admission by guided tour Tue-Sun 1000-1330, 1530-1830 (1600-1900 summer), €2.50,* was founded in the mid-16th century by Juan Téllez Girón, who spared no expense in the construction. It's a beautifully proportioned Renaissance building (although there are later additions) in creamy stone. The Plateresque west portal looks out over the town and rolling plains. The interior is harmoniously arched and has a series of excellent paintings by Ribera, including a Crucifixion and a harried-looking San Jerónimo in the sacristy. The small cloister is another highlight, but the most exciting space is the pantheon of the Dukes of Osuna, an atmospheric and highly ornamented Plateresque crypt.

The university stands behind the church and has a fine patio with a pure Renaissance simplicity to it.

In the town below, there are several other churches worth visiting, including the Iglesia de la Merced, which has a barrel-vaulted ceiling.

Listings Osuna

Where to stay

€€€ Palacio Marqués de la Gomera
C San Pedro 20, T954-812223, www.hotelpalaciodelmarques.es.
Where else would you want to stay in Osuna other than a palace? This place fits the bill perfectly, set around a round-arched patio. The 18th-century building is furnished in period style. Rooms on the upper level are more attractive (and pricier) with wooden ceilings, but all are spacious and good value. The hotel also has 2 restaurants and a small garden.

Transport

Bus
There are 6 daily buses to Osuna from **Sevilla**'s Prado de San Sebastián bus station. There are also buses to **Ecija**, **Antequera** and a couple on to **Málaga** itself.

Huelva

historic sites, scrumptious pork and brilliant birdlife

Andalucía's westernmost province tends to be passed over by visitors, but undeservedly so. While Huelva city is short of attractions, there's a huge diversity of other things to see in the region, from sandy beaches along Costa de la Luz to the hilly, wooded Sierra Morena.

Huelva's coastal areas are connected with Christopher Columbus, who set sail from Palos de la Frontera. East of Huelva city is an alluring stretch of coastline with an almost unbroken stretch of sand backed by pine-clad dunes; this runs past the vast wetlands of the Parque Nacional Coto Doñana, one of Europe's top birdwatching havens. On the park edge is El Rocío, its tranquil Wild West atmosphere interrupted only by its renowned and boisterous pilgrimage.

Along the coast west of Huelva city is a curious blend of traditional fishing villages and sprawling beachside development that ends in Ayamonte, a handsome town facing Portugal over the mighty mouth of the Río Guadiana.

Inland is the Parque Natural Sierra de Aracena, where acorns from the ubiquitous holm oaks fatten up the Iberian porkers, producing some of Spain's finest ham.

Best for
Beaches ▪ Birdwatching ▪ Jamón ▪ Walking

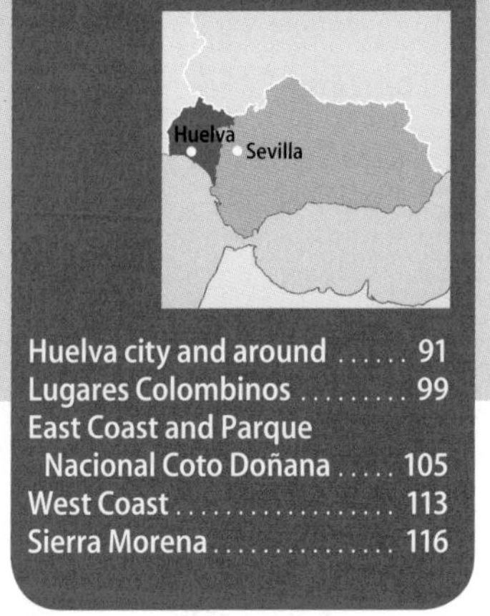

Footprint picks

★ **Niebla**, page 95

Visit this small walled town with a charming church.

★ **Moguer**, page 102

Wander the picturesque streets of the much-loved hometown of Nobel laureate Juan Ramón Jiménez.

★ **Mazagón**, page 106

This low-key town is a changing room for fantastic dune-backed beaches.

★ **Coto Doñana**, page 108

Take the 4WD tour into the unbeatable national park. Book it before reading any further.

★ **Minas de Riotinto**, page 117

Explore Huelva's mining heritage and stay in the colonial English barrio.

★ **Aracena**, page 119

Savour succulent pork in this attractive hill town that's also a great walking base.

★ **Zufre**, page 122

Spend a tranquil night in this relaxing eagles' nest village.

Footprint picks
1 Niebla, page 95
2 Moguer, page 102
3 Mazagón, page 106
4 Coto Doñana, page 108
5 Minas de Riotinto, page 117
6 Aracena, page 119
7 Zufre, page 122
EXTREMADURA
PORTUGAL
HUELVA
SEVILLA
Atlantic Ocean
Sierra Morena
Picos de Aroche
Sierra Madroñera
Sierra del Granado
Embalse de Aracena
Embalse de Sancho
Embalse del Agrio
Río Odiel
Río Guadiana
Río Guadalquivir
Parque Natural las Marismas de Odiel
Parque Nacional Coto Doñana
Encinasola
Cumbres de Enmedio
Rosal de la Frontera
Aroche
Jabugo
Galaroza
Fuenteheridos
Cortegana
Alájar
Aracena
Santa Olalla del Cala
Almonaster la Real
Santa Ana la Real
Linares de la Sierra
Higuera de la Sierra
Zufre
Santa Bárbara de Casa
Paymogo
Cabezas Rubias
Campofrío
Minas de Riotinto
Nerva
Pueblo de Guzmán
Villanueva de las Cruces
Calañas
Zalamea la Real
Castillo de las Guardas
Ronquillo
Puerto de Laja
Alosno
El Granado
El Almendro
Villanueva de los Castillejos
Valverde del Camino
El Garrobo
San Silvestre de Guzmán
San Bartolomé de la Torre
Gerena
Aznalcóllar
Gibraleón
Trigueros
La Palma del Condado
Villablanca
Cartaya
Niebla
Sanlúcar La Mayor
Ayamonte
Huelva
Bonares
Lepe
El Rompido
Moguer
Bollullos del Condado
Palos de la Frontera
La Rábida
Isla Cristina
La Antilla
El Portil
Punta Umbría
Almonte
Hinojos
Pilas
Aznalcázar
Coria del Río
Mazagón
El Rocío
La Rocina
Villafranco del Guadalquivir
El Acebuche
Matalascañas
Lebrija
Bonanza
Sanlúcar de Barrameda
Chipiona
N433
A495
N435
A461
A66
A496
A472
A49
N431
A483
N442
A494
N
10 km
10 miles

Huelva city
& around

Despite its heavily industrialized outskirts, the port of Huelva is neither grim nor workaday, just a little boring. Without outstanding monuments (the 1755 Lisbon earthquake flattened most of them) and lacking many charismatic tapas bars and restaurants, it suffers by comparison with other cities.

Students give its nightlife some muscle and there are long pedestrian shopping streets to stroll down, but, with the best will in the world, Huelva just doesn't deserve a great deal of the visitor's time, in contrast to its province, which has a wealth of attractions, many of which are just a short journey from the capital.

A blue-collar city, Huelva's always been an underdog. It has justifiable pride in its workers' heritage; the best symbol of this is Spain's oldest football club, Recreativo de Huelva. *Colour map 1, C2.*

Historic centre

a fine museum, pedestrian shopping streets and British barrio

While Huelva is well endowed with elegant buildings dating from the early 20th century, its tourist sights are few, though its lengthy pedestrian shopping streets are always good for a stroll. It's also worth making your way to the traditional fish market on Calle Duque de la Victoria in the centre.

Museo de Huelva

Alameda Sundheim 13, T959-650424, www.museosdeandalucia.es. Mid-Sep to May Tue-Sat 1000-2030, Sun 1000-1700, Jun to mid-Sep Tue-Sun 1000-1700.

Stimulated by contact with the Phoenician trading towns, the Tartessian civilization flourished in the south of the Peninsula in the middle of the first millennium BC. Huelva's well-presented museum has a rich and important collection from this period, including Tartessian inscriptions, Phoenician grave goods (look out for the reconstructed funerary cart with a cow's head hubcap) and some Attic pottery. An Iberian gold ring from the fourth century BC also stands out. From earlier periods, there's fourth millennium BC pottery and tools. Roman finds include sculpture and bronzes, some discovered in the Río Tinto mines in the province's interior.

The fine art collection isn't especially remarkable; mostly 20th-century Huelvan artists are represented, such as Daniel Vázquez Díaz, who also has a series of frescoes of Columbus in La Rábida monastery, see page 99.

Nearby on the Alameda is the **Casa Colón** ⓘ *T959-210111*, a late 19th-century former hotel now used for exhibitions. It's a fine architectural legacy from this prosperous period and is strikingly orange and white, with an attractive interior court with palm trees.

Around the turn of the 20th century, the Río Tinto mining company was god in these parts. Indeed, its British workers had an incredible impact on Spanish culture merely by encouraging locals to kick a ball around. These workers were generally housed in suburbs built by the company; the **Barrio Inglés**, also known as Barrio Reina Victoria, is one of them, constructed in 1917. Despite their window sashes painted with southern exuberance, these semi-detached houses are quintessentially British – all that's missing is quaint cottagey names and B&B signs in the windows. A wander around its streets will shift you in time and place for a while until you re-emerge in 21st-century Spain.

Essential Huelva

When to go

As a coastal city Huelva has a balanced maritime climate. You may want to avoid Punta Umbría in summer as it's packed with partying *sevillanos* and accommodation is more expensive.

Time required

Allow one day to see the sights in Huelva city, another day or two to explore Niebla and Punta Umbria.

BACKGROUND

Huelva

Huelva is an ancient port, founded by the Phoenicians in the early first millennium BC, when it was known as Onuba (people from Huelva are still called *onubenses*). Various artefacts from the little-known local Tartessian civilization have been found here, leading to speculation that this was the site of their presumed capital, Tartessos, but this has not been proved, though undoubtedly Huelva would have been an important Tartessian settlement. The Romans used Onuba as a port for the minerals that they extracted from the Río Tinto mines to the north, as did the Moors who named it Guelbah. It was the capital of its own *taifa* state following the collapse of the Córdoba caliphate, before being swallowed by Sevilla in 1051.

Reconquered in 1257 by Alfonso X, its status as a port was enhanced when Columbus, using local crews, set out from this area for the New World. It also prospered as a trading base used by the *conquistadores*, although it later lost ground to Sevilla and Cádiz. The city was almost completely destroyed in the 1755 Lisbon earthquake but with the arrival of the British Río Tinto company in the late 19th century, Huelva again prospered, and the petrochemical industry developed by Franco in the 1950s has kept the city in jobs.

The port and river mouths

From Plaza 12 de Octubre at the edge of the old town, walk through the Jardines del Muelle, populated by white pigeons, down to the port, where there is a graceful sculpture of twisted chrome. Here you can watch ships loading up or, in summer, take a boat to the beach. Turning left, you'll soon come to the Muelle de Riotinto, an iron railway for the unloading of ores built in 1874; it's a fine piece of industrial architecture that you can walk out along. Beyond here at the meeting point of the Odiel and Tinto rivers is a colossal Cubist sculpture, **Monumento a Colón**, looking out to sea. Created in 1929 by the American sculptor Gertrude Vanderbilt Whitney, it depicts a Franciscan friar and is a homage both to Christopher Columbus and the Christian faith that powered Spanish voyages to the New World.

Around Huelva city → *Colour map 1, C2.*

bird-rich wetlands and Huelva's main beach resort

Very close to Huelva, the monastery of La Rábida and towns of Palos de la Frontera and Moguer are all associated with Columbus; see page 99 for more information.

Marismas del Odiel

The river Odiel which runs along Huelva's western edge is significantly cleaner than the overworked Tinto, and harbours a surprisingly large bird population along its banks in the wetlands, particularly in the protected area of the Paraje Natural

Marismas del Odiel. While you'll spot some species from the Paseo Marítimo in the north of town, you can achieve more with your own transport. Head across the Odiel bridge and turn left, following signs for the Dique Juan Carlos I, a dyke stretching out to sea built in an effort to stop silt washing into the river; 2 km along the Dique road is the visitor centre **Anastasio Senra/La Calatilla** ⓘ *T959-524334, Jun-Sep Tue-Sun 0900-1500, Oct-May Tue-Sun 1000-1400, 1600-1800*, with a good exhibition on the wetlands and an adjacent restaurant. Staff can provide you with a map marking various easy signed walking trails. They can also organize guided walks, drives, tourist train routes and boat trips.

Punta Umbría

This one-time fishing village was first developed as a beach resort by British employees of the Rio Tinto mining company in the late 19th century and is still the major beach destination for Huelva city. The strand is long and sandy and there's an even better stretch east of town by the long sea dyke. There are frequent buses

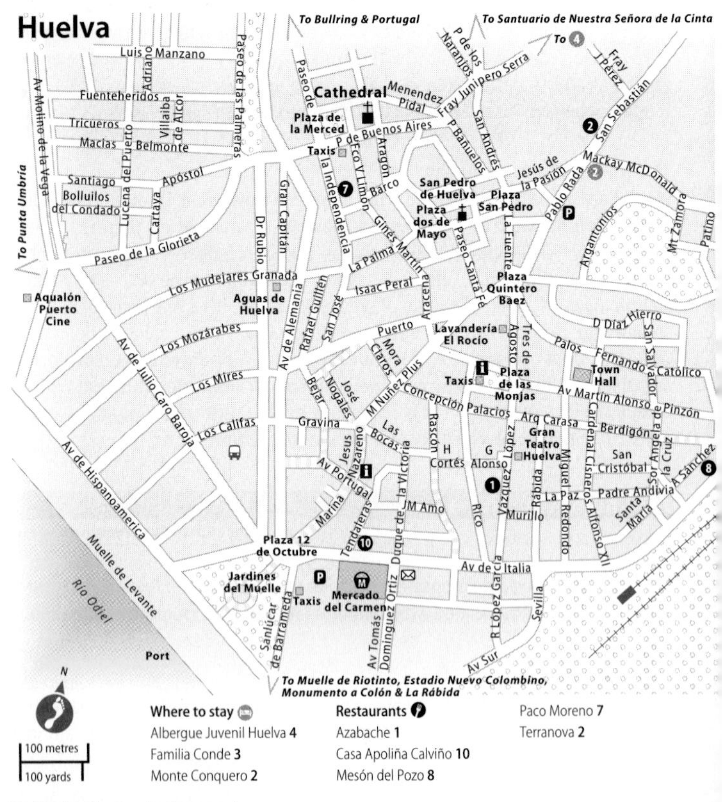

from Huelva and, in summer, there's a boat service too (www.canoadepuntaumbria.es). In summer, there's plenty of nightlife here, with beachside *discotecas* pumping.

★Niebla

On the Sevilla road, 29 km east of Huelva, little-visited Niebla is an amazing sight that has several treasures. It has as proud a history as anywhere in these parts; founded by the Tartessians and named Ilipula, it was then a Roman fortress and centre of a Moorish taifa kingdom, when it was known as Lebla. The initial impression is striking, for the town is completely surrounded by high orange walls, dating mainly from the Almoravid period, although some remains of the original Tartessian and Roman walls have been identified. The walls have 40 square towers and five beautiful gateways.

The city's outstanding monument is the **Iglesia de María de Granada**. Originally a Mozarabic church, it was converted to a mosque by the Almoravids, then back to a church by the conquering Christians. The result is a charming fusion of elements. If it's not open, ask in the Casa de Cultura alongside for the key. On the other side of the old town, the ruined Iglesia de San Martín has a similar blend of styles.

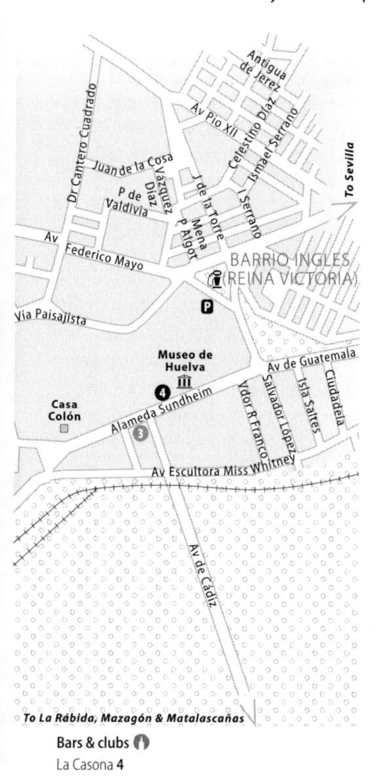

The other main building in town is the **Castillo de los Guzmanes** ⓘ *T959-362270, Mon-Fri 1000-1400, Sat-Sun 1100-1400, some afternoon opening in high season, €4.50*, which also houses the town's **tourist office** ⓘ *turismoniebla@gmail.com*. A huge building that looms over the walls between the Puerta de Sevilla and the Puerta del Embarcadero, it was built over the Roman fortress by the Moors, but was more or less reconstructed in the 15th century by the Count of Niebla. The main tower was destroyed in an earthquake, and the castle suffered damage as a base for Marshal Soult in the Peninsular War. It's been well restored, and the multi-level dungeons, complete with gruesome torture exhibition, are particularly atmospheric.

Tourist information

Huelva regional tourist office
C Jesús Nazareno 21, T959-650200, www.turismohuelva.org. Mon-Fri 0900-1930, Sat and Sun 0900-1500.
In the heart of Huelva city, they are helpful and have a variety of information on the city, province and transport links. The city operates various tourist kiosks around town, the most useful of which is on the central Plaza de las Monjas (Mon-Fri 1000-1400, 1700-2030, Sat 1000-1400) where you can download a multilingual Bluetooth guide to the town.

Where to stay

Accommodation options in unfashionable Huelva are very well priced.

€€€ Hotel Monte Conquero
C Pablo Rada 10, T959-285500, www.hotelesmonte.com.
Huelva has a few business hotels around its centre, and they're a fairly unremarkable bunch, but this is far better, with a good location on a street with lots of eating options, friendly staff, and comfortable, good-sized rooms. You can get substantial discounts online.

€€ Hotel Familia Conde
Av Alameda Sundheim 14, T959-282400, www.hotel familiaconde.com.
Near the museum, this hotel offers reasonable value for spacious modern rooms with OK bathrooms and good facilities. There's free Wi-Fi and internet access in the lobby, and breakfast is also included with a generous time window. Parking available; you can also park in the streets running behind the hotel.

€ Albergue Juvenil Huelva
C Marchena Colombo 14, T959-650010, www.inturjoven.com.
To the northeast of town, this official youth hostel is a hike from the bus station but within 5 mins' walk of the main tapas and bar zones. There's shared accommodation in rooms with 2 decent beds (not bunks) and private bathroom. Breakfast included.

Niebla

€€ Finca Real de Niebla
C Real 5, T959-363206, www.fincarealdeniebla.com.
On the edge of the village, this offers 2 well-equipped houses – 1 large, 1 small – in spacious grounds. There are numerous facilities including a small summer pool.

Restaurants

Huelva's choice of characterful eateries is poor, but there's certainly some good seafood about: the city is famous throughout Spain for its prawns, the best of which don't come cheap. The biggest choice is along Av Pablo Rada and its continuation.

€€ Azabache
C Vázquez López 22, T959-257528, www.restauranteazabache.com.
In the heart of Huelva's commercial centre, this is its star tapas choice, with wonderful fishy creations like tuna chunks tossed in soy sauce served by faultless bar staff to an upmarket crowd who've sometimes dashed straight from the theatre nearby. As well as bar snacking, there's a smart dining room with excellent, imaginative

versions of traditional Huelvan dishes. Recommended.

€€ Mesón del Pozo
C Alonso Sánchez 14, T959-254240.
A place that buzzes with lunchtime workers from the nearby commercial district, this is a rare option that is smart but completely unpretentious. As well as a classy *menú del día* there are good-value à la carte options based on warming Andalucían specialities.

€€ Terranova
Av San Sebastián 19, T959 261507, www.restauranteterranova.com.
This makes up for its less-than-characterful main road location with a caring attitude and a great range of seafood and pork-based dishes. This is one of those spots where you should ask the personable boss for recommendations and just go with the flow.

€ Casa Apoliña Calviño
C Tendaleras 9, T959-249836.
Something of a relic of old Huelva, this bar near the bustling market has a high wooden roof and shapely brick and tile bar, as well as a range of nautical curios and ceramics. There are simple tapas and *raciones*, including very tasty *pulpo* (octopus). It's been open for 50 years and is an unglamorous but worthwhile fixture in these parts.

€ Paco Moreno
Paseo de la Independencia 18, T959-243048.
This is a classic no-frills *freiduría*, serving excellent *raciones* of fried seafood. The *choco* (squid) is great, but the atmosphere is even better – Andalucía at its most typical.

Bars and clubs

Along C Pablo Rada, where it becomes C San Sebastián, are a few drinking bars, while Plaza de la Merced and nearby C Ginés Martín have several lively student-oriented bars. The newish Puerto Sur area has several bars, a *discoteca* and a lively atmosphere.

La Casona
Alameda Sundheim 9, www.lacasonawhite.com.
This *discoteca* in a characterful *indiano* mansion is handy for several Huelva hotels but its best feature is the separate garden bar, shaded by palm and banana trees. Expect regular name changes.

Festivals

Jul/Aug Huelva's major festival is at the end of Jul and beginning of Aug, to celebrate the departure of **Columbus' first voyage**. There are bullfights, live music and street revelry.
8 Sep Fiesta of the town's patron, **Nuestra Señora de la Cinta**.

What to do

Football
Recre play at the **Estadio Nuevo Colombino**, Av Francisco Montenegro s/n, T959-270208, www.recreativohuelva.com, beyond the Río Tinto pier. Stadium tours are available.

Transport

Boat
In summer a pleasant boat service runs from the port to the resort of **Punta Umbría**.

Bus

Huelva city's bus station is to the south-west of town, a short walk to the centre.

The **Damas** company, T959-256900, www.damas-sa.es, serves the province effectively. There are also half-hourly buses to **Sevilla** (1 hr 15 mins via motorway, longer via main road). Some of these continue directly to **Cádiz**, **Málaga** or **Granada**. There are several daily **Socibus** services to **Madrid** (7½ hrs).

There are 2 daily buses on weekdays to **Faro** and **Lagos** in Portugal.

Train

Huelva's fine neo-*mudéjar* train station, Estación de Sevilla, is on Av Italia, from where it is a short walk to the centre.

The train station isn't exactly a hive of activity. There are 4 daily trains to **Sevilla**, 2 via **Niebla** and **La Palma**. For the northern Sierra de Aracena, there is one to **Almonaster** and **Jabugo**. There are 2 daily trains to **Madrid**, taking just 3¾-4 hrs via **Córdoba**.

Niebla

There are 6-9 daily buses to Niebla from **Huelva** and back (30 mins). Most of these are labelled **Sevilla**, their eventual destination, but make sure you get on one that goes along the old road (*por N 431*) and not the motorway (*por autopista*).

Lugares Colombinos

Just across the estuary of the Río Tinto from Huelva are three sites that are intimately connected with the voyages of Cristóbal Colón, or Christopher Columbus. Jointly known as the Lugares Colombinos, they are easily visited on a day trip from Huelva, although it's tempting enough to do it the other way around; there are good places to stay and eat in both Palos de la Frontera and Moguer.

La Rábida and Muelle de las Carabelas → *Colour map 1, C2.*

fascinating 14th-century monastery and replica caravelles

La Rábida

T959-350411, www.monasteriodelarabida.com. Winter Tue-Sat 1000-1300, 1600-1815, Sun 1045-1300, 1600-1815, summer Tue-Sat 1000-1300, 1600-1900, Sun 1045-1300, 1600-1900. €3 includes audio guide in several languages. Park a little bit away from the monastery to avoid paying €1.

Within a large botanical park directly across the river from Huelva, the monastery of La Rábida was where Columbus struggled and schemed with two of the monks for ways to win the support of Fernando and Isabel, the Catholic Monarchs, for his project. He first arrived here with his son Diego in 1484, after João II of Portugal had refused to sponsor his voyage. He was attracted here because one of the Franciscans, Fray Antonio de Marchena, knew Isabel and also because the area was full of mariners with a deep knowledge of the Atlantic.

The monastery has been much altered, but several sections remain as they were when Columbus stayed. The first cloister is decorated with intriguing modern paintings by Juan Manuel Núñez depicting part of the Columbus story. Off here is the stunning chapel, entered through a horseshoe arch: the building was once an Almohad fortress. On the walls are half-preserved 15th-century frescoes, while above the main altar is a replica of the early Gothic crucifixion that hung here until its destruction in the Civil War. The Virgen de la Rábida is a small late 13th-century alabaster Mary in a small chapel opposite the door. She wears a crown placed on her by the Pope during the 500-year celebrations of Columbus' voyage. It seems certain that Columbus and his crew would have prayed here before setting out, and the chapel is one of the spots that most evokes the explorer's memory. The ceiling is a fine neo-*mudéjar artesonado*.

The second cloister is striking; an ensemble of brick *mudéjar* arches with a whitewashed upper level. Off it are a small meeting room where Columbus probably discussed strategies for royal approval with the abbot Juan Pérez, and the refectory, which has been restored. In the former is a small portrait of Columbus by the artist Valeriano Bécquer, brother of the famous poet Gustavo Adolfo. Upstairs is the chapterhouse, where final planning for the voyages took place. Even after gaining royal approval, it was tough for the foreigner Columbus to persuade sceptical local mariners to come along on the voyage. Finally, Alonso Pinzón, an experienced captain from Palos, was brought on board (so to speak), and managed to put together a crew.

Also upstairs is an exhibition, with models of the ships, facsimile documents (including several examples of Columbus' mysterious signature) and samples of soil from the Philippines and all the countries of the Americas. The sword of Hernán Cortés's principal captain, Sandoval, is here. Cortés and Pizarro both came here when planning their journeys.

Muelle de las Carabelas

T959-530597. Mid-Jun to mid-Sep Tue-Sun 1000-2130, mid-Sep to mid-Jun Tue-Sun 0930-2000. €3.55.

Below the monastery, on the water, are replicas of the three ships from the 1492 voyage moored by an exhibition centre. The ships are unadorned and remarkable mainly for their tiny size. The *Santa María* is in the middle: built with a larger, more traditional hull, she proved too unwieldy and was eventually wrecked off Hispaniola. The smaller caravelles (*Niña* on the left, *Pinta* on the right) moved better with the swells and weren't as prone to damage in high seas. There's an unbelievably patronizing display of plastic native Americans, complete with taped soundtrack of screeching parrots. A tokenistic display of South American craft is upstairs in the building, which also contains a more comprehensive exhibition on the voyages.

Also within the park is a large amphitheatre, which, to the council's credit, does make an effort to feature performance groups from Africa and South America during the summer. There's also a large monument to Faith and Exploration, as well as a smaller one to *Plus Ultra*, the first plane to cross the Atlantic (see Palos, below). Unfortunately, the hotel by the monastery takes organized groups only. The park has species from the American continent; as always, it's striking to ponder just how many familiar plants were native to the New World and unknown in Europe until the 16th century.

Palos de la Frontera and Moguer → *Colour map 1, C2.*

attractive whitewashed towns, the birthplaces of Columbus's crew

Palos de la Frontera

This small town was once a heartland of hardened Atlantic mariners but has now been left high and dry as the river Tinto estuary has silted up. Columbus embarked

ON THE ROAD

The voyages of Columbus

Christopher Columbus (Cristóbal Colón, Cristoforo Colombo) was probably born near Genoa in 1451. Little is known of his early life, but he made his way to Portugal and then Madeira, where he married in 1480 and became interested in the popular idea of sailing westwards to Asia. Through various misinterpretations of navigational works, he hypothesized a much lesser distance to Asia than is actually the case and approached João II of Portugal with a plan to challenge Arab domination of the spice trade by forging new routes across the Atlantic. The monarch said no, so Columbus made his way to Spain and petitioned Fernando and Isabel, at first without success. But in 1492, flushed with success in the endgame of the Reconquista, Isabel finally agreed to furnish him with three ships and letters to take to the Great Khan on her behalf. On 3 August that year, Columbus left Palos de la Frontera with three small ships, the *Pinta*, the *Niña* and the *Santa María*, and on 12 October they reached the Bahamas, which they named San Salvador. The expedition then discovered Cuba and Hispaniola, establishing a fort, Navidad, on the latter.

Christopher Columbus arrived back in Spain on 15 March 1493 to great excitement and honour. He brought with him exotic fruits and cereals, as well as six bewildered native Americans.

His second voyage began later the same year, this time equipped with 17 ships and over 1000 men to establish settlements. He discovered several more Caribbean islands, including Puerto Rico and Jamaica, and founded a settlement on Hispaniola. On his third voyage (1498-1500), he actually made landfall on the South American coast, in modern-day Venezuela, but things turned sour when his heavy-handed governorship of the Hispaniola colony led to a revolt. The Spanish government had him imprisoned and brought back to Spain, where he was received well, but lost his position as governor of all the New World Colonies.

On his fourth and final voyage (1502-1504) Columbus reached the Central American isthmus, exploring the coast from Honduras down to Panama. He still believed, against most learned opinion, that he had discovered outlying parts of Asia, and was still hoping to deliver the Great Khan's mail.

He died in Valladolid in 1506, temporarily at least, a forgotten man.

on his first expedition from here, and the three ships were at least a quarter crewed by Palos men. Prominent among those were the Pinzón brothers who did much of the organizing and captained two of the ships that the port had been ordered to provide by royal decree.

Nowadays Palos is a small, pleasant Spanish town devoted to strawberry farming and basically consisting of one long street that rises to the centre and then drops away to where the port used to be. The central square is named Plaza Franco, not after the dictator, but rather his brother, who flew from Palos to Buenos Aires in

1926, thus becoming the first person to cross the Atlantic by plane. Up the hill from here is the house of Martín Alonso Pinzón, captain of the *Pinta* and Columbus' right hand in the organization of the voyage. It's been restored as a **museum** ⓘ *C Cristóbal Colón 24, Mon-Fri 1000-1400, €1*, which includes information about Franco's flight as well as Columbus' first expedition, with facsimile documents and information panels. It's easy to go knocking at the wrong door as there are two number 24s; it's the one opposite number 37.

Further along the main road is the **Iglesia de San Jorge** ⓘ *Mon 0830-1000, Tue-Sun 1930-2100*, which once stood directly above the wharf where Columbus embarked. He surely prayed here before setting sail; an inscription on the church's wall proclaims Palos's pride in its connection with the voyage: *"O Palos, no puede tu gloria igualar ni Menfis ni Tebes ni Roma inmortal"* (Oh Palos, your glory cannot be equalled by Memphis, nor Thebes, nor immortal Rome). The church, built in the 15th century and heavily laden with storks, has the characteristic Andalucían mix of the Gothic and *mudéjar*. The attractive interior features a fine Gothic alabaster sculpture of Santa Ana and some colourful frescoes. Below the church is a small brick fount; it is said that the ships took on their water supply from here before setting sail.

★Moguer

Although the *Niña* was built here, the town provided several of the crew for Columbus' first voyage, and the mariner visited the town several times, Moguer owes more of its fame to its Nobel prize-winning poet Juan Ramón Jiménez (1881-1958), who deeply loved this, his hometown, despite spending the last 20 years of his life across the Atlantic because Franco came to power. An attractive, large town, whitewashed Moguer is worth exploring for its fine buildings and its sites relevant to the life of Jiménez. Quotes from the poet's best-known work are tiled around town in various locations: *Platero y yo* is a lyrical portrait of the town and the region conducted as a conversation between the writer and his donkey, Platero, with whom Jiménez used to wander the town's streets, and who is buried in the grounds of the Casa Fuentepiña, a private residence south of town where the poet spent his summers writing.

Moguer has a good **tourist office** ⓘ *C Andalucía 17, T959-371898, turismo@aytomoguer.es, Mon-Sat 1000-1400, 1700-1900 (1800-2000 summer), Sun 1000-1500.* It's on a central pedestrian street in an ornate theatre building. It makes sense to park your car near here, by the castle, to avoid the narrow maze of streets beyond. Entering the town from the direction of Palos, go straight ahead, then bear left on to Calle Rábida when the road forks. You'll see the car park signposted shortly afterwards to the left. Some buses will drop you off nearby on Avenida América. The castle itself has origins as a Roman tower but was basically built by the Almohads, before being enlarged by the Castillian Monarchs.

Near the tourist office is Plaza del Cabildo on which stands the town hall. So harmonious is its late-Baroque façade with two levels of round arches on marble columns that it used to feature on the 2000 peseta note; you can still watch Spanish visitors start as they try to work out why the building looks vaguely familiar.

Beyond the plaza, down Calle Reyes Católicos, you soon come to the huge parish church, **Santa María de Granada** ⓘ *Mon-Fri 1100-1300, 1830-2100, Sat 1100-1300, Sun 1100-1200, 1930-2130, free*. It is strikingly Sevillian in style with its yellow and blue tiling and a bell tower whose design is clearly based on the Giralda, although on a smaller scale. The statue of the Virgin is in pride of place under a well-proportioned baldachin.

Moguer's finest building is the **Monasterio de Santa Clara** ⓘ *T959-370107, www.monasteriodesantaclara.com, Tue-Sat by guided tour at 1030, 1130, 1230, 1630, 1730, 1830, Sun 1030, 1130, 1230, €3.50*. Founded in the 14th century, it presents a distinctly fortified appearance with its sturdy buttresses, particularly from Plaza de las Monjas, from which it is separated by a low castellated wall. The visit takes you through a pretty *mudéjar* cloister, then a larger Renaissance one, filled with palms and bananas brought back from the New World. After passing through the rooms used in daily life by the nuns, who were here until the 1950s, you enter the church, the highlight of which is the fine carved marble tombs of the Portocarrero family, and the alabaster ones of the founding Tenorio family. A plaque commemorates the fact that Columbus spent a whole night here praying on his return to Palos; something he had promised to the Virgin if she delivered his ships from a terrible Atlantic storm that threatened to send the expedition to the bottom of the sea. Note the choir stalls, excellent *mudéjar* work influenced by the art of Nasrid Granada.

The **Casa Museo Zenobia y Juan Ramón** ⓘ *C Juan Ramón Jiménez 10, T959-372148, fundacion-jrj.es, Tue-Sat 1000-1400, 1700-2000, Sun 1000-1400, reduced hours Oct-Jun, €3.50*, is where Juan Ramón Jiménez lived with his beloved wife Zenobia. This typical Andalucían house with patios has a comprehensive collection of documents, including the telegram notifying of the Nobel Prize for Literature in 1956. The house and furniture have been restored to the way they would have been when the couple lived here; there are optional guided tours lasting around 45 minutes. Jiménez bequeathed the house as a town museum, but only on condition that his wife's name was included in the name of it along with his own. The couple are buried in the cemetery to the east of town in an ornate monument. Jiménez himself was born in the **Casa Natal**, a typically attractive Moguer house with wrought-iron balconies at Calle Ribera 2, north of the Convento de Santa Clara.

Downhill from the town, along the road past the Casa Natal, a palm grove marks where the dock once was. You couldn't launch much more than a paper plane from here these days, but there's enough water to make it a decent birdwatching spot.

Where to stay

Palos de la Frontera

There are a couple of options in Palos, which makes a tranquil base.

€€ Hotel La Pinta
C Rábida 79, T959-350511, www. hotellapinta.com.
In the centre on the main street. Large cool rooms, many with balcony, and free parking opposite; it's the best place to stay in the area. Prices outside of summer are especially reasonable (**€**). The restaurant has warm decor and a good-value *menú*.

Moguer

€€ Hotel Plaza Escribano
Plaza Escribano 5, T959-373063, www. hotelplaza escribano.com.
This rustic hotel occupies one of the many noble white balconied town houses in Moguer's appealing centre. It offers charming patio spaces, well-furnished public areas and comfortable rooms that are snug rather than spacious.

Restaurants

Palos de la Frontera

€€ El Bodegón
Rábida 46, T959-531105.
Delightful family-run restaurant in an old wine bodega with great service, an interesting wine selection, and excellent grilled meats. Try the *verduras a la brasa* (grilled vegetable platter) as a memorable shared starter.

Moguer

€€ El Lobito
C Rábida 31, T959-370660, www. mesonellobito.com.
Ultra-characterful and in sharp contrast to Moguer's elegant whitewashed lanes. Customers scribble on the walls, the ceiling hangs with all kinds of weird and wonderful curios, and the kitchen trucks out decent fish and meat grills, as well as tapas. It used to be a venue for cockfighting.

€€ La Parrala
Plaza de las Monjas 22, T959-370452.
Near the Monasterio de Santa Clara, this sound option is a stylish but warm family-run place with excellent grilled meats and typical local dishes. One tasty speciality is fresh tuna with orange sauce.

Transport

Hourly buses (every 2 hrs Sat and Sun) run from Huelva's bus station to **Moguer**, **Palos**, and **La Rábida**. There are further buses between **Moguer** and **Huelva** only. **Palos** is also a stop on the **Mazagón–Huelva** route.

East Coast & Parque Nacional Coto Doñana

The Huelva section of the Costa de la Luz boasts some extraordinary long Atlantic sandy beaches, backed by protected dune areas that lead up to the magnificent Coto Doñana wetlands, a national park offering wonderful birdwatching opportunities.

The two towns on the coast, Mazagón and Matalascañas, are completely contrasting. There are several campsites and a parador on the beautiful long, dune-backed strand between the two towns.

Back from the coast, the handiest Doñana base is the picturesque sand-street town of El Rocío, home to one of Spain's foremost Virgins.

East Coast → *Colour map 4, A1.*

magnificent beaches backed by extensive sand dunes

★Mazagón

Twenty kilometres east of Huelva, this friendly spot is a fairly low-key place despite its spectacular sandy beach which stretches 10 km east from its marina and centre. Though small, Mazagón bustles year round with seasonal workers from the strawberry plantations and oil refineries to the west, as well as soldiers from the army base nearby. It's one of the best places on the coast off season for this reason, as many of the other beach towns are moribund outside the summer months.

The town itself is centred on the Avenida de la Playa, which descends from the main road down to the beach. The further east you head, the better the beach gets; there are several campsites and, a few kilometres towards Matalascañas, a parador, where the chunky dunes form wooded escarpments backing the strand.

The **tourist office** ⓘ *Mon-Fri 1000-1400 plus Sat in summer*, is in the town hall building in the town centre; near here, the pedestrianized Avenida Fuentepiña is lined with cheap eateries.

Matalascañas

After the quiet charm of Mazagón, the brash development of Matalascañas comes as a shock. Right on the edge of the Coto Doñana national park, it's a moderately ugly strip which nevertheless has a marvellous long beach of fine-grained sand. In summer, *sevillanos* flock here in their thousands to escape the heat in the city. In winter, it's dead.

The Matalascañas beach continues eastwards into the national park itself; you can walk along this beautiful length of beach, but you can't stray inland. You'll see plenty of birdlife and this is the only walking you can actually do within the park boundaries.

At the other end of Matalascañas, near where an old defensive tower, the Torre Higuera, is rapidly getting swallowed by the sea, is a complex of migrating dunes, the **Parque Dunar**, not actually part of the national park, but part of its buffer zone.

The **tourist office** ⓘ *Av de las Adelfas s/n, T959-430086, Mon-Fri 0930-1400, Sat 1000-1400, hours extend in summer*, is at the entrance to the Parque Dunar on the western edge of town (if arriving by car from the north, head straight across the roundabout following signs for the beach).

Listings East Coast

Where to stay

Mazagón

€€€€ Parador de Mazagón
Ctra Huelva–Matalascañas Km 30, T959-536300, www.parador.es.

By far the best option, this modern but sensitively designed hotel nestles in the dunes above a stretch of beach 3 km east of the centre. Its attractive gardens give way to the pines of the dunes. The restaurant is excellent and the rooms cool and well appointed. There's also a tennis court, gym and pool.

€€€ Hotel Martín Alonso Pinzón
Av de los Conquistadores s/n, T959-377875, www.hotelmartinalonsopinzon.com.
This sizeable orange hotel is in town, just a short stroll from the beach. Staff go out of their way to be helpful, and the spacious rooms have balconies to smell the sea air from, and kitchens, making them a good choice for families. There's an adult and kids' pool, and a decent restaurant too.

Camping

Camping Doñana Playa
7 km east of Mazagón, T959-536281, www.campingdonana.com. Open year round.
The best campsite along this coast, this shady site has good facilities, including bike hire, restaurant, bar, tennis courts and a summer-only pool. As well as camping, there are A-frame bungalows and cabins. Crowded during summer, especially at weekends, when non-campers can pay a day fee to use the complex.

Matalascañas

The main reason to stay is the summer nightlife; otherwise choose El Rocío or Mazagón. There are several pricey beach-side complexes 1 km west of town.

€€€ Hotel Doñana Blues
Sector 1, Parcela 129, T959-449817, www.donanablues.com.
Tucked away towards the rear of the town a 5-min walk from the beach, this handsome small hotel and its pretty garden have plenty of charm and a secluded feel. The modern-rustic rooms are comfortable and thoughtful touches add points.

Restaurants

Mazagón

On the pedestrianized Av Fuentepiña there are several bars and restaurants with cheap *raciones* and tapas.

€€ Las Dunas
Av de los Conquistadores 178, T959-377811, www.restaurantelasdunas.com.
At the bottom of Av de la Playa near the beach, this excellent seafood establishment specializes in whole grilled fish; the seafood rice dishes are also memorable. There's a big outdoor terrace.

€ Bar El Choco
Av Fuentepiña 47, T959-536253.
A cheerful spot on this bar-lined street, with a marine-coloured awning shading a sunny terrace, and an interior lined with old fishing photos. There's all kinds of good-value fried seafood, including *raciones* of sea anemones (*ortiguillas*) or hake roe (*huevas de merluza*); unusual dishes that taste much better than they sound.

Matalascañas

€€ Casa Matías
Parque Dunar s/n, T959-449807, www.casamatias.com.
On the roundabout by the tourist office, this large building is impossible to miss. The town's most welcoming restaurant, it has a typically Andalucían interior of whitewashed walls and wooden beams. The bar offers tapas while the restaurant has appetizing choices like *almejas al ajillo* (clams sizzled in garlic) or hake croquettes.

Transport

Mazagón

Buses run to and from **Huelva** via **Palos**. One bus a day runs to **Matalascañas** along the coast; on weekdays only.

Matalascañas

Buses run to **Almonte** via **El Rocío**, to **Sevilla** and to **Huelva** via **Palos** (none at weekends; change at **Almonte** for a connection).

Parque Nacional Coto Doñana → *Colour map 4, A1.*

a vast area of dunes, wetlands and scrub forest

★The Coto Doñana is one of Europe's most important national parks which harbours an incredible array of permanent and migratory birdlife as well as several rare mammals and three distinct botanical zones. For birdwatching, it's a location unparallelled in the peninsula, but anyone with even a passing interest in nature will find it a magical place.

The park

The national park covers an area of just over 500 sq km and was initially created in 1969. It's now a UNESCO World Heritage Site and is surrounded by a 'buffer zone', the Parque Natural, which covers a further 542 sq km.

The parks are divided into distinct zones. Behind the long sandy beaches is a large area of migratory dunes that move inland; the huge sand hills are interspersed with *corrales*, gullies wooded with stone pines and Mediterranean shrubs. Beyond here are areas of fixed dunes; these gradually merge into open woodland of cork oak and stone pines, with clearings (*matorrales*) that have a range of scrub. Beyond here are the *marismas*, marshes that flood with water in winter and spring from the river Guadalquivir. These are freshwater and virtually shielded from the Atlantic by the dune belt and clay soil.

Flora and fauna

The protected conditions and different ecosystems make the park a wildlife paradise. Along the beaches, seabirds and coastal birds thrive; including sandwich terns, oystercatchers, scoters, cormorants, sanderlings and Kentish plover. Turtles and, offshore, whales are also sometimes seen. The dunes are home to small rodents and stands of stone pine, while the woodlands beyond are of lentisks, stone pine and cork trees interspersed with cistus, gorse, lavender and rosemary. This area harbours several larger mammals; herds of fallow and roe deer, genets, wild boar and the Pardel (Iberian) lynx (see box, page 390), a nocturnal beast that is a very rare sighting. The Doñana population of some 85 animals has been helped by the construction of fences running along the main roads, and the construction of various lynx-friendly underpasses to reduce road kill, but the long-term outlook is problematic due to the small population and the difficulty of introducing foreign animals into the existing community.

Essential Parque Nacional Coto Doñana

Access

Apart from an official tour, see page 112, access to the park itself is limited to the beach, and a road along its northern edge. The park cannot be crossed, so there is access from both sides; from Huelva province and from Sanlúcar de Barrameda in Cádiz province (see page 151). On the Huelva side are the best facilities: several visitor centres with walking trails along the edge of the park and excellent hides for birdwatching. From here you can also take a 4WD tour into the park itself. The best base is the town of El Rocío. With your own transport, you could also stay in pleasant Mazagón or along the coast.

When to go

Spring is the best time to visit, as there are huge numbers of breeding birds, unless the winter has been a dry one. Try not to coincide with the Whitsun *romería* to El Rocío (see box, page 110), as all accommodation is booked. In summer, the heat and mosquitoes are intense, the cooler autumn is a better time. Try and book tours, particularly the trip from El Acebuche, as far in advance as you possibly can (see below).

Visitor centres

The principal visitor centre of the national park is at **El Acebuche** (1.5 km off the Matalascañas-El Rocío road, T959-439629, daily 0800-1900, 2100 in summer), an essential stop and starting point of 4WD tours of the park (see What to do, page 112). Passing buses will drop you at the turn-off on request. Situated by a lake, the centre has two circular walks (1.5 km and 3.5 km) and several thatched observatories. The hides have informative panels on the birdlife but no telescopes, so bring binoculars. You'll easily see coots, moorhens, purple gallinules and a range of duck and wader species.

There are four other visitor centres on this side of the park. **Palacio del Acebrón** (daily 0900-1900, summer 1000-1500, 1600-2000) and **La Rocina** (daily 0900-1900, summer 1000-1500, 1600-1800) are close together and within a short walk of El Rocío. La Rocina has a hut with an exhibition on the pilgrimage, an audiovisual display on the area's wildlife and a 3.5-km-long trail along the edge of the wetlands; there are five good hides here. From Palacio del Acebrón, 6 km beyond La Rocina, is a short woodland trail with viewpoints. North of the park, on the edge of the village of Hinojos, **Los Centenales** (1000-1400 and 1600-1900 in winter or 1700-2000 in summer, has an exhibition on the park's ecology and traditional life in and around it. The final centre is **José Antonio Valverde** (1000-1800, summer 2000), a 50-km drive from El Rocío. On the edge of the wetlands, it's one of the best and most isolated spots for observing birds. If you don't have your own transport, you can get there by tour (see page 112).

On the southeastern side of the park, there's another visitor centre; from here you can take a boat tour into the national park. These leave from Sanlúcar de Barrameda (see page 151); luckily no roads cross the park (although there's always a threat that one will be built), so you have to go the very long way around, via Sevilla.

ON THE ROAD

Pilgrimage of the White Dove

The Whitsun *romería* to the Huelvan village of El Rocío is the most colourful and well attended of Spain's many pilgrimages. Nearly a million people descend on the Wild West-like town for the weekend before Pentecost Monday, many arriving on foot and in oxcarts as part of *cofradías* (brotherhoods) from all over Andalucía, each with their own processional float, or *simpecado*, adorned by an image of the Virgin. Many men and women wear traditional *corto* and *flamenca* costumes and the atmosphere is a strange mix of religious solemnity, horsemanship, social bonding and drunken abandonment. On the journey to El Rocío, *rocieras* (flamenco-style songs about the pilgrimage), wine, food and sex meld around the campfires.

The object of the pilgrimage is the Virgen del Rocío (Virgin of the Dew), a 13th-century sculpture housed in a modern sanctuary. The town overspills during the Whitsun weekend and little sleeping goes on between the open-air masses, impromptu parties, galloping horses and competitive *cofradía* rivalries.

On Sunday night, the Virgin, popularly known as the Blanca Paloma (White Dove), leaves her sanctuary and visits the chapels of all the *cofradías*, who aggressively jostle for the honour of carrying her part of the way. 'Viva la Blanca Paloma' is the cry through the streets.

The *romería* is often described as typifying Andalucía in its mixture of pride, emotion, hedonism and sentimentality and is an unforgettable experience that creates lifelong friends and draws people back year after year.

There are also wild cows and horses, as well as mongoose, polecats and, in the *marismas*, otters. The wetlands are home or a stopover point to hundreds of species of birds. Wading birds include white storks, spoonbills, egrets, avocets, stilts, godwits, lapwings and several species of heron. Ducks, coots, moorhens and the park's emblem, the purple gallinule, are present in huge numbers, while wintering greylag geese arrive in their tens of thousands. In the reeds and scrub are nightingales, hoopoes, partridges, bee-eaters and azure-winged magpies, as well as Cettis warblers and great reed-warblers. Birds of prey abound, the rare imperial eagle, as well as booted eagles, short-toed eagles, buzzards, harriers and three types of kite. Good starting spots to see birds are the bridge and walkway at El Rocío and the hides and paths of the visitor centres, but guided birding trips will take you to many further promising locations dotted around the region.

El Rocío

Legendary throughout Spain as the destination of the boisterous Whitsun pilgrimage (see box, above) to adore its famous Virgin, El Rocío perches right on the Doñana wetlands and makes a great base. With its bumpy roads of rutted sand and earth, half its inhabitants seemingly on horseback and its houses built of wooden planks with hitching posts outside, it looks like a film set from a spaghetti western and is a striking place to visit. Birdwatching opportunities start in the heart of the town and the adjacent wetland teems with feathered life.

The town's focal point is the **Ermita del Rocío** ⓘ *daily 0830-2000 (0800-2200 summer), free,* home of the Virgin that inspires the pilgrimage and a whole genre of Andalucían music known as *rocieras*. A shiny white structure built between 1964 and 1969, it has weathered criticism for being overly grand, but in reality is fairly simple and doesn't detract from the Virgin herself. The same can't be said for the ugly *retablo* housing her. The sculpture itself is a work from the 13th century; she's a pale full-faced beauty dressed elaborately and with the appearance of being hooded. There's normally a torrent of flowers at her feet. A picturesque exterior chamber is full of wax and smoke from the thousands of votive candles lit every week; it is difficult to overstate just how important La Blanca Paloma is to Andalucíans. Souvenir stalls abound, selling pictures of the Virgin.

Across from the church is the beginning of the Coto Doñana national park, with wetlands fed by the Río Madre de las Marismas. There are substantial populations of deer and semi-wild horses, along with excellent bird (and mosquito) life. The shallow water teems with flamingos, storks, egrets, and numerous duck and wader species easily viewed from the waterside pathway right in town. Following the water to the left, past Hotel Toruño, is a bird **observation centre** ⓘ *summer Tue-Fri 0900-1400, Sat-Sun 0900-1300, 1800-2100, winter Tue-Sun 0900-1400, 1600-1800, free*; with helpful staff on duty. The road bridge across the water is also a good place for nature-watching.

The area around the church and alongside the *marismas* is studded with *acebuche* (wild olive) trees, some of which are well over half a millennium old. There's a **tourist office** ⓘ *T959-443808, on the main road, just north of the turn-off to the church.*

Listings Parque Nacional Coto Doñana

Where to stay

El Rocío

€€ Hotel Cortijo Las Malvasías
Ctra Lucena-Mazagón, T959-072020, www.las malvasias.com.
Some 7 km from the town of Lucena del Puerto northwest of El Rocío and northeast of Mazagón, this enchanting rural hotel sits in spacious bosky grounds, features endearingly warm hospitality and induces utter relaxation. With your own transport, it's a great base for exploring the Doñana region. They do tasty food and there's a pool and lawn for lounging. There are also 2 self-contained cottages with 3 double rooms and fold-out options. Recommended.

€€ Hotel Toruño
Plaza del Acebuchal 22, T959-442323, www.toruno.es.
Right on the edge of the marshes in the centre of El Rocío, this is an enticing place, if a little overpriced these days. Many of the small but comfortable rooms have views over the wetlands and all have TV, a/c and minibar. The restaurant opposite is also good.

Restaurants

El Rocío

€€€ Toruño
Plaza del Acebuchal s/n, T959-442422, www.toruno.es.
You won't go hungry in the village's best restaurant, opposite the hotel of the same name: the staff seem determined to put a bit of meat on your bones. The place is deceptively large; the main dining area has a great view over the *marismas* and their bird life. The wide selection of meat and fish dishes includes the best of Huelvan pork.

Festivals

El Rocío

May/Jun **Whitsun pilgrimage** in El Rocío, see box, page 110.

What to do

Tours

From El Acebuche visitor centre (see page 109) you can book 4WD bus tours of the park run by **Marismas del Rocío** (see below); this is the best of the three official routes in the park itself. The tours are enjoyable, but serious nature fans may get annoyed at the chattering tourists and limited viewing time available. Take your own binoculars if at all possible; otherwise be sure to hire a pair from the visitor centre before departing. More serious birdwatching excursions are run by other companies; while they are restricted to the road in the national park itself, there are many wonderful birding locations outside the controlled-access zone, and you'll have much more time to appreciate them.

Various companies offer half- and full-day tours from El Rocío through the northern edge of the national park, taking in wetlands, visitor centres and worthwhile birding spots. Highly recommended for birdwatching is English-speaking José Sánchez at **Discovering Doñana**, Av La Canaliega, El Rocío, T620-964369, www.discoveringdonana.com.

Marismas del Rocío, *T959-430432, www.donanavisitas.es. Mid-Sep to Apr Tue-Sun 0830 and 1500, and May to mid-Sep Mon-Sat 0830 and 1700. Tours last 4 hrs and cost €29.50 per person.* It is essential to reserve in advance, or at the centre itself. At short notice, you stand a much better chance midweek; during holiday periods, you should allow a few weeks.

Transport

El Rocío

There are daily buses to and from **Sevilla** (1 hr 30 mins); these continue to **Matalascañas**. 5 additional buses ply the Almonte–Matalascañas route; you'll have to change at one of these towns to reach **Huelva**, but connections are fairly good. All these buses will stop at the **El Acebuche** and **Las Rocinas** visitor centres on request.

West Coast

The long western coastline, part of the Costa de la Luz, of Huelva province is very varied. It's comparatively little visited by foreign tourists and outside of summer just gets on with things, growing strawberries and catching and canning fish. In summer, however, it's popular with holidaying Spaniards, which has led to the creation of kilometres of faceless high-rise development. Dotted around, however, are places such as Isla Cristina that haven't lost their local character.

El Rompido

Beyond Punta Umbría (see page 94) is this appealing fishing village on the estuary of the Río Piedras. On the waterfront are several places to eat top fresh seafood and the nearby beach, 10 km long, is one of the region's best.

La Antilla and El Terrón

South of the thriving strawberry town of Lepe (in Spain, jokes about people from Lepe are like Irish jokes in Britain), La Antilla is one of the more attractive beach destinations on this coast, with low-rise buildings, a super stretch of clean sand and a still-significant fishing industry. Its best part is east of the dividing main road Avenida de la Antilla. The western part merges into the tasteless apartment block sprawl of the newly developed Islantilla, a purpose-built resort whose name sums up its destiny of joining Isla Cristina with La Antilla in a stretch of high-rise buildings. La Antilla has a *mudéjar* church and several places to stay and eat. There's a small **tourist office** ⓘ *Av de Castilla, T959-481479.*

Five kilometres northeast of La Antilla is the small wetland fishing harbour of **El Terrón**, on the Río Piedras. It's more fishing port than village, but boasts a handful of excellent places to eat seafood (as well as a row of *discotecas* to beat La Antilla noise restrictions).

Isla Cristina

Isla Cristina is no longer an island, although it is still largely separated from the mainland by the marshy estuary of the Ría Carreras. Despite being a major summer resort, it's still an important fishing harbour and cannery, and its no-nonsense port area is an appealing contrast to the bland beachside barrios. The town beach, 1 km east from the centre, is magnificent: long, sandy and breezy. Heading east along it, the houses eventually peter out, and the beach is backed by pine-shaded dunes with summer *chiringuitos* (beach bars).

North of the town, the protected area of the *marismas* is excellent for birdwatching. Despite being used for salt extraction, the wetlands also support a large population of waders such as flamingos, avocets and spoonbills as well as smaller waterbirds.

The town is famous for *mechado de atún*, a delicious dish of tuna, pork and garlic baked in wine. There's a good **tourist office** ⓘ *in the old town at C San Francisco 12, T959-332694, Mar-Oct Mon-Fri 1000-1400, 1730-1930, Sat and Sun 1000-1400.*

Ayamonte

The last town in Spain, Ayamonte looks at Portugal across the impressive mouth of the Río Guadiana. There's much charm to its pedestrianized historic centre despite its ugly outskirts. The old town centres on the pretty palm-fringed Plaza de la Laguna (note the Portuguese-style colourfully tiled benches) and the popular marina. The town suffered when its once-important ferry to Portugal was rendered virtually redundant by the large motorway bridge a couple of kilometres upstream. However, cross-border shoppers and tourists, the expat property market, the marina and its fishing industry keep things ticking over.

Ayamonte's closest beach, Isla Canela, is an inconvenient 6 km south, but it's a good one and worth the trip. In summer, frequent buses trundle down there; in winter there's one a day or it's an hour's walk. You could also hire a bike: there are several operators.

Ayamonte's **tourist office** ⓘ *C Huelva 37, T959-320737, Mon 0900-1500, Tue-Fri 0900-2000, Sat 1000-1400*, is opposite the marina in an elegant *indiano* mansion called Casa Grande.

Listings West Coast

Where to stay

There are also numerous chain hotels along this coast that we haven't reviewed here.

El Rompido

€€€€ Hotel Fuerte El Rompido
Urb Marina El Rompido Ctra H-4111, Km 8, CP 21459, T902-343410, www.fuertehoteles.com.
Set in a quiet location surrounded by a protected area, this excellent resort hotel stands out for its family-friendly facilities and staff, sizeable pools, spa complex, good restaurant and ecological credentials. There are spectacular views from most rooms, and the wild 10 km-long El Rompido beach is 10 mins away by free boat service.

Isla Cristina
Camping

Camping Giralda Isla Cristina
near the beach on the eastern edge of town, T959-343318, www.campinggiralda.com. Open year round.
A large complex with good facilities including a pool. Some pitches overlook the river and *marismas*. There are also bungalows and dorms.

Ayamonte

The biggest range of accommodation is by Isla Canela beach, 6 km from town.

€€€ Parador de Ayamonte
T959-320700, www.parador.es.
Situated on a hill where a castle once guarded against Portuguese perfidy. Although it's a modern building, the views are spectacular, and it's a very peaceful place, with all the parador trimmings.

Restaurants

La Antilla and El Terrón

€€€ Coral Playa
C Estrella de Mar 3, La Antilla, T959-481406, www.coralplaya.com.
On the beach in the town centre, this smartish place serves fresh fish by weight and classy seafood. Book in advance in summer as it's pretty popular. There's cheaper tapas eating on the terrace and at the bar.

€€ El Quinto Señora María
El Terrón, T959-380930.
Mid-Mar to mid-Oct. A sound option in El Terrón. Seafood paella, tasty prawns, and whatever's fresh that day. Characterful location.

Isla Cristina

€€ Casa Rufino
Av de la Playa s/n, T959-330810, www.restauranterufino.com. Open lunchtime daily and also dinner on Fri and Sat.
This is an outstanding seafood restaurant with a long tradition of serving excellent fish creations at fair prices. The tuna here is legendary, but if you're hungry, go for the *tonteo*, which serves you 8 fish dishes all cooked with a different sauce. Recommended.

Ayamonte

There are also several good seafood restaurants at the beach and at Punta del Moral.

€€ Casa Luciano
C La Palma 2, T959-471071, www.casaluciano.com.
One of the best options, with a huge range of fish, crustaceans and molluscs. The prices are listed by weight, so be careful when ordering shellfish; you can eat cheaply or splash out on a memorable seafood feast. The *rape* (monkfish) and the *bacalao* (cod) are particularly good.

€ Tasca La Puerta Ancha
Plaza de la Laguna 14, T959-320666.
Near the ferry port on this pretty square, this bar has a characterful brick-arched interior, friendly service, and a fine range of beautifully presented modern tapas.

Transport

Damas, T959-256900, www.damas-sa.es run regular buses from Huelva to all destinations in this section. There are also some services from Sevilla.

Ayamonte

2-3 daily buses head to **Faro**, with some continuing to **Lagos**. More bus options into Portugal can be had from **Vila Real de San Antonio**, across the estuary.

Ferries (www.rioguadiana.net) run across every 40 mins 0930-1900 (2100 summer), €1.75 foot passenger, €5.25 car with driver; 10 mins. Pleasure cruises run from the same dock.

By car you can also cross to Portugal on the motorway via the spectacular Puente del Guadiana suspension bridge.

Sierra Morena

Huelva has by far the most attractive section of the Sierra Morena, the extensive range of low hills that separates Andalucía from the rest of the nation. It's a picturesque region with many charm-laden villages among its gentle slopes and wooded valleys. The town of Aracena is the main one, and the best base to explore the region, which is famous among Spaniards for producing the finest *jamón serrano*. The sierra is an inviting walking destination, with easy stages between villages.

On the way to the Sierra Morena from the coast, a detour to the Río Tinto mines is recommended; the horrifically devastated landscape and otherworldly mineral colours of the river combine to give the feeling the feeling of being on another planet.

Minas de Riotinto → *Colour map 1, B3.*

vast open-cast mines, fascinating mining museum and British barrio

★The Río Tinto (coloured river) is stained yellow and red by the rich ores it carries from this part of the country and not, as is popularly believed, by toxic waste from the mining industry. Its marked acidity mean there's no vegetation, so the rich palette of mineral colours is seen to great effect. If you think it could be Mars, you're not alone: NASA have studied the low-pH waters closely here, believing they could hold clues to the development of micro-organisms on the Red Planet.

This region has been mined for copper for millennia; the Phoenicians exploited the area and the Iberians before that. The Romans, typically, cranked up production, using slave labour to extract every last bit of ore out of flooding shafts. The Moors continued to a lesser degree, but it was the Anglo-German Rio Tinto Mining Company that transformed the area, building a railway to transport the ores to the coast, bringing in foreign engineers and workers and providing employment for thousands of local inhabitants. The operations have continued since the Spanish government bought the concession back in the 1950s. The extensive open-cast mines have made huge concentric craters from what used to be hills; they are an unforgettable sight that inspire varying degrees of awe and horror.

Founded by the Rio Tinto Company, the town of Minas de Riotinto is spread out, lacking a real focus. While rows of terraced cottages built for miners still make up the bulk of the town, most of today's workers are housed in apartment blocks constructed on the town's edges.

The main mining activity now is at Cerro Colorado, 1 km north of town. A mirador overlooks the operations; what was once a hill is now a deep pit, ringed

Essential Sierra Morena

Getting around

There are a few buses a day between the major towns and villages in the Parque Natural Sierra de Aracena, but a car is the best way to explore the park.

Best places to stay

Finca Buen Vino, Aracena, page 120
La Posada de Alájar, Alájar, page 125
La Tahona, Zufre, page 125

When to go

It can be chilly at night in the Sierra Morena except in summer.

Time required

At least a few days to visit the Parque Natural Sierra de Aracena, another day for Minas de Riotinto.

Best restaurants

José Vicente, Aracena, page 121
Casa Sirlache, Aracena, page 121
Arrieros, Linares, page 126

by concentric circles and often filled with water. The colours of the blasted earth are striking, and the vast mining machinery can make for some great industrial photography. In the first stages of open-cast mining, in the early 20th century, blasters descended on ropes to lay their dynamite before being pulled up to hopeful safety.

At the western end of town, the interesting **Museo Minero** ⓘ *Plaza del Museo s/n, T959-590025, www.parquemineroderiotinto.es, daily 1030-1500, 1600-1900 (2000 mid-Jul to Sep), €4, Museo and Peña de Hierro mine €9, plus Ferrocarril Turístico railway trip €17,* is set in what was once the miners' hospital. It covers everything from the area's archaeology and geology to the history of the mining operations. An elegantly restored steam engine stands alongside a beautiful luxury railway carriage known as the Maharajah's Wagon, built for Queen Victoria's prospective visit to India and bought by the mining company when this didn't happen. There's also a reproduction of a Roman mine here, plus your ticket gets you into Casa 21, an ethnographic display in the Barrio Bella Vista (see below). The helpful museum desk also functions as the town's tourist office.

Good guided trips run from the Museo Minero to the **Peña de Hierro mine** ⓘ *T959-590025, daily tours both morning and evening; time depends on bookings, tours should be reserved in advance, €8, for combination tickets, see Museo Minero above.* Unlike most of the modern mines in the area, which are open cast, this one has shafts and galleries, which you enter on the tour. The tour also points out the source of the Río Tinto river.

The **Ferrocarril Minero Turístico** ⓘ *T959-590025, Mar-Nov daily departures, Dec-Feb weekends only, ring for departure times, €10, reservations recommended, for combination tickets, see Museo Minero, above,* a 22-km train ride in elegant carriages originally used by the Rio Tinto company to transport workers from Huelva. The train leaves 1.5 km west of Nerva (3 km from Minas de Rio Tinto) and takes you through a ravaged but eerily beautiful landscape. On the first Sunday of the month from November to April the train is pulled by a steam engine.

Barrio Bella Vista

Daily 1630-1830. Admission is included with entry to the Museo Minero (see above).

Also known as the Barrio Inglés, this is a charmingly atmospheric contrast to the mine works. Built as a sheltered compound for the British mine chiefs and their families, it's an area of lovely gardens and lofty houses, a completely unexpected sight in the Huelvan hills. Hedges, fragrant creepers, a sports club, and a ruined Presbyterian church give it an out-of-place, out-of-time aspect that makes it well worth strolling around. One of the houses, Casa 21, has been lovingly restored to how it would have been at the time. The barrio is just off the main highway, through the gates opposite the football field.

Where to stay

€€ Riotinto Victorian House
Bellavista 43, T959 590262, www.riotintovictorianhouse.com.
One of 2 places to stay in the beautiful Bellavista barrio, this is run by an exceptionally friendly couple and offers great comfort and no little style. There's a back terrace with small pool. Recommended.

Transport

Bus
Nearly all the services mentioned in this section are run by **Damas**, T902-114492, www.damas-sa.es.

Several daily buses (2 on Sun) link **Huelva** with **Minas de Riotinto**. A daily bus runs between Nerva and Aracena via Minas de Riotinto.

Aracena → *Colour map 1, B3.*

handsome settlement with interesting sights and enticing hotels

★The main town in Huelva's Sierra Morena, this is the capital of a region dedicated to production of piggy products; add to this the abundance of locally foraged wild mushrooms and you have an intriguing eating scene. For much of the 13th century, this region was disputed by Castilla and Portugal; the castle overlooking the town is one of numerous examples. Aside from a few intriguing churches, many visitors head to the Gruta de las Maravillas, one of Spain's most spectacular limestone caves.

There are two sources of tourist information. The **Centro de Visitantes El Cabildo** ⓘ *Plaza Alta s/n, T959-129553, cvcabildoviejo@gmail.com, Sep-Jun Thu-Sun 0930-1430, Jul-Aug Fri 1200-1400, 1800-200, Sat 1000-1400, 1800-2000, Sun 1000-1400,* is the visitor centre for the surrounding Parque Natural and has a small exhibition as well as good information on the area. In the Gruta de las Maravillas ticket office is the town's enthusiastic **tourist office** ⓘ *T663-937877, turismo@ayto-aracena.es, daily 1000-1400, 1600-1800,* which has town maps and limited local information.

Sights

Start in Plaza Alta, home to El Cabildo visitor centre in a fortified *mudéjar* mansion. The inscription over the door reads: "Truth grew on earth, and justice watches us from heaven". Opposite is the huge parish church, looking like an arched Fort Knox. Although mostly built in the 16th century, it has never been finished.

Aracena is dominated by its ruined castle, most of which was built in the 13th century over the Moorish one. The French destroyed it during the Peninsular War and although little is left but its curtain wall, it's an enjoyable spot with stunning views, especially at sunset. Next to the castle is an interesting church, **Nuestra Señora de los Dolores** ⓘ *daily summer 1000-1930, winter 1030-1700,* which is a converted mosque. The minaret was changed to a *mudéjar* tower with well-preserved brick tracery. There's a late Gothic side door, and a front Gothic-Renaissance portico with both rounded and pointed arches. The interior has some beautiful rib vaulting.

The principal tourist attraction in Aracena is the **Gruta de las Maravillas** ⓘ *Plaza San Pedro s/n, T663-937876, daily 1030-1330, 1500-1800, €8.50 (€6 for 6-12 year olds, groups leave when 25 people have accumulated; you'll usually have to wait, in summer due to a limit on numbers, in winter because it takes longer for 25 to turn up*. This limestone cave sunk deep under the hill on which the castle stands is undeniably spectacular, one of Spain's finest, although some of the coloured lighting and musical score, not to mention the large visiting groups, takes away from the natural ambience. There are several chambers (some closed to the public) and six eerie underground lakes; the guides always get a laugh from the limestone buttock-like formations in the last cavern. While you're waiting to enter, look at the **geological museum** next to the ticket office with a donated collection of stunning specimens from around the world.

In the town centre, housed in the Ayuntamiento, the **Museo del Jamón** ⓘ *Gran Vía s/n, T959-127995, daily 1045-1415, 1530-1900, €3.50, €10.50 joint entrance with Gruta de las Maravillas, entry by guided tour, limited English information available*, is a well-presented exhibition on the region, and, more particularly, its pigs and their pork products. The guided visit includes interesting displays about the *matanza* (see box, page 123) and a taste of ham.

Walking and cycling

There are many marked trails around Aracena and the villages in the Parque Natural Sierra de Aracena. The visitor centre in Aracena can sell you the *Cuaderno de senderos*, a booklet detailing 24 of the walks in the area (€1); it's also best to buy one of their walking maps. From Aracena to Alájar is an easy morning's walk via Linares de la Sierra; it covers a shady up-and-down 9 km and should take around three hours.

It's also pleasant to cycle in these wooded hills, where the slopes are fairly gentle and climate coolish outside of the summer months.

Listings Aracena

Where to stay

€€€ Finca Buen Vino
Km 95 on the N433, Los Marines, T696-201553, www.fincabuenvino.com.
Family-run farmhouse converted into an elegant and beautifully furnished guesthouse with 5 rooms, set in woodland 6 km west of Aracena. Fabulous views and outstanding food; there are also self-contained cottages available for rent, and a pool. Price includes breakfast; dinners are also available. Must be reserved in advance; it's significantly cheaper for stays of 3 nights or more. Recommended.

€€€ Hotel Convento de Aracena
C Jesús y María 19, T959 126899, www.hotelconventoaracena.es.

This recent conversion of a 17th-century convent makes a most appealing place to stay in central Aracena. Rooms combine modern styling with original features of the building, and there's a great outdoor pool area as well as numerous other facilities. The restaurant is excellent.

€€ Finca Valbono
Ctra de Carboneras Km 1, T959-127711, www.fincavalbono.com.
Located 2 km from Aracena, this is a 20-ha farm with a luxurious 6-room hotel and 20 cottages to rent in a beautiful setting. Each cottage sleeps 3-5 and has a/c, TV, and a small kitchen. It's geared for the sporty with pool, volleyball court and horse- and cycle-riding facilities. They also cook up great dinners with a gourmet touch.

€ Molino del Bombo
Santa Lucía s/n, T959-128478, www.molinodelbombo.com.
An appealingly well-priced choice in the city centre, this is run by sound people and is decorated in the new rustic style typical of *casas rurales*. Rooms aren't huge but still offer great value; pay a bit more for a larger room with a small lounge area.

Restaurants

The quality of Aracena's pork products is outstanding; the area's wild mushrooms are also a must in the autumn.

€€€ José Vicente
Av de Andalucía 53, T959-128455.
The best option for piggy products as well as *setas*, this stylish spot serves up huge portions of succulent pork and ham in a/c comfort. There's also an excellent *menú* and a fine selection of mushroom dishes in season. Recommended.

€ Bar Manzano
Plaza del Marqués de Aracena 9, T959-127513.
The throbbing heart of Aracena, this great spot on the pretty main plaza is a cheery sort of place with cakes, wine, generous tapas, tasty wild mushroom dishes, and efficient service. Take a seat outside for a spot of people watching.

€ Casa Sirlache
Av de Andalucía 49, T959-128888, www.setas-sirlache.com.
An excellent bar with a local feel, welcoming service and low prices. Their cuts of pork are seriously tender and tasty. But the *setas* (wild mushrooms) stand out here: in season they are exquisite. Recommended.

Festivals

Feb/Mar **Carnaval** is a lively affair in which an unlucky egg-shaped figure called *Cebolla* (onion) gets ritually burned.
Mid-Oct The **Feria del Jamón** celebrates all things piggy and coincides with the beginning of the *matanza* (pig slaughtering) season.

Transport

Nearly all the services mentioned in this section are run by **Damas**, T902-114492, www.damas-sa.es.

There are 2 weekday buses from **Huelva** to Aracena, and 1 on Sat and Sun. There are 3 buses daily to and from **Sevilla** (1 hr 30 mins); buses linking Sevilla and Lisboa also stop here. There are also daily buses to **Cortegana**, **Aroche**, **Alájar**, **Linares** and **Almonaster**.

Parque Natural Sierra de Aracena y Picos de Aroche → *Colour map 1, B2/B3/B4.*

hilltop white villages, holm oaks and Iberian pigs

The rolling countryside around Aracena is dotted with handsome villages whose inhabitants make their living from livestock farming. Many places have castles from the times of strife with the Portuguese. The region also boasts the capital of *jamón ibérico*, Jabugo. The Parque Natural Sierra de Aracena y Picos de Aroche is extensively wooded with holm oak, the tree whose acorns fatten the Iberian black pigs used for Spain's best cured ham. Cork trees and sweet chestnut trees as well as smaller shrubs also speckle the slopes.

★Zufre

One of the most picturesque villages you could wish to visit and unspoiled by tourism, the eagle's nest of Zufre east of Aracena is a medley of narrow cobbled streets and whitewashed houses that in any other province would have developers queuing up to take the mayor out to lunch. A crooked stony road winds up the hill to the village, from where there are several spots with marvellous views over the surrounding sierra and the Zufre reservoir. The 16th-century brick **Iglesia de la Purísima Concepción** stands on a quiet square facing the exceptional Renaissance Ayuntamiento, with some of its original Romanesque features. It has an Italianate triple arched *loggia* in sober stone and is a most unusual sight for these parts. Zufre also has two towers, once part of the Almohad fortress. There are appealing places to stay here for a quiet village break in off-the-beaten-track Andalucía.

Linares de la Sierra

Pretty Linares is worth the small detour off the principal road to Alájar west out of Aracena, though don't take your car too far into the village, as its narrow cobbled streets are from another era and mean you'll probably have to head back out the same way ... maybe in reverse.

Alájar and Santa Ana la Real

With a name meaning the stone in Arabic, Alájar is one of the area's most popular villages, reached west from Aracena along a narrow, winding road or by a three-hour walk through the wooded hills. Houses with distinctive cobbled thresholds and colourful trimming cluster around the large stone church of **San Marcos**, a late 18th-century Baroque creation with a pointy spire. Nearby is the pretty Plaza de España overlooked by an elegantly tiled mansion.

Above the village is the spectacular weathered crag of **Peña Arias Montano**, named after a notable 16th-century theologian, natural scientist and thinker. The hilltop now receives thousands of visitors to its **chapel** ⓘ *daily 1100-sunset, Jul 1000-2100, free*, whose image of Nuestra Señora Reina de los Angeles inspires much devotion. The typically white and ochre building has a fine wood-panelled ceiling and bright azulejo tiles, as well as low-quality frescoes. The Virgin herself is surprisingly small, a beautiful 13th-century sculpture heavily gilded and set behind

ON THE ROAD

Ham and the matanza

In racist post-Reconquista Spain, converted Jews (*conversos*) and Muslims (*moriscos*) were under the Inquisition's hammer. It was frequently suspected that the conversions weren't genuine. Proving that you were a good Christian in this paranoid climate was vital insurance against ending up on the barbecue; one of the best ways to do this was to openly eat as much pork as possible. The enduring popularity of Spain's piggy products owes much to those times.

The northern part of Huelva province produces much of Spain's finest *jamón serrano*, literally mountain ham, a general term for cured ham. The finest is known as *ibérico* or *pata negra*, and comes from black-footed Iberian pigs. There are many reasons why the meat is so tasty. The Iberian pigs forage freely in large wooded pastures, eating the acorns from holm oaks. They can easily eat 15% of their weight in a day. Pigs are slaughtered at around 18 months; the traditional method of doing this is the *matanza*, or home butchering ceremony. From November to February, villagers butcher their pigs and preserve the meat by making *jamón*, *chorizo* and *morcilla*, a process accompanied by much drinking and socializing.

The hams are cured in sea salt for a few days, cleaned and then hung up to dry in the cool mountain air for up to two years. Many of the Sierra's houses were traditionally designed for this purpose, with a cool basement for the drying. Pig rearing has, however, become more commercialized and large warehouse-like drying sheds are now the norm.

a red marble screen. There are fine views from the spot and a good restaurant. On 8 September, there's a popular *romería* (pilgrimage) to the spot on horseback and in decorated carts, where locals don traditional colourful flamenco dress. The road continues to Fuenteheridos; stop at the mirador for sweeping views.

Almonaster la Real

The striking settlement of Almonaster is crowned by a unique Moorish *mezquita* (mosque), one of the best-preserved in Spain and well worth a stop. An **information centre** ⓘ *C Llana s/n, T959-143006, daily 1100-1400, 1600-1800, a block down the street next to the town hall*, has a good display in Spanish on the Moorish presence in the region and Andalucía in general, and can give out limited information on the village and region.

The **Ermita de Nuestra Señora de la Concepción** ⓘ *daily 0900-sunset*, is worth a visit in its own right. The Visigoths built a church here over Roman remains in the seventh century; this was rebuilt as a mosque by the Moors in the 10th century. You enter under a marble lintel carved with Visigothic Christian symbols; beyond a font open to the air is the five-aisled mosque, with brick arches balanced on columns. The *mihrab* is framed by a horseshoe arch and points at Mecca. Unusually, although it became a church after the Reconquista, very little of the interior has been altered. The back door leads to the tower, with a Renaissance belfry on Moorish foundations. You can climb to the first level for views over the town; be careful if you're with kids, as there are no guard rails.

Cortegana

This busy town isn't as appealing as some of its neighbours, but is striking from a distance with its restored, squared-off **castle** ⓘ *www.castillocortegana.es, Tue-Sun 1100-1400, 1600-1800 (1700-1900 summer), €2,* high on the hill over town. There's a small information office inside the building, featuring a heavily modified two-level keep as well as the *patio de armas* or parade ground. The Moorish *aljibe* (cistern) is well preserved and still holds water. The castle provides the perfect setting for the annual medieval fair during the first week of August. The *mudéjar* **Iglesia del Salvador** in town is also worth a look.

Aroche

In a region of pretty villages, the hilltop pig farming town of Aroche stands out for its relaxed friendliness and cobbled streets lined with white houses with contrasting black wrought-iron balconies. Only 24 km from the border, there's a distinct Portuguese twang to the local accent.

Although many late Neolithic dolmens and menhirs have been found in the region, the town was originally established and fortified by the Romans, who named it Arruci Vetus; the top of the hill is crowned by a low **castle** ⓘ *Oct to mid-May Sat-Sun 1000-1400, 1500-1700, mid-May to Sep Fri-Sun 1100-1500, €2,* built by the Almohads with 10 rectangular towers. Visits start in the Convento de la Cilla, where you buy tickets and which has information on the area, the *parque natural* and the zone's Roman heritage.

Jabugo

Home of Spain's most famous *jamón*, this village is unashamedly devoted solely to ham, as a series of signs showing the backside of a pig cheerfully affirm. It would take a lot of searching to find a better cured meat than the local *pata negra* (see box, page 123). The key is that Jabugo has a perfect climate for drying the hams. It's a prosperous industry but its large drying warehouses mean that the village itself isn't as postcard-pretty as its *serrano* counterparts.

There's a plethora of shops selling the stuff along the main road through town; several of these places have a bar where you can have a drink and train your palate to appreciate the unique Jabugo flavours. From here, a pretty bow-shaped street leads to the main square (Plaza de Jamón, of course), a lovely space with a central fountain, an elegant former casino and a restored Baroque church with a slim bell tower.

Where to stay

Zufre

€€€ Casa Vesta
www.casa-vesta.com.
Offering simply stunning views from its terrace, infinity pool and the superior rooms, this sizeable *cortijo* makes a fine place to relax in style. Often books out for *sevillano* weddings at weekends.

€€ La Tahona
C Hornillo 10, T676-014025, www.latahonazufre.com.
This *casa rural* in the village itself has been beautifully restored and makes a great base with the bonus of beautiful Zufre views. You rent the whole house, which sleeps up to 6 in 3 rooms, but the price is fair even if there's only 1 or 2 of you. There's a log fire (wood provided) and pool. Recommended.

€ Pensión La Posá
C Barranco 5, T959-198110. Closed for a month in winter.
A very likeable and clean spot to stay, with good rooms in a friendly whitewashed house. Facilities are very good for the price, with a common lounge with DVDs and board games by the fire.

Alájar

€€€ Molino Río Alájar
Finca Cabeza del Molino s/n, 1 km from Alájar signposted off the road to Santa Ana, T959-501282, www.molinorioalajar.com.
Set in a tranquil wooded spot by a mill pond, these are delightful stone *casas rurales* of various sizes individually furnished with antiques and equipped with TV and heating. Pick your own veggies from the organic garden. Pool and good local walks; mule rides also available. The minimum stay is 2 nights but rises to a week in Jul and Aug.

€€ Finca La Fronda
Ctra Aracena–Cortegana Km 22, T959-501247, www.fincalafronda.com.
Tucked away off the road between Linares de la Sierra and Alájar, this classy rural hotel has just 7 spacious rooms and offers plenty of clean hill air and peace and quiet for relaxation. Great views over the undulating landscape, tasty breakfasts, wooded grounds and a pool.

€€ La Posada de Alájar
C Médico Emilio González 2, Alájar, T959-125712, www.posadasalajar.com.
A renovated historic inn that has been furnished in attractive rustic style by its welcoming owners. There's plenty of comfort including a log fire and restaurant, which serves locally produced and organic food. Some rooms have balconies and breakfast is included. The same owners run another *posada* in the village. Recommended.

Almonaster la Real

€€€ Posada El Camino
Just east of town, T959-503166, www.posadaelcamino.es.
A stylish conversion from a humble roadside inn, this has 3 classes of room, the best of which have log fires and spacious lounge areas and can easily sleep a whole family. Good restaurant with elaborate versions of traditional dishes (**€€**).

Cortegana

€€ Posada de Cortegana
Ctra El Repilado-La Corte Km 2.5, T959-503301, www.posadadecortegana.es.
Set in a great location for families and those wanting to escape to the hills, this rural hotel is tucked away in a wooded valley by a stream 4 km from Cortegana. Accommodation is in wooden cabins and there is an inviting restaurant with a terrace and a pool. Archery and bike hire are also available.

Jabugo

€€ Finca La Silladilla
Los Romeros, Jabugo, T959-501350, www.silladilla.com.
A few kilometres from Jabugo towards Los Romeros is this secluded finca, studded with holm and cork oaks. There are 5 cottages, decorated in rustic style without skimping on comfort (some even have jacuzzi) dotted around the farm, which is devoted to producing the finest Iberian *jamón* from the pigs that graze it. There are room-only stays in one of the cottages; facilities include pools, a wine cellar and internet access. Horse riding is also available.

Restaurants

Zufre

€€ Casa Pepa
C Portales 10, T959-190128. Open weekends only in winter.
Tasty and generous servings of local specialities, with pork, game dishes, and tasty stews, as well as delicious chestnut desserts in season. Also has simple rooms.

Linares de la Sierra

€€€ Arrieros
C Arrieros 2, T959-463717, www.arrieros.net. Closed evenings off-season.
On one of Linares's typically narrow, grass-between-the-cobbles streets, this offers local ingredients of super quality, presented with a modern touch, with other Mediterranean influences evident. Recommended. They also run the restaurant at the **Convento de Aracena** hotel in Aracena, see page 120.

Almonaster la Real

The best place to eat is **Posada El Camino**; see Where to stay, above.

Jabugo

€ Asador el Mirador de Jabugo
Ctra Jabugo s/n, T625-517507.
This place has an appealing wooden furnished dining room and a terrace with views over the valley that gets lively on summer evenings. Given that you're in Jabugo and the restaurant is run by a pig producer, we suggest pork, which comes out in generous servings at scandalously low prices. They also do good tapas at the long bar.

Festivals

Almonaster la Real

1st week of May **Las Cruces de Mayo** is one of the best fiestas in the region, with several strange pagan elements as well as excellent flamenco and the usual bullfighting, drinking and funfair.

Transport

Nearly all the services mentioned in this section are run by **Damas**, T902-114492, www.damas-sa.es.

Alájar

There are daily buses from **Aracena**, continuing to **Almonaster** and **Cortegana**.

Almonaster la Real

Buses from **Huelva** Mon-Sat (only one on Sat), as well as two from **Aracena**. The train station is 4 km west of town (signposted off the road to Cortegana), and is served twice daily from **Huelva**.

Aroche

A bus leaves **Huelva** for Aroche at 1500 Mon-Fri. The return is at 0645. There are thankfully other ways to get back, as daily buses link Aroche with **Aracena**.

Jabugo

Buses between **Aracena** and **Aroche** pass through Jabugo.

Cádiz

long, sandy beaches, fine sherry and seafood galore

Of all Spain's provinces, Cádiz perhaps offers the greatest variety; it has everything, whether you're into wine, windsurfing, seafood, horses, architecture, beaches or nightlife. With an Atlantic coastline, Cádiz attracts those who love long, sandy beaches

The very wind that has meant minimal development is what makes Costa de la Luz popular with wind and kitesurfers. Clear views of Morocco add a spicy African feel to relaxed places like Tarifa, while curious Gibraltar marks the entrance to the Mediterranean.

Cádiz city appeals for its promontory setting, maze of narrow streets, fabulous beach and wonderfully irreverent inhabitants. The city that celebrates Spain's most cutting-edge Carnaval still carries whispers of its past maritime greatness; it also has a cracking nightlife. Contrasting Jerez de la Frontera is a staid, dignified place, centre of the wealthy sherry trade and the famed Carthusian horses. There's more sherry in the towns west of Jerez: the favoured summer spots of El Puerto de Santa María and Sanlúcar de Barrameda.

The province's hilly interior is speckled with whitewashed villages; many conserve their original Moorish street plan. The mountains around Grazalema have some of Andalucía's best walking.

Best for
Kitesurfing ■ Seafood ■ Sherry ■ Walking ■ Windsurfing

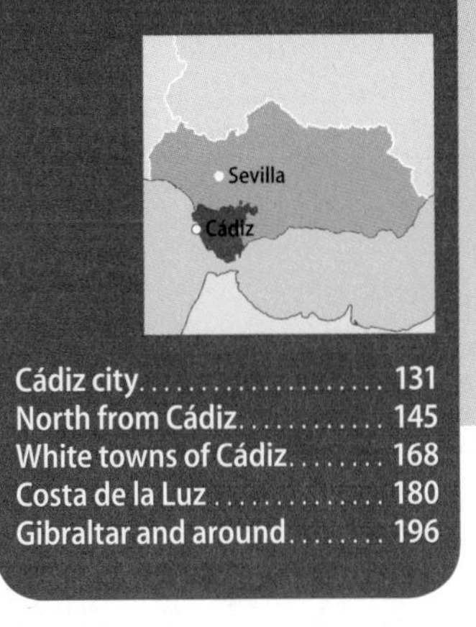

Footprint picks

★ **Cádiz's Barrio del Pópulo**, page 133

Explore the atmospheric fishermen's barrios of this tight-knit promontory city.

★ **Bajo de Guía**, page 152

Sip a *manzanilla* in this beachfront fishermen's suburb and watch the sunset.

★ **Jerez de la Frontera**, page 156

Get absorbed into the world of flamenco in the fascinating Barrio de Santiago.

★ **White Towns**, page 168

Stroll the postcard-perfect streets of these hill towns.

★ **Zahara de los Atunes**, page 187

Enjoy the wild breakers of this tuna-fishing village.

★ **Kitesurfing in Tarifa**, page 190

Soar like a seabird on a kitesurfing course on this long beach.

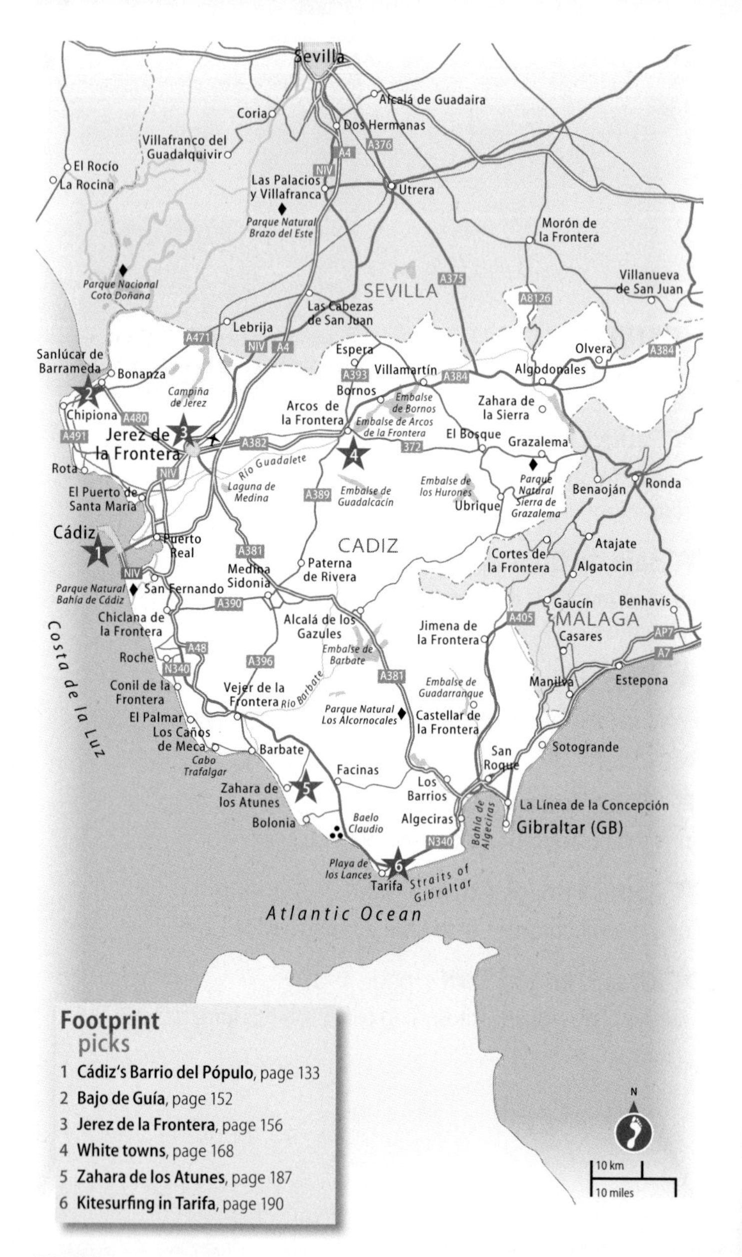
Sevilla
Alcalá de Guadaira
Coria
Dos Hermanas
Villafranco del Guadalquivir
El Rocío
La Rocina
Las Palacios y Villafranca
Utrera
Parque Natural Brazo del Este
Morón de la Frontera
Parque Nacional Coto Doñana
Villanueva de San Juan
SEVILLA
Las Cabezas de San Juan
Lebrija
Espera
Olvera
Sanlúcar de Barrameda
Bonanza
Villamartín
Algodonales
Bornos
Campiña de Jerez
Embalse de Bornos
Zahara de la Sierra
Arcos de la Frontera
Chipiona
Embalse de Arcos de la Frontera
Jerez de la Frontera
El Bosque
Grazalema
Río Guadalete
Rota
Embalse de los Hurones
Parque Natural Sierra de Grazalema
Benaoján
Ronda
Laguna de Medina
Embalse de Guadalcacín
Ubrique
El Puerto de Santa María
Cádiz
Puerto Real
CADIZ
Atajate
Cortes de la Frontera
Algatocin
Paterna de Rivera
Medina Sidonia
Parque Natural Bahía de Cádiz
San Fernando
Gaucín
Benhavís
MALAGA
Chiclana de la Frontera
Alcalá de los Gazules
Jimena de la Frontera
Casares
Embalse de Barbate
Costa de la Luz
Roche
Conil de la Frontera
Vejer de la Frontera
Río Barbate
Embalse de Guadarranque
Manilva
Estepona
Parque Natural Los Alcornocales
Castellar de la Frontera
El Palmar
Los Caños de Meca
Cabo Trafalgar
Barbate
San Roque
Sotogrande
Facinas
Zahara de los Atunes
Los Barrios
Bahía de Algeciras
La Línea de la Concepción
Bolonia
Baelo Claudio
Algeciras
Gibraltar (GB)
Playa de los Lances
Tarifa
Straits of Gibraltar
Atlantic Ocean
A4
A376
NIV
A375
A8126
A471
A384
A393
A480
A491
A382
372
A389
A381
A390
A405
AP7
A7
A48
N340
A396
Footprint picks
1 Cádiz's Barrio del Pópulo, page 133
2 Bajo de Guía, page 152
3 Jerez de la Frontera, page 156
4 White towns, page 168
5 Zahara de los Atunes, page 187
6 Kitesurfing in Tarifa, page 190
N
10 km
10 miles

Cádiz city

Cádiz, one of Spain's most vibrant and lovable cities, was memorably described by Laurie Lee as "a scribble of white on a sheet of blue glass, lying curved on the bay like a scimitar and sparkling with African light". Its location is certainly spectacular, on a long narrow promontory with the Atlantic on one side and the Bahía de Cádiz on the other.

With a proud and long maritime history stretching back to the Phoenicians, it comes as no surprise that Cádiz can seem less conservative and more outward looking than many Andalucían cities; geographically it's not far off being an island, and culturally it's typified by its riotous Carnaval.

Earthquakes and buccaneering have deprived it of monuments, but it's still a cracking place with the sea seemingly at the end of every narrow street. Watching the sunset from the beach or promenade is an experience to compare with any in Andalucía. The architecture of the old town is an elegant blend of 18th- and 19th-century houses, while beyond the old city gates stretches the interminable Avenida de Andalucía, running parallel to the town's long beaches and nightlife zone. *Colour map 4, B1.*

Sights

picturesque narrow streets, lively nightlife and a rich maritime history

One of the charms of Cádiz is simply wandering around its maze of streets; the attractive whitewashed houses typically have glassed-in balconies. Barrio del Pópulo, to the east of the cathedral, is one of the most traditional districts, as is Barrio de la Viña, the blocks behind Castillo de San Sebastián. One of the streets here, Calle Pastora, is picturesquely festooned with flowerpots painted in the colours of the local football team. After a thorough restoration programme these historic barrios are looking rather spruce these days, without having lost their maritime character.

Cathedral

Plaza de la Catedral s/n, T956-286154. Mon-Sat 1000-1830, Sun 1330-1830, €5 including museum, free entry to cathedral only Sun 1130-1230.

Especially picturesque when viewed from further around the waterfront, with its golden dome glinting, Cádiz's cathedral was built in the 18th and 19th centuries. Its main façade on Plaza de la Catedral is a blend of the late Baroque and the neoclassical and flanked by two graceful white towers. The interior is rather sombre and somewhat reminiscent of a Roman necropolis, with huge Corinthian columns looming in the shadows. A fine feature is the wonderful choir of cedar and mahogany, with carved figures of saints. The crypt below is a brilliantly realized space in stone; the architectural precision is reflected by the astonishing echoes produced. The *gaditano* composer Manuel de Falla is buried here.

Also worth looking out for are the elegant sacristy and a large monstrance used in the sober Corpus Christi processions. The effect of the high central dome is rather ruined by the netting that protects visitors from falling masonry.

Entry to the cathedral includes admission to its museum, tucked around the side on Plaza de Fray Félix. This is set in a charming building with an old columned patio that is more interesting than the artwork, particularly as an excavated Roman road runs through it. Of the paintings on display, a picture of the fierce Anglo-Dutch sacking of the town in 1596 stands out, as do two 16th-century works of the Judas Kiss and the Crowning of Thorns. Some massive 16th- to 19th-century pergamines sit in a large bookcase; in the same room is a letter from St Teresa to the Inquisitor-General sealed in an ivory reliquary. A collection of carved 17th- to 18th-century ivory crucifixes show fine craftsmanship.

One of the cathedral's towers, the **Torre de Poniente** ⓘ *T956-251788, www.torredeponiente.com, daily 1000-1800 (2000 in summer), entry by guided tour every 30 mins, €5*, can be climbed as part of a guided tour. There are views over the Atlantic and along the coast.

Tip...

Cádiz city, Jerez de la Frontera and El Puerto de Santa María are all pretty close together and well connected by public transport, so it's easy to base yourself in one to explore all three.

★Barrio del Pópulo

This was the heart of medieval Cádiz and is a small network of charming buildings and narrow streets that has tangibly benefited from recent refurbishment. On the Plaza de la Catedral, look out for the gateway with embrasures that marks the entrance to the district. Near the cathedral on the waterfront is a **Roman theatre** ⓘ *Mon and Wed-Sun 1000-1430, free*, dating to the first century BC, while on Calle San Juan de Dios is another of the gateways to the barrio, as well as a stretch of the old walls. The later walls, built after the attack of 1596, have mostly been taken down.

Tucked away behind the cathedral is the intriguing **Casa del Obispo** ⓘ *Plaza Fray Félix 5, T956-264734, daily 1000-1730 (1930 summer), €5*. The layers beneath this former bishop's residence have been peeled back to reveal remains of buildings from all of Cádiz's phases of occupation. It's an astonishing if sometimes confusing archaeological tour-de-force, exhibiting the foundations of Phoenician walls, fragments of Roman wall painting, part of what was possibly a Punic temple, and more. In one area once the episcopal stables, you can really see the superimposition of one civilization upon the ruins of the last; it's contemplation of this, rather than struggling to understand individual stones, that makes the place fascinating.

At the edge of this barrio, the Plaza San Juan de Dios is dominated by the attractive **Ayuntamiento** (town hall), a typical example of neoclassical *gaditano* architecture. Nearby is a beautiful neo-Moorish former tobacco factory, dating from 1741. Further south is the main entrance to the city, the 18th-century **Puerta de Tierra**

Essential Cádiz

Finding your feet

Cádiz city is forced by geography into being very long and thin. While the old town is reasonably compact and easily explored on foot, the new town is not. The old town occupies the tip of the promontory; the extensive new town stretches several kilometres along the main town beach, Playa de la Victoria. This part of town is known as Puerta de Tierra, named after the city gates that give access to the old town.

Getting around

Bus No 1 runs every five minutes from the Plaza de España in Cádiz right down the length of the new town. You can also head to the new town by the cercanía train, which runs every 40 minutes or so, with several stops along the length of the beach. Segunda Aguada is the closest to the heart of the action. A journey in a cab from Plaza San Juan de Dios in the old town to the bars of the Paseo Marítimo should cost €5-7. There are plenty of ranks; otherwise T956-212121.

When to go

Cádiz's Carnaval in February or March is an unforgettable experience (see box, page 143), but you'll have to book accommodation well ahead. The city is at its liveliest in summer, when the beaches are packed day and night.

Time required

At least a day or two to see the city's main sights.

Cádiz

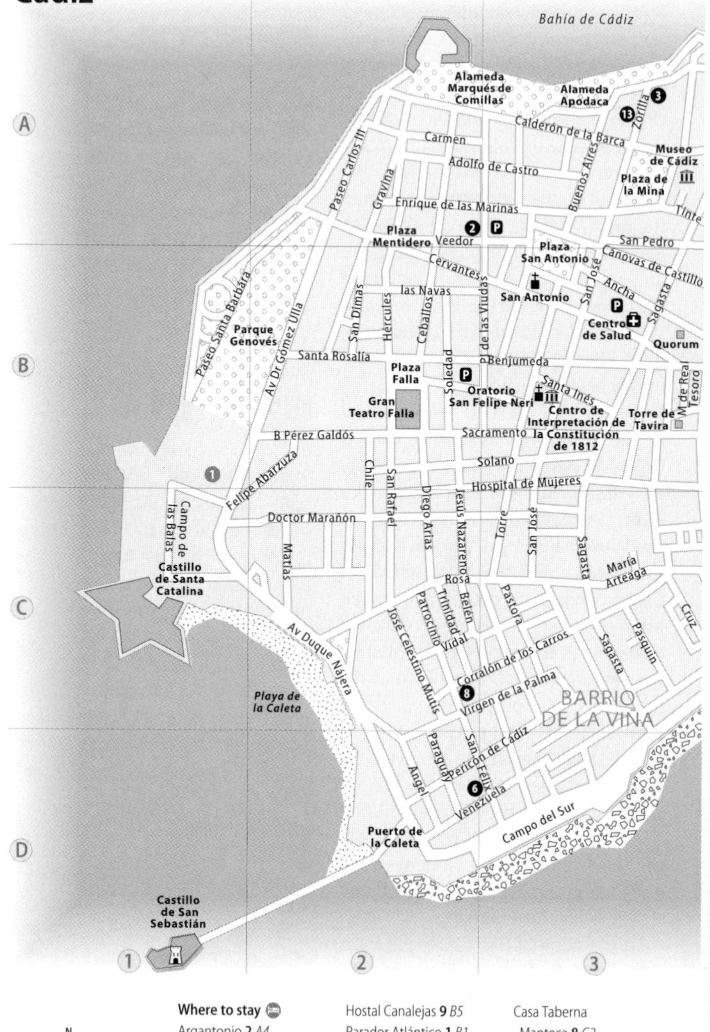

Where to stay
Argantonio **2** *A4*
Casa Caracol **11** *B5*
Convento de Cádiz **12** *B6*
Cuatro Naciones **7** *B5*
Hospedería Las Cortes de Cádiz **8** *A4*
Hostal Canalejas **9** *B5*
Parador Atlántico **1** *B1*
Playa Victoria **19** *C6*
Spa Cádiz Plaza **5** *C6*

Restaurants
Arte Serrano **10** *C6*
Casa Taberna Manteca **8** *C2*
El Balandro **3** *A3*
El Faro **6** *D2*
Freiduría Las Flores **12** *B4, C6*
Habana Café **24** *B4*

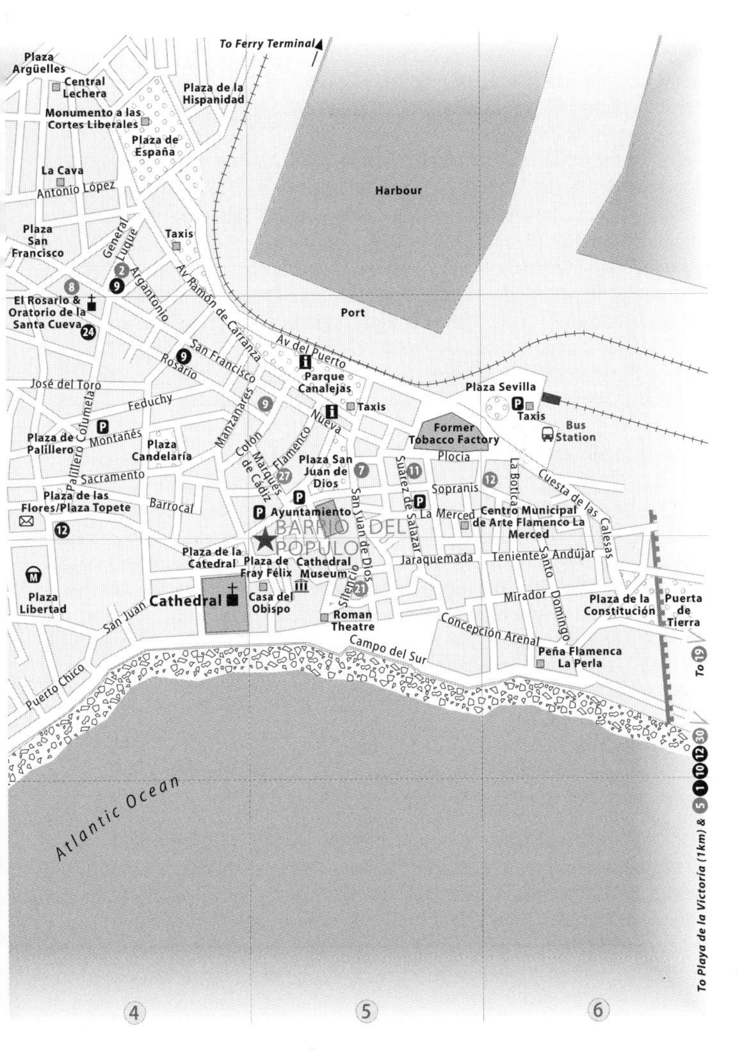

La Gorda te da de Comer **9** *A4, B4*
Mesón Cumbres Mayores **13** *A3*
Ventorillo del Chato **1** *C6*

Bars & clubs
Bar Veedor **2** *A2*
Carbonera **27** *B5*
El Pay-Pay **21** *C5*
Taberna La Hispaniola **30** *C6*

ⓘ *Plaza de la Constitución s/n, T956-288296, Tue-Sun 1000-1400, 1730-2030 (2130 summer), free*, which marks the boundary of the old and new towns. Though still an impressively muscular fortification, it was once much larger, offering the city complete protection from land assault. You can climb to the top of the tower and roam along the sturdy walls.

Moving the other way from the cathedral, and following the waterfront, with rocks pounded by the Atlantic, you'll pass another historic barrio on your right, the **Barrio de la Viña**, before reaching the **Castillo de San Sebastián**. This fort is set on a small islet (joined to the mainland by a causeway in the 19th century) where some say the Phoenician temple of Melqart-Hercules once stood. It's a relaxing stroll out to the castle, now a lighthouse, but you can't enter the building itself.

Beyond is another castle, **Santa Catalina**, constructed after the British attacked. Built in a star shape to maximize firing arcs, it also has a small chapel. Between the two castles is **Playa de la Caleta** beach, backed by massive dragon trees. It's a legendary Cádiz spot, but in truth is not a remarkable beach.

Plaza de la Mina and around

In the north part of the old town, Plaza de la Mina is a large square near which are some of the city's best tapas bars. On the square itself is the excellent Museo de Cádiz (see below). On the south side of the square a plaque marks the house where the composer Manuel de Falla was born. Just east of here is another pleasant square, **Plaza San Francisco**, while to the south the larger **Plaza San Antonio** is dominated by its twin-towered Baroque church. North of Plaza de la Mina are the soothing waterside gardens, the **Alameda Marqués de Comillas**, which end at a defensive gun battery. East of the gardens, the large **Plaza de España** is marked by a monument to the Cádiz *cortes liberales*.

Museo de Cádiz

Plaza de la Mina s/n, T956-203368. Summer Tue-Sun 1000-1700, mid-Sep to mid-Jun Tue-Sat 1000-2030, Sun 1000-1700. Free for EU citizens, €1.50 for others.

This excellent museum, one of the best in Andalucía, comprises both an archaeological and a fine arts section. The former, on the ground floor, is particularly notable for its **Phoenician** collection, with many finds from tombs in Cádiz and the surrounding area. There was an important temple of Melqart-Hercules here, as well as one of Astarte. In this section are some fine votive bronzes and terracotta busts, but the most striking objects are two huge anthropoid sarcophagi, one male, one female, carved from marble, and exhibiting strong stylistic influences from both Egypt and Greece. Found nearly a century apart, they both date from around 400 BC and show that, even this late, the city still had important ties with its founders' homeland in the Eastern Mediterranean; throughout the ages, trade has been Cádiz's lifeline.

The **Roman** collection includes some reconstructed burials and displays of grave goods and funerary plaques. There are also some fine sculptures, particularly a large one of the (Andalucían) Emperor Trajan found at Baelo Claudia.

BACKGROUND

Cádiz

Cádiz has a claim to being Western Europe's oldest city. It was founded as Gadir by the Phoenicians, possibly as early as 1100 BC. Later classical sources claimed that the inhabitants of Tyre were told by an oracle to found a settlement beyond the Pillars of Hercules. The Phoenician name for the city lives on; today's inhabitants are called *gaditanos*. Archaeological discoveries indicate that ties to the Eastern Mediterranean remained strong even once Phoenician sea power had waned. The heirs and descendants of the Phoenicians, the Carthaginians, also established an important presence here. Caesar conferred full Roman citizenship on the *gaditanos* after the town helped him against Pompeii, but the city declined rapidly in the late Roman era and did not play a prominent part in the Moorish era. Cádiz began to benefit from the discovery of the Americas, and prospered greatly once the monopoly for Atlantic trade was moved here from Sevilla in the 18th century. The city's new status attracted the attention of foreign powers, which regularly came to loot the town.

During the Peninsular War, brave liberals invoked the ancient Spanish regional privileges and set up a parliament to rule in the absence of the king. These *cortes* drew up a constitution in 1812, which established a democratic parliamentary monarchy that became a blueprint for constitutional movements throughout Europe. The returning king, Fernando, revoked it, but it was re-proclaimed by a rebellious army colonel, Rafael de Riego, in 1820. Such was his support that the king admitted the legality of the 1812 document, but soon went back on his promise. In the wake of another advancing French army, the *cortes* fled back to Cádiz and surrendered in September 1823. Riego was executed. In the Civil War, Cádiz was firmly on the side of the left, but *Rusia chica* (little Russia), as it was known, couldn't hold out against the Nationalists. Franco banned Cádiz s exuberant Carnaval, but it survived by changing its name and date.

Upstairs, the **art section** has some excellent works. From the 15th century is a fine *Virgin Enthroned* by the Flemish Master of St Ursula, but the highlight is a fine series of Zurbarán's works from the Carthusian monastery at Jerez. The white-robed saints are painted with the artist s usual expressive treatment of cloth; the fact that he used monks as models makes the figures especially realistic. Another series of monastery paintings here are by Francisco Osorio, who took on the job when his teacher, Murillo, died. Murillo is, however, represented by a Stigmata of St Francis. A portrait of a young Carlos II on horseback is a work of the underrated Asturian court painter Juan Carreño de Miranda; in the European section are two fine Giordanos and a small Rubens *Virgin and Child*, looking extremely Dutch. Among more recent works include a portrait by Ignacio Zuloaga, a Miró canvas, and the disturbing *Los Frutos*, by the postmodern *tarifeño* Guillermo Pérez Villalta.

Other sights

Near the museum, the **Oratorio de la Santa Cueva** ⓘ *Rosario s/n, T956-222262, Mon-Fri 1030-1400, 1630-2000, Sat 1030-1400, Sun 1000-1300, €3,* is a small chapel attached to El Rosario church. The two-tiered chapel, the lower sober neoclassical, the upper more extravagant late Baroque, contains three Goya canvases; serious works depicting the *Loaves and the Fishes*, the *Last Supper*, and the *Wedding Guest*.

South of Plaza San Antonio is another oratory, the **Oratorio San Felipe Neri** ⓘ *C Santa Inés s/n, Tue-Fri 1030-1400, 1630-2000, Sat 1030-1400, Sun 1000-1300, €3*. It was in here in 1812 that the historic Constitution was proclaimed and the *cortes* declared in session. The ellipsoid church has two tiers of balconies where the members sat. Plaques on the walls from all over the globe commemorate the event, which had an important impact on politics throughout the world. In the *retablo* is a fine *Immaculate Conception* by Murillo. More information on the period and the Constitution is to be had in the adjacent **Centro de Interpretación de la Constitución de 1812** ⓘ *Pl San Felipe Neri, T697 959 727, Tue-Sun 1100-1400, free*, an innovative modern exhibition with slick multimedia displays.

Near here, it's worth seeking out the neo-Moorish **Gran Teatro Falla**, a striking building with striped horseshoe arches. A couple of blocks east of the Oratorio is the **Plaza de las Flores**, officially called the Plaza Topete and full of flower stalls; next to here is the market.

The **Torre de Tavira** ⓘ *C Marqués del Real Tesoro 10, T956-212910, daily 1000-1800 (2000 summer, last entry 30 mins before closing), €6*, is a slim 18th-century tower with great views over the city. Another perspective is given by the fascinating **Camera Obscura**, a table-top on to which a magnified reflected image of the moving city is projected. There's also a small exhibition on the city.

Beaches

The city's best and biggest beach is **Playa de la Victoria**, a long strip of clean sand and water in the new part of town. Bus No 1 runs here from the old town every five minutes or so; it's also just a short walk from the cathedral to the beginning of the strand. In summer it's a hive of activity with beach bars and *discotecas*; the streets behind are also full of eating and drinking options.

Tourist information

Junta de Andalucía tourist office
C Nueva s/n, T956-258646. Mon-Fri 0900-1900, Sat and Sun 1000-1430.
Handily situated, this helpful tourist office has information on the province. Nearby, the municipal office (T956 241001, www.turismo.cadiz.es, Mon-Fri 0830-1830, to 1900 summer, Sat-Sun 0900-1700), occupies a kiosk in the Parque Canalejas. They also have summer offices at both Playa de la Victoria and Playa de la Caleta, and on Av Carranza near the football stadium.

Where to stay

There's plenty of good accommodation in the old town, mostly in the *hostal* category, but with a growing number of hotels too. The new town has several hotels near or on the beach but little in the budget category. Book ahead in summer and for Carnaval you'll need to reserve several months in advance; prices for even basic rooms are sky high at this time. The following price codes reflect summer rates; things drop substantially outside the beach season.

€€€€ Hotel Playa Victoria
Glorieta Ingeniero de la Cierva 4, T956-205100, www.palafoxhoteles.com.
Luxurious and innovative, this striking large hotel sits in the most lively part of the new town, with the beach an elevator ride away and the best eating and drinking within a minute's stroll. All the rooms have a spacious balcony: the even numbers look out to the ocean, the odds face inland but give you a smidgen of sea view; there's also a pool with plenty of loungers, and various amenities throughout.

€€€€ Parador Atlántico
Av Duque de Nájera 9, T956-226905, www.parador.es.
With an excellent location at the tip of the Cádiz promontory and the Barrio de la Viña's enticing eating options in easy reach, this fabulously renovated hotel offers marvellous views, spacious modern rooms with confident contemporary design, and a brilliant pool area. Recommended.

€€€ Hospedería Las Cortes de Cádiz
C San Francisco 9, T956-220489, www.hotel lascortes.com.
In the heart of the old town, this spot makes a great base. Built around a central patio, it's all yellow ochre and white balcony rails, giving a cool, light feel. The rooms are inviting, with high wooden bedheads and modern comforts like digital TV and a/c. Pick an exterior room if you can: the noise from the bustling street is worth it for the extra light. There are views from the roof as well as a gym and sauna.

€€€ Hotel Spa Cádiz Plaza
Glorieta Ingeniero La Cierva 3, T956-079190, www.hotelcadizplaza.com.
This place offers bright and sparky rooms, some with sea views and balconies, in optimistic colour schemes just a few metres from the beach. Spa complex and upbeat and helpful staff. Bikes and beach gear for hire.

€€ Hotel Argantonio
C Argantonio 3, T956-211640, www.hotelargantonio.com.

This hotel is a sound choice. It occupies a solid old house in a narrow old town street, and has Moorish-inspired decor and very friendly service. Offers good value for this level of comfort. Rates include breakfast. Recommended.

€€ Hostal Canalejas
C Colón 5, T956-264113, www.hostalcanalejas.com.
This *hostal* offers more facilities than most of the choices in this central cluster of accommodation, with a lift and off-street parking (at a cost). The rooms have a/c and heating, though they'll never host the world cat-swinging championships.

€€ Hotel Convento Cádiz
C Santo Domingo 2, T956-200738, www.hotelconventocadiz.com.
Charmingly set around a 17th-century monastery cloister attached to the Santo Domingo church, this hotel has simple modern rooms that offer great value. The location very near the train station is handy too.

€ Casa Caracol
C Suárez de Salazar 4, T956-261166, www.caracolcasa.com.
In a narrow street in the old town, handy for the train station, this backpacker hostel is a cheerful place that wins more points for atmosphere than facilities. It's friendly, but comforts like decent mattresses and lockers are absent. Sleeping is in noisy 4-bed dorms (€17-25) and there's a roof terrace with hammocks. Book ahead. Hard to find; look for the snail sign.

€ Cuatro Naciones
C Plocia 3, T956-255539.
Simple but clean rooms with tartan blankets in a great central location. There's a modern shared bathroom, the place is surprisingly quiet, and the management are friendly. Under different management and in various locations, **Cuatro Naciones** has been a *fonda* for over 150 years.

Restaurants

Cádiz is one of Andalucía's best places to eat, with seafood restaurants jostling with lively tapas bars. The old town's best choices are somewhat scattered, but the area around Plaza de la Mina, especially C Zorilla, is good for tapas, as is the Paseo Marítimo on the beach in the new town, and the streets around C Virgen de la Palma in Barrio de la Viña.

A really enjoyable social snacking scene is to be found in the renovated Plaza Libertad market in the heart of the old town. Here many of the market stalls do tasting plates and tapas, which you can accompany with a beer or glass of wine. It's a top place to be at the weekend.

€€€ El Faro
C San Félix 15, T956-229916, www.elfarodecadiz.com.
This whitewashed little place with a row of tavern lamps outside looks like a humble enough spot at first glance, but is actually one of the region's most celebrated fish restaurants, and deservedly so. The menu and wine list are excellent; some recommendations include *rape con pasas y jerez* (monkfish stewed in raisins and sherry), any of the rice dishes, overflowing with fishy flavours, and the *paté de cabracho*, a tasty scorpionfish mousse. Prices are reasonable for this level of quality; there's also a tapas bar where you can enjoy cheaper but equally perfect fare.

€€ Arte Serrano
Paseo Marítimo 2, T956-277258, www.arteserrano.com.
In a large building on the beachfront promenade, this is one of Puerta de Tierra's most visited spots. In the massive but warm space, you can sit down and enjoy the seafood or browse the extensive tapas menu standing at the long bar. Tapas range from €2 to €3.50 and are delicious. There's also a big covered terrace.

€€ El Balandro
Alameda Apodaca 22, T956-220992, www.restaurantebalandro.com.
A large and sophisticated seafood restaurant and tapas bar with a comfortable dining area overlooking the bay. The fresh local fish and salads are tasty and the prices are very reasonable for the quality. At the bar there's courteous service and fine wines by the glass, among the busy buzz of upmarket *gaditanos*. Tapas here are €4-6 but 2 of them are a meal.

€€ El Ventorrillo del Chato
Ctra Cádiz-San Fernando s/n, T956-257116, www.ventorrilloelchato.com.
By the beach just outside of the city, this place has plenty of character and history but doesn't rest on those. Excellent seafood with innovative touches and warm, friendly service make this worth seeking out. Head out of Cádiz, taking the San Fernando road, and you ll see it on the right shortly after leaving the urban area. Recommended.

€€ Mesón Cumbres Mayores
C Zorilla 4, T856-072242, www.mesoncumbresmayores.com.
This ultra-atmospheric spot is as good as it ever was, and is one of Andalucía's most lovable tapas bars. It oozes character from creaking wooden beams, lively range of customers, hanging ham and garlic. The staff are on the ball, and will recommend from their long tapas list. *Diablillos* are dates wrapped in bacon; the pork *secreto* or a *carrillada* are also worth trying. It's also a fine place to sit down and eat, with efficient service at the tables out the back. You'll never try tastier pork cuts, with the mixed grill for two a good way to try a variety. Recommended.

€ Bar El Veedor
Corner of C Veedor and Vea Murguía, T956-212694.
This long narrow establishment sells delicious hams and cheeses and has a great bar where you can try them, along with a fabulous range of tortillas and other tasty bites.

€ Casa Taberna Manteca
C Corralón de los Carros s/n, T956-213603.
One of the city's favourite tapas bars, this lively spot is decked out with flamenco and bullfighting photos. The tapas are all *chacinas* (hams, sausage, cured pork, cheeses), and are served on squares of greaseproof paper. The ham melts like butter in the mouth and the service is keen and friendly. For atmosphere there are few better bars in Andalucía. Highly recommended.

€ Freiduría Las Flores
C Brasil s/n and Plaza de Topete 4, T956-289378.
Las Flores is a Cádiz institution, with locations in the old and new towns. What they do is fried seafood, and they do it exceptionally well and cheerily. Take away and munch on the beach; you can also graze on tapas at the bar or sit down for larger portions.

€ La Gorda te da de Comer
C General Luque 1, T607-539946.
A busy and friendly bar with chatty staff, brightly painted walls, wooden tables and a touch of the 1970s thrown in. La Gorda (the fat lady) turns out to be the gay chef, and he turns out generous tapas of typical Cádiz dishes for low prices.

Cafés

Habana Café
C Rosario 21, www.habanacafecadiz.com.
In the centre of the shopping district, this light white space offers a serene spot for an early evening drink. Things liven up a little later and the barman makes very decent mojitos and other cocktails.

Bars and clubs

Cádiz has excellent nightlife all year round. In summer, the focus is on the beach, while for the rest of the year it s around Punta San Felipe. This pier jutting into the bay has many bars as well as the city's best *discoteca*. In the new town, the Paseo Marítimo beyond C Brasil has many bars, as does C General Muñoz Arenillas. On the beach in summer are numerous *chiringuitos*, which pump their music late and loud.

Carbonera
C Marqués de Cádiz 1, T956-272800.
This sort of bar is disappearing in Spain, replaced by more fashion-conscious watering holes. The centenarian establishment defines authentic, with its faded tiles, weathered old men and barrels of simple, tasty, and cheap *finos* and *manzanillas*; an exercise in simplicity a few steps from the town hall square.

El Pay-Pay
C Silencio 1, T956-252543, www.cafeteatropaypay.com. Wed-Sat from 2200, also Sun and Tue in summer.
Once an elegant society café, then a high-class brothel, this place has been reopened as a bar and music venue. There are frequent live shows, ranging from flamenco to comedy to jazz and blues, as well as exhibitions of photos and paintings. Whatever's on, there are always plenty of people drinking in the characterful interior until late.

Taberna La Nueva Hispaniola
Paseo Marítimo 23, T956-258458.
Set sail for the Spanish Main! This fabulous beachside bar recreates the glory days of the pirate, but is anything but tacky. Loads of effort has been put into making it feel like a cross between a galleon and a bar of the era, with beer served in tankards. They also do tasty food.

Entertainment

Flamenco

Centro Municipal de Arte Flamenco La Merced, *Plaza Merced s/n, T956-285189, www.cadiz.es.* This performance and rehearsal space normally has a couple of performances a week, most of them free.
La Cava, *C Antonio López 16, T956-211866, www.flamencolacava.com.* Has a good flamenco show on Tue, Thu and Sat (also Wed and Fri Jul-Sep). It's quite a dressy spot. Entry to the show is €22; this includes a drink.
Peña Flamenca La Perla de Cádiz, *C Carlos Ollero s/n, T956-259101, www.perladecadiz.es.* By the sea at the edge of the old town, this spacious venue has regular live performances: check the website for upcoming events. Fri at 2200 (€3) is a fixture.

ON THE ROAD

Cádiz Carnaval

Cádiz has always half faced away from Spain, out to sea, and it's no surprise that the carnival here is very different to those in the rest of the peninsula. Part of this can be ascribed to the independent *gaditanos* themselves, and part to the extensive contact and interchange Cádiz enjoyed with cities such as Venice and Genoa.

The party in Cádiz goes on for nine days, although it centres on Shrove Tuesday. Everyone wears fancy dress and takes to the streets for much drinking and merriment. There's plenty of live music and other performances, but the most famous come from the *agrupaciones*, groups of musicians and comedians who satirize contemporary political figures and events. The best loved are the *chirigotas*, choirs of 10 singers accompanied by guitar, bombo and a wooden box used as a drum. Their songs are usually the most biting and sung to popular folk tunes. During the week, these groups, as well as roaming the streets, compete for a prestigious prize in the Falla theatre. There are plenty of impromptu musical gatherings on the streets too, whether it be flamenco or some of Cádiz's more exotic rhythms such as sambas or creole beats. There are several parades, and a daily ear-splitting explosion of firecrackers in Plaza San Juan de Dios known as *La Toronda* (the thunderclap).

It's difficult and expensive to get accommodation in Cádiz over *Carnaval*. It should be booked several months or more in advance. Even nearby cities like El Puerto de Santa María are usually full. If you can't get a bed try nearby towns like El Puerto de Santa María or San Fernando. Plenty of people stay up all night and then get the train back to Jerez or Sevilla, only to return for the next night's festivities. The atmosphere on this party train can be colourful in itself.

Festivals

Feb/Mar The city is world-famous for its riotous 9-day **Carnaval** (www. carnavalde cadiz.com; see box, above).
7 Oct A smaller fiesta to celebrate the city's patron, **La Virgen del Rosario**.

What to do

Bike hire

Urban Bike Cádiz, *C Marqués de Valdeiñigo 4, T856-170164, Magistral Cabrera 7, T856-170164, www. urbanbikecadiz.es*. In the new town, bikes for hire and guided bike tours of the city. Ring ahead for weekend rentals.

Football

Although outside the top flight at time of writing, going to watch Cádiz football team is one of Spain's more memorable sporting experiences. In contrast to many Spanish teams' hardcore fans, the Cádiz support is leftwing, committedly anti-racist, and prefer their team to lose pretty than to win ugly. The stadium, the Ramón Carranza, is in the new town, close to the beach. The fans' relentless good humour and sportsmanship give the games a fiesta atmosphere.
Estadio Carranza, *T956-070165, www.cadizcf.com.*

Transport

Airport
Cádiz city has no airport, but is close to the international airport of Jerez de la Frontera.

Bus
Intercity buses arrive and depart from next to the train station (see below), close to the centre.

The city is well connected by public transport, and is easily reached by bus from Sevilla or by bus from Málaga. The main company is **Comes**, T956-291168, www.tgcomes.es, who run 9-10 daily buses to **Sevilla** (1 hr 45 mins). **Málaga** is targeted 4 times a day (4 hrs); there are also several daily buses to **Granada, Córdoba** and **Ronda**. **Madrid** is served 4 times daily (8 hrs) by **Socibus**, T956-257415, www.socibus.es.

Within Cádiz province, **Comes** runs roughly hourly to **Jerez** (40 mins) and very frequently to El Puerto de Santa María (30 mins), 6 a day to **Tarifa** (1 hr 30 mins), 8 to **Algeciras** (with 2 continuing to **La Línea** for Gibraltar), and 6-8 to **Barbate**, as well as other coastal destinations. Inland, **Arcos de la Frontera** is reached 3-8 times daily, **Ubrique** 2-4 times and **Medina Sidonia** 2-3 times.

There are also regular buses to **Chipiona** via **Sanlúcar de Barrameda** (1 hr 15 mins).

Car
Most traffic reaches the peninsula of Cádiz via the Ramón de Carranza bridge, with a parallel bridge, Puente de la Pepa, under construction. The latter will make for faster access to the old centre.

Car rental **Bahía**, Plaza de Sevilla s/n, T956-870047, www.bahiarentacar.com.

Ferry
There's a catamaran service that nips across the bay to El Puerto de Santa María more than hourly on weekdays and 5 times at weekends, 30 mins, €2.65 each way. There's also a service to Rota.

Trasmediterránea, Av Ramón de Carranza 26, T956-292811, www.trasmediterranea.es, runs a weekly ferry to the **Canary Islands**, stopping at Arrecife, Las Palmas, **Santa Cruz de Tenerife** and **Santa Cruz de la Palma**. Currently leaving Cádiz on Tue, it takes 38 hrs to Las Palmas and about 48 hrs to Tenerife. The crossing tends to be rough, and it's not great value compared with the flight deals available.

Train
Cádiz's train station is by the port near the city centre, T902-240202.

There are 10-12 daily trains to **Sevilla** (1 hr 45 mins) via **Puerto de Santa María** and **Jerez**. Several of these connect with trains to **Málaga**, **Granada**, or **Almería** in Dos Hermanas; 1 continues to **Jaén** (5 hrs). There are 2 daily fast trains for **Madrid** (5 hrs). **El Puerto de Santa María** and **Jerez** are also served by regular *cercanía* trains every 30 mins. The trip to El Puerto takes 35 mins, and to Jerez 45-50 mins.

North from Cádiz

Across the bay from Cádiz, the sherry-producing town of El Puerto de Santa María is but a short boat trip away and a favourite spot for a seafood lunch. With several notable buildings, this town is an important bullfighting centre and was once home to surrealist poet Rafael Alberti. In summer, this genteel place changes completely, becoming the focus of some of Andalucía's craziest nightlife.

Further west, on the edge of the inspiring Coto Doñana wetlands, Sanlúcar de Barrameda is also a centre for sherry; the dry wines produced here, tangy with sea salt, are called *manzanilla*. Sanlúcar was where Magellan finally set sail from, and it still has the feel of a colonial-era port.

The main city in the region, Jerez de la Frontera, is the elegant capital of the sherry industry, with several worthwhile bodega visits available. It's full of great places to eat and drink as well as several notable sights. It's also an important flamenco centre. *Colour map 4, B1.*

El Puerto de Santa María

sherry bodegas, bullfighting and great seafood

El Puerto de Santa María wears two hats. Its elegant old town testifies to its days as a burgeoning trading and steamer port – Columbus' 1492 flagship, the *Santa María*, was from here – while its fish restaurants on the Ribera del Marisco make a popular and hard-to-beat lunch excursion from Cádiz, Jerez or Sevilla. In summer, though, the nearby beaches rocks to some of Spain's raunchiest nightlife. El Puerto de Santa María is also a sherry town, home to such well-known brands as Osborne and Terry, whose cavernous bodegas impart their distinctive fragrance to the narrow streets.

Sights

The old town lies on the northwest bank of the Río Guadalete, which flows into the Bahía de Cádiz. The town's two beaches are on the bay: Playa de la Puntilla on the city side, and the longer Playa de Valdelagrana on the other side of the river. Several buses link the beaches with the old centre.

First constructed by the Moors in the 10th century, **Castillo de San Marcos** ⓘ *Plaza Alfonso X El Sabio s/n, T627-569335, Tue free by prior arrangement, Wed-Sat 1030, 1130 (English), 1230, 1330, €6*, was rebuilt by Alfonso X in the 13th century, an event he refers to in one of his many writings. The castle has restored heraldic friezes, dogtooth battlements, and Marian inscriptions decorating the walls and towers. The impressive wooden door opens for guided tours that run in English and Spanish. It's worth a visit to see the chapel built over a mosque, whose foundations it preserves. It has a fine 13th-century Gothic sculpture of Santa María de España. The visit includes a sherry tasting, as the castle is owned by Bodegas Caballero.

The **Plaza de España** is dominated by the parish church of **Nuestra Señora de los Milagros** ⓘ *T956-851716, Mon-Fri 0830-1245, 1800-2030, Sat 0830-1200, 1800-2030, Sun 0830-1345, 1830-2030, free*, a late 15th-century Gothic building with flying buttresses and various 17th-century additions. These include the ornate Plateresque/Baroque portal, with intricate vegetal and cherubic decoration, a tympanum with niches holding sculptures of Mary (who is standing atop the town's castle) and the Evangelists, and a strange bearded God atop it all. The side door is an equally elaborate Gothic affair with curious protruding piers.

The **Fundación Rafael Alberti** ⓘ *C Santo Domingo 25, T956-850711, Tue-Sun 1100-1400 (closed weekends from mid-Jun to mid-Sep), €5*, is situated in the house where the 20th-century *portuense* writer lived as a child. There's a collection of objects and documents from his life. A Communist and friend of Federico García Lorca, Alberti was one of the important figures of the Generación del '27, and most famous for his surrealist poetry and lyrical autobiography *La Arboleta Perdida* (The Lost Grove). Alberti fled at the end of the Civil War, and stayed in exile until after the death of Franco in 1975.

The large **bullring** ⓘ *T856-600010, www.plazadetorospuertosantamaria.es, Tue-Fri 1000-1400, 1700-1900, Sat 1000-1400, €4, high-quality fights every Sun in Jul and*

El Puerto de Santa María

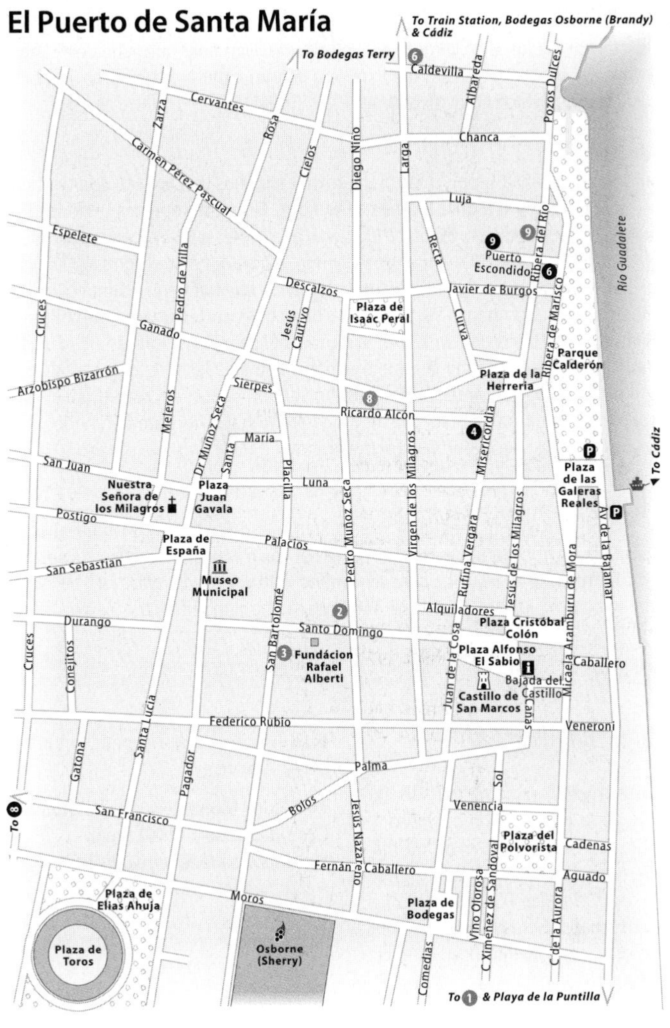

Where to stay
Camping Playa Las Dunas **1**
Casa de Huéspedes Santa María **2**
Casa del Regidor **9**
Hostal Loreto **8**
Monasterio San Miguel **6**
Palacio de San Bartolomé **3**

Restaurants
Aponiente **9**
El Faro de El Puerto **8**
La Antigua **4**
La Taberna del Puerto **6**

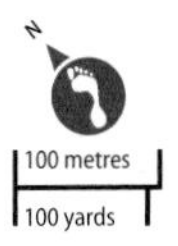

100 metres
100 yards

Aug, looking like a brick Colosseum, is one of the more important in Spain; indeed an inscription by Joselito claims that if you haven't seen bulls here, you don't know bullfighting. When there's no fight on you can visit the arena and have a look round the ring, which holds 15,000.

Bodegas

The tourist office will supply a list of the town's wineries that are open for visiting. Most of them require a prior phone call to book. The best known is undoubtedly **Osborne** ⓘ *sherry bodega, T956-869100, www.osborne.es, tours by prior appointment daily 1030 in English, 1200 Spanish, 1230 German, €8; brandy bodega Ctra NIV Km 651, near the train station, T956-854228, open by prior appointment*. Founded in the 18th century, the company's 90 giant metal black bulls dotted around the country's main roads have become a well-known symbol of Spain. A law forbidding roadside advertising threatened their complete removal in the 1990s (the logo had already been removed for the same reason), but the Supreme Court decreed them as part of the nation's cultural heritage, so they are here to stay. There are two bodegas in town, one for the sherry, and one for the brandy.

Chipiona

Past the huge yachting marina of Puerto Sherry and Rota, with a US naval base, Chipiona, 9 km from Sanlúcar, is a cheery seaside town with fine beaches. It's notable for its **lighthouse** ⓘ *visits by prior reservation with the tourist office, T956-929065, turismo@aytochipiona.es, €5*, whose 344 steps can be climbed for the views.

Listings El Puerto de Santa María *map p147*

Tourist information

Tourist office
By the castle at Plaza Alfonso X/Plaza Castillo s/n, T956-542413, www.turismo elpuerto.com. Daily Oct-Apr 1000-1400, 1730-1930, May-Sep 1730-2030.
Provides maps plus useful printed sheets of accommodation, transport, tapas routes, etc.

Where to stay

Its excellent transport connections mean that El Puerto makes a good base for the Carnaval at Cádiz; there are also festivities going on here. While it's easier to bag a room here than in Cádiz, you'll still need to book well in advance.

€€€ Hotel Monasterio San Miguel
C Larga 27, T956-540440, www. hotelmonasteriodesanmiguel.es.
A place where Spanish royals have laid their heads, this labyrinthine former monastery is now a large and comfortable hotel with a rainforest garden, pool, restaurant and antique furniture. Rooms are large, but at this price you might want to pay the extra and get a suite, which are particularly comfy. In need of a refit at last visit.

€€ Hotel Casa del Regidor
Ribera del Río 30, T956-877333, www. hotelcasadelregidor.com.

Set around a sweetly restored patio, this 2-star hotel offers value, compact rooms with a most affable welcome right in the heart of El Puerto's eat street. That means there's a fair bit of noise in the front rooms at weekends and in summer.

€€ Palacio San Bartolomé
C San Bartolomé 21, T956-850946, www.palaciosanbartolome.com.
The discreet entrance of this caringly restored palace opens on to a lovely interior patio. The rooms live up to the first impression, with carefully chosen fabrics, clever design features and a fine blend of the historic and modern.

€ Casa de Huéspedes Santa María
C Pedro Muñoz Seca 38, T956-853631, www.casadehuespedessantamaria.com.
Offering exceptional value for its spotless, quirkily decorated modern rooms around a pretty patio space, this is a budget star run by friendly people. Recommended.

€ Hostal Loreto
C Ganado 17, T956-542410.
This charming choice is set in a traditional old *portuense* house and is engagingly cluttered with pot plants and old furniture. All rooms have a clean bathroom; it's a good deal and handily located in the shopping area near the tourist office.

Camping

Camping Playa Las Dunas
Paseo Marítimo La Puntilla, T956-872210, www.lasdunas camping.com.
A large site by the beach with excellent facilities including a pool and a party atmosphere in summer. There are also bungalows of various sizes.

Restaurants

El Puerto is a very inviting place to eat. The Ribera de Marísco near the ferry dock has a string of restaurants. There are some excellent tapas bars in the parallel street Ribera del Río and its continuation Misericordia, behind it. It's popular to duck across on the boat from Cádiz for a boozy lunch.

€€€ Aponiente
C Puerto Escondido 6, T956-851870, www.aponiente.com.
The avant-garde cuisine on offer at this central gastronomic highlight may be at odds with El Puerto's conservative core, but remains very much rooted in local tradition, for the chef creates all sorts of new flavours with sherry and the yeast used to produce it. Correct service is complemented by smart contemporary design.

€€€ El Faro de El Puerto
Ctra Fuentebravía Km 0.5, T956-858003, www.elfarodelpuerto.com.
Established by the same owners as **El Faro** in Cádiz (see page 140), this elegant mansion and gardens just outside town showcases the finest of Spanish seafood in refreshingly different ways. You might want to try the black rice with squid and cuttlefish, a lighter dish of red mullet with aubergine, or the utterly sensuous *carabineros* in oloroso sherry. The service is faultless and wine list good.

€€ La Taberna del Puerto
C Ribera del Río s/n, T607-786490.
Just along from the Ribera del Marisco is this likeable stone place with its wood beams and barrels of good *manzanilla* and moscatel. At weekends it's very popular, when there's an in-house seafood stall and folk happily munching away on tasty fare.

€ La Antigua
C Misericordia 8, T687-797709.
Offering an upbeat welcome and tasty vacuum-poured Rioja and Ribera wines in case you've tired of sherry, this convivial place has tasty seafood meatballs and *ensaladilla* with prawns among its various offerings.

Chipiona

€€€ Paco
Puerto Deportivo s/n, T956-374664. Closed Tue and Nov.
At the marina, this is a place for a serious seafood meal; the chef buys his fish direct from the boats outside so it is fresh as can be. Prices are fair (but ask to avoid nasty surprises), and the quality is sky high; you can also come here for tapas. Recommended.

Bars and clubs

There are several bars in the streets behind the Ribera de Marísco, but in summer head to Playa de Valdelagrana, which is one long raucous strip of nightlife, with *chiringuitos*, pubs, and *discotecas* galore. The in places change every summer, so just head down and see where it's all happening.

Festivals

May **Feria de Primavera y Fiestas del Vino Fino**. The town combines a wine festival with typical Andalucían spring horses-and-flamenco merrymaking.

Transport

The tourist office keeps an up-to-date timetable of departures.

Boat
One of the best ways to get to the town is by boat from **Cádiz**. A catamaran service goes to Cádiz 5-17 times daily, 30 mins, €2.65 each way.

Bus
There are buses to **Cádiz** every 30 mins or so (40 mins), leaving from the square outside the bullring. From the same spot are regular departures for **Sanlúcar** and **Chipiona**, while from near the train station, buses also go to **Jerez** hourly or more.

Train
El Puerto is on the Cádiz–Jerez *cercanía* line and there are frequent services in each direction. There are departures every 30 mins or less, taking 12 mins to **Jerez** and 35 mins to **Cádiz**. **Sevilla** is also frequently served (1 hr 20 mins), via **Lebrija** and **Utrera**.

Sanlúcar de Barrameda → *Colour map 4, B1.*

Andalucía's finest seafood, elegant mansions and sherry bodegas

In its heyday this delightful town was an important port for the Americas and was once even touted as a potential capital of Spain. Its narrow streets still proudly bear the mansions of the town's pomp, while Sanlúcar is also famous for serving some of Andalucía's finest seafood. A happy coincidence this, for Sanlúcar produces arguably Spain's finest accompaniment to fresh shellfish, *manzanilla*, a light sherry tangy with the taste of the sea breeze. From Sanlúcar you can take trips to Coto Doñana national park, see page 108.

Sights

The town is divided into an upper and lower barrio, with most of the action in the lower town, around the central pretty Plaza del Cabildo, which is surrounded by terraced cafés, as is the neighbouring Plaza San Roque. From here, you can climb Calle Bretones, which passes the lively food market and Las Covachas, a curious Gothic arcade that is decorated with sea monsters; its original use is unknown but it was likely a market. Continuing up the hill, you get a fine view over the rooftops.

Further up the street, passing the elaborate **Teatro Merced**, housed in an old convent, you come to the **Palacio de Orléans-Borbón** ⓘ *Cuesta de Belén s/n, Mon-Fri 0800-1430, plus Sat and Sun 1030-1300 with free guided visit*, a summer palace built by the Duke and Duchess of Montpensier (the sister of Queen Isabel II of Spain). Now the town hall, it is a fantastic neo-Moorish creation built at the height of Alhambra romanticism. Have a look at the stunning porch and the central patio.

Turning left, you'll come to the church of **Nuestra Señora de la O** ⓘ *Mon-Thu and Sat 1100-1330, €1*, a 14th-century building with a striking main doorway possessed of fine *mudéjar* stonework above a Gothic arch. There's delicate blind arching, heraldic lions and a protruding eave. The round belltower is decorated with paintings of saints; inside, note the star-patterned *mudéjar* ceiling and 16th-century frescoes.

Next to here is the **Palacio de los Duques Medina Sidonia** ⓘ *Plaza Condes de Niebla s/n, T956-360161, www.fcmedinasidonia.com, tours Tue-Fri 1200 and Sun 1130 and 1200, €5, café open Mon-Fri 0900-1300, 1600-2000, Sat-Sun 0900-2100*, an elegant white building mostly dating from the 19th century, but with some chambers remaining from the 15th-century original. It still belongs to the ducal family who are directly descended from the Guzmán family who used to rule the town. There's an important archive of historical documents here, as well as numerous works of art and antique furniture. There are also some rooms available to rent (see Where to stay, below) and a rather charming café. Money raised goes to the late, socially conscious duchess's charitable foundation.

Further along, the **Castillo de Santiago** ⓘ *C Cava de Castillo s/n, T956-088329, www.castillodesantiago.com, summer Tue-Sat 1030-1830, winter Tue-Sat 1000-1430, Sun 1100-1430, €6*, was built in the 15th century into part of the city walls. It was here that Fernando and Isabel stayed when they visited the town. The hexagonal

keep and various Isabelline Gothic details are the most impressive features; there's also a small museum here, as well as a restaurant.

Next door is the bodega of Barbadillo, the biggest of the *manzanilla* producers, see below.

The beach is a 10-minute walk from Plaza del Cabildo and is pleasant, with fine clean sand. It's the scene of a curious spectacle in August, when serious **horse races** are conducted along it. They have all the trimmings: betting tents, binoculars and prize money (check www.carrerassanlucar.es for dates and details).

★Bajo de Guía

Turning right along the waterfront, you'll soon come to Bajo de Guía. This was once the fishermen's quarter and still has a few boats, although the majority of the serious fishing goes on out of nearby Bonanza. There's a string of excellent seafood restaurants here, a fishermen's chapel to **Nuestra Señora del Carmen**, as well as the **Fábrica de Hielo** ⓘ *T956-386577, daily 0900-2000 (1900 winter), free*, a former ice factory that now has a tourist information booth and the booking office for boat trips to the Coto Doñana national park (see What to do, below). There's also a display on different zones of the national park, and a good exhibition upstairs on the history of the region and the voyage of Magellan and his crew; there's a model of the only ship from that expedition to make it back, the *Victoria*.

The *Real Fernando* is a chunky old boat that runs trips from Bajo de Guía across to the Coto Doñana (see What to do, below).

BACKGROUND

Sanlúcar de Barrameda

Sanlúcar was entrusted after the reconquest to Guzmán El Bueno (of Tarifa fame) in the late 13th century. Still resident here today are his descendants, the Dukes of Medina Sidonia. Sanlúcar's superb position facing the Atlantic meant it became an important port once the Americas had been discovered, when wealthy merchants and chandlers built the mansions that still ennoble the town. Columbus sailed from here on his third voyage in 1498, and this was the last place Magellan set foot in Spain. Leaving Sanlúcar on 20 September 1519 with five ships and over 200 men, he attempted to circumnavigate the world. Only one of the ships, the *Victoria*, made it home, three years later. This was skippered by Juan Sebastián Elcano (Elkano), as Magellan himself only got as far as the Philippines before dying in an ill-advised intervention in a local conflict. Sanlúcar, a wealthy and important city in the 16th century, began to decline, but by the 19th and 20th centuries it became a fashionable resort. Today, fishing, *manzanilla* and tourism keep the town in euros.

Bodegas

There are several *manzanilla* bodegas in town, some of which can be visited without phoning ahead. Grab a list of updated visiting hours from the tourist office. The smallest, oldest, and most delightful to visit is right in the heart of town tucked up a side street near the food market. **Bodegas La Cigarrera** ⓘ *Plaza Madre de Dios s/n, T956-381285, www.bodegaslacigarrera.com, Mon-Sat 1000-1500, visits Mon-Fri 1100 Italian, 1200 English, 1300 Spanish, Sat 1100 Spanish, €3 per person*, is housed in part of a former convent, and its atmospheric barrel vaults surround a pretty patio. It was founded in 1758 and is still run by the same family. Visits explain plenty about *manzanilla* and its similarities and differences from other sherries. Their *fino* is unfiltered and delicious; you get a taste at the end of the tour. There's a very pleasant bar-restaurant here, open daily and serving decent tapas.

With a production dozens of times larger, **Barbadillo** ⓘ *next to the castle, T956-385500, www.barbadillo.com, tours Tue-Sat 1100 (English), 1200 and 1300 (Spanish), plus Sun 1200 Spanish from Oct-May, €6*, offers tours as well as a **museum** ⓘ *Tue-Sat 1000-1500, to 1800 Wed, included in tour price.*

Excursions

If you don't manage to visit the Parque Nacional Coto Doñana itself (see page 108), you can get some idea of it (and see a multitude of waterbirds) by driving a circular route along this side of the Guadalquivir estuary. From Sanlúcar, head northeast 23 km to the town of Trebujena. From the centre of Trebujena, follow signs (you may have to ask) to the estuary (*las marismas*). Just past **Chozas Marismeñas** hotel, 6 km from town, the road ends at the water. Here, you can turn left along a poor road, flanked by bird-rich wetlands, which will eventually lead back to Bonanza and Sanlúcar. You can cut through Parque Dunar, an expanse of sand dunes, on your way back.

Tourist information

Tourist office
Calzada de Ejército s/n, T956-366110, www.sanlucardebarrameda.es. Mon 1000-1400, Tue-Fri 1000-1400, 1500-2000, Sat-Sun 1000-1400, 1700-1900, reduced hours winter.
Located on the long avenue that descends to the beach from near Plaza de Cabildo, the tourist office is well organized, with various info sheets on the town. There's also an information desk in the Fábrica de Hielo (see page 152); book trips to the Parque Nacional Coto Doñana there.

Where to stay

There are few options here, and rooms are harder to find in summer.

€€€-€€ Palacio de los Duques Medina Sidonia
Plaza Condes de Niebla 1, T956-360161, www.ruralduquesmedinasidonia.com.
An opportunity to stay in a working palace, ducal seat of the Medina Sidonia family. There's a variety of elegant double rooms, furnished in antique style, and hung with family portraits and ducal heirlooms. The prices include breakfast in the appealing café. Recommended.

€€ Hostal Alcoba
C Alcoba 26, T956-383109, www.hostalalcoba.es.
This is really a boutique hotel, not a *hostal*, and a great spot it is too. The cute rooms, including 1 divine attic suite, are super-comfortable, and there's an utterly relaxing courtyard area with a small pool. The host is super-attentive, and breakfast is excellent. Recommended.

€€ Hotel Barrameda
C Ancha 10, T956-385878, www.hotelbarrameda.com.
An oasis right off the main street in the heart of town, this hotel is built around a pretty patio and decorated with photos of the Doñana wetlands. Rooms are cool, with marble floors and comfortable beds. You pay about €10 extra to get a room overlooking the pedestrian street; a little noisier, but worth it to feel part of the town. A scorching roof terrace gives a chance to take the sun. Recommended.

€ Pensión La Bohemia
C Don Claudio 1, T956-369599, www.pensionlabohemia.com.
Lovely budget accommodation near the Iglesia de Santo Domingo. The place absolutely gleams, so thoroughly are its pretty azulejos scrubbed; the rooms are cosy and have good, if small, modern bathrooms.

Restaurants

The best spot is Bajo de Guía, where a row of seafood restaurants with terraces looking over the river cater to every budget.

€€€ Casa Bigote
Bajo de Guía s/n, T956-362696, www.restaurantecasabigote.com. Closed Sun and Nov.
The *sanluqueño* restaurant with the most formidable reputation. It maintains very high standards and a meal on the terrace by the beach won't be forgotten in a hurry, unless you overindulge on the *manzanilla*. There's efficient service and a fine range of fresh seafood. House specialities include *langostinos* (king

prawns) and *raya* (skate). They also run an excellent tapas bar, the tavern where it all started, a few doors up. Recommended.

€€ Casa Balbino
Plaza del Cabildo 11, T956-360513, www.casabalbino.com.
One of the province's most memorable tapas stops, this main square option is a must, even if you have to use force to get to the bar. The friendly staff will have your *manzanilla* on the bar before you've even asked; the wide range of tapas are excellent, including tasty stuffed potatoes and *tortillita de camarones*. The whole town stops here for a tapa before lunch, and the atmosphere is great; it's an experience just watching bar staff in action. There's an outside terrace too (but no table service). Highly recommended.

€ Bodegas la Cigarrera
Plaza Madre de Dios s/n, T956-381285.
This atmospheric old wine bodega has an equally charismatic bar and patio area to enjoy a glass of their delicious *manzanilla en rama* and traditional tapas.

€ Despacho de Vinos Las Palomas
Plaza de Abastos s/n, T956-368488.
Occupying the ground floor of a fine old mansion, this bar has a beautiful wooden ceiling and a sizeable bull's head watching over proceedings. You'll almost feel guilty paying so little for a glass of local *manzanilla*, which comes with olives; other tapas are mostly tasty *montaditos* and preserved fish snacks.

Cafés

Heladería Bornay
Plaza del Cabildo s/n, T956-877742.
This café and ice cream parlour is a Sanlúcar institution and over a century old. Now with many branches around town, this is still the best spot to sit on the terrace right in the heart of the action.

Bars and clubs

The best zone for bars is the grid of streets around Carril San Diego and C Santa Ana. There are several *discobares* around here.

Festivals

Sanlúcar has a notable **Semana Santa**, with processions through the old town.
End of May The **Feria de la Manzanilla** is a dressy occasion similar to the Feria of Sevilla. It celebrates the town's winemaking tradition by consuming as much as possible of it.
The **Whitsun pilgrimage to El Rocío** (see box, page 110) is also a busy time here, as many of the brotherhoods gather in Bajo de Guía to be ferried across the river.
Aug Horse races (see page 152).
13-15 Aug **Fiesta**, where the local Virgin is carried through the streets in procession over colourful patterns made from dyed salt crystals.

What to do

Tours

The **Real Fernando** is a chunky old boat that runs trips from Sanlúcar across to the **Coto Doñana** (see page 108). These depart daily at 1000; and also at 1600 (Mar, Apr, May, mid-Sep to Oct) and 1700 (Jun to mid-Sep). The trip takes 3½ hrs and includes 2 stops. You can rent binoculars on board (€3). It's essential to reserve a place as far in advance as you can (T956-363813, www.visitasdonana.com). The boats leave from opposite the building and the trip costs €17.27, €8.64 for 5-12 year-olds.

Commentary is also in English. In theory you can combine this boat trip with a 4WD excursion from El Acebuche (€35) if there's space on the vehicle.

Another company, **Viajes Doñana**, C San Juan 20, T956 362540, www.viajesdonana.es, runs 4WD excursions in the park, using a different boat to get across. These cost €40 all included.

Transport

Bus

Buses leave from the station on Av de la Estación. Hourly buses go to **Jerez** (30 mins) on weekdays; every 2 hrs at weekends. 11 daily buses (5 at weekends) run to **Cádiz** (1 hr) via **El Puerto de Santa María**. There are also hourly departures to **Chipiona** (15 mins), and **Sevilla** (2 hrs).

Car

Sanlúcar has limited parking, tight corners and a fiendish one-way system, so park in one of the underground car parks; there's a handy one near the tourist office or near the beach and explore the town on foot.

Jerez de la Frontera → *Colour map 4, B2.*

sherry centre, flamenco and Carthusian horses

★Genteel inland Jerez is quite a contrast to nearby Cádiz. Actually larger than its provincial capital, and Andalucía's fifth largest city, it rarely feels like it. The city is famous for its sherry, the wine that takes its name from the place and known in Falstaff's day as *sack* (see box, page 160). Jerez is also known as an important centre of flamenco and of horsemanship; the dancing white Carthusian mounts have a training base here (see box, opposite). Jerez is also home to a faster steed; it's the venue for the Spanish motorcycling Grand Prix, which sometimes coincides with the town's lively May *feria*.

Sights

The centre of Jerez is the elegant **Plaza del Arenal**, whose southern end is full of tables of poor-quality tourist restaurants. Many of the city's principal sights and several of its best tapas bars are within walking distance of here.

The **Alcázar complex** ⓘ *Alameda Vieja s/n, T956-326923, Nov-Feb Mon-Fri 0930-1500, Sat-Sun 0930-1500, Mar-Jun and mid-Sep Oct Mon-Fri 0930-1800, Sat-Sun 0930-1500, Jul to mid-Sep Mon-Fri 0930-2000, Sat-Sun 0930-1500, €5; €7 including a camera obscura that has shows every 30 mins until 30 mins before closing*, has a bit of everything. A sturdy fortress built by the Almohads, it was a sometime residence of Sevillan kings of that era. It preserves some atmospheric Arab baths as well as the interesting church of Santa María la Real, which retains many features from its days as a mosque, including the *mihrab*. The Palacio de Villavicencio is a mostly 18th-century structure that houses a camera obscura giving views over the city and as far as the coast. The Alcázar's gardens are particularly well maintained and try to lend a Moorish ambience.

BACKGROUND

Jerez de la Frontera

Possibly founded by the Phoenicians, Jerez was an unimportant Roman town called Ceret; what is known is that wine was produced here even back in those times. The Moors took the city, which they named Sherish, after an epic battle in which they defeated a Visigothic army 10 times larger than their own force. It was reconquered in 1251 by Fernando III but subsequently lost in 1264; the commander of the Christian garrison, García Gómez Carillo, so impressed the Moorish victors that they spared his life and set him free. They may have regretted this, for he promptly assembled a force and advanced on the town, taking it back after a five-month siege, this time permanently. The borders of the emirate of Granada lay just to the east, earning Jerez its surname 'de la Frontera' (of the frontier), which it shares with many other towns in this area.

Jerez was already famous for its sherry in 15th-century Britain and the tipple has been popular there ever since, whenever the two countries haven't been at war. Barons is an appropriate word for the heads of the sherry-producing families, who have traditionally treated the town as a private fiefdom. Many of the bodegas are at least partly British in origin, and the town's upper classes today still appear to be a curious hybrid of the two countries. In contrast, Jerez also has a large and close-knit gypsy community, many still living in the old town barrio of Santiago, and is a real centre of flamenco.

Just opposite the Alcázar complex, Jerez's **cathedral** ⓘ *www.diocesisdejerez.org, Mon-Sat 1000-1830, €5*, is built over the site of the former main mosque. There are high stained-glass windows of saints along the central nave and a fine Zurbarán Madonna and Child in the museum, but little else of great artistic merit.

The **Iglesia de San Miguel** ⓘ *Mon-Fri 0930-1330, 1630-1830, €2*, is the most interesting of Jerez's churches. Situated a short way south of Plaza del Arenal, it is immediately noticeable for its ornate 17th-century bell tower, which unusually stands right above the middle of the main entrance, a surprising, ornate, geometrically decorated façade dating from the same period. Around to the left is the original main door, an Isabelline portal with elaborate Gothic pinnacles. Inside, the main *retablo* is a masterpiece by Juan Martínez Montañés. Nearby, on Calle Ramón de Cala, have a look at the powerful monument to the flamenco singer and dancer Lola Flores (1923-1995), who was born in Jerez. It's a fine bit of work by one of Spain's top modern sculptors, Víctor Ochoa. It stands in front of an elegant orange *palacio*.

Another worthwhile churchy visit is to the **Claustros de Santo Domingo** ⓘ *Tue-Fri 1000-1400, 1700-2000, Sat-Sun 1000-1430, free or entry fee if exhibition*. A Moorish military building was given to the Dominicans when the city was reconquered, and the restored complex includes a late-Gothic main cloister, a secondary Baroque one, dormitories, refectory and an Almohad gateway.

Near the cathedral, the **Plaza de Asunción** is a beautiful square with two proud buildings on it: one is the 15th-century church of San Dionisio with yet another *mudéjar* belltower, while the other is the former town hall, with a superbly carved Plateresque façade and curious loggia with two rows of arches.

North of here stretch the narrow streets of the oldest part of the town, part of which is the barrio of Santiago. One of the curious things about Jerez is that alongside its well-heeled sherry population is a large gypsy community whose

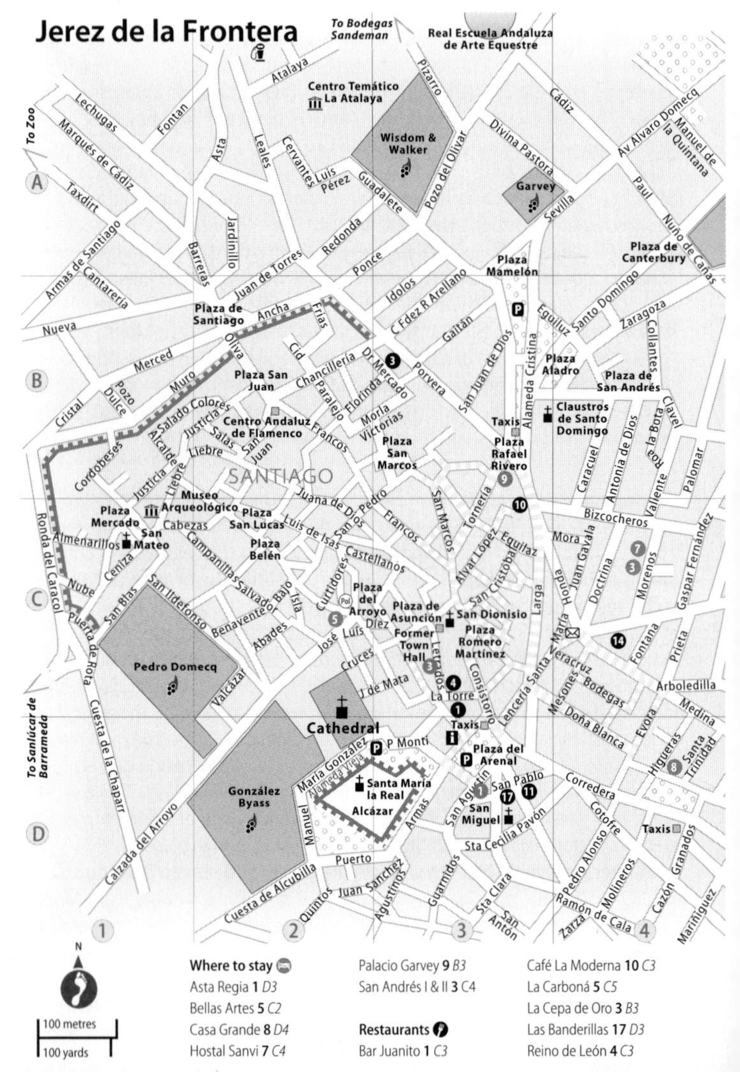

flamenco almost rivals the wine in quality and fame. Santiago is still the centre of the gypsy population and is a good spot for a wander, with several interesting churches and a couple of museums. Of the former, San Mateo is worth a visit primarily for its staggeringly elaborate Baroque *retablo*. The barrio used to have an authentic, seedy charm, but recent renovations and modern apartments have spruced it up but removed some of its character.

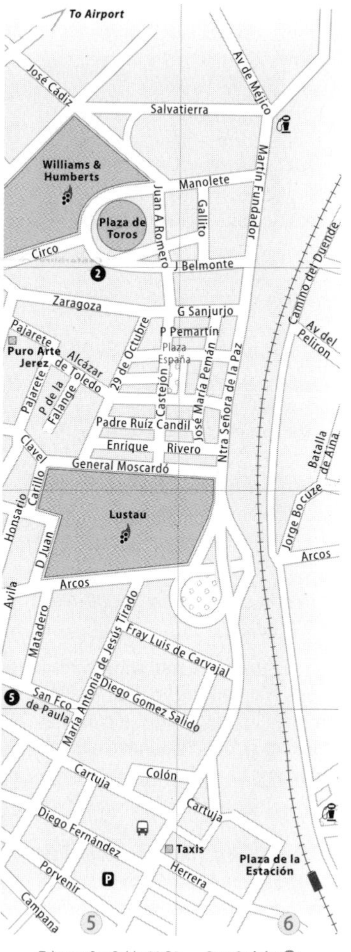

Tabanco San Pablo **11** *D3*
Tendido 6 **2** *B5*
Vinoteca Jerezana **14** *C4*

Bars & clubs
Don Juan **3** *C3*

Museo Arqueológico

Plaza Mercado s/n, T956-333316. Tue-Fri 1000-1400, 1600-1900 (1700-2000 summer), Sat-Sun 1000-1400. €5. Entry includes a multilingual audio guide.

Although not a patch on the excellent museum in Cádiz, Jerez's archaeological museum is very attractive, with its collection laid out around a light patio as well as darker, atmospherically lit chambers. The ground floor is devoted to prehistory, while the first floor has some fine Roman portrait heads, funerary plaques and amphorae as well as the collection's showpiece, a bronze Greek military helmet from the 17th century BC. Upstairs is a Moorish and medieval collection.

Centro Andaluz de Flamenco

Plaza San Juan 1, T856-814132, www.centroandaluzdeflamenco.es. Mon-Fri 0900-1400.

This important centre holds a large archive of printed music, recordings and videos of flamenco; it's Spain's main body for the promotion of the art. As well as temporary exhibitions, screenings of performances by some of the flamenco's greatest names are shown daily; you can also request videos from the archive. The centre is free to enter and is also a good source of information about upcoming events and performances.

ON THE ROAD

Of sherry and other Andalucían nobles

Sherry wines are produced in the area around Jerez de la Frontera, from which their English name derives. The region has a long winemaking history; the wines of Jerez were popular in Britain long before Shakespeare wrote about Falstaff putting away quarts of 'sack' to drown his sorrows or keep out the cold. Britain is still the biggest consumer and there's a distinctly British air to the area's winemaking culture.

The two principal grapes used for the production of sherry wines are the white *Palomino Fino* (the majority) and *Pedro Ximénez*. The region's soils have a massive influence on the final product; the chalky *albariza* tends to produce the finest grapes. Palomino produces the best dry wines, while Pedro Ximénez tends to be dried in the sun before pressing, optimizing its sugar levels for a sweeter wine.

There are two principal styles of sherry, but no decision is taken on which will be produced from each cask's contents until a couple of months after the vintage. This decision is taken by the *capataz* (head cellar person), who tastes the wines, which are poured using the distinctive long-handled *venencia*, designed so as not to disturb the yeast on the wine's surface. Those that will become rich, nutty olorosos are fortified to about 18% to prevent yeast growth; these wines are destined for ageing and may later be sweetened and coloured to produce styles such as cream or amoroso. The best *olorosos* may be aged 25 years or more. *Finos*, on the other hand, are fortified to a lower level and nurtured so as to try and optimize the growth of the naturally

Jerez Zoo

C Taxdirt s/n, T956-182397, www.zoobotanicojerez.com. Summer daily 1000-1900, winter Tue-Sun 1000-1800. €6.20 3-13 year olds, €9.30 adults.

A kilometre or so beyond the Barrio de Santiago is the city's zoo, with animals housed in a peaceful botanic garden. Although, as usual, you find yourself wishing the animals had more space, the organization does its best, and the creatures seem well cared for; there's also a centre for treating sick and wounded animals found in the wild. All in all, it's one of the country's best.

Real Escuela Andaluza de Arte Ecuestre

Av Duque de Abrantes s/n, T956-319635, www.realescuela.org. The show takes place every Thu at 1200, plus Tue Mar-Dec, plus Fri Aug-Sep. In addition, there's a Sat spectacle roughly every 4 weeks; check the website for dates. On weekdays when there's no show, complete visits 1000-1400. Show €21, complete visit €11. Reserve in advance by phone or via the website. There are also 'half-tours' available.

This training centre for the white Carthusian horses (see box, page 162) is a popular attraction. In the show the elegant dancing beasts sashay around to symphony occurring local yeast, *flor*. This produces a pale, dry wine, with a very distinctive clean finish, perfect with seafood tapas.

Manzanillas are *finos* that have been aged in the seaside environment of Sanlúcar de Barrameda; the salty tang is perceptible. Half a million litres of *manzanilla* are drunk during the Sevilla Feria alone, and *manzanilla* sales account for more than half of sales of dry sherry in Spain. At around 15 degrees of alcohol, it's the lightest of the sherries. *Amontillados* are *finos* aged longer than normal so that some oxidation occurs after the protective layer of yeast has died away. Some of these are sweetened for the British market.

Another curiosity of sherry production is the use of the *solera*. This is a system of connected barrels designed to ensure the wine produced is consistent from one year to the next. The wine is bottled from the oldest barrels (butts), which are in turn refilled from the next oldest, until the last are filled with the new wine. While the wine produced has no vintage date, the age of the *solera* is a matter of pride, and there are many around that are well over a century old. The butts can be used for up to 100 years.

Another similar Andalucían wine is *Montilla*, from Córdoba province. Much like a sherry in style, the difference lies in the fact that they are rarely fortified. Málaga wines are fortified and mainly sweet; those from the highest grade, *lágrima*, are pressed using only the weight of the grapes and can be very good.

Brandy is also made in Jerez. Although connoisseurs of French brandies usually sniff at the oaky nature of these coñacs, there are some good ones produced, and even the cheaper varieties are rarely bad. The spirit is produced using sherry casks, and the same *solera* system is employed.

music, with riders dressed in traditional costume. Dubbed an equestrian ballet, it really is quite astounding. When there's no show, you can watch the training sessions; it's very enjoyable to watch horse and rider develop the necessarily close relationship required to perform such complex movements; at these times you can also visit the stables, palace, and two museums – one of equestrian art, one of carriages.

Palacio del Tiempo

C Cervantes 3, www.museosdelaatalaya.com. Entry in groups by time slot. Mon-Fri 0930, 1030, 1130, 1230, 1315. €6.

Jerez's much-loved collection of clocks and watches has been given a contemporary slant and renamed the **Palacio del Tiempo** (Palace of Time). It's an absorbing collection of pieces from all over the world that now takes the form of a voyage through time.

Bodegas

Most of sherry's big names have their bodegas here: Domecq, González Byass, Sandeman, Garvey and many more. Most of the bodegas can be visited, although

ON THE ROAD

All the pretty horses

In Moorish times, there were two basic types of horses in the peninsula: the heavy northern mounts, originally brought by the Celts and of Germanic bloodlines, and the lighter *berberisco* horses of the south, elegant beasts suitable for light cavalry. These were originally brought across from North Africa but were resident in the peninsula well before the Moors' arrival. After the Reconquest, the Castillian crown wished to merge the two species to create an all-purpose Spanish horse. This duly happened, but a few landowners refused to surrender their pure Andalucían horses and gave them into the care of Carthusian monks, who maintained a breeding programme of the elegant creatures that some say are descended from the unicorn, as a bony protrusion on the muzzle is a common genetic trait. Thus the horses came to be known as Carthusians, or *Cartujanos*, and have been very highly prized ever since for their beauty and grace.

Although the monasteries were disentailed in the 1830s, a few breeders kept the line going. They are often fastidiously groomed and dressed and highly trained to 'dance' or walk sideways, a spectacle you can see at *corridas de rejones* (horseback bullfights), or at the Real Escuela de Arte Ecuestre in Jerez, a city historically linked with these horses.

many require a phone call the day before. This is worth the effort (everyone in the Jerez wine trade seems to speak good English) and rarely a problem; if you're lucky you'll get a very personal tour.

The two most-visited bodegas don't require a booking and are handily near the cathedral. The most famous sherry is **Tío Pepe**, a *fino* produced by **González Byass** ⓘ *C Manuel María González 12, T956-357016, www.bodegastiopepe.com, several daily tours in Spanish, English and German, Mon-Sat 1200-1800, Sun 1200-1400, tours from €13*, the biggest of Jerez's producers. Their massive complex can be visited on a slick, slightly Disneyfied tour. You'll learn nothing about the sherry-making process but will have a pleasant ride around the pretty bodega in a small train. Highlights include a pavilion designed by Gustave Eiffel, drunken mice, barrels signed by all manner of celebrities who have visited, and a tasting room left in original early 19th-century state. Although the tour is pricey, there's a generous tasting session at the end of it. Book online at busy periods.

Just up the hill from the cathedral, **Pedro Domecq** ⓘ *C San Ildefonso 3, T956-151500, www.bodegasfundadorpedrodomecq.com, Mon-Fri 1000-1600, Sat 1200-1400, €8, children under 16 free*, is a good bodega to visit. The tour is more informative and personal than González Byass. Staff will happily give explanations in English alongside the Spanish. The tour takes in both the sherry and brandy ageing areas, and has a glass-ended barrel so you can see the thick *flor* yeast. There are signed barrels here too, including one by Franco. When King Alfonso XIII visited the bodega, the Domecq family considered it a discourtesy to make him cross a public street to get from one part of the complex to another. The solution: they bought the street, a typical piece of sherry baron thinking. The tasting here is exceptionally generous – you'll want to have had a decent breakfast – and includes two brandies, one of which, **Fundador**, was Hemingway's standard tipple when in Spain.

The tourist office has a list of other bodegas. One of the smaller but worthwhile ones is **Sandeman** ⓘ *C Pizarro 10, T956-151711, www.sandeman.es, Mon, Wed and Fri 1100-1430, Tue and Thu 1030-1415, €7.50,* who do a good tour, with plenty of English tours. You can pay more for an enlarged tasting with better wines.

Excursions

Ten kilometres from the city on the way to Medina Sidonia, **La Cartuja** ⓘ *Ctra Jerez–Medina Km 9, T956-156465,* a beautiful Carthusian monastery, is still occupied by a community of the white-robed monks. It was here that the *cartujano* breed of horse was developed and refined (see box, opposite). It's well worth dropping by to admire the harmonious Baroque façade and take a stroll in the gardens. Zurbarán's superb series of paintings for the monastery church can now be seen in the Cádiz museum. At time of last research, the monastery was destined for major renovation works, which may close it completely or limit opening times.

One of the most important Carthusian horse studs, **Yeguada de La Cartuja** ⓘ *Ctra Medina Sidonia–El Portal Km 6.5, T956-162809, www.yeguadacartuja.com, every Sat at 1100, €15.50,* is located off the road between Medina Sidonia and El Portal, a few kilometres beyond the La Cartuja monastery. There's a weekly tour of the stables including a show and various runnings; it's advisable to reserve this in advance.

Listings Jerez de la Frontera *map p158*

Tourist information

Tourist office
Pl del Arenal s/n, T956-338874, www.turismojerez.com. Mon-Fri 0900-1500, 1630-1830 (1730-2030 summer), Sat and Sun 0930-1430 (1530 in summer).
You can download an information package to your mobile phone.

Where to stay

€€€ Asta Regia
C San Agustín 9, just off the Plaza del Arenal, T956-327911, www.hotelastaregiajerez.com.
This modern hotel caters to both sherry business visitors and holidaymakers with its spacious modern rooms, roof terrace with plunge pool and semi-spa, plus solicitous staff.

€€€ Hotel Palacio Garvey
C Tornería 24, T956-326700, www.hotelpalaciogarvey.com.
This small hotel is set in a striking neoclassical sherry baron's mansion on Plaza Rafael Rivero and makes an excellent base in the centre. The rooms offer 4-star comfort and are decorated in a modern black and white style that's attractive but seems a little at odds with the noble building, which includes

an elegant patio-lounge. Service is excellent, and the hotel is very good value in summer (**€€**). Recommended.

€€ Hotel Bellas Artes
Plaza del Arroyo 45, T956-348430, www.hotelbellasartes.com.
Opposite the cathedral, this is an elegant but friendly spot set in a beautiful 18th-century house. Its walls are soothing pastel colours and thoughtfully decorated with paintings, including some imaginative woodcut prints in the chambers. The rooms are very attractive, and all a little different. It's worth nabbing one on the street if you can, as they're much lighter. There's a roof terrace looking right at the cathedral. Prices include breakfast.

€€ Hotel Casa Grande
Plaza de las Angustias 3, T956-345070, www.casagrande.com.es.
Excellent value is on offer at this central hotel in an elegantly converted art deco mansion, with cool marble-floored rooms taking the sting out of the Jerez sun. Extra features like an elegant library lounge and spacious roof terrace mean you're not confined to quarters, and the staff are approachable and helpful. Recommended.

€ Hostal Sanvi
C Morenos 10, T956-345624, www.hostalsanvi.com.
Run by a friendly family, this is a very likeable option on a quiet street not far from C Larga. The rooms are small but colourful and have modern bathrooms. They have no exterior windows but open on to the airy central corridor. A bargain *hostal*, with parking available.

€ San Andrés I & II
C Morenos 12, T956-340983, www.hotel-sanandres.com.
This is a 2-in-1 place, a *hostal* and hotel. Both have beautiful patios full of tropical plants and attractive rooms, some with balconies, the hotel's with modern bathroom and both with heating. There are a few rooms without bathroom available but the price is similar. Friendly owners.

Restaurants

The town boasts some excellent restaurants and tapas bars; many of the dishes use sherry, which is also often drunk here as an accompaniment to a meal. Head to Plaza Rafael Rivero for a nice evening scene of outdoor tables at a selection of sherry 'n' cheese bars.

€€€ Tendido 6
C Circo 10, T956-344835, www.tendido6.com.
Closed Sun. With a location opposite the bullring, there's no prizes for guessing the main theme of the decor at this classy restaurant, but it's a warm, comfortable spot with fine service. The meat is good, but there's also excellent fish, such as *urta*, a popular local variety of bream. There's also a worthwhile tapas bar attached.

€€ Bar Juanito
C Pescadería Vieja 4, T956-334838.
One of Jerez's classics, this is a place that must be visited during your stay. With a small bar, large covered patio for dining, and a beautiful terrace shaded by white cloth, it's a welcoming spot, and the quality of the food is excellent. Ask the bar staff what they recommend; suggestions include *carrillada*, artichokes, prawns, *berza*, or calamari, washed down with a selection from a long list of sherries.

€€ La Carboná
C San Francisco de Paula s/n, T956-347475, www.lacarbona.com.
A cavernous restaurant set in an old sherry bodega offering polite service, plenty of space, and, thanks to the high ceiling, a quieter dining experience than in many Spanish restaurants. There's everything from quail to giant *chuletón* steaks here and you're generally better off on the meaty side of things.

€€ La Cepa de Oro
C Porvera 35, T956-344175.
A cosy place popular with all sorts of people and open for years. The homestyle cooking is the big attraction; this is the sort of spot to try classic Andalucían dishes such as *berza* (a spicy stew of beans, sausage and cumin) or *rabo de toro* (bull's tail). There's a small terrace on the lively street. Service can be on the gruff side, particularly if the Xerez football team are on a bad run.

€€ Las Banderillas
C Caballeros 12, T956-350597.
Originally decorated, with breeders' marks on the walls and several clever touches, this bar is decked out like a little *plaza de toros*. The chunky darts that it's named after are everywhere, as are photos of them being stuck into bulls. The icy *fino* is a relief on a typical Jerez summer's day, and the delicious tapas are served with a smile.

€€ Reino de León
C Latorre 8, T956-322915, www.reinodeleongastrobar.com.
Formerly a traditional bar, this has had a serious makeover and now offers a rather stunning dining area with brushed concrete floor, columns, archways and exposed sections of the city wall in what was once used as a cavalry stable. The food is a comfortable blend of bistro favourites with avant-garde touches, and solid meat dishes served on slate. Service is helpful. There are also pleasant tables on the street.

€ Café La Moderna
C Larga 65.
As down to earth as you can get in central Jerez, this popular bar/café is always lively and has an excellent atmosphere. The back room is lovely, with wooden beams and brick vaulting up against a fragment of the old city walls. There are also simple filling tapas available, such as stews of beef, venison or tripe (*menudo*). The beer is cheap, too.

€ Tabanco San Pablo
C San Pablo 12, T956-338436.
An authentic bar, where the sherry barrels are not for decoration but consumption. It's an old-fashioned Spanish spot with yellowing bullfight posters on the walls; the sherry is served in humble glasses and doesn't taste any the worse for it. There's not a big range of food, but the *montaditos* are sensational, especially the ones with *chorizo*. Recommended.

€ Vinoteca Jerezana
C Arcos 6, T956-320288.
This is a no-frills bar to buy decent *fino*, or knock one back rubbing shoulders with wise old locals. The prices and atmosphere confirm you've taken the exit ramp from the touristy part of sherry town.

Bars and clubs

Jerez generally has a quiet nightlife and it can be difficult to find a busy bar midweek. The main nightlife area at weekends is along Av de Méjico, which has a range of bars. C Divina Pastora has a few bars, while on C Zaragoza are a couple of decent *discotecas* and the Plaza de Canterbury, a lively summer square with a few bars around it.

Don Juan
C Letrados 2, T956-343591. Open 2100-0100.
You couldn't get much more Jerez than this elegant little bar. It attracts a dressy young to middle-aged set for quiet drinks and chat.

Entertainment

Flamenco
Jerez is an important centre of flamenco and you can find both the touristy dinner and dance packages as well as classy performances in smoky bars. The best place to find out about upcoming performances is the **Centro Andaluz de Flamenco** (see page 159); the newspaper *Jerez Información* also has a flamenco page.

There are many *peñas* and flamenco bars; some of the most authentic include: **Café El Arriate**, *C Francos 41*. In the heart of the Santiago barrio, the photos on the wall commemorate some of the greats of Jerez flamenco, and there are scheduled and spontaneous performances.
La Bulería, *C Empedrada 20, T856-053772, www.labuleriajerez.com.* Another likely spot to find something good at the weekend.
Puro Arte Jerez, *C Conocedores 28.* Well-known flamenco artist Raul Ortega is the star performer at this atmospheric back street venue, which has a nightly show at 2200, with optional dinner service beforehand.

Festivals

Feb/Mar Festival de Flamenco. Check dates at www.festivaldejerez.es.
Easter Jerez's **Semana Santa** processions are similar to Sevilla's and worth seeing.
First half of May The **Feria del Caballo**, Jerez's main fiesta, runs for a week and a visit during this time is recommended. It's quite similar to Sevilla's Feria de Abril, but has a more serious horsey aspect, and there are more public *casetas*. It's also when the city's best **bullfights** are scheduled and often coincides with the motorcycle grand prix, which fills the city to bursting point at any time. You'll struggle to find accommodation during this time, though. Many revellers come from Sevilla or Cádiz on the train and stay up all night. There are other horse events, either racing, or dressage, throughout the year.
9 Oct The celebration of **San Dionisio**, the town's patron saint.

What to do

Racing
10 km east of Jerez is its **Circuito Permanente de Velocidad**, www. circuito dejerez.com. This racing track has hosted the Spanish Formula 1 Grand Prix, and is the established venue for the motorcycling Grand Prix. All year there are other motor-racing events here at weekends.

Transport

The city is especially well connected with Sevilla and Cádiz.

Air
Jerez's airport is 8 km northeast of town. There are infrequent airport buses; a taxi

will only cost around €13. The train and bus stations are adjacent at the eastern end of town. Frequent local buses (No 10) run to Plaza del Arenal in the centre, or it's about a 15-min walk.

Jerez's airport has a **Ryanair** service to and from **London Stansted** as well as **Frankfurt Hahn** and **Barcelona**. Various other German and European destinations are served by charter airlines.

Bus

The bus station is adjacent to the train station at the eastern end of town. Frequent local buses (No 10) run to Plaza del Arenal in the centre, or it's about a 15-min walk.

Local There are buses every 30 mins to **Cádiz** (40 mins), hourly or more often to **El Puerto de Santa María**, and buses hourly to **Sanlúcar de Barrameda** (30 mins). Going east, hourly buses go to **Arcos de la Frontera** (40 mins), via **Ubrique**. 11 buses daily go to **Algeciras**, 3 of these go via **Tarifa**, some going on to **La Línea**, at the Gibraltar border. 4 buses go to **Conil** daily.

Long distance Buses leave to **Sevilla** (1 hr 15 mins), with 11 weekday departures and 7 at weekends.

There are 4 daily buses to **Ronda** (3 hrs, via **Arcos de la Frontera**), 1 to **Málaga** (5 hrs), 1 to **Granada** (5 hrs), and 1 to **Córdoba** (except Sat).

Car rental

ATESA, Aeropuerto de Jerez, T956-150014, www.atesa.es. One of a few agencies at Jerez airport.

Train

See Bus, above, for details of the train station location.

Jerez is on the main Sevilla-Cádiz train line. There are *cercanía* departures every 30 mins or less to **Cádiz**, taking 50 mins via **El Puerto de Santa María** (12 mins). **Sevilla** is also frequently served (13 or so a day, 1 hr 5 mins), via **Lebrija** and **Utrera**.

White towns
of Cádiz

★East of Jerez, and stretching into Málaga province, the famous white towns of Andalucía preserve much of their original Moorish street plan and are spectacular, whether viewed from afar, perched atop their steep hills, or from up close, lost in their webs of narrow, winding streets. But they are far from being quaint little villages; they were important Moorish and Christian cities and strongholds, the homes of dukes and nobles who have left them with a stunning architectural legacy of palaces and churches. Arcos is the most visited and has an impressive collection of characterful accommodation.

Arcos de la Frontera and around → *Colour map 4, B3.*

one of the most striking white towns, perched on a hilltop

The westernmost white town of the series that runs into Málaga province, Arcos is in a dramatic position on a hill, with many buildings worriedly peering over the edge of the crumbly cliffs. Approaching from Jerez, you won't get this viewpoint; it's worth taking the Avenida Duque de Arcos that runs along the bottom of the cliff for the best view.

Arcos has an ancient history, having been founded by the Romans as Arco Briga; it was expanded by the Moors and even became the seat of its own little *taifa* kingdom. It held out against the Reconquest until 1264; it can't have been the easiest spot on earth to conquer.

Arcos' **tourist office** ⓘ *C Cuesta de Belén 5, T956-702264, turismo@arcosdelafrontera.es, www.arcosdela frontera.es, Mon-Sat 0900-1400, 1500-1930, Sun 1000-1400,* is in the old town, on the main street on the way up to the central Plaza del Cabildo.

Sights

While the new town sprawls unattractively from the main road, the older part is a perfectly preserved network of narrow streets, with a North African feeling of white buildings studded with the sandstone façades of *palacios* and churches. From the new town, the main street, Calle Corredera, climbs along the ridge of the hill up to the heart of the *casco antiguo*, the Plaza del Cabildo, which has a mirador with fine views.

Opposite stands the **Basílica de Santa María** ⓘ *Mon-Fri 1000-1300, 1530-1830 (1600-1900 summer), Sat 1000-1400, €2, closed Jan and Feb*, whose buttresses you had to pass under while ascending the street. The Baroque belfry looks a bit curious tacked on to what is essentially a late Gothic church. It's surprisingly small inside, but you can admire the high panelled golden *retablo* topped by Plateresque stonework. It seems a pity that for some reason the congregation faces the other way these days. The sacristy has a fine frieze and ceiling; but it's the exterior west façade that is the real masterpiece, an Isabelline Gothic work with very ornate piers decorated with niches and pinnacles.

On the west side of Plaza del Cabildo the castle looms. While it was once the Moorish stronghold, it owes its current appearance to the 15th century. Unfortunately, today it's a private residence and not open to the public.

From here, wander to your heart's content through the narrow streets to the east. There are several *palacios*, with delicately carved façades, and another interesting church, **San Pedro** ⓘ *Mon-Fri 0900-1400, 1530-1830, Sat 0900-1400, €1*, which has a fine Baroque bell tower and another excellent painted *retablo*.

Following a lane around the back of San Pedro, the street leads downhill to another fine mirador with 270-degree views over the fertile *vega* below town and the artificial lake that gives citizens relief from the summer heat.

Medina Sidonia

This ancient white town was originally settled by the Phoenicians. The Romans fortified the hilltop and called the colony Asido Caesarina; it later became an important Visigothic and Moorish town. It was recaptured under Guzmán El Bueno, the hero of the defence of Tarifa; the town and lands were granted to him and he thus became the first duke of Medina Sidonia. This aristocratic line has been Spain's most powerful and, for centuries, the dukes were the country s largest private landowners. Medina Sidonia is less touristy than other white towns and only 35 km from Jerez.

The town has preserved a rich array of remnants from its various ruling civilizations, including various Roman ruins. Dominating the small walled precinct at the top of the hill is the church of **Santa María la Mayor la Coronada** ⓘ *daily 1100-1400, 1600-1830 (1700-2000 summer), €2.50*. It preserves the courtyard of the original mosque; the mossy bell tower was once its minaret. The staggering *retablo* dominates the Gothic interior, a memorable 16th-century work with five rows of panels depicting the life of Christ painted and sculpted by Juan Bautista Vásquez and Melchor Turín. There's a fine sculpted Christ by Pedro Roldán.

Opposite the church is a small **information office** ⓘ *T956-412404, oficinadeturismodemedinasidonia@hotmail.es, daily 1030-1400, 1630-1830 (1730-1930 summer)*. Plaza España, the long and elegant main square, has terraced cafés and the Ayuntamiento at one end.

Other things to look out for while wandering around town are the restored 10th-century horseshoe entrance gate, the **Arco de la Pastora**, and lofty vaulted Roman sewers. The castle is poorly preserved.

Off the A396 a couple of kilometres east of Medina Sidonia, **Acampo Abierto** ⓘ *T956-304312, www.acampoabierto.com, visits mid-Mar to Oct Wed, Fri, Sat 1130, €20*, is a bull-breeding ranch which puts on a show (in several languages) of those beasts as well as horse riding.

Listings Arcos de la Frontera and around

Where to stay

Arcos has many worthwhile places to stay, including several *casas rurales* in town and the surrounding region. Email the tourist office for a list.

€€€ Parador Casa del Corregidor
Plaza del Cabildo s/n, T956-700500, www.parador.es.
Right on the main square with fabulous views out from the cliff top, this smart hotel is located in a typical Andalucían mansion, slightly severe from the outside, but with beautiful interior patios. All the rooms are comfortable, but try to get one with views over the *vega* rather than the square.

€€ Hotel El Convento
C Maldonado 2, T956-702333, www.hotelelconvento.es.
A beautifully restored old monastery in the heart of the village, with very hospitable owners. The rooms are elegant and well looked after, with modern bathrooms and a/c; those with a terrace cost more, but they're all good value. Recommended.

€€ La Casa Grande
C Maldonado 10, T956-703930, www.lacasagrande.net.
A tiny, individual hotel with only 4 rooms in a pretty-as-a-picture mansion in the centre of the old town. There are charming doubles and a couple of suites, all decorated with a personal Andalucían touch; the beds have big fluffy pillows and, for a tropical touch, mosquito nets. The roof terrace is the highlight, staring right at San Pedro church. Recommended.

€ Hostal San Marcos
C Marqués de Torresoto 6, T956-700721, www.hostalsanmarcoscadiz.com.
A small and quiet *pensión* with a charming roof terrace and light, clean rooms with a/c and bathroom at a very good price. There's also a washing machine for guests' use.

Medina Sidonia

€€ Hotel Medina Sidonia
Plaza Llanete de Herederos s/n, T956-412317, www.tugasa.com.
A hotel on a quiet street near the church that is set in an elegantly converted *palacio* with an attractive whitewashed patio. The rooms are light on the eye and pleasant. Good value.

Restaurants

Eating choices are limited off-season.

€€ El Convento
C Marqués de Torresoto 7, T956-703222.
Run by the hotel of the same name, this lovable restaurant is set in a

17th-century *palacio* with an elegant patio to dine around. There's a wide selection of meats, including many game dishes; the *albóndigas* (meatballs) are very tasty, as is the *choco a la plancha* (grilled cuttlefish). Don't miss the *tocinillo del cielo* for dessert.

€€ La Taberna de Boabdil
Paseo de Boliches 35, T622-075102.
This curious cavern offers eclectic Maghreb-inspired decor and a secluded location with views over the surrounding countryside. The spot is run with warmth and it's well worth dropping by to check it out, whether for a drink or cup of tea or the Moroccan-style dishes.

Medina Sidonia

€ Paco Ortega
Plaza de España 10, T956-410157.
A typical local bar, this spot opposite the Ayuntamiento is a reader-discovered gem that turns out excellent home cooking; try the crispy croquettes to see what it's all about, or go for the value-packed *menú del día*.

Festivals

Easter The **Holy Week** processions are impressive and the floats have to be specially customized to negotiate the narrow streets.
29 Sep Feria de San Miguel. Bulls with padded horns are let loose in the streets. The locals run before them, dodging into doorways and jumping up on street signs and balconies to evade the horns.

Transport

There are half-hourly buses to and from **Jerez** (45 mins) on weekdays, and a few daily at weekends. There are several daily buses run by 2 different companies to **Cádiz** (1 hr 15 mins), and 4 to **Ronda** (2 hrs), as well as a couple to **Sevilla**. Buses leave from the station on C Los Alcaldes near the main road to Jerez at the bottom of town. There are half-hourly buses from here up into the old town.

Medina Sidonia

There are several buses daily from **Cádiz** and hourly buses from **Jerez**.

Parque Natural Sierra de Grazalema → *Colour map 4, B4.*

one of Andalucía's best walking regions

East of Arcos, the *pueblos blancos* (white towns) continue. Some are situated in the Parque Natural Sierra de Grazalema. Although it's one of Spain's wettest areas, the rain is seasonal and means that a great variety of vegetation, including many pine species, can flourish in the limestone formations. The attractive villages of El Bosque and Grazalema make the best bases for hiking; both offering lots of accommodation and hearty mountain food. There are many other places to explore: north of these villages is the enchanting hamlet of Zahara de la Sierra and beyond that, the marvellously atmospheric towns of Olvera and Setenil de las Bodegas; the other way is the leather-working town of Ubrique; while, further south en route to the coast, the castles of Jimena and Castellar beckon.

El Bosque

Simply named 'the forest' like a place in a fairytale, El Bosque is indeed completely surrounded by trees, mostly pines. It's the gateway to the Parque Natural de Sierra de Grazalema and an important stop for prospective walkers, as you need to get a permit for hiking in most of the park, which is restricted for environmental reasons. It's a notable trout-fishing village; even if you don't fancy casting a fly, you can enjoy other peoples' efforts in the local restaurants. El Bosque is also a centre for hang gliders; there's a popular launch spot in the hills above the town. Otherwise, it doesn't make the most appealing base of the towns in the area.

The main information centre for the natural park is the **Centro de Visitantes** ⓘ *Av de la Diputación s/n, T956-709733, www.juntadeandalucia.es, Feb to mid-Jun and late Sep Tue-Sat 0930-1400, 1600-1800, Sun 0930-1400, mid-Jun to mid-Sep daily 0930-1400, Oct-Jan Wed-Sat 0930-1400, 1600-1800, Sun 0930-1400*. It's on a small square just below the main road. Regulations for park entry change frequently and there are various restricted areas. Permits are free, but should be arranged as far in advance as possible as there are daily quotas for various parts of the park. You can arrange them in person or over the phone.

East of El Bosque, the small village of **Benamahoma** is a peaceful place, also accessible on foot along the river in about an hour.

Grazalema

Hard facts come first in serious guidebooks and it has to be said that Grazalema receives more rainfall than any other spot in Spain. It's a remarkable microclimate, as villages as little as 5 km away receive barely a quarter of the precipitation. Don't be put off, however, as the rain comes down mainly in November, April and May; at other times there's a sporting chance of good weather. Grazalema is one of the prettiest of the *pueblos blancos* and is the major base for walking in the park (see below), with accommodation and eating options to reward a hiker on any budget. The rain, in fact, contributes to the area's appeal, as it's the lushness of the vegetation that makes it such a pleasant spot for rambling about. Although now mostly reliant on tourism, there are still important blanket-making and carpentry industries, just as in the days when the British sociologist Pitt-Rivers wrote his famous study of the town, *People of the Sierra*.

Founded by the Romans, and then expanded by the Moors, it was not reconquered until very late in the day, in 1485. There are four churches in town; the **Iglesia Parroquial** is the most impressive, a 17th-century Baroque work. Wandering around the streets is a pleasure, peering into craft workshops as you go. One of them, on the main road to Ronda, contains a small **museum** ⓘ *www.mantasdegrazalema.com, Mon-Fri 0800-1400, 1500-1830*, on the rug trade.

The town's **tourist office** ⓘ *Plaza de España 11, T956-132225, Tue-Sun 1000-1400, 1600-1800 (1700-2000 Apr-Oct)*, on the central square, is really more of a shop and tour agency, but it is able to provide limited information and can arrange permits for walking in the park.

Practicalities and walking The Parque Natural Sierra de Grazalema is an area of some 500 sq km that has been declared a UNESCO Biosphere Reserve. It's a great haven for birds, including the golden eagle and Egyptian vulture, and huge colonies of the more common griffon vulture. It also sees many migratory species en route to and from the Straits of Gibraltar. Among its lush vegetation is a concentration of *pinsapo*, an increasingly rare variety of native fir. The terrain is extraordinarily varied, with jagged formations of karst giving way to poplar-lined valleys and thick stands of cork and evergreen oaks alternating with olive and almond groves and with wheat and barley fields.

Permits While you can walk in most areas of the park, certain zones require a permit to walk through them. This includes the zone northwest of Grazalema, roughly extending to Benamahoma and Zahara de la Sierra. Permits can be arranged through the visitor centre in El Bosque (see above), but can usually be organized by telephone (you'll need access to a printer), or via the tourist offices in Grazalema or Zahara de la Sierra. As daily numbers entering the park are restricted, try to arrange your permit as far in advance as possible.

Due to the restrictions imposed on walking, the well-marked paths are fairly sparsely hiked; you may well meet nobody on a day out in the hills here. You should obtain the good 1:50,000 map of the area, published by the Junta de Andalucía/Instituto Geográfico Nacional, and stocked by all the tourist offices in the zone.

Grazalema to Benaocáz via El Salto del Cabrero → *Distance: 11-14.5 km. Time: 4-4½ hrs or 5½-6 hrs. Difficulty: medium (short route), medium difficult (long route). At the time of writing, no permit required, but check this situation.*

This is one of the Sierra's most beautiful walks. There are constant changes of terrain, great views to the west across the rolling countryside that leads down towards Jerez and on clear days to the Atlantic. You'll have a steep climb first thing if you leave from Grazalema (longer route) but you can avoid this by taking a taxi up to the Puerto del Boyar (call Rafael at the **Casa de las Piedras**, T617-315765). Due to its popularity this walk is best undertaken on a weekday. Get going by 0930 to allow time for stops and a picnic along the way and to make the 1540 bus from Benaocáz back to Grazalema (Monday-Saturday). You could have lunch in Benaocáz. Beautiful stands of ancient oaks, interesting karst formations, exceptional flora and raptor-spotting possibilities make this a varied trip. **Map**: 1:50,000 Parque Natural Sierra de Grazalema or 1:50,000 Series L 1050 Ubrique.

Benamahoma to Zahara de la Sierra → *Distance: 14 km. Time: 6-6½ hrs. Difficulty: medium-difficult. Permit required.*

If you don't mind walking along tracks rather than paths this makes for a truly great full-day excursion. The hardest part comes first thing, a long pull up from 500 m to 925 m via a well-surfaced track that hugs the course of the Breña del Agua stream. There are great views of the Sierra del Pinar and the Sierra del Labradillo. The second half of the walk is nearly all downhill with views eastwards into the gorges of Garganta Seca and Garganta Verde, home to one of Europe's largest colonies of griffon vultures. You'll almost certainly see several dozen of these enormous raptors during the walk. Steel yourself for a steep final haul up to Zahara. This route links two of the Sierra's prettier villages; if staying overnight, Zahara is recommended. The predominance of track rather than path means that you can forget where your feet are going and concentrate on the amazing views.

Take plenty of water. You'll need to take a taxi to the beginning or end of the walk. This is easily arranged in Zahara (Diego: T956-123109) or Benamahoma (Horacio: T956-716199). **Map**: 1:50,000 Parque Natural Sierra de Grazalema or 1:50,000 1050 Ubrique and 1036 Olvera.

Other walks

El Pinsapar The classic Grazalema itinerary takes you through the heart of the Pinsapo forest. This full-day excursion begins on the road leading from Grazalema to Zahara. After a stiff climb of nearly 300 m a broad path leads through a large stand of *pinsapos*. You need a permit. Start early to avoid school parties and other groups.

Other routes around Grazalema There are two waymarked routes – both half days – which begin near the campsite on the road above the village. A good and easy-to-follow day's walk is to follow the river Campobuche (sometimes called the Gaduares) to Montejaque and then return by taxi. It is also easy to follow the route from Grazalema to Zahara that drops down the Gaidovar valley, skirts round Monte Prieto to Arroyomolinos where a track begins, leading you near to Zahara.

While the A372 heads east from Grazalema straight into Málaga province, there's a little corner of Cádiz that you can explore on your way to Ronda by taking the road north to Zahara de la Sierra, and continuing in a loop round through Olvera and Setenil de las Bodegas. Zahara is reached by a road just west of Grazalema, which climbs north over the austere Puerto de las Palomas mountain pass.

Guy Hunter-Watts's *Walking in Andalucía* (Santana Books) has details of more walks in the area.

Zahara de la Sierra

Zahara is a heart-winning white village crouching under the rock that bears its much-modified Moorish castle. It's spectacular and steep even by white village standards. Below is a large reservoir. The **Iglesia de Santa María** in town is a curious mixture of the Baroque and the neo-Gothic, with an impressive gilt *retablo* inside. It makes another pleasant walking base.

There's an **information office** ⓘ *Plaza del Rey 3, T956-123114, daily 0900-1400, 1600-1900*, which can arrange permits for the Parque Natural and has a display on the local wildlife.

There's plenty to do in the surrounding area, and **Zahara Catur** ⓘ *T657-926394, www.zaharacatur.com*, in association with the visitor centre, organizes many activities, from canoeing and caving to guided walks.

The most interesting walk from the town is the restricted **Sendero de la Garganta Verde**, starting 3 km from Zahara up the road to Grazalema. Within minutes of leaving the car park you enter a pristine, almost prehistoric, valley with no sign of human interference except the odd sign requesting silence in a breeding area for griffon vultures or giving information about nearby rock formations. After about 30 minutes of gentle walking the path descends rapidly, passing a cliff where you can see vultures nesting (during the summer, access to this area may be prohibited by the park authorities), into a canyon with sheer rock faces rising above, up to 400 m in some areas. The air becomes cooler as you follow the old river bed filled with huge boulders and unusual rock formations and descend deeper into the canyon. The route becomes slightly more hazardous at this point as you are required to clamber over rocks to a large cave called the Cueva de la Pileta. It is well worth the effort; the cave is made of an unusual pink rock with stalagmites and stalactites and is some 30 m high and approximately 75 m wide. Rock climbing equipment and a special permit are required to continue beyond this point as the route along the canyon becomes increasingly steep. The return journey is almost entirely uphill. Allow approximately four to five hours from the road for a round trip; only 30 people are allowed access at any one time.

Olvera

In the northeast corner of Cádiz province, and rising high above the surrounding countryside, Olvera is visually dramatic from the moment you espy it. The church looms over the town, and, even higher, its Moorish castle is improbably perched on a small crag. Olvera is an olive-growing town and offers majestic views over the surrounding hills, dappled with trees. It was reconquered by Alfonso XI in 1327 (his first triumph), and was on the frontline until 1482, when most of the sierra towns that remained in Nasrid hands began to fall.

The beige twin-towered church, **Nuestra Señora de la Encarnación**, dominates the plaza at the top of town. Here, by the entrance gate to the fortress, is a helpful **tourist office** ⓘ *T956-120816, Tue-Sun 1030-1400, 1600-1800, 1900 in summer.* They sell tickets (€2) for the castle and a good museum on 14th-century life. There's also an interesting map showing the castles in Andalucía (in Spanish only).

Olvera is also a starting point for a *vía verde*, a disused railway turned into a trail for walkers and cyclists. This heads 36 km to Puerto Serrano through tunnels and over viaducts. The tourist office can provide a map.

Setenil de las Bodegas

One of Andalucía's most intriguing villages, Setenil is set on the sinuous Río Trejo on the edge of Cádiz province near Ronda, see page 253. The river has carved a ravine, and many of Setenil's houses are dug into caves, hence the town's name. Many are overhung by the brooding rock above; in some places the overhang is so great that it covers both sides of the street. There's a 15th-century late Gothic church and the ruins of a Moorish castle, but admiring the extraordinary houses is the real attraction here.

There's an exceedingly helpful **tourist office** ⓘ *in a shop above the central Plaza de Andalucía, C Villa 2, T659-546626, www.setenil.com, Tue-Sun 1000-1400, 1700-1900.* You can arrange guided visits and activities in the region here.

Instead of heading east to Ronda, you may want to drop down to the coast at Algeciras via the impressive white towns of Ubrique, Jimena and Castellar.

Ubrique

South of El Bosque, this busy town is attractively set in a valley under steep limestone crags. It's famous in Spain for being one of the doughtiest Republican towns during the Civil War; its never-say-die guerrillas took to the hills despite overwhelming odds and defied the Nationalist armies for some time. These days it is equally renowned as the home town of bullfighter Jesulín. It's also noted for its leatherwork. Most of the action is in the new town, but the old part is atmospheric for a stroll.

The town was once a Roman settlement, and there are a few remains on the edge of town. Ruins of the Moorish castle, **El Castillo de Fátima**, are located 3 km away.

The town's helpful **tourist office** ⓘ *C Moreno de Mora 19, T956-464900, oficina.turismo@ayuntamientoubrique.es, Mon-Sat 1000-1400, 1600-1800, Sun 1000-1400,* can arrange a visit to one of the leather factories.

Jimena de la Frontera

South of Ubrique, this is another prettily located white village topped by the remains of a Moorish castle. It was a significant Roman town, Oba, which minted its own coinage. Many prehistoric sites have also been found in the immediate vicinity, including the important cave paintings at **Laja Alta**. These Bronze Age artworks depict a variety of stick figures in different positions and, interestingly, ships, the only known depiction of sailing vessels from this period.

Jimena is on the eastern edge of the **Parque Natural Los Alcornocales**, a thickly wooded region of hills and cork trees that is one of Andalucía's largest natural parks. Between the hills are a series of *canutos*, narrow valleys supporting a range of tropical and subtropical ferns and shrubs. The many limestone caverns support an important bat population; it's thought that 18 of the 26 species present in the Iberian Peninsula hang out here. Wild boar, deer, otters and both Egyptian and griffon vultures are also about. The tourist office here can provide a list of walks in the region.

Jimena's **tourist information point** ⓘ *T956-640569, Mon and Wed-Fri 1100-1400, 1600-1800, Sat and Sun 1100-1400,* is located below the castle at the top of the village.

The castle itself stands on the brow of the hill, looking over the town on one side and the cork forests on the other. It's open at all hours to wander around, but preserves little besides its flowerpot-like keep and a fabulous triple-arched entrance gateway. The inspiring view extends to the Rock of Gibraltar.

Castellar de la Frontera

There are actually two towns bearing this name, a legacy of a curious piece of social history. The original, and the one of interest, lies 8 km west of the main road. As the place was so isolated and decayed, Franco's government built the inhabitants a new home on the main road. The original village was later repopulated by mostly German artists and hippies; this caused plenty of conflict once the original inhabitants started drifting back to claim houses that the immigrants had saved, an oft-repeated scenario with abandoned villages throughout Spain.

The old Castellar is a remarkable village that's actually contained within the protective walls of its castle, which is in an utterly dominant position. It's wonderfully atmospheric, with cobbled streets, and little whitewashed houses with window boxes. From the battlements of the castle, you get fabulous views to Gibraltar and Morocco. Many of the houses are *casas rurales* (see page 26 and Where to stay, below). There's an information centre below the castle. There are several art and craft workshops worth a look.

There are no buses to Castellar de la Frontera; you have to get off an Algeciras–Jimena bus (see Transport, below) at the new Castellar and walk or hitch (neither are bad options) the 8 km to the village.

Listings Parque Natural Sierra de Grazalema

Where to stay

El Bosque

€€ Hotel Enrique Calvillo
Av de la Diputación 5, T956-716105, www.hotel enriquecalvillo.com.
Just across the bridge from the visitor centre, this is a likeable, rustic choice with smallish but well-priced rooms that have bathroom, TV and, crucially, heating; there are also cheap meals available.

€ Albergue Juvenil El Bosque
C Molino de Enmedio s/n, T956-716212, www.reaj.com.
An excellent modern youth hostel situated 1 km above the main road; there's a pool and comfortable accommodation mostly in double and triple rooms.

Camping

Camping La Torrecilla
Ctra El Bosque-Ubrique s/n, 1 km south of town on the road to Ubrique, T956-716095, www.campinglatorrecilla.es. Feb-Nov.
A pleasant site with various cabins (€40-65), either with or without kitchen.

Grazalema

€€ Casa de las Piedras
C Las Piedras 32, T956-132014, www. casadelaspiedras.es.
This is a great option in a welcoming white house just off the main square. It's remarkably friendly, and has spruce heated rooms around a courtyard. There's also a cosy lounge with a log fire, and a good restaurant. There are also simple rooms without bath (**€**), and the owners have apartments for rental. Recommended.

€€ Hotel Fuerte Grazalema
Ctra A-372, Km 53, T902-343410, www. fuerte hoteles.com.
This cosy hotel is in the heart of the Parque Natural, and boasts spectacular views of the Sierra and the village of Grazalema, which is 5 km by car or a 25-min walk away. Facilities are excellent; you can hire bikes, or just admire the view from the sizeable pool. Rates include breakfast.

Zahara de la Sierra

There are several places to stay, including *casas rurales*.

€€ Hostal Marqués de Zahara
C San Juan 3, T956-123061, www. marquesdezahara.com.
Of several accommodation options, this is by far the most charismatic, set in a restored 16th-century mansion. The rooms are faded, equipped with TV and bathroom and are heated; you pay a

little more for a room with a balcony. There's also a small cave-like restaurant (dinners only; vegetarian meals available). Horse trekking and guided walks can be arranged.

Setenil de las Bodegas

€€ Hotel Villa de Setenil
C Callejón 10, T956-134261, www.setenil.com.
Commodious and cordial, this newish arrival in the centre makes a very appealing place to stay. Most rooms have pleasant outlooks and the couple who run it couldn't be more helpful. You'll have to park a little walk away though.

Jimena de la Frontera

Jimena and the surrounding area have some good places to stay, including many *casas rurales* to rent; the tourist office has a comprehensive list of these.

€€ Hostal El Anón
C Consuelo 36, T956-640113, www.hostalanon.com.
Beautifully restored complex of 4 joined townhouses, decorated with ceramics, and with a good restaurant. Rooms are attractive and come with heating and a/c, as well as decent bathrooms. Breakfast is included in the price, and there's a pool. Recommended.

Camping

Camping Los Alcornocales
Cruz Blanca s/n, just north of town off the A367 to Ubrique, T956-640060, www.campinglosalcornocales.com. Open all year.
A fairly ecologically minded campsite that has good information about walking in the natural park. There is a pool, bungalows, and a restaurant.

Castellar de la Frontera

In old Castellar, there are several (**€€**) *casas rurales* bookable via the **El Aljibe** restaurant, T956-693150, www.tugasa.com. They make atmospheric places to stay, as they are little village houses tucked within the castle walls.

€€ Casa Convento Almoraima
A few metres north of the turn-off to the old Castellar, T956-693002, www.laalmoraimahotel.com.
Set back from the road in the woods, this excellent rural hotel, a former monastery, has elegant and relaxing rooms set around the cloister, individually decorated with attractive wooden fittings. Excellent restaurant.

Restaurants

El Bosque

€€ El Tabanco
C Huelva 3, T956-716081.
In the old part of town above the main road, this welcoming restaurant is spacious and dark as a good Spanish *mesón* should be. It's a fine option for trout, but there are also yummy venison stews, praiseworthy meat dishes, and paella at weekends. The bar serves great tapas and there's an attractive outdoor eating area. There are also decent rooms available (**€€**).

Grazalema

There are several tapas bars around the main square, in which you can try the local goat's cheese. The accommodation choices also offer good restaurants.

€€ Cádiz El Chico
Plaza España 8, T956-132027.
A warm-hearted restaurant delighting weary walkers with its succulent roast

venison, ample wine list and tasty *revueltos*. It has good service, and also caters for a wide variety of budgets; there's an inexpensive *menú del día*.

€€ La Maroma
C Santa Clara s/n, T617-543756.
Buzzy and friendly, this place uses high-quality local ingredients – the wild mushrooms in season are stunning – to produce toothsome, well-proportioned tapas choices.

Setenil de las Bodegas

€€ El Mirador
C Callejón s/n, T956-134261.
Near the plaza, this offers great views over the town and sierra, and has a generous *menú del día*. They do particularly tasty rice dishes, and there's a great mixed grill for two.

Festivals

Zahara de la Sierra

Jun **Corpus Christi festival**. Streets are strewn with wreaths and bouquets of flowers.

Transport

El Bosque

There are 4 buses Mon-Fri from **Cádiz**, 2 on Sat and Sun (2 hrs) via **Arcos de la Frontera**. There are 1-2 buses on to **Benamahoma** and **Grazalema**. 6 buses run Mon-Fri from **Jerez**.

Grazalema

There are 1-2 buses from **Málaga** to Grazalema via **Ronda**; these continue to **Ubrique**.

Zahara de la Sierra

2 daily buses connect Zahara and **Ronda**.

Olvera and Setenil de las Bodegas

There's 1 bus (Mon-Fri only) from **Cádiz** to Olvera and Setenil (2½ hrs), and 2 from **Jerez**. Setenil is linked to **Ronda** 6 times daily (30 mins) Mon-Sat. You can also access Setenil by train – it's on the Granada–Algeciras line. The station is 5 km from town, so call a taxi (T956-134328).

Ubrique

There are 8 buses on weekdays from **Jerez** to Ubrique, but none at weekends. There are 4 buses from **Cádiz** on weekdays, and 2 on Sat and Sun (2 hrs 15 mins). There are 1-2 daily connections to **Grazalema**, continuing to **Ronda** and **Málaga**.

Jimena de la Frontera

There are 2 buses daily from **Algeciras** (30 mins) as well as trains, and 1-2 to **Ronda**. The RENFE station is 1 km below town; there are 4 daily trains to and from **Algeciras** (36 mins); these continue in the other direction to **Gaucín**, **Ronda** (1 hr 7 mins), **Bobadilla** (an important rail junction), **Antequera** and **Granada** (3 hrs 40 mins).

Costa de la Luz

The most enticing stretch of the Andalucían coast runs south from Cádiz to Gibraltar. It has a range of vast sandy Atlantic beaches, some calm, some with serious surf, and is happily free of much of the overdevelopment that plagues the Mediterranean coast. Backing the beaches are rolling pastures that rise to a chain of green hills.

There's a variety of settlements to choose from: from the bourgeois-bohemian vibe of Los Caños de Meca to the Moorish ambience of Vejer via the windsurfers' haven of Tarifa.

What attracts the sailboarders, however, is the wind, which is more or less a constant presence, from the *poniente* west wind to the wailing *levante* east wind, which howls through town like an avenging Old Testament angel. Don't despair; at least you can exfoliate and suntan at the same time. There's plenty to do away from the sand; the Roman ruins at Baelo Claudia are impressive, the castle at Tarifa was venue for one of the Reconquista's most famous acts of courage, and the alleys of Vejer are a delight to wander.

One of the most exciting aspects of this coast is that you can see the mountains of Morocco looming to the south across the Straits. It's quite feasible to pop across for a day trip or longer.

Conil de la Frontera and El Palmar → *Colour map 4, C2.*

sizeable fishing town with an excellent long beach

Conil de la Frontera

The first place south of Cádiz really worth a stop, likeable Conil is a busy but pleasant resort in summer. The **Torre de Guzmán** near the beach is the town's main monument; it is all that is left of a castle once built by Guzmán El Bueno. A recent over-restoration has converted it into an exhibition space. Opposite, the **Museo de Raíces Conileñas** displays objects from traditional Conil rural and domestic life.

Directly in front of the Paseo Marítimo is the beach of Los Bateles, usually good for families with children as it's calm and shallow. It stretches south to El Palmar – see below – and north to La Fontanilla beach, with plenty of cliff-top development but a couple of fine summer *chiringuitos* and a busy seafood restaurant. North of here, the cliffs follow the curve of the bay round to the fishing port and lighthouse. Just before the port is a turning to **Cala El Aceite**, a secluded and popular cove of perfect sand. Behind the port, the tree-shaded river is a pleasant place for less blustery swimming and picnics. The town's **tourist office** ⓘ *T956-440501, winter Mon-Sun 0830-1430, summer Mon-Fri 0830-1400, 1830-2130 or 1730-2030, Sat-Sun 1000-1400, 1830-2130 or 1730-2030,* is near the **Comes** bus stop on Calle Carretera.

El Palmar

The laid-back village of **El Palmar**, 7 km south of Conil, makes a very appealing place to relax and has a fantastic windswept beach. It's popular for surfing, and several surf schools offering lessons and equipment hire back the length of the strand, particularly north of the main access road to the beach.

Essential Costa de la Luz

When to go

Apart from in the summer, temperatures are a little fresher here on the Atlantic coast, with strong winds a regular feature.

Best beaches

Los Caños de Meca, page 183
Zahara de los Atunes, page 187
Bolonia, page 188
Playa de los Lances, Tarifa, page 190

Time required

At least two or three days to explore a few beaches.

Where to stay

Accommodation becomes pricey in Jul and Aug, but is otherwise reasonable. There are many *hostales* along C Pascual Junquera in Conil.

€€€€ Hotel Fuerte Conil
Playa de la Fontanilla s/n, Conil, T956-443344, www.fuertehoteles.com. Closed Nov to mid-Feb.
Right on the beach, this smart hotel is set in huge, beautiful gardens. It's very family friendly (kids stay free) and has a good pool, spa complex and a diving school. Rooms with sea view cost more, and prices are high in Aug but good value at other times. The hotel has various ecological accreditations. Prices include breakfast. Recommended.

€€€ Hotel Almadraba
C Señores Curas 4, Conil, T956-456037, www.hotelalmadraba conil.com.
This likeable small central hotel is built around a cool patio and has a roof terrace with sea views. The rooms are bright, colourful and furnished with all conveniences. Off-season rates are excellent value.

€€ Casa Francisco
T628-225379, www.casafranciscoelde siempre.com, El Palmar. Closed Jan to mid-Mar.
You can't miss this sturdy tavern in the hamlet of El Palmar; it's the main place to stay, have a coffee, or eat and does all in style. A great place right on the beach with a fine cheap restaurant (see Restaurants). The rooms are modern and all have sea views.

Camping

Camping El Palmar
T956-232161, www.campingelpalmar.es.
Just 1 km back from the sea, with good facilities including a pool, and bungalows available.

Camping la Rosaleda
Ctra del Pradillo, 1.5 km from Conil, T956-443327, www.campinglarosaleda.com.
This is an excellent campsite with a large pool and cute bungalows.

Restaurants

There are good seafood restaurants on the Paseo Marítimo in Conil. Heading up from here, the Plaza Santa Catalina has more bars and restaurants. C Hospital has many more tapas bars.

€€ Casa Francisco
El Palmar, see Where to stay, above.
This restaurant specializes in fish baked in salt, which come out unbelievably succulent and juicy. All the seafood is of the highest quality and freshness, and prices are very reasonable.

€€ La Chanca
Paseo Marítimo s/n, El Palmar, T659-977420, www.casaslachanca.com.
About 500 m south of **Casa Francisco**, this is a sort of ultimate *chiringuito* and one of the best spots in the zone for a drink. It's got a big garden with hessian parasols shading the tables, overlooking the sea. It's the perfect spot for a refreshing something while watching the sunset. It's also an upmarket place to eat, with delicious seafood rice dishes, among others.

€€ Taberna El Retaleo
C Cádiz 12, Conil, T956-456240.
With classic Andalucían decor with hanging plants, this offers a more genuine welcome than most of Conil's restaurants. The food runs from standard fried seafood to more elaborate creations and is reliably delicious.

Transport

Bus

There are 5-10 daily **Comes** buses from **Cádiz** to Conil, and some services from **Jerez**.

Los Caños de Meca and Barbate → *Colour map 4, C2.*

one of Costa de la Luz's finest beaches, with a laid-back atmosphere

Los Caños de Meca

A short way further south from El Palmar, the villages of Zahora and Los Caños de Meca blend into each other. Between them is a beautiful sandy cape with a lighthouse, **Cabo Trafalgar** (accent on the last syllable around here). If you've ever fed the pigeons or waited for a night bus under Nelson's column in London, it's because of what happened just off here on 21 October, 1805. A combined French and Spanish fleet were pulverized by a smaller but technically superior British force; Spanish naval power never really recovered from this devastating defeat. The victorious British commander Horatio Nelson was killed early in the engagement; his Spanish counterpart Admiral Gravina also perished, as did over 6000 men (90% of them Spanish and French) and 18 ships.

Los Caños de Meca is one of the best beaches on this coast and is named for the cascades of water (*caños*) that pour from its low cliffs. The village was once home to a hippy community, and, although now it's also destination of choice for a smart Spanish crowd, there's still an alternative feel to the place, with beach parties, Moroccan-style *jaima* tents erected and plenty of people sleeping rough under the stars. Zahora, too, has a long and inviting stretch of sandy beach.

The road from Los Caños de Meca to Barbate climbs through sand dunes covered with umbrella pines; this zone, known as La Breña, is encompassed in a *parque natural*. Walking in these peaceful woods makes a relaxing break from life on the beach.

Barbate

The road from Los Caños de Meca passes a spectacular sandy beach before winding its way past the modern marina. Barbate is a fishing town: even its staunchest fans (of whom there are many) wouldn't describe it as beautiful, but there's a lot of enjoyment to be had in this friendly, down-to-earth place; this is still the real Spanish seaside, and it's a working town that doesn't shut down off-season. Franco used to spend his summer holidays here; the town is still sometimes referred to as Barbate de Franco.

Barbate makes its living from tuna, and the elaborate traditional fixed nets known as *almadrabas* have changed little since Roman times. At the Barbate marina, there's an **interpretation centre** ⓘ *T956-459804, www.atunalmadraba.com,*

Mon-Fri 0900-1400, 1600-1800, Sat-Sun 0900-1400, free, with information about the *almadraba* tuna fishing. From here, there are boat trips which take you out around the big *almadrabas* outside of town and along the coast.

The town is famous for its tasty *salazones* (salt-cured fish preserves) such as tuna *mojama*; one of the best places to buy these tasty products is the **shop-museum** ⓘ *Av Generalísimo 142, T956-434323*, at the entrance to town from Los Caños de Meca.

Barbate is full of good places to eat; choose one along the beachside Paseo Marítimo for sea views. As well as seafood, it is known for *churrasco*, grilled pork ribs served here in a hot sauce. Also worth a visit is the small **mercado de abastos**, a traditional food market.

Between the beach and the main road is the old part of town; seek out **Calle Real**, a picturesque old street that was once the heart of the community.

Listings Los Caños de Meca and Barbate

Where to stay

Los Caños de Meca

There are many places to stay, mostly overpriced in summer and closed in winter.

€€€ Casas Karen
C Fuente del Madroño 6, T956-437067, www.casaskaren.com. Open year round; prices almost halve off-season.
This quirky and delightful complex has a range of apartments set in characterful buildings that include a barn and thatched houses. There are hammocks to lounge about in and a very friendly owner. The apartments all have a kitchen and, while occasionally available for single-night stays, offer better value by the week.

€€ El Palomar de la Breña
6 km from Los Caños de Meca, taking the Barbate road for 3 km, and then left into the umbrella-pine forest for another 3 km, T956-435003, www.palomardelabrena.com. Closed Nov and only open at weekends Jan-Feb.
A very peaceful spot to stay in the middle of the *parque natural* dunes and excellent value outside of high summer. Also has a restaurant that specializes in chargrilled meats. Prices include breakfast.

€€ Hostal Los Pinos
Ctra Caños de Meca A2233 Km 10, Zahora, T956-437153, www.hostalospinos.com. Open year round.
Opposite the campsite on the main road through Zahora, this doesn't look much from the road side. Don't be fooled; the comfortable rooms are set around an excellent pool area and the complex offers exceptional value. Laid-back, friendly service; it's a great place for a seaside break. Recommended.

Camping

Camping Faro de Trafalgar
Av de las Acacias s/n, T956-437017, www.campingfarodetrafalgar.com. Open year round.
This excellent shady campsite has a great atmosphere in summer. There's a pool, tennis courts and mini-golf.

Barbate

€€ Hotel Adiafa
Av Ruiz de Alda 1, T956-454060, www.adiafahoteles.com.
A few paces from Barbate's beach, this shiny newish hotel makes the best base in town. Rooms are blessed with plenty of natural Atlantic light, some, which cost a little more, have a balcony overlooking the sea. It's much cheaper off-season and they throw in continental breakfast too.

Restaurants

Los Caños de Meca

€€ Castillejos
Av de Trafalgar 10, T956 437 019.
At the southern end of Los Caños, this attractively furnished courtyard restaurant blends a hippy-beachside vibe with some fairly ambitious plates and prices. They mostly succeed, with fresh fish, including red tuna, served with imaginative accompaniments. The upstairs terrace is a romantic place for a pre- or post-dinner drink.

€ El Mero
Ctra Zahora–Los Caños s/n, on the main road 3 km north of Los Caños de Meca in the village of Zahora, T956-437308, www.elmero.com.
A *hostal* with a friendly restaurant. Excellent whole fresh fish cooked with plenty of crisped garlic costs only €10, and there's a cheap *menú del día.*

Barbate

€€€ El Campero
Av Constitución 7, T956-432300, www.restauranteelcampero.es.
If you like tuna, this restaurant is reason enough to come to Barbate. It's all about that fish, and the various exquisite and tender cuts you can enjoy here take it to celestial heights. There's much Japanese influence in the preparation. The menu changes regularly, but such dishes as red tuna *sashimi* and *tataki* make toothsome appetizers before an exquisitely tender *ventresca* or fillet. Recommended.

Transport

Barbate

Buses run between **Conil** and **Barbate** a couple of times a day; on Mon-Fri there are also 2 buses to and from **Cádiz**.

Vejer de la Frontera → *Colour map 4, C2.*

Moorish white town on a high saddle-shaped hill

Set slightly inland this white town is one of the gems of this well-endowed province and is a stunning sight as you approach. The old town is still encircled by its well-preserved 15th-century walls, with gateways from the original Moorish ramparts. Vejer dates back to Roman times, but retains much of its Moorish feel, with narrow streets and glimpses of half-hidden patios. Indeed, until relatively recently, many Vejer women wore a *cobija*, a dark cloak covering the whole face but the eyes. Many scholars feel that the decisive battle between the invading Moorish forces and the Visigoths under King Roderic took place near Vejer in AD 711.

Make your first stop the helpful **tourist office** ⓘ *Av de los Remedios 2, T956-451736, www.turismovejer.es, daily 1000-1500, 1700-2100*, on the way up to the old town. They'll give you a map of Vejer, but ask them for the glossy brochure as well, which has more information on the sights around the place.

In the heart of the old town is the parish church, **Iglesia del Divino Salvador** ⓘ *Mon-Sat 1000-1400, Sun 1100-1400, afternoon opening variable*. Originally built in the 14th century over the town mosque, it is in Gothic-*mudéjar* style; later additions in the 17th century used a sort of neo-Gothic style to stay faithful to the original design. Around the side of the church are part of the town walls and a gateway.

Beyond here is the **castle** ⓘ *daily 1000-1400, 1600-2000*, built by the Moors in the ninth and 10th centuries, but transformed into a 19th-century house. It preserves a horseshoe-arched portal inside the wooden door, but is currently closed to the public. Further along, you come to the Jewish quarter, with gateways in the wall giving fine views across to the new town. At the bottom of the old town is **Plaza de España**, a pretty space with a colourful tiled fountain.

The new part of town has been sensitively designed and doesn't clash at all with the old town. There's little to see apart from a couple of fine whitewashed windmills.

On the N340 south of Vejer is the **Fundación NMAC** ⓘ *Ctra N340 Km 42.5, T956-455134, www.fundacionnmac.org, Tue-Sun winter 1000-1400, summer 1000-2030, €5*, a contemporary art foundation that stages open-air exhibitions in a large wooded park. Some of the pieces are permanent, some temporary, but there are some extraordinary works usually present, and it's well worth visiting. The entrance price includes a drink in the café.

Listings Vejer de la Frontera

Where to stay

€€€-€€ La Casa del Califa

Plaza de España 16, T956-447730, www.lacasadel califa.com.

A bewitching spot, a warren-like place part of which was once where farmers paid their wheat tithes to the authorities, and part of which was once an Inquisition dungeon. It's perfectly fitted in the old structure, with odd-shaped rooms decorated in quiet Moorish style. There's a variety on offer, but all have white walls, plenty of light, varnished wooden furniture, TV, phone, heating and a/c. The pricier ones have a stereo, tea-making facilities and comfy divans. There's a fabulous terrace too. Highly recommended. The same owners have a smaller hotel, No 1 Tripería (**€€€**; www.grupocalifa.com, same phone number), with a sumptuous patio and a pool.

Restaurants

€€ El Jardín del Califa

Plaza de España 16, T956-447730, www.lacasadelcalifa.com.

This amazingly atmospheric place is one of the best places to eat, reached via a series of stairs in **Casa del Califa** hotel (see Where to stay, above). There's a variety of intimate nooks for dining, as well as a garden and an open pavilion. The food is fantastic, with a North African/Lebanese bent. There are many vegetarian options and the prices are very reasonable.

€ Casa Rufino
Outside town, in the village of La Muela, 2 km off the main road opposite Vejer, T956-448481.
An excellent *venta* with Andalucían cooking. The dining area is very simply decorated, but the quality, quantity, and prices of things like mixed fried seafood, grilled king prawns, and steaks are exceptional. The *potajes* (stews) are also particularly good.

Bars and clubs

Janis Joplin
C Marqués de Tamarón 6. Open 2130 to late, weekends only in winter.
A well-known bar that attracts people from all over the region. The decoration is beautiful, a sumptuous neo-Moorish flight of fancy, and the music and company always reliably good.

Peña Flamenca Aguilar de Vejer
C Rosario 29.
An atmospheric cavernous bar with weekend flamenco performances. Check their Facebook page for events.

Transport

Bus
There are 5-7 daily buses to Vejer from **Cádiz** (50 mins), and frequent buses to **Barbate**. For other destinations on the main road such as **Algeciras**, **Tarifa** or **Jerez**, you'll need to descend to La Barca de Vejer, on the N340 below town.

Zahara de los Atunes → *Colour map 4, C2.*

wild and magnificent sandy beach with big breakers

★The name of this somewhat isolated town means 'blossom of the tuna fish' and it is indeed by these large beasts that the town has lived for centuries. The methods of catching the tuna have changed little over the years. Shoals pass along the coast between April and June on their way to spawn in the Mediterranean, returning in July and August. The tuna, which can weigh up to 800 kg, are herded into nets where they are hooked and hauled into the boats. Much of the tuna goes to Japanese and Korean factory ships waiting off shore, but the catch has dwindled in recent years, likely due to overfishing. It's a hard industry, and Cervantes famously commented in *La Ilustre Fregona* that nobody was truly a rogue unless they had fished tuna for two seasons at Zahara.

The centre of town is likeably ordinary, although with some resort development a couple of kilometres to the south, a district called **Atlanterra**. There's nothing to see but the superb beach apart from the ruins of the huge tuna *lonja* (market) that stands by the shore. Very quiet outside of summer, there are always a few places open to try tuna, of which there are many varieties and styles of preparation.

Where to stay

€€€ Hotel Gran Sol
C Sánchez Rodríguez s/n, T956-439309, www.gransolhotel.com.
Right on the beach, with burnished copper domes, this has plenty of comfort and an attractive garden area with a pool. The rooms are showing their age in parts but are comfortable, particularly those facing the sea, whose stupendous views will cost you a little more.

€€ Hostal Marina
C Manuel Mora s/n, T956-439009, www.donalolazahara.com.
Although overpriced in high summer, this is a very good deal for the rest of the year (**€**). Run out of the **Hotel Doña Lola** at the entrance to the town, it has excellent rooms with bathroom and makes a fine base for a beach stay.

Camping

Camping Bahía de la Plata
Ctra Atlanterra s/n, T956-439040, www.campingbahia delaplata.com. Open year round.
A shady spot with plenty of trees on the beach 1.5 km south of Zahara's centre. It can organize a variety of summer watersports. Upmarket bungalows are available for hire.

Restaurants

€ Bar Paquiqui
C Pérez Galdós 4.
This humble backstreet eatery has no pretensions but it's just about the best place in town to try tuna and other local seafood specialities like cuttlefish croquettes. In summer, there's a covered terrace that's a great place for a leisurely lunch.

Transport

Bus
There is 1 daily bus from **Cádiz** to Zahara run by **Comes**.

Bolonia and Baelo Claudia → *Colour map 4, C2-3.*

one of the coast's more alternative places and a Roman site

The small village of Bolonia, on a side road populated by red long-horned cattle, attracts a mixture of summer visitors giving it a great atmosphere. The beach is typical for these parts; beautiful, windswept and with clean sand. In summer, there are several places to stay and eat; off season, there's little open here apart from the interesting Roman ruins of Baelo Claudia. Apart from these Roman ruins, the pleasure of Bolonia is simply lingering on the beach. Walking south, you come to a stone circle that's a fine place to relax by the sea.

Started as a settlement in the late second century BC, **Baelo Claudia** ⓘ *T956-688530, Tue-Sat 1000-1830, to 2030 Apr to mid-Jun, to 1700 mid-Jun to mid-Sep, Sun*

1000-1700, free for EU citizens, €1.50 for others, rapidly became an important Roman town for its market, proximity to North Africa and, later, for its production of salt fish and *garum*, the fish sauce that was much prized in Rome. The geographer Strabo mentions the town as being a port of embarkation for Mauritania; it was given its title of town by Claudius, after whom it is named. You enter the site via the sleek lines of the new museum, which seems too big for its own display, but has well-presented finds and information and a sweet little gift shop. Approaching the ruins, you soon realize that the town was a substantial one: it had a population of about 2000 at its peak. It had a city wall with some 40 defensive towers, and an aqueduct bringing fresh water from 8 km away. Various large villas are in the lower part of town, near the sea; here also are the remains of one of the fish processing plants. Towering over the centre of town were three temples, to Jupiter, Juno, and Minerva. Plagued by earthquakes, Baelo Claudia began to decline in the second half of the second century AD, and was eventually abandoned in the seventh century.

Listings Bolonia and Baelo Claudia

Where to stay

Bolonia

There are many places to stay and eat, nearly all closed in winter.

€€ La Posada de Lola

C El Lentiscal 26, T956-688536, www.laposadadelola.com.

A beautiful choice and excellent value, this welcoming spot is soothingly decorated with cheerful colours and Asian art. The rooms are quirky and comfortable, with mosquito nets, and there's a blooming garden. There's a choice of private or shared bathroom. Recommended. Worth booking well ahead.

Restaurants

Bolonia

€€ Las Rejas

El Lentiscal s/n, T956-688546.

One of Bolonia's smarter eating venues, this beachside restaurant specializes in *atún en manteca*, cold tuna in pork fat that's a famed delicacy of this coastline. They also demonstrate a sure hand with other fish dishes and warming stews.

Transport

Bolonia

In summer, buses run to Bolonia from **Tarifa**, but otherwise it's a 7-km walk from the main road or an hour's walk around the coast from Zahara de los Atunes.

Tarifa → *Colour map 4, C3.*

one of the world's prime destinations for wind- and kitesurfers

★Laid-back, pretty Tarifa, with a distinct Moorish character, is sure to please, not least for the fact that you can nip across to Morocco for lunch on the fast ferry. Due to the almost constant winds that blow across its long, long sandy beach, it's a mecca for wind and kitesurfers. In summer, however, the small town becomes rather congested, and it's difficult to find accommodation.

Tarifa's **tourist office** ⓘ *Paseo de la Alameda s/n, T956-680993, turismo@aytotarifa.com, Mon-Fri 1000-1330, 1600-1800, Sat-Sun 1000-1330, summer 1000-2100*, is just outside the old town. They have lists of accommodation, tour operators, and watersports companies.

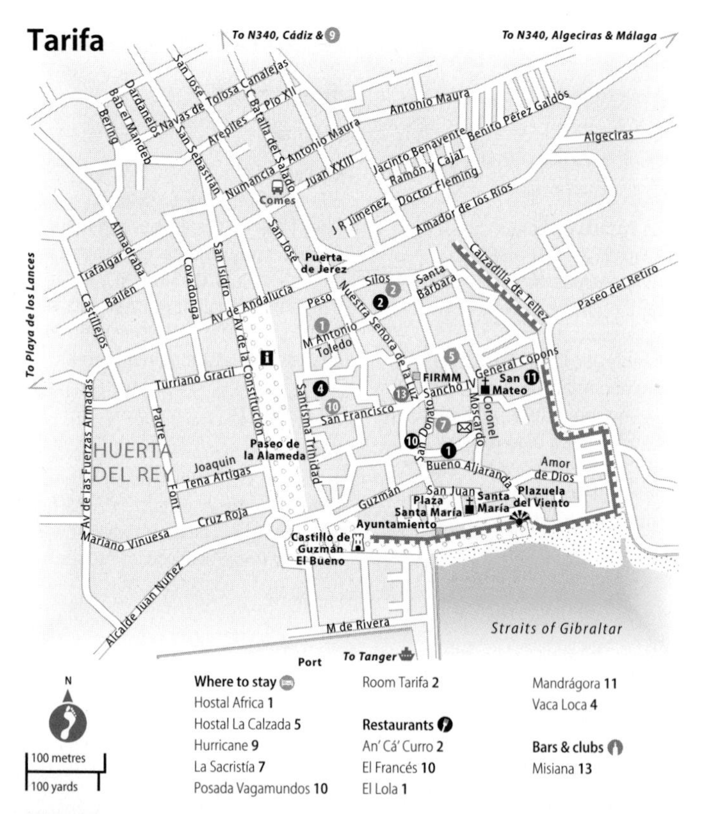

BACKGROUND

Tarifa

Formerly a Roman settlement, and probably a Phoenician one before that, Tarifa is named after the leader of the initial Moorish invasion of Spain, Tarif ibn Malik, who established a base here on his initial exploratory foray to the peninsula in AD 711. The fortress and town were recaptured in the late 13th century, but proved tough to retain. The town's hero is Guzmán El Bueno, a knight from León who was defending the castle against Moorish attackers. The invaders captured his son and threatened to kill him if Guzmán wouldn't yield. The knight allegedly threw down his own dagger to them, saying "I would rather have my honour and no son than my son and no honour". The boy was killed, the city held on, and Guzmán became the first duke of Medina Sidonia for his pains. A similar story occurred during the siege of the Alcázar of Toledo in the Spanish Civil War.

Sights

There's not a huge amount to see in Tarifa, but who'd complain when you've got 10 km of sandy beach with views of Africa thrown in for free? One of the best viewing spots is the small mirador and garden on Plazuela del Viento, a couple of blocks east of the castle. Another fine viewpoint is the **Mirador del Estrecho** a few kilometres east of Tarifa on the main road.

Tarifa's **Castillo de Guzmán El Bueno** ⓘ *Tue-Sat 1100-1930, Sun-Mon 1100-1330, €2*, was built in the 10th century by the Moors, partly because of significant pirate activity in the Straits of Gibraltar. After the town was reconquered by Sancho IV (who sits in sculptured majesty outside the entrance, inadvisably petting a lion), the citadel was commanded by Guzmán El Bueno (see above) and is named after him. Much of the Moorish structure remains, a bit derelict but basically sturdy; there's a foundation tablet in Arabic over one of the entrances. The keep's interior is a little bare, but used for summer concerts; there's a display on the life of Guzmán here, including various newspaper cartoons parodying his famous action. A second castle sits out on a promontory opposite and is used by the Guardia Civil.

The main church in town is the **Iglesia de San Mateo** ⓘ *daily 0830-1300, 1730-2100; free*; whose huge block-built Baroque façade is hard to miss. The interior is more elegant in 15th-century Gothic, brightened by stained-glass windows. The sculpture of the saint himself is an exquisitely rendered piece by Martínez Montañés, several of whose works adorn Sevilla's cathedral. In a side aisle is an interesting Visigothic tombstone.

At the top of the old town, the well-restored Puerta de Jerez lets you into or out of central Tarifa through its horseshoe arches. Once outside, it's worth following around to your right and turning down Calle Calzadilla, where you can admire the best-preserved section of Tarifa's imposing walls.

If you fancy a stroll, Tarifa is the start of the GR7 footpath that leads to ... Athens. If Greece seems like a bit of a hike, you can do a shorter section; the path leads through the pretty natural park of Los Alcornocales to hill villages such as Jimena de la Frontera and beyond.

ON THE ROAD

The coast of death

To vast numbers of North and sub-Saharan Africans, the EU is a place of marvellous opportunity: even with no papers and a menial job, a young Algerian, Mauritanian or Senegalese can send much-needed money home to their family and, in a handful of years, perhaps save enough to buy a place to live back in their motherland. Little wonder then that so many set off on an arduous journey north into the unknown. Andalucía, visible from the Moroccan shore, is an obvious crossing point. Though Spain and the EU get twitchy about the numbers that make it across, a far more serious issue is the alarming number who don't.

Often paying a family's entire life's savings to make the journey – or more, as unscrupulous brokers often take a huge cut of any future earnings – these souls, mostly unable to swim, embark in unseaworthy vessels (known as *pateras*) into one of the narrowest, but most treacherous, stretches of water on the planet. Throw in the fact that the boatmen, to avoid capture by the Guardia Civil land patrols, often shoo their human cargo off the boat dangerously far from shore, and you have a recipe for disaster.

Though coastal patrols have been upped both around Spain and in Senegal and Morocco, this seems to merely drive people to attempt the journey between points further away, exponentially increasing the danger of the crossing.

Listings Tarifa *map p190*

Where to stay

There is also a wide range of apartments and *casas rurales* for weekly rent in and around Tarifa; the tourist office can give you (or email) a full list.

€€€ Hurricane Hotel
Ctra N340 Km78, 6 km north of Tarifa, T956-684919, www.hotelhurricane.com.
This beachside hotel is a deserved favourite, situated in a peaceful leafy garden. Although rooms are overpriced in summer, the hotel's facilities are excellent, including pool, internet, gym, beach bar, restaurant and pool table. There's also an attached kite and windsurfing school (see Windsurfing, below), horse riding and bike hire. The more expensive (and better value) rooms face the beach. Breakfast is included. Book ahead.

€€€ La Sacristía
C San Donato 8, T956-681759, www.lasacristia.net.
Pleasingly refurbished 17th-century building in the heart of town, ideal for a relaxing stay. There's a distinctly Japanese feel to the decor; rooms are simply but attractively furnished, with massive beds, tasteful lamps, floor mats, antique chairs and objets d'art, heating and fine bathrooms. The best one is an attic-like apartment under the dark wooden roof. Downstairs there's an enticing lounge with a fireplace. Some meals can be

arranged (breakfast is included). Live guitar music some evenings.

€€€ Room Tarifa
C Silos 26, T956-682229, www.roomtarifa.com.
Tucked into a great location in the old town, this simple boutique-style place offers small but beautiful rooms with modern bathroom facilities and an exceptionally cordial welcome. The roof terrace is the place to be for views over town in the early evening. A mite overpriced in summer perhaps, but that's Tarifa.

€€ Hostal La Calzada
C Justino Pertínez 7, T956-681492, www.hostallacalzada.com.
Smuggled away up a side street near the church, this offers friendly folk at the front desk and very welcoming rooms, warmly decorated with a caring touch and featuring nice touches like ceramic vases and colourful tilework.

€€ Huerta Grande
Pelayo s/n, T956-679700, www.huertagrande.com.
A very peaceful complex of *casas rurales* set 15 mins' drive east of Tarifa in the Parque Natural de Los Alcornocales. There are wooden cabins and refurbished country houses, all well-equipped and available as complete buildings or per room. The furniture is beautifully wooden and rustic; there are verandas for enjoying the sun, fine views, and a pool and restaurant.

€€ Posada Vagamundos
C San Francisco 18, T956-681513, www.posadavagamundos.com.
This posh *hostal* has a fabulous location in the narrow streets at the heart of old Tarifa. Set in a well-restored old building, the rooms are unobtrusively stylish, if not particularly spacious. Noise can be a problem in summer. The café downstairs has a Zen feel and does pleasing mojitos.

€ Hostal Africa
C María Antonia Toledo 12, T956-680220, www.hostalafrica.com.
This excellent budget choice is just inside the Puerta de Jerez on a quiet street in the old town. The rooms, with or without bath, are warmly welcoming, painted in attractive colours, and with seriously comfortable beds; there's also a roof terrace. The young owners are lively and welcoming; they can store boards or do washing. Recommended.

Camping

There are several campsites near Tarifa, strung out along Playa de los Lances.

Camping Tarifa
Ctra N340 Km 78, T956-684778, www.campingtarifa.es. Open all year.
Near the **Hurricane Hotel** by the beach and has good facilities including well-equipped wooden bungalows (€130) that fit a whole family.

Restaurants

There's a huge range of eating choice in Tarifa during summer, and places are constantly coming and going. In winter far fewer spots are open. Along Playa de los Lances, several of the hotels have excellent restaurants, while in town there are traditional Spanish options, several places offering different international cuisines, and various windsurfer spots with traveller-fusion cuisine and plenty of vegetarian choice.

€€ An 'Cá' Curro
C Moreno de Mora 5, T654-858012.
A classy little establishment with a taurine theme, this tavern doles

out superb *raciones* of high-quality produce. The pork dishes are succulent, the artichokes and the ham are also memorable. Recommended.

€€ El Lola
C Guzmán el Bueno 5, T956-627307, www.ellolatarifa.com.
Bright and upbeat, this is named after the flamenco artist Lola Flores and decorated to match, with red and polka dots all over. Decent wines are served out of magnums, there's flamenco on the stereo, a rock garden feature and delicious tapas cheerfully plated and presented. There's lots of outdoor seating too on this pleasant street of bars. A great place.

€€ Mandrágora
C Independencia 3, T956-681291, www.mandragoratarifa.com.
A romantic restaurant on a secluded street near the church, this is a Tarifa favourite. You can chow down on couscous or tagines, or stick to this side of the straits with Spanish seafood like octopus or sea anemones. There's plenty of vegetarian choice and a thoughtful selection of wines from around the country. The quality of some dishes is spectacular. Recommended.

€€ Vaca Loca
C Cervantes 6, T685-281791.
Tucked away in the heart of old Tarifa, this bar is a popular evening destination. Though it can feel a bit touristy, what keep people coming are the outdoor tables, where sizzling offerings from the barbecue are served: huge steaks, sausages and brochettes.

€ El Francés
C Sancho IV El Bravo 21.
This sweet little French-run tapas bar on the main street through the old town packs 'em in for its delicious, generous servings of tuna and other delicacies. There's also a small side terrace for sit-down dining.

Bars and clubs

In summer action centres around the *chiringuitos* on the beaches and the latest ephemeral *discoteca*; off season the bars in the old town are quiet but the place to be.

Misiana
C Sancho IV El Bravo 18.
This bar under the hotel of the same name is the most stylish spot in town, with designer lighting and chic furniture, including some very snug seating options. It's the most fashionable drinking option in town, but drinks are extremely expensive for Spain.

What to do

There are numerous activity companies, offering windsurfing, kitesurfing, climbing, biking, beach horse riding, quad-biking and whale watching among other things. The tourist office (see page 190) has a full list of operators.

Day trips to Morocco

Numerous agencies offer day trips to Morocco on the ferry; these include a guided visit to Tanger and lunch for around €60. There are more elaborate options with overnight stays, and trips to Fez and Marrakech.

Diving

Aventura Marina, *Av Andalucía 1, T956-681932, www.aventuramarina.org.*
Yellow Sub, *C Covadonga s/n, T655-813304, www.yellowsubtarifa.com.*

Horse riding

Hotel Dos Mares, *Ctra N340 Km 79.5, T626-480019, www.aventuraecuestre.com.*
Hurricane Hípica, *Ctra N340 Km 78, T956-689092, www.tarifahip.com.*

Kitesurfing

Kitesurfing is big in Tarifa and there are 30 or more places to hire equipment or learn the basics, mostly along the main road. It costs around €90-130 for a 2-hr beginners' class. The best conditions depend on the wind, but are typically in the afternoon, so wait until morning before asking about conditions and booking your class.
Tarifa Air Force, *Polígono Industrial La Vega, T672-456664, www.tarifairforce.com.*
Tarifa Max, *C Batalla de Salado s/n, T696-558227, www.tarifamax.net.*

Whale and dolphin watching

Several operators run whale- and dolphin-watching trips out of Tarifa: **FIRMM**, C Pedro Cortés 4, T956-627008, www.firmm.org, is the best, a marine foundation studying the area's cetaceans. They charge €30, run Mar-Oct, and trips should be booked a couple of days in advance. You are more or less guaranteed to see dolphins, and possibly pilot whales, depending on the season. FIRMM offer you another trip free if you don't see anything.

Windsurfing

Tarifa's 2 major winds, the easterly *levante* and the westerly *poniente*, create excellent windsurfing conditions along the beautiful Playa de los Lances, which stretches from town 11 km north. There are heaps of windsurfing schools that give lessons and hire equipment, including **Club Mistral**, at the Hurricane Hotel, Ctra N340 Km 78, T956-689098, www.club-mistral.com, and **Escuela Dos Mares**, at the Hotel Dos Mares, Ctra N340 Km 79.5, T956-684035. Board rental will cost about €60-70 per day, a half-day lesson is around €150.

Transport

Boat

There are 4 daily departures to **Tanger**, taking 45 mins. If planning a day trip, ask in a travel agents, who throw in lunch and a city tour for the same price as a return ticket. Anyone with a right to enter Morocco is allowed on (EU citizens, Australians, Americans, Canadians, New Zealanders and more).
FRS, T956-681830, www.frs.es. Also offers car transport on their fast boats, and charge €37/105 per person/vehicle.

Bus

Comes buses serve Tarifa, and leave from Av Batalla del Salado near the Puerta de Jerez, T956-657555. There are 6 daily buses to **Cádiz** (1 hr 20 mins) 1 to **Jerez** and 4 to **Sevilla**. In an easterly direction, there are regular buses to **Algeciras** (30 mins), and **La Línea**, the entry point for visits to **Gibraltar**. 1 bus on weekdays travels to **Zahara de los Atunes**, **Barbate**, **Los Caños de Meca** and **Conil**. There are 2 buses to **Málaga**. In summer, buses run at weekends to **Bolonia**.

In summer, a local bus company runs a service from town along Playa de los Lances, stopping at hotels en route, and sometimes going as far as Bolonia. The schedule changes each year, so ring or ask at the tourist office for details.

Gibraltar
& around

The controversial British territory of Gibraltar sits on a small headland completely dominated by its famous Rock, a spectacular mountain visible for many miles around.

While one suspects that Britain would, these days, happily hand it over to Spain if it wouldn't lose the incumbent government too many votes, the locals, who are for the most part a curious mix of Mediterranean races, staunchly and understandably demand that their opinion be considered, and an overwhelming majority of them, despite Spanish being their first language, prefer the status quo, with all the economic benefits of being a tax haven and duty-free zone.

There's now barely a British military presence here, but the settlement is busy with tourists, who come to see the monkeys and to buy cheap booze and fags, and sailors from docking warships. If you've just come from Britain, you probably won't see much need to visit, but if you crave a pint of bitter and a pub lunch (think microwaved pies and frozen chips: there's no ham hock terrine or charred sea bass fillets here), it's just the spot. It's well worth heading up to the Upper Rock for the spectacular views as well as the fascinating siege tunnels and the aggressive monkeys. *Colour map 4, C4.*

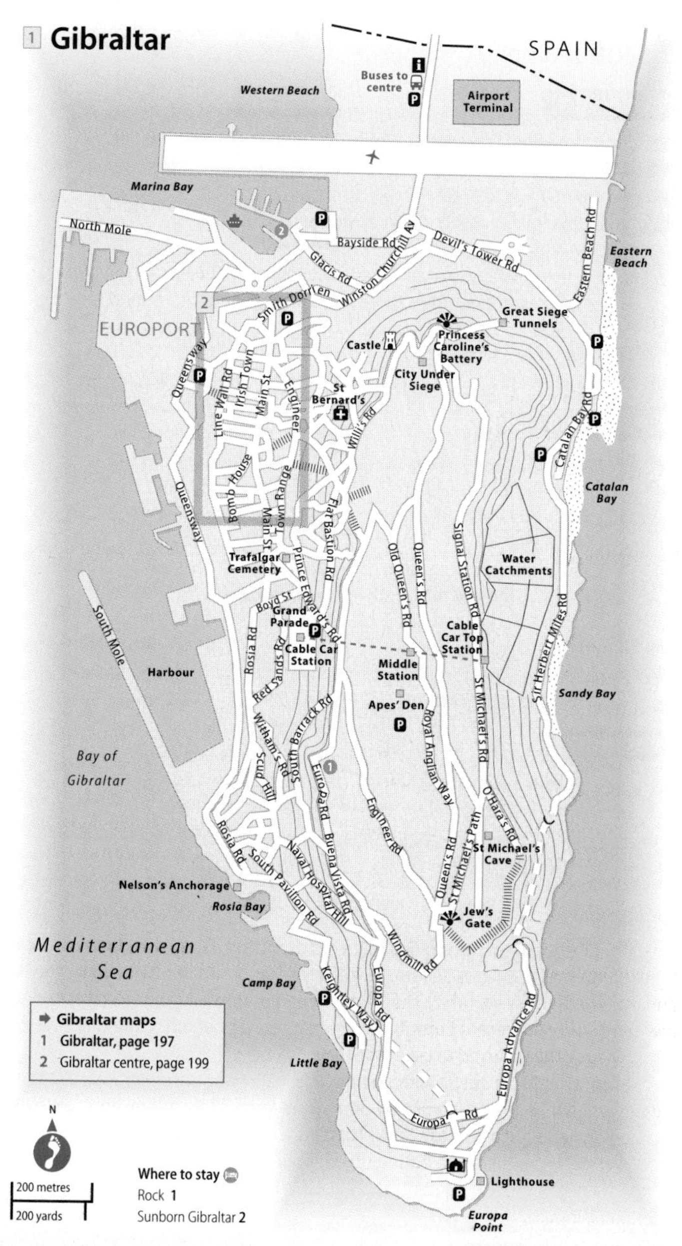
1 Gibraltar
SPAIN
Buses to centre
Western Beach
Airport Terminal
Marina Bay
North Mole
Bayside Rd
Glacis Rd
Winston Churchill Av
Devil's Tower Rd
Eastern Beach Rd
Eastern Beach
Smith Dorrien
EUROPORT
Queensway
Line Wall Rd
Irish Town
Main St
Engineer
Great Siege Tunnels
Princess Caroline's Battery
Castle
City Under Siege
St Bernard's
Willis's Rd
Catalan Bay Rd
Catalan Bay
Bomb House
Town Range
Flat Bastion Rd
Old Queen's Rd
Queen's Rd
Signal Station Rd
Water Catchments
Trafalgar Cemetery
Prince Edward's Rd
Boyd St
Grand Parade
Rosia Rd
Red Sands Rd
Cable Car Station
Middle Station
Cable Car Top Station
Sir Herbert Miles Rd
South Mole
Harbour
Apes' Den
St Michael's Rd
Sandy Bay
Royal Anglian Way
Witham's Rd
Scud Hill
South Barrack Rd
Europa Rd
Bay of Gibraltar
Engineer Rd
O'Hara's Rd
St Michael's Path
St Michael's Cave
Buena Vista Rd
Naval Hospital Hill
South Pavilion Rd
Nelson's Anchorage
Rosia Bay
Jew's Gate
Windmill Rd
Mediterranean Sea
Camp Bay
Keightley Way
Europa Advance Rd
Gibraltar maps
1 Gibraltar, page 197
2 Gibraltar centre, page 199
Little Bay
N
Lighthouse
200 metres
200 yards
Where to stay
Rock 1
Sunborn Gibraltar 2
Europa Point

Essential Gibraltar

Immigration

You'll need a passport to get in, but you don't necessarily need a British visa; citizens of the EU can enter freely. Visit www.gibraltar.gov.uk for details. You can't use a trip to Gibraltar to renew your permitted stay in Spain, as British officials won't stamp your passport. If you've only got a single entry to Spain, check with Spanish officials before crossing.

Finding your feet

The main town stretches in a long line on either side of the pedestrianized Main Street. At the entrance to town is the open Casemates Square, from where the appealing Landport Tunnel runs towards the airport: this was once the only access to the citadel town. The Rock looms over everything; there are two access roads to the upper levels, as well as a cable car at the far end of town.

Electricity

Electricity current is the same as the UK, 230V, with three-pronged sockets. Electrical adaptors for European plugs are easily purchased.

Language

The official language is English, but Gibraltarians mostly speak Spanish among themselves.

Money

Currencies in Gibraltar are the Gibraltar pound and the British pound, although euros are accepted everywhere. It's worth getting pounds if you're going to stay a while, as exchange rates for euros in shops are usually poor. The Gibraltar pound, although equivalent to the sterling, is difficult to use in most of Europe; Spanish banks won't take it, so convert unused Gibraltar pounds into euros or sterling before you leave. There are several ATMs.

Telephone

The country code for Gibraltar is +350, followed by the local number. Dialling Spain from Gibraltar, you must add the +34 international code. Payphones don't take euros. Gibraltar has its own mobile network, Gibtel; if you are using a Spanish mobile phone, you may want to manually select your Spanish operator so as not to be charged roaming rates

Gibraltar

The original entrance to the **Lower Town** old district is through Landport, a tunnel that emerges in Casemates Square. Various fortifications snake their way up the hill and from here the walls run to the southern end of town. All the land west of the walls, including the recent **Europort** development, has been reclaimed during the 20th century; the sea used to lap at the fortifications.

The **Gibraltar Museum** ⓘ *Bomb House Lane, www.gibmuseum.gi, Mon-Fri 1000-1800, Sat 1000-1400 (last admission 30 mins before), £2,* is interesting, covering archaeology and history of the Rock. There's a 15-minute film, as well as superbly preserved 14th-century Arab baths and old photos and prints showing the colony in various stages of development. There's also a replica of the Neanderthal skull of 'Gibraltar Woman'.

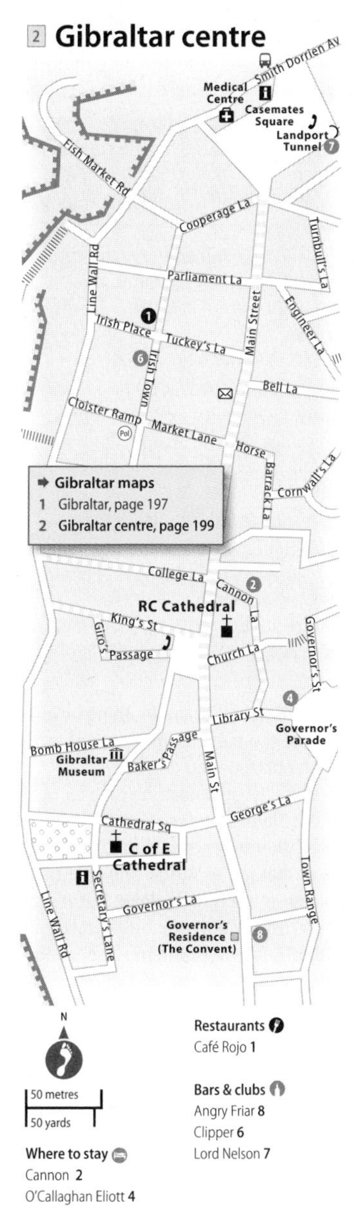

Just outside Southport, the gateway at the southern end of Main Street, is the **Trafalgar Cemetery**, where some of the graves are of British sailors who died in the nearby Battle of Trafalgar in 1805. Beyond here is **Nelson's Anchorage** ⓘ *Rosia Rd, Mon-Sat 0930-1745 (1845 summer), £1, free with Upper Rock Nature Reserve ticket*, where there's the massive 19th-century Hundred Ton Gun. It was here that the body of Nelson himself was brought ashore, allegedly stashed in a rum barrel to preserve it for burial.

At the end of the promontory is **Europa Point**, which has a mosque and a lighthouse. From here, it's easy to see dolphins and it's also a good spot for birdwatching.

The **Upper Rock** ⓘ *daily 0900-1815 (0930-1915 summer), £10 (5-12 year olds £5) for all the sights, £0.50 if you just want to wander around, cars £2 extra*, is a large area that has spectacular views across to Morocco over the Bahía de Algeciras. There are several sights; to see them all in a short time, you're best off taking the taxi tour, see What to do, below. Another option is to take the **cable car** ⓘ *1000-1745 (0930-1945 summer), last ascent 1715 (1915) and last descent 1745 (1945), closed days of high wind (relatively frequent), £10.50 return, £5 children*, leaving the Grand Parade. With your return ticket, you can stop halfway up to visit the Apes' Den. You can also walk up the rock, either following Willi's Road up past the hospital, or the path off Flat Bastion Road. It takes around three hours to cover all the sights on foot.

At the southern end of the Upper Rock, there's a superb viewpoint known as the **Jew's Gate** that looks across to Morocco and Algeciras. A monument commemorates Gibraltar's founding as Mons Calpe by the Phoenicians and its

BACKGROUND

Gibraltar

The rock's numerous defensible caves made it a Millionaires' Row for prehistoric hominids; indeed the 1848 finding of a fossilized female cranium, dubbed Gibraltar Woman, was the first evidence of Neanderthals brought to light. Later, the Phoenicians knew Gibraltar as Calpe and in Greek mythology it formed one of the twin Pillars of Hercules.

When the Moors crossed the Straits in AD 711, they named the rock after their leader; Jebel Tarik (mountain of Tarik), which became Gibraltar. The settlement was founded in 1159 by the Almohads, stayed in Moorish hands until 1309, then was regained in a siege in 1334.

The Moors were finally evicted in 1462; the Spaniards, who added to the fortifications, were to stay for a further 240 years until the War of the Spanish Succession. Britain gained formal sovereignty over the Rock in the Treaty of Utrecht in 1713 and has remained there ever since, despite Spain's diplomatic and military attempts to regain it, most seriously in 1779 when the arduous Great Siege was to last over 3½ years.

At the start of the 1800s, Gibraltar's strategic position was fully utilized during the Napoleonic Wars. After Nelson's victory at nearby Cape Trafalgar, HMS Victory limped into Rosia Bay, with the Admiral's body in a barrel of rum. Some crew members are buried at Trafalgar cemetery.

Gibraltar played an important role in both World Wars. During these times the Rock became honeycombed with passages, augmenting the existing

status as one of the Pillars of Hercules, marking the *non plus ultra* (nothing beyond) of the known world. Ascending from here, note the metal rings attached to the stone; these were used to haul cannon up to the batteries on the rock.

St Michael's Cave is an attractive if over-embellished limestone cave complex that was once believed to be the gateway to Hades, understandably as it sat atop a rock at the end of the known world. Other legends included the belief that it went down to an underground tunnel that led to Africa, and that this is how the monkeys first came over. The stalactites are mostly dead, but it's still worth a visit, especially to see a fascinating cross-section of a huge stalagmite with growth rings like a tree. There's an auditorium inside, and music playing to heighten the atmosphere.

Gibraltar's Barbary apes are in fact macaque monkeys, thought to have been brought over by the Moors. The only wild monkeys in Europe, they have thrived here, and are now wholly accustomed to humankind, to the point where their brand of aggressive cheekiness is something of a problem. They frequently grab tourists' bags if they suspect there are any foodstuffs within, and sometimes bite if they encounter resistance. You can see them all over the Rock, but they tend to hang out at the **Apes' Den**, where they get fed and are encouraged to pose for photos. Be careful around them though. If travelling by cable car, you can get off at caves, making a formidable fortress guarding the western entrance to the Mediterranean. It was during the Second World War that Winston Churchill, on hearing the legend that if the Barbary apes left the Rock, then the British would too, insisted for propaganda reasons that their number should never fall below 35.

In the post-war period, Franco continued to try to persuade the British to give up the Rock, and eventually closed the border in 1965; however, this only served to make the llanitos even more anti-Spanish.

The borders were finally re-opened in 1985. In an attempt to gain economic independence, Gibraltar established a casual attitude to financial regulation that infuriated Spain and the EU. Some controls, including steps to combat money laundering, came into place in 2010. The long-serving chief minister, Peter Caruana, was generally a positive force for change of this sort, clamping down on smuggling and improving relations with Spain. In late 2011, after nearly 16 years as chief minister, Caruana was defeated by a Labour/Liberal coalition led by Fabian Picardo.

Gibraltar has held referendums (declared illegal by Britain) in which a massive majority has affirmed their wish to remain under the British umbrella. While Britain and Spain seem prepared to come to agreement over the Crown Colony, the wishes of the inhabitants have frustrated their designs. The Rajoy PP goverment has been aggressive in its stance towards the enclave, perhaps in part to divert attention from Spain's economic and corruption problems.

Much of today's Gibraltar stands on reclaimed land that has considerably enlarged the area of the colony.

the middle station for the Apes' Den, which is north from St Michael's Cave, on the way towards the siege tunnels.

Princess Caroline's battery offers more excellent views over the north part of Gibraltar and across to La Línea. Up the hill from here are the **Great Siege Tunnels**, the most interesting part of the Upper Rock. These were carved out of the mountain in the Great Siege of the early 1780s to bring guns to bear on the Spanish and French forces. The whole Rock is riddled with similar tunnels. Below the lookout is the mediocre City Under Siege exhibition; the colony has had 14 sieges, and historical documents describe conditions better than do the waxwork soldiers around this ruined bunker.

Near here, the Moorish Castle, used as a prison until 2010, stands guard high above the only landward access to Gibraltar, while the Military Heritage Centre, set in a gun battery, commemorates British services and has a display of weaponry.

Tourist information

Casemates Square tourist office
Casemates Sq s/n, T2005 0762.
Mon-Fri 0900-1730, Sat 1000-1500, Sun 1000-1300.
This is the most useful of several tourist offices in town. There is also a booth (Mon-Fri 0930-1630, plus weekends in summer), in the customs building as you enter Gibraltar. See www.visitgibraltar.gi. There's a police station at 120 Irish Town.

Where to stay

Price codes for Gibraltar are the same as the rest of the book (converted into euros). Better budget options are in La Línea across the border.

€€€€ O'Callaghan Eliott Hotel
Governor's Pde, T2007 0500, www.elliotthotel.com.
Just off the main street but removed from the bustle, this business hotel boasts an impressive array of facilities and great vistas from most of the rooms, though the view from the rooftop bar-restaurant tops the lot.

€€€€ The Rock Hotel
Europa Rd, T2007 3000, www.rockhotelgibraltar.com.
On the slope of The Rock itself at the southern end, this iconic Gibraltar joint is overpriced but has been recently renovated. Rooms have wonderful views over the Algeciras bay, and many have balconies.

€€€€ Sunborn Gibraltar
Ocean Village, T2001 6100, www.sunborn.com.
Perfect for seasickness sufferers, this luxurious cruise ship is parked at Ocean Village and doesn't move. It's not cheap but has an immense amount of facilities, including a pretty pool and several onboard eateries. Rooms are very smart, with seriously comfortable beds. Views are great.

€€ Cannon Hotel
9 Cannon Lane, T2005 1711, www.cannonhotel.gi.
This cheapie is just off the main pedestrian drag. It's pretty basic, but reasonable value for pricey Gibraltar. The rooms come with or without bathroom; a pleasant little patio and a bar are the best features.

Apartments

Email the tourist office (see Tourist information, above) for a list of rental apartments in Gibraltar.

Restaurants

Gibraltar has many mediocre British-style pubs serving unreconstructed bar meals.

€€ Cafe Rojo
54 Irish Town, T2005 1738.
Excellent-value bistro fare served in a friendly, intimate atmosphere. There are tempting mains like tuna steak, a wide range of innovative salads and delicious pastas. Plenty of vegetarian options and super desserts. Worth booking as it often fills.

Bars and clubs

The Angry Friar
287 Main St, T2007 1570.

A busy pub with an outdoor terrace. Average pub meals and decent pints. Opposite the Governor's residence; you can watch the changing of the guard from the pub doorway.

Clipper Bar
78 Irish Town, T2007 9791.
Lively bar with a predictable nautical decor and cheerful bar staff. Several beers on tap and good-value generous dishes. Probably the Rock's best boozer.

Lord Nelson
10 Casemates Sq, T2005 0009.
A trendy bar open later than most with live music, often jazz, with a small cover charge.

Shopping

The astoundingly cheap cigarettes and alcohol attract thousands each day. The drawback is that, as Gibraltar isn't part of the European Economic Zone, you can only take normal duty-free limits back into Spain (ie 200 cigarettes and 1 litre of spirits per adult).

What to do

Dolphin watching

A number of companies offer dolphin-watching trips. These include: **Dolphin Safari**, T2007 1914 (T607-290400 calling from Spain), www.dolphinsafari.gi, and **Dolphin Adventure**, T2005 0650 (T605-608208 from Spain), www.dolphin.gi. The trips last about 2 hrs and cost around £20-25. You should see plenty of dolphins and occasionally whales.

Taxi tours

A handy option for seeing the sights of the Upper Rock is taking a tour by minivan-taxi. This takes you around all the locations up the hill for £15-20 per person (plus the entry fee to the reserve, an additional £10.50 each). Tours require a minimum of 4 people but, if you ask, you'll usually be put in with another group fairly rapidly. This can be arranged at any cab rank; the best is the one outside of Southgate. Make sure the driver takes you to the Great Siege Tunnels, as they'll often try and dissuade you so they can get back quicker. Tour lasts 1½ hrs, longer and shorter tours are negotiable. Try for a discount when things are quiet. The drivers usually are very good sources of information.

Transport

Air

The airport is at the entrance to the colony; you intriguingly have to cross the runway to enter the town.

There are several daily flights to Gibraltar from London and other British cities, mostly with **British Airways** and budget operators **Monarch** and **Easyjet**.

Road

The border with Spain is open 24 hrs. There's usually a long queue of cars, so it's wise to leave your vehicle in La Línea and walk across. From the border to the centre is a 15-min walk. If you do bring your car, drive on the right in Gibraltar, as in Spain. Parking is difficult, but there's often space in free car parks on Line Wall Rd or Queens Way. Petrol is marginally cheaper here.

On leaving Gibraltar by road allow time for delays at the border. **FRS**, T956-681830, www.frs.es, run 3 times a week from Gibraltar to **Tanger**.

Around Gibraltar → *Colour map 4, C3.*

frontier post and busy port with boats to Morocco

La Línea de la Concepción

This place, with the bay of Algeciras on one side and the Atlantic on the other, was built after the dividing line was agreed in the 18th century; the agreement placed the town just beyond cannon range. It's a friendly place that's growing at a fast rate. If you're planning a visit to the Rock, you might consider sleeping in one of the good budget options here. Parking your car here is a good option for visiting Gibraltar, to avoid the border queues. There's plenty of above-ground space (but don't leave any valuables in your car); underground car parks near the border charge around €18 for 24 hours, and have deals for longer stays.

La Línea's handiest **tourist office** ⓘ *Av Príncipe de Asturias s/n, T956-171998, www.ayto-lalinea.org, Mon-Fri 0800-1500*, is opposite the border post. Between here and the beach are numerous Second World War bunkers built by the Spaniards under German supervision for use in a planned attack on Gibraltar, which was codenamed *Operation Felix*. In the wake of the famous stalemate meeting between Franco and Hitler at Hendaye, this never in fact occurred. The **Museo Taurino** ⓘ *C Mateo Inurria 2, T856-225535, Mon-Sat 1200-1500, €4*, is a likeable museum absolutely crammed with bullfighting pictures and memorabilia.

Algeciras

A sizeable city, Algeciras is one of the few places in Andalucía to offer little to the visitor, apart from its busy passenger port with sailings to Ceuta or Tanger. In summer, Algeciras is the destination for thousands of Moroccans, who head home from jobs in Europe to visit friends and family.

Algeciras has an interesting history but, unfortunately, ugly urban expansion has left almost no trace of it. It was an important Roman port, and later the landing point for the first Moorish armies in their invasion of the peninsula in AD 711. Raided by the Vikings in AD 859, it was later seized by raiding Berbers during the collapse of the Córdoba caliphate and became a self-governing *taifa* state until the rulers of Sevilla grabbed control of it. It's now one of Spain's more important ports.

The area around Plaza Alta is the best zone for a bite to eat. The **tourist office** ⓘ *C Juan de la Cierva s/n, T956-571254, otalgeciras@andalucia.org, Mon-Fri 0900-1930, Sat-Sun 0930-1500*, is between the train station and the port; there's also a small tourist kiosk at the entrance to the ferry port area.

Listings Around Gibraltar

Where to stay

If you need to stay in Algeciras, there are numerous cheap options around the port, many of which are distinctly seedy.

Algeciras

€€€ Hotel Reina Cristina
Paseo de la Conferencia s/n, T956-602622, www.hoteles globales.com.
A historic and elegant hotel set in gardens a few mins' walk from the centre. It's had many famous guests and was a hotbed of espionage during the Second World War. It's slightly faded now, but has excellent facilities including a pool and tennis courts. It gets quite busy in summer with package tourists; there's a minimum week's stay in Aug.

Restaurants

Algeciras

€ Las Duelas
Plaza Neda 2, T956-665945, www.mesonlasduelas.es.
With a strong claim to being the city's best tapas bar, this place is adorned with pictures of local bullfighter Fernando Ruíz Miguel in action (signed) and various Semana Santa Christs (not). They do fine smoked fish and a daily tapa special that is always delicious.

Transport

La Línea de la Concepción

Bus

There's no cross-border transport between Spain and Gibraltar, so you have to get to La Línea and cross on foot or in your own vehicle. Buses (line 5) run from near the border post to the centre, a ticket costs £1.30 or €1.80.

As there's no cross-border transport, La Línea is where you get off for Gibraltar. The bus station is a block back from the frontier, and is frequently connected with **Algeciras** (half-hourly, 45 mins), **Málaga** via **Marbella** (4-6 a day, 2 hrs 30 mins), **Tarifa** and **Cádiz** (3-4 daily, 2 hrs 30 mins). There are also daily services to **Sevilla** and **Granada**.

Algeciras

Bus

Comes, near the train station on C San Bernardo, runs half-hourly buses all over the province. From Av Virgen del Carmen 17, opposite the ferry terminal, there are direct services to **Granada**, **Málaga**, and most other Andalucían capitals, as well as coast-hopping buses east along the **Costa del Sol**. There are also services to **Madrid** and **Barcelona**.

Ferry

C San Bernardo leads almost directly to the large modern ferry port, which is close to the town centre. Some buses arrive and depart from the ferry port itself.

There are several ferry companies operating services to **Ceuta** and **Tanger**. There are departures almost half-hourly to both destinations. The ferries take 2 hrs 30 mins, and cost around €45 1 way, and €75-110 for a car. Faster catamarans take 35 mins and are only marginally pricier. You can buy the tickets directly from the companies (**Balearia**, www.balearia.com; **FRS**, www.frs.es; **Trasmediterranea**, www.trasmediterranea.es; and **Intershipping**, www.intershipping.es), from an online broker like www.directferries.co.uk, from a travel agent in town or at the port.

Train

There are 3 daily trains to **Granada** (4 hrs), and 2 to **Madrid** (5 hrs). All go through **Ronda** (1 hr 45 mins), and **Bobadilla**, a junction where you can change for other Andalucían towns.

Málaga

a vibrant provincial capital and rugged mountains

The capital is the vastly underrated Málaga, Andalucía's second largest city with a lively nightlife, Picasso museum, trendy shops and some of the region's best tapas bars. The town's sandy beach is more attractive than many gravelly strips on the Costa del Sol.

Málaga may be Andalucía's smallest province, but it has a significant economy, mostly based on tourism. The Costa del Sol attracts a vast influx of Northern European and Spanish tourists every year, and a large expat population.

The fishing villages along this coast are long gone, swallowed by hotels, bars and golf courses, and towns like the glitzy but notorious resort of Marbella. Venture inland, however, and you'll discover a more authentic Spain. Towns like Antequera with its prehistoric dolmens have an evocative ancient appeal, while Moorish influence is seen in the region's architecture and culture. Also inland is the limestone block of El Torcal, with its surrealistic eroded shapes. The ancient town of Ronda may be on the coach-tour circuit but is still stunning, set on a gorge, while in nearby white villages you still need Spanish to order a beer. The dramatic La Axarquía further east is also dotted with pretty white villages.

Best for
Galleries ▪ History ▪ Tapas ▪ Walking

Footprint picks

★ **Museo Picasso**, page 210

The Picasso Museum has a wealth of works by Málaga's favourite son, while the nearby Carmen Thyssen is a treasure trove of 19th-century Spanish art.

★ **La Axarquía**, page 226

Head for the hills for picturesque Moorish villages and excellent walking.

★ **Marbella**, page 236

Splash the cash at a sumptuous beachside hotel or live it up in one of Spain's best youth hostels.

★ **Bobastro**, page 246

Explore the evocative ruins, stronghold of a ninth-century warlord.

★ **Dolmen de Menga**, page 249

Stop in intriguing Antequera to visit this massive 4500-year-old monument.

★ **Ronda**, page 254

Pace this cloven city, admiring its historic buildings and bullfighting heritage.

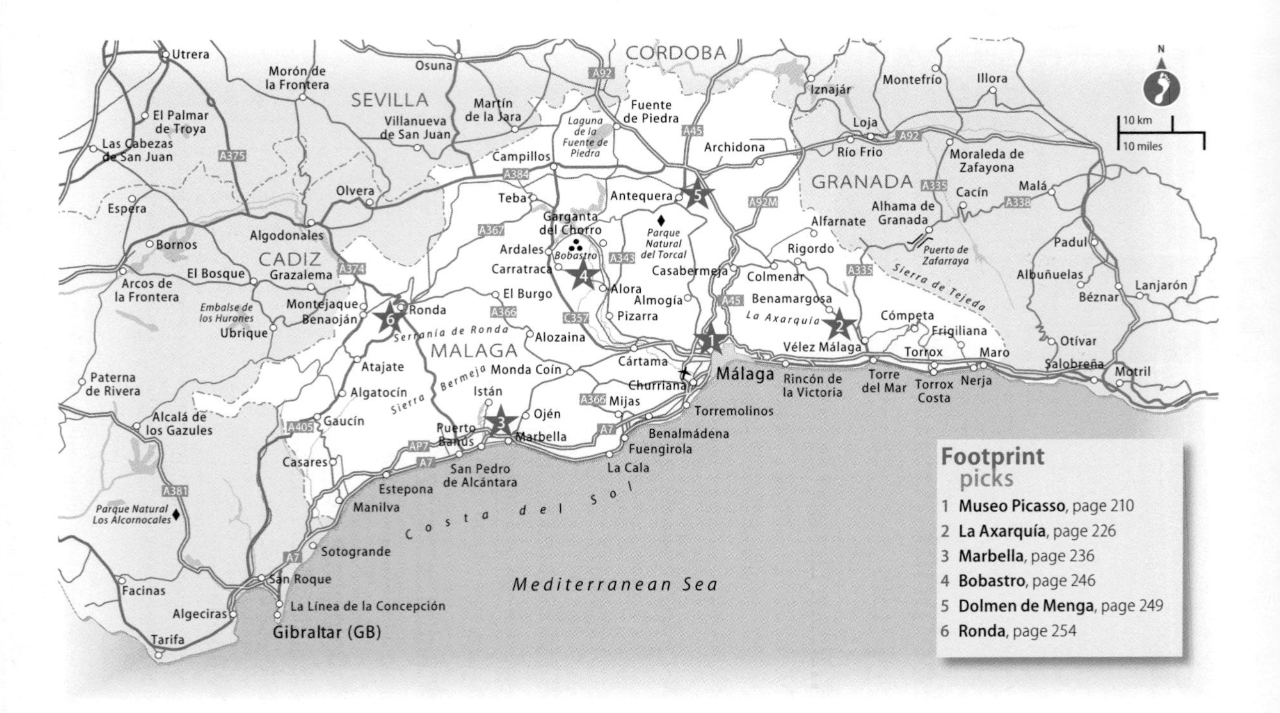

CORDOBA
SEVILLA
CADIZ
MALAGA
GRANADA
Utrera
Morón de la Frontera
Osuna
Martín de la Jara
Villanueva de San Juan
El Palmar de Troya
Las Cabezas de San Juan
Campillos
Laguna de la Fuente de Piedra
Fuente de Piedra
Archidona
Iznajár
Montefrío
Illora
Loja
Río Frio
Moraleda de Zafayona
Olvera
Espera
Teba
Antequera
Garganta del Chorro
Parque Natural del Torcal
Alhama de Granada
Cacín
Malá
Alfarnate
Padul
Algodonales
Bornos
Ardales
Bobastro
Carratraca
Casabermeja
Colmenar
Rigordo
Puerto de Zafarraya
Sierra de Tejeda
Albuñuelas
Lanjarón
Béznar
Arcos de la Frontera
El Bosque
Grazalema
Montejaque
Benaoján
Ronda
Embalse de los Hurones
Ubrique
El Burgo
Alora
Almogía
Pizarra
Benamargosa
La Axarquía
Cómpeta
Frigiliana
Serranía de Ronda
Alozaina
Vélez Málaga
Torrox
Maro
Otívar
Salobreña
Motril
Atajate
Cártama
Málaga
Rincón de la Victoria
Torre del Mar
Torrox Costa
Nerja
Paterna de Rivera
Monda
Coín
Algatocín
Sierra Bermeja
Istán
Churriana
Mijas
Torremolinos
Alcalá de los Gazules
Gaucín
Ojén
Puerto Banús
Marbella
Benalmádena
Fuengirola
Casares
San Pedro de Alcántara
La Cala
Estepona
Manilva
Parque Natural Los Alcornocales
Costa del Sol
Sotogrande
San Roque
Facinas
Mediterranean Sea
La Línea de la Concepción
Algeciras
Gibraltar (GB)
Tarifa
N
10 km
10 miles
A92
A375
A384
A45
A92M
A335
A338
A367
A343
A374
A366
C357
A405
AP7
A7
A381
Footprint picks
1 Museo Picasso, page 210
2 La Axarquía, page 226
3 Marbella, page 236
4 Bobastro, page 246
5 Dolmen de Menga, page 249
6 Ronda, page 254

Málaga city

Though no more than an airport for millions of sunseekers, Málaga is an important Spanish port and city with plenty to offer, perhaps more than the rest of its province's coast put together. Once bypassed by tourists en route to the beach resorts, these days Andalucía's second largest city is a draw of its own with the Picasso Museum as the main crowd-puller.

Málaga's charm lies in the historic city centre with its narrow pedestrian streets. The long town beach is pretty clean, and there's plenty of good-value accommodation. The city is looking very spruce these days, with the designer boutiques of its central streets overlooked by the Moorish castle. It's also got a great tapas scene and one of Andalucía's liveliest fiestas. *Colour map 5, B1.*

Historic centre

majestic cathedral, sun-baked ochre buildings and narrow streets

Most of the places of interest in Málaga are contained within a compact atmospheric area of 19th-century streets and squares north of the main east–west thoroughfare and can be conveniently visited on foot. Look out for the new Museo de Málaga, whose archaeological and art collections are to be located in the sturdy Palacio de la Aduana near the Roman theatre; it's due to open in early 2016.

The cathedral and around

C Molina Lario s/n, T952-215917. Mon-Fri 1000-1800, Sat 1000-1700. €5.

Málaga's cathedral, as with many others in Andalucía, was built on the site of a mosque and dates from the 16th century, with numerous modifications at later dates. One of its two towers was never completed, giving it a lopsided appearance, leading to the nickname of *La Manquita*, or the one-armed lady. The interior is both Gothic and Renaissance, while the exterior is typical 18th-century Baroque, aside from a particularly fine Gothic doorway in Plateresque style that dates from the early 16th century.

Essential Málaga

Getting around

Most of Málaga city's monuments and museums are within a compact area and can be conveniently visited on foot. Taxis, however, are cheap and plentiful.

Best restaurants

Antigua Casa de Guardia, page 218
Isabella Taller de Cocina, page 218
Mesón Astorga, page 218

When to go

Málaga is sun-kissed year-round.

Time required

At least two days to see the main sights.

The highlight of the interior is, without doubt, the **choir**. Behind the stalls are some superb carvings of saints, 42 of which are attributed to Pedro de Mena around 1662 (de Mena's house, now a museum devoted to the painter Revello de Toro, is located in a back street about 500 m from the cathedral). Rearing above the choir stalls are two 18th-century organs. The north entrance, the **Portal of the Chains**, which is usually closed except for Semana Santa processions, is surrounded by a fine screen, carved in mahogany and cedar by Francisco Flores in 1772, with the coats of arms of Felipe II. The admission fee to the cathedral also includes entry to the run-down *museo* near the entrance door, which contains the usual vestments and silver.

There are a number of interesting churches in Málaga centre, the most outstanding being the **Iglesia del Sagrario** ⓘ *Mon-Sat 1000-1200, 1700-1830, Sun 1000-1330*, adjacent to the cathedral with an superb Plateresque *retablo*, and **Nuestra Señora de la Victoria** ⓘ *Mon-Sat 0830-1245, 1800-2030, Sun 0830-1300, €2*, in Calle Victoria, which has further work by de Mena.

Next to the cathedral on Plaza del Obispo, surrounded by open-air bars and cafés, is the 18th-century **Palacio del Obispo**, or Episcopal Palace, with one of the most beautiful façades in the city.

★Museo Picasso Málaga

C San Agustín 8, T952-602731, www.museopicassomalaga.org. Tue-Thu 1000-2000, Fri-Sat 1000-2100, Sun 1000-2000. Collection €8, exhibitions €4.50, both €10.

This museum has made a significant impact on Málaga; it's put it on the map as a destination in its own right rather than a transport hub for the Costa del Sol. The museum is set in the beautiful Buenavista palace, and the juxtaposition of Renaissance architecture and modern painting has been artfully realized. On display are some 150 Picasso works, mostly donated by his daughter-in-law and grandson. Most phases of the artist's trajectory are represented, from formal portraiture – *Olga con Mantilla* (1917) is a portrait of his first wife – to Blue Period and Cubist works, and many from the later stages of Picasso's life. While the collection will disappoint some, as Picasso's best work is in other museums in Spain and around the world, it's an excellent opportunity to see a lot of his oeuvre in one

BACKGROUND

Málaga

Málaga has a long history dating back to the Phoenicians, who founded a settlement called *Malaka*, a word derived from *malac*, meaning to salt fish. Málaga became a busy trading port during Roman times, exporting minerals and agricultural produce from the interior. From the eighth century, Málaga was occupied by the Moors, when it was the main port for the province of Granada. It was they, under Yusef I, who built the Gibralfaro fortress in the 14th century. The city fell to the Catholics in 1487 after a long and violent siege.

After the expulsion of the *morisco* population in the mid-16th century, the fortunes of Málaga declined. It was not until the 19th century, when an agricultural-based revival began, that the situation improved. Gradually, the Costa capital began to become a favoured wintering place for wealthy *madrileños*. During the Civil War, Málaga supported the Republicans and the city suffered from the vicious fighting which included an Italian bombardment that destroyed part of its ancient centre.

Over the last 40 years, mass tourism has transformed the neighbouring Costa del Sol, but has thankfully had little damaging effect on the city itself, which remains intrinsically Spanish.

place. There are regular temporary exhibitions on Picasso or his contemporaries; there is also a café and bookshop here.

Not far away, you can visit the **Casa Natal de Picasso** ⓘ *T952-060215, www.fundacionpicasso.es, 0930-2000, €2,* Picasso's birthplace and now the headquarters of the Picasso Foundation. It is located in the large Plaza de la Merced and has a selection of Picasso's ceramics and lithographs as well as a small selection of his parents' personal objects.

The Alcazaba

T952-216005, Nov-Mar Mon 0900-1800, Tue-Sun 0830-1930, Apr-Oct Mon 0900-2000, Tue-Sun 0900-2015. €2.25, free Sun from 1400 (€3.55 joint entry price with Castillo Gibralfaro).

This former fortress and palace was begun by the Moors in the 700s, but most of the structure dates from the mid-11th century. The site was originally occupied by both the Phoenicians and the Romans and there remains a considerable amount of Roman masonry in the walls. The Alcazaba suffered badly during the Catholic Reconquest, but was restored in the 1930s. Today, it consists of a series of terraced, fortified walls and fine gateways, laid out with gardens and running water in typical Moorish style. There's an archaeological display of pottery and other finds. From the terraces of the main palace building there are fine views over the port and the city.

The Castillo Gibralfaro ⓘ *daily 0900-1800, to 2100 Apr-Oct €2.25 (€3.55 joint-entry price with Alcazaba),* literally 'Lighthouse Hill', is a ruined Moorish castle built by Yusef I of Granada in the early 14th century. It is linked to the Alcazaba below by parallel walls. A path leads up to it from the right side of the Alcazaba or approach it by the road that leads from the city up towards the parador via Calle Victoria. Alternatively, take the No 35 bus from Paseo del Parque.

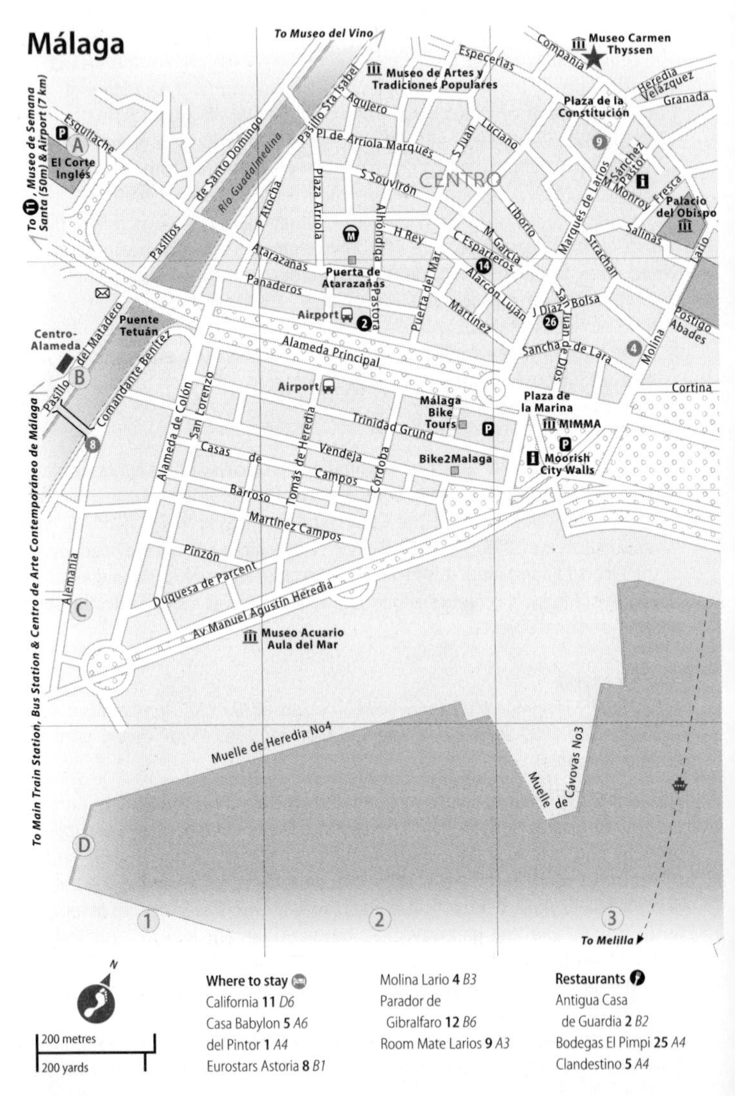

Located close to the entrance of the Alcazaba, the **Teatro Romano** ⓘ *C Alcazabilla 8, Tue 1000-1800, Wed-Sat 0900-1900 (2030 summer), Sun 1000-1600, free*, was built in the early first century AD and used for a couple of centuries. Much of the stone was later used by the Moors for their fortresses above, but restoration

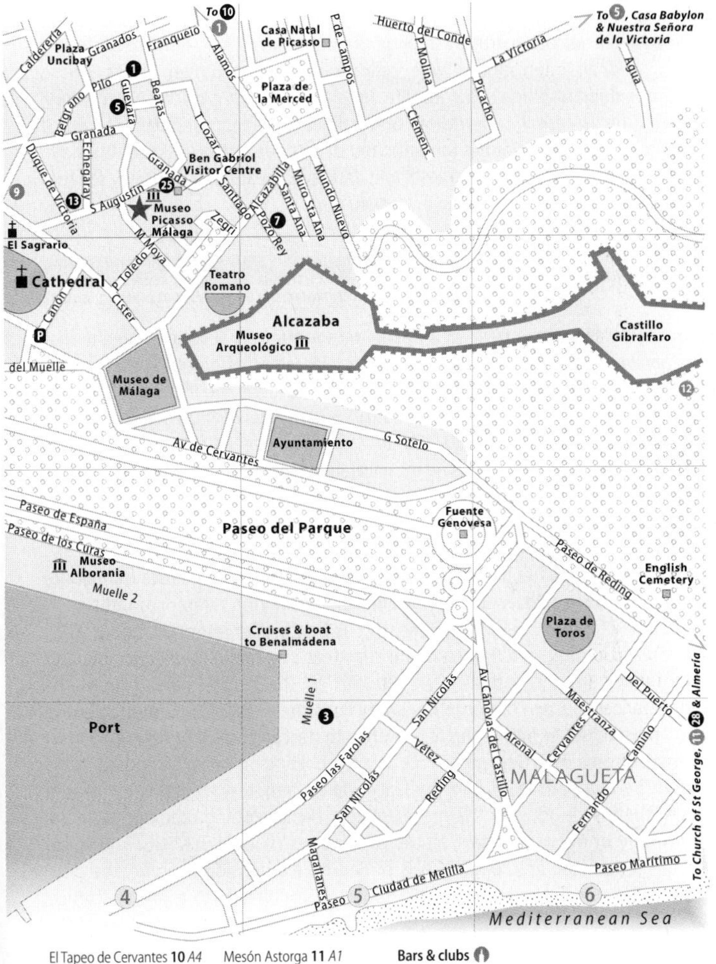

El Tapeo de Cervantes **10** *A4*
El Vegetariano de la Alcazabilla **7** *A5*
Isabella Taller de Cocina **1** *A4*
José Carlos García **3** *D5*
Mesón Astorga **11** *A1*
Mesón el Trillo **26** *B3*
Pitta Bar **13** *A4*
Tintero **28** *D6*

Bars & clubs
Puerta Oscura **9** *A4*

has left the theatre looking rather spruce. There's a small interpretation centre and information in Spanish and English.

★Museo Carmen Thyssen

C Compañía 10, www.carmenthyssenmalaga.org. Tue-Sun 1000-2000. €6.

The excellent Museo Carmen Thyssen in the centre of town holds a fascinating collection of Andalucian artists ranging from Zurbarán to Julio Romero de Torres. There's also an interestingly wide collection of lesser-known artists whose canvases exhibit traditional regional life. The gallery's focus is on the 19th century. It was a difficult century of invasions and political turbulence in Spain, but you'd have no idea of that from the romanticized depictions of the artists of the time. Gypsies, bullfights, muleteers, priests and dark-eyed beauties ... and they say that Andalucía's cliches were a foreign invention?

The waterfront

renovated port area, a great place for a stroll

From the Alcazaba, the tree-lined **Paseo del Parque** is a delightful avenue that runs parallel to the port area and a place of blessed relief on hot summer days. Muelle 2 runs parallel to Paseo del Parque and includes the small and perhaps overpriced **Museo Alborania** ⓘ *Muelle 2, T951-600108, www.museoalborania.com, Oct-Jun Mon-Fri 1000-1400, 1630-2130, to 2330 weekends, Jul-Sep daily 1100-1400, 1700-midnight, €7,* which has some local fish, touch pools, an opening audiovisual and a very constricted turtle tank.

East of here, **Muelle 1** is a new development with shops, boat trips, cycle hire and various eating options.

Further east stretches the city's clean sandy beach, where numerous *chiringuitos* vie for the custom of lovers of seafood and cold beer in the summer months.

A couple of blocks back from the beach, the **English Cemetery** ⓘ *Tue-Sat 1030-1400, Sun 1030-1300, free,* is a beautiful spot that owes its existence to the days when infidels (ie non-Catholics) were buried on the beach, making gruesome reappearances courtesy of storms or hungry dogs. In the mid-18th century, a British consul persuaded the authorities to allow him to start an English cemetery. Look for the small **Church of St George**, a block past the bullring on Paseo de Reding.

From here, a path leads into the leafy walled cemetery, which is a haven of peace. The inscriptions on the gravestones make absorbing reading; there are graves here of many nationalities, the earlier ones covered in shells. The writer Gerald Brenan (see box, page 359) is buried here alongside his wife, the poet Gamel Woolsey; he had wanted his body to be donated to medical science, but was so well respected by the *malagueños* that none of the members of the anatomy faculty could bring themselves to touch him; he finally arrived here in 2000, some 14 years after his death.

Other museums and galleries

social history and contemporary art

Another of Málaga's Moorish curiosities, Puerta de Atarazañas, is at the entrance to the city market. This was originally the gateway into the Moorish dockyard and it displays the crest of the Nasrid dynasty. The market is vibrant and colourful and well worth checking out.

Anyone interested in social history should see the **Museo de Artes y Costumbres Populares** ⓘ *C Pasillo Santa Isabel 10, www.museoartespopulares.com, Mon-Fri 1000-1700, Sat 1000-1400, €4,* which is located by the dried-up bed of the Río Guadalmedina, a two-minute walk from the Alameda. Look for the inn sign labelled Mesón de Victoria, as this museum is housed in an old 17th-century hostelry. The museum consists of a haphazard collection of everyday items from several centuries ago, including fishing boats, an olive press, guns, farming implements and a range of household relics.

The **Centro de Arte Contemporáneo de Málaga** ⓘ *C Alemania s/n, www.cacmalaga.eu, Tue-Sun 1000-2000, summer 1000-1400 and 1700-2100, free,* is dedicated to contemporary art in all its forms. Outside the entrance, a sculpture of a figure with crumpled shirt and trousers (*Man Moving* by German artist Stephen Balkenholl) sets the tone of *vanguardismo*, which includes contemplative photographic studies and paintings, some of them immense in size and all given optimum display space in 2400 m of white, bright exhibition halls. The aim of the centre is to pioneer new artistic trends through four exhibitions which run concurrently: two temporary shows, another for up-and-coming local artists and a changing, permanent exhibition of pieces selected by renowned modern artists.

The **Museo Interactivo de la Música de Málaga (MIMMA)** ⓘ *Plaza de la Marina s/n, www.musicaenaccion.com, Mon 1000-1400, Tue-Sun 1000-1400 and 1600-2000, €4,* is an atmospheric underground space below Plaza de la Marina, the hub of Málaga. Its collection of musical instruments, variety of recordings, and changing exhibitions among the foundations of the Nasrid city walls focus on both traditional and contemporary musical trends.

Málaga's **Museo del Vino** ⓘ *Plaza de los Viñeros 1, www.museovinomalaga.com, €5, Mon-Fri 1000-1700, Sat 1000-1400,* is located in a restored *palacio* a short walk northwest of the old centre. The modern but slightly functional display takes you through the history and actuality of winemaking in the Málaga area through a series of display panels in Spanish. Guided tours leave according to availability for no extra cost and the guide speaks English. The price of admission includes a tasting of a dry and a sweet wine; you can add extra wines for €1 each.

Concepción Botanical Gardens

a cool escape from the heat of the city and beach

4 km north of the city centre, T951-926180, www.laconcepcion.malaga.eu. Tue-Sun 0930-2030, until 1730 in winter, last entry 1 hr before. €5, guided tour, with multilingual guides, for 1½ hrs. Easy access, well signposted off the Málaga–Antequera autovía, just off the Ronda de Málaga; get bus No 2 and walk 10 mins north; city sightseeing tour buses also head out there Tue-Sun from the bus station.

These botanical gardens are well worth a visit and have an interesting history, being created over 150 years ago by Amalia Heredia and her husband, the American George Loring, a mining tycoon, who later became the Marquis of Casa-Loring. They collected plants from many parts of the world and also accumulated an important archaeological collection. The visit leads to a mirador giving stunning views over Málaga (the cathedral and castle are clearly visible) and the enormous stone dam of La Concepción reservoir.

Listings Málaga city *map p212*

Tourist information

Regional tourist office
Pasaje Chinitas 4, T952-213445, otmalaga@andalucia.org. Mon-Fri 0900-1930, Sat and Sun 0930-1500.

Municipal tourist office
Pl de la Marina, T952-926020, www.malagaturismo.com. Daily 0900-1800 (2000 Apr-Oct).
Between the port and the centre, this tourist office has free city audio guides, plus various self-guided walking tours. At C Granada 70, near the Picasso museum, is the Ben Gabirol visitor centre. There are also smaller tourist offices at the airport and bus station, plus several information kiosks in the centre.

Where to stay

There's a good range of accommodation for all budgets in the central area around the Alameda near the port. Prices go up in summer; some cheaper options at this time include university residences, which you can reserve via www.booking.com.

€€€€ Parador de Gibralfaro
Paseo García del Olmo, T952-221902, www.parador.es.
In a dreamy setting, surrounded by pine trees, next to the Moorish castle with panoramic views. The rooms are simply yet tastefully decorated with warm colours, woven rugs and terracotta tiles. There are private entrances and sun terraces. The restaurant dishes up regional and international fare. Have a drink on the terrace even if you're not staying here and take in the vista. Booking essential.

€€€ Hotel Molina Lario
C Molina Lario 20, T952-062002, www.hotelmolinalario.com.
Near the cathedral, this 4-star choice successfully spreads itself to appeal to both the work traveller, with sleek design and business facilities, and families, with kid-friendly staff, and a rooftop pool and

terrace to relax. The rooms are spacious, sparklingly clean and stylishly modern; those facing the street are the most appealing. Recommended.

€€€ Room Mate Larios
Marqués de Larios 2, T952-222200, www.room-mate hotels.com.
This has an upbeat feel to match its top location on Málaga's swanky pedestrian shopping street. The cheerful yet elegant decor features black and white tiles, cream, maroon and warm-toned furnishings and plenty of light wood. Try for a room overlooking the bustling Plaza de la Constitución, although it can be noisy on a Sat night. You can get some very good deals on the website, depending on the date.

€€ Eurostars Astoria
C Comandante Benítez 5, T951-014300, www.eurostars hotels.com.
Slick 3-star hotel near the Contemporary Art Gallery and Alameda train station, for trains to the airport. Rooms are spacious with plenty of gleaming marble and light wood. Excellent value for the price with many extras including hydromassage in the en suite bathrooms and internet access in all rooms. You can get cheaper deals on hotel booking websites.

€€ Hotel California
Paseo de Sancha 17, T952-215164, www.hotelcalifornianet.com.
Near the beach at the eastern end of town, this is a friendly hotel with unremarkable but spacious rooms despite the ominous name. The staff are very helpful and it represents significant value for this coastline.

€€ Hotel del Pintor
C Alamos 27, T952-060980, www.hoteldelpintor.com.
Handily located just on the edge of the old quarter, in easy striking distance of Picasso attractions, this bright white modern place features small but attractive rooms – grab an interior one to avoid the street noise – and friendly staff.

€ Casa Babylon
C Pedro de Quejana 3, T952-267228, www.casababylonhostel.com.
Laid-back but facility packed, this backpackers in a suburban house offers comfortable new bunks, an instant Málaga social life, cheap beer and free internet. The only downside is it's a bit of a trek from the centre of the action. Breakfast included.

Restaurants

There are some very convivial restaurants where you can enjoy traditional local specialities, such as *fritura malagueña* (fried fish), washed down with Málaga's famous wine, a sherry-like substance that comes in sweet and dry varieties. Many of the best fish restaurants as well as *chiringuitos* on the sea can be found in the suburbs of Pedregalejo and El Palo.

€€€€ José Carlos García
Muelle 1, T952-003588, www.restaurantejcg.com.
In a luminous minimalist dining room on Málaga's new waterfront promenade, this takes traditional Andalucían ingredients and gives them a stunning gastro-molecular twist. The degustation menu is €110 plus drinks and, on a good day, it's worth every penny.

€€ Bodegas El Pimpi
C Granada 62, T952-228990, www.elpimpi.com.
Near the Picasso Museum, this labyrinthine former wine warehouse

offers atmosphere in spades, with local sweet and dry drops in barrels signed by famous folk who've been here. If you can grab a table (it's big but often packed), you can snack on traditional Andalucían dishes, but the ambience is better than the food. There's a pleasant terrace around the back opposite the Roman theatre.

€€ Clandestino

C Niño de Guevara 3, T952-219390, www.clandestinomalaga.com. Daily 1300-0100.
This inventive and intensely popular brasserie can resemble a student canteen at first sight, with its chunky wooden tables, relaxed bohemian ambience and scurrying staff. Don't be fooled, as the cuisine is classy and inventive; they aim high, and if they don't always reach, they still comfortably clear most of the places around here.

€€ El Tapeo de Cervantes

C Cárcer 8, T952 609 458, www.eltapeodecervantes.com.
Intimate and charming, one of Málaga's best tapas options is a couple of blocks north of Plaza de la Merced. You might have to wait for one of the few tables, but it's worth it, with excellent traditional dishes backed up by some highly original creations.

€€ Isabella Taller de Cocina

C José Denis Belgrano 25, T951-130018, www.isabellatallerdecocina.com.
This sweet little place can be hard to find but it's worth it. Grab a seat outside if you can – or take a high table by the bar – and enjoy really excellent, innovative and generously proportioned dishes. It's an unusual menu, with North African and other Mediterranean influences, and the originality and quality are outstanding. Recommended.

€€ Mesón Astorga

C Gerona 11, T952-342563, www.mesonastorga.com.
It´s worth the walk out to this welcoming place near the train station for an excellent Málaga dining experience. Top-quality produce, including great grilled meats and fresh fish, is backed up by interesting wines and a genuinely Spanish atmosphere. Recommended.

€€ Mesón el Trillo

C Don Juan Diaz 4, T952-603920, www.grupotrillo.es.
This warm and convivial spot is an atmospheric tapas stop. Excellent wines are available by the glass, and there's a big range of bar food, from *trillos* served on toasted bread, to *revueltos* and delicious chopped steaks. There's also a restaurant menu, served in the spacious interior or on the terrace, but not quite as much love goes into the food, it seems.

€€ Tintero

Playa del Dedo, El Palo, T952-206826, www.restauranteeltintero.com.
One of the most entertaining restaurants (with another branch near Cártama). Waiters bear dishes non-stop into the dining area, shouting what they've got on offer. If you fancy it, grab it from them; nearly all dishes have a standard price. Fried fish is the main thing to try here. It's fast, entertaining and extremely noisy.

€ Antigua Casa de Guardia

Alameda 18, on the corner of C Pastora, T952-214680, www.antiguacasadeguardia.net.
Founded in 1840, this wonderfully atmospheric bar seems to have changed little since then. It opens at 1000 in the morning and starts filling old men's glasses with delicious Málaga wines from the row of barrels behind the bar.

A little seafood stall dishes out prawns and mussels as the perfect accompaniment to a chilled *seco*. A photograph on the wall shows a youthful Picasso knocking one back here. Recommended.

€ El Vegetariano de la Alcazabilla
C Pozo del Rey 5, T952-214858.
One of several vegetarian restaurants around town, this has a handy location at the foot of the Alcazaba and a pleasant quiet terrace. Home-made wholemeal pasta, plenty of salads, vegan dishes and a very tasty mushroom *pil-pil*. On weekdays there's a generous mixed plate for not many euros.

€ Pitta Bar
C Echegaray 8, T952-608675.
Tucked around the corner from the Picasso Museum, you'll find Middle Eastern tapas like falafel, hummus, *baba ghanoush* and tabbouleh. Great for vegetarians. There's a terrace on the street too.

Bars and clubs

The main central nightlife zone is just north of C Granada in the streets around C Luís de Velázquez. Plaza Merced also has some options, while on Plaza Marqués del Vado del Maestre, just off C Caldererίa in the centre, there are also several bars, whose customers merge outside on the square. There is a host of disco-bars south of the bullring, in the Malagueta area, whereas nightlife in the summer months tends to spill out towards El Palo and its beachside discos.

Puerta Oscura
C Molina Lario 5, T952-221900, www.puertaoscuramalaga.com.
One of the classiest in Málaga, this 19th-century bar-café has chandeliers, alcoves and classical music. It's the best – though certainly not the cheapest – place for that late-night coffee and liquor. Recommended.

Festivals

Easter Semana Santa, when religious brotherhoods organize daily processions with huge and elaborate floats carrying sacred *paso* figures through the streets of the city. It's one of Spain's best Easter celebrations.
23 Jun San Juan, sees huge bonfires on the beach, live concerts and all-night partying.
16 Jul Virgen del Carmen's effigy is taken by a procession of boats out to sea by fishermen.
Aug Feria, with bullfights, flamenco, processions and fireworks. There are 2 venues: during the day festivities take place in the streets surrounding C Marqués de Larios; in the evening it moves to the fairgrounds on the outskirts of the city where one of Spain's biggest parties kicks off night after night. All the *casetas* are open to the public, and most serve food as well as drinks.

Shopping

The main shopping area is west of the cathedral and north of the Alameda Principal and in streets around the Plaza de la Constitución. The Larios shopping centre, between El Corte Inglés and the bus station, has over 100 shops, a hypermarket and a multi-cinema.

What to do

Bike tours and hire

Bike2Malaga, *C Vendeja 6, T650-677063, www.bike2malaga.com.* Near the Plaza Merced, these people offer bike hire for €5/10 for a half/full day and also give guided city tours.

Málaga Bike Tours, *Pasaje La Trini 6, T606-978513, www.malagabiketours.eu.* These people take you on good-natured 2-wheeled tours of town for €24, includes a drink in a bar. They also rent bikes for €5/10 for a half/full day.

Boat trips

Cruceros Pelegrín, *Muelle 1, T687-474921, www.barcosdemalaga.es.* Run hour-long cruises from Muelle 1, costing €10, with regular departures throughout the day.

Football

Málaga, now owned by a Qatari investor, have a lot of support, partly from the expat crowd. Games are held at the **Estadio de Fútbol La Rosaleda**, Av de Martiricos, T952-614374, www.malagacf.es.

Golf

There are over 40 golf courses along the Costa del Sol to the west of the city. The nearest, and the oldest course on the coast, is **Real Club de Campo de Málaga**, T952-376677, www.rccm-golf.com, 4 km east of Torremolinos. It's state owned and attached to the Parador de Golf hotel.

Transport

Air

Málaga's international airport, T952-048844, www.aena-aeropuertos.es or the good unofficial page www.malagaairport.eu, is located 7 km west of the centre. A taxi will cost you €15-20. The cheapest transport to centre is the Fuengirola–Málaga train, every 30 mins from 0700 to midnight (€1.70 single). The journey takes 15 mins. There are 2 Málaga stations; the final Centro-Alameda stop is more central. There are also buses (€3) 0700-midnight from the airport (from the Alameda to the airport at 30-min intervals between 0630 and 2330).

Málaga has a busy airport which handles 12 million passengers a year. **Air Europa**, **Vueling** and **Iberia** and its subsidiaries run internal flights to several Spanish cities. Numerous budget airlines from all over Europe fly to Málaga, some only in the summer. See Getting there, page 501, for more details.

Bus

The bus station is conveniently close to the main train station on Paseo de los Tilos, southwest of the centre. It's a 20-min walk to the centre or take a local bus.

A complete timetable is available from the tourist office. There are hourly buses from the bus station (T952-350061, www.estabus.emtsam.es) to **Granada** (2 hrs). Buses to **Sevilla** leave a few times daily (2 hrs 45 mins). Buses to **Córdoba** leave 4 times daily (3 hrs), and there are many buses along the coast in both directions.

Car hire

All the main international firms have offices at the airport. Local Spanish firms are also represented. As ever, the best deals are to be found online via broker websites. Smaller firms have their offices on the airport approach road, to which they will transport customers by minibus (allow 30 mins for this when departing). A reader-recommended operator here is

Helle Hollis, Av del Comandante García Morato, T952-245544, www.hellehollis.com. Offices in the city include: **Avis**, C Cortina del Muelle, T952-216627, www.avis.com; and **Hertz**, Alameda de Colón 17, T952-225597, www.hertz.com.

Ferry

There are regular daily sailings (except Sun mid-Sep to mid-Jun) to **Melilla**, the Spanish enclave in North Africa. The crossing takes around 8 hrs. For further information contact **Trasmediterránea**, C Juan Díaz 4, T902-454645, www.trasmediterranea.es.

Taxi

There are taxi ranks at the bus and train stations and on Alameda Principal. **Radio Taxi**, T952-327950. One of several companies.

Train

The main train station is near the bus station on Paseo de los Tilos, a 20-min walk to the centre, or hop on a bus.

There are 11 daily **AVE** trains to **Madrid** (2 hrs 30 mins, €80), which travel via **Córdoba**, also served by cheaper trains (1 hr). Except on Sun, there's a daily morning train to **Ronda** (2 hrs), stopping at **Alora** and **El Chorro**. There are 6 daily slow trains and 6 daily fast trains to **Sevilla** (1¾-2½ hrs) as well as services to other Andalucían cities.

The **Fuengirola**–Málaga *cercanía* line is planned eventually to extend to **Marbella** and Estepona in the west, and Nerja in the east and has another branch running north to **Alora**. Purchase tickets from the machines on the platform.

East from Málaga

Traditionally more Spanish in character, the eastern Costa del Sol is facing a rapidly increasing influx of tourists and retirees from northern Europe and is changing its nature quickly.

Nevertheless, Nerja is attractive, having not yet been spoiled by the ribbon development that has ruined much of the western part of the province.

Nerja → *Colour map 5, B2.*

spectacular location on a low cliff, backed by impressive mountains

Despite rapid recent growth, Nerja, some 50 km east of its provincial capital, still retains considerable charm in its narrow, winding streets and dramatic setting. There are sandy coves, long beaches and, despite a spiralling increase in residential tourism, most of the new buildings and *urbanizaciones* have been aesthetically designed. Nerja's caves east of town pull the crowds and make a dazzling venue for the annual summer festival. Nerja also has excellent places to stay and eat.

Sights

Today, the local economy is largely reliant on tourism. There is also a large foreign community who have made Nerja their permanent home. Architectural controls here mean that there are few high-rise hotels and the centre is still old fashioned with narrow winding streets flanked by bars, souvenir and speciality shops.

At the heart of the town is the famous **Balcón de Europa**, a balmy, palm-lined promenade with magnificent views over the rocky coastline. To the west of here is the whitewashed **Church of El Salvador**, dwarfed by its Norfolk pine. It has elements of *mudéjar* and baroque work, plus an interesting mural representing the Annunciation on a Nerja beach.

There are still a few fishing boats on the **Playa Calahonda**, just east of the Balcón, but the most popular beach, just out of sight behind the headland, is **Burriana**, which is packed during the summer and offers a whole range of watersports, ranging from waterskiing to kitesurfing. Small cove beaches in town are easily accessed via stairs, and have dark, pebbly sand and quite sharp drop-offs in the water.

BACKGROUND

Nerja

Nerja started life as the Moorish settlement of *Narixa*, but an earthquake in 1884 destroyed much of the town and no Moorish constructions survived. For centuries the inhabitants eked out a living by making silk, growing sugar cane and fishing. None of these activities thrive today and the sugar refining buildings are part of the industrial archaeology. Nerja is famous in Spain for having been the setting for the iconic early 1980s TV series *Verano Azul.*

Cuevas de Nerja

Ctra de Maro s/n, T952-529520, www.cuevadenerja.es. Winter 1000-1300, then guided visits 1300 and 1600-1730, summer 1000-1830, guided 1100-1200, 1830-1930. €9, 6- to 12-year-olds €5. The caves are just above the N340, and clearly signposted from it. Parking costs €1. There are regular buses from Nerja, or it's a 30-min walk or 10-min drive.

These limestone caves 5 km from Nerja were discovered in 1959 by a group of local schoolboys on a bat-hunting expedition and are now a major tourist destination, with busloads rolling up every day of the year. The most important finds were the wall paintings, probably Upper Palaeolithic in age and largely of animals, believed to be part of a magical rite to ensure success in hunting and guarantee the fertility of domestic animals. Regrettably, the paintings are not on public view. The guided visit takes just under an hour; the lighting of the caves and the piped music may appear to some visitors to be somewhat overdone, but the limestone features are genuinely awe-inspiring. The caves are far more extensive than you get to appreciate on the tour, but you can get to grips with further sections by booking a day's caving (October to June, booking via T680-207135 or the website, over-14s only). The day includes drinks, sandwiches, equipment, guide and around five to six hours of exploration. In the summer season, the main chamber of the caves is used as an auditorium for a festival of music.

Listings Nerja

Tourist information

Tourist office
C Carmen 1, T952-521531, www.nerja.es. Mon-Sat 1000-1400, 1700-2045, Sun 1000-1345.
Just across from Balcón de Europa, the tourist office occupies the ground floor of the town hall.

Where to stay

There is a good choice of accommodation to suit all pockets. It is best to book in advance during summer and Semana Santa.

€€€€ Parador de Nerja
C Almuñécar 8, T952-520050, www.parador.es.
The only disappointment here is that, unlike many paradores, the building is not

a historic palace or even that old. On the plus side, the location is perfect: on a cliff edge with rooms overlooking the garden and sea and a lift that drops you right down on the beach. Some rooms have whirlpool baths and private patios. The restaurant is recommended, particularly the seafood; try the giant *langostinos*. There's also a pool and tennis court.

€€€ Balcón de Europa
Paseo Balcón de Europa 1, T952-520800, www.hotelbalcon europa.com.
With an unbeatable location right on the Balcón itself, this has bright and spacious rooms, decorated with elegant simplicity. The hotel is built in the rock face so the entrance is on the 6th floor (from the Balcón), while rooms have direct access to the private beach below. A good place to relax, with a piano bar, sauna and massage. Rooms with views and balcony cost more, but are memorable.

€€€ Hotel Carabeo
C Carabeo 34, T952-525444, www.hotelcarabeo.com.
A delightful English-owned boutique hotel down a quiet side street near the centre. The furniture and decor throughout is sumptuous with tasteful antiques and paintings by acclaimed local artist, David Broadhead. There's a range of rooms (some are **€€**), including sea-view suites with great views and a private terrace. The elegant restaurant serves delicious modern Mediterranean cuisine and tapas. Recommended.

€€-€ Pensión Miguel
C Almirante Ferrándiz 31, T952-521523, www.pensionmiguel.net.
A very appealing option on a pedestrian street near the Balcón de Europa, this renovated Andalucían townhouse offers good-value accommodation in bright and cheerful rooms with fridge and private bathroom. The owners are exceptionally helpful; there's also a lovely roof terrace with views – perfect for tasty breakfast or romantic sunset. Minimum 2-night stay in high summer. Recommended.

€ Hostal Tres Soles
C Carabeo 40, T952-525157, www.hostal3soles.com.
This small, central and helpful option is behind a greenery-covered façade on a pedestrianized central street with easy access to beaches. Rooms are simple and comfortable, offering decent value. A little more gets you an apartment with kitchenette and balcony. Upstairs rooms offer a better outlook. Breakfast available.

€ Mena
C El Barrio 15, T952-520541, www.hostalmena.es.
A good location in the narrow backstreets west of the Balcón. The rooms in this friendly 10-room *hostal* are spotless, bright and cheery with interesting artwork. There's a pretty patio, and the best rooms have a balcony overlooking the cliff-top garden for only €5 more.

Camping

Nerja Camping
T952-529714, www.nerjacamping.com. Closed in Oct.
Located around 5 km east of town on the N-340, the campsite is leafy and spacious, but the place gets busy in summer so book ahead. It's significantly cheaper off season.

Restaurants

There's a wide selection of restaurants to suit all pockets and tastes. Seafood restaurants are moderately priced here. Many restaurants close for part or all of the winter. Beware of inflated prices in the bars and restaurants around the Balcón.

€€€ Oliva
C Pintada 7, T952-522 988, www.restauranteoliva.com.
Stylish and popular, this is a reliable choice for upmarket but unpretentious dining. Plenty of thoughtful touches are allied with well-presented modern cuisine.

€€ El Pulguilla
C Almirante Ferrándiz 26, T952-523872.
Typical of Málaga province with its no-nonsense stainless steel and tiles, this bar pulls in the crowds for its good-quality fried fish and other seafood snacks. There's also ice-cold Cruzcampo beer, generous wine pours, and a free tapa with every drink.

€€ La Marina
Plaza de la Marina, T952-521299.
Famous locally for its fish and seafood, cooked *a la plancha* (grilled), *hervido* (boiled), or *a la sal* (baked in salt). Simple yet uses the freshest ingredients.

€€ Lan Sang
C Málaga 12, T952-528053, www.lansang.com.
This spot is an excellent and authentic Laotian and Thai restaurant with top-notch service, and attractive wooden tables. The food (all coded by spiciness and content) ranges from cracking fish curries to tasty vegetable stir-fries. Try the *khao niew* sticky rice, meant to be eaten balled up in your fingers.

€ Esquina Paulina
C Almirante Ferrándiz 45, T952-522181.
An intimate, well-run and charming place, this offers quality wines, tasty gourmet tapas, fine *tablas* of ham or cheese, as well as coffee, cakes, and cocktails.

Bars and clubs

Disco and karaoke bars cluster around Plaza Tutti Frutti (yes, that is its real name), just west of the main road, running down to the water. By night in summer, the **Papagayo** beachside restaurant turns up the volume with live music (from flamenco to hard rock) and DJs until sun-up.

Entertainment

Flamenco

El Molino, *C San José 4, www.facebook.com/elmolinonerja.* Nightly show at 2100 and a good, not-too-touristy atmosphere.

Festivals

Feb Carnaval for 3 days with parades and singing of *chirigotas* (popular songs).
16 Jul Fiesta de la Virgen del Carmen, the fishermen's fiesta; the statue of the Virgin del Carmen is carried down to the sea at Calahonda beach.
9-13 Oct Feria de Nerja, local saint's day and a week-long festival.

Transport

Bus

There are buses more than hourly to **Málaga** (1 hr) and the coastal towns to the west; and several daily buses eastward to **Almuñécar**, **Granada** and **Almería**. Local buses head to and from the inland villages of the Axarquía, such as **Frigiliana**, **Torrox** and the hospital at **Vélez Málaga**.

Car

It's relatively easy to park on the edges of town or at the underground car park in the centre (follow signs for Balcón de Europa). It's pricey but very handy.

La Axarquía

★This popular walkers' region was once notorious bandit country and later a guerrilla stronghold during and after the Civil War. Like the Alpujarra in Granada province, it preserves a distinctly North African character: the remains of the Moors' labours in creating terracing and irrigation channels can still be seen, while the small villages dotting the area are whitewashed, with narrow streets.

The main settlement of the region, Vélez Málaga, isn't a particularly enticing place, as it is rapidly succumbing to overdevelopment fuelled by expat demand. The same is gradually happening to most of the villages – the only buildings not for sale are the estate agencies – but the region still has ample charms and offers some rewarding walking. It's better to pick up tourist information on the region before arriving; contact the offices in Nerja and Málaga.

Driving through La Axarquía → *Colour map 5, B1/B2.*

North African-influenced whitewashed villages linked by waymarked routes

In an effort to encourage rural tourism, five routes have been devised for visiting La Axarquía by car, each colour coded and waymarked. Owing to the terrain, most of the routes are not circular and involve retracing one's steps in places, but they are, nevertheless, recommended. A detailed brochure describing the routes can be obtained from the tourist office in Nerja. Be prepared, in the more remote parts of La Axarquía, for some erratic signposting.

The Ruta del Sol y del Aguacate (the Sun and Avocado Route) starts at Rincón de la Victoria and visits the agricultural villages of the Vélez valley, including Macharaviaya, Benamacarra and Iznate. The Ruta del Sol y del Vino (the Sun and Wine Route) starts in Nerja and includes the main wine-producing villages, such as Cómpeta and Frigiliana. The Ruta Mudéjar concentrates on architecture, looking at villages, such as Archez, Salares and Sedilla. The Ruta de la Pasa (the Route of the Raisin) looks at the more mountainous villages in the northwest of the area. Finally, the Ruta del Aceite y los Montes (the Route of the Oil and the Mountains) examines the olive-growing villages, such as Periana and Alaucín in the north of the area.

Vélez Málaga

The so-called capital of the Axarquía is only 4 km from the coast and is more of a gateway really, as it has little in common with the villages of the area apart from being steeply located on a hilltop. It wasn't reconquered by the Christians until 1487, and still preserves some of its Moorish fortress on a crag above the town. The parish church of **Santa María la Mayor** was built on the site of the main mosque, whose minaret has been converted into the belltower. There's a fine *mudéjar* ceiling inside.

Vélez Málaga has no tourist office, though there is one on the coast in Torre del Mar, so the offices in the villages of Sayalonga, Cómpeta and Frigiliana are the best places for information on the Axarquía region.

Cómpeta and around

Despite the large numbers of northern European expats, this village is still one of the best spots to relax in the Axarquía. The hills around are stocked with Moscatel grapes that are used to make a sweet wine. The main square is overlooked by the **Iglesia de la Asunción**. Nearby, on the main road, is a small **tourist office** ⓘ *T952-553685, turismo@competa.es, Apr-Oct Mon-Sat 1000-1500, Sun 1000-1400, winter closed Mon-Tue*; this is also where the bus stops. You can obtain local walking maps at the office.

Sayalonga and Archez

From the coast at Caleta de Vélez, a road snakes up into the hills towards Cómpeta via the typically picturesque villages of Sayalonga and Archez. The former has a **tourist office** ⓘ *T952-535206, oficinadeturismo@sayalonga.es, Mon-Fri 1000-1500*. It's in the square at the end of the only road through this narrow village. Leave your car on the main road to explore the village, as you'd probably have to back it out again.

The village's main attraction is the **Cementerio Redondo**, which is indeed round. Sayalonga is also the start of a pleasant walk (see the Sayalonga circuit, below).

Not far beyond, and signposted left off the main road, **Archez** is another sleepy, pleasant place with a good place to stay and eat.

Frigiliana

Frigiliana, a mere 6 km from the coast and steeped in Muslim atmosphere, was the site of one of the last battles between the Christians and the Moors in 1569 and ceramic plaques record the events on the walls of the houses in the older part of the town. With narrow streets and whitewashed houses festooned with hanging plants and geraniums, it's perhaps the region's prettiest village, although also its most touristy. For the best view of the surrounding valley with its Mediterranean backdrop, climb up to the mirador with its handy bar and restaurant. The **tourist office** ⓘ *Plaza del Ingenio, T952-534261, www.turismofrigiliana.es, mid-Sep to Jun Mon-Fri 1000-1730, Sat-Sun 1000-1400, 1600-2000, Jul to mid-Sep Mon-Fri 1000-1530, 1700-2100, Sat-Sun 1000-1400, 1600-2000*, can provide information on accommodation.

Alfarnate

In the northwest of La Axarquía, not far from Antequera, is Alfarnate. On the road outside the village, the **Antigua Venta de Alfarnate** ⓘ *T952 759388, www.ventadealfarnate.es, 1000-1800*, is claimed to be the oldest inn in Andalucía. Once the haunt of assorted highwaymen and robbers, including the notorious El Tempranillo, it now houses a small outlaws' museum including a prison cell. The characterful *venta* serves country food and is cheerfully crowded with Spanish families at weekends.

Walking in La Axarquía

magnificent Mediterranean and mountain views

What makes walking in La Axarquía such a treat is the very marked difference in climate, vegetation and terrain between the higher passes and the coastal fringe. The Mediterranean is often visible, sparkling in the distance, and on most of the walks the Sierra de Tejeda provides a spectacular backdrop, especially during the winter months when there is often snow on its higher reaches. Many walks in the area are waymarked.

The best maps of the area are the standard 1:50,000 map of the Servicio Geográfico del Ejército, Series L. The walks mentioned below are covered by maps: Zafarraya 18-43 and Vélez-Málaga 18-44. The Marco Polo bookstore in Cómpeta generally has both maps in stock.

Sayalonga circuit → *Distance: 10 km. Time: 3½-4 hrs. Difficulty: easy.*

This half-day excursion links two attractive villages, Sayalonga and sleepy Corombela. The walk takes you through the subtropical orchards of Sayalonga's terraced river valley where there is an astonishing variety of fruit trees. Then comes a steep climb up to Corombela passing by several small farmsteads and on the return leg there are excellent views of the Sierra de Tejeda and the Mediterranean.

Nearly all the walk is along tracks and this is an easy circuit to follow. There is a short section of tarmac road when you leave Corombela but there is very little traffic; don't let this put you off this walk. **Map**: 1:50,000 Vélez-Málaga (1054).

Canillas de Albaida circuit → *Distance: 11 km. Time: 4½-5 hrs. Difficulty: medium.*
This enchanting walk takes you out from Canillas de Albaida via a beautiful riverside path, which meanders through thick stands of oleander, crossing back and forth across the Cájula river – easily passable unless there has been heavy rainfall. After a steep climb the middle section of the walk takes you along dirt tracks and is quite different in feel. But it is easy to follow and there are fine views of the Sierra de Tejeda. The final section of the walk – there is a steep climb last thing – is along an ancient cobbled path with gorgeous views of Canillas and the Chapel of Santa Ana. Try to do this walk when the oleander is in flower for a real spectacle. There are some prickly plants on the middle section before you reach the forestry track so you could wear trousers. **Map**: 1:50,000 Zafarraya (1040).

Itinerary The walk begins from the car park at the entrance of Canillas as you come from Cómpeta. Go down the hill from the roundabout past the supermarket and chemist. At the bottom bear left at a sign for 'Finca El Cerrillo'. Head down past the chapel of San Antón then bear right and drop down, cross the river then immediately bear right following a concrete road towards an old mill. The road narrows to a path that runs beside the Cájula river, crossing back and forth several times. Pass a breeze-block building (20 minutes) on your left and continue along the river's right bank. You'll see red waymarking. Cross the river again and climb; there is beautiful old cobbling in places. After passing beneath an overhanging rock face you descend back down to the river, cross it a couple more times, then the path climbs up the river's left bank between two fences and becomes a track. Ahead you will see a white farmhouse.

Be careful! Before you reach it, branch right (by a small orange tree to the left of the track) at a sign 'Camino del Río' along a narrow path that passes by a grove of avocados. It winds, passes the stumps of a line of poplars, then continues on its rather serpentine course, occasionally marked by cairns. Shortly your path is crossed by another, which has black water pipes following its course. Turn right here and then almost immediately left, then wind down to the river that you cross via stepping stones. The path climbs up the other bank and soon becomes better defined (occasional red dots mark the way). Where the path divides go left. A ruined house comes into sight on the other side of the river. Cross the river again and climb the path towards the house. You should pass just to the right of the house then climb steeply up the side of the valley. As you climb you'll see a solitary building on the crown of a hill. Remember this landmark – you'll pass by it later in the walk. The path swings right, descends, crosses a (dry) stream, then bears right again and winds uphill. You come to an area of terracing where you continue to climb. Above you to your right you'll see a small farmhouse. Head up to the farm that you should pass just to its right. You reach a dirt track. Turn right here (one hour, 15 minutes) and head for the solitary building which you saw earlier in the walk. Just past the house the track arcs left towards the head of the Cájula gorge and a small cluster of houses. The track winds, descends, crosses el Arroyo de Luchina via a concrete bridge with rusting railings, then climbs again past olive and citrus groves. After passing a house to your right, where a row of pines has been planted, you cross the river (one hour, 45 minutes). Continue past a row of poplars on the main track: don't turn sharp right on a track leading down towards the river. Follow this track, climbing at first, roughly parallel to the Río Cájula, heading back towards Canillas. Eventually you pass a water tank then a house to the right of the track with a solar panel (two hours). Just past this house the track swings to the left and another track branches right (it has a chain across it). Ignore this turning, continue for 30 m and then – careful! – turn right away from the track on to a beautiful path that zigzags all the way down to the river Llanada de Turvilla. Somewhere to one side of the path would make a memorable picnic spot. Cross the bridge over the river then bear right and wind up towards the Santa Ana chapel. Pass beneath the chapel – the gorge is now down to your right – and after a steep climb the path becomes a track that leads you just beneath the cemetery where a green mesh fence runs to your right. Bear sharp left past house No 35, go to the end of the street then head up the hill past the supermarket and bank to arrive back at your point of departure.

Listings La Axarquía

Where to stay

There are many *casas rurales* in the Axarquía region. Check with local tourist offices or visit www.toprural.com for a good selection.

Cómpeta and around

€€ Hotel Alberdini
Pago la Lomilla 85, T952-516294, www.alberdini.com. If coming from Sayalonga, turn right towards Torrox just before entering Cómpeta.
Perched on a hill with wonderful views over the surrounding valleys, this rustic stone-clad rural hotel makes a relaxing base. Rooms are decorated in individual styles, and there's a restaurant, other good facilities and various activities like Pilates and Spanish classes. There are various free-standing bungalows, including one rather curious cave-like one. Prices are very reasonable.

€ La Vista Cómpeta
C Panaderos 43, T625-857318, www.lavistacompeta.com.
This charming whitewashed place nestled high in the village offers sweet simple rooms and gorgeous roof terraces plus a small plunge pool. Rates are a bargain and include breakfast, served alfresco.

Apartments
There are numerous houses for holiday rentals available in the village; ask at the tourist office or in one of the estate agents.

Sayalonga and Archez

The tourist office in Sayalonga plus online brokers have details of a number of village houses for rent, either for a night or for a longer stay. Prices vary.

Frigiliana

€€€-€€ Hotel Los Caracoles
Ctra Frigiliana-Torrox Km 4.6, around 5 km west of Frigiliana, T616-779339, www.hotelloscaracoles.com.
One of the more unusually designed hotels in southern Spain, this has 5 striking bungalows (*caracoles*, or snails), that are romantic shell-shaped structures blending *modernista* architecture with North Africa via Greece and *Star Wars*. They are equipped with salon, bedroom and bathroom and have a double room and a sofa bed. There are also enchanting doubles with terrace, and a restaurant that has some Mozarabic-style dishes and cracking views over coast, hills, and villages.

€€ La Posada Morisca
Ctra Frigiliana–Torrox Km 2, T952-534151, www.laposada morisca.com.
A couple of kilometres west of Frigiliana, this is an enchanting spot, and utterly relaxing. All rooms have views of the coast from their balconies, and elegant rustic-style decor. They also have wood-burning stoves and decent bathrooms. There's a good restaurant (dinner only) and a small pool.

Restaurants

See also the hotel listings for good eating options.

Cómpeta and around

€€ Museo del Vino
Av Constitución s/n, T952-553314, www.museodelvinocompeta.com.
This isn't a museum but a shop. It deals out generous glasses of local wine, which you can accompany with traditional tapas of ham, chorizo or cheese. There's also a restaurant serving classy roast meats. It's a little tacky, but the food and service is good.

€€ Restaurante El Pilón
C Laberinto s/n, T952-553512, www.restaurantelpilon.com.
On a steep street below C San Antonio, this Brit-run restaurant has an upstairs terrace and dining rooms with great views over the village and the hills beyond. It's warm and busy. Book ahead in summer.

Festivals

Cómpeta and around

15 Aug The boisterous **Noche del Vino** festival where you can enjoy the local wine.

Frigiliana

20 Jan **Fiesta San Sebastián** when villagers walk barefoot through the streets carrying candles and the statue of San Sebastián.
Aug Annual **dance and music festival**, with plenty of *fino* and fiesta spirit.

Transport

Vélez Málaga

There are several daily buses from **Málaga** and frequent connections from **Torre del Mar** and **Nerja** on the coast.

Cómpeta and around

There are 3 daily buses to Cómpeta from **Málaga** via **Vélez Málaga**.

Frigiliana

Regular buses run from Torrox to Frigiliana.

Costa del Sol

The Costa del Sol is a curious mix of paradise and hell, a stretch of ribbon-developed coast where sun-blessed retirees rub shoulders with corrupt mayors and mafiosos looking for the next dodgy property deal.

To impoverished Franco-era Spain the influx of tourists was a blessing; now, with competition from other holiday destinations in the Mediterranean and Caribbean, the concrete jungles can seem more of a curse, and the lack of foresight in approval of developments, not to mention the bribes taken to rubber-stamp them, is staggering.

Nevertheless, despite the timeshares and the crimes against architecture, it remains a good-time zone. Spain's former property boom meant that facilities improved, and it's not just a spot for cheap beer and a lobster tan. The ever-increasing numbers of 'residential tourists', generally middle-aged northern Europeans looking to live out their retirement years with a bit of decent sunshine has boosted the local economy and meant that the seaside towns aren't so reliant on the whims of the sun-seeking package tourist.

While not even the Costa del Sol's biggest fan could describe the beaches as anything more than gritty, nor the cultural attractions anything more than token, the climate remains exceptional, and the ambience cheery. Still, it can seem like the least Spanish of places, with northern European languages dominant. In July and August resorts are very crowded.

Torremolinos and Benalmádena → *Colour map 4, B6.*

fishermen's quarter, beaches and marine attractions

Once a byword for all the worst aspects of Mediterranean tourism, Torremolinos has long been surpassed in crassness by other destinations and, if visited off season, can actually be quite pleasant.

It is difficult to appreciate that 50 years ago there were hardly any buildings here apart from the water mills that gave Torremolinos its name (and which stopped working in 1924), and a few fishermen's cottages behind La Carihuela beach. The centre of what old town existed is Calle San Miguel, now a busy pedestrianized alley full of boutiques, restaurants and a Moorish tower. Torremolinos has four beaches; for the best sand, atmosphere and restaurants head for La Carihuela, the old fishermen's quarter, with the most appealing part of the maritime promenade. There are three **tourist offices** ⓘ *one at Bajondillo beach, Plaza de las Comunidades Autónomas s/n, T952-371909, one in La Carihuela, C Delfines 1, T952-372956, and one in the centre on Plaza Independencia, T952-374231.*

Torremolinos merges imperceptibly into Benalmádena to the west. The name applies to both the pretty *pueblo*, 300 m above sea level, and the beachside development. The beach is one of the Costa's best, and there's an attractive marina where various companies offer boat trips out into the Mediterranean. There are also a couple of family-friendly attractions. Within the marina is **Sea Life** ⓘ *T952-560150, www.visitsealife.com, daily 1000-1800, to 2000 May-Jun and Sep-Oct, to midnight Jul-Aug, €15.50, children €12.50*, a submarine park with plastic tunnels taking you into the aquarium for eyeball-to-eyeball contact with sharks, jellyfish (no eyeballs) and other sea creatures. It's substantially cheaper to book via their website. While travelling along the N340 you'll see the **Teleférico de Benalmádena** ⓘ *T952-577773, www.telefericobenalmadena.com, return trips 1100 until dusk plus night trips Jul-Aug, closed Jan to mid-Feb, €7.40/€13.25 single/return*, a cable car swinging above the road to the top of the Calamorro mountain, 769 m above sea level. The journey takes 15 minutes and there are fantastic views; you can even spot Morocco on a clear day. Hikers can enjoy a choice of several trails when they reach the top. Alternatively, there's a bar, donkey rides and regular bird-of-prey displays.

Listings Torremolinos and Benalmádena

Where to stay

Torremolinos

There are plenty of rooms except at the height of the season. Most large package tour hotels are behind the eastern beaches; you get better rates for these booking through agencies. The best place to be based is La Carihuela.

€€€€ Hotel Amaragua
C Los Nidos 3, T952-384700, www.amaragua.com. 4-day minimum stay in season.
In La Carihuela near Benalmádena marina, this is a sizeable and striking seafront hotel, with plenty of space, decent rooms, all with balcony, most

with sea views (although these can be noisy). The location is good, and it feels more Spanish than British. There's a pool and spa, and standard 4-star facilities.

€€ Hotel Cabello
C Chiriva 28, T952-384505, www.hotelcabello.com.
This small family-run hotel is a block back from La Carihuela beach. Rooms are clean and simply furnished; most have a sea view. There is a small bar with an adjacent small lounge with a pool table. Good value, especially outside of Aug, when it's **€**.

Transport

Bus

Regular buses run along the coast road between **Málaga** and **Fuengirola** (45 mins) via Torremolinos. There are also many services on to **Marbella** and a number of long-distance services from Fuengirola to other Andalucían cities as well as **Madrid**.

Train

Torremolinos is a stop on the **Fuengirola–Málaga** railway, trains run every 30 mins in each direction.

Fuengirola and Mijas → *Colour map 4, B6.*

lively resort and more Spanish than most of this coast

Fuengirola

A mere 20-minute drive from Málaga airport, Fuengirola is both a popular holiday spot and a genuine Spanish working town, with a busy fish dock and light industry in the suburbs to the north. It appeals to northern European retirees in the winter, when it feels fairly staid, and attracts large numbers of Spaniards in the summer, when it doesn't.

The main **tourist office** ⓘ *Av Jesús Rein 6, T952-467457, www.visitafuengirola.com, Mon-Fri 0930-1400, 1630-1900 (2000 in summer), Sat 1000-1300*, at the old railway station, can provide maps and information.

Unlike Torremolinos, Fuengirola has a long history. Extensive Roman remains have been excavated; it was they who probably built the first structure at the **Castillo de Sohail** located on a hill by the river at the west end of the town. The castle was destroyed in 1485 in the Christian reconquest of the area, the Moors surrendering on the day of San Cayetano, the patron saint of Fuengirola today. In 1730, the castle was rebuilt to defend the coast against the British who had taken Gibraltar in 1704. During the Peninsular War in 1810, a British expedition of 800 men under General Blayney landed at the castle and advanced on Mijas, but later they retreated to the castle, where, humiliatingly they were obliged to surrender to 150 Polish mercenaries. At this time the population of Fuengirola was a mere 60 people; today, it is closer to 50,000. The Castillo de Sohail interior is now an outdoor auditorium where concerts take place. There is also a small exhibition centre/museum.

The small zoo **Bioparc Fuengirola** ⓘ *Av José Cela 6, T952-666301, www.bioparcfuengirola.es, daily 1000 until dusk, to midnight in Jul-Aug, €17.90, children €12.50*, is an excellent example of humane treatment. There are no cages and four different habitats create a natural environment for the animals. The zoo is also heavily involved in conservation programmes and focuses particularly on African and Asian rainforest species. A majestic baobab tree is another highlight.

Mijas

Mijas is geared to the tourist (foreign residents outnumber Spaniards by two to one in the Mijas administrative district), with donkey rides, garish souvenirs and English-run restaurants. Despite all this, Mijas has a certain charm and is worth a visit. It has a long history, going back to Roman times, while the Moors built the defensive walls that partially remain today. The village is located 425 m above sea level at the foot of steep mountains. The *vista panorámica* in well-kept gardens above the cliffs gives superb views along the coast. There's a **tourist office** ⓘ *Plaza Virgen de la Peña s/n, T952-589034, www.mijas.es, Mon-Fri 0900-1800 (2000 summer), Sat 1000-1400.*

Housed in the former town hall, the **Mijas Museum** ⓘ *Plaza de la Libertad s/n, daily summer 1000-1500, 1700-2200, winter 0900-1900, €1*, has various themed rooms, such as an old-fashioned bodega and bakery, and regular exhibitions are held in the gallery upstairs.

Donkey 'taxis' are popular in Mijas, and are now being looked after better thanks to the monitoring of a donkey sanctuary. Standard rates are €10-15 for a ride, or €15-20 to be pulled in a donkey cart.

Listings Fuengirola and Mijas

Where to stay

Fuengirola

Many hotels have reduced rates in winter.

€€ Las Islas
C Canela 12, T952 375 598, www.lasislas.info. Easter-Oct.
Unpromisingly set in the narrow lanes of the Torreblanca district, this romantic hotel is quite a surprise with its relaxing tropical vegetation, sizeable pool and colourful, comfortable rooms with views. The on-site restaurant does some Lebanese dishes among other fare. Recommended.

Camping

There are numerous sites close to the sea to the west of Fuengirola.

Mijas

The Mijas area has plenty of hotels.

€€ El Escudo de Mijas
C Trocha de los Pescadores 7, T952-591100, www.el-escudo.com.
Spotless, attractive rooms in a friendly location in the heart of Mijas *pueblo*.

Restaurants

Fuengirola

There is a vast and cosmopolitan range of choice in Fuengirola; however, the standard often leaves much to be desired. Head to C Capitán for a few more traditional eateries. Tapas bars are located mainly in the area to the west of the train station and on C San Rafael, which leads off the main square.

€€ Bodega El Tostón
C San Pancracio, T952-475632, www.bodegaeltoston.com.
A good tapas choice, decked out like a traditional Madrileña bodega with a vast selection of wine, served in enormous goblet-style glasses and accompanied

by complimentary canapés or more filling fare.

€€ Mesón Salamanca
C Capitán 1, T952-473888, www.mesonsalamanca.es.
A reliable option for good solid Castilian cuisine just off the main square on a street with several decent choices. It's traditional in feel and generous in portion.

Mijas
If you head for the Plaza de la Constitución, there are several restaurants with stunning views down to the coast.

Festivals

Fuengirola
16 Jul **Fiesta de la Virgen del Carmen**. The statue of the Virgin is carried from the church in Los Boliches in a 2-hr procession to the beach and into the sea. An amazing spectacle, with half the inhabitants on the beach and the other half either swimming or in boats.
1st 2 weeks of Oct Feria del Rosario takes place on the showground site between Los Boliches and Fuengirola, where there are *casetas* for the various societies and brotherhoods. All this is accompanied by fireworks, bullfights and flamenco.

Transport

Bus
Most of the bus services are run by **Portillo**, T902-450550, www.portillo.avanzabus.com.

Marbella → *Colour map 4, B5.*

the most interesting of the Costa del Sol towns

★In Spain, the name Marbella conjures up a host of images. As the place where many of the country's celebrities spend summer, it has glamorous connotations; Spain's tabloid press relocates here in August to keep track of A-listers hanging out in the latest glitzy nightclub. But Spaniards always knew there was plenty of sleaze behind the diamanté façade – Jesús Gil y Gil, an infinitely corrupt man, was mayor here for years; after his death, the police investigation Operación Malaya opened a stinking can of worms, centred around cash-for-development approval scandals and money-laundering.

Nevertheless, Marbella is still by far the best place to stay along this coast, if you stay in its picturesque old city or on the beach below. Here, there are excellent places to stay and eat, and a lively atmosphere all year. West of the centre, however, a hideous strip of pleasure palaces, plastic surgery clinics, and Ferrari repair shops line the road to Puerto Banús, a luxury marina and hubristic exercise in the poorest of taste. Cracking summer nightlife yes – but it's a depressing triumph of style over substance and reeks of Eastern European mafias and local corruption.

Sights

Marbella's **Casco Antiguo** (Old Town) is a compact area located to the north of Avenida Ramón y Cajal. In its centre is the pretty **Plaza de Naranjos**, opened up in the 16th century by the Christian town planners who demolished the maze of

BACKGROUND

Marbella

Marbella has a long history, having been populated at various times by Phoenicians, Visigoths and Romans, as well as being the most important Moorish town between Málaga and Gibraltar. Historians suggest that Moorish Marbella was a fortified town, with an oval shaped, 2-m-thick encircling wall containing 16 towers and three gates – to Ronda, Málaga and the sea. The town was taken by the Christians in 1485 and they set about remodelling the layout of the fortress, but much of the Moorish street plan remains today.

The changes began in the mid-1950s when a Spanish nobleman named Ricardo Soriano introduced his friends to the area. His nephew, Prince Alfonso von Hohenlohe, built the **Marbella Club**, attracting a wealthy international set to the area. Marbella's inhabitants include Arab royalty, stars of the media, famous sportspeople and members of Russian mafias. A visitor to Marbella might be surprised at its reputation as life seems entirely normal on the surface, but the glitzy social life is there going on behind closed doors in luxury yachts, palatial villas and private clubs.

Former mayor Jesús Gil actively promoted Marbella as a sort of Spanish Montecarlo, but ran up huge debts, and was staggeringly corrupt. He had friends in high places but, once he died in 2004, his lackeys and co-conspirators found themselves in an exposed position. The police investigation Operación Malaya saw some three billion euros in cash and valuables – paid for by illegally appropriated public funds – seized, and over a hundred notables sent to prison at some point, including the late Gil's protégé, Julián Muñoz, and Muñoz's lover, the famous copla singer and darling of the celebrity pages, Isabel Pantoja.

alleyways that comprised the Moorish *médina*. On the north side of the square is the 16th-century **Ayuntamiento** (town hall). In the southwest corner of the square is a delightful stone fountain, the **Fuente de la Plaza**, which dates from 1604. Nearby is the **Ermita de Nuestro Señor Santiago**, Marbella's oldest church, a small and simple building thought to date from the late 15th century. Look also for the **Casa Consistorial**, built in 1572. It has a fine wrought-iron balcony and *mudéjar* entrance, while on its exterior stonework is a coat of arms and inscriptions commemorating the bringing of water to the town. Finally in the square is the **Casa del Corregidor**, with a 16th-century stone façade, now a café.

Head for the northeast corner, particularly around Calle Trinidad, where there are good stretches of the old Moorish walls and at the western end of this street stands one of the towers of the original *Castillo*, built by the Moors in the ninth century. The old walls continue into Calle Carmen and Calle Salinas. Also at the east end of the old town in Calle Misericordia, is **Hospital Real de San Juan de Dios**, which was founded by the Reyes Católicos at the time of the Reconquest to minister to foreign patients. It has a chapel with a panelled *mudéjar* ceiling and a tiny cloister.

The **Museo del Grabado Español Contemporáneo** ⓘ *C Hospital Bazán s/n, T952-765741, www.mgec.es, Mon and Sat 1000-1400, Tue-Fri 1000-1430, 1700-2030 (1800-2200 summer), €3, under 18s free*, an exhibition of contemporary Spanish prints, is housed in the sympathetically restored **Palacio de Bazán**. This Renaissance building with an attractive exterior of pink stone and brickwork was originally bequeathed by its owner Don Alonso de Bazán to be a local hospital.

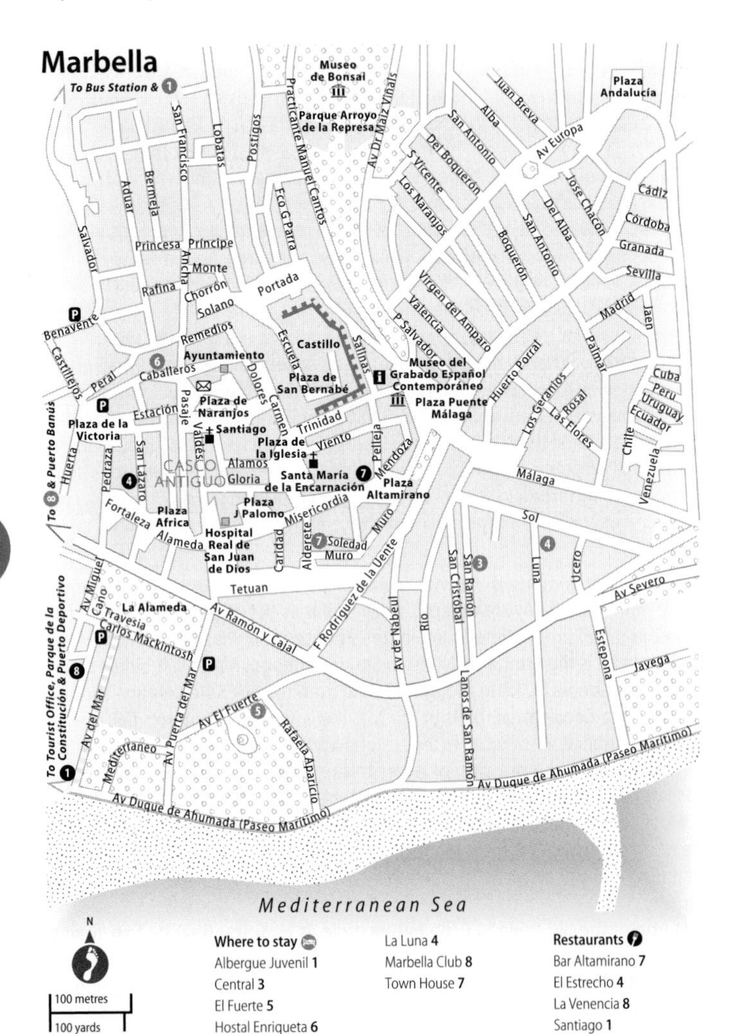

In the Parque Arroyo de la Represa, a series of terraced gardens and lakes to the east of town, the **Museo de Bonsai** ⓘ *Parque Arroyo de la Represa, T952-862926, daily 1030-1330, 1600-1830 (1700-2000 in Jul/Aug), €4*, is housed in a modern building surrounded by landscaped gardens and lakes. The miniature trees are imaginatively displayed on a wooden raft-like structure over water containing turtles and fish in Japanese style.

The **Museo Ralli** ⓘ *CN-340, Km 176, T952-857923, www.rallimuseums.com, Tue-Sat 1000-1500, closed mid-Dec to mid-Jan, free*, located in the Coral Beach complex a few kilometres to the west of Marbella, isn't dedicated to wrestling cars through forests, but is rather a light and airy collection of fine Latin American art and sculptures, as well as some paintings and graphic designs by Picasso, Dalí, Miró and Chagall. It's a very worthwhile visit.

Listings Marbella *map p238*

Tourist information

Tourist office
Glorieta de la Fontanilla s/n, T952-771442, www.marbellaexclusive.com. Mon-Fri 0900-2100, Sat 1000-1400.
On the main promenade, the tourist office is helpful. There's another *turismo* (C Salinas 4, T952-761197, Mon-Fri 0930-2000, Sat 1000-1400) in the old town, with town maps.

Where to stay

Most of Marbella's hotels are on the outskirts. There's good budget accommodation within the old town itself.

€€€€ Hotel El Fuerte
Av El Fuerte, T952-861500, www.fuertehotels.com.
One of the few hotels in the centre, this is a charming older building dating back to the 1950s and renovated recently. Most rooms have balconies with sea views (substantially more expensive) and the furnishings are traditional with plenty of dark wood. There is a lovely palm-filled garden with a pool situated between the hotel and the beach, just a few paces away. Recommended.

€€€€ Marbella Club Hotel
Bulevar Príncipe Alfonso von Hohenlohe s/n, T952-822211, www.marbellaclub.com.
The **Marbella Club** opened its doors almost 60 years ago and has since become part of the Marbella tradition. The level of luxury is exemplary and facilities include a golf resort and riding stables, thalassotherapy spa and exclusive hair salon. The rooms, however, don't always live up to the hype, and you might be better off in one of the villas, which have their own garden area. There's also a smart restaurant, pool, gym, and a host of other 4-star facilities. You may get better rates from a travel agent. Think €450+ for a double in summer.

€€€ The Town House
C Alderete 7, T952-901791, www.townhouse.nu.
An appealing boutique B&B in a great location in the old town. It's very elegant, with white walls and furnishings offset by works of art. The rooms vary

substantially; some are cosy, some more spacious. Best of all is the relaxing roof terrace – a quiet drink after a day at the beach goes down a treat here. Breakfast is included. Recommended.

€€ Hostal Enriqueta
C Los Caballeros 18, T952-827552, www.hostalenriqueta.com.
Close to Plaza los Naranjos, this has spacious, clean, good-value rooms with bathroom and friendly management. It's particularly well priced off season. You can put the car in the underground public car park right by the *hostal*. Recommended.

€€ Hotel Central
C San Ramón 15, T952-902442, www.hotelcentralmarbella.com.
This has a superb location on a pretty flower-flanked pedestrian street in the old town. The rooms are cheery, with chessboard tiles, and small balconies; go for one overlooking the patio garden. All have a/c and free Wi-Fi access; there's also a cosy sitting room with fireplace furnished with antiques. Prices are very reasonable.

€€ La Luna
C La Luna 7, T952-825778, hostallaluna.wordpress.com.
The rooms here are situated around a central terrace. There are fans and fridges and the rooms are a good size and squeaky clean – so much so that owner Salvador will refund your money if you find so much as a speck of dust! Peaceful and friendly. There are several other good budget options in these narrow pedestrian streets east of the centre if it's full.

€ Albergue Juvenil
C Trapiche 2, T951-270301, www.inturjoven.com.
Andalucía's best official youth hostel is just above the old town, and is a great, spacious facility with the bonus of a pool (summer only). Rooms vary in size, but are clean and modern; there's also disabled access, and a more-than-decent kitchen.

Camping

There are a few excellent campsites near Marbella, all on the coast road, close to the beach. All are open year round. Booking is advisable Jul and Aug and during fiesta time.

Restaurants

There is a glittering array of eateries in Marbella, including several of Andalucía's best.

€€€ La Meridiana
Camino de la Cruz, Las Lomas, T952-776190, www.lameridiana.es.
Just west of town near the mosque with upbeat Moroccan-style decor and an enclosed patio for year-round alfresco dining. The menu includes roasts and fish dishes like *lubina grillé al tomillo fresco* (grilled sea bass with fresh thyme). Quality is trumped by high prices here, but the atmosphere can make it worth it for a romantic evening.

€€€ Santiago
Paseo Marítimo 5, T952-770078, www.restaurante santiago.com. Closed Nov.
Appropriately located just across from the beach, this is a Marbella fish classic. The seafood here is catch-of-the-day-fresh with lobster salad a speciality. This is a popular restaurant with well-heeled locals, who wisely ask the professional staff for the day's recommendation. Meat dishes are also available, and the place also runs 2 tapas

bars, 1 specializing in stews, around the corner. Recommended.

€€ Bar Altamirano
Plaza Altamirano 4, T952-824932, www.baraltamirano.es.
This buzzing place is vastly popular with locals and tourists around, so get there early to bag your table and enjoy the well-priced *raciones* of rather tasty seafood and fish bought fresh from the market that morning. It's no-nonsense and traditional in feel and all the better for it. A real highlight is the warm and professional service.

€€ La Venencia
Av Miguel Cano 15, T952-857913, www.bodegaslavenencia.com.
In this promising tapas zone between the old town and the beach, this is the most outstanding choice. There's an excellent range of cold and hot plates; you can't really go wrong. There's cheerful seating around barrels both inside and out, and top service. Recommended.

€ El Estrecho
C San Lázaro 4, T952-770004, www.barelestrecho.es.
This reliable old tapas haunt is a well-established favourite on a narrow street off Plaza de la Victoria. It's full of locals enjoying the cheap and tasty morsels dished over the bar; the *albóndigas* and *ensaladilla rusa* stand out from the herd. Look out for the curious frieze depicting the social life of dogs. The Bartolo, opposite, specializes in fried fish and is also worthwhile.

Bars and clubs

Most of the action in the area takes place in Puerto Banús, rather than Marbella. From Marbella, buses run regularly from Av Ramón y Cajal just below the old town. In Marbella itself, most of the evening action is around Plaza Los Olivos at the top of C Peral in the old town, or in the port area, where there are a couple of dozen bars in a row – take your pick.

Festivals

Easter **Semana Santa** processions.
Jun **Feria y Fiesta de San Bernabé** celebrates Marbella's patron saint with concerts and firework displays.

Shopping

Good-quality shops abound in Marbella, particularly along Av Ricardo Soriano and in the alleyways of the old town. Many specialize in expensive jewellery and fashion goods. There are also numerous art galleries and craft shops.

What to do

Golf

Marbella is surrounded by golf courses, including **Río Real**, T952-765732, www.rioreal.com; **Aloha**, T952-907085, www.clubdegolfaloha.com; **Los Naranjos**, T952-812428, www.losnaranjos.com; **Las Brisas**, T952-813021, www.realclubdegolflasbrisas.es; **Guadalmina**, T952-883375, www.guadalminagolf.com (at San Pedro) and **La Quinta**, T952-762390, www.laquintagolf.com (road to Benahavís).

Transport

Air

The nearest airports are Málaga and Gibraltar, both accessible by road in under an hour. The nearest train stations are Algeciras to the west and Fuengirola to the east.

Bus

Most of these bus services are run by **Portillo**, T902-450550, www.portillo.avanzabus.com.

There are regular buses to and from **Málaga**, some express (50 mins), and some go via **Fuengirola** (45 mins) and **Torremolinos**. There is also a Málaga airport bus that leaves from Marbella bus station 10 times daily between 0530 and 2200. Heading west, there are regular buses to **Algeciras**, some via **Estepona**.

Other cities served include **Sevilla**, **Madrid**, **Granada**, **Ronda**, and **Cádiz**. The main bus station is in C Trapiche, next to the bypass, but most local buses pass through the town centre.

Around Marbella → *Colour map 4, B5.*

laid-back resort, attractive whitewashed settlements and views of North Africa

Ojén

Just 8 km north of Marbella is the expanding village of Ojén, which has a history going back to Roman times. A number of springs rise in the village and this attracted the Moors who were in power here until 1570 and Ojén still retains much of the flavour of that time. It was once famous for the production of *aguardiente*, a powerful *anís*, but its main claim to fame today is the annual **Fiesta de Flamenco** during the first week in August. Ojén also has an interesting parish church that was built on the site of a mosque.

Continue through Ojén and over the pass and after 4 km turn left through the pine forests to the Refugio de Juanar and a walking track that leads through woodland of sweet chestnut, almonds and olives to a mirador at 1000 m, from where there are stupendous views over Marbella, the coast and, on clear days, Morocco. Allow 1½ hours for this walk. The wildlife is incredible, with a wide range of flowers, including orchids, butterflies and birds. Small family groups of ibex are not uncommon; during the spring and autumn, migratory birds of prey can be seen en route to and from the Straits of Gibraltar, while booted and Bonelli's eagles breed in the vicinity. The area can be crowded with picnickers on Sundays.

Estepona

Perhaps the most low-key and relaxed of the Costa del Sol resort towns, likeable and family-friendly Estepona has a long seafront backing a clean shingle beach. It's a quiet place, more a home for the grey diaspora than young funseekers, but has a few picturesque corners. It has an enthusiastic **tourist office** ⓘ *back from the beach at Av San Lorenzo 1, T952-802002, turismo@estepona.es, winter Mon-Fri 0900-1500, Sat 1000-1330, summer Mon-Fri 0900-1930, Sat 1000-1330.*

Outside of town north of the motorway, **Selwo Aventura** ⓘ *Autovía Costa del Sol Km 162.5, T902 190 482, www.selwo.es, €24.50 for over-9s, open 1000-dusk mid-Feb to Oct plus weekends in Nov-Dec*, is a popular safari park where you can see various 'respect' animals from a truck that takes you around the complex. There are also various activities on offer. You can save almost 50% by booking a week in advance online.

Casares

Some 3 km west of Estepona, a winding road leads inland for 18 km to Casares, a lovely white town that attracts many tourists. Its whitewashed houses clothe the side of a hill which is capped by the ruins of a 13th-century **Moorish fortress** on Roman foundations, which was built in the time of Ibn al Jatib. The fort was also a centre of resistance against the French during the Peninsular War. Next to the fort is the **Iglesia de la Encarnación**, built in 1505 and with a brick *mudéjar* tower. There are majestic views from here along the whole coast and, on a good day, across to North Africa.

Casares is said to have derived its name from Julius Caesar, who may have been cured of his liver complaints by the sulphur springs at nearby Manilva. The 17th-century **Iglesia de San Sebastián**, which can be visited on the way to the fortress, is a simple whitewashed 17th-century building containing the image of the Virgen del Rosario del Campo. In the adjacent square is a statue of Blas Infante who was a native of Casares and leader of the Andalucían nationalist movement. He was executed by Falangists shortly after the start of the Civil War.

The **tourist office** ⓘ *C Carreras 46, T952-895521, winter Mon-Fri 1100-1430, 1600-1830, Sat 1100-1600, summer Mon-Sat 0900-1400*, is located in the house where Blas Infante was born, on the main road through town. They can provide details of a number of good circular walks that start from the main road just above the village.

From Casares, it is an exciting 20-minute drive to **Gaucín**, see page 260.

Listings Around Marbella

Where to stay

Benahavís

€€€ Amanhavis Hotel
C Pilar 3, T952-856026, www.amanhavis.com.
This hotel is a real one-off. The rooms are themed, ranging from a Moorish sultan's bedchamber to an astronomer's observatory. They vary substantially in facilities and price, but all are charmingly decorated. The restaurant here is excellent, specializing in fresh seasonal fare. Recommended.

Estepona

Book ahead for accommodation in Jul and Aug. There are numerous hotels, and you tend to get better rates via online hotel websites or travel agencies. Make sure you confirm the location; 'Estepona' can refer to a spot on the main road 5 km from town.

€ Hostal El Pilar
Plaza de las Flores 10, T952-800018, www.hostalelpilar.es.
With a great location on the prettiest square in Estepona and a couple of minutes from the beach, this offers plenty of value. Decoration is simple, airy and cheerful, and the management are kindly. All rooms come with bathroom, and there are a few that sleep 4, good for families or groups.

Casares

€€ Hotel Rural Casares
C Copera 52, T952-895211.
Just off the plaza, this simple hotel has a rather old-fashioned feel but boasts some good views over the village.

Rooms are clean and well-priced, management is formally courteous, and a simple breakfast is included.

Restaurants

Estepona

Apart from the big hotels outside town, the main restaurants are around pedestrianized C Real, a block back from the beach, and C Terraza, which crosses it in the centre.

€€ Los Rosales
C Damas 12, T952-792945, www.restaurantelosrosales.com.
An excellent place in the centre, with high-quality fish given expert, and not too interventionist, treatment by the chef. Recommended.

Casares

€€ The Forge/Restaurante El Forjador
Ctra Casares Km 10, T952-895120, www.forgesrestaurant.com. Book ahead; opens for lunch Wed-Sun in winter and dinner Wed-Sat plus Sun lunch in summer.
Just above the road between Estepona and Casares, this hideaway among larch and cork trees offers a warm welcome, views, and a sweet dining area and indoor terrace. Some British classics take their place on the menu alongside lamb curry, Moroccan chicken and Spanish-influenced plates. Leave room for dessert.

Festivals

Ojén

1st week in Aug Fiesta de Flamenco.

Transport

Most of these bus services are run by **Portillo**, T902-450550, www.portillo.avanzabus.com.

Estepona

Estepona is served by regular daily buses along the coast in both directions.

Casares

The alternative route back to the coast at **Manilva** passes through attractive vineyards and limestone scenery, although the road surface is poor. There are 2 buses a day from **Estepona** to Casares.

North from Málaga

Málaga's hinterland, the province's most interesting zone, is a world away from the busy coast. The main town in the north of the province is Antequera, which has a host of interesting monuments as well as a range of natural attractions. While the most direct route north is via the N331 *autovía*, a more enticing option for those with transport sends you northwest via the El Chorro region, gouged with gorges and redolent with curious local history.

Garganta del Chorro and Bobastro → *Colour map 4, B6.*

a mighty ravine and Moorish ruins

Garganta del Chorro

Taking the Cártama road from Málaga, continue along the course of the Río Guadalhorce to **Pizarra**, and then to the white hilltop town of **Alora**. A 14th-century Alcazaba stands above it, largely in ruins; it now serves as Alora's cemetery. On the town's main square is the huge parish church of La Encarnación, built in the 18th century and said to be the province's second largest place of worship after Málaga's cathedral.

Just north of Alora fork right and after 12 km you will arrive at Garganta del Chorro, or Desfiladero de los Gaitanes, an impressive but narrow ravine cut into the limestone by the Río Guadalhorce. The striking railway cuts in and out of tunnels along the side of the gorge, which in some places is over 300 m deep. Also following the side of the gorge is a narrow path, **El Caminito del Rey**, which was built in the early 1920s and used by King Alfonso XIII when he opened the nearby hydroelectric works. It's a narrow, dramatic path of 3 km, recently rebuilt and reopened after years of dangerous neglect, and is scary but spectacular. An entry fee is due to be charged from mid-2015 onwards.

The gorge is a prime draw for rock climbers, who descend on El Chorro from all over Spain. There are many assisted climbing routes equipped with bolts or rings. Other activities you can arrange include canoeing and abseiling.

The hamlet of **El Chorro** is at the point the river is dammed, and it's where the train stops. It sits in magnificent surroundings; there's a hotel here, *casas rurales* nearby, and several hostels and campsites. It's also a popular lunch destination for malagueños at weekends.

★Bobastro

Six kilometres north of El Chorro, Bobastro is what remains of the stronghold of one of the most interesting characters in the history of Al-Andalus. Ibn Hafsun was a *muwallad* (from a family of Christian converts to Islam) who became a renegade after killing a neighbour in AD 879. Fleeing to North Africa, he returned after a year and set him up here, where he raised a ragtag army and became a real thorn in the side of the Córdoban rulers. Defeating various expeditions sent against him, he was captured in AD 883 and forced to join the army. After serving for a while, he deserted and returned to his fortress, where he rapidly started campaigning and conquering territory. At one point he held most of southern Andalucía with the help of various allies. He was never defeated and seems to have converted to Christianity; at any rate he built a church here. He died in AD 917, but his sons weren't able to keep hold of Bobastro for too long; it was retaken by Córdoba in AD 927.

Ibn Hafsun chose a wild, beautiful and highly defensible spot for his fortress, of which little remains atop the hill. Before reaching it, you pass the Mozarabic church in which later sources claim he was buried. It's a place of great beauty and solitude. It's in ruins, but a horseshoe arch has been preserved and the views are enchanting. Although Bobastro was once a sizeable town, scattered stone is all that remains.

Listings Garganta del Chorro and Bobastro

Where to stay

Garganta del Chorro

There are several *refugios* near the train station charging around €10-14 for a dorm bed. There's also a campsite.

€€€ Cortijo Valverde

Apt 47, Alora, T952-112979, www.cortijovalverde.com. Minimum 2-night stay.

A rural hotel set in olive and almond groves near El Chorro. Each cottage has its own terrace and superb views. There's a pool, the hotel makes an environmental effort and walking and other activities in the area can be arranged. Breakfast is included, and other meals are available.

€€ Complejo Turístico La Garganta

Bda El Chorro s/n, T952-495000, www.lagarganta.com.

Dominating the hamlet, and offering spectacular views over the reservoir and gorge, this former flour mill is now a hotel. Attractive rooms and apartments are compact but fairly priced; it's more for a room with balcony. All have modern rustic decor; there's a pool, and the outdoor restaurant terrace buzzes with contented chatter during weekend lunches.

€ Finca La Campana

T626-963942, www.fincalacampana.com. Reception open 0900-1100, 1900-2100.

A hospitable base run by climbers 2 km from the railway station. They offer climbing, caving and mountain bike trips and have cosy double and family accommodation in a variety of cottages or in the *refugio*, where a dorm bed costs €12. You can also camp. All guests have use of the kitchen and pool, and there's a shop. Mountain bikes, climbing gear and kayaks can be hired here. Recommended.

Transport

Garganta del Chorro

There are no buses to El Chorro, but 2 daily trains arrive from **Málaga** (40 mins). Both stop in **Alora**. One continues to **Ronda**, one to **Sevilla**.

Ardales and Carratraca → *Colour map 4, B5.*

pretty hilltop settlement and spa

The main town in the region, Ardales is 10 km west of El Chorro. It's a pleasant place, capped by a ruined castle that was presumably also built by Ibn Hafsun. Below it is the church, **Nuestra Señora de los Remedios**, which is a mixture of the *mudéjar* and Baroque; from the former style it conserves a fine wooden ceiling. Also in town are a couple of museums, one dedicated to the **Cueva de Ardales** ⓘ *4 km outside of town, T952-458046*. Important Palaeolithic paintings decorate this cave, discovered in the early 19th century. The cave is closed to the public except by prior appointment, which you should arrange well in advance. If you read Spanish, the results of geological and archaeological investigations are summarized on www.cuevadeardales.com.

Some 5 km southeast of Ardales is **Carratraca,** famous for its sulphurous waters which were highly regarded back in Roman times. The village really took off in the 19th century when the despotic King Fernando VII built a mansion here for his personal use. Royal patronage made society sit up and take notice, and numerous famous visitors from all over Europe came here to take the waters, which, with a constant temperature of 18°C, is emphatically a summer-only pastime. There's a luxury spa hotel here, and in recent years, Carratraca has revived the performance of its ancient passion play, which takes place on Good Friday and Easter Saturday in the bullring, with a cast of over 100 villagers.

Listings Ardales and Carratraca

Where to stay

Ardales

€€ Posada del Conde
Pantano del Chorro 16-18, Ardales, T952-112411, www.hotel delconde.com.
This stately old building has been well converted into a comfortable hotel. It has high-quality rooms, with plenty of space and good bathrooms, and a restaurant serving generous and elaborate cuisine including hearty Castilian roasts.

Carratraca

€€€€ Villa Padierna
C Antonio Rioboo 11, Carratraca, T952-489542, villapadiernathermashotel.com.
This luxury spa hotel seeks to recreate the glory days – Roman, Moorish and 19th century – of taking the waters. The installations are magnificently attractive,

as is the building; try to nab a deal that includes spa treatments or meals.

Restaurants

Ardales

On and around the central Plaza de San Isidro are a handful of good tapas bars, including **El Mellizo**.

Transport

Ardales

There are 4 daily buses from **Málaga** to Ardales; these continue to **Ronda**.

Antequera and around → *Colour map 4, A6/B6.*

some of Europe's most impressive prehistoric dolmens

You know a town must be pretty old when even the Romans named it 'ancient place', or Antikaria. It's an excellent place to visit; on the city's edge stand three stunning prehistoric dolmens. The old town has numerous noble buildings of great interest, and the surrounding area offers tempting excursions to the dramatic rockscapes of El Torcal, the Lobo Park wolfery, and the flamingo lake of La Fuente de Piedra.

The dolmens are an obvious indication that the Antequera hilltop was an important prehistoric settlement, and the town's strategic position at the head of one of the easiest routes to the coast also appealed to the Romans. The Moors fortified the town with a citadel and, as part of the kingdom of Granada, Antequera didn't fall to the Christians until 1410. After becoming an important military base for assaults on the remaining Moorish possessions, the city grew in wealth in the 16th and 17th centuries, from which period most of its monuments date.

Sights

The centre of Antequera is Plaza San Sebastián, on which stands the **tourist office** ⓘ *C Encarnación 1, T952-702505, www.turismo.antequera.es, Mon-Sat 0930-1900, Sun 1000-1400*, which has helpful information on the town and area.

At the top of town, the **Arco de los Gigantes**, a triumphal arch built in 1585, gives on to the attractive Plaza de los Escribanos, by which stands the town's most impressive church, **Real Colegiata de Santa María la Mayor** ⓘ *Tue-Sat 1000-1900 (1030-1730 Oct-Apr), Sun 1030-1500, €3*, with a beautiful Renaissance façade worked on, among others, by the master Diego de Siloé in the mid-16th century. The spacious interior is now used for exhibitions and concerts and is a fine space with fat Ionic columns and a wooden ceiling. The cedarwood baldachin is a recent replica of the original. From the terrace beside the church, as well as stirring views, you can examine the excavated **Roman baths** below you.

The hillside above the church is covered with a peaceful hedged garden stretching up to the **Alcazaba** ⓘ *Tue-Sat 1000-1900 (1030-1730 Oct-Apr), Sun 1030-1500, €6 including Santa María la Mayor*, the remains of the Moorish fortress. The best-preserved feature is the **Torre del Homenaje** (keep) from the 13th century.

The castle has been comprehensively restored (actually, completely rebuilt in places, which has raised various authenticity questions) and is an atmospheric spot. From the hilltop you look across to the curiously shaped hill known as the **Peña de los Enamorados** (Lovers' Hill), from which it is said that a pair of star-crossed Moorish lovers threw themselves when their union was prohibited.

Antequera's rich archaeological heritage is represented in the **Museo de la Ciudad de Antequera** ⓘ *Plaza del Coso Viejo, May-Sep Tue-Fri 0930-1400, 1900-2100, Sat 0930-1400, 1800-2100, Sun 1000-1400, Oct-Apr Tue-Fri 0930-1400, 1630-1830, Sat 0930-1400, 1600-1900, Sun 1000-1400, €3*, near the Plaza San Sebastián. Set in a *palacio* dating from the Renaissance, it's a display of mixed quality, but has some outstanding pieces. The pride and joy of the museum is a famous Roman bronze statue dating from the first century AD. A life-sized depiction of a naked boy known as Efebo, it's a fine work. There are also some high-quality Roman mosaics in the museum. Another sculpture worth a look is a beautifully rendered St Francis, which is attributed to Alonso Cano.

There's another museum nearby, in the **Convento de las Carmelitas Descalzas** ⓘ *Plaza de las Descalzas s/n, T606-855792, Tue-Fri 1030-1400, 1700-2000, Sat 0900-1230, 1700-2000, Sun 0900-1230, plus 1700-2000 summer, closed Jul, guided tours on the half hour, €3.30*, the order founded by Teresa of Avila. The visit is by guided tour and as worthwhile for the building as for the artworks, although a Luca Giordano depiction of Teresa herself is a fine work.

Antequera is full of other churches; in fact, although it likes to call itself the Athens of Andalucía, Rome might be (marginally) more accurate. Among them is the **Iglesia del Carmen** ⓘ *May-Sep Mon-Fri 0900-1400, 1630-1900, Sat-Sun 1000-1330, 1700-1900, Oct-Apr Tue-Fri 1100-1330, 1630-1745, Sat-Sun 1100-1400, €2*, which has a *mudéjar* ceiling but is most notable for its excellent wooden *retablo*. Dating from the 18th century, it was carved by Antonio Primo in incredible size and detail; it's decorated with a wealth of scrolls, volutes and cherubs, as well as figures of popes, archbishops, John the Baptist and other prophets. Also look out for the pretty organ in the gallery and some ornate fresco work in one of the side chapels.

On the Plaza del Portichuelo, look out for the highly unusual arched brick façade of the small chapel, the **Tribuna del Portichuelo**. On the same square is the church of **Santa María de Jesús**, a bright white Baroque creation.

★Dolmens

All dolmens Tue-Sat 1000-1830 (summer until 2030), Sun 1000-1700. Free.

The highlight of any visit to Antequera will be a visit to these hugely impressive and moving monuments. They are megalithic in the true sense of the word, consisting of vast slabs of stone, the largest of which weighs a massive 180 tons. The stones were dragged over 1 km from a nearby quarry. After erecting the upright stones, earth ramps were constructed to manoeuvre the covering slabs into place. There are three dolmens, dating from the Chalcolithic period; they were built as burial chambers, presumably for important chiefs.

The adjacent **Menga** and **Viera** dolmens are about 1 km from the centre of town. From Plaza San Sebastián, walk down Calle Encarnación past the tourist office, carry on straight ahead, and follow the road (now Calle Carrera) left. Eventually you'll reach the entrance to the dolmen area on your left. You access the dolmens through an interpretation centre that provides some context. Menga, the oldest of them, dates from approximately 2500 BC, and is an eerily atmospheric chamber roofed with vast stone slabs. Recently, a deep well has been discovered at one end of the chamber. At the entrance, the staff on duty will point out the faint engravings in the portal. On Midsummer's Day, the rising sun shines directly into the chamber from behind the Peña de los Enamorados, clearly of ritual significance. The Viera dolmen dates from some five centuries later and has an access corridor leading to a smaller burial chamber.

El Romeral dolmen stands a further couple of kilometres out past the Menga and Viera dolmens; turn left when you reach the major intersection (head for Córdoba/Sevilla), then turn left after crossing the railway line. It dates to around 1800 BC and presents a very different aspect, with smaller corbelled stones being used to wall the access chamber and half-domed burial chamber, which is entered through a doorway.

El Torcal

This massive chunk of limestone, 16 km south of Antequera, has been weathered into rugged and surreal sculptural karstic formations and is a memorable place to visit, although preferably on a weekday when it's less crowded. The bulk of the massif is a *parque natural* and a **visitor centre** ⓘ *T952-702505, daily 1000-1700 (1900 summer)*, atop it has exhibitions on the formations and wildlife; there's also an audiovisual presentation and café. From here, there's a short path leading to a stunning viewpoint and, from the centre's car park, two marked walking trails of approximately 45 minutes and two hours' duration. Spring is an excellent time to explore El Torcal, as the grey rocky zone is enlivened by a riot of colourful wildflowers.

The closest town is **Villanueva de la Concepción**, 18 km southwest of Antequera and served by buses from there and Málaga. The tourist office in Antequera can arrange a taxi to take you to the visitor centre, wait for you to do the trail, and take you back to town.

Lobo Park

Ctra Antequera–Alora Km 16, T952-031107, www.lobopark.com, daily 1000-1800, tours 1100, 1300, 1500, 1630, €11, children €7.

An intriguing spot to visit in easy striking distance of Antequera, this wolf park houses a variety of lupine residents rescued from the wild or captivity. The tour visits the enclosures of several different packs – Iberian, timber, European, and Arctic wolves are all present. There's heaps of information – enquire ahead if you want an English-speaking guide – and it's fascinating to see the packs' strict hierarchies, plus the group 'bonding' behaviour after being fed. There's a good ecological vibe here, and the visit also includes a look at some domestic animals – a hit with the kids, but also great to see some animals rescued from the wild, including a pair of foxes who literally jump for joy when their handler approaches. A few nights a month from May to October you can pre-book a visit to hear the wolves howling in unison; an eerie moonlit sound. It includes dinner; check the website for dates.

Laguna de la Fuente de Piedra

Twenty kilometres northwest of Antequera, this large saltwater lake is one of Europe's most important breeding grounds for the greater flamingo. The loveably awkward pinkish birds arrive early in the year to rear their chicks and hang around until the water level drops in summer, usually in late July or August. There are dozens of other waterbird species present, including avocets, terns and the rare white-headed duck. There's an **information centre** ⓘ *T952-111715, Wed-Sun 1000-1400, 1600-1800 (1800-2000 Apr-Sep),* by the lake that hires binoculars and provides birdwatching advice.

Nearby, **El Refugio del Burrito** ⓘ *T952-735077, www.elrefugiodelburrito.com, 1000-1800, free,* rescues donkeys and mules from across Europe and brings them here to rehabilitate and enjoy retirement in the Andalucían sunshine. It's great for kids and entry is free, but the organization relies on donations, so you may want to sponsor one of the gentle long-eared beasts for €15 per year.

Archidona

Some 15 km east of Antequera lies this once strategic town. Occupied by the Iberians, the Romans and the Moors and defended by a hilltop castle, it was captured by Christian forces in 1462. Later it was the chief town of the Counts of Ureña and the Dukes of Osuna.

Today, it is a backwater, bypassed by both the main road and the *autovía* to Granada. Its pride and joy, however, is Plaza Ochavada, a late 18th-century octagonal square, surrounded by buildings using ornamental brickwork and stone. It's a lovely space, and on it is the **tourist office** ⓘ *T952-716479, www.archidona.org.* Further up the hill, a palm-shaded plaza is home to the Casa Consistorial, which boasts a beautiful carved façade. It now houses the municipal museum.

Listings Antequera and around

Where to stay

€€€ Parador de Antequera

C García de Olmo s/n, T952-840261, www.parador.es.
The town's modern parador is near the bullring on the edge of town and offers quiet comfort. There's a pool and pleasant gardens; the rooms have polished floors and large beds.

€ Hotel Plaza San Sebastián

Plaza San Sebastián 4, T952-844239, www.hotelplaza sansebastian.com.
Centrally located, this friendly hotel has recently renovated modern rooms

with a/c, heating and good bathrooms. A sound choice lacking character but good value.

Laguna de la Fuente de Piedra

Camping

Camping Fuente Piedra
Camino de la Rábita s/n, T952-735294, www.campingfuentedepiedra.com.
A good base for flamingo-watchers, this well-equipped campsite is close to the lake and open all year. As well as tent and van sites, there are bungalows and rooms available. Pool and bar/restaurant.

Restaurants

€€ Mesón El Escribano
Plaza de los Escribanos 11, T952-706533.
This popular restaurant has a terrace looking out at the collegiate church and specializes in local dishes such as *porra*, a thick tomato cold soup similar to *salmorejo*.

Bars and clubs

Manolo Bar
C Calzada 14, T952-841015. Open 1700-late.
With a Wild West theme, it serves a big mix of Antequera folk, coffee, tapas and mixed drinks late into the night.

Transport

Bus

Antequera is well served by buses from **Málaga**, which run almost hourly (1 hr) from the bus station, a 15-min walk north of Plaza San Sebastián. There are 5 daily buses to **Granada**, and 5 to **Sevilla** via **Osuna**. There are also connections to **Córdoba** and other Andalucían cities.

Train

The train station is 1.5 km north of the town centre. There are 3 daily trains to **Ronda** (1 hr 10 mins) and services to **Sevilla** (4 a day, 1 hr 50 mins), **Granada** and **Algeciras**. Regular fast trains between Málaga and Córdoba stop at Antequera–Santa Ana station, 17 km west of town.

Laguna de la Fuente de Piedra

There are 3 buses daily from **Antequera** to Fuente de Piedra village.

Archidona

6-7 daily buses between **Antequera** and Archidona (20 mins), continuing to **Granada**.

Ronda

★"There is one town that would be better than Aranjuez to see your first bullfight in if you were only going to see one and that is Ronda. That is where you should go if you ever go to Spain on a honeymoon or if you ever bolt with anyone." Ernest Hemingway, *Death in the Afternoon*.

The cradle of bullfighting as we know it, Ronda features high on the must-see list of many visitors to Andalucía because of its picturesque whitewashed streets and, most spectacularly, its position straddling a deep gorge that separates the old and new parts of town. The gorge is spanned by the Puente Nuevo, a late 18th-century bridge that crosses 80 m above the stream below.

These attractions mean that it's overrun with tourists in peak season; to really appreciate the town you should spend a night or two here, as most people come on day trips and by six in the evening the tour buses have rolled back to the coast. Pack a thick coat if you plan to visit in winter. *Colour map 4, B4.*

famous bullring, historic bridge and Moorish old town

Plaza de España and Puente Nuevo

It's likely that you'll make this your first port of call in Ronda, as looking down into the gorge has a magnetic appeal. The plaza itself is dominated by the former town hall, now a parador. After pondering for a moment what idiot allowed a McDonald's to be opened next to it, move over to the Tajo and look down 80 m or so into the narrow gorge.

The Puente Nuevo was built in the late 18th century and designed by José Martín de Aldehuela. Legend says that he died falling into the gorge while carving the date on the bridge, but this is in fact untrue – he died in Málaga several years later. The stones were raised on pulleys from the bottom of the Tajo. Within the bridge itself is an **interpretation centre** ⓘ *Plaza de España s/n, T649-965338, Mon-Fri 1000-1800 or 1900, Sat and Sun 1000-1500, €2,* in what used to be a small prison. Apart from the knowledge that you're standing over the ravine, there's little worthwhile here.

Essential Ronda

Finding your feet

The largest of the white towns in these parts, Ronda sits atop a hill, which is cut in two by the Tajo, a narrow gorge formed by the Río Guadalevín. The centre of town is Plaza de España on the edge of the ravine; from here the Puente Nuevo crosses the drop to the original Moorish part of town, where most of the interesting monuments are located. The larger Christian expansion, known as the Mercadillo, stretches north and east of Plaza de España and is the main focus for the daily life of *rondeños*; it's also where most of the restaurants and bars are located.

Best places to stay

Hotel Montelirio, page 260
Alavera de los Baños, page 261
Hotel Enfrente Arte, page 261
Hotel San Gabriel, page 261

When to go

Ronda gets very icy in autumn and winter.

Plaza de Toros

C Virgen de la Paz s/n, T952-874132. Daily 1000-1900 or 2000 in summer, €6.50, with audioguide €8.

One of the country's oldest, the Ronda bullring has a special appeal to lovers of tauromachy, for it was here that the rules for modern bullfighting were laid down by the Romero clan. While admission isn't cheap, if you have an interest in such things, it's well worth a visit. Apart from the thrill of walking out on to the arena itself, there's a museum with all sorts of memorabilia. You can also visit the stables, and, most interestingly, the bull pens, with their complex system of lifting gates operated from the safety of above.

Most of the other sights are across in the old town, but it's worth seeking out the **Templete de la Virgen de los Dolores**, also known as Los Ahorcados, on Calle Santa Cecilia. Built in the 18th century, it's a small chapel with a highly unusual façade. The Ionic columns

BACKGROUND

Ronda

In the collapse of the Córdoba caliphate, Ronda was seized by a Berber general and became its own *taifa* state before being annexed by Sevilla in 1066. Ronda wasn't reconquered by the Christians until 1485, when it was taken by forces under Fernando, the Catholic monarch. Always a centre for resistance and bandit activity, the Ronda area held out strongly in the 19th century against the invading French forces, leading villagers to chant 'Napoleón, Napoleón, conquistaste toda España, pero no pudiste entrar en la tierra de las castañas' (Napoleon, Napoleon, you conquered all of Spain, but you never could enter the land of the chestnuts).

Later, the town was popularized by Romantic travellers and became a haunt of artists and writers. Gustav Doré, Rainer Maria Rilke and Ernest Hemingway are among those who spent much time here. In the Civil War, many right-wingers were brutally murdered and the town shared its resources along a strict socialist system; reprisals after the Nationalist takeover were also fierce.

are supported by strange birdmen and other figures, a product of late-Baroque mannerism influenced by Latin-American imagery.

Ciudad Vieja

Known simply as La Ciudad, the old part of Ronda is a tight knot of small streets and white houses, including several noble *palacios* and churches. A stretch of the city walls still encircles part of the area, beyond which extend green fields and the mountains of the sierra.

After crossing the bridge over the chasm, take a quick left and you'll soon come to the **Casa del Rey Moro** ⓘ *Barrio de Padre Jesús s/n, T952-187200, daily 1000-1900, €4*. This evocatively faded mansion (also known as La Mina and Jardines de Forestier) with jutting wooden eaves was built in the 18th century over Moorish foundations. The principal attraction here is an impressive staircase hewn 80 m downwards through the rock to the river below. Some scholars say its function was merely so that slaves could fetch water for their Moorish master, but its real purpose is likely to have been as a sally-port in times of siege; legend attributes its construction to the king Abomelic. There are 232 steps down to the river, and they are slippery and steep. Once you're down you can admire the blue-green water from a tranquil small platform and look up at the town above. A fine landscaped garden is the other feature of the (slightly overpriced) attraction.

On exiting the Casa del Rey Moro, you will enjoy the fine views of the town and countryside. Below is an old entrance gate into the city, which commemorates Felipe V. A short distance beyond, following the river away from town, are the 14th-century **Baños Arabes (Arab baths)** ⓘ *Cuesta de Santo Domingo s/n, T656-950937, Mon-Fri 1000-1800 (1900 summer), Sat and Sun 1000-1500, €3*, preserving brick arches and star-shaped skylights.

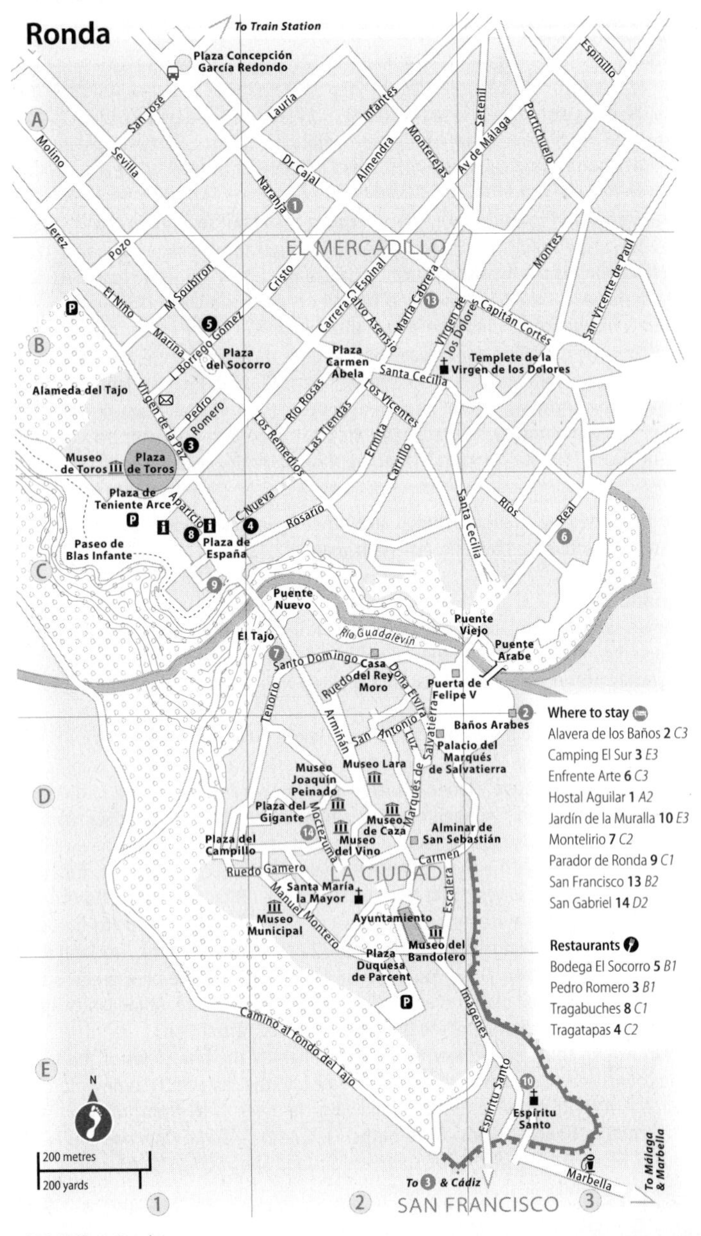
Ronda
To Train Station
Plaza Concepción García Redondo
San José
Lauría
Infantes
Molino
Sevilla
Dr Cajal
Naranja
Almendra
Montereja
Av de Málaga
Setenil
Portichuelo
Espinillo
Jerez
Pozo
EL MERCADILLO
Cristo
M Soubirón
El Niño
Marina
L Borrego Gómez
Carrera C Espinal
Calvo Asensio
María Cabrera
Virgen de los Dolores
Capitán Cortés
Montes
San Vicente de Paul
Plaza del Socorro
Plaza Carmen Abela
Santa Cecilia
Templete de la Virgen de los Dolores
Alameda del Tajo
Virgen de la Paz
Pedro Romero
Río Rosas
Las Tiendas
Los Remedios
Los Vicentes
Ermita
Carrillo
Museo de Toros
Plaza de Toros
Plaza de Teniente Arce
Aparicio
C Nueva
Rosario
Ríos
Real
Paseo de Blas Infante
Plaza de España
Puente Nuevo
El Tajo
Río Guadalevín
Puente Viejo
Puente Arabe
Santo Domingo
Casa del Rey Moro
Doña Elvira
Ruedo
Tenorio
Puerta de Felipe V
Armiñán
San Antonio
Luz
Salvatierra
Baños Arabes
Palacio del Marqués de Salvatierra
Museo Lara
Museo Joaquín Peinado
Marqués de Salvatierra
Plaza del Gigante
Moctezuma
Museo de Caza
Museo del Vino
Alminar de San Sebastián
Plaza del Campillo
Ruedo Gamero
LA CIUDAD
Carmen
Escalera
Santa María la Mayor
Manuel Montero
Museo Municipal
Ayuntamiento
Museo del Bandolero
Plaza Duquesa de Parcent
Imágenes
Camino al fondo del Tajo
Espíritu Santo
Espíritu Santo
Marbella
To Málaga & Marbella
To 3 & Cádiz
SAN FRANCISCO
N
200 metres
200 yards
A
B
C
D
E
1
2
3
Where to stay
Alavera de los Baños 2 C3
Camping El Sur 3 E3
Enfrente Arte 6 C3
Hostal Aguilar 1 A2
Jardín de la Muralla 10 E3
Montelirio 7 C2
Parador de Ronda 9 C1
San Francisco 13 B2
San Gabriel 14 D2
Restaurants
Bodega El Socorro 5 B1
Pedro Romero 3 B1
Tragabuches 8 C1
Tragatapas 4 C2

Just above the Puerta de Felipe V is the **Palacio del Marqués de Salvatierra**, one of the more impressive of Ronda's many elegant buildings. Its 18th-century Baroque façade has been recently restored, and features four columns carved with caryatid-like figures, in this case apparently native American inspired. Outside is a stone *crucero*.

Following this street along, you'll reach a small tower, the **Alminar de San Sebastián**, a former minaret of one of the town's many mosques. It's been capped by a later belfry but still preserves most of its original structure, including a horseshoe-arched window.

Near here, two grand and unusual buildings face each other across Plaza Duquesa de Parcent. The collegiate church of **Santa María la Mayor** ⓘ *Plaza Duquesa de Parcent s/n, T952-874048, daily 1000-1800 (2000 summer), closed Sun 1230-1400 €4*, was once Ronda's principal mosque. Converted into a church by Fernando, the Catholic Monarch, it retains little of its Moorish origins apart from an inscribed archway, the *mihrab* and the minaret, converted into a bell tower. Most striking is its double gallery looking out on to the square. The interior is mostly a blend of late Gothic and Renaissance arching; there's a fine elaborate choir, some poor frescoes, and an inlaid Churrigueresque *retablo*. Upstairs, behind the galleries, is an exhibition of polychrome sculpture.

On the same square are the long arcades of the **Ayuntamiento**, perhaps reminiscent of a row of shops for good reason, as it has been suggested that was once a Moorish market.

Beyond here, the Ciudad comes to an end in the Barrio de San Francisco, which has a well-preserved section of walls and a fine sandstone-block church in **Iglesia del Espíritu Santo**. A gate leads out through the walls towards the countryside beyond.

Back at Plaza Duquesa, head east to the **Museo Municipal** ⓘ *Plaza Mondragón s/n, T952-870818, www.museoderonda.es, Mon-Fri 1000-1800 (1900 summer), Sat and Sun 1000-1500, €3*, which is set in the Palacio de Mondragón, one of Ronda's most beautiful mansions. The building alone is worth the price of admission; it centres around two patios, the first with red arches and a well, the second with a wooden gallery and eaves, as well as colourful tilework. There's also a Moorish-style garden. The collection is a mixture of displays: the flora and fauna of the Sierra de los Nieves; a reconstruction of a late Bronze Age hut with thatched roof on stone foundations; of a cave; and a prehistoric metalworking furnace. One of the most important pieces is a seventh-century BC mould for making swords. There's also a resumé of Muslim funerary customs and a collection of Moorish gravestones.

There are several other museums in the Ciudad Vieja. The **Museo Lara** ⓘ *C Armiñán 29, T952-871263, www.museolara.org, daily 1100-2000 (1900 winter), €4*, could be described as a collection of collections, with a bizarre range of objects housed in yet another attractive *palacio*. There are swords, opera glasses, sewing machines, torture implements, witchcraft displays and typewriters among numerous other curios. There are flamenco shows here on spring and summer evenings. Nearby, the **Centro de Interpretación del Vino** ⓘ *C González Campos 2, T952 879 735, www.bodegaslasangrederonda.es, Mon-Thu and Sat 1030-1900 (2030*

ON THE ROAD

Los toros

The bullfight, or *corrida*, is an emblem of Spanish culture, a reminder of when Roman gladiators fought wild beasts in amphitheatres. It is emphatically not a sport (the result is a given) but a ritual; a display of courage by both animal and human. While to outside observers it can seem as if the bull is being tortured and humiliated, that is not the way many Spaniards perceive it, though there is an ever-increasing lobby against it in the country.

The myth that bullfighting aficionados are a bloodthirsty lot should be dispelled. Nobody likes to see a *torero* hurt, a less-than-clean kill, or overuse of the *pic*. What keeps many people going is that all-too-rare sublime fight, where the *matador* is breathtakingly daring, and the bull strong and courageous.

The fighting bull, or *toro de lidia*, is virtually a wild animal reared in vast ranches where human contact is minimal. It enters the ring when it is about four years old, and weighs about 500 kg.

In a standard bullfight there are six bulls and three *matadores*, who fight two each. The fights take 15 minutes each, so a standard *corrida* lasts about two hours, usually starting in the late afternoon. The fight is divided into three parts, or *tercios*. In the first part, the bull emerges and is then played with the cape by the *matador*, who judges its abilities and tendencies. The bull is then induced to charge a mounted *picador*, who meets it with a sharp lance which is dug into the bull's neck muscles as it tries to toss the horse. Although the horses are thankfully padded these days, it's the most difficult part of the fight to enjoy or comprehend and *picadores* (following the *matador*'s orders) frequently overdo it with the lance, tiring, hurting and dispiriting the animal.

summer), Fri 1100-1800, Sun 1100-1530, €5, is a bodega with a pretty patio; the tour includes a taste of one wine; for an extra fee you can taste more Andalucían drops; the **Museo de Caza** is devoted to hunting, while the **Museo del Bandolero** pays homage to the famous bandits of the region. Lastly, the **Museo Joaquín Peinado** is a gallery with works by that *rondeño* painter of the Paris school.

Around Ronda

The ruins of **Acinipo** ⓘ *Ctra MA-449 s/n, T952-041452, Wed-Sun 1000-1500, opening times are changeable, so ring ahead, free,* also known as **Ronda la Vieja**, lie 12 km northwest of Ronda off the Sevilla road. An important Roman town in its day (the first century AD was its zenith), it later declined as Ronda's fortunes rose. Sprawled across a hilltop, most of the ruins are fragmentary, but what makes the visit worthwhile is the massive theatre with views across the sierra. There are also remains of earlier Iberian and Phoenician structures. Not much further is the strange and beautiful town of **Setenil de las Bodegas** (see page 175).

Cueva de la Pileta ⓘ *Benaoján, T952-167343, daily 1000-1300, 1600-1700 (1800 summer), entry by guided tour on the hour in groups of up to 25, 1 hr,* an important

The second *tercio* involves the placing of three pairs of darts, or *banderillas*, in the bull's neck muscles, to further tire it so that the head is carried low enough to allow the *matador* to reach the point where the sword should go in. The placing of the *banderillas* is usually rapid and skilful, done on foot, occasionally by the *matador* himself.

The last part is the *tercio de la muerte*, the third of death. The *matador* faces the bull with a *muleta* (small cape) and a sword. He passes it a few times then positions himself for the kill. After profiling (turning side on and pointing the sword at the bull), he aims for a point that should kill the bull instantly. But this rarely happens; there are often a few attempts, with the animal wounded and gushing blood, and then a *descabello* (coup de grace), where the spinal cord is severed below the base of the skull.

If the spectators have been impressed by the bullfighter's performance, they stand and wave their handkerchiefs at the president of the ring, who may then award one or two ears and, for exceptional performances, the tail as well. These are then chopped off the animal and paraded around the ring by the fighter, who will be thrown hats and wineskins as gestures of appreciation. Meanwhile, the dead bull has been dragged out in a flurry of dust by mules; if it has fought well, it will be applauded out of the ring.

Andalucía justly claims to be the cradle of bullfighting, and rings at El Puerto de Santa María, Ronda and Sevilla are among the most prestigious in Spain. The famous Ronda school developed the structure of the fight as we see it today. Another type of bullfight is the *corrida de rejones*, where skilled riders fight the bull from horseback atop highly trained mounts; a combination of skill and showmanship.

cave 20 km southwest of Ronda, was discovered in 1905 by a local farmer. On following a stream of bats in the hope of collecting some of their dung as fertilizer, he came across a series of prehistoric paintings. The cave is 2 km long and further exploration has revealed a large quantity of art in various different chambers. While the limestone formations aren't the most spectacular you've ever seen, the visit is fascinating, and guided by a descendant of the original farmer. Commentary, in Spanish, and limited English, is intelligent and humorous. The oldest paintings date from the Palaeolithic and range from 12,000 to 30,000 years old. You can see a horsehead, bulls, goats, a fish, and a seal. The oldest probably represents the earliest phase of Cro-Magnon presence in Europe. There are also Neolithic paintings; mostly geometric patterns and abstract forms, but also what appears to be a form of calendar. It's all the better for being able to peer at these paintings by lantern light before the inevitable interpretation centre is built. To get there, take a left off the A-574 (Sevilla) road not far below Ronda; it's signposted Benaoján. When you get to Benaoján, head through the village, then take a sharp left as you leave it on the other side. The cave is 5 km along this road; bat-phobes should stay in the car.

As well as the excursions listed above, the white towns of Cádiz province, including Grazalema, are close at hand (see page 168).

Ronda to Gaucín

One of the province's more spectacular drives heads from Ronda southwest towards Algeciras through a succession of whitewashed hilltop villages with a distinctly Moorish ambience. **Atajate**, some 18 km from Ronda, is typical, with a high 19th-century church and perspectives over olive groves, grapevines and chestnut woods. **Benadalidad** boasts a castle that was strategically crucial in the Reconquista, while larger **Benalauría** and **Algatocín** have several fine buildings amid their narrow streets. The most interesting of the towns, **Gaucín**, makes a tempting rural base and is dominated by its ruined fortress on a rocky crag high over town. From Gaucín, you can cross a valley via a spectacular road to the pretty town of Casares, near Estepona on the Costa del Sol, see page 243. A 13-km detour south from Algatocín, Genalguacil seems like another typical village from afar, until you arrive and find its streets, parks and plazas stocked full of sculptures of every type imaginable, a legacy of a biennial gathering of artists in the village. It's well worth the detour to see it.

Listings Ronda *map p256*

Tourist information

Regional office
Plaza de España 1, T952-169311. Mon-Fri 0900-1930, Sat and Sun 0930-1500.
Ronda's municipal office (Paseo Blas Infante s/n, T952-187119, Mon-Fri 1000-1800, Sat 1000-1400, 1500-1700, Sun 1000-1430) is near the regional one next to the bullring. Both offices have a wide range of information in several languages on the town and area. There is also a useful tourism website, www.turismoderonda.es.

Where to stay

€€€€ Parador de Ronda
Plaza de España s/n, T952-877500, www.parador.es.
Set in the former town hall on the very edge of the Tajo by the Puente Nuevo bridge, this parador has one of the most memorable locations of any Andalucían hotel. While its public areas still suffer from a municipal feel, the rooms are excellent, with comfortable furniture, polished floorboards, plenty of space and big beds. The pricier ones have balconies overlooking the gorge, and it's hard to beat the hotel pool, which is right on the lip of it.

€€€ Hotel Jardín de la Muralla
C Espíritu Santo 13, T952-872764, www.jardindela muralla.com.
A charming hotel set around a central patio, it has large, light rooms that are cheerfully furnished with curios and pictures. There's a lounge with a piano and a garden terrace. Breakfast is included. Good value.

€€€ Hotel Montelirio
C Tenorio 8, T952-873855, www.hotelmontelirio.com.

Close to the bridge, and with rooms and spacious junior suites offering views (rooms without a view are only €16 less, so you might as well), this boutique hotel impresses on many levels, not least for its welcoming management. The more than decent restaurant has a terrace perched right on the edge of the ravine, and there's also a small pool. Recommended.

€€ Alavera de los Baños
C San Miguel s/n, T952-879143, www.alaveradelosbanos.com.
Delightful small hotel with an organically minded restaurant, located between the town walls and the Baños Arabes. Rooms are charmingly and tastefully decorated and you'll get a warm welcome from the owners. Relaxing garden with a pool. Breakfast included. Recommended.

€€ Hotel Enfrente Arte
C Real 40, T952-879088, www.enfrentearte.com.
This stylish and friendly hotel is painted throughout in bright pastel colours that define the funky mood of the place. The rooms are cheerful and comfortable and vary in size and price; some have views. There's a pool, pool table and internet access and, with a generous breakfast/brunch buffet and all beverages included, it's a delight. Recommended.

€€ Hotel San Francisco
C María Cabrera 18, T952-873299, www.hotelsanfrancisco-ronda.com.
This well-run, central choice has a variety of rooms with colourful bedspreads and padded headboards. They are excellent value, have plenty of light and very good bathrooms, as well as TV, heating and a/c. Rates include breakfast. Recommended for decent sleeping at a low price.

€€ Hotel San Gabriel
C Marqués de Moctezuma 19, T952-190392, www.hotelsan gabriel.com.
Beautifully restored and located townhouse run with real love by 3 siblings who grew up in it. A tastefully old-fashioned lounge has bookcases and old sofas. The rooms are elegant; the larger ones have colourful screens to make the space a bit more intimate. Bathrooms and facilities are top-grade without detracting from the old-world charm. Easy street parking nearby. Excellent continental breakfast for a little extra. Highly recommended.

€ Hostal Aguilar/Doña Carmen
C Naranja 28, T952-871994, www.hostaldonacarmen.com.
Modernized *hostal* with good clean rooms and heating, run by a friendly family. There's another section with older, shabbier rooms that are gradually being renovated; these have shared bathroom and are fine value in summer but iceboxes in winter.

Camping

Camping El Sur
Ctra A369, Km 2, 2 km out of town on the Algeciras road, T952-875939, www.campingelsur.com. Open all the year.
This excellent campsite has a pool, bar, restaurant and tidy modern bungalows.

Ronda to Gaucín

€€ Hotel La Fructuosa
C Convento 67, Gaucín, T617-692784, www.lafructuosa.com.
This excellent rural hotel is an appetizing place right in the heart of pretty Gaucín, 36 km southwest of Ronda, and a base for walking and driving exploration of the surrounding

hills. All the rooms are different, offering great views and decorated with exquisite modern rural style. Facilities include a fabulous roof terrace; the included breakfast and the warm personal service also make this a standout.

Restaurants

Many of Ronda's restaurants are tourist traps. Avoid most of the ones along C Nueva.

€€€ Pedro Romero
C Virgen de la Paz 18, T952-871110, www.rpedroromero.com.
The best of the restaurants along the main street near the bullring and predictably decorated with taurine memorabilia. Although it sees its fair share of tourists, it can't be faulted on quality. The bull's tail is particularly good, but anything with a local flavour is recommended. The lunchtime *menú* is decent but the à la carte is more memorable.

€€€ Tragabuches
C José Aparicio 1, T952-878447, www.tragabuches.com.
With an attractive modern dining area with big plate-glass windows looking out over the gardens by the bullring, this restaurant usually wins the foodies' vote as Ronda's most creative. The menu is a small one and changes often. The prices are high for Spain, but OK for the quality on offer; try anything with local *setas* (wild mushrooms). The best way to eat here is to take the pricey but memorable degustation menu.

€€ Tragatapas
C Nueva 4, T952-877209, www.facebook.com/tragatapas.
The delicious fare at this central tapas bar features plenty of innovation, with ox *tataki* taking its place alongside salmon with vanilla and lime or fried squid with broad beans. Recommended.

€ Bodega El Socorro
C Molina 4, T651-746099, www.facebook.com/bodegasocorro.
Just off Plaza del Socorro, this warm and busy bar is decorated with farm tools. The tapas are excellent; try the spinach croquettes, prawn and bacon brochettes or the cold pasta salad.

Festivals

Early Sep Ronda's main fiesta, named in honour of **Pedro Romero** is celebrated with bullfights in 18th-century costumes. There's also a flamenco festival as part of it.

What to do

Bike hire

CycleRonda, *C Juan José de Puya 21, T952-083553, www.cycleronda.com.* Hires bikes at €15 a day.
Pangea, *Pasaje Cayetano 10, T630-562705, www.pangeacentral.com.* Offers outdoor activities in the surrounding area; check website for details.

Bullfighting

You'll need to be here in mid-May for the *feria* or in early Sep for the fiestas. Book tickets on T952-876967 (fiesta box office opens 1 Jul).

Transport

Ronda's bus and train stations are both on Av de Andalucía on the northern edge of the new town, a 10- to 15-min walk from Plaza de España.

Bus

There are 4 to 10 daily buses to **Málaga** (2 hrs), some direct. **Sevilla** is served 3-5 times daily (2 hrs 30 mins), and there are a couple of daily buses to **Marbella** and **Fuengirola**. Other destinations include **Grazalema** and **Ubrique** (2 a day, none on Sun), **Cádiz** via **Arcos de la Frontera** and **Jerez** 5 times daily, 1 to **Algeciras** via **Gaucín** and **Jimena de la Frontera**, and 6 to nearby **Setenil** (4 on Sat, none on Sun).

Train

Ronda is on the train line running from **Algeciras** to **Granada** via **Jimena de la Frontera** and **Antequera**. There are 3 daily trains to **Granada**, 2 hrs 30 mins, and 5 to **Algeciras**, 1 hr 45 mins, as well as connections to Bobadilla and then **Córdoba**, **Málaga**, **Madrid** and **Sevilla**.

Córdoba

renowned Moorish landmark and craggy mountains

Moorish Spain can sometimes seem a little elusive but in Córdoba some of the splendour of their reign can be appreciated. This is most notable in the Mezquita, the city's main mosque, a massive space which is, a millennium on, still a memorable building.

But Córdoba is far from being a one-monument town. While the narrow streets of the Judería are somewhat touristy, much fertile ground for wandering lies north of the old town. Here, the Palacio de Viana is a stunning ensemble of Córdoba's favourite architectural feature: patios. Add in the distinctive Córdoban cuisine and wines and you've got an enticing mix.

Córdoba's elongated province surprises with its ruggedness. Its northern marches are guarded by fortified villages; south of the city, agricultural towns like Montilla and Baena, redolent with the scent of wine and olive oil respectively, give way to the Sistema Subbética. This chain of mountains holds gems like Zuheros, an absolutely delightful village with an important prehistoric cave in the bare rocks above, and Priego de Córdoba, a hilltop settlement dignified by a rich ensemble of Baroque architecture and one of Andalucía's most delightful barrios.

Best for
Architecture ■ Oil ■ Tapas ■ Wine

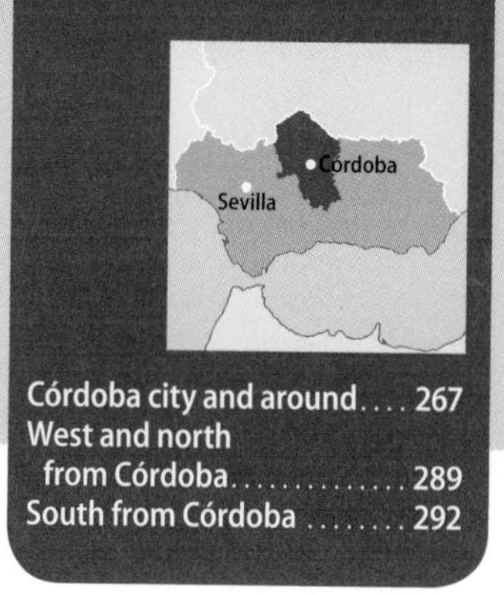

Footprint picks

★ **Mezquita**, page 268

Córdoba's famous mosque, with its distinctive red and white arches, is a must-see.

★ **Palacio de Viana**, page 279

Visit the Tardis-like network of postcard-pretty linked patios.

★ **Montoro**, page 282

This sleepy town is an unspoiled place above the Guadalquivir.

★ **Almodóvar del Río**, page 289

Head west from Córdoba to see this formidable castle.

★ **Baena**, page 294

Taste some of Baena's finest olive oil; you'll never reach for that supermarket cheapie again.

★ **Zuheros**, page 296

Experience mountain hospitality and invigorating walking in this enchanting village.

★ **Priego de Córdoba**, page 299

Wander the narrow whitewashed lanes in one of Andalucía's prettiest barrios.

Footprint
picks
1 Mezquita, page 268
2 Palacio de Viana, page 279
3 Montoro, page 282
4 Almodóvar del Río, page 289
5 Baena, page 294
6 Zuheros, page 296
7 Priego de Córdoba, page 299
N
10 km
10 miles
EXTREMADURA
CASTILLA LA MANCHA
Belalcázar
Los Pedroches
Hinojosa
del Duque
N502a
A422
A449
Torrecampo
Alcaracejos
Fuente
Ovejuna
Peñarroya-
Pueblonuevo
Pozoblanco
A422
Villanueva
de Córdoba
Embalse de
Sierra Boyera
N432
Cardeña
Parque Natural
Sierra Cardeña
Montoro
Sierra
Morena
Espiel
CORDOBA
N420
N432
Adamuz
Montoro
Andújar
Embalse de
Bembézar
Río Bembézar
Medina
Azahara
A4
Arjona
A6175
Hornachuelos
A431
Córdoba
Bujulance
Almodóvar
del Río
Río Gualajoz
Porcuna
Escañuela
Peñaflor
Río Guadalquivir
JAEN
A431
Lora
del Rio
Palma del Río
Torredonjimeno
A4
A45
N432
A453
La Carlota
Castro del Río
Martos
Río Genil
Espejo
SEVILLA
La Rambla
A307
N432
A316
Ecija
Baena
A4
Santaella
Montilla
Aguilar de
la Frontera
Zuheros
Alcaudate
Cueva de los
Murciélagos
N432
A364
A388
A318
A304
A45
Cabra
Parque Natural
Sierra Subbética
Marchena
Puente-Genil
A316
A339
Lucena
Carcabuey
Priego de Córdoba
Estepa
A335
A92
Osuna
Iznajár
Montefrío
Illora
Morón de
La Frontera
Martín
de la Jara
Villanueva
de San Juan
Fuente de
Piedra
Loja
Sierra de
Yuegas
Río Frío
A382
Campillos
Archidona
Olvera

Córdoba city
& around

Córdoba, the glory of Moorish Spain, was in its day the largest and most important city in Western Europe, on a par with Constantinople in the east. Set on the Río Guadalquivir, which was once navigable up to here, Córdoba has recovered from centuries of neglect to be one of Andalucía's largest and most prosperous towns once more.

The refugee Umayyad prince Abd al-Rahman set up his stall here and initiated the construction of the imposing Mezquita, the city's main mosque. Added to by later members of the ruling dynasty, the series of seemingly endless arches of the prayer hall is one of the region's most distinctive sights, despite the fact that after the Reconquest a cathedral was parked in the middle of it.

There are many attractions besides the mosque; a feature of Córdoban architecture is the interior patio and every May hundreds of private patios around the city are opened and garlanded with flowers (see box, page 273). *Colour map 2, B3.*

Essential Córdoba

Getting around

Córdoba's old centre is where most of the monuments and accommodation are located and walking is by far the best option to get around. Horse carriages parked next to the Mezquita will trot you around town for a negotiable fee.

Best places to stay

La Hospedería de El Churrasco, page 282
Casa de los Azulejos, page 283
Las Casas de la Judería, page 283

When to go

Córdoba gets extremely hot in summer so the best time to visit is spring or autumn. It can be chilly in winter. In May in Córdoba city there is the bonus of the Festival of the Patios (see box, page 273) and the provincial capital's major fiesta. Prices rise slightly at this time.

Time required

Two to three days.

Best restaurants

Bodegas Mezquita, page 284
La Cazuela de Espartería, page 285
La Fragua, page 285
La Tinaja, page 285

The Mezquita and around

one of Andalucía's most famous sights

★The Mezquita

T957-470512, www.mezquitadecordoba.org, Mar-Oct Mon-Sat 1000-1900, Sun 0830-1130, 1500-1900, Nov-Feb Mon-Sat 0830-1800, Sun 0830-1130, 1500-1800, €8, 10-14 year-olds half price, under 10s free, free Mon-Sat from 0830-0920, audio guide €3 (good, though a little skewed towards the Christian side).

This is what draws most people to Córdoba. Unlike Granada's Alhambra, the wistful fantasy of an insignificant and doomed dynasty, this mosque is the creation of a civilization at the peak of its power. It is the principal architectural legacy that remains of Al-Andalus and a fitting centrepiece to the city that was once pre-eminent in Western Europe.

The building is no longer a mosque but Córdoba's cathedral, and this fact shows the differences between Christian and Muslim art and architecture, which are in the most pure sense of the word, fundamental. The choir, crossing and high altar, which would be majestic in any other setting, seems a gaudy gatecrasher in the subdued splendour of the vast arched precinct, while the mosque's linear harmony is disrupted by the additions.

That said, the initial impact on entering the building is unforgettable; a couple of seconds of wonderment that won't easily be eclipsed. It's as if, in pursuit of the fleeting ghost of Moorish Spain, the quarry suddenly turns and says 'I am here. This is my home'.

The Moorish construction was actually built in four distinct phases by different rulers, adding each time to the grandeur, but more significantly, the capacity – the capital of the Caliphate was a fast-growing city. In the way such things went, it was originally erected over the Visigothic basilica when the Moors took the Christian city. After the final reconquest in 1236, modifications were made to turn it into a cathedral, but the most significant alterations occurred in the 16th century. The Flemish king Carlos V gave the go-ahead for the crossing and choir to be placed in the middle of the building, but he had never been to Córdoba. When he finally saw the result, he was aghast. "You have built", he harshly commented, "what you or others might have built anywhere, but you have destroyed something that was unique in the world." In the 19th and 20th centuries several of the side chapels were pulled down in an attempt to recreate the mosque's original appearance.

The visit → *Numbers in brackets below refer to the map on page 271.*
Before entering, walk around the walls. Like the homes of Córdoba with their patios, it's an introverted structure, but there is some fine blind horseshoe arching and carved vegetal and geometric motifs along the perimeter. As in Islamic times, the mosque is entered via the Puerta del Perdón (**1**) and the Patio de los Naranjos (orange-tree courtyard). This shady cobbled space was once used for the ritual of washing before prayer. Interspersed among the citrus are cypresses, palms and fountains. The irrigation channels are a characteristic Moorish innovation. The court is overlooked by the beautiful bell tower (**2**), unfortunately no longer accessible.

The initial impression upon entry through the Puerta de las Palmas (**7**) is of a huge and dark space partitioned by seemingly endless rows of red and white arches, the Mezquita's signature. Standing on heterogeneous columns garnered from Visigothic and Roman buildings, they use red brick and white stone to form stripes. The arches are double; a second row stands on top of the lower ones, providing greater support for the ceiling; a technique learned from Roman aqueducts and also used in Damascus. The columns are of marble, jasper and porphyry, and their different colours and capitals subtly dispel the illusion of being in a hall of mirrors. This is the original mosque, built by Abd al-Rahman I and begun in AD 786. Due to the reuse of materials it was erected quickly.

The best way to appreciate the different construction phases is to stroll around in an anticlockwise direction. In so doing, you'll immediately notice the first of the Christian modifications; the side aisles have been closed off to form chapels. Some of these are very fine; in this first quadrant of the mosque notice the Capilla de Nuestra Señora de la Concepción, elaborately decked out in red marble and surmounted by two cupolas, the nearer painted with frescoes of angels and the evangelists. The sculpture of the Virgin in the *retablo* is by Pedro de Mena.

Immediately beyond this the floor slopes slightly – this marks the beginning of the first expansion of the mosque, carried out by Abd al-Rahman II from AD 833 to 848. Most of this expansion is now taken up by the cathedral's devotional spaces, of which more shortly. This part of the mosque is more ornate than the original; flamboyant multi-lobed arches stand out from the more conventional horseshoe ones, and decorative carving is in evidence. It is thought that

Tip...
A useful combined ticket in Córdoba city lets you into the Alcázar, Museo Julio Romero de Torres, Baños Califales and Museo Taurino for €8.40. It's purchasable at any of those sights.

when this section was complete, little more than a century after the city was taken, it could accommodate 10,000 worshippers.

Moving on, the second expansion is soon reached. This third phase was overseen by Al-Hakam II from AD 968 onwards. Apart from the fine panelled Renaissance ceiling to one side, notice the finely decorated Moorish ceiling; presumably the whole mosque was once similarly adorned. In glass cases in the corner of the building are some remains from the Visigothic basilica (**8**). Pause for a moment to inspect these inspired sixth-century carvings, for they will dispel any notions that these people were lager-swilling barbarians.

The jewel of the Mezquita is the *mihrab* (**9**) of Al-Hakam's mosque. It doesn't actually quite face Mecca, but the orientation of the building was already determined before the Moors arrived. Although the niche itself is railed off, elbow your way through the crowds to get the best view you can; the marble ceiling is striking, as is the delicate blind arching. The *maksura* (antechamber) is highly decorative. Floral patterns and gold mosaic work is topped by an octagonal cupola adorned with pieces of coloured marble, the work of Byzantine Christian craftsmen hired for the project. Adjacent are the cathedral's sacristy and tesoro or treasury (**10**). Rendering the collection of processional crosses and chalices puny is a leviathan gold and silver monstrance from the 16th century, the masterwork of the craftsman Enrique de Arfe. The detailing is frighteningly intricate. This monstrance is taken through the streets at Corpus Christi.

The final expansion of the mosque was under the vizier and regent Almanzor, military genius and scourge of the Christian north (see box, page 462). This brought it to its current size of 23,000 sq m, the size of four football pitches. After the *mihrab* and its surrounds, this section of the building seems much more functional. It looks a cheaper job too; the stripes are painted onto the arches.

After examining the classicizing frescoes of the sacrarium in the corner, head for the centre and the cathedral's devotional spaces. The high altar (**13**) and its *retablo* are worked in marble and bronze and feature painted panels by the local artist Antonio Palomino. The central panel on the upper level is of the Assumption of the Virgin, but that's about as unparochial as the Córdobans were going to get in their own cathedral; she's flanked by local favourites St Acisclo, St Victoria, St Digna and St Pelagio. The dome over the altar features Carlos V himself in one of the roundels; he was never ashamed to be seen in the most exalted company.

The standout mahogany choir (**14**) looks like a fantasy in dark chocolate. It was carved in the mid-18th century by Pedro Cornejo, who is deservedly buried in the middle of it. The bishop's throne is topped by another Córdoban favourite, the archangel Rafael. Behind here is the Capilla Real or Royal Chapel (**17**), which holds the tombs (but not the bodies) of Fernando IV and Alfonso XI; it's frustratingly closed off, but you can glimpse the elaborate *mocárabes* of the ceiling. The cathedral is undeniably fine; however, you are likely to be left yearning for a glimpse of what the Mezquita must have been like before its awkward lodger moved in.

Mezquita

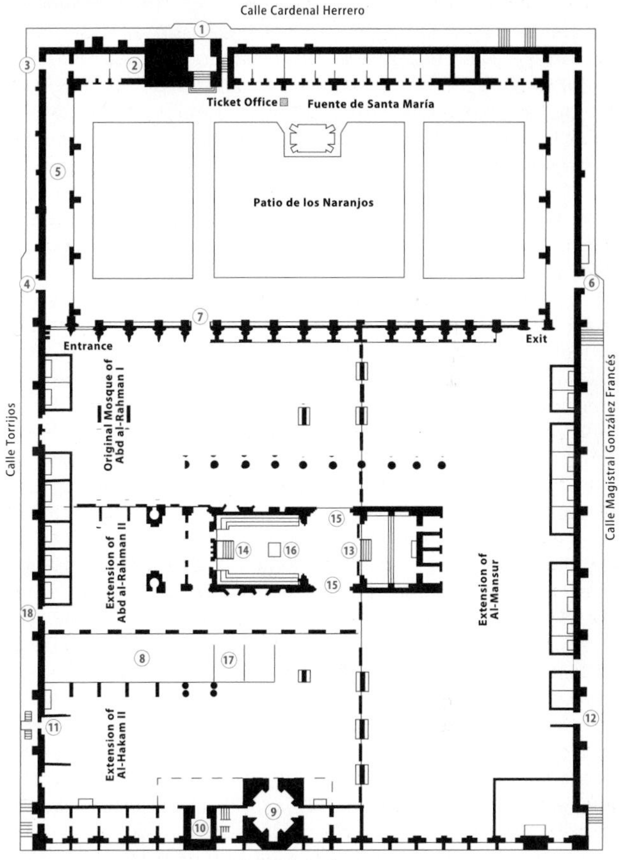

1 Puerta del Perdón
2 Bell Tower
3 Puerta de la Leche
4 Puerta de los Deanes
5 Cloisters
6 Puerta de Santa Catalina
7 Puerta de las Palmas
8 Site of Visigoth basilica
9 Mihrab
10 Tesoro
11 Puerta del Palacio
12 Puerta del Sagrario
13 High Altar
14 Choir
15 Transepts
16 Capilla Mayor
17 Capilla Real
18 Puerta de San Miguel

Not to scale

BACKGROUND

Córdoba

While there were certainly Neolithic and Bronze Age settlements here, it was under the Romans that the city sprang to prominence. Founded in the late third century BC as a military camp, it was developed into a full settlement before the locals took the wrong side in the Caesar-Pompey conflict; Julius destroyed Córdoba in revenge. It was rebuilt and extended by Augustus, who made it the administrative centre for the province of *Baetica*, roughly modern Andalucía. The birthplace of Seneca the Elder and his nephew Lucan, the town had an aqueduct, a large theatre and a particularly grand palace, which was imperial accommodation when Maximiano Hercules toured the provinces in the third century AD. The city proved troublesome to the Visigothic conquerors and it was some time before they could subdue it to their rule.

In late AD 711, Córdoba was captured by Moorish troops and in AD 756 had become the de facto capital of the squabbling Moorish dominions. Once Abd al-Rahman, a refugee Umayyad prince from Damascus, had established himself as emir, order began to be restored and Córdoba began its glory years. For several centuries it was the principal centre of Western European culture and learning, producing poets and philosophers such as Averroes and Maimonides. As well as the Mezquita, Córdoba boasted a library with some 400,000 texts, and the palace complex of Medina Azahara, which Abd al-Rahman III built after declaring himself caliph. With a population of perhaps as much as half a million in the 10th-11th centuries, Córdoba was an equivalent size to Constantinople and several times larger than any other Western European city.

The caliphate disintegrated in civil strife and Córdoba lost its importance as the Moorish domains were divided into a number of *taifa* statelets. The Sevilla *taifa* gained control over Córdoba in 1069, and the Almoravid takeover followed. The Moors briefly lost the city in 1146, when it was captured by Alfonso VII, but the Almohad armies soon recaptured it. By now more of a symbolic prize than a significant city, it was finally reconquered in 1236, almost by accident, as a group of skirmishing Christian mercenaries gained temporary control and called on King Fernando III, who was several hundred miles away, for help. He marched down at speed and managed to hold the city.

Little of the wealth from the New World found its way to Córdoba and, with a particularly severe inquisition ruling the roost, the departure of Jews and Muslims left the traditional silversmithing and leatherworking industries almost derelict. The population dropped rapidly and Córdoba played little part in Habsburg or Bourbon Spain, apart from producing one of the most notable writers of the literary Golden Age in Spain, Luis de Góngora (1561-1627). The city was occupied by the French during the Peninsular War, and suffered terrible atrocities under the Nationalists in the Spanish Civil War. The *cordobeses* proved to have long memories and became the first city in Spain to elect a Communist local council after the return to democracy.

ON THE ROAD

Pretty patios

The patio is a common feature of Andalucían domestic buildings directly inherited from Roman, then Moorish architectural traditions. While they are enchanting spaces wherever you go in the region, in Córdoba the citizens are particularly proud of their enclosed spaces. At any time of year, wandering through the city's streets, you can glimpse the odd patio behind a front door, sparkling clean, tiled, and often bedecked with flowers. To fully appreciate them, you'll have to visit during the city's **Festival of Patios** in May. The owners make a huge effort to make their homes as beautiful as possible and then open the patios to the public at certain hours through the week. The open patios are clearly marked with signs. Some have over a thousand blooming flowerpots, for the festival is also a prestigious contest for the most elegant space.

Museo Diocesano

C Torrijos 6.

Your ticket from the Mezquita gets you into the former bishops' palace next door, which now holds a collection of religious art. The building was originally a Visigothic fortress, then a Moorish palace (linked to the mosque by a covered passageway). The pieces are displayed around a central patio that contains a lovable Iberian stone bear. Ascend to the second floor for a rather fine collection of 13th- and 14th-century religious painting and sculpture, nearly all by anonymous monks. The Renaissance art is more of a mixed bag; some mediocre 17th-century Flemish tapestries are of most interest. The portraits of Bourbon royalty merely highlight how good Goya was by comparison; better are a pair of small canvases by Antonio Palomino, who painted the panels of the cathedral's *retablo*. The building was closed for renovations at time of last research.

Alcázar de los Reyes Cristianos and Baños Califales

www.alcazardelosreyescristianos.cordoba.es, Tue-Fri 0830-2045, Sat 0830-1630, Sun 0830-1430, €4.50, plus Mon 0830-2030, Sat 1630-2030, Sun 1500-2030, €7, includes ticket to sound and light show.

By the Guadalquivir and just south of the Mezquita, this palace was originally built by Alfonso X in the 13th century before being expanded by Fernando and Isabel, the Catholic Monarchs. Annoyed by the noise of the mills on the river, however, Isabel took a dislike to the place and it became the home of the Córdoba Inquisition. What finery those austere gentlemen might have left in place disappeared when the building was converted into a prison, a function it served well into the 20th century. There's now very little to see inside the building apart from some reasonable Roman mosaics found under the Plaza de la Corredera in 1959 and some Arab baths tucked under one corner of the courtyard. Much the best feature is the large garden, surrounded by high toothed walls and filled with

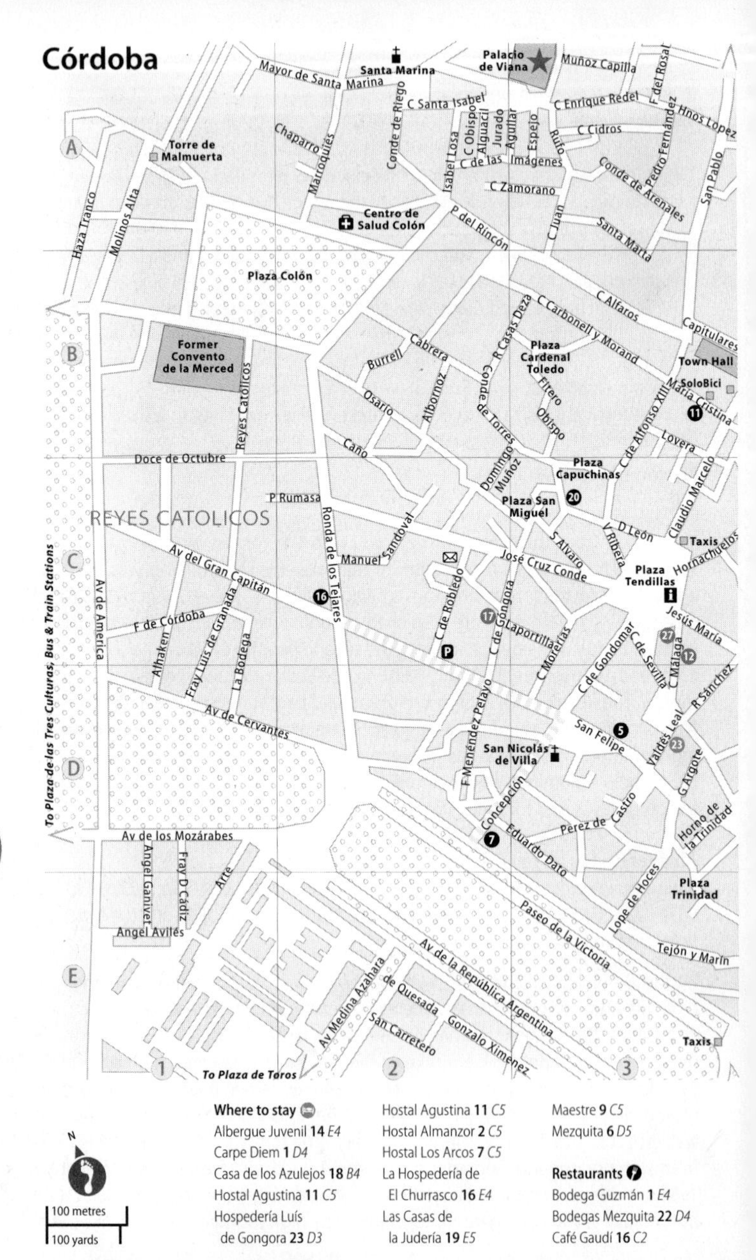
Córdoba
Santa Marina
Palacio de Viana
Mayor de Santa Marina
Muñoz Capilla
F del Rosal
C Santa Isabel
C Enrique Redel
Hnos Lopez
C Cidros
Conde de Riego
Chaparro
Marroquíes
Isabel Losa
C Obispo
Alguacil
Jurado
Aguilar
Espejo
Rufo
C de las Imágenes
Pedro Fernández
Conde de Arenales
San Pablo
C Zamorano
Torre de Malmuerta
Centro de Salud Colón
C Juan
Santa Marta
P del Rincón
Haza Tranco
Molinos Alta
Plaza Colón
C Alfaros
C Casas Deza
C Carbonell y Morand
Capitulares
Town Hall
Former Convento de la Merced
Cabrera
Burrell
Plaza Cardenal Toledo
Fitero
SoloBici
María Cristina
Reyes Católicos
Osario
Albornoz
Conde de Torres
Obispo
C de Alfonso XIII
Lovera
Caño
Doce de Octubre
Domingo Muñoz
Plaza Capuchinas
Claudio Marcelo
P Rumasa
REYES CATOLICOS
Plaza San Miguel
D León
Sandoval
Ronda de los Tejares
S Alvaro
V Ribera
Taxis
Manuel
José Cruz Conde
Hornachuelos
Av del Gran Capitán
Plaza Tendillas
C de Robledo
C de Góngora
Laportilla
Jesús María
Av de América
F de Córdoba
Fray Luis de Granada
C de Gondomar
C de Sevilla
C Málaga
Alhaken
La Bodega
C Morerías
R Sánchez
Av de Cervantes
San Felipe
Valdés Leal
To Plaza de las Tres Culturas, Bus & Train Stations
San Nicolás de Villa
F Menéndez Pelayo
G Argote
Concepción
Perez de Castro
Horno de la Trinidad
Av de los Mozárabes
Eduardo Dato
Angel Ganivet
Fray D Cádiz
Arte
Plaza Trinidad
Lope de Hoces
Angel Avilés
Paseo de la Victoria
Tejón y Marín
Av de la República Argentina
Av Medina Azahara
de Quesada
San Carretero
Gonzalo Ximenez
Taxis
To Plaza de Toros
A
B
C
D
E
1
2
3
N
100 metres
100 yards
Where to stay
Albergue Juvenil 14 E4
Carpe Diem 1 D4
Casa de los Azulejos 18 B4
Hostal Agustina 11 C5
Hospedería Luís de Gongora 23 D3
Hostal Agustina 11 C5
Hostal Almanzor 2 C5
Hostal Los Arcos 7 C5
La Hospedería de El Churrasco 16 E4
Las Casas de la Judería 19 E5
Maestre 9 C5
Mezquita 6 D5
Restaurants
Bodega Guzmán 1 E4
Bodegas Mezquita 22 D4
Café Gaudí 16 C2

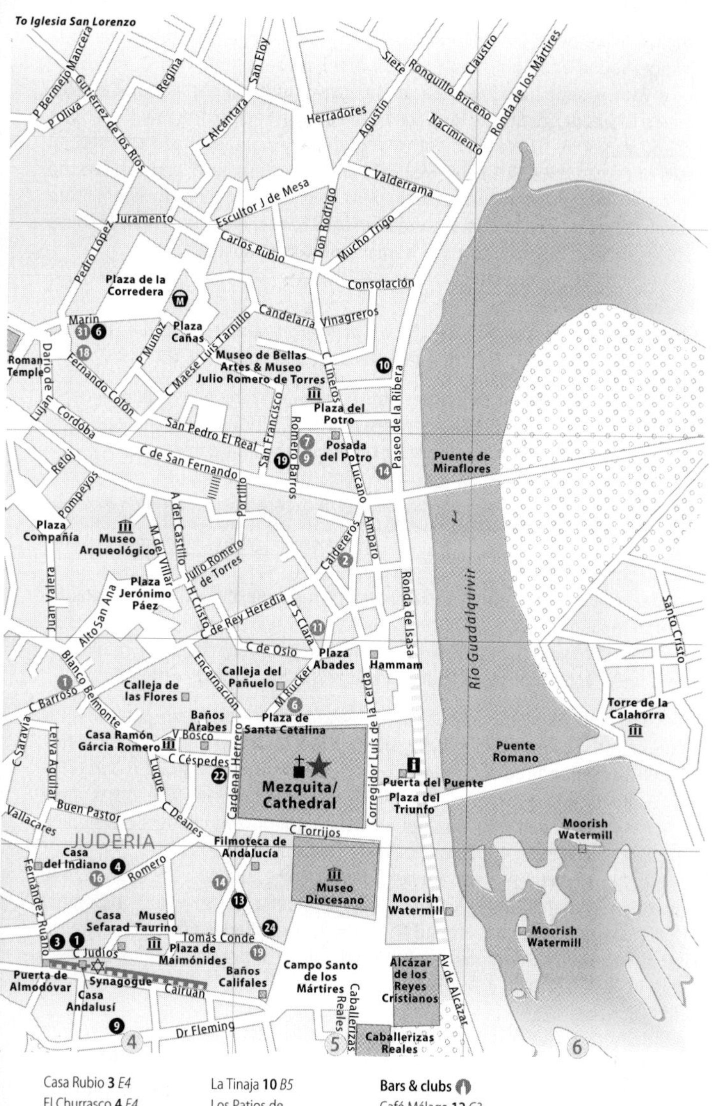

Casa Rubio **3** *E4*
El Churrasco **4** *E4*
El Gallo **11** *B3*
El Pisto **20** *C3*
La Cazuela de Espartería **6** *B4*
La Fragua **24** *E5*
La Tinaja **10** *B5*
Los Patios de la Marquesa **13** *E5*
Mesón Juan Peña **9** *E4*
Roldán **7** *D2*
Taberna El Juncal **5** *D3*
Taberna Plateros **19** *C5*

Bars & clubs

Café Málaga **12** *C3*
Correo **27** *C3*
Góngora Gran Café **17** *C2*
Jazz Café **31** *B4*
Sojo **14** *C5*

fountains, flowerbeds and deep pools sheltering portly carp. In the evenings, a 45-minute sound-and-light show operates in the gardens.

Save your receipt from the Alcázar and use it to enter the **Baños Califales** ⓘ *Tue-Fri 0830-2045, Sat 0830-1630, Sun 0830-1430*, just across the way (otherwise it's €2.50 to get in). These Arab baths were the city's grandest and saw several phases of construction. It's been well excavated and displayed; you can see the cold, warm and hot rooms, with star-shaped air vents in the roof. The warm room has been reconstructed to an approximation of its former glory, with marble pillars and horseshoe arches making it into a small shrine to cleanliness.

Caballerizas Reales

C Caballerizas Reales s/n, T957-497843, www.caballerizasreales.com, Tue-Sat 1100-1330, 1700-1930, Sun 1000-1130, free, show Wed, Fri, Sat 2100, Sun 1200, €15.

Next to the Alcázar, the royal stables housed and bred the finest Spanish horse bloodstock from the 16th century onwards. The horses now housed here perform equestrian spectacles four times weekly; otherwise the visit is free.

Judería

an atmospheric web of narrow medieval lanes

Córdoba's *Judería* (former Jewish Quarter) runs west from the Mezquita. Although most of the buildings currently on show were constructed long after the Catholic Monarchs expelled the Jewish population, the area retains an ancient feel, despite the tacky souvenir shops and tourist-trap restaurants.

Córdoba's most eminent Jewish son, Maimonides (see box, page 484), is commemorated by a statue on Calle Judíos; a few doors up from here is the tiny 14th-century **synagogue** ⓘ *C Judíos 20, T957-202928, Tue-Sat 1000-2030, Sun 1000-1700 EU citizens free, otherwise €0.30*. Heavily restored but evocative, it has some fine plasterwork and Hebrew inscriptions. The local government are developing an interpretation centre on Jewish Spain alongside at number 22.

Near the synagogue is **Casa Sefarad** ⓘ *C Judíos 17, T957-421404, www.casadesefarad.es, daily 1000-1800, €4*, a Judería house whose basement preserves original features. Around the patio is a small exhibition on Sephardic culture, with much biographical information about prominent Córdoban Jews, details of festivals, and a display on musical tradition. There are sometimes evening concerts here.

A little further up the same street is **Casa Andalusi** ⓘ *C Judíos 12, T957-290642, daily 1000-1930, €2.50*, a prettily done reconstruction of a wealthy Moorish home. It's small but has some very pretty touches and peaceful atmosphere with soft medieval music playing. The jewel-like interior can transport you quickly back to Al-Andalus if it's not too full. Downstairs is a Visigothic mosaic floor.

Near the statue of Maimonides, in an attractive building on the square that bears his name, is the **Museo Municipal Taurino** ⓘ *Plaza Maimonides s/n, T957-*

201056, Tue-Fri 0830-2045, Sat 0830-1630, Sun 0830-1430, €4. Córdoba has always been a thriving source of both *matadors* and aficionados, and this museum has the usual range of memorabilia and souvenirs, focusing particularly on the tragic hero Manolete, who died in the ring in 1947, and the more recent El Cordobés, darling of the *prensa rosa* (tabloid press).

Leaving the Judería by the Puerta de Almodóvar west of the synagogue, take a sharp left and stroll along the Almohad city walls towards the Alcázar. It's a beautifully quiet area and is dignified by a statue of Averroes, the eminent Moorish philosopher.

One of Córdoba's most popular nooks is the tourist-choked **Calleja de las Flores**, a narrow alley leading to a tiny cobbled plaza lined with flower-laden balconies. It's near the Mezquita off Calle Velásquez Bosco; the alleyway frames a camera-ready view of the building's bell tower. Nearby are the **Baños Arabes**, a small 10th-century bath complex in a private home. It's a euro well spent for a look. A quieter but equally picturesque alleyway can be found just north of the Mezquita, off Calle Martínez Rücker to the left. The street is so narrow that it's nicknamed Calleja del Pañuelo (Handkerchief Lane).

It's also worth seeking out another Córdoba gem: the **Casa del Indiano**, on Plaza Angel de Torres. Only the façade remains of this noble mansion, but walking through what was once the main door takes you down a dead-end lane flanked by modern but attractive neighbourhood flats. It's an intriguing corner.

Another interesting spot, **Casa Ramón García Romero (Arte Sobre Piel)** ⓘ *Plaza Agrupacíon de Cofradías 2, T957-050131, www.artesobrepiel.com, Mon-Sat 1030-1400, 1630-2000, free*, is a display of the lifetime's work of a local artist who revived the Moorish tradition of *guadameci*, a form of embossed leather artwork, sometimes enriched with silver or gold thread, that developed during the period of the Córdoba caliphate.

Río Guadalquivir

Roman bridge and Moorish watermills

Just below the Mezquita, the Puerta del Puente gateway once led out through the city walls. Originally Roman, but extensively modified over the centuries, it stands next to a monument to San Rafael. Slightly pompous in style, the angel stands atop a pillar that stands on a watchtower which in turn rests on a grotto-like arrangement of stones.

Inside there's a small **exhibition** ⓘ *daily 1000-1400, 1600-1930, €1*, inside, with information on the monument's history, and an observation platform with good perspectives of the river and mosque. The **Puente Romano** (Roman bridge) crosses the Guadalquivir from here. Walking across, you can see the remains of several Moorish watermills among the islets of tangled vegetation. By the near bank one of the mill wheels has been preserved. Upstream, a modern bridge in fashionable rusted iron contrasts effectively with the more classic lines of the Roman one, although new public spaces on the far side have yet to catch on.

Guarding the eastern end of the Roman bridge is the **Torre de la Calahorra** ⓘ *T957-293929, daily 1000-1400 and 1630-2030 (1000-1800 in winter), 5-6 audiovisual shows daily, €4.50, €5.70 including audiovisual*, a defensive installation turned interpretation centre. The visit, conducted via a multilingual headset, is entertaining and focuses on life in Moorish Córdoba, with personalities like Maimonides and Averroes making an appearance, as well as displays on Andalusi music, engineering and court life. The optional slideshow narrates the history of humanity and emphasizes the need for cultural interaction.

North of the Mezquita

picturesque old town streets away from the crowds

The streets north and northwest of the Mezquita make excellent ground for exploration. Medieval Córdoba was a huge place and you can mine a rich vein of pretty streets without heading near the Judería or its tour groups.

A five-minute stroll due north of the Mezquita will bring you to Plaza del Potro (Square of the Colt), named after the 16th-century fountain that complements the elegant buildings lining this elongated space. The Posada del Potro on the south side of the square was once a haunt of Cervantes and is mentioned in *Don Quijote*; it's now a flamenco centre. Opposite, in what was once a Franciscan charity hospital until the monasteries were disentailed in the 1830s, are two art galleries.

The **Museo de Bellas Artes** ⓘ *T957-355550, Tue-Sat 1000-2030, Sun 1000-1700, free to EU nationals, €1.50 others*, has a moderate collection, mostly of Córdoban artists. There are some fine 16th-century religious pieces, including one by Alejo Fernández depicting Christ bound to the column. There are a couple of paintings by the Sevillian master Juan Valdés Leal, a gaudy Inmaculada and a better, earthy Holy Family. These hang alongside works of the Córdoban Antonio del Castillo Saavedra, a local beneficiary of the Golden Age of Sevillian Baroque art.

Among the 20th-century collection are pieces by the Equipo 57 movement, a group of artists who reacted against the stultifying atmosphere of Fascist Spain, and several interesting sculptures by Mateo Inurria Leinosa, a local working in the early 1900s. The museum's highlight, however, is a much earlier piece; an Iberian sculpture of a she-wolf suckling a cub, dating from the second century BC.

Across the patio is the **Museo Julio Romero de Torres** ⓘ *T957-491909, Tue-Fri 0830-2045, Sat 0830-1630, Sun 0830-1430, €4.50*, filled with the works of that Córdoban painter. His subjects are almost exclusively women and by far his best work comes in his smaller portraits; in some of these, such as *Cabeza Vieja* and *Rafaela*, he achieves excellent depictions of Córdoban faces. His most famous works are, however, *Chiquita Piconera*, a sexually charged painting of a girl stoking a fire, and *Cante Hondo*, a much-reproduced portrayal of the dark passions of flamenco.

Museo Arqueológico

Plaza Jerónimo Páez s/n, T957-355517. Tue-Sat 1000-2030, Sun 1000-1700. Free to EU nationals, €1.50 others. Descriptions in Spanish, but reasonable leaflets in English, French and German are available at the entrance.

Tucked away in the narrow streets west of Plaza del Potro is Córdoba's unassuming archaeological museum. It's unusually well put together and sensibly focuses on sculpture, which is picturesquely displayed around a sunny patio.

A to-the-point section on prehistoric ceramics is followed by a fierce array of Iberian lions and other beasts. The Roman pieces are thoughtfully arranged, especially the portrait heads; by following them in date order the important stylistic shift from exaggerated Republican realism to idealized Imperial beauty is clear. A fine second-century AD sculpture of the eastern god Mithra is evidence of oriental tendencies in the Roman Empire, while a range of Visigothic carvings shows just how much these 'barbarians' were successors to the cultural legacy of the Romans. Upstairs is a delicate series of capitals from Al-Andalus, as well as the famous bronze faun found at Medina Azahara. The hind that it was paired with on an ornate fountain is to be found in the Museum of Islamic Art in Qatar.

Plaza de la Corredera and Plaza Tendillas

Moving east from here, make your way to the inspiring Plaza de la Corredera, a surprisingly ample space after the narrow streets. It was once used for burning heretics and also for bullfights, and its 17th-century arcades and balconies are one of Córdoba's finest and least-appreciated sights. Around the square are several antique dealers and shops selling traditional esparto baskets. There are plenty of terraces to enjoy the view with a drink and a tapa; it's also home to the city's typical food market. West of here, the city's town hall has a neighbour, a Roman temple, the columns of which have been re-erected and make a fine sight under floodlights. It is thought to have been devoted to one of the god-emperors. Further west is Plaza Tendillas, the focus of the modern town and adorned with fountains and a statue of the Gran Capitán, Gonzalo de Córdoba, a man born in nearby Montilla who fought for the Catholic Monarchs in the final phase of the Reconquista and then won great fame prosecuting wars in Italy. He is credited as the man who adapted warfare to the gunpowder era, creating small, mobile units of infantry and cavalry that eventually won the kingdom of Naples for Spain.

★Palacio de Viana and around

Plaza Don Gome 2, T957-496741, www.palaciodeviana.com. Sep-Jun Tue-Sat 1000-1900, Sun 1000-1500, Jul-Aug Tue-Sun 0900-1500. €5 patios, €8 for patios and interior.

Whatever time you've allotted to see Córdoba, make a point of visiting the Palacio de Viana. The city is renowned for its patios and this rambling palace has a feast of 13 of them, all resoundingly graceful. The various trees that shade them are named in tiled plaques; the whole is a harmonious and soothing ensemble that (dare we say it) pushes the Mezquita close for top Córdoban attraction.

The interior of the palace is accessible on a guided tour and boasts a wealth of valuable objects, including 19th-century tapestries from the famous Madrid factory and a fine collection of local leatherwork.

Just up the road from the Palacio de Viana, you'll reach the honeyed sandstone **Santa Marina church**, with bulging buttresses, simple Gothic doorways and a somewhat heavy-handed rose window. Opposite is a monument to Manolete, the Córdoban bullfighter slain in the ring at Linares in 1947. Follow this lane and you'll reach **Plaza Colón**, a large square centred on a park. Walking around the plaza, note the gate in the city walls and defensive tower, the Torre de Malmuerta, and the vibrant Baroque façade of the former Convento de la Merced, now used by the local government. Turn down Calle Cabrera and take the next left and you'll reach Plaza de Capuchinos, surrounded by a former monastery complex and featuring the sculpture of Cristo de los Faroles, a much-revered Crucifixion surrounded by lanterns and humble offerings.

Although other sights tend to take precedence, Córdoba has many fine churches, most built in the aftermath of the Christian conquest in the 13th century. Built in local sandstone, they are particularly attractive at sunset, which is coincidentally the only time you can get access to the interiors (around 1830, just before mass, is ideal). Among others, **Iglesia San Lorenzo** is worth seeking out for its superb rose window, while **Iglesia San Nicolás de Villa** features a muscular octagonal defensive tower.

Around Córdoba → *Colour map 2, B3/B4.*

cork tree-studded hills, a Moorish ruin and an olive town

By way of Avenida del Brillante, you can wind your way up into the hills north of Córdoba. There are many fine viewpoints over the city on the plain below.

A signposted left turn just before reaching El Rosal leads to one of the viewpoints, at **Las Ermitas** ⓘ *Tue-Sun 1000-1330, 1630-1930 (1830 winter), €1.50*, a venerable hermit colony. While its official beginnings were in the 17th century when a group of monks came to live here, it was known as a residence of holy men long before, perhaps even as far back as the Visigothic period. Some hermits still live here, enjoying the contemplative life and the views. You can visit the site; their houses are simple, two-roomed cells and one of the houses has been set up as a small exhibition with daily objects used here in the past. The small church has a skull to greet visitors; this was once used as a bowl by a local noble who came to live here.

Continue along the road signposted Santa María de la Trassierra and, after wending through the hills awhile, you'll come to a roundabout, from where it's a further 3 km downhill to Medina Azahara. On the way down, look up and you may get a glimpse of the Gothic monastery of San Jerónimo, a private residence not open to the public.

Medina Azahara (Madinat al-Zahra)

Ctra de Palma de Río Km 8, T957-104933. Tue-Sat 1000-1830 (2030 summer), Sun 1000-1700. EU citizens free, €1.50 others. A tour bus leaves Córdoba 2-3 times daily, departing from Glorieta Cruz Roja, on the main road outside the Puerta de Almodóvar. This costs €8.50 return and gives you 2½ hrs at the site. It should be booked the day before at the tourist office (many hotels also accept bookings).

In AD 936, Abd al-Rahman III began to construct this complex situated 8 km from Córdoba. A visit to the site today is an engaging experience, but don't expect to be confronted with the architectural glory of Al-Andalus. The complex was thoroughly demolished and archaeologists have laboured gamely to create order from the rubble – excavation here is a massive and ongoing task and less than a tenth of the expanse has been trowelled.

More than just a palace, the complex was "a new centre of government of a grandeur fitting to the ruler's new dignity as caliph". The bare statistics are certainly impressive: sources tell us that 10,000 men worked on the site and that, when finished, the caliph and his ministers were attended to by a grand total of 3750 slaves.

Medina Azahara must have been quite a sight, with its extensive gardens, aviaries, menageries, fishponds (one Moorish writer dubiously boasted that 12,000 loaves of bread were needed daily just to feed the fish) and even fountains filled with liquid mercury, filling rooms with an eerie reflected light. It was destined not to last, however.

After Abd al-Malik, son of Almanzor, died young in 1008, civil strife broke out in Córdoba. The powerless caliph Hisham II was deposed and rival claimants battled for supremacy. Medina Azahara, first used as a military base, was soon destroyed by the out-of-control bands of Berber troops that ravaged the city and surrounding countryside. The symbol of the glory of the Córdoba caliphate became a symbol of its disintegration after less than a century.

The entrance is at the top of the site and you enter the compound through the north gate, along a path dog-legged for defensive reasons. Turning left, the road slopes down into the so-called administrative area and its largest building, the partially reconstructed Upper Basilical Building (the name, refreshingly, reflecting the uncertainty over its function). Beyond here are the arches of the principal entrance, which once would have been an imposingly monumental structure. Further south, you can overlook the main mosque, which is accurately aligned towards Mecca.

While most of the site requires a leap of imagination to envisage it in its pomp, the throne room is immediately impressive. Much of the decoration has been reassembled or reconstructed (with textual sources an important aid). The chamber features an elaborate array of colourful moulded patterning and red and white striped horseshoe arches reminiscent of the Mezquita. Mentally add in a few silk hangings and a plump divan and you can well picture the caliph reclining to receive dignitaries, perhaps allowing his bejewelled hand to be kissed if the visitor was of exceptionally high rank.

The western part of the excavated area served a domestic function: here were the homes of guards and slaves, as well as the purported sleeping chambers of the caliph, at present not open to the public.

★Montoro

This beautiful olive town perches above a meander of the lazy Guadalquivir, 45 km east of Córdoba. Its narrow streets are unspoiled and picturesque and it makes an excellent day trip from the city or a stopover en route to Madrid or Jaén, for example.

There's a **tourist office** ⓘ *C Corredera 25, T957-160089, Mon-Fri 0930-1500, Sat 1000-1300, Sun 1000-1400*, which will furnish you with a map of the town.

The parish church of **San Bartolomé**, tower reaching for the heavens, sits on the same square, a picturesque space surrounded by buildings of warm reddish stone. Most of the building dates from the 16th century and combines Gothic, Renaissance and *mudéjar* elements. The fine carved Isabelline portal gives way to a triple-naved interior with a bright wooden *artesonado* ceiling. Beside the church is the town hall, with a fine Plateresque and Baroque façade. There are several fine mansions around the narrow streets.

Listings Córdoba city and around *map p274*

Tourist information

Tourist office

Puerta del Puente s/n, T957-471235, otcordoba@andalucia.org. Mon-Fri 0900-1930, Sat-Sun 0930-1500.

This new office is between the Mezquita and the river. There is a city information kiosk (daily 0900-1400, 1700-1930), on Plaza Tendillas and a booth at the train station. The Córdoba Card offers various packages of attractions and might save you money if you want to see a few sights and a flamenco show in the city, for example. Ask at the tourist office. The tourist office can provide you with the *This.Is:Córdoba* multilingual audio guide to the city, which has detailed information on sights around town including Medina Azahara. It costs €15, but you get it for 48 hrs. There's about 4½ hrs of commentary on it. It comes with 2 headphones, so a couple can listen simultaneously.

Where to stay

There are plenty of excellent-value *hostales* dotted through the streets of old Córdoba; the best zone for budget places is in the streets east of the Mezquita. With a couple of exceptions, the hotels adjacent to the Mezquita are poor value in high season. There are lots of 4-star chain hotels in the newer part of town. Many hotels raise their prices during May.

€€€€ La Hospedería de El Churrasco
C Romero 38, T957-294808, www.elchurrasco.com.

Just down the road from the restaurant of the same name, this charming Judería boutique hotel makes an excellent Córdoba address. It's very seductive, with all rooms a little different, and filled, albeit a little heavily at times, with antique furniture, as well as modern conveniences. The service and location are great, but you'll want to book this one ahead. Breakfast included. Recommended.

€€€ Casa de los Azulejos
Fernando Colón 5, T957-470000, www.casadelos azulejos.com.
In old Córdoba but far from the tourist bottlenecks of the Judería, this charming place is run with enthusiasm and features beautiful tiling, a patio with frondy plants reaching for the sky, and high-ceilinged rooms with pleasing antique features and colourful modern bathrooms. You're within yards of pretty Plaza Corredera and some great local bars. Breakfast is included. Recommended.

€€€ Hotel Las Casas de la Judería
C Tomás Conde 10, T957-202095, www.casasypalacios.com.
This fabulous conversion of historic Judería buildings set around picturesque patios makes a great place to stay in the heart of the historic city. It's close to everything and offers polite service and exceptionally comfortable rooms. The pool is on the small side, but the ambience is everything here.

€€ Carpe Diem
C Barroso 4, T957-476221, www.hotelcordobacarpediem.com.
An easy stroll to the Mezquita and also handy for the centre, but on a quiet side street, this bright, modern choice is set around a central light well and offers comfortable, stylish rooms at a very fair price. The suites cost little more, but have more unused space than extra amenities. Excellent value.

€€ Hotel Maestre
C Romero Barros 4, T957-472410, www.hotelmaestre.com.
This well-run hotel by Plaza del Potro is gleamingly clean, with marble floors and helpful management. The rooms are spotless, adequate and fairly priced. Some have more light than others. A couple of doors down, the hotel also runs a *hostal* (**€**), which is good value, and some immaculate self-catering apartments. Parking available.

€€ Hotel Mezquita
Plaza de Santa Catalina 1, T957-475585, www.hotel mezquita.com.
Offering the best value of the several hotels around the Mezquita, this welcoming spot doesn't offer luxury but is carefully decorated, with some particularly fine gilt mirrors; the rooms are large, with clean marbled floors and pictures of Moorish fantasies on the walls. Some look across to the mosque, others over the interior patio; room 10 is a romantic Baroque fantasy but stuffy in summer. It's a bargain off-season (**€**). You can park in the hotel next door. Recommended.

€ Albergue Juvenil
Plaza Juda Leví s/n, T957-355040, www.inturjoven.com. YHA card required, but can be purchased here.
Unusually for a Spanish youth hostel, this excellent place is in the heart of town, in the Judería. Accommodation is in rooms sleeping 2-5. It's a bit more expensive for over 25s.

€ Hostal Agustina
C Zapateria Vieja 5, T957-470872.
This sweet *pensión* is typically Spanish with cheery no-frills hospitality. Several generations of family run the place, whose handful of rooms are big, polished and have bags of character. Shared bathroom. Good location and well-priced.

€ Hostal Almanzor
C Cardenal González 10, T957-485400, www.hostal-almanzor.es.
About as much value as you can get for this price and location, a couple of minutes' walk from the Mezquita. The

rooms are spick and span, and come with a/c, TV and tiny bathroom. Some have balconies, although those on the street can be noisy in the evenings: avoid Room 1. Parking included if there's room in the nearby car park.

€ Hostal Los Arcos
C Romero Barros 14, T957-485643, www.pensionlosarcos.com.
A patio filled with succulents is the feature of this fine family-run budget place near Plaza del Potro. The place is scrubbed to a healthy shine every morning; copper-coloured azulejos on the stairways are another feature. The rooms are bare but spacious; those on the roof (without bathrooms) are particularly enjoyable. Prices are low.

Montoro

€€ Casa Maika
C Salazar 21, T636-035552, www.casamaika.com.
Right in Montoro itself, this pretty spot offers grand views over the river and hills. Built around an airy patio, it offers inviting rooms (better upstairs) and a couple of self-catering apartments in the heart of the village. Head up the slope from Plaza España.

€€ Molino La Nava
Camino La Nava 6, 8 km northeast of Montoro, T957-336041, www.molinonava.com. Print the directions off their website or programme the Satnav otherwise it's a tough find.
This stylish rural hotel is a handsomely converted old olive mill. It makes a cracking place to stay; the rooms and suites are spacious, pretty and very relaxing, with firm mattresses; even better is the welcome from the cheery owners, who prepare excellent food. There's also a pool. It's a very Andalucían experience and recommended.

Restaurants

There are many excellent restaurants in Córdoba; some of these are in the Judería where there are also several establishments seeking only to fob tourists off with a frozen paella and glass of watery *sangría*.

There's also a proud tapas scene here; the best places are *tabernas*, generally long-standing establishments serving traditional bites with a glass of Montilla or Moriles wine. Things wind up much earlier here than in the rest of Spain; many tapas bars pull the shutters down at 2200 or so midweek.

€€€ El Churrasco
C Romero 16, T957-290819, www.elchurrasco.com. Closed Aug.
One of the city's signature restaurants, this has a solid reputation, but it helps if you stick to the things they are good at, so stock up on vegetables and salads elsewhere. The downstairs dining room is in a pretty patio, with braziers underfoot when things get chillier. The meat is famous here; best is the *chuletón* steak for 2 people; other cuts are tasty if not huge for the price. Fish is also well-prepared, with a delicious salmon carpaccio recommendable. The owner had to buy the house next door to store all the wines on his list, one of the best in the region but not cheap.

€€ Bodegas Mezquita
C Céspedes 12, T957-107859, www.bodegasmezquita.com. The kitchen is open all afternoon.
A cut above most of the other mosque-side options, this cheery spot offers up a range of excellent local tapas and *raciones*,

which you can wash down with a range of fairly priced wines. The *salmorejo* and other cold tapas are generally the best options here. There's another location on the opposite side of the Mezquita at C Corregidor Luis de la Cerda 73.

€€ Casa Rubio
Puerta de Almodóvar 5, T957-420853, www.restaurantecasarubiocordoba.com.
This softly lit Judería restaurant is divided from its tapas bar by elaborate Mezquita-style arches. While it's visited by plenty of tourists, it hasn't let that affect it; service is upright and polite. The kitchen puts a classy spin on traditional dishes; the ubiquitous *rabo de toro* (bull's tail) is great here. The tapas are limited but what's available is very tasty; bars in these parts live or die by their *salmorejo*, and here it's thick and more than generously seeded with *jamón serrano*. The place's sister set-up nearby, **Casa Pepe de la Judería**, is more upmarket and also worthwhile.

€€ La Cazuela de Espartería
C Rodríguez Marín 16, T957-488952, www.lacazueladela esparteria.net.
Just up the hill from Plaza Corredera, this handsome bar has a sizeable Córdoba fan club, but its scurrying staff are nonetheless welcoming and helpful. Grab a table if you can for the toothsome *raciones – alcachofas con rabo* (artichokes with bull's tail) or *revuelto de berenjenas* (scrambled eggs with aubergine) are standouts, but it's all excellent. Recommended.

€€ La Fragua
Calleja del Arco 2, T957-484572.
Tucked away behind the Almudaina restaurant, this tavern is tough to find but worth the effort. Historic and ultra-atmospheric, its brick-arched interior is delightful. Service is very attentive, and there's a delicious range of delicately prepared dishes. Romantic and recommended.

€€ La Tinaja
Paseo de la Ribera 12, T957-047998, www.latinajadecordoba.com.
On the riverside road very close to the Plaza del Potro but pleasantly removed from the tourist hurly-burly, this is a rather lovely place with very pleasant dining areas and a romantic terrace. They deal in good-quality market produce: cheeses, seafood, and seasonal specials.

€€ Mesón Juan Peña
C Doctor Fleming 1, T957-200702.
A block from the Judería in the new town, this homely place appeals immediately with its warm glow, cheerful buzz, and comfortable rustic decor. The food, eaten at no-frills wooden tables (with traditional foot warmers in winter), is excellent, and typically *cordobés*. It's worth arriving early at weekends to get a table.

€€-€ Los Patios de la Marquesa
C Manríquez 4, www. lospatiosdelamarquesa.com.
For an interesting eating scene, drop into this unusual place in the heart of the Judería. It's like an upmarket food court, with delis and tapas bars surrounding a central area, great for a glass of wine and casual snacking. Out the back there's a pleasant terrace area for an after-dinner *copa*.

€ Bodega Guzmán
C Judíos 7.
A huge former wine warehouse and the place to come for authenticity in this part of town. Its local crowd is gruff old Spanish men sipping the cheap *montilla fino* made by the owner and discussing football and the bulls.

€ El Gallo

C María Cristina s/n, T957-482953.

Another bar that hasn't changed a bit for years. Barrels of really good *montilla* are slowly emptied by a row of old blokes standing at the bar, backs firmly turned to the street and the 21st century.

€ El Pisto

C San Miguel 1, T957-478328.

Officially named **Taberna San Miguel**, this is one of the city's crucial tapas joints. Convivial and traditional, it's predictably decked from floor to ceiling with photos of Manolete and other *matadors*, and has a great atmosphere as well as some excellent comfort-tapas like *albóndigas* (meatballs), which come floating in a bowl of soup, or heartwarming bowls of *callos* (tripe) net. Eat at the bar or sit down in a closed patio.

€ Taberna El Juncal

C San Felipe 13, T957-471592.

This warm and unpretentious restaurant is popular with students and lecturers from the university near here. They specialize in tasty, traditional dishes such as *salmorejo*, *pulpo*, and *bacalao*.

€ Taberna Plateros

C San Francisco 6, T957-470042. Closed Mon.

Córdoba's old silversmiths' society runs several worthwhile bars around the city. This, the original, is a low-key sort of place with a large seating area with whitewashed walls and high, varnished wooden ceilings. They don't skimp on the barrelled Montilla, at a bargain rate, and the traditional Córdoban tapas are just as good and also priced to please.

Cafés

For an afternoon *merienda*, head to the terrace at smart, bright **Roldán**, Plaza Grilo s/n, famous for its glistening cakes and tarts.

Café Gaudí

Av Gran Capitán 22, T957-471736.

Done up as a café from the golden art nouveau days, this looks the part, with a brass rail at the horseshoe-shaped bar and chessboard tiles. It's popular with well-dressed Córdobans day and night for its good coffee, range of *pinchos* and more substantial plates, range of imported beers and large terrace: a good launching point for an evening's exploration.

Bars and clubs

The best bar zone is on and around Av del Gran Capitán between Ronda de los Tejares and Av de América, an area known as Reyes Católicos, after one of its streets. The major *discoteca* zone is along Av del Brillante further out. The following are all central options.

Bar Correo

C Jesús María 2.

Correo is little more than a hole-in-the-wall off Plaza Tendillas, but the cheery staff keep the street outside it packed with drinkers until midnight.

Café Málaga

C Málaga 3, T957-474107, www.facebook.com/cafemalagalivemusic.

Just off Plaza Tendillas, this elegant space is a real haven. Solicitous service, well-chosen music and excellent mixed drinks make it the city's finest *copas* bar. They also run a nearby venue with regular live music. Recommended.

Góngora Gran Café

C Góngora 10, T662-352389, www.gongoragrancafe.es.

Decked out with paintings and chandeliers, this bar and *discoteca* is a memorable place for a drink. Quiet by day, it hosts live bands at night midweek, and is one of the more popular *discotecas* at weekends. There's a cover of €8-12, but it includes 2 drinks.

Jazz Café

C Rodríguez Marín 6, T957-485854, www.facebook.com/jazzcafecordoba.

There seem to be only 2 types of jazz bar around; smoky cellars or breezy white walled-style bars. This is of the latter variety, and frequently has live acts. These are free, although drinks prices are higher than usual. The competent bar staff mix a good *caipirinha* – there's also good vermouth served from a barrel.

Sojo

Paseo de la Ribera s/n, T957-492192, www.cafesojo.es.

Rather a surprising find – you have to take the lift in a public car park to the 3rd floor – this striking space offers luxurious Moorish-style furnishings, sofas and a glorious covered terrace, all with magnificent views over the Guadalquivir. They do breakfast and light meals through the day, but the best time to be here is for a sundown drink.

Entertainment

Bullfights

The Plaza de Toros is south of the centre. The best fights are during Córdoba's main fiesta (see Festivals, below), but there are regular fights during the Apr-Sep season.

Cinema

There are several large multiplexes in the new town. Right in the Judería, **Filmoteca de Andalucía**, C Medina y Corella 5, T957-103627, www.filmotecadeandalucia.com, screens new European films and older original version releases.

Festivals

Feb-Mar While not a patch on Cádiz's, Córdoba's **Carnaval**, www.carnavaldecordoba.com, is a boisterous affair and dressing up is definitely recommended. The main days are Shrove Tue, 47 days before Easter Sun, and the weekend before it.

Easter **Semana Santa** in Córdoba features traditional processions similar to the better-known ones in Sevilla. Some 30 *cofradías* parade images of Christ and the Virgin through the city streets.

5-12 May **Festival of Patios** (see box, page 273), www.patios.cordoba.es. In the evenings and all day weekends, beautifully maintained private patios all around the city are open to visitors; entry is free, although small donations are sometimes appreciated. There's also much live music and flamenco.

End May **Feria de Nuestra Señora de la Salud**, Córdoba's major fiesta, is a big event, a week of top bullfights, fireworks, markets and much revelry. Much of the action centres on the Feria ground, which has tents for drinking, eating and dancing; unlike Sevilla, most of these are open to the public.

What to do

The tourist office prints a monthly sheet with details of all the available guided tours, visits and events.

Spa

Hammam, *C Corregidor Luis de la Cerda 51, T957-484746, www.hammamalandalus.com.* A beautiful bathhouse in Moorish style. A 90-min session costs €24, or €36 including a massage; booking is advisable.

Tours

Walking tours of Córdoba, organized by the tourist office (see page 282), leave from the centre of Plaza Tendillas daily. They're conducted in several languages and cover much of the old town, including a stop at a tapas bar. Duration about 1½ hrs. Check tourist office for times.

Transport

For information on intercity buses, T957-404040; for trains T957-400202; for local bus information, get a route map from the tourist office or online at www.aucorsa.es.

Air

Córdoba's airport has no commercial flights; Sevilla and Málaga airports are both within 2 hrs' drive.

Bus

The bus station is 1 km west of the old town on Plaza de las Tres Culturas and city buses link it to the centre. No 3 is the most useful, taking you to the western edge of the Judería and Plaza Tendillas, while No 5 takes you through Plaza Colón and the modern centre. Otherwise it's a 15- to 20-min walk to the heart of the old town or take a taxi (€6).

There are regular buses to **Priego de Córdoba** (13 a day, less at weekends, 1 hr 15 mins), **Zuheros** (5 a day, 2 on Sun, 1 hr), **Montilla** (1 hr) and **Almodóvar del Río** (10 daily, 2-4 at weekends, 30 mins). **Belalcázar** and **Belmez** have 2-4 buses daily.

Sevilla is served hourly (1 hr 45 mins), as is **Granada** (2 hrs 45 mins), while there are 4 daily to **Málaga** (3 hrs). **Jaén** has 8 buses a day (5 at weekends, 1 hr 30 mins). A couple of buses daily go to **Cádiz** and **Algeciras**, and 1 to **Almería**.

Further afield, **Madrid** is served 5 times a day (5 hrs), and there are 2 nightly buses to **Barcelona** (13½ hrs).

Car

If arriving by car, park as soon as you can; negotiating the narrow old town streets is tricky, and most corners bear the paint marks of wounded vehicles. There are lots of supervised parking areas, and many accommodation options offer car spaces for €13-20 per day; you may also be lucky and find a nook in the old town to nose into.

Taxi

There are several cab ranks around the edge of the old town; or T957-764444.

Train

The modern train station is next door to the bus station (see above).

The lack of air traffic is made up for by the **AVE** fast train that connects the city with **Málaga** (1 hr), **Sevilla** (45 mins) and **Madrid** (1 hr 45 mins), with departures more than hourly during the day. It's worth booking these in advance. There's an a/c lounge available with free food and drinks if you have booked in *preferente* class, which costs 50% more. The **Avant** trains to **Sevilla** and **Málaga** are almost as quick but about half the price. Slower trains to Sevilla take 1 hr 20 mins.

Other trains head to **Barcelona** and **Jerez/Cádiz**. For most other Andalucían destinations the bus is cheaper and quicker.

Montoro

There are several daily buses from **Córdoba** to Montoro (40 mins), and some of the Córdoba-bound buses from Jaén stop here.

West & north from Córdoba

Heading west from Córdoba towards Sevilla, you should certainly veer off course to visit the fierce castle of Almodóvar del Río on the Guadalquivir river. Beyond here, the small village of Hornachuelos makes the best base for seeing the Córdoba section of the Sierra Morena range of hills that separates Andalucía from the rest of the country.

North of Córdoba the fertile fields of the Guadalquivir plain and the green hills of the Sierra Morena eventually give way to a bleaker region of hard granite villages, closed mines and quarries, and pig farming. This zone, known as Los Pedroches, already feels like neighbouring Extremadura and is really Andalucían only in name. The villages and towns seem very austere compared with the south of the province, but this is partly just because they are built of the local granite.

West from Córdoba → *Colour map 2, B2.*

fortified town and Sierra Morena hills

★Almodóvar del Río

This small town on the Guadalquivir is 23 km downstream from Córdoba and worth a trip for its fantastic **castle** ⓘ *T957-634055, www.castillodealmodovar.com, mid-Sep to Mar Mon-Fri 1100-1430, 1600-1900, Sat-Sun 1100-1900, Apr-Jun same but to 2000, Jul to mid-Sep Mon-Thu 1000-1500, Fri-Sat 1000-1500, 1900-midnight, Sun 1000-1600, €7.* Bristling with dogtooth castellation, it presents a formidable aspect, partly because of extensive restoration over the years. Originally built in the mid-eighth century by the Moors, it was named *Al Mudawar* (the sturdy), giving its name to the town. Mostly dating from the 14th-century Christian rebuilding, the castle centres around a large *patio de armas* or parade ground, which, as well as the doughty keep, also has more recent buildings from the early 20th century, when it was adapted to be a residence for the Marquises of Motilla, who still own it. It's recently been jollied up for tourism, and now has a bar and restaurant, which puts on medieval feasts in the summer. The normal visit includes several audiovisual elements, and bookable special visits throw in some medieval actors.

Hornachuelos

The sleepy village of Hornachuelos, attractively situated above a small *embalse*, makes the best place to base yourself for investigating the Córdoban section of the Sierra Morena range. While the villages in the area are not quite as appealing as those of the western part of the range in Huelva province, the landscape is similar, with low hills verdant with cork trees, holm oaks and several species of pine. In the large Parque Natural Sierra de Hornachuelos there's a good range of wildlife; among the mammals are small numbers of mongoose, lynx and wolves, while otters fish in the rivers and reservoirs. There are several species of raptor, with three varieties of vulture and five eagles, as well as the rare black stork. In spring, the hills are alive with colourful wildflowers and butterflies.

Hornachuelos itself centres on the main square, Plaza de la Constitución. Here you will find the **tourist office**, who can advise on walking in the area. For more detailed information on the park, a 15-minute walk from the town on the CO-142 heading north towards San Calixto is the **visitor centre** ⓘ *T957-641140, Ctra Hornachuelos–San Calixto Km 1.6, Oct-Jun Wed-Fri 1000-1400, Sat-Sun 1000-1400, 1600-1800 (2000 May-Jun), Jul-Sep Fri-Sun 0800-1400*. Several walks start from here. There's little of great interest to see in the town itself, but it's a relaxed little place with several *miradores* giving views over the hills. The Moorish castle is in ruins, although restoration work is in the pipeline. The keep is still just about standing, as are parts of the walls.

Listings West from Córdoba

Where to stay

Hornachuelos

There are no characterful *pensiones*, although there are several *casas rurales*; the tourist office has a list, and some are on the websites www.escapadarural.com and www.toprural.com.

Restaurants

Hornachuelos

€€-€ Casa Alejandro
Av Guadalquivir 4, T957-640098.
The best place in town. There's lots of seating outside, while inside is cosy with a fireplace and decorated with deer heads and antlers; the same hapless beasts often feature on the menu. Tasty tapas at the bar.

Transport

Almodóvar del Río

Hourly buses run to **Córdoba** Mon-Fri, 1 every 2 hrs on Sat, and 2 on Sun (30 mins).

Hornachuelos

2-4 daily buses run to Hornachuelos from **Córdoba** (1 hr).

North from Córdoba → *Colour map 2, A2.*

wide open spaces, farmland and temperature extremes

Belmez and Belalcázar

In the far north of Córdoba province are a couple more castles for fans of the genre. The landscape is more like Extremadura than Andalucía and is quite bleak compared to the mannered elegance of Córdoba, but this is where the Moors and Christians slugged things out for supremacy.

On the main road to Badajoz (N-432) some 65 km northwest of the provincial capital, Belmez is a farming town with a striking square keep atop a huge rock high above the town. Built by the Moors, it was taken by Fernando III in the 13th century, owned by the Knights of Calatrava and later occupied by the French in the Peninsular War.

Forty kilometres further north, in a remote area, Belalcázar stands alone. The town's name means beautiful castle and the 15th-century structure is indeed strikingly magnificent. Although currently closed to the public, it has been bought by the regional government with the aim of restoring it and opening it to visits. Meanwhile, from outside you can appreciate its finest feature, the lofty keep, extraordinarily decorated with brickwork mouldings that seem rather frivolous for the stern Gutierre de Sotomayor who had it built. He was a knight of the Calatrava order who owned much of south-central Spain. The main façade of the castle is a later Renaissance addition built as a cosy palace for descendants of Gutierre who lacked his knightly rigour.

Listings North from Córdoba

Transport

To Belmez, there are 5 daily buses between **Córdoba** and **Badajoz** that stop here, while to Belálcazar, there are 2-4 daily buses from **Córdoba** and 1 on to **Badajoz**.

South from Córdoba

This economically important region is a traditional Mediterranean agricultural zone, with gentle hills covered with olive trees, whose fruit are pressed for oil, and with vines, from which the tasty Montilla and Moriles wine is made. Beyond here, the land rises into the Sistema Subbética, a lightly wooded expanse of tortured limestone hills and plateaux.

Places such as Priego de Córdoba and Zuheros rank among Andalucía's prettiest white towns; the former has a fine ensemble of Baroque architecture, while the latter is a stunningly attractive spot with an important Neolithic cave above town. Meanwhile, Baena is one of Spain's most heralded olive oil towns.

Montilla and around → *Colour map 2, C3.*

centre of Córdoba's wine production

The centre for the production of Córdoba's favourite wine is a spread-out place with a quiet, reasonably attractive centre and sprawling ugly outskirts. This was the birthplace of the Gran Capitán, the famous Reconquista general Gonzalo de Córdoba, whose name is inescapable in this province. Near here, in 45 BC, the battle of Munda was fought between two rival Roman factions, Julius Caesar's and Pompey's; the battle was decisively won by Caesar.

The largest *montilla* producer is **Bodegas Alvear** ⓣ *T957-022063, www.alvear.es, €7,* whose winery is on the approach to the centre of town, the entrance is on Avenida Boucou off the main Avenida de Andalucía. They do a good tour with a tasting session of three wines at the end; it leaves daily at 1230 but it's best to phone to confirm. The winery shop is also open daily. Opposite the bodega, at Avenida Andalucía 26, the Durán wine shop has a wider selection from the region.

Lagar Blanco ⓘ *T628-319977, www.lagarblanco.es*, is another bodega offering recommended tours. There are no set visiting hours, so you'll have to book via email or phone. The visit includes tasting of several wines and optional tapas lunch.

Aguilar de la Frontera

This typically Andalucían village, 10 km south of Montilla, has a centre of narrow streets and elegant buildings. It's worth a stop for its striking 18th-century **Plaza San José**, a beautiful octagonal space whose green shutters and black iron balconies offset the white walls. There's a small tourist **information centre** ⓘ *Cuesta de Jesús, T957-661567.*

Espejo

Some 33 km southeast of Córdoba (and 13 km east of Montilla) is an attractive white town crowned by a castle. The town was originally an important Iberian settlement known as Ucubi and was further fortified by the Romans and the Moors. The nuggety **castle** ⓘ *T686-311212, www.castillodeespejo.es, visits 1000-1400, 1600-1900 must be prebooked, €5*, however, dates from the early 14th century, and has some *mudéjar* features. It still belongs to the Dukes of Osuna. Near it is the whitewashed church of San Bartolomé, with an *artesonado* ceiling and a simple brick tower. There's tourist information available in the town hall, and a few places to eat strung along the main road below town.

Listings Montilla and around

Where to stay

Montilla

€€ Hostal Bellido
C Enfermería 57, T957-651915, www.hostalbellido.com.
This handsome *hostal* occupies a fine old building, is centrally located and offers refurbished rooms with pleasingly old-fashioned decor and shiny bathrooms. Best, though, they've got their own tiny bodega room, where you can have a tipple straight from the barrel.

Restaurants

Montilla

€€ Las Camachas
Av Europa 3, T957-650004, www.restaurantelascamachas.com.
The noble colonnaded dining room here is the venue for an excellent selection of Córdoban cuisine backed up by cordial service and an ample selection of local wines.

Aguilar de la Frontera

€ La Casona
Ctra Montoro–Puente Genil s/n, T957-660439, www.lacasonarestaurante.es, on the main road that skirts around the village's edge.

You cannot do better than this. As well as tasty tapas, they put on fine plates of regional food and are particularly popular with Córdobans coming down from the city for a big weekend lunch.

What to do

Montilla

Just Explore, *T957-022902, www.just-explore.com.* Based in Montilla, these friendly, English-speaking folk offer winery tours around the region, as well as other trips to various highlights of Córdoba province and beyond.

Transport

Bus

Most buses in southern Córdoba province are run by **Autocares Carrera** (www.autocarescarrera.es). From Córdoba, they run to **Montilla** (more than hourly Mon-Fri, 2 buses Sat-Sun), **Aguilar and Espejo**. Check their website for timetables.

Train

There are trains to **Lucena** and **Córdoba** from Montilla.

Baena → *Colour map 2, C4.*

one of Spain's best-known production centres of olive oil

★Prosperous Baena is famed for its olive oil, for which, like several towns in Andalucía, it has its own *denominación de origen* (DO) classification. Baena is also known for its earsplitting Semana Santa processions, when two rival brotherhoods, the White-Tailed Jews and the Black-Tailed Jews, parade, rolling their drums, on alternate days. Should they meet (and this is usually arranged) they try to out-drum each other; the noise made by upwards of a thousand drums can barely be believed.

Once an Iberian settlement named Iponuba, it was taken over by the Romans, who also produced large quantities of oil here. It became one of the more important Moorish cities in Al-Andalus under the name Bayyana, but declined in population after its reconquest in 1240.

The town's **tourist office** ⓘ *T957-671757, Mon-Fri 0900-1400, Sat 1030-1330, 1700-1900 (1800-2000 summer), Sun 1030-1330,* is just off the main road at Calle Virrey 5. Opposite, the old town runs up the side of a steep hill that rises from the main road to **Plaza de la Constitución**, with the modern Ayuntamiento alongside the beautiful long brick arches of **Casa del Monte**, a building that has served a variety of municipal functions since its construction in the 18th century.

Leaving the square by Calle Santo Domingo Henares, you'll soon reach the **Casa de la Tercia**, built around the same time, and once used to store the tithes collected from farmers. It's a great old building with a patio, low wooden eaves and a cobbled gallery on the top floor. On the floor below is an excellent little **archaeological museum** ⓘ *Tue-Thu and Sun 1030-1330, Fri-Sat 1030-1330, 1700-1900 (1800-2000 summer), €2.* There's a semi-fossilized skull from the Neolithic period and a display of ceramics that clearly shows Greek and Phoenician influences on locals in the first half of the first millennium BC. There's a fine series of Iberian votive anthropomorphic sculptures from the nearby **Sanctuary of Torreparedones**, as well as a carved lioness and wild boar. Roman finds include many gravestones, *terra sigillata* ware, lamps and machinery for making olive oil, while a fine Visigothic rosette plaque and a collection of coins round off the enjoyable display. There's also a small **museum** in the same building about the town's Semana Santa traditions.

Above here, at the top of the town, are what remains of the castle, and the convent of **La Madre de Díos**, which has a fine *mudéjar* portal.

The lower town centres on **Plaza de España**, whose fountain has one of the many modern sculptures commissioned by the council to enliven the town. Not far away, tucked into a backstreet in a former oil factory, is Baena's modern **olive oil museum** ⓘ *C Cañada 7, T957-691641, www.museoaceite.com, Tue-Sun 1000-1500 (0900-1400 summer), €2*. In a former oil mill, it recreates the pressing and bottling stages on the ground floor, with information upstairs on the olive calendar and the use of oil in the Spanish kitchen.

To further your exploration of the olive oil industry, take Calle Cervantes from behind **Primero de la Mañana** café on the main road and you'll soon come to an attractive 19th-century olive oil factory, **Núñez de Prado** ⓘ *C Cervantes 15, T957-670141, Mon-Fri 0900-1330, 1600-1830, Sat 0900-1300, free*. With a prior telephone call, you can visit the olive works on a friendly guided tour (in Spanish, English and French), which lasts 30 minutes and lets you see the original cellars from 1795 as well as the more modern machinery. A small percentage of the oil is still bottled manually. For groups of 15-20, traditional lunches can be arranged.

Listings Baena

Where to stay

€€ La Casa Grande
Av Cervantes 35, T957-671905, www.lacasagrande.es.
Occupying a turn-of-the-20th-century mansion in the lower part of town, this hotel is decorated with farm implements and blacksmiths' tools; the rooms are modern but still reasonably characterful; they come with minibar among other conveniences. Rooms come with hydromassage bathroom; there's an opulent suite, plus simpler doubles with shower (**€€**). Has a bar and restaurant.

€ Pensión Los Claveles
C Juan Valera 15, T957-670174.
Half a block from Plaza de España, this is very trim and clean, with spotless rooms at a low price.

Transport

Most buses in southern Córdoba province are run by **Autocares Carrera** (www.autocarescarrera.es). There are buses between **Córdoba** and Baena, as well as **Montilla**, **Aguilar**, **Zuheros**, **Cabra, Lucena** and **Priego**.

Sierras Subbéticas → *Colour map 5, A1/C4.*

jagged karstic limestone formations and gently wooded valleys

This southern part of Córdoba province has a number of picturesque white villages and towns; part of the region has been demarcated a *parque natural*, with characteristically Mediterranean vegetation, mostly cork oaks, and significant mammal- and birdlife, including shrews, boar, wildcats, golden eagles and peregrine falcons. The old olive oil railway line has been reclaimed and made into a 60-km path or *vía verde*, an excellent walking or cycling route running from Luque in the northeast of the region through Zuheros, Cabra and as far as Lucena.

★Zuheros

The most attractive spot in the Subbética region, Zuheros is a quiet and enchanting white village sandwiched into a pocket of land surrounded by a semi-circle of high limestone crags. Its narrow streets are wonderfully atmospheric and guarded by its spectacular ruined castle, seemingly at one with the rock that it sits on.

The village is a small one, 8 km south of Baena. The ruined **castle** was originally built in the ninth century, although later modifications were made; these included a **Renaissance palace**, whose walls are still visible among the fortifications. Opposite the castle is the **Museo Arqueológico** ⓘ *museum and castle joint entry, Tue-Sun 1000-1400, 1600-1800 (1700-1900 summer), tours on the hour (last tour 1800, 1900 in summer), €2*, with some of the important finds from the cave (see below). The museum guardian will show you around then take you into the castle. You can save a little money by buying a joint entry ticket to the museum and the cave. It's worth phoning ahead if you're visiting on a weekday: T957-694545.

There's a small **tourist office** ⓘ *Pl de la Paz 2*, by the castle, with the same hours. There's an **information centre** ⓘ *summer only*, for the national park 500 m above town on the road to the cave.

At the top end of town, in a large three-storey mansion, is the **Museo de Costumbres y Artes Populares** ⓘ *C Santo 29, T957-694690, Tue-Fri 1200-1400, 1600-1900 (1700-2030 summer), Sat and Sun 1030-1430, 1600-1900 (1730-2030 summer), €3.* With various exhibition rooms and an open patio, it features an interesting array of tools and implements from traditional trades, as well as reconstructed bedrooms, workshops and shops. It's full of interesting objects from all walks of *serrano* life.

Cueva de los Murciélagos

T957-694545, turismo@zuheros.es. Tours Apr-Sep Tue-Fri 1230 and 1730 by advance reservation only, Sat and Sun 1100, 1230, 1400, 1700, 1830, Oct-Mar Tue-Fri 1230 and 1630 by advance reservation only, Sat and Sun 1100, 1230, 1400, 1600, 1730. It's advisable to phone ahead, as the daily number is limited. €6, €7.50 including castle and museum in Zuheros.

Four kilometres above the town is the Cueva de los Murciélagos (Cave of the Bats – there are still a few about but they're pretty shy). It's a stiff hour's walk

ON THE ROAD

Olives and their oil

The olive tree was first introduced to Andalucía by the Romans, and the region developed an important export industry to Rome itself. The Moors extended the cultivation and most Spanish words relating to olives and olive production are taken directly from Arabic, such as the fruit itself, *aceituna* (az-zitouna in Arabic). Today, Spain is the world's largest producer of olive oil and Andalucía, particularly the provinces of Jaén and Córdoba, accounts for 75% of this amount, with some 14,000 sq km of olive groves; nearly a sixth of the region's area.

Some of the trees are over a millennium old and are incredibly hardy and resistant to fire. Methods of harvesting have barely changed since Roman times; it's a hard, labour-intensive process. Teams of four or five use sticks to beat the branches, and spread huge nets (*mantas*) under the tree to catch the olives. Any that escape or have previously fallen are all collected by hand. The green, unripe olives are harvested around October; the ripe black ones are harvested in December or January. Around 90% of the harvest is used for oil.

Until recently, the olives were ground under cone-shaped stones, then pressed on mats and filtered, but now it's usually a more industrial process. The olives have to be pressed quickly, as any fermentation results in an unpleasant flavour. The oil from the first pressing is known as virgin. The best oil, extra *virgen*, must have no more than 1% acidity and only receives the grade after it is tasted by the central authority. Olive oil has denominations of origin like wine. The higher the acidity of the oil, the stronger the flavour, and therefore the lower the price. Lower quality oil is pressed in refineries from the waste matter – *orujo* – from the first pressing. On average, about 4 kg of olives are needed to produce a litre of oil.

Folklore had always claimed that olive oil contributed to good complexion, efficient digestion and strong hearts and modern nutritional theory has emphasized that this liquid, which contains no cholesterol, is probably a significant reason for the fact that the people of Spain, Italy and Greece have a markedly lower incidence of coronary disease than their northern European counterparts.

The other 10% of the olives are eaten. Green olives, often stuffed with bits of anchovy or pepper, are more commonly eaten in Spain than the black ones, which mainly go for oil. Before eating, olives must first be soaked in saltwater so that a bitter chemical, *alpechín*, can be released – trying an olive off the tree is a memorably unpleasant experience.

up to the caves (or a short drive) from Zuheros, but the views are fantastic, first winding above the village, then emerging into a rocky karst landscape. The cave, as well as spectacular limestone cavern formations, has important Chalcolithic and Neolithic wall paintings of humans and animals. Some burials with ceramics were also unearthed here; it's one of the key sites for students of Andalucían prehistory.

As caves weren't really dwelling places by this period (4300-3950 BC), there was perhaps some sort of religious or ritual function to the caves and their artwork.

Cabra

A busy but attractive service centre and market town for the region, Cabra has a real highlight in its tiny but lovely Barrio de la Villa, the old part of town that harbours cobbled squares, ramparts of the city walls and a clutch of historic buildings shaded by palm trees.

Here, the notable parish church, **Iglesia de la Asunción**, is particularly beautiful floodlit, with its soaring narrow spire and corkscrew columns. Although built in the 15th century, its five-naved ground plan is all that really remains from this period; the rest is pure Baroque thanks to reformations in the 17th and 18th centuries. It's only open at mass (doors open around 1800) but is worth a visit for its fine stonework, including exotic-looking red marble on some of its columns. It was built on the site of a mosque, while the small neighbouring castle was once the Moorish fortress before being reformed by the Counts of Cabra; it's now a school.

There's a **tourist office** ⓘ *C Mayor 1, T957-523493, www.turismodecabra.es, daily 1000-1400, 1700-2000*, and, on the outskirts of town, an **olive oil museum** ⓘ *C Vado del Moro 2, T957-521771, Mon-Sat 0900-1400, €1.50*, which has reconstructed Roman presses as well as a thorough explanation of the olive oil manufacturing process.

Lucena

This large town is mostly devoted to the manufacture of wooden furniture; numerous wholesale and retail warehouses are lined along the busy main road.

If you're passing, it's worth delving into the centre, where the **San Mateo church** sits on the focal Plaza Nueva. Mostly built in the 15th and 16th centuries in Renaissance and Gothic styles, its outstanding feature is its octagonal **Capilla del Sagrario** ⓘ *daily 0730-1330, 1830-2100, free*, which is astounding with its very elaborate Baroque decoration. The masterwork of Leonardo de Castro, who worked on it for more than 30 years in the 18th century, it boasts a profusion of painted plasterwork, with incredibly ornate vegetal scrollwork studded with sculptures of cherubs and saints.

On the adjacent Plaza de España the castle houses an ethnographic and archaeological **museum** ⓘ *daily 1000-1800, €3*. The last Moorish king, Boabdil, was once a prisoner here. The town's **tourist office** ⓘ *T957-513282, www.turlucena.com, Mon-Sat 1000-1400, 1700-2000, Sun 1000-1400*, sits in an elegant 18th-century Baroque palace, which contains an interpretative display on the Subbética region (free, same hours, but closed on Mondays).

Six kilometres above town is the much-visited Baroque sanctuary of **Nuestra Señora de Araceli** ⓘ *daily 0900-sunset, free*, with lively and colourful wall paintings and fine views over the hills. The sculpture of the Virgin is revered in the province and explains why Araceli is a common Córdoban girl's name. There's a bar here that serves food.

Where to stay

Zuheros

€€ Hotel Zuhayra
C Mirador 10, T957-694693, www.zercahoteles.com.
A likeable mountain hotel offering fine value for money. They organize walking excursions and have simply furnished and attractive heated rooms, as well as a cosy restaurant. Recommended.

Transport

Bus

Buses in southern Córdoba province are run by **Autocares Carrera** (www.autocarescarrera.es). There are buses between **Córdoba** and **Zuheros**, as well as **Montilla**, **Aguilar**, **Baena**, **Cabra**, **Lucena** and **Priego**.

Train

There are trains to **Córdoba** and **Montilla**.

Priego de Córdoba and around → *Colour map 5, A2.*

twisted warren of narrow white streets filled with colourful flowerpots

★One of Andalucía's most interesting provincial towns, friendly Priego de Córdoba was founded by the Moors as Medina Baguh and soon developed a significant textile industry. This declined after the Reconquest in 1341 (Fernando III had seized Priego for a short period in 1226), but revived in the 18th century, when local velvets became highly prized in the peninsula. The ensuing wealth paid for the building of several fine churches, and Priego now has Córdoba's richest collection of Baroque architecture. The old town perches on a hill, surrounded by steep cliffs with the new town sprawling below. There are several character-packed accommodation choices in the old town, which makes a relaxing base from which to explore the Sierra Subbética, or even the cities of Córdoba and Granada.

The town has a very helpful **tourist office** ⓘ *Pl de la Constitución 3, T957-700625, www.turismodepriego.es, Tue-Sat 1000-1400, 1630-1830 (1700-1930 summer), Sun 1000-1400*, on the main square.

All the town's monuments are located within a short distance of **Plaza de la Constitución**, the hub of the old town. Several are available on a combined entrance ticket. Head first for the **castle** ⓘ *Tue-Fri 1000-1400, 1600-1800 (1700-2000 summer), Sat-Sun 1130-1330, 1600-1800 (1700-2000 summer), €1.50*, a well-preserved Arab fortress that was modified in the 13th and 16th centuries. It boasts a sturdy keep, square towers and embrasures and magnificent views from the ramparts.

Across from the castle is Priego's finest church, **Nuestra Señora de la Asunción** ⓘ *Tue-Sun 1130-1330, and daily from 1915 until mass at 2000, €3*, a Gothic-*mudéjar* creation with a slim stone belfry. Enter to admire the octagonal sacrarium, a fine galleried space with exuberant rococo plasterwork and depictions of saints and biblical events. The artist responsible was Francisco Javier Pedrajas. The church also harbours a Renaissance *retablo*.

Priego's most enchanting area is tucked away behind the church. Follow the small lane (on the left as you face the church) into some of the most picturesque lanes imaginable, the walls all whitewashed and groaning with a wealth of flowerpots. This is the **Barrio de la Villa**, the town's oldest part. Make sure you see tiny **Plaza San Antonio**. On the edge of this small barrio are some viewpoints over the escarpment edge.

The **Iglesia de la Aurora** ⓘ *Tue-Sun 1000-1300, €1.50*, is another Baroque gem, with a small façade adorned with solomonic columns. The bell tower, part of the original 15th-century structure, is thin and crumbling, and looks like it might topple any day now unless someone shores it up. The narrow interior is intricately vaulted and decorated with a wealth of gleaming plasterwork and paint.

There are several other churches that merit a visit. One of these is the **Iglesia de San Francisco** ⓘ *Mon-Fri 1000-1300, 1800-2000, Sat 1000-1300, check for afternoon opening, Sun 0900-1245, free*, a late Gothic affair given a Baroque makeover in the 18th century, and featuring much work by the local master **Juan de Dios Santaella**, who designed the fluid portal. Although it's very beautiful, Gerald Brenan (see box, page 359) had a point when he commented in *The Face of Spain* that "one cannot think of anything Saint Francis would have liked less".

Beyond the tourist office, Calle Río leads to two fountains: the elegant, if bombastic, 19th-century **Fuente del Rey**, with 139 water spouts and a central sculpture of Neptune. It looks at its best at night when lit up. By its side is the older 16th-century Fuente de Salud.

Almedinilla

Nine kilometres southeast of Priego, the small village of Almedinilla boasts an excellent attraction, the Roman villa of El Ruedo. By the main road, the **villa** ⓘ *T957-703317, Mon-Fri 0900-1500, Sat 1000-1400, 1630-1930, Sun 1000-1400, €2.50*, dates from the first century AD and has been beautifully excavated and cleverly presented. Mosaic floors and the remains of wall paintings are well preserved, and the various rooms, heating system, atrium and dining platform are clearly visible. Looking out over the fields and olive-speckled hills, you can imagine that the view from here hasn't fundamentally changed over the last two millennia.

In the village's centre, a small archaeological museum, with the same hours as the villa, displays some of the finds from the site, including a fine bronze of Hypnos, personification of sleep, in 'talk-to-the-hand' mode.

Listings Priego de Córdoba

Where to stay

There are several enchanting *casas rurales* in Priego, some in the desirable Barrio de la Villa. The tourist office (www.turismodepriego.es) has a full list and can make a reservation for you. The hotels are less appealingly situated on the main roads below the town.

€€ Casa Baños de la Villa
C Real 63, T957-547274, www.casabanosdelavilla.com.
Tucked away in the narrow streets of the prettiest part of town, this spot combines rooms with plenty of white and upbeat colours with facilities such as kitchen/dining area for guests' use. The real appeal, though, is the in-house Arab baths, with massage available. The standard rate includes a bath session and breakfast; the baths are open to non-guests (€15) 1000-0130.

€€ Hospedería Zahori
C Real 2, T957-547292, www.hotelzahori.es.
At the entrance to the Barrio de la Villa, this spot has a bar with tranquil terrace and pretty patio tables for breakfast or simple meals. Upstairs are dark, compact new rooms with beamed ceilings, rather attractively decorated in nouveau-rustic and quite a steal for the price.

€ Hostal Rafi
C Isabel la Católica 4, T957-540749, www.hostalrafi.es.
In the centre of the old town, this *hostal* offers remarkable value for money. Rooms have TV, heating, modern showers and a/c and are decorated with artistic photos of Priego sights. Downstairs there's an attractive patio, azulejos and a cheery songbird, as well as a cheap and satisfying restaurant. Recommended.

€ La Posada Real
C Real 14, T957-541910, www.laposadareal.com.
This *casa rural* on a mazy Barrio de la Villa street offers a most hospitable welcome, cosy rooms with balcony that feel underpriced, and sweet patio breakfasts. You can also rent the whole house out for up to 6 people.

Restaurants

See also Hostal Rafi, above, which is a convivial spot for cheap, tasty food.

€€ Balcón del Adarve
Paseo de Colombia 36, T957-547075, www.balcondeladarve.com.
The best place to eat in Priego, this restaurant sits on the edge of the escarpment and has a fabulous terrace perched on the cliffside with great views. You can eat in the bar area or downstairs in the elegant dining room too; the cuisine is typically Córdoban, with tasty cuts of meat, delicious partridge pâté and good wines.

€ El Virrey
C Solana 14, T957-541323.
A local favourite, this central spot buzzes with chatter on weekend evenings. It's famous hereabouts for its potatoes, particularly *patatas con bacalao*, a warming mash of spuds and salt cod.

Transport

Bus

Priego's bus station is inconveniently located on the main road, a 20-min hike from the old town. Local bus No 1 runs from here to Plaza de la Constitución.

From Córdoba, **Autocares Carrera** (www.autocarescarrera.es) run to **Priego**. Check their website for timetables.

As well as Córdoba buses, there are 2-4 buses daily to **Granada** and several links to **Lucena**, **Cabra**, **Baena** and other southern Cordoban towns. 2 daily buses go to **Alcalá la Real** in Jaén province, from where you can continue to **Montefrío**.

Granada

a spectacular and mountainous province

The last outpost of Moorish Spain, Granada city's main attraction and Andalucía's most famous sight, the palace and fortress complex of the Alhambra, is simply magnificent. But Granada the city is no one-hit wonder.

You could happily spend weeks pursuing the spirit of Federico García Lorca, one of Spain's greatest poets, pacing the streets of the Moorish Albayzín district, investigating Renaissance buildings and enjoying the free tapas in the city's bars.

Overlooking the city is the lofty Sierra Nevada, offering year-round outdoor activities. Mulhacén, the peninsula's highest peak, can be climbed in summer, and in winter there's decent skiing. On the south side, the range drops into the Alpujarra, with great hiking between charmingly compact villages.

Further south is the Costa Tropical, with the beachside towns of Almuñécar and Salobreña making tempting stops.

East of Granada is Guadix, whose inhabitants still live in caves, while La Calahorra has one of Andalucía's most memorable castles.

Best for
Architecture ■ Skiing ■ Tapas ■ Walking

Footprint picks

★ **The Alhambra**, page 306

The Moorish palace of the Alhambra is set against a stunning backdrop of the Sierra Nevada.

★ **Federico García Lorca**, page 326

Read some of Lorca's poems, visit the site where he was murdered, then compose your thoughts by the Fountain of Tears.

★ **Ferreirola**, page 352

Dine on fresh trout in Ferreirola, one of many enticing Alpujarran villages, after a day's walking in this area.

★ **Cave dwelling**, page 363

Satisfy your prehistoric urges in one of Guadix's troglodyte hotels.

★ **La Calahorra**, page 365

Visit the dramatic castle, outwardly desolate-looking yet elaborately decorated on the inside.

★ **Alhama**, page 375

Have a night time soak in the hot springs.

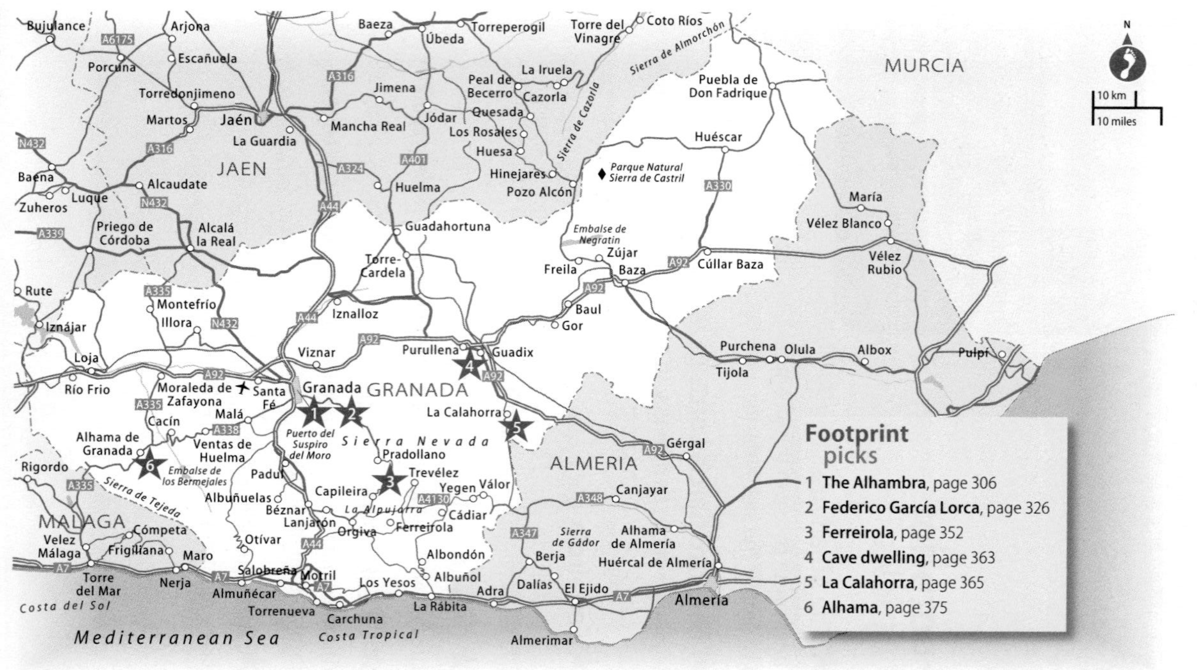

MURCIA
JAEN
GRANADA
ALMERIA
MALAGA
Mediterranean Sea
Costa Tropical
Costa del Sol
N
10 km
10 miles
Sierra de Cazorla
Sierra de Almorchón
Parque Natural Sierra de Castril
Embalse de Negratín
Sierra Nevada
La Alpujarra
Sierra de Gádor
Sierra de Tejeda
Embalse de los Bermejales
Puerto del Suspiro del Moro
Bujalance
Arjona
Escañuela
Porcuna
Torredonjimeno
Martos
Jaén
La Guardia
Baena
Luque
Zuheros
Alcaudate
Priego de Córdoba
Alcalá la Real
Rute
Iznájar
Montefrío
Illora
Loja
Río Frio
Baeza
Úbeda
Torreperogil
Jimena
Mancha Real
Jódar
Peal de Becerro
La Iruela
Cazorla
Quesada
Los Rosales
Huesa
Hinejares
Pozo Alcón
Huelma
Torre del Vinagre
Coto Ríos
Puebla de Don Fadrique
Huéscar
María
Vélez Blanco
Vélez Rubio
Guadahortuna
Torre-Cardela
Iznalloz
Freila
Zújar
Baza
Cúllar Baza
Baul
Gor
Purullena
Guadix
Víznar
Purchena
Olula
Albox
Pulpí
Tijola
Granada
Moraleda de Zafayona
Santa Fé
Malá
Cacín
Alhama de Granada
Ventas de Huelma
Rigordo
La Calahorra
Pradollano
Trevélez
Capileira
Padul
Albuñuelas
Yegen
Válor
Cádiar
Béznar
Lanjarón
Orgiva
Ferreirola
Gérgal
Canjayar
Alhama de Almería
Huércal de Almería
Cómpeta
Velez Málaga
Frigiliana
Maro
Otívar
Albondón
Berja
Torre del Mar
Nerja
Salobreña
Motril
Los Yesos
Albuñol
Dalías
El Ejido
Almuñécar
Torrenueva
Carchuna
La Rábita
Adra
Almería
Almerimar
A6175
A316
N432
A324
A401
A44
A330
A339
A335
A92
A338
A4130
A348
A347
A7
Footprint picks
1 The Alhambra, page 306
2 Federico García Lorca, page 326
3 Ferreirola, page 352
4 Cave dwelling, page 363
5 La Calahorra, page 365
6 Alhama, page 375

Granada city

Most of the popular Western images of Moorish culture – courtyards with delicate fountains, archways sensuously sculpted with arabesques, secluded galleries once paced by viziers and concubines – owe much to the Alhambra, which stands above the city of Granada like a fairyland that might only be accessed by stepping through a wardrobe or by the caprice of a djinn.

It's a place that imposes itself on the visitor's psyche; as well as time spent within its walls, the wanderer in Granada's streets is constantly confronted with a new and unexpectedly sublime view of the fortress and palace, backed (if the weather favours you) by the ridges of the Sierra Nevada. The Alhambra imbues Granada with a tangible romance that this traditionally reactionary city would otherwise struggle to attain.

But while *granadinos* are complaining about the new North African 'invasion', visitors pace the hilltop streets of the Albayzín, discovering atmospheric remnants of Muslim hegemony and Christian conquest. Further into the city, which is studded with bars that lay on free tapas, is some breathtaking Renaissance and Baroque architecture, the tombs of the Catholic Monarchs, as well as the spirit of Federico García Lorca, a giant of 20th-century literature and victim of the thuggery perpetrated away from the frontline of the Spanish Civil War. *Colour map 5, A3.*

La Alhambra

a magical closed world of Moorish palaces

★*www.alhambradegranada.org, daily 0830-2000 (1800 Nov-Feb; closed Christmas Day and New Year's Day). Ticket office open 0800-1900 (1700 Nov-Feb). You'll be assigned either a morning ticket (up until 1400) or an afternoon ticket, and an additional half-hour period during which you must enter the Nasrid Palace complex (although you can stay there as long as you choose). It's best to buy your ticket in advance at www.alhambra-tickets.es, or at the La Caixa bank – visit any Spanish branch (Mon-Fri 0830-1400) or T902-888001 from within Spain or T+34-934-923750 from abroad. Choose the day and time you wish to visit, and then pick up your tickets from any La Caixa cash machine (full-price tickets and kids' tickets only), from the machines at the Alhambra ticket office or from the ticket office itself, though expect to queue. If you just turn up at the ticket office, there are long queues, which you can bypass by buying entry at the machines (€1 extra). Expect long waits until your entry slot or a 'come back tomorrow' in busy periods. Tickets cost €14, with a surcharge of €1.40 for prebooking. Seniors and students €9, 12-15 year-olds and disabled visitors €8, under-12s free. If you want to visit the public areas of the Alhambra as well as the extensive gardens around the Generalife, this costs €7.*

Night visits, Mar-Oct Tue-Sat 2200-2330 (ticket office open 2130-2230), Nov-Feb Fri-Sat 2000-2130 (tickets 1930-2030) can be booked in the same way as other tickets and cost the same, or €8 for just the Nasrid Palace complex. If the moon is up and shining into the courtyards, this is an unforgettable experience.

There's not a lot of information posted about the place, so you may want to consider the audio guide for €3 (though it seems to clash with full appreciation of the palace). The official guidebook is €6 in a variety of languages at the ticket office shop. In the ticket office is also a tourist information kiosk. For the disabled, there is an established route that avoids stairs and takes in as much as possible; the ticket office will supply a map and advice.

The approach

Bus and car It's a fabulous experience to walk up to the palace, but a day at the Alhambra is hard on the feet, so you may well want to ascend on wheels. By far the easiest way to do this is to catch the C3 bus from Plaza Isabel la Católica, which zips up the hill every five minutes or so. If you're thinking of driving, it's likely to take you longer to get to the Alhambra than on foot, but there are two ways; a serpentine route that ascends from off Calle Molinos, or a purpose-built back road that leaves the Ronda Sur bypass, which in turn comes off the *circunvalación* which circles the north and west of the city. It's well signposted; if arriving from outside town, don't leave the bypass until you see the Alhambra signs. Depending on how busy the car parks are, you may have to park a fair walk away from the entrance.

On foot If you are walking up, it's a steepish climb. Most visitors ascend via the Cuesta de Gomérez from the Plaza Nueva; here a different ascent is suggested, and the Cuesta can be used for the return trip.

At one end of Plaza Nueva is the Church of Santa Ana. Keeping it on your right, follow the course of the river along a cobbled street (this walk is detailed on page 317). The Alhambra will soon become visible above you to your right. Reaching the end of the café-lined promenade known as Paseo de los Tristes, turn right and cross the bridge. From here a pretty path called Cuesta del Rey Chico (also known as Cuesta de los Chinos) ascends gently directly to the Alhambra. It's a fine little walk: after passing under the mighty bridge leading to the Generalife, you emerge alongside a restaurant; turn left and you'll be at the ticket office.

If you've pre-purchased your ticket and your entry slot for the Nasrid Palace is a long way off, it's a good idea to head for the Generalife (see page 316) first, before returning to the main centre of the Alhambra. If it is fairly soon, head directly towards the Alcazaba and the principal buildings. That route is followed here.

Follow the signs for the Alcazaba and Palacios Nazaríes. Passing through the checkpoint, you descend the main street of the Alhambra complex, the Calle Real. This used to be the heart of the Moorish town within the Alhambra, and the location of the main mosque and the Baños del Polinario, or public baths. The baths are still in good shape; go in and admire their brickwork and horseshoe arches. There's some stucco work preserved, but best are the typical star-shaped holes in the ceiling. In this building, which was also once a tavern, is a small museum dedicated to the Granadan composer Angel Barrios. Next door, where the mosque once stood, is the early 17th-century church of Santa María, even more out of place here than the Palace of Carlos V, which is the next building.

Essential Granada

Getting around

Walking is the best option for getting about, but Granada is a hilly place so you may want to use public transport. Tired feet will love buses C3 and C4, which ascend from Plaza Isabel la Católica to the Alhambra. Bus C1 does a circuit from Calle Reyes Católicos around the Albayzín, while C2 heads into Sacromonte. The LAC line runs long buses on a high-density loop around the centre of town; all other buses are routed to connect with it at some point, so cross-city journeys typically involve catching the LAC then transferring (free) to another bus, or vice versa. A ticket on a local bus costs €1.20. An online journey planner in Spanish is at www.transportesrober.com. Taxis are also readily available and cheap.

Best places to stay

Carmen de la Alcubilla del Caracol, page 330
Cuevas El Abanico, page 330
Casa Morisca, page 330
Hotel Santa Isabel la Real, page 331
Hotel Párragasiete, page 332

When to go

Like most of inland Andalucía, Granada gets powerfully hot in summer. Winters are cold; general visit to the city, spring and autumn are the best periods.

Best tapas bars

Casa Enrique, page 335
La Brujidera, page 335
Bodegas Espadafor, page 335

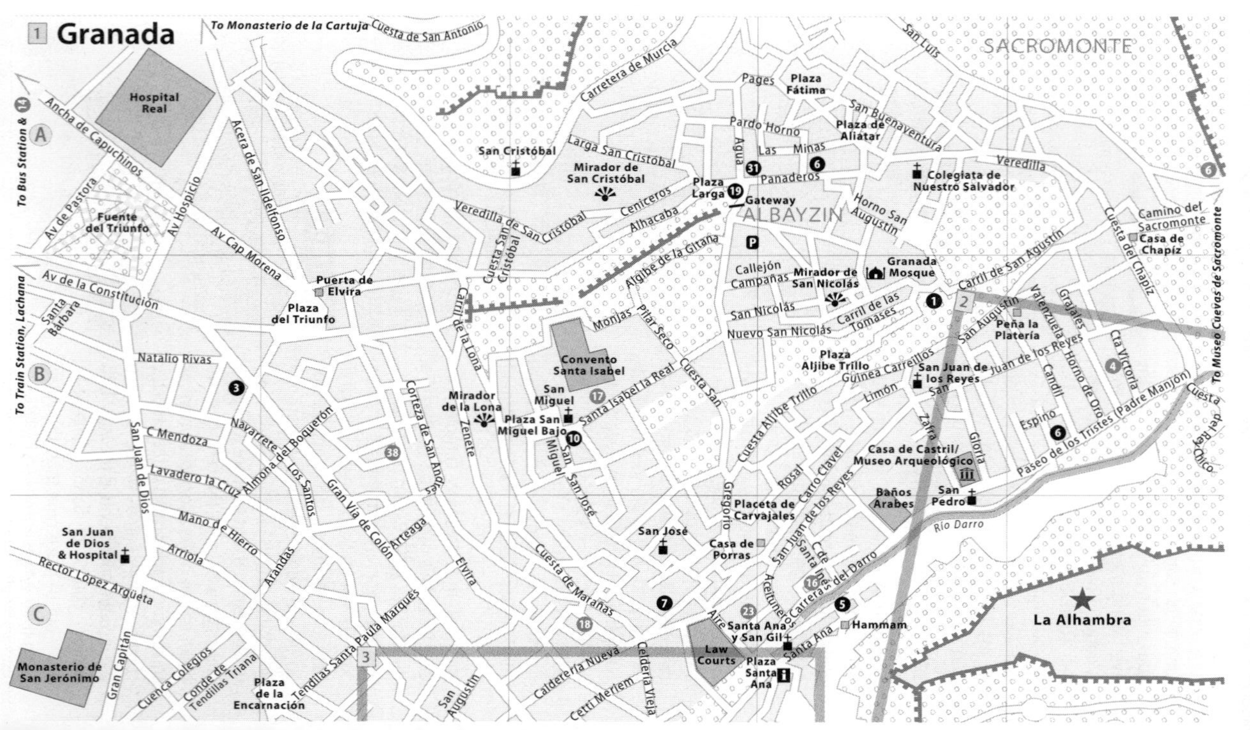
Granada
1
2
3
A
B
C
To Monasterio de la Cartuja
Cuesta de San Antonio
SACROMONTE
ALBAYZIN
La Alhambra
To Museo Cuevas de Sacromonte
To Bus Station & 14
To Train Station, Lachana
Hospital Real
Fuente del Triunfo
Plaza del Triunfo
Puerta de Elvira
San Cristóbal
Mirador de San Cristóbal
Plaza Larga
Gateway
Plaza Fátima
Plaza de Aliatar
Colegiata de Nuestro Salvador
Granada Mosque
Mirador de San Nicolás
Callejón Campanas
Convento Santa Isabel
San Miguel
Plaza San Miguel Bajo
Mirador de la Lona
Plaza Aljibe Trillo
San Juan de los Reyes
Peña la Platería
Casa de Chapiz
Casa de Castril/ Museo Arqueológico
San Pedro
Baños Arabes
Hammam
Placeta de Carvajales
Casa de Porras
San José
Santa Ana y San Gil
Plaza Santa Ana
Law Courts
Plaza de la Encarnación
San Juan de Dios & Hospital
Monasterio de San Jerónimo
Río Darro
Ancha de Capuchinos
Av de Pastora
Av Hospicio
Av de la Constitución
Av Cap Morena
Acera de San Ildelfonso
Santa Bárbara
Natalio Rivas
C Mendoza
Lavadero la Cruz
Mano de Hierro
Arriola
San Juan de Dios
Rector López Argüeta
Gran Capitán
Cuenca Colegios
Conde de Tendillas Triana
Tendilas Santa Paula Marqués
Arandas
Almona del Boquerón
Navarrete
Los Santos
Gran Vía de Colón
Corteza de San Andrés
Elvira
Arteaga
Zenete
Carril de la Lona
Cuesta San Cristóbal
Veredilla de San Cristóbal
Larga San Cristóbal
Carretera de Murcia
Ceniceros
Alhacaba
Aljibe de la Gitana
Monjas
Pilar Seco
Cuesta San
Santa Isabel la Real
San Miguel
San José
Cuesta de Marañas
Caldería Nueva
Cetti Meriem
Caldería Vieja
San Augustín
Agua
Pardo Horno
Pages
Las Minas
Panaderos
San Buenaventura
San Luis
Veredilla
Horno San Augustín
Carril de las Tomasas
San Nicolás
Nuevo San Nicolás
Cuesta Aljibe Trillo
Guinea Carreillos
Limón
Zafra
Gloria
Rosal
Carro Clavel
San Juan de los Reyes
C de Santa Inés
Carrera del Darro
Aceituneros
Aire
Santa Ana
Gregorio
Carril de San Agustín
San Augustín
Valenzuela
Grajales
Horno de Oro
Candil
Espino
Cta Victoria
Juan de los Reyes
Cuesta del Chapiz
Camino del Sacromonte
Paseo de los Tristes (Padre Manjón)
Cuesta del Rey Chico

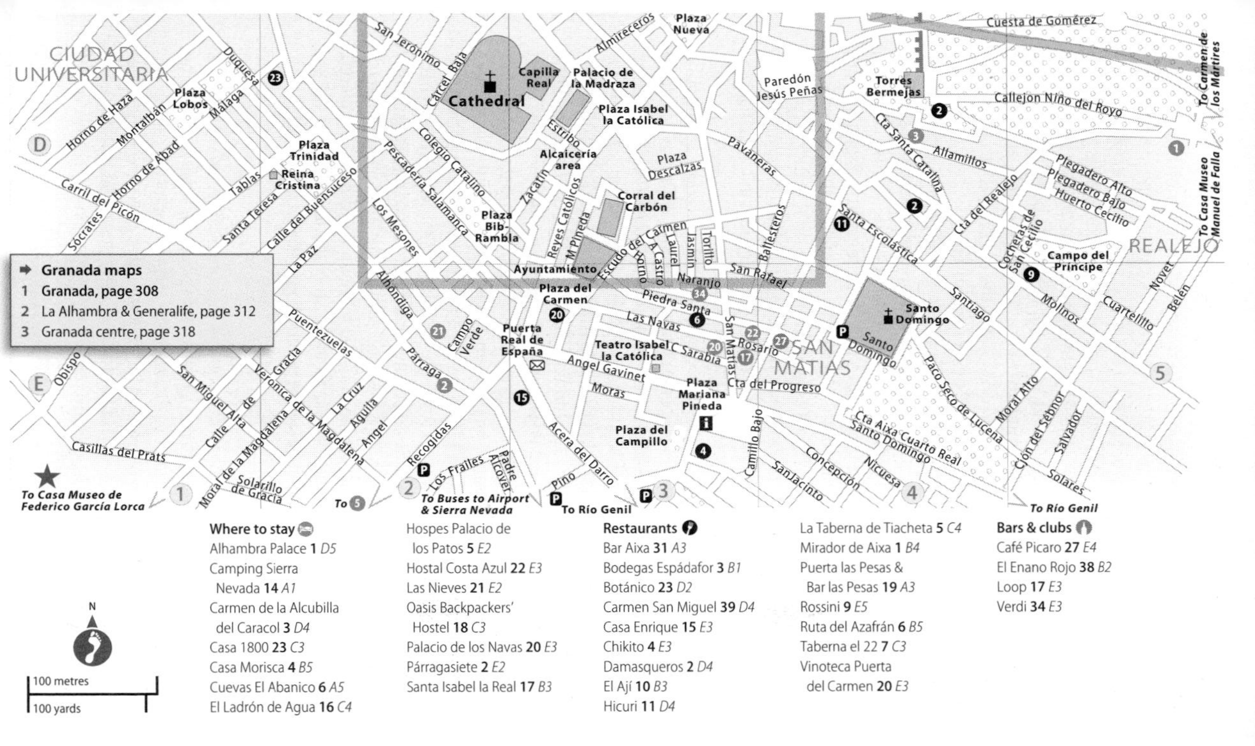

Where to stay

Alhambra Palace **1** *D5*
Camping Sierra Nevada **14** *A1*
Carmen de la Alcubilla del Caracol **3** *D4*
Casa 1800 **23** *C3*
Casa Morisca **4** *B5*
Cuevas El Abanico **6** *A5*
El Ladrón de Agua **16** *C4*
Hospes Palacio de los Patos **5** *E2*
Hostal Costa Azul **22** *E3*
Las Nieves **21** *E2*
Oasis Backpackers' Hostel **18** *C3*
Palacio de los Navas **20** *E3*
Párragasiete **2** *E2*
Santa Isabel la Real **17** *B3*

Restaurants

Bar Aixa **31** *A3*
Bodegas Espádafor **3** *B1*
Botánico **23** *D2*
Carmen San Miguel **39** *D4*
Casa Enrique **15** *E3*
Chikito **4** *E3*
Damasqueros **2** *D4*
El Ají **10** *B3*
Hicuri **11** *D4*
La Taberna de Tiacheta **5** *C4*
Mirador de Aixa **1** *B4*
Puerta las Pesas & Bar las Pesas **19** *A3*
Rossini **9** *E5*
Ruta del Azafrán **6** *B5*
Taberna el 22 **7** *C3*
Vinoteca Puerta del Carmen **20** *E3*

Bars & clubs

Café Picaro **27** *E4*
El Enano Rojo **38** *B2*
Loop **17** *E3*
Verdi **34** *E3*

Palacio de Carlos V

Many words have been written in prosecution and defence of this building, unmistakeable with its massive modern-looking blocks of stone studded with huge rings held in the mouths of lions and eagles. As a Renaissance building in its own right, it has several striking features. The core of most complaints is its heavy-handedness in comparison with the delicate dignity of the Muslim palace, part of which was demolished to accommodate it. But it's easy to be tough on Carlos; he liked the Nasrid Palace well enough to use it as his own quarters, and if he had simply built his palace over the Nasrid one, as was the custom of both Moors and Christians in those days, the issue would never have arisen.

The palace was never finished in Carlos's lifetime – indeed the roof went on only in the 20th century. Construction had been funded by taxes raised from the Moriscos – the nominally converted descendants of the Moors – but with their major rebellion in 1568, it ground to a halt. What remains is impressive, but definitely grandiose rather than subtle. The southern portal is supported on Ionic columns and has figures of Victory, Fame and Fertility over the door, as well as panels with mythological scenes and the arms of Carlos V. This contrasts with the western Doric entrance, with escutcheons carved with Hercules and Atlas flanking the arms of Felipe II; below are scenes of the battle of Pavia.

Most of the building is taken up by the circular central courtyard, an imposing space with superb acoustics; try whispering from the centre. While the octagonal chapel features temporary exhibitions, most of the rooms of the palace are taken up by the **Museo de la Alhambra** ⓘ *Wed-Sat 0830-1800 or 2000, Tue and Sun 0830-1400 or 1430, free with Alhambra ticket*, and **de Bellas Artes** ⓘ *Tue-Sat 1000-1700 summer, 1000-1800 winter, 1000-2030 spring and autumn, Sun 1000-1700; EU citizens free, others €1.50*. The former, on the ground floor, describes itself as having 'the world's best collection of Nasrid art'; not such an impressive claim considering that the Nasrids were purely a Granadan dynasty. The museum, though, is well worth a visit. There are many tiled and stuccoed panels from the site itself, as well as the fine painted Jar of the Gazelles, a 15th-century urn 1.5 m high. The Fine Arts museum upstairs has a collection of works from Granadine artists and some fine religious pieces, especially sculptures by Diego de Siloé, Alonso Cano and Pedro de Mena. An enamel triptych from Limoges features El Gran Capitán, but the museum is unfortunately placed; it's hard to resist the call of the Alhambra's many other attractions. There's also a reasonable book and souvenir shop on the ground floor of the building.

La Alcazaba

From the Palacio de Carlos V, head through the monumental gateway known as the Puerta del Vino – for it was used in Christian times to store wine – to the large open space in front of the Alcazaba. La Alcazaba, the fortress part of the compound, is muscular, unashamedly functional and highly impressive. Older than the rest of the buildings on the site, much of its finer features were destroyed by Napoleon's troops in the Peninsular War. Its effective defensive design is immediately evident upon entering, as you are forced to walk along a narrow passageway overlooked by high towers. Climb the one at the corner, the **Torre del Homenaje** (Tower of

BACKGROUND

Alhambra

Of all Spain's tens of thousands of historical monuments, the Alhambra stands supreme. The final manifestation of the doomed Moorish civilization in the peninsula, its history also mirrors that of Spain in the succeeding six centuries. Taken by Fernando and Isabel in a surge that culminated in Catholic Spain ruling vast tracts of Europe and the New World, it, like the country, eventually fell into dereliction and then use as a barracks in the war-torn 19th century. Rediscovered by Romantic travellers, it is now one of Europe's most-visited destinations, with over two million visitors annually.

The defensible hills were the principal reason why the Zirid rulers moved their town from nearby Elvira to Granada in the early 11th century. A natural fortress, the Sabika hill on which the Alhambra stands had previously been used by the Romans and Visigoths, but only a few remnants have been found from those eras. The Zirids fortified the hill, although their main palace was on the facing Albayzín. The Alhambra as we see it today was principally a construction of the later Nasrid dynasty, who rose to power in the 1230s and established the hill as their seat of power. The Nasrids ruled Granada until 1492 and are responsible for most of the many buildings that form the Alhambra complex. Of these, their royal palace complex is what inspires visitors with the most awe. After Boabdil surrendered the city and fortress to the Catholic Monarchs, many modifications were made to the existing structures, and several new edifices were thrown up, not least of which is the bulky Renaissance Palacio de Carlos V. The name Alhambra is from the Arabic *al-qalat al-hamra*, meaning the red fort, perhaps from the colour of the sandstone, especially in the setting sun.

Homage), for views, before crossing the large central courtyard. This was once covered with dwellings housing the soldiers who defended the complex. The high **Torre de la Vela** (watchtower) looms large over the city and has a spectacular panorama. Directly across from you is the hill of the Albayzín with its flood of white houses, while to the left stretches the modern city. Turning further to the left, you can see an earlier fortification on the next hill; these are the **Torres Bermejas** (Vermilion Towers). They're actually more of a light orange in colour if you walk to them; you can't enter, but there's a good restaurant at the base. The large orange castellated affair further along the ridge is the Alhambra Palace hotel. On 2 January, the Torre de la Vela is filled with *granadinos* queuing to have a go at ringing the bell; if a single woman does so, it's said that she'll be engaged within the year. You exit the Alcazaba through a long formal garden. In the centre of it is a fountain that used to stand atop the fountain in the Court of Lions in the Nasrid Palace.

Palacios Nazaríes

No matter what alterations and restructuring have taken place, even though the original bright colours have completely faded away, this ensemble of Moorish palaces is one of staggering architectural and artistic achievement. Many visitors are left in a sort of amazed incomprehension after passing through the elaborate patios and halls.

To move beyond this, it is helpful to have some understanding of Islamic architectural principles. While it is untrue that Islam prohibits the depiction of human or animal figures (although at certain periods prevailing fundamentalism has certainly discouraged it), they are not a common decorative theme; vegetal and geometric motifs form the bulk of the decoration. Perhaps the fundamental principle of the Alhambra is that of levels, or hierarchy. As certain chambers within the building are clearly attributable by size and ornateness to different strata of

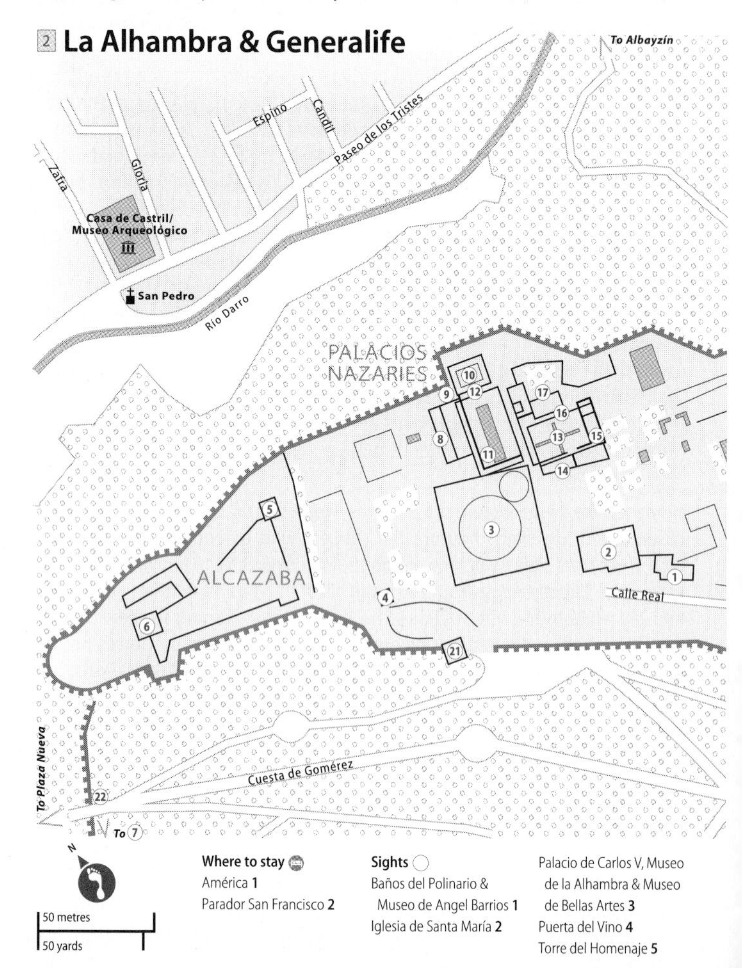

the royal entourage, so the decoration of each room follows this theme. Small and intricate pieces of pattern join to form a larger design; as our focus widens, the design widens with it. A tiny *mocárab* or tiled motif, perfect in itself, becomes merely a star in an entire firmament. This has clear theological overtones, and the message is reinforced by the Arabic phrases repeated over and over around rooms and by visionary poems that clearly describe the Alhambra as a small jewel reflecting the unimaginable grandeur of Allah.

The palaces are entered through the **Mexuar**, still a fine space although much meddled with by both the Nasrid rulers and then the Catholic Monarchs, who

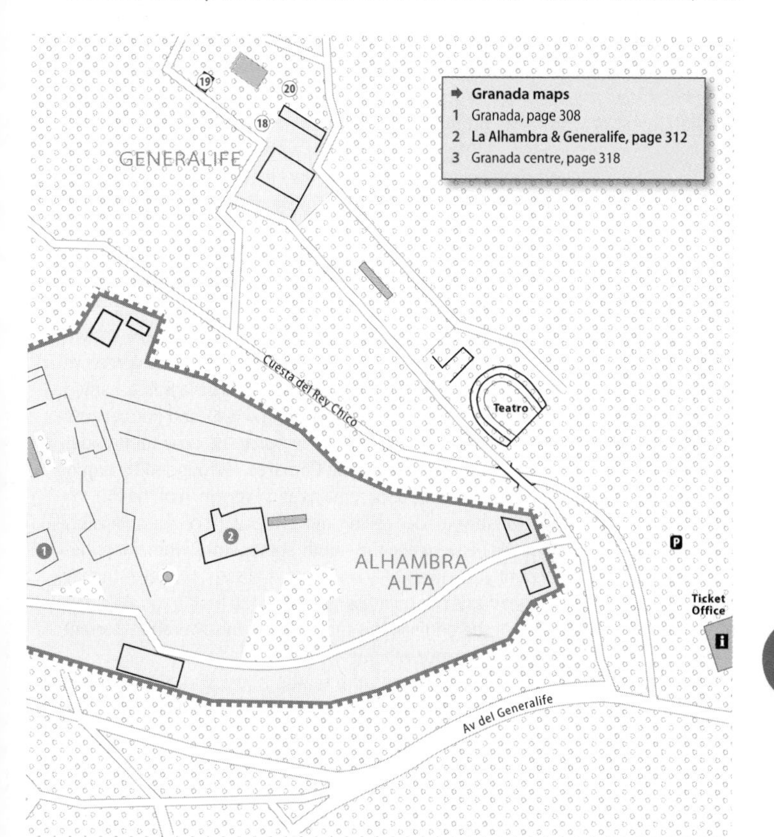

Torre de la Vela **6**
Torres Bermejas **7**
Mexuar **8**
Patio del Cuarto Dorado **9**
Salón de Comares **10**
Patio de los Arrayanes **11**
Sala de la Barca **12**
Patio de los Leones **13**
Sala de los Abencerrajes **14**
Sala de los Reyes **15**
Sala de Dos Hermanas **16**
Mirador de Lindaraja **17**
Patio de la Acequia **18**
Sala Regia **19**
Patio de los Cipreses **20**
Torre de la Justicia **21**
Puerta de las Granadas **22**

converted what was once a reception hall into a chapel. Despite this, you'll notice several features that recur throughout the building. The ceramic dado decorated with coloured polygons is typical, as is the inlaid wooden ceiling (restored) and the arches with their *mocárabes* (concave depressions forming an array of icicle-like points). The capitals of the columns are particularly fine and preserve much original colour. The gallery was put in when the conversion to chapel took place. Beyond the hall is an angled prayer-room with a *mihrab* accurately aligned towards Mecca and windows looking over the Albayzín.

You'll soon arrive at a small courtyard with a fountain, known as the **Patio del Cuarto Dorado**. The northern arcade has impressive stucco and arabesques, while the room off here has a gilt wooden ceiling put in by the Catholic Monarchs. However, the space is dominated by the high façade of the **Salón de Comares**, constructed around 1370. Under its elegant wooden eaves is amazingly intricate decoration, all of which was brightly coloured until as recently as the mid-19th century. Going through this façade, we are faced not with an equally monumental hallway, but with a cramped space with small corridors leading off it. The Nasrids knew that, amid all this earthly delight, their days were numbered, and defence remained an important consideration.

Twisting through to your left, you emerge in the **Patio de los Arrayanes** (Court of the Myrtles), centred on a large pool of water that seems to have been designed to exactly fit the reflections of the two large façades at either end of it. Both of these rest on a portico of seven round arches topped with perforated plasterwork known as *sebka*. The porticos end in alcoves richly adorned with *mocárabes*, which preserve some blue colouring. On the near side, you pass through the **Sala de la Barca**, named for the Arabic inscription *baraka*, or blessing, that adorns the wall (and not because the restored 20th-century ceiling resembles a boat, or *barca*, as some tour guides solicitously point out), and into the high **Salón de Comares**, surrounded by highly adorned alcoves. Part of the gilt ceramic floor remains and every inch of the room is intricately decorated. Gaze on the wooden ceiling and its hierarchy of stars, plausibly claimed to represent the seven heavens and the eighth, at the centre, wherein resides Allah. Although on first count you'll likely only see six rows of stars, the seventh may become clear before you get dizzy. The ceiling is reconstructed from fragments, but has recaptured the impact of the original. It is thought that this was an important state room where the Nasrid rulers received guests.

At the other end of the Court of Myrtles, the façade is just that, since Charles V knocked down that part of the palace to park his own construction alongside. So after examining the other chambers around the court, head through into the most-photographed part of the ensemble, the **Patio de los Leones**, or Court of Lions. Here the grace of the Moorish design reaches new heights. Framing the central fountain propped up by 12 lovable kings of beasts is a fantasy of stonework. Two pavilions supported by the slenderest of columns and most delicate of arches face each other across the courtyard, the whole of which is framed by an elegant colonnade. Stop and linger, then move anti-clockwise around the courtyard. On the first of the long sides is the **Sala de los Abencerrajes**, graced by a cupola of *mocárabes*. It was here that Boabdil was supposed to have had the leading

BACKGROUND

Granada

The site of Granada was originally settled in the first millennium BC, when it was an Iberian hilltop town known as Elybirge. Taken over by the Romans, who named it Illiberis, it grew in importance during the Visigothic period; at this time a Jewish district known as **Garnatha Alheyud** was established on the southern slopes of the Alhambra hill.

After the Moors took control, the town's name became Elvira, based on nearby hills, and the Jewish part **Garnata**; the latter name has persisted. It was under the control of the caliphate of Córdoba, and then became the capital of an important *taifa* state. As the Christians advanced into Andalucía, taking cities such as Córdoba and Sevilla, there was a huge influx of Muslim refugees to Granada, where the nobleman Mohammed Ibn-Yusuf Ibn-Nasr had set himself up as ruler here in 1237, giving his name to the Nasrid dynasty. With the Christians in such bullish mood, it was decided to construct a bigger and better fortification on the hill opposite the Albayzín; its reddish hue led to its name, **Al-Qalat Al-Hamra**, or the red fort. Most of what we see in the Alhambra today was built during the reigns of Yusuf I (1334-1354) and Mohammed V (1354-1391), at which time the city was very prosperous. The Granada emirate was effectively a vassal state of the Christian kingdoms surviving by paying tribute. Once Fernando and Isabel set their sights on conquering it, the city was doomed to fall. After dynastic strife and vacillations that rendered the Moors' last days more comedy than a tragedy, the last emir of Granada, Boabdil, surrendered the keys of the city to the Catholic Monarchs on New Year's Day in 1492 after a siege. The immediate expulsion of the nation's Jews hit Granada hard, and once the Moors and Moriscos had followed, the city had lost vital segments of its population.

The city prospered somewhat with the new American trade routes, and a number of Renaissance and Baroque monuments were erected, but Granada was gradually becoming a provincial backwater. The Peninsular War hit the city especially hard, with French troops heavily damaging the Alhambra while using it as a barracks. It was in this decaying atmosphere that Washington Irving and others visited, raising awareness of the Moorish majesty of the city that has made it enduringly popular with visitors ever since. The 19th century also saw a number of questionable urban projects, such as the covering of the river and the bulldozing of the Gran Vía through part of the old town.

In the early part of the 20th century, Granada had a full-scale cultural revival, with the poet Federico García Lorca and the composer Manuel de Falla prominent and active in promoting Andalucían heritage. This came to an abrupt end. Although Granada had been an actively liberal city early in the 19th century, it was steadfastly nationalist by the time the Civil War came along, and the local fascists slaughtered thousands of moderates and left-wingers, including Lorca.

members of the Abencerraje family murdered one by one; the proof is the 'blood stains' in the fountain.

At the far end of the Court of Lions is the **Sala de los Reyes**, whose alcoves feature a range of paintings on sheepskin, depicting in contrast with the rest of the palace, portraits of seated rulers and a range of knightly scenes. They bear clear Christian influences and some scholars feel that they must have been painted by Italian artists resident in the Nasrid city.

The next chamber, the **Sala de Dos Hermanas** has another grand cupola similar to that of the **Sala de los Abencerrajes** opposite. The adjoining **Sala de los Ajimeces** has perhaps the most romantic of the Alhambra's lookouts, the **Mirador de Lindaraja**, from the original Arabic meaning eyes of Aixa's house (Aixa was the mother of the last Moorish ruler Boabdil). Originally it would have looked over a garden and beyond to the city. The tiny chamber is as perfect as anything here, with its dado of coloured tiles, stucco work and ceiling embedded with stained glass.

Beyond here, the **Imperial chambers** were built as the residence of Carlos V; Washington Irving stayed in a room off here. There are more excellent views over the Albayzín from here; you descend and exit through a pair of patios, off one of which are the original Moorish baths, again with star-shaped skylights for steam to exit.

After exiting, and even though you may well be overwhelmed by stuccoed splendour, keep going ahead and to your left to examine two more small buildings, the **Palacio del Pórtico**, a small, earlier palace fronted by an elegant pool, and next to it, a sublime little oratory with an elaborate *mihrab*.

Generalife

Retracing your steps towards the ticket office, follow the signs for the Generalife. Although it could be an insurance company, the name of this summer palace separated from the bulk of the Alhambra's buildings is usually accepted to mean 'the gardens of the master builder'. It is indeed surrounded by gardens, but these were mostly planted in the 19th and 20th centuries and perhaps bear little resemblance to the original Moorish design. The walk to the Generalife is down a grove of cypress and jasmine; the building is entered through a controversially renovated doorway marked with the symbol of the key of Allah. Passing through a courtyard, you emerge into the **Patio de la Acequia**, an extensive space marked by an array of criss-cross water jets that sprinkle into a long pool. The belvedere, which gives fine views, was a Christian addition, such openness being anathema to the Moors, who preferred to look out only from the small mirador halfway along, decorated with 14th-century stucco. A herb garden along the pool scents the air. At the end of the patio is the **Sala Regia**, or royal hall, accessed via a five-arched portico. The hall is small but well proportioned, with fine *mocárabes* on the capitals and cornice and a small delicate mirador. The repeated inscription reads "There is one and only one conqueror, and that is Allah". The top floor was added by the Catholic Monarchs; from it there are views of the Albayzín and the caves of Sacromonte, but to reach it you first pass through the **Patio de los Cipreses** (Court of the Cypresses). This was once a place to bathe, and the tree is said to have borne witness to the seduction of the luckless Boabdil's wife by a noble of the Abencerraje family, an indiscretion that may have led to the massacre of the clan.

After visiting the top floor, ascend to the upper gardens by way of the water staircase, which has a stream flowing down the banisters, yet another example of Moorish hydrological genius. This garden is full of squirrels, who are keenly watched by the Alhambra's vast population of semi-feral cats.

Leaving the Alhambra

When you're ready to leave the Alhambra, walk back to the courtyard in front of the Alcazaba and turn left to descend through the **Torre de la Justicia** (Gate of Justice), the most impressive of the Alhambra's remaining gateways. Turn as you pass through it and note the Islamic motifs of the key and the hand engraved on the outside. Washington Irving was told that on the day the hand reached down to grasp the key, the Alhambra would crumble to dust and the buried gold of the Moors would be revealed. Below here is an ornate fountain from the time of Carlos V, with three grotesque heads and pomegranate symbols. Descend from here down an avenue lined with elms planted by the Duke of Wellington to the **Puerta de las Granadas**, or Gate of the Pomegranates. From here the Cuesta de Gomérez descends to Plaza Nueva.

Plaza Nueva to Sacromonte

a great walk along the Darro, with spectacular Alhambra views

The Darro is one of Granada's two rivers, but is usually no more than a mountain stream, although it's a mouse that occasionally roars and floods the Albayzín and Sacromonte. It actually flows through much of central Granada but its course has been gradually paved over. You can see it emerge from its tunnel to merge with the larger Río Genil at Puente Blanco, at the end of Acera del Darro. It enters the tunnel just off Plaza Nueva and you can follow its course upstream from here. (Alternatively, you can take bus C2 from Plaza Nueva all the way into Sacromonte.)

Start off in **Plaza Nueva** with its terraced cafés that you're really better off avoiding. On the north side of the plaza is the large building of the law courts. It has a Renaissance patio designed by Diego de Siloé, but you'll probably only get past security if you look like you have a reason to be there.

At the end of the plaza is the church of **Santa Ana y San Gil**, built on the site of a mosque in the early 16th century. The bell tower that peers over the river features fine *mudéjar* tilework, while the doorway (you can discern the bricked-in entrance of the original mosque) is flanked by stately cypresses. If you can get in (it opens for the 1830 mass at around 1800) you'll be struck by the ornate Baroque side chapels and wooden ceiling. The church is crowded with sculpture and paintings, particularly around the gallery. An arch, no doubt part of the original structure, separates the chancel from the nave.

Follow the Darro, leaving the church on your right. Passing picturesque stone bridges, this is one of Granada's nicest walks, and is well stocked with tapas bars.

In its heyday, Granada would have had dozens of bathhouses in the Albayzín, but the **Baños Arabes** ⓘ *Cra del Darro 31, T958-229738, summer daily 0930-1430, 1700-2100, winter 1000-1700, entry free at time of research but due to be charged,* is the only one that retains more than fragments. Many tourists pass by the understated façade; make sure you visit during your stay. While the baths were used as a communal laundry in the 19th century, they became a private residence. After passing through a patio, you enter the baths, which are extraordinarily well preserved. It's a place of marvellous peace with its star-shaped air vents in the ceiling admitting a delicate light. It was open to men and women on alternate days. The Catholic Monarchs shut down the bathhouses pretty rapidly when they took Granada; they were appalled at the unhealthy idea of washing off the protective coating of filth that coated Christians at the time (Isabel claimed to only have washed twice in her life; that was twice more than many people, one suspects); they also feared (more understandably) that the bathhouses would become centres of sedition and plots.

A little beyond the baths, the river is spanned by the remains of a horseshoe arch that once formed part of the Alhambra's fortifications.

Granada's **Museo Arqueológico** ⓘ *Cra del Darro 43, closed for renovations at time of research but hoped to open in 2015 or 2016,* is housed in the Casa de Castril,

a 16th-century mansion with an admirable Plateresque façade that could be a textbook example of the style, with its coats of arms, courtly symbols, shells, beasts and intricate stonework. The collection is strong; many of Andalucía's most interesting prehistoric finds are from caves in this province. There's an ancient fossilized skull of an *elephas meridionalis* mammoth and much material from grave sites, including amazing material from Albuñol, a gold torc and pieces of woven basket that are nearly 6000 years old. Bronze Age pot burials are well displayed, as are a series of alabaster funerary jars originally from Egypt. A bronze astrolabe is the highlight of the Moorish section; dating from 1481, it's a phenomenal piece of craftsmanship and testament to the high-powered scientific tradition of the Muslim world.

The narrow Carrera del Darro widens into the **Paseo de los Tristes**, named because funeral processions used to pass this way en route to the cemetery atop the Alhambra hill. The Alhambra itself looms over it; you can admire it from the terrace of one of the cafés here. Reaching the end of the promenade, you can turn right up the footpath to the Alhambra (see page 306), or left up the hill called the Cuesta del Chapiz. The massive house and gardens on the opposite bank of the river is the **Carmen de los Chapiteles**, once home of El Gran Capitán, the general Gonzalo de Córdoba, and now used for cultural events and conferences.

Ascending the Cuesta, turn right at the Moorish Casa de Chapiz to enter the barrio of **Sacromonte**. Built along a hillside, most of the houses here are caves. Until the 1960s it was home to most of Granada's gypsy population, and a few still live here, though the increasingly fashionable zone is now one of Granada's trendiest and most expensive. There are a number of touristy flamenco shows put on here in the evenings (see Flamenco, page 337). Wandering through the area, you may still be invited into a gypsy cave home, where you'll be treated to a personal flamenco show; you'll be expected to pay heavily.

It's a very picturesque place to stroll in the sun; the homes are all whitewashed; the doors and windows trimmed with blue, and prickly pears stud the hillside. At the top of the district is the **Museo Cuevas del Sacromonte** ⓘ *C Barranco de los Negros s/n, T958-215120, www.sacromontegranada.com, winter 1000-1800, summer 1000-2000, €5*, an ethnographic museum well set out in a series of caves, which is pricey but has some good displays on traditional crafts such as basketwork and weaving. There's also a café and good viewpoint.

El Albayzín

Granada's most fascinating quarter, preserving a significant Islamic feel

The Albayzín (or Albaicín), which rises above the Darro on the opposite bank to the Alhambra, was once the residence of the bulk of the city's population and is filled with Moorish remnants. More than similar quarters in other Andalucían cities, the Albayzín has retained a distinctly Islamic atmosphere. This is partly due to the narrow street plan and whitewashed houses, partly due to the sublime vistas of the Alhambra that open up at unexpected moments, and partly due to the presence of a significant North African population. Moroccan- and Algerian-run craft shops, teahouses and restaurants line the region's lower reaches, while near the top is a mosque.

The best way to ascend to the Albayzín for the first time is from Calle de Elvira, turning up **Calle Caldererîa Nueva**, lined with teahouses and Moroccan shops. At a small square, fork left up the hill following Cuesta San Gregorio. After a short distance, turn right at Calle del Beso (Street of the Kiss) and drop into the small Plaza de Porras.

On this plaza is the 16th-century mansion of **Casa de Porras**, now a cultural centre with art exhibitions. Enter and admire the central patio.

Continuing through the square, you'll come to the **Placeta de Carvajales**, reached by a flight of steps up to your left. This offers a peaceful bench or two to enjoy stunning vistas of the Alcazaba part of the Alhambra. Bookmark the spot as one to come back to at night, when the view is even more memorable.

Leaving the plaza without going down the stairs, turn left, which will bring you back to Cuesta San Gregorio; follow it up the hill to the right. Coming to Plaza Aljibe Trillo, you could take a short detour to your right then left. At the bottom of Calle Limón, look out for the dilapidated church of **San Juan de los Reyes**, with a beautiful ex-minaret with blind arches and delicate tracery. Just beyond, on Calle Zafra, there's a 15th-century Moorish house visible down the slope.

Back in Plaza Aljibe Trillo, follow the *cuesta* of the same name up the hill. Taking your third left, you'll emerge in a square by a church. The **Colegiata de Nuestro Salvador** ⓘ *Mon-Sat 1000-1300, 1630-1830, €1*, was built over the main mosque of the Albayzín in the 16th to 18th centuries. Burned down in the lead-up to the Spanish Civil War, the church is mostly reconstructed and of limited interest apart from a secluded Moorish patio filled with lemon trees and horseshoe arches. It's a simple and likeable space; the strict Almohads who built it in the 12th century had little regard for ornamentation. The other Moorish remnant is the bell tower, transformed from a minaret by Diego de Siloé.

Near here, the **Mirador de San Nicolás** is the most popular spot to sit and enjoy the sun setting on the Alhambra opposite. Despite being crowded with locals and tourists, the views are worth watching, as they are at night, when the complex is floodlit.

Adjacent to the mirador is the **Granada mosque** ⓘ *www.mezquitadegranada.com, gardens open 1000-1400, 1800-2130*, with a formal garden open to the public, and a centre of Islamic studies. The *mihrab* is a replica of that in the Mezquita at Córdoba.

Returning to the Colegiata, follow Calle Panaderos down to the tree-shaded Plaza Larga, a popular locals' hang-out by day but usually deserted at night. There's an impressive Moorish gateway at one end of it. From here head to Plaza San Miguel Bajo. The easy way is through the arch, straight ahead, and take the second right down Camino Nuevo San Nicolás. The hillier route, however, is a better option if you've still got plenty of energy. From Plaza Larga, head straight down the hill, Calle Alhacaba. You'll get a cracking view of the Almohad city walls on your left (the council will one day open a walkway along them, which will be accessed by the gate at the end of Plaza Larga).

ON THE ROAD

The place to be at sunset

Less thronged than the popular Mirador de San Nicolás is one higher up, the Mirador de San Cristóbal, which gives good, if more distant, views of the Alhambra and a spectacular perspective over the city and the mountains that surround it. It's the place to be at sunset.

You can get there by taking a right up Cuesta San Cristóbal as you descend Calle Alhacaba from Plaza Larga. Otherwise follow Cuesta de San Antonio from the Hospital Real (turning right at the crossroads) by following signs for Murcia from the northern part of town, or by catching bus C2 from Gran Vía. Get off at the church of San Cristóbal; the mirador is opposite. The whole of Granada is displayed before you, including the walls of the Albayzínn. Flitting bats are backed by the peaks of the Sierra Nevada. Stunning.

The road eventually leads down to the impressive Puerta de Elvira, which was once the main gateway into the city. Before you've descended the whole way, though, turn left up Carril de la Lona past another gateway (unless sunset is approaching, in which case see box, above). Take the left (steeper) fork and at the top of the hill you'll reach the mirador of La Lona. Turn left to find yourself in **Plaza San Miguel Bajo**.

This is one of the most endearing parts of the Albayzín, a lopsided square lined on one side by chestnut trees. The Diego de Siloé façade of the 16th-century San Miguel church looms over the square; the church preserves its cistern from its early days as a mosque. On the plaza opposite is a *crucero*, Cristo de las Lañas (Christ of the Clamps; after being broken to pieces in the Civil War, he was clamped together and repaired by locals who had guarded the pieces). There are several good places to eat here.

Near Plaza San Miguel Bajo is the convent of Santa Isabel, erected by the Catholic Monarchs, whose symbols of the yoke and arrows can be seen on the lavish Isabelline façade of the church. It's still populated by nuns; the church's opening is irregular, but you can try to sneak a peek just before 1830 mass; note the fine *mudéjar* ceiling.

When you're ready to leave the Albayzín, head down Calle San Miguel, which becomes Calle San José and has a 16th-century church of the same name. Its bell tower was inevitably once a minaret, and is constructed of beautifully irregular stone; there's a horseshoe arched window halfway up dating from the 10th century. The church also preserves its *aljibe*, the cistern used for ritual washing before prayer.

Keep heading straight ahead and you'll come once again to Cuesta San Gregorio, where a right turn will lead you back to Calle de Elvira.

The Catedral and around

home of the sepulchres of Spain's most influential monarchs

Catedral

Gran Vía s/n, T958-222959. Apr-Oct Mon-Sat 1045-1945, Sun 1600-1845, Nov-Mar Mon-Sat 1045-1315, 1600-1845, Sun 1600-1845. €4; audio guide €3.

After the Reconquest, Granada's main mosque was consecrated as a cathedral and used for three decades until it was levelled and a new cathedral begun in 1521. The project changed architectural course several times and wasn't really finished; by the time it was ready for its final touches a couple of centuries later, interest and cash had long since dwindled.

The cathedral leaves many visitors cold, but it needn't. It was largely designed by the great early Renaissance master Diego de Siloé, and much of the artworks are by the hand of the versatile Alonso Cano, a temperamental 17th-century all-rounder equally adept with brush, chisel or graph paper in hand. One unlikely story claims that he was forced to seek asylum in the cathedral after being accused of murdering his wife. The bishop let him stay, but only on condition that he set about decorating the place.

Before entering the building, stroll around to its southwestern façade, best viewed from a couple of blocks down the street. Executed by Cano, its triple arch exudes purity of form and simplicity. Along the northwestern side of the building are some intriguing open-air spice stalls exuding rich aromas.

Inside, you will be immediately struck by the lightness of the white interior, giving it a most un-Spanish feel. In fact, because of its incompleteness, the whole space is a strange mixture of the ornate and the austere, the gilt and the plain. The massive columns provide solidity, but the lack of a main *retablo* gives the church a pleasant sense of openness. There are many sculptures by Cano (who is buried in the crypt) and by Pedro de Mena, and Cano's masterpieces, a series of paintings of the life of the Virgin, hang around the cupola, but are helpfully reproduced around the ambulatory. It's a fine display of Spanish Baroque art, painted over a long period in the mid-17th century.

Capilla Real

C Oficios s/n, T958-229239. Mon-Sat 1030-1315 and 1600-1915, Sun 1100-1315 and 1430-1745, hours vary slightly through year. €4.

If you have travelled a little in Spain, or read something of the nation's history, the very thought of viewing the tombs of the Catholic Monarchs, Fernando and Isabel, who had such an impact on the world's history, might send an anticipatory shiver up your spine.

Although they had originally planned to be buried at Toledo, Fernando and Isabel decided in 1504 that it would be more fitting to rest in peace in Granada, symbolic scene of the triumph of their Catholic faith. Isabel died a few months later, in November of the same year, followed by Fernando (a pragmatic figure, once described by Shakespeare, accurately, as "reckon'd one the wisest prince that

ON THE ROAD

Granada Card

Granada's tourist pass costs €33.50 for the basic version and €37.50 for the 'plus' version. Both include entry to the Alhambra, Catedral, Capilla Real, Monasterio de la Cartuja, Monasterio de San Jerónimo and the Parque de las Ciencias, as well as being valid for five/nine journeys respectively by normal bus. The Plus card also allows one circuit in the tourist bus. It's not a huge saving. Buy it online at www.granadatur.com and pick it up at one of several places. At time of booking you'll have to reserve your time slot for the Alhambra. Some hotels give you one for free if you stay two nights or more, but you'll have to mention it when you check in.

there had reign'd by many a year before") in 1516. Their bodies lay in the monastery (now parador) of San Francisco on the Alhambra hill until their grandson Carlos V could complete the chapel. He added a few modernizing touches to the Isabelline Gothic design, and brought their bodies here in 1521. By Fernando and Isabel's side, he also had tombs carved for his parents, Felipe El Hermoso (the Fair, who died in 1505), and Juana La Loca (the Mad), who was far from dead; she finally passed away in 1555, only three years before Carlos himself.

The burial chapel is entered through one of Carlos's additions to the original design, an inspirational Plateresque *reja* built by Bartolomé de Jaén between 1518 and 1520. Above depictions of the 12 apostles and the arms of Fernando and Isabel are scenes of the Passion and Resurrection of Christ.

The centre of the transept is occupied by the tombs themselves. Although you need to be incredibly tall to fully appreciate them, they are finely carved from Carrara marble. Fernando and Isabel are to the right as you enter, with Juana and Felipe beside them. The former tombs, notable for their realism, were carved by the Italian master Domenico Fancelli; the feet are guarded by tiny lions. Felipe and Juana are works of the Spaniard Bartolomé Ordóñez. An inscription reads: *Mahometice secte prostratores et heretice pervicacie extinctores* (Vanquishers of the Muslim sects and extinguishers of the lies of heretics). Descending a stair below the tombs you view the small crypt with its creepy lead coffins; there is also one for Fernando and Isabel's grandson, Miguel, who died in infancy. Ransacked by troops headed by Napoleon during the Peninsular War, it is doubtful whether the tombs now actually hold the monarchs' remains. The simplicity of the coffins reflects the austere faith of, in particular, Isabel, who desired to be buried unadorned.

The *retablo* is a suitably fine work, created in 1520-1522 by Felipe Vigarny, who was assisted by Jacobo of Florence and Alonso Berruguete among others.

The sacristy museum is entered through a doorway with a notable Isabelline Gothic flourish and an elegant Annunciation. The vaulted museum is fascinating, containing some royal standards and garments and Fernando's sword alongside the battered crown and sceptre of Isabel. Many of the queen's personal effects and paintings are also present, including some fine Flemish pieces, especially the masterly 15th-century *retablo* triptych by Bouts, featuring the Crucifixion, Descent, and Resurrection, and some exquisite Hans Memling paintings. There's also a work widely attributed to Botticelli as well as works by some Spanish masters.

Around the Capilla Real

Opposite the entrance to the Capilla Real is the cheerfully speckled façade of the **Palacio de la Madraza**, an old Islamic college (*madrassa*) now a university building. While the façade is post-Moorish, the building was constructed by the Nasrid king Yusuf I. Wander into the fine patio and examine the octagonal oratory with well-preserved Nasrid decorations adorning the walls, prayer niche and cupola. The colour is well preserved in parts, giving some idea of what the Alhambra palaces might have looked like centuries ago.

Across Calle Reyes Católicos, the **Corral del Carbón** ⓘ *entry fee due to be charged*, was once a Moorish inn, or *caravanserai*, where merchant convoys could hole up and store their goods. You enter the courtyard through a 14th-century arched portal decorated with *mocárabes*.

The **Ayuntamiento** on Plaza del Carmén also has a very fine patio; you're usually allowed to walk in and have a look.

Realejo and San Matías

This interesting zone, southeast of Plaza Nueva and running up the southern face of the Alhambra hill, was once home to much of the city's Jewish population. It's well worth a look, not least because it's still pretty local in character.

Plaza Mariana Pineda is a short walk from Puerta Real and is centred on a statue of the Granadan martyr whom Lorca immortalized in his play about her (see box, page 328). Near here, the **Iglesia de Santo Domingo** stands on a small square and has a high Renaissance portico reminiscent of the cathedral's western façade; the front of the church itself is covered in Romanizing frescoes. Further towards the Alhambra hill, the **Campo del Príncipe** is a large plaza cleared by the Catholic Monarchs to celebrate the wedding of their short-lived son. It's now a popular place for tapas.

Climbing up the hill with the orange-coloured Alhambra Palace hotel looming overhead, a side street leads to the **Casa Museo Manuel de Falla** ⓘ *Casa Museo: C Antequerela Alta 11, T958-228421, www.museomanueldefalla.com, Tue-Fri 0930-1800, Sat-Sun 0900-1400, Jul-Aug Wed-Sun 0900-1330, €3 (guided visit)*. De Falla (1876-1946) was a friend of Lorca's and Spain's most renowned composer. As well as writing *zarzuela* operas, he had a keen interest in flamenco. The *cante jondo* competition he organized in 1922 expressed his desire to revive a fast-disappearing art. The fairly humble *carmen* he lived in from 1921 has been lovingly preserved; much of the man's engaging, obsessive and hypochondriac character can be gleaned here thanks to the tour. Above the house is an exhibition on Falla and an auditorium that has regular live classical music.

Continuing from here past the **Alhambra Palace** hotel and down a narrow lane, you arrive at the Torres Bermejas (see La Alhambra, page 311).

Turning hairpin right at the Alhambra Palace and up the hill past the Falla auditorium brings you to the **Carmen de los Mártires** ⓘ *Mon-Fri 1000-1400,*

1600-1800 (1800-2000 summer), Sat and Sun 1000-1800 (2000 summer), free. This extraordinary place consists of a decaying but opulent 19th-century palace surrounded by a lush and enormous park with various types of gardens. It's due for renovation, but it's a peaceful delight to wander the unkempt estate, finding unexpected fountains, sculptures and duckponds at every turn.

University district

north and west of the cathedral with several outstanding monuments

Hospital Real

Beyond the Puerta de Elvira, once the main gateway into the city, this endearing Renaissance building was commissioned by the Catholic Monarchs as a home for the mentally ill, an enlightened piece of work for those times. Completed by Carlos V, one of its early inmates was a young Portuguese called João, a former soldier who heard God tell him to care for the sick. After recovering from the shock of this, he was released from the madhouse and went about doing exactly that, founding a hospital of his own and becoming revered as a holy man. He is now known as San Juan de Dios, or John of God. If you are interested in his life, there's a small exhibition about him in the house where he died, Casa de los Pisa, in the Albayzín near Plaza Nueva.

Today the building is the main library of Granada's university, which is spread around this district. Set in a palm-filled garden, it features four patios, two of which are superbly harmonious examples of the purest Renaissance. In one of the others is a statue of Charles V, who founded the university.

Monasterio de San Jerónimo

C Gran Capitán s/n, T958-279337. Summer Mon-Fri 1000-1330, 1600-1930, Sat-Sun 1000-1430, 1600-1930, winter afternoons 1500-1830. €4.

Begun by the Catholic Monarchs four years after taking Granada, this monastery, the resting place of El Gran Capitán, Gonzalo de Córdoba, is especially notable for its vividly decorated church, much of which was designed by Diego de Siloé. The monastery suffered grievously at the hands of Napoleon's troops and, after the Disentailment Act of 1835, was used as a cavalry barracks, so it's something of a miracle that it's so well preserved today. It now has a population of 15 cloistered nuns. The cloister is a fine feature, with Renaissance arches offset by an Isabelline balustrade on the upper level. The capitals are worth examining; they are well carved with vegetal and mythical designs. There is an unusual loggia running alongside the church above the cloister level. After viewing some mediocre paintings in the refectory and chapterhouse, the church is like a fireworks display, decorated floor to ceiling with frescoes. One of the artists went berserk with a cherub gun; it would take all day to count how many of the winged innocents there are. The painted side chapels feature scenes from history and lives of the saints, while the huge dusty gold *retablo* (worth a coin to light it up) is dedicated to the Immaculate Conception; its panels feature scenes of Mary's life. In one of the chapels, note Pedro de Mena's fine sculpture of Nuestra Señora de la Soledad; one of Granada's favourites of the Semana Santa processions at Easter. Note the elaborate vaulting, the cupola over the crossing abuzz with cherubs and busts, and the separate gallery and choir for the nuns. The tomb of Gonzalo is before the high altar; the church was completed by his wife to provide a suitable resting place for the great soldier. Statues of the couple at prayer flank the *retablo*.

Monasterio de la Cartuja

Paseo de Cartuja s/n, T958-161932. Daily 1000-1300, 1600-2000 (1500-1800 winter), €4. Bus No 8 will get you here from Gran Vía, or a 30-min walk from the centre, or take the LAC bus westwards and change to the N7.

This former Carthusian monastery merits a visit for its riotous Baroque church. A construction project plagued with problems, the building was commenced in the early 16th century but not completely finished until the monks were booted out by the Disentailment Act of 1835. Walking around the cloister you can sense the austere hard-working, contemplative lives of the 'white robes', and the vaulted chapterhouse features paintings of historical persecutions inflicted on the monks. All of which adds to the contrast that awaits when entering the church, which is a dazzling array of the colourful and the flamboyant.

The nave is divided into three sections; one for the public, one for the lay-brothers, and one for the monks. The last two were separated by an elaborate tortoiseshell door paned with Venetian glass; it's placed in a Baroque screen decorated with canvases by Sánchez Cotón, just two of many fine paintings in here. The choir stalls have beautiful mouldings around them, while the walls in general are covered with polychrome plasterwork. A gilt baldachin sits over the altar and features the Assumption of the Virgin; above is a cupola with well-rendered cherubs peering down on the bewildered visitor. Behind it, a glassed arch leads to the Sanctuary Chapel. The dome and walls are painted by Palomino, who also did much work in Córdoba's cathedral, but the room is dominated by an immense tabernacle in the centre. The whole is a gilt and marble fantasy, executed to perfection, and, once in here, it's decision time: love it or hate it. After this, no visitor could possibly have mixed feelings about Spanish Baroque.

The sacristy is also exceptionally ornamental, but here the straight line has been eschewed, giving the extraordinary sensation that the room is melting, a feeling partly brought about by the unusual Alpujarran marble, which has streaks of colour that make it look like an exotic chocolate cocktail. There are a pair of sculptures of St Bruno, one of the founders of the Carthusian order, and an 18th-century painted dome.

In Federico García Lorca's footsteps

one of Spanish literature's giants, intimately connected with Granada

★There are three museums in and around Granada set up in houses where Federico García Lorca (see box, page 328) once lived.

The first is now in the city itself, but was once a summer house outside town, in the fertile meadows known as La Vega. This is the **Casa Museo de Federico García Lorca** ⓘ *T958-258466, Tue-Sun 0915-1330, 1715-1930 or 1600-1830, closed afternoons mid-Jun to mid-Sep, garden 0800-dusk, tours (mandatory) on the half-hour, €3, free on Wed*. Lorca's father bought it in 1925, when it was a small farmhouse among other such properties. From the age of 27 until his death at 38, Lorca spent most of his summers here and produced much of his best work in the place, which he loved dearly. With the help of Lorca's late sister Isabel, the house has been returned to its original state. Very modern for its time, it's now an interesting period piece. By far the most fascinating part is Lorca's bedroom and writing desk. In the room hangs a Rafael Alberti painting; downstairs is a sketch by Salvador Dalí, who was a very close friend of Lorca's, and a famous portrait by Toledo of the poet in a yellow dressing gown, a typically humorous touch on his part. Lorca's joy for life is tangible in the small remnants of his existence here.

The second museum, **Museo Casa-Natal Federico García Lorca** ⓘ *T958-516453, www.museogarcialorca.org, visits on the hour Oct-Mar Tue-Sun 1000-1300, 1600-1700 Apr-Jun 1000-1300, 1700-1800, Jul-Sep 1000-1400, €1.80*, is in a village 17 km west of Granada called Fuente Vaqueros, surrounded by lands that once belonged to the Duke of Wellington. This is where Lorca was born in 1898 and lived his early years. The house has been painstakingly recreated as it was in those days. The tour will show you the kitchen and bedrooms, including drawings by young Federico that were made into embroidery by his sister, copies of his birth and baptismal certificates, and school photos. Upstairs, the granary has been converted into an exhibition room, while across the grapevine-covered courtyard is another room where you can see video footage of the man himself. Although simple, it's an excellent museum, largely due to the tour being conducted by a man with a deep love for and knowledge of the poet.

To get there by car, exit Granada on the Málaga–Antequera road and, as you pass the airport, take the exit for Fuente Vaqueros. Turning right at the roundabout in the centre of the village, the house is signposted on the left. Buy tickets at the rear, on the parallel street. Buses leave Granada from Avenida de Andaluces by the train station hourly (except 1000) on weekdays, and at 0900, 1100, 1300, 1700, 1900 and 2100 at weekends. Return buses leave Fuente an hour later. The journey takes 20 minutes.

Another site is just outside the village of **Alfacar** north of Granada (regular buses from Calle Capitán Moreno in Granada, next to the Arco de Elvira arch), where the poet was shot in August 1936. A rather unpoetic memorial park has been built on the spot, but the olive tree where he is said to have died and been buried, though his remains were not found there in a recent excavation, is a more sobering place indeed and worth the journey.

Nearby, on the edge of the village, is a spot to clear your thoughts somewhat; the **Fuente Grande**, a natural spring whose combination of clear water and green plants is somehow intensely satisfying. Watch for the bubbles naturally bursting to the surface; the Moors named the site 'the fountain of tears'.

Other Lorca sites you may like to visit in Granada include **Chikito** restaurant (detailed below) where he used to chat with a group of friends, the hotel **Alhambra**

ON THE ROAD

The poet they silenced

One of Spain's finest writers, the poet and dramatist Federico García Lorca was born in 1898 at Fuente Vaqueros, near Granada, to a prosperous farmer and former local schoolteacher. While studying law none too enthusiastically at Granada, he published his first book of poems; at the same time he got to know the composer Manuel de Falla and became an accomplished musician. He then went to study in Madrid, meeting important contemporaries, such as Salvador Dalí, Pablo Neruda, and Juan Ramón Jiménez. Lorca developed a deep interest in Andalucían life and culture and had an enduring passion for gypsy life and flamenco. By the age of 30, he had achieved national fame for a play, *Mariana Pineda*, based on the exploits of Granada's 19th-century liberal martyr, and his book of gypsy ballads, *Romancero Gitano*. *Poema del Cante Jondo* was a long lyric poem that also captured the flamenco mood.

On the strength of the success of *Romancero Gitano*, Lorca went to live in New York for a year, learning English and writing the depressed and alienated poems that were to appear after his death as *Poeta en Nueva York*. On his return to Spain, he ran a popular travelling theatre for the Republican government; in these years he produced his best-known stage works *Bodas de Sangre* (Blood Wedding), *Yerma* and *La Casa de Bernarda Alba*, all dealing with passions, emotions and the female condition in rural Spain. In 1935, his poem *Llanto por Ignacio Sánchez Mejías* (Lament for the Death of a Bullfighter), an elegy for the great *torero* and friend of Lorca's who was gored in the ring in Manzanares in 1934, won great critical acclaim.

Lorca spent as much of his time in Granada as he could, but was openly critical of the city's middle classes, who he labelled as uncultured boors. This attitude, together with his Republican sympathies and his homosexuality, were to see him seized from the house of a Falangist friend shortly after the Civil War started, detained and then driven to the village of Viznar by a group of fascist thugs acting for the military governor. On the morning of 19 or 20 August 1936, he was driven outside the village and forced to dig his own grave by an olive tree. He was then shot several times, a deed which the perpetrators later boasted about in Granada. His books were burned in the town square and were soon banned by Franco. Despite renewed efforts to find his grave in recent years, body has never been identified among the thousands killed.

Lorca's Granada, by biographer Ian Gibson (Faber and Faber, 1992) is a labour of love that leads you on a series of walks through Granada, pointing out spots where Lorca lived, ate and drank and that he wrote about, all the while filling you in with fascinating background information on his life and excerpts of his poetry.

Palace (see below) where he performed readings, Falla's house nearby, where he was a frequent visitor, and the hotel **Reina Cristina** ⓘ *C Tablas 4*. This used to be the residence of the poet Luis Rosales, and it was where Lorca was snatched from in the early days of the Civil War before being driven outside Granada to his murder; however, it's changed much since those days. Unfortunately another of his favourite cafés, the **Gran Café Granada** on Puerta Real, is these days a Burger King.

Listings Granada city *maps p308, p312 and p318*

Tourist information

Tourist office
C Santa Ana 4, T958-225990, otgranada@andalucia.org. Mon-Fri 0900-1930, Sat and Sun 0930-1500.
The city's handiest office is just off Plaza Nueva. The provincial tourist office (Plaza de Mariana Pineda 10, T958-247128, Mon-Fri 0900-2000 (1900 in winter), Sat 1000-1900, Sun 1000-1500) is larger and less crowded. Both have a good information on transport, accommodation and opening hours of sights (which change frequently), as well as city maps and information about the province. Within the Alhambra ticket pavilion is another tourist office; there are also various kiosks around town that are closed in winter. Look for the free guide *Guía de Granada*; a useful monthly 'what's on' publication.

Where to stay

Granada has a huge range of accommodation options, with hundreds of hotels and *pensiones*. Apart from a couple of recommendable hotels around (and in) the Alhambra itself, the choicest and most romantic area to stay is the old Moorish quarter of the Albayzín, where several superbly renovated mansion-hotels offer patios, beamed rooms and Alhambra views.

There's a huge concentration of budget accommodation in the university zone, around C San Juan de Dios, so head there if there are no rooms around Plaza Nueva.

The tourist office and various online resources can provide a list of apartments for rent; also look out for signs around the city, particularly near the Albayzín.

La Alhambra

€€€€ Alhambra Palace
C Peña Partida 2, T958-221468, www.h-alhambrapalace.es.
This huge orange castellated affair is far from subtle, and caused much controversy when it was built in 1910 on the Alhambra hill. That said, once you're inside you can forget about the slightly gauche exterior and concentrate on the luxury of the rooms and installations and the superb views of the city or Alhambra, depending on which side your room is. The bar's terrace is one of Granada's prime spots for a drink; there's also a good restaurant and a small theatre where Lorca recited poetry a few times. Extras like breakfast are expensive.

€€€€ Parador San Francisco
Real de la Alhambra s/n, T958-221440, www.parador.es.
With comparatively few rooms, however, booking well in advance is essential;

think at least several months in peak periods. This is Spain's flagship parador, with an enviable location within the Alhambra complex itself. Built as a monastery by the Catholic Monarchs, it's a magnificent nexus of luxury and history. Bear in mind that you are paying a premium for location here.

€€€ Carmen de la Alcubilla del Caracol
Aire Alta 12, T958-215551, www. alcubilladel caracol.com. Closed Aug.
In a very secluded location on the side of the Alhambra hill below the Torres Bermejas, this boutique hotel doesn't exactly trip off the tongue but has 7 gorgeous rooms, some with balconies overlooking town. It's a lovely traditional Granada *carmen* with a beautiful spacious interior enlivened by thoughtfully selected furniture. Service is warm and personal and numerous caring touches make for a memorable stay. Recommended.

€€€ Hotel América
Real de la Alhambra 53, T958-227471, www.hotelamericagranada.com. Closed Dec-Feb. Booking well in advance is crucial.
Right in the Alhambra, this small hotel doesn't only deliver on location. Set around a vine-covered patio café, it exudes character from every pore; from the creaky wooden staircase decorated with paintings to the snug venerable rooms furnished with rustic vintage sofas and (narrow) beds. It's far from luxurious but intensely charismatic. You have to go elsewhere for meals and park in the Alhambra car park.

Plaza Nueva to Sacromonte

€€ Cuevas El Abanico
Verea de Enmedio 89, T958-226199, T608-848497, www.el-abanico.com. Reservation advisable; minimum stay of 3 nights in busy periods.
A must for those with troglodyte tendencies, these smartly appointed cave apartments are in the heart of Sacromonte. The standard cave is long, white and decorated with tiles and other Andalucían favourites. There's a well-equipped kitchen, bathroom and a bedroom annex. And blankets, as the caves are a cool 18°C all year. You can't park very close, so it's not for those who don't fancy lugging bags. Recommended.

€ Hostal Navarro Ramos
Cuesta de Gomérez 21, T958-250555, www.pension navarroramos.com.
Family-run place whose simple tiled-floored and white-walled rooms are well looked after. Like all the places on this hill, the rooms on the street are very noisy. Priced very low; the shared bathrooms have good showers. Centrally heated in winter. Recommended.

El Albayzín

€€€ Casa Morisca
Cuesta de la Victoria 9, T958-221100, www.hotelcasamorisca.com.
A late 15th-century home in the Albayzín just off the picturesque Paseo de los Tristes, this sumptuous and intimate hotel exudes charm and neo-Moorish grace. A delightful pool in the central patio is surrounded by restored a restored wooden gallery; the rooms and passageways feature inlaid ceilings returned to their original glory. The rooms on the street are especially desirable, but all are classily and

comfortably furnished in the same style as the rest of the building. It's usually possible to park in the street outside. Recommended.

€€€ El Ladrón de Agua
Carrera del Darro 13, T958-215040, www.ladrondeagua.com.
One of several gloriously refurbished historic Albayzín houses, this hotel is among the best. The rooms are lovely, but not overburdened decoratively – they let the attractive brick, tile and wood surfaces create the harmony. As in all these hotels, there are many distinct types and prices of rooms, some quite small, others rather luxurious. There's a literary theme to the rooms here, with each named after a work by Lorca or Juan Ramón Jiménez. Meals are also available for guests.

€€€ Hotel Casa 1800
C Benalúa 11, T958-210700, www.hotelcasa1800granada.com.
This handsome lodging has become one of Granada's most appealing hotels. The rooms, surrounding a typically elegant patio, are romantic and attractively decorated in a sober style. The location is excellent, and some superior rooms have views of the Alhambra. Service is great, and there are loads of thoughtful extras, though no on-site parking. Recommended.

€€ Hotel Santa Isabel la Real
C Santa Isabel la Real 19, T958-294658, www.hotel santaisabellareal.com.
Set in our favourite part of the Albayzín, just off Plaza San Miguel Bajo, this small hotel has a fine, peaceful location by the convent of the same name. With very attractive rooms around a light central patio, helpful staff, and a couple of great restaurants nearby, it's a top option. Very handily, bus C1 stops outside the door. Breakfast included. Recommended.

€ Oasis Backpackers' Hostel
Placeta Correo Viejo 3, T958-215848, www.oasisgranada.com.
This excellent backpackers' hostel is tucked away in the Albayzín, not far from C de Elvira. Exceedingly well run, it offers all the comforts and luxuries a traveller could hope for. Accommodation is in clean and comfortable dorms (doubles also available), and you get your own personal safe – a great feature. There's a lively social scene here, with a roof terrace (top views) and a good kitchen available 24/7. Recommended.

The Catedral and around

€€€€ Hospes Palacio de los Patos
C Solarillo de Gracia 1, T958-535790, www.hospes.com.
Occupying an exquisite 19th-century mansion in the heart of Granada, this 5-star choice has an excellent central location but the quiet and relaxation of a rural hotel. The pretty garden and classy restaurant are complemented by most elegant interior decoration and chic white modern rooms.

€€€ Hotel Palacio de los Navas
C Navas 1, T958-215760, www.palaciodelosnavas.com.
This excellent boutique hotel, set in a 16th-century *mudéjar palacio*, is a real treat at the end of this excellent tapas street. The rooms, of which there are 2 categories, are a little dark but very pleasant and comfortable, and the elegant building, constructed around a pretty patio, is most appealing. The staff are great, and the whole place is kept absolutely spotless, especially the praiseworthy bathrooms. One room has disabled access.

€€ Hotel Las Nieves
C Alhóndiga 8, T958-265311, www.hotellasnieves.com.
A professional and friendly choice in the shopping zone, and handy for just about everything, this has warmly decorated modern rooms with excellent bathrooms. Staff are helpful and prices are particularly attractive; off-season, staying here offers exceptional value. There's a restaurant with a decent *menú*.

€€ Hotel Párragasiete
C Párraga 7, T958-264227, www.hotelparragasiete.com.
This boutique hotel is on a quiet street but is very central. Rooms offer plenty of style and comfortable beds; they include decent singles. There's also a restaurant with gastronomic pretensions. Recommended.

€ Hostal Costa Azul
C Rosario T958-222298, www.hostalcostaazul.com.
This unassuming spot is perfectly situated for sallies forth to the tapas heartland of C Navas, and has a pretty tiled patio, little garden, free Wi-Fi and laundry service. It's a friendly spot, but try not to get shunted across the road to the annexe, where rooms aren't as inviting.

Camping

Camping Sierra Nevada
C Juan Pablo II 23, T958-150062, www.campingsierranevada.com. Mar-Oct. Bus SN2 runs from here to a connection with the central LAC service.
A well-equipped campsite near the bus station in a perfect location. The pool is a godsend in the summer heat. Recommended.

Restaurants

The highlight of Granada's eating scene is its tapas culture. Bars here charge more for drinks, but give free tapas with each, giving different tapas for each round of drinks.

Boisterous C de Elvira just off Plaza Nueva is a popular place to start your tapas trail, but prices are high and you'll find more tourists than locals. C Navas is the favourite for many *granadinos*. The plazas of the Albayzin have sunkissed terraces for alfresco snacking, and the university district has numerous good-value tapas choices and a convivial studenty atmosphere.

Among Granada's restaurants are a selection of mirador eateries with superb views of the Alhambra. The city is well stocked with *teterías*, atmospheric teahouses serving minty Moroccan tea and other infusions, waterpipes and Maghrebi pastries.

Remember that Granada sees a huge number of tourists. Beware any place without prices marked on its menus and always check prices on terraces before ordering.

Plaza Nueva to Sacromonte

€€ La Taberna de Tiacheta
Puente Cabrera s/n.
This bar is romantically set by an old bridge over the river. It's a small set-up with a friendly feel and excellent tapas; try the *morcilla* if you're a fan of blood sausage, or choose from a number of other thoughtfully prepared deli-style plates.

€€ Ruta del Azafrán
Paseo Padre Manjón 1, T958 226 882, www.rutadelazafran.es.

With a lovely setting on Paseo de los Tristes, and views up to the Alhambra from the outdoor tables, this makes a romantic dinner spot. Many dishes are Moroccan-influenced, and portions are healthy rather than hearty, but it's all tasty and served with a smile.

Cafés

Heladería Tiggiani
C Cuchilleros 15, T958-252811.
On Plaza Nueva, this wonderful ice creamery delights with its beautifully presented concoctions, with flavours like Ferrero Rocher or Cointreau. Another branch on Plaza Bib-Rambla.

El Albayzín *map p308*

The Albayzín is fertile ground for tapas, particularly during the day, and has a selection of classy restaurants, many offering Alhambra views. The streets around C de Elvira form the classic tapas zone, but it's often crowded and touristy.

€€€ Mirador de Aixa
Carril de San Agustín 2, T958-223616, www.miradordeaixa.com. Closed Sun night and Mon.
There are several mirador restaurants in the Albayzín, most with wonderful views across to the Alhambra and attractive places to eat by day or night, when the complex is floodlit. In some, you pay mostly for location, but this is one of the better options, just below the Mirador de San Nicolás. The menu is short in length and high on quality, from a delicious house *revuelto* to a sizeable *chuletón* steak; Moorish-inspired dishes like aubergines with honey are a less carnivorous option. Service is friendly, and the terrace is prettily covered with vines.

€€ El Ají
Plaza San Miguel Bajo 9, T958-292930, www.restauranteelaji.com.
This warmly decorated and friendly place has quickly become a favourite with Albayzín locals, who already have several good options on this square. It's modern, but cheerfully so, and this extends to the food, which is thoughtfully concocted and presented. There are vegetarian choices, including good salads, as well as tasty grilled meats. The *menú* is good and low priced, but à la carte is even better. There are outdoor tables.

€€ Taberna Salinas
C de Elvira 13, T958-221411, www.tabernassalinas.com.
This is touristy but has an old-fashioned cavernous bodega atmosphere with hams hanging over the bar and is dimly lit and cosy. The plates that accompany the drinks for free here are excellent, and there are plenty of tables where you can dine on a wide choice of classic tapas and *raciones*.

€ Antigua Bodegas Castañeda
C Almireceros 3, T958-223222.
This long-established classy joint serves classic tapas dishes such as *cazuelas* (stews) as well as mixed plates of cured meats and cheeses. Stepping inside recalls a bygone age. It's always packed; locals enjoy its large selection of barrelled wines. Try the *calicasa*, a potent blend of vermouth and other goodies, which is tasty and strong. There's a newer but equally popular version of the same bar behind it. Not really recommended for a sit-down meal though.

€ Bar Aixa
Plaza Larga 5.
On this appealing square tucked up the back of the Albayzin, this typical local

tapas bar stands out for its big-hearted service, democratic feel, and generous free tapas. Try a *ración* of potatoes or snails on the terrace.

€ Bar León
C Pan 1, www.restaurante barleon.com.
Much more authentic and down-to-earth than most of the bars in the Elvira zone, this has tasty traditional raciones from all around Spain, including such will-I-won't-I delicacies as *sesos* (brains) and *criadillas* (bull testicles), as well as fried fish and *callos* (tripe). It's a welcoming haven of Granada normality.

€ Bodega La Mancha
C Joaquín Costa 10, T958-228968.
A wonderfully traditional spot around the corner from the C de Elvira action and a world away from it. It's a gruffly welcoming, handsome, proper Spanish bar that does cracking tortilla and serves up a range of no-nonsense wines to go with it. They don't usually give a free tapa, but there's a range of cheap ones to choose from – try their tasty *croquetas* (croquettes) or excellent tortilla.

€ Puerta de las Pesas
Plaza Larga s/n.
With a great little terrace right by an impressive Moorish gateway, this is one of the better spots to stop off for a drink and a bite while strolling around the Albayzín. The tiny bar itself is warmly decorated and run by a family. It's not flash, but it's honest, friendly and authentic.

€ Taberna el 22
Cuesta de San Gregorio 5.
A small and hospitable bar with a popular terrace on the way up into the Albayzín. The tapas are fabulous, as are the cheap *raciones*: *revuelto de setas* (scrambled eggs with wild mushrooms) is just one of many changing and recommended choices, with lots of vegetarian options. Try the orange wine too; a curious Andalucían beverage that's very tasty – at least for the first glass.

Cafés

Rising off C de Elvira, C Calderería Nueva is like stepping into a Moroccan souk. There are several atmospheric teahouses, all with comfortable low seating, ambient North African music, and a fine range of teas served in exquisite pots. Everyone has their personal favourite, but they are all good.

The Catedral and around

C Navas off Plaza del Carmen is a pedestrian street almost wholly devoted to bars, many of them excellent.

€€€ Carmen San Miguel
Plaza Torres Bermejas 3, T958-226723, www.carmen sanmiguel.com. Closed Sun.
Right by the Torres Bermejas, this secluded restaurant offers a covered terrace with unbeatable views over the city in a traditional *carmen* where the Russian composer Glinka once lived while studying Spanish musical forms in the 19th century. The menu won't disappoint either; the chef produces creations of great originality and taste. Their vanilla roasted suckling pig is a signature dish.

€€€ Damasqueros
C Damasqueros 3, T958-210550, www.damasqueros.com.
The 5-course degustation menu here (€42) changes weekly and combines both sensational local ingredients with imaginative presentation. A reasonably priced wine flight is offered alongside. Don't confuse with the bar of the same

name on the corner of this street. Recommended.

€€€-€€ Chikito
Plaza del Campillo 9, T958-223364, www.restaurantechikito.com. Closed Wed.
In Lorca's day this was a café, and he used to spend much time in discussion here with friends sitting in a corner; the group thus became known as *El Rinconcillo*. Although it's now a restaurant, one senses the poet would have approved of the warm-coloured dining room hung with photos of Lorca himself and of other famous visitors. A dish the house prides itself upon is its *zarzuela* (casserole) of fish and seafood; in fact the fish dishes here tend to shine brighter than the meat ones; there's a Basque touch to many of the offerings. Book ahead if possible, as it's a long-standing local favourite.

€€€ Vinoteca Puerta del Carmen
Plaza del Carmen 1, T958-223737, www.puerta delcarmenrestaurante.com.
A favourite of the well-dressed *funcionarios* from the town hall opposite, this bar features an excellent selection of fine Spanish wines, helpful service, and tapas and *raciones* of deli products, including excellent ham and *salazones* (salted fish preserves). There are pleasant tables outside on the terrace and an elegant interior.

€€ Casa Enrique
C Acera de Darro 8, T958-255008, www.tabernacasaenrique.es.
Open since 1911, this is a deserved local favourite nicknamed El Elefante perhaps because it's so small. Decked out with dark wood, hanging hams and old wine bottles, and without a seat in the place, it's a classic Spanish bar and has heaps of atmosphere. There are deli products from all over Spain; like Jabugo ham, Galician cheese, Burgos *morcilla* or Bierzo chorizo. There's also tasty house vermouth from the barrel. Tapas are not free here. Highly recommended.

€€ La Brujidera
C Monjas del Carmen 2, T958-202595.
A dark and atmospheric venue with one of the city's best selections of wines by the glass. Work your way through the regions of Spain; the bartender will be happy to give advice on some of the lesser known choices such as Ribeiro, Somontano and Bierzo. These all come well accompanied; the bar specializes in ham and chorizo, and there are tempting mixed platters of pâtés and cheeses available, and some seriously delicious ciabattas, as well as the mouth-watering queen scallops, *zamburiñas*. Draws a loyal Granada crowd who never tire of discussing the significant merits of Spanish food and wine. Tough to find (the name isn't prominent), but worth the effort. Recommended.

€€ Rossini
Campo del Príncipe 15, T686-312118.
An equally good choice for tapas or a full meal, the warm fern-filled interior of this busy and stylish eatery is redolent with the aromas of cheeses. There's a large range of these, as well as pâtés, smoked fish and cured meats and hams (the latter particularly appropriate as Rossini was addicted to hams from nearby Trevélez). Order *raciones* of 100 g or so, or opt for a large mixed dish.

€ Bodegas Espadafor
Gran Vía 59, T958-202138.
Steeped in tradition, this bar is more than a century old and doesn't seem to have changed much. It's a fabulous spot, a big bodega with their own wine

served from barrels, tiles on the walls, *raciones* and tapas of things like cooked ham that really hit the spot, and a patina of generations of contented customers.

€ Hicuri

C Santa Escolástica 4, T858-987473.

This cheerily colourful place is a sound breakfast stop, then puts on delicious non-typical vegetarian and vegan food. Staff are friendly, there's an emphasis on organic produce, and there are some great desserts.

University district

Southwest of the centre, this area bristles with good-value tapas bars that serve a populous residential area as well as students. Plaza Einstein, a couple of blocks west of the D1 square of our map, is the hub, off which run the tapas-rich streets of C Gonzalo Gallas and C Pintor López Mezquita. Parallel C Sol is another with plenty of choice.

€€ Botánico

C Málaga 3, T958-271598, www. botanicocafe.es.

A polished, modern spacious café-restaurant that offers a bit of everything: coffees on its terrace by the small botanical gardens, late-night weekend DJ sessions, but, above all, fantastic food. The menu is avant-garde for Granada, and always features a range of interesting daily specials. There's a lot of vegetarian choice; dishes with tofu or fried goat's cheese take their place alongside meatier things like quail rice or an excellent roast duck. Service is efficient and welcoming, the house Rioja excellent and the atmosphere warm. Recommended.

Granada suburbs

A popular tapas zone that few tourists get to is in the residential suburb of La Chana, just off the Ctra de Málaga in the northwest of the city. There are several bars here in a block known as Las Torres, all with terraces that are popular at weekends. The key factor is that to get people to make the effort to come out here, the free tapas have to be high quality and large – and they are. All the streets here are named after fish; there are enough bars here to make it worth the taxi ride.

Bars and clubs

Granada has excellent nightlife – for year-round reliability it's just about Andalucía's best – including on week nights, when a mix of students and tourists keep things pumping. C de Elvira is an excellent street for bars; the university zone around C Duquesa is fertile ground, and there's a high concentration of weekend bars around C Pedro Antonio de Alarcón and its intersections with C Socrates, C Emperatriz, C Eugenia and C Pintor López Mezquita. Grab vouchers from the people on the street outside the bars for cheaper drinks.

El Albayzín

El Enano Rojo

C de Elvira 91.

One of Granada's best bars, this smoky den is a reliable standby on a night out, being open from 2200 until 0300 on weekdays and 0400 at weekends. The music played depends on the whim of the bar staff, but it centres around 1980s and 1990s alternative rock. The crowd is an appropriate mix of students and people who bought the original singles.

The Catedral and around

Café Pícaro
C Varela 10, T619-203616.
Daily 1600-0300.
Run by a local writer, this is a smart, popular spot with good chat, a relaxing vibe, and regular live jazz. It's handy for a coffee or a *copa* after a visit to the C Navas tapas zone.

La Estrella
C Cuchilleros 7.
A major star in the Granada bar firmament, this dark tunnel-like place tucked away not far from Plaza Nueva has absolutely no pretensions except those to being one of the best bars in the city. A real mix of people and music, and open late every night. Just the ticket for those looking to lurk in an authentic atmosphere. No sign, but the blue neon star marks the spot.

Loop
C San Matías 8.
Popular for a *copa* after tapas on C Navas, this small spot bustles at weekends thanks to its hospitable bar staff and cool white-tiled bar. If you like the music, you can buy it – a wall of vinyl albums hangs for sale behind the bar.

Verdi
C Sacristía de San Matías 18.
Open from 2200 to 0200.
Look behind the San Matías church for this elegantly baroque bar, a quiet, refined little place run by a guy who believes in the art of cocktail making. It's unusual and a great spot for a secluded drink with someone special. Recommended.

Entertainment

Bullfights

There are regular bullfights at **Plaza de Toros** northwest of town, but especially important during Corpus Christi. The box office is on C Escudo del Carmen, open evenings only, when a fight is imminent. You can book tickets in advance on www.mundotoro.com.

Cinemas

Multicines Centro, C Solarillo de Gracia 9, T958-252950, www.multicines-centro.com. The closest of the multiplexes to town.

Flamenco

The Sacromonte area is filled with touristy flamenco shows, in which visitors pay €20-30 for a drink and a performance, with bus transport available for a few extra euros. Though certainly not for aficionados, there can be a good atmosphere, with busloads of tourists being invited up on stage to try a bit of dancing or clapping.

Much better than those, however, are:
La Alboreá, *C Pan 3, T664-362540, www.liveflamencoshow.com.* Tucked away just off Plaza Nueva, this offers 2 decent shows nightly for €20.
Casa del Arte Flamenco, *Cuesta de Gomérez 11, T958-565767, www.casadelarteflamenco.com.* 2 decent-quality shows nightly in a handy central location. Entry €18.
Peña la Platería, *Placeta de Toqueros 7, T958-210650, www.laplateria.org.es,* is a long-established flamenco social club in the Albayzín. While it's officially members-only for the Sat night show, you may get in if you show interest; otherwise it's the public Thu night show for €8. It starts at 2230 and runs from Oct to Jun.

Zambra María la Canastera, *Camino del Sacromonte 89, T958-121183, www.marialacanastera.com.* In Sacromonte, but more professional and intimate than most, €22. Show at 2200 nightly, 2145 in winter.

Theatre

The central **Teatro Isabel la Católica**, C Almona del Campillo 2, T958-221514, www.teatroisabellacatolica.es, is the main theatre. **Auditorio Manuel de Falla**, Paseo de los Mártires s/n, T958-221144, www.manueldefalla.org, has frequent classical concerts.

Festivals

1-2 Jan Día de la Toma, when the reconquest of Granada is celebrated with official processions, while the townsfolk queue up to ring the bell on the Alhambra's Torre de la Vela – tradition has it that any single girl doing so will be engaged within the year.
1st Sun in Feb To celebrate the **Fiesta of San Cecilio**, a *romería* (pilgrimage walk) winds its way up into Sacromonte.
Easter Semana Santa, traditional Holy Processions throughout the week, on a smaller scale to Sevilla or Córdoba but well attended nonetheless. The highlight is the Sat night, when Nuestra Señora de las Angustias is paraded within the Alhambra precinct.
Jun Corpus Christi, Granada's major fiesta, with street parties, bullfights, fireworks and a *feria* in the Almanjayour district in the west of town. The celebrations last 9 days centred on the Thu itself: 4 Jun 2015, 26 May 2016, 15 Jun 2017, 31 May 2018.
Jun/Jul International Festival of Music and Dance (www.granadafestival.org), in various locations in the city.
Last Sun of Sep Fiesta of Nuestra Señora de las Angustias, with bullfights and a procession.
1st 2 weeks in Nov International Jazz Festival (www.jazzgranada.es).

Shopping

Clothes

The main region for clothes shopping is at the top of C Recogidas and the streets around, while **El Corte Inglés** on C Acera del Darro is a well-stocked department store.

Guitars

There are several guitar-makers around the old town, including **Casa Morales**, Cuesta de Gomérez 9, T958-221387.

Souvenirs

Granada abounds in souvenir shops, but not all can be written off as tacky. Many sell ornate Granadan marquetry work, typically jewellery boxes and chess sets, and Spanish and Moorish-style ceramics. C Calderería Nueva, C de Elvira and the streets around have a range of Moroccan-style products, from *chichas/* hookahs to tea sets and slippers. Another area, southeast of the cathedral around Pasaje Zacatín off Plaza Bib-Rambla, has developed into a pretty authentic souk and is well worth a look.

What to do

Baths

Hammam, *C Santa Ana 16, T958-229978, granada.hammamalandalus.com.* A luxuriously appointed Arab bathhouse, whose decoration will take you right back to the glory years of Moorish Granada. With hot- and cold-water pools and optional massage, it's a perfect way to relax. Entry is by

2-hr time slot; it's advisable to book a day or so ahead (by phone, in person or online). Daily 1000-2400; bath only €24, bath plus massage €36, discounts and offers available online.

Bike and scooter hire

Ecoway, *Plaza Cuchilleros 6, T672-228890, www.ecowayrental.com.* Hire bikes from €19 a day at a convenient central location just off Plaza Nueva.

Tours

Cicerone, *T607-691676, www.cicerone granada.com.* Walking tours of Granada leave from the kiosk on Plaza Bib-Rambla, they cost €15 (under-14s free). They leave twice daily; there are separate Spanish and English groups. The tour takes about 2½ hrs and doesn't take in the Alhambra except at a distance. There's no need to book.

There's the inevitable **hop-on, hop-off red bus tour** that does 2 circuits, 1 around the new town (including the Alhambra) in a double decker, and 1 around the Albayzín and Alhambra in a minibus.

From a kiosk on Plaza Nueva near the Cuesta de Gomérez, you can rent an audio guide, **This.Is:Granada**, www.thisis.ws, covering a total of 4 different walking routes, including the Alhambra and Albayzín. It comes with 2 sets of headphones so a couple can listen simultaneously, and has commentary in several languages with a mildly annoying soundtrack. €15 for 5 days.

Language schools

There are dozens of Spanish schools in Granada. All offer accommodation arrangements in host families and a range of cultural activities. Some to try are:

Carmen de las Cuevas, Calle Cueste de los Chinos 15, T958-221062, www.carmencuevas.com. **DeLengua**, Calle Calderería Vieja 20, T958-204535, www.delengua.es. **Escuela Montalbán**, Calle Conde Cifuentes 11, T958-256875, www.escuela-montalban.com. **Instituto Europeo**, Calle Marqués de Mondéjar 40, T958-535760, www.e-institutoeuropeo.com. **Sociedad Hispano Mundial**, Calle San Antón 72, T958-010172, www.shm.edu.

Transport

Air

Granada's airport, named after Lorca, is 17 km west of town. Buses run between the airport and the centre to coincide with flights, stopping on Acera del Darro, near the cathedral, and at the bus station door, 40 mins, €3, T958-490164, www.autocaresjosegonzalez.com.

There are daily flights from Granada's airport to **Madrid** and **Barcelona**, and regular flights to a couple of other domestic destinations as well as a **British Airways** service to **London City**.

Bus

The bus station is a long way from the centre of town, on Ctra de Jaén; a 30-min walk, or take a cab and a combination of buses.

For bus information, T900-710900. **Alsa** (www.alsa.es) is one of the main operators.

Granada is well connected by road with the rest of Andalucía.

Within Granada province, regular daily buses run from here to the coast at **Motril** (1 hr 20 mins) and **Salobreña/Almuñécar** (1 hr 15 mins/1 hr 30 mins).

There are 6-9 daily buses to **Orgiva** (1 hr 15 mins) via Lanjarón, the gateway to the **Alpujarras** (45 mins); 2 of these continue further to **Ugijar** and outlying villages. **Güejar-Sierra** has 10 buses on weekdays, but less at weekends (25 mins), while **Guadix** (1 hr 30 mins) and **Montefrío** are served almost hourly on weekdays but only a couple of times on Sun.

There are 3 daily buses to the **Sierra Nevada** (50 mins). During the ski season, there are extra services leaving from a stand on Paseo del Violón.

Other Andalucían destinations include: **Sevilla** (8 daily, 3 hrs), **Jaén** (more than hourly, 1 hr) and **Málaga** (hourly, 2 hrs), **Córdoba** (8 daily, 2 hrs 30 mins), **Almería** (7 daily, 2 hrs 15 mins), and **Cazorla** (2 daily, 4 hrs).

Long distance Major destinations outside Andalucía include **Valencia** (6 daily; 7 hrs 30 mins to 9 hrs), **Madrid** (10 daily, 5 hrs), and **Barcelona** (5 daily, 13 hrs).

Car

If arriving by car, the best option is to park it as soon as possible. Large tracts of the centre are only accessible to residents or those who are going to stay in the area. These zones are camera controlled; you can enter, but make sure your hotel registers your license plate number to the police, otherwise you'll get fined. If you've booked a hotel within the area blocked off by automated pillars, press the buzzer for your hotel on the console (if there is one), or give the operator the name of the hotel and your reservation number, and you'll be let through.

Parking Many hotels offer pricey parking; underground car parks will cost around €18-30 per day; the more expensive ones are nearest the old centre. Hotels without private parking usually have a discount arrangement with a car park; make sure you check this beforehand, as once you take the ticket from the machine, it may be too late.

Car hire At the airport: **Avis**, T958-446455, www.avis.com and **Europcar**, T958-245275, www.europcar.com, among others. These 2 are also at the train station.

Train

The train station is a 15-min walk west of the centre; a short walk brings you to Av de la Constitución from where the LAC bus will bring you to the centre.

In practice, there aren't many destinations for which this is a handier mode of transport than the bus, but **Ronda** (3 daily, 2 hrs 40 mins) is certainly one, and there are 4 daily trains to **Guadix** (1 hr) which are speedier than going by road. **Antequera** (8 daily, 1 hr 30 mins) is served regularly, as are **Sevilla** (4 daily, 3 hrs), **Algeciras** (3 daily, 4 hrs 30 mins) and **Almería** (4 daily, 2 hrs 15 mins). There are 2 direct fast trains to **Madrid** (4 hrs 30 mins) via **Córdoba** (2 hrs 30 mins) and a night train to **Barcelona** (11 hrs). Use the **Algeciras** lines if you want to reach **Córdoba** (by normal train) or **Málaga**, and change at **Bobadilla**.

Sierra Nevada

The Sierra Nevada, which translates into English more prosaically as Snowy Mountains, is the memorable backdrop to Granada's Alhambra: if you're lucky with the visibility, that is. Hardy climbers used to ascend the Camino de la Nieve (Route of the Snow) to bring back fresh ice for the Moorish rulers' cocktails, but now streams of cars with skis aboard make the journey up a smoothly contoured road.

The range boasts mainland Spain's highest peak and Europe's southernmost ski resort; out of season, the region offers excellent walking opportunities and a chance to bag a few summits without any Alpine training. The upper section is a national park, while the lower reaches are *parque natural*, with lesser degrees of protection. The bleak and rugged peaks are an incredible contrast to much of the scenery of Andalucía and deserve a visit, whatever the season.

Pradollano → Colour map 5, B4.

mountain resort on the slopes of Spain's second highest summit

Pradollano, whose name (which translates literally as 'flat meadow') gives no hint of its dramatic location at 2172 m on the slopes of the crooked witch-hat peak of Veleta. The bustling main resort of the Sierra Nevada is a well-equipped place to ski and is chock full of facilities and (while the snow's around) life. In summer it's still lively with walkers and day trippers, but off season it's a ghost town.

The road through town is one way, so you have to enter at the top of the hill and work your way down, or park in the huge multi-storey at the lower entrance to the settlement.

The ski season usually commences in December and lasts until April or later, although the high temperatures at this low latitude can sometimes disrupt this. Day passes cost a maximum of €47, or €280 for a flexible seven-day pass to be used at your leisure. There are over 100 runs, seven of them black. The ski-lift ascends to **Borreguiles**, where there's a dedicated snowboard slope, before heading up to the top of the runs.

There are heaps of ski schools and equipment hire stores, and competition keeps the prices relatively low. Shop around before taking your pick. Prices for a day's hire of all the kit start at around €25, while a two-hour class for two costs around €40-50. A recommended school, who also do snowboard lessons, kids' classes and equipment hire, is the **Escuela Oficial de Esquí** ⓘ *Edif Telecabina, T958-480011, www.sierranevadaescuela.com*.

Essential Sierra Nevada

When to go

If you're visiting during the ski season, you'll find that prices are sky-high; even unremarkable hotels charge well over €100 for a double. You're much better off pre-booking a package (including lift passes, ski hire and accommodation) online or via a travel agent. Arrive at the resort without having booked anything and you'll pay well over the odds, even if the hotels are half-empty.

Warning

The Sierra Nevada is a significantly high mountain zone. Although it may appear harmless in summer, mist and bad weather can descend at any time. The paths are well marked, so stick to them, and always be equipped for cold weather. On long day hikes, be prepared to stay overnight, just in case. Call 112 in all emergencies.

Walking

For all walks, make sure you are equipped with a decent map. The free sheets from the tourist offices won't do, even for the shortest stroll, so invest a few euros in a 1:25,000 scale map of the area.

Above Pradollano is Veleta, the second highest peak in the Spanish peninsula. A road from the resort leads a further 3 km uphill to Hoya de la Mora, where there are car parks, cafés and a tourist kiosk. It's about three hours to the summit of Veleta (3394 m) from here; it's an easy enough hike in late spring and summer (although take warm clothing), but ask for advice from October onwards. In summer, a bus runs 5 km past Hoya de la Mora a few times a day, cutting an hour off the climb. The road, which continues across the sierra to Capileira in the Alpujarra, is now closed to normal traffic year round. The walk to Capileira from the car park is at least eight to 10 hours but spectacular on both the ascent and descent.

From Hoya de la Mora, you can conquer mainland Spain's two highest mountains, Veleta and Mulhacén, in one go, although you'll have to be prepared to stay in the mountains overnight. Ascend to Veleta and, descending a short way, cut right along the ridge; Mulhacén (3479 m) is about another three hours from here. On the way back, there are two unmanned *refugios* you can make use of, **La Caldera**, on the way down to Capileira, or **La Carihuela**, near the summit of Veleta.

Less challenging hikes run from the car park downhill along ridges towards the information office. The office itself can provide details of these. See La Alpujarra, page 345, for more walking options to the Sierra Nevada peaks. For more detail, **Cicerone** ⓘ *www.cicerone.co.uk*, publish a good walking guide to the Sierra Nevada.

Listings Pradollano

Tourist information

El Dornajo information centre
On the main road 8 km before the ski resort, T958-340625. Daily 0930-1430, 1630-1930.
The centre has maps and walking advice and can book walking, riding and hang-gliding in spring and summer. For skiing conditions, see www.sierranevadaski.es or T902-708090. For information on accommodation contact the tourist offices in Granada.

Where to stay

There are numerous apartments for rent in the resort; see www.turgranada.es for a list. There are a few *hostales*, hotels and restaurants strung along the highway, but most of the accommodation and eating options are in Pradollano itself.

€€€€ Vincci Rumaykiyya
T958-482508, www.vinccihoteles.com. Nov-Apr.
More or less the most luxurious of the resort's options, this is right by a chairlift stop at the top of the settlement. 5-star facilities include pool and spa complex for ironing out the post-slope creases and a creche to look after the younger generation. You can get some excellent deals (**€€**) booking in advance via their website.

€€€ Trevenque
Plaza de Andalucía s/n, T958-465022, www.apartahoteltrevenque.com.
This hotel is one of the resort's better designed, in an attractive vine-covered stone building looking over the valley. Most of the rooms are apartment style – book ahead for the best rates – and there's a comfortable lounge with a view.

€ Albergue Sierra Nevada
C Peñones 22, Pradollano, T955-035886, www.inturjoven.com. Open all year.

Right at the top of town, this spacious modernized official youth hostel has a great position and snowy vistas. There are 4-bed dorms and a few doubles. There are also 6 self-contained apartments sleeping 4.

Restaurants

€€€ Ruta del Veleta
Edificio Bulgaria s/n, T958-486134, www.rutadelveleta.com. Nov-Apr.
The resort's best restaurant should be reserved ahead as its cosy rustic dining room, ceiling festooned with ceramic jugs, is popular after a day on the slopes. Dishes combine local ingredients with a gourmet, French-influenced touch, but the tradition of 30 years of mountain hospitality means there's no over-elaboration.

What to do

Gran Aventour, *C Cerro del Oro 20, Granada, T958-091662, www.granaventour.com.* Apart from ski schools in the resort, this outfit organizes various activities in the Sierra Nevada area, including canyoning, walking, rafting and cross-country skiing.

Transport

Bus

There are 3 daily buses to the Sierra Nevada (50 mins) from Granada. During the ski season, there are extra services (up to 4 a day, depending on conditions) leaving from a stand on Paseo del Violón. In season, there are also special services from Madrid via Granada.

Car

The main road winds 35 km southeast from Granada up to the main ski resort. The easiest way up from Granada by car is to head along C Acera del Darro, cross the bridge and follow the signs straight on up. The road is well ploughed in winter, but there are places to hire snow chains on the way up.

If your car is in reasonable shape and you don't mind steep and narrow roads, there's a spectacular and little-used climb that's not much more than an asphalted footpath (also a great walk). Exit the A395 8 km from Granada and follow the signs for Güejar-Sierra (for those on foot, regular buses run to this town from Granada). From Güejar, follow C Maitena out of town, eventually passing the restaurant of the same name, and follow signs to **El Charcón** restaurant. Keep going, and you'll climb sharply through walnut and chestnut trees, finally emerging above the Sierra Nevada information bureau (turn right to reach it and the main road to Pradollano, turn left for the more picturesque route to the ski resort). If you'd prefer to use this route on the way down (good brakes essential), turn off the main road at the information centre and take a left down the lane signposted to the Seminario. Either way, it's an unforgettable journey, but not to be attempted in icy conditions.

On foot

The road that crosses from the Alpujarra to the Sierra Nevada is closed to traffic, but walkable.

La Alpujarra

★La Alpujarra (or Las Alpujarras) is a fascinating and stunningly beautiful system of valleys and ravines isolated between two mountain ranges, the Sierra Nevada to the north, and the equally rugged Sierra de la Contraviesa to the south.

In Nasrid times, it was an important agricultural region, supplying Granada with vegetables and silk; after the fall of Granada, the Moors, upset with the ever-tightening strictures imposed on by the Catholic Monarchs, rose in two major revolts, both bloodily suppressed. The region then declined into rural poverty and, when the Guadix writer Pedro de Alarcón explored the region in the late 19th century, it was almost unknown.

In 1919, the Englishman Gerald Brenan (see box, page 359), walked in, pack on back and made his home at tiny Yegen. His post-war publication of his experiences, *South from Granada*, awakened foreign interest in the Alpujarra, which has been further put in the spotlight by more recent bestsellers *Driving over Lemons* and its sequels, written by ex-Genesis drummer Chris Stewart, who has made his home on a farm in the area.

While there are a lot of tourists, especially in summer, they come for two good reasons: the hiking through the valleys, hills, and mountains is some of Spain's best, and the villages and hamlets preserve some of the feel of the *morisco* culture that originally built them.

Western Alpujarra → *Colour map 5, B3/B4.*

sprucely whitewashed and atmospheric villages, with a Moorish flavour

Puerto El Suspiro del Moro

Heading to the Alpujarra from Granada, the motorway crosses a low pass over the western foothills of the Sierra Nevada. The pass of the Moor's Last Sigh (Salman Rushdie named a novel after it), this is where Boabdil, last of the Nasrid rulers, turned back for a last look at the city over which the standards of Fernando and Isabel were now flying. His mother told him: "You weep as a woman for what you could not defend as a man." Thanks Mum!

Lanjarón

The first town in the Alpujarra, and one of the largest, Lanjarón's name might look familiar: that's because it adorns the labels of many Andalucían bottles of mineral water. The town gained fame in the early 20th century as a spa; the hillside is also riddled with fountains and springs (*fuentes* or *manantiales*), each of which claims to remedy a specific ailment.

Lanjarón has a different feel to the villages that draw visitors to the region; with its elegant avenue lined with plane trees, it could almost be in France. The spa is still very popular, particularly with people with rheumatic and arthritic complaints; there are various treatments available, from hydrotherapy and massages to mud showers.

At the entry to town, opposite the large spa hotel, is the **tourist office** ⓘ *T958-770462, Mon-Sat 1000-1400, 1630-2030 (1600-1900 winter), Sun 1000-1400,* which is good for specific information on walking routes around Lanjarón as well as maps and more general information on the Alpujarra.

There are several gentle walking trails north of town, as well as some more serious ascents of nearby hills and peaks. The tourist office has a couple of map sheets. You can also join the GR-7 path here and work your way up to the villages of the High Alpujarra. Pampaneira, via Cañar, is about six hours away.

Orgiva

Entering the Alpujarra proper, Orgiva (stress on the first syllable; *or*-hee-va) is the principal town of the western region, and sits in the middle of the valley cut by the river Guadalfeo. Although attractive enough, it's hardly a charming place, with a traffic-choked main street and profusion of expat residents. Nevertheless, it's handy as a service centre; there are a range of shops, a medical centre and a cinema (open weekends only). Just after crossing the bridge to enter town, **tourist information** ⓘ *C Fuente Mariano 1, T958-784484, www.turismoalpujarra.com, Mon-Fri 0900-1400, 1700-1900, Sat 1000-1400,* is tucked away behind the petrol station. They are helpful and can book you accommodation in the whole region.

Orgiva's main monument is its church, with twin pointed towers. Inside, under a florid late Baroque dome and cupola, the ornate gilt pulpit stands out in front of a *retablo* with a recessed Crucifixion. The remains of a Moorish watchtower are nearby.

Essential La Alpujarra

Getting around

The Alpujarra region runs due east from Lanjarón, extending into Almería province, see page 432. The western zone is the most picturesque but also the most touristy. From Orgiva, a road runs along the northern edge of the Alpujarra, winding through some of the most attractive villages that cling to the southern slopes of the Sierra Nevada. The quicker southern route heads east into the heart of the area towards the chief town of the eastern zone, Ugíjar. These parts are more barren and isolated. Another route could take you through the less-visited Sierra de la Contraviesa, further to the south.

There are petrol stations just past Pampaneira and between Pitres and Pórtugos, and then not until Cádiar.

La Alpujarra has many bus services between the main centres, with less frequent ones linking smaller settlements.

See also Transport, pages 349, 356, 358 and 361.

When to go

If you're planning to do some walking, by far the best times are spring, with a riot of wildflowers, and autumn, when temperatures have cooled and villagers are busy picking grapes, peppers and chestnuts. If you plan on walking into the Sierra Nevada, perhaps ascending mainland Spain's highest peak, Mulhacén, be aware that this is a much more serious exercise after September, when the temperature drops sharply at the higher altitudes. Walking in summer is a possibility, but take it easy: the sun is fierce, particularly at altitude. Be warned that during Easter, summer and other major European holiday times, the Alpujarra gets very crowded with visitors.

Tourist information

Tourist offices in Granada, Lanjarón and Orgiva can provide information on the Alpujarra. It's worth stocking up on maps and information in these places as in the smaller villages further into the region, information is sparser. In some places, private tour companies can help visitors with impartial advice. There are also information offices and kiosks in other villages.

Listings Western Alpujarra

Where to stay

Lanjarón

€€ Hotel El Sol
Av de la Alpujarra 30, T958-770130, www.hotelelsol.es.
While most visitors understandably push on through Lanjarón to other villages, this is a fine all-round option. The good-value rooms are clean and comfortable, equipped with heating, phone and TV, and there's a jacuzzi and sauna in the hotel. The café does excellent breakfast.

Orgiva

€€ Casa Rural Jazmín
C Ladera de la Ermita s/n, T958-784795, www.casaruraljazmin.com.

This French/Spanish-run guesthouse is at the top of the town, and a delightfully peaceful hideaway. The rooms are appealingly decorated in rustic style, and there's a garden with fruit trees and a pool. Prices include breakfast. The hosts are incredibly attentive and welcoming. Recommended.

€€ Hotel Taray Botánico
Ctra A-348 Km 18, T958-784525, www.hoteltaray.com.
A kilometre below town, this hotel sits in spacious grounds studded with palms and fruit trees. It boasts a big pool, Orgiva's best restaurant, and a row of well-equipped bungalow-style rooms with minibar; the more expensive of which have a private roof terrace (**€€€**). It's a very welcoming place.

Camping

Camping Orgiva
T958-784307, www.campingorgiva.com, 2 km below town near the river.
The better of the 2 campsites, this offers good facilities including pool and restaurant. It also has pretty and well-equipped bungalows (**€€**) sleeping 2-6, as well as a little cabin (**€**) on a platform for those with treehouse fantasies.

Restaurants

You can eat very well for very little in the Alpujarra. There are few gourmet choices, but nearly all the villages have at least a down-to-earth bar to try the delicious, no-frills Alpujarran cuisine, with dishes like local trout, *migas*, or the mixed platter *plato alpujarreño*, a meat-and-potatoes fix for the chilly nights. All to be washed down with simple but tasty *costa* wine.

Lanjarón

€€ Alcadima
C Tarrega 3, T958-770809, www.alcadima.com.
This romantic hotel restaurant offers great perspectives over the town and turns out very inventive neo-Moorish dishes in substantial portions. It's rapidly become one of the Alpujarra's best places to eat. Recommended.

Festivals

20 Jan **Feast of San Sebastián**, a big event in all Alpujarran villages.
Easter During **Semana Santa**, Orgiva celebrates a livestock fair that draws people from the whole region.
Late Sep Orgiva's fiestas.

What to do

See also page 516 for tour operators who run walking and other trips to the Alpujarra.
Agetrea, *www.andaluciaacaballo.org.* An association of various operators that run horse-riding trips in the Alpujarra and Sierra Nevada areas. Their website links to their pages where you can browse the trips.
Aventura Alpujarra, *T638-597715, www.aventuraalpujarra.es.* Based in Orgiva, organizes quad and mountain bike excursions as well as canyoning.
Aventura Polar, *T952-583945, www.puertodelaragua.com.* Based in winter at the *posada* on the road at the top of the Puerto de la Ragua pass, this set-up offers fun in the snow with activities like horse treks, husky sledging, and snowshoe walking.
Caballo Park, *T606-032005, www.caballopark.com.* 9 km from Orgiva on the Pampaneira road, is

ON THE ROAD

Walking

This area is one of the country's most popular destinations for walking. There are numerous short-distance routes in and around the valleys, as well as the GR-7 long-distance path that crosses the region. Some paths are well waymarked, others less so or not at all.

For any walking in the region, it is essential to have a proper map. The most detailed maps available of the area are the 1:25,000 series of the Instituto Geográfico Nacional but these only cover small areas. It is perhaps best to stick with the Instituto Geográfico Nacional 1:50,000 map (*mapa* or *guía*) *Sierra Nevada*. Alpina's 1:40,000 map *Sierra Nevada/La Alpujarra* isn't bad although some tracks are missing from the map. The best place to pick up maps and guidebooks is in the Pampaneira visitor centre where the excellent Nevadensis guides are based (see What to do, below). Or buy Discovery Walking Guides *Las Alpujarras 1:40,000 Tour & Trail Map*, with detailed GPS information, before you go. You can purchase it from their website www.walking.demon.co.uk or download a digital edition.

Walking in the Alpujarra is mostly easy. Although there's a lot of up-and-down, the gradients aren't that steep and villages are closely spaced. The sun, however, even in spring and autumn, is intense, and you should be properly prepared for it. If walking above village level up towards the Sierra Nevada or similar, be prepared for bad weather at any time of year; if doing longer walks, be ready to stay a night at a *refugio*.

one of several that offer good excursions, from short treks (€35) to longer day or weekend escapes. **Nevadensis**, *Plaza de la Libertad, Pampaneira, T958-763127, www.nevadensis.com*. Highly recommended mountain and walking guides; also offer 4WD excursions, quad biking, and horse riding.

Transport

Bus

From Granada, **Lanjarón** is served by bus 6 to 9 times daily (1-1½ hrs depending on route). These buses continue to **Orgiva** (15 mins more). These buses are run by **Alsa**; timetables and tickets online at www.alsa.es.

High Alpujarra → *Colour map 5, B4.*

La Alpujarra's most popular and delightful villages

Just before Orgiva, a road snakes off into the hills and along the northern edge of the Alpujarra; on this route are some of the region's best places, including Pampaneira, Bubión and Capileira, as well as the ham town of Trevélez.

Ascending above Orgiva, you soon pass a turn-off for Cañar, an untouristy place with fantastic views from its situation high above the central valley. There's a

ON THE ROAD

Architecture, agriculture and crafts

The typical Alpujarran village consists of box-shaped houses traditionally roofed with a thick local clay called *launa*. They are closely packed together along narrow streets and up hillsides. All the villages today are whitewashed, but this is a recent innovation; Gerald Brenan (see box, page 359), on returning to Yegen in the 1950s, was surprised at the prosperity shown by the fact that several houses were now white.

The Alpujarran house is typically fairly large, with a storage/stable area on the ground floor and living quarters upstairs.

The Moors terraced and irrigated the Alpujarra, and their earthworks remain the basis of the region's agriculture. Watercourses (*acequías*) are still of paramount importance; each farm along an *acequía*'s route has rights to divert the waterflow for a couple of hours; this is done with guillotine-like metal slabs. The region is astonishingly fertile, and produces almost every sort of Mediterranean vegetable; staples are grapes, peppers, potatoes, almonds, onions and chestnuts.

The Alpujarra was once famous for its silks (see Brenan's *South from Granada*, for a hilarious description of the fussy silkworm's habits). These days there is a flourishing trade in *artesanía* (handcrafts), of which some are more traditional than others. Ceramics and leather are evident throughout, as well as thick woollen jerseys and socks. The New Age element in the valleys has added a different stylistic trend to the mixture.

whitewashed church and a central plaza with a fountain, but little going on. It's very unspoiled, and many houses still have the livestock living on the ground floor.

Locals are divided on the hippie community of **El Beneficio** that lies between here and Orgiva. A hardy year-round group lives there, bolstered by large numbers of part-time residents in spring and summer. The village, centred on a large and social tepee, runs along simple communal lines.

Pampaneira, Bubión and Capileira

These three villages are deservedly the most visited in the Alpujarra. Closely spaced, they perch on the Pampaneira gorge, a narrow offshoot from the central valley that is blessed with exceptionally fertile soil. All three have small supermarkets, ATMs and pharmacies, as well as a wide choice of eating and lodging options. There's a petrol station just beyond Pampaneira at the turn-off to the other two villages.

With the giant backdrop of the Sierra Nevada looming behind, it's no surprise to find that there's plenty of walking in the area. The Nevadensis office in Pampaneira or the park information office in Capileira can advise; also look out for the cheery walking pamphlets written by Elma Thompson, most of which leave from the villages in this zone.

The first village, Pampaneira, has a small main street and plaza; the rest of the village climbs up behind it. The whitewashed brick church is typical of the region, while the village's fountain dispenses virtue to those in need. **Nevadensis** ⓘ *Plaza Libertad s/n, T958-763127, www.nevadensis.com, Tue-Sat 1000-1400, 1600-1800 (1700-1900 summer), Sun and Mon 1000-1500*, is a helpful tour agency that gives regional information to visitors as well as offering guided walks in the Alpujarra and Sierra Nevada, horse trekking, canyoning and other activities.

A Tibetan monastery, **O Sel Ling** ⓘ *T958-343134, www.oseling.org*, is reached via a turn-off 5 km short of Pampaneira. The badly marked road is a poor one, deliberately so to discourage sightseeing, although interested visitors are welcome to visit part of the monastery. The site is impressive for its natural beauty and the decorative Buddhist elements. You can also arrange to stay on a retreat in simple accommodation or work as a volunteer.

Beyond Pampaneira, a turn-off leads further up the ravine to Bubión and Capileira. Both make good bases. Bubión's whitewashed church is below the main road in the Barrio Bajo; next door is the excellent **Casa Alpujarreña** ⓘ *Wed-Mon 1100-1400, Sat and Sun also 1700-1900, €2*, a museum in a large house that simply displays what a typical Alpujarran dwelling was like not so very long ago. The area only got running water in the 1970s, and many of the medieval farming implements on display are still in use. Note the collection of old newspapers with the Berlin airlift as one of the headlines: the house was acquired by the council from a deceased estate, and nothing had to be changed to convert it to a museum.

Capileira is the highest of the triumvirate, and a 30-minute walk beyond Bubión. Its higher altitude means it has more snow and wind than the lower villages. It is the best base for walking if you want to explore the high sierra, as a road (closed to traffic after a point) continues from here across the range to the Sierra Nevada ski resorts; from it climbs the main route to Spain's highest peak, Mulhacén. There's a helpful **peaks information office** ⓘ *T958-763090, www.magrama.gob.es, daily high summer 1000-1400, 1700-2000, otherwise Easter-early Dec Mon-Thu 1000-1400, Fri-Sun 1000-1400, 1600-1900*, on the main road. Ask them about weather conditions if you plan to walk further up into the mountains. There is a small **museum** ⓘ *C Mentidero, Tue-Sun 1130-1430, Sat also 1700-2000, €1*, about the writer Pedro de Alarcón, one of the first to make the Alpujarra known to a wider audience.

From Capileira, the road ascends a further 14 km up into the Sierra Nevada. A walkers' bus runs from Capileira up into the mountains daily from May to September, and at weekends only when conditions permit in autumn and winter. How far it goes depends on the snow, but in good conditions it climbs to Alto del Chorrillo, at 2700 m, from where it's only a four-hour return climb to the top of Mulhacén, or a seven-hour hike over the mountains and down to the Sierra Nevada ski resort of Solynieve. A useful *refugio* sits not far from Alto del Chorrillo, see Where to stay, below. From here you can also walk down to Trevélez in about 90 minutes, or walk back to Capileira. The information office has a leaflet detailing various suggested walks in conjunction with the bus service.

★Mecina-Fondales and Ferreirola

Beyond the turn-off to Bubión and Capileira, the road continues towards Pitres. Halfway along, a small road leads down to the hamlets of Mecina-Fondales and Ferreirola. The latter has one of the region's most charming places to stay (see Where to stay, below).

Trevélez

This is the highest village in the Alpujarra (although the locals' claim that it's the highest in the country is false), with its highest part standing 1600 m above sea level. The altitude and clean mountain air are beneficial in the curing of hams, and the village's *jamón serrano* has traditionally been so good that the composer Rossini arranged for a constant supply of Trevélez ham to be sent to him.

These days, however, there are few pigs here, so the pig legs arrive in truckloads from elsewhere in Spain to be cured. The ham is still good and the industry employs most of the town's workforce. The main road is wall-to-wall shops selling *jamón* to people passing through, many of whom are anglers attracted by the river's fine trout.

Trevélez has three distinct barrios, a low, a medium and a high, separated by a good 150 m of altitude; it's a stiff climb to the top of the town from the main road.

Walking from Trevélez

Many people use Trevélez as a base for an ascent on Mulhacén, usually stopping at the Poqueira *refugio* en route (see Capileira, above, and Where to stay, below).

Another excellent walk is an all-day circuit from the village, one of the Alpujarra's most spectacular hikes. The distance covered is 14-15 km, and should take five to seven hours. There are some steep stretches, as you ascend to within 600 m of Mulhacén's summit. From Trevélez you have a climb of some 1200 m so to enjoy this walk you should be fairly fit and get going at a reasonable hour. You can shorten the walk by almost 6 km by ending the climb at the ruins of **Cortijo La Campiñuela**. In the colder months there is often snow on the higher sections of the walk so check before leaving Trevélez. The path followed on the circular option from La Campiñuela is steep and loose at times; if in doubt you can simply make this an up-and-down walk for as far as the mood takes you. **Map**: 1:50,000 Sierra Nevada General Map.

Juviles and Bérchules

Juviles is the next village along, after passing the intersection for Torvizcón (a good walk, see Torvizcón, page 356). Juviles is one of the region's most relaxed and welcoming villages, although there's not much in the way of sights.

Bérchules is, like everywhere, a town with good views, and this steep village has many houses prettily decorated with flowering pot plants and, in autumn, drying peppers.

Where to stay

Pampaneira, Bubión and Capileira

€€ Casa Belmonte
C Ermita s/n Bubión, T958-763135, www.ridingandalucia.com.
Happiness in Bubión is a cute little apartment with your own terrace to marvel at the splendour of the view down the valley. With a pretty twin bedroom and a fold-out sofa, this is exactly what is needed. The owner can organize horse riding.

€€ Hotel Estrella de las Nieves
C de los Huertos s/n, Pampaneira, T958-763981, www.estrelladelasnieves.com.
At the top of the village, this attractive recent construction offers spectacular views from its spacious a/c rooms. There's a charming garden pool area and both the staff and the breakfasts are top-notch. Recommended.

€€ Hotel Real de Poqueira
C Doctor Castilla 11, Capileira, T958-763902, www.hotelpoqueira.com.
This sturdy white building by the church in Capileira is an excellent new accommodation option. Very pleasing modern rooms, a sweet pool and warm hospitality make a home-from-home of this enchanting village.

€ Hostal Pampaneira
C José Antonio 1, Pampaneira, T958-763002, www.hostalpampaneira.com.
Spacious rooms with en suite bathroom; the beds are decorated with *jarapa* cloth. Breakfast is included. Downstairs there's a bar and restaurant; the gruff but good-natured boss has been dishing out local food for years. It's good and cheap, especially the fresh trout.

€ Las Terrazas de la Alpujarra
Placeta del Sol 12, Bubión, T958-763034, www.terrazas alpujarra.com.
Excellent budget place, offering fine clean rooms with bathroom complemented by a cosy TV lounge, pool table, and chirpy bird in a cage. There are also well-equipped apartments and whole houses for rent; these have kitchen, central heating and fireplace. Recommended.

€ Refugio Poqueira
Between Capileira and Mulhacén, T958-343349, www.refugiopoqueira.com. Open all year.
Reserve accommodation and meals ahead. At the foot of Mulhacén, this is a large, simple but comfortable refuge for walkers that serves warming meals. Accommodation is in typical mountain-hostel style, with mattresses side by side. Shower and sheets are extra; meals cost €17; they also do packed lunches.

Mecina-Fondales and Ferreirola

€€ Hotel Maravedí
C Fuente Escarda 5, Pitres, T958-766292, www.hotelmaravedi.com.
Eco-friendly and run with a generous personal touch, this is just the spot to wind down for a couple of days. With spacious, welcoming rooms, modern and attractive bathrooms, and several above-the-price-band facilities, it makes a sound Alpujarra base.

€€ Sierra y Mar
Ferreirola, T958-766171, www.sierraymar.com. Normally closed 1-2 months in winter; check the website.

A top place to stay in this tiny village. Accommodation is in one of several self-contained rooms, many of which have a terrace, and all of which are individually decorated. Original Alpujarran furniture has been used as much as possible, and the low beds are designed for comfort. There's a lounge with books and a log fire, use of a kitchen, and a good breakfast included in the price, but the highlight is the genial hospitality of the owners, who are keen walkers. Highly recommended.

Trevélez

There's a wide choice of places to stay, with most of the options on the main road.

€€ Hotel La Fragua

C San Antonio 4, Barrio Medio, T958-858626, www.hotellafragua.com.
Simple and homely rooms in a pretty whitewashed building. Many have balconies. Worth the walk up the hill, but ring ahead, as it's often full with British walking groups. The more modern **Fragua 2** is behind the restaurant (worthwhile; see Restaurants) on the edge of the village and features sunnier, somewhat larger rooms with balconies.

€ Hostal Fernando

Pista del Barrio Medio s/n, T958-858565.
At the entrance to the middle section of town it enjoys a great setting with views, peace and quiet. The rooms are simple, but the balcony makes up for it. Private parking.

€ Pensión Mulhacén

T958-858587.
Run by a charming old couple, this *hostal* has 2 classes of room with a minimal difference in price, so go for the renovated ones, though the others are perfectly serviceable. It's on the main road right at the bottom of things.

Camping

Camping Trevélez

1 km west of town, T958-858735, www.campingtrevelez.net.
Open all year (don't even think about pitching a tent in winter though).
A likeable campsite, one of the best in the Alpujarra. It's got a bar, pool, restaurant and play area for kids. There are several simple cabins sleeping 2 to 4, as well as tent and van sites.

Juviles and Bérchules

€€ Hotel Los Bérchules

Ctra Granada 20, Bérchules, T958-852530, www.hotel berchules.com.
This friendly modern hotel just below the village has well-equipped rooms with balconies, views, a pool and inviting lounge with a fireplace. It is great value, and the cheerful English-speaking owners can organize activities such as horse trekking and offer walking advice. There's a restaurant serving hearty Alpujarran fare; half-board is €21 per person.

€ El Paraje

Ctra Juviles–Bérchules, 500 m above the road between Juviles and Bérchules in the Parque Natural Sierra Nevada, T958-064029, www.elparaje.com.
This lovely spot is a large, traditional whitewashed farmhouse with 5 spacious, heated rooms that offer plenty of simple comfort. There are terrific views over the hills and valleys and acres of peace and quiet. They also have a compact self-catering apartment. Breakfast and other meals can be provided on request and you can rent mountain bikes to explore the area.

Restaurants

Pampaneira, Bubión and Capileira

See also Where to stay, above.
There are several eateries around Pampaneira square.

€€ El Corral del Castaño
Plaza Calvario 16, Capileira, T958-763414.
This atmospheric rustic restaurant is on the main plaza and makes an excellent eating choice. There's a combination of invention and tradition in the attractively presented plates. Fine salads, tasty grilled meats and a great pastry dish with salmon and goat's cheese stand out.

€€ Estación 4
C Estación 4, Bubión, T651-831363. Tue-Fri 1700-2300, Sat 1300-2300.
A winning combination of Mediterranean food, teas and books drives business at this inviting spot, well signposted towards the bottom of the village. Tangy tabbouleh, creamy hummus and seafood spaghetti are among the draws.

€€ Teide
Ctra 2, Bubión, T958-763084, www.restauranteteide.com.
On the main road, this is a redoubt of traditional cooking, with typical Alpujarran cuisine served up in the bar, terrace, and an attractive dining room. Trout with ham, *plato alpujarreño*, or anything else is good. Recommended.

€ Bodega Alacena
Callejón de las Campanas s/n, Capileira, T958-763268.
Tucked away down the side of the church, this little gem sells delicious chestnut honey, ham, wine and other goodies, but also has a delightful little bodega space where you can sit down for wine and simple *raciones*. Recommended.

Trevélez

As in much of the Alpujarra, many places partially or fully close over winter.

€€ Mesón La Fragua
C Posadas s/n, along from the hotel of the same name, T958-858573, www.hotellafragua.com.
A cosy spot on the top floor with views over the valley and very fair prices. Food and service are to be admired here; the *ensalada de jamón* (ham salad) is a meal in itself, but leave room for the house roast lamb, which is superb.

€€ Piedra Ventana
Ctra Ugíjar 36, T958-858599, www.restaurantepiedraventana.com.
Near the bridge right at the bottom of town, this has a traditional bar decorated with cowbells and a dining area with relaxing perspectives over the river. They do a great line in local food.

€ Haraiçel
C Real s/n, T958-858530.
Unpretentious and notably welcoming spot that isn't afraid to break Alpujarran conventions on the menu. Pork loin in raspberry sauce is one surprising but tasty offering. For a real pig experience, though, it has to be the *codillo*, a large pork knuckle boiled to tenderness and served with red cabbage and potatoes. Wash it down with a jug of *costa* wine.

Festivals

20 Jan **Feast of San Sebastián**, a big event in all Alpujarran villages.
13 Jun Trevélez's famous **Moors and Christians fiesta**, with mock battles.
4-5 Aug *Romería* from Trevélez to the top of Mulhacén via the Ermita de San Antonio.
3rd weekend of Oct Trevélez's fiesta.

What to do

Tour operators
See page 348 and page 516 for tour operators who run walking and other trips to the Alpujarra.

Transport

Bus
From Granada, there are buses 3 times daily to **Trevélez** (3 hrs 15 mins) via **Pampaneira**, **Bubión** and **Capileira** (2 hrs 25 mins). These buses are run by **Alsa**; timetables and tickets online at www.alsa.es.

Southern Alpujarra → *Colour map 5, B4.*

superb views of wine-producing white villages and hamlets

From Orgiva, the A348 runs along the southern edge of the Alpujarra, linking up with the northern route again at Cádiar. Like in the song about Loch Lomond, the low road is faster than the high one, and, while not quite as dramatic, provides excellent and expansive views of the valley and the white villages on the other side.

Torvizcón and Cádiar

The only major village on the route is sleepy Torvizcón, prettily situated at the bottom of a *rambla* (stony gully). It's got a bulky church and a ruined Moorish tower, and there's a small *esparto* **museum** at the far end of town. *Esparto* is the sturdy grass traditionally used in Andalucía to make baskets, blinds, mats and wall-hangings.

From just beyond Torvizcón, a narrow road cuts across the valley and up the other side towards Trevélez, passing the tiny hamlet of Almegíjar en route. It's a stunning drive and best done in this direction for your brakes' sake. Walking, it's less arduous to come the other way. Follow the road down from the junction between Trevélez and Juviles, bearing right as soon as you reach the deserted mining village.

The village of **Cádiar**'s central position and the fact that it is the hub of the region's road system mean that at some point you'll likely fetch up here. It's not particularly pretty, but it's a sociable place, particularly at the beginning of October, during its fiesta, when the best of the Alpujurran village fountains, the Fuente del Vino, is set up for a week in the main square dispensing *costa* wine to all comers. The town's name derives from the Arabic word *qadi*, meaning judge; this was probably where the local one resided.

Ugíjar more or less marks the eastern end of the Granadan part of the Alpujarra, but beyond it are more delights in its eastern, Almerían portion, see page 432. It's a busy but not unattractive one-street service town with a couple of cheap lodging options, a tourist office, petrol station and places to eat.

Sierra de la Contraviesa

From the Orgiva–Torvizcón road, you could strike off on another circuit through the southern Sierra de la Contraviesa to Albuñol via several less touristy villages, and then to Cádiar or, indeed, down to the coast a few kilometres away.

From the turn-off some 6 km from Orgiva, the road (signposted Albuñol) ascends a craggy valley to a pass, where magnificent views over the sierra, coast, and sea suddenly open up. From here, the road winds its way eastwards to Albuñol, passing several picturesque wine-growing *pueblos* en route; it's worth making a detour to investigate them, as they are traditional and mostly unspoiled by tourism. There's little in the way of gourmet restaurants, but every village has its little bar where you can try a glass of the local *costa* wine and munch on bread and ham.

Albuñol is a large, sprawling town that has very little appeal and nowhere to stay. It does, however, have the **Cueva de los Murciélagos**, which produced some remarkable neolithic basketwork on display in Granada's archaeological museum (see page 318).

From Albuñol, you can head south to the coast road 7 km away, or head north to **Albondón**, a pleasant wine-producing village, and on to **Cádiar**, the hub of the Alpujarra proper, or to Ugíjar, via the picturesque town of Murtas, another wine centre. The distinctive muddy-coloured *costa* wine here is popular in the Alpujarra region and should be tried at least once; cheaper examples are much better with food than on their own.

Listings Southern Alpujarra

Where to stay

Torvizcón and Cádiar

€€ Alquería de Morayma
Ctra A348, Km 52, 3 km from Cádiar, down the Torvizcón road, T958-343221, www.alqueriamorayma.com.
This is an utterly rustic and peaceful hideaway, surrounded by an ecologically minded farm producing wine and olive oil. There's a variety of rooms designed in traditional Alpujarran style. From apartments equipped with fridge and stove to a room in a whitewashed chapel, all have clay tiled floors, Moorish tracery and prints, ceilings with wooden beams and iron bedheads. There's a pool and a restaurant.

Restaurants

Torvizcón and Cádiar

See also Where to stay, above.

€ Parada Bar
Plaza España 12, Cádiar.
Local in character, this bar on the square is coloured a rather garish orange but is an atmospheric spot for a tapa, with its conversations about the grape harvest and noticeboard with donkeys and tractors for sale.

Festivals

20 Jan **Feast of San Sebastián**, a big event in all Alpujarran villages.
Early Oct Cádiar's knees-up with its fountain of wine.

2nd week of Oct Ugíjar has some well-attended fiestas, revolving around livestock and drinking.

What to do

Tour operators
See page 348 and page 516 for tour operators who run walking and other trips to the Alpujarra.

Transport

Bus
There are 2 daily buses from Granada to **Ugíjar** (4½ hrs) via Torvizcón and Cádiar. Buses to **Almería** via **Berja** leave 2-3 times daily from the centre of Ugíjar, and a couple of daily buses run to Laroles from Ugíjar.

There's a daily bus from Granada to **Albuñol** (3½ hrs), via Orgiva and the road junctions for villages on this route.

Northeastern Alpujarra → *Colour map 5, B4/B5.*

Gerald Brenan's house and spectacular mountain walks

From Cádiar or Bérchules, you can follow the twisty road along the northern edge of the Alpujarra, more interesting than the road that heads due east via Yátor to Ugíjar. The first village is Mecina Bombarón, with several *casas rurales* and a hotel.

Yegen, Válor and Mairena

Described in detail in *South from Granada* by Gerald Brenan (see box, opposite), the village where the author lived is still very typical of the Alpujarra, if you discount the central fountain, which Brenan would be highly amused to see is now a replica of that in the Court of Lions in the Alhambra. Just below this square is Brenan's old house, No 28, marked by a small plaque. If you've seen the film of the book, you'll recognize the village.

Válor, the next town to Yegen, is one of the little-visited gems of the Alpujarra. Still very much reliant on local industry rather than tourism, you can visit the small factories that produce olive oil, cheese and soap or just enjoy wandering around the streets. The whitewashed church has a brick bell tower but an unadorned interior. There's a bank, ATM, pharmacy, and good accommodation and eating.

From Válor, a 15-minute climb will take you to the hamlet of **Nechite**, a tiny place with excellent views from the terrace beside its church. Beyond Válor, you pass through **Mecina Alfahar**, a shady vine-laced village, and arrive at pretty **Mairena**, with views over its plentiful olive groves. From Mairena, you can ascend to lovely **Júbor**, a tiny village reached in 10 minutes on foot through a chestnut grove. There's a red-roofed church as well as a small bar serving food, and a view over the spiny rock ridges below.

Laroles

This seldom-visited town marks the end of the northern route along the Alpujarra; from here you can descend to Ugíjar via Cherín or climb over the Sierra Nevada

ON THE ROAD

Don Gerardo

On the wall of a house, just off a small square in the Alpujarran village of Yegen, is a tiny plaque that proclaims in blue letters that the English writer Gerald Brenan lived here in the 1920s and 1930s. This is a modest tribute to someone whom many consider to be the greatest British Hispanist.

Brenan was born in Malta in 1894 and after a public school education, he fought in the First World War, gaining a Military Medal and the French Croix de Guerre. He became acquainted with the Bloomsbury Group after the war, but soon tired of what he saw as the sexual hypocrisies of British life, and headed for Spain, drawn as much as anything by the cheap wine and cigarettes, his lifelong addictions. He lived in the then remote village of Yegen, with his collection of over 2000 books. Don Gerardo, as locals knew him, intimately describes the village in *South from Granada*, regarded as a sociological masterpiece and now made into a film.

In Yegen he had a steamy relationship with a 15-year-old local girl, Juliana, resulting in a daughter, Elena. In 1930, Brenan, back temporarily in England, met the American poet Gamel Woolsey, whom he married; the couple returned to Spain. Brenan took his daughter from Juliana and renamed her Miranda Helen; he only saw Juliana once more, reintroducing her to her own daughter on the condition that she didn't reveal who she was.

Brenan published several other books about Spain and its people. He developed a strong Andalucían dialect and a love for the Spanish, a two-way rapport as his passionate writing found an appreciative readership in Spain.

Brenan was also an assiduous correspondent and wrote at length to contemporaries in Britain, especially the Bloomsbury circle. Indeed, his biographer, Jonathon Gathorne-Hardy, believes that his brilliant letters will "eventually prove Gerald's most lasting memorial". Gerald Brenan moved to England at the outbreak of the Civil War until 1949, when he settled in Churriana near Málaga. *The Face of Spain* was a personal account of this time. In his later years, Brenan enthusiastically embraced the hippy culture of Torremolinos, despite being in his late sixties. After the death of his wife, he moved in with a much younger woman in the village of Alhaurín el Grande. Finally, at the age of 90, he returned to England, staying in an old people s home in Pinner. Brenan was always more highly regarded in Spain than in England and the Spanish press spread the idea that he had returned to England against his will. Eventually a delegation from Alhaurín came to Pinner and virtually kidnapped Brenan and returned him to Andalucía. He was installed in a home in Alhaurín, the Regional Government providing a nurse and covering his living expenses until he died in 1987. He left his body to medical science but no-one at Málaga university wanted to take a scalpel to such a significant figure, so he was finally buried next to his wife in Málaga's English cemetery in 2001.

north to Guadix (see page 363). The road that reaches Laroles from Mairena is spectacular, in some places offering almost a 360-degree panorama of the valleys below. Laroles makes a good base for the Eastern Alpujarra with its views, accommodation and sociable folk. There's also a small **tourist office** ⓘ *Fri 1700-2100 (1900 winter), Sat-Sun 1000-1400.*

There are several **walking trails** around Laroles, including the one that climbs to the pass of La Ragua (see below), which is a full day's ascent. A fascinating shorter walk of two to three hours runs in a loop up the valley of the Río Laroles, following the main Moorish aqueduct of the region, the Acequia Real. Walk back along the main road towards Mairena and turn right shortly after crossing the Río Laroles, just before the road crosses a gravelly gully, the **Barranco del Arena**. The path climbs along the gully, then cuts right, following the Laroles valley. The *acequia* comes in on your left; at the point where it meets the river a couple of kilometres upstream, cross the small bridge and bear right, following the valley back down to Laroles down what was once the old muleteers' path over the Sierra Nevada. The tourist office has maps of this and other walks, as do the campsites.

Puerto de la Ragua

From Laroles you can ascend to Puerto de la Ragua, a 2000 m-high pass over the Sierra Nevada. It's a memorable drive through increasingly bleak mountain scenery. At the top, where there's a small ski resort, you begin a steep descent to the sheet-like plains east of Guadix, dominated by the highly memorable castle of La Calahorra (see page 365).

You can also climb a forested path from Laroles; this takes six to seven hours, so book a bed up the top and be prepared for poor weather, particularly in spring and autumn. The trail ascends through a fertile corner before climbing through pine forest. The total distance is 18 km, and is of medium difficulty. From the top, the GR-7 trail continues down to La Calahorra, and if you have time, you should walk this leg too; a stunning descent down to the plains. At the pass is a year-round *refugio* (see Where to stay, below).

Listings Northeastern Alpujarra

Where to stay

Yegen, Válor and Mairena

€€ Las Chimeneas
C Amargura 6, Mairena, T958-760089, www.alpujarra-tours.com.
A charming *casa rural* easily accessed at the bottom of this village, this offers valley views and spacious rooms with balcony. There are also self-catering houses and apartments in adjacent buildings. Breakfast is included, other meals are available, and they can do anything from setting you off on a self-guided walk to arranging a week-long extravaganza of guided outdoors and cultural activities.

€ La Fuente
C Real 46, Yegen, T958-851067.
This great-value cheapie in Yegen offers simplicity but authenticity, 3 spotless

cool rooms, and a location right on the square. The attractive *comedor* also does local dishes.

Laroles

See **Balcón de la Alpujarra** in Restaurants, below.

Apartments

€€ Hotel Real de Laroles
C Real 46, T958-760058, www.turismorurallaroles.com.
Near the plaza at the base of the village, this is one of the region's more charming options, a delightfully homely family-run place decorated in simple but appealing rural style with wrought-iron bedsteads and cut-glass lampshades. There are roof spaces with awesome views and the welcome is generous, as is the delicious mountain fare in the adjacent restaurant.

Puerto de la Ragua

€ Albergue Puerto de la Ragua
T950-524020, www.puertodelaragua.com. Open year round.
Right at the top of the pass, this *refugio* is a popular base for cross-country skiing in winter and walkers in summer, and has 32 dorm beds, and a restaurant serving lunches and dinners.

Restaurants

Laroles

As well as the restaurant at the Hotel Real, the **€ Balcón de la Alpujarra**, T958-760217, appeals as a place to eat for its cheap local dishes and inexpensive *menú del día*, but most of all its top views over the valley below. They also have rooms (**€**), some with kitchen.

Festivals

20 Jan **Feast of San Sebastián**, a big event in all Alpujarran villages.
Mid-Sep In Válor you can see another of the region's best **Moros y Cristianos** festivals.

What to do

See page 348 and page 516 for tour operators who run walking and other trips to the Alpujarra.

Transport

Bus

There are 2 daily buses from **Granada** to Yegen, and Válor. A couple of daily buses run to Laroles from **Ugíjar**.

East from Granada

Heading east from Granada into the long 'handle' of the province, the landscape becomes increasingly rugged. At its extremity, it's one of the most rewarding remote regions of Andalucía.

Many of the towns and villages in this area have substantial barrios where people live in caves, which were traditionally a cheap place to live and a way of avoiding temperature extremes. One such town is Guadix, which also has a striking cathedral.

Near here, the extraordinary castle at La Calahorra is a must-see, while the little known valley of Gorafe has hundreds of well-excavated prehistoric tombs to investigate.

From the town of Baza, surrounded by *parque natural*, you can head northwards towards the Sierra de Cazorla through some impressive jagged terrain, or up towards the remote sheep-rearing town of Huéscar and on towards Almería province or Murcia.

Guadix → *Colour map 5, A5.*

famous for its fascinating cave suburbs

★Arriving for the first time, the town of Guadix seems as if it's an offworld colony, set among otherworldly crags sharply eroded into fey formations. When the wind blows through here in winter, you can feel why the rocks have crumbled before it. Troglodyte communities are important parts of Guadix and most of the towns and villages in this area. Guadix also has a stunning cathedral and array of other monuments, but the rest of the town is impoverished, with few employment prospects and tension between its gypsy and *payo* communities.

Guadix's helpful **tourist office** ⓘ *Pl de la Constitución 15, T958-662804, www.guadix.es, Mon-Fri 0900-1400, 1600-1800*, is in the old town near the cathedral.

The centre of Guadix is dominated by its memorable **cathedral** ⓘ *T958-665108, Mon-Sat 1040-1400, 1600-1800, 1700-1930 summer, €5*, built from a dusky orange sandstone and overlooking the bare space that was once Guadix's prosperous Jewish quarter. It was built in different periods: the Isabelline Gothic interior has a Renaissance apse by Diego de Siloé, and there are two exuberantly Baroque façades on the exterior. The brick bell tower adds another ingredient to the mix, but when the sun shines, it's one of the more remarkable buildings in Andalucía. The main façade is pure Spanish Baroque, full of niches and columns. Move to your right to where a street cuts in behind you and observe how the façade suddenly realigns itself with the white saints all in a line.

The interior is gloomy by comparison; the highlight is the very ornately carved choir stalls. The Guadix choirboys have achieved some fame in Spain and sold many albums. Note the contrast between the earlier Gothic part and the simpler Renaissance classicism with its round arches and smooth lines. The museum (included in the admission) is disappointing; among some worthwhile religious art is a surfeit of showy silver and hoarded 'treasures'.

Opposite the cathedral, you can head under an arch into the charming **Plaza Constitución**. In this old part of town are also a couple of fine Renaissance palaces, the **Palacio de Peñaflor** by the Alcazaba, and the **Palacio de Villalegre** behind the cathedral. Both built in the 16th century, they are similarly designed, with twin brick towers flanking a façade decorated with coats of arms. Below the Palacio de Peñaflor, the **Iglesia de Santiago** has an excellent *mudéjar* wooden ceiling. Guadix's most famous citizen, the writer Pedro Antonio de Alarcón, is commemorated with a small statue in the *alameda* below the cathedral.

Guadix's once-proud Moorish **Alcazaba** now has its walls bolstered by decaying concrete. Built in the 10th century, it offers little more than wistful historical reminders of Guadix's more prosperous days and is currently closed to the public. As well as the Alcazaba, significant stretches of Moorish walls still encircle the old town.

Though most spaghetti western filming in Spain took place around Almería, Guadix had its moment in the limelight too – it featured as the Mexican town of Mesa Verde in Sergio Leone's *A Fistful of Dynamite*.

However, Guadix's biggest silver screen celebrity is 'Baldwin', a glorious old 1928 steam train sitting with its four carriages in a shed near the station. It has starred in dozens of films, including *Dr Zhivago*, *The Good, the Bad and the Ugly*, and *Indiana Jones and the Last Crusade*. Despite not being officially open to the public – though plans are afoot – ask around the station, for it is lovingly maintained by train buffs who are delighted to show it off.

The caves

There are several consecutive cave suburbs encircling the town's southern edges. They are bizarrely picturesque, with chimneys emerging from the hillside like comedy toadstools alongside radio aerials hung with washing. It's pleasant to wander around the area, but avoid rubbernecking. You may be lured into 'tours' of private homes; these are best avoided, as nasty scenes can ensue when an exorbitant sum is demanded on your exit.

A couple of caves are open to the public. The **Centro de Interpretación Cuevas de Guadix** ⓘ *Pl Padre Oveda s/n, T958-665569, www.cuevamuseoguadix.com, Mon-Fri 1000-1400, 1600-1800 (1700-1900 summer), Sat 1000-1400, €2.60*, has an interesting display on troglodyte life.

Guadix has several accommodation options in caves, and there are dozens more in surrounding towns and villages; contact the tourist office for details.

Listings Guadix

Where to stay

The main reason to stay in Guadix is to experience one of its several cave hotels, which are rather more luxurious than they may sound. As well as those mentioned here, the tourist office can provide a list of further troglodyte options.

€€ Cuevas de Rolando
Rambla de Baza s/n, 3 km from the centre of Guadix, T670-799138, www.cuevasderolando.com.
These are some of the most atmospheric caves available, with uplifting views to be enjoyed from your little private patio at the cave mouth. Inside, they are decorated with style and charm by the friendly owners.

€€ Cuevas El Abuelo Ventura
Ctra de Lugros s/n, about 1 km out of Guadix T958-664050, www.cuevasabueloventura.com.
This is a fairly luxurious trog option, though the fact that the caves aren't natural might put you off. Spacious, comfortable dens have good facilities and views from the front; there's a restaurant and even a pool half-in and half-out of a cave. It needed a facelift at our last visit.

Restaurants

€€ Boabdil
C Manuel de Falla 3, T958-664883, www.restauranteboabdilguadix.com.
This is one of Guadix's better eateries. Apart from the usual hearty meat dishes, there's some excellent grilled fish, and

a thoughtful selection of mid-priced Spanish wines. Among the starters, the unusual pineapple and asparagus salad has plenty going for it, as does the smoked salmon.

Transport

Bus

Buses run roughly hourly to **Granada** from Guadix's bus station, by the river to the east of town (1 hr), and to **Almería** almost as often (1 hr 20 mins). Trains run the same route 4 times daily (1 hr), or the other way to Almería. Other bus services run regularly to the surrounding villages, including **La Calahorra**. **Madrid** is served 5 times daily (5 hrs), while on Mon, Wed, Fri, a bus heads to Almería over the **Puerta de la Ragua**. **Baza** is served hourly.

La Calahorra → *Colour map 5, A5.*

a compulsory stop for the amazing castle

★The town of La Calahorra is famous for its stunning castle which wholly dominates the surrounding countryside. To call this one of the most dramatic and unexpected castles in Spain is no exaggeration. Although from the outside it may look every inch a purely functional fortification, it is in fact more of a palace than a redoubt.

To visit the **castle** ⓘ *Wed only, 1000-1300, 1600-1800, entrance by gratuity,* outside of the opening times call on the keyholder, Antonio, at Calle Claveles 2, T958-677098, just down from Labella *hostal*. He'll usually be happy to take you up, but he's only doing you a favour, so don't complain if he's got something better to do, and do tip generously if he does. Remember that 1400-1700 are sacred lunch and siesta hours.

The exterior conceals one of the earliest Renaissance interiors in Spain, created on the whim of Rodrigo de Vivar y Mendoza, an illegitimate son of a duke whose life reads like a cheap historical novel. Fleeing persecution by the aristocracy after the death of his father and first wife, he headed to Italy, where he fell under the spell of the pope's daughter, Lucrezia Borgia. He returned to Spain without an Italian consort but with a head full of the new architectural ideas of that region. The palace was a result of that, but no sooner was it completed than Rodrigo was forced to leave the area; old-seated prejudices compounded by the marquis's scandalous private life made residence in Granada province a very hot potato. It's now owned by another ducal family, who are suspicious of the state's attempts to open it to tourism.

The road to the top is a poor one, so if it's your own beloved car you may want to spare it the climb; in any case, the walk to the top heightens the anticipation, as the unlikely building looms menacingly above.

From La Calahorra you can ascend the GR-7 path up to Puerto de la Ragua (see page 360) and down again into the Alpujarra. The ascent to the pass takes some six to eight hours, with spectacular views all the way, and you can stay in the *refugio* up the top (see Where to stay, page 361).

Where to stay

€€ El Castillo/Hospederia del Zenete
Ctra La Ragua s/n, T958-677192, www.hospederiadelzenete.com.
This well-appointed hotel is somewhat tastelessly built to resemble the castle itself, but has a range of comfortable accommodation, ranging from attractive standard doubles to split-level suites and a family apartment. There's also a gym and sauna. The restaurant is the best in town, and serves generous portions of heartily flavoured local fare. Service is lax but willing.

€ Hostal Labella
Ctra de Aldeire 1, T958-677241.
A modern choice offering excellent value, rooms have heating, bathroom, phone and TV. Most importantly, half of them have a balcony that looks directly at the magnificent castle. Downstairs is a convivial bar and restaurant.

Gorafe → *Colour map 5, A5.*

remarkable place with late-Neolithic tombs, hidden deep in Granada province

Gorafe is almost never visited except by *granadinos*, but that will surely change. Crossing a flat arid plain punctuated with olive trees, the ground suddenly gives way and a picturesque canyon opens up. Apart from the walking and photographic opportunities, there are some 200 painstakingly excavated and labelled late-Neolithic tombs in the immediate vicinity to investigate.

You can pick up a map of the tombs at the Gorafe town hall or from the **Centro de Interpretación Sobre El Megalítico** ⓘ *A92, T958-693159, www.gorafe.es, Tue-Sun 1100-1600, €3,* on the motorway 20 km from Guadix towards Murcia. This unusual underground museum is set up to resemble a dolmen burial chamber and brings the tombs to life with information and a flashy 3D audiovisual.

The village of Gorafe itself has plenty of unspoilt charm, including many cave dwellings around its edges. Several of the caves have been converted to comfortable apartments in which you can stay (if travelling by public transport you'll have to). These can get busy with *granadino* families at weekends, so it's better to book ahead.

To get there by car, take the Baza–Murcia road from Guadix and exit the *autopista* 16 km from town; Gorafe is signposted, and is 13 km to the north of the junction. If returning to Guadix or Granada by car, it's worth continuing up the road to Alicún and Villanueva, then descending via the NE51 to Pedro Martínez; the drive is spectacular.

Where to stay

€€-€ Las Cuevas del Pataseca
C La Mina 43, T958-693114.
Ignacio has beautifully done up, colourful cave apartments at reasonable prices.

Transport

Bus
A daily bus leaves **Guadix** for Gorafe at 1430. The return bus leaves at 0730.

Baza → *Colour map 5, A6.*

historic town making a decent stopover

Heading northeast from Guadix the scenery becomes increasingly rugged, and the olive tree increasingly predominant. The road passes through the Parque Natural Sierra de Baza before dramatically descending to the town of Baza, which has a much more peaceful and friendly feel than Guadix.

Baza was once an important Iberian town known as Basti, and it was here that one of the finest pre-Roman pieces unearthed by archaeologists in Spain was found: the *Dama de Baza*, an enigmatic roughly life-size sculpture of a woman of such beauty and importance that it was quickly whisked away to Madrid, where it can be seen in the city's archaeological museum. The Moors held on to Baza until 1489, when Castilian armies finally took its hill fortress. From that period the town has been a peaceful rural backwater and service town for the surrounding agricultural area.

Baza has been wracked by earthquakes over the years, which have damaged and destroyed many of its historic buildings. The old quarter is centred around Plaza Mayor, whose pleasing fountain is surrounded by roses. On this square are two of the most important edifices: the Colegiata, a high fortress-like church adorned with a Plateresque and a Baroque portal and some fine coats of arms. It is much revered for being the resting place of the local patron, San Máximo. Part of it was designed by the budding architect Alonso de Covarrubias, who was to rise to become one of the stars of the Spanish Renaissance. The bell tower dates from later and its chimes can be heard all over town.

Also on the Plaza Mayor is the **Museo Arqueológico** ⓘ *daily 1100-1400, 1600-1830 (1830-2000 summer), €3,* housed in a palace that also contains the tourist office (same opening hours). The museum has a replica of the colourful Dama de Baza as well as a comprehensive prehistoric section, some Roman architectural and ceramic remains and artefacts from the Moorish period.

Above the Colegiata, the **Moorish Alcazaba** is now a concrete compound that offers nothing more than views and a heavily restored section of Renaissance colonnade.

Where to stay

€€€ Cuevas Al Jatib
Arroyo Cúrcal s/n, T958-342248, www.aljatib.com.
The Rolls Royce of troglodyte accommodation in Granada province, this sumptuous complex takes the humble cave into luxury class – has humanity gone full circle? The self-catering caves are appealing – although no more so than others in the area – but it's the classy restaurant, and, most of all, the cave-built hammam that sets this apart. Caves come in various sizes. Romantic, out-of-the-way and fun. Set a little way east of Baza, along the Camino de Oría; take the 'Baza este' exit from the motorway.

€ Hotel Anabel
C María de Luna s/n, a short walk to west of the centre, T958-860998, www.hotelanabelbaza.com.
Central Baza's best option, this hotel is situated above a vast restaurant (*menú del día* very reasonable). The rooms are well decorated with pale wooden floorboards, gratifyingly large beds and well-equipped bathrooms. There's also a lift and easy parking outside.

Restaurants

€€ Los Cántaros
C Arcipreste Juan Hernández s/n, T958-700375, www.restaurantelos cantaros.com.
Baza's best eating option, in the centre of town behind the cinema, combines a long bar stocked with happy tapas-eaters and an elegant dining area with round tables. There's good seafood on offer here – *quisquillas* (miniature shrimp) are worth trying, but it's hard to resist the allure of the wood-fired grill smoking away up the back. The steaks are excellent, but vegetarians are also well catered for with the house salad plump with avocado and artichokes.

€ La Solana
C Serrano 4, T958-861523, up a narrow lane off the Plaza Mayor.
The town's most characterful tapas bar. Packed floor to ceiling with curios, it's a warm and welcoming place. There's a wide choice of *raciones*; recommended are the brochettes, or the grilled cuttlefish.

Festivals

6-15 Sep Baza's **fiesta** is a lively event drawing villagers of the northeast of the province, as well as from Granada and Guadix.

Transport

Bus
Baza's bus station is on C Reyes Católicos, a short way east of the centre. There are hourly buses to **Granada** (1 hr 30 mins) via **Guadix** (30 mins), and there are 3 daily buses to **Huéscar** (1 hr), which continue to **Puebla de Don Fadrique**. There are 2-3 connections to **Almería** and **Jaén** daily: these require a change at Guadix, but the ongoing bus waits for you. There are also daily buses to **Madrid**, **Sevilla** and **Murcia**.

La Costa Tropical

The short coastline of Granada province is a breath of fresh air between the Costa del Sol and the relentless plasticulture of western Almería province. Known as the Costa Tropical, it indeed has a fabulous climate, which is being increasingly sought by northern Europeans. The beach towns of La Herradura, Almuñécar and Salobreña are attractive places to stay.

Almuñécar and La Herradura → *Colour map 5, B3.*

laid-back neighbouring beach towns

Almuñécar is a peaceful resort except in high summer, when its population multiplies by about eight times and it becomes a party capital for *granadinos* and *madrileños*. While the town still has plenty of Spanish character, it's increasingly being taken over by the expat invasion.

Almuñécar was founded as a trading outpost in the eighth century BC by the Phoenicians, who named it Sexi, inadvertently giving today's tourist board a mountain of marketing opportunities. Later a Roman town, it was renamed *Al-Munakkah* by the Moors. In AD 755, the Ummayad prince Abd al-Rahman arrived here after fleeing the massacre of his family in Damascus. He established himself in Córdoba, which under him began its pre-eminence in the western world. The town achieved more recent fame as the town where Laurie Lee fetched up after walking across Spain. His time here is described in *As I Walked Out One Midsummer Morning*; until Franco's death editions disguised the town as Castillo because it had been a hotbed of anarchist and republican sympathizers. When the Civil War started, Lee was picked up by a British destroyer and taken home. *A Rose for Winter* describes his return here after the war.

The **tourist office** ⓘ *Av de Europa s/n, T958-631125, www.turismoalmunecar.es, daily 0930-1330, 1630-1900 (1700-2000 in summer)*, stands in a striking neo-Moorish *palacio* just back from the Playa de San Cristóbal. There's also a tourist kiosk on the Paseo del Altillo between the old town and the beach.

Down the road from the tourist office is the **botanic gardens**, in the centre of which are the ruins of a Carthaginian and Roman factory for the making of the prized fish sauce called *garum*. The ruins are a little difficult to understand, but you can see the tanks where the fish was fermented. Around the gardens are small art workshops, one named for each province of Andalucía. Some of them run short courses in traditional handicrafts of the region.

Above here is the **castle** ⓘ *Tue-Sat 1030-1330, 1600-1830 (1700-1930 summer), Sun 1000-1400, €2.35 joint entry with Museo Arqueológico*. It was originally fortified by the Phoenicians and then used by the Carthaginians and Romans. The Moorish rulers of Granada, the Nasrids, used it as a summer palace and a dungeon for political opponents. Heavily modified by Charles V in the 16th century, the castle was virtually destroyed during the Peninsular War. Until recently it was used as the town's cemetery. There's not a huge amount remaining inside, but some Moorish wall is preserved, as well as a scary dungeon. A small display of artefacts is housed in the central building, including an excellent bronze lion's head with the horns of a goat from the Roman period. There's also a scale model of the area, showing the locations of various ancient sites. Beyond here are some simple Roman tombs. The castle offers spectacular views both ways along the coast.

The **Museo Arqueológico** ⓘ *C Málaga s/n, hours and admission as castle, above*, is housed in reconstructed Roman cisterns dating from the first century AD. Various finds are displayed, but the highlight is a fine Egyptian vase from around 1700 BC, with hieroglyphic inscriptions referring to the pharaoh Apophis/Apepi I, of whom almost nothing is known as he is associated with the mysterious Hyksos period. Its presence here is a mystery; best guess is that the Phoenicians brought it here a millennium after its manufacture. The staff here can tell you about more sites in the area, including various sections of Roman aqueducts and a Phoenician and Roman necropolis a 20-minute walk west of town.

Acuario de Almuñécar ⓘ *Pl Kuwait s/n, T902-109835, www.acuarioalmunecar.es, 1000-1400, 1600-2000, hours change significantly through year, €12, children €9*, is the town's aquarium, a good two-level display of all that swims, sprouts and scuttles under the surface of the Mediterranean. There's information on underwater evolution and adaptation to the marine environment, as well as the obligatory tunnel where you can watch sharks, rays, and sunfish cruising about.

Loro Sexi (Sexy Parrot) ⓘ *C Bikini s/n, open 1030-1400, 1600-1800 (1700-2000 summer), €4*, is a bird park in the middle of town, near the Playa San Cristóbal. There's a very good collection of parrots and their like, but many appear depressed and spend their time pulling their own feathers out. The macaws are particularly fine though, and other attractions include prim mandarin ducks, and striking silver and gold pheasants. The park is shady and makes an enjoyable stroll up and down the hillside.

The central town beach is **Playa Puerta del Mar**, where on the promenade is an imaginative monument to the Phoenicians and, nearby, a homage to Laurie Lee. A rocky outcrop, with a mirador and numerous seabirds, divides this from the better **Playa de San Cristóbal** to the west, which is backed by hotels and restaurants.

West of Almuñécar is the resort village of La Herradura. Between the two, there's some pleasant strolling to be done around the cliffs of the **Punta de la Mona**. The area's very popular for paragliding, and there are several good beaches around here, including **Playa El Muerto**, a relaxed and secluded nudist beach (nudism is mainstream in Spain).

La Herradura is a friendly, low-key place set around a large, sheltered bay with an attractive (if pebbly) beach. In the summer, it's busy with foreign and Spanish beachgoers, but its seafront *chiringuito* bars are still a perfect spot for a cold beer and plate of *boquerones fritos* on a hot day. Just out of La Herradura on the way to Nerja is a protected area, the Acantilados de Maro–Cerro Gordo, with spectacular cliffs, stunning views along the coast and secluded rocky coves with sandy beaches.

Listings Almuñécar and La Herradura

Where to stay

Almuñécar

There are numerous resort hotels along the Playa de San Cristóbal beach. Book ahead in summer. There are good off-season rates.

€€ Hostal Altamar
C Alta del Mar s/n, T958-630346, www.hostalaltamar.com.
Central spot with clean and well-kept rooms in the heart of the old town. It's not bad value in summer, but in winter it's an absolute bargain.

€€ Hotel Casablanca
Plaza San Cristóbal 4, T958-635575, www.hotelcasablanca almunecar.com.
In extravagant neo-Moorish style, this hotel is great value, especially off season and is a pebble's throw from the beach. Rooms are elegant, spacious, a/c, and many have balconies overlooking the sea. The bathrooms are decked out in black marble, and there's also a good restaurant.

€ Hostal Rocamar
C Córdoba 3, T958-630023.
Great value for money, this *hostal* is in the heart of things just off Av Andalucía and run by a friendly young family. Its rooms are decent for the price, and include a small bathroom. Very cheap off season.

Restaurants

Almuñécar

Just off Plaza Madrid, C Buenos Aires leads into a small square, Plaza Kelibia, surrounded by bars. They're all based half-outdoors and serve generous free snacks with each drink.

€€ Los Geraneos
Pl de la Rosa 4, T958-634020.
In a little square just off the waterfront promenade, this is a sweet place offering tasty meals, including a good Caesar salad and delicious fried brie with strawberry sauce.

€€ Mesón Gala
Pl Antonio Gala 5, T958-881455.
Deservedly popular indoor-outdoor venue with a boss who looks after his customers. Generous, interesting plates of free tapas accompany your drink, and tasty full meals never disappoint.

€ Bodega Francisco I
C Real 7.
Stocked with old photos and venerable barrels from which they draw excellent local wines, this bar could appear to be living in the past. But an upbeat attitude, tasty *raciones* and daily *menú*, as well as optimistic Southeast Asian art on the walls mean it's unique and usually packed at mealtimes. They also run a worthwhile meat restaurant further down the street.

€ La Trastienda
Plaza Kelibia s/n.
One of a clutch of appealing tapas bars on this square, this has a large terrace, an attractive indoor-outdoor bar area, and sound staff. There's a fine choice of *raciones*, including *roscas* (ring-shaped loaves of bread filled with *jamón serrano* and cheese), for sharing.

Bars and clubs

Almuñécar
There are 4 or 5 bars on the beach itself, below the Paseo; these get busy in summer with pumping music until late. The *discoteca* action mainly heats up during summer.

Festivals

Almuñécar
Jul Almuñécar hosts a significant **jazz festival** that attracts performers from around the world. Information on programming and ticketing can be found on the town's website, www.almunecar.info.

What to do

Almuñécar
Almuñécar Dive Center, *Paseo de Cotobro s/n, T958-634512, www.scubasur.com.* Run diving courses.
Centro Hípico Taramay, *behind the Hotel Taramay, T609-568966.* Can arrange horse-riding excursions in the area.

Transport

Almuñécar
Almuñécar has good bus connections. They stop at the bus station, a short walk northeast of the centre. Departures are nearly hourly to **Salobreña** and **Motril** (15 mins/30 mins). **Granada** is served by 8 to 9 daily buses (1 hr 15 mins) and other regular destinations include **Málaga** (1 hr 45 mins), some via **Nerja**; and **Almería** (3 hrs 10 mins).

Salobreña → *Colour map 5, B3.*

picturesque white village cascading down a hill to the beach

Dominated by a Moorish castle and once an important Phoenician settlement, inviting Salobreña comprises a hilltop village which extends down past sugarcane plantations to its modern beachside extension. The planting of sugar ensures Salobreña's continued prosperity; indeed it's the only town in Europe with a sugar cane factory, the chimney of which you can see on the west side of town. With the old town preserving its Moorish street plan, and the beachside development fairly restrained, Salobreña is as quiet and pleasant a location as you could wish for.

The town's **tourist office** ⓘ *Plaza de Goya, T958-610314, turismo@ayto-salobrena.org, Mon-Fri 0900-1500, 1630-2000, Sat-Sun 1000-1330,* is below the old town, on the roundabout just as you enter Salobreña if coming off the highway. You can download a guide to the town to your mobile phone.

The major sight is the **Castillo** ⓘ *winter Tue-Sun 1000-1300, 1600-1900; summer daily 1000-1400, 1730-2115, €2.75, or €3.45 including the archaeological museum Museo Villa de Salobreña (same opening hours) on Plaza del Ayuntamiento.* Although fortified by successive occupying civilizations, the castle now dates mainly from the 12th century. It was used by Granada's Nasrid rulers as a palace and a prison, and still preserves much of its structure from this period. With steep cliffs on three sides, the only approach was through the houses, making it very siege resistant, especially as a fountain within the castle gave a reliable water supply. It is kidney shaped and consists of two enclosures, one of which contained the prison, which at one time or another held a number of disgraced Moorish kings such as Muley Hacen and Yusef III. A large flattened tower contained the armoury, while another tower protected the entrance. The Tower of Homage is of square construction and contains two large rooms on two storeys. The windows have decorated arches, and Moorish ceramics and glass have been found on the site. The views are exceptional from the walls.

The town's real pleasure is walking its steep narrow streets, which in parts suddenly give way to spectacular views from sheer drops. The beach is pretty good, and the development around it hasn't spoiled it. A string of bars and eateries along it make fine places for lunch on a hot day or for an evening drink while watching the spectacular sunsets.

Listings Salobreña

Where to stay

There are also various unexceptional mid-range hotels.

€€ Hostal Jayma
C Cristo 24, T958-610231, www.hostaljayma.com.
This *hostal* offers a big welcome and great modern rooms, all with terrace or balcony. The place is spotless, with excellent bathrooms and thoughtful extras like free bottled water. There's also a roof terrace with castle views. It's a great base in the old town, and well signposted. Recommended.

€ Pensión Mari Carmen
C Nueva 30, T958-610906, www.pensionmaricarmen.com.
A simple place with a friendly owner and a terrace with views over the sea. The decor is charming and the rooms, although without frills, are very likeable. Rooms without bathroom are much cheaper.

Restaurants

The best places to eat are on the beachfront, with its terraced cafés, restaurants and bars.

€€ Casa Emilio
Paseo Marítimo 5, T958-349432, www.chiringuitocasaemilio.es.
One of the best of the seaside options, this is right on the beach with a great selection of grilled fish as well as rice dishes and their famous sardine skewers.

Transport

Bus
Buses run regularly from opposite the tourist office. See Almuñécar for routes and distances, which are practically the same.

West from Granada

West of Granada, the motorway speeds into the distance. It's worth taking a bit of time, however, to appreciate two excellent Spanish villages, Alhama de Granada and Montefrío.

Montefrío → *Colour map 5, A2.*

dramatic setting in a craggy valley

This village 30 km north of the main road has a far-flung allure. A high limestone outcrop dominates the town, topped by a church. It's particularly striking at night, when the building is floodlit and seems to float in the air above the town.

The building is called the **Iglesia de la Villa**, and is built inside the old Moorish castle. Attractively early Renaissance in style; it has a **display** ⓘ *Mon-Fri 1200-1400*, on the Moorish culture of the region inside. The town itself is centred around the vast round neoclassical **Iglesia de la Encarnación**, which looks distinctly mosque-like from above. Its interior is a stunning space under the vast bare dome. Nearby is the helpful **tourist office** ⓘ *T958-336004*, in the Casa de Oficios.

Accessed from the road to Illora, **Las Peñas de los Gitanos** (Hills of the Gypsies) is an area of striking natural beauty, with grassy meadows dividing zones of olive trees and low Mediterranean forest. The *peñas* themselves are craggy limestone outcrops. The area harbours archaeological sites; caves occupied in the Neolithic era, several Chalcolithic necropolises with dolmens and the remains of Iberian and Visigothic see below. It's a wonderful area to lose yourself strolling around for a day.

From Montefrío, you have the options of heading east to Alcalá and Jaén province, or north into the Sistema Subbética of southern Córdoba.

Listings Montefrío

Where to stay

Ask at the tourist office for locals who sometimes have rooms available. There are several *casas rurales*; contact the tourist office or search online for information.

€€ Hotel La Enrea
Paraje de Enrea s/n, T958-336662, www.laenreahotel.com.
At the entrance to the village, by a stream, this good-value hotel is in a former olive mill. There's a patio, a good restaurant and a lounge with a cosy fire.

Transport

Bus
3 buses run Mon-Sat between **Granada** and Montefrío (1 hr) ; there's also a daily bus to **Alcalá la Real** in Jaén province.

Alhama de Granada → *Colour map 5, B2.*

an appealing village, a smaller-scale Ronda

★Alhama de Granada is perched on the edge of low cliffs dropping to a grassy ravine. The Moors named it for its natural hot springs. When the governor of the town was away in 1482, Christian forces took Alhama in a bloody battle; his lamenting cry "Ay! De mi Alhama!" is still used as an expression of regret.

The small 19th-century castle incorporates part of the original Moorish fortress but is a private residence. The **tourist office** ⓘ *Carrera de Francisco de Toledo 10, T958-360686, www.turismodealhama.com, Mon 0930-1500, Tue-Fri 0930-1500, 1630-1830, Sat and Sun 1000-1430, 1630-1830*, is on the Paseo near it. Beyond here is the Iglesia del Carmen, from behind which you get excellent views of the *tajo* (ravine).

The church, **Santa María de la Encarnación**, is a chunky Gothic structure erected shortly after the reconquest of the town. Legend has it that the ornate vestments in the interior were embroidered by Isabel herself. The church was designed by Diego de Siloé among others. An inscription by one door commemorates King Alfonso XII helping victims of the 1884 earthquake, which killed 745 people in this region.

The **Moorish baths** ⓘ *daily 1400-1600, €1, free Mon, closed mid-Dec to March*, are well preserved inside the Hotel Balneario, see below. A popular spot for a free hot bath is outside the entrance, where hot waters meet the river.

Listings Alhama de Granada

Where to stay

€€ Hotel Balneario
Ctra del Balneario s/n, 1 km from the centre, T958-350011, www.balnearioalhamade granada.com. Closed mid-Dec to Mar.
This spa hotel sits atop the natural hot springs. Rooms are large and comfy, and there are treatments. Could do with a spruce-up.

€€ La Seguiriya
C Las Peñas 12, T958-360636, www.laseguiriya.com.
Charmingly restored 18th-century house. Comfy rooms are named after flamenco singers. There's a terrace with views; includes breakfast. Recommended.

€ Pensión San José
Plaza de la Constitución 27, T958-350156, www.sanjosealhama.com.
An excellent budget option in the town centre, with a restaurant.

Restaurants

€ Bar Ochoa
Plaza San Sebastián s/n. Closed Tue.
Bursting with character: people always seem to be having a good time. That's largely down to the energetic owner and his *raciones* of local produce. Recommended.

Transport

Bus
There are 3 daily buses to **Granada**.

Jaén

a rugged and sparsely populated region

Word hasn't got around about how much this most Spanish of Andalucía's provinces possesses in its remote corners. Jaén has always been strategically important, as it guards the Despeñaperros Pass, the main route linking Andalucía with the rest of Spain.

The capital city, Jaén, is a quiet, staid place dominated by its fine Renaissance cathedral and, high above, its castle. Two of Spain's most beautiful towns lie to the east: Baeza and Ubeda boast an astonishing collection of elegant Renaissance palaces and churches in warm-coloured stone.

Beyond here, pretty Cazorla is the gateway to the verdant and mountainous natural park of the same name and offers plenty of shady walking and hospitable places to stay.

The province has plenty to offer castle enthusiasts too; north of Jaén, on the way to the Despeñaperros Pass, the village of Baños de la Encina has a particularly muscular example, while the impressive Castillo de la Mota towers above Alcalá la Real.

This is in prime olive country and the wide skies and lonely hills make it worth exploring.

Best for
Architecture ▪ Castles ▪ Oil

Footprint picks

★ **Museo Internacional de Arte Naïf**, page 385

Enjoy the excellent collection, which has more than a hint of rural nostalgia.

★ **Andújar**, page 389

Head here in late April for the busy *romería* to the town's hilltop sanctuary.

★ **Alcalá la Real**, page 391

Climb the steep streets to the imposing castle, perhaps the finest of many that dot the province.

★ **Ubeda and Baeza**, pages 394 and 398

A splendid collection of Renaissance buildings forms the historic centres of these charming towns.

★ **Walking around Cazorla**, page 406

A staggering network of marked trails makes this national park one of Andalucía's finest destinations for hiking.

Footprint picks

1. **Museo Internacional de Arte Naïf**, page 385
2. **Andújar**, page 389
3. **Alcalá la Real**, page 391
4. **Ubeda and Baeza**, pages 394 and 398
5. **Walking around Cazorla**, page 406

Jaén city

The self-styled 'olive oil capital of the world' is a busy provincial centre little visited by tourists. This fact alone, together with its lack of self-consciousness, can come as a distinct relief in high season. Although Jaén isn't Andalucía's most vibrant city, a day or so can happily be spent here taking in the sights.

The cathedral has some excellent Renaissance stonework and appears to have bulked up on steroids in an effort to upstage the castle, perched way up on a rocky hill overlooking the town, which is, of course, surrounded by a sea of olive groves.

Other worthwhile sights include a delightful museum of naive art, in the same building as the city's well-restored Arab baths. *Colour map 2, C5.*

Cathedral

Plaza Santa María s/n, T953-234233. Cathedral Mon-Fri 1000-1400, 1600-1900 (2000 summer), Sat 1000-1400, 1600-1800 (1900 summer) Sun 1000-1200, 1600-1800 (1900 summer), €5.

Jaén's cathedral was often derided by the big names of 20th-century travel writing as being ungainly. Certainly its immense bulk would have Olympic officials scurrying to demand a urine sample, but its clean Renaissance lines will appeal to many.

Originally the site of the city's main mosque, the present structure wasn't started until 1548, supervised by the master architect Andrés de Vandelvira. It wasn't finished until the 18th century; the main façade, flanked by twin towers, dates from the 17th century and is pure Baroque, with massive columns and three panels above its portals of San Miguel, the Assumption and Santa Catalina. Many of the Elders of the Church statues are by Pedro Roldán.

The interior is triple-naved and has fine Renaissance stonework with some Baroque modifications. The intricately carved choir is particularly noteworthy, as are the elegant cupolas, svelte Corinthian columns and Plateresque ceiling dotted with shields and rosettes. The marble retrochoir is carved with the Holy Family. The presbytery is open with a small elegant tabernacle; behind is the Capilla Mayor which holds a gothic sculpture, the Virgen de la Antigua, and a reliquary that holds the much-venerated Santo Rostro. This cloth is said to be that with which Veronica wiped the face of Christ as he carried the cross to Golgotha. The image of a face is imprinted on the cloth, which has been the subject of numerous Spanish paintings. Veronica's action also gave her name to one of the more skilful cape manoeuvres in bullfighting. How the cathedral came into possession of the relic is no longer known, after the destruction of the archives in a 14th-century fire. During the Civil War the Santo Rostro was seized by members of the Communist party; it eventually showed up in a garage near Paris and was returned to Jaén by the French authorities.

Adjacent to the cathedral, sharing the same opening hours and included in the price of admission, is a **museum of religious art**. Most of the pieces are mediocre, but there's a fine early 15th-century Christ attributed by some to Jacob of Florence. A Flemish alabaster sculpture of the Descent also stands out. At the entry to the museum you can also purchase admission to the sacristy and chapterhouse, stunning vaulted chambers in pure Renaissance style and true to the original Vandelvira design.

A few streets northeast of the cathedral is another interesting church, **San Ildefonso** ⓘ *Plaza de San Ildefonso s/n, T953-190346, Mon-Thu and Sat 0830-1230, 1700-2015, Fri 0830-1030, 1700-2015, Sun 0900-1400, 1800-2015, free.* Its rough corbelled stone exterior presents a delightful and fortress-like aspect; the structure is principally a Gothic one from the 15th century, with Renaissance additions, such as the bell tower, and later neoclassical modifications. The interior is bare but houses items intimately concerned with the city of Jaén. In a chapel is the 13th-century sculpture of Nuestra Señora de la Capilla, who is the city's patron. The master Renaissance architect Andrés de Vandelvira, responsible for the design of Jaén's cathedral and for many of the fine palaces of Ubeda and Baeza, is buried here, and the skin of the *lagarto de Jaén*, the pesky lizard that terrorized the city for so many years, also hangs in the church. Also worth noting is the painting of the Last Judgement just inside the side door; among those consigned to the flames is a sinful bishop wearing his mitre.

Essential Jaén

Getting around

Jaén is compact and easily negotiable on foot. Drivers will find that parking in the old town is difficult, but there are underground car parks.

When to go

As elsewhere in inland Andalucía, it's very hot in summer.

Time required

Two days.

Castillo de Santa Catalina

T953-120733, Tue-Sat 1000-1400 and 1530-1930 (1700-2100 summer), Sun 1000-1500, €3.50. The castle is 4 km by a winding road above town (follow C Carrera de Jesús uphill from beside the cathedral), a local bus from Plaza de la Constitución goes halfway, or it's €8 by taxi.

Jaén's castle stands high on the craggy hill overlooking the town. Originally built by Ibn Nasr (who fled to Granada when the city fell and founded the Nasrid dynasty there), it was extensively modified after the reconquest, being divided into three parts, two of which were demolished to make way for the parador that now sits alongside. What remains, the Alcázar Nuevo, is worth a visit, not least for the spectacular views from this lofty position. There's an audiovisual presentation in Spanish, and a number of interactive displays, including a camera that you can zoom in on the people walking the streets in the city far below. As well as the main **Torre del Homenaje** (keep), the long-drop latrine, prison cells and Moorish cistern are well preserved. Investigations have revealed some underground passages leading down to the Moorish barrio of La Magdalena in the town below. From the castle you can walk to a mirador atop the hill, marked by a huge cross, which gives even finer views over the city and hills.

Museo Provincial

Paseo de la Estación 27, T953-250600. Mid-Sep to mid-Jun Tue-Sat 1000-2030, Sun 1000-1700, summer Tue-Sun 1000-1700. Free for EU residents, €1 for other passport holders.

The Museo Provincial houses many of the main archaeological finds of the province, as well as a collection of local artworks. The undisputed highlight, housed in an annex alongside the principal building, is the collection of Porcuna sculptures, some Iberian works dating from the fifth century BC, found in the late 1970s in

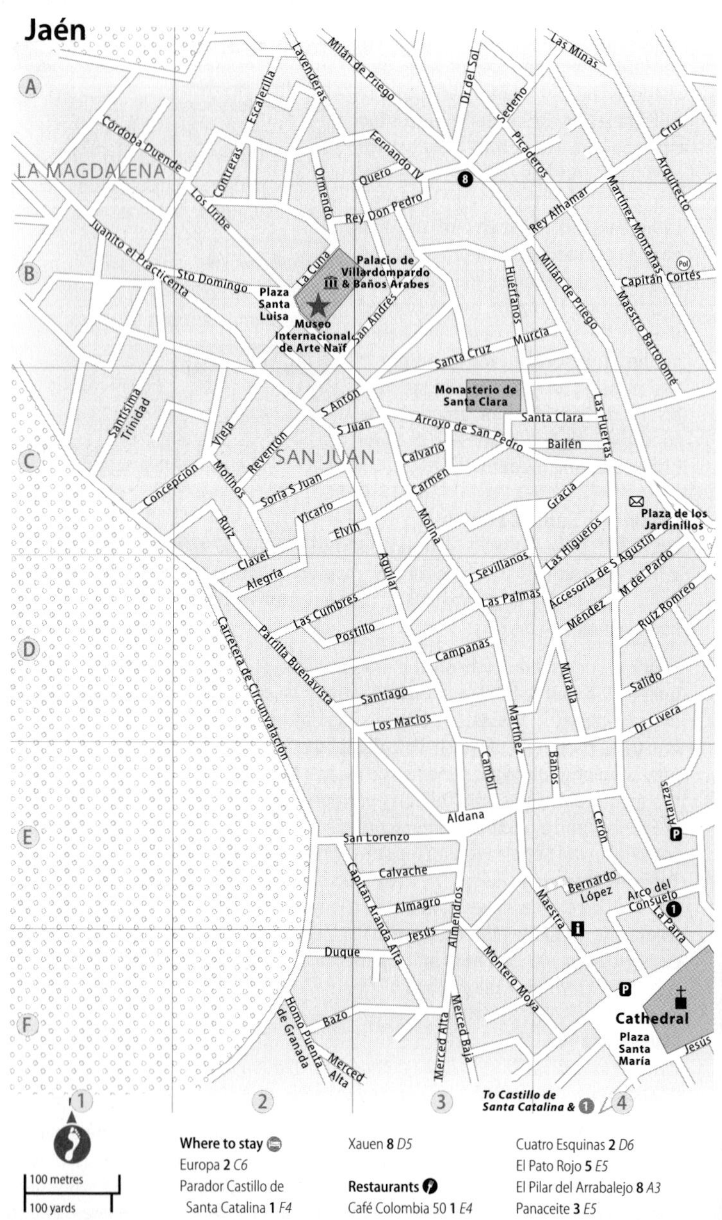
Jaén
A
B
C
D
E
F
1
2
3
4
LA MAGDALENA
SAN JUAN
Lavenderas
Milán de Priego
Dr del Sol
Las Minas
Escalerilla
Sedeño
Córdoba Duende
Contreras
Fernando IV
Picaderos
Cruz
Ormendo
Quero
Arquitecto
Los Uribe
Rey Don Pedro
Rey Alhamar
Martínez Montañas
Juanito el Practicenta
Palacio de Villardompardo & Baños Arabes
La Cuna
Sto Domingo
Plaza Santa Luisa
Museo Internacional de Arte Naïf
San Andrés
Huérfanos
Millán de Priego
Capitán Cortés
Maestro Bartolomé
Murcia
Santa Cruz
Monasterio de Santa Clara
Santísima Trinidad
S Antón
Santa Clara
Las Huertas
S Juan
Arroyo de San Pedro
Bailén
Vieja
Reventón
Calvario
Concepción
Molinos
Soria S Juan
Carmen
Gracia
Plaza de los Jardinillos
Vicario
Ruiz
Elvin
Molina
Las Higueros
Accesoria de S Agustín
Clavel
Aguilar
J Sevillanos
M del Pardo
Alegría
Las Palmas
Méndez
Ruíz Romreo
Las Cumbres
Carretera de Circunvalación
Postillo
Parrilla Buenavista
Campanas
Muralla
Salido
Santiago
Los Macios
Martínez
Dr Civera
Cambil
Baños
Atanzas
Aldana
Cerón
San Lorenzo
Calvache
Bernardo López
Arco del Consuelo
Maestra
Almagro
La Parra
Capitán Aranda Alta
Almendros
Jesús
Duque
Montero Moya
Cathedral
Plaza Santa María
Homo Puenta de Granada
Bazo
Merced Alta
Merced Baja
Jesus
To Castillo de Santa Catalina & 1
100 metres
100 yards
Where to stay
Europa 2 C6
Parador Castillo de Santa Catalina 1 F4
Xauen 8 D5
Restaurants
Café Colombia 50 1 E4
Cuatro Esquinas 2 D6
El Pato Rojo 5 E5
El Pilar del Arrabalejo 8 A3
Panaceite 3 E5

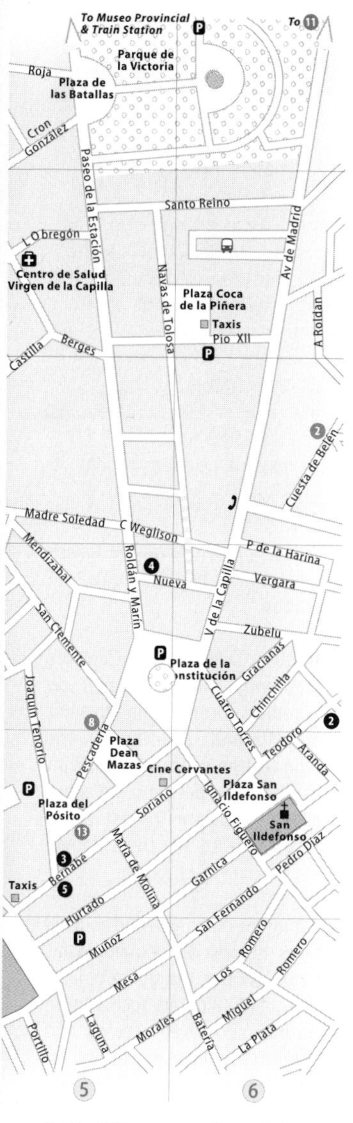

Río Chico **4** *D5*

Kharma **11** *A6*

Bars & clubs

El Pósito **13** *E5*

the west of the province. They were all destroyed in antiquity and buried across a wide area. Painstakingly restored, they are very finely worked, and display clear influences from the Eastern Mediterranean not only in the noble-heroic style but also in the evidence of a developing mythology based around fertility symbols. There are bulls, a wolf and, most famously, a warrior with a superbly crafted inscrutable face.

In the main section of the museum, dull displays showcase Neolithic ceramics and other haphazard prehistoric finds. There are some very fine Attic red-figure kraters and black-slip ware, found in an Iberian necropolis, Castellones de Ceal, a tomb from which has been reconstructed here. From the Roman period there are mosaics and some exceptional silver treasures. A marble sarcophagus dating from the fourth-century carved with Old Testament scenes is also an intriguing work. The mezzanine level has some more Roman and Visigothic items and upstairs the fine art section focuses on local painters but has little of interest in its collection.

To get to this museum from Plaza de la Constitución, head down Paseo de la Estación. Just before reaching it, you cross Plaza de las Batallas, with a memorial to the important battles of Las Navas de Tolosa (1212) and Bailén (1808). The first was a nail in the coffin for Moorish presence in the peninsula, the second a surprising triumph over Napoleon.

Palacio de Villardompardo

The oldest part of Jaén curves around the base of the castle hill to the northwest of the cathedral. These barrios, San Juan and La Magdalena, still preserve their sinuous Moorish street plan and are

BACKGROUND

Jaén

Jaén was probably originally an Iberian settlement, but the first major town here was built by the Romans, who were attracted by local deposits of silver. They named it Aurigi, and it was here, legend has it, that Christianity was introduced to the peninsula by Euphrasius.

The Moors took the city in AD 712, calling it Jayyan. It was strategically important, located near the crucial Despeñaperros pass, and was known as the Iron Door of Al-Andalus. Jaén came under the control of the Nasrid kingdom of Granada before being ceded to Fernando III in 1246 after a tough siege, after which time it played a key role in the final stages of the reconquest.

As in many parts of Andalucía, decline set in, and there was large-scale emigration from the province; a trend that continued right through the 20th century. Today, Jaén is one of the poorest of Andalucía's cities, with chronic unemployment both in town and in the surrounding area.

Jaén is also known for its *lagarto*, a lizard that terrorized the city in ancient times and whose skin is said to be displayed in the church of San Ildefonso.

interesting to wander through. At the heart of the area, in what was the Jewish quarter, is the **Palacio de Villardompardo**, which contains two museums (see below), exhibitions and, in its cellars, the **Baños Arabes**.

Baños Arabes The well-restored **Moorish bathhouse** ⓘ *Plaza Santa Luisa s/n, T953-248068, Tue-Sat 0900-2200, Sun 0900-1500, last entry 1 hr before, free if you show a passport or ID card*, is large, with several chambers corresponding to a hot room, a warm room and a cold room. Built in the 11th and 12th centuries, the chambers are constructed of vaulted brick, with the customary star-shaped light holes and horseshoe arches. After seeing the chambers you pass into the space with the heating system before exiting into the cellar of the palace. The restoration of the baths, which includes a walk over perspex panels to see some Roman remains below, won the Europa Nostra prize.

Museo de Artes y Costumbres Populares On exiting the baths, you find yourself in part of the collection of this museum, which takes up most of the building. It's an ethnographic display, somewhat lifeless but with enough intriguing objects to be worth a visit. Traditional crafts and industries are highlighted, such as olive cultivation (many ceramic vessels used for oil until comparatively recently had changed little from Roman originals), and the *matanza* or annual pig slaying for ham and sausages. There are also local costumes and ceramics, including the colourful glazed pottery of Andújar.

★**Museo Internacional de Arte Naïf** This is the other museum within the building and it's a display that might warm the heart of even the sternest critic of the style. The upper level is mostly Spanish work, including some 19th-century paintings of a Spanish seaside town by Gutier and a large number of works by the local artist Manuel Moral, including a wood sculpture of his family at lunch, and offers some excellent vistas of the olive groves around Jaén. Downstairs is a very inclusive international collection; it's fascinating to see the different approaches of artists from countries as diverse as Haiti and Japan. A recurring theme throughout the collection is a semi-nostalgic portrayal of idyllic rural life perhaps reflecting a loss of traditional values in a changed world.

Listings Jaén city *map p382*

Tourist information

Tourist office
Maestra 13, T953-313281, otjaen@andalucia.org. Mon-Fri 0900-1930, Sat and Sun 0930-1500.
Just below the cathedral is the helpful tourist office. You can download the turjaen.org guide app from Google Play or the AppStore.

Where to stay

€€€ Parador Castillo de Santa Catalina
Castillo de Santa Catalina s/n, T953-230000, www.parador.es.
Jaén's top place to stay is located alongside the castle perched high over the town. Needless to say, there are spectacular views and very atmospheric pseudo-medieval dining room and lounges, but the quality of the rooms, in contrast to some paradores, is also high, with tiled floors, 4-poster beds and attractive rugs. There is also an outdoor pool. Recommended.

€€ Hotel Europa
Plaza Belén 1, T953-222700, www.hoteleuropajaen.es.
This former chain hotel is a bright and breezy modern option, with comfortable rooms and excellent bathrooms a short stroll from the main sights. Breakfast is included in the very reasonable rates, and there's free street parking in the narrow streets around here. The hotel's covered parking is around 250 m away.

€€ Hotel Xauen
Plaza Dean Mazas 3, T953-240789, www.hotelxauenjaen.com.
The central location and recent refurbishment of this 3-star hotel make it a sound option. The modernized rooms are very good for this price category, with big comfortable beds, excellent bathrooms and plenty of space, as well as heating, a/c, TV and phone. There's also a roof terrace with great cathedral views. The price includes breakfast, but it's not exactly served at holidaymakers' hours.

Restaurants

As in all of the province, bars in the capital give you a free tapa with your drink. Jaén's liveliest tapas areas are a few bars on tiny C Nueva, C Teodoro Calvache and the streets near San Ildefonso church, and a knot of no-frills traditional options in the narrow streets – Arco del Consuelo and Bernardo López – near the cathedral. It's quiet midweek.

€€ El Pato Rojo
C Bernabé Soriano 12, T953-234099.
This great-value seafood place is a democratic place with a local vibe. There are well-priced *raciones* of all types of Spanish seafood served over the no-nonsense stainless steel counter. Recommended.

€€ El Pilar del Arrabalejo
C Millán de Priego 49, T953-240781.
This wonderful tapas option is the place to go for typical Jaén dishes and Andalucían region staples at a good price. Recommendable are the partridge pâté and olive pâté; you can also sit down to eat, where an assorted plate of tapas can feed 2 comfortably.

€€ Panaceite
C Bernabé Soriano 1, T953-240630.
Lively and likeable, this makes tapas fun with upbeat, generous creations to accompany your glass of decent wine. There's pleasant indoor-outdoor seating and a good local buzz.

€€ Río Chico
C Nueva 12, T953-240802, www.facebook.com/mesonriochicojaen.
A top option on this little street, this spot consists of a friendly downstairs tapas bar, who pride themselves on *pastel de verduras*, a lasagna-like *ración* that's a hefty meal in itself. Upstairs the small, intimate restaurant has formal service and a changing variety of rich traditional dishes at higher prices. The waiters like to recommend what's good that day rather than giving out the menu.

€ Cuatro Esquinas
C Teodoro Calvache 12.
This ageing, low, corner bar in the tapas zone below San Ildefonso church is refreshingly typical and usually packed with people descending for its tapa of *migas*.

Cafés

Café Colombia 50
C Cerón 5, corner of La Parra, T953-241750, www.facebook.com/colombia50cafe.
With a seductive little terrace on the edge of the old town, this friendly café is an inviting stop at any time of the day. They do good coffee, cheap and filling *tostadas* and efficient, cordial service.

Bars and clubs

Jaén's nightlife is poor by Andalucían standards. C Hurtado has the highest concentration of *bares de copas*, while the *discoteca* action is around the train station.

Bar El Pósito
Plaza del Pósito 10.
Jaén's best option for a drink, this welcoming bar is decorated with arty black and white paintings and has an outdoor terrace on the square, which gets very lively on summer weekends. There's a blend of arty people most nights, enjoying the mojitos, good *copas* and thoughtfully selected music. Recommended.

Kharma
Av Madrid, Km 333, on the edge of town, near the train station, www.discotecakharma.com. Fri-Sat til late.
This popular *discoteca* is the best in town. The roof terrace is the best aspect, with fantastic views across the city.

Festivals

Jun 11 Fiesta de Nuestra Señora de la Capilla, Jaén's patron; there are processions and dances scheduled.
Mid-Oct The city's major celebration is the **Feria de San Lucas**, with bullfights, horsemanship and plenty of Torreperogil wine consumed.
Late Oct-early Dec Festival de Otoño, with classical and jazz concerts, dance spectacles and theatre in city venues.

What to do

Tour operators

Seturja, *T953-236898, www.bonoturisticojaen.com*. Run walking tours of Jaén for €12 including sight admission, lasting 2½ hrs. Book via the tourist office; they leave from Casa Almansa, by the tourist office on C Ramón y Cajal. They also run tours to Ubeda and Baeza.

Transport

Air

Airport The nearest airport is Granada.

Bus

The bus station is a 10-min walk from the centre, on Plaza Coca de la Pinera, just off Av de Madrid (T953-250106).

Timetables are posted on the internet at www.epassa.es/autobus. Within the province, there are regular services to most towns on weekdays, but far fewer at weekends. 15 weekday buses (9 at weekends) go to **Ubeda** (1 hr) via **Baeza** (40 mins), and there are 3 daily departures for **Cazorla** (2½ hrs).

Other Andalucían destinations include **Granada** 14 times daily (1 hr 15 mins), **Córdoba** 8 times daily (5 at weekends, 2 hrs), **Sevilla** 3-4 times daily (4 hrs), **Algeciras** and **Almería** (3 hrs 30 mins-4 hrs) both twice daily, **Cádiz** twice daily (1 at weekends, 5 hrs 45 mins), **Málaga** 4 times daily (3 hrs 15 mins).

Further afield, there are 2 daily departures to **Barcelona** and 6-7 to **Madrid** (5 hrs).

Taxi

There are plenty of ranks or call T953-222222.

Train

The train station, T953-270202, is 1 km north of the centre; just follow Paseo de la Estación downhill from Plaza de la Constitución.

There are 3-4 daily trains to **Madrid** (3 hrs 45 mins), and 4 to **Córdoba** (1 hr 30 mins), which continue to **Sevilla** (2 hrs 55 mins), **Jerez** and **Cádiz**. These trains also stop at **Andújar** (40 mins).

Around Jaén

Jaén province is an undulating ocean of olive trees, over 50 million of them at last count. North of the capital, it's punctuated by the industrial towns of Bailén, Linares and the more interesting Andújar. Near Bailén, the castle village of Baños de la Encina makes an inviting detour, while further north the road heads towards the plains of Castilla-La Mancha, through the Despeñaperros Pass.

The little-visited western and southern reaches of Jaén province guard several attractive towns and villages overlooked by craggy fortresses high over the settlements.

You can visit the region in an appealing circular route from Jaén, or use it as a slower, but much more scenic, way of approaching Granada.

North of Jaén → *Colour map 2, B6.*

striking mountain pass, rich in history and gateway to Andalucía

Bailén and Baños de la Encina

A thriving but unappealing service centre, Bailén is the first major Andalucían town you reach after penetrating the region via the Despeñaperros Pass. It's famous as the site of a battle in 1808, in which the invading French armies were defeated by Spanish forces under the command of General Castaños. A Carthaginian army also suffered a significant reverse against the Romans here in 208 BC. Bailén has a thriving ceramics trade, with several workshops around town churning out traditional household pottery.

Ten kilometres north of Bailén, and only 6 km west of the Madrid–Andalucía motorway, is Baños de la Encina, a beautiful village of honeyed stone whose streets are lined with sensitively restored buildings and overlooked by a massive **Moorish castle** with 14 sturdily bristling towers and high walls. Built in the 10th century, it was a crucial outpost for controlling the Despeñaperros pass to the north, the major gateway between Andalucía and the rest of Spain. Views from the village's high perch stretch far away over the olive groves.

The historic centre of the village is just below the castle. On the main road which winds into town from Bailén, you'll find Enclave Baños, an interpretation centre and guiding company that functions as the **tourist office** ⓘ *Av José Luis Messía 2, T953-613338, www.bdelaencina.com, Wed-Mon 1000-1330, 1630-1930.* Guided visits to the **castle** ⓘ *Mon-Fri 1115, 1315, 1715, Sat-Sun 1030, 1115, 1230, 1345, 1630, 1715, 1830; afternoon visits later in summer, €3,* leave from here. You can also arrange visits at different times by previous reservation. As well as the castle visits they can arrange guided walks around the village.

★Andújar

A largely modern market town, Andújar was once an important Roman settlement, which they named Iliturgi; the town's inhabitants are still known as *iliturgitanos*. The French army surrendered here after the battle of Bailén. The much-vaunted Roman bridge is attractive, but dates mostly from the medieval period, although some foundations are original from the first century AD. But the highlight of a visit to Andújar is the church of **Santa María** on the plaza of the same name. A squat, ruddy affair dating mostly from the 16th century, it preserves an El Greco in situ in a chapel in the left aisle. A depiction of *Christ on the Mount of Olives*, it's one of his finer works, and all the better for being where it was originally painted.

Opposite the church is the impressive bell tower, Torre del Reloj, now home to the **tourist office** ⓘ *T953-504959, turismo@ayto-andujar.es, Oct-May Mon-Fri 0900-1400, 1700-1900, Sat 0900-1330, Jun-Sep Mon-Fri 0800-1500, Sat 0900-1330.*

Andújar is the starting point for a *romería* to the **Santuario of Nuestra Señora de la Cabeza**, 32 km north of town and tucked away deep in the Sierra de Andújar natural park. The Virgen de la Cabeza sculpture, affectionately known as 'la morenita' is one of Spain's three famous Black Virgins, and the *romería* on 30 April is one of the country's oldest and remains phenomenally popular; incredibly, hundreds of thousands of people take part.

Despeñaperros Pass

The main road bypasses the town of **La Carolina**, which was one of the most successful foreign colonies founded in Andalucía in the 18th century by the energetic minister Pablo de Olavide. Although there's nothing much to see, you can appreciate the regular plan of its streets; the creation of these colonies formed an intriguing chapter in Spanish history. On the main road at the north end of La Carolina, a large sculptural group commemorates the nearby battle of Las Navas de Tolosa, a Christian victory over the Moors in 1212 of great significance, see page 464.

Beyond La Carolina, magnificent Despeñaperros Pass has always been a historically important entry route into and out of Andalucía. This status now takes the form of a truck-choked main road and a railway, but the pass was once notorious for the bandits that preyed on passing mule caravans and travellers. The name literally means 'the pass where dogs are thrown from cliffs'; this probably refers either to the defeat of the Moors at Las Navas or to whatever nasty deeds were perpetrated on those Muslims who were captured after fleeing the battle. Numerous vultures circle above the pass, as no doubt their ancestors did six centuries before. A visitor centre, Puerta de Andalucía, on the main road, can provide information about exploring the surrounding *parque*

ON THE ROAD

The Iberian lynx

The Jaén highlands are an important redoubt for the Iberian lynx, *Lynx pardinus*, a predator that was once common across the Iberian peninsula but whose numbers dwindled alarmingly until they were on the point of extinction. Though they remain endangered, things have improved in the past decade, as breeding centres here and in the Coto Doñana have been set up, with the aim of reintroducing the species to other areas across southern Spain; this has been trialled, so far successfully, in Córdoba province. Local awareness of the issue has increased markedly, and the lynx has become something of a symbol for a new conservation-based attitude towards southern Spain's wilder places.

Silvery grey to brownish yellow in colour with cheetah-like black spots, this, also known as the pardel lynx, is the smallest of such species. It dines almost exclusively on rabbits; this has been part of the problem, as diseases in the 20th century wiped out large swathes of Spain's lapine population. Now reintroduction of rabbits is seen as being crucial to sustain a viable lynx presence.

natural but have minimal information on the rest of Andalucía if this is your point of entry to the region.

A kilometre or so north of the border of Andalucía, Spanish flags point the way to Casa Pepe, a shiver-inducing roadside café stuffed full of mementoes and souvenirs of fascism, Franco and the Falange that has to be seen to be believed. And no, they're not joking: it's a frightening glimpse of something that, though by now mostly extinguished in Spain, still lurks in some corners.

Listings North of Jaén

Where to stay

Bailén and Baños de la Encina

€€ Palacio de los Guzmanes
C Trinidad 4, T953-613075, www.palacioguzmanes.com.
Just below the plaza in lovely Baños de Encina, this noble 17th-century palace's historic façade hides a luxurious and relaxing *casa rural* with great views from most of the 20 distinct rooms, as well as a pool. Meals on request.

Restaurants

Andújar

€€ El Mesón
C Isidoro Miñón s/n, T953-511769.
A reliable and much-transited choice, which provides for many different *iliturgitano* needs, serving strong coffee, good beer, tasty tapas and *raciones*, and generous plates of roast goat.

Festivals

Alcalá la Real

Jul Etnosur (www.etnosur.com), a 3-day celebration of global culture, food, handicrafts and music. Well worth visiting.

Transport

Bailén and Baños de la Encina

There are 3 buses from **Jaén** to Baños de la Encina Mon-Fri but none at weekends.

Andújar

There are 12 buses from **Jaén** to Andújar on weekdays, 4 on Sat and 2 on Sun; there are also connections to **Córdoba**. 4 daily trains also run between Jaén and **Córdoba/Sevilla/ Cádiz**, stopping in Andújar.

Despeñaperros Pass

Hourly departures from Jaén Mon-Fri, and 5-8 Sat-Sun for **La Carolina**, with some continuing to **Santa Elena**.

West and south of Jaén → *Colour map 2, C5.*

traditional towns surrounded by a sea of olive trees

Martos and Alcaudete

Twenty four kilometres west of Jaén, the town of Martos surfs a sea and aroma of olive trees. Though its lower town is workaday, Martos boasts two castles, one at the top of the town, and one, rather ruinous, improbably perched atop the 1000-m-high hill, **La Peña**, that looms over the settlement; the views from up here (partway by road then a path to the summit) are phenomenal. The main settlement was once up there, but people moved downhill to save their legs in times of peace after the reconquest. It was from there that the Carvajal brothers were thrown to their deaths (see box, page 392); you can see their tombstone in the late Gothic church of Santa Marta. Also in the old town is the church of Santa María, begun in the 13th century but mostly Renaissance in style, and several towers and noble mansions.

Continuing south through the steadily growing hills, you are surrounded only by olive trees and the largest of skies. The village of Alcaudete has another Moorish castle, which rises spectacularly over the town; the keep and part of the walls are preserved. Below, in the village, which was once an important Visigothic town, the attractive church has a square bell tower with pointed roof and a striking marble portal in Plateresque style. Alcaudete is famous for production of marzipan and other festive sweetmeats.

Martos (28 km) and Alcaudete (55 km) are connected to Jaén via a 55-km *vía verde*, a former railway converted to an attractive, if hot, walking and cycling route.

★Alcalá la Real

The main town in this area of the Sierra Sur, beautiful Alcalá was named by the Moors *Al-Qalat*, meaning 'the fortress', and you'll soon notice why – the formidable-looking **Fortaleza de la Mota** dominates the skyline above this settlement that spreads peacefully along the valley below.

ON THE ROAD

The summoned king

Fernando IV, king of Castilla (1285-1312) is known as *El Emplazado* (the summoned one) because of a curious incident that took place at Martos. He unjustly condemned to death two brothers, Pedro and Alfonso Carvajal; some say they were accused of murdering one of the king's advisors, some say they had been robbed and were taken for vagabonds by the king. In any event, they had their hands cut off and were ordered to be thrown off the cliffs that tower high above the town. They maintained their innocence and pleaded with the king for justice; when he was unmoved, they called on God to judge the unjust monarch within 30 days. The brothers were killed but sure enough, 30 days later, pacing outside his tent after dinner, Fernando dropped down stone dead in the prime of his life. The brothers' last request had been heard and the king was summoned to account for his deeds. The story became the subject of a 16th-century romantic ballad.

The principal **tourist office** ⓘ *Carrera de las Mercedes s/n, T953-582077, www.turismodealcalala real.es, Mon 1000-1500, Tue-Sun 1000-1700*, is in the Palacio Abacial on the main road through town.

From here, the **castle** ⓘ *T953-102717, daily 1030-1930 (1730 winter), €6*, is reached by ascending the steep Calle Real from opposite the **Iglesia de Consolación**. After stopping at the ticket office, which also provides tourist information, you wind your way through a series of gates that culminate in the massive Puerta de la Imagen. Passing through here, you find yourself in a large open space dotted with the foundations of the Moorish town, founded in the eighth century. The town was occupied by the Christians after its reconquest in 1341; the new town that you see cascading down the hill below was only really settled after the Moors were ousted from nearby Granada in 1492.

The castle's keep, or **Torre de Homenaje**, is one of only two original buildings still standing on the hilltop. From its battlements there are excellent views as far as the Sierra Nevada; there is also an exhibition of various archaeological finds from prehistoric to medieval occupation layers.

On the other side of the compound, the austere weather-beaten church of Santa María was once part of a convent; it's now a shell, but excavations in the interior have revealed many medieval tombs, as well as foundations from Moorish and Roman buildings that stood on the site. The work of the archaeologists enabled researchers to put together quite a clear picture of life here, and an impressive new exhibition brings it alive. As well as detailed display panels on life on the frontier between Christendom and Al-Andalus, a wine cellar and, most charmingly, an apothecary's shop, have been recreated atop the excavated foundations of buildings of the time. There's also an audiovisual screened four times daily on the wall of the church. Further developments are in store.

The lower town has several fine *palacios*, one of which once belonged to the abbot. This swish 18th-century building, on the main road through the centre, holds the tourist office as well as the **Museo Abacial** ⓘ *Cra de las Mercedes s/n, T953-582077, Mon 1000-1500, Tue-Sun 1000-1700, €3 (free with castle ticket)*, mostly displaying local customs and archaeological artefacts. Near the museum is a well-crafted, if crumbly, Plateresque fountain dating from the 16th century.

Listings West and South of Jaén

Where to stay

Alcalá la Real

Alcalá appeals as a stop for a couple of days.

€€ Llave de Granada
C Bélgica 49, T953-583691, www.llavedegranada.com.
A 10-min stroll from the heart of town, these modern apartments offer excellent comfort and facilities, including a spa complex and a great roof terrace area. They come in several sizes and are perfect for families.

€ Hostal Río de Oro
C Abad Moya 2, T953-580337.
Cheerful management and good-value rooms, some with balconies overlooking the tree-lined *alameda*. Good food available.

Restaurants

Alcalá la Real

€€ Zacatín
C Pradillo 2, T953-580568, www.hospederiazacatin.com.
In the lower part of town near the tourist office, this amiable local spot has attractive rustic decor, a most unusual urinal in the gents, and great value fish and meat dishes, including local specialities such as *secretaria* (a beef and vegetable stew) at the bar or in its attractive wooden-ceilinged dining room. They also have rooms upstairs. Recommended.

€ Rincón de Pepe
C Fernando el Católico 17, T699-249659.
A great tapas stop for castle-tired legs, this cosy place has classic decor and ingredients, but some quite original combinations. Don't confuse with the restaurant **Casa Pepe**, which also does delicious food.

Transport

Martos and Alcaudete

Buses every 30 mins Mon-Fri, hourly on Sat, 4 times on Sun from **Jaén** to Martos. 5 weekday buses run to **Alcaudete** (1 Sat, 2 Sun).

Alcalá la Real

There are 3 buses weekdays to and from **Jaén**, and 1 bus at weekends.

East from Jaén

The towns of Baeza and Ubeda, within easy reach of Jaén, are among Andalucía's finest sights. These remarkable hilltop settlements are filled with stunning Renaissance buildings, erected by prosperous nobles during the 16th-century wool boom. Many of the palaces and civic buildings were designed by the master architect Andrés de Vandelvira and commissioned by the aristocrat Francisco de los Cobos, private secretary to King Carlos V. Several of the fine buildings have been converted into classy hotels in Ubeda, while quieter Baeza is also a delightful place to stay for a night or two. Both are blessed with excellent restaurants.

Baeza → *Colour map 3, B2.*

a quiet, appealing place, replete with fine Renaissance buildings

★The enticing small town of Baeza has some elegant palaces erected during the town's heyday in the 16th century and an impressive cathedral. Baeza is made for leisurely strolling, and soon has stress levels down a notch or two.

An important Roman and Visigothic city, Baeza, then called Bayasa, was the civilian and religious capital of the upper Guadalquivir region. The town's post-Reconquista wealth came from agriculture; it prospered and so was granted a university, which endured until the 19th century. The poet Antonio Machado lived here for several years teaching in the local school; the town is also known as the training headquarters of the Guardia Civil, the paramilitary police force.

Baeza's **tourist office** ⓘ *T953-779982, Mon-Fri 0900-1930, Sat and Sun 0930-1500,* is in a beautiful building on the Plaza del Pópulo. There are also good information posts around the town in Spanish and English.

On the way to Baeza from Jaén, look out for the striking medieval bridge over the Guadalquivir at Puente del Obispo.

Sights

The main avenue through town is the arcaded Paseo de la Constitución. Just off here is **Plaza del Pópulo**, and you're already in Plateresque heaven. In the centre of the square is the Fuente de los Leones, a fountain populated with carved lions and a female statue. These are Iberian sculptures found in the region; the lady has been traditionally identified with Imilce, a local lass who married Hannibal.

On the square is the Antigua Carnicería, a beautiful Plateresque building, once a butchery, and adorned with the sizeable coat of arms of the Habsburg emperor Carlos V. It's now the law courts. Next to it is the Casa del Pópulo, dating from the same period and now housing the tourist office (see above). Adjoining this building, the Arco de Villalar is a triumphal arch built to commemorate the defeat of the *comunero* revolt, which Ubeda and Baeza strongly opposed. The arch seems a little unnecessary, as there was already one next to it: the Puerta de Jaén, a gate in the old city wall.

Ascending Calle Conde Romanones from Plaza del Pópulo takes you into the heart of monumental Baeza. On your left is the **Antigua Universidad** ⓘ *daily 1000-1400, 1600-1900, closed Fri afternoon, free*, dating from the late 16th century, and with an attractive mannerist façade and attached church. It was a fully functioning university until it was closed in 1824 and, since then, has been devoted to secondary education. Antonio Machado taught French here from 1912 to 1919 and off the elegant double-levelled patio is the room he gave his classes in, marked with a plaque.

Reaching Plaza Santa Cruz, look over your right shoulder to behold the most charismatic of Baeza's buildings, the **Palacio de Jabalquinto** ⓘ *Mon-Fri 0900-1400, free*. Its Isabelline façade, recently restored to full glory, is a heart-liftingly exuberant, almost Gaudí-esque creation of the early 16th century, awash with extravagant detail. The pillars are crowned with Moorish-influenced *mocárabes*, the windows feature delicate tracery, while above is an open Renaissance loggia. The interior patio has two levels of round arching. Both this, and the adjacent building, also with an elegant patio, are used by an international university.

Opposite here, the **Iglesia de la Santa Cruz** ⓘ *1100-1300, 1600-1800, free*, is a rare example of the Romanesque style in Andalucía, having been primarily built in 1227. The endearing and humble simplicity of its design seems a little out of place among all these grand Renaissance structures. Inside, the nave is divided by wall arches from the aisles; the columns have carved vegetal capitals.

Nearby, Baeza's **cathedral** ⓘ *Mon-Fri 1000-1400, 1600-1900, Sat 1000-1900, Sun 1000-1800, €4*, is one of only two in Jaén province, and the building's status was a source of much annoyance to Ubeda, a far larger town that always likes to consider itself more important than its little neighbour. Originally built in the 13th century (over, you guessed it, a mosque), it was given a Renaissance makeover in the 16th century by Andrés de Vandelvira, the supreme technician of many of the buildings of Baeza and Ubeda. Before entering, walk around the building; the narrow streets are picturesque, and you can admire some Gothic round windows at the back, as well as the Puerta de Perdón doorway from the same period. The main portal is also Gothic, with some *mudéjar* influences; it dates from the original construction. The bell tower is also attractive. The interior is spacious and light thanks to Vandelvira's efforts; there's an ornate gilt Baroque *retablo* and, at the other end of the nave, a fine *reja* by Maestro Bartolomé closing off the old choir. Unusually, at the rear of the left aisle you can slip a euro in a slot to provoke a painting to slide aside with a burst of church music, revealing a finely crafted monstrance rotating on a stand; it's an 18th-century work of the Córdoba silversmith Núñez de Castro. There's also a fine Gothic-*mudéjar* cloister that houses the **cathedral museum** with its collection of religious painting, sculpture and processional monstrances. You can also climb the belltower.

Next to the cathedral is one of the most beautiful buildings in Baeza, the **Casa Consistoriales Altas**, also known as the Palacio de los Cabreras and once the town hall. Now a national monument, the walls display the coats of arms of Juana the Mad and her husband Felipe the Fair.

On the other side of the square from the cathedral is yet another fine building, a former seminary, Seminario San Felipe Neri, with a fairly sober façade featuring the faded graffiti that successful students traditionally painted to celebrate. The fountain in front of it, **Fuente de Santa María**, is a small gem, constructed like a miniature triumphal arch complete with columns and a large coat of arms.

Northeast of here is the ruined convent of Santa Clara, behind which you get an excellent perspective from the escarpment on which the town sits across the numerous olive trees to the spectacular mountains of the Sierra Mágina beyond.

On the edge of the old town, the 12th-century Moorish tower at the Puerta de Ubeda gate holds an **exhibition** ⓘ *T953-744370, closed temporarily for restoration at last visit*, on life in medieval Baeza.

On the other side of Paseo de la Constitución are more buildings worth a look. Chief among these is the **Convento San Francisco**, another design by Andrés de Vandelvira. It must have been breathtaking once, but was badly damaged by an earthquake in the 18th century. What remained suffered further indignities, being used as a stable by Napoleon's troops, and suffering total neglect until the late 20th century, when an expensive restoration project was begun, which has converted part of the building into a congress centre and hotel. You can still admire the transept and apses, adorned with excellent Renaissance sculptures. The curved metal frame overhead outlines the dimensions of the former dome.

Listings Baeza

Where to stay

€€€ Hotel Puerta de la Luna
C Raya s/n, T953-747019, www.hotelpuertadelaluna.com.
Discreetly tucked away on a narrow street by the cathedral, this carefully restored *palacio* is decorated with uncluttered elegance. Built around a charming central patio, it has rooms with crisp white sheets, stylish lines and fine bathrooms. Service is excellent, and the overall ambience is classy and romantic. It's much cheaper (**€€**) midweek. There's a pool, and parking underneath the building.

€€ Hospedería Fuentenueva
T953-743100, www.fuentenueva.com.
A couple of blocks beyond the bus station on the way to Ubeda, this enticing, hospitable and unusual

hotel was once a prison. The crumbly creeper-covered façade gives no clue to the gleaming interior which is styled confidently and contemporarily, with bold colours and a minimalist Far Eastern feel. The great rooms have plenty of light, glass, and hydro massage showers. It's a top spot for a romantic break. There's also a delightful sunny terrace and small pool.

€€ La Casona del Arco
C Sacramento 3, T953-747208, www.lacasonadelarco.com.
Offering great value just inside the old town through the Puerta de Ubeda gateway, this boutique hotel is a winner. The rooms are darkly attractive, with characterful features like exposed beams or sloping ceilings, and artistically tiled modern bathrooms. Good service can be expected here, and there are spa treatments on offer, but the secluded patio area around the small pool is the real highlight. Recommended.

Restaurants

€€€ Juanito
Paseo Arca del Agua s/n, T953-740040, www.juanitobaeza.com. Closed 1-20 Jul.
With a deservedly high reputation for traditional dishes taken to exquisite heights, this spot, full of photos of famous diners, has been going for years. The decor is rustic and the food focuses on the finest local produce. Luisa's artichokes are highly acclaimed, as is the *pichón al estilo de mi madre* (squab like mum used to do it). The restaurant is on the eastern edge of town on the way to Ubeda, next to the Campsa petrol station. They also have rooms (**€€**). Highly recommended.

€€ Taberna El Pájaro
Portales Tundidores 5 (Paseo de la Constitución), T953-744348, www.tabernaelpajaro.com.
With a smart line in deli-style tapas such as partridge pâté, cheese platters and tasty marinated artichokes, this attractive tapas bar pulls a loyal local crowd. There's also a dining area elegantly walled with stone, and more substantial dishes (including delicious seafood) to make a meal of it.

€ Tasca Peña Flamenca
C Conde Romanones 11, www.facebook.com/penaflamenca.debaeza.
An unpretentious old-town tapas place with warming dishes such as *callos* (tripe stew) or *fabada* (Asturian bean and sausage casserole). Flamenco on Fri.

What to do

Tours

There are several organizations offering tours of Ubeda, Baeza and environs. You can combine a tour of Ubeda and Baeza for €20, the so-called Bono Turístico (www.bonoturistico.com; buy online for a discount). This also gives you small discounts off admission to some sights. The price doesn't include transport between the 2 towns but this can be arranged for extra.
Pópulo, *Plaza de los Leones 1, T953-744370, www.populo.es.* Offers tours of the town for €10.

Transport

Bus

The bus station is 10 mins' walk to the east of the centre on C Coca de Pinera, on the road to Ubeda. There are 14 weekday buses (9-10 at weekends) to **Jaén** (50 mins), and even more heading to **Ubeda**, only 10 mins away. 5 buses go to **Granada** daily, and 3 to **Málaga**. There are 3 daily buses to **Cazorla**.

Train

Beware catching a train to Baeza, as the so-called Linares–Baeza station is 13 km away; some buses to **Linares** pass it, but it's hardly convenient given the number of bus connections to the town from Jaén.

Ubeda and around → *Colour map 3, B2.*

staggering ensemble of Renaissance architecture virtually unparalleled in Andalucía

★Entering this sprawling agricultural service town there's little hint of the glories awaiting you as you approach the more venerable centre; it's only when you've descended to the older part that you realize you're in a town with the most Renaissance treasures in the region (except in nearby Baeza). Ubeda (stress on the first syllable) is slowly beginning to receive the attention it deserves, and its assortment of delightful *palacio* hotels makes it all the more appealing.

Known to the Romans as Betula because of its location near the river Betis (Guadalquivir), it became a walled Moorish town with important pottery and *esparto* (woven grass) industries that have persisted to the present day. Squabbling among the noble families led Fernando and Isabel to demolish the town's defences in 1503; once things settled, the city became rich on the export of its textiles. Much of the town's cachet in those days came from Francisco de los Cobos, minister to Carlos V and a man of huge influence and power in Spain. Ubeda has a more austere and less intimate feel than Baeza, partly due to the size and quantity of the palaces, which were very much intended as statements of position and wealth, although many were never lived in by their owners.

Ubeda's **tourist office** ⓘ *C Baja del Marqués 4, T953-779204, otubeda@andalucia.org, Mon-Fri 0900-1930, Sat and Sun 0930-1500*, is housed in part of a *palacio* near the Plaza del Ayuntamiento. They can provide town maps.

Sights

Such is Ubeda's wealth of historic buildings that it is impossible to provide a full account of them all here, but part of the fun is wandering around the centre's meandering lanes discovering charming façades and loggias at every turn.

The logical place to begin a visit is in **Plaza de Vázquez de Molina**; at any rate, this will ensure that your first impression of monumental Ubeda won't be soon forgotten. This extensive square is surrounded by noble buildings that may make all but the proudest of spirit feel somewhat insignificant for a while; no doubt an intentional effect on the part of the master architects and their aristocratic patrons.

At the square's southern end is the most imposing building, the **Palacio de Vázquez de Molina**, also known as the Palacio de las Cadenas (Palace of the Chains). It's now Ubeda's **Ayuntamiento** (town hall) ⓘ *Mon-Fri 0800-1430, free entrance around the back on the adjacent Plaza del Ayuntamiento.* The stern three-tiered façade is a model of Renaissance sobriety; the building was designed by Andrés de Vandelvira, master architect and one time pupil of the great Diego de Siloé, in the mid-16th century. The whimsical corner turrets are the only note of exterior levity, but the interior is a more comfortable space, with a patio with arches and a central fountain. On the ground floor is an **exhibition** on Ubeda's Renaissance heritage. The upper level, which has a fine *mudéjar* wooden ceiling, holds the town's important archives. If you're discreet, they don't mind you wandering around.

Opposite is the **Iglesia de Santa María de los Reales Alcázares** ⓘ *Tue-Sat 1100-1400, 1600-1830, Sun 1100-1400, €4 including audioguide*, which was originally built in the 13th century over the old mosque. Its 16th-century façade is superb, with two delicate bell towers framing the central portal, which is capped by a sculptured panel depicting the Adoration of the Magi and flanked by Corinthian columns. The interior is mostly Gothic, and was severely damaged in the Civil War;

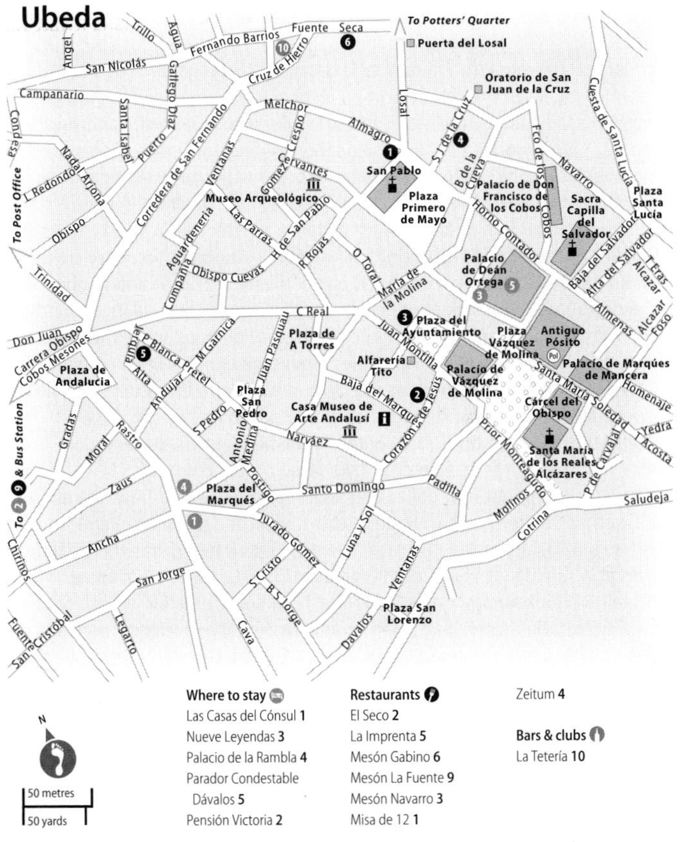

the cloister stands where the ablutions courtyard of the mosque was. There's a fine wrought-iron *reja* by Maestro Bartolomé depicting the Tree of Jesse.

Next to the church are three further elegant structures, as well as a statue of Andrés de Vandelvira himself, very much the Renaissance man with a short belted tunic, leggings and architect's tools in hand. The Cárcel del Obispo was once where errant women were sent by the bishop to do penance with an order of nuns; it's now the courthouse. The Antiguo Pósito, now a police station, was once a communal grain store, while the Palacio de Marqués de Mancera is yet another dapper Renaissance mansion.

At the eastern end of the long square, the delicate and somewhat austere **Palacio del Deán Ortega** is another Vandelvira work with a fine patio. Once the residence of local clerics (not a bad posting), it's now Ubeda's luxurious parador. Non-guests are welcome to investigate the patio.

Next to the parador is Ubeda's most intriguing building. The **Sacra Capilla del Salvador** ⓘ *C Baja del Salvador s/n, T609-279905, Mon-Sat 0930-1400, 1600-1800, Sun 1130-1400, 1600-1900, €5,* was commissioned by Francisco de los Cobos, private secretary to the emperor Carlos V, and designed by Diego de Siloé and Andrés de Vandelvira, Spain's two 16th-century architects who between them share the credit for nearly all of Andalucía's finest Renaissance buildings. Vandelvira was unknown before working under Siloé on this building, but, when Siloé moved on to another project, he entrusted the building's completion to his young apprentice. Constructed between 1536 and 1559, De los Cobos had it built as a funerary chapel for himself and his family. Renaissance religious architecture in Spain always trod a fine line between worship of God and man: the emperor's secretary crossed it without a second thought; the result is one of the most eclectic and symbol-filled façades around. There's plenty of sculptural decoration, particularly around the elaborate portal; the archivolts are filled with small demons, while the underside of the arch has an array of Roman deities. Above is a panel of the Transfiguration, with St Peter and St Paul on either side. Just in case you'd forgotten who had the chapel built, his oversized shield stands to one side, borne by two men; his wife's coat of arms is on the other side. Entering the building via the side door, you'll notice that the altar is screened off by a large ornate *reja*; Carlos V was known to love these wrought-iron grilles. The main *retablo* is a fine Transfiguration by the Castillian master Alonso Berruguete; it mirrors the panel on the façade but was badly damaged in the Civil War. The star at your feet marks the location of the crypt where De los Cobos and his wife are buried. The dome overhead makes the building look somewhat mosque-like from some exterior angles. Squeeze your way into the sacristy to the left to admire the carved ceiling. There are also damaged frescoes in the side chapels which are in the process of restoration. The chapel originally adjoined the Palacio de Don Francisco de los Cobos, but this burned down, and only the façade remains (it's on the street named after the man, which runs along the left side of the chapel as you face the main façade).

The town ends abruptly at Plaza Santa Lucía just beyond the chapel, where you can enjoy the inspiring views. Heading up Calle Navarro, you'll come after a couple of doglegs to the **Oratorio (Museo) de San Juan de la Cruz** ⓘ *T953-750615, C del*

Carmen s/n, www.museosanjuandelacruz.es, Tue-Sun 1100-1300, 1700-1900, €3.50 including audioguide. This mystic saint (St John of the Cross), joint founder of the Discalced Carmelites with St Teresa of Avila, was born in Fontiveros in Avila province in 1542. His best-known verses and commentaries, *The Ascent of Mount Carmel* and *The Dark Night of the Soul*, were written during and after he was imprisoned in Toledo; afterwards he came to Andalucía and ran monasteries in Granada and Baeza, among other places, before he came to Ubeda, seriously ill. Scorned by the clergy here to begin with, his indisputable piety eventually won them over and he died here in 1591 amid great mourning. The basilica here was built in the 20th century after the original was destroyed in the Civil War; part of his remains reside in a glass reliquary. There's a collection of writings and items from his life, including a reconstruction of his cell, in which he sits at a writing desk he used.

Descending the street named after the saint, you arrive at Plaza Primero de Mayo, on which is the striking low church of **San Pablo** ⓘ *Tue-Fri 1100-1300, 1800-1930, Sat 1100-1300, Sun 1200-1330, free,* fronted by orange trees. It has a curious apsidal gallery, below which is a historic public fountain. The main portal of the church is a fine late Gothic work from the early 16th century, with ornate foliage decoration. The side portal is a rare example of the Romanesque (albeit very late) in Andalucía, adorned with blind arching. The interior is simple, with three naves; it features some fine *rejas* and preserves some fresco work. Also on the square is the old town hall, with an Italianate arched façade in perfect proportion. The upper loggia was used by dignitaries to watch the bullfights that used to take place in the plaza.

Just past the church's side portal is the **Museo Arqueológico** ⓘ *C Cervantes 6, T953-108623, free,* set in a *mudéjar* house with pointed horseshoe arches. The collection includes prehistoric finds from the province and Roman, Visigothic and Moorish remains.

One street behind the tourist office is an excellent, if little-visited museum, the **Casa Museo de Arte Andalusí** ⓘ *C Narváez 11, T619-076132, phone to visit or ask at tourist office, €2,* the lifetime's work of an amiable collector who'll show you around this pretty house with a charming patio. There's a wide range of *mudéjar*, Mozarabic, and Moorish pieces, including some stupendous painted doors and other noble wooden objects. It's well worth the effort.

In the new town, near the bus station, you'll likely have already noticed the massive **Hospital de Santiago** ⓘ *Carrera Obispo Cobos s/n, T953-750842, 1000-1400, 1700-2100, closed Sun in Jun and Sat-Sun in Aug,* known hereabouts as the Escorial de Ubeda. It's another Vandelvira work, on an even larger scale to his works in the old town. Its nickname comes as much from its sobriety as its scale; the façade is fairly unadorned, with two tall towers at either end. The patio is two-levelled and sculpted from Italian marble. Now used as a cultural centre, you can wander in; don't miss the chapel, with a fine wooden *retablo*.

The Potters' Quarter

Ubeda has historically had an excellent reputation for its glazed ceramics and there are still some producers plying their trade in the barrio of San Millán. Head out of the old town through the Puerta del Losal gateway near Plaza Primero de Mayo.

Following straight ahead, and crossing Plaza Olleros, you'll reach Calle Valencia, where most of them are located. The Tito family are big names down here: at number 22 you'll find Paco Tito's exhibition and workshop while back in town, on Plaza del Ayuntamiento, a sizeable refurbished *palacio* has been converted into **Alfarería Tito** ⓘ *Plaza del Ayuntamiento 12, T953-751302, www.alfareriatito.com*, a large shop and display where you can see potters at work and admire an old Moorish kiln in the pretty patio.

Around Ubeda

Eight kilometres east of Ubeda, the village of **Sabiote** is little visited but is well worth exploring. Like Ubeda and Baeza, it has many fine Renaissance *palacios*, such as the Palacio de los Melgarejos, better known as the **Casa de las Manillas** (House of the Hands) for its outsized metal knockers. Andrés de Vandelvira lived here for a period and worked on, among other buildings, Sabiote's finest monument, its superb **castle** ⓘ *Sat and Sun 1100-1400, 1600-1830 (1800-2000 summer)*. Originally a Moorish fortress, it was rebuilt after the reconquest in the 13th century, and later remodelled by Vandelvira under the orders of Francisco de los Cobos. Vandelvira added a Plateresque entrance gate, adding nobility to the fierce lines of the castle. Its commanding position and rugged stone walls make it one of the most impressive citadels in the region. South of Sabiote on the main road is **Torreperogil**, whose cheap and cheerful red wines you have likely already sampled in the bars and restaurants of Ubeda, Baeza or Jaén.

On the main road between Ubeda and Torreperogil is the hamlet of **San Bartolomé**, which harbours an excellent *casa rural*; see Where to stay, below. Twenty kilometres south of Ubeda, the olive-farming town (aren't they all, in Jaén province) of **Jódar** is a handsome spot overlooking the surrounding plantations. It has a two-towered castle in the middle of the old town; further up the hill is a barrio of traditional cave dwellings. One of the castle's towers holds an **interpretation centre** ⓘ *T953-779718, normally open Thu-Sun mornings plus Sat afternoons, and daily in Aug but closed at time of research for staffing problems*, with information on visiting the *parque natural* that stretches south from Jódar to the lofty 2000 m-plus Sierra Mágina that rises dramatically in the south.

Listings Ubeda and around *map p399*

Where to stay

Ubeda has a wealth of quality accommodation in refurbished *palacios*.

€€€€ Parador Condestable Dávalos *Plaza Vázquez de Molina 1, T953-750345, www.parador.es*. This is right in the middle (and part of) Ubeda's most stunning ensemble of Renaissance buildings. Although the façade is a later addition, the substance of the *palacio* is from the 16th century, with a typical 2-level round-arched patio. The rooms are large and furnished in dark wood, with some looking over the square.

€€€ Las Casas del Cónsul
Plaza del Marqués 5, T953-795430, www.lascasasdel consul.es.
This boutique spot is yet another sumptuous conversion of a 17th-century palace. There are just 8 rooms, which combine pared-back modern design harmoniously with the sublime architectural features of the building. The rooms have all modern conveniences, appealing bathrooms, and the garden has an attractive plunge pool.

€€€ Palacio de la Rambla
Plaza del Marqués 1, T953-750196, www.palacio delarambla.com.
Character and comfort don't always go hand in hand, but they are best of friends here in Ubeda's most enchanting place to stay. This charming Renaissance *palacio* has huge rooms with high inlaid ceilings and lovely old furniture. Decent bathrooms, Wi-Fi and minibars offer mod cons, but it's the old-world charm that enchants here, as well as the excellent service and knockdown price that includes breakfast. Recommended.

€€ Nueve Leyendas
Pl de López Almagro 3, T953-792297, www.hotelnueveleyendas.com.
Enchanting and romantic, this is a beautiful conversion of an old *palacio.* The couple who run it couldn't be more helpful and have decorated the rooms in vintage style with an expert eye. Some have in-room jacuzzi. Beds are comfortable and the breakfasts great. Recommended.

€ Pensión Victoria
C Alaminos 5, T953-752952.
Comfortably the best budget option, and closer to the sights than other *hostales*, this quiet spot is well run and has rooms that are a bargain for the price, with clean bathroom, TV, heating and a/c, which according to readers works better in some rooms than others. You've a sporting chance of parking on the street outside.

Around Ubeda

€€ La Casería de Tito
Aldea San Bartolomé 33, 7 km east of Ubeda towards Torreperogil, T953-776771, www.lacaseria detito.com.
Facing the crumbling church in the strangely deserted middle of town, this excellent *casa rural* is a peaceful and beautiful stone-built house that offers all the comforts for a relaxing stay. Rooms are welcoming, with cosy colourful beds and good bathrooms, there's a lounge with a roaring fire, as well as a pool. Breakfast is excellent, and there's top home-style cooking at lunch and dinner. Best, though, are the charming hosts. It's 7 km east of Ubeda and 2 km west of Torreperogil. Recommended.

Restaurants

As well as these, there's a small knot of tapas bars behind the bullring on Cronista Pasquau, a small doglegged street between Av Cristo Rey and Constitución.

€€€ Zeitum
C San Juan de la Cruz 10, T953-755800, www.zeitum.com.
Set in yet another stately 16th-century palace, this restaurant offers ambience that is matched by the high-quality gourmet cuisine, with local ingredients given a dash of innovation and flair. Presentation is gorgeous and it all tastes sensational. Recommended.

€€ La Imprenta
Plaza Doctor Quesada 1, T953-755500, www.imprentaubeda.com.
This classy spot is just off Plaza Andalucía at the top of the old town. Once a printers, it now offers exquisite modern tapas, as well as excellent meals in the small dining room. Not-too-big portions of suckling pig take their place alongside sizeable salads and a selection of tasty wines. It's worth asking for the daily specials – and also for their prices.

€€ Mesón Gabino
Fuente Seca s/n, T953-757553, www.mesongabino.es.
Traditional and atmospheric, this spot is tucked away in a cave-like dugout under the old walls that used to be a hideout during the Civil War. The quality of the food is good, with traditional no-frills plates like cuts of pork, fish baked in salt, and decent steaks as well as subtler choices like partridge pâté and avocado salad. Wash them down with cheap and cheerful wines like the smooth young red from down the road in Torreperogil. There's also a bar where you can have tapas. Recommended.

€€ Misa de 12
Plaza 1 de Mayo, T953-828197, www.misade12.com.
In a lovely location, with romantic terraced seating overlooking a pretty plaza, this does delicious tapas and *raciones* out of a tiny kitchen. Because it's so small, service can be slow when they're busy, but it's worth the wait. Recommended.

€€ Restaurante El Seco
Plazuela Juan de Valencia s/n, T953-791452, www.restauranteelseco.com.
A fine eating choice just off the main plaza. Although the atmosphere is quite classy, the food is authentic home-style Andalucían fare for the most part; the *ajo blanco* is tasty, as are the croquettes. There are a few more adventurous dishes too, such as *lenguado* (sole) in cava, lamb cooked in a honey sauce, and *judías con perdiz* (green beans with partridge).

€ Mesón La Fuente
Av Cristo Rey 10, T953-752312.
A reader put us on to this good-value local eatery near the giant Hospital de Santiago building. The *menú del día* is very worthwhile; rustic decor, a warm welcome, and tasty free tapas add to the experience.

€ Mesón Navarro
Plaza del Ayuntamiento 2, T953-790638.
A small and popular tapas bar on this central square. There are many tasty offerings, with the fishy ones the best. There are cheap raciones including warming revueltos (scrambled egg dishes). Great summer terrace but you might have to queue for a seat.

Bars and clubs

Ubeda's nightlife is pretty dead midweek, but cranks up at weekends. There are few options for the gregarious in the old town; head to the new town streets near the bus station and around C Ramón y Cajal.

La Tetería
C Cruz de Hierro 3, www.facebook.com/lateteria.ubeda.
Something of an Ubeda icon, this bar/café attracts a leftish, liberal crowd and has a grungy, relaxed feel. There's frequent live music, from rockabilly to jazz and blues, as well as other events.

Festivals

Late Sep/early Oct Ubeda celebrates its patron **San Miguel** with a week of bullfights, partying and agricultural show.
Late Nov/early Dec Ubeda and Baeza jointly host a high-quality **classical and medieval music festival**. See www.festivalubedaybaeza.org. Concert prices range from €10-15, a little cheaper if bought in advance.

What to do

Tours

See also Tours in Baeza, page 397.
Artificis, *C Baja de El Salvador 14, T953-758150, www.artificis.com*. One of the best; visit their shop by the Capilla de El Salvador or just up from the Plaza del Ayuntamiento. A standard tour costs €12.

Transport

Bus

Ubeda's bus station is near Hospital de Santiago on C San José off the main road entering town. There are 14 weekday buses to **Jaén** (1 hr) via **Baeza** (10 mins), and 9-10 at weekends. There are 8 daily departures for **Granada**, and 3 for **Málaga** (all in the morning, 3 hrs 45 mins-6 hrs 15 mins). 5-7 daily buses go to **Linares** (1 hr), and there are 3-4 daily buses to **Cazorla** and also to **La Puerta de Segura**, near Segura la Sierra.

Sierra de Cazorla, Segura y las Villas

Spain's largest natural park is a heavily wooded zone of mountains and parallel limestone ridges that stretches from Cazorla, gateway to the park, northeast to the edge of the province. The park covers an area of 2143 sq km and is an important water catchment area: the Río Guadalquivir river rises here before reaching the Atlantic via Córdoba and Sevilla. Talk of water catchment and rising rivers is usually enough to furrow the brows of sun lovers and, indeed, Cazorla is one of Spain's wettest places, with over 2000 mm of precipitation annually.

It's a region of undeniable beauty, but somewhat blighted by tourism; there's basically only one road route through the park, and coach loads of visitors make their way along it, stopping at various laid-on attractions. To get away from this and fully appreciate the park, put on your hiking boots and try some of the walks suggested below.

Essential Sierra de Cazorla, Segura y las Villas

Getting around

A leisurely day's drive through the park could take you from Cazorla to Segura la Sierra, allowing plenty of time for strolling and relaxation. Two buses from Cazorla ply this route as far as Coto Ríos every day except Sunday, one leaving early (currently 0545), and one at 1430, but check these times on arrival in town as they change regularly. There are no buses to Segura la Sierra; the closest you can get is La Puerta de Segura, some 9 km away; this is accessible by buses from Jaén or from Ubeda.

When to go

For the most abundant flowers and birdlife the best time to visit the park is May and June. Avoid summer weekends and July and August, when the park is saturated with visitors. Autumn can be very pleasant; disruption from snow is not unknown during the winter months.

Tourist information

The tourist office in Cazorla (see below) has information on the park, as do various tour operators in town. There's an **interpretation centre** at Torre del Vinagre (see page 410) with displays on ecology, wildlife and vegetation. The brochure maps of the park come in cycling and walking versions among others; they're OK but you're better off buying a decent map in Cazorla (available at the tourist office).

Walking in the park

Most walkers base themselves in Cazorla, at the park's southeastern tip. The area immediately to the east has some of the park's most dramatic scenery and somewhere in or close to the town would provide the best base for walking here, although you would be a drive away from the start of the Río Borosa walk described on page 412. If you don't have your own transport, you'll need to rely on taxis or buses to get you up into the park.

The most easily available maps for walking in the park are the Alpina 1:50,000 series. There are three covering different areas: Sierra de Cazorla, Sierra de Segura I, and Sierra de Segura II. Their 1:100,000 map is of more use for drivers than hikers.

Cazorla → *Colour map 3, B3.*

the principal access point for the park and a pretty base for exploring the ranges

Cazorla is sandwiched between the relentless Jaén olive groves and the jagged rocks. Although some development has given it a certain middle-aged sprawl, its centre is peaceful and attractive, overlooked by two Moorish castles and the jagged limestone bluff of the Peña de los Halcones (Mount of the Falcons). As well as being the main destination for buses, Cazorla is also the place to come for maps, park information, tours and budget accommodation.

The **tourist office** ⓘ *C Paseo del Santo Cristo 19, T953-969191, www.turismoencazorla.com, daily summer 1000-1300, 1730-2000, winter 1000-1300, 1700-1930*, is not far from Plaza de la Constitución. Follow the sign uphill to the Parque Natural and take the first left.

The centre of urban Cazorla is **Plaza de la Constitución**, where buses stop and where arriving motorists spin round the roundabout and double back up the hill towards the natural park. From here, the pedestrianized Calle Doctor Múñoz runs southeast to the attractive **Plaza de la Corredera**, which is surrounded by some fine buildings. One of these is the **Iglesia de San José**, a 17th-century church with a somewhat stern gilt *retablo* and poor 1960s fresco copies of El Greco works. On the other side of the square is Cazorla's town hall, a 16th-century edifice that was once a monastery.

The town's largest church, **Santa María la Mayor** ⓘ *T953-710102, Tue-Sun 1000-1300, 1600-1900 (1700-1930 summer)*, is little more than a shell. Severely damaged by flooding in the late 17th century, it received the *coup de grâce* during the Peninsular War. The building was originally designed by Andrés de Vandelvira, and you can still see a segment of the vaulting of what once must have been a structure of enormous elegance. The ruins house the municipal tourist office. At the other end of the square (Plaza Santa María, which has some pleasant summer terraces) from the ruined church, the Gypaetus foundation run **CETEAM** ⓘ *T953-720923, Wed-Sun 1030-1330 plus afternoon hours varying by season*, an exhibition of information on the region's threatened species, such as the lynx and Egyptian vulture.

The castle of **La Yedra**, also called **Las Cuatro Esquinas** ⓘ *T953-101402, Tue 1430-2000, Wed-Sat 0900-2000, Sun 0900-1400, free for EU citizens, theoretically €1.50 others*, stands formidably on a crag above the edge of town. Once a Roman fortress, it was rebuilt by the Moors and now contains an ethnographic museum, the Museo de Artes y Costumbres Populares del Alto Guadalquivir, with a two-part display. One has ceramics and other daily objects like olive presses, and a traditional kitchen. In the keep's atmospheric chambers is an array of religious art, weaponry and Flemish tapestries.

Further above the town is another castle, named **Salvatierra** or **Las Cinco Esquinas** (Five Corners). The latter name derives from the pentagonal shape of its main tower, which is in fact all that survives of the building.

Southwest of Cazorla the road runs on to **Quesada**, another former Moorish settlement and beyond to the **Puerto de Tíscar**. This road winds through spectacular rocky scenery, in some places even more impressive than in the park itself. It eventually reaches the town of **Baza**, on the motorway between Granada to Murcia. It's a wonderfully remote drive.

Listings Cazorla

Where to stay

€€ El Molino la Fárraga
Camino de la Hoz s/n, T953-721249, www.molinolafarraga.com. Closed mid-Dec to Feb. You can't get a car closer than 100 m.
This enchanting *casa rural*, although only just beyond the last houses of the village of Cazorla, is in an utterly peaceful rural setting. It is located in a narrow valley carved by a stream that actually runs under the house, which was formerly a mill. The rooms are extremely cosy, with tiled floors, wooden beams and *esparto* mats. Some have fireplace and balcony. The huge garden is tranquil, and there are great views up the valley, and at night of the floodlit castle. There's also a pool, and a big welcome from the hosts. Breakfast is included. Recommended.

€ Albergue de Cazorla
Plaza Mauricio Martínez 6, T953-711301, www.inturjoven.com. Open year round.
An attractive and well-equipped official hostel in a noble former convent with pretty doubles with bathroom as well as dorm rooms. Good facilities including a pool.

€ La Finca Mercedes
Ctra de la Sierra Km 1, 1 km from Cazorla on the park road in La Iruela, T953-721087, www.lafincamercedes.es.
This great-value place is just and offers simple but comfortable rooms, a lovely garden and pool, filling and cheap home-style *serrano* cooking and expansive views way to the west. The hospitable owners have an excellent *casa rural* with 6 rooms just down the road. Recommended.

Camping

You can also camp at the **Albergue de Cazorla** hostel (see above).

Camping Cortijo San Isicio
T953-721128, www.campingcortijo.com. Mar-Oct.
Set on the road to San Isicio a couple of kilometres from town, this is a small campsite with plenty of shade.

Restaurants

€€ La Sarga
Plaza del Mercado s/n, T953-721507, www.lasarga.com.
One of Cazorla's best tapas options, with excellent specialities from the region using fresh ingredients such as asparagus and *setas* (wild mushrooms). There are also tables to enjoy a full meal; there's an interesting lunch menu and a degustation menu of local produce. There are plenty of choices of vegetable (but not all vegetarian) dishes, as well as more carnivorous options like fallow deer chops.

€€ Mesón Don Chema
C Escaleras del Mercado 2, T953-710529.
In a side alley off Cazorla's main shopping street, this large warm, restaurant is decorated with hunting trophies, old photographs and checked tablecloths. No prizes for guessing

that game dishes are their speciality; venison chops and rabbit in garlic take their place alongside *revueltos* and other mountain fare. Recommended.

Festivals

Jul Taking place over the last weekend of Jul, **Blues Cazorla** is a big international event featuring big names from around the world. See www.bluescazorla.com for details.

3rd week of Sep Cazorla's main fiesta has live bands, bullfights, and market stalls.

What to do

Tour operators

There are numerous operators offering all manner of excursions in the park, by 4WD, mountain bike, quad, foot or on horseback.

Excursiones Puente las Herrerías, *Ctra del Río Guadalquivir Km 3, T953-727090, www.puentedelasherrerias.com.* A little outside town, for horse riding, as well as mountain biking and other adventure sports.

Picadero El Cortijillo, *T690-697850, Ctra de la Sierra Km 39.8, www.turismoencazorla.com/empresas/picaderoelcortijillo.* Down a side turning just out of Arroyo Frío, this is perhaps the best of the local horse-riding set-ups, with noble, well-looked-after beasts. Their webpage has route options (in Spanish).

Turisnat, *Paseo del Santo Cristo 17, T953-721351, www.turisnat.es.* One of the best 4WD operators, located in the same building as the tourist office. They have a licence to take visitors into the restricted zones of the park.

Transport

Bus

Buses arrive and depart from Plaza de la Constitución. There are 3 daily buses to/from **Jaén** (2½ hrs) via **Ubeda** and **Baeza**. One of these continues to **Granada**, and there's a bus on Sun to **Málaga**. 2 buses from Cazorla go into the park as far as **Coto Ríos**.

The Parque Natural → *Colour map 3, B3.*

fabulous scenery and a great new network of walking trails

From the centre of Cazorla, the Burunchel road leads up into the park. Shortly above town, you pass the hamlet of La Iruela, which has an evocative ruined castle. From here you can take a detour along dirt roads to the spectacular El Chorro gorge, and, beyond, the Nacimiento, where the Guadalquivir river rises out of the ground and begins its journey to Sevilla and the Atlantic.

Otherwise, the tarmac road ascends to the Puerta de las Palomas pass, where there's a mirador to admire the views over the valleys below. Shortly afterwards, a right turn leads towards the parador, 8 km away. If you've taken the road to the Nacimiento, you can re-emerge at this point by following signs to El Vadillo.

The main road crisscrosses the Guadalquivir stream and passes through the ugly settlement of Arroyo Frío, where there are several hotels and restaurants, before reaching **Torre del Vinagre**, with an uninteresting interpretation centre and even less enthralling (unless you like antlers) hunting museum, **Museo de la**

ON THE ROAD

Fauna and flora in the Parque Natural Sierra de Cazorla

The park is heavily wooded, with aleppo pines at lower levels and maritime and laricio pines higher up. Patches of mixed woodland include *encinas* (holm oaks), olives and junipers, with poplars and willows in the wetter valleys. The whole area is a naturalist's delight, with some 1300 flowering species, including some 30 endemics, such as the Cazorla violet and the hoop petticoat daffodil. Wild peonies and gladioli plus a host of orchids are among the outstanding flowers.

There is a lot of game; many species were introduced when the park was a shooting reserve. The bellows of the rutting red deer are a typical sound in autumn. Also found are roe and fallow deer, while ibex can be seen, usually above the tree line. Predators include beech martens, polecats and genet and the occasional Pardel (Iberian) lynx. Other mammals include foxes, badgers and wild boars, while otters frequent many of the rivers. Over 100 bird species nest within the park. Raptors include all three vultures, four varieties of eagle, honey buzzards and peregrines. There is also a range of woodland birds, including crossbills and firecrests. There are many butterflies in spring and early summer and the endemic Valverde's lizard is one of several reptile species.

Caza ⓘ *T953-713040, Tue-Sun 1100-1400, 1600-1800 (1600-1900 spring and autumn; 1700-2000 summer), free.* The park was originally a shooting reserve, and Franco, among others, used to come here with rifle and rod in the 1960s. Across the road is a **botanical garden** ⓘ *daily 1000-1400, 1700-1900 (1600-1800 winter), free,* with labelled specimens of the park's native plants and trees.

After passing the settlement of Coto Ríos, you reach the tail of the Embalse del Tranco, a reservoir created by damming the waters of the Guadalquivir and Borroso rivers. On its shore is the **Parque Cinegético**, an animal reserve where you stand a chance of spotting deer or mouflon; a trail leads to some lookout points. The road continues along the reservoir's shore and finally crosses the dam itself, near which you can rent canoes or pedalos. Just beyond, a road turns off to the left towards the park exit and Villanueva del Arzobispo – one of the park's most spectacular stretches of road, with large brooding rock formations frowning all around.

Continuing, however, you reach two of the park's most attractive villages, **Hornos** and **Segura de la Sierra**. Both preserve part of their walls and are topped by a spectacular castle.

Segura de la Sierra is easily reached from Hornos and can be seen from kilometres around, sitting on the top of its conical hill. Offering white houses, a soaring castle and epic views over pine-clad hills and olive groves, it makes a tempting base. Its strategic position meant that it was occupied in turn by all the groups who invaded Andalucía, from the Phoenicians through to the Moors. The **castle** ⓘ *Apr-Oct Tue-Sun 1100-1400, 1700-2000, Nov-Mar Wed-Sun 1100-1400, 1600-1900, €4,* built by the Almoravids and eventually destroyed by French troops during the Peninsular War, consists of two main precincts, several towers, gates, a keep and a well. There are interactive displays and interpretative boards. Ask at the castle or the Ayuntamiento for entrance to the Moorish baths in the main square, where you can see cold, tepid and hot rooms, with double horsehoe arches at each end and a barrel vault with star-shaped ventilation holes.

Sendero Bosques del Sur → *Distance: 480 km.*
Recently inaugurated, the Southern Woodlands Trail, or GR247, is a giant trail with extensions and diversions that does a big circuit around the whole park. It's divided into numbered stages, with easy vehicular access, so you don't have to do it all at once. It's well signposted throughout and much of it is bikeable.

You can get details from park information offices or check route information and download a map from www.sierrasdecazorlaseguraylasvillas.es.

Río Borosa Gorge → *Distance: 21 km. Time: 7-7½ hrs. Difficulty: medium-difficult.*
The Sierra's best-known walk takes you along a beautiful section of the impressive gorge of the Río Borosa. You follow a dirt track and then a spectacular wooden walkway eastwards through the gorge, which opens out into a huge, natural ampitheatre of soaring limestone crags. From here a steep climb takes you to a high reservoir that you reach by following the course of a mill race, tunnelled out of the mountainside. The walk can be as far up and down as you like but remember you'll climb for 600 m should you do the whole lot. It is best done on a weekday out of holiday season. Remember that the upper section of the walk is sometimes impassable in winter; check with the park rangers at Torre de Vinagre centre (see above) or with one of the agencies in Cazorla. Take a torch for negotiating the tunnels and in the warmer months remember your bathing costume – there are lovely river pools for swimming. **Maps**: Alpina 1:40,000 map: Sierra de Segura I.

Itinerary From Cazorla take the road that leads via La Iruela then Burunchel, up into the park, then turn left for Coto Ríos/Embalse del Tranco on the A319. When you reach the Centro de Interpretación Torre del Vinagre, turn right and follow signs for 'Central Eléctrica', the electricity generating station. Cross the river and leave your car in the park to the left of the road just after the *piscifactoría*, or trout farm.

The walk begins from the car park and follows the river the whole way. Cross a bridge, then turn right and follow a track along the left bank of the river. Soon you cross a concrete bridge; swing left along the river's right bank, then cross back again to the left bank via a wooden bridge. Where the track bears left and climbs, you branch right (35 minutes) on a path marked 'Cerrada de Elías'. You twice cross the river via narrow footbridges. The Borosa's gorge narrows and you follow a hanging boardwalk above the river. Eventually the path meets the track again. Continue up the gorge, which begins to open out. There are wonderful views of the twisted strata of La Cuerda de Las Banderillas and La Peña Plumera and, when the track bears slightly right, of the towering massif of Castellón del Haza de Arriba (1504 m). Soon you'll catch sight of the pipeline that funnels the water down the side of the valley to the Central Eléctrica. You cross over a bridge (one hour, 45 minutes) then follow a fence that runs just to the right of the station and its outbuildings. You pass a spring, cross a narrow bridge, then pick up a path at a sign for 'Laguna de Valdeazores'. You now climb steeply up the left bank of the river. Steel yourself: you have a climb of about 300 m if you wish to follow the walk all the way. To the left you'll spot the Picón del Haza; for much of the year a waterfall runs off its eastern flank. The path climbs up into the spectacular ampitheatre of the gorge's higher reaches: the mountains rise almost sheer to 1500 m. Red dots mark your way and soon you'll see a second waterfall to your right: El Salto de los Organos. The path passes over loose scree, bears right and, where you can see the remains of a dam, swings sharply to the left towards an electricity pylon. Just before the pylon bear right at a sign 'Nacimiento de Aguas Negras' and 'Laguna de Valdeazores'. The path leads through one of the tunnels that were cut to bring water to the mill race: this one is almost 350 m long! After passing through a second, shorter tunnel you come to the reservoir called Embalse del Borosa, La Laguna de Aguas Negras or Embalse de los Organos – according to which map you are following (two hours, 45 minutes). Where the path divides, you have a choice. Either bear left and climb away from the water channel and head up the valley of the Arroyo del Infierno to the Nacimiento de Aguas Negras (a further 10 minutes), where the Río Borosa rises from beneath the rocks, or bear right a further 1 km to a pretty and secluded lake. Either makes a perfect spot for a picnic stop. Retrace your footsteps all the way back down the gorge in order to arrive back at your point of departure.

★Vadillo Castril to Cazorla → *Distance: 9 km. Time: 4 hours. Difficulty: medium.*
This walk follows a wonderful mountain trail that cuts up from the Guadalquivir valley through a high pass, before winding its way down and around the Escribano peak, to Cazorla. There are wonderful views up the valley and out across the sea of olive groves that stretches west from Cazorla. Be prepared for a long climb of almost 400 m up and past the Fuente del Oso. **Maps**: Alpina 1:40,000 map: Sierra de Segura I. Because this is a linear walk you'll need a chauffeur or taxi ride from Cazorla to El Puente de la Herrerias. The journey takes about 30 minutes and costs approximately €25 (recommended taxi driver: Urbano García, T608-854701).

Cazorla circuit → *Distance: 16 km. Time: 7-7½ hrs. Difficulty: medium-difficult.*
This circular walk from Cazorla, mostly along high mountain trails, is one of the Sierra's classic itineraries and is well worth its reputation. A long climb of nearly 900 m up from the village leads you to a high pass from where the peak of El Gilillo (1848 m) is easily climbed: the views on a clear day of the distant Sierra Nevada alone make this walk worth the effort. From here a beautiful high mountain trail brings you back to Cazorla in a long, lazy loop – a wonderful reward for your efforts earlier in the day.

If you find the idea of a long climb intimidating, you can avoid the initial 3 km of mountain road above Cazorla by taking a taxi to the barrier by the Hotel Ríogazas. You should be prepared for cold conditions on the higher, often windy, section of this walk. If climbing Gilillo add an hour to the timings below. **Maps**: Alpina 1:40,000 map: Sierra de Segura I.

Where to stay

Apart from basing yourself in Cazorla (see above), there are several hotels and campsites within the park boundaries itself. There are numerous *casas rurales* for rent; www.turismoencazorla.com has a list, or you can search online. Segura de la Sierra makes another excellent base on the other side of the park.

€€€ Parador de Cazorla
Sierra de Cazorla s/n, T953-727075, www.parador.es. Closes from mid-Dec to Jan. On summer weekends you need to reserve for 2 nights.
In an isolated spot high up in the protected area of the sierra, past Vadillo Castril, this cosy lodge makes a great activity base, with bikes, horse riding and hiking available from the doorstep. The restaurant, spacious pool and garden area offer wonderful mountain views, as do some of the rooms.

€€ Los Huertos de Segura
C Castilla 11, Segura de la Sierra, T953-480402, www.loshuertosdesegura.com.
Offering a perfect blend of hospitality and independence, these standout studios and apartments at the top of the village have superlative views and a homely feel to their interiors. All come with kitchen, fireplace and Wi-Fi, but it's the solicitous hosts, full of information about the area, who make the stay memorable.

€€ Santa María de la Sierra
Ctra de la Sierra Km 39.8, T630-346600, www.crsanta maria.com.
A welcoming and peaceful *casa rural* situated a couple of kilometres down a signposted side road just beyond Arroyo Frío. There's a variety of accommodation; the standard doubles and singles are comfortable, with colourful walls and beds, and heating and there are special doubles with fireplace. The most characterful, however, are the *nidos* (nests), treehouse cabins in the wooded gardens. There's a large comfortable lounge, 2 pools and a restaurant serving mountain cuisine. Breakfast included. Recommended.

Camping

There are 8 official campsites in the Sierras de Cazorla and Segura. There are also a number of free camping grounds without facilities; contact the information centre in Cazorla for details. 2 handily located sites are: **Camping Montillana**, T680-158778, beyond the dam at El Tranco on the road to Hornos, and **Camping Fuente de la Pascuala**, T953-713028, www.campinglapascuala.com, which is shaded by pine trees and has a pool; it's near the shore of the reservoir beyond the turn-off for Coto Ríos.

Restaurants

€€ La Mesa Segureña
C Postigo 2, Segura de la Sierra, T953-482101, www.lamesadesegura.com.
In the village centre, this appealing rustically decorated restaurant offers dishes with a local emphasis and generous proportions. They are more elaborate than you'd expect, and utterly delicious. Tender sierra lamb, great daily specials, imaginative salads,

and toothsome home-made desserts make this a winner. They also have enticing rooms and apartments. Great views from the terrace. Recommended.

Transport

Bus

Segura la Sierra has no bus connection, but there are 2-4 daily buses to **La Puerta de Segura**, 17 km away and an appealing town in its own right.

Almería

sun-baked and arid, Spain's driest mainland province

In far east Andalucía, Almería is mostly a desert zone, with less than 250 mm of annual precipitation. A popular film location for American Wild West cinema, the almost constant sunshine also attracts expats from Northern Europe.

The city of Almería makes a pleasant stop with its Alcazaba fortress which defended the major port of Granada's Moorish kingdom; today it overlooks the centre's enjoyable tapas bars.

The western coast with its vast areas scarred by plastic greenhouses is best avoided, but to the east is the supremely barren Cabo de Gata, an ensemble of wild and rugged countryside ending in high cliffs enclosing some of Andalucía's best sandy beaches. Further east, the atmospheric hilltop village of Mojácar was an artists' haven in the 1960s; today tourists are also attracted to its long coastal strip.

Inland Almería is sparsely populated over folded hills and mountains. In the west, the Alpujarra is less touristy than in Granada and substantially greener. Within this relaxing and pretty section of rural Andalucía is the friendly village of Laujar de Andarax.

In the northeast, the castle of Vélez Blanco is worth a trip to see it towering on its crag above the village.

Best for
Beaches ▪ Tapas ▪ Walking

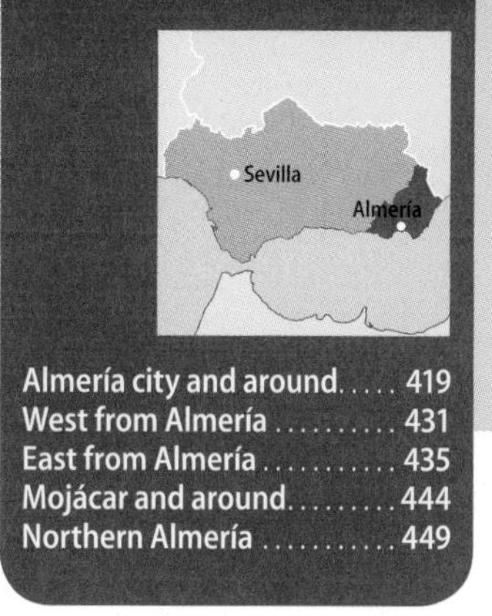

Footprint picks

★ **Los Millares**, page 426

Take a trip to the important and mostly deserted Chalcolithic settlement in the hills northwest of Almería city.

★ **Laujar de Andarax**, page 433

Use this appealing village as a base to explore the lesser-visited Almerian Alpujarra.

★ **Flamingoes**, page 437

Spot flamingoes from the hide near San Miguel de Cabo de Gata.

★ **Playa de los Genoveses**, page 438

Enjoy a refreshing dip, a short walk from San José in Cabo de Gata.

★ **Mojácar**, page 444

Watch the amazing sunset from the remains of the castle in the old town.

★ **Vélez Blanco**, page 450

Photograph the striking outlines of the castle overlooking this village.

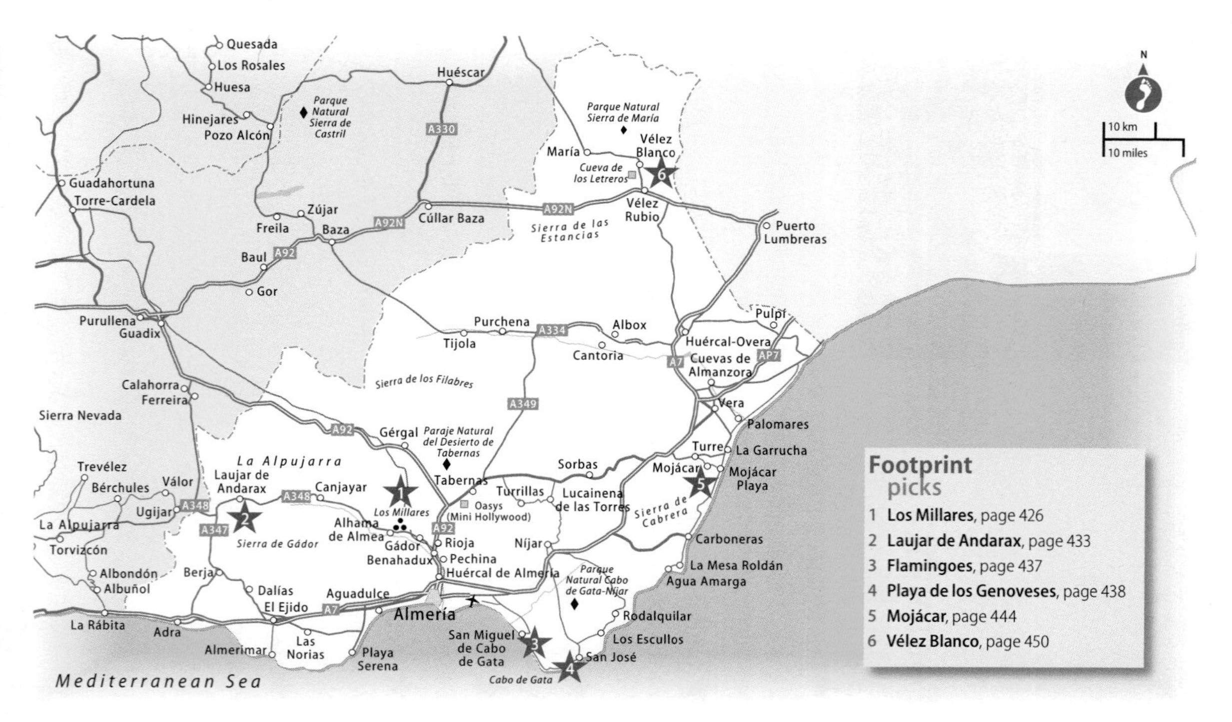

N
10 km
10 miles
Quesada
Los Rosales
Huesa
Hinejares
Pozo Alcón
Parque Natural Sierra de Castril
Huéscar
A330
Parque Natural Sierra de María
María
Vélez Blanco
Cueva de los Letreros
Guadahortuna
Torre-Cardela
Zújar
Freila
Baza
A92N
Cúllar Baza
Vélez Rubio
Sierra de las Estancias
Puerto Lumbreras
Baul
A92
Gor
Purullena
Guadix
Purchena
Tíjola
A334
Albox
Cantoria
Pulpí
Huércal-Overa
A7
Cuevas de Almanzora
AP7
Sierra de los Filabres
Calahorra
Ferreira
A349
Vera
Sierra Nevada
Gérgal
Paraje Natural del Desierto de Tabernas
Palomares
Turre
La Garrucha
Trevélez
La Alpujarra
Laujar de Andarax
Canjayar
A348
Tabernas
Sorbas
Mojácar
Mojácar Playa
Bérchules
Válor
Ugíjar
Los Millares
Oasys (Mini Hollywood)
Turrillas
Lucainena de las Torres
Sierra de Cabrera
La Alpujarra
A347
Alhama de Almea
Sierra de Gádor
Gádor
Rioja
Níjar
Carboneras
Torvizcón
Benahadux
Pechina
Albondón
Albuñol
Berja
Huércal de Almería
Parque Natural Cabo de Gata-Níjar
La Mesa Roldán
Agua Amarga
Dalías
El Ejido
Aguadulce
Almería
Rodalquilar
La Rábita
Adra
Almerimar
Las Norias
Playa Serena
San Miguel de Cabo de Gata
Los Escullos
San José
Cabo de Gata
Mediterranean Sea
Footprint picks
1 Los Millares, page 426
2 Laujar de Andarax, page 433
3 Flamingoes, page 437
4 Playa de los Genoveses, page 438
5 Mojácar, page 444
6 Vélez Blanco, page 450

Almería city
& around

Once one of the Mediterranean's principal cities, sunny Almería now features on most itineraries only as an airport or a hurried stop on the way to a beach holiday. This does it an injustice, for while it has few outstanding attractions, it's an intriguing place, at once very Spanish and quite North African.

An important ferry port for Morocco and Algeria, there's a real Moorish feel here, especially in its striking Alcazaba, a castle rising in sun-baked splendour over the flat-roofed town and desert surroundings. It's one of Spain's fastest-growing cities and has a significant Maghrebi population, drawn by the proximity to home, the superb sunny climate, and work. The Spanish side comes out in a few elegant avenues, but most of all in a high-quality tapas scene and a diverse and populous zone of old-town bars.

Within easy reach of the city are the theme parks near Tabernas, where dozens of spaghetti western classics were made, and the intriguing Chalcolithic site of Los Millares. *Colour map 6, B1.*

Sights

a massive Moorish castle and a fortress cathedral

Alcazaba

C Almanzor, T950-801008. Tue-Sat 0900-1830 (2030 Apr-Oct), Sun 1000-1700. €1.50, free for EU citizens.

Almería's mighty castle rises over three levels of a long rocky outcrop above the port. Built originally in the 10th century when Abd al-Rahman III, first caliph of Córdoba, granted Almería its town charter, it is heavily restored and preserves few of its Moorish features, but makes a fascinating visit nonetheless, if only for its mighty walls and panoramic views of the city and port.

You enter via the horseshoe arch of the Puerta de la Justicia and emerge in the lower level of the compound, now a surprisingly lush garden. This area was once a district of barracks and craftsmen's workshops. From here you can admire the spiky 11th-century curtain wall that runs across a valley and up to the hill of San Cristóbal, which has a decayed fort and a white Christ. Between the two hills you can spot the bouncing gazelles of a reserve for Saharan fauna, not usually open to the public.

Ascending to the second level, after passing through a tower you emerge in an open area that once would have been the heart of the Moorish castle. Here stood the 11th-century palace of the *taifa* city rulers. Only a small window and section of wall of this palace remain. Named Ventana de la Odalisca, it has a concubine story attached to it, like all Moorish windows in Andalucía. One of the king's harem fell in love with a Christian prisoner; when the wicked Moors defenestrated him, she leapt to her death in despair.

In this area you can also see the cisterns, or *aljibes*, which contain a useful scale model of the fortress. Next door is a *mudéjar* chapel constructed by the Catholic Monarchs.

The third level is a fortress complex also built by Fernando and Isabel, at which time they destroyed much of the original Moorish constructions. The impressive main Tower of Homage overlooks the flagstones of the parade ground and strong walls that were built to withstand cannon fire. Some cannons remain here in the Tower of Gunpowder; from here you can look over Almería's cave district, rapidly disappearing as new housing is being built. The barrio below, stretching down to the port, is La Chanca, which was evocatively

Essential Almería

Getting around

Apart from accessing the airport, the only time you are likely to need public transport in Almería city is for day trips in the surrounding area, or to get to the beach zone, Zapillo.

When to go

As Almería is Spain's driest mainland province, you're pretty much guaranteed sunshine year round. But bear in mind it's baking hot in summer.

Time required

Two to three days.

BACKGROUND

Almería

The city of Almería was established as a port by the Córdoban caliph Abd al-Rahman III in the middle of the 10th century. It was he who ordered the construction of its sturdy Alcazaba fortress when he granted the town its charter. In those days it was called Al-Mariyat, translated by some as 'watchtower', and by others, more poetically, as 'by the mirrored sea'.

After the fall of the caliphate, Almería became an important *taifa* state, thriving on shipbuilding, ceramics and the silk trade. Although conquered by the Christians in 1147, it was soon recaptured by the Almohads and was not surrendered by the Moors until the Catholic Monarchs came calling in 1490.

With the Muslims expelled, a rapid decline set in, not helped by a major earthquake in 1522 which destroyed much of the town. By the 17th century, the population was under 600, a far cry from the hundreds of thousands that had called the city home in its pomp. The late 19th and early 20th centuries saw a revival, as Almería became a useful port for exporting the ores mined in the province's interior. Almería was strongly Republican in the Civil War and was shelled by a German battleship and destroyers; the town fell to the Nationalists at the end of March 1939, amid scenes of panic and brutality.

In recent years, however, Almería has shaken off its bleak and poverty-stricken image and looks far smarter thanks to income from tourism and horticulture, and the boost provided by cultural, transport and economic links to the Maghreb. It is now Andalucía's most rapidly growing major city.

described by Gerald Brenan in *South from Granada*. Once seriously poor and a haunt of vagabonds and thieves, it's still a slightly seedy zone, but composed of colourful fishermen's houses, and worth strolling through with a modicum of caution.

Cathedral

Plaza Catedral s/n, T669-913628. Mon-Fri 1000-1400, 1600-1730, Sat 1000-1400, €5.

With apses bulging like castle towers and a high wall of thick sandstone, Almería's cathedral looks more like a stronghold in a debatable and desert borderland than a place of worship. There's a good reason for this: after the Reconquest, raids by Barbary corsairs were a regular problem for the towns and villages along this coast until Spain's naval power in the Mediterranean became more firmly established.

Rebuilt from 1524 after the original was destroyed in an earthquake, the cathedral stands on the site once occupied by the town's main mosque. There are two noteworthy Renaissance portals decorated with royal coats of arms; they were designed by the local architect Juan de Orea. The interior is a fusion of styles, with ornate Baroque features such as the red marble retrochoir and side chapels that contrast with the Isabelline late-Gothic star vaulting.

Among the chapels, see the gilt *retablo* in the Capilla de San Ildefonso; it centres around a painting of the Virgin giving Ildefonso a chasuble (this particular apotheosis is a common subject in Spanish religious painting). The stately walnut choir is also a 16th-century work by Orea; it faces the altar and main chapel, a striking 18th-century work of gilding and marble. Around the structure are paintings from the life of the Virgin, while in the centre are a 16th-century Calvary and Annunciation.

There are three apsidal chapels; the left-hand one has three paintings by the Granadan master Alonso Cano in the *retablo*, while on the side wall hangs a fine Immaculate Conception by that staunch defender of the Virgin's flawlessness,

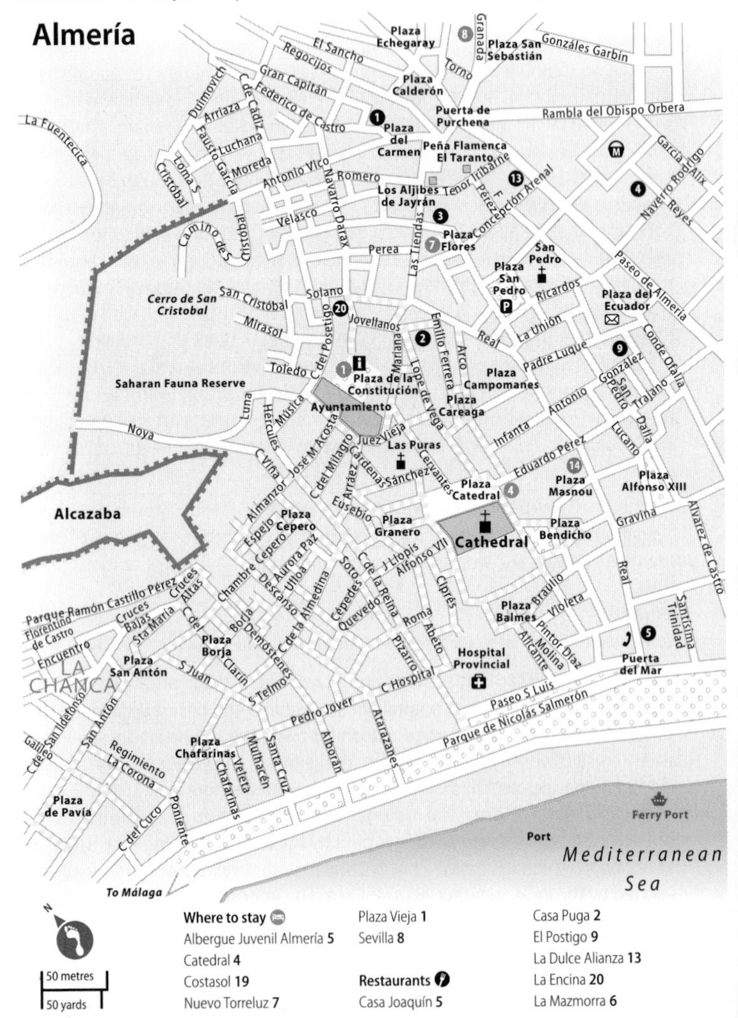

Bartolomé Esteban Murillo of Sevilla. The central chapel has a well-loved Christ, *Santo Cristo de la Escucha* (a copy; the original was destroyed by anticlericals in the Civil War) that is paraded through the streets on Good Friday morning, as well as a marble tomb of the founding archbishop, Fray Diego de Villalán.

The Renaissance sacristy is perhaps the interior's finest feature, again a work of Juan de Orea, with stately arches studded with rosettes. The lushly gardened cloister is entered through an Isabelline portal but itself is neoclassical in style, dating from the late 18th century.

Next door to the cathedral is the convent church of Las Puras, fetchingly built from rough masonry and topped by a small *mudéjar* bell tower.

North of here, the **Plaza de la Constitución** is a fantastic enclosed square (trapezium to be exact). Once the Moorish *souk*, it now features the elegant Ayuntamiento, a 19th-century colonnade, and the squared-off trees that the local council seem to love.

In the centre is a white monument known as *El Pingurucho a los Coloraos. Los coloraos* (the coloureds) were the liberals who during the depredations of the Peninsular War, proclaimed a democratic constitutional monarchy in Spain in 1812. After the war was over, the restoration of Fernando VII resulted in brutal reprisals as he sought to eliminate any traces of anti-monarchism from his kingdom. Riego, one of the prominent later leaders of the movement, was dragged to the gallows in Madrid in a coal basket tied to an ass, and many others were executed, including the Almerians to whom this monument is dedicated. Despite this, the 1812 constitution planted the seeds of democracy in Spain and remains a powerful symbol. The presence of this monument in Almería is a testament to the city's strong republican traditions (although there's a monument to the Falange tucked away in the garden of the adjacent Iglesia de las Claras, burned by leftists during the Civil War).

The original Pingurucho was destroyed by Franco's government but a new one was erected in 1988 by popular demand.

The waterfront

Almería's waterfront is looking much better these days, although it's still a serious commercial port area. The most interesting spot is at the bottom of the Rambla, where a fine piece of 19th-century industrial architecture, the **Cable Inglés**, stands in rusting dignity. Built to ship ores mined in the province's interior, it sports a railway above and a series of funnels to feed the stuff directly into boats moored below. West of here, the Parque Nicolás Salmerón is a shady avenue running alongside the docks and passenger terminal. The industrial port is further along, and finally the fishing port. To the east of the Rambla is the marina, and, a further 1.5 km away, is Almería's grey but reasonable beach and the busy barrio of Zapillo. To reach here, catch one of a few buses from the Paseo de Almería.

Museo de Almería

Ctra de Ronda 91, T950-100409. Tue-Sat 1000-2030, Sun 1000-1700. Free for EU residents, €1.50 for others.

Almería's excellent archaeological museum is a light and airy modern space that sensibly narrows its displays down to a few key items, and lots of explanation. One floor is dedicated to the Los Millares Chalcolithic site, see below, while another display pays homage to the Siret brothers, first excavators there and pioneers of Almerían archaeology. Another floor covers the succeeding Argaric culture, while there's a small Roman and Islamic section at the top. Interactive displays and a neat stratigraphic pillar down the middle add appeal to a place that's full of information but never feels weighty.

Los Aljibes de Jayrán

C Tenor Iribarne s/n, T950-273039. Mon-Fri 0900-1400, closed for refurbishment at time of research.

These Moorish cisterns have been prettily restored with brick arches and marble floors and now regularly hold art exhibitions and, occasionally, live flamenco. They once held enough water to supply the whole city; they were fed by a long channel from a spring 7 km away.

Around Almería → *Colour map 6, B1.*

barren rocky hills and Western film sets

The Wild West

The landscape north of Almería is almost a desert and its arid hills and parched gullies have been a godsend to filmmakers over the years. In economically moribund Francoist Spain, cheap labour led many directors to choose this location to represent America's Wild West, see box, opposite. Hundreds of other films have

ON THE ROAD

Spaghetti westerns

Despite the name, which derives from the fact that these films were mainly financed and directed by Italians, most of the classic spaghetti westerns were filmed in the desert-like landscape north of Almería. Although at the time these low-budget productions were viewed as B movies, over time they have acquired classic status, particularly those involving director Sergio Leone, actor Clint Eastwood or composer Ennio Morricone. *The Good, the Bad and the Ugly* (1966) is regarded as one of the finest of the genre and involves all three, as do the earlier films *A Fistful of Dollars* and *For a Few Dollars More*, where Eastwood memorably plays the Man with No Name. Due to the films being shot here, the plots usually revolved around the Mexican frontier or the Mexican Civil War; there was no shortage of extras with suitable appearances and accents. The genre has inspired countless tributes and is seen these days as having been very influential, particularly in exemplifying the creation of atmosphere with careful choice of musical score and well-selected location.

also been made or partially made in the area, including *Lawrence of Arabia*, *Indiana Jones and the Last Crusade* and the Spanish hit *800 Balas*, a story based on the lives of unemployed extras from the Hollywood classics.

There are three theme parks in the region, built as film sets. All are atmospheric enough, but seriously overpriced and tacky; you may prefer to just cruise around the region, whistling Ennio Morricone scores as you go. A few dilapidated buildings from various other film sets still dot other parts of the countryside hereabouts; there are some on the left as you approach Tabernas from the motorway exit.

The main town is **Tabernas**, easily accessible by bus from Almería. You can walk up the hill to the heavily restored Moorish fort for some spectacular views of the desert scenery around. The fort was an important one, but the Catholic Monarchs took the keys and the title deeds without a fight in 1489. They themselves stayed here shortly thereafter, and later on a church was built on the hilltop.

The following parks are all within a few kilometres of Tabernas: **Oasys/Mini Hollywood** ⓘ *T902-533532, www.oasysparquetematico.com, Apr-Oct daily, Nov-Dec Sat and Sun, open 1000, closes 1800, 1900, 2000 or 2100 depending on season, admission adult/child €22/12.50*, is the oldest of the villages, originally made for Leone's *For a Few Dollars More*. Entry gets you into the township and includes some free events, such as shootouts, bank robberies and underwhelming parrot shows. It's pretty atmospheric, and definitely worth visiting at a weekend if possible, as there seems to be more going on. There's also a zoo here, and a pool. It's easy to access on public transport as buses from Almería to Tabernas will drop you off and pick you up at the door.

Fort Bravo/Texas Hollywood ⓘ *Fort Bravo, T950-066014, www.fortbravo.es, daily 0930-2000 summer, 0930-1800 winter, adults/children €18/10*, is the biggest of the towns and is still used quite often by filmmakers. It features in *The Good, the Bad & the Ugly*, among many others.

Western Leone ⓘ *T950-165405, www.westernleone.es, daily 1000-2000 (1800 winter), adults/children €11/6,* is the third, and smallest of the towns. Originally built for *Once Upon a Time in the West*, it has been added to over the years as further films were made here. It's quite atmospheric, but has far fewer visitors and attractions than the others.

★Los Millares

T677-903404. Wed-Sun 1000-1400, free.

This impressive archaeological site can be visited as a day trip from Almería or en route to the Almerían Alpujarras (see page 432). To get there, leave Almería on the A92 signposted for Guadix and exit for Gádor. The site is in Santa Fé de Mondújar, signposted from Gádor and 4 km beyond it. It's easiest to use your own transport for a visit (although you could get a bus from Almería to Gádor, and walk the 4 km to the site). Gádor station is closer, but the two trains from Almería don't run at convenient times.

Spread over a large hilltop overlooking the Andarax, which in its day would have been a significant river, Los Millares was a Chalcolithic settlement of extraordinary size and sophistication: it's one of Spain's most important archaeological sites. Inhabited from around 3200-2250 BC, it consists of three parts; a sturdily walled town, a large necropolis and a system of defensive towers that included one amazingly complex fort. Though all the material finds from the site are in Almería's archaeological museum, a visit to Los Millares is both memorable and worthwhile. Try and get here before midday, as you'll need at least two hours for the visit, which requires plenty of walking in the powerful Almerían sun.

The visitor centre on the main road has a small display and an excellent video on the principal fort, an ingenious structure that suggests, as do the numerous arrowheads found at the site, that Los Millares was often under attack. From the entrance, the left-hand path leads to an area where replica houses, a forge, an impressive defensive wall and two tombs have been built. It really brings the site to life and is worth visiting first. These structures are highly advanced for this period in Western Europe.

Returning to the centre, take the right-hand path to the site itself, passing through the necropolis area as you go. The necropolis has over 100 tombs of different types that were used for collective burials: elaborate tholoi with corbelled domes, dolmens and simpler chambered tombs. Lovingly excavated by the Belgian railway workers Louis and Henri Siret, funded out of their own pockets, the tombs and site have yielded many finds from fine ceramics to copper tools and jewellery.

The culture that lived at Los Millares made the gradual transition from stone tools to copper ones; a period of civilization known as Chalcolithic that preceded the development of bronze working. Theorists have debated the origins of the people; they may have come by sea from the Eastern Mediterranean and almost certainly had trade contact with that region. The town flourished, as is shown by its expansions, each of which had to be contained by a new, larger, defensive wall. At the centre of the settlement is the foundation of a large rectangular building, some

12 m long; nearby is what was clearly a metalworking forge. The stone foundations of the dwellings run over a large area that may once have housed up to 2000 people.

At strategic points around the larger Los Millares area are the forts, some of which are linked by a walking trail (take water) from the visitor centre. The major fort, on the other side of the road from the visitor centre, is currently closed to the public.

Listings Almería city and around *map p422*

Tourist information

Provincial tourist office
Parque de Nicolás Salmerón s/n, T950-175220, otalmeria@andalucia.org. Mon-Fri 0900-1930, Sat and Sun 0930-1500.
By the park that runs along the waterfront. There is also a municipal office (Pl de la Constitución s/n, T950-210538, Sep-Jun 0900-1500, Jul-Aug 0900-1400, 1800-2000). Offices have well-trained bilingual staff and an excellent range of pamphlets on the city and province. They run regular worthwhile free guided walks.

Where to stay

Many of Almería's business-class hotels lower their rates by around 30% at weekends.

€€€ Hotel Catedral
Plaza de la Catedral 8, T950-278178, www.hotelcatedral.net.
With an enviable location on the quiet cathedral square, this modern, classy hotel in a converted mansion is one of Almería's best. While most rooms don't actually face the cathedral, they are stylish, contemporary and spacious. There's also a small pool/spa on a terrace with views and good internet facilities.

€€€ Plaza Vieja
Pl de la Constitución 4, T950-282096, www.plazaviejahl.com.
On this lovely pedestrian square, this excellent hotel features stylish rooms with arty whole-wall photos of Almería, exposed wall and gleaming modern bathrooms. There's a romantic Arab-style spa as well as other conveniences. Recommended.

€€ Hotel Costasol
Paseo de Almería 58, T950-234011, www.hotelcostasol.com.
This excellent central hotel is right on the main drag, and offers great value for spacious, modern rooms with comfortable beds and good facilities. Attractive design throughout and helpful service make this a real Almería bargain; the only downside is finding a parking space: try the narrow streets in the blocks to the west. Recommended.

€€ Hotel Nuevo Torreluz
Plaza Flores 10, T950-234399, www.torreluz.es.
This confusing plaza has no fewer than 3 places to stay named Torreluz; this is the higher-category hotel, which offers significant value. It's been recently refitted and the business-standard rooms are well appointed. Efficient staff. Parking available.

€€ Hotel Sevilla
C Granada 25, T950-230009, www.hotelsevillaalmeria.net.
This good-value hotel, a block from Puerta de Purchena, offers efficient and

friendly service. Rooms are simple but spotless and comfortable with a decent bathroom, there's Wi-Fi in the 1st-floor salon, laundry service, and non-smoking rooms available. Underground parking is nearby on the plaza or try parking on a backstreet nearby.

€ Albergue Juvenil Almería
C Isla de Fuerteventura s/n, T950-271744, www.inturjoven.com.
Take bus No 1 from Paseo de Almería from the centre. Next to the stadium in the beach suburb of Zapilla, this is a decent official hostel without too many rules or curfews. Accommodation is mostly in double rooms, includes breakfast, and is much cheaper for those aged 26 and under.

Restaurants

Almería's restaurants are comparatively few because the local tapas scene is a booming one. Drinks are more expensive than in other cities (€2-3.50 for a *caña* of beer or a glass of wine), but you can order a free tapa with each one.

The old town west of the Paseo de Almería has many bars, but some of the best are to the east of the Paseo, around C Méndez Núñez. Many tapas bars close early at 1500 and reopen at 2000.

€€ Casa Joaquín
C Real 111, T950-264359.
Amid the aromas of the many Maghrebi cafés in this area near the port, this white, light, traditional spot remains solidly Spanish, with hanging hams and bottles of sherry. They serve up excellent fish dishes at the homely wooden tables.

€€ La Encina
C Marin 16, T950-273429, www.restaurantelaencina.net.
A top-quality eatery, this gem offers honest Almerían cuisine with sophistication but no pretension. Almost everything is tasty; share a *parrillada de verduras* (grilled vegetable platter) to start, move on to venison, *dorada*, or a *zarzuela* (fish stew). Welcoming service. Recommended.

€€ Mediterráneo
Pl Flores 1, T950-281425, www.torreluz.com.
This elegant restaurant makes a very tempting place to dine. The multilevel interior is classically decorated; the food and service are excellent. Particularly worthwhile are the series of inexpensive tapas-style plates; order a few as a shared starter medley.

€ Casa Puga
C Jovellanos 7, T950-231530, www.barcasapuga.es.
An Almerían classic, this 19th-century bar near the Alcazaba oozes traditional character with its dusty bottles and large terracotta vats. The tapas are good; sit in the back (if there's space – this place is reliably packed) to take advantage of cheap *raciones*. Stand on the right side of the bar and watch the cook – order as your tapa whatever happens to be sizzling on the grill at that moment.

€ El Postigo
C Guzmán 1, T950-245652.
Tucked away in the bar area, this great, informal spot is always packed with folk from all strata of Almerían society. There's a shady terrace, but people come mainly for the free tapas, like the generous charcoal-grilled ribs. It's a popular last stop on the trail, as it's open until 0200 at weekends.

€ La Mazmorra
C Javier Sanz 4, T950-624593, www.lamazmorrarestaurants.com.
Get here early to bag a table at lunchtime, because it packs out pretty quickly. Why? Enormous plates of simple, tasty food, with grilled meats a speciality. For under a tenner, grab a brochette, an enormous hanging slab of various meats suspended over salad that will comfortably feed two. The tapas choices are wide and generous also. There's a terrace, but not much shade.

€ Quinto Toro
C Juan Leal (Reyes Católicos) 6, T950-239135.
Well loved by a cross-section of Almerían society, this is decked out with colourful azulejo tiles and numerous photos of bullfighters. There's a huge tapas choice: a local favourite here is the butter-soft chicken liver stewed in sherry; there are also tempting cold plates such as *ensaladilla* or *remojón*.

€ Rincón de Juan Pedro
Plaza del Carmen 5, T950-235184, www.facebook.com/elrincondejuanpedro.
Next to the La Perla hotel, this small but stylish spot has a chatty owner and puts out a very satisfying *menú del día* at lunchtimes, which comes with a flask of wine. In the evenings, simple and effective Almerían classics are the go – try the *gachas*, a spicy clam stew.

Cafés

La Dulce Alianza
Paseo de Almería 6, T950-237379.
A glamorous *confitería* with a sparkling range of pastries, chocolates and deli products. There's also a café where you can enjoy some of them with a cup of coffee.

Bars and clubs

Almería's principal and excellent bar zone is around C Trajano west of the Paseo de Almería. Here there are bars to suit all tastes; many are open until 0400 or so nightly.

Vhada
C Real 54.
A moody bar that's basically just a dark room with a few posters and a relaxed alternative atmosphere. It draws an eclectic mix of people who come to listen to the rock and indie music on the great sound system.

Entertainment

Flamenco
Peña Flamenca El Taranto, *C Tenor Iribarne 20, T950-235057, www.eltaranto.com.* Above the Arab cisterns, this is one of a few enthusiasts' clubs that put on regular live flamenco, usually at weekends. They also do decent, good-value dinners, based around fried fish.

Festivals

2nd half of Aug Virgen del Mar, Almería's major fiesta. There are 10 days of lively partying, bullfights and a large funfair. During the day the tapas bars in the centre are packed with people sampling and voting for the best traditional offerings.
Late Aug Festival de Flamenco.

What to do

Apart from walking tours (see under Tourist information, above), there are regular weekend and summer sailings of small cruise boats. A couple of these run around Almería itself and its ports. The most popular is a 4-hr return trip to the Cabo de Gata, costing €25 per person. It needs to be booked in advance at the tourist office.

Transport

Air

The airport is 8 km east of the city centre and is connected by the No 22 bus (www.surbus.com) to the bus/train station. These run roughly hourly (€1.05). It's €15-20 in a cab.

The airport is served to and from **London** by **Easyjet**. There are other charter flights here from both Britain and **Germany**, as well as other European and Spanish destinations served.

Bus

The bus station is next to the train station, a short walk to the east of the centre.

For bus information, T950-210029.

Within Almería province, there are 4 daily departures (2 on Sun) for **San José** in Cabo de Gata (1 hr), one of which (Mon and Sat only) continues to **Isleta del Moro**. To **Cabo de Gata** village, there are 6 daily buses (45 mins). To **Rodalquilar** and **Las Negras**, a daily bus (except Sun) makes the trip (2 hrs). One also leaves direct to **Agua Amarga** (2 hrs). There are 4 buses to **Carboneras** on weekdays but only 1 on Sat and Sun.

On Mon-Fri, a daily bus leaves to **Laujar**, and there's a daily bus (2 at weekends) to **Ugijar** in the Granadan Alpujarras.

Mojácar is served by 2-5 daily buses (1-2 hrs), while **Tabernas** gets up to 7 weekday buses but fewer at weekends (30 mins).

A couple of daily buses go to **Níjar**, **Sorbas**, **Vélez Blanco** and **Vélez Rubio**.

Within Andalucía, there are daily buses to **Cádiz**, **Córdoba**, **Sevilla** (3 daily) and **Jaén** (2 daily). More frequent connections include **Málaga** (5-7 daily) and **Granada** (5-7 daily, 2 hrs).

Outside Andalucía, there are several daily departures for **Murcia**, **Madrid** (6-7 hrs), and **Barcelona** via **Alicante**.

Car

Car hire Apart from airport agencies, a good local dealer is **Almericar**, T950-334482, www.almericar.com.

Ferry

Almería is an important ferry port that connects Spain with Morocco and Algeria. In summer, there are several daily departures to **Melilla**, a Spanish port on the Moroccan coast, to nearby **Nador** in Morocco itself, and to **Ghazaouet** and **Oran** in Algeria. In winter, ferries are less frequent. It is important to check all departures at the port itself as schedules change frequently. The information desk at the passenger port is very helpful.

Ferries are run by **Trasmediterránea** (T902-454645, www.trasmediterranea.es). The crossing takes 6-9 hrs and costs from €45 for a seat, and from €72 per person for a double cabin.

Taxi

T950-251111.

Train

Almería's beautiful art nouveau train station, which is next to the bus station, unfortunately doesn't see too much action. There are 4 daily departures to **Granada** (2 hrs 15 mins), and **Sevilla** (5 hrs), 2 to **Madrid** (6 hrs 30 mins), and 1 service to **Barcelona** every couple of days (13 hrs).

West from Almería

One of Andalucía's least attractive sections of coast stretches west of Almería, with a couple of high-rise resorts sandwiched into seemingly endless seas of plastic greenhouses. If you're looking for beaches and seafood, it's best to go the other way, or continue into Granada province.

Fortunately, a few kilometres inland is the eastern half of the Alpujarra region; much less explored than the area's valleys in Granada province, these wooded hills offer plenty of walking opportunities. The main settlement in the region is Laujar de Andarax, a lovable village and tranquil place to stay for a couple of days. As a bonus, some of Andalucía's best table wine is produced there.

The west coast of Almería → *Colour map 5, B6.*

ugly coastline with little appeal

What would otherwise be an attractive bit of coastline leading to Granada province has been sacrificed to the demands of productivity. The noble Spanish tomato, once one of the tastiest things on the planet, is now mass-cultivated in vast plastic *invernaderos*, mostly staffed by North African workers without papers, who are treated appallingly. Important as the industry now is for the Almerían economy, it's a tragedy that things have been allowed to get to the stage where half the province's coast has become one of the ugliest sights in the peninsula (see box, page 432).

A short way from Almería is the tasteless resort of **Roquetas del Mar**, whose main redeeming feature is its lively summer nightlife. **El Ejido**, capital of the plasticulture industry, is a sad mix of the wealthy Spaniards making a fortune from the greenhouses and the exploited workers that sweat it out inside them. **Almerimar**

ON THE ROAD

Plasticultura

It seems a curious paradox that Spain's most barren coastline is the site of its most intensive horticultural operations. The irrigation and agricultural infrastructure laid down by the Moors was abandoned in the wake of the Reconquista, and erosion and lack of water soon made it nearly impossible to cultivate.

In the 1950s a technique was developed that involved spreading a layer of clay over the natural soil to prevent losing water through permeation. Over this, a fertile topsoil was placed to enable crops to grow. Plastic sheeting to cover these crops began to be used in the 1960s, and exploded in the 1970s.

Now, Almería province has some 33,000 ha of land under plastic greenhouses, an aesthetic disaster, but one that produces important quantities of flowers, tomatoes, peppers, cucumbers and melons, both for local consumption and export in refrigerated lorries.

The rapid expansion of this industry has led to several problems apart from the scenic havoc. Many of the greenhouses are illegally constructed and environmental laws are generally poorly respected. Illegal immigrants are often used as labourers in the stifling conditions and are frequently abominably treated by employers, the ruthless 'plastic millionaires'. Also, water is paramount to the industry and is pumped from increasingly deeper and chemically compromised aquifers, but appears to be running out. Schemes to pump water from the Alpujarra have alarmed residents in that area, as they fear any lowering of their own water table will have devastating results on the local environment and agriculture. You can be sure that the industry, which has created numerous ruthless 'plastic millionaires' over the past decades, will eventually have its way.

is a resort that for some reason attracts the Mediterranean luxury yacht crowd, while **Adra**, a grimy port, is ugly and seedy.

West of here, a road heads inland to the Alpujarra via Albuñol, see page 357.

Almerían Alpujarra → *Colour map 5, B5.*

forested valleys and hills with plenty of charming villages

Scarcely visited in comparison with its continuation in Granada province, this zone is well worth a visit. From Almería, take the northbound motorway towards Guadix, exiting at Gádor. Passing the fascinating Chalcolithic site of Los Millares (see page 426), the road starts winding up a long, spectacular, and fertile valley formed by the Río Andarax.

The first Alpujarra town, Alhama de Almería, can be safely bypassed, as more traditional villages lie ahead. Little **Instinción** has a hotel and spectacular surrounding hillscapes. Appealing **Canjáyar** comes next, cascading down a burgundy hillside studded with prickly pears. Apart from its small church, there are few sights, but a short walk will bring you to some *miradores* with good views of the valley and rocky hills enclosing it. Canjáyar produces olive oil, which you can try and buy at two *almazaras* (mills) open to visitors in the town; village shops also sell the cheap and cheerful local *costa* wine.

★Laujar de Andarax

This quiet town is the major centre in the region, but is scarcely more than a village. It is exceptionally friendly and makes an excellent place to stay for a couple of days; you'll experience a slice of village life that can't help but be enjoyed. At the western end of town is an **information office** ⓘ *T950-513548, Fri-Sun 0900-1400, 1530-1830*, with an exhibition on the local environment. If it's shut, the La Alacena shop in the centre of town also has some information.

In town, the main square is presided over by the impressive town hall. Built in the late 18th century, it has a distinctive triple-tiered arched façade and a bell tower. Below is a beautiful fountain with much-prized drinking water. Above the town hall, the 17th-century church has an ornate gilt *retablo*.

Just past the town hall, take the first major street on the left, which ascends 1 km to **El Nacimiento**, a pretty picnic area on the river. From here you can take an excellent walk along the Andarax to its source; it's about a four-hour loop (starting from the village) through Mediterranean forest, with birches, pines, chestnuts and ash, and the stream gurgling peacefully alongside. The trail passes an old *cortijo* (farmhouse) with a vast chestnut tree; there's also an unstaffed *refugio* on the path, Monterrey, which you can use as a base for walking further. In the recreation area is an old mill and a couple of traditional country restaurants, great to eat at but open weekends only.

Laujar is famous for its wines, which are the province's best. A drive from town, **Bodega Cortijo El Cura** ⓘ *Paraje de Ojancos s/n, T649-307200, www.cortijoelcura.com*, has a couple of very palatable ecologically produced reds and can be visited by prior appointment.

Listings Almerían Alpujarra

Where to stay

€€ Hotel La Kabila
C Ejido s/n, Instinción, T950-601802, www.lakabila.es.
On the main road at the entrance to Instinción, this blue Moorish fantasy offers simple but good value rooms and lovely views of folded hills. There's also a suite equipped with a jacuzzi, a restaurant serving local produce, and a *tetería* serving Moroccan-style teas.

€€ La Posada de Eustaquio
Plaza de la Constitución 9, Canjáyar, T950-510177, www.posadaeustaquio.com.
A quiet place with simply decorated but well-equipped rustic rooms and

an excellent restaurant with generous portions and prices.

Laujar de Andarax

€€ Villa Turística de Laujar
Cortijo de la Villa s/n, T950-608050, laujardeandarax@reddevillas.es.
Set on a hillside above town, with great views over the verdant valley, this curious complex looks like a monastery from afar. Accommodation is is in well-equipped self-contained apartments, and there's a pretty pool, tennis court, and horse riding and walking opportunities. Good value. Recommended.

€ Hotel Almirez
Ctra Laujar–Orgiva Km 1.6, a 15-min walk from the town centre on the western edge of town, T950-513514, www.hotel-almirez.es.
Excellent value rooms in this quiet, welcoming place with plenty of facilities including a good restaurant. The rooms are spacious and have a balcony.

Camping

Camping La Molineta
1 km east of town, T950-514315, www.campinglamolineta.es. Open all year.
A rural campsite often booked by school groups at weekends. It has basic facilities, but ring ahead as it sometimes closes if they're not expecting anybody.

Restaurants

€€ Asador La Tahá
C Emilio Esteban Hanza 1, Canjáyar, T950-510800. Open lunchtimes plus Sat evenings.
This cavernous restaurant makes a good midday venue for a slap-up Alpujarran meal; they serve hearty portions of local specialities using the town olive oil. The meat dishes like roast lamb leg could feed 2, but try and leave room for their tasty *leche frita* dessert.

Laujar de Andarax

The best places to eat are the 2 restaurants at El Nacimiento, but these are open at weekends only. Of the two, **La Fabriquilla**, T950-513510, beloved of Almerían families, does good tapas and excellent meats grilled over the fire.

€ La Barandilla
C Canalejas 2, on the main road, T655-997673.
The most outstanding place in town, this tapas bar offers a warm welcome, cheap local wine and a delicious selection of free tapas. Difficult to leave. Recommended.

Transport

Laujar de Andarax

Bus
There are 2 daily buses to **Almería**, leaving Laujar at 1100 and 1545 (1½ hrs-2½ hrs), and another weekdays only, leaving at 0735. This last goes via the uninteresting town of **Berja**, from where you can connect to **Ugíjar** in the Granadan Alpujarras.

Hitching
Hitching a lift to Ugíjar is easy and much quicker; or ask in the local bars, as there are usually plenty of people travelling to and fro.

East from Almería

Shortly beyond the provincial capital, the large and memorably scenic promontory of the Cabo de Gata juts out into the Mediterranean. This is one of Andalucía's most intriguing stretches of coast, with jagged cliffs and sparse and arid scenery harbouring several excellent sandy beaches. The shadeless rocky surrounds can get seriously hot in summer, as well as busy with holidaymakers.

San José is the largest of the beachside towns, while there are several more secluded villages, all with inviting accommodation options. North of the cape are the inland towns of Níjar and Sorbas.

Níjar and Sorbas → *Colour map 6, B1/B2.*

towns renowned for their colourful ceramics

Níjar

With an important tradition of ceramics, this small town 30 km northeast of Almería is much visited by tourists. Its one main street rises towards the church and is one long line of shops selling attractive pottery, cheap *jarapa* fabric and souvenirs. At the top of town, after the sharp right-hand curve, is the restored 17th-century church, which preserves an important parish archive dating back to the 16th century. It has three naves divided by stone arches and a noble wooden roof; the Baroque *retablo* has a painting of the Trinity below the Virgin, St Francis and San Sebastián. The potters' workshops are on the west side of town and worth seeking out.

Ceramics apart, there's little to detain you and Níjar certainly appeals more as a day trip from Almería or a short stop en route to another town.

Sorbas

The road from Tabernas heads east through archetypal spaghetti western countryside, where even the most hardy eucalyptus and olive trees struggle to thrive. The impact of the terrain is somewhat spoiled by being dotted with ugly warehouses, bars and brothels.

Sorbas is a town perched on the edge of a cliff; in fact the whole town sits on a sort of island; erosion caused by the changing courses of the seasonal local rivers has created a dramatic landscape of stark ravines. Some of this terrain is the **Parque Natural Karst en Yesos** south of town. The **Centro de Visitantes** ⓘ *at the entrance to the centre of town, T950-364563, Oct-Mar only, Thu-Sun 1030-1430*, has information on local geology, including a recreated cave. There are several caves in the area, which can be explored as part of an organized guided tour (see What to do, below), from simple walking to proper caving.

Sorbas is also famous for its ceramics, including a striking traditional pot whose top half is in the shape of a rooster. A handful of workshops are still operating, but not using the natural glazes described by Gerald Brenan in *South from Granada*. Although it has its share of expat pubs and estate agents, Sorbas is still a local place with a central market and a plaza dominated by the austere neoclassical façade of its church. Opposite is a red-coloured *palacio* built by a Duke of Alba. The pottery barrio lies beyond here on the other side of the hill.

Various *miradores* around town give views over the surrounding ravines, but the best vantage point is from the main road heading east, when the full drama of Sorbas' cliff-top position suddenly reveals itself.

Listings Níjar and Sorbas

Where to stay

There is a great number of *casas rurales* and apartments for rent in the area. Look at www.degata.com and www.toprural.com.

Sorbas

€ Hostal Sorbas
Ctra Tabernas-Murcia s/n, T950-364160. Decent rooms at a cheap rate in a dramatically ugly building on the main road through town.

Restaurants

Sorbas

€€ El Rincón
Plaza Constitución 8, T950-364591. A cheery restaurant on the central square, which is by far the centre's best option for a meal.

What to do

Sorbas

Cuevas de Sorbas, *T950-364704, www.cuevasdesorbas.com.* Runs tours of the Sorbas caves, ranging from basic to expert routes.

Transport

Níjar

Níjar is served by 2 daily buses from **Almería**, but these are inconvenient for day trips.

Sorbas

There are 3 daily buses to and from **Almería** and one on Sat and Sun (1 hr 45 mins).

Cabo de Gata → *Colour map 6, B2.*

bare volcanic hills sheltering fine and remote sandy beaches

The rocky headland of El Cabo de Gata is one of Andalucía's finest natural assets, a striking ensemble of volcanic cliffs that descend dramatically to the sea. A couple of the best are within an easy walk of the main resort, San José, but to escape the summer crowds and high prices, strike off further east to the quieter villages and strands on the eastern side of the promontory.

Much of the area is encompassed by the **Parque Natural Cabo de Gata-Níjar**, which affords the region some protection from the creeping curse of the plastic hothouses. Nevertheless, overdevelopment is already affecting some of the villages; for the moment, though, El Cabo de Gata is a blessed and awe-inspiring relief from the brash strips that blight Andalucía's coastline elsewhere. From Almería city heading east, the sprawling satellite town of Retamar, can be safely ignored as better things lie ahead. Between here and **Ruescas** is a park **information office** ⓘ *T950-160435, Jun-Sep daily 1000-1400, 1600-1800, 1000-1500 the rest of the year.* There are displays here on the local plants and wildlife.

★Cabo de Gata village

Cabo de Gata village, whose full name is **San Miguel de Cabo de Gata**, is a somewhat bleak and not particularly appealing place, although its long, exposed beach is an obvious attraction. An 18th-century fortified tower guards the coast, while the tiny church has a simple interior and a statue of the Virgin of the Sea, whose protection is much invoked by sailors.

From here, the coast stretches south 6 km to the cape itself. It's an excellent walk or drive; the beach has colourful fishing boats drawn up in places and runs alongside some important *salinas*, or salt marshes. A hide a couple of kilometres south of the village allows you to appreciate a range of birdlife, including hundreds of flamingos. Make sure you have a couple of €1 coins to operate the telescope if you don't have binoculars. The flamingos are present most of the year and other seasonal visitors include avocets and storks. In November, the salt pans are drained and the salt mined, but the evicted wildfowl make a return once the water is pumped back. Beyond here, a dilapidated but noble church is visible from miles around. Built in the early 20th century, its tall spire is a pleasing incongruity in this flat expanse. At the end of the beach, the road climbs up to the headland, where there is a lighthouse and, beyond, an 18th-century fort, **Torre de la Vela Blanca**, closed to the public. The spectacular mirador here looks out to a reef where sightings of mermaids have occurred regularly over the centuries.

From just below the fort a track (open to walkers and cyclists only) continues east along the rocky volcanic coast to San José, 8 km away, passing the superb beaches of Monsul and Los Genoveses (see below). Leaving from the beach at La Fabriquilla a mile or so short of the lighthouse, **El Cabo a Fondo** ⓘ *T637-449170, www.elcaboafondo.com*, run hour-long trips eastwards along the coast several times a day in busy periods (ring ahead to reserve a time), costing €20.

★San José

While walkers and cyclists can head directly along the coast from Cabo de Gata to San José, motorists must take a detour inland. Before reaching the town, stop in El Pozo de los Frailes 3 km beforehand. On the main road is a reconstruction of the old communal well; operated by a mule, the water was raised in ceramic jugs that emptied themselves into a basin for collection. It's a beautiful piece of village life preserved.

San José is the largest town on this section of the coast and the principal summer resort. It's substantially developed these days although it hasn't been that way for long; a glance at a photo of the village in the 1950s reveals a few dilapidated and scattered houses and little else. Though thronged with holidaymakers in summer, it doesn't lose its relaxed feel; at other times it's an appealingly quiet base for exploring the Cabo de Gata. The town beach is wide, sandy and sheltered; to the east is a small marina and a string of seafood restaurants, while the headland to the west offers wonderful perspectives over the town and the sea.

Southwest of the village are two of Almería's most enchanting beaches, **Playa de los Genoveses** and **Playa de Mónsul**. The former is about a 20-minute walk along a dirt road (although you can scramble around the rocks at low tide) and is an excellent stretch of sand around a horseshoe-shaped bay backed by meadows and rocky hills. Overlooking the beach is one of the area's best-preserved windmills. The beach is named because it once sheltered a Genoese fleet that attacked Moorish Almería in the 12th century. Some 2.5 km further, Monsul is dominated by a large rock; the coastline here is very wild and erosion has sculpted some startling shapes. From Monsul, walkers and cyclists can continue along the coast to the Cabo de Gata lighthouse and beyond.

San José has a worthwhile **information office** ⓘ *in the centre of town, T950-380299, daily winter 1000-1400, summer 1000-1400, 1800-2200*. They stock walking maps of the region (€10) and map guides (€2).

North of San José

North of San José, the road leads past **Los Escullos**, which has a pretty beach and places to stay, and past a couple of windmills, a characteristic feature of this area. **Isleta del Moro** is a hamlet so named because it once sheltered North African pirate ships. Past here, the road turns inland via **Rodalquilar**, before heading back to the coast.

The village of **Las Negras** with a pebbly beach is undergoing rapid development but still has a tranquil, laid-back character. You can walk from here along the coast to Agua Amarga (see below), via the village of San Pedro, 4 km north, rounding the volcanic mass of Cerro Negro. Abandoned reasonably recently by its original inhabitants, San Pedro is still home to a hippy community, which gets quite busy in summer. The village is worth a visit anyway for its small tower and beautiful dovecote whose interior is studded with pots for nesting birds.

Agua Amarga

Inland from Las Negras, a paved road (not marked on many maps) leads from Fernán Pérez north, where it hits the main road a few kilometres inland. Turning towards the coast, you arrive at Agua Amarga, a small village that was once the terminus of a railway built to ship iron ore from the interior. Little remains these days; the mine was closed in 1942. The sheltered cove has a pleasant beach, on which the tiny local fishing fleet is drawn up. The western end of the strand is given over to recommendable hotels.

Carboneras and around

Despite having a large and ugly cement factory at its western end, Carboneras is a likeable and low-key resort and fishing port with a fine sandy beach and waterfront promenade. It's a refreshing dose of Spain if you're coming from Mojácar; offshore is the small Isla de San Andrés, which necessitated the building of a fort in Carboneras itself so that corsairs couldn't use the islet as a base for attacks on the town.

The castle is closed to the public, but the nearby gardens are very enjoyable, with impressive cacti and date palms. West of town past the factory, is busy **Playa de los Muertos** (Beach of the Dead). On the beach is a bunker from the Civil War, but it's nevertheless a beautiful stretch of sand and sea. Above, a 1.5-km walk leads up to a lighthouse and 18th-century defensive tower, from where there are superb long views of the coast.

Between Carboneras and Mojácar is a spectacular coastal road that passes one of the region's best beaches, **Playa del Algarrobico**, which has been somewhat blighted by the now-halted construction of a massive modern hotel on the cape; **Playa de Macenas**, close to Mojácar itself, is also being overdeveloped.

Listings Cabo de Gata

Where to stay

Cabo de Gata village

€€ Hostal Las Dunas
C Barrionuevo 58, T950-370072, www. hostallasdunas.es.
This *hostal* is a well-maintained place with cool marble fittings and a small bar. It has fine rooms with comfortable beds. Some rooms have a terrace; those without are slightly bigger. The decor is a wee bit kitsch and the bathrooms are small, but the price includes a simple breakfast and all rooms have TV, heating and a/c.

€€ Hostal Navas
Plaza de la Iglesia 3, T680-910176, www. barnavas.com.
On a plaza in the heart of the village, this cordial place is a tapas bar (the seafood is simple and good here) with clean modern rooms that offer plenty of value and have that crucial Almería ingredient: a/c.

€€ Hotel Blanca Brisa
Las Joricas 49, T950-370001, www. blancabrisa.com.

This hotel at the entrance to town has spacious, commodious rooms with a/c, as well as a restaurant. It offers excellent value and a friendly welcome.

Camping

Camping Cabo de Gata
Ctra Cabo de Gata s/n, accessed off the road north after passing the hamlet of Pujaire, T950-160443, www.campingcabode gata.com. Open all year.
The nearest campsite, but is actually nowhere near the village. It's got a pool, shop and restaurant, and also has good cabins sleeping up to 4 people. If you haven't got a car it's a 6-km trudge to Pujaire. Buses going to Cabo de Gata will drop you off at the turn-off, from where it's a 10-min walk.

San José

There's a wide range of accommodation in San José, but rooms are priced high in summer and you'll need to book ahead at that time to be sure of getting a bed.

€€€ Cortijo El Sotillo
Ctra San José s/n, T950-611100, www.cortijoelsotillo.es.
On the edge of town as you enter, this modern *cortijo* offers high-class rustic Andalucían comfort. Rooms are individually decorated and equipped with all conveniences, including a private terrace. There are good communal facilities too; a large lounge, pool table, table tennis and an outdoor pool. The *cortijo* also has a number of very well-kept horses; excursions with these are available at reasonable rates for guests and non-guests.

€€€ MC San José
C El Faro 2, T950-611111, www.hotelesmcsanjose.com.
Currently the best hotel in San José, this offers appealing modern rooms with a balcony or terrace space, professional staff and decent facilities. A number of thoughtful extras raise the experience from good to excellent.

€€ Hostal Puerto Genovés
C Balandro s/n, 5 mins' walk from the beach, off the main road just before reaching the centre of town, T950-380320, www.puertogenoves.com.
At the low end of this price bracket and with breakfast included, this clean modern place is decorated with charm. Many of the rooms have balconies, all have a/c, TV and heating and the beds are attractive and large.

€€ Pensión Aloha
C Cala Higuera s/n, T950-611050, www.pensionaloha.com. Closed Nov-Easter.
This long-established spot is something of a find, for it unexpectedly has a large pool overlooked by palm trees. The rooms are recently renovated and great value. All have bathroom, and many have big balconies; these cost marginally more.

€ Albergue Juvenil
C Montemar s/n, T950-380353, www.alberguesanjose.com.
A friendly hostel opposite the town's cemetery above the eastern end of the beach. With a small bar and shady terrace, it's a relaxed spot; the rooms all have 2 bunk beds and prices include linen. Bathrooms are clean and the atmosphere very good. €12-15 per person per night. Reception open 0900-1300, 1700-2100.

Camping

Camping Tau
San José s/n, T950-380166, www.campingtau.com. Easter-Sep.

A small shady campsite on the eastern edge of town.

North of San José

€€€ Hotel Cala Chica
C Hélice s/n, Las Negras, T950-388181, www.calachica.com.
Chic yet comfortable, this hotel sits just off the elongated roundabout at the top of town and commands views over the village and the sea. Most of the rooms have a private balcony with comfy seats and views; if you take the junior suite you get a jacuzzi out there too. The public areas are decorated with a sure-handed minimalism but always feel homely. Facilities include a pool and restaurant.

€€ Casa Emilio
Los Escullos, T950-389761, www.hostalcasaemilio.es.
Good value even in the height of summer, this is 1 min's stroll from the appealing clean-watered beach in Los Escullos and offers 9 clean, simple and bright whitewashed rooms, many with their own terrace, as well as a café-restaurant downstairs.

Camping

Camping La Caleta
1 km south of Las Negras, T950-525237, www.campinglacaleta.com. Open all year.
There's a pool, restaurant and shop, and a party atmosphere.

Agua Amarga

€€€€ El Tío Kiko
C Embarque s/n, T950-138080, www.eltiokiko.com. Closed mid-Dec to mid-Feb.
Indisputably the best hotel in Agua Amarga, this whitewashed establishment is designed with an elegant minimalism, the rooms are a treat with polished wooden furniture, *esparto* mats on the floors and personal touches such as fresh fruit and something to read. There's a large pool and an excellent breakfast is included in the price. Recommended.

€€ Hotel Family
C La Lomilla s/n, T950-138014, www.hotelfamily.es. Weekends only Nov-Mar.
This peaceful and welcoming home is tucked away in the middle of the development at the western end of the beach. It's a quiet, leafy spot with a pool with plenty of lounging space. The rooms are all appealingly decorated, without luxury. There's a restaurant too, serving excellent French food. Reserve well in advance, as they get plenty of repeat custom. Recommended.

Carboneras and around

€€ Hoteles Felipe
C Sorbas 13, T950-454565, www.hotelesfelipe.com.
Felipe is the Godfather of accommodation in central Carboneras, with 2 adjacent hotels and a *hostal* right in the centre of town. The *hostal* offers good value (**€€**) even in the height of summer, while of the hotels, the newer rooms of the **Tío Felipe** cost little more than those of the **Don Felipe** next door.

Restaurants

Cabo de Gata village

€€ Las Salinas
T950-370103, on the road to the lighthouse, about halfway along.
From the battered old sign and unremarkable outdoor tables, you

wouldn't expect much but reliably fresh, tasty seafood will soon win you over. They've also got bright rooms (**€€**).

San José

€€ Casa Miguel
Av San José 43, T950-380329, www.casamiguelentierradecine.es.
On the main street, this fine choice has a shady terrace and a grotto-like interior. An attentive host and waiters serve you with an excellent selection of Andalucían produce, including excellent ham, juicy grilled sardines, tasty little fried *chipirones*, and steak, fish and game dishes.

€€ El Otro Parque
C La Testa 1, T950-380111.
There are several Italian-run restaurants in San José, but this is a standout. Romantically lit outdoor seating is the best place to enjoy the succulent home-made pastas, generous carpaccios and tasty meats coming out of the open kitchen. Grill-your-own tuna steaks are another highlight. Recommended.

North of San José

€€ Restaurante Toresano
C Bahía de las Negras s/n, Las Negras, T950-388196.
They offer great tapas of seafood – pick your favourite – which they cook for you fresh on the *plancha*, but leave room for a fuller meal in the cool dining room, where more seafood is on offer, as well as a most acceptable *menú del día*.

Agua Amarga

€€€ La Villa
Ctra Carboneras 18, T950-138090. Dinner Wed-Mon.
On a beach holiday in little Agua Amarga, it's nice to be able to choose between tasty beachside fried fish or more refined dining. The setting here is great; as the name suggests, it's a villa, and tables are memorably set around the pool. The fish is reliably good, with dishes like poached hake in cava and clam sauce standing out. Like its hotel stable mate **Mikasa**, value isn't always apparent, but it's nevertheless a romantic place to eat.

What to do

San José

Alpha, *Puerto Deportivo s/n, T950-380321, www.alphabuceo.com.* Runs diving trips and courses from their office in the San José marina.
Cabo de Gata Kayak, *T689-812773, www.cabodegatakayak.es.* Excursions in sea kayak around the beaches and headlands of the national park.
Cortijo El Sotillo *(see Where to stay, above).* Has some fine horses that you can hire for trekking in the region.
Grupo J126, *Av San José 27, T950-380299, www.cabodegata-nijar.com.* A professional set-up that runs good 4WD trips in the region with qualified guides who know plenty about the park's geology and wildlife. They also run various 3-hr walking trips from San José.
Isub, *C Babor 3, T950-380004, www.isubsanjose.com.* Runs diving excursions, hires bicycles, and can also arrange guided bike trips.

Transport

Cabo de Gata village

Almería there are buses to Cabo de Gata village, to **San José**, to **Las Negras** and to **Carboneras**. There are 6 daily buses to Cabo de Gata (45 mins).

San José

4 daily buses (only 2 on Sun) connect **Almería** and **San José**. They are run by **Autocares Bernardo**, T950-250422, 1 hr. If you need a cab, call **Manuel** on T649-129068 or **Pedro** on T600-596596.

North of San José

A bus runs to and from **Almería** and **Isleta del Moro** on Mon and Sat. There's a bus from Almería to Las Negras Mon-Sat. The return leaves for Almería at about 0730.

Carboneras and around

There are 4 buses from **Almería** to Carboneras on weekdays (2 hrs), but only 1 on Sat and Sun.

Mojácar
& around

The popular destination of Mojácar has two distinct parts: a white hilltop village and a long beachside strip. Nearby are several other seaside towns, including the fishing village of Garrucha and several naturist beaches. Inland, Cuevas de Almanzora is a relaxed small town topped by a castle.

Mojácar → *Colour map 6, B2.*

white hilltop village and beach resort

★The two Mojácars are wildly different. The original, known as Mojácar Pueblo, is a whitewashed village that perches on a hill 3 km inland. Heavily colonized by artists in the 1950s and 1960s, some of this influence remains, although about half the inhabitants are more recent arrivals, mostly from Britain. While it's hardly very Spanish, it's nevertheless a very open and pleasant place; the expats here are generally people looking for something a little different than the typical villa on the beach.

Mojácar number two, Mojácar Playa, is the beachfront development, a long sprawl of hotels and bars extending for kilometres along the waterfront. It's not as bad as it could have been; the buildings are mostly low-rise and there's a distinct air of relaxed enjoyment. The beach itself is mediocre compared with those further west around Carboneras and the Cabo de Gata. The road from the village meets the coast at a roundabout, besides which is the Centro Comercial (shopping centre), an essential reference point.

With its defensive hilltop location, it's no surprise that settlement of Mojácar Pueblo goes way back to Iberian times. The Romans occupied the town and it became a major fortified outpost, Murgis. The Moors then renamed it Muxacra and it fell to the Catholic Monarchs in 1488 after stout resistance. The town governor begged the monarchs that the Muslims should be allowed to keep their customs; this wish was granted, at least in the short term. After the Civil War, Mojácar suffered from massive depopulation and poverty; it was only after the artists came, lured by free land grants, that it resumed its prosperous appearance. The town still preserves a Moorish street plan and its whitewashed square houses evoke North Africa.

In Mojácar Pueblo, there's a good **tourist office** ⓘ *T950-475162, turismo@mojacar.es, Mon-Fri 1000-1400, 1730-2030, Sat 1000-1330, 1730-2030, Sun 1000-1330,* just off Plaza Frontón near the church. Mojácar Playa has a tourist information kiosk on the beach opposite the Centro Comercial, at the roundabout where the road from Mojácar Pueblo meets the coast. Both can supply a useful map of the village and beachfront.

Mojácar Playa's beach strip of hotels, restaurants and estate agents has a cheerful feel, despite the busy road. There's not much to do here except sit on the beach, eat, drink, play golf and enjoy the sun. Mojácar Pueblo, on the other hand, has considerable charm. Although more than half the population is made up of expats, it's a much better integrated, friendlier scene than along most of the coast. The village stands proud atop a high hill and has a complex configuration of narrow, steep streets among its whitewashed houses. Although this gives it a somewhat Moorish feel, this is a little deceptive, as many of the buildings are modern and those that aren't were probably only whitened a couple of decades ago. It's a pretty place for strolling anyway, with bougainvillea garlanding many of the houses.

There are few actual sights; the keep-like **church** has 16th-century origins, while the old Moorish castle at the top of the town no longer exists. Climb up at sunset anyway for some magnificent views. On Calle La Fuente is the famous, but over-restored **Fuente Mora**, a pretty Moorish fountain, with an inscription remembering the dignified Alavez, last Moorish ruler of the town.

Listings Mojácar

Where to stay

The beachfront strip has a few dozen hotels and *hostales*, but most are lacking in character and have prices that bear little relation to the services on offer. Mojácar *pueblo* has more for the budget traveller and offers a different atmosphere to the coast 3 km below.

Mojácar Playa

€€€-€€ Hotel El Puntazo
Paseo del Mediterráneo 257, T950-478265, www.hotel elpuntazo.com.
This is actually 2 adjacent hotels of different grades, a short way south of the Centro Comercial. The grander one is a friendly, modern place with a pool and pleasant well-equipped rooms. They are significantly cheaper off season. The 1-star hotel has clean white rooms with bathroom, phone and TV and some with balcony. You can use the pool, too. Recommended.

€€ Hotel Río Abajo
Av Mediterráneo s/n, T950-478928, www.rioabajomojacar.com.
A curious complex of dark rooms set in a sweet tropical garden between Mojácar and Garrucha, this place is actually on the beach itself and offers not luxury but character and low prices. There's a pool in the complex, as well as a diving school. You pay a bit more for lighter rooms with a sea view.

€€ Hotel Sal Marina
Av del Mediterráneo s/n, T950-472404, www.hotelsalmarina.com. Closed Jan-Feb.

This friendly choice is perhaps the best value on the beachfront. While the outside doesn't look great, the rooms are superb, with lots of natural light, large comfy beds, great bathrooms, and a little terrace with sea views. In summer there's a restaurant open. Top off-season prices.

Mojácar Pueblo

€€ El Mirador del Castillo
Plaza Castillo s/n, T950-473022, www.elcastillomojacar.com.
At the top of the town, where the castle once stood, this spot has a wonderful location, with views and sunsets to linger long in the memory. The 5 rooms vary in quality and price, but all have views of some sort, and the rates are good value for this spectacular location; there's also a pool in the courtyard. Even if you don't stay, it's worth coming up here for the vistas.

€€ Hostal Arco Plaza
Plaza Nueva s/n, T950-472777, www.hostalarcoplaza.es.
With a great location looking over the main square, this is a decent year-round option. The a/c rooms are modern and have small but adequate bathrooms. Some have balconies overlooking the plaza.

Camping

El Quinto
Just below Mojácar pueblo, *head 2 km along the Turre road from the bus stop at the bottom of the* pueblo, *T950-478704. Open all year, but quickly fills up at peak periods.*
This campsite is the best in the area, although pretty hot and dusty in summer.

Restaurants

Mojácar Playa is one long strip of places to eat and drink, particularly in its southern reaches; there are several international restaurants, as well as good old British fish'n'chips on offer, although quality Spanish fare is a little harder to track down. The *pueblo* is a bit quieter, particularly out of season when many bars and restaurants close down. Eating hours tend to be early.

€€ La Cabaña
Paseo Mediterráneo s/n, T950-615179.
At the western end of the seaside strip, this barn of a place is an Argentine *parrilla* restaurant, serving various pricey but tasty cuts of beef, backed up by salads, various types of *empanadas*, and a few brochettes for those who like their meat (there is a vegetable one too) bite-sized. Friendly and informal.

€€-€ El Reclamo
Plaza Frontón s/n, T950-472881.
This excellent husband-and-wife set-up offers traditional local fare using high-quality products. The owner will tell you what's good that day; he's justifiably proud of his ham croquettes. Or try the snails or *cuajadera de pescado* (baked fish stew). Recommended.

€€-€ El Viento del Desierto
Plaza Frontón s/n, T950-478626.
Buzzing little restaurant in the centre of the old town, which does some fine no-frills dishes at cheap prices, as well as classier fare, some of it North African-inspired.

Bars and clubs

There's plenty of action along the seaside strip, and a knot of locals' bars around Plaza Frontón in the *pueblo*.

Mandala
Paseo Mediterráneo 391, www.facebook.com/mandalabeachmojacar.
Open 2000-late.
Done up as an Indochinese fantasy, this sizeable bar and *discoteca* is the current trendiest spot on the beach, and is well worth stopping by for a drink, if only to admire the decor. There are several bars, including one on the beach; it also opens as a restaurant at lunchtimes, serving Japanese-influenced fare.

What to do

Water sports

Samoa Surf, *in the Pueblo Indalo section of the strip south of the Centro Comercial, T950-478490, www.facebook.com/samoasurfmojacar.* Organizes sailing and diving courses, as well as boat excursions (including rides on a 'banana') and hire of sea canoes.

Transport

Bus

An hourly bus runs right along the beach-front and also up and down to Mojácar *pueblo*. Stops are clearly signposted.

2-5 buses run daily from **Almería** to Mojácar, stopping at the Centro Comercial on the beach and at the bottom of the *pueblo* (1-2 hrs). In the other direction there are 3 daily services to **Murcia** (2 hrs 30 mins). There are also a couple of buses to **Granada** (4 hrs).

North from Mojácar → *Colour map 6, B2-A3.*

fishing port with excellent seafood restaurants, and an interesting town

La Garrucha

The next town along the coast from Mojácar is La Garrucha, which still has a functioning fishing harbour and much less of a resort feel. The beach isn't particularly good, but it's enjoyable to sit in one of the town's many high-standard seafood restaurants and watch the Mediterranean. The Casa de Cultura can provide tourist information.

Further along the coast, on the road to **Villaricos**, is a stretch of beach and apartment complexes popular with nudists. This area includes a four-star naturist hotel, see Where to stay, below.

Cuevas de Almanzora

Cuevas is the largest and most interesting town in the area east of Mojácar. It takes its name from form a small cave suburb like those of Granada province, but there's not a great deal to see there. A curious historical note: the town used to be called Cuevas de Vera, but locals, who had a strong local rivalry with the nearby Vera, demanded to have it changed because they felt that it implied they were just a barrio of caves belonging to the other town. Their pleas were duly answered.

Below the main square is the **Iglesia de la Encarnación**, built in red brick, with a sundial on its façade. Inside, a high gallery runs right around, while the tabernacle behind the altar is backed with *trompe l'oeil* wall paintings. The most impressive feature is the beautiful marble baptismal font.

Cuevas has many fine houses from the 19th and early 20th centuries. One of the most endearing is a few steps from the church, following Calle El Pilar (signposted to the *correos*). At No 17, it's a frenzy of tile and mosaic work.

Above the plaza is the **castle** ⓘ *Tue-Sat 0930-1330, 1600-1900 or 1700-2000, Sun 1000-1330, Jul-Aug Tue-Sat 0800-1400, free*, built in the 16th century by the Marqués de Vélez. By this time, castles were on their way out as defensive needs were less important. This can be seen from the keep inside the walls, which is a very curious building with embrasures and castellation, but with corner turrets barely higher than a person. There's a charming old metal door that will lead you in to a mediocre museum of modern art. Opposite, the **Museo Arqueológico** ⓘ *same opening hours as the castle, free*, is more interesting, displaying a range of prehistoric finds from the region.

Listings North from Mojácar

Where to stay

€€€€ Hotel Vera Playa Club
Ctra Garrucha–Villaricos s/n, T950-467475, www.veraplayaclubhotel.com. Closed Nov-Mar.
This naturist hotel, very light and pleasant with plenty of running water and some noisy green parrots at the entrance, is built around a pool that's surrounded by a huge number of palm trees and sun loungers. The beach is directly in front and the compound the hotel is housed in includes bars and supermarkets. The only dress regulations are: nudity compulsory in the pool area and clothing compulsory after 2000 in the restaurant. Prices range according to the season (much cheaper in May, Jun and Oct; prices rise sharply in Jul). Breakfast included in rates.

Restaurants

There are many fine seafood restaurants along the seafront in the port of Garrucha.

€€ Rincón del Puerto
Puerto Deportivo s/n, T950-133042.
One of the most likeable choices, this has a terrace right by the marina, a great light nautical-blue dining room, and a more intimate indoor *comedor*; you can also eat tapas at the bar. Everything's delicious, from crispy *cazón* to octopus, prawns and seafood salads. At weekends, try the *cuajadera*, a local speciality that can be made from meat, cuttlefish or fish.

Northern Almería

Right at the end of Andalucía, the top corner of Almería province is one of its most intriguing nooks. The village of Vélez Blanco is memorably situated among rocky pinnacles and crags; perched on one of these above the town is one of Andalucía's most spectacular castles. Nearby is a cave with important prehistoric paintings, while the neighbouring town of Vélez Rubio is stocked with noble 18th- and 19th-century architecture. Beyond them is the Sierra de María natural park, a remote region of wooded hills with satisfying walking and spectacular wildflowers.

Vélez Rubio → *Colour map 3, C5.*

tranquil country town with many fine mansions

Although lacking the memorable setting and castle of its neighbour Vélez Blanco, it's worth stopping at this laid-back town; if the two were further apart, more people would definitely do so. Although Boabdil sought refuge here in times of trouble, almost nothing remains of the Moorish castle: the town's appeal lies in its elegant ensemble of 18th- and 19th-century mansions.

First stop should be the **tourist office** ⓘ *T950-412560, Tue-Sun 0900-1400, plus Tue and Thu 1630-1830, Fri/Sat 1630-1900*, on Carrera del Carmen. Housed in the 18th-century Hospital Real, they'll provide you with a very well-produced map of the town and its principal sights. Within this building is a small ethnographic museum with a collection of household objects and farming implements.

Continuing down this street you'll absorb the farming town atmosphere; at the end, after passing the horrific Edificio del Carmen (the self-destructive architectural tendencies of the province even once reached this far), turn left and you'll arrive at the **Iglesia de la Encarnación** ⓘ *Tue-Sun 1000-2000*, essentially built from 1751 to 1768 after an earthquake razed the previous church. The decorative white Baroque façade contrasts strikingly with the pale red brick towers to either side, topped by octagonal bell chambers. The large coat of arms is topped by a scene of the Annunciation. Inside is a fine wooden *retablo* carved by Francisco Zesta, while the organ and cupola are also of note.

Listings Vélez Rubio

Transport

Bus

Vélez Rubio is well connected by bus to several towns. Buses stop outside the **Hostal Zurich**. 4 daily buses head to **Granada** (2 hrs 30 mins) via **Baza** and **Guadix**; 2 continue to **Sevilla** and **Cádiz**.

In the other direction, 4-6 head to **Murcia** daily. There are 4 buses daily to **Almería** (4 hrs 15 mins) via **Mojácar** (1 hr 10 mins), stopping at all places. 1 bus from **Almería** continues to **Vélez Blanco** and **María**; otherwise it's an hour's walk to the former, or a taxi ride. Other buses head to **Málaga**, **Valencia** and **Barcelona**.

Vélez Blanco → *Colour map 3, B5.*

striking castle-topped town, a Neolithic cave and a wildlife-rich park

★One of the most dramatic of Spain's castles perches over this village, seeking to defy its facing mountain, La Muela, a flat-topped peak that surely merits at least a small circling dragon. The castle, which on approach seems a fearsome castellated stronghold, reveals a more sensitive side when viewed from Vélez, for an elegant loggia reveals it to be one of the earliest flowerings of Spanish Renaissance architecture. A considerably older dwelling nearby holds important cave paintings.

Housed in an old grain store is an **information office** ⓘ *T950-415354, Apr-Sep Thu-Sun 1000-1400, 1800-2000, Oct-Mar Tue-Sun 1000-1400, also Fri-Sat 1600-1800.* As well as a small display on the area's history and some replica mills, they can help with brochures and maps of the area, including walking options in the Sierra de María. The worryingly low level of protection accorded to a *parque natural* compared with a *parque nacional* is summed up in a panel that lists the functions of the zone: these include pasturing, farming, hunting, logging, sport and bar-restaurants.

The village itself is centred on a long, winding main street. Perching over the town is the **castle** ⓘ *T607-415055, Wed-Sun 1000-1400, 1600-1800 (1700-2000 summer), free.* This area was taken late by the Christians in 1488, and was ceded to the man who would become the first marquis, Pedro Facardo y Chacón. He built his castle over the remains of the Moorish fortress and incorporated the new Italian ideas into his design. Built between 1506 and 1515, the military aspect and function were combined with a luxurious Renaissance interior, designed by a team of Italian architects. The marble patio, regrettably, was sold off in the early 20th century and now lives in the Metropolitan Museum of Art in New York. The

Junta de Andalucía regional government bought the deteriorating castle from the ducal family, and have completed a restoration programme.

The castle-palace proper is entered by way of a fortified outbuilding; the bridge you cross to enter the main section was once a proper drawbridge. The best rooms of the castle are on the second floor, but the atmosphere of the halls is misleadingly medieval without the plush 16th-century furniture that once would have made these rooms the latest in comfortable Christian fashion. Climbing the main tower gives a superb view over the town and the plains below it. Even the castellation has a suspiciously unmilitary touch, being adorned with onion-like pompoms.

Below the castle, on the steep road down to the village, are the ruins of a church; this was the first in the village and replaced the mosque, some walls of which remain.

Cueva de los Letreros

T671-999269. Visits Jun-Aug Wed, Sat, Sun 1900, Sep-May Wed, Sat, Sun 1630, €2 from the kiosk opposite and along from the petrol station at the exit of town on the Vélez Rubio road. Groups can arrange visits outside the normal opening hours, €2.

Located just outside Vélez Blanco on the road to Vélez Rubio, the Cueva is more a rock shelf than a cave, but preserves some faded neolithic paintings, dating from around 4000 BC. The shadows of animals and hunters can be made out, including a scary 'sorcerer', a male figure with horns, tail, and sickles in each hand, and also the famous **Indalo**, a stick figure thought by some to be directly related to the very similar character painted until recently on houses in Mojácar to ward off the evil eye. The Indalo has become a symbol of Almería so you'll see it everywhere.

María and the Parque Natural Sierra de María

For Andalucía at least, María is the end of the line, in its eastern extremity, close to the province of Murcia. It's a quiet and welcoming place visited chiefly for the *parque natural* that surrounds it. The park is made up of limestone hills and valleys dotted with caves while the lower levels are covered with Mediterranean shrubs, oaks and Aleppo pines, and contrast with the bare slopes above. The spring wildflowers are superb and it's a noted haven for birds of prey, including the golden eagle. The park has a **visitor centre** ⓘ *off the Puebla de Don Fadrique road 2 km from the centre, T950-527005, Sat and Sun 1000-1400, 1600-1800 (Apr-Sep 1800-2000), for information at other times, see the Ayuntamiento in the town.* Outside town is a **botanical garden** ⓘ *T950-011364, Apr-Oct Tue-Sun 1000-1600*, which offers a chance to identify local plant species before heading off to the park. There are a couple of labelled walking trails.

Where to stay

Vélez Blanco

€€ Hotel Los Arcos
C San Francisco 2, T950-614805, www.hotelcasadelosarcos.com.
An attractively restored *palacio* in the heart of town and on the edge of the hill with spectacular panoramas. Exceptional value.

€ Hostal Sociedad
C Corredera 14, T950-415027.
Run out of the bar of the same name nearby, this is a budget gem, with small and simple rooms that come with bathroom and TV. They're clean as a whistle.

María and the Parque Natural Sierra de María

€ Hostal Torrente
Camino Real 10, T950-417399, www.hostalrestaurantetorrente.com.
Clean rooms, some with a small balcony and all with modern bathroom and heating. There's a restaurant downstairs specializing in charcoal-grilled steak and lamb.

Camping

Camping Sierra de María
7 km from town in the natural park, T950-167045, www.campingsierrademaria.com.
Equipped with bar/restaurant. They can organize horse excursions and also have a good knowledge about walking in the region.

Restaurants

Vélez Blanco

€€€ Molino del Reloj
Between Vélez Blanco and Vélez Rubio, T950-415600, www.molinodelreloj.com.
For classy dining, try this modern but countrified restaurant. It features formal service and stylish cuisine; you might want to try the abundant *cabrito al horno*, roast kid –one of the region's signature dishes.

Transport

Vélez Blanco

1 bus a day runs to Vélez Blanco from **Almería** via **Mojácar** (3 hrs); otherwise the village is a 1-hr walk (or €10 by taxi) from nearby **Vélez Rubio**, which is much better connected (see above).

María and the Parque Natural Sierra de María

The daily bus that serves **Vélez Blanco** continues to María, arriving 10 mins later.

Background Andalucía

History

Spain's proximity to Africa meant that Andalucía was one of Europe's frontlines for migrating hominids from the south. Discoveries near Burgos, in Spain's north attest that prehistoric humans inhabited the peninsula 1.3 million years ago; these are the oldest known hominid remains in Western Europe. Andalucía was a likely entry point.

One of the most important prehistoric European finds was discovered in **Gibraltar**; the finding of a woman's skull in one of the enclave's numerous caves was the first evidence of Neanderthals. The fossilized cranium has been dated to some 60,000 years.

While these fragments from an inconceivably distant past do little more than tantalize, there is substantial archaeological evidence of extensive occupation of Andalucía in the Upper Palaeolithic period. Several caves across the region have painting dating from this period, such as **La Pileta** near Ronda, and **Nerja** on the Málaga coast. Although not as sophisticated as the roughly contemporary works at Altamira in northern Spain, the depictions of horses, deer, fish and other animals are almost 20,000 years old and give a valuable insight into the lives of these early groups.

In 6000 BC, waves of immigration in the Almería area seem to have to ushered southern Spain rapidly into the Neolithic era. The Granada archaeological museum (see page 318), has some stunning finds from the **Cueva de los Murciélagos** in the south of the province, where burial goods include finely worked gold jewellery and some happily preserved woven *esparto* objects. From the same period are a new series of cave paintings at sites such as the **Cueva de los Letreros** near Vélez Blanco; one of the motifs here is the *Indalo*, a stick figure that was still used in the region until relatively recently as protection against evil spirits.

Around the middle of the third millennium, megalithic architecture began to appear in the form of dolmens, stone burial chambers whose most impressive exemplars are the massive structures at **Antequera**. At around the same time, the site of **Los Millares** in Almería province reveals a thriving and expanding society with an economy based on animal husbandry and working of copper; there is clear evidence of some form of contact with other Mediterranean peoples.

The Almería area is in a favoured geographical position for this type of cultural interchange, and it is no coincidence that the peninsula's first Bronze Age culture, known as **Agaric**, emerged in this region. Although almost nothing remains of the hilltop settlements themselves, excavations have retrieved bronze artefacts of a high technical standard and material that suggests extensive sea trading networks around the beginning of 2000 BC.

Around the turn of the first millennium, the face of the region was changing significantly. The people named as **Iberians** in later texts, and probably of local origin, inhabited the area and were joined by some **Celts**, although these peoples predominantly settled in the north of the peninsula. The Iberians had two distinct languages, unrelated to the Indo-European family, and benefited significantly from the arrival of another group, the **Phoenicians**.

These master sailors and merchants from the Levant set up many trading stations on the Andalucían coast. These included modern Huelva, Málaga and Cádiz; the latter, which they named **Gadir**, was possibly founded around 1100 BC, which would make it Western Europe's most venerable city. The Phoenicians set about trading with the Iberians, and began extensive mining operations, extracting gold, silver and copper from Andalucía's richly endowed soils.

Profitable contact with this maritime superpower led to the emergence of the wealthy local **Tartessian** civilization. Famed in classical sources as a mystical region where demigods walked streets paved with gold, precious little is actually known about this culture. Although they developed writing, it is undeciphered. Although it seems that they had an efficiently controlled society, no site worthy of being identified as the capital, Tartessos, has been excavated. Seemingly based in the region around the Guadalquivir valley, including in such settlements as Carmona, Niebla and Huelva, the Tartessians were highly skilled craftsmen; the Carambolo hoard found in Sevilla province consists of astonishingly intricate and beautiful gold jewellery.

Towards the end of the sixth century BC, the Tartessian culture seems to disappear and Iberian settlements appear to have reverted to self-governing towns, usually fortified places on hilltops. Continued contact with the Mediterranean, including with the **Greeks**, who had a brief presence on Spanish shores in the middle of the millennium, meant that these towns produced coins, texts and, particularly, fine sculpture, including such examples as the Dama de Baza, a lifesize seated goddess found in Granada province, and the Porcuna sculptures displayed in the provincial museum in Jaén.

As Phoenician power waned, their heirs and descendants, the **Carthaginians**, increased their operations in the western Mediterranean and settled throughout Andalucía, particularly at Cádiz. While the Phoenicians had enjoyed a mostly prosperous and peaceful relationship with the local peoples, the Carthaginians were more concerned with conquest and, under **Hamilcar Barca** and his relatives **Hasdrubal** and **Hannibal**, they took control of much of southern Spain and increased mining operations. The Iberian tribes, who included the **Turdetanians**, the group that had inherited the Tartessian mantle in the Guadalquivir basin, seem to have had mixed relations with the Barcid rulers. Some towns accepted Carthaginian control, while others resisted it.

Hispania

The Romans were bent on ending Punic power in the Mediterranean and soon realized that the peninsula was rapidly becoming a second Carthage. Roman troops arrived in Spain in 218 BC and Andalucía became one of the major theatres of the Second Punic War. Some of the local tribes, such as the Turdetanians, sided with the Romans against the Carthaginians and the final Roman victory came in

206 BC, at the Battle of Ilipa near Sevilla. The Carthaginians were kicked out of the peninsula.

During the war, the Romans had established the city of Itálica near Sevilla as a rest camp for dissatisfied Italian troops but it was only some time after the end of hostilities that the Romans appear to have developed an interest in the peninsula itself. Realizing the vast resources of the region, they set about conquering the whole of Hispania, a feat that they did not accomplish until late in the first century BC. It was the Romans that first created the idea of Spain as a single geographical entity, a concept it has struggled with ever since.

Rome initially divided the peninsula into two provinces, **Hispania Citerior** in the north and **Hispania Ulterior** in the south. Here, the military faced immediate problems from their one-time allies, the Turdetanians, who were not happy that the invaders hadn't returned home after defeating the Carthaginians. This rebellion was quelled brutally by Cato the Elder around 195 BC and, although there were several uprisings over the succeeding centuries, the Romans had far fewer problems in Andalucía than in the rest of the peninsula.

Part of this was due to the region's wealth. The ever-increasing mining operations mostly used slave labour and gave little back to the locals, but exports of olive oil, wine and *garum* meant the local economy thrived, despite the heavy tributes exacted by the Republic. Roman customs rubbed off on the Iberians and the local languages gradually disappeared as Latin became predominant.

The wealth of Hispania meant that it became an important pawn in the power struggles of the Roman republic and it was in Andalucía, near modern Bailén, that **Julius Caesar** finally defeated Pompey's forces in 45 BC. With peace established, Caesar set about establishing colonies in earnest; many of Andalucía's towns and cities were built or rebuilt by the Romans in this period. Julius knew the region pretty well; he had campaigned here in 68 BC and later had been governor of Hispania Ulterior. The contacts he had made during this period served him well and Caesar rewarded the towns that had helped him against Pompey, such as Sevilla and Cádiz, by conferring full Roman citizenship on the inhabitants. Later, Vespasian granted these rights to the whole of the peninsula.

Augustus redivided Hispania into three provinces; the southernmost, **Baetica**, roughly corresponded to modern Andalucía. Initially administered from Córdoba, the capital was switched to Hispalis (Sevilla), which, along with neighbouring Itálica, prospered under the Imperial regime. The south of Spain became a real Roman heartland, the most Roman of the Roman colonies. Itálica was the birthplace of the Emperor Trajan and sometime home of his protegé Hadrian, while the Seneca family originated in Córdoba. The first century AD was a time of much peace and prosperity and Andalucía's grandest Roman remains date largely from this period.

It was probably during this century that the bustling Andalucían ports heard their first whisperings of Christianity, which arrived early in the peninsula. Around this time, too, a Jewish population began to build up; the beginnings of what was a crucial segment of Andalucían society for 1500 years.

A gradual decline began late in the second century AD, with raids from North Africa nibbling at the edges of a weakening empire. The Iberian provinces took the wrong side in struggles for the emperorship and suffered as a result; by the fourth century, Cádiz was virtually in ruins and the lack of control meant that an almost feudal system developed, with wealthy citizens controlling local production from fortified villas. Christianity had become a dominant force, but religious squabblings exacerbated rather than eased the tension.

In the fifth century, as the Roman order tottered, various barbarian groups streamed across the Pyrenees and created havoc. **Alans** and **Vandals** established themselves in the south of Spain; it has been (almost certainly erroneously) suggested that the latter group lent their name to Andalucía. The Romans enlisted the Visigoths to restore order on their behalf. This they succeeded in doing, but they liked the look of the land and returned for good after they lost control of their French territories. After a period of much destruction and chaos, a fairly tenuous Visigothic control ensued. They used Sevilla as an early capital, but later transferred their seat of power to Toledo.

The Visigoths

While there is little enough archaeological and historical evidence from this period, what has been found shows that the Visigoths had inherited Roman customs and architecture to a large degree, while many finds exhibit highly sophisticated carving and metalworking techniques. The bishop and writer San Isidoro produced some of Europe's most important post-Roman texts from his base in Sevilla. There were likely comparatively few Visigoths; a small warrior class ruling with military strength best fits the evidence, and they seem to have fairly rapidly become absorbed into the local culture.

The politics of the Visigothic period are characterized by kinstrife and wranglings over Christian doctrine. Some of the numerous dynastic struggles were fought across a religious divide: the Visigothic monarchs were initially adherents of Arianism, a branch of Christianity that denied the coëval status of the Son in the Trinity. While the general population was Catholic, this wasn't necessarily a major stumbling block, but various pretenders to the throne used the theological question as a means for gaining support for a usurpment. During these struggles in the mid-sixth century, various of the pretenders called upon Byzantine support and Emperor Justinian I took advantage of the situation to annex the entire Andalucían coastline as a province, which was held for some 70 years. Inland Andalucía had proved difficult to keep in line for the Visigothic monarchs: King Agila was defeated by a rising in Córdoba and the Sevilla-based businessman Athanagild managed to maneouvre his way on to the throne. He and his successor Leovigild finally pacified the unruly Córdobans, but Leovigild faced a revolt in Andalucía from his own son, Hermenegild, who had converted to Catholicism. Father defeated offspring and the kingdom passed to Leovigild's younger son Reccared (AD 586-601), who wisely converted to Catholicism and established a period of relative peace and prosperity for the people of the peninsula.

BACKGROUND

San Isidoro

"No one can gain a full understanding of Spain without a knowledge of Saint Isidore" - Richard Ford

Born in AD 560, Isidoro succeeded his brother Leandro as Bishop of Sevilla. One of the most important intellectual figures of the Middle Ages, his prolific writings cover all subjects and were still popular at the time of the Renaissance. His *Etymologiae* was one of the first secular books in print when it appeared in AD 1472. The first encyclopedia written in the Christian west, it became the primary source for the 154 classical authors that Isidoro quoted. He also wrote on music, law, history and jurisprudence as well as doctrinal matters.

Isidoro is also recognized as an important church reformer and was responsible for the production of the so-called Mozarabic rite which is still practised in Toledo Cathedral today. His writings were an attempt to restore vigour and direction to a church that was in decline following the Visigothic invasions.

Another important element to Isidoro's writings were his prophecies, based both on the Bible and classical references. This element of his writings appealed to later generations living in the shadow of the Muslim conquests and was to be the source of many stories and legends. Following the expulsion of the Moors it seemed to some that an ancient prophecy was about to be fulfilled.

Isidoro died in Sevilla in AD 636 and his writings continued to inspire Spain for the next nine centuries. His body is now in León, moved there by Fernando I of Castilla who repatriated it to the Christian north around AD 1060.

The seventh century saw numerous changes of rulers, many of whom imposed increasingly severe strictures on the substantial Jewish population of the peninsula. Restrictions on owning property, attempted forced conversions and other impositions foreshadowed much later events in Spain. The Visigoths possibly paid a heavy price for this persecution; several historians opine that the Moorish invasion was substantially aided by the support of Jewish communities that (rightly, as it turned out) viewed the conquerors as liberators.

Al-Andalus

In AD 711 an event occurred that was to define Spanish history for the next eight centuries. The teachings of Mohammed had swept across North Africa and the Moors were to take most of Spain before the prophet had been dead for even a century. After a number of exploratory raids, Tarik, governor of Tanger, crossed the straits with a small force of mostly Berber soldiers. It is said that he named the large rock he found after himself; Jebel Tarik (the mountain of Tarik), a name which over time evolved into Gibraltar. Joined by a larger force under the command of the governor of North Africa, Musa ibn-Nusair, the Moors then defeated and slew the Visigothic king Roderic somewhere near Tarifa. The conquests continued under Musa's son Abd al-Aziz until almost the whole peninsula was in Moorish hands: the conquest had taken less than three years, an extraordinary feat. Soon the Muslim armies were well advanced on the *autoroutes* of southern France.

The Moors named their Iberian dominions Al-Andalus and while these lands grew and shrunk over time, the heartland was always in the south. After the conquest, Al-Andalus was administered by governors based in Córdoba, who ultimately answered to the Ummayad caliph in distant Damascus. This shift of the effective capital south from Toledo to Córdoba meant that the peninsula's focus was much more in Andalucía and, consequently, the Mediterranean and North Africa.

In AD 750, an event occurred in distant Damascus that was to shape the destiny of Moorish Spain. The Abbasid dynasty ousted the ruling Umayyad family and proceeded to massacre them. One prince, Abd al-Rahman, managed to escape the carnage and made his way to Spain in AD 756. Arriving in Córdoba, he contrived to gain and hold power in the city. Gradually taking control over more and more of Al-Andalus, he established the emirate of Córdoba, which was to rule the Moorish dominions in Spain for nearly three centuries.

Romantic depictions of Al-Andalus as a multicultural paradise are way off the mark; the situation is best described by Richard Fletcher as one of "grudging toleration, but toleration nonetheless". Christians and Jews were allowed relative freedom of worship and examples of persecution are comparatively few. Moorish texts throughout the history of Al-Andalus reveal a condescending attitude towards non-Muslims (and vice-versa in Christian parts of Spain), but it is probable that in day-to-day life there was large-scale cultural contact, a process described by Spanish historians as *convivencia* (cohabitation). The conversion of Christians and Jews to Islam was a gradual but constant process; this was no doubt given additional impetus by the fact that Muslims didn't pay any tax beyond the alms required as part of their faith. Christian converts to Islam were known as *muwallads*, while those who remained Christian under the rule of the Moors are called *mozárabes* or Mozarabs.

Arabic rapidly became the major language of southern Spain, even among non-Muslims. The number of Arabic words in modern Spanish attests to this. Many of them refer to agriculture and crops; the Moors brought with them vastly improved farming and irrigation methods, as well as a host of fruits and vegetables not grown before on the peninsula's soil. This, combined with wide and profitable trading routes in the Mediterranean, meant that Al-Andalus began to thrive economically, which must have assisted in the pacification of the region. Córdoba's Mezquita, begun in the eighth century, was expanded and made richer in various phases through this period; this can be seen as reflecting both the growing wealth and the increasing number of worshippers.

Christian kingdoms

Geography divides Spain into distinct regions, which have tended to persist through time, and it was one of these – Asturias – that the Moors had trouble with. They were defeated in what was presumably a minor skirmish in AD 717 at Covadonga, in the far northern mountains. While the Moors weren't too rattled by this at the time, Spain views it today as a happening of immense significance, a victory against all odds and even a sort of mystical watershed where God proved himself to be on the Christian side. It was hardly a crippling blow to the Moors, but it probably sowed the seeds of what became the **Asturian** and **Leonese** monarchy. A curious development in many ways, this royal line emerged unconquered from the shadowy northern hills and forests. Whether they were a last bastion of Visigothic resistance, or whether they were just local folk ready to defend their lands, they established an organized little kingdom of sorts with a capital that shifted about but settled on Oviedo in AD 808.

The Asturian kingdom began to grow in strength and the long process of the *Reconquista*, the Christian reconquest of the peninsula, began. The northerners took advantage of cultural interchange with the south, which remained significant during the period despite the militarized zone in between, and were soon strong enough to begin pushing back. The loose Moorish authority in these lands certainly helped; the northern zone was more or less administered by warlords who were only partially controlled by the emirs and caliphs in Córdoba. Galicia and much of the north coast was reclaimed and in AD 914 the Asturian king Ordoño II reconquered León; the capital shortly moved to here and the line of kings took on the name of that town. As the Christians moved south, they re-settled many towns and villages that had lain in ruins since Roman times.

By the 10th century, the economy was booming in Córdoba and its dominions. A growing sophistication in politics and the arts was partly driven by cultured expats from Damascus and Baghdad who brought learning and fashions from the great cities of the Arab world. It was a time of achievement in literature, the sciences and engineering, including the works of classical writers such as Aristotle and Arabic treatises on subjects such as astronomy and engineering. The whole of Europe felt the benefit as knowledge permeated to the Christian north.

Little wonder then, that the emir Abd al-Rahman III (AD 912-961) felt in bullish mood. In AD 929 he gave himself the title of *caliph*, signalling a definitive break with the east as there can only be one caliph (ordained successor to Mohammed) and he was in Baghdad. Although he had no basis to name himself caliph, the declaration served to establish Al-Andalus as a free-standing Islamic kingdom in the west. Córdoba at this time probably had over 100,000 inhabitants, which would have put it at the same level as Constantinople and far above any other European city. Abd al-Rahman celebrated the new status by building an incredibly lavish palace and administration complex, Madinat al-Zahra (Medina Azahara), to the west of the city.

But Asturias/León wasn't the only Christian power to have developed. The Basques had been quietly pushing outwards too and their small mountain

BACKGROUND

The Conqueror

Mohammed ibn-Abi al Ma'afari was born to a poor family near Algeciras around AD 938. Known to latter generations as Al-Manzur or 'the conqueror', he is one of the most remarkable figures of the Middle Ages, representing both the strength of Muslim Spain and its ultimate failure. A lawyer, he succeeded in reforming the administration of the Caliphate and in modernizing its army before getting his chance at power as one of three co-regents named to govern while the child-caliph Hisham II grew to maturity. Al-Manzur managed to manoeuvre the other co-regents out of the way, having one imprisoned and murdered and engaging the forces of the other in battle. Meanwhile, he beguiled Hisham with wine, women, and song so successfully that once the caliph grew up he never made a political decision, letting Al-Manzur rule in his stead. The regent was so sure of his position that he even took the title of king in AD 996.

While regent, he launched a series of lightning raids across the Christian north. His army, made up of mercenary Slavs, Christian renegades and North African Berbers, sacked Zamora and Simancas in AD 981, Barcelona in AD 985 and León in AD 987. The Leonese king Bermudo had broken an agreement to pay tribute and was forced to flee to the Asturian mountains. In AD 997 he embarked on his final campaign to extinguish Christian opposition. He took A Coruña and the holy city of Santiago where he removed the bells of the cathedral to the mosque of Córdoba. On encountering a lone priest protecting the shrine of St James he is said to have ordered his men to leave the holy relics of the city untouched.

While his military exploits were undoubtedly one of the period's great feats of generalship, Al-Manzur was not really a bloodthirsty tyrant. Under his guidance a university was established in Córdoba and he was a great patron of the arts and science. On his many military campaigns both in Spain and North Africa he took a library of books. It was under Al-Manzur that the final expansion of the Mezquita took place.

After an inconclusive battle in 1002 at Calatañazor in Castilla, Al-Manzur died of natural causes. The relief of the Christians was immense, even more so when the caliphate, without the Conqueror at the helm, disintegrated six years later.

kingdom of Navarra grew rapidly. Aragón emerged and gained power and size via a dynastic union with Catalunya. The entity that came to dominate Spain, Castilla, was born at this time too. In the middle of the 10th century, a Burgos noble, Fernán González, declared independence from the kingdom of León and began to rally disparate Christian groups in the region. He was so successful in this endeavour that it wasn't long before his successors labelled themselves kings.

Both the Christian and Muslim powers were painfully aware of their vulnerability and constructed a series of massive fortresses that faced each other across the central plains. The Muslim fortresses were particularly formidable; high eyries with commanding positions, accurately named the 'front teeth' of Al-Andalus. Relations between Christian and Muslim Spain were curious. While there were frequent campaigns, raids and battles, there was also a high level of peaceful contact and diplomacy. Even the fighting was far from being a confrontation of implacably opposed rivals: Christian knights and Moorish mercenaries hired themselves out to either side, none more so than the famous El Cid.

The caliphate faced a very real threat from the Fatimid dynasty in North Africa and campaigning in the Christian north was one way to fund the fortification of the Mediterranean coast. No-one campaigned more successfully than the formidable Al-Manzur (see box, above), who, while regent for the child-caliph Hisham II, conducted no fewer than 57 victorious sallies into the peninsula, succeeding in sacking almost every city in Northern Spain in a 30-year campaign of terror. Al-Manzur was succeeded by his equally adept son Abd al-Malik, but when he died young in 1008, the caliphate disintegrated with two rival Ummayad claimants seeking to fill the power vacuum.

Twenty years of civil war followed and Córdoba was more or less destroyed. Both sides employed a variety of Christian and Muslim mercenaries to prosecute their claims to the caliphal throne; the situation was bloody and chaotic in the extreme. When the latest puppet caliph was deposed in 1031, any pretence of centralized government evaporated and Berber generals, regional administrators and local opportunists seized power in towns across Al-Andalus, forming the small city-states known as the *taifa* kingdoms; *taifa* means faction in Arabic.

This first *taifa* period lasted for most of the rest of the 11th century and in many ways sounded an early death-knell for Muslim Spain. Petty rivalries between the neighbouring *taifas* led to recruitment of Christian military aid in exchange for large sums of cash. This influx led in turn to the strengthening of the northern kingdoms and many *taifas* were then forced to pay tribute, or protection money, to Christian rulers or face obliteration.

The major *taifas* in Andalucía were Sevilla and Granada, which gradually swallowed up several of their smaller neighbours. The Abbadid rulers of Sevilla led a hedonistic life, the kings Al-Mu'tadid and his son Al-Mu'tamid penning poetry between revelries and romantic liaisons. A pogrom against the Jewish population in 1066 indicated that there was little urban contentment behind the luxuriant façade.

The Christian north lost little time in taking advantage of the weak *taifa* states. As well as exacting punitive tribute, the Castilian king Alfonso VI had his eye on conquests and crossed far beyond the former frontline of the Duero valley. His capture of highly symbolic Toledo, the old Visigothic capital and Christian centre, in 1085, finally set alarm bells ringing in the verse-addled brains of the *taifa* kings.

They realized they needed help, and they called for it across the Straits to Morocco. Since the middle of the 11th century, a group of tribesmen known as the **Almoravids** had been establishing control there and their leader, Yusuf, was invited across to Al-Andalus to help combat Alfonso VI. A more unlikely alliance is hard to imagine; the Almoravids were barely-literate desert warriors with a strong and fundamentalist Islamic faith, a complete contrast to the *taifa* rulers in their blossom-scented pleasure domes. The Almoravid armies defeated Alfonso near Badajoz in 1086 but were appalled at the state of Islam in Al-Andalus, so Yusuf decided to stay and establish a stricter observance. He rapidly destroyed the *taifa* system and established governors, answerable to Marrakech, in the major towns, including Sevilla, having whisked the poet-king off to wistful confinement in Fez.

Almoravid rule was marked by a more aggressive approach to the Christian north, which was matched by the other side. Any hope of retaking much territory soon subsided, as rebellions from the local Andalusi and pressure from another dynasty, the Almohads in Morocco, soon took their toll. This was compounded by another factor: tempted no doubt by big lunches, tapas, siestas and free-poured spirits, the hardline Almoravids were lapsing into softer ways. Control again dissolved into local *taifas*; Alfonso VII took advantage, seizing Córdoba in 1146 and Almería in 1147.

They weren't held for long, though. The Almohads, who by now controlled Morocco, began crossing the Straits to intervene in Andalusi military affairs. Although similarly named and equally hard line in their Islamism, the Almohads were significantly different to the Almoravids, with a canny grasp of politics and advanced military tactics. They founded the settlement of Gibraltar in 1159, took back Almería and Córdoba and gained control over the whole of what is now Andalucía by about 1172. Much surviving military architecture in Andalucía was built by the Almohads, including the great walls and towers of Sevilla. Yet they too lapsed into decadence, and bungled planning led to the very costly military defeat at Las Navas de Tolosa at the hands of Alfonso VIII in 1212. This was a major blow. Alfonso's son Fernando III (1217-1252) capitalized on his father's success, taking Córdoba in 1236, Jaén, the 'Iron Gate' of Andalucía, in 1246, and then Sevilla, the Almohad capital, in 1248, after a two-year siege. The loss of the most important city of Al-Andalus, mourned across the whole Muslim world, was effectively the end of Moorish power in Spain, although the emirate of Granada lingered on for another 250 years. Fernando, sainted for his efforts, kicked out all Sevilla's Moorish inhabitants, setting a pattern of intolerance towards the *mudéjares*, as those Muslims who lived under Christian rule came to be called.

What was left of Muslim Spain was the emirate of Granada. The nobleman Mohammed Ibn-Yusuf Ibn-Nasr set himself up here as ruler in 1237 and gave his name to the Nasrid dynasty. Although nominally independent, it was to a large extent merely a vassal of the Castilian kings. Mohammed surrendered Jaén and began paying tribute to Fernando III in exchange for not being attacked in Granada. He even sent a detachment of troops to help besiege Sevilla, a humiliation that eloquently shows how little real power he had. His territory included a long stretch of the Andalucían coastline from the Atlantic eastwards past Almería and a small inland area that included Granada itself, Antequera and Ronda.

Meanwhile, the Christians were consolidating their hold on most of Andalucía, building churches and cathedrals over the mosques they found and trying to find settlers to work the vast new lands at their disposal as many of the Moors had fled to the kingdom of Granada or across the sea to North Africa. Nobles involved in the *Reconquista* claimed vast tracts of territory; estates known as *latifundias* that still exist today and that have been the cause of numerous social problems in Andalucía over the centuries.

The Christians still had some fighting to do. The Marinid rulers of Morocco were a constant menace and managed to take Algeciras in the late 13th century. Tarifa was recaptured in 1292 and became the scene of the famous heroic actions of Guzmán 'El Bueno' who defended it against another siege two years later. There were also regular, if half-hearted, Christian campaigns agaist Nasrid Granada, one of which involved Sir James 'the Black' Douglas, who met his death carrying the embalmed heart of Robert the Bruce into combat at Teba in 1329.

The Nasrid kingdom continued to survive, partly because its boundaries were extremely well fortified with a series of thousands of defensive towers. The Alhambra as we know it was mostly built under Mohammad V in the second half of the 14th century; at the same time, the enlightened Castilian king Pedro I was employing Moorish craftsmen to recreate Sevilla's Alcázar in sumptuous style.

The Golden Age

In the 15th century, there were regular rebellions and much kinstrife over succession in the Nasrid kingdom, which was beginning to seem ripe for the plucking. One of the reasons this hadn't yet happened was that the Christian kingdoms were involved in similar succession disputes. Then, in 1469, an event occurred that was to spell the end for the Moorish kingdom and have a massive impact on the history of the world. The heir to the Aragonese throne, Fernando, married Isabel, heiress of Castilla, in a secret ceremony in Valladolid. The implications were enormous. Aragón was still a power in the Mediterranean (Fernando was also king of Sicily) and Castilla's domain covered much of the peninsula. The unification under the *Reyes Católicos*, as the monarchs became known, marked the beginnings of Spain as we know it today. Things didn't go smoothly at first, however. There were plenty of opponents to the union and forces in support of Juana, Isabel's elder (but claimed by her to be illegitimate) sister waged wars across Castilla.

When the north was once more at peace, the monarchs found that they ruled the entire peninsula except for Portugal, with which a peace had just been negotiated, the small mountain kingdom of Navarra, which Fernando stood a decent chance of inheriting at some stage anyway, and the decidedly un-Catholic Nasrids in their sumptuous southern palaces. The writing was on the wall and Fernando and Isabel began their campaign. Taking Málaga in 1487 and Almería in 1490, they were soon at Granada's gates. The end came with a whimper, as the vacillating King Boabdil, who had briefly allied himself with the monarchs in a struggle against his father, elected not to go down fighting and surrendered the keys of the great city on New Year's Day in 1492 in exchange for a small principality in the Alpujarra region (which in the end he decided not to take and left for Morocco). His mother had little sympathy as he looked back longingly at the city he had left. "You weep like a woman," she allegedly scolded, "for what you could not defend like a man".

The Catholic Monarchs had put an end to Al-Andalus, which had endured in various forms for the best part of 800 years. They celebrated in true Christian style by kicking the Jews out of Spain. Andalucía's Jewish population had been hugely significant for a millennium and a half, heavily involved in commerce, shipping and literature throughout the peninsula. But hatred of them had begun to grow in the 14th century and there had been many pogroms, including an especially vicious one in 1391, which began in Sevilla and spread to most other cities in Christian Spain. Many converted during these years to escape the murderous atmosphere; they became known as *conversos*. The decision to expel those who hadn't converted was far more that of the pious Isabel than the pragmatic Fernando and has to be seen in the light of the paranoid Christianizing climate. The Jews were given four months to leave the kingdom and even the *conversos* soon found themselves under the iron hammer of the Inquisition.

The valleys of the Alpujarra region south of Granada were where many refugees from previously conquered Moorish areas had fled to from the Christians. When Granada itself fell, many Muslims came here to settle on the rich agricultural land. Although under the dominion of the Catholic Monarchs, it was still largely Muslim in character and it is no surprise that, as new anti-Islamic legislation began to bite, it was here that rebellion broke out. From 1499, the inhabitants fought the superior Christian armies for over two years until the revolt was bloodily put down. In no mood for conciliation, Fernando and Isabel gave the Moors the choice of baptism (converts became known as *moriscos*) or expulsion. Emigration wasn't feasible for most; a vast sum of money had to be handed over for the 'privilege' and in most cases parents weren't allowed to take their children with them.

There was another *morisco* revolt in 1568, again centred on the Alpujarra region. After this, there was forcible dispersal and resettlement of their population throughout Spain. Finally, the *moriscos* too were expelled (in 1609) by Felipe III. It is thought that the country lost some 300,000 of its population and parts of Spain have perhaps still not wholly recovered from this self-inflicted purge of the majority of its intellectual, commercial and professional talent. The lack of cultural diversity led to long-term stagnation. The ridiculous doctrine of *limpieza de sangre* (purity of blood) became all-important; the enduring popularity of pig meat surely owes something to these days, when openly eating these foods proved that one wasn't Muslim or Jewish.

But we move back for a moment to 1492. One of the crowd watching Boabdil hand the keys to Granada over to Fernando and Isabel was Cristóbal Colón (Christopher Columbus), who had been petitioning the royal couple for ships and funds to mount an expedition to sail westwards to the Indies. Finally granted his request, he set off from Palos de la Frontera near Huelva and, after a deal of hardship, reached what he thought was his goal. In the wake of Columbus's discovery, the treaty of Tordesillas in 1494 partitioned the Atlantic between Spain and Portugal and led to the era of Spanish colonization of the Americas. In many ways, this was an extension of the *Reconquista* as young men hardened on the Castilian and Extremaduran *meseta* crossed the seas with zeal for conquest, riches and land. Andalucía was both enriched and crippled by this exodus: while the cities flourished on the New World booty and trade, the countryside was denuded of people to work the land. The biggest winner proved to be Sevilla, which was granted a monopoly over New World trade by the Catholic Monarchs in 1503. It grew rapidly and became one of Western Europe's foremost cities. In 1519 another notable endeavour began here. Ferdinand Magellan set sail from Triana, via Sanlúcar de Barrameda, in an attempt to circumnavigate the world. He didn't make it, dying halfway, but one of the expedition's ships did. Skippered by a Basque, Juan Sebastián Elkano, it arrived some three years later.

Isabel died in 1504, but refused to settle her Castilian throne on her husband, Fernando, to his understandable annoyance, as the two had succeeded in uniting virtually the whole of modern Spain under their joint rule. The inheritance passed to their mad daughter, Juana la Loca, and her husband, Felipe of Burgundy (el Hermoso or the Fair), who came to Spain in 1506 to claim their inheritance. Felipe soon died, however, and his wife's obvious inability to govern led to Fernando being recalled as regent of the united Spain until the couple's son, Carlos, came of age. During this period Fernando completed the boundaries of modern Spain by annexing Navarra. On his deathbed he reluctantly agreed to name Carlos heir to Aragón and its territories, thus preserving the unity he and Isabel had forged. Carlos I of Spain (Carlos V) inherited vast tracts of European land; Spain and southern Italy from his maternal grandparents, and Austria, Burgundy and the Low Countries from his paternal ones. He was shortly named Holy Roman Emperor and if all that worldly power weren't enough, his friend, aide and tutor, Adrian of Utrecht, was soon elected Pope.

The first two Habsburg monarchs, Carlos V and then his son Felipe II relied on the income from the colonies to pursue wars (often unwillingly) on several European fronts. It couldn't last; Spain's Golden Age has been likened by historian Felipe Fernández-Armesto to a dog walking on its hind legs. While Sevilla prospered from the American expansion, the provinces declined, hastened by a drain of citizens to the New World. The *comunero* revolt expressed the frustrations of a region that was once the focus of optimistic Christian conquest and agricultural wealth, but had now become peripheral to the designs of a 'foreign' monarchy. Resentment was exacerbated by the fact that the king still found it difficult to extract taxes from the *cortes* of Aragón or Catalunya, so Castilla (of which Andalucía was a part) bankrolled a disproportionate amount of the crippling costs of the running of a worldwide empire. The growing administrative requirements of managing an empire had forced the previously itinerant Castilian monarchs to choose a capital and Felipe II picked the small town of Madrid in 1561, something of a surprise, as Sevilla or Valladolid were more obvious choices. Although central, Madrid was remote, tucked away behind a shield of hills in the interior. This seemed in keeping with the somewhat paranoid nature of Habsburg rule. And beyond all other things, they were paranoid about threats to the Catholic religion; the biggest of which, of course, they perceived to be Protestantism. This paranoia was costly in the extreme.

Decline of the empire

The struggle of the Spanish monarchy to control the spread of Protestantism was a major factor in the decline of the empire. Felipe II fought expensive and ultimately unwinnable wars in Flanders that bankrupted the state; while within the country the absolute ban on the works of heretical philosophers, scientists and theologists left Spain behind in Renaissance Europe. In the 18th century, for example, the so-called Age of Enlightenment in Western Europe, theologists at the noble old university of Salamanca debated what language the angels spoke; that Castilian was proposed as a likely answer is certain. Felipe II's successors didn't have his strength of character; Felipe III was ineffectual and dominated by his advisors, while Felipe IV, so sensitively portrayed by Velázquez, tried hard but was indecisive and unfortunate, despite the best efforts of his favourite, the remarkable Conde-Duque de Olivares. As well as being unwillingly involved in several costly wars overseas, there was also a major rebellion in Catalunya in the mid-17th century. The decline of the monarchy parallelled a physical decline in the monarchs, as the inbred Habsburgs became more and more deformed and weak; the last of them, Carlos II, was a tragic victim of contorted genetics who died childless and plunged the nation into a war of succession. "Castilla has made Spain and Castilla has destroyed it," commented early 20th century essayist José Ortega y Gasset. While the early 17th century saw the zenith of the Seville school of painting, the city was in decline; the expulsion of the *moriscos* had removed a vital labour force and merchants and bankers were packing up and going elsewhere as the crown's economic problems led to increasingly punitive taxation. The century saw several plagues in Andalucían cities and Sevilla lost an incredible half of its inhabitants in 1649.

The death of poor heirless Carlos II was a long time coming and foreign powers were circling to try and secure a favourable succession to the throne of Spain. Carlos eventually named the French duke Felipe de Bourbon as his successor, much to the concern of England and Holland, who declared war on France. War broke out throughout Spain until the conflict's eventual resolution at the Treaty of Utrecht; at which Britain received Gibraltar, and Spain also lost its Italian and Low Country possessions.

The Bourbon dynasty succeeded in bringing back a measure of stability and wealth to Spain in the 18th century. Sevilla's decline and the silting up of the Guadalquivir led to the monarchs establishing Cádiz as the centre for New World trade in its place and Spain's oldest city prospered again. The Catholic church, however, was in a poor state intellectually and came to rely more and more on cults and fiestas to keep up the interest of the populace: many of Andalucía's colourful religious celebrations were formed during this period. The 18th century also saw the energetic reformer Pedro de Olavide, chief adviser to King Carlos III, try to repopulate rural Andalucía by creating planned towns and encouraging foreign settlers to live in them.

The 19th century in Andalucía and Spain was turbulent to say the least. The 18th century had ended with a Spanish-French conflict in the wake of the French revolution. Peace was made after two years, but worse was to follow. First was a heavy defeat for a joint Spanish-French navy by Nelson off Cabo Trafalgar near Cádiz. Next Napoleon tricked Carlos IV. Partitioning Portugal between France and Spain seemed like a good idea to Spain, which had always coveted its western neighbour. It wasn't until the French armies seemed more interested in Madrid than Lisbon that Carlos IV got the message. Forced to abdicate in favour of his rebellious son Fernando, he was then summoned to a conference with Bonaparte at Bayonne, with his son, wife and Manuel Godoy, his able and trusted adviser (who is often said to have been loved even more by the queen than the king). Napoleon had his own brother Joseph (known among Spaniards as *Pepe Botellas* for his heavy drinking) installed on the throne.

On 2 May 1808 (still a red-letter day in Spain), the people revolted against this arrogant gesture and Napoleon sent in the troops later that year. Soon after, a hastily assembled Spanish army inflicted a stunning defeat on the French at Bailén, near Jaén; the Spaniards were then joined by British and Portuguese forces and the ensuing few years are known in Spain as the Guerra de Independencia (War of Independence). The allied forces under Wellington won important battles after the initiative had been taken by the French. The behaviour of both sides was brutal both on and off the battlefield. Marshal Soult's long retreat across the region saw him loot town after town; his men robbed tombs and burned priceless archives. The allied forces were little better; the men Wellington had referred to as the 'scum of the earth' sacked the towns they conquered with similar destructiveness.

Significant numbers of Spaniards had been in favour of the French invasion and were opposed to the liberal republican movements that sprang up in its wake. In 1812, a revolutionary council in Cádiz, on the point of falling to the French, drafted a constitution proclaiming a democratic parliamentary monarchy of sorts. Liberals had high hopes that this would be brought into effect at the end of the war, but the returning king, Fernando, revoked it. Meanwhile, Spain was on the point of losing its South American colonies, which were being mobilized under *libertadores* such as Simón Bolívar. Spain sent troops to restore control; a thankless assignment for the soldiers involved. One of the armies was preparing to leave Cádiz in 1820 when the commander, Rafael de Riego, invoked the 1812 constitution and refused to fight under the 'unconstitutional' monarchy. Much of the army joined him and the king was forced to recognize the legality of the constitution. Things soon dissolved though, with the 'liberals' (the first use of the word) being split into factions and opposed by the church and aristocracy. Eventually, king Fernando called on the king of France to send an invading army; the liberals were driven backwards to Sevilla, then to Cádiz, where they were defeated and Riego taken to his execution in Madrid. In many ways this conflict mirrored the later Spanish Civil War. Riego, who remained (and remains) a hero of the democratically minded, did not die in vain; his stand impelled much of Europe on the road to constitutional democracy, although it took Spain itself over a century and a half to find democratic stability.

The remainder of the century was to see clash after clash of liberals against conservatives, progressive cities against reactionary countryside, restrictive centre against outward-looking periphery. Spain finally lost its empire, as the strife-torn homeland could do little against the independence movements of Latin America.

When Fernando died, another war of succession broke out, this time between supporters of his brother Don Carlos and his infant daughter Isabella. The so-called Carlist Wars of 1833-1839, 1847-1849 (although this is sometimes not counted as one) and 1872-1876 were politically complex. Don Carlos represented conservatism and his support was drawn from a number of sources. Wealthy landowners, the church and the reactionary peasantry, with significant French support, lined up against the loyalist army, the liberals and the urban middle and working classes. In between and during the wars, a series of *pronunciamientos* (coups d'état) plagued the monarchy. In 1834, after Fernando's death, another, far less liberal constitution was drawn up. An important development for Andalucía took place in 1835 when the Prime Minister, desperate for funds to prosecute the war against the Carlists, confiscated church and monastery property in the Disentailment Act. The resulting sale of the vast estates aided nobody but the large landowners, who bought them up at bargain prices, further skewing the distribution of arable land in Andalucía towards the wealthy.

Despite the grinding poverty, the middle years of the 19th century saw the beginnings of what was eventually to save Andalucía: tourism. Travellers, such as Washington Irving, Richard Ford and Prosper Merimée, came to the region and enthralled the world with tales of sighing Moorish princesses, feisty *sevillanas*, bullfights, gypsies, bandits and passion. While to the 21st-century eye, the uncritical romanticism of these accounts is evident, they captured much of the magic that contemporary visitors still find in the region and have inspired generations of travellers to investigate Spain's south.

During the third Carlist war, the king abdicated and the short-lived First Spanish Republic was proclaimed, ended by a military-led restoration a year later. The Carlists were defeated but remained strong and played a prominent part in the Spanish Civil War. (Indeed, there's still a Carlist party.) As if generations of war weren't enough, the wine industry of Andalucía received a crippling blow with the arrival of the phylloxera pest, which devastated the region.

The 1876 constitution proclaimed by the restored monarchy after the third Carlist war provided for a peaceful alternation of power between liberal and conservative parties. In the wake of decades of strikes and *pronunciamientos* this was not a bad solution and the introduction of the vote for the whole male population in 1892 offered much hope. The ongoing curse, however, was *caciquismo*, a system whereby elections and governments were hopelessly rigged by influential local groups of 'mates'.

Spain lost its last overseas possessions; Cuba, Puerto Rico and the Phillippines, in the 'Disaster' of 1898. The introspective turmoil caused by this event gave the name to the '1898 generation', a forward-thinking movement of artists, philosophers and poets among whom were numbered the poets Antonio Machado and Juan Ramón Jiménez, the philosophers José Ortega y Gasset and Miguel de Unamuno and the painter Ignacio de Zuloaga. It was a time of discontent, with regular strikes culminating in the Semana Trágica (tragic week) in Barcelona in 1909, a week of church-burning and rioting sparked by the government's decision to send a regiment of Catalan conscripts to fight in the 'dirty war' in Morocco; the revolt was then brutally suppressed by the army. The growing disaffectation of farmworkers in Andalucía, forced for centuries into seasonal labour on the vast *latifundias* with no security and minimal earnings, led to a strong anarchist movement in the region. The CNT, the most prominent of the 20th-century anarchist confederations, was founded in Sevilla in 1910.

The Second Republic

The early years of the 20th century saw repeated changes of government under King Alfonso XIII. A massive defeat in Morocco in 1921 increased the discontent with the monarch, but General Miguel Primo de Rivera, a native of Jerez de la Frontera, led a coup and installed himself as dictator under Alfonso in 1923. One of his projects was the grandiose Ibero-American exhibition in Sevilla. The preparation for this lavish event effectively created the modern city we know today and, despite bankrupting the city, set the framework for a 20th-century urban centre.

Primo de Rivera's rule was relatively benign, but growing discontent eventually forced the king to dismiss him. Having broken his coronation oath to uphold the constitution, Alfonso himself was soon toppled as republicanism swept the country. The anti-royalists achieved excellent results in elections in 1931 and the king drove to Cartagena and took a boat out of the country to exile. The Second Republic was joyfully proclaimed by the left.

Things moved quickly in the short period of the republic. The new leftist government moved fast to drastically reduce the church's power. The haste was ill-advised and triumphalist and served to severely antagonize the conservatives and the military. The granting of home rule to Catalunya was even more of a blow to the establishment and their belief in Spain as an indissoluble *patria*, or fatherland.

Through this period, there was increasing anarchist activity in Andalucía, where land was seized as a reaction to the archaic *latifundia* system under which prospects for the workers, who were virtually serfs, were nil. Anarchist cooperatives were formed to share labour and produce in many of the region's rural areas. Squabbling among leftist factions contributed to the government's lack of control of the country, which propelled the right to substantial gains in elections in 1933. Government was eventually formed by a centrist coalition, with the right powerful enough to heavily influence lawmaking. The 1933 elections also saw José Antonio Primo de Rivera, son of the old dictator, elected to a seat on a fascist platform. Although an idealist and no man of violence, he founded the Falange, a group of fascist youth that became an increasingly powerful force and one which was responsible for some of the most brutal deeds before, during and immediately after the Spanish Civil War.

The new government set about reversing the reforms of its predecessors; provocative and illegal infractions of labour laws by employers didn't help the workers' moods. Independence rumblings in Catalunya and the Basque country began to gather momentum, but it was in Asturias that the major confrontation took place. The left, mainly consisting of armed miners, seized the civil buildings of the province and the government response was harsh, with generals Goded and Franco embarking on a brutal spree of retribution with their well-trained Moroccan troops.

The left was outraged and the right feared complete revolution; the centre ceased to exist, as citizens and politicians were forced to one side or the other. The elections of February 1936 were very close, but the left unexpectedly defeated the right. In an increasingly violent climate, mobilized Socialist youth and the Falange were clashing daily, while land seizures continued. A group of generals began to plan a coup and in July 1936 a military conspiracy saw garrisons throughout Spain rise against the government and try to seize control of their provinces and towns. Within a few days, battle lines were clearly drawn between the Republicans (government) and the Nationalists, a coalition of military, Carlists, fascists and the Christian right. Most of northern Spain rapidly went under Nationalist control, while Madrid remained Republican. In Andalucía, Córdoba, Cádiz, Sevilla, Huelva and Granada were taken by Nationalists, but the remainder was in loyalist hands.

In the immediate aftermath of the uprising, frightening numbers of civilians were shot behind the lines, including the Granadan poet, Federico García Lorca. This brutality continued throughout the war, with chilling atrocities committed on both sides.

The most crucial blow of the war was struck early. Francisco Franco, one of the army's best generals, had been posted to the Canary Islands by the government, who were rightly fearful of coup attempts. As the uprising occurred, Franco was flown to Morocco where he took command of the crack North African legions. The difficulty was crossing into Spain: this was achieved in August in an airlift across the Straits of Gibraltar by German planes. Franco swiftly advanced through Andalucía where his battle-hardened troops met with little resistance. Meanwhile, the other main battle lines were north of Madrid and in Aragón, where the Republicans made a determined early push for Zaragoza.

At a meeting of the revolutionary generals in October 1936, Franco had himself declared *generalísimo*, the supreme commander of the Nationalists. Few could have suspected that he would rule the nation for nearly four decades. Although he had conquered swathes of Andalucía and Extremadura with little difficulty, the war wasn't to be as short as it might have appeared. Advancing on Madrid, he detoured to relieve the besieged garrison at Toledo; by the time he turned his attention back to the capital, the defences had been shored up and Madrid resisted throughout the war.

A key aspect of the Spanish Civil War was international involvement. Fascist Germany and Italy had troops to test, and a range of weaponry to play with; these countries gave massive aid to the Nationalist cause as a rehearsal for the Second World War, which was appearing increasingly inevitable. Russia provided the Republicans with some material, but inscrutable Stalin never committed his full support. Other countries, such as Britain, USA and France, disgracefully maintained a charade of international non-intervention despite the flagrant breaches by the above nations. Notwithstanding, thousands of volunteers mobilized to form the international brigades to help out the Republicans. Enlisting for idealistic reasons to combat the rise of fascism, many of these soldiers were writers and poets such as George Orwell and WH Auden.

Although Republican territory was split geographically, far more damage was done to their cause by ongoing and bitter infighting between anarchists, socialists, Soviet-backed communists and independent communists. There was constant struggling for power, political manoeuvring, backstabbing and outright violence, which the well-organized Nationalists must have watched with glee. The climax came in Barcelona in May 1937, when the Communist party took up arms against the anarchists and the POUM, an independent communist group. The city declined into a mini civil war of its own until order was restored. Morale, however, had taken a fatal blow.

Cities continued to fall to the Nationalists, for whom the German Condor legion proved a decisive force. In the south, the armies were under the command of Gonzalo Queipo de Llano, who though of broadly republican sympathies, was one of the original conspirators, and had expertly taken Sevilla at the beginning of things. Although his propaganda broadcasts throughout the war revealed him to be a kind of psychopathic humourist, this charismatic aristocrat was an impressive general and took Málaga in early 1937. Fleeing refugees were massacred by tanks and aircraft. Republican hopes now rested solely in the outbreak of a Europe-wide war. Franco had set up base appropriately in deeply conservative Burgos; Nationalist territory was the venue for many brutal reprisals against civilians perceived as leftist, unionist, democratic, or owning a tasty little piece of land on the edge of the village. Republican atrocities in many areas were equally appalling although rarely sanctioned or perpetrated by the government.

The Republicans made a couple of last-ditch efforts in early 1938 at Teruel and in the Ebro valley but were beaten in some of the most gruelling fighting of the Civil War. The Nationalists reached the Mediterranean, dividing Catalunya from the rest of Republican territory and, after the ill-fated Republican offensive over the Ebro, putting Barcelona under intense pressure; it finally fell in January 1939. Even at this late stage, given united resistance, the Republicans could have held out a while longer and the World War might have prevented a Franco victory, but it wasn't to be. The fighting spirit had largely dissipated and the infighting led to meek capitulation. Franco entered Madrid and the war was declared over on 1 April 1939.

If Republicans were hoping that this would signal the end of the slaughter and bloodshed, they didn't know the *generalísimo* well enough. A vengeful spate of executions, lynchings, imprisonments and torture ensued and the dull weight of the new regime stifled growth and optimism. Although many thousands of Spaniards fought in the Second World War (on both sides), Spain remained nominally neutral. After meeting Franco at Hendaye, Hitler declared that he would prefer to have three or four teeth removed than have to do so again. Franco had his eye on French Morocco and was hoping to be granted it for minimal Spanish involvement; Hitler accurately realized that the country had little more to give in the way of war effort and didn't offer an alliance.

The post-war years were tough in Spain, particularly in poverty-stricken Andalucía, where the old system was back in place and the workers penniless. Franco was an international outcast and the 1940s and 1950s were bleak times. Thousands of Andalucíans left in search of employment and a better life in Europe, the USA and Latin America. The Cold War was to prove Spain's saviour. Franco was nothing if not anti-communist and the USA began to see his potential as an ally.

Eisenhower offered to provide a massive aid package in exchange for Spanish support against the Eastern Bloc. In practice, this meant the creation of American airbases on Spanish soil; one of the biggest is at Rota, just outside Cádiz.

The dollars were dirty, but the country made the most of them; Spain boomed in the 1960s as industry finally took off and the flood of tourism to the Andalucían coasts began in earnest. But dictatorship was no longer fashionable in western Europe and Spain was regarded as a slightly embarassing cousin. It was not invited to join the European Economic Community (EEC) and it seemed as if nothing was going to really change until Franco died. He finally did, in 1975, and his appointed successor, King Juan Carlos I, the grandson of Alfonso XIII, took the throne of a country burning with democratic desires.

La Transición

The king was initially predicted to be just a pet of Franco's and therefore committed to maintaining the stultifying status quo, but he surprised everyone by acting swiftly to appoint the young Adolfo Suárez as prime minister. Suárez bullied the parliament into approving a new parliamentary system; political parties were legalized in 1977 and elections held in June that year. The return to democracy was known as *la transición*; the accompanying cultural explosion became known as *la movida (madrileña)*. Suárez's centrist party triumphed and he continued his reforms. The 1978 constitution declared Spain a parliamentary monarchy with no official religion; Franco must have turned in his grave and Suárez faced increasing opposition from the conservative elements in his own party. He resigned in 1981 and as his successor was preparing to take power, the good old Spanish tradition of the *pronunciamiento* came to the fore once again. A detachment of *Guardia Civil* stormed parliament in their comedy hats and Lieutenant Colonel Tejero, pistol waving and moustache twitching, demanded everyone hit the floor. After a tense few hours in which it seemed that the army might come out in support of Tejero, the king remained calm and, dressed in his capacity as head of the armed forces, assured the people of his commitment to democracy. The coup attempt thus failed and Juan Carlos was seen in an even better light.

In 1982, the Socialist government (PSOE) of Felipe González was elected. Hailing from Sevilla, he was committed to improving conditions and infrastructure in his native Andalucía. The single most important legislation since the return to democracy was the creation of the *comunidades autónomas*, in which the regions of Spain were given their own parliaments, which operate with varying degrees of freedom from the central government. This came to bear in 1983, although it was a process initiated by Suárez. Sevilla became the capital of the Andalucían region.

The Socialists held power for 14 years and oversaw Spain's entry into the EEC (now EU) in 1986, from which it has benefited immeasurably, although rural Andalucía remains poor by western European standards. But mutterings of several scandals began to plague the PSOE government and González was really disgraced when he was implicated in having commissioned death squads with the aim of terrorizing the Basques into renouncing terrorism, which few of them supported in any case.

Modern Andalucía

In 1996, the rightist PP (Partido Popular) formed a government under the young former tax inspector José María Aznar López, and was re-elected in 2000. Economically conservative, Aznar strengthened Spain's ties with Europe and set a platform for strong financial performance. He then used the prevailing international climate to take strong action against ETA. This seemed to have paid off, but his heavy-handed and undemocratic methods appalled international observers and stirred the ghosts of Francoism in Spain. Aznar then took the country to war in Iraq against the wishes of a massive majority of the population. On 11 March 2004, three days before the general election, a series of 10 bombs exploded in four commuter trains approaching Madrid's Atocha station; nearly 200 people were killed. The government was quick to blame ETA for the attack despite that group's denial and substantial evidence for involvement by Islamic extremists. The electorate was outraged at what was perceived as a vote-minded cover-up and punished Aznar's hand-picked successor, Mariano Rajoy, at the election. Far adrift in the polling only a few days before, the PSOE were elected to government and the new prime minister, 43 year-old José Luis Rodríguez Zapatero, immediately pledged to withdraw Spanish troops from Iraq and re-align the country with 'old Europe'.

Zapatero's government pursued a decidedly liberal course. Spain's religious right were outraged by the legalization of same-sex marriage, and when Zapatero agreed to pass a statute granting the Catalan government more autonomy (approved in a local referendum in Catalunya) the PP, who maintain the ideal that Spain is indissoluble, were furious. Zapatero also pursued peaceful solutions to the Gibraltar question and was responsible for a major crackdown on ETA, which eventually led to a peace which persisted at time of writing. Re-elected in 2008, Zapatero then came under increasing criticism for his uncertain handling of 'la crisis', the economic downturn that severely affected Andalucía and Spain with the key industries of construction and tourism suffering significant reverses, and unemployment skyrocketing to over 20%. A hastily concocted reform package designed to placate the EU and the money masters led to widespread indignation in 2010 as people perceived they were being forced to tighten their belts while the banks and corporations continued on their merry way. Massive protests through 2011 demanded wholesale changes to the system. The PSOE were defeated in the November elections and the PP's Mariano Rajoy took the reins with troubled economic waters to negotiate.

Despite initial optimism, faith in Rajoy's rule quickly declined as further austerity measures were imposed and his government seemed to be powerless to resist the diktats of Germany and the EU. A major corruption scandal left scars, and sabre-rattling over Gibraltar was employed to deflect some attention. Catalunya's wish for a referendum on independence – unthinkable for the Spanish right – emphasized divisions in the country. At time of writing, the crisis was still biting deep in Andalucía, and, despite some upturn in the economic outlook, it looked like being a long road back for much of southern Spain.

Culture

Architecture

Spain's architectural heritage is one of Europe's richest and certainly its most diverse, due in large part to the dual influences of European Christian and Islamic styles during the eight centuries of Moorish presence in the peninsula. Another factor is economic: both during the *Reconquista* and in the wake of the discovery of the Americas, money seemed limitless and vast building projects were undertaken. Entire treasure fleets were spent in erecting lavish churches and monasteries on previously Muslim soil, while the relationships with Islamic civilization spawned some fascinating styles unique to Spain. The Moors adorned their towns with sensuous palaces, such as Granada's Alhambra, and elegant mosques, as well as employing compact climate-driven urban planning that still forms the hearts of most towns. In modern times Spain has shaken off the ponderous monumentalism of the Franco era and become something of a powerhouse of modern architecture.

Andalucía's finest early stone structures are in Antequera, whose dolmens are extraordinarily monumental burial spaces built from vast slabs of stone. The dwellings of the period were less permanent structures of which little evidence remains, except at the remarkable site of **Los Millares** near Almería, a large Chalcolithic settlement, necropolis, and sophisticated associated fortifications that has provided valuable information about society in the third millennium BC. The first millennium BC saw the construction of further fortified settlements, usually on hilltops. Little remains of this period in Andalucía, as the towns were then occupied by the Romans and Moors.

Similarly, while the Phoenicians established many towns in southern Spain, their remains are few; they were so adept at spotting natural harbours that nearly all have been in continual use ever since, leaving only the odd foundations or breakwater. There are also few Carthaginian remains of note. Their principal base in Andalucía was Cádiz, but two millennia of subsequent occupation have taken their toll on the archaeological record.

The story of Spanish architecture really begins with the Romans, who colonized the peninsula and imposed their culture on it to a significant degree. More significant still is the legacy they left; architectural principles that endured and to some extent formed the basis for later peninsular styles.

There's not a wealth of outstanding monuments; **Itálica**, just outside Sevilla, and **Baelo Claudia**, on the Costa de la Luz, are impressive, if not especially well-preserved Roman towns. **Acinipo**, near Ronda, has a large and spectacularly sited theatre, **Carmona** has a beautifully excavated necropolis and **Almuñécar** has the ruins of its fish sauce factory on display. In many towns and villages you can see Roman fortifications and foundations under existing structures.

There are few architectural reminders of the Visigothic period, although it was far from a time of lawless barbarism. Germanic elements were added to Roman and local traditions and there was widespread building; the kings of the period commissioned many churches, but in Andalucía these were all demolished to make way for mosques.

The first distinct period of Moorish architecture in Spain is that of the Umayyads who ruled as emirs, then as caliphs, from Córdoba from the eighth to 11th centuries. Although the Moors immediately set about building mosques, the earliest building still standing is Córdoba's **Mezquita**. Dating from the late ninth century, the ruined church at the mountain stronghold of Bobastro exhibits clear stylistic similarities with parts of the Mezquita and indicates that already a specifically *Andalusi* architecture was extant.

The period of the caliphate was the high point of Al-Andalus and some suitably sumptuous architecture remains. Having declared himself caliph, Abd al-Rahman III had the palace complex of **Madinat az-Zahra** built just outside of Córdoba. Now in ruins, excavation and reconstruction have revealed some of the one-time splendour, particularly of the throne room, which has arcades somewhat similar to those of the Mezquita and ornate relief designs depicting the Tree of Life and other vegetal motifs. The residential areas are centred around courtyards, a feature of Roman and Moorish domestic architecture that persists in Andalucía to this day.

The Mezquita had been added to by succeeding rulers, who enlarged it but didn't stray far from the original design. What is noticeable is a growing ornamentality, with use of multi-lobed arches, sometimes interlocking, and blind arcading on gateways. The *mihrab* was resituated and topped with a recessed dome, decorated with lavish mosaic work, possibly realized by Byzantine craftsmen. A less ornate mosque from this period can be seen in a beautiful hilltop setting at **Almonaster la Real** in the north of Huelva province.

Many defensive installations were also put up at this time: the castles of Tarifa and Baños de la Encina mostly date from this period. Bathhouses such as those of Jaén were also in use, although were modified in succeeding centuries. The typical Moorish *hammam* had a domed central space and vaulted chambers with star-shaped holes in the ceiling to admit natural light.

The *taifa* period, although politically chaotic, continued the rich architectural tradition of the caliphate. Málaga's **Alcazaba** preserved an 11th-century pavilion with delicate triple arches on slender columns. Elaborate stucco decoration, usually with repeating geometric or vegetal motifs, began to be used commonly during this time.

The Almoravids contributed little to Andalucían architecture, but the Almohads brought their own architectural modifications with them. Based in Sevilla, their styles were not as flamboyant and relied heavily on ornamental brickwork. The supreme example of the period is the **Giralda tower** that once belonged to the Mosque in Sevilla and now forms part of the cathedral. The use of intricate wood-panelled ceilings began to be popular and the characteristic Andalucían azulejo decorative tiles were first used at this time. Over this period the horseshoe arch developed a point. The Almohads were great military architects and built or improved a large number of walls, fortresses and towers; these often have characteristic pointed battlements. The **Torre del Oro** in Sevilla is one of the most famous and attractive examples.

The climax of Moorish architecture ironically came when Al-Andalus was already doomed and had been reduced to the emirate of Granada. Under the Nasrid rulers of that city the sublime **Alhambra** was constructed; a palace and pleasure garden that took elegance and sophistication in architecture to previously unseen levels. Nearly all the attention was focused on the interior of the buildings, which consisted of galleries and courtyards offset by water features and elegant gardens. The architectural high point of this and other buildings is the sheer intricacy of the stucco decoration in panels surrounding the windows and doorways. Another ennobling feature is *mocárabes*, a curious concave decoration of prisms placed in a cupola or ceiling and resembling natural crystal formations in caves. The Alcázar in Sevilla is also a good example of the period, though actually constructed in Christian Spain; it is very Nasrid in character and Granadan craftsmen certainly worked on it.

As the Christians gradually took back Andalucía, they introduced their own styles, developed in the north with substantial influence from France and Italy. The Romanesque barely features in Andalucía; it was the Gothic style that influenced post-Reconquista church building in the 13th, 14th and 15th centuries. It was combined with styles learned under the Moors to form an Andalucían fusion known as Gothic-*mudéjar*. Many of the region's churches are constructed on these lines, typically featuring a rectangular floor plan with a triple nave surrounded by pillars, a polygonal chancel and square chapels. Gothic exterior buttresses were used and many had a bell tower decorated with ornate brickwork reminiscent of the Giralda, which was also rebuilt during this period.

The Andalucían Gothic style differs from the rest of the peninsula in its basic principles. Whereas in the north, the 'more space, less stone, more light' philosophy pervaded, practical considerations demanded different solutions in the south. One of these was space; the cathedrals normally occupied the site of the former mosque, which had square ground plans and were hemmed in by other buildings. Another was defence – on the coast in particular, churches and cathedrals had to be ready to double as fortresses in case of attack, so sturdy walls were of more importance than stained glass. The redoubt of a cathedral at Almería is a typical example. Many of Andalucía's churches, built in the Gothic style, were heavily modified in succeeding centuries and present a blend of different architectures.

Mudéjar architecture spread quickly across Spain. Moorish architects and those who worked with them began to meld their Islamic tradition with the northern influences. The result is distinctive and pleasing, typified by the decorative use of brick and coloured tiles, with tall elegant bell towers a particular highlight. Another common feature is the highly elaborate wooden panelled ceilings, some of which are masterpieces. The word *artesonado* describes the most characteristic type of these. The style became popular nationwide; in certain areas, *mudéjar* remained a constant feature for over 500 years of building.

The final phase of Spanish Gothic was the Isabelline, or Flamboyant. Produced during and immediately after the reign of the Catholic Monarchs (hence the name), it borrowed decorative motifs from Islamic architecture to create an exuberant form characterized by highly elaborate façades carved with tendrils, sweeping curves and geometrical patterns. The Capilla Real in Granada is an example and the Palacio de Jabalquinto in Baeza is a superb demonstration of the style.

The 16th century was a high point in Spanish power and wealth, when it expanded across the Atlantic, tapping riches that must have seemed limitless. Spanish Renaissance architecture reflected this, leading from the late Gothic style into the elaborate peninsular style known as Plateresque. Although the style originally relied heavily on Italian models, it soon took on specifically Spanish features. The word refers particularly to the façades of civil and religious buildings, characterized by decoration of shields and other heraldic motifs, as well as geometric and naturalistic patterns such as shells. The term comes from the word for silversmith, *platero*, as the level of intricacy of the stonework approached that of jewellery. Arches went back to the rounded and columns and piers became a riot of foliage and 'grotesque' scenes.

A classical revival put an end to much of the elaboration, as Renaissance architects concentrated on purity. To classical Greek features such as fluted columns and pediments were added large Italianate cupolas and domes. Spanish architects were apprenticed to Italian masters and returned to Spain with their ideas. Elegant interior patios in *palacios* are an especially attractive feature of the style, to be found across the country. Andalucía is a particularly rich storehouse of this style, where the master Diego de Siloé designed numerous cathedrals and churches. The palace of Carlos V in the Alhambra grounds is often cited as one of the finest examples of Renaissance purity. One of Diego de Siloé's understudies, Andrés de Vandelvira, evolved into the über-architect of the Spanish Renaissance. The ensemble of palaces and churches he designed in Jaén province, particularly in the towns of Ubeda and Baeza, are unsurpassed in their sober beauty. Other fine 16th-century *palacios* can be found in nearly every town and city of Andalucía; often built in honey-coloured sandstone, these noble buildings were the homes of the aristocrats who had reaped the riches of the Reconquista and the new trade routes to the Americas.

The pure lines of this Renaissance classicism were soon to be transformed into a new style, Spanish Baroque. Although it started fairly soberly, it soon became rather ornamental, often being used to add elements to existing buildings. The Baroque was a time of great genius in architecture as in the other arts in Spain, as masters playfully explored the reaches of their imaginations; a strong reaction against the sober preceding style. Churches became ever larger, in part to justify the huge façades, and nobles indulged in one-upmanship, building ever-grander *palacios*. The façades themselves are typified by such features as pilasters (narrow piers descending to a point) and niches to hold statues. Andalucía has a vast array of Baroque churches; Sevilla in particular bristles with them, while Cádiz cathedral is almost wholly built in this style. Smaller towns, such as Priego de Córdoba and Ecija, are also well endowed, as they both enjoyed significant agriculture-based prosperity during the period.

The Baroque became more ornate as time went on, reaching the extremes of Churrigueresque, named for the Churriguera brothers who worked in the late 17th and early 18th centuries. The result can be overelaborate but on occasion transcendentally beautiful. Vine tendrils and cherubs decorate façades and *retablos*, which seem intent on breaking every classical norm, twisting here, upside-down there and at their best seeming to capture motion.

Neoclassicism, encouraged by a new interest in the ancient civilizations of Greece and Rome, was an inevitable reaction to such *joie de vivre*. It again resorted to the cleaner lines of antiquity, which were used this time for public spaces as well as civic and religious buildings. Many plazas and town halls in Spain are in this style, which tended to flourish in the cities that were thriving in the late 18th and 19th centuries, such as Cádiz, whose elegant old town is largely in this style. The best examples use symmetry to achieve beauty and elegance, such as the Prado in Madrid, or Sevilla's tobacco factory, which bridges Baroque and neoclassical styles.

The late 19th century saw Catalan *modernista* architecture break the moulds in a startling way. At the forefront of the movement was Antoni Gaudí. Essentially a highly original interpretation of art nouveau, Gaudí's style featured naturalistic curves and contours enlivened with stylistic elements inspired by Muslim and Gothic architecture. There is little *modernista* influence in Andalucía, but more sober *fin de siècle* architecture can be seen in Almería, which was a prosperous industrial powerhouse at the time.

Awakened interest in the days of Al-Andalus led to the neo-Moorish (or neo-*mudéjar*) style being used for public buildings and private residences. The most evident example of this is the fine ensemble of buildings constructed in Sevilla for the 1929 Ibero-American exhibition. Budgets were thrown out the window and the lavish pavilions are sumptuously decorated. Similarly ornate is the theatre in Cádiz.

Elegance and whimsy never seemed to play much part in fascist architecture and during the Franco era Andalucía was subjected to an appalling series of ponderous concrete monoliths, all in the name of progress. A few avant-garde buildings managed to escape the drudgery from the 1950s on, but it was the dictator's death in 1975, followed by EEC membership in 1986, that really provided the impetus for change.

Andalucía is not at the forefront of Spain's modern architectural movements, but the World Expo in Sevilla in 1992 brought some of the big names in. Among the various innovative pavilions, Santiago Calatrava's sublime bridges stand out. The impressive Teatro de la Maestranza and public library also date from this period, while the newer Olympic stadium, and Málaga's Picasso Museum and Centro de Arte Contemporáneo – both successful adaptations of older buildings – are more recent offerings. Sevilla's fantastic Parasol building, daringly built over a square in the old town, is the latest spectacular construction. Elsewhere, the focus has been on softening the harsh Francoist lines of the cities' 20th-century expansions. In most places this has been quietly successful. Much of the coast, however, is still plagued by the concrete curse, where planning laws haven't been strict enough in some places, and have been circumvented with a well-placed bribe in others.

Art

In the first millennium BC, Iberian cultures produced fine jewellery from gold and silver, as well as some remarkable sculpture and ceramics.These influences derived from contact with trading posts set up by the Phoenicians, who also left artistic evidence of their presence, mostly in the port cities they established. Similarly, the Romans brought their own artistic styles to the peninsula and there are many cultural remnants, including some fine sculpture and a number of elaborate mosaic floors. Later, the Visigoths were skilled artists and craftspeople and produced many fine pieces, most notably in metalwork.

The majority of the artistic heritage left by the Moors is tied up in their architecture (see below). As Islamic tradition has tended to veer away from the portrayal of human or animal figures, the norm was intricate applied decoration with calligraphic, geometric and vegetal themes predominating. Superb panelled ceilings are a feature of Almohad architecture; a particularly attractive style being that known as *artesonado*, in which the concave panels are bordered with elaborate inlay work. During this period, glazed tiles known as azulejos began to be produced; these continue to be a feature of Andalucían craftsmanship.

The gradual process of the *Reconquista* brought Christian styles into Andalucía. Generally speaking, the Gothic, which had arrived in Spain both overland from France and across the Mediterranean from Italy, was the first post-Moorish style in Andalucía. Over time, Gothic sculpture achieved greater naturalism and became more ornate, culminating in the technical mastery of sculptors and painters, such as Pedro Millán, Pieter Dancart (who is responsible for the massive altarpiece of Sevilla's cathedral) and Alejo Fernández, all of whom were from or heavily influenced by northern Europe.

Though to begin with, the finest artists were working in Northern Spain, Andalucía soon could boast several notable figures of its own. In the wake of the Christian conquest of Granada, the Catholic Monarchs and their successor Carlos V went on a building spree. The Spanish Renaissance drew heavily on the Italian but developed its own style. Perhaps the finest 16th-century figure is Pedro de Campaña, a Fleming whose exalted talent went largely unrecognized in his own time. His altarpiece of the Purification of Mary in Sevilla's cathedral is particularly outstanding. The Italian sculptor Domenico Fancelli was entrusted by Carlos to carve the tombs of Fernando and Isabel in Granada; these are screened by a fine *reja* (grille) by Maestro Bartolomé, a Jaén-born artist who has several such pieces in Andalucían churches. The best-known 16th-century Spanish artist, the Cretan Domenikos Theotokopoulos (El Greco), has a few works in Andalucía, but the majority are in Toledo and Madrid.

As the Renaissance progressed, naturalism in painting increased, leading into the Golden Age of Spanish art. As Sevilla prospered on New World riches, the city became a centre for artists, who found wealthy patrons in abundance. Pre-eminent among all was Diego Rodríguez de Silva Velázquez (1599-1660), who started his career there before moving to Madrid to become a court painter. Another remarkable painter working in Sevilla was Francisco de Zurbarán

(1598-1664) whose idiosyncratic style often focuses on superbly rendered white garments in a dark, brooding background, a metaphor for the subjects themselves, who were frequently priests. During Zurbarán's later years, he was eclipsed in the Sevilla popularity stakes by Bartolomé Esteban Murillo (1618-1682). While at first glance his paintings can seem heavy on the sentimentality, they tend to focus on the space between the central characters, who interact with glances or gestures of great power and meaning. Juan Valdés Leal painted many churches and monasteries in Sevilla; his greatest works are the macabre realist paintings in the Hospital de la Caridad. The sombre tone struck by these works reflects the decline of the once-great mercantile city.

At this time, the sculptor Juan Martínez Montañés carved numerous figures, *retablos* and *pasos* (ornamental floats for religious processions) in wood. Pedro Roldán, Juan de Mesa and Pedro de Mena were other important Baroque sculptors from this period, as was Alonso Cano, a crotchety but talented painter and sculptor working from Granada. The main focus of this medium continued to be ecclesiastic; *retablos* became ever larger and more ornate, commissioned by nobles to gain favour with the church and improve their chances in the afterlife.

The 18th and early 19th centuries saw fairly characterless art produced under the new dynasty of Bourbon kings. Tapestry production increased markedly but never scaled the heights of the earlier Flemish masterpieces. One man who produced pictures for tapestries was the master of 19th-century art, Francisco Goya. Goya was a remarkable figure whose finest works included both paintings and etchings; there's a handful of his work scattered around Andalucía's galleries, but the best examples are in Madrid's Prado and in the north.

After Goya, the 19th century produced few works of note as Spain tore itself apart in a series of brutal wars and conflicts. Perhaps in reaction to this, the *costumbrista* tradition developed; these painters and writers focused on portraying Spanish life; their depictions often revolving around nostalgia and stereotypes. Among the best were the Bécquer family: José; his cousin Joaquín; and his son Valeriano, whose brother Gustavo Adolfo was one of the period's best-known poets.

The early 20th century saw the rise of Spanish modernism and surrealism, much of it driven from Catalunya. While architects such as Gaudí managed to combine their discipline with art, it was one man from Málaga who had such an influence on 20th-century painting that he is arguably the most famous artist in the world. Pablo Ruiz Picasso (1881-1973) is notable not just for his artistic genius, but also for his evolution through different styles. Training in Barcelona, but doing much of his work in Paris, his initial Blue Period was fairly sober and subdued, named for predominant use of that colour. His best early work, however, came in his succeeding Pink Period, where he used brighter tones to depict the French capital. He moved on from this to become a pioneer of cubism. Drawing on non-western forms, cubism forsook realism for a new form of three-dimensionality, trying to show subjects from as many different angles as possible. Picasso then moved on to more surrealist forms. He continued painting right throughout his lifetime and produced an incredible number of works. One of his best-known paintings is *Guernica*, a nightmarish ensemble of terror-struck animals and people that he produced in abhorrence of the Nationalist bombing of the defenceless Basque market town in April 1937. The Picasso Museum in Málaga displays a range of his works.

A completely different contemporary was the Córdoban Julio Romero de Torres, a painter who specialized in sensuous depictions of Andalucían women, usually fairly unencumbered by clothing. A more sober 20th-century painter was Daniel Vázquez Díaz, a Huelvan who adorned the walls of La Rábida monastery with murals on the life of Columbus.

The Civil War was to have a serious effect on art in Spain, as a majority of artists sided with the Republic and fled Spain with their defeat. Franco was far from an enlightened patron of the arts and his occupancy was a monotonous time. Times have changed, however, and the regional governments, including the Andalucían, are extremely supportive of local artists these days and the museums in each provincial capital usually have a good collection of modern works.

Literature

The peninsula's earliest known writers lived under the Roman occupation. Of these, two of the best known hailed from Córdoba; Seneca the Younger (3 BC-AD 65), the Stoic poet, philosopher and statesman who lived most of his life in Rome, and his nephew Lucan (AD 39-AD 65), who is known for his verse history of the wars between Caesar and Pompey, *Bellum Civile*. Both were forced to commit suicide for plotting against the emperor Nero. After the fall of Rome, one of the most remarkable of all Spain's literary figures was the bishop of Sevilla, San Isidoro, whose works were classic texts for over a millennium, see box, page 459.

In Al-Andalus a flourishing literary culture existed under the Córdoba caliphate and later. Many important works were produced by Muslim and Jewish authors; some were to have a large influence on European knowledge and thought. The writings of Ibn Rushd (Averroes; 1126-1198) were of fundamental importance, asserting that the study of philosophy was not incompatible with religion and commentating extensively on Aristotle; see box, page 484. The discovery of his works a couple of centuries on by Christian scholars led to the rediscovery of Aristotle and played a triggering role in the Renaissance. His contemporary in Córdoba, Maimonides (1135-1204) was one of the foremost Jewish writers of all time; writing on Jewish law, religion and spirituality in general and medicine, he remains an immense and much-studied figure; see box, page 484. Another important Jewish writer was the philosopher and poet Judah ha-Levi (1075-1141); although born in the north, he spent much of his time writing in Granada and Córdoba. Throughout the Moorish period, there were many chronicles, treatises and studies written by Arab authors, but poetry was the favoured form of literary expression. Well-crafted verses, often about love and frequently quite explicit, were penned by such authors as the Sevilla king Al-Mu'tamid and the Córdoban Ibn Hazm.

After the Moors, however, Andalucía didn't really produce any literature of note until the so-called Golden Age of Spanish writing, which came in the wake of the

BACKGROUND

Averroes and Maimonides

Two of Córdoba's most famous sons, and scholars of immense historical significance, were born within a few years of each other in the city in the 12th century.

Ibn Rushd, better known as Averroes (1126-1198), was from a high-ranking Moorish family. An extraordinary polymath, he was a doctor, theologist, philosopher, mathematician and lawyer. He was well respected by the rulers of Córdoba until a backlash against philosophers saw him banished to Morocco and many of his texts burned. Averroes' primary thesis was that the study of philosophy was not incompatible with religion. He commentated extensively on Aristotle and the rediscovery of some of these works played a triggering role in the Christian Renaissance.

Moses Maimonides (Moses ben Maimun; 1135-1204) was born of Jewish parents in Córdoba, but moved on at a fairly young age, finishing up in Cairo. Like Averroes, he was a physician, and became an absolute authority on Jewish law, religion, and spirituality. He wrote several commentaries on the ancient Hebrew texts; such was his influence that it has been said that "Between Moses and Moses, there was no one like unto Moses". As with Averroes, he had a great influence on the development of philosophy in succeeding centuries.

discovery of the Americas and the flourishing of trade and wealth; patronage was crucial for writers in those days. The most notable poet of the period is the Córdoban Luis de Góngora (1561-1627), whose exaggerated, affected style is deeply symbolic (and sometimes almost inaccessible). His work has been widely appreciated recently and critics tend to label him the greatest of all Spanish poets, though he still turns quite a few people off.

The extraordinary life of Miguel de Cervantes (1547-1616) marks the start of a rich period of Spanish literature. *Don Quijote* came out in serial form in 1606 and is rightly considered one of the finest novels ever written; it's certainly the widest-read Spanish work. Cervantes spent plenty of time in Andalucía and some of his *Novelas Ejemplares* are short stories set in Sevilla.

The Sevillian, Lope de Rueda (1505-1565), was in many ways Spain's first playwright. He wrote comedies and paved the way for the explosion of Spanish drama under the big three – Lope de Vega, Tirso de la Molina and Calderón de la Barca – when public theatres opened in the early 17th century.

The 18th century was not such a rich period for Andalucían or Spanish writing but in the 19th century the *costumbrista* movement (see page 482) produced several fine works, among them *La Gaviota* (the Seagull), by Fernán Caballero, who was actually a Sevilla-raised woman named Cecilia Böhl von Faber, and *Escenas Andaluzas* (Andalucían Scenes), by Serafín Estébanez Calderón. Gustavo Adolfo Bécquer died young having published a famous series of legends and just one volume of poetry, popular, yearning works about love. Pedro Antonio de Alarcón

BACKGROUND

Antonio Machado

Mi infancia son recuerdos de un patio de Sevilla, / y un huerto claro donde madura el limonero; / mi juventud, veinte años en tierras de Castilla; / mi historia, algunos casos que recordar no quiero

My childhood is memories of a patio in Sevilla, / and of a light-filled garden where the lemon tree grows / My youth, twenty years in the lands of Castilla / My story, some happenings I wish not to remember

Along with Federico García Lorca, Antonio Machado was Spain's greatest 20th-century poet. Part of the so-called Generation of '98 who struggled to re-evaluate Spain in the wake of losing its last colonial possessions in 1898, he was born in 1875 in Sevilla.

Growing up mostly in Madrid, he spent time in France and then lived and worked in Soria, in Castilla; much of his poetry is redolent of the harsh landscapes of that region. His solitude was exacerbated when his young wife Leonor died after three years of marriage. He then moved to Baeza, where he taught French in a local school. Like the poetry written in Soria, his work in Andalucía reflected his profound feelings for the landscape.

Machado was a staunch defender of the Republic and became something of a bard of the Civil War. Forced to flee with thousands of refugees as the Republic fell, he died not long after, in 1939, in a pensión in southern France. His will to live was dealt a bitter blow by the triumph of fascism, while his health had suffered badly during the trying journey.

(1833-1901), who hailed from Guadix, is most famous for his work *The Three-Cornered Hat*, a light and amusing tale which draws heavily on Andalucían customs and characters; it was also made into a popular ballet.

At the end of the 19th century, Spain lost the last of its colonial possessions after revolts and a war with the USA. This event, known as the Disaster, had a profound impact on the nation and its date 1898 gave its name to a generation of writers and artists. This group sought to express what Spain was and had been and to achieve new perspectives for the 20th century. One of their number was Antonio Machado (1875-1939), one of Spain's greatest poets; see box, above.

Another excellent poet of this time was Juan Ramón Jiménez (1881-1958), from Moguer in Huelva province, who won the Nobel Prize in 1956. His best-known work is the long prose poem *Platero y Yo*, a lyrical portrait of the town and the region conducted as a conversation between the writer and his donkey. He was forced into exile by the Spanish Civil War.

The Granadan Federico García Lorca (see box, page 328) was a young poet and playwright of great ability and lyricism with a gypsy streak in his soul. His play *Bodas de Sangre* (Blood Wedding) sits among the finest Spanish drama ever written and his verse ranges from the joyous to the haunted and draws heavily on

Andalucían folk traditions. Lorca was shot by fascist thugs in Granada just after the outbreak of hostilities in the Civil War; one of the most poignant of the thousands of atrocities committed in that bloody conflict.

Lorca was associated with the so-called Generation of 27, another loose grouping of artists and writers. One of their number was Rafael Alberti (1902-1999), a poet from El Puerto de Santa María and a close friend of Lorca's. Achieving recognition with his first book of poems, *Mar y Tierra*, Alberti was a Communist (who once met Stalin) and fought on the Republican side in the Civil War. He was forced into exile at the end of the war, only returning to Spain in 1978. Other Andalucían poets associated with this movement were the neo-romantic Luis Cernuda (1902-1963) and Vicente Aleixandre (1898-1984), winner of the 1977 Nobel Prize for his surrealist-influenced free verse. Both men were from Sevilla.

Although Aleixandre stayed in Spain, despite his poems being banned for a decade, the exodus and murder of the country's most talented writers was a heavy blow for literature. The greatest novelists of the Franco period, Camilo José Cela and Miguel Delibes, both hailed from the north, but in more recent times Andalucía has come to the fore again with Antonio Múñoz Molina (born 1956) from Ubeda in Jaén province. His *Ardor Guerrero* (*Warrior Lust*) is a bitter look at military service, while his highly acclaimed *Sepharad* is a collection of interwoven stories broadly about the Diaspora and Jewish Spain and set in various locations ranging from concentration camps to rural Andalucían villages. In 2013 he won the prestigious Prince of Asturias prize, Spain's top literary award.

Cinema

After years under the cultural anaesthetic of the fascist dictatorship, Spanish cinema has belatedly made a strong impression on the world stage. With an enthusiastic home audience of cinema-goers, increased funding, and a huge global Spanish-speaking population, it was perhaps only a matter of time.

Andalucía's major film body is the **Andalucía Film Commission** ⓘ *www.andaluciafilm.com*; the website has English pages and is a good way to keep up with what's going on in the world of cinema down south.

Music and dance

Flamenco

Few things symbolize the mysteries of Andalucía like flamenco but, as with the region itself, much has been written that is over-romanticized, patronizing or just plain untrue. Like bullfighting, flamenco as we know it is a fairly young art, having basically developed in the 19th century. It is constantly evolving and there have been significant changes in its performance in the last century, which makes the search for classic flamenco a bit of a wild goose chase. Rather, the element to search for is authentic emotion and, beyond this, *duende*, an undefinable passion that carries singer and watchers away in a whirlwind of raw feeling, with a devil-may-care sneer at destiny.

Though there have been many excellent *payo* flamenco artists, its history is primarily a gypsy one. It was developed among the gypsy population in the Sevilla and Cádiz area but clearly includes elements of cultures encountered further away.

Flamenco consists of three basic components: *el cante* (the song), *el toque* (the guitar) and *el baile* (the dance). In addition, *el jaleo* provides percussion sounds through shouts, clicking fingers, clapping and footwork (and, less traditionally, castanets). Flamenco can be divided into four basic types: *tonás*, *siguiriyas*, *soleá* and *tangos*, which are characterized by their *comps* or form, rhythm and accentuation and are either *cante jondo* (emotionally deep)/*cante grande* (big) or *cante ligero* (lighter)/*cante chico* (small). Related to flamenco, but not in a pure form, are *sevillanas*, danced till you drop at Feria, and *rocieras*, which are sung on (and about) the annual *romería* pilgrimage to El Rocío.

For a foreigner, perhaps the classic image of flamenco is a woman in a theatrical dress clicking castanets. A more authentic image is of a singer and guitarist, both sitting rather disconsolately on ramshackle chairs, or perhaps on a wooden box to tap out a rhythm. The singer and the guitarist work together, sensing the mood of the other and improvising. A beat is provided by clapping of hands or tapping of feet. If there's a dancer, he or she will lock into the mood of the others and vice versa. The dancing is stop-start, frenetic: the flamenco can reach crescendoes of frightening intensity when it seems the singer will have a stroke, the dancer is about to commit murder, and the guitarist may never find it back to the world of the sane. These outbursts of passion are seen to their fullest in *cante jondo*, the deepest and saddest form of flamenco.

After going through a moribund period during the mid-20th century, flamenco was revived by such artists as Paco de Lucía, and the gaunt, heroin-addicted genius Camarón de la Isla, while the flamenco theatre of Joaquín Cortés put purists' noses firmly out of joint but achieved worldwide popularity. More recently, Diego 'El Cigala' carries on Camarón's angst-ridden tradition. Fusions of flamenco with other styles have been a feature of recent years, with the flamenco-rock of Ketama and the flamenco-chillout of Málaga-based Chambao achieving notable success. Granada's late Enrique Morente, a flamenco artist from the old school, outraged purists with his willingness to experiment with other artists and musical forms; his release Omega brought in a punk band to accompany him and featured flamenco covers of Leonard Cohen hits.

Other music

Music formed a large part of cultural life in the days of the Córdoba emirate and caliphate. The earliest known depiction of a lute comes from an ivory bottle dated around AD 968; the musician Ziryab, living in the 11th century, made many important modifications to the lute, including the addition of a fifth double-string.

Like other art forms, music enjoyed something of a golden age under the early Habsburg monarchs. It was during this period that the five-string Spanish guitar came to be developed and the emergence of a separate repertoire for this instrument.

In 1629 Lope de Vega wrote the libretto for the first Spanish opera, which was to become a popular form. A particular Spanish innovation was the *zarzuela*, a musical play with speech and dancing. It became widely popular in the 19th century and is still performed in the larger cities. Spain's contribution to opera has been very important and has produced in recent times a number of world-class singers such as Montserrat Caballé, Plácido Domingo, José Carreras and Teresa Berganza.

The Cádiz-born Manuel de Falla is the greatest figure in the history of a country that has produced few classical composers. He drew heavily on Andalucían themes and culture and also helped keep flamenco traditions alive.

De Falla's friendship with Debussy in Paris led to the latter's work *Ibéria*, which, although the Frenchman never visited Spain, was described by Lorca as very evocative of Andalucía. It was the latest of many Andalucía-inspired compositions, which include Bizet's *Carmen*, from the story by Prosper Merimée and Rossini's *The Barber of Seville*, based on the play by Beaumarchais.

Contemporary music

Flamenco aside, Andalucía doesn't have a cutting-edge contemporary music scene. Most bars and *discotecas* play a repetitive selection of Spanish pop, much of it derived from the phenomenally successful TV show *Operación Triunfo*, a star-creation programme that spawned *Fame Academy* in the UK.

In contrast, the Andalucían Joaquín Sabina is a heavyweight singer-songwriter who works both solo and in collaboration with other musicians. His songs draw on Andalucían folk traditions and he is deeply critical of modern popular culture. His gravelly voice is distinctive and has deservedly won him worldwide fame.

Religion

The history of Spain and the history of the Spanish Catholic church are barely separable but, in 1978, Article 16 of the new constitution declared that Spain was now a nation without an official religion, less than a decade after Franco's right hand man, Admiral Luis Carrero Blanco, had declared that "Spain is Catholic or she is nothing".

From the sixth-century writings of San Isidoro (see box, page 459) onwards, the destiny of Spain was a specifically Catholic one. The *Reconquista* was a territorial war inspired by holy zeal, Jews and Moors were expelled in the quest for pure Catholic blood, the Inquisition demonstrated the young nation's religious insecurities and paranoias and Felipe II bled Spain dry pursuing futile wars in a vain attempt to protect his beloved Church from the spread of Protestantism. Much of the strife of the 1800s was caused by groups attempting to end or defend the power of the church, while in the 20th century the fall of the Second Republic and the Civil War was engendered to a large extent by the provocatively anticlerical actions of the leftists.

Faced with a census form, a massive 94% of Spaniards claim to be Catholics, but less than a third of them cut regular figures in the parish church. Although regular churchgoing is increasingly confined to an aged (mostly female) segment of society and seminaries struggle to produce enough priests to stock churches, it's not the whole picture. *Romerías* (religious processions to rural chapels and sites) and religious fiestas are well attended – the most famous being the boisterous Whitsun journey to El Rocío (see box, page 110) and places of pilgrimage, usually chapels housing venerated statues of the Virgin, are flooded with Spanish visitors during the summer months. Very few weddings are conducted away from the church's bosom and, come Easter, a big percentage of the male population of some towns participates in solemn processions of religious *cofradías* (brotherhoods), most famously in Sevilla. Nevertheless, the church plays an increasingly minor role in most Spaniards' lives, especially those of those born after the return to democracy.

Land & environment

Geography

Andalucía's 87,000 sq km makes it somewhat larger than Scotland and about the size of Indiana or Maine. It comprises just under a fifth of Spain's total land area. Its 700 km of coastline encompass both the Mediterranean Sea and the Atlantic Ocean. Administratively, Andalucía is a semi-autonomous community with the regional government in Sevilla. It is divided into eight provinces, named after their capital cities. Geographically, Andalucía can be more or less split into four zones. It is divided from the rest of Spain by the Sierra Morena range, a low chain of rugged hills wooded with holm oak and cork trees rarely rising above 1000 m in height. It stretches across the northern parts of Huelva, Sevilla, Córdoba and Jaén provinces and forms a natural barrier across which the Despeñaperros Pass, north of Jaén, has traditionally been the principal crossing. There are some mining areas, particularly in Córdoba province and in Huelva, where the massive Rio Tinto copper mines have created a moonscape over the millennia. The area also produces some of the world's finest ham from the black-footed porkers that feed on acorns.

The valley of the Guadalquivir river has historically been the agricultural and demographic centre of Andalucía. The river is Spain's fifth longest, rising in the Sierra de Cazorla in Jaén province and flowing for 657 km via the cities of Córdoba and Sevilla to its destiny with the Atlantic, where it creates the fabulous wetlands of the Coto Doñana. In Roman times the river was known as the *Betis* (giving its name to one of Sevilla's football teams), but the Moors imaginatively renamed it *al wadi al kibir* (the big river) which has stuck. The valley is rich in alluvial soils; this combined with ready water for irrigation made this part of Andalucía the major settlement zone for Iberians, Romans, Moors and Christians. The river has silted up over the centuries: it was once navigable as far as Córdoba, but these days you could just about stroll across it in the city of the caliphs.

The Cordillera Bética is one of Spain's principal ranges and runs close to the coast eastwards from the west of Málaga province across Granada province and into Jaén and beyond to Murcia. The sierra can be divided into the Sistema Subbética in the northeast of Andalucía and the Sistema Penibética in the south. The former is situated in the east of the region and rises to its highest point of 3398 m in the Cazorla natural park in Jaén province. The Sistema Cordillera Penibética includes the Sierra Nevada, which boasts the nation's highest peak, Mulhacén, which stands at 3479 m. The Sierra Nevada houses Europe's most southerly ski resort and is fairly reliably snowbound from December through to

April. The slopes of the ranges in Jaén and Córdoba provinces are studded with olive groves and there are several *parques naturales* (protected natural parks) covering the upland areas.

The coastal plain has the highest population density of the region, due mainly to the tourist industry. The Mediterranean coastline is heavily built up, particularly betweeen Gibraltar and Málaga. West of Gibraltar, the Atlantic coast is known as the Costa de la Luz and is less developed, partly on account of the strong *levante* and *poniente* winds that make it such a sought-after windsurfing destination. In Almería, where the coastal plain is wider, there are huge numbers of plastic greenhouses for the production of fruit and vegetables for export. Huelva province also produces strawberries in this manner, mainly around the towns of Lepe and Mazagón. There is substantial variation within these four zones. The eastern stretch of coast in Almería province is very arid, with desert-like badlands stretching inland, while at the junction of Cádiz and Huelva provinces, the freshwater marshes of the Coto Doñana are a wetland haven for animals and birds. Andalucía is characterized by its large number of lakes – over 300, as well as several *embalses* (reservoirs). These projects have deprived the rivers of their former majesty and have been socially and environmentally extremely controversial in some cases. Natural habitats, towns and villages have been flooded by the *embalses*; enforced eviction and laughable compensation for property was a feature of these projects, particularly in Franco's later years. Nevertheless, the water is much needed. Apart from the Guadalquivir, Andalucía's major watercourses are the **Guadiana**, in the extreme west and forming part of the border with Portugal, the **Tinto** and **Odiel** which meet at Huelva and the shorter central and eastern rivers such as the **Guadalhorce**, near Málaga and the **Almanzora**, east of Almería.

Climate

In an area that extends 400 km from west to east and an average of 225 km from north to south and with altitudes varying from sea level to 3479 m in the Sierra Nevada, it is hardly surprising that there are wide variations in climate. In fact, Andalucía is home to both the wettest place in Spain, the Sierra de Grazalema, and the driest place, the Cabo de Gata area of Almería province.

Andalucía has, in general, what is known as a Mediterranean climate: hot dry summers and mild wet winters, with high sunshine totals. The south of Spain is its sunniest part and is also one of Europe's sunniest regions. Winter temperatures on the coast are very forgiving and the summers are hot but not overly so. Inland Andalucía, however, is a furnace in the summer months, with frequent centigrade temperatures in the high 30s and low 40s. On the coast, summer temperatures hover around 30°C, while winter temperatures are typically about 15°C during the day. Inland, however, it gets chillier, as places such as Ronda and Granada often drop below zero.

Wildlife and vegetation

The wide diversity of wildlife found in Andalucía is truly amazing. Because of the geographical isolation of the Iberian Peninsula and in particular Andalucía, cut off to the north by high ranges, the area is rich in endemic species. Reasons for this abundance include the region's diversity of habitats and climatic zones and its position at the crossroads of Europe and Africa.

Plants and trees

There are more than 5000 species of flowering plant found in Andalucía, a total that includes over 150 that are endemic, mainly found in the Sierra Nevada and the Cazorla range. A favoured spot for botanists is the so-called painted fields area between Vejer and Tarifa, where meadows that have never known pesticides are a riot of colour in spring, with mallows, convolvulus, lupins, irises and squills in abundance. There are, however, flowers to be seen in all seasons, with roadside verges covered with Bermuda buttercups and narcissi as early as January. Even in the aridity of August, coastal dunes can produce surprising numbers of sea daffodils. Alpine plants are found in the Sierra Nevada, where by early summer the snow is melting from the upper slopes. In the *maquis* areas, cistus, rock roses and aromatic herbs, like lavender, rosemary, thyme and oregano, are abundant. A wide range of orchids can be found in all the habitats, but particularly on the limestone soils. The rare and ancient Spanish fir, the *pinsapo*, is becoming more common in the Parque Natural de Grazalema, thanks to conservation efforts. Woodlands of *encina* (holm oak), sweet chestnut and cork trees are also widespread in certain areas, particularly in the Sierra Morena.

Birds

While Andalucía is attractive for many forms of wildlife, it is the wide selection of birds that is a magnet for naturalists. There are over 400 birds on the systematic list and nearly half of these breed. It is the only place in Europe where you will find, for example, white-headed ducks, marbled ducks, black-shouldered kites, Spanish imperial eagles, purple gallinules, black-bellied sand grouses, red-necked nightjars, Dupont's larks, black wheatears, azure-winged magpies, spotless starlings and trumpeter finches. This is enough to whet the appetite of all keen birdwatchers, let alone the most fanatical twitchers.

Winter visitors include a range of wildfowl and gulls, plus passerines, such as meadow pipits, white wagtails, blackcaps and chiffchaffs. **Summer visitors** include such spectacular species as little bitterns, purple herons, black storks, white storks, short-toed eagles, booted eagles, collared pratincoles, bee eaters, rollers and golden orioles. Other birds simply pass through Andalucía on their way north and south; these are called **passage migrants** and include a whole range of warblers, terns, waders and raptors.

It is the wetlands that attract most birds and birdwatchers. The incomparable Parque Nacional Coto Doñana at the mouth of the Río Guadalquivir is arguably Europe's best wetland reserve. Apart from over 300,000 wintering wildfowl, its breeding species include cattle and little egrets, grey, night and purple herons, spoonbills and white storks. Raptors include black and red kites, short-toed eagles and marsh harriers, while there are some 15 pairs of the rare Spanish imperial eagle within the park boundary. Among other coastal wetlands are the Odiel and Isla Cristina marshes west of Huelva city and the Cabo de Gata-Níjar in Almería province. There are also a number of inland wetlands, such as the group of freshwater lakes south of Córdoba and the Laguna de Medina east of Cádiz. The salt lake of Fuente de Piedra in Málaga province can have as many as 40,000 breeding flamingoes when conditions are right.

The mountain areas have their own bird communities, which include raptors such as golden eagles, griffon vultures and Bonelli's eagles. Blue rock thrushes and black wheatears are typical of rocky slopes, while at the highest levels ravens, choughs, Alpine accenters and rock buntings are the specialities.

There are many roads in Andalucía with telephone wires and these make excellent vantage points and song posts for corn buntings, stonechats, rollers, bee eaters and shrikes, while in the adjacent farmland with its extensive methods of production are great and little bustards, red-legged partridges and Montagu's harriers. The forests, olive groves and *maquis* are also rich in birdlife. The soaring birds, such as raptors and storks, which migrate to Africa for their winter quarters, face the problem of crossing the Mediterranean Sea. They are obliged to head for the narrowest point, which is the Straits of Gibraltar. Here they gain height in thermals over the land and then attempt to glide over the water (where thermals are usually lacking) to the other side. Observing this movement when conditions are right and numbers are high can be an unforgettable sight.

Mammals

There is a wide variety of mammals in Andalucía, although it must be said that many of the species are either very scarce or nocturnal and therefore highly unlikely to be seen. Of the three North African species, the mongoose and genet are quite common, while Barbary macaques have been introduced to Gibraltar. Of the more endangered 'respect' species, the wolf hangs on in small numbers in the Sierra Morena, while the pardel or Iberian lynx (see box, page 390) can occasionally be spotted in the Parque Nacional Coto Doñana and in the highlands of Jaén and Córdoba provinces. Otters, on the other hand, whilst rarely seen are still common. Of the herbivores, both red and fallow deer appear in a number of locations, as do wild boar. The Spanish ibex seems to be increasing its numbers and can easily be seen in the Sierra Nevada, Cazorla and the Serranía de Ronda, while *mouflon* – a type of wild sheep – have been introduced in some areas like Cazorla as a game species.There are numerous varieties of bat including the small pipistrelle type, which will often fly during the day. Both common and bottle nosed dolphins can always be seen in the Straits of Gibraltar, where there are also regular sightings of pilot whales and occasionally orcas.

Reptiles, amphibians, butterflies and other insects

With over 130 species of butterfly, including more than 30 types of blue alone, Andalucía is a lepidopterist's nirvana. Many of the butterflies seen in northern

Europe have bred in Andalucía, such as clouded yellows, while others migrate to the area from north Africa, like painted ladies. There are also a small number of endemics, including Nevada blues and Nevada graylings. Among the more spectacular and common butterflies are two varieties of swallowtail, Spanish festoons, Cleopatras, the ubiquitous speckled wood and the Moroccan orange tip. Most striking of all is the huge two-tailed pasha, which you could easily mistake for a small bird when it is in flight. On occasions, large numbers of American vagrants turn up, including the monarch. There are also a number of day-flying moths, of which great peacock moths and hummingbird moths are most likely to be noticed.

Among the insects the most fascinating is the praying mantis, which may be brown or green. Noisy cicadas, crickets and grasshoppers are heard everywhere during the summer. Dung beetles make fascinating watching. The plethora of ants and flies are less welcome.

There are some 17 species of amphibian, including a variety of frogs, toads and newts. Of these, the noisy marsh frog and the delightful little green tree frog are notable, while salamanders can often be seen.

Reptiles are widespread, particularly lizards, which vary from the iguana-like ocellated lizard, which can grow up to 1 m in length, down to common wall lizards and geckoes. In the southern coastal fringes of Andalucía, the highly protected chameleon may still be seen in a few places if you're lucky.

Of the eight species of snake, only one, the latastes viper, is venomous, while the largest is the Montpellier snake, which can grow up to 2 m. Most common are the familiar grass snake and the southern smooth snake.

Protected areas

The Andalucían government has made a strong commitment to protecting the environment by creating 150 protected areas, including two *parques nacionales* (national parks), 24 *parques naturales* (natural parks), mostly in upland regions, and numerous smaller areas, even down to protected coastal features and individual trees. Collectively, these make up nearly 20% of the region's surface area and, although protection for the species within these areas in some cases isn't absolute, it is significant and crucial in many cases for survival. The two national parks, situated in the contrasting zones of the Coto Doñana wetlands and the Sierra Nevada mountains, are administered by the national government and have very high levels of protection. Most of the parks have good systems of information centres, access routes, nature trails and helpful wardens. Hiking is very popular in Spain and the majority of the parks have marked trails and a variety of maps and route suggestions. Two of the best parks for walking are the Sierra de Grazalema in eastern Cádiz province and the Sierra de Cazorla in Jaén province. Most of the parks have a good range of accommodation available in the vicinity, including *casas rurales* (rural cottages) and sometimes *refugios* (simple hostels for climbers and walkers).

Reservas de caza are protected areas that also have significant coverage but for less noble reasons: so that there'll be plenty of animals to shoot when the hunting season comes around.

Environmental issues

One of Spain's most pressing environmental issues is the significant and growing level of desertification, a problem that is most evident in Andalucía. Parts of the region, particularly around Almería, are officially classified as arid, and the worry is that these are rapidly increasing and expanding. Though climate change and reduced precipitation is playing a part in this, a major factor has been, and continues to be, farming practices in the region. Andalucía's Mediterranean climate has been a bountiful provider for farmers over the millennia, but aggressive agricultural methods haven't repaid it with kindness. In ancient times, the Romans began to change the landscape, replacing the indigenous Mediterranean forest with intensive zones of olive cultivation, a practice that has continued over the years. Now, numerous parallel lines of olive trees stretch to the horizon all over the interior, and the bare earth between each tree is easily borne away by rainfall, wind, and over-irrigation. Erosion and overuse have led to massive degradation of the soil, which is now basically dirt with no organic content. This means that farmers rely increasingly on fertilization. These chemicals eventually find their way into the water supply, and in many areas the aquifers are worryingly compromised, placing a further strain on water resources. The vast fields of plasticultura (see box, page 432) hothouses use irresponsible amounts of water for such a dry zone, and use it in an inefficient, outdated manner. Similarly, the ever-increasing number of golf courses demanded by tourism would be better located in Spain's north, where rainfall, not sputtering hoses, could keep the greens green.

The golf courses are just one aspect of a general, serious overdevelopment of the coast that is especially worrying. Described by writer and environmental activist Chris Stewart as a "collar of concrete", it continues despite having the handbrake applied somewhat by the ongoing financial crisis. The growing demand for residential tourism, as retirees from northern Europe seek to live in the glorious Andalucían sunshine, has been a strong driver of development in the last decades. Developers are kings, with local authorities frequently in their pockets. The *política del ladrillo* (the law of the brick) inevitably takes precedence over environmental concerns, with numerous housing developments, and resorts being built in areas that should be protected, or lack the natural resources – especially water – to support them.

As are other parts of the world, Andalucía is also looking nervously at the climate change issue. Apart from the decreasing precipitation, a rise in sea levels would mean trouble for coastal cities like Cádiz and severely affect regions like the Coto Doñana wetlands. Higher temperatures would imply a loss of biodiversity in highland regions like the Sierra Nevada, and environmental scientists fear that changed conditions in southern Spain could provide a bridge to Europe for various potentially devastating plant and animal diseases endemic in Africa but hitherto not present in the peninsula.

Books

History and politics

Beevor, A *The Battle for Spain (2007).* Detailed but readable, it's not perhaps as good as Hugh Thomas's, but it's shorter and benefits from recent research.
Brenan, G *The Spanish Labyrinth (1943).* A good explanation of the background to the Spanish Civil War, particularly in Andalucía.
Carr, R (ed) *Spain: A History (2000).* An interesting compilation of recent writing on Spanish history, with entertaining and contributions from leading academics.
Elliott, J *Imperial Spain (1963).* History as it should be: precise, sympathetic and very readable.
Fletcher, R *Moorish Spain (1992).* A simple and approachable history of the Moorish presence in Spain with an attempt to gauge how life was for the average citizen.
Sánchez Montero, R *A Short History of Seville (1992).* Succinct, readable and intelligent.
Thomas, H *The Spanish Civil War (1961/77).* The first unbiased account of the war read by many Spaniards in the censored Franco years, this is large but always readable. A superbly researched work.

Literature

Alarcón, P *The Three-Cornered Hat (1874).* Tales of colourful characters and political corruption from 19th-century Spain.
Alberti, R *Concerning the Angels (1995).* Some of this writer's finest poems, written in the late 1920s.
Aleixandre, V *A Longing for the Light (1985).* The collected poems of the Sevillian Nobel Prize winner.
Burns, J *Spain: A Literary Companion (1995).* Good anthology of Spanish writers.
Jiménez, J *Platero and I (1994).* Lyric prose poem about a conversation between the poet and his donkey.
Lorca, F *The Collected Poems (2002).* Complete bilingual edition of Lorca's poems.
Lorca, F *Three Plays (1993).* A translation of the plays *Blood Wedding*, *Yerma* and *The House of Bernarda Alba*.
Machado, A *Border of a Dream: Selected Poems of Antonio Machado (2003).* A good bilingual collection of Machado's work.
Muñoz Molina, A *Sepharad (2003).* One of Spain's best contemporary novelists. This weaves together tales from the Holocaust and rural Andalucía to examine the Diaspora and Sephardic Spain.
Pérez-Reverte, A *The Seville Communion (1995).* Entertaining novel of renegade priests and shifty Sevilla characters who spend their time in various cafés and tapas bars.

The outdoors

Farino, T and Grunfeld, F *Wild Spain.* Knowledgeable book on Spain's wildlife and the quiet corners where you find it.
García, Ernest and Patterson, Andrew *Where to Watch Birds in Southern Spain.*
Hunter-Watts, Guy *Walking in Andalucía (2010).* Details of specific walks, background information and accommodation. GPS compatible.
Molesworth Allen, Betty *Wildflowers of Southern Spain.*

Palmer, Michael *A Birdwatching Guide to Southern Spain.*

Travelogues

Bohme, L *Granada: City of my Dreams (2000).* Entertaining and personal account of the city of Granada. Full of entertaining anecdotes and observations.

Borrow, G *The Bible in Spain (1842).* Amusing account of a remarkable 19th-century traveller who travelled widely through Spain trying to distribute Bibles during the first Carlist war and spent much time with the gypsy population.

Brenan, G *The Face of Spain (1950).* Worth a read for Brenan's insights into the people he lived among for many years. Returning after the Civil War, he seeks to rediscover his country and probe Lorca's death.

Brenan,G *South from Granada (1957).* An account of this writer's time living in the remote Alpujarran village of Yegen. Incisive commentary on local culture; recently made into a faithful film.

Chetwode, P *Two Middle-Aged Ladies in Andalusia (1963).* Likeable account of an English lady's solo ride through the little visited upland areas of Granada on the back of the Marquesa, an elderly mare.

Ford, R *A Hand-Book for Travellers in Spain (1845).* Difficult to get hold of (there have been several editions) but worth it; amazingly comprehensive and entertaining guide written by a 19th-century British gentleman who spent 5 years in Spain.

Ford, R *Gatherings from Spain (1846).* Superb and sweeping overview of Spanish culture and customs; Richard Ford was something of a genius and has been surpassed by few if any travel writers since.

Gibson, I *Lorca's Granada (1992).* A superb collection of walks through Granada, evoking the ghosts of Lorca at every corner. Written by his pre-eminent biographer and including a wealth of detail about the poet's life. Recommended. Gibson has also recently published an excellent Spanish biography of Antonio Machado, which may be translated into English.

Irving, W *Tales of the Alhambra (1832),* Ed Miguel Sánchez. This American diplomat travelled to Granada and stayed in the Alhambra itself. He describes the colourful characters he found there and recounts tales he heard of sighing Moorish princesses and ardent lovers.

Jacobs, M *Andalucía (1998).* An excellent series of essays and information by a British writer who knew the region deeply. Never straying into sentimentality, the writer captures much of the magic and history of the region.

Jacobs, M *The Factory of Light (2003).* A class above any of the other expat-in-Andalucía experiences, this biography of the remote village of Frailes in Jaén province brings out the humanity and quirkiness of a typical yet unusual rural settlement. Recommended.

Lee, L *As I Walked Out One Midsummer Morning (1969).* A poignant account of a romantic walk across pre-Civil War Spain, ending with a spell in Almuñécar. *A Rose in Winter* is the same author's story about returning after the war.

Nooteboom, C *Roads to Santiago (1992).* An offbeat travelogue that never fails to entertain. One of the best travel books around; it manages to be soulful, literary and moving. It's written by a Dutch author with a deep love of architecture and solitude. Highly recommended.

Stewart, C *Driving over Lemons (1999).* The account of an ex-Genesis drummer and itinerant sheep-shearer settling in the Alpujarra. Candid and unpretentious and a better read than the sequel, *A Parrot in the Pepper Tree*. His third account of Alpujarra life is *The Almond Blossom Appreciation Society*, while his latest, *The Last Days of the Bus Club*, makes for an entertaining read.

Other

Ball, P *¡Morbo! (2001)*. Entertaining review of rivalry in Spanish football with plenty to say on Sevilla-Betis and the creation of *Recreativo de Huelva*, the first Spanish club.

Barrucand, M and Bednorz, A *Moorish Architecture (2002)*. Updated edition of this beautifully illustrated handbook to the principal Islamic buildings of the peninsula. Excellent detail and incisive historical background.

Casas, Penelope *The Foods and Wines of Spain (1982)*. Considered by many as the definitive book on Spanish cooking, the author is married to a Madrileño and covers regional cuisine as well as tapas and traditional desserts.

Collins, L and Lapierre, D *Or I'll Dress You in Mourning (1968)*. Fascinating biography for those into tauromachy, on the rags-to-riches tale of the famous bullfighter, known as El Cordobés. Apart from the superb insight into bullfighting, the account documents the shocking poverty of life under Franco.

Davidson, A *Guide to the Seafood of Spain and Portugal (1992)*. A comprehensive guide to any of the finny tribes that may turn up on your plate in restaurants and tapas bars.

Hemingway, E *Death in the Afternoon (1939)*. Superb book on bullfighting by a man who fell heavily for it.

Radford, J & Torres, M *The New Spain: A Complete Guide to Contemporary Spanish Wine (2006)*. A guide to Spain's wines and wineries.

Webster, J *Duende (2004)*. A no-punches-pulled exploration of the world of flamenco. The same author's *Andalus* is a light and easy read on the investigation of Moorish Spain.

Woodall, J *In Search of the Firedance (1992)*. An excellent and impassioned history and travelogue of flamenco, if inclined to over-romanticize.

Footprint Mini Atlas

Andalucía

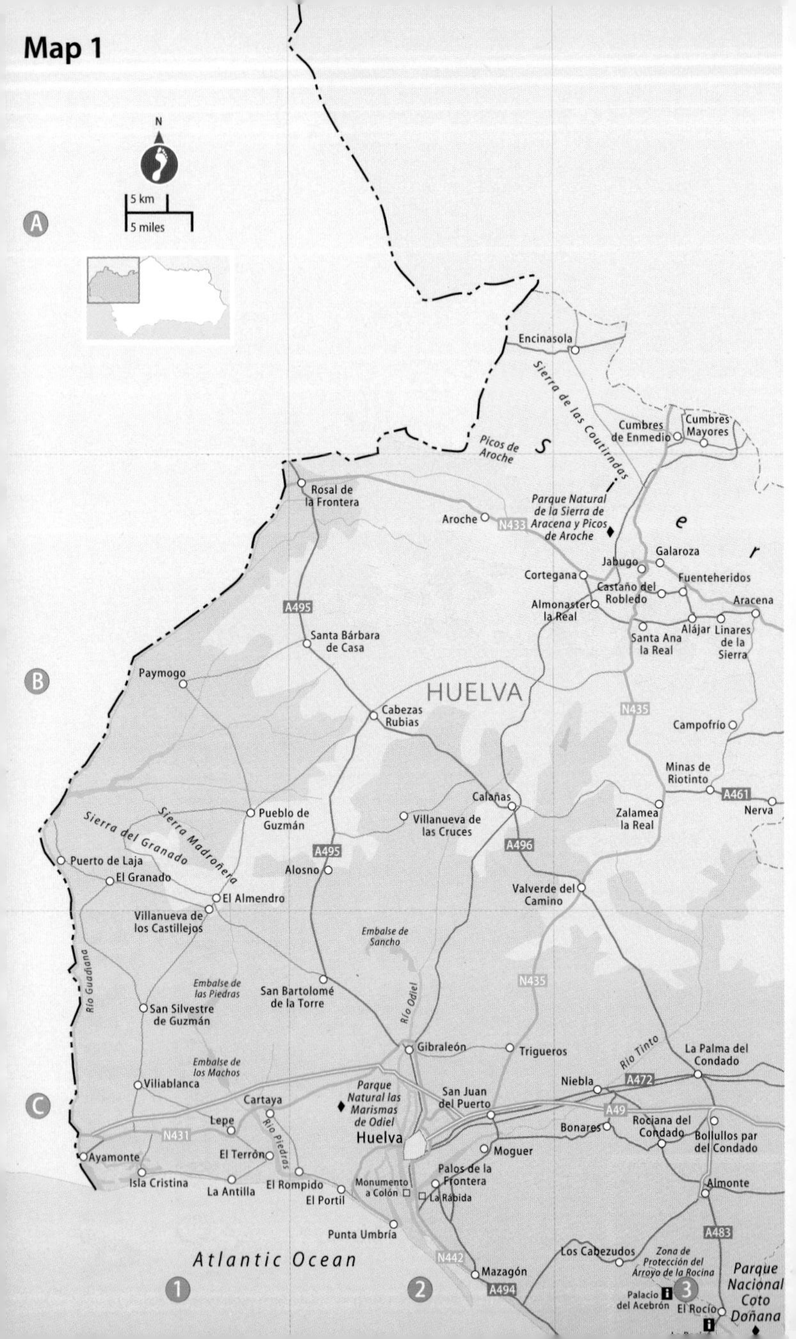

Map 1
N
5 km
5 miles
A
B
C
1
2
3
Encinasola
Sierra de las Coutirndas
Cumbres de Enmedio
Cumbres Mayores
Picos de Aroche
S
e
r
Rosal de la Frontera
Aroche
N433
Parque Natural de la Sierra de Aracena y Picos de Aroche
Galaroza
Jabugo
Cortegana
Fuenteheridos
Castaño del Robledo
Almonaster la Real
Aracena
Santa Ana la Real
Alájar
Linares de la Sierra
A495
Santa Bárbara de Casa
Paymogo
HUELVA
Cabezas Rubias
N435
Campofrío
Minas de Riotinto
A461
Nerva
Calañas
Zalamea la Real
Pueblo de Guzmán
Villanueva de las Cruces
Sierra Madroñera
Sierra del Granado
A496
Puerto de Laja
El Granado
Alosno
El Almendro
Valverde del Camino
Villanueva de los Castillejos
Embalse de Sancho
Río Guadiana
Embalse de las Piedras
San Bartolomé de la Torre
San Silvestre de Guzmán
Río Odiel
Gibraleón
Trigueros
Río Tinto
La Palma del Condado
Embalse de los Machos
Viliablanca
Parque Natural las Marismas de Odiel
Niebla
A472
San Juan del Puerto
Cartaya
A49
Lepe
Bonares
Rociana del Condado
Bollullos par del Condado
N431
Río Piedras
Huelva
Ayamonte
El Terrón
Moguer
Isla Cristina
La Antilla
El Rompido
Palos de la Frontera
Monumento a Colón
La Rábida
El Portil
Almonte
Punta Umbría
A483
Atlantic Ocean
N442
Mazagón
A494
Los Cabezudos
Zona de Protección del Arroyo de la Rocina
Parque Nacional Coto Doñana
Palacio del Acebrón
El Rocío

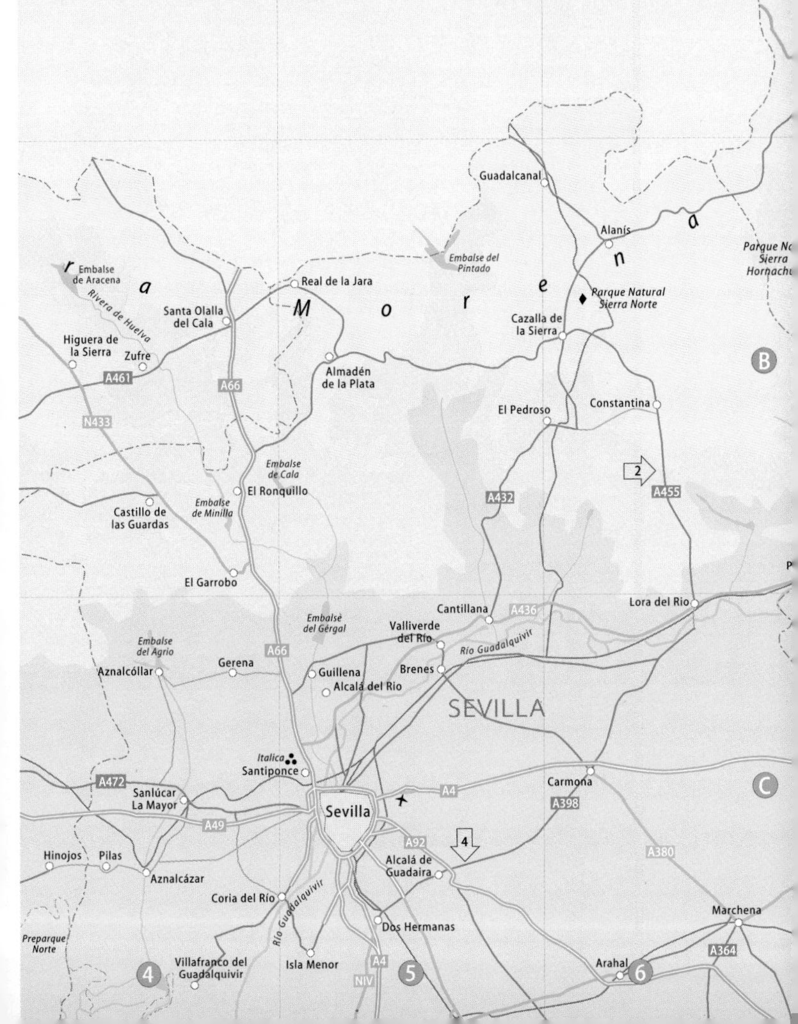
EXTREMADURA
A
B
C
Guadalcanal
Alanís
Embalse del Pintado
Parque Natural Sierra Norte
Embalse de Aracena
Rivera de Huelva
Real de la Jara
Santa Olalla del Cala
Higuera de la Sierra
Zufre
A461
A66
N433
Almadén de la Plata
Cazalla de la Sierra
Constantina
El Pedroso
2
A455
A432
Embalse de Cala
El Ronquillo
Embalse de Minilla
Castillo de las Guardas
El Garrobo
Cantillana
A436
Lora del Rio
Embalse del Gergal
Valliverde del Río
Río Guadalquivir
Embalse del Agrio
Aznalcóllar
Gerena
Guillena
Alcalá del Rio
Brenes
SEVILLA
Italica
Santiponce
A472
Sanlúcar La Mayor
A49
Sevilla
A4
Carmona
A398
A92
4
Hinojos
Pilas
Aznalcázar
Alcalá de Guadaira
A380
Coria del Río
Río Guadalquivir
Dos Hermanas
Marchena
Preparque Norte
A364
Villafranco del Guadalquivir
Isla Menor
NIV
Arahal
5
6

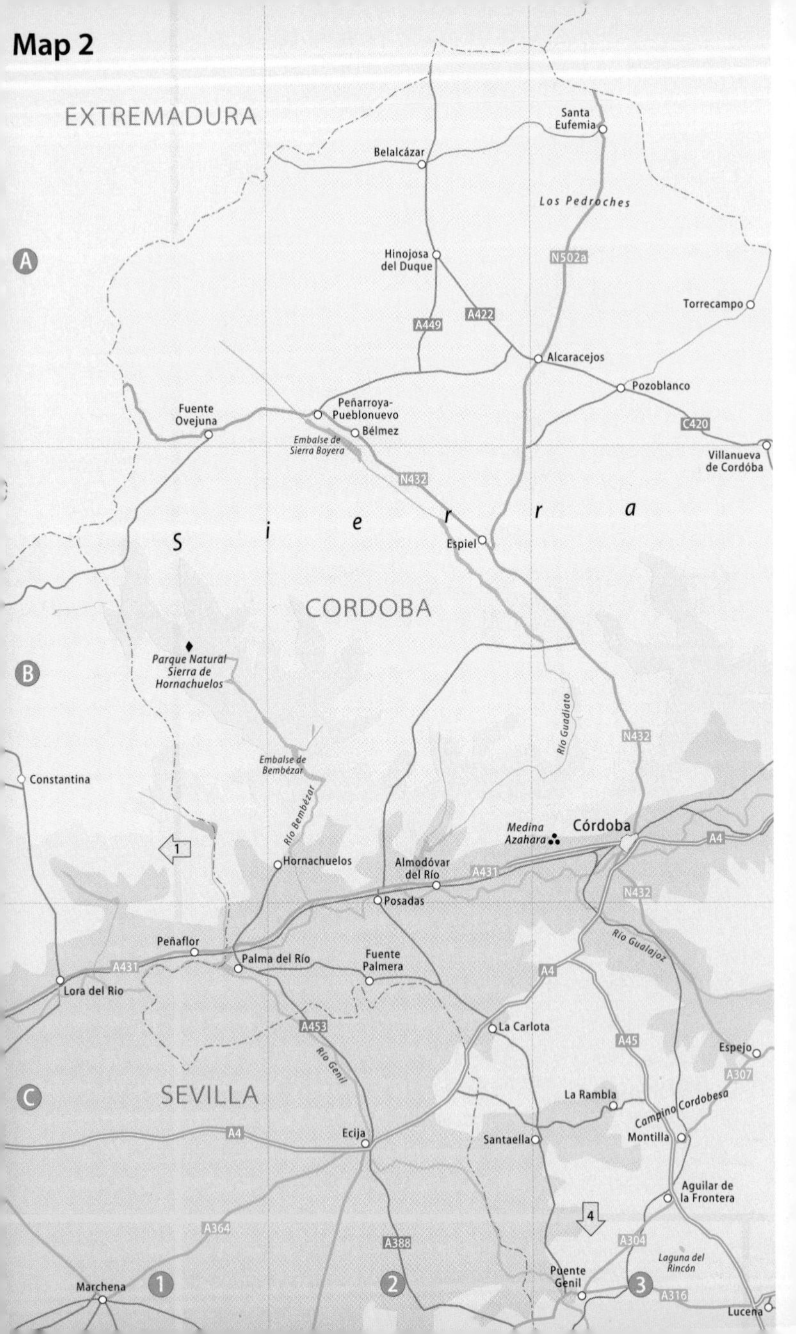
Map 2
EXTREMADURA
Santa Eufemia
Belalcázar
Los Pedroches
A
Hinojosa del Duque
N502a
Torrecampo
A422
A449
Alcaracejos
Pozoblanco
Peñarroya-Pueblonuevo
Fuente Ovejuna
Bélmez
Embalse de Sierra Boyera
C420
Villanueva de Cordóba
N432
S i e r r a
Espiel
CORDOBA
Parque Natural Sierra de Hornachuelos
B
Río Guadiato
N432
Embalse de Bembézar
Constantina
Río Bembézar
Medina Azahara
Córdoba
1
A4
Hornachuelos
Almodóvar del Río
A431
Posadas
N432
Peñaflor
Río Gualajoz
A431
Palma del Río
Fuente Palmera
A4
Lora del Rio
A453
La Carlota
Río Genil
A45
Espejo
A307
C
SEVILLA
La Rambla
Campino Cordobesa
A4
Ecija
Santaella
Montilla
Aguilar de la Frontera
4
A364
A388
A304
Laguna del Rincón
Marchena
1
2
Puente Genil
3
A316
Lucena

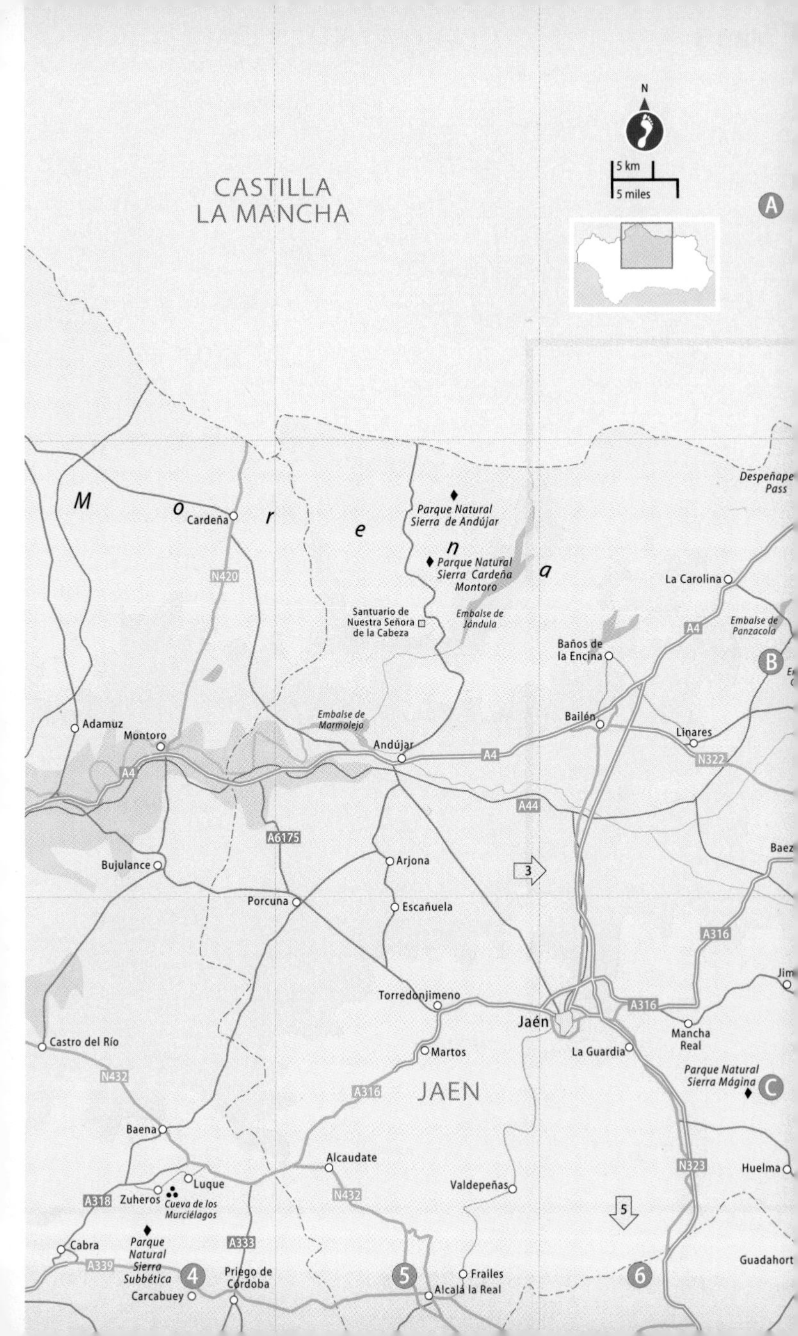

N
5 km
5 miles
CASTILLA
LA MANCHA
A
B
C
M o r e n a
Cardeña
N420
Parque Natural
Sierra de Andújar
Parque Natural
Sierra Cardeña
Montoro
Santuario de
Nuestra Señora
de la Cabeza
Embalse de
Jándula
Despeñape
Pass
La Carolina
Embalse de
Panzacola
A4
Baños de
la Encina
Adamuz
Montoro
Embalse de
Marmolejo
Andújar
Bailén
Linares
N322
A44
A6175
Bujulance
Arjona
3
Baez
Porcuna
Escañuela
A316
Torredonjimeno
Jaén
Mancha
Real
Castro del Río
Martos
La Guardia
N432
A316
JAEN
Parque Natural
Sierra Mágina
Baena
Alcaudate
N323
Huelma
Luque
Zuheros
A318
Cueva de los
Murciélagos
N432
Valdepeñas
5
Parque
Natural
Sierra
Subbética
A333
Cabra
A339
4
Priego de
Córdoba
5
Frailes
6
Guadahort
Carcabuey
Alcalá la Real

Map 3

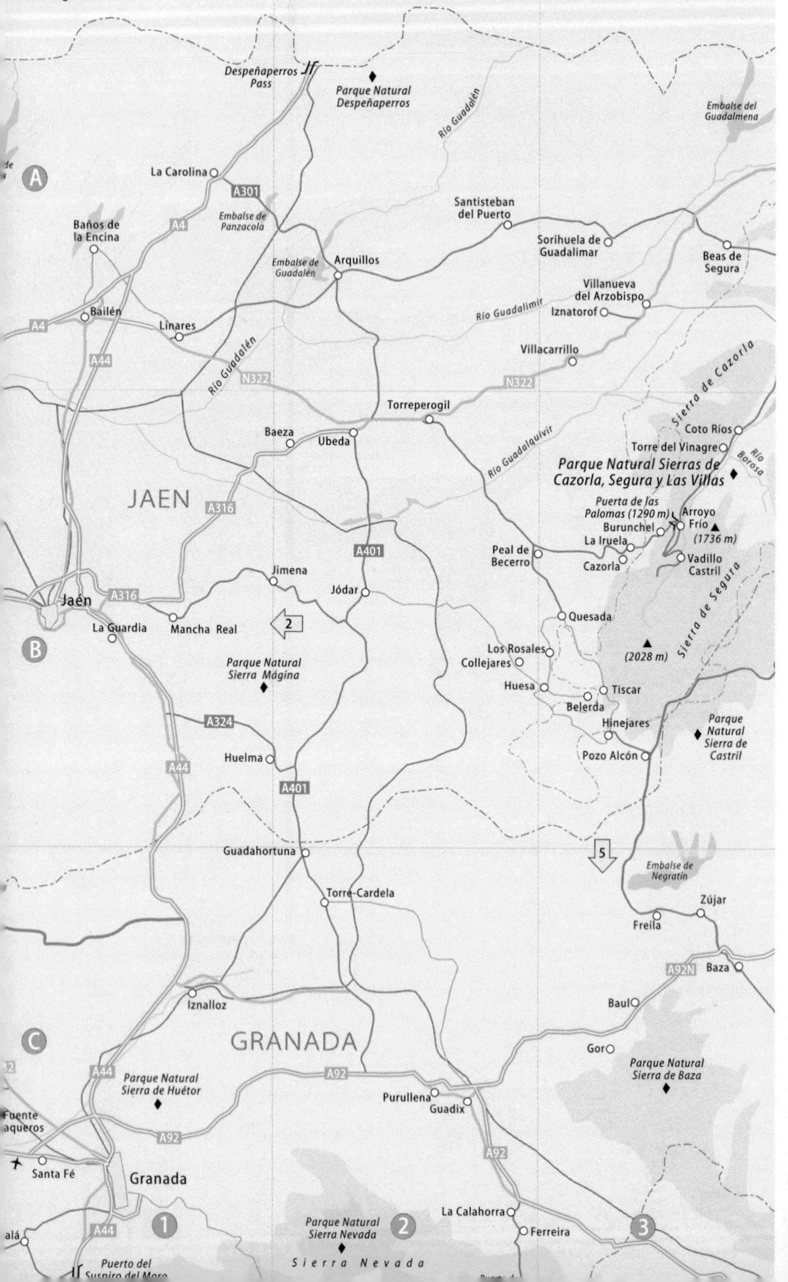
CASTILLA LA MANCHA
Despeñaperros Pass
Parque Natural Despeñaperros
Río Guadalén
Embalse del Guadalmena
A
La Carolina
A301
Embalse de Panzacola
A4
Baños de la Encina
Santisteban del Puerto
Sorihuela de Guadalimar
Beas de Segura
Embalse de Guadalén
Arquillos
Villanueva del Arzobispo
Río Guadalimir
Iznatorof
Bailén
A4
Linares
A44
Río Guadalén
N322
Villacarrillo
N322
Sierra de Cazorla
Torreperogil
Coto Ríos
Baeza
Ubeda
Torre del Vinagre
Río Borosa
Río Guadalquivir
Parque Natural Sierras de Cazorla, Segura y Las Villas
JAEN
A316
Puerta de las Palomas (1290 m)
Arroyo Frío
(1736 m)
Burunchel
La Iruela
A401
Peal de Becerro
Cazorla
Vadillo Castril
Jimena
A316
Jódar
Jaén
Sierra de Segura
La Guardia
Mancha Real
2
Quesada
B
Los Rosales
(2028 m)
Collejares
Parque Natural Sierra Mágina
Huesa
Tiscar
Belerda
A324
Hinejares
Parque Natural Sierra de Castril
Huelma
Pozo Alcón
A44
A401
Guadahortuna
5
Embalse de Negratín
Torre-Cardela
Zújar
Freila
A92N
Baza
Iznalloz
Baul
C
GRANADA
Gor
A44
Parque Natural Sierra de Huétor
A92
Parque Natural Sierra de Baza
Purullena
Guadix
Fuente Vaqueros
A92
A92
Santa Fé
Granada
La Calahorra
1
Parque Natural Sierra Nevada
2
3
Ferreira
A44
Sierra Nevada
Puerto del Suspiro del Moro

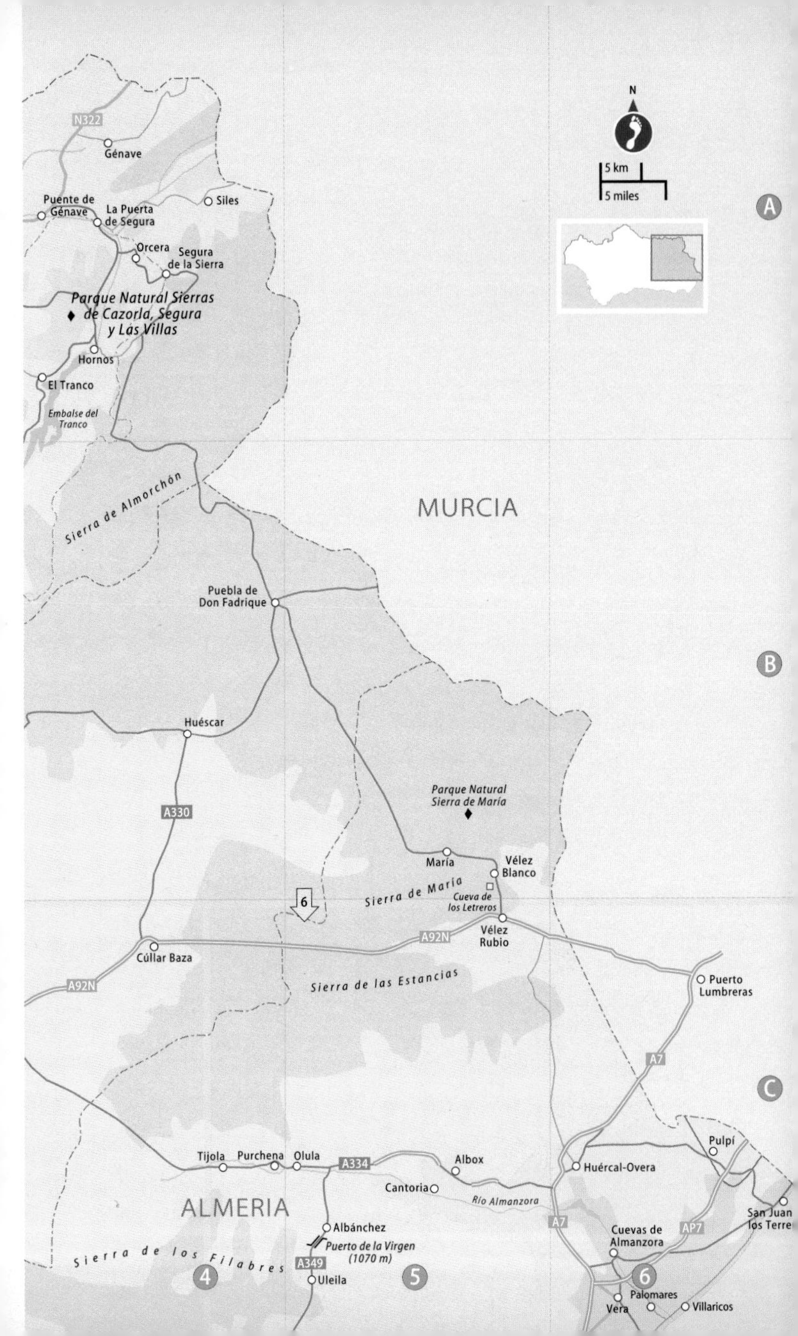
N322
Génave
Puente de Génave
La Puerta de Segura
Siles
Orcera
Segura de la Sierra
Parque Natural Sierras de Cazorla, Segura y Las Villas
Hornos
El Tranco
Embalse del Tranco
Sierra de Almorchón
MURCIA
Puebla de Don Fadrique
Huéscar
A330
Parque Natural Sierra de María
María
Vélez Blanco
Sierra de María
Cueva de los Letreros
6
Vélez Rubio
A92N
Cúllar Baza
A92N
Sierra de las Estancias
Puerto Lumbreras
A7
Tijola
Purchena
Olula
A334
Albox
Huércal-Overa
Pulpí
Cantoria
Río Almanzora
ALMERIA
A7
Albánchez
Puerto de la Virgen (1070 m)
Cuevas de Almanzora
AP7
San Juan los Terre
Sierra de los Filabres
A349
Uleila
4
5
6
Vera
Palomares
Villaricos
5 km
5 miles
A
B
C

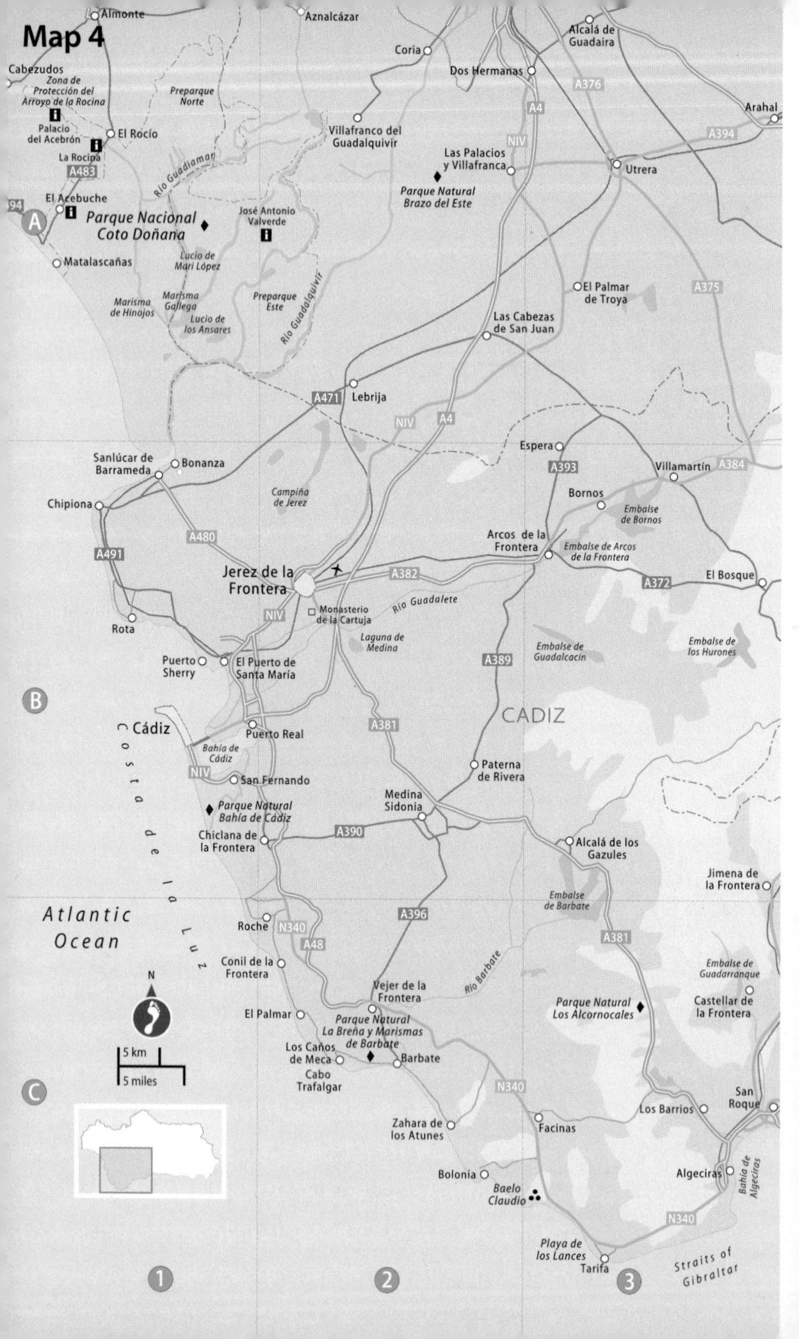

Map 4
Almonte
Aznalcázar
Alcalá de Guadaira
Coria
Dos Hermanas
Cabezudos
Zona de Protección del Arroyo de la Rocina
Preparque Norte
A376
A4
Arahal
Palacio del Acebrón
El Rocío
Villafranco del Guadalquivir
NIV
A394
La Rocina
Las Palacios y Villafranca
Utrera
A483
Río Guadiamar
Parque Natural Brazo del Este
El Acebuche
José Antonio Valverde
Parque Nacional Coto Doñana
Matalascañas
Lucio de Mari López
El Palmar de Troya
A375
Marisma de Hinojos
Marisma Gallega
Preparque Este
Lucio de los Ansares
Río Guadalquivir
Las Cabezas de San Juan
A471
Lebrija
NIV
A4
Espera
Sanlúcar de Barrameda
Bonanza
A393
Villamartín
A384
Campiña de Jerez
Bornos
Chipiona
Embalse de Bornos
A480
Arcos de la Frontera
A491
Embalse de Arcos de la Frontera
Jerez de la Frontera
A382
El Bosque
A372
Monasterio de la Cartuja
Río Guadalete
Rota
NIV
Laguna de Medina
Embalse de Guadalcacín
Embalse de los Hurones
Puerto Sherry
El Puerto de Santa María
A389
CADIZ
Cádiz
Puerto Real
A381
Bahía de Cádiz
Paterna de Rivera
NIV
San Fernando
Medina Sidonia
Parque Natural Bahía de Cádiz
Chiclana de la Frontera
A390
Alcalá de los Gazules
Costa de la Luz
Jimena de la Frontera
Embalse de Barbate
Atlantic Ocean
A396
Roche
N340
A48
A381
Conil de la Frontera
Río Barbate
Embalse de Guadarranque
Vejer de la Frontera
Castellar de la Frontera
El Palmar
Parque Natural Los Alcornocales
Parque Natural La Breña y Marismas de Barbate
Los Caños de Meca
Barbate
5 km
5 miles
Cabo Trafalgar
N340
San Roque
Los Barrios
Zahara de los Atunes
Facinas
Bolonia
Algeciras
Bahía de Algeciras
Baelo Claudio
N340
Playa de los Lances
Tarifa
Straits of Gibraltar
A
B
C
1
2
3

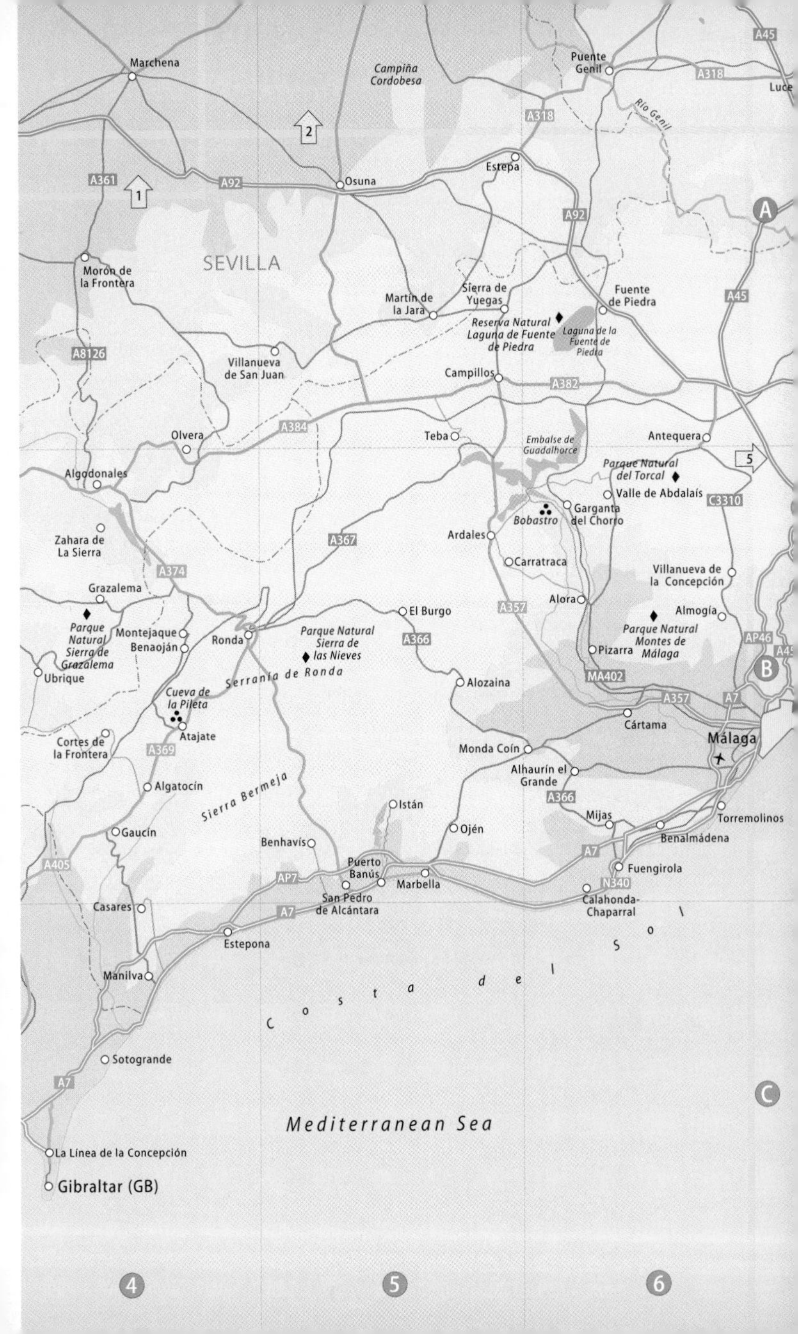
Marchena
Campiña Cordobesa
Puente Genil
A45
A318
Luce
Río Genil
2
1
A361
A92
Osuna
Estepa
SEVILLA
Morón de la Frontera
Martín de la Jara
Sierra de Yuegas
Fuente de Piedra
A45
Reserva Natural Laguna de Fuente de Piedra
Laguna de la Fuente de Piedra
A8126
Villanueva de San Juan
Campillos
A382
A384
Olvera
Teba
Embalse de Guadalhorce
Antequera
5
Parque Natural del Torcal
Valle de Abdalaís
C3310
Algodonales
Garganta del Chorro
Bobastro
Ardales
Zahara de La Sierra
A367
A374
Carratraca
Villanueva de la Concepción
Grazalema
Alora
A357
El Burgo
Almogía
Parque Natural Sierra de Grazalema
Montejaque
Benaoján
Ronda
Parque Natural Sierra de las Nieves
A366
Parque Natural Montes de Málaga
Pizarra
AP46
Ubrique
Serranía de Ronda
Alozaina
MA402
Cueva de la Pileta
A357
A7
Atajate
Cártama
Cortes de la Frontera
A369
Monda
Coín
Málaga
Alhaurín el Grande
Algatocín
Sierra Bermeja
A366
Istán
Mijas
Torremolinos
Gaucín
Ojén
Benalmádena
Benhavís
A405
A7
Puerto Banús
Fuengirola
AP7
Marbella
N340
San Pedro de Alcántara
Calahonda-Chaparral
Casares
A7
Estepona
Manilva
Costa del Sol
Sotogrande
A7
Mediterranean Sea
La Línea de la Concepción
Gibraltar (GB)
A
B
C
4
5
6

Map 5

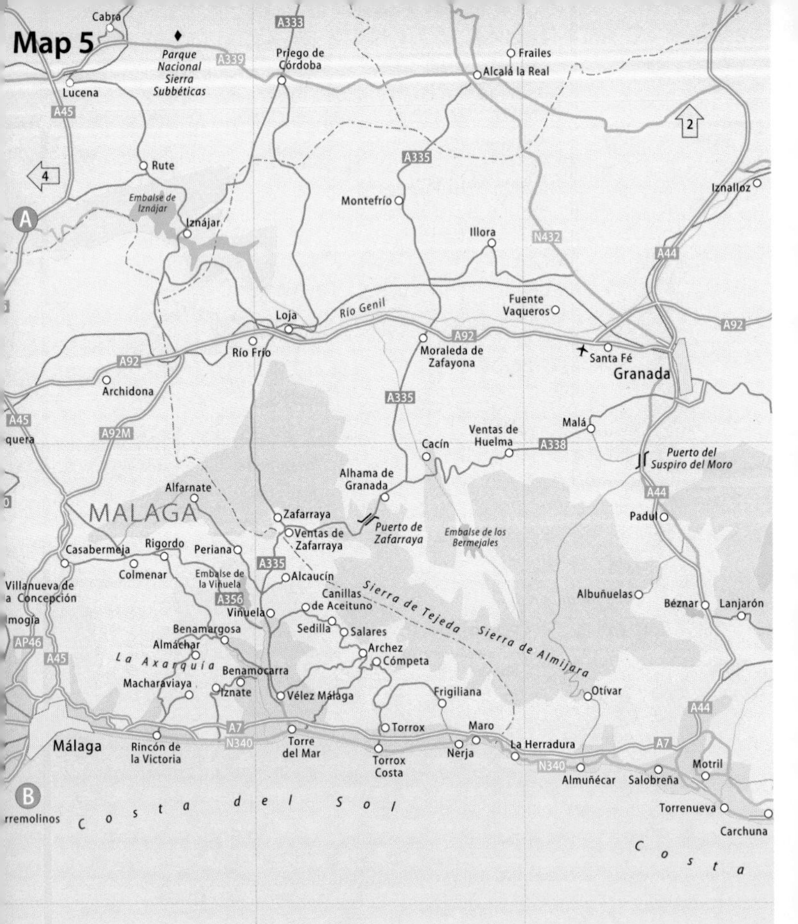

Mediterranean Sea

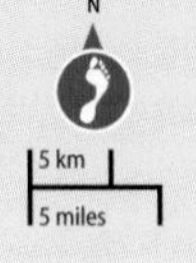

C

1 2 3

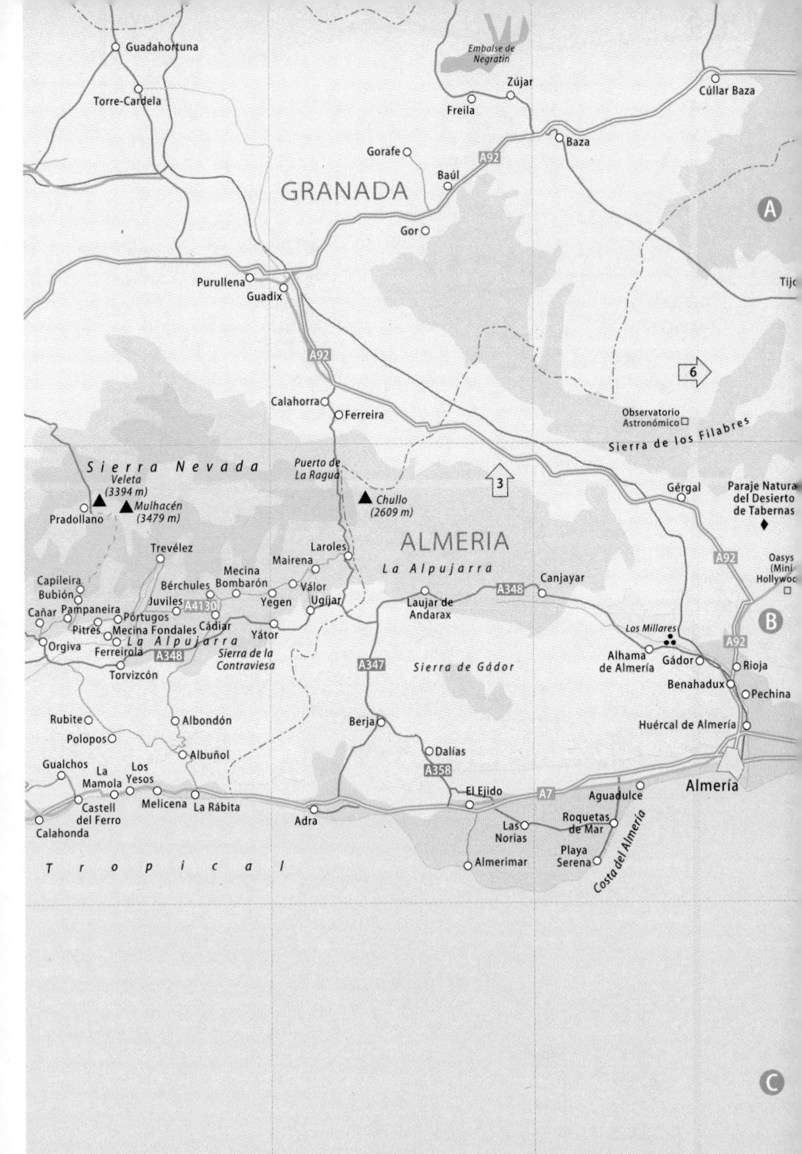

Guadahortuna
Torre-Cardela
Embalse de Negratín
Zújar
Freila
Cúllar Baza
Baza
Gorafe
A92
Baúl
GRANADA
A
Gor
Purullena
Guadix
Tíj
A92
6
Calahorra
Ferreira
Observatorio Astronómico
Sierra de los Filabres
Sierra Nevada
Puerto de La Ragua
Veleta (3394 m)
3
Gérgal
Paraje Natural del Desierto de Tabernas
Chullo (2609 m)
Pradollano
Mulhacén (3479 m)
ALMERIA
Trevélez
Laroles
A92
Oasys (Mini Hollywood)
Mairena
La Alpujarra
Mecina Bombarón
Capileira
Bérchules
Válor
Canjayar
Bubión
A348
Juviles
Yegen
Laujar de Andarax
A4130
Ugíjar
Cañar
Pampaneira
Pórtugos
B
Cádiar
Pitres
Mecina Fondales
Yátor
Los Millares
Orgiva
La Alpujarra
A92
Ferreirola
Alhama de Almería
Gádor
Rioja
A348
Sierra de la Contraviesa
A347
Sierra de Gádor
Torvizcón
Benahadux
Pechina
Rubite
Albondón
Berja
Huércal de Almería
Polopos
Dalías
Albuñol
Gualchos
La Mamola
Los Yesos
A358
Almería
El Ejido
A7
Aguadulce
Castell del Ferro
Melicena
La Rábita
Adra
Calahonda
Las Norias
Roquetas de Mar
Playa Serena
Almerimar
Costa del Almería
Tropical
C
4
5
6

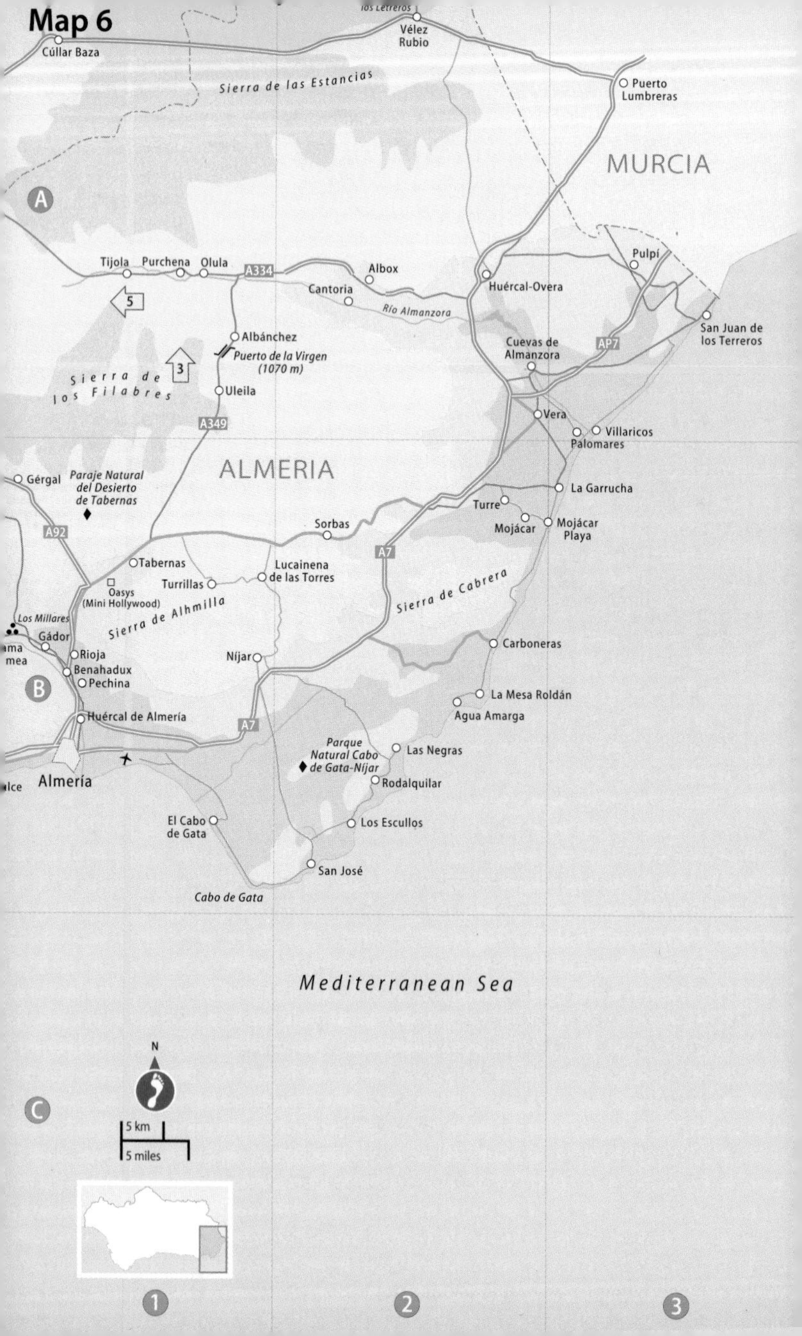

Map 6
los Letreros
Vélez Rubio
Cúllar Baza
Sierra de las Estancias
Puerto Lumbreras
MURCIA
A
Tijola
Purchena
Olula
A334
Albox
Cantoria
Huércal-Overa
Pulpí
Río Almanzora
5
Albánchez
Puerto de la Virgen (1070 m)
3
Sierra de los Filabres
Uleila
A349
San Juan de los Terreros
AP7
Cuevas de Almanzora
Vera
Villaricos
Palomares
ALMERIA
Gérgal
Paraje Natural del Desierto de Tabernas
A92
La Garrucha
Turre
Mojácar
Mojácar Playa
Sorbas
A7
Tabernas
Lucainena de las Torres
Turrillas
Oasys (Mini Hollywood)
Sierra de Alhmilla
Sierra de Cabrera
Los Millares
Gádor
Rioja
Benahadux
Pechina
Níjar
Carboneras
B
La Mesa Roldán
Agua Amarga
Huércal de Almería
Parque Natural Cabo de Gata-Níjar
Las Negras
Almería
Rodalquilar
El Cabo de Gata
Los Escullos
San José
Cabo de Gata
Mediterranean Sea
N
C
5 km
5 miles
1
2
3

Practicalities Andalucía

Getting there

Air

There are numerous options for reaching Andalucía. Six airports in the region (Sevilla, Málaga, Almería, Granada and Jerez de la Frontera, as well as Gibraltar) are served regularly by flights from a wide variety of European cities; add in all the standard and charter flights, and it's one of Europe's easiest destinations to reach.

Charter flights are cheaper and are run by package holiday firms. You can find bargains through travel agencies or online. The drawback of these flights is that they usually have a fixed return flight, often only a week or a fortnight later, and they frequently depart at antisocial hours. An upside is that charter flights operate from many regional airports.

Before booking, it's worth doing a bit of online research. Three of the best search engines for flight comparisons are www.opodo.com, www.skyscanner.com and www.kayak.com, which compare prices from a range of agencies. To keep up to date with the ever-changing routes available, sites like www.flightmapper.net are handy. Flightchecker (http://flightchecker.moneysavingexpert.com) is handy for checking multiple dates for budget airline deals.

Flights from the UK

Competition has benefited travellers in recent years. Budget operators have taken a significant slice of the market and forced other airlines to compete.

Budget There are numerous budget connections from the UK to Málaga. **Easyjet** and **Ryanair** connect Andalucía – particularly Málaga – with over a dozen UK airports, while other budget airlines running various routes from the UK to Andalucía include **Flybe**, **Vueling**, **Norwegian**, **Jet2**, **Thomson** and **Monarch**. Apart from Málaga, there are lots of flights to Almería, several to Sevilla and Granada, and some to Jerez de la Frontera and Gibraltar.

Charter There are numerous charter flights to Málaga (and some to Almería) from many British and Irish airports. **Avro** ⓘ *www.avro.co.uk*, **Thomas Cook** ⓘ *www.thomascook.com*, and **Thomson** ⓘ *www.thomson.co.uk*, are some of the best charter flight providers, but it's also worth checking the travel pages of newspapers for cheap deals. The website www.flightsdirect.com is also a good tool to search for charter flights.

Non-budget flights Málaga again has the most scheduled flights, with several airlines including **Iberia** and **British Airways** flying direct from London airports and a few other UK cities. From London, there are daily direct flights to Sevilla and Granada with **Iberia/BA** and connections via Madrid and Barcelona to several other Andalucian airports.

TRAVEL TIP

Packing for Andalucía

Spain is a modern European country, and you can buy almost everything you'll need here; packing light is the way to go. If you're venturing inland, remember that it can get distinctly chilly outside of summer in places like Granada and Ronda. Pack a beach towel, sunscreen and swimsuit for the coast. A GPS device is handy for navigating and a European adaptor (plug a double adaptor into it) is a must for recharging electrical goods (see page 509).

Flights from the rest of Europe

There are numerous budget airlines operating from European and Spanish cities to Málaga and Almería.

Numerous charter flights operate to Málaga and some to Almería from Germany, Scandinavia, France, the Netherlands and Belgium.

There are non-stop flights to Málaga with non-budget airlines from many major European cities. There are daily non-stop flights to Sevilla from a few European capitals. Flying from these or other western European cities via Madrid or Barcelona usually costs about the same.

Flights from North America and Canada

Delta fly direct from New York to Málaga, while there are fortnightly charter flights from Montreal and Toronto with **Air Transat**. Otherwise, you'll have to connect via Madrid, Barcelona, Lisbon, London or another European city to Andalucían airports. Although sometimes you'll pay little extra to Andalucía than the Madrid flight, you can often save considerably by flying to Madrid and getting the bus down south or book a domestic connection on the local no-frills airline **Vueling** ⓘ *www.vueling.com*, or **Ryanair** ⓘ *www.ryanair.com*.

Flights from Australia and New Zealand

There are no direct flights to Spain from Australia or New Zealand; the cheapest and quickest way is to connect via Frankfurt, Paris or London. It might turn out cheaper to book the Europe–Spain leg separately via a budget operator.

Road

Bus

Eurolines ⓘ *T01582-404511, www.eurolines.com*, runs several buses from major European cities to a variety of destinations in Andalucía, but you won't get there cheaper than a flight.

Car and sea

It's a long haul to Andalucía by road if you're not already in the peninsula. From the UK, you have two options if you want to take the car: take a ferry to northern Spain (www.brittany-ferries.co.uk), or cross the Channel to France and then drive down. The former option is much more expensive; it would usually work out far cheaper to fly to Andalucía and hire a car once you get there. For competitive fares by sea to France and Spain, check with **Ferrysavers** ⓘ *www.ferrysavers.com*, or **Direct Ferries** ⓘ *www.directferries.com*.

Andalucía is about 2000 km from London by road; a dedicated drive will get you there in 20-24 driving hours. By far the fastest route is to head down the west coast of France and to Burgos via San Sebastián. From here, for eastern and central Andalucía head south via Madríd, for western Andalucía, head for Salamanca then south.

Train

Unless you've got a rail pass, love train travel or aren't too keen on planes, forget about getting to Andalucía by train from anywhere further than France; you'll save no money over the plane fare and use up days of time better spent in tapas bars. You'll have to connect via either Barcelona or Madrid. Getting to Madrid/Barcelona from London takes about a day using **Eurostar** ⓘ *www.eurostar.com, £100-250 return to Paris, and another €130 or more return to reach Madrid/Barcelona from there*. Using the train/Channel ferry combination will more or less halve the cost and double the time to Paris.

If you are planning the train journey, **Voyages-SNCF** ⓘ *www.voyages-sncf.com*, is a useful company. **RENFE**, Spain's rail network, has online timetables at www.renfe.com. Best of all is the extremely useful www.seat61.com.

Getting around

Public transport between the cities of Andalucía is good, with lots of bus services, and several fast train connections.

Air

Andalucía has several airports that are serviced regularly from Barcelona and Madrid, but there are no flights between the cities themselves, so once you're in the region, you're better off staying on the ground rather than backtracking through Madrid. Full-fare domestic flights are expensive, but budget airlines **Vueling** and **Ryanair** offer domestic routes. Most internal flights in Spain are operated by **Iberia**; **Air Europa** also run some routes. If you're flying into Spain from overseas, a domestic leg can often be added at comparatively little cost.

If you're flying into Spain from outside Europe on a **OneWorld** affiliate airline, you may want to consider the OneWorld Visit Europe airpass, which offers set-rate flights with Iberia. The same rates apply for flights all around Europe. See www.oneworld.com for more details.

Road

Bus

Buses are the staple of Spanish public transport. Services between major cities are fast, frequent, reliable and fairly cheap; the six-hour trip from Madrid to Sevilla, for example, costs €23. When buying a ticket, always check how long the journey will take, as the odd bus will be an 'all stations to' job, calling in at villages that seem surprised to even see it.

Most cities have a single terminal, the *estación de autobuses*. Buy your tickets at the relevant window; if there isn't one, buy it from the driver. Superior classes may cost up to 60% more but offer lounge access and onboard service. Newer buses in all classes may offer Wi-Fi, personal entertainment system and sockets. Most tickets will have an *asiento* (seat number) on them; ask when buying the ticket if you prefer a *ventana* (window) or *pasillo* (aisle) seat. Some of the companies allow booking online or by phone. If you're travelling at busy times (particularly a fiesta or national holiday) always book the bus ticket in advance.

Rural bus services are slower, less frequent and more difficult to coordinate.

All bus services are reduced on Sundays and, to a lesser extent, on Saturdays; some services don't run at all on weekends.

Car

Roads and motorways The roads in Andalucía are good, excellent in many parts. While driving isn't as sedate as in parts of northern Europe, it's generally pretty good and you'll have few problems. The roads near the coast, dense with partygoers and sunseekers, can be dangerous in summer, particularly the stretch along the Costa del Sol.

There are two types of motorway in Spain, *autovías* and *autopistas*; for drivers, they are little different. They are signposted in blue and may have tolls payable, in which case there'll be a red warning circle on the blue sign when you're entering the motorway. Tolls are generally reasonable; the quality of motorway is generally excellent. The speed limit on motorways is 120 kph, though it is scheduled to rise to 130 kph on some stretches.

Rutas Nacionales form the backbone of the country's road network. Centrally administered, they vary wildly in quality. Typically, they are choked with traffic backed up behind trucks, and there are few stretches of dual carriageway. Driving at siesta time is a good idea if you're going to be on a busy stretch. *Rutas Nacionales* are marked with a red N followed by a number. The speed limit is 100 kph outside built-up areas, as it is for secondary roads, which are usually marked with an A (Andalucía), or C (*comarcal*, or local) prefix.

In urban areas, the speed limit is 50 kph. City driving can be confusing, with signposting generally poor and traffic heavy; it's worth using a Satnav or printing off the directions that your hotel may send you with a reservation. In some towns and cities, many of the hotels are officially signposted, making things easier. Larger cities may have their historic quarter blocked off by barriers; if your hotel lies within these, ring the buzzer and say the name of the hotel, and the barriers will open. Other cities enforce restrictions by camera, so you'll have to give your number plate details to the hotel so they can register it.

Police are increasingly enforcing speed limits in Spain, and foreign drivers are liable to a large on-the-spot fine. Drivers can also be punished for not carrying two red warning triangles to place on the road in case of breakdown, a bulb-replacement kit and a fluorescent green waistcoat to wear if you break down by the side of the road. Drink driving is being cracked down on; the limit is 0.5 g/l of blood, a little lower than the equivalent in the UK, for example.

Parking Parking is a problem in nearly every town and city in Andalucía. Red or yellow lines on the side of the street mean no parking. Blue or white lines mean that some restrictions are in place; a sign will indicate what these are (typically it means that the parking is metered). Parking meters can usually only be dosed up for a maximum of two hours, but they take a siesta at lunchtime too. Print the ticket off and display it in the car. If you overstay and get fined, you can pay it off for minimal cost at the machine if you do it within an hour of the fine being issued. Parking fines are never pursued for foreign vehicles, but if it's a hire car you'll likely be liable for it. Underground car parks are common, but pricey; €15-20 a day is normal. The website www.parkopedia.es is useful for locating underground car parks and comparing their rates.

Documentation To drive in Spain, you'll need a full driving licence from your home country. This applies to virtually all foreign nationals but, in practice, if you're from an 'unusual' country, consider an International Driving Licence or official translation of your licence into Spanish.

Liability insurance is required for every car driven in Spain and you must carry proof of it. If bringing your own car, check carefully with your insurers that you're covered and get a certificate (green card).

Car hire Hiring a car in Andalucía is easy and cheap. The major multinationals have offices at all large towns and airports. Prices start at around €150 per week for a small car with unlimited mileage. You'll need a credit card and most agencies will either not accept under-25s or demand a surcharge. By far the cheapest place to hire a car is Málaga, where even at the airport there are competitive rates. With the bigger companies, it's always cheaper to book over the internet. The best way to look for a deal is using a price-comparison website like www.kayak.com. Drop-offs in other cities, which used to be ridiculously punitive, are now often much more affordable.

There are often hidden charges, the most common being compulsory purchase of a tank of petrol at an overpriced rate. You then have to return the car with the tank empty.

Cycling and motorcycling

Motorcycling is a good way to enjoy Andalucía and there are few difficulties to trouble the biker; bike shops and mechanics are relatively common. There are comparatively few outlets for motorcycle hire.

Cycling presents a curious contrast; Spaniards are mad for the competitive sport, but essentially disinterested in cycling as a means of transport, though local governments are trying to encourage it with new bike lanes and free borrowable bikes in cities. Thus there are plenty of cycling shops but few cycle-friendly features on the roads. Taking your own bike to Andalucía is well worth the effort as most airlines are happy to accept them, providing they come within your baggage allowance. Bikes can be taken on the train, but have to travel in the guard's van and must be registered.

Hitchhiking

Hitchhiking is fairly easy in Spain, although not much practised. The police aren't too keen on it, but with sensible placement and a clearly written sign, you'll usually get a lift without a problem, particularly in rural areas, where, in the absence of bus services, it's a more common way for locals to get about.

Taxi and bus

Most Andalucían cities have their sights closely packed into the centre, so you won't find local buses particularly necessary. There's a fairly comprehensive network in most towns, though; the travel text indicates where they come in handy. Taxis are a good option; the minimum charge is around €2.50 in most places (it increases slightly at night and on Sundays). A taxi is available if its green light is lit; hail one on the street, call, or ask for the nearest *parada de taxis* (rank). If you're using a cab to get to somewhere beyond the city limits, there are fixed tariffs.

Train

The Spanish national rail network, **RENFE** ⓘ *T902-240202 (English-speaking operators), www.renfe.com for timetables and tickets*, is, thanks to its growing network of high-speed trains, a useful option. **AVE** trains run from Madrid to Córdoba, Sevilla and Málaga and, though expensive, cover these large distances impressively quickly and reliably. Elsewhere in Andalucía though, you'll find the bus is often quicker and cheaper.

Prices vary significantly according to the type of service you are using. The standard high-speed intercity service is called *Talgo*, while other intercity services are labelled *Altaria*, *Intercity*, *Diurno* and *Estrella* (overnight). Slower local trains are called *regionales*. Alvia is a mixed AVE-Talgo service.

It's always worth buying a ticket in advance for long-distance travel, as trains are often full. The best option is to buy them via the website, which sometimes offers advance purchase discounts. The website is notoriously unreliable, with not all services appearing, and a clunky mechanism for finding connections. You can print out the ticket yourself, or print it at a railway station using the reservation code. If buying your ticket at the station, allow plenty of time for queuing. Ticket windows are labelled *venta anticipada* (in advance) and *venta inmediata* (six hours or less before the journey).

All Spanish trains are non-smoking. The faster trains will have a first-class (*preferente*) and second-class sections as well as a cafeteria. First class costs about 30% more than standard and can be a worthwhile deal on a crowded long journey. Families and groups can take advantage of the cheap 'mesa' tickets, where you reserve four seats around a table. Buying a return ticket is 10% to 20% cheaper than two singles, but you qualify for this discount even if you buy the return leg later (but not on every service).

An **ISIC student card** or **youth card** grants a discount of 20% to 25% on train services. If you're using a European railpass, be aware that you'll still have to make a reservation on Spanish trains and pay the small reservation fee (which covers your insurance). If you have turned 60, it's worth paying €6 for a Tarjeta Dorada, a seniors' card that gets you a discount of 40% on trains from Monday to Thursday, and 25% at other times.

Maps

A useful website for route planning is www.guiarepsol.com. Car hire companies have Satnavs available, though they cost a hefty supplement.

Essentials A-Z

Accidents and emergencies

General emergencies 112.

Children

Kids are kings in Spain and it's one of the easiest places to take them along on holiday. Children socialize with their parents from an early age and you'll see them eating in restaurants and out in bars well after midnight. Outdoor summer life and pedestrianized areas of cities make for a stress-free time for both you and the kids.

Spaniards are friendly and accommodating towards children and you'll undoubtedly get treated better with them than without them, except perhaps in the most expensive restaurants and hotels. Few places, however, are equipped with highchairs or baby-changing facilities. Children are expected to eat the same sort of things as their parents, although you'll sometimes see a *menú infantil* at a restaurant, which typically has simpler dishes and smaller portions. As for attractions, beaches are an obvious highlight, but many of the newer museums are hands-on. Spanish campsites are well set up; the larger ones often with child-minding facilities.

The cut-off age for children paying half or being free on public transport and in tourist attractions varies widely. RENFE trains let under-4s on free and offer discounts of around 50% for 4-12 year-olds. Most car-rental companies have child seats available, but it's wise to book these in advance, particularly in summer.

Bear in mind that Andalucía can get unbearably hot in the summer, particularly in certain spots like Sevilla.

Customs and duty free

Non-EU citizens are allowed to import 1 litre of spirits, 2 litres of wine and 200 cigarettes or 250 g of tobacco or 50 cigars. EU citizens are theoretically limited by personal use only. Gibraltar is not part of the EU economic zone, so normal duty-free limits apply.

Disabled travellers

Spain isn't the best equipped of countries in terms of disabled travel, but things are improving rapidly. By law, all new public buildings have to have full disabled access and facilities, but disabled toilets are rare elsewhere. Facilities generally are significantly better in Andalucía than in the rest of the country.

Most trains and stations are wheelchair friendly to some degree, as are many urban buses, but intercity buses are largely not accessible. **Hertz** in Málaga and Sevilla have a small range of cars set up with hand controls, but be sure to book them well in advance. Nearly all underground and municipal car parks have lifts and disabled spaces, as do many museums, castles, etc.

An invaluable resource for finding a bed are the regional accommodation lists, available from tourist offices and the www.andalucia.org website. Most of these include a disabled-access criterion. Many *hostales* are in buildings with ramps and lifts, but there are many that are not, and the lifts can be very small. Nearly all paradores and chain hotels are fully accessible by wheelchair, as is any accommodation built since 1995, but it's best to phone. Be sure to check details as many hotels' claims are well intentioned but not fully thought through.

While major cities are relatively straightforward, smaller towns and villages frequently have uneven footpaths, steep streets (often cobbled) and little, if any, disabled infrastructure.

Useful contacts

Confederación Nacional de Sordos de España (CNSE), www.cnse.es, has links to local associations for the deaf.
Global Access, www.globalaccessnews.com, has regular reports from disabled travellers as well as links to other sites.
Mobility Abroad, T0871-277 0888 (UK) or T+34-952 447764 (Spain), www.mobilityabroad.com, is a Málaga-based organization that provides support and hire of wheelchairs and disabled vehicles throughout the Costa del Sol area.
ONCE, www.once.es. The blind are well catered for as a result of the efforts of ONCE, the national organization for the blind, which runs a lucrative daily lottery. It can provide information on accessible attractions for blind travellers.

Electricity

230V. A round 2-pin plug is used (European standard).

Embassies and consulates

For a list of Spanish embassies abroad, see http://embassy.goabroad.com.

Gay and lesbian travellers

Homosexuality is legal, as is gay marriage, though it's just the sort of thing the incumbent Partido Popular would like to revoke. There are different levels of tolerance and open-mindedness towards gays and lesbians in Andalucía. In the larger cities and on the coast (particularly in summer), there's a substantial amount of gay life, although not on a par with Barcelona or Madrid. Inland, however, it can be a different story, and a couple walking hand-in-hand will likely be greeted with incredulous stares, although rarely anything worse.. The most active scenes can be found in Cádiz, Torremolinos, Marbella and, in summer, El Puerto de Santa María.

Useful contacts

COLEGA, www.colegaweb.org. A gay and lesbian association with offices in many cities.
Shangay/Shanguide, www.shangay.com, is a useful magazine with reviews, events, information and city-by-city listings for the whole country.

Useful websites

www.damron.com Subscription listings and travel info.

Health

Medical facilities in Andalucía are very good. However, EU citizens should make sure they have the **European Health Insurance Card** (EHIC) to prove reciprocal rights to medical care. These are available free of charge in the UK from the Department of Health (www.dh.gov.uk) or post offices.

Non-EU citizens should consider travel insurance to cover emergency and routine medical needs; be sure that it covers any sports or activities you may do. Check for reciprocal cover with your private or public health scheme first.

Water is safe to drink. The **sun** in southern Spain can be harsh, so take precautions to avoid heat exhaustion and sunburn.

Many medications that require a prescription in other countries are available over the counter at pharmacies in Spain. Pharmacists are highly trained and usually speak some English. In medium-sized towns and cities, at least one pharmacy is open 24 hrs; this is performed on a rota system (posted in the window of all pharmacies and listed in local newspapers).

No vaccinations are needed.

Insurance

Insurance is a good idea to cover you for theft. In the unlucky event of theft, you'll have to make a report at the local police station within 24 hrs and obtain a *denuncia* (report) to show your insurers. See above for health cover for EU citizens.

Internet

Cyber cafés are increasingly rare in Spain, though you'll still find them in large cities. Other places that often offer access are *locutorios* (call shops), which are common in areas with a high immigrant population. Most accommodation and an increasing number of cafés and restaurants offer Wi-Fi. Internet places tend to appear and disappear rapidly, so we have minimized listings in this guide; ask the tourist information office for the latest place to get online. Mobile phone providers offer pay-as-you-go data SIM cards and USB modems at a reasonable rate. Roaming charges within the EU are set to be abolished in late 2015, so mobile data usage will cost EU residents no more in Andalucía than it would in your home country.

Language

Everyone in Andalucía – except many of the large expat population – speaks Spanish, known either as *castellano* or *español*, and it's a huge help to know some. The local accent, *andaluz*, is characterized by dropping consonants left, right and centre, thus *dos tapas* tends to be pronounced *dotapa*. Unlike in the rest of Spain, the letters 'c' and 'z' in words such as *cerveza* aren't pronounced 'th' (although in Cádiz province, perversely, they tend to pronounce 's' with that sound).

Most young people know some English, and standards are rising fast, but don't assume that people aged 40 or over know any at all. Spaniards are often shy to attempt to speak English. On the coast, high numbers of expats and tourists mean that bartenders and shopkeepers know some English. While many visitor attractions have some sort of information available in English (and to a lesser extent French and German), many don't, or have English tours only in times of high demand. Most tourist office staff will speak at least some English and there's a good range of translated information available in most places. People are used to speaking English in well-visited areas, but trying even a couple of words of Spanish is basic politeness. Small courtesies grease the wheels of everyday interaction here: greet the proprietor or waiting staff when entering a shop or bar, and say *hasta luego* when leaving. See page 518, for useful words and phrases in Spanish.

Language schools

Sevilla and Granada have the most language schools; see boxes on pages 78 and 339.

Amerispan, www.amerispan.com. Immersion programmes throughout Spain.

Escuela Hispalense, Av Fuerzas Armadas 1, T956-680927, www.hispalense.com, Tarifa.

Instituto Picasso, Pl de la Merced 20, Málaga, T952-213932, www.instituto-picasso.com.

Languages Abroad, www.languagesabroad.com. Immersion courses in Andalucían cities.

Linguae Mundi, C Enrique Rivero 18, Jerez de la Frontera, T956-349696, www.linguae-mundi.com.

Spanish Abroad, www.spanishabroad.com. 2-week immersion language courses in several Andalucían locations including Granada, Málaga, Sevilla, Marbella and Vejer de la Frontera.

Media

Newspapers and magazines

The Spanish press is generally of a high journalistic standard. The national dailies, *El País* (still a qualitative leap ahead), *El Mundo* and the rightist *ABC*, are read throughout the country, but local papers are widely read in Andalucía. Overall circulation is low, partly because many people read newspapers provided in cafés and bars. Each major city has its own newspaper; in Sevilla, *El Correo* is one of the best. Large cities will also have 'what's on' magazines, often distributed in tourist offices or bars.

The terribly Real Madrid-biased sports dailies *Marca* and *As*, dedicated mostly to football, have a large readership that rivals any of the broadsheets. There's no tabloid press as such; the closest equivalent is the *prensa de corazón* and the gossip magazines such as *¡Hola!*, forerunner of Britain's *Hello!* English-language newspapers are widely available in kiosks in larger towns and tourist resorts. Several English dailies now have European editions available on the day of publication; the same goes for major European dailies. There are a number of free English-language newspapers, which are usually vehicles only for details on local events, real estate listings and idle gossip. An exception is the English edition of Málaga's newspaper *Sur*, www.surinenglish.com.

Radio

Radio is big in Spain, with audience figures relatively higher than most of Europe. There's a huge range of stations, mainly on FM wavelengths, many of them broadcasting to a fairly small regional area. You'll be unlikely to get much exposure to it (beyond the top-40 music stations blaring in bars) unless you're in a car.

TV

TV is the dominant medium in Spain, with audience figures well above most of the EU. The main channels are the state-run *TVE1*, with standard programming, and *TVE2*, with a more cultural/sporting bent alongside the private *Antena 3*, *Cuatro* and *Tele 5*, *La Sexta (6)*, and *Canal Plus*. Regional stations also draw audiences. Overall quality is low, with reality shows and lowest-common-denominator kitsch as popular here as anywhere. Cable TV is widespread, and satellite and digital have a wide market.

Money

Currency and exchange

For up-to-the-minute exchange rates visit www.xe.com.

In 2002, Spain switched to the euro, bidding farewell to the peseta. The euro (€) is divided into 100 *céntimos*. Euro notes are standard across the whole euro zone and come in denominations of 5, 10, 20, 50, 100, and the rarely seen 200 and 500. Coins have one standard face and one national face; all coins are, however, acceptable in all countries. The coins are slightly difficult to tell apart when you're not used to them. The coppers are 1, 2 and 5 cent pieces, the golds are 10, 20 and 50, and the silver/gold combinations are €1 and €2. The exchange rate was approximately €6 to 1000 pesetas or 166 pesetas to the euro. Some people still quote large amounts, like house prices, in pesetas.

ATMs and banks

The best way to get money in Spain is by plastic. ATMs are plentiful and accept all the major international debit and credit cards. The Spanish bank won't charge for the transaction, though they will charge a mark-up on the exchange rate, but beware of your own bank hitting you for a hefty fee: check with them before leaving home. Even if they do, it's likely to be a better deal than changing cash over a counter.

Banks are usually open Mon-Fri (and Sat in winter) 0830-1430 and many change foreign money (sometimes only the central branch in a town will do it). Commission rates vary widely; it's usually best to change large amounts, as there's often a minimum commission. The website www.moneysavingexpert.com has a good rundown on the most economical ways of accessing cash while travelling.

Cost of living

Prices have soared since the euro was introduced; some basics rose by 50-80% in 3 years, and hotel and restaurant prices can even seem dear by Western European standards these days. Nevertheless, Andalucía still offers value for money, and you can get by cheaply if you forgo a few luxuries. If you're travelling as a pair, staying in cheap *pensiones*, eating a set meal at lunchtime, travelling short distances by bus or train daily, and snacking on tapas in the evenings, €65 per person per day is reasonable. If you camp and grab picnic lunches from shops, you could reduce this somewhat. In a good *hostal* or cheap hotel and using a car, €150 a day and you'll not be counting pennies; €300 per day and you'll be very comfy indeed unless you're staying in 5-star accommodation.

Accommodation is usually more expensive in summer than winter, particularly on the coast, where hotels and *hostales* in seaside towns are overpriced. Sevilla is noticeably pricier than elsewhere in Andalucía.

Public transport is generally cheap; intercity bus services are quick and low-priced, though the new fast trains are expensive. If you're hiring a car, Málaga is the cheapest place in Andalucía. Standard unleaded petrol is around 150 cents per litre. In some places, particularly in tourist areas, you may be charged up to 20% more to sit outside a restaurant. It's also worth checking if the 10% IVA (sales tax) is included in menu prices, especially in the more expensive restaurants; it should say on the menu.

Opening hours

Business hours Mon-Fri 1000-1400, 1700-2000; Sat 1000-1400. **Banks** Mon-Fri, plus sometimes Sat in winter, 0830-1430. **Government offices** Mornings only.

Post

The Spanish post is still notoriously inefficient and slow by European standards. *Correos* (post offices) generally open Mon-Fri 0800-1300, 1700-2000; Sat 0800-1300, although main offices in large towns will stay open all day. Stamps can be bought here or at *estancos* (tobacconists).

Public holidays

1 Jan **Año Nuevo**, New Year's Day.
6 Jan **Reyes Magos/Epifanía**, Epiphany, when Christmas presents are given.
28 Feb **Andalucía day**.
Easter **Jueves Santo, Viernes Santo, Día de Pascua** (Maundy Thu, Good Fri, Easter Sun).
1 May **Fiesta del Trabajo** (Labour Day).
24 Jun **Fiesta de San Juan** (Feast of St John and name-day of the king Juan Carlos I).
25 Jul **Día del Apostol Santiago**, Feast of St James.
15 Aug **Asunción**, Feast of the Assumption.
12 Oct **Día de la Hispanidad**, Spanish National Day (Columbus Day, Feast of the Virgin of the Pillar).
1 Nov **Todos los Santos**, All Saints' Day.
6 Dec **El Día de la Constitución Española**, Constitution Day.
8 Dec **Inmaculada Concepción**, Feast of the Immaculate Conception.
25 Dec **Navidad**, Christmas Day.

Safety

Andalucía is a very safe place to travel. There's been a crackdown on tourist crime in recent years and even large cities like Sevilla and Málaga feel much safer than their equivalents in, say, England.

What tourist crime there is tends to be of the opportunistic kind. Robberies from parked cars (particularly those with foreign plates) or snatch-and-run thefts from vehicles stopped at traffic lights are not unknown, and the occasional mugger operates in the cities of Sevilla, Málaga and Granada. Keep car doors locked when driving in those big cities. If parking in a city or a popular hiking zone, make it clear there's nothing worth robbing in a car by opening the glove compartment.

If you are unfortunate enough to be robbed, you should report the theft immediately at the nearest police station, as insurance companies will require a copy of the *denuncia* (police report).

Smoking

Smoking is widespread in Spain, but it's been banned in all enclosed public spaces (ie bars and restaurants) since 2011. There are still rooms for smokers in some hotels, but these are limited to 30% of the total rooms. Prices are standardized; you can buy cigarettes at tobacconists or at machines in cafés and bars (with a small surcharge).

Student travellers

An **International Student Identity Card** (ISIC; www.isic.org), for full-time students, is worth having in Spain. Get one at your place of study, or at many travel agencies both in and outside Spain. The cost varies from country to country, but is generally about €6-10 – a good investment, providing discounts of up to 20% on some plane fares, train tickets, museum entries, bus tickets and some accommodation. A **European Youth Card** (www.eyca.org) card gives similar discounts for anyone under 30 years of age.

Taxes

Nearly all goods and services in Spain are subject to a value-added tax (IVA). This is 10% for things like supermarket supplies, hotels and restaurant meals, but is 21% on luxury goods such as computer equipment. IVA is normally included in the stated prices. You're technically entitled to claim it back if you're a non-EU citizen, for purchases over €90. If you're buying something pricey, make sure you get a stamped receipt clearly showing the IVA component, as well as your name and passport number; you can claim the amount back at major airports on departure. Some shops will have a form to smooth the process.

Telephone

Country code +34; **IDD Code** 00
Phone booths on the street are dwindling. Those that remain are mostly operated by **Telefónica**, and all have international direct dialling. They accept coins from €0.05 upwards and phone cards, which can be bought from *kioscos* (newspaper kiosks).

Domestic landlines have 9-digit numbers beginning with 9. Although the first 3 digits indicate the province, you have to dial the full number from wherever you are calling, including abroad. Mobile numbers start with 6.

Most foreign mobiles will work in Spain (although older North American ones won't); check with your service provider about what the call costs will be like. Roaming charges within the EU are set to be abolished from late 2015. Many mobile networks require you to call before leaving your home country to activate overseas service (roaming). If you're staying a while and have an unlocked phone, it's pretty cheap to buy a Spanish SIM card.

Time

1 hr ahead of GMT. Clocks go forward an hour in late Mar and back in late Oct with the rest of the EU.

Tipping

Tipping in Spain is far from compulsory. A 10% tip would be considered extremely generous in a restaurant; 3% to 5% is more usual. It's rare for a service charge to be added to a bill. Waiters don't expect tips but in bars and cafés people will sometimes leave small change, especially for table service. Taxi drivers don't expect a tip, but will be pleased to receive one.

Tourist information

The tourist information infrastructure in Andalucía is organized by the Junta (the regional government) and is generally excellent, with a wide range of information, often in English, German and French as well as Spanish. The website www.andalucia.org has comprehensive information and *Oficinas de turismo* (local government tourist offices) are in all the major towns, providing more specific local information. In addition, many towns run a municipal *turismo*, offering locally produced material. The tourist offices are generally open during normal office hours and in the main holiday areas normally have enthusiastic, multilingual staff. The tourist offices can provide local maps and town plans and a full list of registered accommodation. Staff are not allowed to make recommendations. If you're in a car, it's especially worth asking for a listing of *casas rurales* (rural accommodation). In villages with no *turismo* you could try asking for local information on accommodation and sights in the *ayuntamiento* (town hall). Some city tourist offices offer downloadable smartphone content.

There is a substantial amount of tourist information on the internet. Apart from the websites listed (see below), many towns and villages have their own site with information on sights, hotels and restaurants, although this may be in Spanish.

The **Spanish Tourist Board** (www.spain.info) produces a mass of information that you can obtain before you leave from their offices located in many countries abroad.

Useful websites

www.alsa.es One of the country's main bus companies with online booking.
www.andalucia.com Excellent site with comprehensive practical and background information on Andalucía, covering everything from accommodation to zoos.
www.andalucia.org The official tourist-board site, with details of even the smallest villages, accommodation and tourist offices.
www.booking.com The most useful online accommodation booker for Spain.
www.dgt.es The transport department website has up-to-date information in Spanish on road conditions throughout the country.
www.elpais.com Online edition of Spain's biggest-selling daily paper. Also in English.
www.guiarepsol.com Online route planner for Spanish roads, also available in English.
www.inm.es Site of the national metereological institute, with the day's weather and next-day forecasts.
www.inturjoven.com Details of youth hostel locations, facilities and prices.
maps.google.es Street maps of most Spanish towns and cities.
www.movelia.es Online timetables and ticketing for some bus companies.
www.paginasamarillas.es Yellow Pages.
www.paginasblancas.es White Pages.
www.parador.es Parador information, including locations, prices and photos.
www.raar.es Andalucían rural accommodation network with details of mainly self-catering accommodation to rent, including cottages and farmhouses.
www.renfe.com Online timetables and tickets for RENFE train network.
www.spain.info The official website of the Spanish tourist board.
www.soccer-spain.com A website in English dedicated to Spanish football.
www.surinenglish.com The weekly English edition of the Málaga *Sur* paper.
www.ticketmaster.es Spain's biggest ticketing agency for concerts and more, with online purchase.
www.toprural.com and **www.todoturismorural.com** 2 of many sites for *casas rurales*.
www.tourspain.es A useful website run by the Spanish tourist board.
www.typicallyspanish.com News and links on all things Spanish.

Tour operators

UK and Ireland

Abercrombie and Kent, www.abercrombiekent.com. Upmarket operator offering tailor-made itineraries in Andalucía as well as the rest of Spain.
ACE Cultural Tours, www.acecultural tours.co.uk. Trips focusing on Moorish culture, as well as wildlife.
Andante Travels, www.andantetravels.com. Popular operator running a variety of different cultural and active holidays in Andalucía. They focus on archaeology and the Roman presence.
Arblaster & Clarke, www.winetours.co.uk. Experienced operator of wine tours, including a sherry-tasting extravaganza in Jerez, Sanlúcar de Barrameda, and El Puerto de Santa María.
Cycling Safaris, www.cyclingsafaris.com. Irish operator offering well-priced tours to Andalucía.
Exodus, www.exodus.co.uk. Walking and adventure tours to suit all pockets.
Iberocycle, www.iberocycle.com. Recommended bike tours, guided or self-guided, of Moorish heritage and the white towns.
In the Saddle, www.inthesaddle.com. Runs riding trips in the Costa de la Luz and the Sierra Nevada/Alpujarra regions.
Martin Randall Travel, www.martinrandall.com. Excellent cultural itineraries accompanied by lectures. Covers all the main cities, and also has an off-beat tour visiting some out-of-the-way spots.
Naturetrek, www.naturetrek.co.uk. Birdwatching and botanical tours in Andalucía, including the Coto Doñana national park.
Ornitholidays, www.ornitholidays.co.uk. Well-established set-up for birding trips to the Coto Doñana.
Step in Time Tours, www.stepintime tours.com. Tours that focus on Moorish culture and the cities of Córdoba, Granada, and Ronda. Inclusive ethos.

Rest of Europe

Bootlace Walking Holidays, www.bootlace.com. Down-to-earth Alpujarran walking trips with vegetarian food.
Bravo Bike Travel, www.bravobike.com. Runs 8-day bike tours of Andalucía.
Finca El Moro, www.fincaelmoro.com. Recommended walking and riding holidays in the Sierra de Aracena with accommodation and food on the farm.
Las Chimeneas, www.alpujarra-tours.com. Based in Mairena in the Alpujarra region, organize packages including sweet village accommodation and self-guided hikes as well as other activities.
Los Alamos Equestrian Holidays, www.losalamosriding.co.uk. Horse-riding trips around the beaches and forests of the Costa de la Luz.
Spain Birds, www.spain birds.com. Birdwatching tours and trips.

North America

Cycling Through The Centuries, www.cycling-centuries.com. Runs guided cycling tours of Andalucía.
Epiculinary Tours, www.epiculinary.com. Tours to delight foodies, with lessons on making tapas and other Andalucían food interspersed with plenty of tastings and cultural visits.
Heritage Tours, www.htprivatetravel.com. Interesting, classy itineraries around the south of Spain.
Magical Spain, www.magicalspain.com. American-run tour agency based in Sevilla, who runs a variety of tours.
Spain Adventures, www.spain adventures.com. Organizes a range of hiking and biking tours, including the

Sierra de Grazalema, Ronda and the Sierra de Aracena.

Australia

Ibertours,www.ibertours.com.au. Spanish specialist and booking agent for **Parador** and **Rusticae** hotels.

Timeless Tours & Travel, www.timeless.com.au. Specializes in tailored itineraries for Spain.

Visas and immigration

EU citizens and those from countries within the Schengen agreement can enter Spain freely. UK and Irish citizens will need to carry a passport, while an identity card suffices for other EU/Schengen nationals. Citizens of Australia, the USA, Canada, New Zealand, several Latin American countries and Israel can enter without a visa for up to 90 days. Other citizens will require a visa, obtainable from Spanish consulates or embassies. These are usually issued quickly and are valid for all Schengen countries. The basic visa is valid for 90 days, and you'll need 2 passport photos, proof of funds covering your stay, and possibly evidence of medical cover (ie insurance).

For extensions of visas, apply to an *oficina de extranjeros* in a major city (usually in the *comisaría*, main police station).

Weights and measures

Metric.

Women travellers

While there's still the odd wolf-whistling dinosaur lurking around Andalucía, female travellers shouldn't encounter any harassment at all. Topless sunbathing is common along the Andalucían coast on many beaches.

Working in the country

The most obvious paid work for English speakers is through teaching the language. Even the smallest towns usually have an English college or two. Rates of pay aren't great except in the large cities, but you can live quite comfortably. The best way of finding work is by trawling around the schools, but there are dozens of useful internet sites; check www.eslcafe.com for links and listings. There's also a more casual scene of private teaching; noticeboards in universities and student cafés are the best way to find work of this sort, or to advertise your own services. Standard rates for 1-to-1 classes are €15-30 per hr.

Bar work is also relatively easy to find, particularly in summer on the coast. Live-in English-speaking au pairs and childminders are also popular with wealthier city families. The **International Au Pair Association** (www.iapa.org) lists reliable agencies that arrange placements. The online forum **Au Pair World** (www.aupairworld.net) is a popular free service.

EU citizens are at an advantage when it comes to working in Spain; they can work without a permit. Non-EU citizens need a working visa, obtainable from Spanish embassies or consulates, but you'll need to have a firm offer of work to obtain it. Most English schools can organize this for you but make sure you arrange it before arriving in the country.

Another popular line of work for travellers is crewing on yachts; the best places to pick up work of this sort are Marbella/Puerto Banús, Ayamonte and Gibraltar.

Basic Spanish

Learning Spanish is a useful part of the preparation for a trip to Spain and no volumes of dictionaries, phrase books or word lists will provide the same enjoyment as being able to communicate directly with the people of the country you are visiting. It is a good idea to make an effort to grasp the basics before you go. As you travel you will pick up more of the language and the more you know, the more you will benefit from your stay. Regional accents and usages vary, but the basic language is essentially the same everywhere.

Vowels

a as in English *cat*
e as in English *best*
i as the ee in English *feet*
o as in English *shop*
u as the oo in English *food*
ai as the i in English *ride*
ei as ey in English *they*
oi as oy in English *toy*

Consonants

Most consonants can be pronounced more or less as they are in English. The exceptions are:

g before *e* or *i* is the same as *j*
h is always silent (except in *ch* as in *chair*)
j as the *ch* in Scottish *loch*
ll as the *y* in *yellow*
ñ as the *ni* in English *onion*
rr trilled much more than in English
x depending on its location, pronounced *x*, *s*, *sh* or *j*

Spanish words and phrases

Greetings, courtesies

hello *hola*
good morning *buenos días*
good afternoon/evening *buenas tardes/noches*
goodbye *adiós/hasta luego*
pleased to meet you *encantado/a*
how are you? *¿cómo estás?*
I'm called ... *me llamo ...*
what is your name? *¿cómo te llamas?*
I'm fine, thanks *muy bien, gracias*
yes/no *sí/no*
please *por favor*
thank you (very much) *(muchas) gracias*
I speak a little Spanish *hablo un poco de español*
I don't speak Spanish *no hablo español*
do you speak English? *¿hablas inglés?*
I don't understand *no entiendo*
please speak slowly *habla despacio por favor*
I am very sorry *lo siento mucho/discúlpame*
what do you want? *¿qué quieres?*
I want/would like *quiero/quería*
I don't want it *no lo quiero*
good/bad *bueno/malo*

Basic questions and requests

have you got a room for two people?
¿tienes una habitación para dos personas?
how do I get to_? *¿cómo llego a_?*
how much does it cost?
¿cuánto cuesta? ¿cuánto es?
is VAT included? *¿el IVA está incluido?*
when does the bus leave (arrive)?
¿a qué hora sale (llega) el autobús?
when? *¿cuándo?*
where is_? *¿dónde está_?*
where can I buy? *¿dónde puedo comprar...?*
where is the nearest petrol station?
¿dónde está la gasolinera más cercana?
why? *¿por qué?*

Basic words and phrases

bank *el banco*
bathroom/toilet *el baño*
to be *ser, estar*
bill *la factura/la cuenta*
cash *efectivo*
cheap *barato/a*
credit card *la tarjeta de crédito*
exchange rate *el tipo de cambio*
expensive *caro/a*
to go *ir*
to have *tener, haber*
market *el mercado*
note/coin *el billete/la moneda*
police (policeman) *la policía (el policía)*
post office *el correo*
public telephone *el teléfono público*
shop *la tienda*
supermarket *el supermercado*
there is/are *hay*
there isn't/aren't *no hay*
ticket office *la taquilla*
traveller's cheques *los cheques de viaje*

Getting around

aeroplane *el avión*
airport *el aeropuerto*
arrival/departure *la llegada/salida*
avenue *la avenida*
border *la frontera*
bus station *la estación de autobuses*
bus *el bus/el autobús/el camión*
corner *la esquina*
customs *la aduana*
left/right *izquierda/derecha*
ticket *el billete*
empty/full *vacío/lleno*
highway, main road *la carretera*
insurance *el seguro*
insured person *el asegurado/la asegurada*
luggage *el equipaje*
motorway, freeway *el autopista/autovía*
north/south/west/east *el norte, el sur, el oeste, el este*
oil *el aceite*
to park *aparcar*
passport *el pasaporte*
petrol/gasoline *la gasolina*
puncture *el pinchazo*
street *la calle*
that way *por allí*
this way *por aquí*
tyre *el neumático*
unleaded *sin plomo*
waiting room *la sala de espera*
to walk *caminar/andar*

Accommodation

air conditioning	*el aire acondicionado*
all-inclusive	*todo incluido*
bathroom, private	*el baño privado*
bed, double	*la cama matrimonial*
blankets	*las mantas*
to clean	*limpiar*
dining room	*el comedor*
hotel	*el hotel*
noisy	*ruidoso*
pillows	*las almohadas*
restaurant	*el restaurante*
room/bedroom	*la habitación*
sheets	*las sábanas*
shower	*la ducha*
soap	*el jabón*
toilet	*el inódoro*
toilet paper	*el papel higiénico*
towels, clean/dirty	*las toallas limpias sucias*
water, hot/cold	*el agua caliente/fría*

Health

aspirin	*la aspirina*
blood	*la sangre*
chemist	*la farmacia*
condoms	*los preservativos, los condones*
contact lenses	*los lentes de contacto*
contraceptives	*los anticonceptivos*
contraceptive pill	*la píldora anticonceptiva*
diarrhoea	*la diarrea*
doctor	*el médico*
fever/sweat	*la fiebre/el sudor*
pain	*el dolor*
head	*la cabeza*
period	*la regla*
sanitary towels	*las toallas femininas*
stomach	*el estómago*

Family

family	*la familia*
brother/sister	*el hermano/la hermana*
daughter/son	*la hija/el hijo*
father/mother	*el padre/la madre*
husband/wife	*el esposo (marido)/la mujer*
boyfriend/girlfriend	*el novio/la novia*
friend	*el amigo/la amiga*
married	*casado/a*
single/unmarried	*soltero/a*

Months, days and time

January	*enero*
February	*febrero*
March	*marzo*
April	*abril*
May	*mayo*
June	*junio*
July	*julio*
August	*agosto*
September	*septiembre*
October	*octubre*
November	*noviembre*
December	*diciembre*

Monday	*lunes*	it's one o'clock	*es la una*
Tuesday	*martes*	it's seven o'clock	*son las siete*
Wednesday	*miércoles*	it's six twenty	*son las seis y veinte*
Thursday	*jueves*		
Friday	*viernes*	it's five to nine	*son las nueve menos cinco*
Saturday	*sábado*		
Sunday	*domingo*	in ten minutes	*en diez minutos*
at one o'clock	*a la una*	five hours	*cinco horas*
at half past two	*a las dos y media*	does it take long?	*¿tarda mucho?*
at a quarter to three	*a las tres menos cuarto*		

Numbers

one	*uno*	sixteen	*dieciséis*
two	*dos*	seventeen	*diecisiete*
three	*tres*	eighteen	*dieciocho*
four	*cuatro*	nineteen	*diecinueve*
five	*cinco*	twenty	*veinte*
six	*seis*	twenty-one	*veintiuno*
seven	*siete*	thirty	*treinta*
eight	*ocho*	forty	*cuarenta*
nine	*nueve*	fifty	*cincuenta*
ten	*diez*	sixty	*sesenta*
eleven	*once*	seventy	*setenta*
twelve	*doce*	eighty	*ochenta*
thirteen	*trece*	ninety	*noventa*
fourteen	*catorce*	hundred	*cien/ciento*
fifteen	*quince*	thousand	*mil*

Food glossary

A

acedía small wedge sole

aceite oil; *aceite de oliva* is olive oil and *aceite de girasol* is sunflower oil

aceitunas olives, also sometimes called *olivas*. The best kind are unripe green *manzanilla*, particularly when stuffed with anchovy, *rellenas con anchoas*

adobo marinated fried nuggets usually of shark (*tiburón*) or dogfish (*cazón*); delicious

agua water

aguacate avocado

ahumado smoked; *tabla de ahumados* is a mixed plate of smoked fish

ajillo (al) cooked in garlic, most commonly *gambas* or *pollo*

ajo garlic, *ajetes* are young garlic shoots, often in a *revuelto*

ajo arriero a simple sauce of garlic, paprika and parsley

ajo blanco a chilled garlic and almond soup, a speciality of Málaga

albóndigas meatballs

alcachofa/ alcaucil artichoke

alcaparras capers

aliño any salad marinated in vinegar, olive oil and salt; often made with egg or potato, with chopped onion, peppers and tomato

alioli a tasty sauce made from raw garlic blended with oil and egg yolk; also called *ajoaceite*

almejas name applied to various species of small clams, often cooked with garlic, parsley and white wine

almendra almond

alubias broad beans

anchoa preserved anchovy

anchoba/ anjova bluefish

añejo aged (of cheeses, rums, etc)

angulas baby eels, a delicacy that has become scarce and expensive. Far more common are *gulas*, false *angulas* made from putting processed fish through a spaghetti machine; squid ink is used for authentic colouring

anís aniseed, commonly used to flavour biscuits and liqueurs

arroz rice; *arroz con leche* is a sweet rice pudding

asado roast. An *asador* is a restaurant specializing in charcoal-roasted meat and fish

atún blue-fin tuna

azúcar sugar

B

bacalao salted cod, either superb or leathery
berberechos cockles
berenjena aubergine/eggplant
besugo red bream
bistec steak. *Poco hecho* is rare, *al punto* is medium rare, *regular* is medium, *muy hecho* is well done
bizcocho sponge cake or biscuit
bocadillo/bocata a crusty filled roll
bogavante lobster
bonito atlantic bonito, a small tuna fish
boquerones fresh anchovies, often served filleted in garlic and oil
botella bottle
(a la) brasa cooked on a griddle over coals
buey ox

C

caballa mackerel
cacahuetes peanuts
café coffee; *solo* is black, served espresso-style; *cortado* adds a dash of milk, *con leche* more; *americano* is a long black coffee
calamares squid
caldereta a stew of meat or fish usually made with sherry; *venao* (venison) is commonly used, and delicious
caldo a thin soup
callos tripe
caña a glass of draught beer
cangrejo crab; occasionally river crayfish
caracol snail; very popular in Sevilla *cabrillas*, *burgaos*, and *blanquillos* are popular varieties
caramelos boiled sweets
carne meat
carta menu
casero home-made
castañas chestnuts
cava sparkling wine, mostly produced in Catalunya
cazuela a stew, often of fish or seafood
cebolla onion
cena dinner
centollo spider crab
cerdo pork
cerezas cherries
cerveza beer
champiñón mushroom
chipirones small squid, often served *en su tinta*, in its own ink, mixed with butter and garlic
chocolate a popular afternoon drink; also slang for hashish
choco cuttlefish
chorizo a red sausage, versatile and of varying spiciness (*picante*)
choto roast kid
chuleta/chuletilla chop
chuletón a massive T-bone steak, often sold by weight
churrasco barbecued meat, often ribs with a spicy sauce
churro a fried dough-stick usually eaten with hot chocolate (*chocolate con churros*). Usually eaten as a late afternoon snack (*merienda*), but sometimes for breakfast

cigala Dublin Bay prawn/ Norway lobster
ciruela plum
cochinillo suckling pig
cocido a heavy stew, usually of meat and chickpeas/beans; *sopa de cocido* is the broth
codorniz quail
cogollo lettuce heart
comida lunch
conejo rabbit
congrio conger eel
cordero lamb
costillas ribs
crema catalana a lemony crème brûlée
criadillas hog or bull testicles
croquetas deep-fried crumbed balls of meat, béchamel, seafood, or vegetables
cuchara spoon
cuchillo knife
cuenta (la) the bill

D

desayuno breakfast
dorada a species of bream (gilthead)
dulce sweet

E

ecológico organic
embutido any salami-type sausage
empanada a pie, pasty-like (*empanadilla*) or in large flat tins and sold by the slice; *atun* or *bonito* is a common filling, as is ham, mince or seafood
ensalada salad; *mixta* is usually a large serve of a bit of everything; excellent option
ensaladilla rusa Russian salad, with potato, peas and carrots in mayonnaise
escabeche pickled in wine and vinegar
espárragos asparagus, white and usually canned
espinacas spinach
estofado braised, often in stew form

F

fabada the most famous of Asturian dishes, a hearty stew of beans, *chorizo*, and *morcilla*
fideuá a bit like a paella but with noodles
filete steak
fino the classic dry sherry
flamenquín a fried and crumbed finger of meat stuffed with ham
flan the ubiquitous crème caramel, great when home-made (*casero*), awful when it's not
foie fattened goose liver; often made into a thick gravy sauce
frambuesas raspberries
fresas strawberries
frito/a fried
fruta fruit

G

galletas biscuits
gallo rooster, also the flatfish megrim
gambas prawns
garbanzos chickpeas, often served in *espinacas con garbanzos*, a spicy spinach dish that is a signature of Seville
gazpacho a cold garlicky tomato soup, very refreshing

granizado	popular summer drink, like a frappé fruit milkshake
guisado/ guiso	stewed/a stew
guisantes	peas

H

habas	broad beans, often deliciously stewed *con jamón*, with ham
harina	flour
helado	ice cream
hígado	liver
higo	fig
hojaldre	puff pastry
horno (al)	oven (baked)
hueva	fish roe
huevo	egg

I/J

ibérico	see *jamón*; the term can also refer to other pork products
infusión	herbal tea
jabalí	wild boar
jamón	ham; *jamón York* is cooked British-style ham. Far better is cured *jamón serrano*; *ibérico* ham comes from Iberian pigs in western Spain fed on acorns (*bellotas*). Some places, like Jabugo, are famous for their hams, which can be expensive
judías verdes	green beans
jerez (al)	cooked in sherry

L

langosta	crayfish
langostinos	king prawns
lechazo	milk-fed lamb
leche	milk
lechuga	lettuce
lengua	tongue
lenguado	sole
lentejas	lentils
limón	lemon
lomo	loin, usually sliced pork, sometimes tuna
lubina	sea bass

M

macedonia de frutas	fruit salad, usually tinned
manchego	Spain's national cheese; hard, whitish and made from ewe's milk
manitas (de cerdo)	pork trotters
mantequilla	butter
manzana	apple
manzanilla	the dry, salty sherry from Sanlúcar de Barrameda; also, confusingly, camomile tea and the tastiest type of olive
marisco	shellfish
mejillones	mussels
melocotón	peach, usually canned and served in *almíbar* (syrup)
melva	frigate mackerel, often served tinned or semi-dried
menestra	a vegetable stew, usually served like a minestrone without the liquid; vegetarians will be annoyed to find that it's often seeded with ham and bits of pork
menú	a set meal, usually consisting of three or more courses, bread and wine or water

menudo tripe stew, usually with chickpeas and mint

merluza hake is to Spain as rice is to southeast Asia

mero grouper

miel honey

migas breadcrumbs, fried and often mixed with lard and meat to form a delicious rural dish of the same name

Mojama salt-cured tuna, most common in Cádiz province

mollejas sweetbreads; ie the pancreas of a calf or lamb

montadito a small toasted filled roll

morcilla blood sausage, either solid or semi-liquid

morro cheek, pork or lamb

mostaza mustard

mosto grape juice. Can also refer to a young wine, from 3 months old

N

naranja orange

nata sweet whipped cream

natillas rich custard dessert

navajas razor shells

nécora small sea crab, sometimes called a velvet crab

nueces walnuts

O

orejas ears, usually of a pig

orujo a fiery grape spirit, often brought to add to black coffee if the waiter likes you

ostras oysters, also a common expression of dismay

P

paella rice dish with saffron, seafood and/or meat

pan bread

parrilla grill; a *parrillada* is a mixed grill

pastel cake/pastry

patatas potatoes; often chips (*patatas fritas*, which confusingly can also refer to crisps); *bravas* are with a spicy tomato sauce

pato duck

pavía a crumbed and fried nugget of fish, usually *bacalao* or *merluza*

pavo turkey

pechuga breast (usually chicken)

perdiz partridge

pescado fish

pescaíto frito Andalucían deep-fried fish and seafood

pestiños an Arabic-style confection of pastry and honey, traditionally eaten during Semana Santa

pez espada swordfish; delicious; sometimes called *emperador*

picadillo a dish of spicy mincemeat

picante hot, ie spicy

pichón squab

pijota whiting

pimienta pepper

pimientos peppers; there are many kinds, *piquillos* are the trademark thin Basque red pepper; Padrón produces sweet green mini ones. A popular tapa is *pimientos aliñados* (marinated roasted peppers, often with onion, sometimes with tuna)

pincho a small snack or grilled meat on a skewer (or *pinchito*)
pipas sunflower seeds, a common snack
pisto a ratatouille-like vegetable concoction
plancha (a la) grilled on a hot iron or fried in a pan without oil
plátano banana
pluma a cut of pork next to the loin
pollo chicken
postre dessert
potaje a soup or stew
pringá a tasty paste of stewed meats usually eaten in a *montadito* and a traditional final tapa of the evening
puerros leeks
pulpo octopus, particularly delicious *a la gallega*, boiled Galician style and garnished with olive oil, salt and paprika
puntillitas small squid, often served crumbed and deep fried

Q/R

queso cheese; *de cabra* (goat's), *oveja* (sheep's) or *vaca* (cow's). It comes fresh (*fresco*), medium (*semi-curado*) or strong (*curado*)
rabo de buey/toro oxtail
ración a portion of food served in cafés and bars; check the size and order a half (*media*) if you want less
rana frog; *ancas de rana* is frogs' legs
rape monkfish/anglerfish
raya any of a variety of rays and skates
rebujito a weak mix of *manzanilla* and lemonade, consumed by the bucketload during Andalucían festivals
relleno/a stuffed
reserva, gran reserva, crianza terms relating to the age of wines; *gran reserva* is the oldest and finest, then *reserva* followed by *crianza*
revuelto scrambled eggs, usually with wild mushrooms (*setas*) or seafood; often a speciality
riñones kidneys
rodaballo turbot; pricey and delicious
romana (à la) fried in batter
rosca a large round dish, a cross between sandwich and pizza
rosquilla doughnut

S

sal salt
salchicha sausage
salchichón a salami-like sausage
salmón salmon
salmonete red mullet
salmorejo a delicious thicker version of gazpacho, often garnished with egg and cured ham
salpicón a seafood salad with plenty of onion and vinegar
salsa sauce
San Jacobo a steak cooked with ham and cheese
sandía watermelon
sardinas sardines, delicious grilled

sargo white sea bream
seco dry
secreto a cut of pork loin
sepia cuttlefish
serrano see *jamón*
setas wild mushrooms, often superb
sidra cider
solomillo beef or pork steak cut from the sirloin bone, deliciously fried in whisky and garlic in Sevilla (*solomillo al whisky*)
sopa soup; *sopa castellana* is a broth with a fried egg, noodles, and bits of ham

T

tapa a saucer-sized portion of bar food
tarta tart or cake
té tea
tenedor fork
ternera veal or young beef
tinto red wine is *vino tinto*; a *tinto de verano* is mixed with lemonade and ice, a refreshing option
tocino pork lard; *tocinillo de cielo* is a caramelized egg dessert
tomate tomato
torrijas a Semana Santa dessert, bread fried in milk and covered in honey and cinnamon
tortilla a Spanish omelette, with potato, egg, olive oil and optional onion; *tortilla francesa* is a French omelette
tostada toasted, also a toasted breakfast roll eaten with olive oil, tomato or pâté
trucha trout

U/V

uva grape
vaso glass
venado/ venao venison
verduras vegetables
vieiras scallops, also called *veneras*
vino wine; *blanco* is white, *rosado* or *clarete* is rosé, *tinto* is red

Z

zanahoria carrot
zumo fruit juice, usually bottled and pricey

Glossary of architectural terms

A

alcázar	a Moorish fort
ambulatory	a gallery round the chancel and behind the altar
apse	vaulted square or rounded recess at the back of a church
archivolt	decorative carving around the outer surface of an arch
art deco	a style that evolved between the World Wars, based on geometric forms
artesonado ceiling	ceiling of carved wooden panels with Islamic motifs popular throughout Spain in the 15th and 16th centuries
ayuntamiento	a town hall
azulejo	an ornamental ceramic tile

B

Baldacchino	an ornate carved canopy above an altar or tomb
Baroque	ornate architectural style of the 17th and 18th centuries
bodega	a cellar where wine is kept or made; the term also refers to modern wineries and wine shops
buttress	a pillar built into a wall to reinforce areas of greatest stress. A flying buttress is set away from the wall; a feature of Gothic architecture

C

capilla	a chapel within a church or cathedral
capital	the top of column, joining it to another section. Often highly decorated
castillo	a castle or fort
catedral	a cathedral, ie the seat of a bishop
chancel	the area of a church which contains the main altar, usually at the eastern end
chapterhouse	area reserved for Bible study in monastery or church
Churrigueresque	a particularly ornate form of Spanish Baroque, named after the Churriguera brothers
colegiata	a collegiate church, ie one ruled by a chapter of canons
conjunto histórico	a tourist-board term referring to an area of historic buildings

convento	a monastery or convent
coro	the area enclosing the choirstalls, often central and completely closed off in Spanish churches
crossing	the centre of a church, where the 'arms' of the cross join

E

ermita	a hermitage or rural chapel

G

Gothic	13th-15th-century style formerly known as pointed style; distinguished externally by pinnacles and tracery around windows, Gothic architecture lays stress on the presence of light

H

hospital	in pilgrimage terms, a place where pilgrims used to be able to rest, receive nourishment and receive medical attention

I

iglesia	a church

L

lobed arch	Moorish arch with depressions in the shape of simple arches
lonja	a guildhall or fish market

M

mocárabes	small concave spaces used as a decorative feature on Moorish ceilings and archways
modernista	a particularly imaginative variant of art nouveau that came out of Catalonia; exemplified by Gaudí
monasterio	a large monastery usually located in a rural area
monstrance	a ceremonial container for displaying the host
Mozarabic	the style of Christian artisans living under Moorish rule
mudéjar	the work of Muslims living under Christian rule after the Reconquest, characterized by ornate brickwork
multifoil	a type of Muslim-influenced arch with consecutive circular depressions
muralla	a city wall

N

nave	the main body of the church, a single or multiple passageway leading (usually) from the western end up to the crossing or high altar
neoclassical	a reaction against the excesses of Spanish Baroque, this 18th- and 19th-century style saw clean lines and symmetry valued above all things

P

palacio	a palace or large residence
patio	an interior courtyard
pediment	triangular section between top of collums and gables
pilaster	pillar attached to the wall
Plateresque	derived from *platero* (silversmith); used to describe a Spanish Renaissance style characterized by finely carved decoration

R

reliquary	a container to hold bones or remains of saints and other holy things
Renaissance	Spanish Renaissance architecture began when classical motifs were used in combination with Gothic elements in the 16th century
retablo	altarpiece or retable formed by many panels often rising to roof level; can be painted or sculptured
Romanesque (románico)	style spread from France in the 11th and 12th centuries, characterized by barrel vaulting, rounded apses and semicircular arches
Romano	Roman

S

sacristy (sacristía)	part of church reserved for priests to prepare for services
soportales	wooden or stone supports for the 1st floor of civic buildings, forming an arcade underneath
stucco (yesería)	moulding mix consisting mainly of plaster; fundamental part of Moorish architecture

Index

→ *Entries in* **bold** *refer to maps*

print story

een partitioned, the
'e striking for more
ation of British
ea. Exports were
America – how
k for businessmen
away continent?
American
rn that year,
el, the most prolific
erica of his day.

the book was
1924, in the
l, the steamship
America, it
American
d 'South America
nnual publication
for generations
h America
is day. In the
s by sea and
all the details
j voyage from
ar for dinner; how
match with the
ff on the Cape
full account of
erpool up the
5898 miles
abin!

ened up,
Handbook
n Am flying
e fortnightly
Rio to Europe
. For reasons
extraordinary
nnual editions
he Second

1970s

Many more people discovered South America and the backpacking trail started to develop. All the while the Handbook was gathering fans, including literary vagabonds such as Paul Theroux and Graham Greene (who once sent some updates addressed to "The publishers of the best travel guide in the world, Bath, England").

1990s

During the 1990s the company set about developing a new travel guide series using this legendary title as the flagship. By 1997 there were over a dozen guides in the series and the Footprint imprint was launched.

2000s

The series grew quickly and there were soon Footprint travel guides covering more than 150 countries. In 2004, Footprint launched its first thematic guide: *Surfing Europe*, packed with colour photographs, maps and charts. This was followed by further thematic guides such as *Diving the World*, *Snowboarding the World*, *Body and Soul escapes*, *Travel with Kids* and *European City Breaks*.

2015

Today we continue the traditions of the last 94 years that have served legions of travellers so well. We believe that these help to make Footprint guides different. Our policy is to use authors who are genuine experts who write for independent travellers; people possessing a spirit of adventure, looking to get off the beaten track.

Credits

Footprint credits
Editor: Jo Williams
Production and layout: Emma Bryers
Maps: Kevin Feeney

Publisher: Patrick Dawson
Managing Editor: Felicity Laughton
Advertising: Elizabeth Taylor
Sales and Marketing Executive:
Kirsty Holmes

Photography credits
Front cover: StevanZZ/Shutterstock.com
Back cover: Top: NaughtyNut/Shutterstock.com. Bottom: Subbotina Anna/Shutterstock.com

Colour section
Page i: José Fuste Raga/age fotostock; age footstock/age footstock. **Page 1**: age fotostock/age footstock. **Page 2-3**: Radius/Radius. **Page 4**: Hemis.fr/Hemis.fr; Tips Images/Tips Images; Frischknecht Patrick/Prisma. **Page 5**: age fotostock/age footstock; age fotostock/age footstock; Design Pics/Design Pics; Lucas Vallecillos/age footstock.**Page 6**: Eduardo Grund/age footstock; Rolf Hicker/All Canada Photos; Travel Library Limited/Travel Library Limited. **Page 7**: Lucas Vallecillos/age footstock; Eduardo Grund/age footstock; Lucas Vallecillos/age footstock; José Antonio Moreno/age footstock. **Page 10**: MATTES Ren/Hemis.fr. **Page 11**: Luis Domingo/age footstock; Ben Welsh/age footstock. **Page 13**: imageBROKER/imageBROKER; Christian Handl/imageBROKER. **Page 14**: Robert Harding Picture Library/Robert Harding Picture Library. **Page 15**: age fotostock/age footstock; Design Pics/Design Pics; age fotostock/age footstock. **Page 16**: Lucas Vallecillos/age footstock; Peter M Wilson/Axiom Photographic/Design Pics; Eye Ubiquitous/Eye Ubiquitous. **Page 17**: Cubo Images/Cubo Images; Hilary Jane Morgan/age footstock; Salva Garrigues/age footstock. **Page 18**: Wolf Winter/age fotostock

Printed in India by Thomson Press Ltd, Faridabad, Haryana

Publishing information
Footprint Andalucía
8th edition

ISBN: 978 1 910120 26 2
CIP DATA: A catalogue record for this book is available from the British Library

Published by Footprint
6 Riverside Court
Lower Bristol Road
Bath BA2 3DZ, UK
T +44 (0)1225 469141
F +44 (0)1225 469461
footprinttravelguides.com

Distributed in the USA by
National Book Network, Inc.

	Almería	Cádiz	Córdoba	Gibraltar	Granada	Huelva	Jaén	Madrid	Málaga	Marbe	S
Cádiz	484										
Córdoba	332	263									
Gibraltar	343	141	293								
Granada	166	335	166	260							
Huelva	516	219	232	289	350						
Jaén	228	367	104	338	99	336					
Madrid	563	663	400	672	434	632	335				
Málaga	219	265	187	137	129	313	209	544			
Marbe	340	199	215	82	190	345	261	592	59		
S	422	125	138	199	256	94	242	538	219	255	
	366	106	315	47	290	296	362	692	159	105	2

Distances in kilometres 1 kilometre = 0.62 miles

Map symbols
- Capital city
- Other city, town
- International border
- Regional border
- Customs
- Contours (approx)
- Mountain, volcano
- Mountain pass
- Escarpment
- Glacier
- Salt flat
- Rocks
- Seasonal marshland
- Beach, sandbank
- Waterfall
- Reef
- Motorway
- Main road
- Unpaved or ripio (gravel) road
- Track
- Footpath
- Railway
- Railway with station
- Airport
- Bus station
- Metro station
- Cable car
- Funicular
- Ferry
- Pedestrianized street
- Tunnel
- One way-street
- Steps
- Bridge
- Fortified wall
- Park, garden, stadiu
- Where to stay
- Restaurants
- Bars & clubs
- Building
- Sight
- Cathedral, church
- Chinese temple
- Hindu temple
- Meru
- Mosque
- Stupa
- Synagogue
- Tourist office
- Museum
- Post office

Foo

It was 1921
Ireland had just
British miners w
pay and the fe
industry had an
booming in Sou
about a handbo
trading in that f
The Anglo-Sout
Handbook was
written by W Ko
writer on Latin A

1924
Two editions late
'privatized' and i
hands of Royal M
company for Sou
became The Sou
Handbook, subti
in a nutshell'. Thi
became the 'bib
of travellers to S
and remains so t
early days travel
the Handbook ga
needed for the lo
Europe. What to v
to arrange a crick
Cable & Wireless s
Verde Islands and
the journey from
Amazon to Mana
without changin

1939
As the continent
the South Americ
reported the new
boat services, and
airship service fro
on the Graf Zepp
still unclear but w
determination, the
continued throug
World War.